DAPHNE DU MAURIER

THREE COMPLETE NOVELS

AND FIVE SHORT STORIES

DAPHNE DU MAURIER

THREE COMPLETE NOVELS
AND FIVE SHORT STORIES

The King's General

The Glass Blowers

The House on the Strand

Don't Look Now
And Other Stories

AVENEL BOOKS · NEW YORK

This edition is published by Avenel Books
distributed by Crown Publishers, Inc.
by arrangement with Doubleday & Company, Inc.

h g f e d c b a

AVENEL 1981 EDITION

Manufactured in the United States of America

Library of Congress Cataloging in Publication Data

Du Maurier, Daphne, Dame, 1907-
    Three complete novels and five short stories.

    Contents: The King's general—The glass blowers—
The house on the strand—[etc.]
    I. Title.
PR6007.U47A6   1981   823'.912   81-12891
ISBN 0-517-34917-5 (Crown)   AACR2

CONTENTS

The King's General

1

The Glass Blowers

193

The House on the Strand

371

Don't Look Now

535

DAPHNE DU MAURIER

THREE COMPLETE NOVELS

AND FIVE SHORT STORIES

The King's General

To My Husband
Also a General, but, I trust, a more discreet one.

Menabilly,
May 5–July 19, 1945

1

SEPTEMBER 1653. The last of summer. The first chill winds of autumn. The sun no longer strikes my eastern window as I wake, but, turning laggard, does not top the hill before eight o'clock. A white mist hides the bay sometimes until noon and hangs about the marshes, too, leaving, when it lifts, a breath of cold air behind it. Because of this the long grass in the meadow never dries, but long past midday shimmers and glistens in the sun, the great drops of moisture hanging motionless upon the stems. I notice the tides more than I did once. They seem to make a pattern to the day. When the water drains from the marshes and little by little the yellow sands appear, rippling and hard and firm, it seems to my foolish fancy lying here that I, too, go seaward with the tide, and my old hidden dreams that I thought buried for all time lie bare and naked to the day, just as the shells and the stones do on the sands.

It is a strange, joyous feeling, this streak back to the past. Nothing is regretted, and I am happy and proud. The mist and cloud have gone, and the sun, high now and full of warmth, holds revel with my ebb tide. How blue and hard the sea as it curls westward from the bay, and the Blackhead, darkly purple, leans to the deep water like a sloping shoulder. Once again—and this I know is fancy—it seems to me the tide ebbs always in the middle of the day, when hope is highest and my mood is still. Then, half consciously, I become aware of a shadow, of a sudden droop of the spirit. The first clouds of evening are gathering beyond the Dodman. They cast long fingers on the sea. And the surge of the sea, once far off and faint, comes louder now, creeping towards the sands. The tide has turned. Gone are the white stones and the cowrie shells. The sands are covered. My dreams are buried. And as the darkness falls the flood tide sweeps over the marshes and the land is covered. . . . Then Matty will come in to light the candles and to stir the fire, making a bustle with her presence, and if I am short with her or do not answer, she looks at me with a shake of her head and reminds me that the fall of the year was always my bad time. My autumn melancholy. Even in the distant days, when I was young, the menace of it became an institution, and Matty, like a fierce clucking hen, would chase away the casual visitor. "Miss Honor can see nobody today."

My family soon learnt to understand and left me in peace. Though "peace" is an ill word to describe the moods of black despair that used to grip me. Ah well . . . they're over now. Those moods at least. Rebellion of the spirit against the chafing flesh, and the moments of real pain when I could not rest. Those were the battles of youth. And I am a rebel no longer. The middle years have me in thrall, and there is much to be said for them. Resignation brings its own reward.

The trouble is that I cannot read now as I used to do. At twenty-five, at thirty, books were my great consolation. Like a true scholar, I worked away at my Latin and Greek so that learning was part of my existence. Now it seems profitless. A cynic when I was young, I am in danger of becoming a worse one now I am old. So Robin says. Poor Robin. God knows I must often make a poor companion. The years have not spared him either. He has aged much this year. Possibly his anxiety over me. I know they discuss the future, he and Matty, when they think I sleep. I can hear their voices droning in the parlour. But when he is with me he feigns his little air of cheerfulness, and my heart bleeds for him. My brother . . . Looking at him as he sits beside me, coldly critical as I always am towards the people I love, I note the pouches beneath his eyes and the way his hands tremble when he lights his pipe. Can it be that he was ever light of heart and passionate of mind? Did he really ride into battle with a hawk on his wrist, and was it only ten years ago that he led his men to Braddock Down, side by side with Bevil Grenvile, flaunting that scarlet standard with the three gold rests in the eyes of the enemy? Was this the man I saw once, in the moonlight, fighting his rival for a faithless woman?

Looking at him now, it seems a mockery. Poor Robin, with his greying locks shaggy on his shoulders. Yes, the agony of the war has left its mark on both of us. The war—and the Grenviles. Maybe Robin is bound to Gartred still, even as I am to Richard. We never speak of these things. Ours is the dull, drab life of day by day.

Looking back, there can be very few amongst our friends who have not suffered. So many gone, so many penniless. I don't forget that Robin and I both live on charity. If Jonathan Rashleigh had not given us this house we should have had no home, with Lanrest gone and Radford occupied. Jonathan looks very old and tired. It was that last grim year of imprisonment in St. Mawes that broke him, that and John's death. Mary looks much the same. It would take more than a civil war to break her quiet composure and her faith in God. Alice is still with them, and her children, but the feckless Peter never visits her.

I think of the time when we were all assembled in the long gallery, and Alice and Peter sang, and John and Joan held hands before the fire—they were all so young, such children. Even Gartred with her calculated malevolence could not have changed the atmosphere that evening. Then Richard, my Richard, broke the spell deliberately with one of his devastating cruel remarks, smiling as he did so, and the gaiety went, and the careless joy vanished from the evening. I hated him for doing it, yet understood the mood that prompted him.

Oh, God confound and damn these Grenviles, I thought afterwards, for harming everything they touch, for twisting happiness into pain with a mere inflection of the voice. Why were they made thus, he and Gartred, so that cruelty for its own sake was almost a vice to be indulged in, affording a sensuous delight? What evil genius presided at their cradle? Bevil had been so different. The flower of the flock, with his grave courtesy, his thoughtfulness, his rigid code of morality, his tenderness to his own and to other people's children. And his boys take after him. There is no vice in Jack or Bunny that I have ever seen. But Gartred . . . Those serpent's eyes beneath the red-gold hair; that hard, voluptuous mouth; how incredible it seemed to me, even in the early days when she was married to my brother Kit, that anyone could be deceived by her. Her power to charm was devastating. My father and my mother were jelly in her hands, and as for poor Kit, he was lost from the beginning, like Robin later. But I was never won, not for a moment.

Well, her beauty is marred now, and I suppose forever. She will carry that scar to the grave. A thin scarlet line from eye to mouth where the blade slashed her.

Rumour has it that she can still find lovers, and one of the Careys is her latest conquest, having come to live near by her at Bideford. I can well believe it. No neighbour would be safe from her if he had a charm of manner, and the Careys were always presentable. . . . I can even find it in my heart to forgive her, now that everything is over. The idea of her dallying with George Carey—she must be at least twenty years the elder—brings a flash of colour into a grey world. And what a world! Long faces and worsted garments, bad harvests and sinking trade, everywhere men poorer than they were before, and the people miserable. The happy aftermath of war. Spies of the Lord Protector (God, what an ironic designation!) in every town and village, and if a breath of protest against the state is heard the murmurer is borne straight away to jail. The Presbyterians hold the reins in their grasping hands, and the only men to benefit are upstarts like Dick Buller and Robert Bennett and our old enemy John Robartes, all of them out for what they can get and damn the common man. Manners are rough, courtesy a forgotten quality; we are each one of us suspicious of our neighbour. O brave new world!

The docile English may endure it for a while, but not we Cornish. They cannot take our independence from us, and in a year or so, when we have licked our wounds, we'll have another rising, and there'll be more blood spilt and more hearts broken. But we shall still lack our leader. . . . Ah, Richard—my Richard—what evil spirit in you urged you to quarrel with all men, so that even the King now is your enemy? My heart aches for you in this last disgrace. I picture you sitting lonely and bitter at your window, gazing out across the dull, flat lands of Holland, and you put the final words to the Defence that you are writing and of which Bunny brought me a rough draft when he came to see me last.

"Oh, put not your trust in princes, nor in any child of man, for there is no help in them."

Bitter, hopeless words that will do no good and only breed further mischief.

> Sir Richard Grenvile for his presuming loyalty must be by a public declaration defamed as a Banditto and his very loyalty understood a crime. However, seeing it must be so, let God be prayed to bless the King with faithful Councillors, and that none may be prevalent to be any way hurtful to him or to any of his relations. As for Sir Richard Grenvile, let him go with the reward of an old soldier of the King's. There is no present use for him. When there shall be the Council will think on it, if not too late. Vale.

Resentful, proud, and bitter to the end. For this is the end. I know it and you know it too. There will be no recovery for you now; you have destroyed yourself forever. Feared and hated by friend and foe.

The King's General in the West. The only man I love . . .

It was after the Scillies fell to the Parliament, and both Jack and Bunny were home for a while, having visited Holland and France, that they rode over from Stowe to see the Rashleighs at Menabilly and came down to Tywardreath to pay their respects to me. We talked of Richard, and almost immediately Jack said, "My uncle is greatly altered; you would hardly know him. He sits for hours in silence, looking out of the window of his dismal lodging watching the eternal rain—God, how it rains in Holland—and he has no wish for company. You remember how he used to quip and jest with us and with all youngsters? Now if he does speak it is to find fault, like a testy old man, and crab his visitor."

"The King will never make use of him again, and he knows it," said Bunny. "The quarrel with the Court has turned him sour. It was madness to fan the flame of his old enmity with Hyde."

Then Jack, with more perception, seeing my eyes, said quickly, "Uncle was always his own worst enemy; Honor knows that. He is damnably lonely, that's the truth of it. And the years ahead are blank."

We were all silent for a moment. My heart was aching for Richard, and the boys perceived it.

Presently Bunny said in a low tone, "My uncle never speaks of Dick. I suppose we shall never know now what wretched misfortune overtook him."

I felt myself grow cold and the old sick horror grip me. I turned my head so that the boys should not see my eyes.

"No," I said slowly. "No, we shall never know."

Bunny drummed with his fingers on the table, and Jack played idly with the pages of a book. I was watching the calm waters of the bay and the little fishing boats creeping round the Blackhead from Gorran Haven. Their sails were amber in the setting sun.

"If," pursued Bunny, as though arguing with himself, "he had fallen into the hands of the enemy, why was the fact concealed? That is what always puzzles me. The son of Richard Grenvile was a prize indeed."

I did not answer. I felt Jack move restlessly beside me. Perhaps marriage had given him perception—he was a bridegroom of a few months' standing at that time—or maybe he was always more intuitive than Bunny, but I knew he was aware of my distress.

"There is little use," he said, "in going over the past. We are making Honor tired."

Soon after they kissed my hands and left, promising to come to see me again before they returned to France. I watched them gallop away, young and free and untouched by the years that had gone. The future was theirs to seize. One day the King would come back to his waiting country, and Jack and Bunny, who had fought so valiantly for him, would be rewarded. I could picture them at Stowe, and up in London at Whitehall, growing sleek and prosperous, with a whole new age of splendour opening before them.

The civil war would be forgotten, and forgotten, too, the generation which had preceded them, which had fallen in the cause, or which had failed. My generation, which would enter into no inheritance.

I lay there in my chair, watching the deepening shadows, and presently Robin came in and sat beside me, enquiring, in his gruff, tender way, if I were tired, regretting that he had missed the Grenvile brothers, and going on to tell me of some small pother in the courthouse at Tywardreath. I made pretence of listening, aware with a queer sense of pity how the trifling events of day by day were now his one concern. I thought how once he and his companions had won immortality for their gallant and so useless defence of Pendennis Castle in those tragic summer months in '46—how proud we were of them, how full our hearts—and here he was rambling on about five fowls that had been stolen from a widow in St. Blazey.

Perhaps I was no cynic after all, but rotten with sentiment. . . .

It was then that the idea came first to me, that by writing down the events of those few years I would rid myself of a burden. The war and how it changed our lives, how we were all caught up in it, and broken by it, and our lives hopelessly intermingled one with another. Gartred and Robin, Richard and I, the whole Rashleigh family, pent up together in that house of secrets, small wonder that we came to be defeated.

Even today Robin goes every Sunday to dine at Menabilly, but not I. My health pleads its own excuse. Knowing what I know, I could not return.

Menabilly, where the drama of our lives was played, is vivid enough to me three miles distant here in Tywardreath. The house stands as bare and desolate as it did when I saw it last in '48. Jonathan has neither the heart nor the money to restore it to its former condition. He and Mary and the grandchildren live in one wing only. I pray God they will always remain in ignorance of that final tragedy. Two people will carry the secret to the grave. Richard and I. He sits in Holland, many hundred miles away, and I lie upon my couch in Tywardreath, and the shadow of the buttress is upon us both.

When Robin rides each Sunday to Menabilly I go with him, in imagination, across the park and come to the high walls surrounding the house. The courtyard lies open; the west front stares down at me. The last rays of the sun shine into my old room above the gatehouse, for the lattice is open, but the windows of the room beside it are closed. Ivy tendrils creep across it. The smooth stone of the buttress outside the window is incrusted with lichen.

The sun vanishes, and the west front takes once more to the shadows. The Rashleighs eat and sleep within, and go by candlelight to bed, and dream; but I, down here three miles away in Tywardreath, wake in the night to the sound of a boy's voice calling my name in terror, to a boy's hands beating against the walls, and there in the pitch-black night before me, vivid, terrible, and accusing, is the ghost of Richard's son. I sit up in bed, sweating with horror, and faithful Matty, hearing me stir, comes to me and lights the candle.

She brews me a warm drink, rubs my aching back, and puts a shawl about my shoulders. Robin, in the room adjoining, sleeps on undisturbed. I try to read awhile, but my thoughts are too violent to allow repose. Matty brings me paper and a pen, and I begin to write. There is so much to say and so little time in which to say it.

For I do not fool myself about the future. My own instinct, quite apart from Robin's face, warns me that this autumn will be the last. So while my Richard's Defence is discussed by the world and placed on record for all time amongst the archives of this seventeenth century, my apologia will go with me to the grave, and by rotting there with me, unread, will serve its purpose.

I will say for Richard what he never said for himself, and I will show how, despite his bitter faults and failings, it was possible for a woman to love him with all her heart, and mind, and body, and I that woman.

I write at midnight then, by candlelight, while the church clock at Tywardreath chimes the small hours, and the only sounds I hear are the sigh of the wind beneath my window and the murmur of the sea as the tide comes sweeping across the sands to the marshes below St. Blazey Bridge.

2

THE FIRST TIME I saw Gartred was when my eldest brother Kit brought her home to Lanrest as his bride. She was twenty-two and I, the baby of the family except for Percy, a child of ten.

We were a happy, sprawling family, very intimate and free, and my father, John Harris, cared nothing for the affairs of the world, but lived for his horses, his dogs, and the peaceful concerns of his small estate Lanrest, which was no large property, but lay high amidst a sheltering ring of trees, looking down upon the Looe Valley, and was one of those placid, kindly houses that seem to slumber through the years, and we loved it well.

Even now, some thirty years after, I have only to close my eyes and think of home, and there comes to my nostrils the well-remembered scent of hay, hot with the sun, blown by a lazy wind; and I see the great wheel thrashing the water down at the mills at Lametton, and I smell the fusty-dusty golden grain. The sky was always white with pigeons. They circled and flew above our heads and were so tame that they would take grain from our hands. Strutting and cooing, puffed and proud, they created an atmosphere of comfort. Their gentle chattering amongst themselves through a long summer's afternoon brought much peace to me in the later years, when the others would go hawking and ride away laughing and talking and I could no longer follow them.

But that is another chapter. . . . I was talking of Gartred as I saw her first. The wedding had taken place at Stowe, her home, and Percy and I, because of some childish ailment or other, had not been present at it. This, very foolishly, created a resentment in me from the first. I was undoubtedly spoilt, being so much younger than my brothers and sisters, who made a great pet of me, as did my parents, too, but I had it firmly in my mind that my brother's bride did not wish to be bothered with children at her wedding and that she feared we might have some infection.

I can remember sitting upright in bed, my eyes bright with fever, remonstrating with my mother.

"When Cecilia was married Percy and I carried the train," I said. (Cecilia was my eldest sister.) "And we all of us went to Maddercombe, and the Pollexefens welcomed us, although Percy and I both made ourselves sick with overeating."

All that my mother could say in reply was that this time it was different, and Stowe was quite another place to Maddercombe, and the Grenviles were not the Pollexefens—which seemed to me the most feeble of arguments—and she would never forgive herself if we took the fever to Gartred. Everything was Gartred. Nobody else mattered. There was a great fuss and commotion, too, about preparing the spare chamber for when the bride and bridegroom should come to stay. New hangings were bought, and rugs and tapestries, and it was all because Gartred must not be made to feel Lanrest was shabby or in poor repair. The servants were made to sweep and dust, the place was put into a bustle, and everyone made uncomfortable in the process.

If it had been because of Kit, my dear, easygoing brother, I should never have grudged it for a moment. But Kit himself might never have existed. It was for Gartred. And, like all children, I listened to the gossip of the servants.

"It's on account of his being heir to Sir Christopher at Radford that she's marrying our young master," was the sentence I heard amidst the clatter in the kitchen.

I seized upon this piece of information and brooded on it, together with the reply from my father's steward.

"It's not like a Grenvile to match with a plain Harris of Lanrest."

The words angered me and confused me too. The word "plain" seemed a reflection on my brother's looks, whom I considered handsome, and why should a Harris of Lanrest be a poor bargain for a Grenvile? It was true that Kit was heir to our uncle Christopher at Radford—a great barracks of a place the other side of Plymouth—but I had never thought much of the fact until now. For the first time I realised, with something of a shock, that marriage was not the romantic fairy legend I had imagined it to be, but a great institution, a bargain between important families, with the tying up of property. When Cecilia married John Pollexefen, whom she had known since childhood, it had not struck me in this way, but now with my father riding over to Stowe continually, and holding long conferences with lawyers, and wearing a worried frown between his brows, Kit's marriage was becoming like some frightening affair of state, which, if worded wrong, would throw the country into chaos.

Eavesdropping again, I heard the lawyer say, "It is not Sir Bernard Grenvile who is holding out about the settlement, but the daughter herself. She has her father wound round her finger."

I pondered over this awhile and then repeated it to my sister Mary.

"Is it usual," I asked, with no doubt irritating precocity, "for a bride to argue thus about her portion?"

Mary did not answer for a moment. Although she was twenty, life had barely brushed her as yet, and I doubt if she knew more than I did. But I could see that she was shocked.

"Gartred is the only daughter," she said after a moment. "It is perhaps necessary for her to discuss the settlement."

"I wonder if Kit knows of it," I said. "I somehow don't think he would like it."

Mary then bade me hold my tongue and warned me that I was fast becoming a shrew and no one would admire me for it. I was not to be discouraged, though, and while I refrained from mentioning the marriage settlement to my brothers I went to plague Robin—my favourite even in those days—to tell me something of the Grenviles. He had just ridden in from hawking and stood in the stable yard, his dear, handsome face flushed and happy, the falcon on his wrist, and I remember drawing back, scared always by the bird's deep, venomous eyes and the blood on her beak. She would permit no one to touch her but Robin, and he was stroking her feathers. There was a clatter in the stable yard, with the men rubbing down the horses, and in one corner by the well the dogs were feeding.

"I am pleased it is Kit and not you that has gone away to find a bride for himself," I said, while the bird watched me from beneath its great hooded lids, and Robin smiled and reached out his other hand to touch my curls, while the falcon ruffled in anger.

"If I had been the eldest son," said Robin gently, "I would have been the bridegroom at this wedding."

I stole a glance at him and saw that his smile had gone, and in its place a look of sadness.

"Why, did she like you best?" I asked.

He turned away then and, placing the hood over his bird, gave her to the keeper. When he picked me up in his arms he was smiling again.

"Come and pick cherries," he said, "and never mind my brother's bride."

"But the Grenviles," I persisted as he bore me on his shoulders to the orchard, "why must we be so mighty proud about them?"

"Bevil Grenvile is the best fellow in the world," said Robin. "Kit and Jo and I were at Oxford with him. And his sister is very beautiful."

More than that I could not drag from him. But my brother Jo, to whose rather sarcastic, penetrating mind I put the same question later in the day, expressed surprise at my ignorance.

"Have you reached the ripe age of ten, Honor," he enquired, "without knowing that in Cornwall there are only two families who count for anything? The Grenviles and the Arundells. Naturally we humble Harris brood are overwhelmed that our dear brother Kit has been honoured by the august hand of the so ravishing Gartred." Then he buried his nose in a book and there was an end of the matter.

The next week they were all gone to Stowe for the wedding. I had to hug my soul in patience until their return, and then, as I feared, my mother pleaded fatigue, as did the rest of them, and everyone seemed a little jaded and out of sorts with so much feasting and rejoicing, and only my third sister Bridget unbent to me at all. She was in raptures over the magnificence of Stowe and the hospitality of the Grenviles.

"This place is like a steward's lodge compared to Stowe," she told me. "You could put Lanrest in one pocket of the grounds there, and it would not be noticed. Two servants waited behind my chair at supper, and all the while musicians played to us from the gallery."

"But Gartred, what of Gartred?" I said with impatience.

"Wait while I tell you," she said. "There were more than two hundred people staying there, and Mary and I slept together in a chamber bigger by far than any we possess here. There was a woman to tend us and dress our hair. And the bedding was changed every day, and perfumed."

"What else then?" I asked, consumed with jealousy.

"I think Father was a little lost," she whispered. "I saw him from time to time with the older people, endeavouring to talk, but he looked stifled, as though he could not breathe. And all the men were so richly attired, somehow he seemed drab beside them. Sir Bernard is a very fine-looking man. He wore a blue velvet doublet, slashed with silver, the day of the wedding, and Father was in his green that fits him a little too well. He overtops him, too—Sir Bernard, I mean—and they looked odd standing together."

"Never mind my father," I said. "I want to hear of Gartred."

My sister Bridget smiled, superior with her knowledge.

"I liked Bevil the best," she said, "and so does everyone. He was in the midst of it all, seeing that no one lacked for anything. I thought Lady Grenvile a little stiff, but Bevil was the soul of courtesy, gracious in all he did." She paused a moment. "They are all auburn-haired, you know," she said with some inconsequence; "if we saw anyone with auburn hair it was sure to be a Grenvile. I did not care for the one they called Richard," she added with a frown.

"Why not? Was he so ugly?" I asked.

"No," she answered, puzzled, "he was more handsome than Bevil. But he looked at us all in a mocking, contemptuous way, and when he trod on my gown in the crush he made no apology. 'You are to blame,' he had the impudence to tell me, 'for letting it trail thus in the dust.' They told me at Stowe he was a soldier."

"But there is still Gartred," I said; "you have not described her." And then, to my mortification, Bridget yawned and rose to her feet.

"Oh, I am too weary to tell you any more," she said. "Wait until the morning. But Mary and Cecilia and I are all agreed upon one thing, that we would sooner resemble Gartred than any other woman."

So in the end I had to form my own judgment with my own eyes. We were all gathered in the hall to receive them—they had gone first from Stowe to my uncle's estate at Radford—and the dogs ran out into the courtyard as they heard the horses.

We were a large party because the Pollexefens were with us too. Cecilia had her baby Joan in her arms—my first godchild, and I was proud of the honour—and we were all happy and laughing and talking because we were one family and knew ourselves so well. Kit swung himself down from the saddle—he looked very debonair and gay—and I saw Gartred. She murmured something to Kit, who laughed and coloured and held his arms to help her dismount, and in a flash of intuition I knew she had said something to him which was part of their life together and had nought to do with us, his family. Kit was not ours any more, but belonged to her.

I hung back, reluctant to be introduced, and suddenly she was beside me, her cool hand under my chin.

"So you are Honor?" she said.

The inflection in her voice suggested that I was small for my age, or ill-looking, or disappointing in some special way, and she passed on through to the big parlour, taking precedence of my mother with a confident smile, while the remainder of the family followed like fascinated moths. Percy, being a boy and goggle-eyed at beauty, went to her at once, and she put a sweetmeat in his mouth. She has them ready, I thought, to bribe us children as one bribes strange dogs.

"Would Honor like one too?" she said, and there was a note of mockery in her voice, as though she knew instinctively that this treating of me as a baby was what I hated most.

I could not take my eyes from her face. She reminded me of something, and suddenly I knew. I was a tiny child again at Radford, my uncle's home, and he was walking me through the glasshouses in the gardens. There was one flower, an orchid, that grew alone; it was the colour of pale ivory, with one little vein of crimson running through the petals. The scent filled the house, honeyed and sickly sweet. It was the loveliest flower I had ever seen. I stretched out my hand to stroke the soft velvet sheen, and swiftly my uncle pulled me by the shoulder. "Don't touch it, child. The stem is poisonous." I drew back, frightened. Sure enough, I could see the myriad hairs bristling, sharp and sticky, like a thousand swords.

Gartred was like that orchid. When she offered me the sweetmeat I turned away, shaking my head, and my father, who had never spoken to me harshly in his life, said sharply, "Honor, where are your manners?"

Gartred laughed and shrugged her shoulders. Everyone present turned reproving eyes upon me; even Robin frowned. My mother bade me go upstairs to my room. That was how Gartred came to Lanrest. . . .

The marriage lasted for three years, and it is not my purpose now to write about it. So much has happened since to make the later life of Gartred the more vivid, and in the battles we have waged the early years loom dim now and unimportant. There was always war between us, that much is certain. She, young and confident and proud, and I a sullen child, peering at her from behind doors and screens, and both of us aware of a mutual hostility. They were more often at Radford and Stowe than at Lanrest, but when she came home I swear she cast a blight upon the place. I was still a child and I could not reason, but a child, like an animal, has an instinct that does not lie.

There were no children of the marriage. That was the first blow, and I know that was a disappointment to my parents because I heard them talk of it. My sister Cecilia came to us regularly for her lying-in, but there was never a rumour of Gartred. She rode and went hawking as we did; she did not keep to her room or complain of fatigue, which we had come to expect from Cecilia. Once my mother had the hardihood to say, "When I was first wed, Gartred, I neither rode nor hunted, for fear I should miscarry," and Gartred, trimming her nails with a tiny pair of scissors made of mother-of-pearl, looked up at her and said, "I have nothing within me to lose, madam, and for that you had better blame your son." Her voice was low and full of venom, and my mother stared at her for a moment, bewildered, then rose and left the room in distress. It was the first time the poison had touched her. I did not understand the talk between them, but I sensed that Gartred was bitter against my brother, for soon afterwards Kit came in and, going to Gartred, said to her in a tone loaded with reproach, "Have you accused me to my mother?"

They both looked at me, and I knew I had to leave the room. I went out into the garden and fed the pigeons, but the peace was gone from the place. From that moment all went ill with them and with us all. Kit's nature seemed to change. He wore a harassed air, wretchedly unlike himself, and a coolness grew up between him and my father, who had hitherto agreed so well.

Kit showed himself suddenly aggressive to my father and to us all, finding fault with the working of Lanrest and comparing it to Radford, and in contrast to this was his abject humility before Gartred, a humility that had nothing fine about it but made him despicable to my intolerant eyes.

The next year he stood for West Looe in Parliament and they went often to London, so we did not see them much, but when they came to Lanrest there seemed to be this continual strain about their presence, and once a heated quarrel between Kit and Robin, one night when my parents were from home. It was midsummer, very stifling and warm, and I, playing truant from my nursery, crept down to the garden in my nightgown. The household were abed. I remember flitting like a little ghost before the windows. The casement of the guest chamber was open wide, and I heard Kit's voice, louder than usual, lifted in argument. Some devil interest in me made me listen.

"It is always the same," he said, "wherever we go. You make a fool of me before all men, and now tonight before my very brother. I tell you I cannot endure it longer."

I heard Gartred laugh and I saw Kit's shadow reflected on the ceiling by the quivering candlelight. Their voices were low for a moment, then Kit spoke again for me to hear.

"You think I remark nothing," he said. "You think I have sunk so low that to keep you near me, and to be allowed to touch you sometimes, I will shut my eyes to everyone. Do you think it was pleasant for me at Stowe to see how you looked upon Antony Denys that night when I returned so suddenly from London? A man with grown children, and his wife scarce cold in her grave? Are you entirely without mercy for me?"

That terrible pleading note I so detested had crept back into his voice again, and I heard Gartred laugh once more. "And this evening," he said, "I saw you smiling here across the table at him, my own brother." I felt sick and rather frightened, but curiously excited, and my heart thumped within me as I heard a step beside me on the paving and, looking over my shoulder, I saw Robin standing beside me in the darkness.

"Go away," he whispered to me, "go away at once."

I pointed to the open window.

"It is Kit and Gartred," I said. "He is angry with her for smiling at you."

I heard Robin catch his breath and he turned as if to go, when suddenly Kit's voice cried out, loud and horrible, as though he, a grown man, were sobbing like a child. "If that happens I shall kill you. I swear to God I shall kill you." Then Robin, swift as an arrow, stooped to a stone and, taking it in his hand, he flung it against the casement, shivering the glass to fragments.

"Damn you for a coward, then," he shouted. "Come and kill me instead."

I looked up and saw Kit's face, white and tortured, and behind him Gartred with her hair loose on her shoulders. It was a picture to be imprinted always on my mind, those two there at the window, and Robin suddenly different from the brother I had always known and loved, breathing defiance and contempt. I felt ashamed for him, for Kit, for myself, but mostly I was filled with hatred for Gartred who had brought the storm to pass and remained untouched by it.

I turned and ran, with my fingers in my ears, and crept up to bed with never a word to anyone and drew the covers well over my head, fearing that by morning they would all three of them be discovered slain there in the grass. But what passed between them further I never knew. Day broke and all was as before, except that Robin rode away soon after breakfast and he did not return until after Kit and Gartred took their departure to Radford, some five days later. Whether anyone else in the family knew of the incident I never discovered. I was too scared to ask, and since Gartred had come amongst us we had all lost our old manner of sharing troubles and had each one of us grown more polite and secretive.

Next year, in '23, the smallpox swept through Cornwall like a scourge, and few families were spared. In Liskeard the people closed their doors and the shopkeepers put up their shutters and would do no trade, for fear of the infection.

In June my father was stricken, dying within a few days, and we had scarcely recovered from the blow before messages came to us from my uncle at Radford to say that Kit had been seized with the same dread disease, and there was no hope of his recovery.

Father and son thus died within a few weeks of each other, and Jo, the scholar, became the head of the family. We were all too unhappy with our double loss to think of Gartred, who had fled to Stowe at the first sign of infection and so escaped a similar fate, but when the two wills came to be read, both Kit's and my father's, we learnt that although Lanrest, with Radford later, passed to Jo, the rich pasture lands of Lametton and the Mill were to remain in Gartred's keeping for her lifetime.

She came down with her brother Bevil for the reading, and even Cecilia, the gentlest of my sisters, remarked afterwards with shocked surprise upon her composure, her icy confidence, and the niggardly manner with which she saw to the measuring of every acre down at Lametton. Bevil, married himself now and a near neighbour to us at Killigarth, did his utmost to smooth away the ill feeling that he sensed amongst us; and although I was still little more than a child, I remember feeling unhappy and embarrassed that he was put to so much awkwardness on our account. It was small wonder that he was loved by everyone, and I wondered to myself what opinion he held in his secret heart about his sister, or whether her beauty amazed him as it did every man.

When affairs were settled and they went away I think we all of us breathed relief that no actual breach had come to pass, causing a feud between the families, and that Lanrest belonged to Jo was a weight off my mother's mind, although she said nothing.

Robin remained from home during the whole period of the visit, and maybe no one but myself could guess the reason. The morning before she left some impulse prompted me to hesitate before her chamber, the door of which was open, and look at her within. She had claimed that the contents of the room belonged to Kit, and so to her, and the servants had been employed the day before in taking down the hangings and removing the pieces of furniture she most desired. At this last moment she was alone, turning out a little *secrétaire* that stood in one corner. Nor did she observe that I was watching her, and I saw the mask off her lovely face at last. The eyes were narrow, the lips protruding, and she wrenched at a little drawer with such force that the hinge came to pieces in her hands. There were some trinkets at the back of the drawer—none, I think, of great value—but she had remembered them. Suddenly she saw my face reflected in the mirror.

"If you leave to us the bare walls we shall be well content," I said as her eyes met mine.

My father would have whipped me for it had he been alive, and my brothers, too, but we were alone.

"You always played the spy, from the first," she said softly, but because I was no man she did not smile.

"I was born with eyes in my head," I said to her.

Slowly she put the jewels in a little pouch she wore hanging from her waist.

"Take comfort and be thankful, you are quit of me now," she said. "We are not likely to see each other again."

"I hope not," I told her.

Suddenly she laughed.

"It were a pity," she said, "that your brother did not have a little of your spirit."

"Which brother?" I asked.

She paused a moment, uncertain what I knew, and then, smiling, she tapped my cheek with her long slim finger.

"All of them," she said, and then she turned her back on me and called to her servant from the adjoining room.

Slowly I went downstairs, my mind on fire with questions, and, coming into the hallway, I saw Jo fingering the great map hanging on the wall. I did not talk to him but walked out past him into the garden.

She left Lanrest at noon, herself in a litter, and a great train of horses and servants from Stowe to carry her belongings. I watched them, from a hiding place in the trees, pass away up the road to Liskeard in a cloud of dust.

"That's over," I said to myself. "That's the last of them. We have done with the Grenviles."

But fate willed otherwise.

3

MY EIGHTEENTH BIRTHDAY. A bright December day. My spirits soaring like a bird as, looking out across the dazzling sea from Radford, I watched His Majesty's fleet sail into Plymouth Sound.

It concerned me not that the expedition now returning had been a failure and that far away in France La Rochelle remained unconquered; these were matters for older people to discuss.

Here in Devon there was laughing and rejoicing and the young folk held high holiday. What a sight they were, some eighty ships or more, crowding together between Drake's Island and the Mount, the white sails bellying in the west wind, the coloured pennants streaming from the golden spars. As each vessel drew opposite the fort at Mount Batten she would be greeted with a salvo from the great guns and, dipping her colours in a return salute, let fly her anchor and bring up opposite the entrance to the Cattwater. The people gathered on the cliffs waved and shouted, and from the vessels themselves came a mighty cheer, while the drums beat and the bugles sounded, and the sides of the ships were seen to be thronged with soldiers pressing against the high bulwarks, clinging to the stout rigging. The sun shone upon their breastplates and their swords, which they waved to the crowds in greeting, and gathered on the poop would be the officers, flashes of crimson, blue, and Lincoln green, as they moved amongst the men.

Each ship carried on her mainmast the standard of the officer in command, and as the crowd recognised the colours and the arms of a Devon leader, or a Cornishman, another great shout would fill the air and be echoed back to us from the cheering fellows in the vessel. There was the two-headed eagle of the Godolphins, the running stag of the Trevannions from Carhayes, the six swallows of the numerous Arundell clan, and, perhaps loveliest of all, the crest of the Devon Champernownes, a sitting swan holding in her beak a horseshoe of gold.

The little ships, too, threaded their way amongst their larger sisters, a vivid flash of colour with their narrow decks black with troopers, and I recognised vessels I had seen last lying in Looe Harbour or in Fowey, now weather-stained and battered, but bearing triumphantly aloft the standards of the men who had built them, and manned them, and commissioned them for war—there was the wolf's head of our neighbour Trelawney, and the Cornish chough of the Menabilly Rashleighs.

The leading ship, a great three-masted vessel, carried the commander of the expedition, the Duke of Buckingham, and when she was saluted from Mount Batten she replied with an answering salvo from her own six guns, and we could see the duke's pennant fluttering from the masthead. She dropped anchor, swinging to the wind, and the fleet followed her, and the rattle of nigh a hundred cables through a hundred hawsers must have filled the air from where we stood on the cliffs below Radford, away beyond the Sound to Saltash, at the entrance of the Tamar River.

Slowly their bows swung round, pointing to Cawsand and the Cornish coast, and their sterns came into line, the sun flashing in their windows and gleaming upon the ornamental carving, the writhing serpents and the lion's paws.

And still the bugles echoed across the water and the drums thundered. Suddenly there was silence, the clamour and the cheering died away, and on the flagship commanded by the Duke of Buckingham someone snapped forth an order in a high clear voice. The soldiers who had crowded the bulwarks were there no longer; they moved as one man, forming into line amidships; there was no jostling, no thrusting into position. There came another order and the single tattoo of a drum, and in one movement, it seemed, the boats were manned and lowered into the water, the coloured blades poised as though to strike, and the men who waited on the thwarts sat rigid as automatons.

The manoeuvre had taken perhaps three minutes from the first order; and the timing of it, the precision, the perfect discipline of the whole proceeding drew from the crowd about us the biggest cheer yet from the day, while for no reason I felt the idiotic tears course down my cheeks.

"I thought as much," said a fellow below me. "There's only one man in the West who could turn an unruly rabble into soldiers fit for His Majesty's Bodyguard. There go the Grenvile coat of arms; do you see them, hoisted beneath the Duke of Buckingham's standard?"

Even as he spoke I saw the scarlet pennant run up to the masthead, and as it streamed into the wind and flattened, the sun shone upon the three gold rests.

The boats drew away from the ship's side, the officers seated in the stern sheets, and suddenly it was high holiday again, with crowded Plymouth boats putting out from the Cattwater to greet the fleet—the whole Sound dotted at once with little craft—and the people watching upon the cliffs began to run towards Mount Batten, calling and shouting, pushing against one another to be the first to greet the landing boats. The spell was broken, and we returned to Radford.

"A fine finish to your birthday," said my brother with a smile. "We are all bidden to a banquet at the castle, at the command of the Duke of Buckingham."

He stood on the steps of the house to greet us, having ridden back from the fortress at Mount Batten. Jo had succeeded to the estate at Radford, my uncle Christopher having died a few years back, and much of our time now was spent between Plymouth and Lanrest. Jo had become indeed a person of some importance, in Devon especially, and besides being undersheriff for the county, he had married an heiress into the bargain, Elizabeth Champernowne, whose pleasant manner and equable disposition made up for her lack of looks. My sister Bridget, too, had followed Cecilia's example and married into a Devon family, and Mary and I were the only daughters left unwed.

"There will be ten thousand fellows roaming the streets of Plymouth tonight," jested Robin. "I warrant if we turned the girls loose amongst them they'd soon find husbands."

"Best clip Honor's tongue then," replied Jo, "for they'll soon forget her blue eyes and her curls once she begins to flay them."

"Let me alone. I can look after myself," I told them. For I was still the spoilt darling, the *enfant terrible,* possessing unbounding health and vigour and a tongue that ran away with me. I was, moreover (and how long ago it seems), the beauty of the family, though my features, such as they were, were more impudent than classical, and I still had to stand on tiptoe to reach Robin's shoulder.

I remember, that night, how we embarked below the fortress and took boat across the Cattwater to the castle, and all Plymouth seemed to be upon the water or on the battlements, while away to the westward gleamed the soft lights of the fleet at anchor, the stern windows shining, and the glow from the poop lanterns casting a dull beam upon the water. When we landed we found the townsfolk pressing about the castle entrance, and everywhere were the soldiers, laughing and talking, strung about with girls, who had them decked with flowers and ribbons for festivity. There were casks of ale standing on the cobbles beside the braziers, and barrow loads of pies and cakes and cheeses, and I remember thinking that the maids who roystered there with their soldier lovers would maybe have more value from their evening than we who must behave with dignity within the precincts of the castle.

In a moment we were out of hearing of the joyful noises of the town, and the air was close and heavy with rich scent, and velvet, and silk, and spicy food, and we were in the great banqueting hall with voices sounding hollow and strange beneath the vaulted roof. Now and again would ring out the clear voice of a gentleman-at-arms, "Way for the Duke of Buckingham," and a passage would be cleared for the commander as he passed to and fro amongst the guests, holding court even as His Majesty himself might do.

The scene was colourful, exciting, and I—more accustomed to the lazy quietude of Lanrest—felt my heart beating and my cheeks flush, and to my youthful irresponsible fancy it seemed to me that all this glittering display was somehow a tribute to my eighteenth birthday.

"How lovely it is. Are you not glad we came?" I said to Mary, and she, always reserved amid strangers, touched my arm and murmured, "Speak softer, Honor, you draw attention to us," and was for pressing back against the wall. I pressed forward, greedy for colour, devouring everything with my eyes, and smiling even at strangers and caring not at all that I seemed bold, when suddenly the crowd parted, a way was cleared, and here was the duke's retinue upon us, with the duke himself not half a yard away.

Mary was gone, and I was left alone to bar his path. I remember standing an instant in dismay, and then, losing my composure, I curtseyed low, as though to King Charles himself, while a little of laughter floated above my head. Raising my eyes, I saw my brother Jo, his face a strange mixture of amusement and dismay, come forward from amongst those who thronged the duke and, leaning towards me, he helped me to my feet, for I had curtseyed so low that I was hard upon my heels and could not rise.

"May I present my sister Honor, Your Grace," I heard him say. "This is, in point of fact, her eighteenth birthday, and her first venture into society."

The Duke of Buckingham bowed gravely and, lifting my hand to his lips, wished me good fortune. "It may be your sister's first venture, my dear Harris," he said graciously, "but with beauty such as she possesses you must see to it that it is not the last." He passed on in a wave of perfume and velvet, with my brother hemmed in beside him, frowning at me over his shoulder, and as I swore under my breath, or possibly not under my breath but indiscreetly—and a stable oath learned from Robin at that—I heard someone say behind me, "If you care to come out onto the battlements I will show you how to do that as it should be done." I whipped round, scarlet and indignant, and looking down upon me from six feet or more, with a sardonic smile upon his face, was an officer still clad in his breastplate of silver, worn over a blue tunic, with a blue-and-silver sash about his waist. His eyes were golden brown, his hair dark auburn, and I saw that his ears were pierced with small gold rings, for all the world like a Turkish bandit.

"Do you mean you would show me how to curtsey or how to swear?" I said to him in fury.

"Why, both, if you wish it," he answered. "Your performance at the first was lamentable, and at the second merely amateur."

His rudeness rendered me speechless, and I could hardly believe my ears. I glanced about me for Mary or for Elizabeth, Jo's serene and comfortable wife, but they had withdrawn in the crush, and I was hemmed about with strangers. The most fitting thing then was to withdraw with dignity. I turned on my heel and pushed my way through the crowd, making for the entrance, and then I heard the mocking voice behind me once again, "Way for Mistress Honor Harris of Lanrest," proclaimed in high clear tones, while people looked at me astonished, falling back in spite of themselves, and so a passageway was cleared. I walked on with flaming cheeks, scarce knowing what I was doing, and found myself, not in the great entrance as I had hoped, but in the cold air upon the battlements, looking out on to Plymouth Sound, while away below me, in the cobbled square, the townsfolk danced and sang. My odious companion was with me still, and he stood now, with his hand upon his sword, looking down upon me with that same mocking smile on his face.

"So you are the little maid my sister so much detested," he said.

"What the devil do you mean?" I asked.

"I would have spanked you for it had I been her," he said. Something in the clip of his voice and the droop of his eye struck a chord in my memory.

"Who are you?" I said to him.

"Sir Richard Grenvile," he replied, "a colonel in His Majesty's Army, and knighted some little while ago for extreme gallantry in the field."

He hummed a little, playing with his sash.

"It is a pity," I said, "that your manners do not match your courage."

"And that your deportment," he said, "does not equal your looks."

This reference to my height—always a sore point, for I had not grown an inch since I was thirteen—stung me to fresh fury. I let fly a string of oaths that Jo and Robin, under the greatest provocation, might have loosed upon the stablemen, though certainly not in my presence, and which I had only learnt through my inveterate habit of eavesdropping; but if I hoped to make Richard Grenvile blanch I was wasting my breath. He waited until I had finished, his head cocked as though he were a tutor hearing me repeat a lesson, and then he shook his head.

"There is a certain coarseness about the English tongue that does not do for the occasion," he said. "Spanish is more graceful and far more satisfying to the temper. Listen to this." And he began to swear in Spanish, loosing upon me a stream of lovely-sounding oaths that would certainly have won admiration had they come from Jo or Robin.

As I listened I looked again for that resemblance to Gartred, but it was gone. He was like his brother Bevil, but with more dash, and certainly more swagger, and I felt he cared not a tinker's curse for anyone's opinion but his own.

"You must admit," he said, breaking off suddenly, "that I have you beaten." His smile, no longer sardonic but disarming, had me beaten, too, and I felt my anger die within me. "Come and look at the fleet," he said. "A ship at anchor is a lovely thing."

We went to the battlements and stared out across the Sound. It was a still, clear night and the moon had risen. The ships were motionless upon the water, and they stood out in the moonlight carved and clear. The men were singing; the sound of their voices was borne to us across the water, distinct from the rough jollity of the crowds in the street below.

"Were your losses very great at La Rochelle?" I asked him.

"No more than I expected in an expedition that was bound to be abortive," he answered, shrugging his shoulders. "Those ships yonder are filled with wounded men who won't recover. It would be more humane to throw them overboard." I looked at him in doubt, wondering if this was a further instalment of his peculiar sense of humour. "The only fellows who distinguished themselves were those in the regiment I have the honour to command," he continued, "but as no other officer but myself insists on discipline, it was small wonder that the attack proved a failure."

His self-assurance was as astounding to me as his former rudeness.

"Do you talk thus to your superiors?" I asked him.

"If you mean superior to me in matters military, such a man does not exist," he answered, "but superiors in rank, why, yes, invariably. That is why, although I am not yet twenty-nine, I am already the most detested officer in His Majesty's Army." He looked down at me, smiling, and once again I was at a loss for words.

I thought of my sister Bridget and how he had trodden upon her dress at Kit's wedding, and I wondered if there was anyone in the world who liked him. "And the Duke of Buckingham?" I said. "Do you speak to him in this way too?"

"Oh, George and I are old friends," he answered. "He does what he is told. He gives me no trouble. Look at those drunken fellows in the courtyard there. My heaven, if they were under my command I'd hang the bastards." He pointed down to the square below, where a group of brawling soldiers were squabbling around a cask of ale, accompanied by a pack of squealing women.

"You might excuse them," I said, "pent up at sea so long."

"They may drain the cask dry and rape every woman in Plymouth, for all I care," he answered, "but let them do it like men and not like beasts, and clean their filthy jerkins first." He turned away from the battlement in disgust. "Come now," he said, "let us see if you can curtsey better to me than you did to the duke. Take your gown in your hands, thus. Bend your right knee, thus. And allow your somewhat insignificant posterior to sink upon your left leg, thus."

I obeyed him, shaking with laughter, for it seemed to me supremely ridiculous that a colonel in His Majesty's Army should be teaching me deportment upon the battlements of Plymouth Castle.

"I assure you it is no laughing matter," he said gravely. "A clumsy woman looks so damnably ill bred. There now, that is excellent. Once again. . . . Perfection. You can do it if you try. The truth is you are an idle little baggage and have never been beaten by your brothers." With appalling coolness he straightened my gown and rearranged the lace around my shoulders. "I object to dining with untidy women," he murmured.

"I have no intention of sitting down with you to dine," I replied with spirit.

"No one else will ask you, I can vouch for that," he answered. "Come, take my arm; I am hungry if you are not."

He marched me back into the castle, and to my consternation I found that the guests were already seated at the long tables in the banqueting hall, and the servants were bearing in the dishes. We were conspicuous as we entered, and my usual composure fled from me. It was, it may be remembered, my first venture in the social world. "Let us go back," I pleaded, tugging at his arm. "See, there is no place for us; the seats are all filled."

"Go back? Not on your life. I want my dinner," he replied.

He pushed his way past the servants, nearly lifting me from my feet. I could see hundreds of faces stare up at us amidst a hum of conversation, and for one brief moment I caught a glimpse of my sister Mary, seated next to Robin, 'way down in the centre of the hall. I saw the look of horror and astonishment in her eyes and her mouth frame the word "Honor" as she whispered hurriedly to my brother. I could do nothing but hurry forward, tripping over my gown, borne on the relentless arm of Richard Grenvile to the high table at the far end of the hall where the Duke of Buckingham sat beside the Countess of Mount Edgcumbe, and the nobility of Cornwall and Devon, such as they were, feasted with decorum, above the common herd.

"You are taking me to the high table," I protested, dragging at his arm with all my force.

"What of it?" he asked, looking down at me in astonishment. "I'm damned if I'm going to dine anywhere else. Way there, please, for Sir Richard Grenvile." At his voice the servants flattened themselves against the wall, and heads were turned, and I saw the Duke of Buckingham break off from his conversation with the countess. Chairs were pulled forward, people were squeezed aside, and somehow we were seated at the table a hand's stretch from the duke himself, while the Lady Mount Edgcumbe peered round at me with stony eyes. Richard Grenvile leaned forward with a smile. "You are perhaps acquainted with Honor Harris, Countess," he said, "my sister-in-law. This is her eighteenth birthday." The countess bowed and appeared unmoved. "You can disregard her," said Richard Grenvile to me. "She's as deaf as a post. But for God's sake smile and take that glassy stare out of your eyes."

I prayed for death, but it did not come to me. Instead I took the roast swan that was heaped upon my platter. The Duke of Buckingham turned to me, his glass in his hand. "I wish you many many happy returns of the day," he said. I murmured my thanks and shook my curls to hide my flaming cheeks.

"Merely a formality," said Richard Grenvile in my ear. "Don't let it go to your head. George has a dozen mistresses already and is in love with the Queen of France."

He ate with evident enjoyment, villifying his neighbours with every mouthful, and because he did not trouble to lower his voice I could swear that his words were heard. I tasted nothing of what I ate or drank, but sat like a bewildered fish throughout the long repast. At length the ordeal was over, and I felt myself pulled to my feet by my companion. The wine, which I had swallowed as though it were water, had made jelly of my legs, and I was obliged to lean upon him for support. I have scant memory indeed of what followed next. There were music and singing, and some Sicilian dancers, strung about with ribbons, performed a tarantella, but their final dizzy whirling was my undoing, and I have shaming recollection of being assisted to some inner apartment of the castle, suitably darkened and discreet, where nature took her toll of me and the roast swan knew me no more. I opened my eyes and found myself upon a couch, with Richard Grenvile holding my hand and dabbing my forehead with his kerchief.

"You must learn to carry your wine," he said severely. I felt very ill and very shamed, and tears were near the surface. "Ah, no," he said, and his voice, hitherto so clipped and harsh, was oddly tender, "you must not cry. Not on your birthday." He continued dabbing at my forehead with the kerchief.

"I have n-never eaten roast swan b-before," I stammered, closing my eyes in agony at the memory.

"It was not so much the swan as the burgundy," he murmured. "Lie still now, you will be easier by and by."

In truth, my head was still reeling, and I was as grateful for his strong hand as I would have been for my mother's. It seemed to me in no wise strange that I should be lying sick in a darkened unknown room with Richard Grenvile tending me, proving himself so comforting a nurse.

"I hated you at first. I like you better now," I told him.

"It's hard that I had to make you vomit before I won your approval," he answered.

I laughed and then fell to groaning again, for the swan was not entirely dissipated.

"Lean against my shoulder so," he said to me. "Poor little one, what an ending to an eighteenth birthday." I could feel him shake with silent laughter, and yet his voice and hands were strangely tender, and I was happy with him.

"You are like your brother Bevil after all," I said.

"Not I," he answered. "Bevil is a gentleman, and I a scoundrel. I have always been the black sheep of the family."

"What of Gartred?" I asked.

"Gartred is a law unto herself," he replied. "You must have learnt that when you were a little child and she wedded to your brother."

"I hated her with all my heart," I told him.

"Small blame to you for that," he answered me.

"And is she content, now that she is wed again?" I asked him.

"Gartred will never be content," he said. "She was born greedy, not only for money, but for men too. She had an eye to Antony Denys, her husband now, long before your brother died."

"And not only Antony Denys," I said.

"You had long ears for a little maid," he answered.

I sat up, rearranging my curls, while he helped me with my gown. "You have been kind to me," I said, grown suddenly prim and conscious of my eighteen years. "I shall not forget this evening."

"Nor I either," he replied.

"Perhaps," I said, "you had better take me to my brothers."

"Perhaps I had," he said.

I stumbled out of the little dark chamber to the lighted corridor.

"Where were we all this while?" I asked in doubt, glancing over my shoulder.

He laughed and shook his head. "The good God only knows," he answered, "but I wager it is the closet where Mount Edgcumbe combs his hair." He looked down at me, smiling, and for one instant touched my curls with his hands. "I will tell you one thing," he said, "I have never sat with a woman before while she vomited."

"Nor I so disgraced myself before a man," I said with dignity.

Then he bent suddenly and lifted me in his arms like a child. "Nor have I ever lay hidden in a darkened room with anyone so fair as you, Honor, and not made love to her," he told me, and, holding me for a moment against his heart, he set me on my feet again.

"And now if you permit it, I will take you home," he said.

That is, I think, a very clear and truthful account of my first meeting with Richard Grenvile.

4

WITHIN A WEEK of the encounter just recorded I was sent back to my mother at Lanrest, supposedly in disgrace for my ill behaviour, and once home I had to be admonished all over again and hear for the twentieth time how a maid of my age and breeding should conduct herself. It seemed that I had done mischief to everyone. I had shamed my brother Jo by that foolish curtsey to the Duke of Buckingham and, further to this, had offended his wife Elizabeth by taking precedence of her and dining at the high table, to which she had not been invited. I had neglected to remain with my sister Mary during the evening, had been observed by sundry persons cavorting oddly on the battlements with an officer, and had finally appeared sometime after midnight from the private rooms within the castle in a sad state of disarray.

Such conduct would, my mother said severely, condemn me possibly for all time in the eyes of the world, and had my father been alive he would more than likely have packed me off to the nuns for two or three years, in the hope that my absence for a space of time would cause the incident to be forgotten. As it was. . . . And here invention failed her, and she was left lamenting that, as both my married sisters Cecilia and Bridget were expecting to lie-in again and could not receive me, I would be obliged to stay at home.

It seemed to me very dull after Radford, for Robin had remained there, and my young brother Percy was still at Oxford. I was therefore alone in my disgrace.

I remember it was some weeks after I returned, a day in early spring, and I had gone out to sulk by the apple tree, that favourite hiding place of childhood, when I observed a horseman riding up the valley. The trees hid him for a space, and then the sound of horse's hoofs drew nearer, and I realised that he was coming to Lanrest. Thinking it was Robin, I scrambled down from my apple tree and went to the stables, but when I arrived there I found the servant leading a strange horse to the stall—a fine grey—and I caught a glimpse of a tall figure passing into the house. I was for following my old trick of eavesdropping at the parlour door, but just as I was about to do so I observed my mother on the stairs.

"You will please to go to your chamber, Honor, and remain there until my visitor has gone," she said gravely.

My first impulse was to demand the visitor's name, but I remembered my manners in time and, afire with curiosity, went silently upstairs. Once there I rang for Matty, the maid who had served me and my sisters for some years now and was become my special ally. Her ears were nearly as long as mine, and her nose as keen, and her round plain face was now alight with mischief. She guessed what I wanted her for before I asked her.

"I'll bide in the hallway when he comes out and get his name for you," she said; "a tall, big gentleman he was, a fine man."

"Not the prior from Bodmin," I said with sudden misgiving, for fear my mother should, after all, intend to send me to the nuns.

"Why, bless you, no," she answered. "This is a young master, wearing a blue cloak slashed with silver."

Blue and silver. The Grenvile colours.

"Was his hair red, Matty?" I asked in some excitement.

"You could warm your hands at it," she answered.

This was an adventure then, and no more dullness to the day. I sent Matty below, and myself paced up and down my chamber in great impatience. The interview must have been a short one, for very soon I heard the door of the parlour open and the clear, clipped voice that I remembered well taking leave of my mother, and I heard his footsteps pass away through the hallway to the courtyard. My chamber window looked out on to the garden, and I thus had no glimpse of him, and it seemed eternity before Matty reappeared, her eyes bright with information. She brought forth a screwed-up piece of paper from beneath her apron, and with it a silver piece.

"He told me to give you the note and keep the crown," she said.

I unfolded the note, furtive as a criminal, and read:

> Dear Sister, although Gartred has exchanged a Harris for a Denys, I count myself still your brother, and reserve for myself the right of calling upon you. Your good mother, it seems, thinks otherwise, tells me you are indisposed, and has bidden me good day in no uncertain terms. It is not my custom to ride some ten miles or so to no purpose, therefore, you will direct your maid forthwith to conduct me to some part of your domain where we can converse together unobserved, for I dare swear you are no more indisposed than is your brother and servant Richard Grenvile.

My first thought was to send no answer, for he took my compliance so much for granted, but curiosity and a beating heart got the better of my pride, and I bade Matty show the visitor the orchard, but that he should not go too directly for fear of being seen from the house. When she had gone I listened for my mother's footsteps, and sure enough they sounded up the stairs, and she came into the room. She found me sitting by the window with a book of prayers open on my knee.

"I am happy to see you so devout, Honor," she said.

I did not answer, but kept my eyes meekly upon the page.

"Sir Richard Grenvile, with whom you conducted yourself in so unseemly a fashion in Plymouth, has just departed," she continued. "It seems he has left the Army for a while and intends to reside near to us at Killigarth, standing as member of Parliament for Fowey. A somewhat sudden decision."

Still I did not answer.

"I have never heard any good of him," said my mother. "He has always caused his family concern and been a sore trial to his brother Bevil, being constantly in debt. He will hardly make us a pleasant neighbour."

"He is, at least, a very gallant soldier," I said warmly.

"I know nothing about that," she answered, "but I have no wish for him to ride over here, demanding to see you, when your brothers are from home. It shows great want of delicacy on his part."

With that she left me, and I heard her pass into her chamber and close the door. In a few moments I had my shoes in my hands and was tiptoeing down the stairs into the garden. I then flew like the wind to the orchard and was safe in the apple tree before many minutes had passed. Presently I heard someone moving about under the trees and, parting the blossoms in my hiding place, I saw Richard Grenvile stooping under the low branches. I broke off a piece of twig and threw it at him. He shook his head and looked about him. I threw another, and this one hit him a sharp crack upon the nose. "Damn it——" he began, and, looking up, he saw me laughing at him from the apple tree. In a moment he had swung himself up beside me and with one arm around my waist had me pinned against the trunk. The branch cracked most ominously.

"Descend at once; the branch will not hold us both," I said.

"It will if you keep still," he told me.

One false move would have seen us both upon the ground, some ten feet below, but to remain still meant that I must continue to lie crushed against his chest, with his arm around me, and his face not six inches away from mine.

"We cannot possibly converse in such a fashion," I protested.

"Why not? I find it very pleasant," he answered. Cautiously he stretched his legs along the full length of the branch to give himself more ease and pulled me closer. "Now what have you to tell me?" he said, for all the world as though it were I who had demanded the interview and not he.

I then recounted my disgrace, and how my brother and sister-in-law had sent me packing home from Plymouth, and it seemed as if I must now be treated as a prisoner in my own home.

"And it is no use your coming here again," I added, "for my mother will never let me see you. It seems you are a person of ill repute."

"How so?" he demanded.

"You are constantly in debt; those were her words."

"The Grenviles are never not in debt. It is the great failing of the family. Even Bevil has to borrow from the Jews."

"You are a sore trial to him and to all your relatives."

"On the contrary, it is they who are a sore trial to me. I can seldom get a penny out of them. What else did your mother say?"

"That it showed want of delicacy to come here asking to see me when my brothers are from home."

"She is wrong. It showed great cunning, born of long experience."

"And as for your gallantry in the field, she knows nothing about that."

"I hardly suppose she does. Like all mothers, it is my gallantry in other spheres that concerns her at the present."

"I don't know what you mean," I said.

"Then you have less perception than I thought," he answered, and, loosening his hold upon the branch, he flicked at the collar of my gown. "You have an earwig running down your bosom," he said.

I drew back, disconcerted, the abrupt change from the romantic to the prosaic putting me out of countenance.

"I believe my mother to be right," I said stiffly. "I think there is very little to be gained from our further acquaintance, and it would be best to put an end to it now." It was difficult to show dignity in my cramped position, but I made some show to sitting upright and braced back my shoulders.

"You cannot descend unless I let you," he said, and in truth I was locked there, with his legs across the branch.

"The moment is opportune to teach you Spanish," he murmured.

"I have no wish to learn it," I answered.

Then he laughed and, taking my face in his hands, he kissed me very suddenly, which, being a novelty to me and strangely pleasant, rendered me for a few moments incapable of speech or action. I turned away my head and began to play with the blossoms.

"You can go now if you desire it," he said.

I did not desire it but had too much pride to tell him so. He swung himself to the ground and lifted me down beside him.

"It is not easy," he said, "to be gallant in an apple tree. Perhaps you will tell your mother." He wore upon his face that same sardonic smile that I had first seen in Plymouth.

"I shall tell my mother nothing," I said, hurt by this abrupt dismissal.

He looked down on me for a moment in silence, and then he said, "If you bid your gardener trim that upper branch we would do better another time."

"I am not certain," I answered, "that I wish for another time."

"Ah, but you do," he said, "and so do I. Besides, my horse needs exercise." He turned through the trees, making for the gate where he had left his horse, and I followed him silently through the long grass. He reached for the bridle and climbed into the saddle.

"Ten miles between Lanrest and Killigarth," he said. "If I did this twice a week Daniel would be in fine condition by the summer. I will come again on Tuesday. Remember those instructions to the gardener." He waved his gauntlet at me and was gone.

I stood staring after him, telling myself that he was quite as detestable as Gartred and that I would never see him more; but for all my resolutions I was at the apple tree again on Tuesday. . . .

There followed then as strange and, to my mind, as sweet a wooing as ever maiden of my generation had. Looking back on it now, after a quarter of a century, when the sequel to it fills my mind with greater clarity, it has become the hazy unreality of an elusive dream. Once a week, and sometimes twice, he would ride over to Lanrest from Killigarth, and there, cradled in the apple tree—with the offending branch lopped as he demanded—he tutored me in love, and I responded. He was but twenty-eight, and I eighteen. Those March and April afternoons, with the bees humming above our heads and the little blackcap singing, and the grass in the orchard growing longer day by day, there seemed no end to them and no beginning.

Of what we discoursed, when we did not kiss, I have forgotten. He must have told me much about himself, for Richard's thoughts were ever centred about his person, more then than latterly, and I had a picture of a red-haired lad rebellious of authority, flaunting his elders, staring out across the storm-tossed Atlantic from the towering craggy cliffs of his north Cornish coast, so different from our southern shore, with its coves and valleys.

We have, I think, a more happy disposition here in southeast Cornwall, for the very softness of the air, come rain or sun, and the gentle contour of the land make for a lazy feeling of content. Whereas in the Grenvile country, bare of hedgerow, bereft of trees, exposed to all four winds of heaven, and those winds laden as it were with surf and spray, the mind develops with a quick perception, with more fire to it, more anger, and life itself is hazardous and cruel. Here we have few tragedies at sea, but there the coast is strewn with the bleached bones of vessels wrecked without hope of haven, and about the torn, unburied bodies of the drowned the seals do play and the falcons hover. It holds us more than we ever reckon, the few square miles of territory where we are born and bred, and I understand what devils of unrest surged in the blood of Richard Grenvile.

These thoughts of mine came at a later date, but then, when we were young, they concerned me not, nor he either, and whether he talked to me of soldiering or Stowe, of fighting the French or battling with his own family, it sounded happy in my ears, and all his bitter jests were forgotten when he kissed me and held me close. It seems odd that our hiding place was not discovered. Maybe in his careless, lavish fashion he showered gold pieces on the servants; certainly my mother passed her days in placid ignorance.

And then, one day in early April, my brothers rode from Radford, bringing with them young Edward Champernowne, a younger brother of Elizabeth's. I was happy to see Jo and Robin, but in no mood to exchange courtesies with a stranger—besides, his teeth protruded, which seemed to me unpardonable—and also I was filled with furtive fear that my secret meetings would be discovered. After we had dined Jo and Robin and my mother, with Edward Champernowne, withdrew to the bookroom that had been my father's, and I was left alone to entertain Elizabeth. She made no mention of my discourtesy at Plymouth, for which I was grateful, but proceeded to lavish great praise upon her brother Edward, who, she told me, was but a year older than myself and recently left Oxford. I listened with but half an ear, my thoughts full of Richard, who, in debt as usual, had talked at our last meeting of selling lands in Killigarth and Tywardreath that he had inherited from his mother, and bearing me off with him to Spain or Naples, where we would live like princes and turn bandit.

Later in the evening I was summoned to my mother's room. Jo was with her, and Robin, too, but Edward Champernowne had gone to join his sister. All three of them wore an air of well-being.

My mother drew me to her and kissed me fondly and said at once that great happiness was in store for me, that Edward Champernowne had asked for my hand in marriage, that she and my brothers had accepted, the formalities had been settled, my portion agreed to with Jo adding to it most handsomely, and nothing remained now but to determine upon the date. I believe I stared at them all a moment, stupefied, and then broke out wildly in a torrent of protestation, declaring that I would not wed him, that I would wed no man who was not of my own choice, and that sooner than do it I would throw myself from the roof. In vain my mother argued with me; in vain Jo enthused upon the virtues of young Champernowne, of his steadiness, of his noble bearing, and of how my conduct had been such, a few months back, that it was amazing he should have asked for my hand at all. "You have come to the age, Honor," he said, "when we believe marriage to be the only means to settle you, and in this matter Mother and myself are the best judges." I shook my head; I dug my nails into my hands.

"I tell you I will not marry him," I said.

Robin had not taken part in the conversation; he sat a space away, but now he rose and stood beside me.

"I told you, Jo, it would be little use to drive Honor if she had not the inclination," he said. "Give her time to accustom herself to the project, and she will think better of it."

"Edward Champernowne might think better of it too," replied Jo.

"It were best to settle it now while he is here," said my mother.

I looked at their worried, indecisive faces—for they all loved me well and were distressed at my obduracy—but "No" I told them, "I would sooner die," and I flounced from the room in feverish anger and, going to my chamber, thrust the bolt through the door. To my imagination, strained and overwrought, it seemed to me that my brother and my mother had become the wicked parents in a fairy tale and I the luckless princess whom they were bent on wedding to an ogre, though I believe the inoffensive Edward Champernowne would not have dared lay a finger upon me. I waited till the whole brood of them were abed, and then, changing my gown and wrapping a cloak about me, I stole from the house. For I was bent upon a harebrained scheme, which was no less than walking through the night to Killigarth, and so to Richard. The thunder had passed, and the night was clear enough, and I set off with beating heart down the roadway to the river, which I forded a mile or so below Lanrest. Then I struck westward on the road to Pelynt, but the way was rough and crossed with intersecting lanes, and my mind misgave me for the fool I was, for without star lore I had no knowledge of direction. I was ill used to walking any distance, and my shoes were thin. The night seemed endless and the road interminable, and the sounds and murmurs of the countryside filled me with apprehension, though I pretended to myself I did not care. Dawn found me stranded by another stream and encompassed about by woods; and, weary and bedraggled, I climbed a farther hill and saw at last my first glimpse of the sea and the hump of Looe Island away to the eastward.

I knew then that some inner sense had led me to the coast, and I was not walking north as I had feared, but the curl of smoke through the trees and the sound of barking dogs warned me that I was trespassing, and I had no wish to be caught by keepers.

About six o'clock I met a ploughman tramping along the highway, who stared at me amazed and took me for a witch, for I saw him cross his fingers and spit when I had passed, but he pointed out the lane that led to Killigarth. The sun was high now above the sea, and the fishing vessels strung out in a line in Talland Bay. I saw the tall chimneys of the house of Killigarth, and once again my heart misgave me for the sorry figure I should make before Richard. If he were there alone it would not matter, but what if Bevil were at home, and Grace his wife, and a whole tribe of Grenviles whom I did not know? I came to the house then like a thief and stood before the windows, uncertain what to do. It wore the brisk air of early morning. Servants were astir. I heard a clatter in the kitchens and the murmur of voices, and I could smell the fatty smell of bacon and smoky ham. Windows were open to the sun, and the sound of laughter came, and men talking.

I wished with all my heart that I were back in my bedchamber in Lanrest, but there was no returning. I pulled the bell and heard the clanging echo through the house. Then I drew back as a servant came into the hall. He wore the Grenvile livery and had a stern, forbidding air.

"What do you want?" he asked of me.

"I wish to see Sir Richard," I said.

"Sir Richard and the rest of the gentlemen are at breakfast," he answered. "Away with you now, he won't be troubled with you."

The door of the dining room was open, and I heard more sound of talk and laughter, and Richard's voice topping the rest.

"I must see Sir Richard," I insisted, desperate now and near to tears, and then, as the fellow was about to lay his hands upon me and thrust me from the door, Richard himself came out into the hall. He was laughing, calling something over his shoulder to the gentlemen within. He was eating still and had a napkin in his hand.

"Richard," I called, "Richard, it is I, Honor." And he came forward, amazement on his face, and "What the devil——" he began; then, cursing his servant to be gone, who vanished instantly, he drew me into a little anteroom beside the hall.

"What is it, what is the matter?" he said swiftly, and I, weak and utterly worn out, fell into his arms and wept upon his shoulder.

"Softly, my little love, be easy then," he murmured, and held me close and stroked my hair, until I was calm enough to tell my story.

"They want to marry me to Edward Champernowne," I stammered—how foolish it sounded to be blurted thus—"and I have told them I will not do so, and I have wandered all night on the roads to tell you of it."

I felt him shake with laughter as he had done that first evening weeks ago when I had sickened of the swan.

"Is that all?" he asked. "And did you tramp ten miles or more to tell me that? Oh, Honor, my little love, my dear."

I looked up at him, bewildered that he found so serious a matter food for laughter. "What am I to do then?" I said.

"Why, tell them to go to the devil, of course," he answered, "and if you dare not say it, then I will say it for you. Come in to breakfast."

I tugged at his hand in consternation, for if the ploughman had taken me for a witch, and the servants for a beggar, God only knew what his friends would say to me. He would not listen to my protests, but dragged me into the dining room where the gentlemen were breakfasting, and there was I, with my bedraggled gown and cloak and my torn slippers, faced with Ranald Mohun and young Trelawney, Tom Treffry and Jonathan Rashleigh, and some half dozen others whom I did not know.

"This is Honor Harris of Lanrest," said Richard. "I think you gentlemen are possibly acquainted with her," and they one and all stood up and bowed to me, astonishment and embarrassment written plain upon their faces. "She has run away from home," said Richard, in no way put out by the situation. "Would you credit it, Tom? They want to marry her to Edward Champernowne."

"Indeed," replied Tom Treffry, quite at a loss, and he bent to stroke his dog's ear to hide his confusion.

"Will you have some bacon, Honor?" said Richard, proffering me a platter heaped with fatty pork, but I was too tired and faint to desire anything more than to be taken upstairs and put to rest.

Then Jonathan Rashleigh, a man of family and older than Richard and the others, said quietly, "Mistress Honor would prefer to withdraw, I fancy. I would summon one of your serving-women, Richard."

"Damn it, this is a bachelor household," answered Richard, his mouth crammed with bacon; "there isn't a woman in the place."

I heard a snort from Ranald Mohun, who put a handkerchief to his face, and I saw also the baleful eye that Richard cast upon him, and then somehow they one and all made their excuses and got themselves from the room, and we were alone at last.

"I was a fool to come," I said. "Now I have disgraced you before all your friends."

"I was disgraced long since," he said, pulling himself another tankard of ale, "but it was well you came after breakfast rather than before."

"Why so?" I asked.

He smiled and drew a document from his breast.

"I have sold Killigarth, and also the lands I hold in Tywardreath," he answered. "Rashleigh gave me a fair price for them. Had you blundered in sooner he might have stayed his hand."

"Will the money pay your debts?" I said.

He laughed derisively. "A drop in the ocean," he said, "but it will suffice for a week or so, until we can borrow elsewhere."

"Why 'we'?" I enquired.

"Well, we shall be together," he answered. "You do not think I am going to permit this ridiculous match with Edward Champernowne?"

He wiped his mouth and pushed aside his plate, as though he had not a care in the world. He held out his arms to me and I went to him.

"Dear love," I said, feeling in sudden very old and very wise, "you have told me often that you must marry an heiress or you could not live."

"I should have no wish to live if you were wedded to another man," he answered.

Some little time was wasted while assuring me of this.

"But, Richard," I said presently, "if I wed you instead of Edward Champernowne my brother may refuse his sanction."

"I'll fight him if he does."

"We shall be penniless," I protested.

"Not if I know it," he said. "I have several relatives as yet unfleeced. Mrs. Abbot, my old aunt Katherine up at Hartland, she has a thousand pounds or so she does not want."

"But we cannot live thus all our lives," I said.

"I have never lived any way else," he answered.

I thought of the formalities and deeds that went with marriage, the lawyers and the documents.

"I am the youngest daughter, Richard," I said, hesitating. "You must bear in mind that my portion will be very small."

At this he shouted with laughter and, lifting me in his arms, carried me from the room.

"It's your person I have designs upon," he said. "Damn your portion."

5

O WILD BETROTHAL, startling and swift, decided on an instant without rhyme or reason, and all objections swept aside like a forest in a fire! My mother helpless before the onslaught, my brothers powerless to obstruct. The Champernownes, offended, withdrew to Radford, and Jo, washing his hands of me, went with them. His wife would not receive me now, having refused her brother, and I was led to understand that the scandal of my conduct had spread through the whole of Devon.

Bridget's husband come posting down from Holbeton, and John Pollexefen from Maddercombe, and all the West, it seemed, said I had eloped with Richard Grenvile and was to wed him now through dire necessity.

He had shamed me in a room at Plymouth—he had carried me by force to Killigarth—I had lived there as his mistress for three months—all these and other tales were spread abroad, and Richard and I, in the gladness of our hearts, did nought but laugh at them.

He was for taking horse to London and giving me refuge with the Duke of Buckingham, who would, he declared, eat out of his hand and give me a dowery into the bargain, but at this moment of folly came his brother Bevil riding to Lanrest, and with his usual grace and courtesy insisted that I should go to Stowe and be married from the Grenvile home. Bevil brought law and order into chaos; his approval lent some smacking of decency to the whole proceeding, a quality which had been lacking hitherto, and within a few days of his taking charge my mother and I were safely housed at Stowe, where Kit had gone as a bridegroom nearly eight years before. I was too much in love by then to care a whit for anyone, and like someone who has feasted too wisely and too well, I swam through the great rooms at Stowe aglow with confidence, smiling at old Sir Bernard, bowing to all his kinsmen, in no more awe of the grandeur about me than I had been of the familiar dusty corners in Lanrest. I have small recollection now of what I did or whom I saw—save that there were Grenviles everywhere and all of them auburn-haired as Bridget had once told me—but I remember pacing up and down the great gardens while Sir Bernard discoursed solemnly upon the troubles brewing between His Majesty and Parliament, and I remember, too, standing for hours in a chamber, that of the Lady Grace, Bevil's wife, while her woman pinned my wedding gown upon me, and gathered it, and tuckered it, and pinned it yet again, she and my mother giving advice, while it seemed a heap of children played about the floor.

Richard was not much with me. I belonged to the women, he said, during these last days; we would have enough of each other by and by. These last days—what world of prophecy.

Nothing then remains out of the fog of recollection but that final afternoon in May, and the sun that came and went behind the clouds, and a high wind blowing. I can see now the guests assembled on the lawns, and how we all proceeded to the falconry, for the afternoon of sport was to precede a banquet in the evening.

There were the goshawks on their perches, preening their feathers, stretching their wings, the tamer of them permitting our approach, and further removed, solitary upon their blocks in the sand, their larger brethren, the wild-eyed peregrines.

The falconers came to leash and jess the hawks, and hood them ready for the chase, and as they did this the stablemen brought the horses for us, and the dogs that were to flush the game yelped and pranced about their heels. Richard mounted me upon the little chestnut mare that was to be mine hereafter, and as he turned to speak a moment to his falconer about the hooding of his bird I looked over my shoulder and saw a conclave of horsemen gathered about the gate to welcome a new arrival. "What now?" said Richard, and the falconer, shading his eyes from the sun, turned to his master with a smile.

"It's Mrs. Denys," he said, "from Orley Court. Now you can match your red hawk with her tiercel."

Richard looked up at me and smiled. "So it has happened after all," he said, "and Gartred has chose to visit us."

They were riding down the path towards us, and I wondered how she would seem to me, my enemy of childhood, to whom in so strange a fashion I was to be related once again. No word had come from her, no message of congratulation, but her natural curiosity had won her in the end.

"Greetings, sister," called Richard, the old sardonic mockery in his voice. "So you have come to dance at my wedding after all."

"Perhaps," she answered. "I have not yet decided. Two of the children are not well at home." She rode abreast of me, that slow smile that I remembered on her face. "How are you, Honor?"

"Well enough," I answered.

"I never thought to see you become a Grenvile."

"Nor I either."

"The ways of Providence are strange indeed. . . . You have not met my husband."

I bowed to the stranger at her side, a big, bluff, hearty man, a good deal older than herself. So this was the Antony Denys who had caused poor Kit so much anguish before he died. Maybe it was his weight that had won her.

"Where do we ride?" she asked, turning from me to Richard.

"In the open country, towards the shore," he answered.

She glanced at the falcon on his wrist. "A red hawk," she said, one eyebrow lifted, "not in her full plumage. Do you think to make anything of her?"

"She has taken kite and bustard, and I propose to put her to a heron today if we can flush one."

Gartred smiled. "A red hawk at a heron," she mocked. "You will see her check at a magpie and nothing larger."

"Will you match her with your tiercel?"

"My tiercel will destroy her, and the heron afterwards."

"That is a matter of opinion."

They watched each other like duellists about to strike, and I remembered how Richard had told me they had fought with each other from the cradle. I had my first shadow of misgiving that the day would turn in some way to disaster. For a moment I wondered whether I would plead fatigue and stay behind. I rode for pleasure, not for slaughter, and hawking was never my favourite pastime.

Gartred must have observed my hesitation, for she laughed and said, "Your bride loses her courage. The pace will be too strong for her."

"What?" said Richard, his face falling. "You are coming, aren't you?"

"Why, yes," I said swiftly. "I will see you kill your heron."

We rode out to the open country, with the wind blowing in our faces, and the sound of the Atlantic coming to us as the long surf rollers spilt themselves with a roar onto the shore far below.

At first the sport was poor, for no quarry larger than a woodcock was flushed, and to this was flown the goshawks, who clutch their prey between their claws and do not kill outright like the large-winged peregrines.

Richard's falcon and Gartred's tiercel were still hooded and not slipped, for we were not yet come upon the herons' feeding ground.

My little mare pawed restlessly at the ground, for up to the present we had had no run, and the pace was slow. Hard by a little copse the falconers flushed three magpies, and a cast of goshawks were flown at them, but the cunning magpies, making up for the lack of wing power by shiftiness, scuttled from hedge to hedge, and after some twenty minutes or so of hovering by the hawks, and shouting and driving by the falconers, only one magpie was taken.

"Come, this is poor indeed," said Gartred scornfully. "Can we find no better quarry, and so let fly the falcons?"

Richard shaded his eyes from the sun and looked towards the west. A long strip of moorland lay before us, rough and uneven, and at the far end of it a narrow, soggy marsh, where the duck would fly to feed in stormy weather, and at all seasons of the year, so Richard told me, the sea birds came, curlews, and gulls, and herons.

There was no bird as yet on passage through the sky, save a small lark high above our heads, and the marsh, where the herons might be found, was still two miles away.

"I'll match my horse to yours, and my red hawk to your tiercel," said Richard suddenly, and even as he spoke he let fly the hood of his falcon and slipped her, putting spurs to his horse upon the gesture. Within ten seconds Gartred had followed suit, her grey-winged peregrine soaring into the sun, and she and Richard were galloping across the moors towards the marsh, with the two hawks like black specks in the sky above them. My mare, excited by the clattering hoofs of her companions, took charge of me, nigh pulling my arms out of their sockets, and she raced like a mad thing in pursuit of the horses ahead of us, the yelping of the dogs and the cries of the falconers whipping her speed. My last ride . . . The sun in my eyes, the wind in my face, the movement of the mare beneath me, the thunder of her hoofs, the scent of the golden gorse, the sound of the sea . . . Unforgettable, unforgotten, deep in my soul for all time. I could see Richard and Gartred racing neck to neck, flinging insults at each other as they rode, and in the sky the male and female falcons pitched and hovered, when suddenly away from the marsh ahead of us rose a heron, his great grey wings unfolding, his legs trailing. I heard a shout from Richard, and an answering cry from Gartred, and in an instant it seemed the hawks had seen their quarry, for they both began to circle above the heron, climbing higher and still higher, swinging out in rings until they were like black dots against the sun. The watchful heron, rising, too, but in a narrower circle, turned down-wind, his queer ungainly body strangely light and supple, and like a flash the first hawk dived to him—whether it was Richard's young falcon or Gartred's tiercel I could not tell—and missed the heron by a hair's breadth. At once, recovering himself, he began to soar again, in ever higher circles, to recover his lost pitch, and the second hawk swooped, missing in like manner.

I tried to rein in my mare but could not stop her, and now Gartred and Richard had turned eastward, too, following the course of the heron, and we were galloping three abreast, the ground ever rising towards a circle of stones in the midst of the moor.

"Beware the chasm," shouted Richard in my ear, pointing with his whip, but he was past me like the wind and I could not call to him.

The heron was now direct above my head, and the falcon lost to view, and I heard Gartred shout in triumph, "They bind—they bind—my tiercel has her," and I saw silhouetted against the sun one of the falcons locked against the heron and the two come swinging down to earth not twenty yards ahead.

I tried to swerve, but the mare had the mastery, and I shouted to Gartred as she passed me, "Which way the chasm?" but she did not answer me. On we flew towards the circle of stones, the sun blinding my eyes, and out of the darkening sky fell the dying heron and the blood-bespattered falcon, straight into the yawning crevice that opened out before me. I heard Richard shout and a thousand voices singing in my ears as I fell.

It was thus, then, that I, Honor Harris of Lanrest, became a cripple, losing all power in my legs from that day forward until this day on which I write, so that for some twenty-five years now I have been upon my back, or upright in a chair, never walking more or feeling the ground beneath my feet. If anyone, therefore, thinks that a cripple makes an indifferent heroine to a tale, now is the time to close these pages and desist from reading. For you will never see me wed to the man I love, nor become the mother of his children. But you will learn how that love never faltered, for all its strange vicissitudes, becoming to both of us, in later years, more deep and tender than if we had been wed, and you will learn also how, for all my helplessness, I took the leading part in the drama that unfolded, my very immobility sharpening my senses, quickening my perception, and chance itself forcing me to my role of judge and witness. The play goes on then—what you have just read is but the prologue.

6

IT IS NOT my purpose to survey, in these after years, the suffering, bodily and mental, that I underwent during those early months when my life seemed finished. They would make poor reading. And I myself have no inclination to drag from the depths of my being a bitterness that is best forgotten. It is enough to say that they feared at first for my brain, and I lived for many weeks in a state of darkness. As little by little clarity returned and I was able to understand the full significance of my physical state, I asked for Richard; and I learnt that after having waited in vain for some sign from me, some thread of hope from the doctors that I might recover, he had been persuaded by his brother Bevil to rejoin his regiment. This was for the best. It was impossible for him to remain inactive. The assassination at Portsmouth of his friend the Duke of Buckingham was an added horror, and he set sail for France with the rest of the expedition in that final halfhearted attack on La Rochelle. By the time he returned I was home again at Lanrest and had sufficient strength of will to make my decision for the future. This was never to see Richard again. I wrote him first a letter, which he disregarded, riding down from London expressly to see me. I would not see him. He endeavoured to force his way into my room, but my brothers barred the way. It was only when the doctors told him that his presence could but injure me further that he realised the finality of all bonds between us. He rode away without a word. I received from him one last letter, wild, bitter, reproachful—then silence.

In November of that year he married Lady Howard of Fitzford, a rich widow, three times wed already, and four years older than himself. The news came to me indirectly, an incautious word let slip from Matty and at once confusedly covered, and I asked my mother the truth. She had wished to hide it from me, fearing a relapse, and I think my calm acceptance of the fact baffled her understanding.

It was hard for her, and for the rest of them, to realise that I looked upon myself now as a different being. The Honor that was had died as surely as the heron had that afternoon in May, when the falcon slew him.

That she would live forever in her lover's heart was possible, no doubt, and a lovely fantasy, but the Richard that I knew and loved was made of flesh and blood; he had to endure, even as I had.

I remember smiling as I lay upon my bed, to think that after all he had found his heiress, and such a notorious one at that. I only hoped that her experience would make him happy, and her wealth ensure him some security.

Meanwhile, I had to school myself to a new way of living and a day-by-day immobility. The mind must atone for the body's helplessness. Percy returned from Oxford about this time, bringing his books of learning, and with his aid I set myself the task of learning Greek and Latin. He made an indifferent though a kindly tutor, and I had not the heart to keep him long from his dogs and his horses, but at least he set me on the road to reading, and I made good progress.

My family were all most good and tender. My sisters and their children, tearful and strung with pity as they were at first, soon became easy in my presence, when I laughed and chatted with them, and little by little I—the hitherto spoilt darling— became the guide and mediator in their affairs, and their problems would be brought to me to solve. I am speaking now of years and not of months, for all this did not happen in a day. Matty, my little maid, became from the first moment my untiring slave and bondswoman. It was she who learnt to read the signs of fatigue about my eyes and would hustle my visitors from my room. It was she who attended to my wants, to my feeding and my washing, though after some little while I learnt to do this for myself; and after three years, I think it was, my back had so far strengthened that I was able to sit upright and move my body.

I was helpless, though, in my legs, and during the autumn and the winter months, when the damp settled in the walls of the house, I would feel it also in my bones, causing me great pain at times, and then I would be hard put to it to keep to the standard of behaviour I had set myself. Self-pity, that most insidious of poisons, would filter into my veins and the black devils fill my mind, and then it was that Matty would stand like a sentinel at the door and bar the way to all intruders. Poor Matty, I cursed her often enough when the dark moods had me in thrall, but she bore with me unflinching.

It was Robin, my dear, good Robin and most constant companion, who first had the thought of making me my chair, and this chair that was to propel me from room to room became his pet invention. He took some months in the designing of it, and when it was built and I was carried to it and could sit up straight and move the rolling wheels without assistance, his joy, I think, was even greater than my own.

It made all the difference to my daily life, and in that summer I could even venture to the garden and propel myself a little distance, up and down before the house, winning some measure of independence.

In '32 we had another wedding in the family. My sister Mary, whom we had long teased for her devoutness and gentle, sober ways, accepted the offer of Jonathan Rashleigh of Menabilly, who had lost his first wife in childbed the year before and was left with a growing family upon his hands. It was a most suitable match in all respects, Jonathan being then some forty years of age and Mary thirty-two. She was married from Lanrest, and with their father to the wedding came his three children, Alice, Elizabeth, and John, whom later I was to come to know so well, but even now—as shy and diffident children—they won my affection.

To the wedding also came Bevil Grenvile, close friend to Jonathan as he was to all of us, and it was when the celebrating was over, and Mary departed to her new home the other side of Fowey, that I had a chance to speak with him alone. We spoke for a few moments about his own children and his life at Stowe, and then I asked him, not without some tremulation, for all my calm assurance, how Richard did.

For a moment he did not answer, and, glancing at him, I saw his brow was troubled.

"I had not wished to speak of it," he said at length, "but since you ask me—all has gone very ill with him, Honor, ever since his marriage."

Some devil of satisfaction rose in my breast, which I could not crush, and:
"How so?" I asked. "Has he not a son?"

For I had heard that a boy was born to them a year or so before, on May 16 to be exact, which date, ironically enough, was the same as that on which I had been crippled.

A new life for the one that is wasted, I had thought at the time, when I was told of it, and like a spoilt child that has learnt no wisdom after all, I remember crying all night upon my pillow, thinking of the boy who, but for mischance and the workings of destiny, might have been mine. That was a day, if I recollect aright, when Matty kept guard at my door, and I made picture after picture in my mind of Richard's wife propped upon pillows with a baby in her arms, and Richard smiling beside her. The fantasy was one which, for all my disciplined indifference, I found most damnable. But to return to Bevil.

"Yes," he answered, "it is true he has a son, and a daughter, too, but whether Richard sees them or not I cannot say. The truth is he has quarrelled with his wife, treated her in a barbarous fashion, even laid violent hands upon her, so she says, and she is now petitioning for a divorce against him. Furthermore, he slandered the Earl of Suffolk, his wife's kinsman, who brought an action against him in the Star Chamber and won the case, and Richard, refusing to pay the fine—and in truth he could not, possessing not a penny—is likely to be cast into the Fleet Prison for debt at any moment."

Oh God, I thought, what a contrast to the life we would have made together. Or was I wrong, and was this symbolic of what might have been?

"He was always violent-natured, even as a lad," continued Bevil. "You knew so little of him, Honor; alas, three months of happy wooing is no time in which to judge a man."

I could not answer this, for reason was on his side. But I thought of the spring days, lost to me forever, and the apple blossoms in the orchard. No maid could have had more tender or more intuitive a lover.

"How was Richard violent?" I asked. "Irresponsible and wild, perhaps, but nothing worse. His wife must have provoked him."

"As to that, I know nothing," answered Bevil. "But I can well believe it. She is a woman of some malice and of doubtful morals. She was a close friend to Gartred—perhaps you did not know—and it was when she was visiting at Orley Court that the match was made between them. Richard—as no one knows better than yourself—could not have been his best self at that time."

I said nothing, feeling behind Bevil's gentle manner some faint reproach, unconscious though it was.

"The truth is," said Bevil, "that Richard married Mary Howard for her money, but, once wed, found he had no control over her purse or her property, the whole being in the power of trustees who act solely in her interest."

"Then he is no whit better off than he was before?" I asked.

"Rather worse, if anything," replied Bevil. "For the Star Chamber will not release him from his debt for slander, and I have too many claims upon me at this time to help him either."

It was a sorry picture that he painted, and though to my jealous fancy more preferable than the idyllic scene of family bliss that I had in imagination conjured, it was no consolation to learn of his distress. That Richard should ill-use his wife because he could not trifle with her property was an ugly fact to face, but, having some inkling of his worser self, I guessed this to be true. He had married her without love and in much bitterness of heart, and she, suspecting his motive, had taken care to disappoint him. What a rock of mutual trust on which to build a lasting union! I held to my resolve, though, and sent him no word of sympathy or understanding. Nor was it my own pride and self-pity that kept me from it, but a firm belief that such a course was wisest. He must lead his own life, in which I had no further part.

He remained, we heard later, for many months in prison, and then in the autumn of the following year he left England for the continent, where he saw service with the King of Sweden.

How much I thought of him and yearned for him, during those intervening years, does not matter to this story. I was weakest during the long watches of the night, when my body pained me. During the day I drilled my feelings to obedience, and what with my progress in my studies—I was by way of becoming a fair Greek scholar—and my interest in the lives of my brothers and sisters, the days and the seasons passed with some fair measure of content.

Time heals all wounds, say the complacent, but I think it is not so much time that does it, but determination of the spirit. And the spirit can often turn to devil in the darkness.

Five, ten, fifteen years; a large slice out of a woman's life, and a man's too, for that matter. We change from the awakening questing creatures we were once, afire with wonder, and expectancy, and doubt, to persons of opinion and authority, our habits formed, our characters moulded in a pattern.

I was a maid, and a rebellious, disorderly one at that, when I was first crippled; but in the year of '42, when the war that was to alter all our lives broke forth, I was a woman of some two and thirty years, the "good aunt Honor" to my numerous nephews and nieces, and a figure of some importance to the family at large.

A person who is forever chair-bound or bedridden can become a tyrant if she so desires, and though I never sought to play the despot, I came to be, after my mother died, the one who made decisions, whose authority was asked on all occasions, and in some strange fashion it seemed that a legendary quality was wove about my personality, as though my physical helplessness must give me greater wisdom.

I accepted the homage with my tongue in my cheek but was careful not to destroy the fond illusion. The young people liked me, I think, because they knew me to be a rebel still, and when there was strife within the family I was sure to take their part. Cynical on the surface, I was an incurable romantic underneath, and if there were messages to be given, or meetings to arrange, or secrets to be whispered, my chamber at Lanrest would become trysting place, rendezvous, and confessional in turn. Mary's stepchildren, the Rashleighs, were my constant visitors, and I found myself involved in many a youthful squabble, defending their escapades with a ready tongue, and soon acting go-between to their love affairs. Jonathan, my brother-in-law, was a good, just man, but stern; a firm believer in the settled marriage as against the impulsive prompting of the heart.

No doubt he was right, but there was something distasteful to my mind in the bargaining between parents and the counting of every farthing, so that when Alice, his eldest daughter, turned thin and pale for languishing after that young rake Peter Courtney—the parents disputing for months whether they should wed or no—I had them both to Lanrest and bade them be happy while the chance was theirs, and no one was a whit the wiser.

They married in due course, and although it ended in separation (for this I blame the war), at least they had some early happiness together, for which I hold myself responsible.

My godchild Joan was another of my victims. She was, it may be remembered, the child of my sister Cecilia, and some ten years my junior. When John Rashleigh, Mary's stepson, came down from Oxford to visit us, he found Joan at my bedside, and I soon guessed which way the wind was blowing. I had half a thought of sending them to the apple tree, but some inner sentimentality forbade me, and I suggested the bluebell wood instead. They were betrothed within a week and married before the bluebells had faded, and not even Jonathan Rashleigh could find fault with the marriage settlement.

But the war years were upon us before we were aware, and Jonathan, like all the county gentlemen, my brothers included, had more anxious problems put before him.

Trouble had been brewing for a long while now, and we in Cornwall were much divided in opinion, some holding that His Majesty was justified in passing what laws he pleased (though one and all grumbled at the taxes), and others holding to it that

Parliament was right in opposing any measure that smacked of despotism. How often I heard my brothers argue the point with Jack Trelawney, Ranald Mohun, Dick Buller, and other of our neighbours—my brothers holding firmly for the King, and Jo already in a position of authority, as his business was to superintend the defences of the coast—and as the months passed tempers became shorter and friendships grew colder, an unpleasing spirit of distrust walking abroad.

Civil war was talked of openly, and each gentleman in the county began to look to his weapons, his servants, and his horses, so that he could make some contribution to the cause he favoured when the moment came. The women, too, were not idle, many—like Cecilia at Maddercombe—tearing strips of bed linen into bandages and packing their storerooms with preserves for fear of siege. Arguments were fiercer then, I do believe, than later when the fighting was amongst us. Friends who had supped with us the week before became of a sudden suspect, and long-forgotten scandals were brought forth to blacken their names, merely because of the present opposition to their views.

The whole business made me sick at heart, and this whipping up of tempers between neighbours who for generations had lived at peace seemed a policy of the devil. I hated to hear Robin, my dearly loved brother with his tenderness for dogs and horses, slander Dick Buller for upholding Parliament, vowing he took bribes and made spies of his own servants, when Dick and he had gone hawking together not six months before. While Rob Bennett, another of our neighbours and a friend of Buller's, began to spread damning rumours in return against my brother-in-law Jonathan Rashleigh, saying Jonathan's father and elder brother, who had died very suddenly within a week of each other many years before, during the smallpox scourge, had not succumbed to the disease at all but had been poisoned. These tales showed how in a few months we had changed from neighbours into wolves at one another's throats.

At the first open rupture between His Majesty and Parliament in '42, my brothers Jo and Robin and most of our friends, including Jonathan Rashleigh, his son-in-law Peter Courtney, the Trelawneys, the Arundells, and of course Bevil Grenvile, declared for the King. There was an end at once to family life and any settled way of living. Robin went off to York to join His Majesty's Army, taking Peter Courtney with him, and they were both given command of a company almost immediately. Peter, showing much dash and courage in his first action, was knighted on the field.

My brother Jo and my brother-in-law Jonathan went about the county raising money, troops, and ammunition for the royal cause, the first no easy matter, Cornwall being a poor county at the best of times, and lately the taxes had well-nigh broken us; but many families, with little ready money to spare, gave their plate to be melted down to silver, a loyal if wasteful gesture which I had many qualms about before following it myself, but in the end was obliged to do so, as Jonathan Rashleigh was collector for the district. My attitude to the war was somewhat cynical, holding no belief in great causes; and, living alone now at Lanrest with only Matty and the servants to tend me, I felt myself curiously detached.

The successes of the first year did not go to my head, as they did to the rest of my family, for I could not believe, which they were inclined to do, that the Parliament would give way so easily. For they had many powerful men at their command, and much money—all the rich merchants of London being strongly in their favour— besides which I had an uneasy suspicion, which I kept to myself, that their army was incomparably the better of the two. God knows our leaders wanted nothing in courage, but they lacked experience; equipment, too, was poor, and discipline non-existent in the ranks. By the autumn the war was getting rather too close for comfort, and the two armies were ranged east and west along the Tamar. I had an uneasy Christmas, and in the third week of January I learnt that the worst had happened and the enemy had crossed the Tamar into Cornwall. I was at breakfast when the news was brought us, and by none other than Peter Courtney, who had ridden hot-foot from Bodmin to warn me that the opposing army was even now on the road to Liskeard, he with his regiment, under the command of Sir Ralph Hopton, being drawn up to oppose them, and Hopton at the moment holding a council of war at Boconnoc, only a few miles distant.

"With any luck," he told us, "the fighting will not touch you here at Lanrest, but will be between Liskeard and Lostwithiel. If we can break them now and drive them out of Cornwall the war will be as good as won."

He looked handsome, flushed and excited, his dark curls falling about his face.

"I have no time to go to Menabilly," he told me. "Should I fall in battle, will you tell Alice that I love her well?"

He was gone like a flash, and I and Matty, with the two elderly menservants and three lads, all that were left to us, were alone, unarmed and unprepared. There was nothing to do but get the cattle and the sheep in from pasture and secure them in the farmstead, and likewise bolt and bar ourselves within the house. Then we waited, all gathered round the fireside in my chamber upstairs, and once or twice, opening the casement, we thought we heard the sound of cannon shot, dull and intermittent, sounding strangely distant in the cold clear air of January. Somewhere about three in the afternoon one of the farm lads came running to the house and hammered loud upon the entrance door.

"The enemy are routed," he called excitedly. "The whole pack of them scattering like whipped dogs along the road to Liskeard. There's been a great battle fought today on Braddock Down."

More stragglers appeared, who had taken refuge in the hedges, and one and all told the same story, that the King's men had won a victory, fighting like furies and taking nigh a thousand prisoners.

Knowing that rumour was a lying jade, I bade the household bide awhile and keep the doors fast until the story should be probed, but before nightfall we knew the victory was certain, for Robin himself came riding home to cheer us, covered in dust, with a bloodstained bandage on his arm, and with him the Trelawney brothers and Ranald Mohun. They were all of them laughing and triumphant, for the two Parliament divisions had fled in dire disorder straight for Saltash and would never, said Jack Trelawney, show their faces more this side of Tamar.

"And this fellow," he said, clapping Robin on the shoulder, "rode into battle with a hawk on his wrist, which he let fly at Ruthin's musketeers, and by God, the bird so startled them that the lot of them shot wide and started taking to their legs before they'd spent their powder."

"It was a wager I had with Peter," smiled Robin, "which, if I lost, I'd forfeit my spurs and be godfather to his next baby."

They rocked with laughter, caring not a whit for the spilt blood and the torn bodies they had trampled, and they sat down, all of them, and drank great jugs of ale, wiping the sweat from their foreheads and discussing every move of the battle they had won, like gamesters after a cockfight.

Bevil Grenvile had been the hero of the day in this, his first engagement, and they described to us how he led the Cornish foot down one hill and up another in so fierce a charge that the enemy could not withstand them.

"You should have seen him, Honor," said Robin, "with his servants and his tenants drawn up in solemn prayer before him, his sword in his hand, his dear, honest face lifted to the sky, and they all clad in the blue-and-silver livery, as if it were high holiday. And down the hill they followed him, shouting, 'A Grenvile, a Grenvile,' with his servant Tony Paine waving his standard with the griffin's head upon it. My God, I tell you, it made me proud to be a Cornishman."

"It's in his blood," said Jack Trelawney. "Here's Bevil been a country squire for all his life, and you put a weapon in his hand and he turns tiger. The Grenviles are all alike at heart."

"I wish to heaven," said Ranald Mohun, "that Richard Grenvile would return from slaughtering the savages in Ireland and come and join his brother."

There was a moment's awkward silence, while some of them remembered the past and recollected my presence in the room, and then Robin rose to his feet and said they must be riding back to Liskeard. Thus, in southeast Cornwall, war touched us for a brief space in '43 and so departed, and many of us who had not even smelt the battle talked very big of what we had heard and seen, while those who had taken part in it, like Robin, boasted that the summer would see the rebels in Parliament laying down their arms forever.

Alas, his optimism was foolish and ill judged. Victories we had indeed that year, throughout the West, as far as Bristol, with our own Cornishmen covering themselves with glory, but we lost, in that first summer, the flower of our Cornish manhood.

Sydney Godolphin, Jack Trevannion, Nick Slanning, Nick Kendall, one by one their faces come back to me as I review the past, and I remember the sinking feeling in the heart with which I would take up the list of the fallen that would be brought to me from Liskeard.

All of them were men of noble conduct and high principle, whom we could ill spare in the county and whose loss would make its mark upon the Army. The worse tragedy of the year, or so it seemed to us, was when Bevil Grenvile was slain at Lansdowne. Matty came running to my chamber with tears falling down her cheeks.

"They've killed Sir Bevil," she said.

Bevil, with his grace and courtesy, his sympathy and charm, was worth all the other Cornish leaders put together. I felt it as if he had been my own brother, but I was too stunned to weep for him.

"They say," said Matty, "that he was struck down by a pole-axe just as he and his men had won the day and the enemy were scattering. And big Tony Paine, his servant, mounted young Master Jack upon his father's horse, and the men followed the lad, all of them fighting mad with rage and grief to see their master slain."

Yes, I could picture it. Bevil killed on an instant, his head split in two by some damned useless rebel, while his boy Jack, barely fourteen, climbed onto Bevil's white charger that I knew so well, and with the tears smarting his eyes brandished a sword that was too big for him. And the men, with the blue-and-silver colours, following him down the hill, their hearts black with hatred for the enemy.

Oh, God, the Grenviles . . . There was some quality in the race, some white, undaunted spirit bred in their bones and surging through their blood, that put them, as Cornishmen and leaders, 'way ahead above the rest of us. So, outwardly triumphant and inwardly bleeding, we royalists watched the year draw to its close, and 1644—that fateful year for Cornwall—opened with His Majesty master of the West, but the large and powerful forces of the Parliament in great strength elsewhere and still unbeaten.

In the spring of the year a soldier of fortune returning from Ireland rode to London to receive payment for his services. He gave the gentlemen in Parliament to understand that in return for this he would join forces with them, and they, being pleased to receive so doughty a warrior amongst their ranks, gave him six hundred pounds and told him their plans for the spring campaign. He bowed and smiled—a dangerous sign had they but known it—and straightway set forth in a coach and six, with a host of troopers at his side and a banner carried in front of him, the banner being a great map of England and Wales on a crimson ground, with the words "England Bleeding" written across it in letters of gold. When this equipage arrived at Bagshot Heath the leader of it descended from his coach and, calling his troopers about him, suggested to them calmly that they should all now proceed to Oxford and fight for His Majesty and not against him.

The troopers, nothing loath, accepted, and the train proceeded on its way to Oxford, bearing with it a quantity of money, arms, and silver plate, bequeathed by Parliament, and all the minutes of the secret council that had just been held in London.

The name of this soldier of fortune, who had hoodwinked the Parliament in so scurrilous a fashion, was Richard Grenvile.

7

ONE DAY TOWARDS the end of April '44 Robin came over from Radford to see me, urging me to leave Lanrest and to take up residence, for a time at any rate, with our sister Mary Rashleigh at Menabilly. Robin was at that time commanding a regiment of foot, for he had been promoted colonel, under Sir John Digby, and was taking part in the long-drawn-out siege of Plymouth, which alone among the cities in the West still held out for Parliament.

"Jo and I are both agreed," said Robin, "that while the war continues you should not live here alone. It is not fit for any woman, let alone one as helpless as yourself. Deserters and stragglers are constantly abroad, robbing on the highway, and the thought of you here, with a few old men and Matty, is a constant disturbance to our peace of mind."

"There is nothing here to rob," I protested, "with the plate gone to the mint at Truro, and as to harm to my person—a crippled woman can give little satisfaction."

"That is not the point," said Robin. "It is impossible for Jo and I and Percy to do our duty, remembering all the while that you are here alone."

He argued for half a day before I reluctantly gave way, and then with an ill grace and much disturbance in my mind.

For some fifteen years—ever since I had been crippled—I had not left Lanrest, and to set forth now, to another person's house, even though that person was my own sister, filled me with misgiving.

Menabilly was already packed with Rashleigh relatives who had taken refuge there with Jonathan, seizing the war as an excuse, and I had no wish to add to their number. I had a great dislike for strangers, or conversing with anyone for the sake of courtesy; besides, I was set now in my ways, my days were my own, I followed a personal routine.

"You can live at Menabilly exactly as you do here at Lanrest," protested Robin, "save that you will be more comfortable. Matty will attend you; you will have your own apartment and your meals brought to you, if you do not wish to mix with the company. Set on the hill there, with the sea air blowing and the fine gardens for you to be wheeled about in, nothing could be more pleasant, to my opinion."

I disagreed, but, seeing his anxiety, I said no more; and within a week my few belongings were packed, the house was closed, and I was being carried in a litter to Menabilly.

How disturbing it was, and strange, to be on the road again. To pass through Lostwithiel, to see the people walking in the market place—the normal daily life of a community to which I had been so long absent, living in my own world at Lanrest. I felt oddly nervous and ill at ease as I peered through the curtains of my litter, as if I had been suddenly transplanted to a foreign land, where the language and the customs were unknown to me. My spirits rose as we climbed the long hill out of the town, and as we came abreast of the old redoubt at Castledore and I saw the great blue bay of Tywardreath spread out before me, I thought that maybe after all the change of place and scene might yet be bearable. John Rashleigh came riding along the highway to meet me, waving his hat, a broad smile on his thin, colourless face. He was just twenty-three, and the tragedy of his life was that he had not the health or strength to join the Army, but must bide at home and take orders from his father, being cursed from babyhood with a malignant form of ague that kept him shivering and helpless sometimes for days on end. He was a dear, lovable fellow, with a strong sense of duty, yet in great awe of his father; and his wife—my goddaughter Joan—with her merry eyes and mischievous prattle, made him a good foil. Riding with him now was his companion and second cousin, Frank Penrose, a young man of the same age as himself and who was employed by my brother-in-law as secretary and junior agent about the estate.

"All is prepared for you, Honor," smiled John as he rode beside my litter. "There are over twenty of us in the house at present, and the lot of them gathered in the courtyard to greet you. Tonight a dinner is to be given for your reception."

"Very well then," I answered, "you may tell these fellows to turn back again towards Lostwithiel."

At this he confessed that Joan had bade him tease me, and all the company were in the east wing of the house, and no one would worry me.

"My stepmother has put you," he said, "in the gatehouse, for she says you like much light and air, and the chamber there has a window looking both ways, over the outer courtyard to the west, and on to the inner court that surrounds the house. Thus you will see all that goes on about the place and have your own private peep show."

"It sounds," I answered, "like a garrison, with twenty people crammed within the walls."

"Nearly fifty altogether, counting the servants," laughed John, "but they sleep head to toe up in the attics."

My spirits sank again, and as we turned down from the highway into the park and I saw the great stone mansion at the end of it, flanked by high walls and outbuildings, I cursed myself for a fool for coming. We turned left into the outer court, surrounded by bake houses and larders and dairies, and, passing under the low archway of the gatehouse—my future dwelling—drew up within the inner court. The house was thus foursquare, built around the court, with a big clock tower or belfry at the northern end, and the entrance to the south. On the steps stood Mary now to greet me, and Alice Courtney, her eldest stepdaughter, and Joan, my godchild, both of them with their babies tugging at their skirts.

"Welcome, dearest Honor, to Menabilly," said Mary, her dear face puckered already in nervousness that I should hate it.

"The place is full of children, Honor; you must not mind," smiled Alice, who since her marriage to Peter had produced a baby every year.

"We are thinking out a plan to attach a rope of your own to the bell in the belfry," said Joan, "so that if the noise becomes too deafening you can pull it in warning and the household will be silenced."

"I am already established, then, as a dragon," I replied, "which is all to the good, for I mean to do as I please, as Robin may have warned you."

They carried me into the dark-panelled hall and, ignoring the long gallery which ran the whole length of the house and from which I could hear the ominous sound of voices, bore me up the broad staircase and along a passage to the western wing. I was, I must confess, immediately delighted with my apartment, which, though low-ceilinged, was wide and full of light. There were windows at each end, as John had said, the western one looking down over the archway to the outer court and the park beyond, and the eastern one facing the inner court. There was a small room to the right for Matty, and nothing had been forgotten for my comfort.

"You will be bothered by no one," said Mary. "The apartments beyond the dressing room belong to the Sawles—cousins of Jonathan's—who are very sober and retiring and will not worry you. The chamber to your left is never occupied."

They left me then, and with Matty's aid I undressed and got myself to bed, a good deal exhausted from my journey and glad to be alone.

The first few days passed in becoming accustomed to my new surroundings and settling down, like an old hound to a change of kennel.

My chamber was very pleasant, and I had no wish to leave it; also, I liked the chiming of the clock in the belfry, and once I told myself firmly that the quietude of

Lanrest must be forgotten, I came to listen to the comings and goings that were part of this big house, the bustle in the outer court, the footsteps passing under the arch below me, and also—though I would have denied the accusation—taking peep from my curtains at the windows opposite that, like mine, looked down upon the inner court and from which, now and again, people would lean, talking to others within. At intervals during the day the young people would come and converse with me and I would get a picture of the other inmates of the house, the two families of Sawle and Sparke, cousins to the Rashleighs, between whom passed, it seemed, perpetual bickering. When my brother-in-law Jonathan was from home it fell upon his son John to keep the peace, a heavy burden for his none too brawny shoulders, there being nothing so irritating to a young man as scolding spinsters and short-tempered elderly folk, while Mary, in a fever of unending housekeeping, was from dawn to dusk superintending dairy, store, and stillroom to keep her household fed. There were the grandchildren, too, to keep in order—Alice had three small daughters, and Joan a boy and girl, with another baby expected in the autumn—so one way and another Menabilly was a colony to itself, with a different family in every wing.

By the fifth day I was sufficiently at home and mistress of my nerves to leave my chamber and take to my chair, in which, with John propelling it and Joan and Alice on either side and the children running before, I made a tour of the domain. The gardens were extensive, surrounded by high walls and laid out to the eastward on rising ground, which, when the summit was reached, looked down over dense woodland across to farther hills and the highway that ran to Fowey, three miles distant. To the south lay pasture land and farm buildings and another pleasure garden, also walled, which had above it a high causeway leading to a summerhouse, fashioned like a tower with long leaded windows, commanding a fine view of the sea and the Gribbin Head.

"This," said Alice, "is my father's sanctum. Here he does his writing and accounts and, watching from the windows, can observe every ship that passes, bound for Fowey."

She tried the door of the summerhouse, but it was locked.

"We must ask him for the key when he returns," she said. "It would be just the place for Honor and her chair, when the wind is too fresh upon the causeway."

But John did not answer, and it occurred to him, perhaps, as it had to me, that his father might not wish me for companion. We made a circle of the grounds, returning by the steward's house and the bowling green, and so through the warren at the back to the outer court. I looked up at the gatehouse, already grown familiar with the vase of flowers set in my window, and noticed for the first time the barred window of the apartment next to mine and the great buttress that jutted out beside it.

"Why is that apartment never used?" I asked idly, and John waited for a moment or two before replying. "My father goes to it at times," he said. "He has furniture and valuables shut away."

"It was my uncle's room," said Alice, hesitating, with a glance at John. "He died very suddenly, you know, when we were children."

Their manner was diffident, and I did not press the question, remembering all at once Jonathan's elder brother, who had died within eight days of his old father, supposedly of smallpox, and about whom the Parliamentarian Rob Bennett had spread his poison rumour.

We then went below the archway, and I schooled myself to an introduction to the Rashleigh cousins. They were all assembled in the long gallery, a great dark-panelled chamber with windows looking out on to the court and also eastward to the gardens. There were fireplaces at either end, with the Sawles seated before the first and the Sparkes circled round the other, glaring at one another like animals in a cage, while in the centre of the gallery my sister Mary held the balance with her other stepdaughter Elizabeth, who was twice a Rashleigh, having married her first cousin a mile away at Coombe. John propelled me up the gallery and with fitting solemnity presented me to the rival factions.

There were but two Sawles to three Sparkes, and my godchild Joan had made a pun upon their names, saying that what the Sparkes possessed in flame the Sawles made up in soul. They were indeed a dour, forbidding couple, old Nick Sawle doubled up with rheumatics and almost as great a cripple as I was myself, while Temperance, his wife, came of Puritan stock, as her name suggested, and was never without a prayer book in her hand. She fell to prayer as soon as she observed me—God knows I had never had that effect before on man or woman—and when she had finished asked me if I knew that we were all of us, saving herself, damned to eternity. It was a startling greeting, but I replied cheerfully enough that this was something I had long suspected, whereupon she proceeded to tell me in a rapid whisper, with many spiteful glances at the farther fireplace, that anti-Christ was come into the world. I looked over my shoulder and saw the rounded shoulders of Will Sparke engaged in a harmless game of cribbage with his sisters.

"Providence has sent you amongst us to keep watch," hissed Temperance Sawle, and while she tore to shreds the characters of her cousins, piece by piece, her husband, Nick Sawle, droned in my left ear a full account of his rheumatic history, from the first twinge in his left toe some forty years ago to his present dire incapacity to lift either elbow above the perpendicular. Half stupefied, I made a signal to John, who propelled me to the Sparkes—two sisters and a brother—Will being one of those unfortunate high-voiced old fellows with a woman's mincing ways, whom I felt instinctively must be malformed beneath his clothes. His tongue seemed as two-edged as his cousin Temperance's, and he fell to jesting with me at once about the habits of the Sawles, as though I were an ally. Deborah made up in masculinity what her brother lacked, being heavily moustached and speaking from her shoes, while Gillian, the younger sister, was all coy prettiness in spite of her forty years, bedecked with rouge and ribbons and having a high thin laugh that pierced my eardrums like a sword.

"This dread war," said Deborah in bass tones, "has brought us all together," which seemed to me a hollow sentiment, as none of them were on speaking terms with one another, and while Gillian praised my looks and my gown I saw Will, out of the tail of my eye, make a cheating move upon the cribbage board.

The air seemed purer somehow in the gatehouse than in the gallery, and after I had visited the apartments of Alice and Joan and Elizabeth, and watched the rompings of the children and the kicking of the babies, I was thankful enough to retire to my own chamber and blissful solitude. Matty brought me my dinner—this being a privilege to which I clung—and was full of gossip, as was her nature, about the servants in the house and what they said of their masters.

Jonathan, my brother-in-law, was respected, feared, but not much loved. They were all easier when he was from home. He kept an account of every penny spent, and any servant wasting food or produce was instantly dismissed. Mary, my sister, was more liked, though she was said to be a tyrant in the stillroom. The young people were all in high favour, especially Alice, whose sweet face and temper would have endeared her to the devil himself, but there was much shaking of heads over her handsome husband Peter, who had a hot eye for a fine leg, as Matty put it, and was apt to put his arm round the kitchen girls if he had the chance. I could well believe this, having flung a pillow at Peter often enough myself for taking liberties.

"Master John and Mistress Joan are also liked," said Matty, "but they say Master John should stand up more to his father."

Her words put me in mind of the afternoon, and I asked her what she knew of the apartment next to mine.

"It is a lumber room, they tell me," she answered. "Mr. Rashleigh has the key and has valuables shut away."

My curiosity was piqued, though, and I bade her search for a crack in the door. She put her face to the keyhole but saw nothing. I gave her a pair of scissors, both of us giggling like children, and she worked away at the panelling for ten minutes or so until she had scraped a wide enough crack at which to place one eye.

She knelt before it for a moment or two, then turned to me in disappointment. "There's nothing there," she said. "It is a plain chamber, much the same as this, with a bed in one corner and hangings on the wall."

I felt quite aggrieved, having hoped—in my idiot romantic fashion—for a heap of treasure. I bade her hang a picture over the crack and turned to my dinner. But later, when Joan came to sit with me at sunset and the shadows began to fall, she said suddenly, with a shiver:

"You know, Honor, I slept once in this room when John had the ague, and I did not care for it."

"Why so?" I asked, drinking my wine.

"I thought I heard footsteps in the chamber next door."

I glanced at the picture over the crack, but it was well hidden. "What sort of footsteps?" I said.

She shook her head, puzzled. "Soft ones," she said, "like someone who walks with slippered soles for fear he shall be heard."

"How long ago was this?" I asked.

"During the winter," she said. "I did not tell anyone."

"A servant, perhaps," I suggested, "who had no business to be there."

"No," she said. "None of the servants have a key; no one has but my father-in-law, and he was from home then." She waited a moment and then she said, glancing over her shoulder, "I believe it was a ghost."

"Why should a ghost walk at Menabilly?" I answered. "The house has not been built fifty years."

"People have died here, though," she said. "John's old grandfather and his uncle John." She watched me with bright eyes, and, knowing my Joan, I wagered there was more to come.

"So you, too, have heard the poison story," I said, drawing a bow at a venture.

She nodded. "But I don't believe it," she said. "It would be wicked, horrible. He is too good and kind a man. But I do think it was a ghost that I heard, the ghost of the elder brother whom they call Uncle John."

"Why should he pace the room with padded soles?" I asked.

She did not answer for a moment, and then, guiltily, she whispered, "They never speak of it. John made me promise not to tell, but he was mad—a hopeless idiot—they used to keep him shut up in the chamber there."

This was something I had never heard before. I found it horrible.

"Are you certain?" I said.

"Oh, yes," she replied. "There is a bit about it in old Mr. Rashleigh's will, John told me. Old Mr. Rashleigh, before he died, made my father-in-law promise to look after the elder brother, give him food and drink and shelter in the house. They say the chamber there was set aside for him, built in a special way—I don't exactly know. And then he died, you see, very suddenly of the smallpox. John and Alice and Elizabeth don't remember him; they were only babies."

"What a disagreeable tale," I said. "Give me some more wine and let's forget it."

After a while she went away, and Matty came to draw the curtains. I had no more visitors that night. But as the shadows lengthened and the owls began to hoot down in the warren I found my thoughts returning to the idiot Uncle John, shut up in the chamber there, year after year, from the first building of the house, a prisoner of the mind, as I was of the body.

But in the morning I heard news that made me forget for a while this talk of footsteps in the night.

8

THE DAY BEING fine, I ventured forth in my chair once more upon the causeway, returning to the house at midday to find that a messenger had ridden to Menabilly during my absence, bearing letters from Plymouth and elsewhere to members of the household, and the family were now gathered in the gallery discussing the latest information from the war. Alice was seated in one of the long windows overlooking the garden, reading aloud a lengthy epistle from her Peter.

"Sir John Digby has been wounded," she said, "and the siege is now to be conducted by a new commander who has them all by the ears at once. Poor Peter—this will mean an end to hawking excursions and supper parties; they will have to wage war more seriously." She turned the page of scrawled writing, shaking her head.

"And who is to command them?" enquired John, who once more was acting as attendant to my chair.

"Sir Richard Grenvile," answered Alice.

Mary was not in the gallery at the time, and she being the only person at Menabilly to know of the romance long finished and forgotten, I was able to hear mention of his name without embarrassment, it being a strange truth, I had by then discovered, that we only become aware of hot discomfort when others are made awkward for our sakes.

I knew, from something that Robin had let slip, that Richard was come into the West, his purpose being to raise troops for the King, so I understood, and his now being placed in command of the siege of Plymouth meant promotion. He had already become notorious, of course, for the manner in which he had hoodwinked Parliament and joined His Majesty.

"And what," I heard myself saying, "does Peter think of his new commander?" Alice folded up her letter.

"As a soldier he admires him," she answered, "but I think he has not such a great opinion of him as a man."

"I have heard," said John, "that he hasn't a scruple in the world, and once an injury is done to him he will never forget it or forgive."

"I believe," said Alice, "that when in Ireland he inflicted great cruelty on the people—though some say it was no more than they deserved. But I fear he is very different from his brother."

It made strange hearing to have discussed in so calm and cool a fashion the lover who had held me once against his heart.

At this moment Will Sparke came up to us, also with a letter in his hand.

"So Richard Grenvile is commanding now at Plymouth," he said. "I have the news here from my kinsman in Tavistock, who is with Prince Maurice. It seems the prince thinks highly of his ability, but my heaven—what a scoundrel."

I began to burn silently, my old love and loyalty rising to the surface.

"We were just talking of him," said John.

"You heard his first action on coming West, I suppose?" said Will Sparke, warming, like all his kind, to malicious gossip. "I had it direct from my kinsman at the time. Grenvile rode straight to Fitzford, his wife's property, turned out the caretakers, seized all the contents, had the agent flung into jail, and took all the money owed by the tenants to his wife for his own use."

"I thought," said Alice, "that he had been divorced from his wife."

"So he is divorced," replied Will. "He is not entitled to a penny from the property. But that is Richard Grenvile for you."

"I wonder," I said calmly, "what has happened to his children."

"I can tell you that," said Will. "The daughter is with the mother in London—whether she has friends in Parliament or not I cannot say. But the lad was at Fitzford with his tutor when Grenvile seized the place and by all accounts is with him now. They say the poor boy is in fear and trembling of his father, and small blame to him."

"No doubt," I said, "he was brought up to hate him by his mother."

"Any woman," retorted Will, "who had been as ill-used as she, unhappy lady, would hardly paint her spouse in pretty colours."

Logic was with him, as it always was with the persons who maligned Richard, and presently I bade John carry me upstairs to my apartment, but the day that had started so well when I set forth upon the causeway turned sour on me, and I lay on my bed for the rest of it, telling Matty I would see no visitors.

For fifteen years the Honor that had been lay dead and buried, and here she was struggling beneath the surface once again at the mere mention of a name that was best forgotten. Richard in Germany, Richard in Ireland, was too remote a person to swim into my daily thoughts. When I thought of him or dreamt of him—which was often—it was always as he had been in the past. And now he must break into the present, being some thirty miles away only, and there would be constant talk of him, criticism and discussion; I would be forced to hear his name bandied and besmirched, as Will Sparke had bandied it this morning.

"You know," he had said before I went upstairs, "the Roundheads call him Skellum Grenvile and have put a price upon his head. The nickname suits him well, and even his own soldiers whisper it behind his back."

"And what does it signify?" I asked.

"Oh," he said, "I thought you were a German scholar, Mistress Harris, as well as learned in the Greek and Latin." He paused. "It means a vicious beast," he sniggered.

Oh yes, there was much reason for me to lie moody on my bed, with the memory of a young man smiling at me from the branches of an apple tree and the humming of the bees in the blossoms.

Fifteen years . . . He would be forty-four now, ten years older than myself.

"Matty," I said, before she lit the candles, "bring me a mirror."

She glanced at me suspiciously, her long nose twitching.

"What do you want a mirror for?" she asked.

"Damn you, that's my business," I answered.

We snapped at each other continually, she and I, but it meant nothing. She brought me the mirror, and I examined my appearance as though seeing myself as a stranger would.

There were my two eyes, my nose, my mouth, much as they had always been, but I was fuller in the face now than I had been as a maid—sluggish from lying on my back, I told myself. There were little lines, too, beneath my eyes, lines that had grown there from pain when my legs hurt me. I had less colour than I had once. My hair was the best point, for this was Matty's special pride, and she would brush for hours to make it glossy. I handed back the mirror to Matty with a sigh.

"What do you make of it?" she asked.

"In ten years," I said, "I'll be an old woman."

She sniffed and began to fold my garments on a chair.

"I'll tell you one thing," she said, drawing in her underlip.

"What's that?"

"You're fairer now as a woman than you ever were as a prinking blushing maid, and I'm not the only one that thinks it."

This was encouraging, and I had an immediate vision of a long train of suitors all tiptoeing up the stairs to pay me homage. A pretty fancy, but where the devil were they?

"You're like an old hen," I said to Matty, "who always thinks her poorest chick the loveliest. Go to bed."

I lay there for some time, thinking of Richard, wondering, too, about his little son, who must be a lad now of fourteen. Could it be true, as Will Sparke had said, that the boy went in fear of his father? Supposing we had wedded, Richard and I, and this had been our son? Would we have sported with him as a child, danced him upon our knees, gone down with him on all fours on the ground and played at tigers? Would he have come running to me with muddied hands, his hair about his face, laughing? Would he be auburn-haired like Richard? Would we all three have ridden to the chase, and Richard showed him how to sit straight in the saddle? Vain idle supposition, drenched in sentiment, like buttercups by the dew on a wet morning. I was half asleep, muzzy with a dream, when I heard a movement in the next chamber. I raised my head from the pillow, thinking it might be Matty in the dressing room, but the sound came from the other side. I held my breath and waited. Yes, there it was again. A stealthy footstep padding to and fro. I remembered in a flash the tale that Joan had told me of the mad Rashleigh uncle confined in there for years. Was it his ghost, in truth, that stole there in the shadows? The night was pitch, for it was only quarter moon, and no glimmer came to me from either casement. The clock in the belfry struck one. The footsteps ceased, then proceeded once again, and for the first time, too, I was aware of a cold current of air coming to my apartment from the chamber beyond.

My own casements were closed, save the one that looked into the inner court, and this was only open to a few inches; besides, the draught did not come from that direction. I remembered then that the closed-up door into the empty chamber did not meet the floor with its base but was raised two inches or so from the ground, for Matty had tried to look under it before she made the crack with the scissors.

It was from beneath this door that the current of air blew now—and to my certain knowledge there had never been a draught from there before. Something, then, had happened in the empty chamber next to mine to cause the current. The muffled tread continued, stealthy, soft, and with the sweat running down my face I thought of the ghost stories my brothers had recounted to me as a child, of how an earth-bound spirit would haunt the place he hated, bringing with him from the darker regions a whisper of chill dank air. . . . One of the dogs barked from the stables, and this homely sound brought me to my senses. Was it not more likely that a living person was responsible for the cold current that swept beneath the door, and that the cause of it was the opening of the barred window that, like my western one, looked out on to the outer court? The ghost of poor idiot Uncle John would have kept me in my bed forever, but a living soul treading furtively in the night hours in a locked chamber was something to stir to fire the curiosity of one who, it may be remembered, had from early childhood shown a propensity to eavesdrop where she was not wanted.

Secretly, stealthily, I reached my hand out to the flint that Matty from long custom left beside my bed, and lit my candle. My chair was also within reach. I pulled it close to me, and with the usual labour that years of practice had never mitigated lowered myself into it. The footsteps ceased abruptly. So I am right, I thought in triumph. No ghost would hesitate at the sound of a creaking chair. I waited perhaps for as long as five minutes, and then the intruder must have recovered himself, for I heard the faint pulling noise of the opening of a drawer. Softly I wheeled myself across the room. Whoever is there, I smiled grimly, is not aware that a cripple can be mobile, granted she has a resourceful brother with a talent for invention. I came abreast of the door and waited once again. The picture that Matty had hung over the crack was on a level with my eye. I blew my candle, trusting to fortune to blunder my way back to bed when my curiosity was satisfied. Then, very softly, holding my breath, I lifted the picture from the nail and, framing my face with my hands for cover, I peered with one eye into the slit. The chamber was in half darkness, lit by a single candle on a bare table. I could not see to right or left—the crack was not large enough—but the table was in direct line with my eye. A man was sitting at the table, his back turned to me. He was booted and spurred and wore a riding cloak about his shoulders. He had a pen in his hand and was writing on a long white slip of paper, consulting now and again another list propped up before him on the table. Here was flesh and blood indeed, and no ghost, and the intruder writing away as calmly as though he were a clerk on a copying stool. I watched him come to the end of the long slip of paper, and then he folded it and, going to the cabinet in the wall, opened the drawer with the same pulling sound I had heard before. The light was murky, as I have said, and with his back turned to me and his hat upon his head, I could make little of him except that his riding cloak was a dark crimson. He then moved out of my line of view, taking the candle, and softly walked to the far corner of the room. I heard nothing after that and no further footsteps, and while I waited, puzzled, with my eye still to the crack, I became aware suddenly that the draught of air was no longer blowing beneath the door. Yet I had heard no sound of a closing window. I bent down from my chair, testing the bottom of the door with my hand, but no current came. The intruder, therefore, had, by some action unperceived by me, cut off the draught, making his exit at the same time. He had left the chamber, as he had entered it, by some entrance other than the door that led into the corridor. I blundered back across my room in clumsy fashion, having first replaced the picture on its nail, and, knocking into a table on the way, woke that light sleeper Matty.

"Have you lost your senses," she scolded, "circling round your chamber in the pitch black?" And she lifted me like a child and dumped me in my bed.

"I had a nightmare," I lied, "and thought I heard footsteps. Is there anyone moving in the courtyard, Matty?"

She drew aside the curtain. "Not a soul," she grumbled, "not even a cat scratching on the cobbles. Everyone is asleep."

"You will think me mazed, I don't doubt," I answered, "but venture with your candle a moment into the passage and try the door of the locked apartment next to this."

"Mazed it is," she snapped. "This comes of looking into the mirror on a Friday night."

In a moment she was back again. "The door is locked like it always is," she said, "and, judging by the dust upon the latch, it has not been opened for months or more."

"No," I mused, "that is just what I supposed."

She stared at me and shook her head.

"I'd best brew you a hot cordial," she said.

"I do not want a hot cordial," I answered.

"There's nothing like it for putting a stop to bad dreams," she said. She tucked in my blankets and after grumbling a moment or two went back to her own room. But my mind was far too lively to find sleep for several hours. I kept trying to remember the formation of the house, seen from without, and what it was that struck me as peculiar the day before, when John had wheeled me in my chair towards the gatehouse. It was past four in the morning when the answer came to me. Menabilly was built foursquare around the courtyard, with clean straight lines and no protruding wings. But at the northwest corner of the house, jutting from the wall outside the fastened chamber, was a buttress, running tall and straight from the roof down to the cobbles.

Why in the name of heaven, when old John Rashleigh built his house in 1600, did he build the northwest corner with a buttress? And had it some connection with the fact that the apartment behind it was designed for the special use of his idiot elder son?

Some lunatics were harmless; some were not. But even the worst, the truly animal, were given air and exercise at certain periods of the day and would hardly be paraded through the corridors of the house itself. I smiled to myself in the darkness, for I had guessed, after three restless hours of tossing on my back, how the intruder had crept into the apartment next to mine without using the locked door into the passage. He had come and he had gone, as poor Uncle John had doubtless done nearly half a century before, by a hidden stairway in the buttress.

But why he had come, and what was his business, I had yet to discover.

9

It TURNED TO rain the next morning, and I was unable to take my usual airing in the grounds, but later in the day the fitful sun peeked through the low clouds and, wrapping my cloak about me, I announced to Matty my intention of going abroad.

John Rashleigh was out riding round the farms on the estate with the steward Langdon, whose house it was I had observed beyond the bowling green, thus I had not my faithful chair attendant. Joan came with me instead, and it was an easy enough matter to persuade her to wheel me first through the archway to the outer court, where I made pretence of looking up to admire my quarters in the gatehouse.

In reality I was observing the formation of the buttress, which ran, as I thought it did, the whole depth of the house on the northwest corner, immediately behind it being the barred chamber.

The width of the buttress was a little over four feet, so I judged, and, if hollow behind a false façade of stone, could easily contain a stair. There was, however, no outlet to the court; this was certain. I bade Joan wheel me to the base on pretence of touching the lichen, which already, after only some forty years, was forming on the stone, and I satisfied myself that the outside of the buttress, at any rate, was solid. If my supposition was correct, then there must be a stairway within the buttress leading underground, far beneath the foundations of the house, and a passage running some distance to an outlet in the grounds. Poor Uncle John . . . It was significant that there was no portrait of him in the gallery, alongside the rest of the family. If so much trouble was taken by his father that he should not be seen, he must have been an object of either fear or horror.

We left the outer court and, traversing the warren, came by the path outside the steward's lodge. The door was open to the parlour, and Mrs. Langdon, the steward's wife, was standing in the entrance, a comfortable homely woman, who on being introduced to me insisted that I take a glass of milk. While she was absent we glanced about the trim room, and Joan, laughing, pointed to a bunch of keys that hung on a nail beside the door.

"Old Langdon is like a jailer," she whispered. "As a rule he is never parted from that bunch but dangles them at his belt. John tells me he has a duplicate of each key belonging to my father-in-law."

"Has he been steward long?" I asked.

"Oh yes," said Joan. "He came here as a young man when the house was built. There is no corner of Menabilly that he does not know."

I wager, then, I thought to myself, that he knows, too, the secret of the buttress, if there is a secret. Joan, with a curiosity much like mine, was examining the labels on the keys.

"'Summerhouse,'" she read, and with a mischievous smile at me she slipped it from the bunch and dangled it before my eyes. "You expressed a wish to peep into the tower on the causeway, did you not?" she teased.

At this moment Mrs. Langdon returned with the milk and, fearful of discovery, Joan, like a guilty child, reddened and concealed the key within her gown. We chatted for a few moments, I drinking my milk in haste, and Joan gazing with great innocence at the ceiling. Then we bade the good woman farewell and turned into the gardens, through the gate in the high wall.

"Now you have done for yourself," I said. "How in the world will you return the key?"

Joan was laughing under her breath.

"I'll give it to John," she said. "He must devise some tale or other to satisfy old

Langdon. But seeing that we have the key, Honor, it were a pity not to make some use of it."

She was an accomplice after my own heart, and a true godchild.

"I make no promise," I murmured. "Wheel me along the causeway, and we will see which way the wind is blowing."

We crossed the gardens, passing the house as we did so and waving to Alice at the window of her apartment above the gallery. I caught sight, too, of Temperance Sawle peering like a witch from the side door, evidently in half a mind to risk the damp ground and join us.

"I am the best off in my chair," I called to her. "The walks are wringing wet, and clouds coming up again from the Gribbin."

She bolted like a rabbit withindoors again, and I saw her pass into the gallery, while Joan, smothering her laughter, propelled me through the gate on to the causeway.

It was only when mounted thus some ten feet from the ground that the fine view of the sea could be obtained, for down on a level the sloping ground masked all sight of it. Menabilly, though built on a hill, lay, therefore, in a saucer, and I commented on the fact to Joan as she wheeled me towards the towered summerhouse at the far end of the causeway.

"Yes," she said, "John has explained to me that the house was so built that no glimpse of it should be sighted from the sea. Old Mr. Rashleigh lived in great fear of pirates. But if the truth be told, he was not above piracy himself, and in the old days, when he was alive, there were bales of silk and bars of silver concealed somewhere within the house, stolen from the French and brought hither by his own ships, then landed down at Pridmouth yonder."

In which case, I thought privately, a passage known to no one but himself, and perhaps his steward, would prove of great advantage.

But we had reached the summerhouse, and Joan, glancing first over her shoulder to see that no one came, produced her key and turned it in the lock.

"I must tell you," she confessed, "that there is nothing great to see. I have been here once or twice with my father-in-law, and it is nought but a rather musty room, the shelves lined with books and papers, and a fine view from the windows."

She wheeled me through the door, and I glanced about me, half hoping in a most childish manner to find trace of piracy. But all was in order. The walls of the summerhouse were lined with books, save for the windows, which even as she had said, commanded the whole stretch of the bay to the Gribbin, and to the east showed the steep coast road that led to Fowey. Anyone, on horse or on foot, approaching Menabilly from the east, would be observed by a watcher at the window, likewise a vessel sailing close inshore. Old Mr. Rashleigh had shown great cunning as a builder.

The flagged floor was carpeted, save in one corner by my brother-in-law's writing table, where a strip of heavy matting served for his feet. It was like his particular character that the papers on his desk were neatly documented and filed in order. Joan left me in my chair to browse up at the books, while she herself kept watch out on the causeway. There was nothing much to tempt my interest. Books of law, dry as dust, books of accountancy, and many volumes docketed as *County Affairs*, no doubt filed when Jonathan was sheriff for the Duchy of Cornwall. On a lower shelf, near to the writing table, were volumes labelled *My Town House* and another, *Menabilly,* while close beside these he had *Marriage Settlements* and *Wills.* He was nothing if not methodical about his business. The volume marked *Wills* was nearest to me and surprisingly tempting to my hand. I looked over my shoulder and saw through the window that Joan, humming a tune, was busily engaged in picking posies for her children. I reached out my hand and took the volume. Page after page was covered in my brother-in-law's meticulously careful hand. I turned to the entries headed by the words, "My father, John Rashleigh, born 1554. Died May 6th, 1624," and folded close to this—perhaps it had slipped in by accident—was an account of a case brought to the Star Chamber in the year 1616 by one Charles Bennett against the above John Rashleigh. This Charles Bennett I remembered was father to Robert Bennett, our neighbour at Looe, who had spread the poison rumour. The case, had I time to peruse it, would have made good reading, for it was of a highly scandalous nature; Charles Bennett accusing John Rashleigh of "leading a most incontinent course of life, lying with divers women, over forty-five in number, uttering blasphemies, etc., etc., and his wife dying through grief at his behaviour, she being a sober, virtuous woman." I was somewhat surprised after this, when glancing at the end, to find that John Rashleigh had been acquitted. What a lovely weapon, though, to hold over the head of my self-righteous brother-in-law when he made boast, as he sometimes did, about the high morals of his family. But I turned a page and came to the will I had been seeking. So John Rashleigh had not done too badly for his relatives. Nick Sawle had got fifty pounds (which I dare say Temperance had snatched from him), and the Sparkes had benefited to the same extent. The poor of Fowey had some twenty pounds bestowed upon them. It is really most iniquitous, I told myself, that I should be prying thus into matters that concern me not at all, but I read on. All lands in Cornwall, his house in Fowey, his house at Menabilly, and the residue of his estate to his second son, Jonathan, his executor. And then the codicil at the end: "Thirty pounds annuity out of Fowey to the use of my elder son John's maintenance, to be paid after the death of my second son Jonathan, who during his life will maintain him and allow him a chamber with meat, drink, and apparel." I caught a glimpse of Joan's shadow passing the window, and with a hurried guilty movement I shut the volume and put it back upon the shelf.

There was no doubt then about the disability of poor Uncle John. . . . I turned my chair from the desk, and as I did so the right wheel stuck against some obstruction on the ground beneath the heavy matting. I bent down from my chair to free the wheel, turning up the edge of the mat as I did so. I saw then that the obstruction was a ring in the flagstone, which, though flat to the ground and unnoticeable possibly to a foot treading upon it, had been enough to obstruct the smooth running of my chair.

I leant from my chair as far as I could and, seizing the ring with my two hands, succeeded in lifting the stone some three inches from the ground, before the weight of it caused me to drop it once again. But not before I had caught a glimpse of the sharp corner of a step descending into the darkness. . . . I replaced the mat just as my godchild came into the summerhouse.

"Well, Honor," she said, "have you seen all you have a mind to for the present?"

"I rather think I have," I answered, and in a few moments she had closed the door, turned the key once more in the lock, and we were bowling back along the causeway. She prattled away about this and that, but I paid but scant attention, for my mind was full of my latest discovery. It seemed fairly certain that there was a pit tunnel underneath the flagstone in the summerhouse, and the placing of a mat on top of it and the position of the desk suggested that the hiding of it was deliberate. There was no rust about the ringbolt to show disuse, and the easiness with which I, helpless in my chair, had lifted the stone a few inches proved to me that this was no cobwebby corner of concealment long forgotten. The flagstone had been lifted frequently and recently. I looked over my shoulder down the pathway to the beach, or Pridmouth Cove, as Joan had termed it. It was narrow and steep, flanked about with stubby trees, and I thought how easy it would be for an incoming vessel, anchored in deep water, to send a boat ashore with some half dozen men, and they to climb up the path to where it ended beneath the summerhouse on the causeway, and for a watcher at the window of the summerhouse to relieve the men of any burden they should bear upon their backs. Was this what old John Rashleigh had foreseen when he built his tower, and did bales of silk and bars of silver lie stacked beneath the flagstone some forty years before? It seemed very probable, but whether the step beneath the flagstone had any connection with my suspicions of the buttress it was difficult to say. One thing was certain. There was a secret way of entrance to Menabilly, through the chamber next to mine, and someone had passed that way only the night before, for I had seen him with my own eyes. . . .

"You are silent, Honor," said Joan, breaking in upon my thoughts. "Of what are you thinking?"

"I have just come to the opinion," I answered, "that I was somewhat rash to leave Lanrest, where each day was alike, and come amongst you all at Menabilly, where something different happens every day."

"I wish I thought as you did," she replied. "To me the days and weeks seem much the same, with the Sawles backbiting at the Sparkes, and the children fretful, and my dear John grousing all the while that he cannot go fighting with Peter and the rest."

We came to the end of the causeway and were about to turn in through the gate into the walled gardens, when little Jonathan, her son, a child of barely three years, came running across the path to greet us.

"Uncle Peter is come," he cried, "and another gentleman, and many soldiers. We have been stroking the horses."

I smiled up at his mother.

"What did I tell you?" I said. "Not a day passes but there is some excitement at Menabilly."

I had no wish to run the gauntlet of the long windows in the gallery, where the company would be assembled, and bade Joan wheel me to the entrance in front of the house, which was usually deserted at this time of the day, no one being within the dining chamber. Once indoors, one of the servants could carry me to my apartment in the gatehouse, and later I could send for Peter, always a favourite with me, and have his news of Robin. We passed in then through the door, little Jonathan running in front, and at once we heard laughter and talk coming from the gallery, and, the wide arched door to the inner courtyard being open, we could see some half dozen troopers with their horses watering at the well beneath the belfry. There was much bustle and clatter, a pleasant lively sound, and I saw one of the troopers look up to a casement in the attic and wave his hand in greeting to a blushing kitchen girl. He was a big strong-looking fellow with a broad grin on his face, and then he turned and signalled to his companions to follow him, which they did, each one leading his horse away from the well and following him through the archway beneath my gatehouse to the outer courtyard and the stables.

It was when they turned thus and clattered through the court that I noticed how each fellow wore upon his shoulder a scarlet shield with three gold rests upon it. . . .

For a moment I thought my heart would stop beating, and I was seized with sudden panic.

"Find one of the servants quickly," I said to Joan. "I wish to be carried straightway to my room."

But it was too late. Even as she sent little Jonathan scampering hurriedly towards the servants' quarters Peter Courtney came out into the hall, his arm about his Alice, in company with two or three brother officers.

"Why, Honor," he cried, "this is a joy indeed. Knowing your habits, I feared to find you hiding in your apartment, with Matty standing like a dragon at the door. Gentlemen, I present to you Mistress Honor Harris, who has not the slightest desire to make your acquaintance."

I could have slain him for his lack of discretion, but he was one of those gay, lighthearted creatures with a love of jesting and poking fun, and no more true perception than a bumblebee. In a moment his friends were bowing before my chair and exchanging introductions, and Peter, still laughing and talking in his haphazard strident way, was pushing my chair through to the gallery. Alice, who made up in intuition all he lacked, would have stopped him had I caught her eye, but she was too glad to have a glimpse of him to do anything else but smile and hold his arm. The gallery seemed full of people, Sawles and Sparkes and Rashleighs, all chatting at the top of their voices, and at the far end by the window I caught sight of Mary in conversation with someone whose tall back and broad shoulders were painfully, almost terrifyingly, familiar.

Mary's expression, preoccupied and distrait, told me that she was at that moment wondering if I had returned yet from my promenade, for I saw her eyes search the gardens; and then she saw me, and her brow wrinkled in a well-known way and she began talking sixteen to the dozen. Her loss of composure gave me back my own, and what in hell's name do I care, after fifteen years? I told myself. There is no need to swoon at an encounter; God knows I have breeding enough to be mistress of the situation, here in Mary's house at Menabilly, with nigh a score of people in the room.

Peter, impervious to any doubtful atmosphere, propelled me slowly towards the window, and out of the corner of my eye I saw my sister Mary, overcome by cowardice, do something I dare swear I might have done myself had I been she, and that was to murmur a hasty excuse to her companion about summoning the servants to bring further refreshment, and she fled from the gallery without looking once in my direction. Richard turned and saw me. And as he looked at me it was as if my whole heart moved over in my body and was mine no longer.

"Sir," said Peter, "I am pleased to present to you my dearly loved kinswoman, Mistress Honor Harris of Lanrest."

"My kinswoman also," said Richard, and then he bent forward and kissed my hand.

"Oh, is that so, sir?" said Peter vaguely, looking from one to the other of us. "I suppose all we Cornish families are in some way near related. Let me fill your glass, sir. Honor, will you drink with us?'

"I will," I answered.

In truth, a glass of wine seemed to me my only salvation at the moment. While Peter filled the glasses I had my first long look at Richard. He had altered. There was no doubt of it. He had grown much broader, for one thing, not only in the body, but about the neck and shoulders. His face was somehow heavier than it had been. There was a brown weather-beaten air about him that was not there before, and lines beneath his eyes. It was, after all, fifteen years. . . .

And then he turned to me, giving me my glass, and I saw that there was only one white streak in his auburn hair, high above the temple, and the eyes that looked at me were quite unchanged.

"Your health and fortune," he said quietly, and, draining his glass, he held it out with mine to be refilled. I saw the little telltale pulse beating in his right temple, and I knew then that the encounter was as startling and as moving to him as it was to me.

"I did not know," he said, "that you were at Menabilly."

I saw Peter glance at him curiously, and I wondered if this was the first time he had ever seen his commanding officer show any sign of nervousness or strain. The hand that held the glass trembled very slightly, and the voice that spoke was hard, queerly abrupt.

"I came here a few days since from Lanrest," I answered, my voice perhaps as oddly flat as his. "My brothers said I must not live alone, not while the war continues."

"They showed wisdom," he replied. "Essex is moving westward all the time. It is very probable we shall see fighting once again this side the Tamar."

At this moment Peter's small daughters came running to his knees, shrieking with joy to see their father, and Peter, laughing an apology, was swept into family life upon the instant, taking one apiece upon his shoulders and moving down the gallery in triumph. Richard and I were thus left alone beside the window. I looked out on to the garden, noting the trim yew hedges and the smooth lawns, while a score of trivial observations ran insanely through my head.

"How green the grass is after the morning rain" and "It is something chilly for the time of year" were phrases I had never yet used in my life, even to a stranger, but they seemed, at that moment, to be what was needed to the occasion. Yet though they rose unbidden to my tongue I did not frame them, but continued looking out upon the garden in silence, with Richard as dumb as myself. And then in a low voice, clipped and hard, he said:

"If I am silent you must forgive me. I had not thought, after fifteen years, to find you so damnably unchanged."

This streak back to the intimate past from the indifferent present was a new shock to be borne, but a curiously exciting one.

"Why damnably?" I said, watching him over the rim of my glass.

"I had become used, over a long period, to a very different picture," he said. "I thought of you as an invalid, wan and pale, a sort of shadow without substance, hedged about with doctors and attendants. And instead I find—this." He looked me then full in the face, with a directness and a lack of reserve that I remembered well.

"I am sorry," I answered, "to disappoint you."

"You misinterpret me," he said. "I have not said I was disappointed. I am merely speechless." He drained his glass once more and put it back upon the table. "I shall recover," he said, "in a moment or two. Where can we talk?"

"Talk?" I asked. "Why, we can talk here, I suppose, if you wish to."

"Amidst a host of babbling fools and screaming children? Not on your life," he answered. "Have you not your own apartment?"

"I have," I replied with some small attempt at dignity, "but it would be considered somewhat odd if we retired there."

"You were not used to quibble at similar suggestions in the past," he replied.

This was something of a blow beneath the belt, and I had no answer for him.

"I would have you remember," I said with lameness, "that we have been strangers to each other for fifteen years."

"Do you think," he said, "that I forget it for a moment?"

At this juncture we were interrupted by Temperance Sawle, who with baleful eyes had been watching us from a distance and now moved within our orbit.

"Sir Richard Grenvile, I believe," she said.

"Your servant, ma'am," replied Richard with a look that would have slain anyone less soul-absorbed than Temperance.

"The Evil One seeks you for his own," she announced. "Even at this moment I see his talons at your throat and his jaws open to devour you. Repent, repent, before it is too late."

"What the devil does she mean?" said Richard.

I shook my head and pointed to the heavens, but Temperance, warming to her theme, continued:

"The mark of the Beast is on your forehead," she declared; "the men you lead are become as ravening wolves. You will all perish, every one of you, in the bottomless pit."

"Tell the old fool to go to hell," said Richard.

I offered Mistress Sawle a glass of wine, but she flinched as if it had been boiling oil. "There shall be a weeping and a gnashing of teeth," she continued.

"My God, you're right," said Richard, and, taking her by the shoulders, he twisted her round like a top and walked her across the room to the fireplace and her husband.

"Keep this woman under control," he ordered, and there was an immediate silence, followed by a little flutter of embarrassed conversation. Peter Courtney, very red about the neck, hurried forward with a brimming decanter.

"Some more wine, sir?" he said.

"Thank you, no, I've had about as much as I can stand," said Richard.

I noticed the young officers, all their backs turned, examining the portraits on the walls with amazing interest. Will Sparkes was one of the little crowd about the fireplace, staring hard at the King's general, his mouth wide open.

"A good day for catching flies, sir," said Richard pleasantly.

A little ripple of laughter came from Joan, hastily suppressed as Richard turned his eyes upon her.

Will Sparkes pressed forward.

"I have a young kinsman under your command," he said, "an ensign of the twenty-third regiment of foot—"

"Very probably," said Richard. "I never speak to ensigns." He beckoned to John Rashleigh, who had returned but a few moments ago from his day's ride and was now hovering at the entrance to the gallery, somewhat mudstained and splashed, bewildered by the unexpected company.

"Hi, you," called Richard, "will you summon one of your fellow servants and carry Mistress Harris's chair to her apartment? She has had enough of the company downstairs."

"That is John Rashleigh, sir," whispered Peter hurriedly, "the son of the house, and your host in his father's absence."

"Ha! My apologies," said Richard, walking forward with a smile. "Your dress being somewhat in disorder, I mistook you for a menial. My own young officers lose their rank if they appear so before me. How is your father?"

"Well, sir, I believe," stammered John in great nervousness.

"I am delighted to hear it," said Richard. "Tell him so when you see him. And tell him, too, that now I am come into the West I propose to visit here very frequently—the course of the war permitting it."

"Yes sir."

"You have accommodation for my officers, I suppose, and for a number of my men out in the park, should we wish to bivouac at any time?"

"Yes indeed, sir."

"Excellent. And now I propose to dine upstairs with Mistress Harris, who is a close kinswoman of mine, a fact of which you may not be aware. What is the usual method with her chair?"

"We carry it, sir. It is quite a simple matter."

John gave a nod to Peter, who, astonishingly subdued for him, came forward, and the pair of them each seized an arm of my chair on either side.

"It were an easier matter," said Richard, "if the occupant were bodily removed and carried separately." And before I could protest he had placed his arms about me and had lifted me from the chair.

"Lead on, gentlemen," commanded Richard.

The strange procession proceeded up the stairs, watched by the company in the gallery and by some of the servants, too, who, with their backs straight against the wall and their eyes lowered, permitted us to pass. John and Peter tramped on ahead with the chair between them, step by step, and both of them red about the neck, while I, with my head on Richard's shoulder and my arms tight about him for fear of falling, thought the way seemed overlong.

"I was in error just now," said Richard in my ear. "You have changed after all."

"In what way?" I asked.

"You are two stone heavier," he answered.

And so we came to my chamber in the gatehouse.

10

I CAN RECOLLECT that supper as if it were yesterday: I lying on my bed with the pillows packed behind me, and Richard seated on the end of it, with a low table in front of us both.

It might have been a day since we had parted instead of fifteen years. When Matty came into the room bearing the platters, her mouth pursed and disapproving, for she had never understood how we came to lose each other but imagined he had deserted me because of my crippled state, Richard burst out laughing on the instant, calling her "old go-between," which had been his nickname for her in those distant days, and asked her how many hearts she had broken since he saw her last. She was for replying to him shortly, but it was no use—he would have none of it—and, taking the platters from her and putting them on the table, he soon had her reconciled—blushing from head to toe—while he poked fun at her broadening figure and the frizzed curl on her forehead.

"There are some half dozen troopers in the court," he told her, "waiting to make your acquaintance. Go and prove to them that Cornishwomen are better than the frousts in Devon." And she went off, closing the door behind her, guessing, no doubt, that for the first time in fifteen years I had no need of her services. He fell to eating right away, being always a good trencherman, and soon clearing all that had been put before us, while I—still weak with the shock of seeing him—toyed with the wishbone of a chicken. He started walking about the chamber before he had finished, a habit I remembered well, with a great bone in one hand and a pie in the other, talking all the while about the defences at Plymouth which his predecessor had allowed to become formidable instead of razing them to the ground on first setting siege to the place.

"You'd hardly credit it, Honor," he said, "but there's that fat idiot Digby been sitting on his arse nine months before the walls of Plymouth, allowing the garrison to sortie as they please, fetch food and firewood, build up barricades, while he played cards with his junior officers. Thank God a bullet in his head will keep him to his bed for a month or two and allow me to conduct the siege instead."

"And what do you propose to do?" I asked.

"My first two tasks were simple," he replied, "and should have been done last October. I threw up a new earthwork at Mount Batten, and the guns I have placed there so damage the shipping that endeavours to pass through the Sound that the garrison are hard put to it for supplies. Secondly, I have cut off their water power, and the mills within the city can no longer grind flour for the inhabitants. Give me a month or two to play with, and I'll have 'em starved."

He took a great bite out of his pie and winked at me.

"And the blockade by land, is that effective now?" I questioned.

"It will be when I've had time to organise it," he answered. "The trouble is that I've arrived to find most of the officers in my command are worse than useless—I've sacked more than half of them already. I have a good fellow in charge at Saltash, who sent the rebels flying back to Plymouth with several fleas in their ears when they tried a sortie a week or two back—a sharp engagement in which my nephew Jack, Bevil's eldest boy—you remember him—did very well. Last week we sprang a little surprise on one of their outposts close to Maudlyn. We beat them out of their position there and took a hundred prisoners. I rather think the gentlemen of Plymouth sleep not entirely easy in their beds."

"Prisoners must be something of a problem," I said, "it being hard enough to find forage in the country for your own men. You are obliged to feed them, I suppose?"

"Feed them be damned," he answered. "I send the lot to Lydford Castle, where they are hanged without trial for high treason." He threw his drumstick out of the window and tore the other from the carcass.

"But, Richard," I said, hesitating, "that is hardly justice, is it? I mean—they are only fighting for what they believe to be a better cause than ours."

"I don't give a fig for justice," he replied. "The method is effective, and that's the only thing that matters."

"I am told the Parliament has put a price upon your head already," I said. "I am told you are much feared and hated by the rebels."

"What would you have them do, kiss my backside?" he asked. He smiled and came and sat beside me on the bed.

"The war is too much with us. Let us talk about ourselves," he said.

I had not wished for that but hoped to keep him busy with the siege of Plymouth. "Where are you living at the moment?" I parried. "In tents about the fields?"

"What would I be doing in a tent," he mocked, "with the best houses in Devon at my disposal? Nay, my headquarters are at Buckland Abbey, which my grandfather sold to Francis Drake half a century ago, and I do not mind telling you that I live there very well. I have seized all the sheep and cattle upon the estate, and the tenants pay their rents to me or else are hanged. They call me the Red Fox behind my back, and the women, I understand, use the name as a threat to their children when they misbehave, saying, 'Grenvile is coming; the Red Fox will have you.'"

He laughed as if this were a fine jest, but I was watching the line of his jaw that was heavier than before, and the curve of his mouth that narrowed at the corners.

"It was not thus," I said softly, "that your brother Bevil's reputation spread throughout the West."

"No," he said, "and I have not a wife like Bevil had, nor a home I love, nor a great brood of happy children."

His voice was harsh suddenly and strangely bitter. I turned my face away and lay back on my pillows.

"Do you have your son with you at Buckland?" I asked quietly.

"My spawn?" he said. "Yes, he is somewhere about the place with his tutor."

"What is he like?"

"Dick? Oh, he's a little handful of a chap with mournful eyes. I call him 'whelp' and make him sing to me at supper. But there's no sign of Grenvile in him—he's the spit of his damned mother."

The boy we would have played with and taught and loved . . . I felt suddenly sad and oddly depressed that his father should dismiss him with this careless shrug of a shoulder.

"It went wrong with you then, Richard, from the beginning?" I said.

"It did," he answered.

There was a long silence, for we had entered upon dangerous ground.

"Did you never try," I asked, "to make some life of happiness?"

"Happiness was not in question," he said; "that went with you, a factor you refused to recognise."

"I am sorry," I said.

"So am I," he answered.

The shadows were creeping across the floor. Soon Matty would come to light the candles.

"When you refused to see me that last time," he said, "I knew that nothing mattered any more but bare existence. You have heard the story of my marriage with much embellishment, no doubt, but the bones of it are true."

"Had you no affection for her?"

"None whatever. I wanted her money, that was all."

"Which you did not get."

"Not then. I have it now. And her property and her son—whom I fathered in a moment of black insensibility. The girl is with her mother up in London. I shall get her, too, one day when she can be of use to me."

"You are very altered, Richard, from the man I loved."

"If I am so, you know the reason why."

The sun had gone from the windows; the chamber seemed bleak and bare. Every bit of those fifteen years was now between us. Suddenly he reached out his hand to mine and, taking it, held it against his lips. The touch I so well remembered was very hard to bear.

"Why, in the name of God," he said, rising to his feet, "were you and I marked down for such a tragedy?"

"It's no use being angry," I said. "I gave that up long ago. At first, yes, but not now. Not for many years. Lying on my back has taught me some discipline—but not the kind you engender in your troops."

He came and stood beside my bed, looking down upon me.

"Has no one told you," he said, "that you are more lovely now than you were then?"

I smiled, thinking of Matty and the mirror.

"I think you flatter me," I answered, "or maybe I have more time now. I lie idle to play with paint and powder."

No doubt he thought me cool and at my ease and had no knowledge that his tone of voice ripped wide the dusty years and sent them scattering.

"There is no part of you," he said, "that I do not now remember. You had a mole in the small of your back which gave you much distress; you thought it ugly—but I liked it well."

"Is it not time," I said, "that you went downstairs to join your officers? I heard one of them say you were to sleep this night at Grampound."

"There was a bruise on your left thigh," he said, "caused by that confounded branch that protruded halfway up the apple tree. I compared it to a dark-sized plum, and you were much offended."

"I can hear the horses in the courtyard," I said. "Your troopers are preparing for the journey. You will never reach your destination before morning."

"You lie there," he said, "so smug and so complacent on your bed, very certain of yourself now you are thirty-four. I tell you, Honor, I care not two straws for your civility."

And he knelt then at my bed with his arms about me, and the fifteen years went whistling down the wind.

"Are you still queasy when you eat roast swan?" he whispered.

He wiped away the silly childish tears that pricked my eyes and laughed at me and smoothed my hair.

"Beloved half-wit, with your damned pride," he said, "do you understand now that you blighted both our lives?"

"I understood that then," I told him.

"Why, then, in the name of heaven, did you do it?"

"Had I not done so, you would soon have hated me, as you hated Mary Howard."

"That is a lie, Honor."

"Perhaps. What does it matter? There is no reason now to harp back on the past."

"There I agree with you. The past is over. But we have the future with us. My marriage is annulled; you know that, I suppose? I am free to wed again."

"Then do so, to another heiress."

"I have no need of another heiress now, with all the estates in Devon to my plunder. I have become a gentleman of fortune, to be looked upon with favour by the spinsters of the West."

"There are many you might choose from, all agog for husbands."

"In all probability. But I want one spinster only, and that yourself."

I put my two hands on his shoulders and stared straight at him. The auburn hair, the hazel eyes, the little pulse that beat in his right temple. He was not the only one with recollections. I had my memories, too, and could have reminded him—had I the mind and lack of modesty—of a patch of freckles that had been as much a matter for discussion as the mole upon my back.

"No, Richard."

"Why?"

"Because I will not have you wedded to a cripple."

"You will never change your mind?"

"Never."

"And if I carry you by force to Buckland?"

"Do so, if you will; I can't prevent you. But I shall still be a cripple."

I leant back on my pillows, faint suddenly, and exhausted. It had not been a light thing to bear, this strain of seeing him, of beating down the years. Very gently he released me and smoothed my blankets, and when I asked for a glass of water he gave me one in silence.

It was nearly dark; the clock in the belfry had struck eight a long while since. I could hear the jingling of harness from the courtyard and the scraping sound of horses.

"I must ride to Grampound," he said at length.

"Yes," I said.

He stood for a moment looking down on to the court. The candles were lit now throughout the house. The west windows of the gallery were open, sending a beam of light into my chamber. There was a sound of music. Alice was playing her lute and Peter singing. Richard came once more and knelt beside my bed.

"I understand," he said, "what you have tried so hard to tell me. There can never be between us what there was once. Is that it?"

"Yes," I said.

"I knew that all along, but it would make no difference," he said.

"It would," I said, "after a little while."

Peter had a young voice, clear and gay, and his song was happy. I thought how Alice would be looking at him over her lute.

"I shall always love you," said Richard, "and you will love me too. We cannot lose each other now, not since I have found you again. May I come and see you often, that we may be together?"

"Whenever you wish," I answered.

There came a burst of clapping from the gallery, and the voices of the officers and the rest of the company asking for more. Alice struck up a lively jigging air upon her lute—a soldiers' drinking song, much whistled at the moment by our men—and they one and all chimed in upon the chorus, with the troopers in the courtyard making echo to the song.

"Do you have as much pain now as when you were first hurt?" he said.

"Sometimes," I answered, "when the air is damp. Matty calls me her weatherglass."

"Is there nothing can be done for it?"

"She rubs my legs and my back with lotion that the doctors gave her, but it is of little use. You see, the bones were all smashed and twisted; they cannot knit together."

"Will you show me, Honor?"

"It is not a pretty sight, Richard."

"I have seen worse in battle."

I pulled aside my blanket and let him look upon the crumpled limbs that he had once known whole and clean. He was thus the only person in the world to see me so, except Matty and the doctors. I put my hands over my eyes, for I did not care to see his face.

"There is no need for that," he said. "Whatever you suffer you shall share with me from this day forward." He bent then and kissed my ugly twisted legs and after a moment covered me again with the blanket. "Will you promise," he said, "never to send me from you again?"

"I promise," I said.

"Farewell, then, sweetheart, and sleep sound this night."

He stood for a moment, his figure carved clear against the beam of light from the windows opposite, and then turned and went away down the passage. Presently I heard them all come out into the courtyard and mount their horses; there was sound of leave-taking and laughter. Richard's voice high above the others telling John Rashleigh he would come again. Suddenly, clipped and curt, he called an order to his men, and they went riding through the archway beneath the gatehouse where I lay, and I heard the sound of the hoofbeats echo across the park.

11

THAT RICHARD GRENVILE should become suddenly, within a few hours, part of my life again was a mental shock that for a day or two threw me out of balance. The first excitement over and the stimulation of his presence that evening fading away, reaction swung me to a low ebb. It was all too late. No good could come of it. Memory of what had been, nostalgia of the past coupled with sentiment, had stirred us both to passion for a moment; but reason came with daylight. There could never be a life for us together, only the doubtful pleasure of brief meetings which the hazards of war at any time might render quite impracticable. What then? For me a lifetime of lying on my back, waiting for a chance encounter, for a message, for a word of greeting; and for him, after a space, a nagging irritation that I existed in the background of his life, that he had not visited me for three months and must make some effort to do so, that I expected some message from him which he found difficult to send—in short, a friendship that would become as wearisome to him as it would be painful to me. Although his physical presence, his ways, his tenderness, however momentary it may have been, had been enough to engender in me once again all the old love and yearning in my heart, cold criticism told me he had altered for the worse.

Faults that I had caught glimpses of in youth were now increased tenfold. His pride, his arrogance, his contempt for anyone's opinion but his own—these were more glaring than they had ever been. His knowledge of matters military was great—that I well believed—but I doubted if he would ever work in harmony with the other leaders, and his quick temper was such that he would have every royalist leader by the ears if he did not control it, and in the end give offence to His Majesty himself.

The callous attitude to prisoners—dumped within Lydford Castle and hung without trial—showed me that streak of cruelty I had always known was in his nature; and his contemptuous dismissal of his little son, who must, I felt sure, be baffled and bewildered at the sudden change in his existence, betrayed a deliberate want of understanding that was almost vile. That suffering and bitterness had turned him hard, I granted. Mine was the fault, perhaps; mine was the blame.

But the hardness had bitten into his nature now, and it was too late to alter it. Richard Grenvile at forty-four was what fate and circumstance and his own will had made him.

So I judged him without mercy, in those first days after our encounter, and was within half a mind of writing to him once again, putting an end to all further meetings. Then I remembered how he had knelt beside my bed, and I had shared with him my terrible disfigurement, and he, more tender than any father, more understanding than any brother, had kissed me and bade me sleep.

If he had this gentleness and intuition with me, a woman, how was it that he showed to others, even to his son, a character at once so proud and cruel, so deliberately disdainful?

I felt torn between two courses, lying there on my bed in the gatehouse. One was to see him no more, never, at any time. Leave him to carve his own future, as I had done before. And the other was to ignore the great probability of my own personal suffering, spurn my own weak body that would be tortured incessantly by his physical presence, and give to him wholeheartedly and without any reservation all the small wisdom I had learnt, all the love, all the understanding that might yet bring to him some measure of peace.

This second course seemed to me more positive than the first, for if I renounced him now, as I had done before, it would be through cowardice, a sneaking fear of being hurt in more intolerable a fashion, if it were possible, than I had been fifteen years ago.

Strange how all arguments in solitude, sorted, sifted, and thrashed in the quietude of one's own chamber, shrivel to nothing when the subject of them is close once more instead of separated by distance. And so it was with Richard, for when he rode to Menabilly on his return from Grampound to Plymouth and, coming out on to the causeway to me, found me in my chair looking out towards the Gribbin and, bending to me, kissed my hand with all the old fire and love and ardour—haranguing me straightforth upon the gross inefficiency of every Cornishman he had so far encountered except those under his immediate command—I knew that we were bound together for all time and I could not send him from me. His faults were my faults, his arrogance my burden, and he stood there, Richard Grenvile, what my tragedy had made him.

"I cannot stay long," he said to me. "I have word from Saltash that those damned rebels have made a sortie in my absence, effecting a landing at Cawsand and taking the fort at Inceworth. The sentries were asleep, of course, and if the enemy haven't shot them, I will do so. I'll have my army purged before I'm finished."

"And no one left to fight for you, Richard," I said.

"I'd sooner have hired mercenaries from Germany or France than these own soft-bellied fools," he answered. And he was gone in a flash, leaving me half happy, half bewildered, with an ache in my heart that I knew now was to be forever part of my existence.

That evening my brother-in-law, Jonathan Rashleigh, returned to Menabilly, having been some little while in Exeter on the King's affairs. He had come by way of Fowey, having spent, so he informed us, the last few days at his town house there on the quay, where he had found much business to transact and some loss amongst his shipping, for the Parliament having at this time command of the sea and seizing every vessel they could find, it was hard for any merchant ship unarmed to run the gauntlet.

Some feeling of constraint came upon the place at his return, of which even I, secure in my gatehouse, could not but be aware.

The servants were more prompt about their business, but less willing. The grandchildren, who had run about the passages in his absence, were closeted in their quarters with the doors well shut. The voices in the gallery were more subdued. It was indeed obvious that the master had returned. Alice and John and Joan found their way more often to the gatehouse, as if it had become in some sort a sanctuary. John looked harassed and preoccupied, and Joan whispered to me in confidence that his father found fault with his running of the estate and said he had no head for figures.

I could see that Joan was burning to enquire about my friendship with Richard Grenvile, which they must have thought strangely sudden, and I saw Alice look at me, though she said nothing, with a new warm glance of understanding. "I knew him well long ago when I was eighteen," I told them, but to plunge back into the whole history was not my wish. I think Mary had given them a hint or two in private. She herself said little of the visit, beyond remarking he had grown much stouter, a true sisterly remark, and then she showed me the letter he had left for Jonathan, which ended with these words:

> I here conclude, praying you to present once more my best respects to your good wife, being truly glad she is yours, for a more likely good wife was in former time hardly to be found, and I wish my fortune had been as good—but patience is a virtue, and so I am your ready servant and kinsman, Richard Grenvile.

Patience is a virtue. . . . I saw Mary glance at me as I read the lines.

"You do not intend, Honor," she said in a low voice, "to take up with him again?"

"In what way, Mary?"

"Why, wed with him, to be blunt. This letter is somewhat significant."

"Rest easy, sister. I shall never marry Richard Grenvile or any man."

"I should not be comfortable, nor Jonathan either, if Sir Richard should come here and give an impression of intimacy. He may be a fine soldier, but his reputation is anything but that."

"I know, Mary."

"Jo writes from Radford that they say hard things of him in Devon."

"I can well believe it."

"I know it is not my business, but it would sadden me much, it would greatly grieve us all, if—if you felt bound yourself to him in some way."

"Being a cripple, Mary, makes one strangely free of bonds."

She looked at me doubtfully and then said no more, but I think the bitterness was lost on her.

Presently Jonathan himself came up to pay his respects to me. He hoped I was comfortable, that I had everything I needed and did not find the place too noisy after the quiet of Lanrest.

"And you sleep well, I trust, and are not disturbed at all?"

His manner, when he asked this, was somewhat odd, a trifle evasive, which was strange for him who was so self-possessed a person.

"I am not a heavy sleeper," I told him; "a creaking board or a hooting owl is enough to waken me."

"I rather feared so," he said abruptly. "It was foolish of Mary to put you in this room, facing as it does a court on either side. You would have been better in the south front, next to our own apartment. Would you prefer this?"

"Indeed, no, I am very happy here."

I noticed that he stared hard at the picture on the door, hiding the crack, and once or twice seemed as if he would ask a question but could not bring himself to the point; then after chat upon no subject in particular he took his leave of me.

That night, between twelve and one, being wakeful, I sat up in bed to drink a glass of water. I did not light my candle, for the glass was within my reach. But as I replaced it on the table I became aware of a cold draught of air blowing beneath the door of the empty room. That same chill draught I had noticed once before. . . . I waited, motionless, for the sound of footsteps, but none came. And then, faint and hesitating, came a little scratching sound upon the panel of the door where I had hung the picture. Someone, then, was in the empty room, clad in his stockinged feet, with his hands upon the door. . . .

The sound continued for five minutes, certainly not longer, and then ceased as suddenly as it had started, and once again the telltale draught of air was cut in a trice and all was as before.

A horrid suspicion formed then in my mind, which in the morning became certainty. When I was dressed and in my chair and Matty busy in the dressing room I wheeled myself to the door and lifted the picture from the nail. It was as I thought. The crack had been filled in. . . . I knew then that my presence in the gatehouse had been a blunder on the part of my sister and that I caused annoyance to that unknown visitor who prowled by night in the adjoining chamber.

The secret was Jonathan Rashleigh's and not mine to know. Suspecting my prying eyes, he had given orders for my peephole to be covered.

I pondered then upon the possibility, which had entered my head earlier, that Jonathan's elder brother had not died of the smallpox some twenty years before but was still alive—in some horrid state of preservation, blind and dumb—living in animal fashion in a lair beneath the buttress, and that the only persons to know of this were my brother-in-law and his steward Langdon and some stranger—a keeper, possibly—clad in a crimson cloak.

If it were indeed so, and my sister Mary and her stepchildren were in ignorance of the fact, while I, a stranger, had stumbled upon it, then I knew I must make some excuse and return home to Lanrest, for to live day by day with a secret of this kind upon my conscience was something I could not do. It was too sinister, too horrible.

I wondered if I should confide my fears to Richard when he next came, or whether, in his ruthless fashion, he would immediately give orders to his men to break open the room and force the buttress, so bringing ruin, perhaps, to my brother-in-law and host.

Fortunately the problem was solved for me in a very different way, which I will now disclose. It will be remembered that on the day of Richard's first visit my godchild Joan had mischievously borrowed the key of the summerhouse, belonging to the steward, and allowed me to explore the interior. The flurry and excitement of receiving visitors had put all thoughts of the key from her little scatterbrained head, and it was not until two days after my brother-in-law's return that she remembered the key's existence.

She came to me with it in her hands in great perturbation, for, she said, John was already so much out of favour with his father for some neglect on the estate that she was loath now to tell him of her theft of the key for fear it should bring him into greater trouble.

As for herself, she had not the courage to take the key back to Langdon's house and confess the foolery. What was she then to do?

"You mean," I said, "what am I to do? For you wish to absolve yourself of all responsibility, isn't that so?"

"You are so clever, Honor," she pleaded, "and I so ignorant. Let me leave the key with you and so forget it. Baby Mary has a cough and poor John a touch of his ague; I really have so much on my mind."

"Very well then," I answered, "we will see what can be done."

I had some idea of taking Matty into my confidence and weaving a tale by which Matty would visit Mrs. Langdon and say how she had found the key thrown down on a path in the warren, which would be plausible enough, and while I turned this over in my mind I dangled the key between my fingers. It was of medium size, not larger, in fact, than the one in my own door. I compared the two and found them very similar. A sudden thought then struck me and, wheeling my chair into the passage, I listened for a moment to discover who stirred about the house.

It was a little before nine o'clock, with the servants all at their dinner and the rest of the household either talking in the gallery or already retired to their rooms for the night. The moment seemed well chosen for a very daring gamble, which might, or might not, prove nothing to me. I turned down the passage and halted outside the door of the locked chamber. I listened again, but no one stirred. Then very stealthily I pushed the key into the rusty lock. It fitted. It turned. And the door creaked open. . . .

I was so carried away for a moment by the success of my own scheme that I was nonplussed. I sat in my chair, uncertain what to do. But that there was a link between this chamber and the summerhouse now seemed definite, for the key turned both locks.

The chance to examine the room might never come again, and for all my fear, I was devoured with horrid curiosity.

I edged my chair within the room and, kindling my candle, for it was of course in darkness with the windows barred, I looked about me. The chamber was simple enough. Two windows, one to the north and the other to the west, both with iron bars across them.

A bed in the far corner, a few pieces of heavy furniture, and the table and chair I had already seen from the crack. The walls were hung about with a heavy arras, rather old and worn in many parts. It was indeed a disappointing room, with little that seemed strange in its appointments. It had the faded, musty smell that always clings about disused apartments. I laid the candle on the table and wheeled myself to the corner that gave upon the buttress. This, too, had arras hanging from the ceiling, which I lifted—and found nothing but bare stone behind it. I ran my hands over the surface but could find no join. The wall seemed smooth to my touch. But it was murky and I could not see, so I returned to the table to fetch my candle, first listening at the door to make certain that the servants were still at supper.

It was while I waited there, with an eye to the passage that turned at right angles running beneath the belfry, that I felt a sudden breath of cold air on the back of my head.

I looked swiftly over my shoulder and noticed that the arras on the wall beside the buttress was blowing to and fro, as though a cavity had opened, letting through a blast of air; and even as I watched I saw, to my great horror, a hand appear from behind a slit in the arras and lift it to one side. There was no time to wheel my chair into the passage, no time even to reach my hand out to the table and blow out the candle.

Someone came into the room with a crimson cloak about his shoulders and stood for a moment with the arras pushed aside and a great black hole in the wall behind him. He considered me a moment and then spoke.

"Close the door gently, Honor," he said, "and leave the candle. Since you are here it is best that we should have an explanation and no further mischief."

He advanced into the room, letting the arras drop behind him, and I saw then that the man was my brother-in-law, Jonathan Rashleigh.

12

I FELT LIKE a child caught out in some misdemeanour and was hot with shame and sick embarrassment. If he, then, was the stranger in the crimson cloak, walking his house in the small hours, it was not for me to question it; and to be discovered thus, prying in his secrets, with the key not only of this door but of his summerhouse as well, was surely something he could never pardon.

"Forgive me," I said, "I have acted very ill."

He did not answer at once, but first made certain that the door was closed. Then he lit further candles and, laying aside his cloak, drew a chair up to the table.

"It was you," he said, "who made a crack there in the panel? It was not there before you came to Menabilly."

His blunt question showed me what a shrewd grasp he had of my gaping curiosity, and I confessed that I was indeed the culprit. "I will not attempt to defend myself," I said. "I know I had no right to tamper with your walls. There was some talk of ghosts, otherwise I would not have done it. And one night during last week I heard footsteps."

"Yes," he said. "I had not thought to find your chamber occupied. I heard you stir and guessed then what had happened. We are somewhat pushed for room, as you no doubt realise, otherwise you would not have been put into the gatehouse."

He waited a moment and then, looking closely at me, he said, "You have understood, then, that there is a secret entry to this chamber?"

"Yes."

"And the reason you are here this evening is that you wished to find whither it led?"

"I knew it must be within the buttress."

"How did you come upon that key?"

This was the very devil, but there was nothing for it but to tell him the whole story, putting the blame heavily upon myself and saying little of Joan's share in the matter.

I said that I had looked about the summerhouse and admired the view, but as to my peering at his books and his father's will and lifting the heavy mat and finding the flagstone—nay, he would have to put me on the rack before I confessed to that.

He listened in silence, regarding me coldly all the while, and I knew what an interfering fool he must consider me.

"And what do you make of it now you know that the nightly intruder is none other than myself?" he questioned.

Here was a stumbling block. For I could make nothing of it. And I did not dare voice that secret, very fearful supposition that I kept hidden at the back of my mind.

"I cannot tell, Jonathan," I answered, "except that you use this entry for some purpose of your own and that your family know nothing of it."

At this he was silent, considering me slowly, and then after a long pause he said to me, "John has some knowledge of the subject, but no one else, except my steward Langdon. Indeed, the success of the royal cause we have at heart would gravely suffer should the truth become known."

This last surprised me. I did not see that his family secrets could be of any concern to His Majesty. But I said nothing.

"Since you already know something of the truth," he said, "I will acquaint you further, desiring you first to guard all knowledge of it to yourself."

I promised after a moment's hesitation, being uncertain what dire secret I might now be asked to share.

"You know," he said, "that at the beginning of hostilities I, with certain other gentlemen, was appointed by His Majesty's Council to collect and receive the plate given to the royal cause in Cornwall and arrange for it to be taken to the mint at Truro and there melted down?"

"I knew you were collector, Jonathan, no more than that."

"Last year another mint was erected at Exeter, under the supervision of my kinsman, Sir Richard Vyvyan, hence my constant business with that city. You will appreciate, Honor, that to receive a great quantity of very valuable plate and be responsible for its safety until it reaches the mint lies a heavy burden upon my shoulders."

"Yes, Jonathan."

"Spies abound, as you are well aware. Neighbours have long ears, and even a close friend can turn informer. If some member of the rebel army could but lay his hands upon the treasure that so frequently passes into my keeping the Parliament would be ten times the richer and His Majesty ten times the poorer. Therefore, all cartage of the plate has to be done at night, when the roads are quiet. Also, it is necessary to have depots throughout the county, where the plate can be stored until the necessary transport can be arranged. You have followed me so far?"

"Yes, Jonathan, and with interest."

"Very well then. These depots must be secret. As few people as possible must know their whereabouts. It is therefore imperative that the houses or buildings that serve as depots should contain hiding places known only to their owners. Menabilly, as you have already discovered, has such a hiding place."

I found myself getting hot under the skin, not at the implied sarcasm of his words, but because his revelation was so very different from what I—with excess of imagination—had supposed.

"The buttress against the far corner of this room," he continued, "is hollow in the centre. A flight of narrow steps leads to a small room, built in the thickness of the wall and beneath the courtyard, where it is possible for a man to stand and sit, though it is but five feet square. This room is connected with a passage, or rather tunnel, which runs under the house and so beneath the causeway to an outlet in the summerhouse.

"It is in this small buttress room that I have been accustomed, during the past year, to hide the plate. You understand me?"

I nodded, gripped by his story and deeply interested.

"When bringing the plate to this depot, or taking it away, we work by night, my steward, John Langdon, and I. The wagons wait down at Pridmouth, and we bring the plate from the buttress room, along the tunnel to the summerhouse, and so down to the cove in one of my handcarts, from where it is placed in the wagons. The men who conduct the procession from here to Exeter are all trustworthy, but none of them, naturally, know where abouts at Menabilly I have kept the plate hidden. That is not their business. No one knows that but myself and Langdon, and now you, Honor, who—I regret to say—have really no right at all to share the secret."

I said nothing, for there was no possible defence.

"John knows the plate has been concealed in the house but has never enquired where. He is, as yet, ignorant of the room beneath the buttress, likewise the tunnel to the summerhouse."

Here I risked offence by interrupting him.

"It was providential," I said, "that Menabilly possessed so excellent a hiding place."

"Very providential," he agreed. "Had it not been so, I could hardly have set about the business. You wonder, no doubt, why the house should have been so constructed?"

I confessed to some small wonder on the subject.

"My father," he said briefly, "had certain—how shall I put it?—shipping transactions which necessitated privacy. The tunnel was, therefore, useful in many ways."

In other words, I said to myself, your father, dear Jonathan, was nothing more or less than a pirate of the first order, whatever his standing and reputation in Fowey and the county.

"It happened, also," he said in a lower tone, "that my unfortunate elder brother was not in full possession of his faculties. This was his chamber from the time the house was built, in 1600, until his death, poor fellow, twenty-four years later. At times he was violent, hence the reason for the little cell beneath the buttress, where lack of air and close confinement soon rendered him unconscious and easy then to handle."

He spoke naturally and without restraint, but the picture that his words conjured turned me sick. I saw the wretched, shivering maniac choking for air in the dark room beneath the buttress, with the four walls closing in upon him. And now this same room stacked with silver plate like a treasure house in a fairy tale.

Jonathan must have seen my change of face, for he looked kindly at me and rose from his chair.

"I know," he said, "it is not a pretty story. It was a relief to me, I must admit, when the smallpox that carried off my father took my brother too. It was not a happy business, caring for him, with young children in the house. You have heard, no doubt, the malicious tales that Robert Bennett spread abroad?"

I mentioned vaguely that some rumour had passed me by.

"He took the disease some five days after my father," said Jonathan. "Why he should have taken it, and my wife and I escaped, we shall never know. But so he did, and, becoming violent at the same time with one of his periodic fits, he stood not a chance. It was over very quickly."

There were sounds now of the servants moving from the kitchens.

"You will return now to your apartment," he said, "and I will go back the way I came. You may give me John Langdon's key. If in future you hear me come to this apartment you will understand what I am about. I keep accounts here of the plate temporarily in my possession which I refer to from time to time. I need hardly tell you that not a word of what has this night passed between us must be spoken about to any other person."

"I give you my solemn promise, Jonathan."

"Good night then, Honor."

He helped me turn my chair into the passage and then, very softly, closed the door behind me. I got to my room a few moments before Matty came upstairs to draw the curtains.

13

ALTHOUGH THERE NEVER were any ties of affection between me and my brother-in-law, I certainly held him in greater respect and regard after our encounter of that evening. I knew now that "the King's business" on which he travelled to and fro was no light matter, and it was small wonder he was often short-tempered with his family.

Men with less sense of duty would have long since shelved the responsibility to other shoulders. I respected him, too, for having taken me into his confidence after my unwarrantable intrusion into his locked chamber. I was left only with a sneaking regret that he had not shown me the staircase in the buttress nor the cell beneath it, but this would have been too much to expect. I had a vivid picture, though, of the flapping arras and the black gulf behind.

Meanwhile, the progress of the war was causing each one of us no small concern. Our Western army was under the supreme command of the King's nephew, Prince Maurice, who was in great need of reinforcements, especially of cavalry, if he was ever to strike a decisive blow against the enemy. But the plan of the summer campaign appeared unsettled, and although Maurice's brother, Prince Rupert, endeavoured to persuade the King to send some two thousand horses into the West, there was the usual obstruction from the council, and the cavalry were not forthcoming. This, of course, we heard from Richard, who, fuming with impatience because he had as yet no guns that had been promised him, told us with grim candour that our Western army was, anyhow, worn with sickness and quite useless, Prince Maurice himself with but one bee in his bonnet, and that to sit before Lyme Regis, waiting for the place to open up to him. "If Essex and the rebel army choose to march West," said Richard, "there is nothing to stop him except a mob of sick men all lying on their backs and a handful of drunken generals. I can do nothing with my miserable two men and a boy squatting before Plymouth." Essex did choose to march West and was in Weymouth and Bridport by the third week of June, and Prince Maurice, with great loss of prestige, retreated in haste to Exeter.

Here he found his aunt, the Queen, who had arrived in a litter from Bristol, being fearful of the approaching enemy, and it was here at Exeter that she gave birth to her youngest child, which did not lessen the responsibilities of Prince Maurice and his staff. He decided that the wisest course was to get her away to France as speedily as possible, and she set forth for Falmouth, very weak and nervous, two weeks after the baby had been born.

My brother-in-law Jonathan was amongst those who waited on her as she passed through Bodmin on her way South, and came back telling very pitiful tales of her appearance, she being much worn and shaken by her ordeal. "She may have ill-advised His Majesty on many an occasion," said Jonathan, "but at least she is a woman, and I tremble to think of her fate if she fell into the hands of the rebels." It was a sore relief to all the royalists in Cornwall when she reached Falmouth without mishap and embarked for France.

But Essex and the rebel army were gathering in numbers all the while, and we felt it was but a matter of weeks before he passed through Dorset into Devon, with nothing but the Tamar then between him and Cornwall. The only one who viewed the approaching struggle with relish was Richard. "If we can but draw the beggar into Cornwall," he said, "a country of which he knows nothing and whose narrow lanes and high hedges would befog him completely, and then with the King's and Rupert's armies coming up in the rear and cutting off all retreat, we will have Essex surrounded and destroyed."

I remember him rubbing his hands gleefully and laughing at the prospect like a boy on holiday, but the idea did not much appeal to Jonathan and other gentlemen, who were dining at Menabilly on that day. "If we have fighting in Cornwall the country will be devastated," said Francis Bassett, who, with my brother-in-law, was engaged at that time in trying to raise troops for the King's service and finding it mighty hard. "The land is too poor to feed an army; we cannot do it. The fighting must be kept the other side the Tamar, and we look to you and your troops, Grenvile, to engage the enemy in Devon and keep us from invasion."

"My good fool," said Richard—at which Francis Bassett coloured, and we all felt uncomfortable—"you are a country squire, and I respect your knowledge of cattle and pigs. But for God's sake leave the art of war to professional soldiers like myself. Our aim at present is to destroy the enemy, which we cannot do in Devon, where there is no hope of encirclement. Once across the Tamar, he will run his head into a noose. My only fear is that he will not do so but will use his superior cavalry on the open Devon moors against Maurice and his hopeless team of half-wits, in which case we shall have lost one of the greatest chances this war has yet produced."

"You are prepared, then," said Jonathan, "to see Cornwall laid waste, people homeless, and much sickness and suffering spread abroad. It does not appear to be a prospect of much comfort."

"Damn your comfort," said Richard. "It will do my fellow countrymen a world of good to see a spot of bloodshed. If you cannot suffer that for the King's cause, then we may as well treat with the enemy forthwith."

There was some atmosphere of strain in the dining chamber when he had spoken, and shortly afterwards my brother-in-law gave the host's signal for dispersal. It was an oddity I could not explain even to myself that since Richard had come back into my life I could face company with greater equanimity than I had done before and had now formed the habit of eating downstairs rather than in my chamber. Solitude was no longer my one aim. After dining, it still being light, he took a turn with me upon the causeway, making himself attendant to my chair.

"If Essex draws near to Tavistock," he said, "and I am forced to raise the siege of Plymouth and retreat, can I send the whelp to you?"

I was puzzled for a moment, thinking he alluded to his dog.

"What whelp?" I asked. "I did not know you possessed one."

"The Southwest makes you slow of brain," he said. "My spawn, I mean, my pup, my son and heir. Will you have him here under your wing and put some sense into his frightened head?"

"Why, yes indeed, if you think he would be happy with me."

"I think he would be happier with you than any other person in the world. My aunt Abbot at Hartland is too old, and Bevil's wife at Stowe is so slung about with her own brood that I do not care to ask her. Besides, she has never thought much of me."

"Have you spoken to Jonathan?"

"Yes, he is willing. But I wonder what you will make of Dick. He is a scrubby object."

"I will love him, Richard, because he is your son."

"I doubt that sometimes when I look at him. He has a shrinking, timid way with him, and his tutor tells me that he cries for a finger scratch. I would exchange him any day for young Joe Grenvile, a kinsman whom I have as aide-de-camp at Buckland. He is up to any daring scheme, that lad, and a fellow after my own heart, like Bevil's eldest boy."

"Dick is barely turned fourteen," I said to him. "You must not expect too much. Give him a year or two to learn confidence."

"If he takes after his mother, then I'll turn him off and let him starve," said Richard. "I won't have frogs' spawn about me."

"Perhaps," I said, "your example does not greatly encourage him to take after yourself. Were I a child I would not want a red fox for a father."

"He is the wrong age for me," said Richard, "too big to dandle and too small to talk to. He is yours, Honor, from this day forward. I declare I will bring him over to you this day week."

And so it was arranged, with Jonathan's permission, that Dick Grenvile and his tutor, Herbert Ashley, should add to the numbers at Menabilly. I was strangely happy and excited the day they were expected and went with my sister Mary to inspect the room that had been put to their service beneath the clock tower.

I took pains with my toilet, wearing my blue gown that was my favourite and bidding Matty brush my hair for half the morning. And all the while I told myself what a sentimental fool I was to waste such time and trouble for a little lad who would not look at me. . . .

It was about one o'clock when I heard the horses trotting across the park and I called in a fever to Matty to fetch the servants to carry me downstairs, for I wished to be in the garden when I greeted them, having a firm belief that it is always easier to become acquainted with anyone out of doors in the sun than to be shut fast within four walls.

I was seated, then, in the walled garden beneath the causeway when the gate opened and a lad came walking across the lawn towards me. He was taller than I had imagined, with the flaming Grenvile locks and an impudent snub nose and a swagger about him that reminded me instantly of Richard. And then as he spoke I realised my mistake.

"My name is Joe Grenvile," he said. "They have sent me from the house to bring you back. There has been a slight mishap. Poor Dick tumbled from his horse as we drew rein in the courtyard—the stones were somewhat slippery—and he has cut his head. They have taken him to your chamber, and your maid is washing the blood."

This was very different from the picture I had painted, and I was at once distressed that the arrival should have gone awry.

"Is Sir Richard come with you?" I asked as he wheeled me down the path.

"Yes," said young Joe, "and in a great state of irritation, cursing poor Dick for incompetence, which made the little fellow worse. We have to leave again within the hour. Essex has reached Tiverton, you know, and Taunton Castle is also in the rebels' hands. Prince Maurice has withdrawn several units from our command, and there is to be a conference at Okehampton, which Sir Richard must attend. Ours are the only troops that are now left outside Plymouth."

"And you find all this greatly stirring, do you, Joe?" I asked.

"Yes, madam. I can hardly wait to have a crack at the enemy myself."

We turned in at the garden entrance and found Richard pacing up and down the hall. "You would hardly believe it possible," he said, "but the whelp must go and tumble from his horse, right on the very doorstep. Sometimes I think he has softening of the brain, to act in so boobyish a fashion. What do you think of Joe?" He clapped the youngster on the shoulder, who looked up at him with pride and devotion. "We shall make a soldier of this chap anyway," he said. "Go and draw me some ale, Joe, and a tankard for yourself. I'm as thirsty as a drowning man."

"What of Dick?" I asked. "Shall I not go to him?"

"Leave him to the women and his useless tutor," said Richard. "You'll soon have enough of him. I have one hour to spend at Menabilly and I want you to myself."

We went to the little anteroom beyond the gallery, and there he sat with me while he drank his ale and told me that Essex would be at Tavistock before the week was out.

"If he marches on Cornwall, then we have him trapped," said Richard, "and if the King will only follow fast enough on his heels the game is ours. It will be unpleasant while it lasts, my sweetheart, but it will not be for long; that I can promise you."

"Shall we see fighting in this district?" I asked with some misgiving.

"Impossible to answer. It depends on Essex, whether he strikes north or south. He will make for Liskeard and Bodmin, where we shall try to hold him. Pray for a dirty August, Honor, and they will be up to their eyes in mud. I must go. I sleep tonight in Launceston if I can make it." He put his tankard on the table and, first closing the door, he knelt beside my chair. "Look after the little whelp," he said, "and teach him manners. If the worst should happen and there be fighting in the neighbourhood hide him under your bed—Essex would take any son of mine as hostage. Do you love me still?"

"I love you always."

"Then cease listening for footsteps in the gallery and kiss me as though you meant it."

It was easy for him, no doubt, to hold me close for five minutes and have me in a turmoil with his love-making and then ride away to Launceston, his mind aflame with other matters; but for me, left with my hair and gown in disarray, and no method of escape and long hours stretching before me to think about it all, it was rather more disturbing. I had chosen the course, though; I had let him come back into my life, and I must put up with the fever he engendered in me which could never more be stilled.

So calling to his aide-de-camp, he waved his hand to me and rode away to Launceston, where, I told myself with nagging jealousy, he and young Joe would in all probability dine overwell and find some momentary distraction before the more serious business of tomorrow, for I knew my Richard too well to believe he lived a life of austerity simply because he loved me.

I patted my curls and smoothed my lace collar, then pulled the bell rope for a servant, who, with the aid of another, bore me in my chair to my apartment. I did not pass through the front of the house, as was my custom, but through the back rooms beneath the belfry, and here in a passage I found Frank Penrose, my brother-in-law's cousin and dependent, engaged in earnest conversation with a young man of about his own age who had a sallow complexion and retreating chin and who appeared to be recounting the story of his life.

"This is Mr. Ashley, Mistress Honor," said Frank with the smarming manner peculiar to him. "He has left his charge resting in your apartment. Mr. Ashley is about to take refreshment with me below."

Mr. Ashley bowed and scraped his heels.

"Sir Richard informed me you are the boy's godmother, madam," he said, "and that I am to take my commands from you. It is, of course, rather irregular, but I will endeavour to adapt myself to the circumstances."

You are a fool, I thought, and a prig, and I don't think I am going to like you, but aloud I said, "Please continue, Mr. Ashley, as you have been accustomed to at Buckland. I have no intention of interfering in any way, except to see that the boy is happy."

I left them both bowing and scraping and ready to pull me to pieces as soon as my back was turned, and so was brought to the gatehouse. I met Matty coming forth with a basin of water and strips of bandage on her arm.

"Is he much hurt?" I asked.

Her lips were drawn in the tight line I knew meant disapproval of the whole proceeding.

"More frightened than anything else," she said. "He'll fall to pieces if you look at him."

The servants set me down in the room and withdrew, closing the door.

He was sitting hunched up in a chair beside the hearth, a white shrimp of a boy with great dark eyes and tight black locks, his pallor worsened by the bandage on his head. He watched me, nervously biting his nails all the while.

"Are you better?" I said gently.

He stared at me for a moment and then said with a queer jerk of his head, "Has he gone?"

"Has who gone?" I asked.

"My father."

"Yes, he has ridden away to Launceston with your cousin."

He considered this a moment.

"When will he be back?" he asked.

"He will not be back. He has to attend a meeting at Okehampton tomorrow or the following day. You are to stay here for the present. Did he not tell you who I am?"

"I think you must be Honor. He said I was to be with a lady who was beautiful. Why do you sit in that chair?"

"Because I cannot walk. I am a cripple."

"Does it hurt?"

"No, not very much. I am used to it. Does your head hurt you?"

He touched the bandage warily. "It bled," he said. "There is blood under the bandage."

"Never mind, it will soon heal."

"I will keep the bandage on or it will bleed afresh," he said. "You must tell the servant who washes it not to move the bandage."

"Very well," I said, "I will tell her."

I took a piece of tapestry and began to work on it so he should not think I watched him and would grow accustomed to my presence.

"My mother used to work at tapestry," he said after a lengthy pause. "She worked a forest scene with stags running."

"That was pretty," I said.

"She made three covers for her chairs," he went on. "They were much admired at Fitzford. You never came to Fitzford, I believe?"

"No, Dick."

"My mother had many friends, but I did not hear her speak of you."

"I do not know your mother, Dick. I only know your father."

"Do you like him?" The question was suspicious, sharply put.

"Why do you ask?" I said, evading it.

"Because I don't. I hate him. I wish he would be killed in battle."

The tone was savage, venomous. I stole a glance at him and saw him once more biting at the back of his hand.

"Why do you hate him?" I asked quietly.

"He is a devil, that's why. He tried to kill my mother. He tried to steal her house and money and then kill her."

"Why do you think that?"

"My mother told me."

"Do you love her very much?"

"I don't know. I think so. She was beautiful. More beautiful than you. She is in London now with my sister. I wish I could be with her."

"Perhaps," I said, "when the war is finished with, you will go back to her."

"I would run away," he said, "but for London being so far, and I might get caught in the fighting. There is fighting everywhere. There is no talk of anything at Buckland but the fighting. I will tell you something."

"What is that?"

"Last week I saw a wounded man brought into the house upon a stretcher. There was blood upon him."

The way he said this puzzled me. His manner was so shrinking.

"Why," I asked, "are you so much afraid of blood?"

The colour flamed into his pale face.

"I did not say I was afraid," he answered quickly.

"No, but you do not like it. Neither do I. It is most unpleasant. But I am not fearful if I see it spilt."

"I cannot bear to see it spilt at all," he said after a moment. "I have always been thus since a little child. It is not my fault."

"Perhaps you were frightened as a baby."

"That's what my mother brought me up to understand. She told me that when she had me in her arms once my father came into the room and quarrelled violently with her upon some matter and that he struck her on the face and she bled. The blood ran onto my hands. I cannot remember it, but that is how it was."

I began to feel very sick at heart and despondent but was careful that he should not notice it.

"We won't talk about it any more then, Dick, unless you want to. What shall we discuss instead?"

"Tell me what you did when you were my age, how you looked, and what you said, and had you brothers, and had you sisters?"

And so I wove him a tale about the past, thus making him forget his own, while he sat watching me; and by the time Matty came, bringing us refreshment, he had lost so much of his nervousness as to chat with her, too, and make big eyes at the pasties which soon disappeared, while I sat and looked at his little chiselled features, so unlike his father's, and the close black curls upon his head. Afterwards I read to him for a while, and he left his chair and came and curled on the floor beside my chair, like a small dog that would make friends in a strange house, and when I closed the book he looked up at me and smiled—and the smile for the first time was Richard's smile and not his mother's.

14

FROM THAT DAY forward Dick became my shadow. He arrived early with my breakfast, never my best moment of the day, but because he was Richard's son I suffered him. He then left to do his lessons with the sallow Mr. Ashley while I made my toilet, and later in the morning came to walk beside my chair upon the causeway.

He sat beside me in the dining chamber and brought a stool to the gallery when I went there after dinner; seldom speaking, always watchful, he hovered continually about me like a small phantom.

"Why do you not run and play in the gardens," I asked, "or desire Mr. Ashley to take you down to Pridmouth? There are fine shells there on the beach and, the weather being warm, you could swim if you had the mind. There's a young cob, too, in the stables you could ride across the park."

"I would rather stay with you," he said.

And he was firm on this and would not be dissuaded. Even Alice, who had the warmest way with children I ever saw, failed with him, for he would shake his head and take his stool behind my chair.

"He has certainly taken a fancy to you, madam," said the tutor, relieved, I am sure, to find his charge so little trouble. "I have found it very hard to interest him."

"He is your conquest," said Joan, "and you will never more be rid of him. Poor Honor. What a burden to the end of your days!"

But it did not worry me. If Dick was happy with me that was all that mattered, and if I could bring some feeling of security to his poor lonely little heart and puzzled mind I should not feel my days were wasted. Meanwhile, the news worsened, and some five days after Dick's arrival word came from Fowey that Essex had reached Tavistock, and the siege of Plymouth had been raised, with Richard withdrawing his troops from Saltash, Mount Stampford, and Plympton, and retreating to the Tamar bridges.

That evening a council was held in Tywardreath amongst the gentry in the district, at which my brother-in-law presided, and one and all decided to muster what men and arms and ammunition they could and ride to Launceston to help defend the county.

We were at once in a state of consternation and the following morning saw the preparations for departure. All those on the estate who were able-bodied and fit to carry arms paraded before my brother-in-law with their horses and their kits packed on the saddles, and amongst them were the youngest of the house servants who could be spared and all the grooms. Jonathan and his son-in-law, John Rashleigh of Coombe, and Oliver Sawle from Penrice—brother to old Nick Sawle—and many other gentlemen from round about Fowey and St. Austell gathered at Menabilly before setting forth, while my poor sister Mary went from one to the other with her face set in a smile I knew was sadly forced, handing them cake and fruit and pasties to cheer them on their way. John was left with many long instructions, which I could swear he would never carry in his head, and then we watched them set off across the park, a strange, pathetic little band full of ignorance and high courage, the tenants wielding their muskets as though they were hay forks, and with considerably more danger to themselves than to the enemy they might encounter. It was '43 all over again, with the rebels not thirty miles away, and although Richard might declare that Essex and his army were running into a trap, I was disloyal enough to wish they might keep out of it.

Those last days of July were clammy and warm, a sticky breeze blowing from the southwest that threatened rain and never brought it, while a tumbled sea rolled past the Gribbin white and grey. At Menabilly we made a pretence of continuing as though all were as usual, and nothing untoward likely to happen, and even forced a little gaiety when dining that we must wait upon ourselves, now that there were none but womenfolk to serve us. But for all this deception, intended to convey a sense of courage, we were tense and watchful—our ears always pricked for the rumble of cannon or the sound of horses. I can remember how we all sat beside the long table in the dining chamber, the portrait of His Majesty gazing calmly down upon us from the dark panelling above the open hearth, and how at the end of a strained, tedious meal Nick Sawle, who was the eldest amongst us, conquered his rheumatics and rose to his feet in great solemnity, saying, "It were well that in this time of stress and trouble we should give a toast unto His Majesty. Let us drink to our beloved King and may God protect him and all who have gone forth from this house to fight for him."

They all then rose to their feet, too, except myself, and looked up at his portrait— those melancholy eyes, that small, obstinate mouth—and I saw the tears run down Alice's cheeks—she was thinking of Peter—and sad resignation come to Mary's face, her thoughts with Jonathan, yet none of them gazing at the King's portrait thought to blame him for the trouble that had come upon them. God knows I had no sympathy for the rebels, who each one of them was out for feathering his own nest and building up a fortune, caring nothing for the common people whose lot they pretended would be bettered by their victory; but nor could I, in my heart, recognise the King as the fountain of all truth, but thought of him always as a stiff, proud man, small in intelligence as he was in stature, yet commanding by his grace of manner, his dignity, and his moral virtue a wild devotion in his followers that sprang from their warm hearts and not their reason.

We were a quiet, subdued party who sat in the long gallery that evening. Even the sharp tongue of Temperance Sawle was stilled, her thin features were pinched and anxious, while the Sparkes forewent their usual game of cribbage and sat talking in low voices, Will, the rumour-monger, without much heart now for his hobby.

"Have the rebels crossed the Tamar?" This was, I think, the thought in all our minds, and while Mary, Alice, and Joan worked at their tapestry and I read in a soft voice to Dick, my brain, busy all the while, was reckoning the shortest distance that the enemy would take and whether they would cross by Saltash or by Gunnislake. John had left the dining chamber as soon as the King's health had been drunk, saying he could stand this waiting about no longer but must ride to Fowey for news. He returned about nine o'clock, saying that the town was well-nigh empty, with so many ridden north to join the Army, but those who were left were standing at their doors, glum and despondent, saying that word had come that Grenvile and his troops had been defeated at Newbridge below Gunnislake, while Essex and some ten thousand men were riding toward Launceston.

I remember Will Sparke leaping to his feet at hearing this and breaking out into a tirade against Richard, his shrill voice sharp and nervous. "What have I been saying all along?" he cried. "When it comes to a test like this the fellow is no commander. The pass at Gunnislake should be easy to defend, no matter the strength of the opponent, and here is Grenvile pulled out and in full retreat without having struck a blow to defend Cornwall. Heaven, what a contrast to his brother."

"It is only rumour, Cousin Will," said John with an uncomfortable glance in my direction. "There was no one in Fowey able to swear to the truth of it."

"I tell you, everything is lost," said Will. "Cornwall will be ruined and overrun, even as Sir Francis Bassett said the other day. And if it is so, then Richard Grenvile will be to blame for it."

I watched young Dick swallow the words with eager eyes and, pulling at my arm, he whispered, "What is it he says? What has happened?"

"John Rashleigh hears that the Earl of Essex has passed into Cornwall," I told him softly, "finding little opposition. We must wait until the tale be verified."

"Then my father has been slain in battle?"

"No, Dick, nothing has been said of that. Do you wish me to continue reading?"

"Yes, please, if you will do so."

And I went on with the tale, taking no notice of his biting of his hand, for my anxiety was such that I could have done the same myself. Anything might have happened during these past eight and forty hours. Richard left for slain upon the steep road down from Gunnislake and his men fled in all directions, or taken prisoner, perhaps, and at this moment being put to torture in Launceston Castle that he might betray the plan of battle.

It was always my fault to let imagination do its worst, and although I guessed enough of Richard's strategy to know that a retreat on the Tamar bank was probably his intention from the first, in order to lure Essex into Cornwall, yet I longed to hear the opposite and that a victory had been gained that day and the rebels pushed back into Devon.

I slept ill that night, for to be ignorant of the truth is, I shall always believe, the worst sort of mental torture, and for a powerless woman who cannot forget her fears in taking action there is no remedy.

The next day was as hot and airless as the one preceding, and when I came down after breakfast I wondered if I looked as haggard and as careworn to the rest of the company as they looked to me. And still no news. But everything strangely silent, even the jackdaws that usually clustered in the trees down in the warren had flown and settled elsewhere.

Shortly before noon, when some of us were assembled in the dining chamber to take cold meat, Mary, coming from her sun parlour across the hall, cried, "There is a horseman riding across the park towards the house."

Everyone began talking at once and pushing to the windows, and John, something white about the lips, went to the courtyard to receive whoever it should be.

The rider clattered into the inner court, with all of us watching from the windows, and though he was covered from head to foot with dust and had a great slash across his boot I recognised him at once as young Joe Grenvile.

"I have a message for Mistress Harris," he said, flinging himself from his horse, and my throat went dry and my hands went wet, and he is dead, I thought, for certain.

"But the battle, how goes the battle?" and "What of the rebels?" "What has happened?" Questions on all sides were put to him, with Nick Sawle on one side and Will Sparke on the other, so that he had to push his way through them to reach me in the hall.

"Essex will be in Bodmin by nightfall," he said briefly. "We have just had a brush with Lord Robartes and his brigade above Lostwithiel, who have now turned back to meet him. We ourselves are in hot retreat to Truro, where Sir Richard plans to raise more troops. I am come from the road but to bring this message to Mistress Harris."

"Essex at Bodmin?" A cry of alarm went up from all the company, and Temperance Sawle went straightway on her knees and called upon her Maker. But I was busy tearing open Richard's letter. I read:

> My sweet love, the hook is nicely baited, and the poor misguided
> fish gapes at it with his mouth wide open. He will be in Bodmin
> tonight, and most probably in Fowey tomorrow. His chief adviser
> in the business is that crass idiot, Jack Robartes, whose mansion at

Lanhydrock I have just had infinite pleasure in pillaging. They will swallow the bait, hook, line, and sinker. We shall come up on them from Truro, and His Majesty, Maurice, and Ralph Hopton from the east. The King has already advanced as far as Tavistock, so the fish will be most prettily landed. Your immediate future at Menabilly being somewhat unpleasant, it will be best if you return the whelp to me, with his tutor. I have given Joe instructions on the matter. Keep to your chamber, my dear love, and have no fear. We will come to your succour as soon as may be. My respects to your sister and the company.

Your devoted servant,
RICHARD GRENVILE

I placed the letter in my gown and turned to Joe.
"Is the general well?" I asked.
"Never better." He grinned. "I have just left him eating roast pork on the road to Grampound, while his servant cleaned his boots. We seized a score of pigs from Lord Robartes's park, and a herd of sheep, and some twenty head of cattle—the troops are in high fettle. If you hear rumours of our losses at Newbridge pay no attention to them; the higher figure they are put at by the enemy, the better pleased will be Sir Richard."
I motioned then that I should like to speak with him apart, and he withdrew alone with me to the sun parlour.
"What is the plan for Dick?" I asked.
"Sir Richard thinks it best if the boy and Mr. Ashley embark by fishing boat for St. Mawes, if arrangements can be made with one of the fellows at Polkerris. They can keep close inshore, and once around the Dodman the passage will not be long. I have money here to pay the fishermen, and pay them well, for their trouble."
"When should they depart?"
"As soon as possible. I shall see to it and go with them to the beach. Then I shall return to join Sir Richard and, with any luck, catch up with him on the Grampound-Truro road. The trouble is the roads are already choked with people in headlong flight from Essex, all making for the West, and it will not be long now before the rebel cavalry reach the district."
"There is, then, no time to lose," I answered, "and I will ask Mr. John Rashleigh to go with you to Polkerris; he will know the men there who are most likely to be trusted."
I called John to come to me and hurriedly explained the plan, whereupon he set forth straightway to Polkerris with Joe Grenvile, while I sent word to Herbert Ashley that I wished to speak to him. He arrived looking very white about the gills, for rumour had run riot in the place that the Grenvile troops were flying in disorder with the rebels on their heels and the war was irrevocably lost. He looked much relieved when I told him that he and Dick were to depart upon the instant, by sea and not by road, and went immediately to pack their things, promising to be ready within the hour. The task then fell upon me to break the news to my shadow. He was standing by the side door, looking out on to the garden, and I beckoned him to my side.
"Dick," I said to him. "I want you to be brave and sensible. The neighbourhood is likely to be surrounded by the enemy before another day, and Menabilly will be seized. Your father thinks it better you should not be found here, and I have arranged, therefore, with Mr. Rashleigh, that you and your tutor go by boat to St. Mawes, where you will be safe."
"Are you coming too?" he asked.
"No, Dick. This is a very sudden plan, made only for yourselves. I and the rest of the company will remain at Menabilly."

"Then so will I."

"No, Dick. You must let me judge for you. And it is best for you to go."

"Does it mean that I must join my father?"

"That I cannot tell. All I do know is that the fishing boat is to take you to St. Mawes."

He said nothing but looked queerly sulky and strange, and after a moment or two went up to join his tutor.

I had a pain at the pit of my stomach all the while, for there is nothing so contagious as panic, and the atmosphere of sharp anxiety was rife in the air. In the gallery little groups of people were gathered, with strained eyes and drawn faces, and Alice's children, aware of tension, chose—poor dears—this moment to be fretful and were clinging to her skirts, crying bitterly.

"There is time yet to reach Truro if only we had a conveyance," I heard Will say, his face grey with fear, "but Jonathan took all the horses with him, and the farm wagons would be too slow. Where has John gone? Is it not possible for John to arrange in some manner that we be conducted to Truro?"

His sisters watched him with anxious eyes, and I saw Gillian whisper hurriedly to Deborah that none of their things were ready, it would take her till evening to sort out what was necessary for travel. Then Nick Sawle, drawing himself up proudly, said in a loud voice, "My wife and I propose to stay at Menabilly. If cowards care to clatter on the roads as fugitives they are welcome to do so, but I find it a poor return to our cousin Jonathan to desert his house like rats in time of trouble."

My sister Mary looked towards me in distress.

"What do you counsel, Honor?" she asked. "Should we set forth or should we stay? Jonathan gave me no commands. He assured me that the enemy would not cross the Tamar, or, at the worst, be turned back after a few miles."

"My God," I said, "if you care to hide in the ditches with the driven cattle, then by all means go, but I swear you will fare worse upon the road than you are likely to do at home. Better to starve under your own roof than in the hedges."

"We have plenty of provisions," said Mary, snatching a ray of hope. "We are not likely to want for anything unless the siege be long."

She turned in consultation to her stepdaughters, who were all of them still occupied in calming the children, and I thought it wisest not to spread further consternation by telling her that once the rebels held the house they would make short work of her provisions.

The clock in the belfry had just struck three when Dick and his tutor came down ready for departure. The lad was still sulky and turned his head from me when I would say good-bye. This was better than the rebellious tears I had expected, and with a cheerful voice I wished him a speedy journey and that a week or less would see the end of all our troubles. He did not answer, and I signed to Herbert Ashley to take his arm and to start walking across the park with Frank Penrose, who would conduct them to Polkerris, and there fall in with John Rashleigh and Joe Grenvile, who must by this time have matters well arranged.

Anxiety and strain had brought an aching back upon me, and I desired now nothing so much as to retire to the gatehouse and lie upon my bed. I sent for Matty, and she, with the help of Joan and Alice, carried me upstairs. The sun was coming strongly through my western casement and the room was hot and airless. I lay upon my bed sticky wet, wishing with all my heart that I were a man and could ride with Joe Grenvile on the road to Truro, instead of lying there, a woman and a cripple, waiting for the relentless tramp of enemy feet. I had been there but an hour, I suppose, snatching brief oblivion, when I heard once more the sound of a horse galloping across the park, and, calling to Matty, I enquired who it should be. She went to the casement and looked out.

"It's Mr. John," she said, "in great distress by his expression. Something has gone amiss."

My heart sank at her words. Perhaps, after all, the fishermen at Polkerris could not be tempted to set sail. In a moment or two I heard his footstep on the stairs and he flung into my room, forgetting even to knock upon the door.

"We have lost Dick," he said; "he has vanished. He is nowhere to be found." He stood staring at me, the sweat pouring down his face, and I could see that his whole frame was trembling.

"What do you mean? What has happened?" I asked swiftly, raising myself in my bed.

"We were all assembled on the beach," he said, his breath coming quickly, "and the boat was launched. There was a little cuddy below deck, and I saw Dick descend to it with my own eyes, his bundle under his arm. There was no trouble to engage the boat, and the men—both of them stout fellows and well known to me—were willing. Just before they drew anchor we heard a clatter on the cobbles beside the cottages, and some lads came running down in great alarm to tell us that the first body of rebel horse had cut the road from Castledore to Tywardreath and that Polmear Hill was already blocked with troops. At this the men began to make sail, and young Joe Grenvile turned to me with a wink and said, 'It looks as if I must go by water too,' and before I could answer him he had urged his horse into the sea and was making for the sand flats half a mile away to the westward. It was half low tide, but he had reached them and turned in his saddle to wave to us within five and twenty minutes. He'll be on Gosmoor by now and halfway to St. Austell."

"But Dick?" I said. "You say you have lost Dick?"

"He was in the boat," he said stubbornly, "I swear he was in the boat, but we turned to listen to the lads and their tale of the troops at Tywardreath, and then with one accord we watched young Joe put his horse to the water and swim for it. By heaven, Honor, it was the boldest thing I have ever seen a youngster do, for the tide can run swiftly between Polkerris and the flats. And then Ashley, the tutor, looking about him, called for Dick but could not find him. We searched the vessel from stem to stern, but he wasn't there. He was not on the beach. He was not anywhere. For God's sake, Honor, what are we now to do?"

I felt as helpless as he did, and sick with anxiety, for here was I, having failed utterly in my trust, and the rebel troops not two miles away.

"Where is the boat now?" I asked.

"Lying off the Gribbin, waiting for a signal from me," said John, "with that useless tutor aboard with no other thought in his mind but getting to St. Mawes. But even if we find the boy, Honor, I fear it will be too late."

"Search the cliffs in all directions," I said, "and the grounds, and the park, and pasture. Was anything said to the lad upon the way?"

"I cannot say. I think not. I only heard Frank Penrose tell him that by nightfall he would be with his father."

So that was it, I thought. A moment's indiscretion but enough to turn Dick from his journey and play truant like a child from school. I could do nothing in the search but bade John set forth once more with Frank Penrose, saying no word to anyone of what had happened. And, calling to Matty, I bade her take me to the causeway.

15

ONCE ON THE high ground I had as good a view of the surrounding country as I could wish, and I saw Frank Penrose and John Rashleigh strike out across the beef park to the beacon fields and then divide. All the while I had a fear in my heart that the boy had drowned himself and would be found with the rising tide floating face downwards in the wash below Polkerris cliffs. There was no sign of the boat, and I judged it to be to the westward beyond Polkerris and the Gribbin.

Back and forth we went along the causeway, with Matty pushing my chair, and still no sign of a living soul, nothing but the cattle grazing on the farther hills and the ripple of a breeze blowing the corn upon the sky line.

Presently I sent Matty withindoors for a cloak, for the breeze was freshening, and on her return she told me that stragglers were already pouring into the park from the roads, women and children and old men, all with makeshift bundles on their backs, begging for shelter, for the route was cut to Truro and the rebels everywhere. My sister Mary was at her wit's end to know what to say to them, and many of them were already kindling fires down in the warren and making rough shelter for the night.

"As I came out just now," said Matty, "there was a litter borne by four horses come to rest in the courtyard, and a lady within demanding harbourage for herself and her young daughters. I heard the servant say they had been nine hours upon the road."

I thanked God in my heart that we had remained at Menabilly and not lost our heads like these other poor unfortunates.

"Go back, Matty," I said, "and see what you can do to help my sister. None of the servants have any sense left in their heads."

She had not been gone more than ten minutes before I saw two figures coming across the fields towards me, and one of them, seeing me upon the causeway, waved his arm, while with the other he held fast to his companion.

It was John Rashleigh, and he had Dick with him.

When they reached me I saw the boy was dripping wet and scratched about the face and hands by brambles, but for once he was not bothered by the sight of blood but stared at me defiantly.

"I will not go," he said; "you cannot make me go."

John Rashleigh shook his head at me and shrugged his shoulders in resignation. "It's no use, Honor," he said. "We shall have to keep him. There's a wash on the beaches now and I've signalled to the boat to make sail and take the tutor across the bay to Mevagissey or Gorran, where he must make shift for himself. As for this lad—I found him halfway up the cliff, a mile from Polkerris, having been waist-deep in water for the past three hours. God only knows what Sir Richard will say to the bungle we have made."

"Never mind Sir Richard, I will take care of him," I said, "when—and if—we ever clap eyes on him again. That boy must return to the house with me and be shifted into dry clothes before anything else be done with him."

Now the causeway at Menabilly is set high, as I have said, commanding a fine view both to east and west, and at this moment—I know not why—I turned my head towards the coast road that descended down to Pridmouth from Coombe and Fowey, and I saw, silhouetted on the sky line above the valley, a single horseman. In a moment he was joined by others who paused an instant on the hill and then, following their leader, plunged down the narrow roadway to the cove.

John saw them, too, for our eyes met and we looked at each other long and silently, while Dick stood between us, his eyes downcast, his teeth chattering.

Richard in the old days was wont to tease me for my southcoast blood, so sluggish, he averred, to that which ran through his own north-coast veins, but I swear I thought, in the next few seconds, as rapidly as he had ever done or was likely yet to do.

"Have you your father's keys?" I said to John.

"Yes," he said.

"All of them?"

"All of them."

"On your person now?"

"Yes."

"Open, then, the door of the summerhouse."

He obeyed me without question—thank God his stern father had taught him discipline—and in an instant we stood at the threshold with the door flung open.

"Lift the mat from beneath the desk there," I said, "and raise the flagstone."

He looked at me then in wonder but went without a word to do as I had bidden him. In a moment the mat was lifted and the flagstone, too, and the flight of steps betrayed to view.

"Don't ask me any questions, John," I said; "there is no time. A passage runs underground from those steps to the house. Take Dick with you now, first replacing the flagstone above your heads, and crawl with him along the passage to the farther end. You will come then to a small room like a cell, and another flight of steps. At the top of the steps is a door which opens, I believe, from the passage end. But do not try to open it until I give you warning from the house."

I could read the sense of what I had said go slowly to his mind and a dawn of comprehension come into his eyes.

"The chamber next to yours?" he said. "My uncle John—"

"Yes," I said. "Give me the keys. Go quickly."

There was no trouble now with Dick. He had gathered from my manner that danger was deadly near and the time for truancy was over. He bolted down into the hole like a frightened rabbit. I watched John settle the mat over the flagstone and, descending after Dick, he lowered the stone above his head and disappeared.

The summerhouse was as it had been, empty and untouched. I leant over in my chair and turned the key in the lock and then put the keys inside my gown. I looked out to the eastward and saw that the sky line was empty. The troopers would have reached the cove by now and after watering their horses at the mill would climb up the farther side and be at Menabilly within ten minutes.

The sweat was running down my forehead clammy cold, and as I waited for Matty to fetch me—and God only knew how much longer she would be—I thought how I would give all I possessed in the world at that moment for but one good swig of brandy.

Far out on the beacon hills I could see Frank Penrose still searching hopelessly for Dick, while in the meadows to the west one of the women from the farm went calling to the cows, all oblivious of the troopers who were riding up the lane.

And at that moment my godchild Joan came hurrying along the causeway to fetch me, her pretty face all strained and anxious, her soft dark hair blowing in the wind.

"They are coming," she said. "We have seen them from the windows. Scores of them, on horseback, riding now across the park."

Her breath caught in a sob, and she began running with me along the causeway, so that I, too, was suddenly caught in panic and could think of nothing but the wide door of Menabilly still open to enfold me. "I have searched everywhere for John," she faltered, "but I cannot find him. One of the servants said they saw him walking out towards the Gribbin. Oh, Honor—the children—what will become of us? What is going to happen?"

I could hear shouting from the park, and out on the hard ground beyond the gates came the steady rhythmic beat of horses trotting; not the light clatter of a company, but line upon line of them, the relentless measure of a regiment, the jingle of harness, the thin alien sound of a bugle.

They were waiting for us by the windows of the gallery, Alice and Mary, the Sawles, the Sparkes, a little tremulous gathering of frightened people, united now in danger, and two other faces that I did not know, the peeky, startled faces of strange children with lace caps upon their heads and wide lace collars. I remembered then the unknown lady who had flung herself upon my sister's mercy, and as we turned into the hall, slamming the door behind us, I saw the horses that had drawn the litter still standing untended in the courtyard, save that the grooms had thrown blankets upon them, coloured white and crimson, and the corners of the blankets were stamped with a dragon's head. . . . A dragon's head . . . But even as my memory swung back into the past I heard her voice, cold and clear, rising above the others in the gallery: "If only it can be Lord Robartes I can assure you all no harm will come to us. I have known him well these many years and am quite prepared to speak on your behalf."

"I forgot to tell you," whispered Joan, "she came with her two daughters scarce an hour ago. The road was held; they could not pass St. Blazey. It is Mrs. Denys of Orley Court."

Her eyes swung round to me. Those same eyes, narrow, heavy-lidded, that I had seen often in my more troubled dreams, and her gold hair, golder than it had been in the past, for art had taken council with nature and outstripped it. She stared at sight of me, and for one second only I caught a flash of odd discomfiture run in a flicker through her eyes, and then she smiled her slow, false, well-remembered smile, and, stretching out her hands, she said, "Why, Honor, this is indeed a pleasure. Mary did not tell me that you, too, were here at Menabilly."

I ignored the proffered hand, for a cripple in a chair can be as ill mannered as she pleases, and as I stared back at her in my own fashion, with suspicion and foreboding in my heart, we heard the horses ride into the courtyard and the bugles blow. Poor Temperance Sawle went down upon her knees, the children whimpered, and my sister Mary, with her arm about Joan and Alice, stood very white and still. Only Gartred watched with cool eyes, her hands playing gently with her girdle.

"Pray hard and pray fast, Mrs. Sawle," I said; "the vultures are gathering. . . ."

And there being no brandy in the room, I poured myself some water from a jug and raised my glass to Gartred.

16

IT WAS WILL Sparke, I remember, who went to unbar the door, having been the first to bolt it earlier, and as he did so excused himself in his high-pitched shaking voice, saying, "It is useless to start by offending them. Our only hope lies in placating them."

We could see through the windows how the troopers dismounted, staring about them with confident hard faces beneath their close-fitting skull helmets, and it seemed to me that one and all they looked the same, with their cropped heads, their drab brown leather jerkins, and this ruthless similarity was both startling and grim. There were more of them on the eastward side now, in the gardens, the horses' hoofs trampling the green lawns and the little yew trees as a first symbol of destruction, and all the while the thin high note of the bugle, like a huntsman summoning his hounds to slaughter. In a moment we heard their heavy footsteps in the house, clamping through the dining chamber and up the stairs, and into the gallery returned Will Sparke, a nervous smile on his face which was drained of all colour, and behind him three officers, the first a big burly man with a long nose and heavy jaw, wearing a green sash about his waist. I recognised him at once as Lord Robartes, the owner of Lanhydrock, a big estate on the Bodmin road, and who in days gone by had gone riding and hawking with my brother Kit, but was not much known to the rest of us. He was now our enemy and could dispose of us as he wished.

"Where is the owner of the house?" he asked, and looked toward old Nick Sawle, who turned his back.

"My husband is from home," said Mary, coming forward, "and my stepson somewhere in the grounds."

"Is everyone living in the place assembled here?"

"All except the servants."

"You have no malignants in hiding?"

"None."

Lord Robartes turned to the staff officer at his side. "Make a thorough search of the house and grounds," he said. "Break down any door you find locked and test the panelling for places of concealment. Give orders to the farm people to round up all sheep and cattle and other livestock, and place men in charge of them and the granaries. We will take over this gallery and all other rooms on the ground floor for our personal use. Troops to bivouac in the park."

"Very good, sir." The officer stood to attention and then departed about his business.

Lord Robartes drew up a chair to the table, and the remaining officer gave him paper and a quill.

"Now, madam," he said to Mary, "give me your full name and the name and occupation of each member of your household."

One by one he had us documented, looking at each victim keenly, as though the very admission of name and age betrayed some sign of guilt. Only when he came to Gartred did his manner relax something of its hard suspicion. "A foolish time to journey, Mrs. Denys," he said. "You would have done better to remain at Orley Court."

"There are so many soldiery abroad of little discipline and small respect," said Gartred languidly; "it is not very pleasant for a widow with young daughters to live alone, as I do. I hoped by travelling South to escape the fighting."

"You thought wrong," he answered, "and, I am afraid, must abide by the consequences of such an error. You will have to remain here in custody with Mrs. Rashleigh and her household."

Gartred bowed and did not answer. Lord Robartes rose to his feet. "When the apartments above have been searched you may go to them," he said, addressing Mary and the rest of us, "and I must request you to remain in them until further orders. Exercise once a day will be permitted in the garden here under close escort. You must prepare your food as, and how, you are able. We shall take command of the kitchens, and certain stores will be allotted to you. Your keys, madam."

I saw Mary falter and then, slowly and reluctantly, she unfastened the string from her girdle. "Can I not have entry there myself?" she asked.

"No, madam. The stores are no longer yours but the possession of the Parliament, likewise everything pertaining to this estate."

I thought of the jars of preserves upon Mary's shelves, the honeys and the jams and the salted pilchards in the larders and the smoked hams and the sides of salted mutton. I thought of the bread in the bakeries, the flour in the bins, the grain in the granaries, the young fruit setting in the orchards. And all the while I thought of this the sound of heavy feet came tramping from above and out in the grounds came the bugle's cry.

"I thank you, madam. And I must warn you and the rest of the company that any attempt at escape, any contravention of my orders will be punished with extreme severity."

"What about milk for the children?" said Joan, her cheeks very flushed, her head high. "We must have milk and butter and eggs. My little son is delicate and inclined to croup."

"Certain stores will be given you daily, madam. I have already said so," said Lord Robartes. "If the children need more nourishment you must do without yourselves. I have some five hundred men to quarter here, and their needs come before yours or your children. Now you may go to your apartments."

This was the moment I had waited for and, catching Joan's eye, I summoned her to my side. "You must give up your apartment to Mrs. Denys," I murmured, "and come to me in the gatehouse. I shall move my bed into the adjoining chamber."

Her lips framed a question, but I shook my head. She had sense enough to accept it, for all her agitation, and went at once to Mary with the proposition, who was so bewildered by the loss of her keys that her natural hospitality had deserted her.

"I beg of you, make no move because of me," said Gartred, smiling, her arms about her children. "May and Gertie and I can fit in anywhere. The house is something like a warren; I remember it of old."

I looked at her thoughtfully and remembered then how Kit had been at Oxford the same time as my brother-in-law, when old Mr. Rashleigh was still alive, and during the days of Jonathan's first marriage Kit had ridden over to Menabilly often from Lanrest.

"You have been here then before?" I said to Gartred, speaking to her for the first time since I had come into the gallery.

"Why, bless me, yes." She yawned. "Some five and twenty years ago Kit and I came for a harvest supper and lost ourselves about the passages." But at this moment Lord Robartes, who had been conferring with his officer, turned from the door.

"You will now please," he said, "retire to your apartments."

We went out of the farther door where the servants were huddled like a flock of startled sheep, and Matty and two others seized the arms of my chair. Already the troopers were in the kitchens, in full command, and the round of beef that had been roasting for our dinner was being cut into great slices and served out amongst them while down the stairs came three more of them, two fellows and a non-commissioned officer, bearing loads of Mary's precious stores in their arms. Another had a great pile of blankets and a rich embroidered cover that had been put aside until winter in the linen room.

"Oh, but they cannot have that," said Mary. "Where is an officer? I must speak to someone of authority."

"I have authority," replied the sergeant, "to remove all linen, blankets, and covers that we find. So keep a cool temper, lady, for you'll find no redress." They stared us coolly in the face, and one of them favoured Alice with a bold familiar stare and then whispered something in the ear of his companion.

Oh God, how I hated them upon the instant. I, who had regarded the war with irony and cynicism hitherto and a bitter shrug of the shoulder, was now filled with burning anger when it touched me close. Their muddied boots had trampled the floors and, once above, wanton damage could at once be seen where they had thrust their pikes into the panelling and stripped the hangings from the walls. In Alice's apartment the presses had been overturned and the contents spilled upon the floor, and already a broken casement hung upon its hinge with the glass shattered. Alice's nurse was standing in the centre of the room crying and wringing her hands, for the troopers had carried off some of the children's bedding, and one clumsy oaf had trodden his heel upon the children's favourite doll and smashed its head to pieces. At the sight of this, their precious toy, the little girls burst into torrents of crying, and I knew then the idiot rage that surges within a man in wartime and compels him to commit murder. In the gardens the troopers were trampling down the formal beds and with their horses had knocked down the growing flowers, whose strewn petals lay crumpled now and muddied by the horses' hoofs.

I took one glance and then bade Matty and her companions bear me to my room. It had suffered like disturbance, with the bed tumbled and the stuffing ripped from the chairs for no rhyme or reason, and they had saved me the trouble of unlocking the barred chamber, for the door was broken in and pieces of planking strewn about the floor. The arras was torn in places, but the arras that hung before the buttress was still and undisturbed.

I thanked God in my heart for the cunning of old John Rashleigh and, desiring Matty to set me down beside the window, I looked out into the courtyard and saw the soldiers all gathered below, line upon line of them, with their horses tethered and the tents gleaming white already in process of erection in the park, with the campfires burning and the cattle lowing as they were driven by the soldiers to a pen, and all the while that damned bugle blowing, high-pitched and insistent in a single key. I turned from the window and told Matty that Joan and her children would now be coming to the gatehouse and I remain here in the chamber that had been barred.

"The troopers have made short work of mystery," said Matty, looking about her and at the broken door. "There was nothing put away here, after all, then."

I did not answer, and while she busied herself with moving my bed and my own belongings I wheeled myself to the cabinet and saw that Jonathan had taken the precaution of removing his papers before he went, leaving the cabinet bare.

When the two rooms were in order and the servants had helped Matty to repair the door, thus giving me my privacy from Joan, I sent them from me to give assistance to Joan in making place for Gartred in the southern front. All was now quiet save for the constant tramping of soldiers in the court below and the comings and goings beneath me in the kitchens. Very cautiously I drew near the northeast corner of my new apartment and lifted the arras. I ran my hands over the stone wall as I had done that time before in the darkness when Jonathan had discovered me, and once again I could find no outlet, no division in the stone.

I realised then that the means for entry must be from without only, a great handicap to us who used it now, but no doubt cunningly intended by the builder of the house, who had no desire for his idiot elder son to come and go at pleasure. I knocked with my fists against the wall, but they sounded not at all. I called, "John," in a low voice, expecting no answer; nor did I receive one.

This, then, was a new and hideous dilemma, for I had warned John not to attempt an entry to the chamber before I warned him first, being confident at the time that I would be able to find the entrance from inside. This I could not do, and John and Dick were in the meantime waiting in the cell below the buttress for a signal from me. I placed my face against the stone wall, crying, "John . . . John . . ." as loudly as I dared, but I guessed, with failing heart, that the sound of my voice would never carry through the implacable stone.

Hearing footsteps in the corridor, I let the arras fall and returned to the window, where I made pretence of looking down into the court. I heard movement in my old apartment in the gatehouse and a moment later a loud knocking on the door between. "Please enter," I called, and the roughly repaired door was pushed aside, tottering on its hinges, and Lord Robartes himself came into the room accompanied by one of his officers and also Frank Penrose, with his arms bound tight behind him.

"I regret my sudden intrusion," said Lord Robartes, "but we have just found this man in the grounds who volunteered information I find interesting, which you may add to, if you please."

I glanced at Frank Penrose, who, half frightened out of his wits, stared about him like a hare, passing his tongue over his lips.

I did not answer but waited for Lord Robartes to continue.

"It seems you have had living here, until today, the son of Skellum Grenvile," he said, watching me intently, "also his tutor. They were to have left by fishing boat for St. Mawes a few hours since. You were the boy's godmother and had the care of him, I understand. Where are they now?"

"Somewhere off the Dodman, I hope," I answered.

"I am told that as the boat set sail from Polkerris the boy could not be found," he replied, "and Penrose here and John Rashleigh went in search of him. My men have not yet come upon John Rashleigh or the boy. Do you know what has become of them?"

"I do not," I answered. "I only trust they are aboard the boat."

"You realise," he said harshly, "that there is a heavy price upon the head of Skellum Grenvile, and to harbour him or any of his family would count as treason to Parliament. The Earl of Essex has given me strict orders as to this."

"That being the case," I said, "you had better take Mrs. Denys into closer custody. She is Sir Richard's sister, as you no doubt know."

I had caught him off his guard with this, and he looked at me nonplussed. Then he began tapping on the table in sudden irritation. "Mrs. Denys has, I understand, little or no friendship with her brother," he said stiffly. "Her late husband, Mr. Antony Denys, was known to be a good friend to Parliament and an opposer of Charles Stuart. Have you nothing further to tell me about your godson?"

"Nothing at all," I said, "except that I have every belief that he is upon that fishing boat, and with the wind in the right quarter he will be, by this time, nigh halfway to St. Mawes."

He turned his back on me at that and left the room, with the luckless Frank Penrose shuffling at his heels, and I realised, with relief, that the agent was ignorant as to Dick's whereabouts, like everybody else in Menabilly, and for all he knew my tale might be quite true and both Dick and John some ten miles out to sea.

Not one soul then, in the place, knew the secret of the buttress but myself, for Langdon, the steward, had accompanied my brother-in-law to Launceston. This was a great advantage, making betrayal an impossibility. But I still could not solve the problem of how to get food and drink and reassurance to the two fugitives I had myself imprisoned. And another fear began to nag at me with a recollection of my brother-in-law's words: "Lack of air and close confinement soon rendered him unconscious and easy to handle." Uncle John gasping for breath in the little cell beneath the buttress . . . How much air, then, came through to the cell from the tunnel beyond? *Enough for how many hours?*

Once again, as earlier in the day, the sweat began to trickle down my face, and half consciously I wiped it away with my hand. I felt myself defeated. There was no course for me to take. A little bustle from the adjoining room and a child's cry told me that Joan and her babies had come to my old apartment, and in a moment she came through with little Mary whimpering in her arms and small Jonathan clinging to her skirts.

"Why did you move, Honor dear?" she said. "There was no need." And, like Matty, she gazed about the room in curiosity. "It is very plain and bare," she added, "nothing valuable at all. I am much relieved, for these brutes would have got it. Come back in your own chamber, Honor, if you can bear with the babies."

"No," I said, "I am well enough."

"You look so tired and drawn," she said, "but I dare swear I do the same. I feel I have aged ten years these last two hours. What will they do to us?"

"Nothing," I said, "if we keep to our rooms."

"If only John would return," she said, tears rising to her eyes. "Supposing he has had some skirmish on the road and has been hurt? I cannot understand what can have become of him."

The children began to whimper, hearing the anxiety in her voice, and then Matty, who loved children, came and coaxed the baby and proceeded to undress her for her cot, while little Jonathan, with a small boy's sharp, nervous way, began to plague us all with questions: why did they come to their aunt Honor's room, and who were all the soldiers, and how long would they stay?

The hours wore on with horrid dragging tedium, and the sun began to sink behind the trees at the far end of the park, while the air was thick with smoke from the fires lit by the troopers.

All the time there was tramping below and orders called and the pacing to and fro of horses, with the insistent bugle sometimes far distant in the park, echoed by a fellow bugle, and sometimes directly beneath the windows. The children were restless, turning continually in their cots and calling for either Matty or their mother, and when Joan was not hushing them she was gazing from my window, reporting fresh actions of destruction, her cheeks aflame with indignation.

"They have rounded up all the cattle from the beef park and the beacon fields and driven them into the park here with a pen about them," she said, "and they are dividing up the steers now to another pen." Suddenly she gave a little cry of dismay. "They have slaughtered three of them," she said; "the men are quartering them already by the fires. Now they are driving the sheep."

We could hear the anxious baaing of the ewes to the sturdy lambs and the lowing of the cattle. I thought of the five hundred men encamped there in the park and the many hundreds more between us and Lostwithiel and how they and their horses must be fed, but I said nothing. Joan shut the window, for the smoke from the campfires blew thick about the room, and the noise of the men shouting and calling orders made a vile and sickening clamour. The sun set in a dull crimson sky and the shadows lengthened.

About half-past eight Matty brought us a small portion of a pie upon one plate with a carafe of water. Her lips were grimly set.

"This for the two of you," she said. "Mrs. Rashleigh and Mrs. Courtney fare no better. Lady Courtney is making a little broth for the children's breakfast in case they give us no eggs."

Joan ate my piece of pie as well as hers, for I had no appetite. I could think of one thing only, and that was that it was now nearly five hours since her husband and Richard's son had lain hidden in the buttress. Matty brought candles, and presently Alice and Mary came to say good night, poor Mary looking suddenly like an old woman from anxiety and shock, with great shadows under her eyes.

"They're axing the trees in the orchard," she said. "I saw them myself sawing the branches and stripping the young fruit that has scarce formed. I sent down a message to Lord Robartes, but he returned no answer. The servants have been told by the soldiers that tomorrow they are going to cut the corn, strip all the barley from eighteen acres and the wheat from the Great Meadow. And it wants three weeks to harvest."

The tears began to course down her cheeks and she turned to Joan. "Why does John not come?" she said in useless reproach. "Why is he not here to stand up for his father's home?"

"If John were here he could do nothing," I said swiftly before Joan could lash back in anger. "Don't you understand, Mary, that this is war? This is what has been happening all over England, and we in Cornwall are having our first taste of it."

Even as I spoke there came a great burst of laughter from the courtyard and a tongue of flame shot up to the windows. The troopers were roasting an ox in the clearing above the warren, and because they were too idle to search for firewood they had broken down the doors from the dairy and the bakery and were piling them upon the fire.

"There must have been thirty officers or more at dinner in the gallery," said Alice quietly. "We saw them from our windows afterwards walk up and down the terrace before the house. One or two were Cornish—I remember meeting them before the war—but most of them were strangers."

"They say the Earl of Essex is in Fowey," said Joan, "and set up his headquarters at Place. Whether it is true or not I do not know."

"They Treffrys will not suffer," said Mary bitterly. "They have too many relatives fighting for the rebels. You won't find Bridget has her stores pillaged and her larders ransacked."

"Come to bed, Mother," said Alice gently. "Honor is right; it does no good to worry. We have been spared so happily until now. If my father and Peter are somewhere safe with the King's Army, nothing else can matter."

They went to their own apartments and Joan to the children next door, while Matty—all oblivious of my own hidden fears—helped me undress for bed.

"There's one discovery I've made this night, anyway," she said grimly as she brushed my hair.

"What is that, Matty?"

"Mrs. Denys hasn't lost her taste for gentlemen."

I said nothing, waiting for what would follow.

"You and the others and Mrs. Sawle and Mistress Sparke had pie for your suppers," she said, "but there was roast beef and burgundy taken up to Mrs. Denys and places set for two upon the tray. Her children were put together in the dressing room and had a chicken between them."

I realised that Matty's partiality for eavesdropping and her nose for gossip might stand us in good stead in the immediate future.

"And who was the fortunate who dined with Mrs. Denys?" I asked.

"Lord Robartes himself," said Matty with sour triumph.

My first suspicion became a certainty. It was not mere chance that had so strangely brought Gartred to Menabilly after five and twenty years. She was here for a purpose.

"Lord Robartes is not an ill-looking man," I said. "I might invite him to share cold pie with me another evening."

Matty snorted and lifted me to bed. "I'd like to see Sir Richard's face if you did," she snapped.

"Sir Richard would not mind," I answered, "not if there was something to be gained from it."

I feigned a lightness I was far from feeling, and when she had blown the candles and was gone I lay back in my bed with my nerves tense and strained. The flames outside my window died away, and slowly the shouting and the laughter ceased and the trampling of feet and the movement of the horses and the calling bugles. I heard the clock in the belfry strike ten, then eleven, and then midnight. The people within the house were still and silent, and so was the alien enemy. At a quarter after midnight a dog howled in the far distance, and as though it were a signal I felt suddenly upon my cheek a current of cold chill air. I sat up in bed and waited. The draught continued, blowing straight from the torn arras on the wall.

"John," I whispered, and "John," I whispered again. I heard a movement from behind the arras like a scratching mouse; slowly, stealthily, I saw the hand come from behind the arras, lifting it aside, and a figure step out, dropping on all fours and creeping to my bed. "It is I, Honor," I said, and the cold froggy hand touched me, icy cold, and the hands clung to me and the dark figure climbed onto my bed and lay trembling beside me.

It was Dick, the clothes still dank and chill upon him, and he began to weep, long and silently, from exhaustion and from fear.

I held him close, warming him as best I could, and when he was still I whispered, "Where is John?"

"In the little room," he said, "below the steps. We sat there waiting, hour after hour, and you did not come. I wanted to turn back, but Mr. Rashleigh would not let me." He began to sob again, and I drew the covers over his head.

"He has fainted down there on the steps," he said; "he's lying there now, his head between his hands. I got hold of the long rope that hangs there above the steps and pulled at it, and the hinged stone gave way and I came up into this room. I did not care. I could not stay there longer, Honor; it's black as pitch and closer than a grave."

He was still trembling, his head buried in my shoulder. I went on lying there, wondering what to do, whether to summon Joan and thus betray the secret to another, or wait until Dick was calmer and then send him back there with a candle to John's aid. And as I waited, my heart thumping, my ears strained to all sounds, I heard from without the tiptoe of a footstep in the passage, the noise of the latch of the door gently lifted and then let fall again as the door was seen to be fastened, and a moment's pause; then the footstep tiptoeing gently away once more and the soft departing rustle of a gown. Someone had crept to the chamber in the stillness of the night, and that someone was a woman.

I went on lying there with my arms wrapped close about the sleeping boy, and the clock in the belfry struck one, then two, then three. . . .

17

As THE FIRST grey chinks of light came through the casement I roused Dick, who lay sleeping with his head upon my shoulder like a baby, and when he had blinked a moment and got his wits restored to him I bade him light the candle and creep back again to the cell. The fear that gripped me was that lack of air had so caused John to faint and, he being by nature far from strong, anything might have happened. Never, in all the sixteen years I had been crippled, had I so needed the use of my legs as now, but I was helpless. In a few moments Dick was back again, his little ghost's face looking more pallid than ever in the grey morning light.

"He is awake," he said, "but very ill, I think. Shaking all over and seeming not to know what has been happening. His head is burning hot, but his limbs are cold."

At least he was alive, and a wave of thankfulness swept over me. But from Dick's description I realised what had happened. The ague that was his legacy from birth had attacked John once again with its usual ferocity, and small wonder after more than ten hours crouching beneath the buttress. I made up my mind swiftly. I bade Dick bring the chair beside my bed and with his assistance I lowered myself into it. Then I went to the door communicating with the gatehouse chamber and very gently called for Matty. Joan answered sleepily, and one of the children stirred.

"It is nothing," I said; "it is only Matty that I want."

In a moment or two she came from the little dressing room, her round plain face yawning beneath her nightcap, and would have chided me for rising had I not placed my finger on my lips.

The urgency of the situation was such that my promise to my brother-in-law must finally be broken, though little of it held as it was. And without Matty it would be impossible to act. She came in then, her eyes round with wonder when she saw Dick.

"You love me, Matty, I believe," I said to her. "Now I ask you to prove that love as never before. This boy's safety and life are in our hands."

She nodded, saying nothing.

"Dick and Mr. John have been hiding since last evening," I said. "There is a staircase and a little room built within the thickness of these walls. Mr. John is ill. I want you to go to him and bring him here. Dick will show you the way."

He pulled aside the arras, and now for the first time I saw how the entrance was effected. A block of stone, about four feet square, worked on a hinge, moved by a lever and a rope if pulled from beneath the narrow stair. This gave an opening just wide enough for a man to crawl through. When shut, the stone was so closely fitting that it was impossible to find it from within the chamber, nor could it be pushed open, for the lever held it. The little stairway, set inside the buttress, twisted steeply to the cell below, which had height enough for a man to stand upright. More I could not see, craning from my chair, save for a dark heap that must be John lying on the lower step.

There was something weird and fearful in the scene with the grey light of morning coming through the casement, and Matty, a fantastic figure in her night clothes and cap, edging her way through the gap in the buttress. As she disappeared with Dick I heard the first high call of the bugle from the park and I knew that for the rebel army the day had now begun.

Soon the soldiers within the house would also be astir, and we had little time in hand. It was, I believe, some fifteen minutes before they were all three within the chamber, though it seemed an hour, and in those fifteen minutes the daylight had filled the room and the troopers were moving in the courtyard down below.

John was quite conscious, thank God, and his mind lucid, but he was trembling all over and in a high fever, fit for nothing but his own bed and his wife's care. We held rapid consultation in which I held firmly to one thing, and that was that no further person, not Joan, his wife, nor Mary, his stepmother, should be told how he had come into the house or that Dick was with us still.

John's story then was to be that the fishing boat came into one of the coves beneath the Gribbin, where he put Dick aboard, and then on returning across the fields he had seen the arrival of the troopers and hid until nightfall. But, his fever coming upon him, he decided to return and therefore climbed by the lead piping and the creeper that ran the south front of the house outside his father's window. For corroboration of this John must go at once to his father's room, where his stepmother was sleeping, and waken her and win her acceptance of the story. And this immediately, before the household were awake. It was like a nightmare to arrange, with Joan, his wife, in the adjoining chamber through which he must pass to gain the southern portion of the house. For if he went by the passage beneath the belfry he might risk encounter with the servants or the troopers. Matty went first, and when there was no question from Joan nor any movement from the children, we judged them to be sleeping, and poor John, his body on fire with fever, crept swiftly after her. I bethought me of the games of hide-and-seek I had played with my brothers and sisters at Lanrest as children and how now that it was played in earnest there was no excitement but a sickening strain that brought sweat to the forehead and a pain to the belly. When Matty returned and reported John in safety in his father's rooms the first stage of the proceeding was completed. The next I had to break to Dick with great misgiving and an assumption of sternness and authority that I was far from feeling. It was that he could remain with me in my apartment but must be prepared to stay, perhaps for long hours at a time, within the secret cell beneath the buttress and must have a palliasse there to sleep upon, if need be, should there be visitors to my room.

He fell to crying at once, as I had expected, and beseeching me not to let him stay alone in the dark cell; he would go mad, he said, he could not stand it, he would rather die.

I was well-nigh desperate, with the movement now within the house and the children beginning to talk in the adjoining chamber.

"Very well then," I said, "open the door, Matty. Call the troopers. Tell them that Richard Grenvile's son is here and wishes to surrender himself to their mercy. They have sharp swords and the pain will soon be over." God forgive me that I could find it in my heart to so terrify the lad, but it was his only salvation.

The mention of the swords sent the colour draining from his face, as I knew it would, bringing the thought of blood, and he turned to me, his dark eyes desperate, and he said, "Very well. I will do as you ask me." It is those same dark eyes that haunt me still and will always do so to the day I die.

I bade Matty take the mattress from my bed and the stool beside the window and some blankets and bundle them through the open gap into the stair. When it is safe for you to come I will let you know," I said.

"But how can you," said Dick, "when the gap is closed?"

Here was I forced back again into the old dilemma of the night before. I could have wept with strain and weariness and looked at Matty in despair.

"If you do not quite close the gap," she said, "but let it stay open to three inches, Master Dick, with his ear put close to it, would hear your voice."

We tried it, and although I was not happy with the plan, it seemed the one solution, and we found, too, that with a gap of two or three inches he could hear me strike with a stick upon the floor, once, twice, or thrice, which we arranged as signals. Thrice meant real danger, and then the stone must be pulled flush to the wall.

He had gone to his cell with his mattress and his blankets and half a loaf that Matty had found for him, as the clock in the belfry struck six, and almost immediately little Jonathan from the adjoining room came pushing through the door, his toys under his arm, calling in loud tones for me to play with him. The day had started. When I look back now to the intolerable strain and anguish of that time I wonder how in God's name I had the power to endure it. For I had not only to be on guard against the rebels but against my friends, too, and those I loved. Mary, Alice, Joan must all three remain in ignorance of what was happening; and their visits to my chamber, which should have been a comfort and a consolation in this time of strain, merely added to my anxiety.

What I would have done without Matty I do not know. It was she, acting sentinel as she had done in the past, who kept them from the door when Dick was with me; and poor lad, I had to have him often, for the best part of the day. Luckily my crippled state served as a good excuse, for it was known that often in the past I had "bad days" and had to be alone, and this lie was now my only safeguard.

John's story had been accepted as full truth, and since he was quite obviously ill and in high fever he was allowed to remain in his father's rooms with Joan to care for him and was not removed to closer custody under guard. Severe questioning from Lord Robartes could not shake John from his story, and thank heaven Robartes had other cares upon his shoulders gathering fast to worry any further what had happened to Skellum Grenvile's son.

I remember Matty saying to me on that first day, Friday, the second of August, "How long will they be here, Miss Honor? When will the royalist army come to relieve us?" And I, thinking of Richard down at Truro and His Majesty already, so the rumour ran, entering Launceston, told her four days at the longest. But I was wrong. And for four whole weeks the rebels were our masters.

It is now nearly ten years since that August of '44, but every day of that agelong month is printed firm upon my memory. The first week was hot and stifling, with a glazed blue sky and not a cloud upon it, and in my nostrils now I can recapture the smell of horseflesh and the stink of sweating soldiery, borne upwards to my open casement from the fetid court below.

Day in, day out, came the jingle of harness, the clattering of hoofs, the march of tramping feet, the grinding sound of wagon wheels, and ever insistent above the shouting of orders and the voices of the men, the bugle call hammering its single note.

The children, Alice's and Joan's, unused to being withindoors at high summer, hung fretful from the windows, adding to the babel; and Alice, who had the care of all of them, whilst Joan nursed John in the greater quietude of the south front, would take them from room to room to make distraction. Imprisonment made cronies of us all, and no sooner had Alice and the brood departed than the Sparke sisters would come enquiring for me, who had hitherto preferred cribbage to my company, both with some wild rumour to unfold, gleaned from a frightened servant, of how the house was to be burnt down with all its inmates when Essex gave the order, but first the women ravaged. I dare say I was the only woman in the house to be unmoved by such a threat, for God knows I could not be more bruised and broken than I was already. But for Deborah and Gillian it was another matter, and Deborah, whom I judged to be even safer from assault than I was myself, showed me with trembling hands the silver bodkin with which she would defend her honour. Their brother Will was become a sort of toady to the officers, thinking by smiling and by wishing them good morning he would win their favour and his safety, but as soon as their backs were turned he was whispering some slander about their persons and repeating snatches of conversation he had overheard, bits and pieces that were no use to anyone. Once or twice Nick Sawle came tapping slowly to my room, leaning on his two sticks, a look of lost bewilderment in his eyes and muddled resentment that the rebels had not been flung from Menabilly within four and twenty hours of their arrival; and I was forced to listen to his theories that His Majesty must be now at Launceston, now at Liskeard, now back again at Exeter, which suppositions brought our release no nearer. And while he argued poor Temperance, his wife, stared at him dully, in a kind of trance, her religious eloquence pent up at last from shock and fear so that she could do no more than clutch her prayer book without quoting from it.

Once a day we were allowed within the garden for some thirty minutes, and I would leave Matty in my room on an excuse and have Alice push my chair while her nurse walked with the children.

The poor gardens were laid waste already with the yew trees broken and the flower beds trampled, and up and down the muddied paths we went, stared at by the sentries at the gate and by the officers gathered at the long windows in the gallery. Their appraising hostile eyes burnt through our backs but must be endured for the sake of the fresh air we craved, and sometimes their laughter came to us and their voices hard and ugly, for they were mostly from London and the Eastern counties, except those staff officers of Lord Robartes, and I never could abide the London twang, made doubly alien now through enmity. Never once did we see Gartred when we took our exercise, though her two daughters, reserved and unfriendly, played in the far corner of the garden, watching us and the children with blank eyes.

They had neither of them inherited her beauty, but were brown-haired and heavy-looking like their dead father, Antony Denys.

"I don't know what to make of it," said Alice in my ear. "She is supposed to be a prisoner like us, but she is not treated so. I have watched her from my window walk in the walled garden beneath the summerhouse, talking and smiling to Lord Robartes, and the servants say he dines with her most evenings."

"She only does what many other women do in wartime," I said, "and has turned the stress of the day to her advantage."

"You mean she is for the Parliament?" asked Alice.

"Neither for the Parliament nor for the King but for Gartred Denys," I answered. "Do you not know the saying—to race with the hare and to run with the hounds? She will smile on Lord Robartes and sleep with him, too, if she has a mind, just as long as it suits her. He would let her leave tomorrow if she asked him."

"Why, then," said Alice, "does she not do so and return in safety to Orley Court?"

"That," I answered, "is what I would give a great deal to find out."

And as we paced up and down, up and down, before the staring hostile eyes of the London officers I thought of the footstep I had heard at midnight in the passage, the soft hand on the latch, and the rustle of a gown. Why should Gartred, while the house slept, find her way to my apartment in the northeast corner of the building and try my door unless she knew her way already; and, granting that she knew her way, what, then, was her motive?

It was ten days before I had my answer.

On Sunday, August the eleventh, came the first break in the weather. The sun shone watery in a mackerel sky and a bank of cloud gathered in the southwest. There had been much coming and going all the day, with fresh regiments of troopers riding to the park, bringing with them many carts of wounded who were carried to the farm buildings before the house. Their cries of distress were very real and terrible and gave to us, who were their enemies, a sick dread and apprehension. The shouting and calling of orders were persistent on that day, and the bugle never ceased from dawn to sundown.

For the first time we were given soup only for our dinner and a portion of stale bread, and this, we were told, would be the best we could hope for from henceforward. No reason was given, but Matty, with her ears pricked, had hung about the kitchens with her tray under her arm and gleaned some gossip from the courtyard.

"There was a battle yesterday on Braddock Down," she said. "They've lost a lot of men." She spoke softly, for with our enemies about us we had grown to speak in whispers, our eyes upon the door.

I poured half my soup into Dick's bowl and watched him drink it greedily, running his tongue round the rim like a hungry dog.

"The King is only three miles from Lostwithiel," she said; "he and Price Maurice have joined forces and set up their headquarters at Boconnoc. Sir Richard has advanced with nigh a thousand men from Truro and is coming up on Bodmin from the west. 'Your fellows are trying to squeeze us dry,' said the trooper in the kitchen, 'like a bloody orange. But they won't do it.'"

"And what did you answer him?" I said to Matty.

She smiled grimly and cut Dick the largest slice of bread.

"I told him I'd pray for him when Sir Richard got him," she answered.

After eating I sat in my chair looking out across the park and watched the clouds gathering thick and fast. There were scarce a dozen bullocks left in the pen out of the fine herds that had been the week before and only a small flock of sheep. The rest had all been slaughtered. These remaining few would be gone within the next eight and forty hours. Not a stem of corn remained in the far meadows. The whole had been cut and ground and the ricks pulled. The grass in the park was now bare earth where the horses had grazed upon it. Not a tree stood in the orchard beyond the warren. If Matty's tale was true and the King and Richard to east and west of Lostwithiel, then the Earl of Essex and ten thousand men were pent up in a narrow strip of land some three miles long with no way of escape except the sea.

Ten thousand men with provisions getting low and only the bare land to live on, while three armies waited in their rear.

There was no laughter tonight from the courtyard, no shouting and no chatter; only a blazing fire as they heaped the cut trees and the kitchen benches upon it, the doors torn from the larder and the tables from the steward's room, and I could see their sullen faces lit by the leaping flames.

The sky darkened and slowly, silently, the rain began to fall. And as I listened to it, remembering Richard's words, I heard the rustle of a gown and a tap upon my door.

18

DICK WAS GONE in a flash to his hiding place and Matty clearing his bowl and platter. I sat still in my chair with my back to the arras and bade them enter who knocked upon the door.

It was Gartred. She was wearing, if I remember right, a gown of emerald green, and there were emeralds round her throat and in her ears. She stood a moment within the doorway, a half-smile on her face.

"The good Matty," she said, "always so devoted. What ease of mind a faithful servant brings."

I saw Matty sniff and rattle the plates upon her tray while her lips tightened in ominous fashion.

"Am I disturbing you, Honor?" said Gartred, that same smile still on her face. "The hour is possibly inconvenient; you go early, no doubt, to bed?"

All meaning is in the inflexion of the voice, and when rendered on paper words seem harmless enough and plain. I give the remarks as Gartred phrased them, but the veiled contempt, the mockery, the suggestion that because I was crippled I must be tucked down and in the dark by half-past nine, these were in her voice and in her eyes as they swept over me.

"My going to bed depends upon my mood, as doubtless it does with you," I answered; "also, it depends upon my company."

"You must find the hours most horribly tedious," she said, "but then, no doubt, you are used to it by now. You have lived in custody so long that to be made prisoner is no new experience. I must confess I find it unamusing." She came closer in the room, looking about her, although I had given her no invitation.

"You have heard the news, I suppose?" she said.

"That the King is at Boconnoc and a skirmish was fought yesterday in which the rebels got the worst of it? Yes, I have heard that," I answered.

The last of the fruit picked before the rebels came was standing on a platter in the window. Gartred took a fig and began to eat it, still looking about her in the room. Matty gave a snort of indignation which passed unnoticed and, taking her tray, went from the chamber with a glance at Gartred's back that would have slain her had it been perceived.

"If this business continues long," said Gartred, "we none of us here will find it very pleasant. The men are already in an ugly mood. Defeat may turn them into brutes."

"Very probably," I said.

She threw away the skin of her fig and took another.

"Richard is at Lanhydrock," she said. "Word came today through a captured prisoner. It is rather ironic that we have the owner of Lanhydrock in possession here. Richard will leave little of it for him by the time this campaign is settled, whichever way the battle goes. Jack Robartes is black as thunder."

"It is his own fault," I said, "for advising the Earl of Essex to come into Cornwall and run ten thousand men into a trap."

"So it is a trap," she said, "and my unscrupulous brother the baiter of it? I rather thought it must be."

I did not answer. I had said too much already, and Gartred was in quest of information. "Well, we shall see," she said, eating her fig with relish, "but if the process lasts much longer the rebels will turn cannibal. They have the country stripped already between here and Lostwithiel, and Fowey is without provisions. I shudder to think what Jack Robartes would do to Richard if he could get hold of him."

"The reverse equally holds good," I told her.

She laughed and squeezed the last drop of juice into her mouth. "All men are idiots," she said, "and more especially in wartime. They lose all sense of values."

"It depends," I said, "upon the meaning of values."

"I value one thing only," she said, "my own security."

"In that case," I said, "you showed neglect of it when you travelled upon the road ten days ago."

She watched me under heavy lids and smiled.

"Your tongue hasn't blunted with the years," she said, "nor tribulation softened you. Tell me, do you still care for Richard?"

"That is my affair," I said.

"He is detested by his brother officers; I suppose you know that," she said, "and loathed equally in Cornwall as in Devon. In fact, the only creatures he can count as friends are sprigs of boys who daren't be rude to him. He has a little train of them nosing his shadow."

Oh God, I thought, you bloody woman, seizing upon the one insinuation in the world to make me mad. I watched her play with her rings.

"Poor Mary Howard," she said, "what she endured. . . . You were spared intolerable indignities, you know, Honor, by not being his wife. I suppose Richard has made great play lately of loving you the same, and no doubt he does, in his vicious fashion. Rather a rare new pastime, a woman who can't respond."

She yawned and strolled over to the window. "His treatment of Dick is really most distressing," she said. "The poor boy adored his mother, and now I understand Richard intends to rear him as a freak just to spite her. What did you think of him when he was here?"

"He was young and sensitive, like many other children," I said.

"It was a wonder to me he was ever born at all," said Gartred, "when I think of the revolting story Mary told me. However, I will spare your feelings, if you still put Richard on a pedestal. I am glad, for the lad's sake, that Jack Robartes did not find him here at Menabilly. He has sworn an oath to hang any relative of Richard's."

"Except yourself," I said.

"Ah, I don't count," she answered. "Mrs. Denys of Orley Court is not the same as Gartred Grenvile." Once more she looked up at the walls and then again into the courtyard. "This is the room, isn't it," she said, "where they used to keep the idiot? I can remember his mouthing down at Kit when we rode here five and twenty years ago."

"I have no idea," I said. "The subject is not discussed among the family."

"There was something odd about the formation of the house," she said carelessly. "I cannot recollect exactly what it was. Some cupboard, I believe, where they used to shut him up when he grew violent, so Kit told me. Have you discovered it?"

"There are no cupboards here," I said, "except the cabinet over yonder."

"I am so sorry," she said, "that my coming here forced you to give your room to Joan Rashleigh. I could so easily have made do with this one, which one of the servants told me was never used until you took it over."

"It was much simpler," I said, "to place you and your daughters in a larger room, where you can entertain visitors to dinner."

"You always did like servants' gossip, did you not?" she answered. "The hobby of all old maids. It whips their appetite to imagine what goes on behind closed doors."

"I don't know," I said. "I hardly think my broth tastes any better for picturing you hip to hip with Lord Robartes."

She looked down at me, her gown in her hands, and I wondered who had the greater capacity for hatred, she or I.

"My being here," she said, "has at least spared you all, so far, from worse unpleasantness. I have known Jack Robartes for many years."

"Keep him busy, then," I said; "that's all we ask of you."

I was beginning to enjoy myself at last, and, realising it, she turned towards the door. "I cannot guarantee," she said, "that his good temper will continue. He was in a filthy mood tonight at dinner when he heard of Richard at Lanhydrock and has gone off now to a conference at Fowey with Essex and the chiefs of staff."

"I look to you, then," I said, "to have him mellow by the morning."

She stood with her hand on the door, her eyes sweeping the hangings on the wall. "If they lose the campaign," she said, "they will lose their tempers too. A defeated soldier is a dangerous animal. Jack Robartes will give orders to sack Menabilly and destroy inside and without."

"Yes," I said, "we are all aware of that."

"Everything will be taken," she said, "clothes, jewels, furniture, food—and not much left of the inhabitants. He must be a curious man, your brother-in-law, Jonathan Rashleigh, to desert his home, knowing full well what must happen to it in the end."

I shrugged my shoulders. And then, as she left, she gave herself away.

"Does he still act as collector for the mint?" she said.

Then for the first time I smiled, for I had my answer to the problem of her presence.

"I cannot tell you," I said. "I have no idea. But if you wait long enough for the house to be ransacked you may come upon the plate you think he has concealed. Good night, Gartred."

She stared at me a moment and then went from the room. At last I knew her business, and had I been less preoccupied with my own problem of concealing Dick I might have guessed it sooner. Whoever won or lost the campaign in the West, it would not matter much to Gartred; she would see to it that she had a footing on the winning side. She could play the spy for both. Like Temperance Sawle, I was in a mood to quote the Scriptures and declaim, "Where the body lies, there will the eagles be gathered together." If there were pickings to be scavenged in the aftermath of battle, Gartred Denys would not stay at home in Orley Court. I remembered her grip upon the marriage settlement with Kit; I remembered that last feverish search for a lost trinket on the morning she left Lanrest, a widow; and I remembered, too, the rumours I had heard since she was widowed for the second time, how Orley Court was much burdened with debt and must be settled between her daughters when they came of age. Gartred had not yet found a third husband to her liking, but in the meantime she must live. The silver plate of Cornwall would be a prize indeed, could she lay hands on it.

This, then, was her motive, with suspicion already centred on my room. She did not know the secret of the buttress, but memory had reminded her that there was, within the walls of Menabilly, some such hiding place. And with sharp guesswork she had reached the conclusion that my brother-in-law would make a wartime use of it. That the hiding place might also conceal her nephew had, I was certain, never entered her head. Nor—and this was supposition on my part—was she working in partnership with Lord Robartes. She was playing her own game, and if the game was likely to be advantaged by letting him make love to her, that was only by the way. It was far pleasanter to eat roast meat than watered broth; besides, she had a taste for burly men.

But if she found she could not get what she wanted by playing a lone hand, then she would lay her cards upon the table and damn the consequences.

This, then, was what we had to fear, and no one in the house knew of it but myself. So Sunday, August the eleventh, came and went, and we woke next morning to another problematical week in which anything might happen, with the three royalist armies squeezing the rebels tighter hour by hour, the strip of country left to them becoming daily more bare and devastated, while a steady sweeping rain turned all the roads to mud.

Gone was the hot weather, the glazed sky, and the sun. No longer did the children hang from the windows and listen to the bugles and watch the troopers come and go. No more did we take our daily exercise before the windows of the gallery. A high blustering wind drove across the park, and from my tightshut casement I could see the closed, dripping tents, the horses tethered line upon line beneath the trees at the far end, their heads disconsolate, while the men stood about in huddled, melancholy groups, their fires dead as soon as kindled.

Many of the wounded died in the farm buildings. Mary saw the burial parties go forth at dawn, a silent grey procession in the early morning mist, and we heard they took them to the Long Mead, the valley beneath the woods at Pridmouth.

No more wounded came to the farm buildings, and we guessed from this that the heavy weather had put a stop to fighting, but we heard also that His Majesty's Army now held the east bank of the Fowey River, from St. Veep down to the fortress at Polruan, which commanded the harbour entrance. The rebels in Fowey thus were cut off from their shipping in the Channel and could receive no supplies by sea, except from such small boats as could land at Pridmouth or Polkerris or on the sand flats at Tywardreath, which the heavy run from the southwest now made impossible.

There was little laughter or chatter now from the messroom in the gallery, so Alice said, and the officers, with grim faces, clamped back and forth from the dining chamber, which Lord Robartes had taken for his own use, while every now and then his voice would be raised in irritation and anger as a messenger would ride through the pouring rain bearing some counterorder from the Earl of Essex in Lostwithiel or some fresh item of disaster.

Whether Gartred moved about the house or not I do not know. Alice said she thought she kept to her own chamber. I saw little of Joan, for poor John's ague was still unabated, but Mary came from time to time to visit me, her face each day more drawn and agonised as she learnt of further devastation to the estate. More than three hundred of the sheep had already been slaughtered, thirty fatted bullocks, and sixty store bullocks. All the draught oxen taken and all the farm horses—some forty of these in number—some dozen hogs were left out of the eighty there had been; these would all be gone before the week was out. The last year's corn had vanished the first week of the rebel occupation, and now they had stripped the new, leaving no single blade to be harvested. There was nothing left, of course, of the farm wagons or carts or farming tools; these had all been taken. And the sheds where the winter fuel had been stored were as bare as the granaries. There was, in fact, so the servants in fear and trembling reported to Mary, scarce anything left of the great estate that Jonathan Rashleigh had left in her keeping but a fortnight since. The gardens spoilt, the orchards ruined, the timber felled, the livestock eaten. Whichever way the war in the West should go, my brother-in-law would be a bankrupt man.

And they had not yet started upon the house or the inhabitants. . . . Our feeding was already a sore problem. At midday we gathered one and all to the main meal of the day. This was served to us in Alice's apartment in the east wing, John lying ill in his father's chamber, and there some twenty of us herded side by side, the children clamouring and fretful, while we dipped stale bread in the mess of watery soup provided, helped sometimes by swollen beans and cabbage. The children had their milk, but no more than two cupfuls for the day, and already I noticed a stary look about them, their eyes overlarge in the pale faces, while their play had become listless, and they yawned often. Young Jonathan started his croup, bringing fresh anxiety to Joan, already nursing her husband, and Alice had to go below to the kitchens and beg for rhubarb sticks to broil for him, which were only given her because her gentle ways won sympathy from the trooper in charge. The old people suffered like the children and complained fretfully with the same misunderstanding of what war brings. Nick Sawle would stare long at his empty bowl when he had finished and mutter, "Disgraceful. Quite unpardonable," under his beard, and look malevolently about him as though it were the fault of someone present, while Will Sparke, with sly cunning, would seat himself amongst the younger children and, under pretence of making friends, sneak crumbs from them when Alice and her nurse had turned their backs. The women were less selfish, and Deborah, whom I had thought as great a freak in her own way as her brother was in his, showed great tenderness, on a sudden, for all those about her who seemed helpless, nor did her deep voice and incipient moustache discourage the smallest children.

It was solely with Matty's aid that I was able to feed Dick at all. By some means, fair or foul, which I did not enquire into, she had made an ally of the second scullion, to whom she pulled a long tale about her ailing crippled mistress, with the result that further soup was smuggled to my chamber beneath Matty's apron, and no one the wiser for it. It was this same scullion who fed us with rumours, too, and most of them disastrous to his own side, which made me wonder if a bribe would make him a deserter.

At midweek we heard that Richard had seized Restormel Castle by Lostwithiel and that Lord Goring, who commanded the King's horse, held the bridge and the road below St. Blazey. Essex was now pinned up in our peninsula, some seven miles long and two broad, with ten thousand men to feed and the guns from Polruan trained on Fowey Harbour. It could not last much longer. Either Essex and the rebels must be relieved by a further force marching to them from the East, or they must stand and make a fight of it. And we would sit, day after day, with cold hearts and empty bellies, staring out upon the sullen soldiery as they stood huddled in the rain outside their tents, while their leaders within the house held councils of despondency.

Another Sunday came, and with it a whisper of alarm among the rebels that the country people were stealing forth at night and doing murder. Sentries were found strangled at their posts; men woke to find their comrades with cut throats; others would stagger to headquarters from the highroad, their hands lopped from their wrists, their eyes blinded. The Cornish were rising. . . .

On Tuesday, the twenty-seventh, there was no soup for our midday dinner, only half a dozen loaves amongst the twenty of us. On Wednesday one jugful of milk for the children, instead of three, and the milk much watered.

On Thursday, Alice and Joan and Mary and the two Sparke sisters and I divided our bread amongst the children and made for ourselves a brew of herb tea with scalding water. We were not hungry. Desire for food left us when we saw the children tear at the stale bread and cram it in their mouths, then turn and ask for more which we could not give to them. And all the while the southwest wind tore and blustered in the teeming sky, and the rebel bugle that had haunted us so long sounded across the park like a challenge of despair.

19

ON FRIDAY, THE thirtieth of August, I lay all day upon my bed, for to gather with the others now would be a farce, nor had I the strength to do so. My cowardly soul forbade me watch the children beg and cry for their one crust of bread. Matty brewed me a cup of tea, and even that seemed wrong to swallow. Hunger had made me listless, and, heedless of danger, I let Dick come and lie upon his mattress next my bed while he gnawed a bone that Matty had scavenged for him. His eyes looked larger than ever in his pale face, and his black curls were lank and lustreless. It seemed to me that in his hunger he grew more like his mother, and sometimes, looking down on him, I would fancy she had stepped into his place and it was Mary Howard I fed and sheltered from the enemy, who licked the bone with little pointed teeth and tore at the strips of flesh with small carnivorous paws.

Matty herself was hollow-eyed and sallow. Gone were the buxom hips and the apple cheeks. Whatever food she could purloin from her friend the scullion—and there was precious little now for the men themselves—she smuggled to Dick or to the children.

During the day while I slipped from one more tearing dream into another, with Dick curled at my feet like a puppy, Matty leaned up against the window, staring at the mist that had followed now upon the rain and hid the tents and horses from us.

The hoofbeats woke me shortly after two, and Matty, opening the window, peered down into the outer court and watched them pass under the gatehouse to the courtyard; some dozen officers, she said, with an escort of troopers, and the leader, on a great black horse, wearing a dark grey cloak. She slipped from the room and watched them descend from their horses in the inner court and came back to say that Lord Robartes had stood himself on the steps to receive them, and they all passed into the dining chamber with sentries before the doors.

Even my tired brain seized the salient possibility that this was the last council to be held and the Earl of Essex had come to it in person. I pressed my hands over my eyes to still my aching head. "Go find your scullion," I said to Matty. "Do what you will to him, but make him talk."

She nodded, tightening her lips, and before she went she brought another bone to Dick from some lair within her own small room and, luring him with it like a dog to his kennel, she got him to his cell beneath the buttress.

Three, four, five, and it was already murky, the evening drawing in early because of the mist and rain, when I heard the horses pass beneath the archway once again and so out across the park. At half-past five Matty returned, and what she had been doing those intervening hours I never asked her from that day to this, but she told me the scullion was without and wished to speak to me. She lit the candles, for I was in darkness, and as I raised myself upon my elbow I questioned her with my eyes, and she gave a jerk of her head towards the passage.

"If you give him money," she whispered, "he will do anything you ask him."

I bade her fetch my purse, which she did, and then, going to the door, she beckoned him within.

He stood blinking in the dim light, a sheepish grin on his face, but that face, like ours, was lean and hungry. I beckoned him to my bed, and he came near, with a furtive glance over his shoulder. I gave him a gold piece, which he pocketed upon the instant.

"What news have you?" I asked.

He looked at Matty, and she nodded. He ran his tongue over his lips.

"'Tis only rumour," he said, "but it's what they're saying in the courtyard." He paused and looked again towards the door. "The retreat begins tonight," he said. "There'll be five thousand of them marching through the darkness to the beaches. You'll hear them if you listen. They'll come this way, down to Pridmouth and Polkerris. The boats will take them off when the wind eases."

"Horses can't embark in small boats," I said. "What will your generals do with their two thousand horse?"

He shook his head and glanced at Matty. I gave him another gold piece.

"I had but a word with Sir William Balfour's groom," he said. "There's talk of breaking through the royalist lines tonight when the foot retreat. I can't answer for the truth of it, nor could he."

"What will happen to you and the other cooks?" I asked.

"We'll go by sea, same as the rest," he said.

"Not likely," I said. "Listen to the wind."

It was soughing through the trees in the warren, and the rain spattered against my casement.

"I can tell you what will happen to you," I said. "The morning will come and there won't be any boats to take you from the beaches. You will huddle there, in the driving wind and rain, with a thundering great southwest sea breaking down at Pridmouth and the country people coming down on you all from the cliffs with pitchforks in their hands. Cornish folk are not pleasant when they are hungry."

The man was silent and passed his tongue over his lips once again.

"Why don't you desert?" I said. "Go off tonight before worse can happen to you. I can give you a note to a royalist leader."

"That's what I told him," said Matty. "A word from you to Sir Richard Grenvile would see him through to our lines."

The man looked from one to the other of us, foolish, doubtful, greedy. I gave him a third gold piece.

"If you break through to the King's Army," I said, "within an hour, and tell them there what you have just told me—about the horse trying to run for it before morning—they'll give you plenty more of these gold pieces and a full supper into the bargain."

He scratched his head and looked again at Matty.

"If the worst comes to the worst and you're held prisoner," I told him, "it would be better than having the bowels torn out of you by Cornishmen."

It was these last words that settled him. "I'll go," he said, "if you'll write a word for me."

I scribbled a few words to Richard, which were as like as not never to reach his hands, nor did they do so, as I afterwards discovered, and I bade the fellow find his way through the woods to Fowey if he could and in the growing darkness get a boat to Bodinnick, which was held by the royalists, and there give warning of the rebel plan.

It would be too late, no doubt, to do much good, but was at least a venture worth the trying. When he had gone, with Matty to speed him on his way, I lay back on my bed and listened to the rain, and as it fell I heard in the far distance, from the highroad beyond the park, the tramp of marching feet. Hour after hour they sounded, tramp, tramp, without a pause, through the long hours of the night, with the bugle crying thin and clear above the moaning of the wind; and when the morning broke, misty and wet and grey, they were still marching there upon the highroad, bedraggled, damp, and dirty, hundred upon hundred straggling in broken lines across the park and making for the beaches.

Order was gone by midday Saturday; discipline was broken, for as a watery sun gleamed through the scurrying clouds we heard the first sounds of gunfire from Lostwithiel as Richard's army broke upon them from the rear. We sat at our windows, hunger at last forgotten, with the rain blowing in our weary faces, and all day long they trudged across the park, a hopeless tangle now of men and horses and wagons; voices yelling orders that were not once obeyed, men falling to the ground in weariness and refusing to move further, horses, carts, and the few cattle that remained, all jammed and bogged together in the sea of mud that once had been a park.

The sound of the gunfire drew nearer, and the rattle of musket shot, and one of the servants, climbing to the belfry, reported that the high ground near Castledore was black with troops and smoke and flame, while down from the fields came little running figures, first a score, then fifty, then a hundred, then a hundred more, to join the swelling throng about the lanes and in the park.

And the rain went on, and the retreat continued.

At five o'clock word went round the house that we were every one of us to descend to the gallery. Even John from his sickbed must obey the order. The rest had little strength enough to drag their feet, and I found difficulty holding to my chair. Nothing had passed our lips now but weak herb tea for two whole days. Alice looked like a ghost, for I think she had denied herself entirely for the sake of her three little girls. Her sister Elizabeth was scarcely better, and her year-old baby in her arms was still as a waxen doll.

Before I left my chamber I saw that Dick was safe within his cell, and this time, in spite of protestations, I closed the stone that formed the entrance. . . .

A strange band we were, huddled there together in the gallery with wan faces; the children strangely quiet and an ominous heavy look about their hollow eyes. It was the first time I had seen John since that morning a month ago, and he looked most wretchedly ill, his skin a dull yellow colour, and he was shaking still in every limb. He looked across at me as though to ask a question, and I nodded to him, summoning a smile. We sat there waiting, no one with the heart or strength to speak. A little apart from us, near the centre window, sat Gartred with her daughters. They, too, were thinner and paler than before and, I think, had not tasted chicken now for many days, but compared to the poor Rashleigh and Courtney babies, they were not ill nourished.

I noticed that Gartred wore no jewels and was very plainly dressed, and somehow the sight of this gave me a strange foreboding. She took no notice of us, beyond a few words to Mary on her entrance, and, seated beside the little table in the window, she proceeded to play patience. She turned the cards with faces uppermost, considering them with great intent of mind, and this, I thought, is the moment she has been waiting for for over thirty days.

Suddenly there was a tramping in the hall, and into the gallery came Lord Robartes, his boots besplashed with mud, the rain running from his coat. His staff officers stood beside him, and one and all wore faces grim and purposeful.

"Is everybody in the household here?" he called harshly.

Some sort of murmur rose from amongst us, which he took to be assent.

"Very well then," he said, and, walking towards my sister Mary and her stepson John, he stood confronting them.

"It has come to my knowledge," he said, "that your malignant husband, madam, and your father, sir, has concealed upon his premises large quantities of silver, which silver should by right belong to Parliament. The time has ended for any trifling or protestation. Pressure is being brought to bear upon our armies at this moment, forcing us to a temporary withdrawal. The Parliament needs every ounce of silver in the land to bring this war to a successful conclusion. I ask you, madam, therefore, to tell me where the silver is concealed."

Mary, God bless her ignorance, turned up her bewildered face to him. "I know nothing of any silver," she said, "except what few plate we have kept of our own, and that you now possess, having my keys."

"I talk of great quantities, madam, stored in some place of hiding before it is transported by your husband to the mint."

"My husband was collector for Cornwall, that is true, my lord. But he has never said a word to me about concealing it at Menabilly."

He turned from her to John. "And you, sir? No doubt your father told you all his affairs?"

"No," said John firmly, "I know nothing of my father's business, nor have I any knowledge of a hiding place. My father's only confidant is his steward, Langdon, who is with him at his present. No one here at Menabilly can tell you anything at all."

For a moment Lord Robartes stared down at John, then, turning away, he called to his three officers. "Sack the house," he said briefly; "strip the hangings and all furnishings. Destroy everything you find. Take all jewels, clothes, and valuables. Leave nothing of Menabilly but the bare walls."

At this poor John struggled to his feet. "You cannot do this," he said. "What authority has Parliament given you to commit such wanton damage? I protest, my lord, in the name of common decency and humanity."

And my sister Mary, coming forward, threw herself upon her knees. "My lord Robartes," she said, "I swear to you by all I hold most dear that there is nothing concealed within my house. If it were so I would have known of it. I do implore you to show mercy to my home."

Lord Robartes stared down at her, his eyes hard.

"Madam," he said, "why should I show your house mercy, when none was shown to mine? Both victor and loser pay the penalty in civil war. Be thankful that I have heart enough to spare your lives." And with that he turned on his heel and went from us, taking his officers with him and leaving two sentries at the door.

Once again he mounted his horse in the courtyard and rode away, back to the useless rear-guard action that was being fought in the hedges and ditches up at Castledore, with the mizzle rain still falling thick and fast; and we heard the major he had left in charge snap forth an order to his men—and straightway they started tearing at the panelling in the dining chamber. We could hear the woodwork rip and the glass shatter as they smashed the mullioned windows.

At this first warning of destruction Mary turned to John, the tears ravaging her face. "For God's sake," she said, "if you know of any hiding place tell them of it so that we save the house. I will take full blame upon myself when your father comes."

John did not answer. He looked at me. And no one of the company there present saw the look save Gartred, who at that moment raised her head. I made no motion of my lips. I stared back at him as hard and merciless as Lord Robartes. He waited a moment, then answered very slowly: "I know nought of any hiding place."

I think had the rebels gone about their work with shouts and merriment, or even drunken laughter, the destruction of the house would have been less hard to bear. But because they were defeated troops and knew it well, they had cold savage murder in their hearts and did what they had to do in silence.

The door of the gallery was open, with the two sentries standing on guard beside it, and no voices were uplifted, no words spoken, only the sound of the ripping wood, the breaking of the furniture, the hacking to pieces of the great dining table, and the grunts of the men as they lifted their axes. The first thing that was thrown down to us across the hall, torn and split, was the portrait of the King, and even the muddied heel that had been ground upon the features and the great crack across the mouth had not distorted those melancholy eyes that stared up at us without complaint from the wrecked canvas.

We heard them climb the stairs and break into the south rooms, and as they tore down the door of Mary's chamber she began to weep, long and silently, and Alice took her in her arms and hushed her like a child. The rest of us did nothing but sat like spectres, inarticulate. Then Gartred looked towards me from her window.

"You and I, Honor, being the only members of the company without a drop of Rashleigh blood, must pass the time somehow. Tell me, do you play piquet?"

"I haven't played it since your brother taught me sixteen years ago," I answered.

"The odds are in my favour then," she said. "Will you risk a *partie?*" As she spoke she smiled, shuffling her cards, and I guessed the double meaning she would bring to it.

"Perhaps," I said, "there is more at stake than a few pieces of silver."

We heard them tramping overhead and the sound of the splitting axe, while the shivering glass from the casements fell to the terrace outside.

"You are afraid to match your cards against mine?" said Gartred.

"No," I said. "No, I am not afraid."

I pushed my chair towards her and sat opposite her at the table. She handed the cards for me to cut and shuffle, and when I had done so I returned them to her for the dealing, twelve apiece. There started then the strangest partie of piquet that I have ever played, before or since, for while Gartred risked a fortune I wagered for Richard's son, and no one knew it but myself.

The rest of the company, dumb and apathetic, were too weak even to wonder at us, and if they did it was with shocked distaste and shuddering dislike that we—because we did not belong to Menabilly—could show ourselves so heartless.

"Five cards," called Gartred.

"What do they make?" I said.

"Making nine."

"Good."

"Five."

"A quart major, nine. Three knaves."

"Not good."

She led with the ace of hearts, to which I played the ten, and as she took the trick we heard the rebels wrenching the tapestry from the bedroom walls above. There was a dull, smouldering smell, and a wisp of smoke blew past the windows of the gallery.

"They are setting fire," said John quietly, "to the stables and the farm buildings before the house."

"The rain will surely quench the flames," whispered Joan. "They cannot burn fiercely, not in the rain."

One of the children began to wail, and I saw gruff Deborah take her on her knee and murmur to her. The smoke of the burning buildings was rank and bitter in the steady rain, and the sound of the axes overhead and the tramping of the men was as though they were felling trees in a thick forest, instead of breaking to pieces the great four-poster bed where Alice had borne her babies. They threw the glass mirror out onto the terrace, where it splintered to a thousand fragments, and with it came the broken candlesticks, the tall vases, and the tapestried chairs.

"Fifteen," said Gartred, leading the king of diamonds, and "Eighteen," I answered, trumping it with my ace.

Some of the rebels, with a sergeant in charge of them, came down the staircase, and they had with them all the clothing they had found in Jonathan's and Mary's bedroom, and her jewels, too, and combs, and the fine figured arras that had hung upon the walls. This they loaded in bundles upon the pack horses that waited in the courtyard. When they were fully laden a trooper led them through the archway, and two more took their places.

Through the broken windows of the wrecked dining chamber, the room being open to the hall, we could see the disordered rebel bands still straggling past the smouldering farm buildings towards the meadows and the beach, and as they gazed up at the house, grinning, their fellows at the house windows, warming to their work and growing reckless, shouted down to them with jeers and catcalls, throwing the mattresses, the chairs, the tables, all they could seize hands upon which would make fodder for the flames that rose reluctantly in the slow drizzle from the blackened farm buildings.

There was one fellow making a bundle of all the clothing and the linen. Alice's wedding gown, and the little frocks she had embroidered for her children, and all Peter's rich apparel that she had kept with such care in her press till he should need it.

The tramping ceased from overhead, and we heard them pass into the rooms beneath the belfry. Some fellow, for mockery, began to toll the bell, and the mournful clanging made a new sound in our ears, mingling with the shouting and yelling and rumble of wagon wheels that still came to us from the park, and the ever-increasing bark of cannon shot, now barely two miles distant.

"They will be in the gatehouse now," said Joan. "All your books and your possessions, Honor, they will not spare them any more than ours." There was reproach in her voice and disillusionment that her favourite aunt and godmother should show no sign of grief.

"My cousin Jonathan would never have permitted this," said Will Sparke, his voice high with hysteria. "Had there been plate concealed about the premises he would have given it, and willingly, rather than have his whole house robbed and we his relatives lose everything."

Still the bell tolled, and the ceilings shook with heavy, murderous feet, and down into the inner court now they threw the debris from the west part of the building—portraits and benches, rugs and hangings, all piled on top of one another in hideous confusion—while those below discarded the less valuable and fed them to the flames.

We started upon the third hand of the partie, and "A tierce to a king," called Gartred, and "Good," I replied, following her lead of spades, and all the while I knew that the rebels were now come to the last room of the house and were tearing down the arras before the buttress.

I saw Mary raise her grief-stricken face and look towards us.

"If you would but say one word to the officer," she said to Gartred, "he might prevent the men from further damage. You are a friend of Lord Robartes and have some sway with him. Is there nothing you can do?"

"I could do much," said Gartred, "if I were permitted. But Honor tells me it is better for the house to fall about our ears. . . . Fifteen, sixteen, seventeen, and eighteen. My trick, I fancy."

She wrote her score on the tablet by her side.

"Honor," said Mary, "you know that it will break Jonathan's heart to see his home laid desolate. All that he has toiled and lived for, and his father before him, for nearly fifty years. If Gartred can in some way save us and you are trying to prevent her, I can never forgive you, nor will Jonathan when he knows of it."

"Gartred can save no one, unless she likes to save herself," I answered, and began to deal for the fourth hand.

"Five cards," called Gartred.

"Equal," I answered.

"A quart to a king."

"A quart to a knave."

We were in our last game, each winning two apiece, when we heard them crashing down the stairs, with the major in the lead.

The terrace and the courtyard were heaped high with wreckage, the loved possessions and treasures of nearly fifty years, even as Mary had said, and what had not been packed upon the horses was left now to destroy. They set fire to this remainder and watched it burn, the men leaning upon their axes and breathing hard now that the work was over; and when the pile was well alight the major turned his back upon it and, coming into the gallery, clicked his heels and bowed derisively to John.

"The orders given me by Lord Robartes have been carried out with implicit fidelity," he announced. "There is nothing left within Menabilly house but yourselves, ladies and gentlemen, and the bare walls."

"And you found no silver hidden?" asked Mary.

"None, madam, but your own—now happily in our possession."

"Then this wanton damage, this wicked destruction, has been for nothing?"

"A brave blow has been struck for Parliament, madam, and that is all that we, her soldiers and her servants, need consider."

He bowed and left us, and in a moment we heard him call further orders, and the horses were brought, and he mounted and rode away even as Lord Robartes had done an hour before. The flames licked the rubble in the courtyard, and save for their dull hissing and the patter of the rain, there was suddenly no other sound. A strange silence had fallen upon the place. Even the sentries stood no longer by the door. Will Sparke crept to the hall.

"They've gone," he said. "They've ridden all away. The house is bare, deserted."

I looked up at Gartred, and this time it was I who smiled and I who spread my cards upon the table.

"Discard for carte blanche," I said softly and, adding ten thus to my score, I led her for the first time and with my next hand drew three aces to her one and gained the partie.

She rose then from the table without a word, save for one mock curtsey to me, and, calling her daughters to her, went upstairs.

I sat alone, shuffling the cards as she had done, while out into the hall faltered the poor weak members of our company to gaze about them, stricken at the sight that met their eyes.

The panels ripped, the floors torn open, the windows shattered from their frames, and all the while the driving rain that had neither doors nor windows now to bar it blew in upon their faces, soft and silent, with great flakes of charred timber and dull soot from the burning rubble in the courtyard.

The last rebels had retreated to the beaches, save for the few who still made their stand at Castledore, and there was no trace of them left now at Menabilly but the devastation they had wrought and the black, churning slough that once was road and park.

As I sat there listening, still shuffling the cards in my hands, I heard for the first time a new note above the cannon and the musket shot and the steady pattering rain. Never clamouring, never insistent, like the bugle that had haunted me so long, but sharp, quick, triumphant, coming ever nearer, was the brisk tattoo of the royalist drums.

20

THE REBEL ARMY capitulated to the King in the early hours of Sunday morning. There was no escape by sea for the hundreds of men herded on the beaches. Only one fishing boat put forth from Fowey bound for Plymouth in the dim light before dawn, and she carried in her cabin the Lord General the Earl of Essex and his adviser Lord Robartes. So much we learnt later, and we learnt, too, that Matty's scullion had indeed proved faithful to his promise and borne his message to Sir Jacob Astley at Bodinnick on the Friday evening, but by the time word had reached His Majesty and the outposts upon the road were warned, the Parliament horse had successfully broken through the royalist lines and made good their escape to Saltash. So, by a lag in time, more than two thousand rebel horse got clean away to fight another day, which serious mishap was glossed over by our forces in the heat and excitement of the big surrender, and I think the only one of our commanders to go nearly hopping mad at the escape was Richard Grenvile.

It was, I think, most typical of his character, that when he sent a regiment of his foot to come to our succour on that Sunday morning, bringing us food from their own wagons, he did not come himself but forwarded me this brief message, stopping not to consider whether I lived or died or whether his son was with me still. He wrote:

> You will soon learn that my plan has only partially succeeded. The horse have got away, all owing to that besotted idiot Goring lying in a stupor at his headquarters and permitting—you will scarcely credit it—the rebels to slip through his lines without so much as a musket shot at their backsides. May God preserve us from our own commanders. I go now in haste to Saltash in pursuit, but we have little hope of overtaking the sods, if Goring, with his cavalry, has already failed.

First a soldier, last a lover, my Richard had no time to waste over a starving household and a crippled woman who had let a whole house be laid to waste about her for the sake of the son he did not love.

So it was not the father, after all, who carried the fainting lad into my chamber once again and laid him down, but poor sick John Rashleigh who, crawling for the second time into the tunnel beneath the summerhouse and, finding Dick unconscious in the buttress cell, tugged at the rope, and so opened the hinged stone into the room.

This was about nine o'clock on the Saturday night, after the house had been abandoned by the rebels, and we were all too weak to do little more than smile at them when the royalist foot beat their drums under our gaping windows on the Sunday morning.

The first necessity was milk for the children and bread for ourselves, and later in the day, when we had regained a little measure of our strength and the soldiers had kindled a fire for us in the gallery—the only room left livable—we heard once more the sound of horses, but this time heartening and welcome, for they were our own men coming home. I suppose I had been through a deal of strain those past four weeks, something harder than the others because of the secret I had guarded, and so, when it was over, I suffered a strange relapse, accentuated maybe by natural weakness, and had not the strength for several days to lift my head.

The scenes of joy and reunion then were not for me. Alice had her Peter, Elizabeth her John of Coombe, Mary had her Jonathan, and there was kissing, and crying, and kissing again, and all the horrors of our past days to be described, and the desolation to be witnessed. But I had no shoulder on which to lean my head and no breast to weep upon. A truckle bed from the attic served me for support, this being one of the few things found that the rebels had not destroyed. I do recollect that my brother-in-law bent over me when he returned and praised me for my courage, saying that John had told him everything and I had acted as he would have done himself had he been home. But I did not want my brother-in-law; I wanted Richard. And Richard had gone to Saltash, chasing rebels.

All the rejoicing came as an anticlimax. The bells pealing in Fowey Church, echoed by the bells at Tywardreath, and His Majesty summoning the gentlemen of the county to his headquarters at Boconnoc and thanking them for their support—he presented Jonathan with his own lace handkerchief and prayer book—and a sudden wild thanksgiving for deliverance and for victory seemed premature to me and strangely sour. Perhaps it was some fault in my own character, some cripple quality, but I turned my face to the wall and my heart was heavy. The war was not over, for all the triumphs in the West. Only Essex had been defeated and his eight thousand men. There were many thousands in the North and East of England who had yet to show their heels. And what is it all for? I thought. Why can they not make peace? Is it to continue thus, with the land laid waste and the houses devastated, until we are all grown old?

Victory had a hollow sound, with our enemy Lord Robartes in command at Plymouth, still stubbornly defended, and there was something narrow and parochial in thinking the war over because Cornwall was now free.

It was the second day of our release, when the menfolk had ridden off to Boconnoc to take leave of His Majesty, that I heard the sound of wheels in the outer court and preparation for departure and then those wheels creaking over the cobbles and disappearing through the park. I was too tired then to question it, but later in the day, when Matty came to me, I asked her who it was that went away from Menabilly in so confident a fashion.

"Who else could it be," Matty answered me, "but Mrs. Denys?"

So Gartred, like a true gambler, had thought best to cut her losses and be quit of us.

"How did she find the transport?" I enquired.

Matty sniffed as she wrung out a piece of cloth to bathe my back.

"There was a gentleman she knew, it seems, amongst the royalist party who rode hither yesterday with Mr. Rashleigh, a Mr. Ambrose Manaton, and it's he who has provided her the escort for today."

I smiled in spite of myself. However much I hated Gartred, I had to bow to the fashion in which she landed on her feet in all and every circumstance.

"Did she see Dick," I asked, "before she left?"

"Aye," said Matty. "He went up to her at breakfast and saluted her. She stared at him, amazed; I watched her. And then she asked him, 'Did you come in the morning with the infantry?' And he grinned like a little imp and answered, 'I have been here all the time.' "

"Imprudent lad," I said. "What did she say to him?"

"She did not answer for a moment, Miss Honor, and then she smiled—you know her way—and said, 'I might have known it. You may tell your jailer you are now worth one bar of silver.' "

"And was that all?"

"That was all. She went soon after. She'll never come again to Menabilly." And Matty rubbed my sore back with her hard familiar hands. But Matty was wrong, for Gartred did come again to Menabilly, as you shall hear, and the man who brought her was my own brother. . . . But I run ahead of my story, for we are still in September '44.

The first week while we recovered our strength my brother-in-law and his steward set to work to find out what it would cost to make good the damage that had been wrought upon his house and his estate. The figure was colossal and beyond his means. I can see him now, seated in one corner of the gallery, reading from his great account book, every penny he had lost meticulously counted and entered in the margin. It would take months—nay, years—he said, to restore the house and bring back the estate to its original condition. While the war lasted no redress would be forthcoming. After the war, so he was told, the Crown would see that he was not the loser.

I think Jonathan knew the value of such promises, and, like me, he thought the rejoicings in the West were premature. One day the rebels might return again and next time the scales be turned.

In the meantime all that could be done was to save what was left of the harvest—and that but one meadow of fourteen acres that the rebels had left uncut but the rain had well-nigh ruined.

His house in Fowey being left bare in the same miserable state as Menabilly, his family, in their turn, were become homeless, and the decision was now made amongst us to divide. The Sawles went to their brother at Penrice, the Sparkes to other relatives at Tavistock. The Rashleighs themselves, with the children, split up amongst near neighbours until a wing of Menabilly should be repaired. I was for returning to Lanrest until I learnt, with a sick heart, that the whole house had suffered a worse fate than Menabilly and was wrecked beyond hope of restoration.

There was nothing for it but to take shelter, for the time being, with my brother Jo at Radford, for although Plymouth was still held by Parliament, the surrounding country was safe in royalist hands, and the subduing of the garrison and harbour was only, according to our optimists, a matter of three months at the most.

I should have preferred, had the choice been offered me, to live alone in one bare room at Menabilly than repair to Radford and the stiff household of my brother, but alas, I had become in a few summer months but another of the vast number of homeless people turned wanderer through war, and must swallow pride and be grateful for hospitality, from whatever direction it might come.

I might have gone to my sister Cecilia at Maddercombe, or my sister Bridget at Holbeton, both of whom were pleasanter companions than my brother Jo, whose official position in the county of Devon had turned him somewhat cold and proud, but I chose Radford for the very reason that it was close to Plymouth—and Richard was once more commander of the siege. What hopes had I of seeing him? God only knew, but I was sunk deep now in the mesh I had made for myself, when waiting for a word from him or a visit of an hour was to become sole reason for existence.

"Why cannot you come with me to Buckland?" pleaded Dick, for the tutor, Herbert Ashley, had been sent to fetch him home. "I would be content at Buckland and not mind my father if you could come, too, and stand between us."

"Your father," I answered him, "has enough work on his hands without keeping house for a crippled woman."

"You are not crippled," declared the boy with passion. "You are only weak about the legs and so must sit confined to your chair. I would tend you and wait upon you, hour by hour with Matty, if you would but come with me to Buckland."

I smiled and ran my hand through his dark curls.

"You shall come and visit me at Radford," I said, "and tell me of your lessons. How you fence, and how you dance, and what progress you make in speaking French."

"It will not be the same," he said, "as living with you in the house. Shall I tell you something? I like you best of all the people that I know—next to my own mother."

Ah well, it was achievement to be second once again to Mary Howard.

The next day he rode away in company with his tutor, turning back to wave at me all the way across the park, and I shed a useless sentimental tear when he was gone from me.

What might have been—what could have been—the saddest phrases in our English tongue, and back again, pell-mell, would come the fantasies: the baby I had never borne, the husband I would never hold. The sickly figures in an old maid's dream, so Gartred would have told me.

Yes, I was thirty-four, an old maid and a cripple; but sixteen years ago I had had my moment, which was with me still, vivid and enduring, and by God, I swear I was happier with my one lover than Gartred ever had been with her twenty.

So I set forth upon the road again and turned my back on Menabilly, little thinking that the final drama of the house must yet be played with blood and tears, and I kissed my dear Rashleighs one and all and vowed I would return to them as soon as they could have me.

Jonathan escorted me in my litter as far as Saltash, where Robin came to meet me. I was much shaken, not by the roughness of the journey, but by the sights I had witnessed on the road. The aftermath of war was not a pleasant sight to the beholder.

The country was laid waste, for one thing, and that the fault of the enemy. The corn ruined, the orchards devastated, the houses smoking. And in return for this the Cornish people had taken toll upon the rebel prisoners. There were many of them still lying in the ditches, with the dust and flies upon them. Some without hands and feet, some hanging downwards from the trees. And there were stragglers who had died upon the road in the last retreat, too faint to march from Cornwall—and these had been set upon and stripped of their clothing and left for the hungry dogs to lick.

I knew then as I peered forth from the curtains of my litter that war can make beasts of every one of us and that the men and women of my own breed could act even worse in warfare than the men and women of the Eastern counties. We had, each one of us, because of the civil war, streaked back two centuries in time and were become like those half savages of the fourteen hundreds who, during the Wars of the Roses, slit one another's throats without compunction.

At Saltash there were gibbets in the market square, with the bodies of rebel troopers hanging upon them scarcely cold, and as I turned my sickened eyes away from them I heard Jonathan enquire of a passing soldier what faults they had committed.

He grinned, a fine tall fellow with the Grenvile shield on his shoulder. "No fault," he said, "except that they are rebels and so must be hanged like the dogs they are."

"Who gave the order, then?"

"Our general, of course, Sir Richard Grenvile."

Jonathan said nothing, but I saw that he looked grave, and I leant back upon my cushions, feeling, because it was Richard's doing and I loved him, that the fault was somehow mine, and I responsible.

We halted there that night, and in the morning Robin came with an escort to conduct me across the Tamar, and so through the royalist lines outside the Plymouth defences, round to Radford.

Robin looked well and bronzed, and I thought again with cynicism how men, in spite of protestations about peace, are really bred to war and thrive upon it. He was not under Richard's command but was colonel of foot under Sir John Berkeley, in the army of Prince Maurice, and he told us that the King had decided not to make a determined and immediate assault upon Plymouth after all, but to leave it to Grenvile to subdue by slow starvation, while he and Prince Maurice marched east out of Devon towards Somerset and Wiltshire, there to join forces with Prince Rupert and engage the Parliament forces hitherto unsubdued. I thought to myself that Richard would reckon this bad strategy, for Plymouth was no pooping little town, but the finest harbour in all England next to Portsmouth, and for His Majesty to gain the garrison and have command also of the sea was of very great importance. Slow starvation had not conquered it before; why, then, should it do so now? What Richard needed for assault were guns and men. But I was a woman and not supposed to have knowledge of these matters. I watched Robin and Jonathan in conversation and caught a murmur of the word "Grenvile" and Robin saying something about "harsh treatment of the prisoners" and "Irish methods not suiting Devon men," and I guessed that Richard was already getting up against the county. No doubt I would hear more of this at Radford.

No one hated cruelty more than I did, nor deplored the streak of it in Richard with greater sickness of heart, but as we travelled towards Radford, making a great circuit of the forts around Plymouth, I noticed with secret pride that the only men who carried themselves like soldiers were those who wore the Grenvile shield on their shoulders. Some of Goring's horse were quartered by St. Budeaux, and they were lolling about the village, drinking with the inhabitants, while a sentry squatted on a stool, his great mouth gaping in a yawn, his musket lying at his feet, and from the neary-by inn came a group of officers, laughing and very flushed, nor did the sentry leap to his feet when he observed them. Robin joined the officers a moment, exchanged greetings, and as we passed through the village he told me the most flushed of the group was Lord Goring himself, a very good fellow and a most excellent judge of horses.

"Does that make him a good commander?" I asked.

"He is full of courage," said Robin, "will ride at anything. That is all that matters." And he proceeded to tell me about a race that had been run the day before, under the very noses of the rebels, and how Lord Goring's chestnut had beaten Lord Wentworth's roan by half a neck.

"Is that how Prince Maurice's army conducts its war?" I asked.

Robin laughed; he thought it all very fine sport.

But the next post we passed was held by Grenvile men. And here there was a barrier across the road and armed sentries standing by it, and Robin had to show his piece of paper, signed by Sir John Berkeley, before we could pass through. An officer barked an order to the men, and they removed the barrier. There were perhaps a score of them standing by the postern, cleaning their equipment; they looked lean and tough, with an indefinable quality about them that stamped them Grenvile men. I would have known them on the instant had I not seen the scarlet pennant by the postern door, with the three golden rests staring from the centre, capped by a laughing griffin.

We came at length by Plymstock into Radford and my brother's house, and as I was shown to my apartment looking north over the river towards the Cattwater and Plymouth, I thought of my eighteenth birthday long ago, and how Richard had sailed into the Sound with the Duke of Buckingham. It seemed a world ago, and I another woman.

My brother was now a widower, Elizabeth Champernowne having died a few years before the war in childbed, and my youngest brother Percy, with his wife Phillippa, was come to live with him and look after Jo's son John, a child of seven, they themselves being childless. I had never cared much for Radford, even as a girl, and now within its austere barrack precincts I found myself homesick, not so much for Lanrest and the days that were gone, but for my last few months at Menabilly. The danger I had known there and the tension I had shared had, in some strange fashion, rendered the place dear to me. The gatehouse between the courtyards, the long gallery, the causeway that looked out to the Gribbin and the sea seemed now to me, in retrospect, my own possession, and even Temperance Sawle with her prayers and Will Sparke with his high-pitched voice were people for whom I felt affection because of the siege we had each one of us endured. The fighting did not touch them at Radford, for all its proximity to Plymouth, and the talk was all of the discomfort they had to bear by living within military control.

I, straight from a sacked house and starvation, wondered that they should think themselves ill-used, with plenty of food upon the table, but no sooner had we sat down to dinner (I had not the face to demand it, the first evening, in my room) than Jo began to hold forth, with great heat, upon the dictatorial manners of the Army.

"His Majesty has thought fit," he said, "to confer upon Richard Grenvile the designation of General in the West. Very good. I have no word to say against the appointment. But when Grenvile trades upon the title to commandeer all the cattle within a radius of thirty miles or more to feed his army, and rides roughshod over the feelings of the county gentry with the one sentence, 'Military necessities come first,' it is time that we all protested."

If Jo remembered my old alliance with Richard, the excitement of the moment had made him conveniently forget it; nor did he know that young Dick had been in my care at Menabilly the past weeks. Robin, too, full of his own commander Berkeley, was pleased to agree with Jo.

"The trouble with Grenvile," said Robin, "is that he insists upon his fellows being paid. The men in his command are like hired mercenaries. No free quarter, no looting, no foraging as they please, and all this comes very hard upon the pockets of people like yourself who must provide the money."

"Do you know," continued Jo, "that the commissioners of Devon have been obliged to allot him one thousand pounds a week for the maintenance of his troops? I tell you, it hits us very hard."

"It would hit you harder," I said, "if your house was burnt down by the Parliament."

They stared at me in surprise, and I saw young Phillippa look at me in wonder for my boldness. Woman's talk was not encouraged at Radford.

"That, my dear Honor," said Jo coldly, "is not likely to happen." And, turning his shoulder to me, he harped on about the outraged Devon gentry, and how this new-styled General in the West had coolly told them that he had need of all their horses and their muskets in this siege of Plymouth, and if they did not give them to him voluntarily he would send a company of his soldiers to collect them.

"The fellow is entirely without scruples, no doubt of that," said Percy, "but in fairness to him I must say that all the country people tell me they would rather have Grenvile men in their villages than Goring's. If Grenvile finds one of his own fellows looting he is shot upon the instant. But Goring's men are quite out of control and drunk from dawn to dusk."

"Oh, come," frowned Robin. "Goring and his cavalry are entitled to a little relaxation, now that the worst is over. No sense in keeping fellows standing to attention all day long."

"Robin is right," said Jo. "A certain amount of licence must be permitted to keep the men in heart. We shall never win the war otherwise."

"You are more likely to lose it," I said, "by letting them loll about the villages with their tunics all undone."

The statement was rendered the more unfortunate by a servant entering the room upon this instant and announcing Sir Richard Grenvile. He strode in, with his boots ringing on the stone flags, in that brisk way I knew so well, totally unconscious of himself or the effect he might produce, and with a cool nod to Jo, the master of the house, he came at once to me and kissed my hand.

"Why the devil," he said, "did you come here and not to Buckland?"

That he at once put me at a disadvantage amongst my relatives did not worry him. I mumured something about my brother's invitation and attempted to introduce him to the company. He bowed to Phillippa but turned back immediately to me.

"You've lost that weight that so improved your person," he said. "You're as thin as a church mouse."

"So would you be," I answered, "if you'd been held prisoner by the rebels for four weeks."

"The whelp is asking for you all day long" said Richard. "He dins your praises in my ears till I am sick of them. I have him outside with Joseph. Hi, spawn!" He turned on his heels, bawling for his son.

I think I never knew of any man, save Richard, who could in so brief a moment fill a room with his presence and become, as it were, the master of a house that was in no way his. Jo stood at his own table, his napkin in his hand, and Robin, too, and Percy, and they were like dumb servants waiting for the occasion, while Richard took command. Dick crept in cautiously, timid and scared as ever, his dark eyes lighting at the sight of me, and behind him strode young Joseph Grenvile, Richard's kinsman and aide-de-camp, his features and his colouring so like his general's as to make me wonder, and not for the first time, God forgive my prying mind, whether Richard had been purposely vague about the relationship between them and whether he was not as much his son as Dick was. And damn you, I thought, begetting sons about the countryside before I was even crippled, and what woman in Cornwall or in Devon cradled this youngster some sixteen years ago?

"Have you all dined?" said Richard, reaching for a plum. "These lads and I could eat another dinner."

And Jo, with heightened colour and a flea in his ear, as the saying goes, called the servants to bring back the mutton. Dick squeezed himself beside me, like a small dog regaining his lost mistress, and while they ate Richard declaimed upon the ill advisability of the King having marched East without first seeing Plymouth was subdued.

"It's like talking to a brick wall, God bless him," said Richard, his mouth full of mutton. "He knows no more of warfare than this dead sheep I swallow."

I saw my brothers look at one another in askance, that a general should dare to criticise his King.

"I'll fight in his service until there's no breath left in my body," said Richard, "but it would make it so much simpler for the country if he would ask advice of soldiers. . . . Put some food into your belly, spawn. Don't you want to grow as fine a man as Joe here?"

I saw Dick glance under his eyes at Joseph with a flicker of jealousy. Joe, then, was the favourite, no doubt of that. What a world of difference between them, too, the one so broadshouldered, big, and auburn-haired; the other little, with black hair and eyes. I wonder, I thought grudgingly, what buxom country girl is Joseph's mother, and if she still lives, and what has happened to her.

But while I pondered the question, as jealous as young Dick, Richard continued talking. "It's that damned lawyer who's to blame," he said, "that fellow Hyde, an upstart from God knows what snivelling country town, and now jumped into favour as Chancellor of the Exchequer. His Majesty won't move a finger without asking his advice. I hear Rupert has all but chucked his hand in and returned to Germany. Depend upon it, it's fellows like this who will lose the war for us."

"I have met Sir Edward Hyde," said my brother. "He seemed to me a very able man."

"Able my arse," said Richard. "Anyone who jiggles with the Treasury must be double-faced to start with. I've never met a lawyer yet who didn't line his own pockets before he fleeced his clients." He tapped young Joseph on the shoulder. "Give me some tobacco," he said.

The youngster produced a pipe and pouch from his coat.

"Yes, I hate the breed," said Richard, blowing a cloud of smoke across the table, "and nothing affords me greater pleasure than to see them trounced. There was a fellow called Braband who acted as attorney for my wife against me in the Star Chamber in the year '33, a neighbour of yours, Harris, I believe?"

"Yes," said my brother coldly, "and a man of great integrity and devoted to the King's cause in this war."

"Well, he'll never prove that now," said Richard. "I found him creeping about the Devon lanes disguised the other day and seized the occasion to arrest him as a spy. I've waited eleven years to catch that blackguard."

"What have you done to him, sir?" asked Robin.

"He was disposed of," said Richard, "in the usual fashion. No doubt he is doing comfortably in the next world."

I saw young Joseph hide his laughter in his wineglass, but my three brothers gazed steadfastly at their plates.

"I dare say," said my eldest brother slowly, "that I should be very ill advised if I attempted to address to you, General, a single word of criticism, but——"

"You would, sir," said Richard, "be extremely ill advised," and laying his hand a moment on Joseph's shoulder, he rose from the table. "Go on, lads, and get your horses. Honor, I will conduct you to your apartment. Good evening, gentlemen."

I felt that whatever reputation I might have for dignity in the eyes of my family was gone to the winds forever as he swept me to my room. Matty was sent packing to the kitchen, and he laid me on my bed and sat beside me.

"You had far better," he said, "return with me to Buckland. Your brothers are all asses. And as for the Champernownes, I have a couple of them on my staff, and both are useless. You remember Edward, the one they wanted you to marry? Dead from the neck upwards."

"And what would I do at Buckland," I said, "among a mass of soldiers? What would be thought of me?"

"You could look after the whelp," he said, "and minister to me in the evening. I get very tired of soldiers' company."

"There are plenty of women," I said, "who could give you satisfaction."

"I have not met any," he said.

"Bring them in from the hedgerows," I said, "and send them back again in the morning. It would be far less trouble than having me upon your hands from dawn till dusk."

"My God," he said, "if you think I want to bounce about with some fat female after a hard day's work sweating my guts out before the walls of Plymouth, you flatter my powers of resilience. Keep still, can't you, while I kiss you."

Below the window, in the drive, Joe and Dick paced the horses up and down. "Someone," I said, "will come into the room."

"Let them," he answered. "What the hell do I care?"

I wished that I could have the same contempt for my brother's house as he had. . . . It was dark by the time he left, and I felt as furtive as I had done at eighteen when slipping from the apple tree.

"I did not come to Radford," I said weakly, "to behave like this."

"I have a very poor opinion," he answered, "of whatever else you came for."

I thought of Jo and Robin, Percy and Phillippa, all sitting in the hall below, and the two lads pacing their horses under the stars.

"You have placed me," I said, "in a most embarrassing position."

"Don't worry, sweetheart," he said. "I did that to you sixteen years ago." As he stood there laughing at me, with his hand upon the door, I had half a mind to throw my pillow at him.

"You and your double-faced attorneys," I said. "What about your own two faces? That boy out there—your precious Joseph—you told me he was your kinsman."

"So he is." He grinned.

"Who is his mother?"

"A dairymaid at Killigarth. A most obliging soul. Married now to a farmer and mother of his twelve sturdy children."

"When did you discover Joseph?"

"A year or so ago, on returning from Germany and before I went to Ireland. The likeness was unmistakable. I took some cheeses and a bowl of cream off his mother, and she recalled the incident, laughing with me in her kitchen. She bore no malice. The boy was a fine boy. The least I could do was to take him off her hands. Now I wouldn't be without him for the world."

"It is the sort of tale," I said sulkily, "that leaves a sour taste in the mouth."

"In yours, perhaps," he said, "but not in mine. Don't be so mealymouthed, my loved one."

"You lived at Killigarth," I said, "when you were courting me."

"Damn it," he said, "I didn't ride to see you every day."

I heard them all in a moment laughing beneath my window and then mount their horses and gallop away down the avenue, and as I lay upon my bed, staring at the ceiling, I thought how the blossom of my apple tree, so long dazzling and fragrant white, had a little lost its sheen and was become, after all, a common apple tree; but that the realisation of this, instead of driving me to torments as it would have done in the past, could now, because of my four and thirty years, be borne with equanimity.

21

I WAS FULLY prepared the following morning to have my brother call upon me at an early hour and inform me icily that he could not have his home treated as a bawdyhouse for soldiery. I knew so well the form of such a discourse. The honour of his position, the welfare of his young son, the delicate feelings of Phillippa, our sister-in-law, and although the times were strange and war had done odd things to conduct, certain standards of behaviour were necessary for people of our standing.

I was, in fact, already planning to throw myself upon my sister Cecilia's mercy over at Maddercombe and had my excuses already framed, when I heard the familiar sound of tramping feet; and, bidding Matty look from the window, I was told that a company of infantry was marching up the drive, and they were wearing the Grenvile shield. This, I felt, would add fuel to the flames that must already be burning in my brother's breast.

Curiosity, however, was too much for me, and instead of remaining in my apartment like a child who had misbehaved, I bade the servants carry me downstairs to the hall. Here I discovered my brother Jo in heated argument with a fresh-faced young officer who declared coolly and with no sign of perturbation that his general, having decided that Radford was most excellently placed for keeping close observation on the enemy battery at Mount Batten, wished to commandeer certain rooms of the house for himself as a temporary headquarters, and would Mr. John Harris be good enough to show the officer a suite of rooms commanding a northwestern view?

Mr. Harris, added the officer, would be put to no inconvenience, as the general would be bringing his own servants, cooks, and provisions.

"I must protest," I heard my brother say, "that this is a highly irregular proceeding. There are no facilities here for soldiers; I myself am hard-pressed with work about the county, and——"

"The general told me," said the young officer, cutting him short, "that he had a warrant from His Majesty authorising him to take over any place of residence in Devon or Cornwall that should please him. He already has a headquarters at Buckland, Werrington, and Fitzford, and there the inhabitants were not permitted to remain but were forced to find room elsewhere. Of course he does not propose to deal thus summarily with you, sir. May I see the rooms?"

My brother stared at him tight-lipped for a moment, then, turning on his heel, escorted him up the stairs which I had just descended. I was very careful to avoid his eye.

During the morning the company of foot proceeded to establish themselves in the north wing of the mansion and, watching from the long window in the hall, I saw the cooks and pantry boys stagger towards the kitchen entrance bearing plucked fowls and ducks and sides of bacon, besides crate after crate of wine. Phillippa sat at my side, stitching her sampler.

"The King's general," she said meekly, "believes in doing himself well. I have not seen such fare since the siege of Plymouth started. Where do you suppose he obtains all his supplies?"

I examined my nails, which were in need of trimming, and so did not have to look her in the face.

"From the many houses," I answered, "that he commandeers."

"But I thought," said Phillippa with maddening persistency, "that Percy told us Sir Richard never permitted his men to loot."

"Possibly," I said with great detachment, "Sir Richard looks upon ducks and burgundy as perquisites of war."

She went to her room soon after, and I was alone when my brother Jo came down the stairs.

"Well," he said grimly, "I suppose I have you to thank for this invasion."

"I know nothing about it," I answered.

"Nonsense, you planned it together last night."

"Indeed we did not."

"What were you doing, then, closeted with him in your chamber?"

"The time seemed to pass," I said, "in reviving old memories."

"I thought," he said after a moment's pause, "that your present condition, my dear Honor, would make talk of your former intimacy quite intolerable, and any renewal of it beyond question."

"So did I," I answered.

He looked down at me, his lips pursed.

"You were always shameless as a girl," he said. "We spoilt you most abominably, Robin, your sisters, and I. And now at thirty-four to behave like a dairymaid."

He could not have chosen an epithet, to my mind, more unfortunate.

"My behaviour last night," I said, "was very different from a dairymaid."

"I am glad to hear it. But the impression upon us here below was to the contrary. Sir Richard's reputation is notorious, and for him to remain within a closed apartment for nearly an hour and three quarters alone with a woman can conjure, to my mind, one thing and one thing only."

"To my mind," I answered, "it can conjure at least a dozen."

After that I knew I must be damned forever and was not surprised when he left me without further argument, except to express a wish that I might have some respect for his roof, though "ceiling" would have been the apter word in my opinion.

I felt brazen and unrepentant all the day, and when Richard appeared that evening in tearing spirits, commanding dinner for two in the apartment his soldiers had prepared for him, I had a glow of wicked satisfaction that my relatives sat below in gloomy silence while I ate roast duck with the general overhead.

"Since you would not come to Buckland," he said, "I had perforce to come to you."

"It is always a mistake," I said, "to fall out with a woman's brothers."

"Your brother Robin has ridden off with Berkeley's horse to Tavistock," he answered, "and Percy I am sending on a delegation to the King. That leaves only Jo to be disposed of. It might be possible to get him over to the Queen in France."

He tied a knot in his handkerchief as a reminder.

"And how long," I asked, "will it take before Plymouth falls before you?"

He shook his head and looked dubious.

"They have the whole place strengthened," he said, "since our campaign in Cornwall, and that's the devil of it. Had His Majesty abided by my advice and tarried here a fortnight only with his army, we would have the place today. But no. He must listen to Hyde and march to Dorset, and here I am, back again where I was last Easter, with less than a thousand men to do the job."

"You'll never take it then," I asked, "by direct assault?"

"Not unless I can increase my force," he said, "by nearly another thousand. I'm already recruiting hard up and down the county. Rounding up deserters and enlisting new levies. But the fellows must be paid. They won't fight otherwise, and I don't blame 'em. Why the devil should they?"

"Where," I said, "did you get this burgundy?"

"From Lanhydrock," he answered. "I had no idea Jack Robartes had laid down so good a cellar. I've had every bottle of it removed to Buckland."

He held his goblet to the candlelight and smiled.

"You know that Lord Robartes sacked Menabilly simply and solely because you pillaged his estate?"

"He is an extremely dull-witted fellow."

"There is not a pin to choose between you, where pillaging is concerned. A royalist does as much damage as a rebel. I suppose Dick told you that Gartred was one of us at Menabilly?"

"What was she after?"

"The duchy silver plate."

"More power to her. I could do with some of it myself to pay my troops."

"She was very friendly with Lord Robartes."

"I have yet to meet the man she dislikes."

"I think it very probable that she acts spy for Parliament."

"There you misjudge her. She would do anything to gain her own ends but that. You forget the old saying that of the three families in Cornwall a Godolphin was never wanting in wit, a Trelawney in courage, or a Grenvile in loyalty. Gartred was born and bred a Grenvile, no matter if she beds with every fellow in the duchy."

A brother, I thought, will always hold a brief for a sister. Perhaps Robin at this moment was doing the same thing for me.

Richard had risen and was looking through the window towards the distant Cattwater and Plymouth.

"Tonight," he said quietly, "I've made a gambler's throw. It may come off. It may be hopeless. If it succeeds Plymouth can be ours by daybreak."

"What do you mean?"

He continued looking through the window to where the lights of Plymouth flickered.

"I am in touch with the second-in-command in the garrison," he said softly, "a certain Colonel Searle. There is a possibility that for the sum of three thousand pounds he will surrender the city. Before wasting further lives I thought it worth my while to essay bribery."

I was silent. The prospect was hazardous and somehow smelt unclean.

"How have you set about it?" I asked at length.

"Young Joe slipped through the lines tonight at sunset," he answered, "and will, by now, be hidden in the town. He bears upon him my message to the colonel and a firm promise of three thousand pounds."

"I don't like it," I said. "No good will come of it."

"Maybe not," he said indifferently, "but at least it was worth trying. I don't relish the prospect of battering my head against the gates of Plymouth the whole winter."

I thought of young Joe and his impudent brown eyes.

"Supposing," I said slowly, "that they catch your Joseph?"

Richard smiled.

"That lad," he answered, "is quite capable of looking after himself."

But I thought of Lord Robartes as I had seen him last, with muddied boots and the rain upon his shoulders, sour and surly in defeat, and I knew how much he must detest the name of Grenvile.

"I shall be rising early," said Richard, "before you are awake. If by midday you hear a salvo from every gun inside the garrison, you will know that I have entered Plymouth after one swift and very bloody battle."

He took my face in his hands and kissed it and then bade me good night. But I found it hard to sleep. The excitement of his presence in the house had turned to anxiety and strain. I knew, with all the intuition in my body, that he had gambled wrong.

I heard him ride off with his staff about five-thirty in the morning, and then, dead tired, my brain chasing itself in circles, I fell into a heavy sleep.

When I awoke it was past ten o'clock. A grey day with a nip of autumn in the air. I had no wish for breakfast, nor even to get up, but stayed there in my bed. I heard the noises of the house and the coming and going of the soldiers in their wing, and at twelve o'clock I raised myself upon my elbow and looked out towards the river. Five past twelve. A quarter past. Half-past twelve. There was no salvo from the guns. There was not even a musket shot. It rained at two, then cleared, then rained again. The day dragged on, dull, interminable. I had a sick feeling of suspension all·the while. At five o'clock Matty brought me my dinner on a tray, which I picked at with faint appetite. I asked her if she had heard of any news, but she said she knew of none. But later, when she had taken away my tray, and come to draw my curtains, her face was troubled.

"What is the matter?" I asked.

"It's what one of Sir Richard's men was saying down there to the sentry," she answered. "Some trouble today in Plymouth. One of their best young officers taken prisoner by Lord Robartes and condemned to death by council of war. Sir Richard has been endeavouring all day to ransom him but has not succeeded."

"Who is it?"

"I don't know."

"What will happen to the officer?"

"The soldier did not say."

I lay back again on my bed, my hands over my eyes to dim the candle. Foreboding never played me wrong, not when I was seized with it for a whole night and day. Maybe perception was a cripple quality.

Later I heard the horses coming up the drive and the sentries standing to attention. Footsteps climbed the stairs, slowly, heavily, and passed along to the rooms in the northern wing. A door slammed, and there was silence. It was a long while that I waited there, lying on my back. Just before midnight I heard him walk along the passage, and his hand fumbled a moment on the latch of my door. The candles were blown, and it was darkness. The household slept. He came to my side and knelt before the bed. I put my hand on his head and held him close to me. He knelt thus many moments without speaking.

"Tell me," I whispered, "if it will help you."

"They hanged him," he said, "above the gates of the town where we could see him. I sent a company to cut him down, but they were mown down by gunfire. They hanged him before my eyes."

Now that suspense was broken and the long day of strain behind me, I was aware of the feeling of detachment that possesses all of us when a crisis has been passed and the suffering not one's own.

This was Richard's battle. I could not fight it for him. I could only hold him in the darkness.

"That rat Searle," he said, his voice broken, strangely unlike my Richard, "betrayed the scheme, and so they caught the lad. I went myself beneath the walls of the garrison to parley with Robartes. I offered him any terms of ransom or exchange.

He gave no answer. And while I stood there waiting, they strung him up above the gate. . . ."

He could not continue. He lay his head upon me, and I held his hands that clutched so fiercely at the patchwork quilt upon the bed.

"Tomorrow," I said, "it might have been the same. A bullet through the head. A thrust from a pike. An unlucky stumble from his horse. This happens every day. An act of war. Look upon it in that way. Joe died in your service, as he would wish to do."

"No," he said, his voice muffled. "It was my fault. On me the blame, now, tonight, for all eternity. An error in judgment. The wrong decision."

"Joe would forgive you. Joe would understand."

"I can't forgive myself. That's where the torture lies."

I thought then of all the things that I would want to bring before him. How he was not infallible and never had been, and that this stroke of fate was but a grim reminder of the fact. His own harsh measures to the enemy had been repaid, measure for measure. Cruelty begat cruelty; betrayal gave birth to treachery; the qualities that he had fostered in himself these past years were now recoiled upon him.

The men of Parliament had not forgotten his act of perfidy in the spring, when, feigning to be their friend, he had deserted to the King, bearing their secrets. They had not forgotten the executions without trial, the prisoners condemned to death in Lydford Castle, nor the long line of troopers hanging from the gibbets in the market square in Saltash. And Lord Robartes, with his home Lanhydrock ravaged and laid waste, his goods seized, had seen rough justice and revenge in taking the life of the messenger who bore an offer of bribery and corruption in his pocket.

It was the irony of the devil, or Almighty God, that the messenger should have been no distant kinsman but Richard Grenvile's son. All this came before me in that moment when I held Richard in my arms. And now, I thought, we have come to a crisis in his life. The dividing of the ways. Either to learn from this single tragedy of a boy's death that cruelty was not the answer, that dishonesty dealt a returning blow, that accepting no other judgment but his own would in a space of time make every friend an enemy; or to learn nothing, to continue through the months and years deaf to all counsel, unscrupulous, embittered, the Skellum Grenvile with a price upon his head, the Red Fox who would be pointed to forevermore as lacking chivalry, a hated contrast to his well-beloved brother.

"Richard," I whispered, "Richard, my dear and only love. . ." But he rose to his feet; he went slowly to the window and, pulling aside the curtains, stood there with the moonlight on his hands that held the sword but his face in shadow.

"I shall avenge him," he said, "with every life I take. No quarter any more. No pardons. Not one of them shall be spared. From this moment I shall have one aim only in my life, to kill rebels. And to do it as I wish I must have command of the Army; otherwise I fail. I will brook no dispute with my equals; I will tolerate no orders from those senior to me. His Majesty made me General in the West, and by God, I swear that the whole world shall know it."

I knew then that his worse self possessed him, soul and body, and that nothing I could say or do could help him in the future. Had we been man and wife or truly lovers, I might, through the close intimacy of day by day, have learnt to soften him; but fate and circumstance had made me no more than a shadow in his life, a phantom of what might have been. He had come to me tonight because he needed me, but neither tears nor protestations nor assurances of my love and tenderness to all eternity would stay him now from the pursuit of the dim and evil star that beckoned to him.

22

RICHARD WAS CONSTANTLY at Radford during the six months that followed. Although his main headquarters was at Buckland and he rode frequently through both Devon and Cornwall raising new recruits to his command, a company of his men was kept at my brother's house throughout, and his rooms always in preparation.

The reason given that watch must be kept upon the fortresses of Mount Batten and Mount Stampford was true enough, but I could tell from my brother's tightened lips and Percy's and Phillippa's determined discussion upon other matters when the general's name was mentioned that my presence in the house was considered to be the reason for the somewhat singular choice of residence; and when Richard with his staff arrived to spend a night or two and I was bidden to a dinner tête-à-tête immediately upon his coming into the house, havoc at once was played with what shred of reputation might be left to me. The friendship was considered odd, unfortunate; I think had I thrown my cap over the mills and gone to live with him at Buckland it might have been better for the lot of us. But this I steadfastly refused to do, and even now, in retrospect, I cannot give the reason, for it will not formulate in words. Always, at the back of my mind, was the fear that by sharing his life with too great intimacy I would become a burden to him and the love we bore for each other slip to disenchantment. Here at Radford he could seek me out upon his visits, and being with me would bring him peace and relaxation, tonic and stimulation; whatever mood he would be in, weary or high-spirited, I could attune myself accordingly. But had I made myself persistently available in some corner of his house, little by little he would have felt the tug of an invisible chain, the claim that a wife brings to bear upon a husband, and the lovely freedom that there was between us would exist no more. The knowledge of my crippled state, so happily glossed over and indeed forgotten when he came to me at Radford, would have nagged me, a perpetual reproach, had I lived beneath his roof at Buckland. The sense of helplessness, of ugly inferiority, would have worked like a maggot in my mind, and even when he was most gentle and most tender I should have thought—with some devil flash of intuition—This is not what he is wanting.

That was my greatest fault; I lacked humility. Though sixteen years of discipline had taught me to accept crippledom and become resigned to it, I was too proud to share the stigma of it with my lover. Oh God, what would I have given to have walked with him and ridden, to move and turn before him, to have liveliness and grace.

Even a gypsy in the hedges, a beggarwoman in the gutters had more dignity than I. He would say to me, smiling over his wine:

"Next week you shall come to me at Buckland. There is a chamber, high up in the tower, looking out across the valley to the hills. This was once my grandfather's, who fought in the *Revenge,* and when Drake purchased Buckland he used the chamber as his own and hung maps upon the wall. You could lie there, Honor, dreaming of the past and the Armada. And in the evening I would come to you and kneel beside your bed, and we would make believe that the apple tree at Lanrest was still in bloom and you eighteen."

I could see the room as he described it. And the window looking to the hills. And the tents of the soldiery below. And the pennant flying from the tower, scarlet and gold. I could see, too, the other Honor, walking by his side upon the terrace, who might have been his lady.

And I smiled at him and shook my head.

"No, Richard," I said. "I will not come to Buckland."

And so the autumn passed and a new year came upon us once again. The whole of the West Country was held firmly for the King, save Plymouth, Lyme, and Taunton, which three garrisons stubbornly defied all attempt at subjugation, and the two seaports, relieved constantly by the Parliament shipping, were still in no great danger of starvation. So long as these garrisons were unsubdued, the West could not be counted truly safe for His Majesty, and although the royalist leaders were of good heart and expressed great confidence, the people throughout the whole country were already sick and tired of war, which had brought them nothing but loss and high taxation. I believe it was the same for Parliament, that troops deserted from the Army every day. Men wanted to be home again upon their rightful business. The quarrel was not theirs. They had no wish to fight for King or Parliament, and "A plague on both your houses!" was the common cry.

In January, Richard became sheriff for Devon, and with this additional authority he could raise fresh troops and levies, but the way he set about it was never pleasing to the commissioners of the county. He rode roughshod over their feelings, demanding men and money as a right, and for the smallest pretext he would have a gentleman arrested and clapped into jail until such time as a ransom would be paid.

This would not be hearsay from my brother, but frank admissions on the part of Richard himself. Always unscrupulous where money was concerned, now that he had an army to pay, any sense of caution flew to the winds. Again and again I would hear his justification:

"The country is at war. I am a professional soldier and I will not command men who are not paid. While I hold this appointment from His Majesty I will undertake to feed, clothe, and arm the forces at my disposal, so that they hold themselves like men and warriors and not roam the countryside, raping and looting and in rags, like the disorderly rabble under the so-called command of Berkeley, Goring, and the rest. To do this I must have money. And to get money I must demand it from the pockets of the merchants and the gentry of Cornwall and Devon."

I think, by them, he became more hated every day, but by the common people more respected. His troops won such credit for high discipline that their fame spread far abroad to the Eastern counties, and it was, I believe, because of this that the first seeds of jealousy began to sow themselves in the hearts and in the minds of his brother commanders. None of them were professionals like himself but men of estate and fortune who, by their rank, had immediately, upon the outbreak of war, been given high commands and expected to lead newly raised armies into battle. They were gentlemen of leisure, of no experience, and though many of them were gallant and courageous, warfare to them consisted of a furious charge upon blood horses, dangerous and exciting, with more speed to it than a day's hawking, and when the fray was over, back to their quarters to eat and drink and play cards, while the men they had led could fend for themselves. Let them loot the villages and strip the poor inhabitants; it saved the leaders a vast amount of unpleasantness and the trouble that must come from organisation. But it was irritating, I imagine, to hear how Grenvile's men were praised and how Grenvile's men were paid and fed and clothed; and Sir John Berkeley, who commanded the troops at Exeter and was forever hearing complaints from the common people about Lord Goring's cavalry and Lord Wentworth's foot, was glad enough, I imagine, to report to his supreme commander, Prince Maurice, that even if Grenvile's men were disciplined, the commissioners of Devon and Cornwall had no good word to say of Grenvile himself, and that in spite of all the fire-eating and hanging of rebel prisoners Plymouth was still not taken.

In the despatches that passed between John Berkeley and Richard, which from time to time he quoted to me with a laugh, I could read the veiled hint that Jo Berkeley at Exeter, with nothing much to do, would think it far preferable for himself and for the royal cause if he should change commands with Richard.

"They expect me," Richard would say, "to hurl my fellows at the defences without any regard for their lives, and having lost three quarters of them in one assault, recruit another five hundred the following week. Had I command of unlimited forces and possessed God's quantity of ammunition, a bombardment of three days would reduce Plymouth to ashes, but with the little I have at my disposal I cannot hope to reduce the garrison before the spring. In the meanwhile I can keep the swine harassed night and day, which is more than Digby ever did."

His blockade of Plymouth was complete by land, but the rebels having command of the Sound, provisions and relief could be brought to them by sea, and this was the real secret of their success. All that Richard as commander of the siege could hope to do was to so wear out the defenders by constant surprise attack upon the outward positions that in time they would, from very weariness, surrender.

It was a hopeless, gruelling task, and the only people to win glory and praise for their stout hearts were the men who were besieged within the city.

It was shortly after Christmas that Richard decided to send Dick to Normandy with his tutor, Herbert Ashley.

"It's no life for him at Buckland," he said. "Ever since Joe went I've had a guard watch him day and night, and the thought of him so close to the enemy should they try a sally becomes a constant anxiety. He can go to Caen or Rouen, and when the business is well over I shall send for him again."

"Would you never," I said with diffidence, "consider returning him to London to his mother?"

He stared at me as though I had lost my senses.

"Let him go back to that bitch-faced hag," he said, astounded, "and become more of a little reptile than he is already? I would sooner send him this moment to Robartes and let him hang."

"He loves her," I said; "she is his mother."

"So does a pup snuggle to the cur that suckled him," he answered, "but soon forgets her smell once he is weaned. I have but one son, Honor, and if he can't be a credit to me and become the man I want, I have no use for him."

He changed the subject abruptly, and I was reminded once again how I had chosen to be friend, not wife, companion and not mistress, and to meddle with his child was not my business. So Dick rode to Radford to bid me good-bye and put his arms about me and said he loved me well.

"If only," he said, "you could come with me into Normandy."

"Perhaps," I said, "you will not remain there long. And anyway, it will be fresh and new to you, and you will make friends there and be happy."

"My father does not wish me to make friends," he said. "I heard him say as much to Mr. Ashley. He said that in Caen there were few English, therefore it would be better to go there than to Rouen, and that I was to speak to no one and go nowhere without Mr. Ashley's knowledge and permission. I know what it is. He is afraid that I might fall in with some person who should be friendly to my mother."

I had no answer to this argument, for I felt it to be true.

"I shall not know you," I said, summoning a smile, "the next time that I lay eyes on you. I know how boys grow once they are turned fifteen. I saw it with my brother Percy. You will be a young man with lovelocks on your shoulder and a turn for poetry in six months' time."

"Fine poetry I shall write," he sulked, "conversing in French day by day with Mr. Ashley."

If I were in truth his stepmother, I thought, I could prevent this; and if I were in truth his stepmother, he would have hated me. So whichever way I looked upon the matter there was no solution to Dick's problem. He had to face the future, like his father. And so Dick and the timid, unconvincing Herbert Ashley set sail for Normandy the last day of December, taking with them a bill of exchange for twenty pounds, which was all that the General in the West could spare them, Dick taking, besides, my love and blessing, which would not help at all. And while they rocked upon the Channel between Falmouth and Saint-Malo, Richard launched an attack upon Plymouth which this time, so he promised, would not fail. I can see him now, in his room in that north block at Radford, poring over his map of the Plymouth defences, and when I asked to look at it he tossed it over to me with a laugh, saying no woman could make head or tail of his marks and crosses.

And he was right, for never had I seen a chart more scribbled upon with dots and scratches. But even my unpracticed eye could note that the network of defences was formidable indeed, for before the town and garrison could be attacked a chain of outer forts or "works," as he termed them, had firstly to be breached. He came and stood beside me and with his pen pointed to the scarlet crosses on the map.

"There are four works here to the north, in line abreast," he said, "the Pennycome-quick, the Maudlyn, the Holiwell, and the Lipson forts. I propose to seize them all. Once established there, we shall turn the guns against the garrison itself. My main strength will fall upon the Maudlyn works, the others being more in the nature of a feint to draw their fire."

He was in tearing spirits, as always before a big engagement, and suddenly, folding his map, he said to me:

"You have never seen my fellows, have you, in their full war paint prior to a battle? Would you like to do so?"

I smiled.

"Do you propose to make me your aide-de-camp?"

"No. I am going to take you round the posts."

It was three o'clock, a cold, fine afternoon in January. One of the wagons was fitted as a litter for my person, and with Richard riding at my side we set forth to view his army. It was a sight that even now, when all is over and done with and the siege of Plymouth a forgotten thing except for the official records in the archives of the town, I can call before me with wonder and with pride. The main body of his army was drawn up in the fields behind the little parish of Egg Buckland (not to be confused with the Buckland Monachorum where Richard had his headquarters) and there being no warning of our coming, the men were not summoned to parade but were going about their business in preparation for the attack ahead.

The first signal that the general had come in person was a springing to attention of the guards before the camp, and straightway there came a roll upon the drums from within, followed by a second more distant, and then a third, and then a fourth, so that in the space of a few moments, so it seemed to me, the air around me rung with a tattoo as the drums of every company sounded the alert. And swiftly, unfolding in crisp cold air, the scarlet pennant broke from the pole head, with the three golden rests staring from the centre.

Two officers approached and, saluting with their swords, stood before us. This Richard acknowledged with a half gesture of his hand, and then my chair was lifted from the wagon, and with a stalwart young corporal to propel me we proceeded round the camp.

I can smell now the wood smoke from the fires as the blue rings rose into the air, and I can see the men bending over their washtubs or kneeling before the cooking pots, straightening themselves with a jerk as we approached and standing to attention like steel rods. The foot were quartered separate from the horse, and these we inspected first, great brawny fellows of five feet ten or more, for Richard had disdain for little men and would not recruit them. They had a bronzed clean look about them, the result, so Richard said, of living in the open.

"No billeting in cottages amongst the village folk for Grenvile troops," he said. "The result is always the same, slackness and loss of discipline."

I had fresh in my mind a picture of the rebel regiment who had taken Menabilly, and although they had worn a formidable air upon first sight, with their close helmets and uniform jerkins, they had soon lost their sheen after a few days or so, and as the weeks wore on became dirty-looking and rough, and with the threat of defeat had one and all reverted to a London mob in panic.

Richard's men had another stamp upon them, and though drawn mostly from the farms and moors of Cornwall and Devon, rustic in speech and origin, they had become knit, in the few months of his command, into a professional body of soldiers, quick of thought and swift of limb, with an admiration for their leader that showed at once in the upward tilt of their heads as he addressed them and the flash of pride in their eyes. A strange review. Me in my chair, a hooded cloak about my shoulders, and Richard walking by my side; the campfires burning, the white frost gleaming on the clipped turf, the drums beating their tattoo as we approached each different company.

The horse were drawn up on the farther field, and we watched them groomed and watered for the night, fine sleek animals—many of them seized from rebel estates, I was fully aware—and they stamped on the hard ground, the harness jingling, their breath rising in the cold air like the smoke did from the fires.

The sun was setting, fiery red, beyond the Tamar into Cornwall, and as it sank beyond the hills it threw a last dull, sullen glow upon the forts of Plymouth to the south of us.

We could see the tiny figures of the rebel sentries, like black dots, upon the outer defences, and I wondered how many of the Grenvile men about me would make themselves a sacrifice to the spitting thunder of the rebel guns. Lastly, as evening fell, we visited the forward posts, and here there was no more cleaning of equipment, no grooming of horses, but men stripped bare for battle, silent, motionless, and we talked in whispers, for we were scarce two hundred yards from the enemy defences.

The silence was grim, uncanny. The assault force seemed dim figures in the gathering darkness, for they had blacked their faces to make themselves less visible, and I could make nothing of them but white eyes gleaming and the show of teeth when they smiled.

Their breastplates were discarded for a night attack, and in their hands they carried pikes, steely sharp. I felt the edge of one of them and shuddered.

At the last post we visited the men were not so prompt to challenge us as hitherto, and I heard Richard administer a sharp reproof to the young officer in charge. The colonel of the regiment of foot, in command of the post, came forth to excuse himself, and I saw that it was my old suitor of the past, Jo's brother-in-law, Edward Champernowne. He bowed to me somewhat stiffly, and then, turning to Richard, he stammered several attempts at explanation, and the two withdrew to a little distance. On his return Richard was silent, and we straightway turned back towards my wagon and the escort, and I knew that the review was finished.

"You must return alone to Radford," he said. "I will send the escort with you. There will be no danger."

"And the coming battle?" I asked. "Are you confident and pleased?"

He paused a moment before replying.

"Yes," he answered, "yes, I am hopeful. The plan is sound, and there is nothing wanting in the men. If only my seconds were more dependable."

He jerked his head towards the post from which we had just lately come.

"Your old lover, Edward Champernowne," he said, "I sometimes think he would do better to command a squad of ducks. He has a flickering of reason when his long nose is glued upon a map ten miles from the enemy, but give him a piece of work to do upon the field a hundred yards away and he is lost."

"Can you not replace him with some other?" I questioned.

"Not at this juncture," he said. "I have to risk him now."

He kissed my hand and smiled, and it was not until he had turned his back on me and vanished that I remembered I had never asked him whether the reason for not returning with me to Radford was because he proposed to lead the assault in person.

I jogged back in the wagon to my brother's house, my spirits sinking. Shortly before daybreak next morning the attack began. The first we heard of it at Radford was the echo of the guns across the Cattwater, whether from within the garrison or from the outer defences we could not tell, but by midday we had the news that three of the works had been seized and held by the royalist troops, and the most formidable of the forts, the Maudlyn, had been stormed by the commanding general in person.

The guns were turned, and the men of Plymouth felt for the first time their own fire fall upon the walls of the city. I could see nothing from my window but a pall of smoke hanging like a curtain in the sky, and now and again, the wind being northerly, I thought to hear the sound of distant shouting from the besieged within the garrison.

At three o'clock, with barely three hours of daylight left, the news was not so good. The rebels had counterattacked, and two of the forts had been recaptured. The fate of Plymouth now depended upon the rebels gaining back the ground they had lost and driving the royalists from their foothold all along the line, and most specially from the Maudlyn works. I watched the setting sun, as I had done the day before, and I thought of all those, both rebel men and royalist, whose lives had been held forfeit within these past four and twenty hours.

We dined in the hall at half-past five, with my brother Jo seated at the head of his table as was his custom, and Phillippa at his right hand, and his little motherless son, young John, upon his left. We ate in silence, none of us having much heart for conversation, while the battle only a few miles away hung in the balance. We were nearly finished when my brother Percy, who had ridden down to Plymstock to get news, came bursting in upon us.

"The rebels have gained the day," he said grimly, "and driven off Grenvile with the loss of three hundred men. They stormed the fort on all sides and finally recaptured it barely an hour ago. It seems that Grenvile's covering troops, who should have come to his support and turned the scale to success, failed to reach him. A tremendous blunder on the part of someone."

"No doubt the fault of the general himself," said Jo drily, "in having too much confidence."

"They say down in Plymstock that the officer responsible has been shot by Grenvile for contravention of orders," said Percy, "and is lying now in his tent with a bullet through his head. Who it is they would not tell me, but we shall hear anon."

I could think of nothing but those three hundred men who were lying now upon their faces under the stars, and I was filled with a great war-sickness, a loathing for guns and pikes and blood and battle cries. The brave fellows who had smiled at me the night before, so strong, so young and confident, were now carrion for the sea gulls that swooped and dived in Plymouth Sound, and it was Richard, my Richard, who had led them to their death. I could not blame him. He had only, by attacking, done his duty. He was a soldier. . . .

As I turned away to call a servant for my chair, a young secretary employed by my eldest brother on the Devon Commission came into the room, much agitated, with a request to speak to him.

"What is the matter?" said Jo tersely. "There is no one but my family present."

"Colonel Champernowne lies at Egg Buckland mortally wounded," said the secretary. "He was not hurt in battle but pistolled by the general himself on returning to headquarters."

There was a moment of great silence. Jo rose slowly from his chair, very white and tense, and I saw him turn round and look at me, as did my brother Percy. In a moment of perception I knew what they were thinking. Jo's brother-in-law, Edward Champernowne, had been my suitor seventeen years before, and they both saw, in this sudden terrible dispute after the heat of battle, no military cause but some private jealous wrangle, the settling of a feud.

"This," said my eldest brother slowly, "is the beginning of the end for Richard Grenvile."

His words fell upon my ear cold as steel, and calling softly to the servant, I bade him take me to my room.

The next day I left for Maddercombe, to my sister Cecilia, for to remain under my brother's roof one moment longer would have been impossible. The vendetta had begun. . . .

My eldest brother, with the vast family of Champernowne behind him, and supported by the leading families in the county of Devon, most of them members of the commission, pressed for the removal of Sir Richard Grenvile from his position as sheriff and commander of the King's forces in the West. Richard retaliated by turning my brother out of Radford and using the house and estate as a jumping ground to a fresh assault upon Plymouth.

Snowed up in Maddercombe with the Pollexefens, I knew little of what was happening, and Cecilia, with consummate tact and delicacy, avoided the subject. I myself had had no word from Richard since the night I had bidden him good-bye before the battle, and now that he was engaged in a struggle with foe and former friends as well, I thought it best to keep silent. He knew my whereabouts, for I had sent word of it, and should he want me he would come to me.

The thaw burst at the end of March, and we had the first tidings of the outside world for many weeks.

The peace moves between King and Parliament had come to nothing, the Treaty of Uxbridge having failed, and the war, it seemed, was to be carried on more ruthlessly than ever.

The Parliament, so we heard, was forming a new model army, likely to sweep all before it, in the opinion of the judges, while His Majesty had sent forth an edict to his enemies, saying that unless the rebels repented, their end must be damnation, ruin, and infamy. The young Prince of Wales, it seemed, was now to bear the title of supreme commander of all the forces in the West and was gone to Bristol, but being a lad of only fifteen years or so, the real authority would be vested in his advisory council, at the head of which was Hyde, the Chancellor of the Exchequer.

I remember John Pollexefen shaking his head as he heard the news.

"There will be nothing but wrangles now between the prince's council and the generals," he said. "Each will countermand the orders of the other. Lawyers and soldiers never agree. And while they wrangle the King's cause will suffer. I do not like it."

I thought of Richard and how he had once vouchsafed the same opinion.

"What is happening at Plymouth?" asked my sister.

"Stalemate," said her husband. "A token force of less than a thousand men left to blockade the garrison, and Grenvile with the remainder gone to join Goring in Somerset and lay siege to Taunton. The spring campaign has started."

Soon a year would have come and gone since I left Lanrest for Menabilly. . . . The snow melted down in the Devon valley where Cecilia had her home, and the crocus and the daffodil appeared. I made no plans. I sat and waited. Someone brought a rumour that there was great disaffection in the high command and that Grenvile, Goring, and Berkeley were all at loggerheads.

March turned to April; the golden gorse was in full bloom. And on Easter Day a horseman came riding down the valley, wearing the Grenvile badge. He asked at once for Mistress Harris and, saluting gravely, handed me a letter.

"What is it?" I asked before I broke the seal. "Something has happened?"

My throat felt dry and strange, and my hands trembled.

"The general has been gravely wounded," replied the soldier, "in a battle before Wellington House, at Taunton. They fear for his life."

I tore open the letter and read Richard's shaky scrawl:

> Dear heart, this is the very devil. I am like to lose my leg, if not my life, with a great gaping hole in my thigh below the groin. I know now what you suffer. Come teach me patience. I love you.

I folded the letter and, turning to the messenger, asked him where the general lay.

"They were bringing him from Taunton down to Exeter when I left," he answered. "His Majesty had despatched his own chirurgeon to attend upon Sir Richard. He was very weak and bade me ride without delay to bring you this."

I looked at Cecilia, who was standing by the window.

"Would you summon Matty to pack my clothes," I said, "and ask John if he would arrange for a litter and for horses? I am going to Exeter."

23

WE TOOK THE southern route to Exeter, and at every halt upon the journey I thought to hear the news of Richard's death.

Totnes, Newton Abbot, Ashburton; each delay seemed longer than the last, and when at length after six days I reached the capital of Devon and saw the great cathedral rising high above the city and the river it seemed to me I had been weeks upon the road.

Richard still lived. This was my first enquiry and the only thing that mattered. He was lodging at the hostelry in the cathedral square, to where I immediately repaired. He had taken the whole building to his personal use and had a sentry before the door.

On giving my name a young officer immediately appeared from within, and something ruddy about his colouring and familiar in his bearing made me pause a moment before addressing him correctly.

Then his courteous smile gave me the clue.

"You are Jack Grenvile, Bevil's boy," I said, and he reminded me of how he had come once with his father to Lanrest in the days before the war. I remembered, too, how I had washed him as a baby on that memorable visit to Stowe in '28, but this I did not tell him.

"My uncle will be most heartily glad to see you," he said as I was lifted from my litter. "He has talked of little else since writing to you. He has sent at least ten women flying from his side since coming here, swearing they were rough and did not know their business, nor how to dress his wound. 'Matty shall do it,' he said, 'while Honor talks to me.'"

I saw Matty colour up with pleasure at these words and assume at once an air of authority before the corporal who shouldered our trunks.

"And how is he?" I asked as I was set down within the great inn parlour, which had been, judging by the long table in the centre, turned into a messroom for the general's staff.

"Better these last three days than hitherto," replied his nephew. "But at first we thought to lose him. Directly he was wounded I applied to the Prince of Wales to wait on him and I attended him here from Taunton. Now he declares he will not send me back. Nor have I any wish to go."

"Your uncle," I said, "likes to have a Grenvile by his side."

"I know one thing," said the young man; "he finds fellows of my age better company than his contemporaries, which I take as a great compliment."

At this moment Richard's servant came down the stairs, saying the general wished to see Mistress Harris upon this instant. I went first to my room, where Matty washed me and changed my gown, and then with Jack Grenvile to escort me I went along the corridor in my wheeled chair to Richard's room.

It looked out upon the cobbled square, and as we entered the great bell from the cathedral chimed four o'clock.

"God confound that blasted bell," said a familiar voice, sounding stronger than I had dared hope, from the dark curtained bed in the far corner. "A dozen times I have asked the mayor of this damned city to have it silenced, and nothing has been done. Harry, for God's sake, make a note of it."

"Sir," answered hurriedly a tall youth at the foot of the bed, scribbling a word upon his tablet.

"And move these pillows, can't you? Not that way, you clumsy lout. Behind my head, thus. Where the devil is Jack? Jack is the only lad who knows how I like them placed."

"Here I am, Uncle," said his nephew, "but you will not need me now. I have brought you someone with gentler hands than I."

He pushed my chair towards the bed, smiling, and I saw Richard's hand reach out to pull back the curtains.

"Ah!" he said, sighing deeply. "You have come at last."

He was deathly white. And his eyes had grown larger, perhaps in contrast to the pallor of his face. His auburn locks were clipped short, giving him a strangely youthful look. For the first time I noticed in him a resemblance to Dick. I took his hand and held it.

"I did not wait," I said, "once I had read your letter."

He turned to the two lads standing at the foot of the bed, his nephew and the one he had named Harry.

"Get out, both of you," he said, "and if that damned chirurgeon shows his face, tell him to go to the devil."

"Sir," they replied, clicking their heels, and I could swear that as they left the room young Jack Grenvile winked an eye at his companion.

Richard lifted my hand to his lips and then cradled it beside his cheek.

"This is a good jest," he said, "on the part of the Almighty. You and I both smitten in the thigh."

"Does it pain you much?" I asked.

"Pain me? My God, splinters from a cannon ball striking below the groin burn something fiercer than a woman's kiss. Of course it pains me."

"Who has seen the wound?"

"Every chirurgeon in the Army, and each one makes more mess of it than his fellow."

I called for Matty, who was waiting outside the door, and she came in at once with a basin of warm water and bandages and towels.

"Good day to you, mutton-face," said Richard. "How many corporals have you bedded with en route?"

"No time to bed with anyone," snapped Matty, "carried at the rate we were, with Miss Honor delaying only to sleep a few snatched hours every night. Now we've come here to be insulted."

"I'll not insult you, unless you tie my bandages too tight."

"Come, then," she said, "let's see what they have done to you."

She unfolded the bandages with expert fingers and exposed the wound. It was deep, in truth, the splinters having penetrated the bone and lodging there. With every probe of her fingers he winced and groaned, calling her every name under the sun, which did not worry her.

"It's clean, that's one thing," she said. "I fully expected to find it gangrenous. But you'll have some of those splinters to the end of your days, unless you let them take your leg off."

"They'll not do that," he answered, "I'd rather keep the splinters and bear the pain."

"It will give you an excuse, at any rate, for your bad temper," she replied.

She washed the wound and dressed it once again, and all the while he held my hand as Dick might do. Then she finished, and he thumbed his finger to his nose as she left the room.

"Over three months," he said, "since I have seen you. Are the Pollexefens as unpleasant as the rest of your family?"

"My family were not unpleasant till you made them so."

"They always disliked me from the first. Now they pursue their dislike across the county. You know the commissioners of Devon are in Exeter at this moment, with a list of complaints a mile long to launch at me?"

"I did not know."

"It's all a plot hatched by your brother. Three members of the prince's council are
to come down from Bristol and discuss the business with the commissioners; and as
soon as I am fit enough to move I am to go before them. Jack Berkeley, commanding
here at Exeter, is up to his neck in the intrigue."

"And what exactly is the intrigue?"

"Why, to have me shifted from my command, of course, and for Berkeley to take
my place."

"Would you mind so very much? The blockade of Plymouth has not brought you
much satisfaction."

"Jack Berkeley is welcome to Plymouth. But I'm not going to lie down and accept
some secondary command, dished out to me by the prince's council, while I hold
authority from His Majesty himself."

"His Majesty," I said, "appears by all accounts to have his own troubles. Who is
this General Cromwell we hear so much about?"

"Another damned Puritan with a mission," said Richard. "They say he talks with
the Almighty every evening, but I think it far more likely that he drinks. He's a good
soldier, though. So is Fairfax. Their new model army will make mincemeat of our
disorganised rabble."

"And knowing this, you choose to quarrel with your friends?"

"They are not my friends. They are a set of low backbiting blackguards. And I have
told them all so to their faces."

It was useless to argue with him. And his wound made him more sensitive on every
point. I asked if he had news of Dick, and he showed me a stilted letter from the tutor,
also copies of instructions that he had sent to Herbert Ashley. There was nothing very
friendly or encouraging amongst them. I caught a glimpse of the words, "For his
education I desire he may constantly and diligently be kept to the learning of the
French tongue; reading, writing, and arithmetic, also riding, fencing, and dancing.
All this I shall expect of him, which if he follow according to my desire for his own
good, he shall not want anything. But if I understand that he neglects in any kind what
I have herein commanded him to do, truly I will neither allow him a penny to maintain
him, nor look on him again as my son." I folded the instructions and put them back
into the case, which he locked and kept beside him.

"Do you think," I said, "to win his affection in that way?"

"I don't ask for his affection," he said. "I ask for his obedience."

"You were not harsh thus with Joe. Nor are you so unrelenting to your nephew
Jack."

"Joe was one in a million, and Jack has some likeness to him. That lad fought at
Lansdowne like a tiger when poor Bevil fell. And he was but fifteen, as Dick is now.
All these lads I have affection for because they hold themselves like men. But Dick,
my son and heir, shudders when I speak to him and whimpers at the sight of blood. It
does not make for pride in his father."

An argument. A blow. A baby's cry. And fifteen years of poison seeping through a
child's blood. . . . There was no panacea that I could think of to staunch the flood of
resentment. Time and distance might bring a measure of healing that close contact
only served to wound. Once again Richard kissed my hand.

"Never mind young Dick," he said. "It is not he who has a dozen splinters through
his thigh."

No man, I think, was ever a worse patient than Richard Grenvile, and no nurse
more impervious to his threats and groans and curses than was Matty. My role, if less
exacting, called for great equanimity of temperament. Being a woman, I did not have
his spurs hurled at my head, as did his luckless officers, but I suffered many a bitter
accusation because my name was Harris, and he liked to taunt me, too, because I had
been born and bred in southeast Cornwall, where the women all were hags and scolds,
so he averred, and the men cowards and deserters.

"Nothing good came out of Cornwall yet," he said, "save from the north coast." And seeing that this failed to rouse me, he sought by other means to make me rankle, a strange and unprofitable pastime for a sick man, but one I would understand in full measure, having often wished so to indulge myself some seventeen years before but never having the courage of my moods.

He kept to his bed for some five weeks, and then, by the end of May, was sufficiently recovered to walk his chamber with a stick and at the same time curse his harassed staff for idleness.

The feathers flew when he first came downstairs, for all the world like a turkey fight, and I never saw high-ranking officers more red about the ears than the colonels and the majors he addressed that May morning. They looked at the door with longing eyes, like schoolboys, with but one thought in their minds, to win freedom from his lashing tongue, or so I judged from their expressions. But when, after I had taken my airing in the square, I conversed with them, sympathy on the tip of my tongue, they one and all remarked upon the excellence of the general's health and spirits.

"It does one good," said a colonel of foot, "to see the general is himself again. I hardly dared to hope for it a month since."

"Do you bear no malice, then," I said, "for his words to you this morning?"

"Malice?" said the colonel, looking puzzled. "Why should I bear malice? The general was merely taking exercise."

The ways of professional soldiers were beyond me.

"It is a splendid sign," said Richard's nephew Jack, "when my uncle gives vent to frowns and curses. It mostly means he is well pleased. But see him smile and speak with courtesy, and you may well reckon that the luckless receiver of his favours is halfway to the guardroom. I once saw him curse a fellow for fifteen minutes without respite and that evening promote him to the rank of captain. The next day he received a prisoner—a country squire, I think, from Barnstaple, who owed him money—and my uncle plied him with wine and smiles and favours. He was hanging from a tree at Buckland two hours afterwards."

I remember asking Richard if these tales were true. He laughed.

"It pleases my staff," he said, "to weave a legend about my person."

But he did not deny them.

Meanwhile, the prince's council had come to Exeter to have discussion with the Devon commissioners and to hear the complaints they had to make against Sir Richard Grenvile. It was unfortunate, I felt, that the head of the prince's council was that same Sir Edward Hyde whom Richard had described to me at Radford as a jumped-up lawyer. I think the remark had been repeated to him, for when he arrived at the hostelry to call upon Richard, accompanied by Lords Culpepper and Capel, I thought his manner very cold and formal, and I could see he bore little cordiality towards the general who had so scornfully dubbed him upstart. I was presented to them and immediately withdrew. What they thought of me I neither knew nor cared. It would be but another scandalous tale to spread, that Sir Richard Grenvile had a crippled mistress.

What, in truth, transpired behind those closed doors I never discovered. As soon as the three members of the prince's council tried to speak they would be drowned by Richard, with a tirade of accusations against the governor of the city, Sir John Berkeley, who, so he avowed, had done nothing for nine months now but put obstructions in his path. As to the commissioners of Devon, they were traitors, one and all, and tried to keep their money in their pockets rather than pay the army that defended them.

"Let Berkeley take over Plymouth if he so desires it," Richard declared (this he told me afterwards). "God knows it troubles me to be confined to blocking up a place when there is likely to be action in the field. Give me power to raise men in Cornwall and in Devon, without fear of obstruction, and I will place an army at the disposal of the Prince of Wales that will be a match for Cromwell's Puritans."

Whereupon he formally handed over his resignation as commander of the siege of Plymouth and sent the lords of the council packing off back to Bristol to receive the prince's authority sanctioning him to a new command.

"I handled them," he said to me gleefully, "with silken gloves. Let Jack Berkeley stew at Plymouth, and good luck to him."

And he drank a bottle and a half of burgundy at supper, which played havoc with his wound next morning.

I have forgotten how many days we waited for the royal warrant to arrive, confirming him in the appointment to raise troops, but it must have been ten days or more. At last Richard declared that he would not kick his heels waiting for a piece of paper that few people would take the trouble to read, and he proceeded to raise recruits for the new army. His staff were despatched about the countryside rounding up the men who had been idle or had deserted and gone home during his illness. All were promised pay and clothing. And as sheriff of Devon (for this post he had not resigned with his command) Richard commanded his old enemies, the commissioners, to raise fresh money for the purpose. I guessed this would bring a hornets' nest about his ears again, but I was only a woman, and it was not my business.

I sat one day beside my window looking out on to the cathedral and I saw Sir John Berkeley, who had not yet gone to Plymouth, ride away from the hostelry looking like a thundercloud. There had been a stormy meeting down below and, according to young Jack, Sir John had got the worst of it.

"I yield to no man," said Richard's nephew, "in my admiration for my uncle. He has the better of his opponents every time. But I wish he would guard his tongue."

"What," I asked wearily, "are they disputing now?"

"It is always the same story," said Jack. "My uncle says that as sheriff of the county he can compel the commissioners to pay his troops. Sir John declares the contrary. That it is to him, as governor of the city and commander before Plymouth, to whom the money should be paid. They'll fight a duel about it before they have finished."

Shortly afterwards Richard came to my room, white with passion.

"My God," he said, "I cannot stand this hopeless mess an instant longer. I shall ride at once to Bristol to see the prince. When in doubt, go to the highest authority. That has always been my rule. Unless I can get satisfaction out of His Highness, I shall chuck the whole affair."

"You are not well enough to ride," I said.

"I can't help that. I won't stay here and have that hopeless nincompoop Jack Berkeley obstruct every move I make. He is hand in glove with your blasted brother, that's the trouble."

"You began the trouble," I said, "by making an enemy of my brother. All this has come about because you shot Edward Champernowne."

"What would you have had me do, promote the sod?" he stormed. "A weak-bellied rat who caused the death of three hundred of my finest troops because he was too lily-livered to face the rebel guns and come to my support. Shooting was too good for him. A hundred years ago he would have been drawn and quartered."

The next day he left for Barnstaple, where the Prince of Wales had gone to escape the plague at Bristol, and I was thankful that he took his nephew Jack as aide-de-camp. He had three men to hoist him in the saddle and he still looked most damnably unwell. He smiled up at me as I leant from my window in the hostelry, and saluted with his sword.

"Have no fear," he said, "I'll return within a fortnight. Keep well. Be happy."

But he never did return, and that was the end of my sojourn as a nurse and comforter at Exeter. . . .

On the eighteenth of June the King and Prince Rupert were heavily defeated by General Cromwell at Naseby, and the rebel army, under the supreme command of General Fairfax, was marching once again towards the West. The whole of the royalist strategy had now to be changed to meet this new menace, and while rumours ran rife that Fairfax was coming upon Taunton, I had a message from Richard to say that he had been ordered by the Prince of Wales to besiege Lyme and had the commission of field marshal in his pocket.

"I will send for you," he said, "when I have fixed my headquarters. In the meantime, rest where you are. I think it very likely that we shall all of us, before the summer is out, be on the run again."

This news was hardly pleasant hearing, and I bethought me of the relentless marching feet that I had heard a year ago at Menabilly. Was the whole horror of invasion to be endured once again?

I did as he bade me and stayed at Exeter. I had no home, and one roof was as good to me now as another. If I lacked humility, I also had no pride. I was nothing more nor less, by this time, than a camp follower. A pursuivant of the drum.

The last day of June, Jack Grenvile came for me with a troop of horse to bear my litter. Matty and I were already packed and ready. We had been waiting since the message a fortnight before.

"Where are we bound," I said gaily, "for Lyme or London?"

"For neither," he said grimly. "For a tumbled-down residence in Ottery St. Mary. The general has thrown up his comission."

He could tell me little of what had happened, except that the bulk of the new forces that had been assigned to Richard's new command, and who were to rendezvous at Tiverton, had suddenly been withdrawn by the orders of the prince's council and diverted to the defence of Barnstaple, without a word of explanation to the general.

We came to Ottery St. Mary, a sleepy Devon village where the inhabitants stared at the strange equipage that drew before the manor house as though the world were suddenly grown crazy, in which they showed good reason, and in the meadows behind the village were drawn Richard's own horse and foot that had followed him from the beginning.

Richard himself was seated in the dining chamber of his headquarters, his wounded leg propped up on a chair before him.

"Greetings," he said maliciously, "from one cripple to another. Let us retire to bed and see who has the greatest talent for invention."

"If that," I said, "is your mood, we will discuss it presently. At the moment I am tired, hungry, and thirsty. But would you care to tell me what the devil you are doing in Ottery St. Mary?"

"I am become a free man," he answered, smiling, "beholden to neither man nor beast. Let them fight the new model army in their own fashion. If they won't give me the troops I do not propose to ride alone with Nephew Jack against Fairfax and some twenty thousand men."

"I thought," I said, "that you were become field marshal."

"An empty honour," he said, "signifying nothing. I have returned the commission to the Prince of Wales in an empty envelope, desiring him to place it up a certain portion of his person. What shall we drink for supper, hock or burgundy?"

24

THAT WAS, I think, the most fantastic fortnight I have ever known. Richard, with no command and no commission, lived like a royal prince in the humble village of Ottery St. Mary, the people for miles around bringing their produce to the camp, their corn, their cattle, in the firm belief that he was the supreme commander of His Majesty's troops from Lyme to Land's End. For payment he referred them graciously to the commissioners of Devon. The first Sunday after his arrival he caused an edict to be read in the church of Ottery St. Mary, and other churches in the neighbouring parishes, desiring that all those persons who had been plundered by the governor of Exeter, Sir John Berkeley, when quartering troops upon them, should bring to him, Sir Richard Grenvile, the King's General in the West, an account of their losses, and he would see that they would be righted.

The humble village folk, thinking that a saviour had come to dwell amongst them, came on foot from a distance of twenty miles or more, each one bearing in his hands a list of crimes and excesses committed, according to them, by Lord Goring's troopers and Sir John Berkeley's men, and I can see Richard now, standing in the village place before the church, distributing largesse in princely fashion, which sum of money he had discovered behind a panel in his headquarters, the house belonging to an unfortunate squire with vague Parliamentary tendencies, whom Richard had immediately arrested. On the Wednesday, being fine, he held a review of his troops— the sight being free to the villagers—and the drums sounded, and the church bells pealed, and in the evening bonfires were lit and a great supper served at the headquarters to the officers, at which I presided like a queen.

"We may as well be merry," said Richard, "while the money lasts."

And I thought of that letter to the Prince of Wales, which must by now have reached the prince's council, and I pictured the Chancellor of the Exchequer, Edward Hyde, opening the paper before the assembly. I thought also of Sir John Berkeley and what he would say when he heard about the edict in the churches, and it seemed to me that my rash and indiscreet lover would be wiser if he struck his camp and hid in the mists on Darkmoor, for he could not bluff the world much longer in Ottery St. Mary.

The bluff was superb while it lasted, and the Parliamentary squire whom we had superseded keeping a well-stocked cellar, we soon had every bottle sampled, and Richard drank perdition to the supporters of both Parliament and Crown.

"What will you do," I asked, "if the council sends for you?"

"Exactly nothing," he answered, "unless I have a letter, in his own handwriting, from the Prince of Wales himself."

And with a smile that his nephew would call ominous he opened yet another bottle.

"If we continue thus," I said, turning my glass down upon the table, "you will become as great a sot as Goring."

"Goring cannot stand after five glasses," said Richard, "I can drill a whole division after twelve."

And rising from the table, he called to the orderly who stood without the door. "Summon Sir John Grenvile," he said.

In a moment Jack appeared, also a little flushed and gay about the eyes.

"My compliments," said Richard. "to Colonels Roscarrick and Arundell. I wish the troops to be paraded on the green. I intend to drill them."

His nephew did not flicker an eyelid, but I saw his lips quiver.

"Sir," he said, "it is past eight o'clock. The men have been dismissed to their quarters."

"I am well aware of the fact," replied his uncle. "It was for the purpose of rousing them that drums were first bestowed upon the Army. My compliments to Colonels Roscarrick and Arundell."

Jack clicked his heels and left the room. Richard walked slowly and very solemnly towards the chair were lay his sling and sword. He proceeded to buckle them about his waist.

"The sling," I said softly, "is upside down."

He bowed gravely in acknowledgment and made the necessary adjustment. And from without the drums began to beat, sharp and alert, in the gathering twilight. . . .

I was, I must confess, only a trifle less dazed about the head than I had been on that memorable occasion long before, when I had indulged too heavily in burgundy and swan. This time, and it was my only safeguard, I had my chair to sit in and I can remember, through a sort of haze, being propelled towards the village green with the drums sounding in my ears and the soldiers running from all directions to form lines upon the grass sward. Villagers leant from their casements, and I remember one old fellow in a nightcap shrieking out that Fairfax was come upon them and they would all be murdered in their beds.

It was, I dare swear, the one and only occasion in the annals of His Majesty's Army when two divisions have been drawn up and drilled by their commanding general in the dusk after too good a dinner.

"My God," I heard Jack Grenvile choke behind me, whether with laughter or emotion I never discovered, "this is magnificent. This will live forever."

And when the drums were silent I heard Richard's voice, loud and clear, ring out across the village green.

It was a fitting climax to a crazy fourteen days. . . .

At breakfast the next morning a messenger came riding to the door of the headquarters with the news that Bridgwater had been stormed and captured by Fairfax and his rebel forces, the prince's council had fled to Launceston, and the Prince of Wales bade Sir Richard Grenvile depart upon the instant with what troops he had and come to him in Cornwall.

"Is the message a request or a command?" asked my general.

"A command, sir," replied the officer, handing him a document, "not from the council, but from the prince himself."

Once again the drums were sounded, but this time for the march, and as the long line of troops wound their way through the village and on to the highway to Okehampton I wondered how many years would pass before the people of Ottery St. Mary would forget Sir Richard Grenvile and his men.

We followed, Matty and I, within a day or two, with an escort to our litter and orders to proceed to Werrington House, near Launceston, which was yet another property that Richard had seized without a scruple from the owner of Buckland Monachorum, Francis Drake. We arrived to find Richard in fair spirits, restored to the prince's favour after a very awkward three hours before the council.

It might have been more awkward had not the council been in so immediate a need of his services.

"And what has been decided?" I asked.

"Goring is to go north to intercept the rebels," he said, "while I remain in Cornwall and endeavour to raise a force of some three thousand foot. It were better if they had sent me to deal with Fairfax, as Goring is certain to make a hash of it."

"There is no one but you," I said, "who can raise troops in Cornwall. Men will rally to a Grenvile, but none other. Be thankful that the council sent for you at all, after your impudence."

"They cannot afford," said Richard, "to do without me. And anyway, I don't give a fig for the council and that snake Hyde. I am only doing this business to oblige the prince. He's a lad after my own heart. If His Majesty continues to haver as he does at present, with no coherent plan of strategy, I am not at all sure that the best move would not be to hold all Cornwall for the prince, live within it like a fortress, and let the rest of England go to blazes."

"You have only to phrase that a little differently," I said, "and a malicious friend who wished you ill would call it treason."

"Treason be damned," he said, "but it is sound common sense. No man has greater loyalty to His Majesty than I, but he does more to wreck his own cause than any who serve under him."

While Matty and I remained at Werrington, Richard travelled the length and breadth of Cornwall recruiting troops for the prince's army. It was no easy business. The last invasion had been enough for Cornishmen. Men wished only to be left alone to tend their land and business. Money was as hard to raise as it had been in Devon, and with some misgiving I watched Richard use the same highhanded measures with the commissioners of the duchy as he had done with those of the sister county. Those who might have yielded with some grace to tact gave way grudgingly to pressure, and

Richard, during that summer and early autumn of 1645, made as many enemies amongst the Cornish landowners as he had done in Devon.

On the north coast men rallied to his call because of his link with Stowe, the very name of Grenvile sounding like a clarion. They came to him from beyond the border, even from Appledore and Bideford, and down the length of that storm-bound Atlantic coast from Hartland Point to Padstow. They were his best recruits. Clear-eyed, long-limbed, wearing with pride the scarlet shield with the three gold rests upon their shoulders. Men from Bude and Stratton and Tintagel, men from Boscastle and Camelford. And with great cunning Richard introduced his prince as Duke of Cornwall, who had come into the West to save them from the savage rebel hordes beyond the Tamar.

But farther south he met with more rebuffs. Danger seemed more remote to people west of Truro, and even the fall of Bristol to Fairfax and the Parliament, which came like a clap of doom on the tenth of September, failed to rouse them from their lethargy.

"Truro, Helston, and St. Ives," said Richard, "are the three most rotten towns in Cornwall," and he rode down, I remember, with some six hundred horse to quell a rising of the townsfolk, who had protested against a levy he had raised the week before.

He hanged at least three men, while the remainder were either fined or imprisoned, and he took the opportunity, too, of visiting the castle at St. Mawes and severely reprimanding its commander, Major Bonython, because he had failed to pay the soldiers under his command within the garrison.

"Whoever I find halfhearted in the prince's cause must change his tune or suffer disciplinary action," declared Richard. "Whoever fails to pay his men shall contribute from his own pocket, and whoever shows one flicker of disloyalty to me as commander, or to the prince I serve, shall answer for it with his life."

I heard him say this myself in the market place at Launceston before a great crowd assembled there, the last day in September, and while his own men cheered so that the echo came ringing back to us from the walls of the houses I saw few smiles upon the faces of the townsfolk gathered there.

"You forget," I said that night to him at Werrington, "that Cornishmen are independent and love freedom better than their fellows."

"I remember one thing," he answered with that thin, bitter smile of his I knew too well, "that Cornishmen are cowards and love their comfort better than their King."

As autumn drew on I began to wonder if either freedom or comfort would belong to any of us by the end of the year.

Chard, Crediton, Lyme, and finally Tiverton fell before Fairfax in October, and Lord Goring had done nothing to stop them. Many of his men deserted and came flocking to join Richard's army, having greater faith in him as a commander. This led to further jealousy, further recriminations, and it looked as though Richard would fall as foul with Goring as he had done with Sir John Berkeley three months earlier. There was constant fault-finding, too, by the prince's council in Launceston, and scarcely a day would pass without some interfering measure from the Chancellor, Edward Hyde.

"If they would but leave me alone," stormed Richard, "to recruit my army and to train my troops, instead of flooding my headquarters day by day with despatches written by lawyers with smudged fingers who have never so much as smelt gunpowder, there would be greater likelihood of my being able to withstand Fairfax when he comes."

Money was getting scarce again, and the equipping of the Army for the winter was another nightmare for my general.

Boots and stockings were worn through and hard to replace, while the most vital necessity of all, ammunition, was very low in stock, the chief reason for this being that the royalist magazine for the Western forces had been captured at the beginning of the autumn by the rebels when they took Bristol, and all that Richard had at his disposal were the small reserves at Bodmin and at Truro.

Then suddenly, without any warning, Lord Goring threw up his command and went to France, giving as reason that his health had cracked and he could no longer shoulder any responsibility.

"The rats," said Richard slowly, "are beginning, one by one, to desert the sinking ship."

Goring took several of his best officers with him, and the command in Devon was given to Lord Wentworth, an officer with little experience, whose ideas of discipline were even worse than Goring's. He immediately went into winter quarters at Bovey Tracey and declared that nothing could be done against the enemy until the spring. It was at this moment, I think, that the prince's council first lost heart and realised the full magnitude of what might happen. They were fighting a losing cause. . . .

Preparations were made to move from Launceston and go farther west to Truro. This, said Richard grimly when he told me, could mean but one thing. They wanted to be near Falmouth, so that when the crisis came the Prince of Wales and the leaders of the council could take ship to France. It was then I asked him bluntly what he wished to do.

"Hold a line," he answered, "from the Bristol Channel to the Tamar and keep Cornwall for the prince. It can be done. There is no other answer."

"And His Majesty?"

Richard did not answer for a moment. He was standing, I remember well, with his back turned to the blazing log fire and his hands behind his back. He had grown more worn and lined during the past few months, the result of the endless anxieties that pressed upon him, and the silver streak that ran through his auburn locks had broadened above his brow. The raw November weather nipped his wounded leg, and I guessed, with my experience, what he must suffer.

"There is no hope for His Majesty," he said at length, "unless he can come to some agreement with the Scots and raise an army from them. If he fails, his cause is doomed."

'Forty-three, '44, '45, and, approaching us, '46. For more than three years men had fought and suffered and died for that proud, stiff little man and his rigid principles, and I thought of the picture that had hung in the dining chamber at Menabilly, which had afterwards been torn and trampled by the rebels. Would his end be as inglorious as the fate that befell his picture? Everything seemed doubtful, suddenly, and grim and hopeless.

"Richard," I said, and he caught the inflection in my voice and came beside me. "Would you, too," I asked, "leave the sinking ship?"

"Not," he said, "if there is any chance of holding Cornwall for the prince."

"But if the prince should sail for France," I persisted, "and the whole of Cornwall be overrun—what then?"

"I would follow him," he answered, "and raise a French army of fifty thousand men and land again in Cornwall."

He came and knelt beside me, and I held his face between my hands.

"We have been happy in our strange way, you and I," I said.

"My camp follower"—he smiled—"my trailer of the drum."

"You know that I am given up as lost to all perdition by good persons," I said. "My family have cast me off and do not speak of me. Even my dear Robin is ashamed of his sister. I had a letter from him this very morning. He is serving with Sir John Digby before Plymouth. He implores me to leave you and return to the Rashleighs at Menabilly."

"Do you want to go?"

"No. Not if you still need me."

"I shall always need you. I shall never part with you again. But if Fairfax comes you would be safer in Menabilly than in Launceston."

"That is what was said to me last time, and you know what happened."

"Yes, you suffered for four weeks, and the experience made a woman of you."

He looked down at me in his cruel, mocking way, and I remember how he had never thanked me yet for succouring his son.

"Next time it might be for four years," I said, "and I think I would be white-haired at the end of it."

"I shall take you with me if I lose my battle," he said. "When the crisis comes and Fairfax crosses the Tamar I will send you and Matty to Menabilly. If we win the day, so far so good. If we lose and I know the cause is lost, then I will come riding to you at your Rashleighs', and we will get a fishing boat from Polkerris and sail across the Channel to Saint-Malo and find Dick."

"Do you promise?"

"Yes, sweetheart, I promise."

And when he had reassured me and held me close I was something comforted, yet always, nagging at my mind, was the reminder that I was not only a woman but a cripple and would make a sorry burden to a fugitive. The next day the prince's council summoned him to Truro and asked him there, before the whole assembly, what advice he could give them for the defence of Cornwall against the enemy and how the safety of the Prince of Wales could be best assured.

He did not answer at once, but the next day, in his lodging, he composed a letter to the Secretary-at-War and gave full details of the plan, so far only breathed to me in confidence, of what he believed imperative to be done. He showed me the draft of it on his return, and much of what he proposed filled me with misgiving, not because of its impracticability, but because the kernel of it was so likely to be misconstrued. He proposed, in short, to make a treaty with the Parliament, by which Cornwall would become separate from the remainder of the country and be ruled by the Prince of Wales, as Duke of the Duchy. The duchy would contain its own army, its own fortifications, and control its own shipping. In return the Cornish would give a guarantee not to attack the forces of the Parliament. Thus gaining a respite, the people of Cornwall, and especially the Western army, would become so strong that in the space of a year or more they would be in ripe condition to give once more effective aid unto His Majesty.

(This last, it may be realised, was not to be one of the clauses in the treaty.)

Failing an agreement with Parliament, then Richard advised that a line be held from Barnstaple to the English Channel and ditches dug from the north coast to the Tamar, so that the whole of Cornwall became virtually an island. On this riverbank would be the first line of defence, and all the bridges would be destroyed. This line, he averred, could be held for an indefinite period and any attempt at an invasion be immediately repulsed. When he had finished his report and sent it to the council he returned to me at Werrington to await an answer. Five days, a week, and no reply. And then at last a cold message from the Chancellor and the Secretary-at-War, to say that his plan had been considered but had not found approval. The prince's council would thus consider other measures and acquaint Sir Richard Grenvile when his services would be required.

"So," said Richard, throwing the letter onto my lap, "a smack in the eye for Grenvile and a warning not to rise above his station. The council prefer to lose the war in their own fashion. Let them do so. Time is getting short, and if I judge Fairfax rightly, neither snow nor hail nor frost will hamper him in Devon. It would be wise, my Honor, if you sent word of warning to Mary Rashleigh and told her that you would spend Christmas with her."

The sands were running out. I could tell it by his easy manner, his shrugging of his shoulders.

"And you?" I said with that old sick twist of foreboding in my heart.

"I will come later," he said, "and we will see the new year in together in that room above the gatehouse."

And so on the third morning of December I set forth again, after fifteen months, for my brother-in-law's house of Menabilly.

25

MY SECOND COMING was very different from my first. Then it had been spring, with the golden gorse in bloom and young John Rashleigh coming to meet me on the highway before the park. War had not touched the neighbourhood, and in the park were cattle grazing and flocks of sheep with their young lambs and the last of the blossoms falling from the fruit trees in the orchards.

Now it was December, a biting wind cutting across the hills and valleys, and no young laughing cavalier came out to greet me. As we turned in at the park gates I saw at once that the walls were still tumbled and had not been repaired since the destruction wrought there by the rebels. Where the acres dipped to the sea above Polkerris a labourer with a team of oxen ploughed a single narrow enclosure, but about it to east and west the land was left uncultivated. Where should be rich brown ploughland was left to thistle. A few lean cattle grazed within the park, and even now, after a full year or more had come and gone, I noticed the great bare patches of grassland where the rebel tents had stood, and the blackened roots of the trees they had felled for firewood. As we climbed the hill towards the house I would see the reassuring curl of smoke rise from the chimneys and could hear the barking of the stable dogs, and I wondered, with a strange feeling of sadness and regret, whether I should be as welcome now as I had been fifteen months before. Once again my litter passed into the outer court and, glancing up at my old apartment in the gatehouse, I saw that it was shuttered and untenanted, even as the barred room beside it, and that the whole west wing wore the same forlorn appearance. Mary had warned me in her letter that only the eastern portion of the house had as yet been put in order, and they were living in some half a dozen rooms, for which they had found hangings and the bare necessities of furniture. Once more into the inner court, with a glance upward at the belfry and the tall weather vane, and then—reminiscent of my former visit—came my sister Mary out upon the steps, and I noticed with a shock that her hair had gone quite white. Yet she greeted me with her same grave smile and gentle kiss, and I was taken straightway to the gallery, where I found my dear Alice strung about as always with her mob of babies, and the newest of the brood, just turned twelve months, clutching at her knee in her first steps. This was now all our party. The Sawles had returned to Penrice and the Sparkes to Devon, and my goddaughter Joan, with John and the children, were living in the Rashleigh town house at Fowey. My brother-in-law, it seemed, was somewhere about the grounds, and at once, as they plied me with refreshment, I had to hear all the news of the past year, of how Jonathan had not yet received one penny piece from the Crown to help him in the restoration of his property, and whatever had been done he had done himself, with the aid of his servants and tenants.

"Cornwall is become totally impoverished," said my sister sadly, "and everyone dissatisfied. The harvest of this summer could not make up for all we lost last year, and each man with an estate to foster said the same. Unless the war ends swiftly we shall all be ruined."

"It may end swiftly," I answered, "but not as you would wish it."

I saw Mary glance at Alice, and Alice made as though to say something and then desisted. And I realised that as yet no mention had been made of Richard, my relationship to him being something that the Rashleighs possibly preferred should be ignored. I had not been questioned once about the past twelve months.

"They say, who know about these things" said Mary, "that His Majesty is very hopeful and will soon send an army to the West to help us drive Fairfax out of Devon."

"His Majesty is too preoccupied in keeping his own troops together in the midlands," I answered, "to concern himself about the West."

"You do not think," said Alice anxiously, "that Cornwall is likely to suffer invasion once again?"

"I do not see how we can avoid it."

"But—we have plenty of troops, have we not?" said Mary, still shying from mention of their general. "I know we have been taxed hard enough to provide for them."

"Troops without boots or stockings make poor fighters," I said, "especially if they have no powder for their muskets."

"Jonathan says everything has been mismanaged," said Mary. "There is no supreme authority in the West to take command. The prince's council say one thing—the commanders say another. I, for my part, understand nothing of it. I only wish it were all over."

I could tell from their expressions, even Alice's, usually so fair and generous, that Sir Richard Grenvile had been as badly blamed at Menabilly as elsewhere for his highhanded ways and indiscretions, and that unless I broached his name now, upon the instant, there would be an uneasy silence on the subject for the whole duration of my visit. Not one of them would take the first step, and there would be an awkward barrier between us all, making for discomfort.

"Perhaps," I said, "having dwelt with Richard Grenvile for the past eight months, ever since he was wounded, I am prejudiced in his favour. I know he has many faults, but he is the best soldier that we have in the whole of His Majesty's Army. The prince's council would do well to listen to his advice on military matters, if on nothing else."

They neither of them said anything for a moment, and then Alice, colouring a little, said, "Peter is with your brother Robin, you know, under Sir John Digby, before Plymouth. He told us, when he was last here, that Sir Richard constantly sent orders to Sir John which he had no right to do."

"What sort of orders, good or bad?" I asked.

"I hardly think the orders themselves were points of dispute," said Alice; "they were possibly quite necessary. But the very fact that he gave them to Sir John, who is not subordinate, caused irritation."

At this juncture my brother-in-law came to the gallery and the discussion broke, but I wondered, with a heavy heart, how many friends were now left to my Richard, who had at first sworn fealty to his leadership.

After I had been at Menabilly a few days my brother-in-law himself put the case more bluntly. There was no discreet avoidance, on his part, of Richard's name. He asked me straight out if he had recovered of his wound, as he had heard report from Truro that on the last visit to the council the general looked far from well and very tired.

"I think he is tired," I said, "and unwell. And the present situation gives him little cause for confidence or good spirits."

"He has done himself irreparable harm here in Cornwall," said my brother-in-law, "by commanding assistance rather than requesting it."

"Hard times require hard measures," I said. "It is no moment to go cap in hand for money to pay troops, when the enemy is in the next county."

"He would have won far better response had he gone about his business with courtesy and an understanding of the general poverty of all of us. The whole duchy would have rallied to his side had he but half the understanding that was his brother Bevil's." And to this I could give no answer, for I knew it to be true.

The weather was cold and dreary, and I spent much of my time within my chamber, which was the same that Gartred had been given fifteen months before. It had suffered little in the general damage, for which, I suppose, thanks had to be rendered to her, and was a pleasant room with one window to the gardens, still shorn of their glory, the new grass seeds that had been sown very clipped yet and thin, and two windows to the south, from where I could see the causeway sloping to rising ground and the view upon the bay.

I was content enough, yet strangely empty, for it comes hard to be alone again after eight months in company with the man you love. I had shared his troubles and misfortunes and his follies too. His moods were become familiar, loved, and understood. The cruel quip, the swift malicious answer to a question, and the sudden fleeting tenderness, so unaccountable, so warming, that would change him in one moment from a ruthless soldier to a lover.

When I was with him the days were momentous and full; now they had all the chill drabness of December, when as I took my breakfast the candles must be lit, and for my brief outing on the causeway I must be wrapped in cloak and coverture. The fall of the year, always to me a moment of regret, was now become a period of tension and foreboding.

At Christmas came John and Joan from Fowey, and Peter Courtney, given a few days' grace from Sir John Digby in the watch on Plymouth, and we all made merry for the children's sake and maybe for our own as well. Fairfax was forgotten and Cromwell, too, the doughty second-in-command who led his men to battle, so we were told, with a prayer upon his lips. We roasted chestnuts before the two fires in the gallery and burnt our fingers snatching sugar plums from the flames, and I remember, too, an old blind harper who was given shelter for the night on Christmas Eve and came and played to us in the soft candlelight. There were many such wanderers on the road now, since the war, calling no home their own, straggling from village to village, receiving curses more often than silver pieces. Maybe the season had made Jonathan more generous, for this old fellow was not turned away, and I can see him now in his threadbare jerkin and torn hose, with a black shade over his eyes, sitting in the far corner of the gallery, his nimble fingers drumming the strings of his harp, his quivering old voice strangely sweet and true. I asked Jonathan if he were not afraid of thieves in these difficult times and, shaking his head, he gestured grimly to the faded tapestries on the panels and the worn chairs.

"I have nothing left of value," he said. "You yourself saw it all destroyed a year since." And then, with a half-smile and a lowered voice, "Even the secret chamber and the tunnel contain nothing now but rats and cobwebs."

I shuddered, thinking in a sudden of all I had been through when Dick had hidden there, and I turned with relief to the sight of Peter Courtney playing leapfrog with his children, the sound of their merry laughter rising above the melancholy strains of the harper's lament. The servants came to fasten the shutters, and for a moment my brother-in-law stood before the window, looking out upon the lead sky, so soon to darken, and together we watched the first pale snowflakes fall.

"The gulls are flying inland," he said; "we shall have a hard winter." And there was something ominous in his words, harmless in themselves, that rang like a premonition of disaster. Even as he spoke the wind began to rise, echoing in the chimneys, and circling above the gardens wheeled the crying gulls which came so seldom from their ledges in the cliffs, and with them the scattered flocks of redwing from the North, birds of passage seeking sanctuary. Next morning we woke to a white world, strangely still, and a sunless sky teeming with further snow to come, while clear and compelling through the silence came the Christmas bells from the church at Tywardreath.

I thought of Richard, alone with his staff at Werrington, and I feared that he would never keep his promise now, with the weather broken and the snowdrifts maybe ten feet deep upon the Bodmin moors.

But he did come, at midday on the ninth of January, when for four and twenty hours a thaw had made a slush of the frozen snow, and the road from Launceston to Bodmin was just passable to an intrepid horseman. He brought Jack Grenvile with him and Jack's younger brother Bunny, a youngster of about the age of Dick, with a pugnacious jaw and merry eyes, who had spent Christmas with his uncle and now never left his side, vowing he would not return to Stowe again to his mother and his tutor, but would join the Army and kill rebels. As I watched Richard tweak his ear and laugh and jest with him I felt a pang of sorrow in my heart for Dick, lonely and unloved, save for that dreary Herbert Ashley, across the sea in Normandy, and I wondered if it must always be that Richard should show himself so considerate and kind to other lads, winning their devotion, and remain a stranger to his own son.

My brother-in-law, who had known Bevil well, bade welcome Bevil's boys, and after a first fleeting moment of constraint, for the visit was unexpected, he welcomed Richard, too, with courtesy. Richard looked better, I thought, the hard weather suited him; and after five minutes his was the only voice we heard in the long gallery, a sort of hush coming upon the Rashleigh family with his presence, and my conscience told me that his coming had put an end to their festivity. Peter Courtney, the jester in chief, was stricken dumb upon the instant, and I saw him frown to Alice to chide their eldest little girl, who, unafraid, ventured to Richard's side and pulled his sash.

None of them were natural any more because of the general and, glancing at my sister Mary, I saw the well-known frown upon her face as she wondered about her larder and what fare she could provide, and I guessed, too, that she was puzzling as to which apartment could be given to him, for we were all crammed into one wing as it was.

"You are on the way to Truro, I suppose?" she said to him, thinking he would be gone by morning.

"No," he answered, "I thought, while the hard weather lasted, I might bide with you a week at Menabilly and shoot duck instead of rebels."

I saw her dart a look of consternation at Jonathan, and there was a silence which Richard found not at all unusual, as he was unused to other voices but his own, and he continued cursing, with great heartiness, the irritating slowness of the Cornish people.

"On the north coast," he said, "where these lads and myself were born and bred, response is swift and sudden, as it should be. But the duchy falls to pieces south of Bodmin, and the men become like snails."

The fact that the Rashleighs had been born and bred in southeast Cornwall did not worry him at all.

"I could never," he continued, "have resided long at Killigarth. Give a fellow a command at Polperro or at Looe on Christmas Day, and with a slice of luck it will be obeyed by midsummer."

Jonathan Rashleigh, who owned land in both places, stared steadily before him.

"But whistle a fellow overnight at Stratton," said Richard, "or from Moorwinstow or Bude, and he is at your side by morning. I tell you frankly that had I none other but Atlantic men in my army I would face Fairfax tomorrow with composure. But at the first sight of cold steel the rats from Truro and beyond will turn and run."

"I think you underestimate your fellow countrymen and mine," said Jonathan quietly.

"Not a bit of it; I know them all too well."

If, I considered, the conversation of the week was to continue in this strain, the atmosphere of Menabilly would be far from easy, but Jack Grenvile, with a discretion born of long practice, tapped his uncle on the shoulder.

"Look, sir," he said, "there are your duck." And, pointing to the sky above the garden, still grey and heavy with unfallen snow, he showed the teal in flight, heading to the Gribbin.

Richard was at once a boy again, laughing, jesting, clapping his hands upon his nephew's shoulders, and in a moment the men of the household fell under the spell of his change of mood, and John and Peter, and even my brother-in-law, were making for the shore. We wrapped ourselves in cloaks and went out upon the causeway to watch the sport, and it seemed to me, in a sudden, that the years had rolled away, as I saw Richard, with Peter's goshawk on his wrist, turn to laugh at me. The boys were running across the thistle park to the long mead in the Pridmouth Valley, they were shouting and calling to one another, and the dogs were barking. The snow still lay upon the fields, and the cattle in the beef park nosed hungrily for fodder. The flocks of lapwing, growing tame and bold, wheeled screaming round our heads. For a brief moment the sun came from the white sky and shone upon us, and the world was dazzling.

This, I thought, is an interlude, lasting a single second. I have my Richard, Alice has her Peter, Joan her John. Nothing can touch us for today. There is no war. The enemy are not in Devon, waiting for the word to march.

The events of '44 seemed but an evil dream in retrospect that could never be repeated, and as I looked across the valley to the farther hill and saw the coast road winding down the fields of Tregares and Culver Close to the beach at Pridmouth, I remembered the troopers who had appeared there on the sky line on that fateful August day. Surely Richard was mistaken. They could not come again. There was a shouting from the valley, and up from the marshes rose the duck, with the hawks above them, circling, and I shivered of a sudden for no reason. Then the sun went blank, and a cat's paw rippled the sea, while a great shadow passed across the Gribbin Hill. Something fell upon my cheek, soft and clammy white. It was snowing once again. . . .

That night we made a circle by the fire in the gallery, while Jonathan and Mary retired early to their room.

The blind harper had departed with the new year, so there was none to make music for us save Alice and her lute and Peter with his singing, while the two Grenvile brothers, Jack and Bunny, whistled softly together, a schoolboy trick learnt from their father Bevil long ago, when the great house at Stowe had rung with singing and with music.

John heaped logs upon the fire and blew the candles, and the flames lit the long room from end to end, shining upon the panelling and on the faces of us, one and all, as we sat around the hearth.

I can see Alice as she was that night, fingering her lute, looking up adoringly at her Peter, who was to prove, alas, so faithless in the years to come, while he, with his constraint before his general melting with the firelight and the late hour, threw back his head and sang to us:

> "And wilt thou leave me thus?
> Say nay, say nay, for shame.
> To save thee from the blame
> Of all my grief and shame,
> And wilt thou leave me thus?
> Say nay! Say nay!"

I saw Joan and John hold hands and smile; John, with his dear, honest face, who would never be unfaithful and a deserter to his Joan, as Peter would to Alice, but was destined to slip away from her for all that, to the land from which no one of us returns, in barely six years' time.

> "And wilt thou leave me thus,
> And have no more pity
> Of him that loveth thee?
> Alas, thy cruelty.
> And wilt thou leave me thus?
> Say nay! Say nay!"

Plaintive and gentle were Alice's fingers upon the lute, and Jack and Bunny, cupping their mouths with their hands, whistled softly to her lead. I stole a glance at Richard. He was staring into the flames, his wounded leg propped on a stool before him. The flickering firelight cast shadows on his features, distorting them to a grimace, and I could not tell whether he smiled or wept.

"You used to sing that once long ago," I whispered, but if he heard me he made no move; he only waited for the last verse of Peter's song. Then he laid aside his pipe, blowing a long ribbon of smoke into the air, and reached across the circle for Alice's lute.

"We are all lovers here, are we not?" he said. "Each in his own fashion, except for these sprigs of boys."

He smiled maliciously and began to drum the strings of the lute.

> *"Your most beautiful bride who with garlands is crowned,*
> *And kills with each glance as she treads on the ground,*
> *Whose lightness and brightness doth shine in such splendour*
> > *That none but the stars*
> > *Are thought fit to attend her,*
> *Though now she be pleasant and sweet to the sense,*
> *Will be damnably mouldy a hundred years hence."*

He paused, cocking an eye at them, and I saw Alice shrink back in her chair, glancing uncertainly at Peter. Joan was picking at her gown, biting her lips. Oh God, I thought, why do you break the spell? Why do you hurt them? They are none of them much more than children.

> *"Then why should we turmoil in cares and in fears,*
> *Turn all our tranquillity to sighs and to tears?*
> *Let's eat, drink and play till the worms do corrupt us,*
> > *'Tis certain, Post Mortem*
> > *Nulla voluptas*
> *For health, wealth, and beauty, wit, learning and sense,*
> *Must all come to nothing a hundred years hence."*

He rippled a final chord upon the strings and, rising to his feet, handed the lute to Alice with a bow.

"Your turn again, Lady Courtney," he said, "or would you prefer to play at spillikins?"

Someone—Peter, I think it was—forced a laugh, and then John rose to light the candles. Joan leant forward and raked apart the fire, so that the logs no longer burnt a flame. They flickered dully and went dark. The spell was broken.

"It is snowing still," said Jack Grenvile, opening a shutter. "Let us hope it falls twenty feet in depth in Devon and stifles Fairfax and his merry men."

"It will more likely stifle Wentworth," said Richard, "sitting on his arse in Bovey Tracey."

"Why does everyone stand up?" asked young Bunny. "Is there to be no more music?"

But no one answered. The war was upon us once again, the fear, the doubt, the nagging insecurity, and all the quiet had vanished from the evening.

26

I SLEPT UNEASILY that night, passing from one troubled dream into another, and at one moment I thought to hear the sound of horses' hoofs riding across the park, but my windows facing east, I told myself it was but fancy, and the wind stirring in the snowladen trees. But when Matty came to me with breakfast she bore a note in her hands from Richard, and I learnt that my fancy was in truth reality, and that he and the two Grenviles and Peter Courtney had all ridden from the house shortly after daybreak.

A messenger had come to Menabilly with the news that Cromwell had made a night attack on Lord Wentworth in Bovey Tracey and, finding the royalist army asleep, had captured four hundred of the horse, while the remainder of the foot who had not been captured had fled to Tavistock in complete disorder and confusion.

"Wentworth has been caught napping," Richard had scribbled on a torn sheet of paper, "which is exactly what I feared would happen. What might have been a small reverse is likely to turn into disaster, if a general order is given to retreat. I propose riding forthwith to the prince's council and offering my services. Unless they appoint a supreme commander to take over Wentworth's rabble, we shall have Fairfax and Cromwell across the Tamar."

Mary need not have worried after all. Sir Richard Grenvile had passed but a single night under her roof, and not the week that she had dreaded. . . .

I rose that morning with a heavy heart and, going downstairs to the gallery, found Alice in tears, for she knew that Peter would be foremost in the fighting when the moment came. My brother-in-law looked grave and departed at midday, also bound for Launceston, to discover what help might be needed from the landowners and gentry in the possibility of invasion. John, with Frank Penrose, set forth to warn the tenants on the estate that once again their services might be needed, and the day was wretchedly reminiscent of that other day in August, nearly eighteen months before. But now it was not midsummer, but midwinter. And there was no strong Cornish army to lure the rebels to a trap, with another royalist army marching in the rear.

Our men stood alone—with His Majesty three hundred miles away or more, and General Fairfax was a very different leader from the Earl of Essex. He would walk into no trap, but if he came would cross the Tamar with a certainty.

In the afternoon Elizabeth from Coombe came to join us, her husband having gone, and told us that the rumour ran in Fowey that the siege of Plymouth had been raised, and Digby's troops, along with Wentworth's, were retreating fast to the Tamar bridges.

We sat before the mouldering fire in the gallery, a little group of wretched women, and I stared at that same branch of ash that had burnt so brightly the preceding night, when our men were here with us, and was now a blackened log amongst the ashes.

We had faced invasion before, had endured the brief horrors of enemy occupation, but we had never known defeat. Alice and Mary were talking of the children, the necessity this time of husbanding supplies beneath the floor boards of the rooms, as though a siege were all that was before us. But I said nothing, only stared into the fire. And I wondered who would suffer most, the men who died swiftly in battle, or those who would remain to face imprisonment and torture. I knew then that I would rather Richard fought and died than stayed to fall into the hands of Parliament. It did not bear much thinking, what they would do to Skellum Grenvile if they caught him.

"The King will march West, of course," Elizabeth was saying. "He could not leave Cornwall in the lurch. They say he is raising a great body of men in Oxfordshire this moment. When the thaw breaks——"

"Our defences will withstand the rebels," Joan said. "John was talking to a man in Tywardreath. Much has been accomplished since last time. They say we have a new musket—with a longer barrel—I do not know exactly, but the rebels will not face it, so John says. . . ."

"They have no money," said Mary. "Jonathan tells me the Parliament is desperate for money. In London the people are starving. They have no bread. The Parliament are bound to seek terms from the King, for they will be unable to continue the war. When the spring comes . . ."

I wanted to put my fingers in my ears and muffle the sound of their voices. On and on, one against the other, the old false tales that had been told so often. It cannot go on. . . . They must give in. . . . They are worse off than we. . . . When the thaw breaks, when the spring comes . . . And suddenly I saw Elizabeth look towards me. She had less reserve than Alice, and I did not know her so well.

"What does Sir Richard Grenvile say?" she asked. "You must hear everything of what goes on. Will he attack and drive the rebels back to Dorset?"

Her ignorance and theirs was so supreme, I had not the heart nor the will to enlighten her.

"Attack?" I said. "With what force do you suggest that he attack?"

"Why, with those at his disposal," she answered. "We have many able-bodied men in Cornwall."

I thought of the sullen bands I had seen sulking in the square at Launceston and the handful of brawny fellows in the fields below Werrington, wearing the Grenvile shield on their shoulders.

"A little force of pressed men," I said, "and volunteers, against some fifty thousand men, trained soldiers?"

"But man for man we are superior," urged Elizabeth. "Everyone says that. The rebels are well equipped, no doubt, but when our fellows meet them face to face in fair fight, in open country——"

"Have you not heard," I said softly, "of Cromwell and the new model army? Do you not realise that never, in England, until now, has there been raised an army like it?"

They stared at me, nonplussed, and Elizabeth, shrugging her shoulders, said I had greatly altered since the year before and was now become defeatist.

"If we all talked in that fashion," she said, "we would have been beaten long ago. I suppose you have caught it from Sir Richard. I do not wonder that he is unpopular."

Alice looked embarrassed, and I saw Mary press Elizabeth with her foot.

"Don't worry," I said. "I know his faults far better than you all. But I think if the council of the prince would only listen to him this time, we might save Cornwall from invasion."

That evening, on going to my room, I looked out on the weather and saw that the night was clear and the stars were shining. There would be no more snow, not yet awhile. I called Matty to me and told her my resolve. This was to follow Richard back to Werrington, if transport could be gotten for me at Tywardreath, and to set forth at noon the following day, passing the night at Bodmin, and so to Werrington the day after. By doing this I would disobey his last instructions, but I had, in my heart, a premonition that unless I saw him now I would never see him more. What I thought, what I feared, I cannot tell. But it came to me that he might fall in battle and that by following him I would be with him at the last.

The next morning was fine, as I expected, and I rose early and went down to breakfast and informed the Rashleigh family of my plan. They one and all begged me to remain, saying it was folly to travel the roads at such a season, but I was firm; and at length John Rashleigh, dear, faithful friend, arranged matters for me and accompanied me as far as Bodmin.

It was bitter cold upon the moors, and I had little stomach for my journey as, with Matty at my side, I left the hostelry at Bodmin at daybreak. The long road to Launceston stretched before us, bleak and dreary, with great snowdrifts on either side of us, and one false step of our horses would send the litter to destruction. Although we were wrapped about with blankets, the nipping, nagging wind penetrated the curtains, freezing our faces, and when we halted at Five Lanes for hot soup and wine to warm us, I had half a mind to go no farther, but find lodging for the night at Altarnun. The man at the inn, though, put an end to my hesitation.

"We have had soldiers here these past two days," he said, "deserters from the army before Plymouth. Some of Sir John Digby's men. They were making for their homes in west Cornwall. They were not going to stay on the Tamar banks to be butchered, so they told me."

"What news had they?" I asked, my heart heavy.

"Nothing good," he answered. "Confusion everywhere. Orders and counterorders. Sir Richard Grenvile was down on Tamar-side, inspecting bridges, giving instructions to blow them when the need arose, and a colonel of foot refused to take the order, saying he would obey none other than Sir John Digby. What is to become of us if the generals start fighting amongst themselves?"

I felt sick and turned away. There would be no biding for me this night at Altarnun. I must reach Werrington by nightfall.

On then, across the snow-covered moors, wind-swept and desolate, and every now and then we would pass straggling figures making for the west, their apparel proclaiming to the world that once they were King's men, but now deserters. They were blue from cold and hunger, and yet they wore a brazen, sullen look, as though they cared no longer what became of them, and some of them shouted as we passed, "To hell with the war, we're going home," and shook their fists at my litter, jeering, "You're driving to the devil."

The short winter afternoon closed in, and by the time we came to Launceston and turned out of the town to St. Stephens it was grown pitch-dark and snowing once again. An hour or so later I would have been snowbound on the road, with nothing but waste moorland on either side of me. At last we came to Werrington, which I had not thought to see again, and when the startled sentry at the gates recognised me and let the horses pass through the park, I thought that even he, a Grenvile man, had lost his look of certainty and pride and would become, granted ill fortune, no better than the deserters on the road.

We drew up into the cobbled court, and an officer came forth whose face was new to me. His expression was blank when I gave him my name, and he told me that the general was in conference and could not be disturbed. I thought that Jack might help me and asked, therefore, if Sir John Grenvile or his brother Mr. Bernard could see Mistress Honor Harris on a matter of great urgency.

"Sir John is no longer with the general," answered the officer. "The Prince of Wales recalled him to his entourage yesterday. And Bernard Grenvile has returned to Stowe. I am the general's aide-de-camp at present."

This was not hopeful, for he did not know me, and as I watched the figures of the soldiers passing backwards and forwards in the hall within the house and heard the tattoo of a drum in the far distance, I thought how ill-timed and crazy was my visit, for what could they do with me, a woman and a cripple, in this moment of great stress and urgency?

I heard a murmur of voices.

"They are coming out now," said the officer; "the conference is over."

And I caught sight of Colonel Roscarrick, whom I knew well, a loyal friend of Richard's, and in my desperation I leant from my litter and called to him. He came to my side at once, in great astonishment, but at once, with true courtesy, covered his consternation and gave orders for me to be carried into the house.

"Ask me no questions," I said. "I have come at a bad moment, I can guess that. Can I see him?"

He hesitated for a fraction of a minute.

"Why, of course," he said, "he will want to see you. But I must warn you, things are not going well for him. We are all concerned."

He broke off in confusion, looking most desperately embarrassed and unhappy.

"Please," I said, avoiding his eyes, "please tell him I am here."

He went at once into the room that Richard used as his own and where we had sat together, night after night, for more than seven months. He stayed a moment, then came for me. My chair had been lifted from the litter, and he took me to the room, then closed the door. Richard was standing by the table. His face was hard, set in the firm lines that I knew well. I could tell that of all things in the world I was, at that moment, farthest from his thoughts.

"What the devil," he said wearily, "are you doing here?"

It was not the welcome that I yearned for but was that which I deserved.

"I am sorry," I said. "I could not rest once you were gone. If anything is going to happen—which I know it must—I want to share it with you. The danger, I mean. And the aftermath."

He laughed shortly and tossed a paper onto my lap.

"There'll be no danger," he said, "not for you or me. Perhaps, after all, it is as well you came. We can travel west together."

"What do you mean?" I said.

"That letter, you can read it," he said. "It is a copy of a message I have just sent to the prince's council, resigning from His Majesty's Army. They will have it in an hour's time."

I did not answer for a moment. I sat quite cold and still.

"What do you mean?" I asked at length. "What has happened?"

He went to the fire and stood with his hands behind his back.

"I went to them," he said, "as soon as I returned from Menabilly. I told them that if they wished to save Cornwall and the prince they must appoint a supreme commander. Men are deserting in hundreds, discipline is non-existent. This would be the only hope, the last and final chance. They thanked me. They said they would consider the matter. I went away. I rode next morning to Gunnislake and Callington; I inspected the defences. There I commanded a certain colonel of foot to blow a bridge when need arose. He disputed my authority, saying his orders were to the contrary. Would you like to know his name?"

I said nothing. Some inner sense had told me.

"It was your brother, Robin Harris," he said. "He even dared to bring your name into a military matter. 'I cannot take orders from a man,' he said, 'who has ruined the life and reputation of my sister. Sir John Digby is my commander, and Sir John has bidden me to leave this bridge intact.'"

Richard stared at me an instant and then began to pace up and down the strip of carpet by the fire.

"You would hardly credit it," he said, "such lunacy, such gross incompetence. It matters not that he is your brother, that he drags a private quarrel into the King's business. But to leave that bridge for Fairfax, to have the impertinence to tell me, a Grenvile, that John Digby knows his business best——"

I could see Robin, very red about the neck, with beating heart and swelling anger, thinking, dear damned idiot, that by defying his commander he was somehow defending me and downing, in some bewildering hothead fashion, the seducer of his sister.

"What then?" I asked. "Did you see Digby?"

"No," he answered. "What would have been the use, if he defied me, as your brother did? I returned here to Launceston to take my commission from the council as supreme commander, and thus show my powers to the whole Army, and be damned to them."

"And have you the commission?"

He leant to the table and, seizing a small piece of parchment, held it before my eyes. "'The council of the prince,'" he read, "'appoints Lord Hopton in supreme command of His Majesty's forces in the West and desires that Sir Richard Grenvile should serve under him as lieutenant general of the foot.'"

He read slowly, with deadly emphasis and scorn, and then tore the document to tiny shreds and threw the pieces in the fire.

"This is my answer to them," he said; "they may do as they please. Tomorrow you and I will return to shoot duck at Menabilly." He pulled the bell beside the fire, and his new aide-de-camp appeared. "Bid the servants bring some supper," he said. "Mistress Harris has travelled long and has not dined."

When the officer had gone I put out my hand to Richard.

"You can't do this," I said. "You must do as they tell you."

He turned round on me in anger.

"Must?" he said. "There is no must. Do you think that I shall truckle to that damned lawyer at this juncture? It is he who is at the bottom of this, he who is to blame. I can see him, with his bland attorney's manner, talking to the members of the council. 'This man is dangerous,' he says to them, 'this soldier, this Grenvile. If we give him the supreme command he will take precedence of us and send us about our business. We will give Hopton the command; Hopton will not dare to disobey. And when the enemy cross the Tamar, Hopton will withstand them just long enough for us to slip across to Guernsey with the prince.' That is how the lawyer talks; that is what he has in mind. The traitor, the damned disloyal coward."

He faced me, white with anger.

"But, Richard," I persisted, "don't you understand, my love, my dear, that it is you they will call disloyal at this moment? To refuse to serve under another man, with the enemy in Devon? It is you who will be pointed at, reviled? You, and not Hyde?"

He would not listen; he brushed me away with his hand.

"This is not a question of pride, but concerns my honour," he said. "They do not trust me. Therefore, I resign. Now for God's sake let us dine and say no more. Tell me, was it snowing still at Menabilly?"

I failed him that last evening. Failed him miserably. I made no effort to enter into his mood that switched now so suddenly from black anger to forced jollity. I wanted to talk about the future, about what he proposed to do, but he would have none of it. I asked what his officers thought, what Colonel Roscarrick had said, and Colonel Arundell, and Fortescue? Did they, too, uphold him in his grave, unorthodox decision? But he would not speak of it. He bade the servants open another bottle of wine, and with a smile he drained it all, as he had done seven months before at Ottery St. Mary. It was nearly midnight when the new aide-de-camp knocked upon the door, bearing a letter in his hand.

Richard took it and read the message, then with a laugh threw it in the fire.

"A summons from the council," he said, "to appear before them at ten tomorrow in the Castle Court at Launceston. Perchance they plan some simple ceremony and will dub me earl. That is the customary reward for soldiers who have failed."

"Will you go?" I asked.

"I shall go," he said, "and then proceed with you to Menabilly."

"You will not relent," I asked, "not swallow your pride—or honour, as you call it—and consent to do as they demand of you?"

He looked at me a moment and he did not smile.

"No," he said slowly, "I shall not relent."

I went to bed, to my old room next to his, and left the door open between our chambers, should he be restless and wish to come to me. But at past three in the morning I heard his footstep on the stair.

I slept one hour, perhaps, or two; I do not remember. It was still snowing when I woke, and dull and grey. I bade Matty dress me in great haste and sent word to Richard, asking if he would see me.

He came instead to my room and with great tenderness told me to stay abed, at any rate until he should return from Launceston.

"I will be gone an hour," he said, "two at the utmost. I shall but delay to tell the council what I think of them and then come back to breakfast with you. My anger is all spent. This morning I feel free and light of heart. It is an odd sensation, you know, to be, at long last, without responsibility."

He kissed my two hands and then went away. I heard the sound of his horse trotting across the park. There was a single drum and then a silence. Nothing but the footsteps of the sentry pacing up and down before the house. I went and sat in my chair beside the window, with a rug under my knees. It was snowing steadily. There would be a white carpet in the Castle Green at Launceston. Here at Werrington the wind was desolate. The deer stood huddled under the trees down by the river. At midday Matty brought me meat, but I did not fancy it. I went on sitting at the window, gazing out across the park, and presently the snow had covered all trace of the horses, where they had passed, and the soft white flakes began to freeze upon the glass of the casement, clouding my view.

It must have been past three when I heard the sentry standing to attention, and once again the muffled tattoo of a drum. Some horses were coming to the house by the northern entrance, and because my window did not face that way I could not see them. I waited. Richard might not come at once; there would be many matters to see to in that room downstairs. At a quarter to four there came a knock upon my door, and a servant demanded in a hushed tone if Colonel Roscarrick could wait on Mistress Harris. I told him certainly, and sat there with my hands clasped on my lap, filled with that apprehension that I knew too well. He came and stood before the door, disaster written plainly on his face.

"Tell me," I said. "I would know the worst at once."

"They have arrested him," he said slowly, "on a charge of disloyalty to his prince and to His Majesty. They seized him there before us, his staff, and all his officers."

"Where have they imprisoned him?"

"There in Launceston Castle. The governor and an escort of men were waiting to take him. I rode to his side and begged him to give fight. His staff, his command, the whole Army, I told him, would stand by him if he would but give the word. But he refused. 'The prince,' he said, 'must be obeyed.' He smiled at us there on the Castle Green and bade us be of good cheer. Then he handed his sword to the governor, and they took him away."

"Nothing else?" I asked. "No other word, no message of farewell?"

"Nothing else," he said, "except he bade me take good care of you and see you safely to your sister."

I sat quite still, my heart numb, all feeling and all passion spent.

"This is the end," said Colonel Roscarrick. "There is no other man in the Army fit to lead us but Richard Grenvile. When Fairfax chooses to strike he will find no opposition. This is the end."

Yes, I thought. This is the end. Many had fought and died, and all in vain. The bridges would not be blown now; the roads would not be guarded, nor the defences held. When Fairfax gave the word to march the word would be obeyed, and his troops would cross the Tamar, never to depart. The end of liberty in Cornwall, for many months, for many years, perhaps for generations. And Richard Grenvile, who might have saved his country, was now a prisoner of his own side in Launceston Castle.

"If we only had time," Colonel Roscarrick was saying, "we could have a petition signed by every man in the duchy, seeking for his release. We could send messengers, in some way, to His Majesty himself, imploring pardon, insisting that the sentence of the council is unjust. If we only had time."

If we only had time, when the thaw broke, when the spring came . . . But it was that day, the nineteenth of January, and the snow was falling still.

27

MY FIRST ACTION was to leave Werrington, which I did that evening before Sir Charles Trevannion, on Lord Hopton's staff, came to take over for his commander. I no longer had any claim to be there and I had no wish to embarrass Charles Trevannion, who had known my father well. I went, therefore, to the hostelry in Broad Street, Launceston, near to the castle; and Colonel Roscarrick, having installed me there, took a letter for me to the governor, requesting an interview with Richard for the following morning. He returned at nine o'clock with a courteous but firm refusal. No one, said the governor, was to be permitted to see Sir Richard Grenvile, by the strict order of the prince's council.

"We intend," said Colonel Roscarrick to me, "sending a deputation to the prince himself at Truro. Jack Grenvile, I know, will speak for his uncle, and many more besides. Already, since the news has gone abroad, the troops are murmuring and have been confined to their quarters for twenty-four hours, in consequence. I can tell by what the governor said that rioting is feared."

There was no more I could ask him to do that day—I had trespassed too greatly on his time already—so I bade him a good night and went to bed, to pass a wretched night, wondering all the while in what dungeon they had lodged Richard, or if he had been given lodging according to his rank.

The next day, the twentieth, driving sleet came to dispel the snow, and I think, because of this and because of my unhappiness, I have never hated any place so much as Launceston. The very name sounds like a jail. Just before noon Colonel Roscarrick called on me with the news that there were proclamations everywhere about the town that Sir Richard Grenvile had been cashiered from every regiment he had commanded and was dismissed from His Majesty's Army—and all without court-martial.

"It cannot be done," he said with vehemence; "it is against every military code and tradition. There will be a mutiny in all ranks at such gross injustice. We are to hold a meeting of protest today, and I will let you know, directly it is over, what is decided."

Meetings and conferences, somehow I had no faith in them. Yet how I cursed my impotence, sitting in my hired room above the cobbled street in Launceston.

Matty, too, fed me with tales of optimism.

"There is no other talk about the town," she said, "but Sir Richard's imprisonment. Those who grumbled at his severity before are now clamouring for his release. This afternoon a thousand people went before the castle and shouted for the governor. He is bound to let him go, unless he wants the castle burnt about his ears."

"The governor is only acting under orders," I said. "He can do nothing. It is to Sir Edward Hyde and the council that they should direct their appeals."

"They say, in the town," she answered, "that the council have gone back to Truro, so fearful they are of mutiny."

That evening, when darkness fell, I could hear the tramping of many feet in the market square, and distant shouting, while flares and torches were tossed into the sky. Stones were thrown at the windows of the Town Hall, and the landlord of my hostelry, fearing for his own, barred the shutters early, and the doors.

"They've put a double guard at the castle," he told Matty, "and the troops are still confined to their quarters."

How typical it was, I thought with bitterness, that now, in his adversity, my Richard should become so popular a figure. Fear was the whip that drove the people on. They had no faith in Lord Hopton or any other commander. Only a Grenvile, they believed, could keep the enemy from crossing the Tamar.

When Colonel Roscarrick came at last to see me I could tell from his weary countenance that nothing much had been accomplished.

"The general has sent word to us," he said, "that he will be no party to release by force. He asked for a court-martial and a chance to defend himself before the prince and to be heard. As to us and to his army, he bids us serve under Lord Hopton."

Why, in God's name, I wondered, could he not do the same himself but twelve hours since?

"So there will be no mutiny," I said, "no storming of the castle?"

"Not by the Army," said Colonel Roscarrick in dejection. "We have taken an oath to remain loyal to Lord Hopton. You have heard the latest news?"

"No."

"Dartmouth has fallen. The governor, Sir Hugh Pollard, and over a thousand men are taken prisoner. Fairfax has a line across Devon now from north to south."

This would be no time, then, to hold courts-martial.

"What orders have you," I asked wearily, "from your new commander?"

"None as yet. He is at Stratton, you know, in the process of taking over and assembling his command. We expect to hear nothing for a day or two. Therefore, I am at your disposal. And I think—forgive me—there is little purpose in your remaining here at Launceston."

Poor Colonel Roscarrick. He felt me to be a burden, and small blame to him. But the thought of leaving Richard a prisoner in Launceston Castle was more than I could bear.

"Perhaps," I said, "if I saw the governor myself?"

But he gave me little hope. The governor, he said, was not the type of man to melt before a woman.

"I will go again," he assured me, "tomorrow morning, and ascertain at least that the general's health is good and that he lacks for nothing."

And with that assurance he left me to pass another lonely night, but in the morning I woke to the sound of distant drums and then heard the clattering of horses and troopers pass my window, and I wondered whether orders had come from Lord Hopton at Stratton during the night and the Army was on the march again. I sent Matty below for news, and the landlord told her that the troops had been on the move since before daybreak.

All the horse, he said, had ridden away north already.

I had just finished breakfast when a runner brought me a hurried word, full of apology, from Colonel Roscarrick, saying that he had received orders to proceed at once to Stratton, as Lord Hopton intended marching north to Torrington, and that if I had any friend or relative in the district it would be best for me to go to them immediately. I had no friend or relative, nor would I seek them if I had, and summoning the landlord, I told him to have me carried to Launceston Castle, for I wished to see the governor. I set forth, therefore, well wrapped against the weather, with Matty walking by my side and four fellows bearing my litter, and when I came to the castle gate I demanded to see the captain of the guard. He came from his room, unshaven, buckling his sword, and I thought how Richard would have dealt with him.

"I would be grateful," I said to him, "if you would give a message from me to the governor."

"The governor sees no one," he said at once, "without a written appointment."

"I have a letter here in my hands," I said. "Perhaps it could be given to him."

He turned it over, looking doubtful, and then he looked at me again.

"What exactly, madam, is your business?" he said.

He looked not unkindly, for all his blotched appearance, and I took a chance.

"I have come," I said, "to enquire after Sir Richard Grenvile."

At this he handed back my letter.

"I regret, madam," he said, "but you have come on a useless errand. Sir Richard is no longer here."

Panic seized me on the instant, and I pictured a sudden, secret execution.

"What do you mean," I asked, "no longer here?"

"He left this morning under escort for St. Michael's Mount," replied the captain of the guard. "Some of his men broke from their quarters last night and demonstrated here before the castle. The governor judged it best to remove him from Launceston."

At once the captain of the guard, the castle walls, the frowning battlements lost all significance. Richard was no more imprisoned there.

"Thank you," I said. "Good day." And I saw the officer staring after me and then return to his room beneath the gate.

St. Michael's Mount . . . Some seventy miles away, in the western toe of Cornwall. At least he was far removed from Fairfax, but how in the world was I to reach him there? I returned to the hostelry, with only one thought in my head now, and that to get from Launceston as soon as possible.

As I entered the door the landlord came to meet me, and said that an officer had called to enquire for me and was even now waiting my return. I thought it must be Colonel Roscarrick and went at once to see—and found instead my brother Robin.

"Thank God," he said, "I have sight of you at last. As soon as I had news of Sir Richard's arrest, Sir John gave me leave of absence to ride to Werrington. They told me at the house you had been gone two days."

I was not sure whether I was glad to see him. It seemed to me, at this moment, that no man was my friend, unless he was friend to Richard also.

"Why have you come?" I said coolly. "What is your purpose?"

"To take you back to Mary," he said. "You cannot possibly stay here."

"Perhaps," I answered, "I have no wish to go."

"That is neither here nor there," he said stubbornly. "The entire Army is in the process of reorganising, and you cannot remain in Launceston without protection. I myself have orders to join Sir John Digby at Truro, where he has gone with a force to protect the prince in the event of invasion. My idea is to leave you at Menabilly on my way thither."

I thought rapidly. Truro was the headquarters of the council, and if I went there, too, there was a chance, faint yet not impossible, that I could have an audience with the prince himself.

"Very well," I said to Robin, shrugging my shoulders. "I will come with you, but on one condition. And that is that you do not leave me at Menabilly but let me come with you all the way to Truro."

He looked at me doubtfully.

"What," he said, "is to be gained by that?"

"Nothing gained nor lost," I answered, "only for old time's sake, do what I demand."

At that he came and took my hand and held it a minute.

"Honor," he said, his blue eyes full upon my face, "I want you to believe me when I say that no action of mine had any bearing on his arrest. The whole Army is appalled. Sir John himself, who had many a bitter dispute with him, has written to the council, appealing for his swift release. He is needed at this moment more than any other man in Cornwall."

"Why," I said bitterly, "did you not think of it before? Why did you refuse to obey his orders about the bridge?"

Robin looked startled for a moment and then discomfited.

"I lost my temper," he admitted. "We were all rankled that day, and Sir John, the best of men, had given me my orders. . . . You don't understand, Honor, what it has meant to me and Jo and all your family to have your name a byword in the county. Ever since you left Radford last spring to go to Exeter people have hinted and whispered and even dared to say aloud the foulest things."

"Is it so foul," I said, "to love a man and go to him when he lies wounded?"

"Why are you not married to him then?" said Robin. "Then in God's conscience you would have earned the right now to share in his disgrace. But to follow from camp to camp, like a loose woman . . . I tell you what they say, Honor, in Devon. That he well earns his name of Skellum to trifle thus with a woman who is crippled."

Yes, I thought, they would say that in Devon. . . .

"If I am not Lady Grenvile," I said, "it is because I do not choose to be so."

"You have no pride then, no feeling for your name?"

"My name is Honor, and I do not hold it tarnished," I answered him.

"This is the finish, you know that?" he said after a moment's pause. "In spite of a petition signed by all our names, I hardly think the council will agree to his release. Not unless they receive some counterorder from His Majesty."

"And His Majesty," I said, "has other fish to fry. . . . Yes, Robin, I understand. And what will be the outcome?"

"Imprisonment at His Majesty's pleasure, with a pardon, possibly, at the end of the war."

"And what if the war does not go the way we wish, but the rebels gain Cornwall for the Parliament?"

Robin hesitated, so I gave the answer for him.

"Sir Richard Grenvile is handed over, a prisoner, to General Fairfax," I said, "and sentenced to death as a criminal of war."

I pleaded fatigue then and went to my room and slept easily for the first time for many nights, for no other reason but because I was bound for Truro, which was some thirty miles distant from St. Michael's Mount. . . .

The snow of the preceding days had wrought havoc on the road, and we were obliged to go a longer route, by the coast, for the moors were now impassable. Thus, with many halts and delays, it was well over a week before we came to Truro, only to discover that the council was now removed to Pendennis Castle, at the mouth of the Fal, and Sir John Digby and his forces were now also within the garrison.

Robin found me and Matty a lodging at Penryn and went at once to wait on his commander, bearing a letter from me to Jack Grenvile, whom I believed to be in close attendance on the prince.

The following day Jack rode to see me—and I felt as though years had passed since I had last set eyes upon a Grenvile, yet it was barely three weeks since he and Richard and young Bunny had ridden all three to Menabilly. I nearly wept when he came into the room.

"Have no fear," he said at once, "my uncle is in good heart and sturdy health. I have received messages from him from the Mount, and he bade me write you not to be anxious for him. It is rather he who is likely to be anxious on your part, for he believes you with your sister, Mrs. Rashleigh."

I determined to take young Jack into my confidence.

"Tell me first," I said, "what is the opinion on the war?"

He made a face and shrugged his shoulders.

"You see we are at Pendennis," he said quietly. "That in itself is ominous. There is a frigate at anchor in the roads, fully manned and provisioned, with orders to set sail for the Scillies when the word is given. The prince himself will never give the word—he is all for fighting to the last—but the council lack his courage. Sir Edward Hyde will have the last word, not the Prince of Wales."

"How long, then, have we till the word be given?"

"Hopton and the Army have marched to Torrington," answered Jack, "and there is hope—but I fear a faint one—that by attacking first, Hopton will take the initiative and force a decision. He is a brave fellow but lacks my uncle's power, and the troops care nothing for him. If he fails at Torrington and Fairfax wins the day—then you may expect that frigate to set sail."

"And your uncle?"

"He will remain, I fear, at the Mount. He has no other choice. But Fairfax is a soldier and a gentleman. He will receive fair treatment."

This was no answer for me. However much a soldier and a gentleman Fairfax himself might be, his duty was to Parliament, and Parliament had decreed in '43 that Richard Grenvile was a traitor.

"Jack," I said, "would you do something for me, for your uncle's sake?"

"Anything in the world," he answered, "for the pair of you."

Ah, bless you, I thought, true son of Bevil.

"Get me an audience with the Prince of Wales," I said to him.

He whistled and scratched his cheek, a very Grenvile gesture.

"I'll do my best, I swear it," he said, "but it may take time and patience, and I cannot promise you success. He is so hemmed about with members of the council and dares do nothing but what he is told to do by Sir Edward Hyde. I tell you, Honor, he's led a dog's life until now. First his mother, and now the Chancellor. When he does come of age and can act for himself, I'll wager he'll set the stars on fire."

"Make up some story," I urged. "You are his age and a close companion. You know what would move him. I give you full licence."

He smiled—his father's smile.

"As to that," he said, "he has only to hear your story and how you followed my uncle to Exeter to be on tenterhooks to look at you. Nothing pleases him better than a love affair. But Sir Edward Hyde—he's the danger."

He left me, with an earnest promise to do all he could, and with that I was forced to be content. Then came a period of waiting that seemed like centuries but was, in all reality, little longer than a fortnight. During this time Robin came several times to visit me, imploring me to leave Penryn and return to Menabilly. Jonathan Rashleigh, he said, would come himself to fetch me, would I but send the word.

"I must warn you, in confidence," he said, "that the council have little expectation of Hopton's withstanding Fairfax. The prince, with his personal household, will sail for Scilly. The rest of us within the garrison will hold Pendennis until we are burnt out of it. Let the whole rebel army come. We will not surrender."

Dear Robin. As you said that, with your blue eyes blazing and your jaw set, I forgave you for your enmity for Richard and the silly useless harm you did in disobeying him.

Death or glory, I reflected. That was the way my Richard might have chosen. And here was I, plotting one thing only, that he should steal away like a thief in the night.

"I will go back to Menabilly," I said slowly, "when the Prince of Wales sets sail for the Scillies."

"By then," said Robin, "I shall not be able to assist you. I shall be inside the garrison at Pendennis, with our guns turned east upon Penryn."

"Your guns will not frighten me," I said, "any more than Fairfax's horse thundering across the moors from the Tamar. It will look well in after years, in the annals of the Harris family, to say that Honor died in the last stand in '46."

Brave words, spoken in hardihood, ringing so little true. . . .

On the fourteenth of February, the feast of St. Valentine, that patron saint of lovers, I had a message from Jack Grenvile. The wording was vague and purposely omitted names. "The snake is gone to Truro," he said, "and my friend and I will be able to receive you for a brief space this afternoon. I will send an escort for you. Say nothing of the matter to your brother."

I went alone, without Matty, deeming in a matter of such delicacy it were better to have no confidante at all. True to his word, the escort came, and Jack himself awaited me at the entrance to the castle. No haggling this time with a captain of the guard. But a swift word to the sentry, and we were through the arch and within the precincts of the garrison before a single soul, save the sentry, was a whit the wiser.

The thought occurred to me that this perhaps was not the first time Jack Grenvile had smuggled a woman into the fortress. Such swift handling came possibly from long experience. Two servants in the prince's livery came to carry me, and after passing up some stairs (which I told myself were back ones and suitable to my person) I was brought to a small room within a tower and placed upon a couch. I would have relished the experience were not the matter upon which I sought an audience so deadly serious. There were wine and fruit at my elbow, and a posy of fresh flowers, and His Highness, I thought, for all his mother, has gained something by inheriting French blood.

I was left for a few moments to refresh myself, and then the door opened again, and Jack stood aside to let a youngster of about his own age pass before him. He was far from handsome, more like a gypsy than a prince, with his black locks and swarthy skin, but the instant he smiled I loved him better than all the famous portraits of his father that my generation had known for thirty years.

"Have my servants looked after you?" he said at once. "Given you all you want? This is garrison fare, you know; you must excuse it."

And as he spoke I felt his bold eyes look me up and down in cool appraising fashion, as though I were a maid and not fifteen years his senior.

"Come, Jack," he said, "present me to your kinswoman," and I wondered what the devil of a story Jack had spun.

We ate and drank, and all the while he talked he stared, and I wondered if his boy's imagination was running riot on the thought of his notorious and rebellious general making love to me, a cripple.

"I have no claim to trespass upon your time, sir," I said at length, "but Sir Richard, Jack's uncle, is my dear friend, and has been so now over a span of years. His faults are many; I have not come to dispute them. But his loyalty to yourself has never, I believe, been the issue in question."

"I don't doubt it," said the prince, "but you know how it was. He got up against the council, and Sir Edward in particular. I like him immensely myself, but personal feeling cannot count in these matters. There was no choice but to sign the warrant for his arrest."

"Sir Richard did very wrong not to serve under Lord Hopton," I said. "His worst fault is his temper, and much, I think, had gone wrong that day to kindle it. Given reflection, he would have acted otherwise."

"He made no attempt, you know, sir," cut in Jack, "to resist arrest. The whole staff would have gone to his aid had he given them the word. That I have on good authority. But he told all of them he wished to abide by Your Highness's command."

The prince rose to his feet and paced up and down the room.

"It's a wretched affair all round," he said. "There's Grenvile at the Mount, the one fellow who might have saved Cornwall, while Hopton fights a hopeless battle up in Torrington. I can't do anything about it, you know. That's the devil of it. I shall be whisked away myself before I know what is happening."

"There is one thing you can do, sir, if you will forgive my saying so," I said.

"What then?"

"Send word to the Mount that when you and the council sail for the Scillies Sir Richard Grenvile shall be permitted to escape at the same time and commandeer a fishing boat for France."

The Prince of Wales stared at me for a moment, and then that same smile I had remarked upon his face before lit his whole ugly countenance.

"Sir Richard Grenvile is most fortunate," he said, "to have so *fidèle* an ally as yourself. If I am ever in his shoes and find myself a fugitive, I hope I can rely on half so good a friend." He glanced across at Jack. "You can arrange that, can't you?" he said. "I will write a letter to Sir Arthur Bassett at the Mount, and you can take it there and see your uncle at the same time. I don't suggest we ask for his company in the frigate when we sail, because I hardly think the ship would bear his weight alongside Sir Edward Hyde."

The two lads laughed, for all the world like a pair of schoolboys caught in mischief. Then the prince turned and, coming to the couch, bent low and kissed my hand.

"Have no fear," he said, "I will arrange it. Sir Richard shall be free the instant we sail for the Scillies. And when I return—for I shall return, you know, one day—I shall hope to see you, and him also, at Whitehall."

He bowed and went, forgetting me, I dare say, forevermore, but leaving with me an impression of black eyes and gypsy features that I have not forgotten to this day. . . .

Jack escorted me to the castle entrance once again.

"He will remember his promise," he said; "that I swear to you. I have never known him go back on his word. Tomorrow I shall ride with that letter to the Mount."

I returned to Penryn, worn out and utterly exhausted now that my mission was fulfilled. I wanted nothing but my bed and silence. Matty received me with sour looks and the grim pursed mouth that spelt disapproval.

"You have wanted to be ill for weeks," she said. "Now that we are here, in a strange lodging, with no comforts, you decide to do so. Very well, I'll not answer for the consequences."

"No one asks you to," I said, turning my face to the wall. "For God's sake, if I want to, let me sleep or die."

Two days later Lord Hopton was defeated outside Torrington and the whole Western army in full retreat across the Tamar. It concerned me little, lying in that lodging at Penryn with a high fever. On the twenty-fifth of February Fairfax had marched and taken Launceston and on the second of March had crossed the moors to Bodmin. That night the Prince of Wales, with his council, set sail in the frigate *Phoenix*—and the war in the West was over.

The day Lord Hopton signed the treaty in Truro with General Fairfax, my brother-in-law, Jonathan Rashleigh, by permission of the Parliament, came down to Penryn to fetch me back to Menabilly. The streets were lined with soldiers, not ours, but theirs, and the whole route from Truro to St. Austell bore signs of surrender and defeat. I sat with stony face, looking out of the curtains of my litter, while Jonathan Rashleigh rode by my side, his shoulders bowed, his face set in deep grim lines.

We did not converse. We had no words to say. We crossed St. Blazey Bridge, and Jonathan handed his pass to the rebel sentry at the post, who stared at us with insolence and then jerked his head to let us pass. They were everywhere. In the road, in the cottage doors at Tywardreath, at the barrier, at the foot of Polmear Hill.

This was our future then, forevermore, to ask, in deep humility, if we might travel our own roads. That it should be so worried me no longer, for my days of journeying were over.

I was returning to Menabilly to be no longer a camp follower, no longer a lady of the drum, but plain Honor Harris, a cripple on her back.

And it did not matter to me; I did not care.

For Richard Grenvile had escaped to France.

28

DEFEAT AND THE aftermath of war . . . Not pleasant for the losers. God knows that we endure it still, and I write in the autumn of '53, but in the year '46 we were new to defeat and had not yet begun to learn our lessons. It was, I think, the loss of freedom that hit the Cornish hardest. We had been used, for generations, to minding our own affairs, and each man living after his fashion. Landlords were fair and usually well liked, with tenant and labourer living in amity together. We had our local disagreements, as every man will with his neighbour, and our family feuds, but no body of persons had ever before interfered with our way of living, nor given us commands. Now all was changed. Our orders came to us from Whitehall, and a Cornish County Committee, way up in London, sat in judgment upon us. We could no longer pass our own measures and decide by local consultation what was suited to each town and village. The County Committee made our decisions for us.

Their first action was to demand a weekly payment from the people of Cornwall to the revenue, and this weekly assessment was rated so high that it was impossible to find the money, for the ravages of war had stripped the country bare. Their next move was to sequester the estate of every landlord who had fought for the King, and because the County Committee had not the time or the persons to administer these estates, the owners were allowed to dwell there, if they so desired, but pay to the committee, month by month, the full and total value of the property. This crippling injunction was made the harder because the estates were assessed at the value they had held before the war, and now that most of them were fallen into ruin through the fighting, it would take generations before the land gave a return once more.

A host of petty officials, the only men at these times to have their pockets well lined, and they were paid fixed salaries by the Parliament, came down from Whitehall to collect the sums due to the County Committee; and these agents were found in every town and borough, forming themselves in their turns in committees and subcommittees, so that no man could buy as little as a loaf of bread without first going cap in hand to one of these fellows and signing his name to a piece of paper. Besides these civil employees of the Parliament, we had the military to contend with, and whosoever should wish to pass from one village to another must first have a pass from the officer in charge, and then his motives were questioned, his family history gone into, detail for detail, and as likely as not he would find himself arrested for delinquency at the end of it.

I truly believe that Cornwall was, in that first summer of '46, the most wretched county in the kingdom. The harvest was bad, another bitter blow to landlord and labourer alike, and the price of wheat immediately rose to fantastic prices. The price of tin, on the contrary, fell low, and many mines closed down on this account. Poverty and sickness were rife by the autumn, and our old enemy the plague appeared, killing great numbers in St. Ives and in the western districts. Another burden was the care of the many wounded and disabled soldiers who, half naked and half starved, roamed the villages begging for charity. There was no single man or woman or little child who benefited, in any way, by this new handling of affairs by Parliament, and the only ones to live well were those Whitehall agents, who poked their noses into our affairs from dawn to dusk, and their wealthy masters, the big Parliamentary landlords. We had grumbled in the old days at the high taxes of the King, but the taxes were intermittent. Now they were continuous. Salt, meat, starch, lead, iron—all came under the control of Parliament, and the poor man had to pay accordingly.

What happened upcountry I cannot say—I speak for Cornwall. No news came to us much beyond the Tamar. If living was hard, leisure was equally restricted. The Puritans had the upper hand of us. No man must be seen out of doors upon a Sunday, unless he were bound for church. Dancing was forbidden—not that many had the heart to dance, but youngsters have light hearts and lighter feet—and any game of chance or village festival was frowned upon.

Gaiety meant licence, and licence spelt the abomination of the Lord. I often thought how Temperance Sawle would have rejoiced in the brave new world, for all her royalist traditions, but poor Temperance fell an early victim to the plague.

The one glory of that most dismal year of '46 was the gallant, though, alas, so useless, holding of Pendennis Castle for the King through five long months of siege. The rest of us were long conquered and subdued, caught fast in the meshes of Whitehall, while Pendennis still defied the enemy. Their commander was Jack Arundell, who had been in the old days a close friend as well as kinsman to the Grenviles, and Sir John Digby was his second-in-command. My own brother Robin was made a major general under him. It gave to us, I think, some last measure of pride in our defeat that this little body of men, with no hope of rescue and scarce a boatload of provisions, should fly the King's flag from March the second until August the seventeenth, and even then they wished to blow themselves and the whole garrison to eternity rather than surrender, but starvation and sickness had made weaklings of the men, and for their sakes only did Jack Arundell haul down his flag. Even the enemy respected their courage, and the garrison were permitted to march out, so Robin told us afterwards, with the full honours of war, drums beating, colours flying, trumpets sounding. . . . Yes, we have had our moments here in Cornwall. . . .

When they surrendered, though, our last hopes vanished, and there was nothing now to do but sigh and look into the black well of the future.

My brother-in-law, Jonathan Rashleigh, like the rest of the royalist landlords, had his lands sequestrated by the County Committee and was told, when he went down to Truro in June, that he must pay a fine of some one thousand and eighty pounds to the committee before he could redeem them. His losses, after the '44 campaign, were already above eight thousand, but there was nothing for it but to bow his head to the victors and agree to pay the ransom during the years to come. He might have quitted the country and gone to France, as many of our neighbours did, but the ties of his own soil were too strong, and in July, broken and dispirited, he took the National Covenant, by which he vowed never again to take arms against the Parliament. This bitter blow to his pride, self-inflicted though it was, did not satisfy the committee, and shortly afterwards he was summoned to London and ordered to remain there, nor to return to Cornwall until his full fine was paid. So yet another home was broken, and we at Menabilly tasted the full flavour of defeat. He left us one day in September, when the last of the poor harvest had been gathered in, looking a good ten years older than his five and fifty years, and I knew then, watching his eyes, how loss of freedom can so blight the human soul that a man cares no longer if he lives or dies.

It remained for Mary, my poor sister, and John, his son, to so husband his estate that the debt could month by month be paid, but we well knew that it might take years, even the remainder of his life. His last words to me before he went to London were kind and deeply generous.

"Menabilly is your home," he said, "for as long a time as you should so desire it. We are, one and all, sufferers in this misfortune. Guard your sister for me, share her troubles. And help John, I pray you. You have a wiser head than all I leave behind."

A wiser head . . . I doubted it. It needed a pettifogging mind, with every low lawyer's trick at the finger's end, to break even with the County Committee and the paid agents of Parliament. There was none to help us. My brother Robin, after the surrender at Pendennis, had gone to Radford to my brother Jo, who was in much the same straits as ourselves, while Peter Courtney, loathing inactivity, left the West Country altogether, and the next we heard from him was that he had gone abroad to join the Prince of Wales. Many young men followed this example—living was good at the French court. I think, had they loved their homes better, they would have stayed behind and shared the burdens of defeat with their womenfolk. Alice never spoke a word of blame, but I think her heart broke when we heard that he had gone. . . . It was strange, at first, to watch John and Frank Penrose work in the fields side by side with the tenants, for every hand was needed if the land was to be tilled entirely and to yield a full return. Even our womenfolk went out at harvesting, Mary herself, and Alice and Elizabeth, while the children, thinking it fine sport, helped to carry the corn.

Left to ourselves, we would have soon grown reconciled and even well content with our labours, but the Parliament agents were forever coming to spy upon us, to question us on this and that, to count the sheep and cattle, to reckon, it almost seemed, each ear of corn, and nothing must be gathered, nothing spent, nothing distributed amongst ourselves, but all laid before the smug, well-satisfied officials in Fowey town, who held their licence from Parliament. The Parliament . . . The Parliament . . . From day to day the word rang in our ears. The Parliament decrees that produce shall be brought to market only upon a Tuesday. . . . The Parliament has ordered that all fairs shall from henceforth be discontinued. . . . The Parliament warns every inhabitant within the above-prescribed area that no one, save by permission, shall walk abroad one hour after sunset. . . . The Parliament warns each householder that every dwelling will be searched each week for concealed firearms, weapons, and ammunition, from this day forward, and any holder of the same shall be immediately imprisoned.

"The Parliament," said John Rashleigh wearily, "decrees that no man may breathe God's air, save by a special licence, and then one hour in every other day. My God, Honor, no man can stand this long."

"You forget," I said, "that Cornwall is only one portion of the kingdom. The whole of England, before long, will suffer the same fate."

"They will not, they cannot, endure it," he said.

"What is their alternative? The King is virtually a prisoner. The party with the most money and the strongest army rules the country. For those who share their views life is doubtless very pleasant."

"No one can share their views and call his soul his own."

"There you are wrong. It is merely a matter of being accommodating and shaking hands with the right people. Lord Robartes lives in great comfort at Lanhydrock. The Treffrys—being related to Hugh Peters and Jack Trefusis—live very well at Place. If you chose to follow their example and truckle to the Parliament, doubtless you would find life here at Menabilly so much the easier."

He stared at me suspiciously.

"Would you have me go to them and fawn, while my father lives a pauper up in London, watched every moment of his day? I would sooner die."

I knew he would sooner die and loved him for it. Dear John, you might have had more years beside your Joan and be alive today, had you spared yourself and your poor health in those first few months of aftermath. . . . I watched him toil, and the women, too, and there was little I could do to help but figure the accounts, an unpaid clerk with smudgy fingers, and tot up the debts we owed on quarter days. I did not suffer as the Rashleighs did, pride being, I believe, a quality long lost in me, and I was sad only in their sadness. To see Alice gazing wistfully from a window brought a pain to my heart, and when Mary read a letter from her Jonathan, deep shadows beneath her eyes, I think I hated the Parliament every whit as much as they did.

But that first year of defeat was, in some queer fashion, quiet and peaceful to me who bore no burden on my shoulders. Danger was no more. Armies were disbanded. The strain of war was lifted. The man I loved was safe across the sea in France, and then in Italy, in the company of his son, and now and then I would have word of him, from some foreign city, in good heart and spirits, and missing me, it would seem, not at all. He talked of going to fight the Turks with great enthusiasm, as if, I thought with a shrug of my shoulders, he had not had enough of fighting after three hard years of civil war. "Doubtless," he wrote, "you find your days monotonous in Cornwall." Doubtless I did. To women who have known close siege and stern privation, monotony can be a pleasant thing. . . .

A wanderer for so many months, it was restful to find a home at last and to share it with people whom I loved, even if we were all companions in defeat. God bless the Rashleighs, who permitted me those months at Menabilly. The house was bare and shorn of its former glory, but at least I had a room I called my own. The Parliament could strip the place of its possessions, take the sheep and cattle, glean the harvest, but they could not take from me, nor from the Rashleighs, the beauty that we looked on every day. The devastation of the gardens was forgotten when the primrose came in spring, and the young green-budded trees. We, the defeated, could still listen to the birds on a May morning and watch the clumsy cuckoo wing his way to the little wood beside the Gribbin Hill. The Gribbin Hill . . . I watched it, from my chair upon the causeway, in every mood from winter to midsummer. I have seen the shadows creep on an autumn afternoon from the deep Pridmouth Valley to the summit of the hill, and there stay a moment, waiting on the sun.

I have seen, too, the white sea mists of early summer turn the hill to fantasy, so that it becomes, in a single second, a ghost land of enchantment, with no sound coming but the wash of breakers on the hidden beach, where, at high noon, the children gather cowrie shells. Dark moods, too, of bleak November, when the rain sweeps in a curtain from the southwest. But quietest of all, the evenings of late summer, when the sun has set and the moon has not yet risen, but the dew is heavy in the long grass.

The sea is very white and still, without a breath upon it, and only a single thread of wash upon the covered Cannis Rock. The jackdaws fly homeward to their nests in the warren. The sheep crop the short turf before they, too, rub together beneath the stone wall by the winnowing place. Dusk comes slowly to the Gribbin Hill, the woods turn black, and suddenly, with stealthy pad, a fox creeps from the trees in the thistle park and stands watching me, his ears pricked. . . . Then his brush twitches and he is gone, for here is Matty tapping along the causeway to bring me home; and another day is over. Yes, Richard, there is comfort in monotony. . . .

I return to Menabilly to find that all have gone to bed and the candles extinguished in the gallery. Matty carries me upstairs, and as she brushes my hair and ties the curling rags I think I am almost happy. A year has come and gone, and though we are defeated, we live, we still survive. I am lonely, yes, but that has been my portion since I turned eighteen. And loneliness has compensations. Better to live inwardly alone than together in constant fear. And as I think thus, my curl rag in my hand, I see Matty's round face looking at me from the mirror opposite.

"There were strange rumours in Fowey today," she says quietly.

"What rumours, Matty? There are always rumours." She moistens a rag with her tongue, then whips it round a curl.

"Our men are creeping back," she murmurs, "first one, then two, then three. Those who fled to France a year ago."

I rubbed some lotion on my hands and face.

"Why should they return? They can do nothing."

"Not alone, but if they band together, in secret, one with another . . ."

I sit still, my hands in my lap, and suddenly I remember a phrase in the last letter that came to me from Italy. "You may hear from me," he said, "before the summer closes, by a different route." I thought him to mean he was going to fight the Turks.

"Do they mention names?" I say to Matty, and for the first time for many months a little seed of anxiety and fear springs to my heart. She does not answer for a moment; she is busy with a curl. Then at last she speaks, her voice low and hushed.

"They talk of a great leader," she says, "landing in secret at Plymouth from the Continent. He wore a dark wig, they said, to disguise his colouring. But they did not mention any names. . . ."

A bat brushes itself against my window, lost and frightened, and close to the house an owl shrieks in warning.

And it seemed to me, that moment, that the bat was no airy mouse of midsummer, but the sacred symbol of all hunted things.

29

RUMOURS. ALWAYS RUMOURS. Never anything of certainty. This was our portion during the early autumn of '47 to '48. So strict was the Parliamentary hold on news that nothing but the bare official statements were given to us down in Cornwall, and these had no value, being simply what Whitehall thought good for us to know.

So the whispers started, handed from one to the other, and when the whispers came to us fifth-hand we had to sift the welter of extravagance to find the seed of truth. The royalists were arming. This was the firm base of all the allegations. Weapons were being smuggled into the country from France, and places of concealment were found for them. Gentlemen were meeting in one another's houses. The labourers were conversing together in the field. A fellow at a street corner would beckon to another, for the purpose, it would seem, of discussing market prices; there would be a question, a swift answer, and then the two would separate, but information had been passed, and another link forged.

Outside the parish church of Tywardreath would stand a Parliamentary soldier leaning on his musket, while the busybody agent who had beneath his arm a fold of documents listing each member of the parish and his private affairs gave him good morning; and while he did so, the old sexton, with his back turned, prepared a new grave, not for a corpse this time, but for weapons. . . .

They could have told a tale, those burial grounds of Cornwall. Cold steel beneath the green turf and the daisies, locked muskets in the dark family vaults. Let a fellow climb to repair his cottage roof against the rains of winter, and he will pause an instant, glancing over his shoulder, and, thrusting his hand under the thatch, feel for the sharp edge of a sword. These would be Matty's tales. . . . Mary would come to me with a letter from Jonathan in London. "Fighting is likely to start again at any moment," would be his guarded words. "Discontent is rife, even here, against our masters. Many Londoners who fought in opposition to the King would swear loyalty to him now. I can say no more than this. Bid John have a care whom he meets and where he goes. Remember, I am bound to my oath. If we meddle in these matters, I and he would answer for it with our lives." Mary would fold the letter anxiously and place it in her gown.

"What does it mean?" she would say. "What matters does he refer to?"

And to this there could be one answer only. The royalists were rising. . . .

Names that had not been spoken for two years were now whispered by cautious tongues. Trelawney . . . Trevannion . . . Arundell . . . Bassett . . . Grenvile . . . Yes, above all, Grenvile. He had been seen at Stowe, said one. Nay, that was false; it was not Stowe, but at his sister's house near Bideford. The Isle of Wight, said another. The Red Fox was gone to Carisbrooke to take secret counsel of the King. He had not come to the West Country. He had been seen in Scotland. He had been spoken to in Ireland. Sir Richard Grenvile was returned. Sir Richard Grenvile was in Cornwall. . . .

I made myself deaf to these tales; for once too often, in my life, I had had a bellyful of rumours. Yet it was strange no letter came any more from Italy or from France. . . .

John Rashleigh kept silent on these matters. His father had bidden him not meddle, but to work night and day on the husbanding of the estate, so that the groaning debt to Parliament be paid. But I could guess his thoughts. If there were in truth a rising and the prince landed and Cornwall freed once more, there would be no debt to pay. If the Trelawneys were a party to the plan, and the Trevannions also, and all those who in the county swore loyalty to the King, in secret, then was it not something like cowardice, something like shame, for a Rashleigh to remain outside the company? Poor John. He was restless and sharp-tempered often, those first weeks of spring, after the ploughing had been done. And Joan was not with us to encourage him, for her twin boys, born the year before, were sickly, and she was with them and the elder children at Maddercombe in Devon. Then Jonathan fell ill up in London, and though he asked permission of the Parliament to return to Cornwall, they would not grant it, so he sent for Mary and she went to him. Alice was the next to leave. Peter wrote to her from France, desiring that she should take the children to Trethurfe, his home, that was—so he had heard—in sad state of repair, and would she go there, now spring was at hand, and see what could be done?

She went the first day of March, and it became, on a sudden, strangely quiet at Menabilly. I had been used so long to children's voices, that now to be without them, and the sound of Alice's voice calling to them, and the rustle of Mary's gown, made me more solitary than usual, even a little sad. There was no one but John now for company, and I wondered what we should make of it together, he and I, through the long evenings.

"I have half a mind," he said to me, the third day we sat together, "to leave Menabilly in your care and go to Maddercombe."

"I'll tell no tales of you if you do," I said to him.

"I dislike to go against my father's wishes," he admitted, "but it is over six months now since I have seen Joan and the children, and not a word comes to us here of what is passing in the country. Only that the war has broken out again. Fighting in places as far apart as Wales and the Eastern counties. I tell you, Honor, I am sick of inactivity. For very little I would take horse and ride to Wales."

"No need to ride to Wales," I said quietly, "when there is likely to be a rising in your own county."

He glanced at the half-open door of the gallery. Queer instinctive move, unnecessary when the few servants that we had could all be trusted, yet since we were ruled by

Parliament this gesture would be force of habit.

"Have you heard anything?" he said guardedly. "Some word of truth, I mean, not idle rumour?"

"Nothing," I answered, "beyond what you hear yourself."

"I thought perhaps Sir Richard—" he began, but I shook my head.

"Since last year," I said, "rumour has it that he has been hiding in the country. I've had no message."

He sighed and glanced once more towards the door.

"If only," he said, "I could be certain what to do. If there should be a rising and I took no part in it, how lacking in loyalty to the King I then would seem. What trash the name of Rashleigh."

"If there should be a rising and it fail," I said, "how damp your prison walls, how uneasy your head upon your shoulders."

He smiled, for all his earnestness.

"Trust a woman," he said, "to damp a fellow's ardour."

"Trust a woman," I replied, "to keep war out of her home."

"Do you wish to sit down indefinitely, then, under the rule of Parliament?" he asked.

"Not so. But spit in their faces before the time is ripe, and we shall find ourselves one and all under their feet forever."

Once again he sighed, rumpling his hair and looking dubious.

"Get yourself permission," I said, "and go to Maddercombe. It's your wife you need and not a rising. But I warn you, once you are in Devon, you may not find it so easy to return."

This warning had been repeated often during the past weeks. Those who had gone into Devon or to Somerset upon their lawful business, bearing a permit from the local Parliamentary official, would find great delay upon the homeward journey, much scrutiny and questioning, and this would be followed by search of their persons for documents or weapons, and possibly a night or more under arrest. We, the defeated, were not the only ones to hear the rumours. . . .

The sheriff of Cornwall at this time was a neighbour, Sir Thomas Herle of Prideaux, near St. Blazey, who, though firm for Parliament, was a just man and fair. He had done all he could to mitigate the heavy fine placed upon the Rashleigh estate, through respect for my brother-in-law, but Whitehall was too strong for his local powers. It was he now, in kindness, who granted John Rashleigh permission to visit his wife in Maddercombe in Devon; so it happened, that fateful spring, I was, of all our party, the only one remaining at Menabilly. A woman and a cripple, it was not likely that such a one could foster, all alone, a grim rebellion. The Rashleighs had taken the oath. Menabilly was now above suspicion. And though the garrison at Fowey and other harbours on the coast were strengthened, and more troops quartered in the towns and villages, our little neck of land seemed undisturbed. The sheep grazed on the Gribbin Hill. The cattle browsed in the beef park. The wheat was sown in eighteen acres. And smoke from a single fire, and that my own, rose from the Menabilly chimneys. Even the steward's house was desolate, now old John Langdon had been gathered to his fathers, for with the crushing burden on the estate his place had not been filled. His keys, once so important and mysterious, were now in my keeping, and the summerhouse, so sacred to my brother-in-law, was become my routine shelter on a windy afternoon. I had no wish these days to pry into the Rashleigh papers. Most of the books were gone, stored in the house, or packed and sent after him to London. The desk was bare and empty. Cobwebs hung from the walls. Green patches of mould upon the ceiling. But the torn matting on the floor still hid the flagstone with the iron ring. . . . I saw a rat once creep from his corner and stare at me a moment with beady, unwinking eyes. A great black spider spun a web from a broken pane of glass in the east window, while ivy, spreading from the ground, thrust a tendril to the sill. A few years more, I thought, and nature would take toll of all. The stones of the summerhouse would crumble, the nettles force themselves through the floor, and no one would remember the flagstone with the ring upon it, nor the flight of steps and the earthy, mouldering tunnel.

Well, it had served its purpose. Those days would not return.

I looked out towards the sea one day in March and watched the shadows darken, for an instant, the pale ripple of water beyond Pridmouth. The clock in the belfry, from the house, struck four o'clock. Matty was gone to Fowey and should be back by now. I heard a footstep on the path beneath the causeway and called, thinking it one of the farm labourers returning home who could bear a message for me to the house. The footsteps ceased, but there came no word in answer.

I called again, and this time I heard a rustle in the undergrowth. My friend the fox, perhaps, was out upon his prowl. Then I saw a hand fasten to the sill and cling there for an instant, gripping for support, but the walls of the summerhouse were smooth, giving no foothold, and in a second the hand had slipped and was gone.

Someone was playing spy upon me. . . . If one of the long-nosed Parliamentary agents who spent their days scaring the wits out of the simple country people wished to try the game on me, he would receive short measure.

"If anyone wishes to speak with Mr. Rashleigh, he is from home," I called loudly. "There is no one but myself in charge at Menabilly. Mistress Honor Harris, at your service."

I waited a moment, my eyes still on the window, and then a shadow falling suddenly upon my right shoulder told me there was someone at the door. I whipped round in an instant, my hands on the wheels of my chair, and saw the figure of a man, small and slight, clad in plain dark clothes like a London clerk, with a hat pulled low over his face. He stood watching me, his hands upon the lintel of the door.

"Who are you?" I said. "What do you want?"

There was something in his manner struck a chord. . . . The way he hesitated, standing on one foot, then bit his thumbnail. . . . I groped for the answer, my heart beating, when he whipped his hat from his close black curls, and I saw him smile, tremulous at first, uncertain, until he saw my eyes, and my arms outstretched towards him.

"Dick," I whispered.

He came and knelt by me at once, covering my hands with kisses. I forgot the intervening years and had in my arms a little frightened boy who gnawed a bone and swore he was a dog and I his mistress. And then as he raised his head I saw he was a boy no longer, but a young man, with hair upon his lip and his curls no longer riotous but sleek and close. His voice was low and soft, a man's voice.

"Four years," I said. "Have you grown thus in four small years?"

"I shall be eighteen in two months' time," he answered, smiling. "Have you forgotten? You wrote the first year for my birthday, but never since."

"Writing has not been possible, Dick, these past two years."

I could not take my eyes from him, he was so grown, so altered. Yet that way of watching with dark eyes, wary and suspicious, was the same, and the trick of gnawing at his hand.

"Tell me quickly," I said, "before they come to fetch me from the house, what you are doing here and why."

He looked at me doubtfully.

"I am the first to come, then?" he asked. "My father is not here?"

My heart leapt, but whether in excitement or in fear, I could not tell. In a flash of intuition it seemed that I knew everything. The waiting of the past few months was over. It was all to begin afresh. . . . It was all to start again. . . .

"No one is here," I answered, "but yourself. Even the Rashleighs are from home."

"Yes, we knew that," he said. "That is why Menabilly has been chosen."

"Chosen for what?"

He did not answer. He started his old trick of gnawing at his hand.

"They will tell you," he said, blinking his eyelids, "when they come."

"Who are they?" I asked.

"My father, firstly," he answered, with his eyes upon the door, "and Peter Courtney another, and Ambrose Manaton of Trecarrel, and your own brother Robin, and of course my aunt Gartred."

Gartred. . . . At this I felt like someone who has been ill overlong, or withdrawn from the world, leading another life. There had been rumours enough, God knows, in southeast Cornwall, to stun the senses, but none so formidable as fell now upon my ears.

"I think it best," I said slowly, "if you tell me what has happened since you came to England."

He rose then from his knees and, dusting the dirt from his clothes with a fastidious hand, swept a place upon the window sill to sit.

"We left Italy last autumn," he said, "and came first of all to London, my father disguised as a Dutch merchant, I as his secretary. Since then we have travelled England from south to north, outwardly as foreign men of business, secretly as agents for the prince. At Christmas we crossed the Tamar into Cornwall and went first of all to Stowe. My aunt is dead, you know, and no one was there but the steward and my cousin Bunny and the others. My father made himself known to the steward, and since then many secret meetings have been held throughout the county. From Stowe it is but a step to Bideford and Orley Court. There we found my aunt Gartred, who, falling out with her Parliamentary friends, was hot to join us, and your brother Robin also."

Truly the world had passed us by at Menabilly. The Parliament had one grace to its credit, that the stoppage of news stopped gossip also.

"I did not know," I said, "that my brother Robin lived at Bideford."

Dick shrugged his shoulders.

"He and my aunt are very thick," he answered. "I understand that your brother has made himself her bailiff. She owns land, does she not, that belonged to your eldest brother who is dead?"

Yes, they could have met again that way. The ground upon which Lanrest had stood, the fields below the Mill at Lametton. Why should I blame Robin, grown weary and idle in defeat?

"And so?" I asked.

"And so the plans matured, the clans gathered. They are all in it, you know, from east to west, the length and breadth of Cornwall. The Trelawneys, the Trevannions, the Bassetts, the Arundells. And now the time draws near. The muskets are being loaded and the swords sharpened. You will have a front seat at the slaughter."

There was a strange note of bitterness in his soft voice, and I saw him clench his hands upon the sill.

"And you?" I asked. "Are you not excited at the prospect? Are you not happy to be one of them?"

He did not answer for a moment, and when he did I saw his eyes look large and black in his pale face, even as they had done as a boy four years before.

"I tell you one thing, Honor," he said passionately, "I would give all I possess in the world, which is precious little, to be out of it!"

The force with which he spoke shocked me an instant, but I took care that he should not guess it.

"Why so?" I asked. "Have you no faith that they will succeed?"

"Faith," he said wearily. "I have no faith in anything. I begged him to let me stay in Italy, where I was content, after my fashion, but he would not let me. I found that I could paint, Honor. I wished to make painting my trade. I had friends, too, fellows of my age, for whom I felt affection. But no. Painting was womanish, a pastime fit for foreigners. My friends were womanish, too, and would degrade me. If I wished to live, if I hoped to have a penny to my name, I must follow him, do his bidding, ape his ways, grow like my Grenvile cousins. God in Heaven, how I have come to loathe the very name of Grenvile."

Eighteen, but he had not changed. Eighteen, but he was still fourteen. This was the little boy who sobbed his hatred of his father.

"And your mother?" I asked gently. He shrugged his shoulders.

"Yes, I have seen her," he said listlessly, "but it's too late now to make amends. She cares nothing for me. She has other interests. Four years ago she would have loved me still. Not now. It's too late. His fault. Always his fault."

"Perhaps," I said, "when—when this present business is concluded, you will be free. I will speak for you; I will ask that you may return to Italy, to your painting, to your friends."

He picked at the fringe of his coat with his long slim hands, too long, I thought, too finely slim for a Grenvile.

"There will be fighting," he said slowly, "men killing one another for no purpose, save to spill blood. Always to spill blood. . . ."

It was growing murky in the summerhouse, and still I had heard no more about their plans. The fear that I read in his eyes found an echo in my heart, and the old strain and anxiety were with me once again.

"When did you leave Bideford?" I asked.

"Two days ago," he answered; "those were my orders. We were to proceed separately, each by a different route. Lady Courtney has gone to Trethurfe, I presume?"

"She went at the beginning of the month."

"So Peter intended. It was part of the ruse, you see, for emptying the house. He has been in Cornwall, Peter Courtney, and amongst us since before Christmas."

Another prey for Gartred? A second bailiff to attend on Orley Court? And Alice here, with wan cheeks and chin upon her hand, at an open window. . . . Richard did not choose his *serviteurs* for kindness.

"Mrs. Rashleigh was inveigled up to London for the same purpose," said Dick. "The scheme has been cunningly planned, like all schemes of my father's. And the last cast of all, to rid the house of John, was quite in keeping with his character."

"John went of his own accord," I answered, "to see his wife at Maddercombe in Devon."

"Aye, but he had a message first," said Dick. "A scrap of paper, passed to him in Fowey, saying his wife was overfond of a neighbour living in her father's house. I know, because I saw my father pen the letter, laughing as he did so, with Aunt Gartred at his back."

I was silent at that. Damn them both, I thought, for cruelty. And I knew Richard's answer, even as I accused him in my thoughts. "Any means to secure the end that I desire."

Well, what was to come was no affair of mine. The house was empty. Let them make it a place of assignation; I could not stop them. Let Menabilly become, in one brief hour, the headquarters of the royalist rising. Whether they succeeded or failed was not my business.

"Did your father," I said, "send any word to me? Did he know that I was here?"

Dick stared at me blankly for a moment, as though I were in truth the half-wit I now believed myself to be.

"Why, yes, of course," he said. "That is why he picked on Menabilly rather than Carhayes. There was no woman at Carhayes to give him comfort."

"Does your father," I said, "still need comfort after two long years in Italy?"

"It depends," he answered, "what you intend by comfort. I never saw my father hold converse with Italian women. It might have made him better-tempered if he had."

I saw Richard, in my mind's eye, pen in hand, with a map of Cornwall spread on a table before him. And dotted upon the map were the houses by the coast that offered sanctuary. Trelawne—too deeply wooded. Penrice—not close enough to the sea. Carhayes—yes, good landing ground for troops, but not a single Miss Trevannion. Menabilly—with a beach and a hiding place and an old love into the bargain who had shared his life before and might be induced, even now, after long silence, to smile on him a moment after supper. . . . And the pen would make a circle round the name of Menabilly.

So I was become cynic in defeat. The rule of Parliament had taught me a lesson. But as I sat there, watching Dick and thinking how little he resembled his father, I knew that all my anger was but a piece of bluff deceiving no one, not even my harder self, and that there was nothing I wanted in the world so much but to play hostess once more to Richard, by candlelight, in secret, and to live again that life of strain and folly, anguish and enchantment.

30

IT FELL ON me to warn the servants. I summoned each one to my chamber in turn.

"We are entering upon dangerous days," I said to them. "Things will pass here at Menabilly which you do not see and do not hear. Visitors will come and go. Ask no questions. Seek no answer. I believe you are one and all faithful subjects of His Majesty?"

This was sworn upon the Book of Common Prayer.

"One incautious word that leaves this house," I said, "and your master up in London will lose his life, and ourselves also, in all probability. That is all I have to say. See that there is clean linen on the beds and sufficient food for guests. But be deaf and dumb and blind to those who come here."

It was on Matty's advice that I took them thus into my confidence.

"Each one can be trusted," she said, "but a word of faith from you will bind them together, and not all the agents in the West Country will make them blab."

The household had lived sparsely now since the siege of '44, and there were few comforts for our prospective visitors.

No hangings to the walls, no carpets to the floors in the upper chambers. Straw mattresses in place of beds. They must take what shift they could and be grateful.

Peter Courtney was the first to come. No secrecy for him. He flaunted openly his pretended return from France, dining with the Treffrys at Place upon the way and announcing loudly his desire to see his children. Gone to Trethurfe? But all his belongings were at Menabilly. Alice had misunderstood his letter. . . .

Nothing wan or pale about Peter. He wore a velvet coat that must have cost a fortune. Poor Alice and her dowry. . . .

"You might," I said to him, "have sent her a whisper of your safe return. She would have kept it secret."

But he shrugged a careless shoulder. "A wife can be a cursed appendage in times like these," he said, "when a man must live from day to day, from hand to mouth. To tell the truth, Honor, I am so plagued with debts that one glimpse of her reproachful eyes would drive me crazy."

"You look well on it," I said. "I doubt if your conscience worries you unduly."

He winked, his tongue in his cheek, and I thought how the looks that I had once admired were coarsened now with licence and good living. Too much French wine, too little exercise.

"And what are your plans," I asked, "when Parliament is overthrown?"

Once again he shrugged his shoulder. "I shall never settle at Trethurfe," he said. "Alice can live there if she pleases. As for myself, why, war has made me restless."

He whistled under his breath and strolled towards the window. The aftermath of war, the legacy of losing it. One more marriage in the melting pot. . . .

The next to come was Bunny Grenvile. Bunny, at seventeen, already head and shoulders taller than his cousin Dick. Bunny with snub nose and freckles. Bunny with eager questing eyes and a map of the coast under his arm.

"Where are the beaches? Where are the landing places? No, I want no refreshment; I have work to do. I want to see the ground."

And he was off to the Gribbin, a hound to scent, another budding soldier like his brother Jack.

"You see," said Dick cynically, his black eyes fastened on me, "how all the Grenvile men but me are bred with a nose for blood? You despise me, don't you, because I do not go with him?"

"No, Dick," I answered gently.

"Ah, but you will in time. Bunny will win your affection, as he has won my father's. Bunny has courage. Bunny has guts. Poor Dick has neither. He is only fit for painting, like a woman."

He threw himself on his back upon the couch, staring upwards at the ceiling. And this, too, I thought has to be contended with. The demon jealousy sapping his strength. The wish to excel, the wish to shine before his father. His father whom he pretended to detest.

Our third arrival was Mr. Ambrose Manaton. A long familiar name to me, for my family of Harris had for generations past had lawsuits with the Manatons, respecting that same property of theirs, Trecarrel. What it was all about I could not say, but I know my father never spoke to any of them. There was an Ambrose Manaton who stood for Parliament before the war, at Launceston. This man was his son. He was, I suppose, a few years older than Peter Courtney, some four and thirty years. Sleek and suave, with a certain latent charm. He wore his own fair hair, curling to his shoulders. Thinking it best spoken and so dismissed forever, I plunged into the family dispute, on setting eyes on him.

"Our families," I said, "have waged a private war for generations. Something to do with property. Being the youngest daughter, you are safe with me. I can lay claim to nothing."

"I could not refuse so fair a pleader if you did," he answered.

I considered him thoughtfully as he kissed my hand. Too ready with his compliment, too easy with his smile. What exactly, I wondered, was his part in this campaign? I had not heard of him ever as a soldier. Money? Property? Those lands at Trecarrel and at Southill that my father could not claim?

Richard had no doubt assessed the value. A royalist rising cannot be conducted without funds. Did Ambrose Manaton, then, hold the purse? I wondered what had induced him to risk his life and fortune. He gave me the clue a moment afterwards.

"Mrs. Denys has not yet arrived?"

"Not yet. You know her well?"

"We count ourselves near neighbours in north Cornwall and north Devon."

The tone was easy and the smile confident. Oh, Richard, my love of little scruple. So Gartred was the bait to catch the tiger.

What in the name of thunder had been going on all these long winter months at Bideford? I could imagine, with Gartred playing hostess. Well, I was hostess now at Menabilly. And the straw mattresses upstairs would be hard cheer after the feather beds of Orley Court.

"My brother, Major General Harris, acts as bailiff to Mrs. Denys, so I understand?"

"Why, yes, something of the sort," said Ambrose Manaton. He studied the toe of his boot. His voice was a shade overcasual.

"Have you seen your brother lately?" he asked.

"Not for two years. Not since Pendennis fell."

"You will see a change in him then. His nerves have gone to pieces. The result of the siege, no doubt."

Robin never had a nerve in his body. Robin rode to battle with a falcon on his wrist. If Robin was changed, it was not the fault of five months' siege.

They came together shortly before dark. I was alone in the gallery to receive them. The rule of Parliament had fallen lightly on Gartred. She was, I think, a little fuller in the bosom, but it became her well. And, chancing fate, she had let nature do its damnedest with her hair, which was no longer gleaming gold, but streaked with silver white, making her look more lovely and more frail.

She tossed her cloak to Robin as she came into the room, proclaiming in that first careless gesture all that I cared to know of their relationship. The years slipped backward in a flash, and there was she, a bride of twenty-three, already tired of Kit, her slave and bondsman, who had not the strength of will to play the master.

It might have been Kit once again, standing there in the gallery at Menabilly, with a dog's look of adoration in his eyes.

But Ambrose Manton was right. There was not only adoration in Robin's eyes. There was strain, too, doubt, anxiety. And the heavy jowls and puffy cheeks betrayed the easy drinker. Defeat and Gartred had taken toll, then, of my brother.

"We seem fated, you and I, to come together at moments of great crisis," I said to Gartred. "Do you still play piquet?"

I saw Robin look from one to the other of us, mystified, but Gartred smiled, drawing off her lacen gloves.

"Piquet is out of fashion," she answered. "Dice is a later craze, but must be done in secret, all games of chance being frowned upon by Parliament."

"I shall not join you then," I said. "You will have to play with Robin or with Ambrose Manaton."

Her glance at me was swift, but I let it pass over my head.

"I have at least the consolation," she said, "of knowing that for once we shall not play in opposition. We are all partners on a winning side."

"Are we?" I said. But only four years had passed since she had come here as a spy for Lord Robartes.

"If you doubt my loyalty," said Gartred, "you must tell Richard when he comes. But it is rather late to make amends. I know all the secrets."

She smiled again, and as I looked at her I felt like a knight of old saluting his opponent before combat.

"I have put you," I said, "in the long chamber overhead, which Alice has with her children when she is home."

"Thank you," she said.

"Robin is on your left," I said, "and Ambrose Manaton upon your right, at the small bedroom at the stair's head. With two strong men to guard you, I think it hardly likely you'll be nervous."

She gave not a flicker of the eyelid but, turning to Robin, gave him some commands about her baggage. He went at once to obey her, like a servant.

"It has been fortunate for you," I said, "that the menfolk of my breed have proved accommodating."

"It would be more fortunate still," she answered, "if they could be at the same time less possessive."

"A family failing," I replied, "like the motto of our house, 'What we have, we hold.'"

She looked at me a moment thoughtfully.

"It is a strange power," she said, "this magnetism that you have for Richard. I give you full credit."

I bowed to her from my chair.

"Give me no credit, Gartred," I answered. "Menabilly is but a name upon a map that will do as well as any other. An empty house, a near-by shore."

"And a secret hiding place into the bargain," she said shrewdly.

But now it was my time to smile. "The mint had the silver long ago," I said, "and what was left has gone to swell the Parliament exchequer. What are you playing for this time, Gartred?"

She did not answer for a moment, but I saw her cat's eyes watching Robin's shadow in the hall.

"My daughters are grown up," she said. "Orley Court becomes a burden. Perhaps I would like a third husband and security."

Which my brother could not give her, I thought, but which a man some fifteen years younger than herself, with lands and fortune, might be pleased to do. Mrs. Harris. . . . Mrs. Denys. . . . Mrs. Manaton?

"You broke one man in my family," I said. "Take care that you do not seek to break another."

"You think you can prevent me?"

"Not I. You may do as you please. I only give you warning."

"Warning of what?"

"You will never play fast and loose with Robin, as you did with Kit. Robin would be capable of murder."

She stared at me a moment, uncomprehending. And then my brother came into the room.

Well, for the love of God, I thought that night, here was a royalist rising, planned to kindle Cornwall from east to west, but there was enough material for explosive purposes gathered beneath the roof of Menabilly to set light to the whole country. . . .

We made a strange company for dinner. Gartred, her silver hair bejeweled, at the head of the table, and those two men on either side of her, my brother with ever-reaching hand to the decanter, his eyes feasting on her face, while Ambrose Manaton, cool and self-possessed, kept up a flow of conversation in her right ear, excluding Robin, about the corrupt practices of Parliament that made me suspect he must have a share in it, from knowing so much detail.

On my left sat Peter Courtney, who from time to time caught Gartred's eye and smiled accordingly, in knowing fashion, but as he did the same to the serving maid who passed his place, and to me when I chanced to look his way, I guessed it to be habit rather than conspiracy. I knew my Peter. . . .

Dick glowered in the centre, throwing black looks towards his cousin opposite, who rattled on about the letters he had received from his brother Jack, who was grown so high in favour with the Prince of Wales in France that they were never parted.

And as I looked at each in turn, seeing they were served with food and wine, playing the hostess in this house that was not mine, frowned upon, no doubt, by the ghost of old John Rashleigh, I thought with some misgiving that, had Richard sought his hardest in the county, he could not have found six people more likely to fall out and disagree than those who sat around the table now.

Gartred, his sister, had never wished him well. Robin, my brother, had disobeyed his orders in the past. Peter Courtney was one of those who had muttered at his leadership. Dick, his son, feared and hated him. Ambrose Manaton was an unknown quantity, and Bunny, his nephew, a pawn who could read a map. Were these to be the leaders of the rising? If so, God help poor Cornwall and the Prince of Wales. . . .

"My uncle," Bunny was saying, arranging the salt cellars in the fashion of a fort, "never forgets an injury. He told me once if a man does him an ill turn he will serve him with a worse one." He went on to describe some battle of the past, to which no one listened, I think, but Peter, who did so from good nature, but the words Bunny had spoken so lightly, without thinking, rang strangely in my head. "My uncle never forgets an injury."

He must have been injured by all of us, at one time or other, seated at the table now at Menabilly. What a time to choose to pay old scores, Richard, my lover, mocking and malevolent . . . The eve of a rising, and these six people deep in it to the hilt.

There was something symbolic in the empty chair beside me.

Then we fell silent, one and all, for the door opened of a sudden, and he stood there, watching us, his hat upon his head, his long cloak hanging from his shoulders. Gone was the auburn hair I loved so well, and the curled wig that fell below his ears gave him a dark satanic look that matched his smile.

"What a bunch of prizes," he said, "for the sheriff of the duchy if he chose to call. Each one of you a traitor."

They stared at him blankly, even Gartred, for once, slow to follow his swift mind. But I saw Dick start and gnaw his fingernails. Then Richard tossed his hat and cloak to the waiting servant in the hall and came to the empty chair at my right side.

"Have you been waiting long?" he said to me.

"Two years and three months," I answered him.

He filled the glass from the decanter at my side.

"In January '46," he said, "I broke a promise to our hostess here. I left her one morning at Werrington, saying I would be back again to breakfast with her. Unfortunately the Prince of Wales willed otherwise. And I breakfasted instead in Launceston Castle. I propose to make amends for this tomorrow."

He lifted his glass, draining it in one measure, then put out his hand to mine and held it on the table.

"Thank God," he said, "for a woman who does not give a damn for punctuality."

31

IT WAS LIKE Werrington once more. The old routine. The old haphazard sharing of our days and nights. He bursting into my chamber as I breakfasted, my toilet yet undone, my hair in curl rags, while he paced about the room, talking incessantly, touching my brushes, my combs, my bracelets on the table, cursing all the while at some delay in the plans he was proposing. Trevannion was too slow. Trelawney the elder too cautious. And those who were to lead the insurrection farther west had none of them big names; they were all small fry, lacking the right qualities for leadership.

"Grosse of St. Buryan, Maddern of Penzance, Keigwin of Mousehole," said Richard, "none of them held a higher rank than captain in '46 and have never led troops in action. But we have to use them now. It is a case of *faute de mieux*. The trouble is that I can't be in fifty places at the same time."

Like Werrington once more. A log fire in the dining chamber. A heap of papers scattered on the table, and a large map in the centre. Richard seated in his chair, with Bunny, instead of Jack, at his elbow. The red crosses on the beaches where the invading troops should land. Crinnis . . . Pentewan . . . Veryan . . . The beacons on the headlands to warn the ships at sea . . . The Gribbin . . . The Dodman . . . The Nare . . . My brother Robin standing by the door, where Colonel Roscarrick would have stood. And Peter Courtney, riding into the courtyard, bearing messages from John Trelawney.

"What news from Talland?"

"All well. They will wait upon our signal. Looe can easily be held. There will be no opposition there to matter."

The messages sifted, one by one. Like all defeated peoples, those who had crumbled first in '46 were now the most eager to rebel.

Helston . . . Penzance . . . St. Ives . . . The confidence was supreme. Grenvile, as supreme commander, had but to give the word.

I sat in my chair by the fireside, listening to it all, and I was no longer in the dining chamber at Menabilly, but back at Werrington, at Ottery St. Mary, at Exeter. . . . The same problems, the same arguments, the same doubtings of the commanders, the same swift decisions. Richard's pen pointing to the Scillies.

"This will be the main base for the prince's army. No trouble about seizing the islands. Your brother Jack can do it with two men and a boy." And Bunny, grinning, nodding his auburn head. "Then the main landings to be where we have our strongest hold. A line between here and Falmouth, I should fancy, with St. Mawes the main objective. Hopton has sent me obstructive messages from Guernsey, tearing my proposals to pieces. He can swallow them, for all I care. If he would have his way he would send a driblet here, a driblet there, some score of pissing landings scattered round the whole of Cornwall, in order, he says, to confuse the enemy. Confuse, my arse. One big punch at a given centre, with us holding it in strength, and Hopton can land his whole army in four and twenty hours. . . ."

The big conferences would be held at night. It was easier then to move about the roads. The Trelawneys from Trelawne, Sir Charles Trevannion from Carhayes, the Arundells from Trerice, Sir Arthur Bassett from Tehidy. I would lie in my chamber overhead and hear the drone of voices from the dining room below and always that clear tone of Richard's that would overtop them all. Was it certain that the French would play? This was the universal doubt, expressed by the whole assembly, that Richard would brush impatiently aside.

"Damn the French! What the hell does it matter if they don't? We can do without them. Never a Frenchman yet but was not a liability to his own side."

"But," murmured Sir Charles Trevannion, "if we at least had the promise of their support and a token force to assist the prince in landing, the moral effect upon Parliament would be as valuable as ten divisions put against them."

"Don't you believe it," said Richard. "The French hate fighting on any soil but their own. Show a frog an English pike and he will show you his backside. Leave the French alone. We won't need them once we hold the Scillies and the Cornish forts. The Mount . . . Pendennis . . . St. Mawes . . . Bunny, where are my notes giving the present disposition of the enemy troops? Now, gentlemen . . ."

And so it would continue. Midnight, one, two, three o'clock, and what hour they went, and what hour he came to bed, I would not know, for exhaustion would lay claim to me long since.

Robin, who had proved his worth those five weeks at Pendennis, had much responsibility on his shoulders. The episode of the bridge had been forgotten. Or had it? I would wonder sometimes, when I watched Richard's eyes upon him. Saw him smile, for no reason. Saw him tap his pen upon his chin. . . .

"Have you the latest news from Helston?"

"Here, sir. To hand."

"I shall want you to act as deputy for me tomorrow at Penrice. You can be away two nights, no more. I must have the exact number of men they can put upon the roads between Helston and Penryn."

"Sir."

And I would see Robin hesitate a moment, his eyes drift towards the door leading to the gallery, where Gartred's laugh, of a sudden, would ring out, and clear. Later, his flushed face and bloodshot eyes told their own tale. . . .

"Come, Robin," Richard would say curtly after supper, "we must burn the midnight candle once again. Peter has brought me messages in cipher from Penzance, and you are my expert. If I can do with four hours' sleep, so can the rest of you."

Richard, Robin, Peter, and Bunny crowded round the table in the dining room, with Dick standing sentinel at the door, watching them wearily, resentfully. Ambrose Manaton standing by the fire, consulting a great sheaf of figures.

"All right, Ambrose," Richard would say. "I shan't need your assistance over this problem. Go and talk high finance to the women in the gallery."

And Ambrose Manaton, smiling, bowing his thanks. Walking from the room with a shade too great confidence, humming under his breath.

"Will you be late?" I said to Richard.

"H'm . . . H'm . . ." he answered absently. "Fetch me that file of papers, Bunny." Then of a sudden, looking up at Dick, "Stand up straight, can't you? Don't slop over your feet," he said harshly. Dick's black eyes blinking, his slim hands clutching at his coat. He would open the door for me to pass through in my chair, and all I could do to give him confidence was to smile and touch his hand. No gallery for me. Three makes poor company. But upstairs to my chamber, knowing that the voices underneath would drone for four hours more. An hour, perhaps, would pass, with I reading on my bed, and then the swish of a skirt upon the landing as Gartred passed into her room. Silence. Then that telltale creaking stair. The soft closing of a door. But beneath me in the dining room the voice would drone on till after midnight.

One evening, when the conference broke early and Richard sat with me awhile before retiring, I told him bluntly what I heard. He laughed, trimming his fingernails by the open window.

"Have you turned prude, sweetheart, in your middle years?" he said.

"Prudery be damned," I answered, "but my brother hopes to marry her. I know it, from his hints and shy allusions about rebuilding the property at Lanrest."

"Then hope will fail him," replied Richard. "Gartred will never throw herself away upon a penniless colonel. She has other fish to fry, and small blame to her."

"You mean," I asked, "this fish she is in the process of frying at this moment?"

"Why, yes, I suppose so," he answered with a shrug. "Ambrose has a pretty inheritance from his Trefusis mother, besides what he will come into when his father dies. Gartred would be a fool if she let him slip from her."

How calmly the Grenviles seized fortunes for themselves.

"What exactly," I said, "does he contribute to your present business?"

He cocked an eye at me and grinned.

"Don't poke your snub nose into my affairs," he said. "I know what I'm about. I'll tell you one thing, though: we'd have difficulty in paying for this affair without him."

"So I thought," I answered.

"Taking me all round," he said, "I'm a pretty cunning fellow."

"If you call it cunning," I said, "to play one member of your staff against another. For my part, I would call it knavery."

"A *ruse de guerre*," he countered.

"Pawky politics," I argued.

"Ah, well," he said, "if the manoeuvre serves my purpose, it matters not how many lives be broken in the process."

"Take care they're broken afterwards, not before," I said.

He came and sat beside me on the bed.

"I think you mislike me much, now my hair is black," he suggested.

"It becomes your beauty but not your disposition."

"Dark foxes leave no trail behind them."

"Red ones are more lovable."

"When the whole future of a country is at stake, emotions are thrown overboard."

"Emotions, but not honour."

"Is that a pun upon your name?"

"If you like to take it so."

He took my hands in his and pressed them backwards on the pillow, smiling.

"Your resistance was stronger at eighteen," he said.

"And your approach more subtle."

"It had to be in that confounded apple tree."

He lay his head upon my shoulder and turned my face to his.

"I can swear in Italian now as well as Spanish," he said to me.

"Turkish also?"

"A word or two. The bare necessities."

He settled himself against me in contentment. One eye drooped. The other
regarded me malevolently from the pillow.

"There was a woman I encountered once in Naples . . ."

"With whom you passed an hour?"

"Three, to be exact."

"Tell the tale to Peter." I yawned. "It doesn't interest me."

He lifted his hands to my hair and took the curlers from it.

"If you placed these rags upon you in the day it would be more to your advantage
and to mine," he mused. "Where was I, though? Ah, yes, the Neapolitan."

"Let her sleep, Richard, and me also."

"I only wished to tell you her remark to me on leaving. 'So it is true, what I have
always heard,' she said to me, 'that Cornishmen are famed for one thing only, which
is wrestling.' 'Signorina,' I replied, 'there is a lady waiting for me in Cornwall who
would give me credit for something else besides.'" He stretched and yawned and,
propping himself on his elbow, blew the candle. "But there," he said, "these southern
women were as dull as milk. My vulpine methods were too much for them."

The nights passed thus, and the days as I have described them. Little by little the
plans fell into line, the schemes were tabulated. The final message came from the
prince in France that the French fleet had been put at his disposal, and an army, under
the command of Lord Hopton, would land in force in Cornwall, while the prince with
Sir John Grenvile seized the Scillies. The landing to coincide with the insurrection of
the royalists, under Sir Richard Grenvile, who would take and hold the key points in
the duchy.

Saturday, the thirteenth of May, was the date chosen for the Cornish rising. . . .
The daffodils had bloomed, the blossom was all blown, and the first hot days of
summer came without warning on the first of May. The sea below the Gribbin was
glassy calm. The sky deep blue, without a single cloud. The labourers worked in the
fields, and the fishing boats put out to sea from Gorran and Polperro.

In Fowey all was quiet. The townsfolk went about their business, the Parliamentary
agents scribbled their roll upon roll of useless records to be filed in dusty piles up in
Whitehall, and the sentries at the castle stared yawning out to sea. I sat out on the
causeway, watching the young lambs, thinking, as the hot sun shone upon my bare
head, how in a bare week now the whole peaceful countryside would be in uproar
once again. Men shouting, fighting, dying. . . . The sheep scattered, the cattle driven,
the people running homeless on the roads. Gunfire once again, the rattle of musketry.
The galloping of horses, the tramp of marching feet. Wounded men, dragging
themselves into the hedges, there to die untended. The young corn trampled, the
cottage thatch in flames. All the old anxiety, the old strain and terror. The enemy are
advancing. . . . The enemy are in retreat. . . . Hopton has landed in force. . . . Hopton
has been repulsed. . . . The Cornish are triumphant. . . . The Cornish have been driven
back. . . . Rumours, counter-rumours. . . . The bloody stench of war. . . .

The planning was all over now, and the long wait had begun. A week of nerves,
sitting one by one, with eyes upon the clock, at Menabilly. Richard, in high spirits as
always before battle, played bowls with Bunny in the little walled green beside the
steward's empty lodge. Peter, with sudden realisation of his flabby stomach muscles,
rode furiously up and down the sands at Par to reduce his weight. Robin was very
silent. He took long walks alone down in the woods, and on returning went first to the
dining room, where the wine decanter stood. I would find him there sometimes, glass
in hand, brooding; and when I questioned him he would answer me evasively, his eye
strangely watchful, like a dog listening for the footstep of a stranger. Gartred, usually
so cool and indifferent when having the whip hand in a love affair, showed herself,
for the first time, less certain and less sure. Whether it was because Ambrose
Manaton was fifteen years her junior, and the possibility of marriage with him hung
upon a thread, I do not know, but a new carelessness had come upon her which was,
to my mind, the symbol of a losing touch. That she was heavily in debt at Orley Court

I knew for certain. Richard had told me as much. Youth lay behind her. And a future without a third husband to support her would be hard going, once her beauty went. A dowager, living in retirement with her married daughters, dependent on the charity of a son-in-law? What an end for Gartred Grenvile! So she became careless. She smiled too openly at Ambrose Manaton. She put her hand in his at the dining table. She watched him over the rim of her glass with that same greed I had noticed years before, when, peeping through her chamber door, I had seen her stuff the trinkets in her gown. And Ambrose Manaton, flattered, confident, raised his glass to her in return.

"Send her away," I said to Richard. "God knows she has caused ill feeling enough already. What possible use can she be to you now here at Menabilly?"

"If Gartred went, Ambrose would follow her," he answered. "I can't afford to lose my treasurer. You don't know the fellow as I do. He's as slippery as an eel and as close-fisted as a Jew. Once back with her in Bideford, and he might pull out of the business altogether."

"Then send Robin packing. He will be no use to you anyway, if he continues drinking in this manner."

"Nonsense. Drink in his case is stimulation. The only way to ginger him. When the day comes I'll ply him so full of brandy that he will take St. Mawes Castle single-handed."

"I don't enjoy watching my brother go to pieces."

"He isn't here for your enjoyment. He is here because he is of use to me, and one of the few officers that I know who doesn't lose his head in battle. The more rattled he becomes here at Menabilly, the better he will fight outside it."

He watched me balefully, blowing a cloud of smoke into the air.

"My God," I said, "have you no pity at all?"

"None," he said, "where military matters are concerned."

"You can sit here quite contentedly, with your sister behaving like a whore upstairs, holding one string of Manaton's purse, and you the other, while my brother, who loves her, drinks himself to death and breaks his heart?"

"Bugger his heart. His sword is all I care about, and his ability to wield it."

And leaning from the window in the gallery, he whistled his nephew Bunny to a game of bowls. I watched them both jesting with each other like a pair of schoolboys without a care, casting their coats upon the short green turf.

"Damn the Grenviles one and all," I said, my nerves in ribbons, and as I spoke, thinking myself alone, I felt a slim hand touch me on the shoulder and heard a boy's voice whisper in my ear:

"That's what my mother said eighteen years ago."

And there was Dick behind me, his black eyes glowing in his pale face, gazing out across the lawn towards his father and young Bunny.

32

THURSDAY, THE ELEVENTH of May, dawned hot and sticky as its predecessors. Eight and forty hours to go before the torch of war was lit once more in Cornwall.... Even Richard was on edge that morning, when word came from a messenger at noon to say spies had reported a meeting a few days since at Saltash between the Parliamentary commander in the West, Sir Hardress Waller, and several of the Parliamentary gentlemen, and instructions had been given to double the guards at the chief towns throughout the duchy. Some members of the Cornish County Committee had gone themselves to Helston to see if all was quiet.

"One false move now," said Richard quietly, "and all our plans will have been made in vain."

We were gathered in the dining room, I well remember, save only Gartred, who was in her chamber, and I can see now the drawn, anxious faces of the men as they gazed in silence at their leader. Robin, heavy, brooding; Peter, tapping his hand upon his knee; Bunny, with knitted brows; and Dick, as ever, gnawing at his hand.

"The one thing I have feared all along," said Richard, "those fellows in the West can't hold their tongues. Like ill-trained redhawks, too keen to sight the quarry. I warned Keigwin and Grosse to stay this last week withindoors, as we have done, and hold no conferences. No doubt they have been out upon the roads, and whispers have the speed of lightning."

He stood by the window, his hands behind his back. We were all, I believe, a little sick with apprehension. I saw Ambrose Manaton rub his hands nervously together, his usual calm composure momentarily lost to him.

"If anything should go wrong," he ventured, hesitating, "what arrangements can be made for our own security?"

Richard threw him a contemptuous glance.

"None," he said briefly. He returned to the table and gathered up his papers. "You have your orders, one and all," he said. "You know what you have to do. Let us rid ourselves then of all this junk, useless to us once the battle starts." He began to throw the maps and documents into the fire, while the others still stared at him, uncertain. "Come," said Richard, "you look, the whole damned lot of you, like a flock of crows before a funeral. On Saturday we make a bid for freedom. If any man is afraid let him say so now, and I'll put a halter round his neck for treason to the Prince of Wales."

Not one of us made answer. Richard turned to Robin.

"I want you to ride to Trelawne," he said, "and tell Trelawney and his son that the rendezvous for the thirteenth is changed. They and Sir Arthur Bassett must join Sir Charles Trevannion at Carhayes. Tell them to go tonight, skirting the highroads, and accompany them there."

"Sir," said Robin slowly, rising to his feet, and I think I was the only one who saw the flicker of his glance at Ambrose Manaton. As for myself, a weight was lifted from me. With Robin gone from the house I, his sister, might safely breathe again. Let Gartred and her lover make what they could of the few hours remaining; I did not care a jot, so long as Robin was not there to listen to them.

"Bunny," said his uncle, "you have the boat at Pridmouth standing by in readiness?"

"Sir," said Bunny, his grey eyes dancing. He was, I think, the only one who still believed he played at soldiers.

"Then we shall rendezvous also at Carhayes," said Richard, "at daybreak on the thirteenth. You can sail to Gorran tomorrow and give my last directions about the beacon on the Dodman. A few hours on salt water in this weather will be good practice for your stomach."

He smiled at the lad, who answered it with boyish adoration, and I saw Dick lower his head and trace imaginary lines upon the table with a slow, hesitating hand.

"Peter?" said Richard.

Alice's husband leapt to his feet, drawn from some pleasant reverie of French wine and women to the harsh reality of the world about him.

"My orders, sir?"

"Go to Carhayes and warn Trevannion that the plans are changed. Tell him the Trelawneys and Bassett will be joining him. Then return here to Menabilly in the morning. And a word of warning, Peter."

"What is that, sir?"

"Don't go a-Courtneying on the way there. There is not a woman worth it from Tywardrath to Dodman."

Peter turned pink, for all his bravado, but nerved himself to answer, "Sir," with great punctilio.

He and Robin left the room together, followed by Bunny and by Ambrose

Manaton. Richard yawned and stretched his arms above his head, and then, wandering to the hearth, stirred the black embers of his papers in the ashes.

"Have you no commands for me?" said Dick slowly.

"Why, yes," said Richard without turning his head. "Alice Courtney's daughters must have left some dolls behind them. Go search in the attics and fashion them new dresses."

Dick did not answer, but he went, I think, a little whiter than before and, turning on his heel, left the room.

"One day," I said, "you will provoke him once too often."

"That is my intention," answered Richard.

"Does it please you, then, to see him writhe in torment?"

"I hope to see him stand up to me at last, not take it lying down, like a coward."

"Sometimes," I said, "I think that after twenty years I know even less about you than I did when I was eighteen."

"Very probably."

"No other father in the world would act as harshly to his son as you do to your Dick."

"I only act harshly because I wish to purge his mother's whore blood from his veins."

"You will more likely kindle it."

He shrugged his shoulders, and we fell silent a moment, listening to the sound of the horses' hoofs echoing across the park as Robin and Peter rode to their separate destinations.

"I saw my daughter up in London, when I lay concealed there for a while," said Richard suddenly.

Foolishly a pang of jealousy shot through my heart, and I answered like a wasp. "Freckled, I suppose? A prancing miss?"

"Nay. Rather studious and quiet. Dependable. She put me in mind of my mother. 'Bess,' I said to her, 'will you look after me in my declining years?' 'Why, yes,' she answered, 'if you send for me.' I think she cares as little for that bitch as I do."

"Daughters," I said, "are never favourites with their mothers. Especially when they come to be of age. How old is she?"

"Near seventeen," he said, "with all that natural bloom upon her that young people have. . . ." He stared absently before him, and this moment, I thought with great lucidity and calm above the anguish, is in a sense our moment of farewell, our parting of the ways, but he does not know it. Now his daughter is of age he will not need me.

"Heigh-ho," he said, "I think I start to feel my eight and forty years. My leg hurts damnably today, and no excuse for it, with the sun blazing in the sky."

"Suspense," I said, "and all that goes along with it."

"When this campaign is over," he said, "and we hold all Cornwall for the Prince of Wales, I'll say good-bye to soldiering. I'll build a palace on the north coast, near to Stowe, and live in quiet retirement, like a gentleman."

"Not you," I said. "You'd quarrel with all your neighbours."

"I'd have no neighbours," he answered, "save my own Grenvile clan. My God, we'd make a clean sweep of the duchy. Jack, and Bunny, and I. D'you think the prince would make me Earl of Launceston?"

He lay his hand upon my head an instant and then was gone, whistling for Bunny, and I sat there alone in the empty dining room, despondent, oddly sad. . . .

That evening we all went early to our beds, with the thunder that would not come still heavy in the air. Richard had taken Jonathan Rashleigh's chamber for his own, with Dick and Bunny in the dressing rooms between.

Now Peter and Robin had gone, the one to Carhayes, the other to Trelawne, I thought, with cynicism, that Ambrose Manaton and Gartred could indulge their separate talents for invention until the morning, should the spirit move them.

A single door between their chambers, and I the only neighbour, at the head of the stairs. I heard Gartred come first, and Ambrose follow her—then all was silent on the landing.

Ah, well, I thought, wrapping my shawl about me, thank God I can grow old with some complacency. White hairs could come, and lines and crow's-feet, and they would not worry me. I did not have to struggle for a third husband, not having had a first. But it was hard to sleep, with the blackbird singing on the tree beside the causeway and the full moon creeping to my window.

I could not hear the clock in the belfry from my present chamber, as I used to in the gatehouse, but it must have been near midnight, or just after, when I woke suddenly from the light sleep into which I had fallen, it seemed, but a few moments earlier, with a fancy that I had heard someone moving in the dining room below. Yes, there it was distinctly. The furtive sound of one who blundered his way in darkness and bumped into a table or a chair. I raised myself in my bed and listened. All was silent once again. But I was not easy. I put my hand out to my chair and dragged it to me, then listened once again. Then suddenly, unmistakably, came the stealthy tread of a footstep on the creaking telltale stair. Some intuition, subconscious, perhaps, from early in the day, warned me of disaster. I lowered myself into my chair, and without waiting to light a candle—nor was there need with the moon casting a white beam on the carpet—I propelled myself across the room and turned the handle of my door.

"Who is there?" I whispered.

There was no answer, and, coming to the landing, I looked down upon the stair and saw a dark figure crouching there, his back against the wall, the moonlight gleaming on the naked sword in his hand. He stood in stockinged feet, his shirt sleeves rolled above his elbows, my brother Robin, with murder in his eyes.

He said nothing to me, only waited what I should do.

"Two years ago," I said softly, "you disobeyed an order given you by your commander because of a private quarrel. That was in January '46. Do you seek to do the same in May of '48?

He crept close and stood on the top stair beside me, breathing strangely. I could smell the brandy on his breath.

"I have disobeyed no one," he said. "I gave my message. I parted with the Trelawneys at the top of Polmear Hill."

"Richard bade you accompany them to Carhayes," I said.

"No need to do so, Trelawney told me; two horsemen pass more easily than three. Let me pass, Honor."

"No, Robin. Not yet. Give me first your sword."

He did not answer. He stood staring at me, looking, with his tumbled hair and troubled eyes, so like a ghost of our dead brother Kit that I trembled, even as his hands did on his sword.

"You cannot fool me," he said, "you nor Richard Grenvile. This business was but a pretext to send me from the house so that they could be together."

He looked upward to the landing and the closed door of the room beyond the stairs.

"Go to bed, Robin," I said, "or come and sit with me in my chamber. Let me talk with you awhile."

"No," he said, "this is my moment. They will be together now. If you try to prevent me I shall hurt you also."

He brushed past my chair and made across the landing, tip-toeing, furtive, in his stockinged feet, and whether he was drunk or mad I do not know, only that I guessed his purpose in his eyes.

"For God's sake, Robin," I said, "do not go into that room. Reason with them in the morning, if you must, but not now, not at this hour."

For answer he turned the handle, a smile upon his lips both horrible and strange, and I wheeled then, sobbing, and went back into my room and hammered loudly on the dressing rooms where Dick and Bunny slept.

"Call Richard," I said, "bid him come quickly, now, this instant. And you, too, both of you. There is no time to lose."

A startled voice—Bunny's, I believe—made answer, and I heard him clamber from his bed. But I had turned again and crossed my room towards the landing, where all was silent still and undisturbed. Nothing but the moonlight shining strong into the eastern windows.

And then there came that sound for which I waited, piercing the silence with its shrill intensity. Not an oath, not a man's voice raised in anger. But the shocking horror of a woman's scream.

33

ACROSS THE LANDING, through Ambrose Manaton's empty room, to Gartred's chamber that lay beyond. The wheels of my chair turning slow, for all my labour, and all the while calling, "Richard . . . Richard . . ." with a note in my voice I did not recognise.

Oh God, that fight there in the moonlight, the cold white light pouring into the unshuttered windows, and Gartred with a crimson gash upon her face clinging to the hangings of the bed. Ambrose Manaton, his silk nightshirt stained with blood, warding off with his bare hands the desperate blows that Robin aimed at him, until, with a despairing cry, he reached the sword that lay amongst his heap of clothes upon a chair. Their bare feet padded on the boards, their breath came quick and short, and they seemed, the two of them, like phantom figures, lunging, thrusting, now in moonlight, now in shadow, with no word uttered. And "Richard . . ." I called again, for this was murder, here before my eyes, with the two men between me and the bed where Gartred crouched, her hands to her face, the blood running down between her fingers.

He came at last, half clad, carrying his sword, with Dick and Bunny at his heels bearing candles, and "An end to this, you damned idiots!" he shouted, forcing himself between them, his own sword shivering their blades, and there was Robin, his right wrist hanging limp, with Richard holding him, and Ambrose Manaton back against the farther wall, with Bunny by his side.

They stared at each other, Robin and Ambrose Manaton, like animals in battle. Robin, seeing Gartred's face, opened his mouth to speak, but no words came; he trembled, powerless to move or utter, and Richard pushed him to a chair and held him there.

"Call Matty," said Richard to me swiftly. "Get water, bandages . . ." And I was once more turning to the landing, but already the household were astir, the frightened servants gathering in the hall below, the candles lit. "Go back to bed," said Richard harshly. "No one of you is needed save Mistress Honor's woman. There has been a trifling accident but no harm done."

I heard them shuffle, whisper, retire to their own quarters, and here was Matty, staunch, dependable, seizing the situation in a glance and fetching bowls of water, strips of clean linen. The room was lit now by some half dozen candles. The phantom scene was done; the grim reality was with us still.

Those tumbled clothes upon the floor, Gartred's and his. Manaton leaning upon Bunny's arm, staunching the cuts he had received, his fair curls lank and damp with sweat. Robin upon a chair, his head buried in his hands, all passion spent. Richard standing by his side, grim and purposeful. And one and all we looked at Gartred on the bed with that great gash upon her face from her right eyebrow to her chin.

It was then, for the first time, I noticed Dick. His face was ashen white, his eyes transfixed in horror, and suddenly he reeled and fell as the blood that stained the clean white linen spread and trickled onto Matty's hands.

Richard made no move. He said to Bunny, between clenched teeth, his eyes averted from his son's limp body, "Carry the spawn to his bed and leave him."

Bunny obeyed, and as I watched him stagger from the room, his cousin in his arms, I thought with cold and deadly weariness, this is the end. This is finality.

Someone brought brandy. Bunny, I suppose, on his return. We had our measure, all of us. Robin drinking slow and deep, his hands shaking as he held his glass. Ambrose Manaton, quick and nervous, the colour that had gone soon coming to his face again. Then Gartred, moaning faintly with her head on Matty's shoulder, her silver hair still horribly bespattered with her blood.

"I do not propose," said Richard slowly, "to hold an inquest. What has been, has been. We are on the eve of deadly matters, with the whole future of a kingdom now at stake. This is no time for any man to seek private vengeance in a quarrel. When men have sworn an oath to my command I demand obedience."

Not one of them made answer. Robin gazed, limp and shattered, at the floor.

"We will snatch," said Richard, "what hours of sleep we can until the morning. I will remain with Ambrose in his room and, Bunny, you shall stay with Robin. In the morning you will go together to Carhayes where I shall join you. Can I ask you, Matty, to remain here with Mrs. Denys?"

"Yes, Sir Richard," said Matty steadily.

"How is her pulse? Has she lost much blood?"

"She is well enough now, Sir Richard. The bandages are firm. Sleep and rest will work wonders by the morning."

"No danger to her life?"

"No, Sir Richard. The cut was jagged, but not deep. The only damage done is to her beauty." Matty's lips twitched in the way I knew, and I wondered how much she guessed of what had happened.

Ambrose Manaton did not look towards the bed. The woman who lay upon it might have been a stranger. This is their finish too, I thought. Gartred will never become Mrs. Manaton and own Trecarrel.

I turned my eyes from Gartred, white and still, and felt Richard's hands upon my chair. "You," he said quietly, "have had enough for one night to contend with." He took me to my room and, lifting me from my chair, laid me down upon my bed.

"Will you sleep?" he said.

"I think not," I answered.

"Rest easy. We shall be gone so soon. A few hours more, it will be over. War makes a good substitute for private quarrels."

"I wonder . . ."

He left me and went back to Ambrose Manaton, not, I reflected, for love to share his slumbers, but to make sure his treasurer did not slip from him in the few remaining hours left to us till daylight. Bunny had gone with Robin to his room, and this also, I surmised, was a precaution. Remorse and brandy have driven stronger men than Robin to their suicide.

What hope of sleep had any of us? There was the full moon, high now in the heavens, and you, I thought, shining there in the hushed gardens with your pale cold face above the shadows, have witnessed strange things this night at Menabilly. We Harrises and Grenviles had paid ill return for Rashleigh hospitality. . . .

The hours slipped by, and I remembered Dick of a sudden, who slept in the dressing room next door to me, alone. Poor lad, faint at the sight of blood as he had been in the past, was he now lying wakeful like me, with shame upon his conscience? I thought I heard him stir and I wondered if dreams haunted him as they did me, and if he wished for company. "Dick," I called softly, and "Dick," I called again, but there was no answer. Later a little breeze rising from the sea made a draught come to my room from the open window, and playing with the latch upon the door, shook it free, so it swung to and fro, banging every instant like a loosened shutter. He must sleep deep, then, if it did not waken him.

The moon went, and the morning light stole in and cleared the shadows, and still the door between our two rooms creaked and closed and creaked again, making a nagging accompaniment to my uneasy slumbers.

Maddened at last, I climbed to my chair to shut it, and as my hand fastened on the latch I saw through the crack of the door that Dick's bed was empty. He was not in the room. . . . Numb and exhausted, I stumbled to my bed. He has gone to find Bunny I thought. He has gone to Bunny and to Robin. But before my eyes swung the memory of his white anguished face, which sleep, when it did come, could not banish from me.

Next morning when I woke to find the broad sun streaming in my room, the scenes of the hours before held a nightmare quality. I longed for them to dissipate, as nightmares do, but when Matty bore me in my breakfast I knew them to be true.

"Yes, Mrs. Denys had some sleep," she answered to my query, "and will, to my mind, be little worse for her adventure until she lifts her bandage." Matty, with a sniff, had small pity in her bosom.

"Will the gash not heal in time?" I asked.

"Aye, it will heal," she said, "but she'll bear the scar there for her lifetime. She'll find it hard to trade her beauty now." She spoke with certain relish, as though the events of the preceding night had wiped away a legion of old scores. "Mrs. Denys," said Matty, "has got what she deserved."

Had she? Was this a chessboard move, long planned by the Almighty, or were we one and all just fools to fortune? I knew one thing, and that was that since I had seen the gash on Gartred's face I hated her no longer.

"Were all the gentlemen to breakfast?" I said suddenly.

"I believe so."

"And Master Dick as well?"

"Yes. He came somewhat later than the others, but I saw him in the dining room an hour ago."

A wave of relief came to me, for no reason except that he was safely in the house. "Help me to dress," I said to Matty.

Friday, the twelfth of May. A hazard might have made it the thirteenth. Some sense of delicacy kept me from Gartred's chamber. She with her beauty marred and I a cripple would now hold equal ground, and I had no wish to press the matter home. Other women might have gone to her, feigning commiseration but with triumph in their hearts, but Honor Harris was not one of them. I sent messages by Matty that she should ask for what she wanted and left her to her thoughts. . . . I found Robin in the gallery, standing with moody face beside the window, his right arm hanging in a sling. He turned his head at my approach, then looked away again in silence.

"I thought you had departed with Bunny to Carhayes," I said to him.

"We wait for Peter Courtney," he answered dully. "He has not yet returned."

"Does your wrist pain you?" I asked gently.

He shook his head and went on staring from the window.

"When the shouting is over and the turmoil done," I said, "we will keep house together, you and I, as we did once at Lanrest."

Still he did not answer, but I saw the tears start in his eyes.

"We have loved the Grenviles long enough," I said, "each in our separate fashion. The time has come when they must learn to live without us."

"They have done that," he said, his voice low, "for nearly thirty years. It is we who are dependent upon them."

These were the last words we ever held upon the subject, Robin and I, from that day unto this in which I write. Reserve has kept us silent, though we have lived together for five years.

The door opened, and Richard came into the gallery, Bunny at his shoulder like a shadow.

"I cannot understand it," he said, pacing the floor in irritation. "Here it is nearly noon and no sign yet of Peter. If he left Carhayes at daybreak he should have been here long since. I suppose, like every other fool, he has thought best to ignore my orders."

The barb was lost on Robin, who was too far gone in misery to mind.

"If you permit me," he said humbly, "I can ride in search of him. He may have stayed to breakfast with the Sawles at Penrice."

"He is more likely behind a haystack with a wench," said Richard. "My God, I will have eunuchs on my staff next time I go to war. Go then, if you like, but keep a watch upon the roads. I have heard reports of troops riding through St. Blazey. The rumour may be false, and yet . . ." He broke off in the middle of his speech and resumed his pacing of the room.

Presently we heard Robin mount his horse and ride away. The hours wore on; the clock in the belfry struck twelve, and later one. The servants brought cold meat and ale, and we helped ourselves, haphazard, all of us with little appetite, our ears strained for sound. At half-past one there was a footfall on the stairs, slow and laboured, and I noticed Ambrose Manaton glance subconsciously to the chamber overhead, then draw back against the window.

The handle of the door was turned, and Gartred stood before us, dressed for travel, the one side of her face shrouded with a veil, a cloak around her shoulders. No one spoke as she stood there like a spectre.

"I wish," she said at length, "to return to Orley Court. Conveyance must be found for me."

"You ask for the impossible," said Richard shortly, "and no one knows it better now than you. In a few hours the roads will be impassable."

"I'll take my chance of that," she said. "If I fall fighting with the rabble, I think I shall not greatly care. I have done what you asked me to do. My part is played."

Her eyes were upon Richard all the while and never once on Ambrose Manaton. Richard and Gartred . . . Robin and I . . . Which sister had the most to forgive, the most to pay for? God knows I had no answer.

"I am sorry," said Richard briefly, "I cannot help you. You must stay here until arrangements can be made. We have more serious matters on our hands than the transport of a sick widow."

Bunny was the first to catch the sound of the horse's hoofs galloping across the park. He went to the small mullioned window that gave on to the inner court and threw it wide; and as we waited, tense, expectant, the sound came closer, nearing to the house, and suddenly the rider and his horse came through the arch beneath the gatehouse, and there was Peter Courtney, dust-covered and dishevelled, his hat gone, his dark curls straggling on his shoulders. He flung the reins to a startled waiting groom and came straightway to the gallery.

"For God's sake, save yourselves, we are betrayed," he said.

I think I did not show the same fear and horror on my face as they did, for although my heart went cold and dead within me, I knew with wretched certainty that this was the thing I had waited for all day. Peter looked from one to the other of us, and his breath came quickly.

"They have all been seized," he said, "Trelawney, his son, Charles Trevannion, Arthur Bassett, and the rest. At ten this morning they came riding to the house, the sheriff, Sir Thomas Herle, and a whole company of soldiers. We made a fight for it, but there were more than thirty of them. I leapt from an upper window, by Almighty Providence escaping with no worse than a wrenched ankle. I got the first horse to hand and put spurs to him without mercy. Had I not known the by-lanes as I know my own hand I could not have reached you now. There are soldiers everywhere. The bridge at St. Blazey blocked and guarded. Guards on Polmear Hill."

He looked around the gallery as though in search of someone.

"Robin gone?" he asked. "I thought so. It was he then I saw, when I was skirting the sands, engaged in fighting with five of the enemy or more. I dared not go to his assistance. My first duty was to you. What now then? Can we save ourselves?"

We all turned now to look at our commander. He stood before us, calm and cool, giving no outward sign that all he had striven for lay crushed and broken.

"Did you see their colours?" he asked swiftly. "What troops were they? Of whose command?"

"Some were from Bodmin, sir," said Peter, "the rest advance guards of Sir Hardress Waller's. There were line upon line of them, stretching down the road towards St. Austell. This is no chance encounter, sir. The enemy are in strength."

Richard nodded, turning quickly to Bunny. "Go to Pridmouth," he said; "make sail instantly. Set a course due south until you come in contact with the first outlying vessel of the French fleet. They will be cruising eastward of the Scillies by this time tomorrow evening. Ask for Lord Hopton's ship. Give him this message." He scribbled rapidly upon a piece of paper.

"Do you bid them come?" said Ambrose Manaton. "Can they get to us in time?" He was white to the lips, his hands clenched tight.

"Why, no," said Richard, folding his scrap of paper. "I bid them alter course and sail for France again. There will be no rising. The Prince of Wales does not land this month in Cornwall."

He gave the paper to his nephew. "Good chance, my Bunny," he said, smiling. "Give greetings to your brother Jack, and with a spice of luck you will find the Scillies fall to you like a plum a little later in the summer. But the prince must say good-bye to Cornwall for the present."

"And you, Uncle?" said Bunny. "Will you not come with me? It is madness to delay if the house is likely to be surrounded."

"I'll join you in my own time," said Richard. "For this once I ask that my orders be obeyed."

Bunny stared at him an instant, then turned and went, his head high, bidding none of us farewell.

"But what are we to do? Where are we to go?" said Ambrose Manaton. "Oh God, what a fool I have been to let myself be led into this business. Are the roads all watched?" He turned to Peter, who stood shrugging his shoulders watching his commander. "Who is to blame? Who is the traitor? That is what I want to know," said Ambrose Manaton, all composure gone, a new note of suspicion in his voice. "None but ourselves knew the change in rendezvous. How did the sheriff time his moment with such devilish accuracy that he could seize every leader worth a curse?"

"Does it matter," said Richard gently, "who the traitor is? Once the deed is done?"

"Matter?" said Ambrose Manaton. "Good God, you take it coolly. Trevannion, the Trelawneys, the Arundells, and Bassett, all of them in the sheriff's hands, and you ask does it matter who betrayed them? Here are we, ruined men, likely to be arrested within the hour, and you stand there like a fox and smile at me."

"My enemies call me fox, but not my friends," said Richard softly. He turned to Peter. "Tell the fellows to saddle a horse for Mr. Manaton," he said, "and for you also. I guarantee no safe conduct for the pair of you, but at least you have a sporting chance, as hares do from a pack of hounds."

"You will not come with us, sir?"

"No, I will not come with you."

Peter hesitated, looking first at him and then at me.

"It will go ill with you, sir, if they should find you."

"I am well aware of that."

"The sheriff, Sir Thomas Herle, suspects your presence here in Cornwall. His first challenge, when he came before Carhayes and called Trevannion, was, 'Have you Sir Richard Grenvile here in hiding? If so, produce him and you shall go free.'"

"A pity, for their sakes, I was not there."

"He said that a messenger had left a note at his house at Prideaux early before dawn, warning him that the whole party, yourself included, would be gathered later at

Carhayes. Some wretch had seen you, sir, and with a devil intuition guessed your plans."

"Some wretch indeed," said Richard, smiling still, "who thought it sport to try the Judas touch. Let us forget him."

Was it his nephew Jack, who long ago at Exeter said once to me, "Beware my uncle when you see him smile?"

Then Ambrose Manaton came forward, his finger stabbing at the air.

"It is you," he said to Richard, "you who are the traitor, you who have betrayed us. From the first to last, from beginning to the end, you knew it would end thus. The French fleet never were to come to our aid; there never was to be a rising. This is your revenge for that arrest four years ago at Launceston. Oh God, what perfidy!"

He stood before him, trembling, a high note of hysteria in his voice, and I saw Peter fall back a pace, the colour draining from his face, bewilderment, then horror, coming to his eyes.

Richard watched them, never moving, then slowly pointed to the door. The horses were brought to the courtyard; we heard the jingle of the harness.

"Put back the clock," I whispered savagely. "Make it four years ago, and Gartred acting spy for Lord Robartes. Let her take the blame. Fix the crime on her. She is the one who will emerge from this unscathed, for all her spoilt beauty."

I looked towards her and saw, to my wonder, she was looking at me also. Her scarf had slipped, showing the vivid wound upon her cheek. The sight of it and the memory of the night before filled me, not with anger or with pity, but despair. She went on looking at me, and I saw her smile.

"It's no use," she said. "I know what you are thinking. Poor Honor, I have cheated you again. Gartred alone has the perfect alibi."

The horses were galloping from the courtyard. I saw Ambrose Manaton go first, his hat pulled low, his cloak bellying, and Peter follow him, with one brief glance towards our windows.

The clock in the belfry struck two. A pigeon, dazzling white against the sky, fluttered to the court below. Gartred lay back against the couch, the smile on her lips a strange contrast to the gash upon her face. Richard stood by the window, his hands behind his back. And Dick, who had never moved once in all the past half-hour, waited, like a dumb thing, in his corner.

"Do the three Grenviles," I said slowly, "wish to take council alone amongst themselves?"

34

RICHARD WENT ON standing by the window. Now that the horses were gone and the sound of their galloping had died away, it was strangely hushed and still within the house. The sun blazed down upon the gardens; the pigeons pricked the grass seeds on the lawn. It was the hottest hour of a warm summer day, when bumblebees go humming in the limes and the young birds fall silent. When Richard spoke he kept his back turned to us, and his voice was soft and low.

"My grandfather," he said, "was named Richard also. He came of a long line of Grenviles who sought to serve their country and their King. Enemies he had in plenty, friends as well. It was my misfortune and my loss that he died in battle nine years before my birth. But I remember, as a lad, asking for tales of him and looking up at that great portrait which hung in the long gallery at Stowe. He was stern, they said, and hard, and smiled not often, so I have heard tell, but his eyes that looked down upon me from that portrait were hawk's eyes, fearless and far-seeing. There were many great names in those days—Drake, Raleigh, Sydney—and Grenvile was of their company. He fell, mortally wounded, you may remember, on the decks of his own ship, called the *Revenge*. He fought alone with the Spanish fleet about him, and when they asked him to surrender he went on fighting still. Masts gone—sails gone—the decks torn beneath his feet, but the Grenvile of that day had courage and preferred to have his vessel blown to pieces than sell his life for silver to the pirate hordes of Spain." He fell silent a moment, watching the pigeons on the lawn, and then he went on talking, with his hands behind his back. "My uncle John," he said, "explored the Indies with Sir Francis Drake. He was a man of courage too. They were no weaklings, those young men who braved the winter storms of the Atlantic in search of savage lands beyond the seas. Their ships were frail, they were tossed week after week at the mercy of wind and sea, but some salt tang in their blood kept them undaunted. He was killed there, in the Indies, was my uncle John, and my father, who loved him well, built a shrine to him at Stowe."

There was no sound from any one of us in the gallery. Gartred lay on the couch, her hands behind her head, and Dick stood motionless in his dark corner.

"There was a saying born about this time," continued Richard, "that no Grenvile was ever wanting in loyalty to his King. We were bred to it, my brothers and I; and Gartred, too, I think will well remember those evenings in my father's room at Stowe, when he, though not a fighting man, for he lived in days of peace, read to us from an old volume with great clasps about it of the wars of the past and how our forebears fought in them."

A gull wheeled overhead above the gardens, his wings white against the dark blue sky, and I remembered of a sudden the kittiwakes at Stowe riding the rough Atlantic beneath Richard's home.

"My brother Bevil," said Richard, "was a man who loved his family and his home. He was not bred to war. He desired, in his brief life, nothing so much as to rear his children with his wife's care and live at peace amongst his neighbours. When war came he knew what it would mean and did not turn his back upon it. Wrangling he detested, bloodshed he abhorred, but because he bore the name of Grenvile he knew, in 1642, where his duty lay. He wrote a letter at that time to our friend and neighbour John Trelawney, who has this day been arrested, as you know, and because I believe that letter to be the finest thing my brother ever penned I asked Trelawney for a copy of it. I have it with me now. Shall I read it to you?"

We did not answer. He felt in his pocket slowly for a paper and, holding it before the window, read aloud:

> "I cannot contain myself within my doors when the King of England's standard waves in the field upon so just occasion, the cause being such as must make all those who die in it little inferior to martyrs. And for mine own part I desire to acquire an honest name or an honourable grave. I never loved my life or ease so much as to shun such an occasion, which if I should, I were unworthy of the profession I have held, or to succeed those ancestors of mine who have so many of them, in several ages, sacrificed their lives for their country."

Richard folded the letter again and put it once more into his pocket.

"My brother Bevil died at Lansdowne," he said, "leading his men to battle, and his young son Jack, a lad of but fifteen, straightway mounted his father's horse and charged the enemy. That youngster who has just left us, Bunny, ran from his tutor last autumn, playing truant, that he might place himself at my disposal and hold a sword for this cause we all hold dear. I have no brief for myself. I am a soldier. My faults are many and my virtues few. But no quarrel, no dispute, no petty act of vengeance has ever turned me, or will turn me now, from loyalty to my country and my King. In the long and often bloody history of the Grenviles, not one of them until this day has proved a traitor."

His voice had sunk now, deadly quiet. The pigeons had flown from the lawns. The bees had hummed their way below the thistle park.

"One day," said Richard, "we may hope that His Majesty will be restored to his throne, or if not he, then the Prince of Wales instead. In that proud day, should any of us live to see it, the name of Grenvile will be held in honour, not only here in Cornwall, but in all England too. I am judge enough of character, for all my other failings, to know that my nephew Jack will prove himself as great a man of peace as he has been a youth of war, nor will young Bunny ever lag behind. They can tell their sons in the years to come, 'We Grenviles fought to bring about the restoration of our King,' and their names will rank in that great book at Stowe my father read to us, beside that of my grandfather Richard who fought in the *Revenge*." He paused a moment, then spoke lower still. "I care not," he said, "if my name be written in that book in smaller characters. 'He was a soldier,' they may say, 'the King's General in the West.' Let that be my epitaph. But there will be no other Richard in that book at Stowe. For the King's general died without a son."

A long silence followed his last words. He went on standing at the window, and I sat still in my chair, my hands folded in my lap. Soon now it would come, I thought, the outburst, the angry frightened words, or the torrent of wild weeping. For eighteen years the storm had been pent up, and the full tide of emotion could not wait longer now.

This is our fault, I whispered to myself, not his. Had Richard been more forgiving, had I been less proud, had our hearts been filled with love and not yet hatred, had we been blessed with greater understanding . . . Too late. Full twenty years too late. And now the little scapegoat of our sins went bleeding to his doom. . . .

But the cry I waited for was never uttered. Nor did the tears fall. Instead, he came out from his corner and stood alone an instant in the centre of the room. The fear was gone now from the dark eyes, and the slim hands did not tremble. He looked older than he had done hitherto, older and more wise. As though, while his father had been speaking, a whole span of years had passed him by.

Yet when he spoke his voice was a boy's voice, young and simple.

"What must I do?" he said. "Will you do it for me, or must I kill myself?"

It was Gartred who moved first. Gartred, my lifelong foe and enemy. She rose from her couch, pulling the veil about her face, and came up to my chair. She put her hands upon it, and still with no word spoken she wheeled me from the room. We went out into the garden under the sun, our backs turned to the house, and we said no words to each other, for there were none to say. But neither she nor I nor any man or woman, alive or dead, will ever know what was said there in the long gallery at Menabilly by Richard Grenvile to his only son.

That evening the insurrection broke out in the west. There had been no way to warn the royalists of Helston and Penzance that the leaders in the east had been arrested, and the prospective rising was now doomed to failure. They struck at the appointed hour, as had been planned, and found themselves faced, not with the startled troops they had expected, but the strong forces, fully prepared and armed, that came riding posthaste into Cornwall for the purpose.

No French fleet beyond the Scillies came coasting to the Land's End and the Lizard. No landing of twenty thousand men upon the beaches beneath Dodman and the Nare. And the leaders who should have come riding to the west were shackled, wrist to wrist, in the garrison at Plymouth. No Trelawney, no Arundell, no Trevannion, no Bassett. What was to have been the torch to light all England was no more than a sudden quivering flame, spurting to nothing, spluttering for a single moment in the damp Cornish air.

A few shops looted at Penzance . . . a smattering of houses pillaged at Mullion . . . a wild unruly charge upon Goonbilly Downs, with no man knowing whither he rode or wherefore he was fighting . . . and then the last hopeless, desperate stand at Mawgan Creek, with the Parliamentary troops driving the ill-led royalists to destruction, down over the rocks and stones to the deep Helford River.

The rebellion of '48. The last time men shall ever fight, please God, upon our

Cornish soil. It lasted but a week, but for those who died and suffered it lasted for eternity. The battles were west of Truro, so we at Menabilly smelt no powder; but every road and every lane was guarded, and not even the servants ventured out of doors.

That first evening a company of soldiers, under the command of Colonel Robert Bennett, our old neighbour near to Looe, rode to Menabilly and made a perfunctory search throughout the house, finding no one present but myself and Gartred. He little knew that had he come ten minutes earlier he would have found the greatest prize of all.

I can see Richard now, his arms folded, seated in the dining chamber with the empty chairs about him, deaf to all my pleading.

"When they come," he said, "they shall take me as I am. Mine is the blame. I am the man for whom my friends now suffer. Very well then. Let them do their worst upon me, and by surrendering my person I may yet save Cornwall from destruction!"

Gartred, with all her old cool composure back again, shrugged her shoulders in disdain. "Is it not a little late now in the day to play the martyr?" she suggested. "What good will your surrender do at this juncture? You flatter yourself, poor Richard, if you think the mere holding of a Grenvile will spare the rest from imprisonment and death. I hate these last-minute gestures. These sublime salutes. Show yourself a man and escape, the pair of you, as Bunny did."

She did not look towards Dick. Nor did I. But he sat there, silent as ever, at his father's side.

"We will make fine figures on the scaffold, Dick and I," said Richard; "my neck is somewhat thicker, I know, than his, and may need two blows from the axe instead of one."

"You may not have the pleasure, nor the parade, of a martyr's execution," said Gartred, yawning, "but instead a knotted rope in a dank dungeon. Not the usual finish for a Grenvile."

"It were better," said Richard quietly, "if these two Grenviles did die in obscurity."

There was a pause then, for all our thoughts to stab the air, unspoken; and then Dick spoke, for the first time since that unforgettable moment in the gallery.

"How do we stand," he said jerkily, "with the Rashleighs? If my father and I are found here by the enemy, will it be possible to prove to them that the Rashleighs are innocent in the matter?"

I seized upon his words for all the world like a drowning woman.

"You have not thought of that," I said to Richard. "You have not considered for one moment what will become of them. Who will ever believe that Jonathan Rashleigh and John, too, were not party also to your plan? Their absence from Menabilly is no proof. They will be dragged into the matter, and my sister Mary also. Poor Alice at Trethurfe, Joan at Maddercombe, a legion of young children. They will all of them, from Jonathan in London to the baby on Joan's knee, suffer imprisonment, and maybe death into the bargain, if you are taken here."

It was at this moment that a servant came into the room, much agitated, his hands clasped before him.

"I think it best to tell you," he said, "a lad has come running across the park to say the troopers are gathered together at the top of Polmear Hill. Some have gone down toward Polkerris. The rest are making for Tregaminion and the park gates."

"Thank you," said Richard, bowing. "I am much obliged to you for your discretion."

The servant left the room, hoping, I dare say, to feign sickness in his quarters when the troopers came. Richard rose slowly to his feet and looked at me.

"So you fear for your Rashleighs?" he said. "And because of them you have no wish to throw me to the wolves? Very well then. For this once I will prove accommodating. Where is the famous hiding palce that four years ago proved so beneficial to us all?"

I saw Dick flinch and look away from me towards his father.

"Dick knows," I answered. "Would you condescend to share it with him?"

"A hunted rat," said Richard, "has no choice. He must take the companion that is thrust upon him."

Whether the place was rank with cobwebs, mould, or mildew, I neither knew nor cared. At least it would give concealment while the troopers came. And no one, not even Gartred, knew the secret.

"Do you remember," I said to Dick, "where the passage led? I warn you, no one has been there for four years."

He nodded, deathly pale. And I wondered what bug of fear had seized him now, when but an hour ago he had offered himself, like a little lamb, for slaughter.

"Go, then," I said, "and take your father. Now, this instant, while there is still time."

He came to me then, his new-found courage wavering, looking so like the little boy who loved me once that my heart went out to him.

"The rope," he said, "the rope upon the hinge. What if it has frayed now, with disuse, and the hinge rusted?"

"It will not matter," I said. "You will not need to use it now. I shall not be waiting for you in the chamber overhead."

He stared at me, lost for a moment, dull, uncomprehending, and I verily believe that for one brief second he thought himself a child again. Then Richard broke the spell with his hard clear voice.

"Well?" he said. "If it must be done, this is the moment. There is no other method of escape."

Dick went on staring at me, and there came into his eyes a strange new look I had not seen before. Why did he stare at me thus, or was it not me he stared at but some other, some ghost of a dead past that tapped him on the shoulder?

"Yes," he said slowly, "if it must be done, this is the moment. . . ." He turned to his father, opening first the door of the dining room. "Will you follow me, sir?" he said to Richard.

Richard paused a moment on the threshold. He looked first at Gartred, then back at me again.

"When the hounds are in full cry," he said, "and the coverts guarded, the Red Fox goes to earth."

He smiled, holding my eyes for a single second, and was gone, after Dick, on to the causeway. . . . Gartred watched them disappear, then shrugged her shoulders.

"I thought," she said, "the hiding place was in the house. Near your old apartment in the gatehouse."

"Did you?" I said.

"I wasted hours, four years ago, searching in the passages, tiptoeing outside your door," she said.

There was a mirror hanging on the wall beside the window. She went to it and stared, pulling her veil aside. The deep crimson gash ran from her eyebrow to her chin, jagged, irregular, and the smooth contour of her face was gone forever. I watched her eyes, and she saw me watching them through the misty glass of the little mirror.

"I could have stopped you," she said, "from falling with your horse to the ravine. You knew that, didn't you?"

"Yes," I said.

"You called to me, asking for the way, and I did not answer you."

"You did not," I said.

"It has taken a long time to call it quits," she said to me. She came away from the mirror and, taking from her sack the little pack of cards I well remembered, sat down by the table, close to my wheeled chair. She dealt the cards face downwards on the table.

"We will play patience, you and I, until the troopers come," said Gartred Grenvile.

35

I DOUBT, IF Colonel Bennett had searched all Cornwall, could he have found a quieter couple, when he came, than the two women playing cards in the dining hall at Menabilly. One with a great scar upon her face and silver hair, the other a hopeless cripple.

Yes, there had been guests with us until today, we admitted it. Mr. Rashleigh's son-in-law, Sir Peter Courtney, and my own brother, Robin Harris. No, we knew nothing of their movements. They came and went as they pleased. Mr. Trelawney had called once, we understood, but we had not seen him. Why was I left alone at Menabilly by the Rashleighs? From necessity, and not from choice. Perhaps you have forgotten, Colonel Bennett, that my home at Lanrest was burnt down four years ago, by your orders, someone told me once? A strange action for a neighbour. And why was Mrs. Denys from Orley Court near Bideford a guest of mine at the present season? Well, she was once my sister-in-law and we had long been friends. . . . Yes, it was true my name had been connected with Sir Richard Grenvile in the past. There are gossips in the West Country as well as at Whitehall. No, Mrs. Denys had never been very friendly with her brother. No, we had no knowledge of his movements. We believed him to be in Naples. Yes, search the house, from the cellar to the attics; search the grounds. Here are the keys. Do what you will. We have no power to stop you. Menabilly is no property of ours. We are merely guests, in the absence of Mr. Rashleigh. . . .

"Well, you appear to speak the truth, Mistress Harris," he said to me on the conclusion of his visit (he had called me Honor once, when we were neighbours near to Looe), "but the fact that your brother and Sir Peter Courtney are implicated in the rising that is now breaking out, abortively, praise heaven, at Helston and Penzance, renders this house suspect. I shall leave a guard behind me, and I rather think, when Sir Hardress Waller comes into the district, he will make a more thorough search of the premises than I have had time to do today. Meanwhile—" He broke off abruptly, his eyes drifting, as if in curiosity, back to Gartred.

"Pardon my indelicacy, madam," he said, "but that cut is recent?"

"An accident," said Gartred, shrugging, "a clumsy movement and some broken glass."

"Surely—not self-inflicted?"

"What else would you suggest?"

"It has more the appearance of a sword cut, forgive my rudeness. Were you a man, I would say you had fought a duel and received the hurt from an opponent."

"I am not a man, Colonel Bennett. If you doubt me, why not come upstairs to my chamber and let me prove it to you?"

Robert Bennett was a Puritan. He stepped back a pace, colouring to his ears.

"I thank you, madam," he said stiffly. "My eyes are sufficient evidence."

"If promotion came by gallantry," said Gartred, "you would still be in the ranks. I can think of no other officer in Cornwall, or in Devon either, who would decline to walk upstairs with Gartred Denys."

She made as though to deal the cards again, but Colonel Bennett made a motion of his hands.

"I regret," he said shortly, "but whether you are Mrs. Denys or Mrs. Harris these days does not greatly matter. What does matter is that your maiden name is Grenvile."

"And so?" said Gartred, shuffling her cards.

"And so I must ask you to come with me and accept an escort down to Truro. There you will be held, pending investigation, and when the roads are quieter you will have to leave to depart to Orley Court."

Gartred dropped her cards into her sack and rose slowly to her feet.

"As you will," she said, shrugging her shoulders. "You have some conveyance, I presume? I have no dress for riding."

"You will have every comfort, madam." He turned then to me. "You are permitted to remain here until I receive further orders from Sir Hardress Waller. These may be forthcoming in the morning. But I must ask you to be in readiness to move upon the instant, should the order come. You understand?"

"Yes," I answered. "Yes, I understand."

"Very good then. I will leave a guard before the house, with instructions to shoot on sight, should his suspicions be in any way aroused. Good evening. You are ready, Mrs. Denys?"

"Yes, I am ready." Gartred turned to me and touched me lightly on the shoulder. "I am sorry," she said, "to cut my visit short. Remember me to the Rashleighs when you see them. And tell Jonathan what I said about the gardens. If he wishes to plant flowering shrubs he must first rid himself of foxes. . . ."

"Not so easy," I answered. "They are hard to catch. Especially when they go underground."

"Smoke them out," she said. "It is the only way. Do it by night; they leave less scent behind them. . . . Good-bye, Honor."

"Good-bye, Gartred."

She went, throwing her veil back from her face to show the vivid scar, and I have not seen her from that day to this.

I heard the troopers ride away from the courtyard and out across the park. Before the two entrance doors stood sentries, with muskets at their sides. And a sentry stood also at the outer gate and by the steps leading to the causeway. I sat watching them, then pulled the bellrope by the hearth for Matty.

"Ask them," I said, "if Colonel Bennett left permission for me to take exercise in my chair within the grounds."

She was back in a moment with the message that I feared.

"He is sorry," she answered, "but Colonel Bennett gave strict orders that you were not to leave the house."

I looked at Matty, and she looked at me. The thoughts chased round my head in wild confusion. "What hour is it?" I asked.

"Near five o'clock," she answered.

"Four hours of daylight still," I said.

"Yes," she answered.

From the window of the dining hall I could see the sentry pacing up and down before the gates of the south garden. Now and then he paused to look about him and to chat with his fellow at the causeway steps. The sun, high in the southwest, shone down upon their muskets.

"Take me upstairs, Matty," I said slowly.

"To your own chamber?"

"No, Matty. To my old room beyond the gatehouse."

I had not been there in all the past two years of my stay at Menabilly. The west wing was still bare, untouched. Desolate and stripped as when the rebels had come pillaging in '44. The hangings were gone from the walls. The room had neither bed, nor chair, nor table. One shutter hung limp from the farther window, giving a faint crack of light. The room had a dead, fusty smell, and in the far corner lay the bleached bones of a rat. The west wing was very silent. Very still. No sound came from the deserted kitchens underneath.

"Go to the stone," I whispered. "Put your hands against it."

Matty did so, kneeling on the floor. She pressed against the square stone by the buttress, but it did not move.

"No good," she murmured. "It is hard fixed. Have you forgotten that it only opened on the other side?"

Had I forgotten? It was the one thing that I remembered. "Smoke them out," said Gartred. "It is the only way." Yes, but she did not understand. She thought them hidden somewhere in the woods. Not behind stone walls three feet thick.

"Fetch wood and paper," I said to Matty. "Kindle a fire. Not in the chimney, here against the wall."

There was a chance, a faint one, God knew well, that the smoke would penetrate the cracks in the stones and make a signal. They might not be there, though. They might be crouching in the tunnel at the farther end, beneath the summer house, not having come up to the buttress cell. . . .

How slow she was, good Matty, faithful Matty, fetching the dried grass and the twigs. How carefully she blew the fire, how methodically she added twig to twig.

"Hurry," I said. "More wood, more flame."

"Patience," she whispered. "It will go in its own time."

In its own time. Not my time. Not Richard's time. . . . The room was filled with smoke. It seeped into our eyes, our hair; it clung about the windows. But whether it seeped into the stones we could not tell. Matty went to the window and opened the crack two inches farther. I held a long stick in my hands, poking helplessly at the slow sizzling fire, pushing the sticks against the buttress wall.

"There are four horsemen riding across the park," said Matty suddenly, "troopers, like those who came just now."

My hands were wet with sweat. I threw away my useless stick and rubbed my eyes, stung and red with smoke. I think I was nearer panic at that moment than any other in my eight and thirty years.

"Oh, God," I whispered, "what are we to do?"

Matty closed the window gently. She stamped upon the embers of the fire.

"Come back to your chamber," she said. "Later tonight I will try here once again. But we must not be found here now."

She carried me in her broad arms from the dark musty room, through the gatehouse, to the corridor beyond, and down to my own chamber in the eastern wing. She laid me on my bed, bringing water for my face and hands. We heard the troopers ride into the courtyard, and then the sound of footsteps down below. Impervious to man or situation, the clock beneath the belfry struck six, hammering its silly leaden notes with mechanical precision. Matty brushed the soot from my hair and changed my gown, and when she had finished there came a tap at the door. A servant with frightened face whispered that Mistress Harris was wanted down below. They put me in my chair and carried me downstairs. There had been four troopers, Matty said, riding across the park, but only three stood here, in the side hall, looking out across the gardens. They cast a curious glance upon me as Matty and the servant put me down inside the door of the dining hall. The fourth man stood by the fireplace, leaning upon a stick. And it was not another trooper like themselves, but my brother-in-law, Jonathan Rashleigh.

For a moment I was too stunned to speak, then relief, bewilderment, and something of utter helplessness swept over me and I began to cry. He took my hand and held it, saying nothing. In a minute or two I had recovered and, looking up at him, I saw what the years had done. Two, was it, he had been away in London? It might be twenty. He was, I believe, at that time but fifty-eight. He looked seventy. His hair was gone quite white; his shoulders, once so broad, were shrunk and drooping. His very eyes seemed sunk deep in his skull.

"What has happened?" I asked. "Why have you come back?"

"The debt is paid," he said, and even his voice was an old man's voice, slow and weary. "The debt is paid; the fine is now wiped out. I am free to come to Cornwall once again."

"You have chosen an ill moment to return," I answered.

"So they have warned me," he said slowly.

He looked at me, and I knew, I think, in that moment, that he had been, after all, a party to the plan. That all the guests who had crept like robbers to his house had come with his connivance, and that he, a prisoner in London, had risked his life because of them.

"You came by road?" I asked him.

"Nay, by ship," he answered, "my own ship, the *Frances,* which plies between Fowey and the Continent, you may remember."

"Yes, I remember."

"Her merchandise has helped me to pay my debt. She fetched me from Gravesend a week ago, when the County Committee gave me leave to go from London and return to Fowey. We came to harbour but a few hours since."

"Is Mary with you?"

"No. She went ashore at Plymouth to see Joan at Maddercombe. The guards at Plymouth told us that a rising was feared in Cornwall and troops were gone in strength to quell it. I made all haste to come to Fowey, fearing for your safety."

"You knew then that John was not here? You knew I was—alone?"

"I knew you were—alone."

We both fell silent, our eyes upon the door.

"They have arrested Robin," I said softly, "and Peter also, I fear."

"Yes," he said, "so my guards tell me."

"No suspicion can fall upon yourself?"

"Not yet," he answered strangely.

I saw him look to the window, where the broad back of the sentry blocked the view. Then slowly, from his pocket, he drew a folded paper, which when he straightened it I saw to be a poster, such as they stick upon the walls for wanted men. He read it to me.

" 'Anyone who has harboured at any time, or seeks to harbour in the future, the malignant known as Richard Grenvile, shall, upon discovery, be arrested for high treason, his lands sequestered finally and forever, and his family imprisoned.' "

He folded the paper once again.

"This," he said, "is posted upon every wall in every town in Cornwall."

For a moment I did not speak, and then I said:

"They have searched this house already. Two hours ago. They found nothing."

"They will come again," he answered, "in the morning." He went back to the hearth and stood in deep thought, leaning on his stick. "My ship the *Frances,*" he said slowly, "anchors in Fowey only for the night. Tomorrow, on the first tide, she sails for Holland."

"For Holland?"

"She carries a light cargo as far as Flushing. The master of the vessel is an honest man, faithful to any trust that I might lay upon him. Already in his charge is a young woman, whom I thought fit to call my kinswoman. Had matters been other than they are, she might have landed with me here in Fowey. But fate and circumstance decided otherwise. Therefore, she will proceed to Flushing also, in my ship the *Frances.*"

"I don't see," I said after a moment's hesitation, "what this young woman has to do with me. Let her go to Holland, by all means."

"She would be easier in mind," said Jonathan Rashleigh, "if she had her father with her."

I was still too blind to understand his meaning, until he felt in his breast pocket for a note, which he handed to me.

I opened it and read the few words scribbled in an unformed youthful hand. "If you still need a daughter in your declining years," ran the message, "she waits for you on board the good ship *Frances.* Holland, they say, is healthier than England. Will you try the climate with me? My mother christened me Elizabeth, but I prefer to sign myself your daughter, Bess."

I said nothing for a little while, but held the note there in my hands. I could have asked a hundred questions, had I the time or inclination. Woman's questions, such as my sister Mary might have answered, and perhaps understood. Was she pretty? Was she kind? Had she his eyes, his mouth, his auburn hair? Would she have comprehension of his lonely moods? Would she laugh with him when his moods were gay? But none of them mattered or were appropriate to the moment. Since I should never see her, it was not my affair.

"You have given me this note," I said to Jonathan, "in the hope that I can pass it to her father?"

"Yes," he answered.

Once again he looked at the broad back of the sentry at the window.

"I have told you that the *Frances* leaves Fowey on the early tide," he said. "A boat will put off to Pridmouth, as they go from harbour, to lift lobster pots dropped between the shore and the Cannis Rock. It would be a simple matter to pick up a passenger in the half-light of morning."

"A simple matter," I answered, "if the passenger is there."

"It is your business," he said, "to see then that he is."

He guessed then that Richard was concealed within the buttress; so much I could tell from his eyes and the look he fastened now upon me.

"The sentries," I said, "keep watch upon the causeway."

"At this end only," he said softly, "not the other."

"The risk is very great," I said, "even by night, even by early morning."

"I know that," he answered, "but I think the person of whom we speak will dare that risk." Once again he drew the poster from his pocket. "If you should deliver the note," he said quietly, "you could give him this as well."

I took the poster in silence and placed it in my gown.

"There is one other thing that I would have you do," he said to me.

"What is that?"

"Destroy all trace of what has been. The men who will come tomorrow have keener noses than the troops who came today. They are scent hounds, trained to the business."

"They can find nothing from within," I answered, "you know that. Your father had the cunning of all time when he built his buttress."

"But from without," he said, "the secret is less sure. I give you leave to finish the work begun by the Parliament in '44. I shall not seek to use the summerhouse again."

I guessed his meaning as he stood there watching me, leaning on his stick.

"Timber burns fiercely in dry weather," he said to me, "and rubble makes a pile, and the nettles and the thistles grow apace in midsummer. There will be no need to clear those nettles in my lifetime, nor in John's either."

"Why do you not stay," I whispered, "and do this work yourself?"

But even as I spoke the door of the dining hall was opened, and the leader of the three troopers waiting in the hall entered the room.

"I am sorry, sir," he said, "but you have already had fifteen minutes of the ten allotted to you. I cannot go against my orders. Will you please make your farewell now and return with me to Fowey?"

I stared at him blankly, my heart sinking in my breast again.

"I thought Mr. Rashleigh was a free agent once again?"

"The times being troublesome, my dear Honor," said Jonathan quietly, "the gentlemen in authority deem it best that I should remain at present under surveillance, if not exactly custody. I am to spend the night, therefore, in my town house at Fowey. I regret if I did not make myself more clear." He turned to the trooper. "I am grateful to you," he said, "for allowing me this interview with my sister-in-law. She suffers from poor health, and we have all been anxious for her."

And without another word he went from me, and I was left there, with the note in my hand and the poster in my gown, and the lives not only of Richard and his son, but those of the whole family of Rashleigh, depending upon my wits and my sagacity.

I waited for Matty, but she did not come to me, and, impatient at last, I rang the bell beside the hearth, and the startled servant who came running at the sound told me that

Matty was not to be found; he had sought for her in the kitchen, in her bedroom, but she had not answered.

"No matter," I said, and made a pretence of taking up a book and turning the pages.

"Will you dine now, madam?" he said to me. "It is nearly seven. Long past your usual hour."

"Why, yes," I said, "if you care to bring it," feigning intensity upon my book, yet all the while counting the hours to darkness and wondering with an anxious, heavy heart what had become of Matty.

I ate my meat and drank my wine, tasting them not at all, and as I sat there in the dark-panelled dining hall with the portrait of old John Rashleigh and his wife frowning down upon me, I watched the shadows lengthen and the murky evening creep and the great banked clouds of evening steal across the sky.

It was close on nine o'clock when I heard the door open with a creak and, turning in my chair, I saw Matty standing there, her gown stained green and brown with earth. She put her finger to her lips, and I said nothing. She came across the room and closed the shutters. As she folded the last one into place she spoke softly over her shoulder.

"He is not ill-looking, the sentry on the causeway."

"No?"

"He knows my cousin's wife at Liskeard."

"Introductions have been made on less than that."

She fastened the hasp of the shutter and drew the heavy curtains.

"It was somewhat damp in the thistle park," she said.

"So I perceive," I answered.

"But he found a sheltered place beneath a bush, where we could talk about my cousin's wife. . . . While he was looking for it I waited in the summerhouse."

"That," I said, "was understandable."

The curtains were now all drawn before the shutters and the dining hall in darkness. Matty came and stood beside my chair.

"I lifted the flagstone," she said. "I left a letter on the steps. I said, if the rope be still in place upon the hinge, would they open the stone entrance in the buttress tonight at twelve o'clock? We would be waiting for them."

I felt her strong comforting hand and held it between mine.

"I pray they find it," she said slowly. "There must have been a fall of earth since the tunnel last was used. The place smelt of the tomb."

We clung to each other in the darkness, and as I listened I could hear the steady thumping of her heart.

36

I LAY UPON my bed upstairs from half-past nine until a quarter before twelve. When Matty came to rouse me the house was deadly still. The servants had gone to their beds in the attics, and the sentries were at their posts about the grounds. I could hear one of them pacing the walk beneath my window. The treacherous moon, never an ally to a fugitive, rose slowly above the trees in the thistle park. We lit no candles. Matty crept to the door and listened. Then she lifted me in her arms, and we trod the long twisting corridor to the empty gatehouse. How bare were the rooms, how silent and accusing, and there was no moonlight here on the western side to throw a beam of light upon the floor.

Inside the room that was our destination the ashes of our poor fire, kindled that afternoon, flickered feebly still, and the smoke hung in clouds about the ceiling. We sat down beside the wall in the far corner and we waited. . . . It was uncanny still. The stillness of a place that has not known a footstep or a voice for many years. The quietude of a long-forgotten prison where no sunlight ever penetrates, where all seasons seem alike.

Winter, summer, spring, and autumn would all come and go, but never here, never in this room. Here was eternal night. And I thought, sitting there beside the cold wall of the buttress, that this must be the darkness that so frightened the poor idiot Uncle John when he lay here, long ago, in the first building of the house. Perhaps he lay upon this very spot on which I sat, his hands feeling the air, his wide eyes searching. . . .

Then I felt Matty touch me on the shoulder, and as she did so the stone behind me moved. . . . There came, upon my back, the current of cold air I well remembered, and now, turning, I could see the yawning gulf and the narrow flight of steps behind, and I could hear the creaking of the rope upon its rusty hinge.

Although it was the sound I wanted most in all the world to hear, it struck a note of horror, like a summons from a grave. Now Matty lit her candle, and when she threw the beam onto the steps I saw him standing there, earth upon his face, his hands, his shoulders, giving him, in that weird, unnatural, ghostly light, the features of a corpse new-risen from his grave. He smiled, and the smile had in it something grim and terrible.

"I feared," he said, "you would not come. A few hours more and it would be too late."

"What do you mean? I asked.

"No air," he said. "There is only room here from the tunnel for a dog to crawl. I have no great opinion of your Rashleigh builder."

I leant forward, peering down the steps, and there was Dick, huddled at the bottom, his face as ghostly as his father's.

"It was not thus," I said, "four years ago."

"Come," said Richard, "I will show you. A jailer should have some knowledge of the cell where she puts her prisoners."

He took me in his arms and, crawling sideways, dragged me through the little stone entrance to the steps and down into the cell below. I saw it for the first time, and the last, that secret room beneath the buttress. Six feet high, four square, it was no larger than a closet, and the stone walls, clammy with years, felt icy to my touch.

There was a little stool in the corner, and by its side an empty trencher with a wooden spoon. Cobwebs and mould were thick upon them, and I thought of the last meal that had been eaten there, a quarter of a century before, by idiot Uncle John. Above the stool hung the rope, near frayed, upon its rusty hinge, and beyond this the opening to the tunnel, a round black hole, about eighteen inches high, through which a man must crawl and wriggle if he wished to reach the farther end.

"I don't understand," I said, shuddering. "It cannot have been thus before. Jonathan would never have used it, had it been so."

"There has been a fall of earth and stones," said Richard, "from the foundations of the house. It blocks the tunnel but for a small space through which we burrowed. I think, when the tunnel was used before, the way was cleared regularly with pick and spade. Now that it has not been used for several years, Nature has claimed it for her own again. My enemies can find me a new name. Henceforth I will be badger, and not fox."

I saw Dick's white face watching me, and what is he telling me, I wondered, with his dark eyes? What is he trying to say?

"Take me back," I said to Richard. "I have to talk to you."

He carried me to the room above, and it seemed to me, as I sat there breathing deep, that the bare boards and smoky ceiling were paradise compared to the black hole from which we had come.

Had I in truth forced Dick to lie there, hour after hour, as a lad four years ago? Was it because of this that his eyes accused me now? God forgive me, but I thought to save his life.

We sat there, by the light of a single candle, Richard and Dick and I, while Matty kept a watch upon the door.

"Jonathan Rashleigh has returned," I said.

Dick threw me a questing glance, but Richard answered nothing.

"The fine is paid," I said. "The County Committee have allowed him to come home. He will be able to live in Cornwall, henceforth, a free man, unencumbered, if he does nothing more to rouse the suspicions of the Parliament."

"That is well for him," said Richard. "I wish him good fortune."

"Jonathan Rashleigh is a man of peace," I said, "who, though he loves his King, loves his home better. He has endured two years of suffering and privation. I think he has earned repose now, and has but one desire, to live amongst his family, in his own house, without anxiety."

"The desire," said Richard, "of almost every man."

"His desire will not be granted," I said, "if it should be proved he was a party to the rising."

Richard glanced at me, then shrugged his shoulders.

"That is something that the Parliament would find difficult to lay upon him," he said. "Rashleigh has been two years in London."

For answer I took the bill from my gown and, spreading it on the floor, put the candlestick upon it. I read it aloud, as my brother-in-law had read it to me that afternoon.

"'Anyone who has harboured at any time, or seeks to harbour in the future, the malignant known as Richard Grenvile, shall, upon discovery, be arrested for high treason, his lands sequestered finally and forever, and his family imprisoned.'"

I waited a moment, and then I said, "They will come in the morning, Jonathan said, to search again."

A blob of grease from the candle fell upon the paper, and the edges curled. Richard placed it to the flame, and the paper caught and burnt, wisping to nothing in his hands, then fell and scattered.

"You see?" said Richard to his son. "Life is like that. A flicker and a spark, and then it's over. No trace remains."

It seemed to me that Dick looked at his father as a dumb dog gazes at his master. Tell me, said his eyes, what you are asking me to do?

"Ah, well," said Richard with a sigh, "there's nothing for it but to run our necks into cold steel. A dreary finish. A scrap upon the road, some dozen men upon us, handcuffs and rope, and then the marching through the streets of London, jeered at by the mob. Are you ready, Dick? Yours was the master hand that brought us to this pass. I trust you profit by it now." He rose to his feet and stretched his arms above his head. "At least," he said, "they keep a sharp axe in Whitehall. I have watched the executioner do justice before now. A little crabbed fellow, he was, last time I saw him, but with biceps in his arms like cannon balls. He only takes a single stroke." He paused a moment, thoughtful. "But," he said slowly, "the blood makes a pretty mess upon the straw."

I saw Dick grip his ankle with his hand, and I turned like a fury on the man I loved.

"Will you be silent?" I said. "Hasn't he suffered enough these eighteen years?"

Richard stared down at me, one eyebrow lifted.

"What?" he said, smiling. "Do you turn against me too?"

For answer I threw him the note I was clutching in my hand. It was smeared by now and scarcely legible.

"There is no need for your fox head to lie upon the block," I said to him. "Read that and change your tune."

He bent low to the candle, and I saw his eyes change in a strange manner as he read, from black malevolence to wonder.

"I've bred a Grenvile after all," he answered softly.

"The *Frances* leaves Fowey on the morning tide," I said. "She is bound for

Flushing and has room for passengers. The master can be trusted. The voyage will be swift."

"And how," asked Richard, "do the passengers go aboard?"

"A boat, in quest of lobsters and not foxes, will call at Pridmouth," I said lightly, "as the vessel sails from harbour. The passengers will be waiting for it. I suggest that they conceal themselves for the remainder of the night till dawn on the cowrie beach, near to the Gribbin Hill, and when the boat creeps to its pots in the early morning light, a signal will bring it to the shore."

"It would seem," said Richard, "that nothing could be more easy."

"You agree, then, to this method of escape? Adieu to your fine heroics of surrender?"

I think he had forgotten them already, for his eyes were travelling beyond my head to plans and schemes in which I played no part.

"From Holland to France," he murmured, "and once there, to see the prince. A new plan of campaign better than this last. A landing, perchance, in Ireland, and from Ireland to Scotland. . . ." His eyes fell back upon the note screwed in his hand. "'My mother christened me Elizabeth,'" he read, "'but I prefer to sign myself your daughter, Bess.'"

He whistled under his breath and tossed the note to Dick. The boy read it slowly, then handed it back in silence to his father.

"Well?" said Richard. "Shall I like your sister?"

"I think," said Dick slowly, "you will like her very well."

"It took courage, did it not," pursued his father, "to leave her home, find herself a ship, and be prepared to land alone in Holland, without friends or fortune?"

"Yes," I said, "it took courage, and something else besides."

"What was that?"

"Faith in the man she is proud to call her father. Confidence that he will not desert her should she prove unworthy."

They stared at each other, Richard and his son, brooding, watchful, as though between them both was some dark secret understanding that I, a woman, could not hope to share. Then Richard put the note into his pocket and turned, hesitating, to the entrance in the buttress.

"Do we go," he said, "the same way by which we came?"

"The house is guarded," I said. "It is your only chance."

"And when the watchdogs come tomorrow," he said, "and seek to sniff our tracks, how will you deal with them?"

"As Jonathan Rashleigh suggested," I replied. "Dry timber in midsummer burns easily and fast. I think the family of Rashleigh will not use their summerhouse again."

"And the entrance here?"

"The stone cannot be forced. Not from this side. See the rope there and the hinge?"

We peered, all three of us, into the murky depths. And Dick, of a sudden reached out to the rope and pulled upon it, and the hinge also. He gave three tugs, and then they broke, useless forevermore.

"There," he said, smiling oddly, "no one will ever force the stone again, once you have closed it from this side."

"One day," said Richard, "a Rashleigh will come and pull the buttress down. What shall we leave them for a legacy?" His eyes wandered to the bones in the corner. "The skeleton of a rat," he said, and with a smile he threw it down the stair.

"Go first, Dick," he said. "I will follow you."

Dick put out his hand to me, and I held it for a moment.

"Be brave," I said. "The journey will be swift. Once safe in Holland, you will make good friends."

He did not answer. He gazed at me with his great dark eyes, then turned to the little stair.

I was alone with Richard. We had had several partings, he and I. Each time I told myself it was the last. Each time we had found each other again.

"How long this time?" I said.

"Two years," he said. "Perhaps eternity."

He took my face in his hands and kissed me long.

"When I come back," he said, "we'll build that house at Stowe. You shall sink your pride at last and become a Grenvile."

I smiled and shook my head.

"Be happy with your daughter," I said to him.

He paused at the entrance to the buttress.

"I tell you one thing," he said. "Once out in Holland, I'll put pen to paper and write the truth about the civil war. My God, I'll flay my fellow generals and show them for the sods they are. Perhaps when I have done so the Prince of Wales will take the hint and make me at last supreme commander of his forces."

"He is more likely," I said, "to degrade you to the ranks."

He climbed through the entrance and knelt upon the stair, where Dick waited for him.

"I'll do your destruction for you," he said. "Watch from your chamber in the eastern wing, and you will see the Rashleigh summerhouse make its last bow to Cornwall, and the Grenviles also."

"Beware the sentry," I said. "He stands below the causeway."

"Do you love me still, Honor?"

"For my sins, Richard."

"Are they many?"

"You know them all."

And as he waited there, his hand upon the stone, I made my last request.

"You know why Dick betrayed you to the enemy?"

"I think so."

"Not from resentment, not from revenge. But because he saw the blood on Gartred's cheek. . . ."

He stared at me thoughtfully, and I whispered, "Forgive him, for my sake, if not for your own."

"I have forgiven him," he said slowly, "but the Grenviles are strangely fashioned. I think you will find that he cannot forgive himself."

I saw them both, father and son, standing upon the stair, with the little cell below, and then Richard pushed the stone flush against the buttress wall, and it was closed forever. I waited there beside it for a moment, then I called for Matty.

"It's all over," I said. "Finished now, and done with."

She came across the room and lifted me in her arms.

"No one," I said to her, "will ever hide in the buttress cell again." I put my hand onto my cheek. It was wet. I did not know I had been crying. "Take me to my room," I said to Matty.

I sat there, by the far window, looking out across the gardens. The moon was high now, not white as last night, but with a yellow rim about it. Clouds had gathered in the evening and were banking curled and dark against the sky. The sentry had left the causeway steps and was leaning against the hatch door of the farm buildings opposite, watching the windows of the house. He did not see me sitting there, in the darkness, with my chin upon my hand.

Hours long, it seemed, I waited there, staring to the east, with Matty crouching at my side, and at length I saw a little spurt of flame rise above the trees in the thistle park. The wind was westerly, blowing the smoke away, and the sentry down below, leaning against the barn, could not see it from where he stood.

Now, I said to myself, it will burn steadily till morning, and when daylight comes they will say poachers have lit a bonfire in the night that spread, unwittingly, catching the summerhouse alight, and someone from the estate here must go, cap in hand, with apologies for carelessness, to Jonathan Rashleigh in his house at Fowey. Now, I said also, two figures wend their way across the cowrie beach and wait there, in the shelter of the cliff. They are safe; they are together. I can go to bed and sleep and so forget them. And yet I went on sitting there, beside my bedroom window, looking out upon the lawns, and I did not see the moon, nor the trees, nor the thin column of smoke rising into the air, but all the while Dick's eyes looking up at me, for the last time, as Richard closed the stone in the buttress wall.

37

AT NINE IN the morning came a line of troopers riding through the park. They dismounted in the courtyard, and the officer in charge, a colonel from the staff of Sir Hardress Waller at Saltash, sent word up to me that I must dress and descend immediately and be ready to accompany him to Fowey. I was dressed already, and when the servants carried me downstairs I saw the troopers he had brought prising the panelling in the long gallery. The watchdogs had arrived. . . .

"This house was sacked once already," I said to the officer, "and it has taken my brother-in-law four years to make what small repairs he could. Must his work begin again?"

"I am sorry," said the officer, "but the Parliament can afford to take no chances with a man like Richard Grenvile."

"You think to find him here?"

"There are a score of houses in Cornwall where he might be hidden," he replied. "Menabilly is but one of them. This being so, I am compelled to search the house, rather too thoroughly for the comfort of those who dwell beneath its roof. I am afraid that Menabilly will not be habitable for some little while. . . . Therefore, I must ask you to come with me to Fowey."

I looked about me, at the place that had been my home now for two years. I had seen it sacked before. I had no wish to witness the sight again.

"I am ready," I said to the officer.

As I was placed in the litter, with Matty at my side, I heard the old sound I well remembered of axes tearing the floor boards, of swords ripping the wood, and another jester, like his predecessor in '44, had already climbed to the belfry and hung crosslegged from the beam, the rope between his hands, swinging the great bell from side to side. It tolled us from the gatehouse, tolled us from the outer court, and this, I thought to myself in premonition, is my farewell to Menabilly. I shall not live here again.

"We will go by the coast," said the officer, looking in the window of my litter. "The highway is choked with troops bound for Helston and Penzance."

"Do you need so many," I asked, "to quell but a little rising?"

"The rising will be over in a day or so," he answered, "but the troops have come to stay. There will be no more insurrections in Cornwall, east or west, from this day forward."

And as he spoke the Menabilly bell swung backwards, forwards, in a mournful knell, echoing his words.

I looked up from the path beneath the causeway, and the summerhouse that had stood there yesterday, a little tower with its long windows, was now charred rubble, a heap of sticks and stones.

"By whose orders," called the officer, "was that fire kindled?"

I heard him take counsel of his men, and they climbed to the causeway to investigate the pile, while Matty and I waited in the litter. In a few moments the officer returned.

"What building stood there?" he asked me. "I can make nothing of it from the mess. But the fire is recent and smoulders still."

"A summerhouse," I said. "My sister, Mrs. Rashleigh, loved it well. We sat there often when she was home . . . This will vex her sorely. Colonel Bennett, when he came here yesterday, gave orders, I believe, for its destruction."

"Colonel Bennett," said the officer, frowning, "had no authority without permission of the sheriff, Sir Thomas Herle."

I shrugged my shoulders.

"He may have had permission, I cannot tell you. But he is a member of the County Committee, and therefore can do much as he pleases."

"The County Committee takes too much upon itself," said the officer. "One day they will have trouble with us in the Army."

He mounted his horse in high ill temper and shouted an order to his men. A civil war within a civil war. Did no faction ever keep the peace amongst themselves? Let the Army and the Parliament quarrel as they pleased, it would help our cause in the end, in the long run. . . . And as I turned and looked for the last time to the smouldering pile upon the causeway and the tall trees in the thistle park I thought of the words that had been whispered two years ago in '46: When the snow melts, when the thaw breaks, when the spring comes . . .

We descended the steep path to Pridmouth. The tide was low, the Cannis Rock showed big and clear, and on the far horizon was the black smudge of a sail. The millstream gurgled out upon the stones and ran sharply to the beach, and from the marsh at the farther end a swan rose suddenly, thrashing his way across the water, and, circling in the air a moment, winged his way out to sea.

We climbed the farther hill, past Coombe Manor, where the Rashleigh cousins lived, and so down to my brother-in-law's town house on Fowey quay. The first thing I looked for was a ship at anchor in the Rashleigh roads, but none was there. The harbour water was still and grey, and no vessels but little fishing craft anchored at Polruan. The people on the quayside watched with curiosity as I was lifted from my litter and taken to the house.

My brother-in-law was waiting for me in the parlour. The room was dark-panelled, like the dining hall at Menabilly, with great windows looking out upon the quay. On the ledge stood a model of a ship. The same ship that his father had built and commissioned forty years before, to sail with Drake against the Armada. She, too, was named the *Frances*.

"I regret," said the officer, "that for a day or so, until the trouble in the West has quietened down, it will be necessary to keep a watch upon this house. I must ask you, sir, and this lady here, to stay within your doors."

"I understand," said Jonathan. "I have been so long accustomed to surveillance that a few more days of it will not hurt me now."

The officer withdrew, and I saw a sentry take up his position outside the window, as his fellow had done the night before at Menabilly.

"I have news of Robin," said my brother-in-law. "He is detained in Plymouth, but I think they can fasten little upon him. When this matter has blown over he will be released, on condition that he take the oath of allegiance to the Parliament, as I was forced to do."

"And then?" I said.

"Why, then he can become his own master and settle down to peace and quietude. I have a little house in Tywardreath that would suit him well, and you too, Honor, if you should wish to share it with him. That is—if you have no other plan."

"No," I said. "No, I have no other plan."

He rose from his chair and walked slowly to the window, looking out upon the quay, white-haired and bent, leaning heavily upon his stick. The sound of gulls came to us as they wheeled and dived above the harbour.

"The *Frances* sailed at five this morning," he said slowly.

I did not answer.

"The fishing lad who went to lift his pots pulled first into Pridmouth for his passenger. He found him waiting on the beach as he expected. He looked tired and wan, the lad said, but otherwise little the worse for his ordeal."

"One passenger?" I said.

"Why, yes, there was but one," said Jonathan, staring at me. "Is anything the matter? You look wisht and strange."

I went on listening to the gulls above the harbour, and now there were children's voices also, laughing and crying, as they played upon the steps of the quay.

"There is nothing the matter," I said. "What else have you to tell me?"

He went to his desk in the far corner and, opening a drawer, took out a length of rope with a rusted hinge upon it.

"As the passenger was about to board the vessel," said my brother-in-law, "he gave the fisher-lad this piece of rope and bade him hand it, on his return, to Mr. Rashleigh. The lad brought it to me as I breakfasted just now. There was a piece of paper wrapped about it, with these words written on the face: 'Tell Honor that the least of the Grenviles chose his own method of escape.'" He handed me the little scrap of paper.

"What does it mean?" he asked. "Do you understand it?"

For a long while I did not answer. I sat there with the paper in my hands, and I saw once more the ashes of the summerhouse blocking forevermore the secret tunnel, and I saw, too, the silent cell, like a dark tomb, in the thick buttress wall.

"Yes, Jonathan," I said, "I understand."

He looked at me a moment and then went to the table and put the rope and hinge back in the drawer.

"Well," he said, "it's over now, praise heaven. The danger and the strain. There is nothing more we can do."

"No," I answered, "nothing more that we can do."

He fetched two glasses from the sideboard and filled them with wine from the decanter. Then he handed one to me. "Drink this," he said kindly, his hand upon my arm. "You have been through great anxiety." He took his glass and lifted it to the ship that had carried his father to the Armada. "To the other *Frances,*" he said, "and to the King's General in the West. May he find sanctuary and happiness in Holland."

I drank the toast in silence, then put the glass back upon the table.

"You have not finished it," he said. "That spells ill luck to him whom we have toasted."

I took the glass again, and this time I held it up against the light so the wine shone clear and red.

"Did you ever hear," I said, "those words that Bevil Grenvile wrote to John Trelawney?"

"What words were those?"

Once more we were assembled, four and twenty hours ago, in the long gallery at Menabilly. Richard at the window, Gartred on the couch, and Dick, in his dark corner, with his eyes upon his father.

"'And for mine own part,'" I quoted slowly, "'I desire to acquire an honest name or an honourable grave. I never loved my life or ease so much as to shun such occasion, which, if I should, I were unworthy of the profession I have held, or to succeed those ancestors of mine who have so many of them, in several ages, sacrificed their lives for their country.'"

I drank my wine then to the dregs and gave the glass to Jonathan.

"Great words," said my brother-in-law, "and the Grenviles were all great men. As long as the name endures we shall be proud of them in Cornwall. But Bevil was the finest of them. He showed great courage at the last."

"The least of them," I said, "showed great courage also."

"Which one was that?" he asked.

"Only a boy," I said, "whose name will never now be written in the great book at Stowe, nor his grave be found in the little churchyard in Kilkhampton."

"You are crying," said Jonathan slowly. "This time has been hard and long for you. There is a bed prepared for you above. Let Matty take you to it. Come now, take heart. The worst is over. The best is yet to be. One day the King will come into his own again; one day your Richard will return."

I looked up at the model of the ship upon the ledge and across the masts to the blue harbour water. The fishing boats were making sail, and the gulls flew above them, crying, white wings against the sky.

"One day," I said, "when the snow melts, when the thaw breaks, when the spring comes . . ."

What Happened to the People in the Story

Sir Richard Grenvile   The King's general never returned to England again. He bought a house in Holland, where he lived with his daughter Elizabeth, until his death in 1659, just a year before the Restoration. He offered his services to the Prince of Wales in exile (afterwards Charles II), but they were not accepted, owing to the ill feeling between himself and Sir Edward Hyde, later Earl of Clarendon. The exact date of his death is uncertain, but he is said to have died in Ghent, lonely and embittered, with these words only for his epitaph: "Sir Richard Grenvile, the King's General in the West."

Sir John Grenvile (Jack), Bernard Grenvile (Bunny)   These two brothers were largely instrumental in bringing about the restoration of Charles II in 1660. They both married, lived happily, and were in high favour with the King. John was created Earl of Bath.

Gartred Denys   She never married again, but, leaving Orley Court, went to live with one of her married daughters, Lady Hampson, at Taplow, where she died at the ripe age of eighty-five.

Jonathan Rashleigh   He suffered further imprisonment for debt, at the hands of the Parliament, but lived to see the Restoration. He died in 1675, a year after his wife Mary.

John Rashleigh   He died in 1651, aged only thirty, in Devon, when on the road home to Menabilly, after a visit to London about his father's business. His widow Joan lived in Fowey until her death in 1668, aged forty-eight. Her son Jonathan succeeded to his grandfather's estate at Menabilly.

Sir Peter Courtney   He deserted his wife, ran hopelessly into debt, married a second time, and died in 1670.

Alice Courtney   Lived the remainder of her life at Menabilly and died there, in 1659, aged forty. There is a tablet to her memory in the church at Tywardreath.

Ambrose Manaton   Little is known about him, except that he was M.P. for Camelford in 1668. His estate, Trecarrel, fell into decay.

Robin and Honor Harris   The brother and sister lived in quiet retirement at Tywardreath, in a house provided for them by Jonathan Rashleigh. Honor died on the seventeenth day of November 1653, and Robin in June 1655. Thus they never lived to see the Restoration. The tablet to their memory in the church runs thus:

"In memory of Robert Harris, sometime Major-General of His Majesty's forces before Plymouth, who was buried here under the 29th day of June 1655. And of Honor Harris his sister, who was likewise here under-neath buried, the 17th day of November, in the year of our Lord 1653.

Loyall and stout; thy Crime this—this thy praise,

Thou'rt here with Honour laid—though without Bayes."

The Glass Blowers

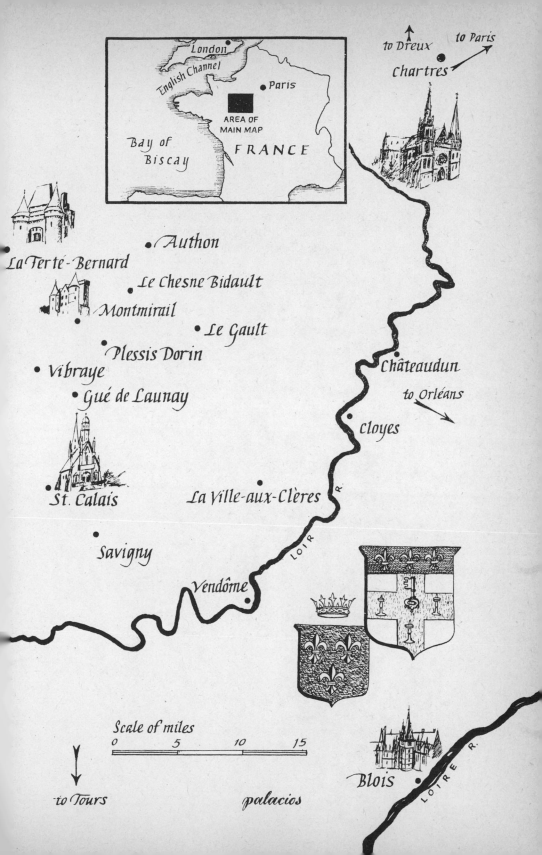

to Dreux   to Paris

Chartres

London

English Channel

Paris

AREA OF
MAIN MAP

FRANCE

Bay of
Biscay

Authon

La Ferté-Bernard

Le Chesne Bidault

Montmirail

Le Gault

Plessis Dorin

Vibraye

Châteaudun

Gué de Launay

to Orléans

Cloyes

St. Calais

La Ville-aux-Clères

LOIR R.

Savigny

Vendôme

Scale of miles

0   5   10   15

to Tours

palacios

Blois

LOIRE R.

To my forebears, the master glass-blowers of
la Brûlonnerie, Chérigny, la Pierre and
le Chesne-Bidault.

Prologue

ONE DAY IN the June of 1844 Madame Sophie Duval, née Busson, eighty years of age and mother of the mayor of Vibraye, a small commune in the département of Sarthe, rose from her chair in the salon of her property at le Gué de Launay, chose her favourite walking-stick from a stand in the hall, and calling to her dog made her way, as was her custom at this hour of the afternoon every Tuesday, down the short approach drive to the entrance gate.

She walked briskly, with the quick step of one who did not suffer, or perhaps refused to suffer, any of the inconveniences of old age; and her bright blue eyes—the noticeable feature of her otherwise unremarkable face—looked keenly to right and left, pin-pointing signs of negligence on the part of the gardener: the gravel under her feet not raked this morning as it should have been, the careless staking of a lily, the grass verges of the formal flower-bed raggedly clipped.

These matters would be corrected at their proper time, either by her son the mayor or by herself; for although Pierre-François had been mayor of Vibraye for some fourteen years, and was approaching his forty-seventh birthday, he knew very well that the house and grounds at le Gué de Launay were his mother's property, that in all matters referring to their upkeep and maintenance she must be the final judge and arbitrator. This small estate which Madame Duval and her husband had settled upon for their retirement at the turn of the century was no great domain, a few acres of ground only, and the house was of medium size; but it was their own, bought and paid for by themselves, so giving them both the status of land-owners and making them the proud equal of any outdated seigneur who still boasted that he held a property by right of birth.

Madame Duval adjusted the widow's cap upon her crown of white hair, set in pin-curls high on her forehead. As she arrived at the end of the approach drive she heard the sound she was expecting, the click of the fastened iron gate and the rasp of the hinge as it swung open, while the gardener—later to be reprimanded—who also served as odd-man, groom, messenger, came towards her with the mail he had fetched from Vibraye.

Her son the mayor usually brought the letters back with him of an evening, if there were any to bring, but once a week, every Tuesday, there came the very special letter written to Madame Duval from her married daughter in Paris, Madame Rosiau; and since this was the most precious moment of her week the old lady could not bear to wait for it. She had given special orders to the gardener for many months now, ever since the Rosiaus had left Mamers for Paris, to go himself on foot the few kilometres to Vibraye, and enquire for the letters addressed to le Gué de Launay, and give them into her hands.

This he now did, doffing his hat, and placing uppermost in her hands the expected letter, with his customary remark, "Now Madame is content". "Thank you, Joseph," she replied. "Find your way to the kitchen and see if there is some coffee for you"—as though the gardener, who had worked for her at le Gué de Launay for thirty years, was looking for the kitchen for the first time. She waited until he was out of sight before she followed him, for it was part of the ritual to be preceded by the servant and walk herself, with measured step, at a certain distance in the rear, the unopened envelope clutched tightly to her, the dog at her heels; and then up the steps and into the house, and to the salon, where she would seat herself once more in her chair by the window, and give herself up to the long-awaited pleasure of the weekly letter.

The tie between mother and daughter was close, as it had been once, so many years ago, between Sophie Duval and her own mother Magdaleine. Sons, even if they lived under one's roof, had their own preoccupations, their business, their wives, political interests; but a daughter, even if she took to herself a husband as Zoë had done, and a very able doctor at that, remained always part of the mother, a nestling, intimate and confiding, a sharer of ills and joys, using the same family expressions long forgotten by the sons. The pains of the daughter were the pains the mother herself knew, or had known: the trifling differences between husband and wife that occurred from time to time had all been endured by Madame Duval in days gone by, along with housekeeping troubles, high prices in the market, sudden illnesses, the dismissal of a servant, the numerous trifles that went with a woman's day.

This letter was the answer to the one she had written over a week ago on her daughter's birthday. Zoë had been fifty-one on the 27th of May. It seemed scarcely credible. Over half a century had passed since she had held that scrap of humanity in her arms—her third child, and the first to survive infancy—and how well she remembered that summer's day too, with the window wide open to the orchard, the pungent smoke from the glass foundry chimney filling the languid air, and the sound and clatter of the workmen as they crossed from the furnace-house to the yard drowning her own cries in labour.

What a moment to bring a child into the world, that summer of '93, the first year of the Republic; with the Vendée in revolt, the country at war, the traitorous Girondins endeavouring to bring down the Convention, the patriot Marat to be assassinated by an hysterical girl, and the unhappy ex-Queen Marie Antoinette confined in the Temple and later guillotined for all the misery she had brought upon France.

So many bitter and exciting days. Such exultation, triumph, and despair. All part of history now, forgotten by most people, over-shadowed by the achievements of the Emperor and his era. Only remembered by herself when she learnt of the death of a contemporary, and so was reminded suddenly, as though it were yesterday, that this same contemporary just laid to rest in the cemetery at Vibraye had been a member of the National Guard under her brother Michel, that the pair of them, with her husband François, had led the foundry workmen on the march in November '90 to sack the château of Charbonnières.

It did not do to speak of these things in front of her son the mayor. After all, he was a loyal subject of King Louis-Philippe, and hardly liked to be reminded of the part his father and uncle had played in the troubled days of the Revolution before he was born; though heaven knows it tempted her sometimes to do so, when he showed himself more than usually pompous and full of bourgeois principle.

Madame Duval opened her letter and straightened out the closely-written pages, crossed and re-crossed in her daughter's cramped hand. Thank God she did not need spectacles, despite her eighty years. "My very dear Maman. . . ."

First, Zoë's grateful thanks for the birthday gift (a patchwork quilt, worked at home during the winter and spring), followed by the usual small items of family news, her husband the doctor producing a paper on asthma to be read before the medical authorities, her daughter Clementine making excellent progress with piano lessons under a good master, and then—the handwriting becoming more careless because of excitement—the main content of the letter, reserved as a final surprise.

"We spent Sunday evening with near neighbours of ours in the Faubourg St. Germain," she wrote, "and as usual there was quite a gathering of doctors and scientists, and much interesting conversation. We were both impressed by the fluent talk and engaging manners of a stranger to our particular circle, an inventor who has apparently patented a portable lamp and expects to make his fortune from it. We were introduced, and imagine my surprise when we learnt that his name was Louis-Mathurin Busson, that he had been born and brought up in England of émigré parents, had come to Paris at some period after the Restoration of the monarchy when he was quite a young man, in company with his mother, now dead, and his surviving brother and sister, and had since lived—chiefly by his wits, I gathered, and his powers as an inventor—between the two countries, sometimes in London, sometimes in Paris, with business in both cities. He is married to an Englishwoman, has a young family, a house in the rue de la Pompe, and a laboratory in the Faubourg Poissonnière. Now, all this might have passed me by but for the singularity of the two names Busson and Mathurin, and the mention of émigré parents. I was careful not to commit myself immediately, or acquaint him of the fact that your maiden name was Busson and Mathurin a family first name, but when I casually enquired if his father, the émigré, had followed any particular profession or had been a man of leisure he answered me at once, and with great pride, 'Oh yes, indeed. He was a gentleman glass-blower, and owned several foundries before the Revolution. At one time he was first engraver in crystal at St. Cloud, the royal foundry patronised by the Queen herself. Naturally, at the outbreak of the Revolution he followed the example of the clergy and the aristocracy and emigrated to England with his young bride, my mother, and suffered much penury in consequence. His full name was Robert-Mathurin Busson du Maurier, and he died tragically and suddenly in 1802, after the Peace of Amiens, on returning to France in the hopes of restoring the family fortunes. My poor mother, left behind in England with her young children, little guessed, when she said good-bye to him, that it was for the last time. I was five years old then, and have no recollection of him, but my mother brought us up to understand that he was a man of tremendous principle and integrity, and of course a Royalist to his finger-tips.'

"Maman . . . I nodded my head, and made some remark or other, while I tried to collect my thoughts. I am right, am I not? This man, this inventor, must be my cousin, son of your beloved brother my uncle Robert. But what is all this talk of his being called du Maurier, leaving a family in England and dying in 1802, when you and I know perfectly well that he died in 1811, and was a widower anyway, with his son Jacques a corporal in the Grande Armée? Why, I was eighteen years old when uncle Robert died, a schoolmaster in Tours, yet here is this inventor, Monsieur Busson, who must be his son, giving a very different account of his father from the one you gave us, and apparently in complete ignorance of his father's true end, or of your existence.

"I asked if he had relatives. He said he believed not. They had all been guillotined during the Terror, and the château Maurier and the glass-foundries destroyed. He had made no enquiries. It was better not. What was past was past. Then my hostess interrupted us, and we were parted. I did not speak to him again. But I have discovered his address—31, rue de la Pompe, in Passy—should you wish me to get in touch with him. Maman, what would you have me do?" ·

Madame Duval laid her daughter's letter aside, and stared out of the window. So . . . It had happened at last. It had taken more than thirty years, but it had happened. What Robert had believed would never be.

"Those children will be brought up in England, and make their life there," he had told her. "What should bring them to France, especially if they believe their father dead? No, that phase of my life, like all the others, is over and done with."

Madame Duval picked up the letter and read it through once again. Two courses were open to her. The first, to write to her daughter Zoë and tell her to make no further attempt to get in touch with the man who had declared himself to be Louis-Mathurin Busson. The second, to go herself to Paris immediately, to call upon Monsieur Busson at 31, rue de la Pompe and acknowledge their relationship, and so see at last, before she died, her brother's child.

The first course she dismissed almost as soon as it entered her head. By following it she would deny all family feeling, and so go against everything she held most dear. The second course must be embarked upon forthwith, or as soon as it could be put into practice.

That evening, when her son the mayor returned from Vibraye, Madame Duval told him her news, and it was arranged that she should travel to Paris within the week to stay with her daughter in the Faubourg St. Germain. All attempts on the part of her son to dissuade her were useless. She remained firm. "If this man is an imposter I shall know it directly I set eyes on him," she said. "If not, then I shall have done my duty."

The night before she left for Paris, she went to the cabinet in the corner of the salon, unlocked it with the key she wore in a locket round her neck, and took out a leather case. This case she packed carefully amongst the few clothes she took with her.

It was about four o'clock on the Sunday of the following week when Madame Duval and her daughter Madame Rosiau called at 31, rue de la Pompe, in Passy. The house was well placed, on the corner of the rue de la Pompe and the rue de la Tour, opposite a boys' school, with a garden behind and a long avenue leading directly to the Bois de Boulogne.

A cheerful femme de ménage opened the door, took their cards, and showed the visitors into a pleasant room facing the garden, from where they could hear the cries of children at play. In a moment or two a figure stepped through the long windows giving on to the garden, and Madame Rosiau, with a brief word of explanation and apology for the intrusion, introduced her mother to the inventor.

One look was enough. The blue eyes, the light hair, the tilt of the head, the quick courteous smile, showing an instant wish to please combined with a desire to turn the occasion to his own advantage if it were possible here was Robert in the flesh as she remembered him, forty, fifty, sixty years ago.

Madame Duval took his extended hand in both of hers and held it, her eyes, the mirror of his own, dwelling at length upon his face. "Forgive me," she said, "but I have every reason to believe that you are my nephew, and the son of my eldest brother Robert-Mathurin."

"Your nephew?" He looked from one to the other in astonishment. "I'm afraid I don't understand. I met Madame . . . Madame Rosiau for the first time nearly two weeks ago. I had not the pleasure of her acquaintance before, and . . . "

"Yes, yes," interrupted Madame Duval. "I know just how you met, but she was too overwhelmed when she learnt your name, and your history, to tell you that her mother's maiden name was Busson, that her uncle was Robert-Mathurin Busson, a master glass-engraver who emigrated . . . I am, in short, her mother, and your aunt Sophie, and have been waiting for this moment for nearly half a century."

They led her to a chair and made her sit down, and she wiped the tears from her eyes—so foolish, she told him, to break down, and how Robert would have mocked her. In a few minutes she was composed, and sufficiently mistress of herself to seize upon the fact that, although her nephew expressed himself delighted to find that he had relatives, he was at the same time a trifle disconcerted that his aunt and his cousin were not great ladies, but ordinary provincial folk with no claim to vast estates or ruined châteaux.

"But the name Busson," he insisted. "I was brought up to understand that we were descended from an aristocratic Breton family going back to the fourteenth century, that my father became a gentleman glass-engraver merely for his own amusement, that our motto—Abret ag Aroag, First and Foremost—belonged to the old knights of Brittany. Do you mean to tell me none of this is true?"

Madame Duval considered her nephew with a sceptical eye. "Your father Robert was first and foremost the most incorrigible farceur I have ever known," she said drily, "and if he told these tales in England no doubt it suited his purpose at the time."

"But the château Maurier," protested the inventor, "the château Maurier that was burnt to the ground by the peasants during the Revolution?"

"A farmhouse," replied his aunt, "unchanged since your father was born there in 1749. We have cousins there still."

Her nephew stared at her aghast. "There must be some misunderstanding," he said. "My mother can have known nothing of this. Unless . . . " He broke off, at a loss how to continue, and she understood from his expression that her blunt words had shattered an illusion held since childhood, that his self-confidence was shaken, that he might now even doubt himself and his own powers for the future.

"Tell me one thing," she asked. "Was she a good mother to you?"

"Oh, yes," he replied, "the best in the world. And she had a hard struggle, I can tell you, with my father gone. But she had wonderful friends amongst the French colony. A fund was started to help us. We received the best of educations in one of the schools founded by the Abbé Carron, along with the children of other émigrés, the de Polignacs, the de Labourdomains, etc." A note of pride crept into his voice, and he did not notice his aunt flinch as he pronounced names reviled and detested by herself and her brothers over fifty years before.

"My sister," he continued, "is companion to the daughter of the Duke of Palmella in Lisbon. My brother James is in business in Hamburg. I myself, with the help of influential friends, intend placing upon the markets of the world a lamp of my own invention. Indeed, we none of us have anything to be ashamed of, we have great hopes . . . " Once again he broke off in mid-sentence. There was a speculative look in his eye strangely reminiscent of his father. This aunt from the provinces was, alas, no aristocrat, but had she money tucked away in a stocking?

Madame Duval could read his thoughts as once she had read her brother Robert's. "You are an optimist, like your father," she told him. "So much the better. It makes life comparatively easy."

He smiled. The look of speculation vanished. The charm returned, Robert's charm, winning, endearing, that could never be withstood.

"Tell me about him," he said. "I must know everything. From the very beginning. Even if he was born in a farmhouse, as you say, and not a château. And far from being a nobleman was in reality . . . "

"An adventurer?" she finished for him.

At that moment her nephew's wife came in from the garden, followed by the three children. The femme de ménage brought in tea. Conversation became general. Madame Rosiau, who felt that her mother had already been far too indiscreet, pressed the wife of her newly found cousin to comparisons between life in London and in Paris. The inventor produced a model of his portable lamp that was to make all their fortunes. Madame Duval remained silent, watching each of the chidren in turn for a family likeness. Yes, the little girl Isobel, pert and quick, was something like her own young sister Edmé at the same age. The second boy, Eugène, or Gyggy, reminded her of nobody. But the eldest, George, nicknamed Kicky, a lad of ten, was her brother Pierre in miniature, the same dreamy reflective eyes, the same way of standing with his feet crossed, his hands in his pockets.

"And you, Kicky," she said, "what do you intend to do when you grow up?"

"My father hopes I'll become a chemist," he said, "but I doubt if I'd pass the exams. I like to draw best of all."

"Show me your drawings," she whispered.

He ran out of the room, pleased at her interest, and returned in a moment with a portfolio full of sketches. She examined them carefully, one by one.

"You have talent," she said. "One day you'll put it to good purpose. It's in your blood."

Madame Duval then turned to her nephew the inventor, interrupting the flow of conversation. "I wish to make a gift to your son George," she announced. "It must be his, by right of inheritance." She felt in the lining pocket of her voluminous cape, and drew forth a package which she proceeded to unwrap. The paper dropped to the floor.

From a leather case she produced a crystal tumbler, engraved with the fleur-de-lys, and with the interlaced letters L.R.XV.

"This glass was made in the foundry of la Pierre, Coudrecieux," she said, "engraved by my father, Mathurin Busson, on the occasion of the visit of King Louis XV. It has had a chequered history, but has been in my safekeeping for many years. My father used to say that as long as it remained unbroken, treasured in the family, the creative talent of the Bussons would continue, in some form or other, through the succeeding generations."

Silently, her newly found nephew and his wife and children gazed upon the glass. Then Madame Duval replaced it in the leather case. "There," she said to the boy George, "remain true to your talent, and the glass will bring you luck. Abuse your talent, or neglect it, as my brother did, and the luck will run out of the glass."

She gave him the leather case and smiled, then turned to her nephew the inventor. "I shall return home to le Gué de Launay tomorrow," she told him. "Perhaps we shall not see each other again. I will write to you, though, and tell you, as best as I can, the story of your family. A glass-blower, remember, breathes life into a vessel, giving it shape and form and sometimes beauty; but he can, with that same breath, shatter and destroy it. If what I write displeases you, it will not matter. Throw my letters in the fire unread, and keep your illusions. For myself, I have always preferred to know the truth."

Madame Duval nodded to her daughter Madame Rosiau and, rising from her chair, embraced her nephew and her nephew's children.

The next day she left Paris and returned home. She said little about her visit to her son the mayor of Vibraye, beyond remarking that looking upon her nephew and his children for the first and perhaps the last time had revived old memories. During the weeks that followed, instead of giving orders at le Gué de Launay and inspecting her fruit-trees, vegetables and flowers, she spent all her time at her bureau in the salon, covering sheet after sheet of writing-paper in her formal, upright hand.

PART ONE

La Reyne d'Hongrie

1

"IF YOU MARRY into glass," Pierre Labbé warned my mother, his daughter Magdaleine, in 1747, "you will say good-bye to everything familiar, and enter a closed world."

She was twenty-two years old, and her prospective bridegroom, Mathurin Busson, master glass-maker from the neighbouring village of Chenu, was a childhood sweetheart, four years older than herself. They had never had eyes for anyone but each other from the day they met, and my father, the son of a merchant in glass, orphaned at an early age, had been apprenticed with his brother Michel to the glass-house known as la Brûlonnerie, in the Vendôme, between Busloup and la Ville-aux-Clercs. Both brothers showed great promise, and my father Mathurin had risen rapidly to the rank of master glass-maker, working directly under Robert Brossard the proprietor, who was a member of one of the four great glass-making families in France.

"I have no doubt Mathurin Busson will succeed in everything he undertakes," continued Pierre Labbé, who was himself bailiff at St. Christophe and law-officer to the district, and a man of some importance. "He is steady, hard-working, and a very fine craftsman; but it is breaking with tradition for a glass-maker to marry outside his own community. As his bride you will find it hard to adapt yourself to their way of life."

He knew what he was talking about. So did she. She was not afraid. The glass world was unique, a law unto itself. It had its own rules and customs, and a separate language too, handed down not only from father to son but from master to apprentice, instituted heaven knows how many centuries ago wherever the glass-makers settled—in Normandy, in Lorraine, by the Loire—but always, naturally, by forests, for wood was the glass-foundry's food, the mainstay of its existence.

The laws, customs, and privileges of the glass-makers were more strictly observed than the feudal rights of the aristocracy; they had more justice, too, and they made more sense. Theirs was indeed a closed community, with every man, woman and child knowing his place within the walls, from the director himself, who worked beside his men, sharing their labour, wearing the same apparel, yet looked upon by all as lord and master, to the little child of six or seven who fetched and carried, taking his shift with his elders, seizing his chance to approach the foundry fire.

"What I do," said Magdaleine Labbé, my mother, "I do with my eyes open, without any vain ideas of an easy life, or believing I can sit back and be waited upon. Mathurin has already disabused me about that."

Nevertheless, as she stood beside her bridegroom on that 18th day of September in the year 1747, in the church of her native village of St. Christophe in the Touraine, and looked from her own relatives—her wealthy uncle Georget, her lawyer uncle Thiezie, her own father in his bailiff's dress—to the opposite side of the nave, where her bridegroom's relatives were assembled, and a number of his workmen and their wives, all glass-makers, all watching her with suspicion, almost with hostility, she

203

certainly experienced—so she told us children years afterwards—a brief moment of doubt; she refused to call it fear.

"I felt," she said, "as a white man must feel when he is surrounded for the first time by American Indians, and knows that by sundown he must enter their encampment, never to return."

The workmen from the glass-house were certainly not in war-paint, but their uniform of black coat and breeches and black flat hat, worn on saints' days and holidays, set them apart from my mother's relatives, giving them the appearance of a religious sect.

Nor did they mix with the rest of the company afterwards at the wedding breakfast, which, because Pierre Labbé was a man of standing in St. Christophe, was necessarily a big event, with almost everyone in the neighbourhood present. They stood aside in a group of their own, too proud, perhaps, to exchange the usual quips and compliments with the rest of the guests, laughing and joking amongst themselves and making a great deal of noise about it too.

The only one to be perfectly at ease was Monsieur Brossard, my father's employer, but then, he was not only a seigneur by birth but the proprietor of three or four other glass-houses besides la Brûlonnerie, and it was a great condescension on his part to be present at the wedding. He did so because of the regard he had for my father: he had already promised him, within the year, the directorship of la Brûlonnerie.

The wedding was held at midday, so that the happy pair and their cortège could reach their destination the other side of Vendôme before midnight. When the last toast had been given my mother had to take off her finery and put on a travelling dress, then mount one of the foundry waggons with the rest of them, and so drive away to her new home in the forest of Fréteval. Monsieur Brossard did not accompany them. He was bound in the opposite direction. My father Mathurin and my mother Magdaleine, with his sister Françoise and her husband Louis Démére—a master glass-maker like himself—seated themselves in the front of the waggon beside the driver, and behind them, in order of precedence, came the various craftsmen with their wives: the souffleurs, or blowers, the melters, and the flux-burners. The stokers, along with the driers, came in the second waggon, and a crowd of apprentices filled the third, with my father's brother Michel in charge.

During the first half of the journey, my mother Magdaleine said, she listened to the singing, for all glass-makers are musicians after their own fashion, and play some instrument or other, and have the special songs of their trade. When they ceased singing they began to discuss the plans for the day ahead, and the week's work. None of it as yet made sense to her, the newcomer, and when darkness fell she was so worn out with excitement and expectation, and the motion of the waggon, that she fell asleep on her bridegroom's shoulder, and did not wake up until they were past Vendôme and entering the forest of Fréteval.

She awoke suddenly, for the waggon had left the road, and she was aware of an immense darkness all about her, seemingly impenetrable. Even the stars were lost, for the interlaced branches of the forest trees made a vault where the sky had been. The silence was as deep as the darkness. The waggon wheels made no sound on the muddied track. As they lurched on into even greater depths of forest she was reminded once more of her fancy of an approach to an Indian encampment.

Then of a sudden she saw the fires of the charcoal-burners, and smelt, for the first time, the bitter-sweet smell of blackened wood and ashes that would remain with her throughout the whole of her married life—the smell that all of us were to know as children and inhale with our first breath, that would become synonymous with our very existence.

The silence ceased. Figures came out of the forest clearing and ran towards the waggons. There was sudden shouting, sudden laughter. "Then indeed," my mother Magdaleine said, "I thought I was amongst the Indians, for the charcoal-burners, their faces blackened with the smoke, their long hair falling about their shoulders, had their huts as outposts to the glass-house itself, and they were the first to greet me, the bride. What I took to be an assault upon all of us in the waggon was in reality their welcome."

This astonished us as children, for we grew up beside the charcoal-burners, called them by their Christian names, watched them at work; visited them in their log huts when they were ill; but to my mother, the bailiff's daughter from St. Christophe, gently nurtured, educated and well-spoken, the rude shouts of these wild men of the woods at midnight must have sounded like devils in hell.

They had to look at her, of course, by the light of their flaring torches, and then with a friendly laugh and a wave of his hand my father Mathurin bade them goodnight, and the waggon plunged on again out of the clearing into the forest, and along the remainder of the track to the glass-house itself. La Brûlonnerie, in those days, consisted of the big furnace house itself, surrounded by the work-buildings, the potting rooms, store-rooms and drying-rooms, and behind these the living quarters of the workmen; while further across the big yard were the small houses for the masters. The first thought to strike my mother was that the furnace chimney was on fire. Tongues of flame shot into the air, with sparks flying in all directions; a belching volcano could not be more malevolent.

"We have arrived just in time," she said abruptly.

"In time for what?" asked my father.

"To put out the fire," she said, pointing to the chimney. A moment later she realised her mistake, and could have bitten out her tongue for making a fool of herself before she had even set foot within the glass-house precincts. Of course her remark was repeated, amidst laughter to everyone else within the waggon, and so back to the other waggons. Her arrival, instead of being a dignified affair with the workmen standing aside to let her pass, became a triumphant procession into the furnace-house itself, hemmed about with grinning faces, so that she could see for herself the "fire" upon which the livelihood of them all depended.

"There I stood," she told us, "on the threshold of the great vaulted space, some ninety feet long, with the two furnaces in the centre, enclosed, of course, so that I could not see the fire. It was the rest period, between midnight and one-thirty, and some of the workmen were sleeping, wherever they could find space upon the floor, and as close to the furnaces as possible, little children amongst them, while the rest were drinking great jugfuls of strong black coffee brewed by the women, and the stokers, naked to the waist, stood ready to feed the two fires before the next shift. I thought I had entered an inferno, and that the curled-up bodies of the children were sacrifices, to be shovelled into the pots and melted. The men stopped drinking their coffee and stared at me, and the women too, and they all waited to see what I would do."

"And what did you do?" we asked, for this was a favourite story, one which we never tired of hearing.

"There was only one thing I could do," she told us. "I took off my travelling-cloak and walked over to the women, and asked them if I could help with the coffee. They were so surprised at my boldness that they handed a jug to me without a word. It was not much of a start to a bridal night, perhaps, but nobody afterwards ever called me too delicate for work, or mocked at me for being a bailiff's daughter."

I do not think they would have mocked my mother whatever she had done. She had a look in her eye, our father told us, even in those days, when she was twenty-two, that would silence anyone who thought to take a liberty. She was immensely tall for a woman, five foot ten or thereabouts, with square shoulders, dwarfing the other foundry women; she even made my father, who was of medium height, look small. She dressed her blonde hair high, which added to her stature, and she kept this style throughout her life; I believe it was her secret vanity.

"Such was my introduction to glass," she told us. "The next morning another shift began, and I watched my bridegroom dress in his working blouse and go off to the furnace-house, leaving me to get accustomed to the smell of the wood-smoke, with worksheds all about me, and nothing outside the foundry fence but forest for ever and ever."

When her sister-in-law Françoise Déméré came to the house at mid-morning to help her unpack she found everything put away and the linen sorted, and my mother Magdaleine gone across to the workshops to talk to the flux-burner, the craftsman who prepared the potash. She wanted to see how the ash was sieved and mixed with the lime, and then placed in the cauldron to boil, before being passed on to the melter.

My aunt Déméré was shocked. Her husband, my uncle Déméré, was one of the most important men in the foundry. He was a master-melter, that is to say he prepared the mixture for the pots, and saw to it that the pots were filled with the right amount for the furnaces before the day's melt, and never, since they had been married, had my aunt Déméré watched the potash being prepared by the flux-burner.

"The first duty of a master's wife is to have food ready for her husband between shifts," she told my mother, "and then to attend to any women or children directly employed by her husband who may be sick. The work in the furnace-house, or outside it, is nothing to do with us."

My mother Magdeleine was silent for a moment. She had sense enough not to argue with someone well versed in glass-house law. "Mathurin's dinner will be ready for him when he comes in," she said at last, "and if I broke one of the rules I'm sorry for it."

"It is not a question of rule," replied my aunt Déméré, "but a matter of principle."

During the next few days my mother remained within doors, where she could not cause gossip, but later in the week curiosity became too strong for her, and she made another break with tradition. She went down to the stamping mill, as they called it, where the blocks of quartz were ground to powder which, after sieving, formed the core of the glass. Before the quartz was ground it had to be sorted and freed from all impurities, and this was one of the tasks of the women, who knelt by the stream, sorting the quartz on large flat boards. My mother Magdaleine went straight to the woman who seemed to be in charge, introduced herself, and asked if she might take her place in the line and learn how the work was done.

They must have been too overcome by her manner and her appearance to say much, but they let her sort the quartz side by side with them until midday, when the ringer-boy sounded the great bell, and those amongst the women who expected their husbands back from morning shift went home. By this time, of course, word had gone round what had happened, for news spreads fast in a glass-house, and when my father came back to the house, and changed from his working-blouse into his Sunday coat and breeches, she sensed that something was wrong. He looked grave too.

"I have to see Monsieur Brossard," he told her, "on account of your behaviour this morning. It seems that he has heard all about it, and demands an explanation."

Here was an issue, my mother Magdaleine told us, upon which the whole of their future might depend, and it had to come up during their first week of married life.

"Did I do anything wrong by working with the women?" she asked him.

"No," he answered, "but a master's wife is on a different footing from the workmen's wives. She is not expected to do manual work, and only loses face by doing so."

Once again my mother did not argue the point. But she too changed her dress, and when my father left the house to see Monsieur Brossard she went with him.

Monsieur Brossard received them in the entrance lodge, which he reserved for his own use when he visited the glass-house. He never spent more than a few days in any place, and was proceeding to another of his foundries later that evening. His manner was more distant than it had been at the wedding, my mother said, when he had given the toast to the bride and kissed her cheek. Now he was the proprietor of la Brûlonnerie, and my father Mathurin one of the master glass-makers in his employ.

"You know why I have sent for you, Monsieur Busson," he said. He had called my father Mathurin at the wedding, but in the glass-house precincts formality between proprietor and master was strictly observed.

"Yes, Monsieur Brossard," replied my father, "and I come to apologise for what was observed down by the stamping mill this morning. My wife let her curiosity overcome her sense of propriety, and what is due to my position. As you know, she has only lived amongst us for a week."

Monsieur Brossard nodded, and turned to my mother.

"You will soon learn our ways," he said, "and come to understand our traditions. If you are in any quandary as to procedure, and your husband is at work, you have only to ask your sister-in-law Madame Démeré, who is well acquainted with every facet of glass-house life."

He rose to his feet, the interview at an end. He was a small man, with great presence and dignity, but he had to look up at my mother, who overtopped him by a good four inches.

"Am I permitted to speak?" she enquired.

Monsieur Brossard bowed. "Naturally, Madame Busson," he replied.

"I'm a bailiff's daughter, as you know," she said. "I have grown up with some experience of the law. I used to help my father sort his papers and make out his assessments, before cases were brought to trial."

Monsieur Brossard bowed again. "I have no doubt you were very helpful to him," he remarked.

"I was," answered my mother, "and I want to be helpful to my husband, too. You have promised him a directorship before long, either here or in a glass-house of his own. When this happens, and he is obliged to be absent from time to time I want to be able to direct the glass-house myself. I cannot do that without first knowing how all the work is done. This morning I took my first lesson in sorting the quartz."

Monsieur Brossard stared at her. So did my father. She did not give them time to answer, but continued her speech.

"Mathurin, as you know, is a designer," she went on. "His head is full of his inventions. Even now he is not thinking about me, but about some new design. When he has a glass-house of his own he will be too busy to occupy himself with day-to-day business. I intend to do that for him."

Monsieur Brossard was nonplussed. None of his master glass-makers, until now, had taken unto themselves so formidable a wife.

"Madame Busson," he said, "all this is very praiseworthy, but you forget your first duty, which is that of rearing a family."

"I have not forgotten," she replied. "A large family will be only part of my work. Thank God I am strong. Child-bearing will not worry me. I will stop working with the women if you consider that it makes Mathurin lose face, but, if I consent to this, perhaps you will do something for me in return. I should like to know how to keep the glass-house records, and how to deal with the merchant buyers. This seems to me the most important business of all."

My mother achieved her purpose. Whether it was her looks that did it, or her tenacity of will, she never disclosed, and I don't think my father knew either; but within the month she had surrounded herself with books and ledgers, and Monsieur Brossard himself gave orders to the store-keeper to instruct her in all matters relating to finance. Perhaps he thought it the best way of keeping her within doors, and from distracting the attention of the workmen and their wives. It did not prevent her, though, from rising at midnight, with the rest of the women, when my father was on night-shift, and crossing to the furnace-house to brew coffee. This was part of the tradition she believed in following, and I doubt if she missed a night-shift during the whole of her married life. Whether there was any small jealousy or not on the part of the other craftsmen's wives because of my mother's superior intelligence, and the favour she had found with Monsieur Brossard, I cannot say, but I hardly think so. None of them, except my aunt Démeré, could read or write, and they certainly did not know how to keep figures in a ledger.

However it may have been with the women, it was during the first year at la Brûlonnerie, in the forest of Fréteval, that she came by the nickname which stayed with her to the end of her days and by which she was known, not only there and in later houses, but throughout the whole of the glass-trade, wherever my father did business.

It was his particular ambition, in these early days as a young man, to design for the Paris market, and for the American continent too, scientific instruments to be used in chemistry and astronomy—for it was the start of an age when new ideas were spreading fast. Because he was ahead of his time he succeeded in inventing, during this period at la Brûlonnerie, certain pieces of an entirely new form. These instruments are now made in bulk and used by doctors and chemists all over France, while my father's name is forgotten, but a hundred years ago the "instruments de chimie" designed at la Brûlonnerie were sought after by all the apothecaries in Paris.

The demand spread to the perfumery trade. The great ladies at Court wished for bottles and flasks of unusual designs to place on their dressing-tables—the more extravagant the better, for this was the moment when the Pompadour had such sway over the King, and all luxury goods were very much in fashion. Monsieur Brossard, bombarded on all sides by tradesmen and merchants eager to make their fortune, implored my father to forget for a moment his scientific instruments, and design a flask to please the highest in the land.

It began as a jest on my father's part. He told my mother to stand up before him while he drew the outline of her figure. First the head, then the square shoulders—so singular in a woman—then the slim hips, the long straight body. He compared his drawing with the last apothecary's bottle he had designed; they were almost identical. "You know what it is," he said to my mother. "I thought I was working to a mathematical formula, when all the while I've been drawing my inspiration from you."

He put on his blouse and went over to the furnace-house to see about his moulds. No one to this day will know whether it was the apothecary's bottle he shaped into a new form or my mother's body—he said it was the latter—but the flask he designed for the perfumeries of Paris delighted the merchants, and the buyers too. They filled the flask with eau-de-toilette, calling it the perfume of "la Reyne d'hongrie" after Elizabeth of Hungary, who had remained beautiful until she was past seventy, and my father laughed so much that he went and told everybody in the glass-house. My mother was very much annoyed. Nevertheless, she became la Reyne d'hongrie from that moment, and was affectionately known as this throughout the glass-trade until the Revolution, when she became la citoyenne Busson, and the title was prudently dropped.

Even then it was revived, from time to time, by my youngest brother Michel, when he wished to be particularly offensive. He would tell his workmen, within earshot of my mother, that all Paris knew that the odour emanating from the corpses of those ladies whose heads had but recently rolled into the basket was none other than that of a famous eau-de-toilette, distilled by the mistress of the glass-house some forty years before, and bottled by her own fair hands for the use of the beauties of Versailles.

2

ONE OF MONSIEUR Brossard's associates was the marquis de Cherbon, whose family had, in the previous century, constructed a small glass-house in the grounds of their château of Chérigny, only a few miles from my father's native village of Chenu and my mother's home at St. Christophe. This little foundry was at present in a poor state, through indifferent supervision, and the marquis de Cherbon, who had lately married and succeeded to his estate at the same time, was determined to put his glass-house to rights and make a profit from it. He consulted Monsieur Brossard, who at once recommended my father as director and lessee, the idea being that my father would thus have his first chance to prove himself a good organiser and business man, as well as a fine craftsman.

The marquis de Cherbon was well satisfied. He already knew my father, and my mother's uncle Georget of St. Paterne, and felt sure that the administration of his glass-house would be in capable hands.

My mother Magdaleine and my father moved to Chérigny in the spring of 1749, and it was here in September that my brother Robert was born, and three years later my brother Pierre.

The setting was very different from la Brûlonnerie. Here at Chérigny the glass-house was on a nobleman's private estate, and consisted of a small furnace-house, with work buildings attached, and workmen's cabins alongside, only a few hundred yards distant from the château itself. There was barely a quarter of the men employed here compared with la Brûlonnerie, and it was truly a family affair, with the marquis de Cherbon taking a personal interest in all that went on, though he never interfered with the work.

My uncle Démére had remained at la Brûlonnerie, but my father's brother Michel Busson had moved to Chérigny with my parents, and about this time another sister, Anne, married Jacques Viau, the melting master at Chérigny. All the members of this small community were closely related, but the differences in status were still strictly kept, and my father and mother lived apart from the others in the farmhouse known as le Maurier, about five minutes' walk from the glass-house. This gave them not only privacy, which had been lacking at la Brûlonnerie, but the necessary degree of importance and privilege which was so strictly adhered to in the glass-trade.

It meant more hard work for my mother, though. Besides keeping the records and writing to the merchants—for she had taken upon herself this part of the business—she had to manage the whole of the farm, see that the cattle were milked and put to pasture, the chickens reared, the pigs killed, and the few acres of ground about the farmstead tilled. None of this dismayed her. She was capable of writing three pages disputing the amount paid for a consignment of goods to Paris—and this at ten o'clock at night after a long day's work in the house and about the farm—of walking across to the glass-house and brewing coffee for my father and those on night-shift, returning and snatching a few hours of sleep, and then rising at five to see that the cows were milked.

The fact that she was carrying my brother Robert, and later nursing him, made no difference to her activities. Here, at le Maurier, she was free to organise her own day as she pleased. There were no watchful eyes about her, no one to criticise or accuse her of breaking with tradition; and if any of my father's relatives should venture to do so, she was the wife of the director, and they never did so twice.

One of the pleasantest things about life at the glass-house of Chérigny was the relationship between my parents and the marquis and marquise de Cherbon. Unlike many aristocrats at that time they were seldom absent from their property for long periods, never went to Court, and were respected and loved by their tenants and the peasantry. The marquise, in particular, made a great favourite of my mother Magdaleine—for they were about the same age, the de Cherbons having been married two years before my parents—and when my mother could spare the time from the farm she would go across to the château, taking my brother with her, and there in the salon the pair of them, my mother and the marquise, would read together, or play and sing, with my brother Robert crawling about the floor between them or taking his first unsteady steps.

It has always seemed to me significant that Robert's first memories, whenever he spoke of them, should not be of the farmhouse le Maurier, or of the lowing of cattle, the scratching of hens and other homely sounds, or even of the roar of the furnace chimney and the bustle of the glass-house; but always of an immense salon, so he described it, filled with mirrors and satin-covered chairs, with a harpsichord standing in one corner, and a fine lady, not my mother, picking him up in her arms and kissing him, then feeding him with little sugared cakes.

"You cannot imagine," he used to tell me in after years, "how vivid is that memory still. The sensation of perfect delight it would be to sit upon that lady's lap, to touch her gown, to smell her perfume, and then for her to set me down upon the floor and to hear her applaud me as I walked from one end of that seemingly immense salon to the other. The long windows gave on to a terrace, and from that terrace paths stretched into the infinite distance. I felt that it was all mine—château, park, harpsichord, and the fine lady too."

If my mother had known what small seed of longing she was sowing in my brother's being, to develop into a folie de grandeur that nearly broke my father's heart, and certainly was partly responsible for his death, she would not have taken Robert so often to the château at Chérigny, to be fed and fondled by the marquise. She would have put him to play amongst the hens and pigs in the muddied farm-yard of le Maurier.

My mother was to blame, but how could she foresee that her indulgence then would help to destroy this first-born son of hers whom she so fiercely loved? And what more natural than to accept the grace and hospitality of so gentle a lady as the marquise de Cherbon?

It was not solely for the pleasure of her society that my mother prized the friendship of the marquise, but also because it gave her the opportunity, when occasion favoured, to speak about my father and his ambitions; how he hoped in time to become just such another as Monsieur Brossard—who was, of course, Robert's godfather—and direct a glass-house, or glass-houses, which should be among the finest in the land.

"We know this will take time," my mother told the marquise, "but already, since Mathurin has been director here at Chérigny, we have doubled our consignments to Paris and have taken on more workmen, and the foundry itself has had a favourable mention in the *Almanach des Marchands.*"

This was no boast. It was all true. The little glass-house at Chérigny had now established itself as one of the foremost "small houses", as they were known, in the trade, specialising in glass for the table, goblets and wine decanters.

The marquis de Cherbon and Monsieur Brossard united in developing further glass-houses, not only la Brûlonnerie, where my uncle Démére was now director in partnership with my father—who alternated between there and Chérigny—but also at la Pierre, Coudrecieux, situated in the midst of the forests of la Pierre and Vibraye, an immense property belonging to a widow, Madame le Gras de Luart. Here, for a time, the marquis de Cherbon installed as director my uncle Michel Busson, who had married a niece of my uncle Démére, but uncle Michel, though a fine engraver of crystal, was no use as an administrator, and the foundry at la Pierre began to fall away and lose money.

Some time between the birth of my brother Pierre in 1752 and my brother Michel in '56 the marquise de Cherbon died in childbirth, to my mother's great distress. The marquis married a second time—for which she never forgave him, though she never failed in civility toward him—choosing his wife from a neighbouring parish to Coudrecieux. His new father-in-law's land adjoined Madame le Gras de Luart's extensive property at la Pierre, and the marquis had, therefore, no wish to see the glass-house there run at a loss. After many months of discussion between all parties, my father dared a very great venture. He, my uncle Démére, and a Monsieur Eloy le Riche, a Paris merchant, entered into partnership, taking on the lease of la Pierre from the marquis de Cherbon and dealing direct with Madame le Gras de Luart, who fortunately for my parents, with their growing family, did not inhabit her late husband's property.

The lease, which was to enter into force on All Saints' Day, 1760, gave the partners the full rights for nine years to develop the glass-house on the domain and everything belonging to it, with the use of timber for the furnace, and to retain the château for their own use. For this they were to pay yearly the sum of 880 livres, and in addition to supply Madame le Gras de Luart with eight dozen crystal glasses for her dining-table. The fact that my uncle Déméré would continue to live at la Brûlonnerie, and Monsieur Eloy le Riche in Paris, meant that my parents, on their own, became tenants of the immense château of la Pierre. Here was a change from the farmhouse le Maurier, and from the master's lodging at la Brûlonnerie!

I believe the shade of the first marquise de Cherbon must have been with my mother when she took possession of la Pierre and surveyed the great staircase and the enormous rooms opening out from one to the other, over which she would now have complete jurisdiction. She chose for herself and my father the big bedroom with its view of the park and the forest beyond, and she knew that her children would grow up here, free to roam wherever they pleased, having the right to do so, just as the children of previous seigneurs had done through the centuries. They would have an added freedom, too. For there were no cooks and scullions here, no powdered footmen and lackeys, but only my mother herself to keep order, and those few wives of the glass-house workmen whom she cared to employ. Half of the château remained dust-sheeted and shuttered, but not always silent; for here my brothers romped and shouted, chasing one another in and out of the great rooms stacked with furniture, halloing along the corridors, finding their way to the attics under the massive roof.

To Robert, now ten years old, la Pierre was an enhancement of his dream. Not only did he live in a château that was larger and grander than Chérigny, but our parents possessed it—or so it seemed to him. He would manage somehow or other to obtain the key of the grande salle from my mother's key-ring, and creep into the room alone. Lifting a corner of a dust-sheet, he would seat himself on one of the brocaded chairs and make believe that the shrouded, silent room was full of guests, and he the host.

Pierre and Michel had no such fancies. The forest lay outside their windows, and this was all they asked for, Pierre especially. Unlike the pleasant woodlands and paths of Chérigny, the forest here was deep and even dangerous, stretching further than the eye could see from the turret windows of the château; it was the haunt of wild boars, perhaps of robbers. Pierre was always in trouble. Pierre climbed highest and fell furthest. Pierre tumbled into streams and soaked his clothes. He was the collector of all wild things, bats, birds, voles, foxes, and would try to tame each one of them in turn, hiding them in the disused rooms of the château, to my mother's fury.

Here, at la Pierre, she was mistress of the glass-house and châtelaine as well. She was responsible, not only for the well-being of the workmen and their wives—and there must have been well over a hundred of them, not counting the charcoal-burners in the forest—but for any damage done in the precincts of the château. The presence of her three lively sons did not make this any easier for her, although Robert, thanks to the recommendation of Monsieur Brossard and the marquis de Cherbon, was being instructed in French and Latin grammar by the curé at Coudrecieux, who had also taught the son of Madame le Gras de Luart.

My mother lost two babies in infancy, a girl and a boy, before I was born in November of '63, followed by my sister Edmé three years later. Our family was now complete, and a very united one at that, with the two youngest members of it, the girls, alternately teased and petted by the older brothers.

If there was any difference of opinion between children and parents, the cause was generally my brother Michel's stammer. Edmé and I grew up with it—we never heard him speak otherwise, and we thought nothing of it—but my mother told us that it came about after the birth of the two babies Françoise and Prosper, who had followed closely upon each other and died as infants, when Michel himself was between four and five years old.

Whether it bewildered him to see these unfortunates come into the world, be nursed

by my mother, and as suddenly depart, causing her great grief, nobody ever discovered. Children do not speak of these things. Perhaps he thought that he too would
disappear, and so lose all he knew. In any event, he began to stammer badly about this
time, soon after my parents came to la Pierre, and there was nothing they could do to
cure him. Michel was exceptionally bright and intelligent, apart from this defect, and
it exasperated my parents, especially my father, to see the boy struggle with his
words, fighting, as it were, for breath, almost as though in this very effort he imitated
the convulsions of the poor babies who had died.

"He does it on purpose," my father would say sternly. "He can pronounce his
words perfectly well if he chooses to do so." He would send Michel from the room
with a book, from which he must learn a page and then repeat it aloud afterwards, but
it never did any good. Michel would turn sullen and rebellious, and sometimes he
would run off for hours at a time and seek out the charcoal-burners in the forest. They
did not mind how much he stammered, for it amused them to teach him their own
rough speech and see what he made of it.

Naturally, Michel was punished for this. My father was a great disciplinarian, and
then my mother would intervene, and ask forgiveness for him, and he would be
allowed to go with my father to the glass-house and watch the men at work, for this
was what he liked to do most of all. Edmé and I were so much younger than our
brothers that our lives were quite different from theirs. To us, the little girls, our
father seemed a most gentle, tender parent, taking the pair of us upon his knees,
bringing us presents after his visits to Paris, laughing with us, singing and playing
with us, and in every way treating us as though we were his one relaxation from daily
cares.

It was very different for the boys. They must all stand up when he entered the room,
wait to sit until he seated himself, never speak at table unless spoken to. When their
turn came to be apprenticed at the glass-house they were obliged to obey the rules
more rigidly, and were given more menial work to do, sweeping the furnace-house
floors, and so on, than the apprentice sons of my father's workmen.

My brother Robert, despite his fine education at the hands of the good curé at
Coudrecieux, did not object to this harsh treatment. He wished to be a master
glass-maker like his father, or, better still, like his godfather Monsieur Brossard, who
had so many friends amongst the aristocracy; and to achieve this end he knew he must
start at the bottom.

Michel too, although he rebelled against his father in other ways, never minded
hard work, indeed, the rougher and dirtier the work the better it was for him. He liked
to mix with the workmen and share their worst duties, and he was never in so good a
humour as when he came back from the furnace-house, his blouse scorched and
bespattered, for it meant that he had taken his shift beside his comrades, and had fared
as well or ill as they.

It was Pierre who gave my father the biggest problem—good-tempered, a perfect
sans-souci, impossible to train to anything. He was apprenticed, of course, to the
glass-house, but was forever slipping away and playing truant—gathering wild
strawberries in the forest, or merely wandering at will, and then returning when fancy
pleased him. Beating him did no good at all. He accepted punishment or praise with
equanimity.

"He is an eccentric," my father would say, dismissing his second son with a shrug
of the shoulders. "He will never make anything of himself. Since he seems to prefer
life in the open he had best go off to the American colonies and settle there."

This was when Pierre was about seventeen years old, and my father, whose
business dealings now ranged far and wide, arranged for Pierre to be shipped off to a
rich planter in Martinique. I was about six years old at the time, and I well remember
the tears and consternation at home—for the three brothers were devoted to one
another—and my mother's tight-lipped silence as she packed a trunk for Pierre,
wondering in her heart if she would ever see her son again. Even my father appeared

remorseful now that the actual moment of departure had arrived, and himself escorted Pierre to Nantes, where my brother was to embark, and shipped a large consignment of glass of inferior quality abroad with him, which, he told Pierre, he could sell to the colonists and make his fortune.

It seemed very dull at the château without Pierre. His cheerful ways and original antics had enlivened the atmosphere, which was sometimes rather solemn for Edmé and myself, two small children left on our own to play, with our brothers at work at the glass-house next door and our mother continually preoccupied, either with my father's business or with the management of the château itself. We were soon to forget him, though, in the months that followed, for two events stand out in my memory as markers to that time.

The first was when my brother Robert became a master glass-maker, after his three years' apprenticeship. The second was the visit of the King to the glass-house of la Pierre. Both events took place during the year of 1769.

The first happened on a Sunday afternoon in June, with every craftsman and workman assembled in his holiday clothes by two o'clock to await the arrival of the musicians. The previous day my mother, and the other masters' wives, had prepared the long trestle tables in the furnace-house—it was between heats, as we termed it, the fires having been allowed to go out—and the tables were now laden with food for all the workers at the glass-house, and for the guests as well.

Numbers of people were invited. All our relatives, of course, and those merchants and tradesmen with whom my father did business, but besides these were the mayor of Coudrecieux, the bailiff, the curé, and the keepers and foresters on the estate, with every woman and child in the district.

A procession was formed, headed by the musicians, and then the two senior masters—in this case my uncle Michel and another engraver—led the master-to-be, my brother Robert, between them, with all the members of the glass-house following behind in strict order of precedence. First the masters, next the journeymen and carriers, then the stokers, apprentices, and so on, and finally the women and children. They processed from the glass-house, through the great park gates, and so to the steps of the château itself, where my father and mother, with the curé, the mayor and other officials, waited to receive them.

A short ceremony followed. The new master was sworn in and blessed by the priest, and then there were speeches. After this the whole procession turned round and marched back to the glass-house. I remember glancing up at my mother and seeing the tears come into her eyes as she watched my brother Robert take his oath.

Both my father and mother had powdered their hair for the occasion—perhaps they felt they were representing the absent family of le Gras de Luart—and my mother wore a brocade gown and my father satin breeches.

"He'll make a fine man," I heard the curé murmur to my father as they waited for the procession to stop in front of them. "I have every confidence in his ability, and I hope you have the same."

My father did not reply immediately. He too was moved by the sight of his eldest son taking the same oath as he had done some twenty-five years before.

"He'll do well enough," he said at last, "providing he keeps his head."

These words were lost on me. I had eyes only for Robert, who, to his six-year-old sister, was the outstanding figure in the whole procession. Tall, slim, fair-haired (my mother had stopped him from powdering it at the last moment), he did not appear to me to be in danger of losing anything. He carried himself erect, and walked as proudly to the steps of the château as though he were to be made a marquis, and not merely a master glass-maker.

A great burst of cheering followed the swearing-in. Robert bowed to the assembled company, the guests and the whole crowd of craftsmen and their families gathered there, and I noticed that he threw a quick glance up at my mother Magdaleine, impetuous, proud, as though to say, "This is what you expected of me, isn't it? This is what both of us wanted?" It seemed to me that she bowed in return, half to my brother, half to herself, and as she towered above me, magnificent in her brocade gown, her whole aspect strangely changed with the powder in her hair, I felt, child as I was, that she was more than my mother; she was some sort of deity, more powerful than the gentle statue of the Blessed Virgin standing in the church at Coudrecieux, the equal of God himself.

The second event gave me a very different impression, and this was, I think, because my parents were relegated to a minor rôle. My father came in one evening and announced in solemn tones, "We are to be much honoured. The King is hunting in the forest of Vibraye next week, and intends paying a visit to the glass-house of la Pierre."

Everyone was at once in consternation. The King . . . What would he say, what would he do, how was he to be fed, to be entertained? My mother at once began preparing the great rooms that were never used, and every woman on the estate and in the glass-house precincts was summoned to scrub, to polish, to sweep. And then, within a few days of the King's visit, Madame le Gras de Luart and her son arrived to do the honours themselves.

"Naturally," she said to my mother—I was there at the time and heard every word—"it is only right that my son and myself should be in residence on this great occasion. No doubt you and your family will find quarters in the glass-house."

"Naturally," replied my mother, who, to tell the truth, had been secretly looking forward to acting châtelaine. "I hope you will find the rooms prepared as they should be. We did not have much warning."

"Oh, as to that, don't concern yourself," replied Madame le Gras de Luart. "The servants will see to it."

Then from carriage, coach and every sort of vehicle tumbled a great crowd of footmen, lackeys, cooks, scullions, all marching through the château as though the place belonged to them, turning the kitchen upside down, stripping the beds of covers and spreading others they had brought with them, speaking rudely to my mother as if she were a lower-paid servant who had been dismissed. We, the family, were turned out of doors and sent packing, with only time enough to thrust our own belongings into one room and turn the key in the lock, and then make our way across to the glass-house to beg shelter from my uncle Michel and his wife.

"It was only to be expected," said my father quietly. "Madame le Gras de Luart is perfectly within her rights."

"Her r-r-rights," stammered my brother Michel, who would then have been about fourteen years old. "What r-r-rights has an old r-r-raddled woman like that to t-t-turn us out of our home?"

"Hold your tongue," commanded my father sharply, "and remember that the château of la Pierre is held on lease only. It never can be, and never will be, ours, any more than the glass-house itself."

Poor Michel looked dumbfounded. He must have believed, as I did, that la Pierre was ours forever. He turned very white, as he always did when he was angry and unable to express himself, and went off to the furnace-house to try and explain the situation to his friends the stokers.

The only member of the family who looked forward to the King's visit with all his heart was my eldest brother Robert. He was to be on show for the occasion, and act as glass-blower beside the other masters, for the King had expressed a wish, so my father said, to see every part of the work at the foundry, from the moment when the liquid first formed in the blow-pipe to the engraving of a finished glass by my father and my uncle Michel.

The great day dawned. We were all of us astir early, myself and my sister Edmé prinked out in our best white frocks. Then, to my great disappointment, my mother did not put on her beautiful brocade gown, but wore her ordinary dark Sunday dress, with the addition of a lace collar. I was about to protest, but she silenced me. "Let those who wish to be peacocks do as they please," she said. "I feel more dignified as I am."

I did not understand why she should put on a brocade gown for my brother and wear nothing but her Sunday dress for the King. My father must have approved, though, for he nodded his head when he saw her, and said. "It's better so." For my part, I thought otherwise. Then, almost before we were aware of it, the party from the château was upon us. Madame le Gras de Luart had driven to the entrance gates of the park in her coach, and her son was on horseback, and there were a lot of other noblemen on horseback too, and several ladies, all in hunting-costume, and, to my critical eye, rather disordered too. There were grooms and keepers all around, and barking dogs; it was not at all my idea of a royal party.

"The King," I whispered to my mother, "where is the King?"

"Hush!" she murmured. "That is he there, dismounting now, talking to Madame le Gras de Luart."

I was almost in tears with disappointment, for the elderly gentleman to whom Madame le Gras de Luart made a great sweeping curtsey looked just like anybody else, in hunting coat and breeches, with his wig not even curled—perhaps, I consoled myself, because he had been hunting all morning he kept his best one in a box. Then, as he looked about him, and the great crowd of craftsmen and workmen's wives gathered to applaud him, he waved his hand in a half-salute and said wearily to his hostess, "My party is famished, we breakfasted early. Where do we eat?"

So instead of the glass-house being visited first, the programme had to be changed. Orders were quickly given and the work rearranged in the glass-house at great inconvenience, and the royal party went off to the château to dine a full three hours before they were due to do so. We were told afterwards that Madame le Gras de Luart was so flustered that she had to be given restoratives, and I thought it served her right for having been discourteous to my mother. Then, later in the day, when all the workmen at the glass-house had been kept waiting for hours, the royal party returned, their stomachs well-lined when ours were empty. They were laughing and talking and in great humour, the ladies exclaiming at everything they saw but quickly turning aside to examine something else, giving the impression that they understood nothing.

My mother was presented to the King, who said something over his shoulder to one of the gentlemen attending him—I think it was a reference to her height, for she certainly dwarfed the pair of them—and then they passed on, and we followed, and they stood and watched my brother Robert use his blow-pipe. He managed it with infinite grace, turning it this way and that, manipulating the long rod with his hands, just as though no one was looking at him, while I knew very well he could see that the King was standing a short distance away, and all the ladies admiring him.

"What a beauty," one of them said, and even at six years old I knew that they were not referring to the blow-pipe but to my brother Robert. Then a dreadful thing happened. My brother Michel, who had been standing in the background amidst a crowd of apprentices, leant forward to get a better view of the royal party, and he slipped and measured his length before the very feet of the King himself. Scarlet with shame he picked himself up, and the King, good-naturedly, patted him on the shoulder.

"Better not do that when you become a glass-blower," he said. "How long have you worked in the glass-house?"

The inevitable happened. Poor Michel tried to speak, but instead one of his worst attempts at speech followed.

He gasped and spluttered, his head jerking at every sound just as it always did when he was nervous, and everyone in the royal party burst out laughing.

"There is a lad who must save his breath for his blow-pipe," said the King, moving on amidst great merriment, and I saw one of the older apprentices, a comrade of Michel's, pull my brother back into line and hide him from view.

After this, it was all spoilt for me. Even the sight of my Uncle Michel engraving the glass, which generally was so great a treat, could not make amends for my brother's shame, and when my father presented the King with a goblet taken from the finished batch they had worked upon for the occasion, with the royal initials and the fleur-de-lys upon it, I almost wished it would shiver to fragments at his feet.

It was over. The royal party left the glass-house and remounted outside the château gates close by, and we watched them disappear into the forest in the direction of Semur. Weary and dispirited, I trailed after my mother to my uncle's house. Edmé was already asleep upon her shoulder. We were soon joined by my father, my uncle and my brothers, the grown men looking much relieved that the great ordeal was over.

"It went well," my father said, with satisfaction. "The King was most gracious. He seemed very pleased with all he saw."

"I never thought to engrave a goblet for the King himself," said my uncle, a shy man, who thought only of his work. "This is a day to remember all my life."

"Very true," rejoined my father, turning to his sons. "We have been greatly honoured today, and we must never forget it." He took one of the goblets in his hand and examined it. "We'll never do finer work than this, Michel," he said to my uncle. "We should be well content. If you can ever equal it, Robert, you will have good reason to be satisfied. I suggest we preserve this goblet as a family symbol, and if it does not bring us fame and fortune it shall serve as a reminder of high craftsmanship through succeeding generations. When you marry, Robert, you may pass it on to your sons."

Robert examined the goblet in his turn. He seemed much impressed. "To anyone who was ignorant," he observed, "the royal insignia might be taken for a family device, and our own at that. I suppose we can never aspire to such an honour." He sighed, and gave the goblet back into my father's hands.

"We have no need of insignias," replied my father. "What we Bussons create with our brains and with our hands is proof of our honour. Here, Michel, don't you want to touch the goblet for luck?" He made as though to hand the precious glass to my youngest brother, but Michel shrank back from him, shaking his head violently.

"It's b-b-bad luck it would bring me," he stammered, "b-b-bad luck, not good. I d-d-d-don't want to touch it."

He turned suddenly and ran out of the room. I immediately began to cry and would have followed him, but my mother prevented me.

"Let him alone," she said quietly, "you will only irritate him further." She then told my father and my uncle of the incident in the glass-house, which they had not seen.

"A pity," observed my father. "Nevertheless, he must learn self-control."

He turned to my uncle and began discussing other matters, but I heard Robert whisper to my mother, "Michel is an idiot. He should have cut some caper and made the King laugh with him, instead of against him. By acting so he would have delighted everyone, including himself, and been the crowning success of the royal visit."

My mother was not impressed. "Not all of us," she said, "have your capacity for turning a situation to his own advantage."

She must have noticed his striking pose with the blow-pipe, and heard the gasps of admiration from the ladies of the Court party. In any event, despite poor Michel's misfortune the goblet did bring us luck. I was convinced of that the very next day.

Madame le Gras de Luart departed from the château with her retinue of servants, and the mud from her carriage wheels had barely settled in when we saw a very different equipage approaching the iron gates from the direction of Coudrecieux. It was a pedlar's cart, strung about with pots and pans, the kind of cart that would roam the countryside, plying between la Ferté-Bernard and Le Mans, and seated beside the driver, or rather standing and waving his hand joyously, was a familiar figure in a multicoloured jacket and a crimson waistcoat, with—unbelievably—a squawking parrot on either shoulder. It was my brother Pierre. My father, who was with us, stood rooted to the ground.

"Where in the world have you come from?" he called sternly, as my brother jumped from the pedlar's cart and ran towards us.

"From Martinique," said Pierre. "It was much too warm, I could not endure it. I have decided, after all, I would rather work in the glass-house." He bent to embrace us, and, happy as we were to see him, we all stepped back a pace, for fear of the squawking parrots.

"I take it," said my mother, "that you have not made your fortune with the packages of glass your father gave you?"

Pierre smiled. "I sold none of it," he said. "I gave it all away."

The pedlar handed down his trunk, which Pierre, despite my father's remonstrances, insisted on opening upon the spot. It contained nothing from the Martinique of any value; only quantities of gaudy coloured waistcoats, woven in the native bazaars, which he had brought as presents for each member of his family.

3

BY THE TIME I was twelve or thirteen years old my father Mathurin Busson had control of four glass-houses. He had obtained an extension of his lease of la Pierre and was still associated with la Brûlonnerie and Chérigny, and now he added the glass-house of le Chesne-Bidault, between Montmirail and le Plessis-Dorin. Here, as at la Pierre, the owner, Monsieur Pesant de Bois-Guilbert, simply leased the foundry to my father, having no say in the management, living himself in his château at Montmirail.

The glass-house of le Chesne-Bidault, like la Pierre, was set in mid-forest, though it was a smaller concern, with the master's house and the farm standing close to the single furnace-house, and the long row of workmen's dwellings opposite.

The grandeur of la Pierre, with the vast château in its fine park, was very different from the rough, somewhat rustic appearance of le Chesne-Bidault; but my mother loved it from the first, and at once set about making the master's house fit and habitable for Robert, the idea being that he should act as manager for my father, and so gain experience for the future.

Le Chesne-Bidault was not more than an hour's ride from la Pierre, and it was one of my great delights to go over there with my mother, for two or three days at a time, to see how Robert was progressing.

He had by now grown into a strikingly handsome young man, with great self-assurance and an excellent manner. In fact, my father used to say that his manners were over-polished, and if he was not careful he would be taken for a flunkey. This annoyed Robert exceedingly.

"My father is quite out of touch with the manners of today," he would say to me, after there had been some words on the subject. "Just because he has spent his life dealing with merchants and traders he assumes that I must do the same, and never move out of the glass milieu. What he does not understand is that by mixing in a more refined society I shall obtain many more orders for glass than he ever does."

When he had been working at la Pierre, and my father was absent, Robert would go as often as he dared to Le Mans, for during the past years the social life of the town had become very gay; there were concerts and balls and plays, and many aristocrats who usually spent all their time at Versailles would now think it fashionable to open up houses and châteaux in the country, and vie with one another as to who would hold the wittiest salon. Freemasonry was all the rage, and whether it was now or later that Robert became a Freemason I am not sure, but certainly, from his talk, he had obtained a foothold in this smart Manceaux society and elsewhere, and once away from the immediate jurisdiction of my father, and on his own at le Chesne-Bidault, it was easier for him to slip off and meet his friends. My mother, very naturally, was quite unaware of this. Robert was never absent when we arrived for a visit, and she would at once become absorbed in all the work of the glass-house, from keeping the books to managing the farm and the house, and seeing that the workmen and their wives lacked for nothing. Also, Robert was by now a fine craftsman on his own account, and she was proud of the wares that he dispatched weekly to Paris.

Nothing pleased me more than to be Robert's confidante, to hear of his amours and his escapades. In return for listening to him, he would give me lessons in history and grammar, for since Edmé and I were girls, and certain to marry within the industry, my father did not think it necessry to teach us anything but the rudiments of education.

"He is quite wrong," Robert would argue. "Every young woman should know how to comport herself, and how to mix in society."

"Surely it depends upon the society?" I would reply, despite my anxiety to learn. "Take aunt Anne at Chérigny. Neither she, nor my uncle Viau, can sign their names properly, and they do very well as they are."

"No doubt," said Robert, "and they will never move from Chérigny to the end of their days. You wait until I have a glass-house of my own, in Paris, and you come to visit me there. I can't introduce my sister to society unless she does me credit."

A glass-house in Paris . . . What ambition! I wondered what my parents would think of it if they knew.

Meanwhile Robert continued as manager of le Chesne-Bidault without running into trouble, and presently Pierre, who had become a master in his turn, joined him there—chiefly, I think, so that Robert could slip off into what he called "society" when he had the mind, but naturally neither my father nor my mother had any idea of this.

Pierre had his head filled with new ideas also, but of a rather different sort. He had returned from Martinique with great stories of the hardships the natives endured there, and he had begun to read a great deal, forever quoting Rousseau and saying, "Man is born free, but is everywhere in chains," much to my father's irritation.

"If you must read philosophy," he would say, "read someone of merit, not a scoundrel who allowed his illegitimate children to be brought up in an orphanage."

Pierre would not be dissuaded. Every state, he declared, should be conducted according to the theories of Jean-Jacques, for the good of all, without distinction of persons. Boys should be educated "naturally", living in the open air, receiving no tuition until they were past fifteen.

"A pity," my father would reply, "that you did not stay in Martinique and turn native. The life would have suited you better than becoming the indifferent craftsman in the glass-trade which you are at present."

The sarcasm was lost on Pierre. He was forever bubbling over with some new enthusiasm, some new cause, and infecting Michel with his ideas, so that my father, who had been so progressive himself as a young man with his chemical and scientific inventions, could not understand what had come over his sons.

My mother took it more calmly. "They are young," she said. "The young always have some new fad or other. It will pass."

One day my brother Robert rode over to la Pierre with the excuse of business between the two foundries, but in reality to swear me to secrecy over a new project, which nobody must know but myself and Pierre.

"I've joined the corps d'élite of the Arquebusiers," he told me, in a state of great excitement. "Only as a temporary officer, of course, but it means doing my turn of service in Paris for three months in the year. Some of my friends at Le Mans persuaded me, and I've received the necessary recommendation. The point is, somehow or other my father must be kept from visiting le Chesne-Bidault during my absence."

I shook my head. "It can never be done," I said. "He is bound to find out."

"No," said Robert. "Pierre is also sworn to secrecy, and the workmen too. If my father should ride over to le Chesne-Bidault, then he will be told I have gone to Le

Mans on some necessity. He never stays more than a day."

During the next few weeks I did everything possible to make myself indispensable to my father. I would accompany him to the foundry in the morning, and be waiting for him when he returned, and I feigned to take a great interest all of a sudden in the day's work. He was both flattered and surprised, and told me I was growing into a sensible girl, and that one of these days I should make a fine wife for a master of a glass-house.

My plans were so successful, and he enjoyed my company at la Pierre so much, that he never once rode over to le Chesne-Bidault. But towards the end of the period of my brother's absence he looked across at me, during the evening meal, and said; "How would you like to pay your first visit to Paris?"

I thought immediately that all had been discovered, and this was a stratagem to make me speak out. I glanced quickly at my mother, but she smiled at me encouragingly.

"Yes, why not?" she nodded to my father. "Sophie is quite old enough to be your companion. Besides, I shall be all the easier if she goes with you." The little pretence that my father might come to no good alone in the capital was a standing joke between my parents.

"Nothing in the world would please me better," I told them, gaining confidence. At once Edmé clamoured to come too, but here my mother was firm. "Your turn will come later," she said to my sister, "but if you behave yourself we will drive over to see Robert at le Chesne-Bidault while your father and Sophie are away."

This was the last thing I wanted, but there was nothing to be done about it, and I soon forgot my anxiety two days later when we were seated side by side in the diligence on our way to the capital. Paris . . . My first visit . . . And I an ignorant country girl not yet fourteen, who had only seen one city in her life so far, Le Mans. We were twelve hours or more upon the road, having left very early in the morning, and it must have been six or seven in the evening as we approached the capital, and I sat with my face pressed to the window, half sick with excitement and exhaustion.

It was June, I remember, and there was a warm haze over the city and a dusty radiance everywhere, with the trees in full leaf, and people thronging the streets, and line upon line of carriages all returning to Versailles from the races. King Louis XVI and his young Queen Marie Antoinette had only been crowned a year, but already, my father said, there had been changes at Court, the old formality was going, the Queen was setting the fashion for balls and opera-going, and the King's brother, the comte d'Artois, and his cousin the duc de Chartres vied with one another in horse-racing, a sport very popular in England. Perhaps, I thought, staring eagerly from the diligence, I too would see some duke or duchess coming away from the races; perhaps those young gallants picking their way across the crowded Place Louis XV in front of the Palais des Tuileries were the King's brothers? I pointed them out to my father, but he only laughed.

"Lackeys," he said, "or coiffeurs. They all ape their masters. But you don't catch a prince of the blood royal on his feet."

The diligence deposited us at its terminus in the rue Boulay. Here all was jostling and confusion, with no one I could possibly call a gallant, or even a coiffeur. The streets were narrow and evil-smelling, with a broad stream running down the centre to carry the sewage, and beggars holding out their hands for alms. I remember my sudden feeling of fright when my father's back was turned to see to our luggage, and in a moment a woman had thrust her way between us, with two little barefooted children beside her, clamouring for money. When I drew back she shook her fist at me, and cursed. This was not the Paris I had expected, where all was gaiety, laughter, driving to the Opera, and bright lights.

It was my father's custom to put up at the Hotel du Cheval Rouge in the rue St. Denis, close to the Church of St. Leu and the great central market of les Halles, and this was where he took me now, and where we stayed during our three days' visit.

I confess I found myself disenchanted. We hardly moved from this quarter, so crowded, so ill-smelling, among the poorest of the people, and when we did walk out it was only to call at the various warehouses where my father did his business. I thought our charcoal-burners at home in the forest of la Pierre were rough, but they were gentle and courteous compared with the people in the streets of Paris, who jostled us without apology, staring rudely all the while. Child as I was, I dared not venture out alone, but was obliged to stay beside my father the whole time, or remain in the bedroom at the Cheval Rouge.

The last evening of our visit my father took me to the Porte St. Martin to see coaches and carriages arriving for the Opera, and here was a change indeed from the poor quarter by our hotel. Glittering ladies, their bare bosoms gleaming with jewels, stepped down from their carriages escorted by gallants as gorgeously dressed as they were themselves. All was colour and brilliance and high affected voices—it was as though they spoke a French totally unlike our own—and the very way the ladies moved, and held their skirts, and the gentlemen swaggered by their side, calling out, "Make way, there, make way for madame la marquise", thrusting the crowds aside before the steps of the Opera, seemed to me like make-believe. A wave of perfume came from these fine folk, a strange exotic scent like flowers no longer fresh, whose petals curl, and this stale richness somehow mingled with the drab dirt of those beside us, pressing forward even as we did, in a dumb desire to see the Queen.

Her coach arrived at last, drawn by four magnificent horses, and the footmen sprang from behind to open the doors, while attendants brandishing staves appeared from nowhere to push back the staring crowds.

The King's brother, the comte d'Artois, descended first, for the King himself was said to dislike opera, and never went. A plump young man, with a pink and white complexion, his satin coat covered with stars and decorations, he was immediately followed by a young lady all in rose, with a jewel glistening in her powdered hair and a haughty, disdainful expression on her face. We heard afterwards that she was the comtesse de Polignac, the intimate friend of the Queen. Then, for a brief moment, I saw the young Queen herself, the last to descend. Dressed all in white, diamonds about her throat and in her hair, her pale blue eyes sweeping past us in complete indifference as she gave her hand to the comte d'Artois and disappeared from view, she looked as exquisite, and as fragile, as those porcelain figures my father had pointed out to me that morning, reposing side by side in one of the warehouses of a merchant friend.

"There we are," said my father. "Now are you content?"

Content or not, I could not say. It was a glimpse into another world. Did these folk really eat, I wondered, and undress, and perform the same functions as we did ourselves? It was hardly credible.

We walked the streets the rest of the evening, to "cool off", as my father expressed himself, and it was when we had stopped in the rue St. Honoré a moment, to chat to one of his business acquaintances, that I saw a familiar figure approaching us, clad in the splendid uniform of an officer in the corps d'Arquebusiers. It was my brother Robert.

He saw us instantly, paused for a moment, then pirouetted swiftly like a ballet-dancer, leaping the stream that ran down the centre of the rue St. Honoré, and disappeared into the gardens of the Palais des Tuileries. My father, who happened to turn his head at this moment, stared after the retreating figure.

"Did I not know my eldest son to be at the glass-house of le Chesne-Bidault," he observed drily to his companion, "I would think that I had recognised him in the person of that young officer whom you can see vanishing into the distance there."

"All young men," remarked my father's acquaintance, "look much the same in uniform."

"Possibly," replied my father, "and have an equal facility for getting themselves out of a scrape."

No more was said. We turned and walked back to our hotel in the rue St. Denis, and the following day returned home to the château at la Pierre. My father never again alluded to the incident, but when I asked my mother if she had visited le Chesne-Bidault during our absence she looked me straight in the eye and said, "I am impressed by the manner in which Robert manages the glass-house and succeeds in amusing himself at the same time."

Playing at soldiers was one thing; dispatching consignments of glassware to Chartres without entering them in the foundry books was another. Anyone who attempted to fool my mother where the merchandise was concerned would be sorry for it.

We were spending our customary two days at le Chesne-Bidault for my mother to check on the orders, and all went smoothly until my mother suddenly announced her intention of counting the empty crates which had returned from Paris the previous week.

"That is quite unnecessary," said my brother Robert, who this time was not on leave of absence. "The crates are piled one on top of the other in the store until our next batch is ready for the road. Besides, we know the figure is two hundred."

"It should be two hundred," replied my mother. "That is what I want to find out."

My brother continued his protestations. "I cannot vouch for the order in the store," he continued, glancing at me with warning in his eye. "Blaise has been sick, and the crates were stacked anyhow, as they came in. I can promise you everything will be satisfactory in time for the next batch."

My mother disregarded him. "I shall need two strong labourers," she said, "to shift the crates so that I can count them. Perhaps you will see about it now. And I shall want you to come with me."

She found fifty crates missing, and as ill-luck had it the journeyman-carrier called at the glass-house that afternoon. On being questioned by my mother he explained to her, in all innocence, that the missing crates were at the moment in Chartres with a consignment of very special table-glass for the regiment of the Dragons de Monsieur, which was just then stationed in that city.

My mother thanked the journeyman for his information, and then asked my brother Robert to accompany her back to the master's house.

"And now," she said, "I should like your explanation as to why this consignment of 'special table-glass' has not been entered in the books?"

It might have helped my eldest brother then had he been cursed with a defect of speech like my youngest brother Michel.

"You must realise," he said glibly, "that in dealing with noblemen like the colonel of the regiment, the comte de la Châtre—who, as everyone knows, is an intimate friend of Monsieur, the King's brother—one does not expect payment on the spot. To have the honour of his custom is almost sufficient payment in itself."

My mother stabbed at the open ledger with her quill.

"Very probably," she said, "but your father and I have not had the doubtful pleasure to date of doing business with him. All I know of the comte de la Châtre is that his château at Malicorne is famous for every extravagance and intrigue, and he is said to have ruined himself and every tradesman in the district, none of whom can get a sou out of him."

"Quite untrue," said my brother, with a disdainful shrug. "I am surprised you should listen to spiteful gossip."

"I don't call it spiteful gossip when honest tradesmen, whom your father knows, are obliged to beg for assistance or go hungry," replied my mother, "because your nobleman friend builds a private theatre on his domain."

"It is very necessary to encourage the arts," protested my brother.

"It is more imperative to pay one's debts," replied my mother. "What was the value of the consignment of glass dispatched to this regiment?"

My brother hesitated. "I am not sure," he began.

My mother insisted.

"Some fifteen hundred livres," he admitted.

I was glad not to be in my brother's shoes. My mother's blue eyes turned as frozen as a northern lake.

"Then I shall myself write to the comte de la Châtre," she said, "and if I do not obtain satisfaction from him I had better address myself to Monsieur, the King's brother. Surely one or the other of them will have the courtesy to reply and honour the debt."

I could tell by Robert's face that this extreme measure would not do at all.

"You can spare yourself the pains," he said. "To be brief—the money has already been spent."

Here was trouble indeed. I began to tremble for my brother. How in the world could he have disposed of fifteen hundred livres? My mother remained calm. She glanced about her at the plain furnishings of the master's house, which she and my father had supplied.

"As far as I am aware," she said, "there has been no expenditure here or in any of the buildings on these premises."

"You are perfectly right," replied Robert. "The money was not spent at le Chesne-Bidault."

"Then where?"

"I refuse to answer."

My mother closed the ledger, and rising to her feet walked towards the door. "You will account for every sou within three weeks," she said. "If I have not an explanation by that time I shall tell your father that we are closing down the glass-house here at le Chesne-Bidault because of fraud, and I shall have your name erased from the list of master glass-makers within the trade."

She left the room. My brother forced a laugh, and, seating himself in the chair she had just relinquished, lounged back with his feet upon the table.

"She would never dare do such a thing," he said. "It would be my ruin."

"Don't be too sure," I warned him. "The money will have to be found, that's certain. How *did* you spend it?"

He shook his head. "I shan't tell you," he said, beginning to smile despite his serious situation. "The point is that the money has gone, beyond recovery."

The truth came out in an unlikely way. About a week later my uncle and aunt Déméré paid us a visit at la Pierre from la Brûlonnerie, and as usual there was much talk of local affairs, besides gossip from Paris, Chartres, Vendôme and other big cities.

"I am told there was great excitement in Chartres with the masked ball," began my aunt Déméré. "All the young good-for-nothings in town were present, with or without their husbands."

I became all attention at the mention of Chartres, and glanced at my brother Robert, who was also present.

"Is that so?" asked my father. "We heard nothing of any ball. But we are a long way from such frivolities out here in the country."

My aunt, who disapproved of gaiety on principle, made a moue of disdain.

"All Chartres was discussing it when we were there two weeks ago," she continued. "It appears there was some sort of wager between the officers of the Dragons de Monsieur and the young blades in the corps d'Arquebusiers as to which regiment could best entertain the ladies of the district."

My uncle Déméré winked at my father. "The ladies of Chartres are known for their enjoyment of hospitality," he said. My father bowed in mock understanding.

"It appears they kept it up to all hours in the morning," went on my aunt, "drinking, dancing, and chasing each other round about the cathedral in a disgraceful manner. They say the officers of the Arquebusiers squandered a fortune providing for the affair."

"I am not surprised," said my father, "but as these gentlemen have the fashion set for them by a young Court at Versailles it is only to be expected. Let us hope they can afford it."

Robert had his eyes fixed upon the ceiling, suggesting he was either plunged in thought or had noticed a patch of worn plaster.

"And the Dragons de Monsieur," enquired my mother, "what part did they play in the business?"

"We were told they had lost their wager," replied my uncle. "The dinner they gave was no match for the masked ball. In any event, the Dragons are now quartered elsewhere and the Arquebusiers, who have a short term of service, are presumably resting on their laurels."

It was to my mother's credit that not a word of this escapade ever reached my father's ears, but she left me, young as I was, in charge of the château at la Pierre, while she returned with my brother Robert to the glass-house at le Chesne-Bidault, and remained with him there until he had himself replaced, by his own craftsmanship, the table-glass he had dispatched to the Dragons de Monsieur.

It was now the spring of the year 1777. The long lease of the château and glass-house of la Pierre, which had been our home for so long, had come to an end. The son of Madame le Gras de Luart, who had succeeded to the property, wished to make other arrangements, and with sad hearts we bade good-bye to the beautiful home where both Edmé and I had been born, and where our three brothers had grown from small boys to young men.

It was impossible for Edmé and myself, and certainly for Pierre and Michel, not to look upon le Gras de Luart as an interloper who, just because he was the seigneur and owner of la Pierre, had the right to turn over his property to a new tenant, or live in it himself for a few months in the year. As to the glass-house itself, which my father had developed from a small family affair to one of the foremost houses in the country, this must now be given up into other hands, and perhaps allowed once more to fall into decay or be exploited by outsiders. Our parents were more philosophical than we were. A master glass-maker must accustom himself to moving on. In old days they had always been wanderers, going from one forest to another, settling for a few years only. We had to consider ourselves fortunates to have been brought up at la Pierre, and to have such happiness there through our childhood years. Luckily the lease of le Chesne-Bidault had many years to run, la Brûlonnerie too, and the family could divide itself up between the two.

My father, mother, Edmé and I removed ourselves to le Chesne-Bidault, and Robert and Pierre went to la Brûlonnerie. Michel, who was twenty-one this year, had elected to go out of the family altogether for a time to gain experience, and was working as master glass-maker near Bourges, at le Berry. My three brothers, to distinguish themselves in the trade one from the other, had added suffixes to their names: Robert signed himself Busson l'Aîné, Pierre Busson du Charme, and Michel Busson-Challoir. These marks of distinction were, needless to say, Robert's idea. Le Charme and le Challoir were small farm properties owned by our parents, forming part of their original marriage portion.

The use of these names struck my mother as extravgant. "Your father and his brother," she said to me, "never thought it necessary to distinguish themselves. They were the Busson brothers, and that was good enough for them. However, now that it pleases Robert to call himself Busson l'Aîné perhaps he will realise his responsibilities at last and settle down. If he can't pick a wife to keep him in order, I must find one for him."

I thought she was joking, for Robert at twenty-seven was surely old enough to choose for himself. Nor did I at first see the connection between my mother's more frequent visits to Paris with my father on business, and her sudden expressed wish to meet the families of some of his trade acquaintances, with the decision on her part that my brother must marry.

It was only when the three of them began to put up at the Cheval Rouge, ostensibly to discuss matters relating to both glass-houses, and my mother mentioned casually on her return that Monsieur Fiat, a well-to-do merchant, had an only daughter, that I began to suspect the motive for her visit.

"What is the daughter like?" I asked.

"Very pretty," replied my mother, which was strong praise for her, "and seemed very much taken with Robert and he with her. At least, they had plenty to say to each other. I heard him ask permission to call next time he is in Paris, which will be next week."

This was match-making with a vengeance. I felt jealous, for up to the present I had been Robert's sole confidante.

"He will soon become tired of her," I ventured.

"Perhaps," shrugged my mother. "She is the very opposite of Robert, apart from her good humour. Dark, petite, large brown eyes, and a quantity of ringlets. Your father was much impressed."

"Robert will never marry a tradesman's daughter," I pursued, "not even if she is the prettiest girl in the whole of Paris. He would lose face among his fine friends."

My mother smiled. "What if she brought him a dot of ten thousand livres," she returned, "and we guaranteed a similar sum, and your father made over to them the lease of la Brûlonnerie?"

This time I had no answer. I went off to my own room to sulk. But such promises, with the addition of pretty, twenty-year-old Catherine Adèle into the bargain, proved too much for my brother Robert to resist.

The agreements were drawn up between the parents of bride and groom, and on the 21st day of July, 1777, the marriage took place at the church of St. Sauveur, Paris, between Robert Mathurin Busson and Catherine Adèle Fiat.

4

THE FIRST SHOCK came about three months after the wedding. My uncle Démére rode over to le Chesne-Bidault to tell my father that Robert had leased la Brûlonnerie to a master glass-maker by the name of Caumont, and had himself rented the magnificent glass-house of Rougemont, which, with its superb château alongside, belonged to the marquis de la Touche, in the parish of St. Jean Froidmentel.

My father was at first stunned by the news, and refused to believe it.

"It is true," insisted my uncle. "I have seen the documents, signed and sealed. The marquis, like so many others of his kind, is an absentee landlord, caring nothing about his property as long as it brings him rent. You know what the place is like. They've been losing money there for years."

"It must be stopped," my father said. "Robert will ruin himself. He will lose everything he possesses, and his reputation into the bargain."

We set forth the very next day, my father, my mother, my uncle Démére and myself—I was determined to be of the company, and my parents were too concerned with what had happened to consider that I made quite an unnecessary fourth. We stayed an hour or two at la Brûlonnerie for my father to speak to the new lessee, Monsieur Caumont, and see the signed documents for himself, and then we drove on through the forest to Rougemont, which stood in the valley across the high road between Châteaudun and Vendôme.

"He is mad," my father kept repeating, "mad . . . mad . . . "

"We are to blame," said my mother. "He cannot forget la Pierre. He imagines he can do at twenty-seven what you only achieved after years of hard work. We are to blame. We have spoilt him."

Rougemont was truly a stupendous place. The glass-house itself consisted of four separate buildings fronting an enormous courtyard. The right-hand building was the lodging of the master glass-makers, and beside it stood the great furnace-house with two chimneys, and beyond this the depots and storehouses, the workrooms for the engravers, and opposite again the workmen's dwellings. Through the courtyard were massive iron gates, and the château itself, splendid, imposing, set amidst formal gardens. My father had hoped to surprise my brother, but as always in our glass-world someone had whispered news of our approach and Robert came forward to meet us as soon soon as we drove into the courtyard, gay and smiling, brimming with self-confidence as usual.

"Welcome to Rougemont," he called. "You could not have come at a better moment. We started a melt this morning and both furnaces are in use, as you can see from the chimneys, with every workman on the place employed. Come and see for yourselves."

He was not himself wearing a working blouse as my father always did during a shift, but sported a blue velvet coat of extravagant cut, more suited to a young nobleman parading the terraces of Versailles than to a master glass-maker about to enter his furnace-house. I thought myself that he looked remarkably well in it, but was abashed for him because of my father's expression.

"Cathie will receive my mother and Sophie in the château," Robert continued. "We keep some of the rooms there for our personal use." He clapped his hands and shouted, like an Eastern potentate summoning a blackamoor, and a servant appeared from nowhere, bowed deeply, and flung open the iron gates leading to the château.

My mother's face was a study as we followed the servant to the entrance door of the château, through ante-rooms to a great salon with stiff-backed chairs ranged against the wall, long mirrors reflecting us as we walked. There awaiting us—she must have perceived our arrival from the window—was Robert's bride, Cathie, Mademoiselle Fiat the merchant's daughter, dressed in a flimsy muslin gown with pink and white bows upon it, as delicious as a piece of confectionary from her own wedding-cake.

"What a pleasant surprise," she fluttered, running to embrace us, and then, remembering the presence of the servant, stood stiffly, and requested him to bring us some refreshment, after which she relaxed and asked us to sit down, and the three of us sat staring at each other.

"You look very pretty," said my mother at last, opening the conversation. "And how do you like being the wife of a master glass-maker here at Rougemont?"

"Well enough," replied Cathie, "but I find it rather fatiguing."

"No doubt," said my mother, "and a great responsibility. How many workmen are employed here, and how many of them are married with families?"

Cathie opened large eyes. "I have no idea," she said. "I have never spoken to any of them."

I thought this would silence my mother, but she quickly recovered.

"In that case," she continued, "what do you do with your time?"

Cathie hesitated. "I give orders to the servants," she said, "and I watch them polish the floors. The rooms are very spacious, as you can see."

"I can indeed," replied my mother. "No wonder you are fatigued."

"Then there is the entertaining," pursued Cathie. "Sometimes ten or twelve to dinner, and all at a moment's notice. It means stocking the larders with food that may be wasted. It is a very different matter from living in the rue des Petits-Carreaux in Paris, and going to the market if we had unexpected company."

Poor Cathie. It was true. She *was* fatigued. It was not so easy after all for a merchant's daughter to adopt the ways of a châtelaine.

"Whom do you entertain?" asked my mother. "It has never been the custom of masters and their wives to eat in each other's lodgings."

Once again Cathie opened large eyes. "Oh, we don't entertain amongst the people here," she explained, "but those friends and acquaintances of Robert's from Paris, who either come to visit us for that purpose, or are travelling between the capital and Blois. It was the same at la Brûlonnerie. One of Robert's chief reasons for moving to Rougemont was so that we could use the rooms in the château for entertaining."

"I see," said my mother.

I felt sorry for Cathie. Although I did not doubt her love for my brother, I sensed that she would be more at her ease back in the rue des Petits-Carreaux. Presently she asked us if we would care to see the rooms that had been put at their disposal, and we wandered through them, each one larger than any we had had at la Pierre. Cathie, trotting ahead of us, pointed out the two great chandeliers in the dining-hall, which, she told us, held thirty candles each, and must be replenished every time they dined there.

"It is a very fine sight when they are lighted," said Cathie proudly. "Robert sits at one end of the table and I at the other, English-fashion, with the guests on either side of us, and he gives me the signal when it is time to withdraw to the salon."

She closed the shutter so that the sunlight should not harm the long strip of carpet that ran down one side of the room.

"She is like a child playing at houses," whispered my mother. "What I ask myself is this—where will it all end?"

It ended precisely eleven months afterwards. The upkeep of the glass-house and the château of Rougemont mounted to a figure far in excess of my brother's reckoning, and the situation was made worse by certain miscalculations in the amount of goods sold to the Paris trading-houses. The greater part of Cathie's "dot" had thus been swallowed up in less than a year, with Robert's portion likewise, and the one merciful thing about the whole affair was that the lease of Rougemont had been for a twelvemonth only.

My father, despite his bitter disappointment at Robert's folly, and the throwing away of so much money, implored my brother to return to le Chesne-Bidault and work beside him as manager. There, with my father on the spot, he could come to no harm. Robert refused. "It is not that I am ungrateful for the suggestion," he explained to my parents when he came home to discuss the matter, bringing with him a subdued and rather wistful Cathie, who had had a hard time of it explaining matters to an irate Monsieur and Madame Fiat in the rue des Petits-Carreaux, "but I already have prospects in Paris—I can't say more than that at the moment—which promise to turn out well. A certain Monsieur Cannette, one of the bankers to the Court of Versailles, is thinking of setting up a glass-house in the quartier St. Antoine, in the rue des Boulets, at my recommendation, and of course if all works out well he will appoint me as director."

My father and mother looked at one another and then back to my brother's eager, smiling face, which showed no trace of anxiety or any other mark after his late disaster.

"You have just lost a small fortune," said my father. "How can you guarantee that it won't happen again?"

"Easily," Robert replied. "This will be Monsieur Cannette's venture, not mine. I shall be paid for my services."

"And if the venture fails?"

"Monsieur Cannette, not I, will be the poorer."

I was not more than fifteen at the time, but even a child of that age could see that there was some sense lacking in my brother—call it moral, call it what you will, but whatever it was it betrayed itself in his very manner of speaking, his carelessness where the property or the feelings of others were concerned, and an inability to understand any viewpoint but his own.

My mother made a last attempt to dissuade him from this new course. "Give up the idea," she pleaded. "Come home, or, if you will, go back to la Brûlonnerie and work under your own tenant. Here in the country everyone knows one another, we are all established. In Paris new houses are continually being set up that come to nothing."

Robert turned to her impatiently. "That's just it," he said. "In the country you are set in your ways, the life here is—well, frankly provincial. Nothing will ever advance. Whereas in Paris . . ."

"In Paris," my mother finished for him, "a man can be ruined in less than a month, with or without friends."

"Heaven be thanked I have friends," returned Robert, "men of influence—Monsieur Cannette is a case in point, but there are others—men even closer to Court circles who have only to say the right word in the right quarter and I am made for life."

"Or finished," said my mother.

"As you will. But I would rather play for high stakes than for none at all."

"Let him go," said my father. "Argument is useless."

The glass-house was set up in the rue des Boulets, Robert was made director of it, and in six months' time Monsieur Cannette, the Court banker, had lost so much money that he sold the enterprise over my brother's head, and Robert was asking Cathie's father Monsieur Fiat for a substantial loan to tide him over "temporary" difficulties.

Then came a long silence. Robert did not write to us at le Chesne-Bidault, nor did we visit Paris, for all of us at home were in a state of agitation over my father's health. He had fallen from his horse riding back one day from Châteaudun, and was in bed six weeks or more, with my mother and Edmé and I taking it in turn to nurse him. The news came at last, not by word of mouth or by letter, but in a trade journal that my father took monthly, which one of us bore up to his bedroom when he was but partially recovered.

The journal was dated November, 1779, and the item ran as follows:

"Monsieur de Quévremont-Delamotte, a banker in Paris, has asked permission of the Minister of the Interior to manufacture glass in the English method at the glass-house of Villeneuve-St. Georges, outside Paris, formerly maintained by the Bohemian glass-manufacturer Joseph Koenig. Monsieur de Quévremont-Delamotte has already spent the sum of 24,000 livres upon this establishment, while it was under the direction of Monsieur Koenig, whose talent and intelligence proved, however, to be smaller than Monsieur de Quévremont-Delamotte had anticipated. He reserves to himself the usual privileges and letters patent, and intends to install as director of this enterprise Monsieur Busson l'Aîné, who has wide connections in the region. Monsieur Busson was brought up in the glass-house of la Pierre by his father Monsieur Mathurin Busson, who has written papers for the Académie on flint glass. Thus Monsieur Quévremont-Delamotte has every expectation that work of the highest possible standard will be forthcoming from the glass-house of Villeneuve-St. Georges, thanks to the care and skill of his young director."

Edmé and I did not read the piece in the journal until later. The first we knew of it was when the furious clanging of the bell in the passage below sent us both hurrying up to my father's bedside. He was lying half across the bed, the front of his nightshirt stained with blood, and blood on the sheet as well.

"Call your mother," he gasped, and Edmé flew downstairs, while I tried to support him on the pillow. It was the second time he had suffered such a haemorrhage; the first was immediately after he had fallen from his horse. My mother came instantly, the surgeon was sent for, and although he pronounced my father to be in no immediate danger he warned my mother that any undue shock or excitement might prove fatal.

Presently, when my father was easier, he pointed to the journal which had fallen on the floor during all this commotion, and we guessed the reason for his sudden attack.

"As soon as I can safely leave him," my mother told me later, "I shall go myself to Paris and see if anything can be done to prevent further mischief. If Robert has agreed to go to Villeneuve as manager only, no great harm may have been done. If, on the other hand, he has committed himself financially, then he is heading for a disaster worse than the one he sustained at Rougemont."

We could but wait and see. My father's health appeared to improve, and my mother left him in my care and proceeded to Paris. When she returned home a week later we learnt at once from her face that the worst had happened. Robert had not only become director of the glass-house at Villeneuve-St. Georges, but had agreed to purchase the property from Monsieur de Quévremont-Delamotte for the sum of 18,000 livres, payable within six months of the date of signature.

"He has until May of next year to find the money," said my mother, and I had never seen her before with tears in her eyes. "He will never do it. Thousands have already been sunk in this particular foundry, and it would need many more thousands spent on it before it could begin to show a profit. It needs a new furnace and new sheds, and the workmen's lodgings are worse than pig-sties. Most of the money spent so far has gone in putting up temporary buildings for the English craftsmen brought over by the last owner, Koenig, who, it now seems, did nothing but drink all the time."

"But why has Robert attempted it?" I asked. "Did he give any excuse at all?"

"The usual one," replied my mother. "He is supported, so he said, by 'influential' friends. A certain marquis de Vichy is interested in the project, and according to your brother may ultimately buy the glass-works from him."

"In that case," put in Edmé, "why did Robert bother with the property in the first place?"

"Because," returned my mother fiercely, "what he has done is known in trade circles as speculation. Your brother is a gambler. There is the crux of the matter."

Then she softened. She put out her arms to us both and we tried to console her. "I am to blame," she said. "All this high-handed folly is due to me. We are both too proud."

Now Edmé was near to tears. "You are not proud," she protested. "How can you accuse yourself? Robert's behaviour has nothing to do with you."

"Oh, yes, it has," replied my mother. "I taught him to aim high, and he knows it. It's too late to expect him to change now." She paused, and looked at each of us in turn.

"Do you know what grieved me most," she said, "more than my anxiety for his future? He never let me know, during all these past months of silence, that Cathie was expecting a baby. They had a little girl, born on the 1st of September. My first grandchild."

Robert a father . . . I could not imagine him in the rôle, any more than I could see Cathie as a nurse. She would be better pleased with a doll.

"What have they called her?" asked Edmé.

My mother's face changed very slightly. "Elizabeth Henriette," she replied, "after Madame Fiat, naturally."

Then she went upstairs to break the news to my father.

During the next few months we heard rumours, but no more. The marquis de Vichy had lost interest in the glass-house at Villeneuve-St. Georges . . . My brother had approached another banker . . . Monsieur de Quévremont-Delamotte was said to be considering an association with his former partner, Joseph Koenig, in a foundry at Sèvres . . .

My father was still not well enough to travel, and he sent Pierre up to Villeneuve-St. Georges early in February to bring back news.

Pierre at twenty-seven, no longer the carefree youth he had been at seventeen, was yet hopeful enough that Robert would succeed in his new undertaking.

"If he does not succeed," he told my father, "he can have all my savings, for I don't need them"—proof that his heart had not changed, despite his maturer years. Alas, it needed more than Pierre's savings to protect my oldest brother from the shame of bankruptcy.

Pierre returned from Villeneuve-St. Georges at the end of the month with a lock of the baby's hair for my mother, a clock of exquisite workmanship whose crystal surround had been designed at the glass-house there by Robert himself for my father—and a copy of a deposition signed before the judges of the Royal Court at the

Châtelet in Paris, admitting Robert's insolvency.

My father, ill as he was, accompanied by my mother and myself, and leaving Pierre in charge of Edmé and le Chesne-Bidault, set forth a fortnight later for Paris. I looked out of the windows of the diligence with very different feelings from those upon my first visit nearly four years before. Then, with my father hale and hearty, and I myself full of expectation and excitement, the journey, though exhausting, had been all pleasure; now, in bitter weather, my father ill, my mother anxious, I had nothing to look forward to but my brother's public disgrace.

Villeneuve-St. Georges lay in the suburbs of Paris to the southeast, and we proceeded directly there, after resting one night at the hotel du Chevel Rouge in the rue St. Denis.

This time, unlike the day of our unannounced arrival at Rougemont, Robert was not standing in the courtyard to welcome us, and here was no imposing structure or grandiose château alongside, but a straggling collection of buildings in a poor state of repair, with two furnace-houses separated from one another by a wide ditch full of broken masonry and rejected glass. There was no sign of life. No smoke came from the chimneys. The place had already been abandoned.

My father tapped on the window of our hired vehicle and hailed a passing labourer. "Has work ceased entirely at the foundry?" he asked.

The fellow shrugged his shoulders. "You can see for yourself it has," he replied. "I was paid off a week ago, like the rest, and we were told we were lucky to get what we did. A hundred and fifty of us suddenly without work, and families to keep. Not a word of warning. Yet there was stuff going out of here to Rouen and other cities in the north, crates of it, every day—someone's been paid for it, that's what we say, but where's the money gone?"

My father was much distressed, but there was nothing he could do. "Can you find other employment?" he enquired.

The workman shrugged again. "What do you expect? There's nothing here for any of us, with the foundry closed. We'll have to take to the roads."

He was staring at my mother all the while, and suddenly he said, "You were here before, weren't you? You're the director's mother?"

"I am," replied my mother.

"Well, you won't find him in the master's house, I can tell you that. We broke the windows for him, and he legged out of it, taking his wife and child."

My father was already reaching for coins to give the workman, and the fellow accepted them with an ill grace, not to be wondered at under the circumstances.

"Return to the rue St. Denis," my father told the driver and we turned about, away from the desolation of my poor brother's foundry, where he had left behind him not only a failed venture but the ill-will of one hundred and fifty hungry workmen.

"What do we do now?" asked my mother.

"What we might have done in the first place," said my father. "Enquire of Cathie's father in the rue des Petits-Carreaux. She and the child will be there, if Robert is not."

He was mistaken. The Fiats knew nothing of what had happened, and had not seen Robert or Cathie for at least two months. Coolness on the part of the Fiats—doubtless because of the loan made to their son-in-law, and pride and loyalty on the part of their daughter—had caused this temporary estrangement.

When we arrived back at the hotel du Cheval Rouge we found a message from Robert awaiting us. It was addressed to my mother.

"Word has reached me that you are in Paris," it said. "No need to worry my father, but I am at present confined in the hotel du St. Esprit, in the rue Montorgueil, pending the hearing of my case. I am engaged in drawing up a list of my debts and assets, and should like your opinion. I am confident that the assets will amount to more than the debts, particularly as la Brûlonnerie is still mine, and there is also a portion of Cathie's 'dot' due to me from her parents. The marquis de Vichy let me down, as doubtless you have already heard, but I am not concerned about the future. English flint glass is all the rage, especially in Court circles, and I have it on good authority that Messieurs Lambert and Boyer are to obtain permission to set up a glass-house for the purpose of developing flint glass in the park of St. Cloud, under the direct patronage of the Queen. If I can get out of this present scrape without too much difficulty, I have every hope of being employed there as first engraver, as I am the only Frenchman in the country to understand anything of the process. Your affectionate son, Robert."

Not a word about Cathie and the child, nor any expression of sorrow for what had happened.

My mother passed the letter in silence to my father—it was useless to attempt to hide the truth from him—and together they went to see my brother in his hotel. They found him well and in excellent spirits, totally unmoved by his insolvency.

"He had the effrontery to tell us," my father—who appeared to me to have aged ten years during his hour with his son—told me afterwards, "that it was good experience to fall into such misfortune. He has given power of attorney to some associate at Villeneuve, as he is forbidden to sign any bills himself."

My father showed me the statement, signed by the judges, of the preliminary hearing on the very day we had travelled to Paris.

"In the year 1780, on March 15th, in the Chambre de Conseil, before us, judges of the Court, appointed by the King, in Paris, appeared le sieur Tréspaigné, resident in Paris and at the glass foundry of Villeneuve-St. Georges, having power of Attorney for sieur Robert Busson the owner of the glass-works at Villeneuve-St. Georges, who was ordered to appear before us and has asked us to appoint whomever we shall judge right to carry out the examination of the accounts of the above named Busson, declared insolvent from the statements deposed of at the Record office, conforming to the Ordinance of 1673 and the Edict of the King, dated November 13th, 1739. For this matter we have called the sieur Tréspaigné named above, giving him power to call all the creditors of the said Busson to appear in person by special order, in this Court, before us, Judges of the Council, and to show and establish their titles of creditors, in order to have them examined and verified as the case may demand.

"This is the official verbatim report of the Court which was made. Signed. Guyot."

I handed the document back to my father, who was preparing to go out once more and seek further advice from the best lawyers in Paris, but my mother dissuaded him.

"You will kill yourself," she told him, "and that would help neither Robert nor anyone else. The first step is to consider what he calls his assets, and I have the papers here with me."

As she sat herself down in the hotel bedroom, she might have been home at le Chesne-Bidault reckoning up the weekly expenditure in her ledger. Something had to be salvaged from the wreck of her son's affairs, and no one was better suited to the task than his mother.

"Where is poor Cathie and the baby in all this?" I asked.

"Hiding in lodgings," she replied, "in Villeneuve-St. Georges."

"Then the sooner somebody brings them here to Paris the better," I said, having more sympathy at this moment for his wife and child than for my brother.

We went to Villeneuve the following day, and found Cathie and the little Elizabeth Henriette lodging with one of the journeyman-carriers and his wife, a couple named Boudin, who had taken no part in the window-breaking at the master's house, but had been seized with pity for the master's family. Cathie herself had been too upset, and too proud, to go home to her parents.

She looked wretched, her pretty face spoilt with weeping, her hair tangled and unkempt, a very altered Cathie from the young bride who had shown us round the château at Rougemont. To make matters worse the baby was ill, too ill, she declared, to be moved. My mother dared not leave my father alone at the Cheval Rouge, so it was decided, with the consent of the good couple Boudin, that I should remain in the lodgings at Villeneuve-St. Georges to help Cathie.

A most miserable few weeks followed. Cathie, already distraught over Robert's disgrace, was in no way capable of looking after her baby, whose sickness, I felt sure, had come about through wrong feeding and neglect. I was only sixteen, and hardly wiser than my sister-in-law. We had to depend upon Madame Boudin for advice, and although she did everything possible for the baby the poor little thing died on the 18th of April. I think I was even more upset than Cathie. It was so needless a loss. The baby lay in the small coffin like a waxen doll, having known seven months of life, and would have been living still, I felt certain, if Robert had never gone to Villeneuve-St. Georges.

My mother came for us the day after the baby died, and we took poor Cathie home to her parents in the rue des Petits-Carreaux, for, although Robert was now staying at the Cheval Rouge with my parents, his affairs were still unsettled and the final reckoning would not be until the end of May.

Robert's list of creditors was formidable, even greater than my father had feared. Quite apart from the 18,000 livres owed to Monsieur Quévremont-Delamotte for the glass-house at Villeneuve-St. Georges, he had debts of nearly 50,000 livres to merchants and dealers all over Paris. The total amounted to something like 70,000 livres, and to meet this appalling sum there was only one answer, and that was to sell the single worthwhile asset he possessed—namely, the glass-house at la Brûlonnerie, given to him in trust at his wedding, valued by my father at 80,000 livres.

It was a bitter blow to my parents. Here was the glass-house where my father had first served as apprentice under Monsieur Brossard, and where he had taken my mother as a bride, which he had later developed with my uncle Démeré as one of the foremost foundries in the country, now to be sold to strangers to pay my brother's debts.

As to the smaller creditors, the wine-merchants, the clothiers, the house-furnishers—even the livery-man who had supplied a carriage for Robert to drive to Rouen and back on some extravagant purchase of material never used—all these debts were paid by my mother out of her own private income, derived from small farm-rents in her native village of St. Christophe.

Even then, when he appeared before the judges for the last time at the end of May, and was given clearance, I do not believe my brother understood the magnitude of what he had done.

"It's really a matter of knowing the right people," he confided to me when we were packing up to return home to le Chesne-Bidault. "I have been unlucky to date, but it will be very different in the future. You wait and see. I won't attempt to direct a foundry, the responsibility is too wearing. But as first engraver at a high salary—and they'll have to pay me well, or I won't accept the position—there is no telling where I might not end up, perhaps at le Petit Trianon itself! I am sorry my father has been so put out about it all, but then, as I have so often said, his outlook is provincial."

He smiled at me, as confident, as gay and as self-possessed as he had always been. Thirty years old and a brilliant craftsman, he had no more sense of responsibility than a child of ten.

"You must know," I said to him with all the weight of my sixteen years, and with the sight of his poor dead baby fresh in my memory, "that you have nearly broken Cathie's heart, and my father's too."

"Nonsense," he replied. "Cathie is already looking forward to living at St. Cloud, and another baby will console her. She will have a son next time. As to my father, once he is back at le Chesne-Bidault and away from Paris, which he has always detested, he will soon be himself again."

My brother was mistaken. The very next day, when we were due to take the diligence and travel home, my father was seized with another haemorrhage. My mother got him to bed at once and sent for the surgeon. There was little he could do. Too weak to travel home, yet conscious enough to know that he was dying, my father lingered on in that hotel bedroom of the Cheval Rouge for another seven days.

My mother never left his side, or when she did it was only to snatch some sleep in my adjoining room, while I took her place. Those faded red hangings to the bed, the cracks on the plastered walls, the chipped ewer and basin in the corner of the room, these things became planted in my memory as I watched my father's progress toward death.

A stifling heat had descended upon Paris too, adding to his suffering, but the window giving on to the noisy, narrow rue St. Denis below did not open more than a few inches only, bringing a turmoil of sound and a fetid air that only turned the room more sour.

How he longed for home—not only the dear familiarity of his surroundings at le Chesne-Bidault, but for his own terrain, the forests and the fields where he had been born and bred. Robert might call his attitude provincial, but our father, and our mother with him, had their roots deep in the soil; and from this same soil which had nurtured them both, the lush Touraine, the very core of France, he had built up his glass-houses, creating with his hands and with his life's breath symbols of beauty that would outlast his time. Now his life was ebbing from him, vanishing like the air in a blow-pipe laid aside, and the last night we were together, while my mother was sleeping, he looked at me and said, "Take care of your brothers. Keep the family one."

He died on the 8th of June, 1780, aged fifty-nine, and was buried close by in the church of St. Leu in the rue St. Denis.

We were too worn out with weeping to notice it at the time, but later it was a source of pride to all of us that every merchant, trader and workman in the glass-trade with whom he had ever done business came to St. Leu that day as a mark of respect to his memory.

5

MY FATHER'S PERSONAL estate amounted to some 167,000 livres gross, and it took my mother and Monsieur Beaussier, the notary of Montmirail, until the end of July to sort out his papers, complete the inventory and the list of debts and assets, and finalise the net figure of 145,804 livres. Half of this sum was my mother's, and the other half was divided equally amongst us, the five children. Robert and Pierre, having attained their majority, received their portion at once, while Michel, Edmé and I, as minors living at home, had our one-fifth in trust, our mother acting trustee. The lease of le Chesne-Bidault, held jointly by our parents, would continue now in my mother's name alone, and she decided to manage the foundry herself as "maîtresse verrière", a title held by no other woman in the trade. She decided to keep for her eventual retirement the small properties in St. Christophe which she had inherited from her father Pierre Labbé; meanwhile she would reign over the community at le Chesne-Bidault.

I well remember how we all assembled, in the August of 1780, in the master's room at home, and discussed the future. My mother sat at the head of the table, the widow's cap topping her grey-gold hair somehow adding to her dignity; and the mock title, la Reyne d'hongrie, seemed better suited to her now at fifty-five than ever before.

Robert stood at her right hand, or paced the room, continually restless, forever touching some ornament which he thought must be his by right of inheritance; while to the left sat Pierre, deep in his own dreams, which I felt sure had little to do with laws or legacies.

Michel, at the end of the table, had grown the most like our father in appearance. Small, dark, thickset, he was now twenty-four years old, and a master glass-maker at Aubigny in le Berry. We had not seen him for many months, and I do not know whether it was absence from home that had matured him, or the sudden realisation of my father's death, but he seemed to have lost his old reserve, and was the first of us to volunteer an opinion upon the future.

"S-s-speaking for myself," he began, with far less hesitation than usual, "I have no more to l-learn at Aubigny. I am now w-willing to work here, if my mother will have me."

I watched him with some curiosity. Here was indeed a new Michel, who, instead of sitting with a sullen expression on his face and eyes firmly fixed upon the floor, looked straight at my mother as though to challenge her.

"Very well, my son," she replied, "if you feel that way I am equally willing to employ you. Remember that I am mistress of le Chesne-Bidault, and while I remain so I expect my orders to be obeyed and carried out."

"That s-s-suits me," he answered, "providing the orders are s-sensible."

He would never have spoken thus a year ago, and although I was surprised at his daring I was secretly filled with admiration. Robert ceased his incessant prowling to throw a glance in Michel's direction, and nodded approvingly.

"I have never given an order yet," my mother remarked, "which was not of immediate benefit to the glass-house under my control. The only error in judgement was to advise your father to give la Brûlonnerie to Robert as his marriage portion."

Michel was silenced. The sale of la Brûlonnerie to meet Robert's debts had been a blow to the interests of all of us.

"I see no necessity," said Robert, when the silence had become too long for comfort, "to revive the old business of my marriage portion. It's over and done with. And my debts are paid. As you all know, and my mother as well, my immediate future has great promise. I become first engraver in crystal at this new establishment in St. Cloud within a few months. Should I wish to have a small financial interest in the place it will now be possible."

Here was a dig at my mother. As a beneficiary under my father's will he was now independent of her and could use his money as he pleased. The will had been drawn up long before my father's illness, and before Robert had started his career of extravagance. My mother wisely ignored his remark and turned to Pierre.

"Well, dreamer?" she said. "We have all known since you came home ten years ago from Martinique that you followed your father's trade through want of ability at anything else. As it has turned out, you have done very well. But don't imagine I shall force you to remain a master glass-maker now that you have your share of the inheritance. You can go and live à la Jean-Jacques if you care to—become a hermit in the forest and exist on hazel-nuts and goat's milk."

Pierre awoke from his dream, yawned, stretched, and gave her a long, slow smile.

"You are perfectly right," he said. "I have no desire to stay in the glass-trade. I thought seriously some months back of going out to North America and fighting for the colonies in their War of Independence against England. It's a tremendous cause. But I have decided to remain in France. I can do more good amongst my own people."

We all stared. This was indeed a statement from dear, lazy Pierre, the "eccentric", as my father used to call him.

"So?" My mother nodded encouragement. "What's in your mind?"

Pierre leant forward in his chair with a determined air.

"I shall buy a notary's practice in Le Mans," he said, "and offer my services to any client who cannot afford lawyer's fees. There are hundreds of poor fellows who cannot read or write and need legal advice, and I shall make it my business to help them."

Pierre a notary! Had he said a lion-tamer I should have been less astonished.

"Very philanthropic," replied my mother, "but I warn you, you won't make a fortune out of it."

"I have no desire to make a fortune," returned Pierre. "Whoever enriches himself does so at the expense of some poor beggar or other. Let those who wish to be wealthy reconcile themselves to their conscience first."

I noticed that he did not look at Robert as he spoke, and I wondered suddenly whether his brother's disasters, first at Rougemont and then at Villeneuve-St. Georges, had affected Pierre more than the rest of us had realised, so that now, in this strange fashion of his own, he had decided to make amends for it.

It was Michel, despite his stammer, who found his tongue first.

"My c-congratulations, Pierre," he said. "As I am never likely to m-make a fortune either, I shall p-probably be among your early clients. In any event, if no one wants your advice, you can always d-d-draw up marriage contracts for Sophie and Aimée."

He could never manage the Ed in Edmé, and Aimée she had become through long habit. My young sister, indulged by all of us, and my father in particular, had remained remarkably quiet throughout these proceedings, but now she spoke up in her own defence.

"Pierre can draw up my marriage contract if he likes," she announced, "but I make the stipulation that I may choose my own husband. He will be fifty years old and as rich as Croesus."

This, said with the determined authority of fourteen years, helped to relax the tension—I asked her afterwards, and she told me that she did it on purpose, for we were all becoming too serious—and so it was that the future of my three brothers was discussed and arranged without ill-feeling among any of us.

One final point remained to be settled. Robert walked over to the glass cabinet standing in one corner of the room, opened the doors, and took out the precious goblet that had been made at la Pierre on the famous occasion of the late King's visit.

"This," he announced, "is mine by right of heritage."

For a moment nobody spoke; we all looked at my mother.

"Do you think you deserve it?" she asked.

"Possibly not," Robert answered, "but my father said it should be mine to hand down to my children, and I have no reason to believe that he would have gone back on his word. It will look very well in my new house at St. Cloud . . . By the way, Cathie expects another baby in the spring."

This was enough for my mother. "Take it," she said, "but remember your father's words when he promised it to you. It was to serve as a reminder of high crafts-manship, and was not intended to bring either fame or fortune."

"Perhaps not," said Robert, "but it rather depends on the hands that hold it."

When Robert left us to return to Paris he had the goblet wrapped up with the rest of his possessions, and the following April, when his son Jacques was born, he and the many fine friends at St. Cloud who were invited to the christening toasted the child in champagne drunk from the goblet.

Meanwhile the rest of us settled down to life at le Chesne-Bidault without my father—with the exception, of course, of Pierre our eccentric, who, true to his decision, bought a notary's practice in Le Mans and gave himself up to helping those less fortunate than himself. I thought myself that he should have had the goblet rather than Robert, for although he would no longer make glass he was a craftsman in his own way, and deliberately chose to live up to the high standard set by my father. Certainly he never lacked clients, and the poorer they were the better pleased was Pierre; he always had a string of unfortunates waiting on his doorstep. I had it in mind to go to Le Mans and keep house for him—it was practically settled between my mother and myself—and then, without a word to either of us, he went and got himself betrothed to a merchant's daughter, a Mlle. Dumesnil of Bonnétable, and was married within the month.

"So exactly like Pierre," observed my mother. "He extricates the merchant from a difficult deal and gets landed with the daughter."

The fact that Marie Dumesnil was older than Pierre, and brought him nothing very much in the way of a "dot", prejudiced her in my mother's eyes. However, she was a good creature and an excellent cook, and if she had not been suited to my brother he would never have taken her.

"Let us hope," said my mother, "that Michel will not allow himself to be caught so easily."

"Don't f-f-fret yourself," replied her youngest son. "I have enough to do at le Chesne-Bidault k-keeping out of your way without s-saddling myself with a wife."

The truth was that Michel and my mother had settled down remarkably well together, and now my father was no longer there to find fault with him, or become exasperated with his stammer, Michel was proving himself an excellent master—under my mother's direction, needless to say. Two or three of the craftsmen who had worked with Michel at Aubigny in le Berry had followed him to le Chesne-Bidault, which showed the influence he must have had upon them. Others had been either workmen or apprentices at la Pierre, and had known him from boyhood.

We were indeed a community at le Chesne-Bidault, with my mother the ruling spirit, and Michel more of a comrade to the men than manager. He was a natural leader, as my father had been before him, but his ways were very different. When my father had entered the furnace-house at the start of a melt, the noisy clatter and rough joking that went with a crowd of men living at close quarters would instantly cease; each man went to his appointed task in silence, without further ado. It was not that they feared the master, but they held him in deep respect. Michel expected neither silence nor respect. His theory was that the greater the clatter the better the response to work, especially if the loudest singing—for all glass-workers are natural singers—and the broadest jokes were started by himself.

He always knew when my mother was likely to make her rounds, which she did every day as matter of principle; then he would give the signal for order, and the men would respond. I think she suspected what went on in her absence, but the output from the glass-house remained steady, so she had no cause for complaint.

The chemical and scientific instruments that had been perfected by my father at la Brûlonnerie continued to be made at le Chesne-Bidault—we would send them locally to Saumur and to Tours, and naturally to Paris too. The fine table-glass that my uncle Michel had designed at la Pierre was not made by us at the smaller foundry. For one thing we had not the craftsmen, although we employed over eighty men, and for another the instruments were less costly to produce. Here at le Chesne-Bidault my mother had the farm to attend to, besides the orchard and garden, and well over forty families in her care, some of whom lived down the hill at le Plessis-Dorin and others through the forest near Montmirail, though the majority were housed in lodgings around the glass-house itself.

Edmé and I were brought up to care for the families just as our mother did. This meant visiting some of them every day and seeing to their needs—for none of the wives could read or write, and perhaps needed letters sent to distant relatives which we would write for them. Often it would be necessary to drive to la Ferté-Bernard or even to Le Mans on some errand for the families, for their lodgings were bare enough; they had little in the way of comforts, and wages were low.

We were continually asked to be godparents, which meant that more than usual attention had to be paid to our godchildren. Edmé and I found this something of an added burden, but our mother insisted. She must have had thirty godchildren at least, and she never forgot the birthday of one of them.

We were never idle at le Chesne-Bidault. If we were not visiting the families we were employed by my mother about the house, sewing, mending, making preserves; or gardening and fruit-picking, depending on the season of the year. My mother would never allow anyone to be idle, and in the winter, when there was snow on the ground and we could not get out, she would set us to stitching blankets for the women and children.

I expected no other life, and was never dissatisfied. All the same, I looked upon it as a great treat when I was allowed to visit Robert and Cathie in Paris perhaps two or three times a year.

So far there had been no repetition of his former folly. His position as first engraver in crystal to the glass-house in the park of St. Cloud, near the pont de Sèvres, had brought him some renown, and in 1784 the foundry had for title "Manufacture des Cristaux et Emaux de la Reine". My brother and Cathie had lodgings close to the glass-house, and although they only had two or three rooms of a very different size from those at Rougemont Robert had furnished them in the latest style, and Cathie herself was prinked out like a lady of the Court. She was pretty and as affectionate as ever, always delighted to see me, and the baby Jacques was a fine little fellow.

As to Robert himself, I never could help contrasting his appearance, and his manner too, with those of Pierre and Michel. If I stayed overnight at Le Mans, as I sometimes did, Pierre would invariably return from his office late, having been detained by one of his unfortunate clients. His hair would be unbrushed and his neckerchief anyhow, and there would be a patch on his coat as likely as not, and he would snatch something to eat, hardly aware of what he tasted, while he recounted to me some tale of poverty that had been unfolded to him, which he was determined to redress.

Michel, too, cared little for his appearance. My mother was forever at him to shave close, and to trim his nails, and to cut his hair, for he would go about looking as rough as the charcoal-burners.

But Robert . . . For one thing, his hair was always powdered, which instantly gave him distinction. His jackets and breeches were from the best tailors. His stockings were silk, never worsted, and his shoes either pointed or square, according to the current fashion. He would return to Cathie and me in the evening as immaculate as when he had sallied forth in the morning—or the other way round, depending upon the shift—and his conversation, instead of being about his working day, which I was accustomed to from both Pierre and Michel, would be fresh and amusing, frequently scandalous, more often than not malicious, and generally bearing upon some lively topic of Court circles.

These were the days when gossip was becoming rife about the Queen. Her extravagance, and love of balls and theatre-going, were well known; and although the birth of the Dauphin had caused general rejoicing, and made a fine occasion for festivities and firework displays throughout the capital, there was much sniggering and chatter at the same time, with whispers that the child had been sired by anybody but the King himself.

"They say . . . " Objectionable phrase, a hundred times repeated by my brother, who, with the Queen as patron of the glass-house at St. Cloud, ought to have known better.

"They say" the Queen has half-a-dozen lovers, the King's brothers amongst them, and doesn't even know herself who is the father of her son . . .

"They say" that her latest ball-gown cost two thousand livres, and the dressmaking-girls who made it were so worn out with getting it put together in time that half of them died in the process . . .

"They say" that when the King comes home exhausted from hunting and goes straight to bed, the Queen disappears into Paris with her brother-in-law le comte d'Artois and her friends the de Polignacs and the princesse de Lamballe, and that they wander in the worst quarters disguised as prostitutes . . .

Who started the rumours nobody knew. It certainly amused my brother to spread them, and he always insisted that he got them at first hand.

When I was staying with Robert and Cathie in the spring of 1784, I was the unwitting cause of an incident that was to have a marked effect upon my brother's future. I was due to leave Paris on the 28th of April, and on the day before, the 27th, the author Beaumarchais was to present the first performance of a new play *Le Mariage de Figaro* at the theatre. Robert was determined to see the play—all Paris would be there, and it was said to be profoundly shocking, full of allusions to happenings at Versailles though disguised in a Spanish setting—and nothing would content him but that I must be present too.

"It will be an education, Sophie," he insisted. "You are far too provincial, and

Beaumarchais is all the rage. If you see this piece you may spend the rest of the year discussing it at home."

This last was quite unlikely. Michel would mock, my mother would raise her eyebrows, and as to Pierre, he would only tell me that here was further proof of the decadence of society.

However, as it was my last day I allowed myself to be persuaded. We left Cathie in St. Cloud in charge of young Jacques and set forth ourselves in a hired carriage, myself in a gown made up by the dressmaker in Montmirail, but Robert a perfect dandy.

The crowds were immense outside the theatre, and I was all for driving straight back again to St. Cloud, but Robert would have none of it.

"Take my arm," he said. "We'll get ourselves inside at least, if you promise not to faint. Afterwards, leave all to me."

We pushed, we struggled, we finally gained entry. Needless to say, not a seat to be found.

"Stay here, and do not move," commanded my brother, placing me beside a pillar. "I will contrive something. There is sure to be someone I know," and with this he disappeared into the crowd.

I would have given anything to be in Cathie's shoes, minding young Jacques. The heat was intolerable, and so was the stench of paint and powder from the chattering women about me, all of them in grande tenue, dressed up in frills and furbelows.

I watched the orchestra come in and take their places. Soon the overture would begin, and still there was no sign of my brother. Then, over the heads of the crowd, I saw him beckon me, and stammering almost as badly as my brother Michel I made my excuses, and edged my way towards him.

"Couldn't be better," he murmured in my ear. "You shall have the best seat in the theatre."

"Where . . . what?" I began, and to my horror he led me towards a box close to the stage, where a magnificently dressed nobleman, wearing the grand cordon bleu, was seated entirely alone.

"The duc de Chartres," whispered Robert, "Grand Master of the Supreme Orient and of all Fremasonry in France. I belong to the same Lodge."

He knocked on the door before I could stop him, made a secret masonic sign of recognition, so he told me afterwards, and in a few hurried words explained the situation to the King's cousin.

"If you could possibly give my sister a seat," my brother said, pushing me forward, and before I knew what was happening the duc de Chartres was offering me his hand, and smiling, and pointing to the chair beside him.

The orchestra started the overture. The curtain rose. The play began. I saw nothing, heard nothing, too acutely conscious of my brother's audacity and my own agony of embarrassment to be aware of anything that happened on the stage. Never before, or since, have I endured hours of such misery. I could not join in either the laughter or the applause; and when the entr'actes came—there were four of them—and the box filled with friends of the duc de Chartres, all of them splendidly dressed, eager to discuss the play, I sat motionless, my face scarlet, never daring once to lift my head.

The duke himself must have been conscious of my confusion, for he wisely left me to myself, and did not again address me; it was only when the play was over, and Robert advanced from the back of the box to fetch me, that I caught his eye, managed to dip a curtsey, and retreated with my brother into the crowds below.

"Well?" said Robert, his eyes shining with pleasure and excitement. "Wasn't that the most delightful evening you have ever spent in your life?"

"On the contrary," I replied, bursting into tears, "the most hateful."

I remember him standing there in the foyer, staring at me in utter bewilderment, while the hordes of painted, powdered and bejewelled ladies filed out past us to their waiting carriages.

"I just don't understand you," Robert repeated again and again, as we rattled back to St. Cloud in our hired conveyance. "To have the chance of a seat beside the future duc d'Orléans, who happens to be the most influential and popular man in the whole of France at this present time, and when one little word in his ear might make your brother for life—and all you can do is to blub like a baby."

No, Robert did not understand. Handsome, gay, debonair, perfectly self-possessed, he had yet not grasped the fact that his young sister, with her smattering of education and her provincial dress, belonged to a world that he had long left behind him, a world which, despite its apparent backwardness and rustic simplicity, had greater depth than his.

"I would rather," I said to my brother, "work a whole shift before the furnace in le Chesne-Bidault than spend another such evening."

The adventure had its sequel. The duc de Chartres, who was to succeed his father as duc d'Orléans in the following year, lived at the Palais-Royal, and in face of much opposition he pulled down a number of properties overlooking his gardens and designed an entirely new lay-out. His palace was now surrounded with arcades, where the people of Paris could wander at will, and beneath these arcades were cafés, boutiques, restaurants, billiard-rooms, "salles de spectacles", and every sort of device to catch the public eye. Above these ground-floor premises were gambling-rooms and clubs.

To wander in the Palais-Royal, to look in the boutique windows, to mount the stairs or even to penetrate to the back-quarters to see the peculiar temptations more than occasionally lurking there, had become the most popular pastime in Paris. My brother took me there one Sunday, and, although I pretended to be amused, I was never more shocked in my life. It did not altogether surprise me therefore, knowing Robert's audacity, that having once dared the presence of the future duc d'Orléans he should venture to do so again. The soirée at the theatre, and renewed thanks for the great honour bestowed upon his little sister from the provinces, furnished the excuse for a visit to the Palais-Royal. He took care to leave beind him some two dozen crystal glasses for the personal use of the prince, which were accepted with a further exchange of masonic signs and symbols.

Some three months after the presentation of *Le Mariage de Figaro*—which was later banned by the King because of its shocking allusions to Court society, all of which had passed over my head—my brother Robert, while continuing to act as first engraver in crystal at the glass-house of St. Cloud, also became the proprietor of a boutique, No. 255, Palais-Royal.

Here he displayed not only objets d'art engraved by himself at St. Cloud, but certain other curiosities of oriental design, rather more costly, for the purchase of which the prospective customer needed a special introduction, and was then obliged to step into a curtained inner room.

"I suppose," remarked my mother in all innocence, when she heard about the Eastern bric-à-brac, "that Freemasons like to exchange objects of a ritual nature."

I did not disabuse her.

6

WHEN THE LEASE of le Chesne-Bidault became due for renewal in the autumn of 1784, my mother decided that the time had come for Michel to take full responsibility. For one thing, we had a new landlord. The whole property of Montmirail and its dependencies, including the glass-house, had passed out of the hands of the Bois-Guilberts into those of a Monsieur de Mangin, a rich young speculator who threatened to spoil the forests by selling timber at exorbitant prices and making all sorts of changes. He held some high position at Court, calling himself Grand Audiencier de France, and had been instrumental in buying St. Cloud for the Queen.

My mother disliked speculators on principle—she had seen too much of it with her eldest son, and the ruin it could bring—and she preferred to retire from the management of the glass-house before she saw the whole forest destroyed before her eyes. As it turned out, the new owner of Montmirail let the forest and the foundry alone and ruined himself over another property in Bordeaux, but my mother was not to know this when she made over the lease of le Chesne-Bidault to my brother Michel.

Michel at once went into partnership with a lively young friend of his called François Duval, who, although hailing originally from Evreux in Normandy, had been managing the ironworks near Vibraye for the past few years. The pair had struck up a great friendship, Michel, who was the older by three years, always the more forceful of the two, and his partner the aider and abetter of all his schemes.

My mother raised no objection to the partnership. Indeed, young Duval was a favourite of hers, making a point of asking her opinion on every sort of topic from iron-work to market prices, all done with tact and an air of modesty. That he had been primed by my brother did not strike my mother until the deed of partnership had been signed, but it would have made no difference had it done so.

"I like young Duval," she continued to say. "He respects superior knowledge, and has pleasant manners to his elders and betters. We shall all get along together very well."

The fact that she intended to stay on for a while at le Chesne-Bidault, despite having handed over the lease, had not occurred either to my brother or to his friend, and they were hard put to it to get rid of her.

"They are starting to f-fell the f-forest," Michel would say. "Soon almost all the area b-between here and Montmirail will be d-devastated."

It was not true, of course. Not an axe had been taken to a single tree, beyond what was usual in the ordinary course of felling.

"That doesn't concern us," replied my mother calmly. "Under the terms of our lease we have a long-term arrangement for the supply of timber for fuel."

"I was th-thinking," continued my brother, "of the natural b-beauty of the surroundings. You had b-better move to St. Christophe before it is all s-spoilt."

My mother would smile and make no comment, knowing pefectly well what was in his mind. Then young Duval would have his turn, going about the business in a different way.

"I wonder, madame," he would begin, "that you are not more anxious about your properties in the Touraine. I am told the frosts have been exceptionally severe this winter, and many of the vines destroyed."

"I have relatives," my mother would answer, "who take care of my vines for me."

"No doubt, madame," young Duval would shake his head, "but it is not the same as being on the spot oneself. You know how it is if one leaves one's possessions to others."

My mother would regard him steadily, and thank him for his concern, but I could tell from the twitch at the corner of her mouth that he had not deceived her. She was careful never to interfere in any way with the management of the foundry, but she continued to care for the welfare of the families, besides surpervising the household for her son and his friend.

Edmé spent most of her time these days with Pierre and his wife in Le Mans, for she was much more intellectual than I was, and Pierre used to instruct her in the evenings in history and geography and grammar, with more than a smattering of the philosophy of Jean-Jacques.

Thus I remained the daughter at home, acting as general aide to my mother and confidante at the same time to my brother Michel and his friend.

"You know w-what you must do," Michel said one evening when the three of us were alone—it was between melts, so that there was no night shift for either of them, and my mother had gone early to bed—"you must pretend to f-f-fall in love with

F-François here, and he with you, and then my mother will be in such a f-fright she will take you off to St. Christophe instantly."

The idea was brilliant, no doubt, but personally I had no desire to leave le Chesne-Bidault and disappear with my mother to the Touraine.

"Thank you," I replied. "I am quite incapable of acting a part."

Michel seemed disappointed. "You w-wouldn't have to d-do anything," he urged, "just sit about s-sighing a great deal and not eating m-much, and when François entered the room you would look d-distressed."

It was really too much. First Robert using me to advance his affairs in Paris, and now Michel trying to push me into a pretended infatuation for his friend.

"I'll have no part in it," I said, in great indignation. "You should be ashamed of yourself for thinking of such a deception."

"Don't tease your sister," put in young Duval. "We will excuse her if it is such an ordeal. But you cannot prevent my paying attention to you, can you, mademoiselle Sophie? Seeming red and uncomfortable in your presence one moment, and desirous of sitting close to you the next. It may well have the right effect upon your mother."

How this reprehensible conduct affected my mother mattered very little, as it turned out; what mattered was the change it brought about in both François Duval and myself.

The game began with all sorts of private jokes and winks, nods between Michel and his friend, and various stratagems to leave us alone together, later to be surprised by my mother. But instead of being outraged at the discovery of her daughter sitting either in silence or in conversation with a young man, she appeared quite unmoved, even conniving, and would say, on entering the room, "Don't let me disturb you. I have only come for some writing paper, and will write my letters upstairs."

This resulted in François and myself taking advantage of our opportunities to get to know one another better. He proved not so entirely under Michel's influence as I had imagined, and was very willing to exchange that influence for mine. Nor did I turn out to be the homely daughter-of-the-house and general go-between that he had at first envisaged, but instead a young woman with plenty to say for herself, and a capacity for affection into the bargain. In short, we *did* fall in love, and there was no play-acting about it. We went hand-in-hand to my mother and asked for her blessing on our betrothal. She was delighted.

"I saw it coming," she declared. "I said nothing, but I saw it coming. Now I know that le Chesne-Bidault will be in safe hands."

François and I looked at one another. Could it be that, unknown to us, my mother had been busy planning this from the start?

"You shall be married as soon as Sophie attains her majority," said my mother, "which will not be until the autumn of '88. She will then come into her portion of the inheritance, and I will add to it from my own settlement. Meanwhile, you will continue to grow in mutual affection and understanding. It never hurts young people to wait."

I thought this unfair. My mother had been married herself at twenty-two. We were both about to protest, but she cut us short.

"You have forgotten Michel, haven't you?" she asked. "It will taken him some time to adjust to this new state of affairs. If you take my advice you will keep your betrothal secret, and let him get used to the idea by degrees."

So Michel remained in perfect ignorance of the fact that François and I had become attached to each other, and did not discover the truth until much later.

Meantime, my brother Robert was in trouble again, and serious trouble, too. It dated back to the sale of la Brûlonnerie. He had, it now appeared, entirely without my father's or my mother's knowledge, mortgaged that property and all its contents to a merchant in the rue St. Denis in exchange for a jeweller's shop called Le Lustre Royal. At the time of his bankruptcy, when he had sold la Brûlonnerie to pay his debts, he had ignored, or conveniently forgotten, this mortgage. Now, the arrears of rent for the shop in the rue St. Denis having mounted, the merchant, a Monsieur Rouillon, wished to foreclose on the mortgage of la Brûlonnerie, and discovered that the property had already been sold in 1780. He at once sued my brother for fraud. The first we heard of the affair was a desperate letter from Cathie to tell us that Robert was imprisoned in La Force. This was in July, 1785.

Once again my mother and I made the long journey to Paris, with Pierre to support us, and the whole wretched business of litigation had to begin all over again—and this time with Robert, a proven fraud, living side by side with common criminals.

Pierre and I refused to allow my mother to visit her son in prison. She remained in the house with Cathie and little Jacques, but we went ourselves; and I felt as if I were back again in the theatre foyer . . . My brother was still the perfect dandy, dressed as though for a reception, with a clean shirt and neckerchief brought to him every day by one of his servers from the boutique in the Palais-Royal, along with wine and provisions, which he shared out with his fellow-prisoners—a mixed bunch of debtors, rogues and petty thieves.

These gentlemen, some dozen of them, were confined in a space about half the size of the master's room at le Chesne-Bidault, with a grille for air high up in the dank walls and straw pallets for beds.

"I do apologise," said Robert, advancing with his usual smile and waving a hand at his surroundings. "Rather close quarters, but charming fellows, every one of them!" He then proceeded to introduce us to his companions as if he were host in some salon, and they his guests.

I bowed, and said nothing; but Pierre, instead of remaining on his dignity, immediately shook hands with each rascal, enquiring if he could do anything to aid them, as well as my brother. They all fell to talking and discussing their cases, while I remained standing by the door, a target for the eyes of those who could not get close enough to Pierre, until one of them, bolder than his companions, approached me close and dared to seize my hand.

"Robert!" I cried—as loud as I dared, for I had no wish to be the centre of attention—and my brother, aware for the first time of my distress, moved blandly to my rescue.

"We are not renowned for courtesy in La Force," he said, "But don't let it worry you. So long as you left your jewellry at home . . ."

"You know very well I don't possess any," I told him, more angry now than frightened. "The point is—how do you intend to get out of this calamity?"

"I shall leave it to Pierre," he replied. "Pierre has an answer to everything. I have friends too, in the right quarters, who will do everything possible . . ."

I had heard all this before. I had never met any of his influential friends—with the exception of his highness the duc d'Orléans, who was very unlikely to come to his assistance in La Force.

"I will tell you one thing," I said. "My mother will not raise the money to help you out of this new scrape, nor can you expect anything from my portion of the inheritance."

Robert patted my shoulder. "I wouldn't dream of asking either of you," he replied. "Something will turn up. It always does."

Pierre's eloquence could not save his brother, or any special pleading before the judges. It was Cathie who proved Robert's saviour. She went herself and served behind the counter in the boutique of No. 255, Palais-Royal, for three months, leaving Jacques in the care of her parents. By October she had put enough money aside to stand surety for Robert, to come to an agreement with his creditor Monsieur Rouillon, and to obtain her husband's release.

"I knew Cathie had it in her to rise to a crisis," declared my mother when we heard the news—for by this time we were back at le Chesne-Bidault. "If I had not been sure of her character I would never have chosen her for Robert. Your father would have been proud of her."

The months of anxiety had taken their toll of my mother, with the journeys backwards and forwards to Paris which had continued during the summer. She had never cared for the capital; and now, she told us, she had no desire to set foot in it again.

"I have one desire left," she said, "and that is to see both you and Edmé settled. Then I shall retire to St. Christophe and end my days alone amongst my vines."

It was said without rancour or regret. Her working life was over, and she knew it. Little by little she would go more often to the Touraine, taking Edmé and me with her, preparing her small property l'Antinière, an inheritance from her father Pierre Labbé, in readiness for the future.

"Lonely?" she would say to us, scoffing, when we argued gently that her farmstead was isolated, some little way from the village itself. "How can anyone be lonely who has as many interests as I have? Cows, chickens, pigs, my few acres to till, an orchard, and vines on the hillside. Anyone who cannot occupy herself with such things and be content had best give up living altogether."

There was one further blow to her pride before she could turn her back on le Chesne-Bidault and leave the glass-house in our care. This time it was not Robert who was at fault, but Michel.

François had thought it best to tell him of our betrothal, on one of the occasions when my mother and I were absent in St. Christophe. He took it well, better than François had expected, saying that the joke had been on him, and served him right.

"There's only one s-solution now," he told me, when I returned, "and that's for Aimée to live with us here, and make a quartet of it. She always t-took my part when we were children."

It was as though the prospective marriage between François and myself had reminded him of the old forgotten days when my father was alive and he the odd man out, rejected by his parents.

"It won't make any difference, Michel," I assured him. "François loves you dearly, and so do I. Everything will go on exactly as it has always done, with you as master here, and he your partner."

"Easy s-s-said," replied my brother bitterly, "you and he like t-turtle doves above, and I alone down here."

I was upset, and went to François, but he made light of it.

"It's nothing," he said. "He'll soon get over it."

I approached Edmé on the subject of living with us at le Chesne-Bidault and taking on my mother's work of managing the books—for she had a good head for figures—but she would have none of it.

"I have other plans," she told me, "and since you have brought up the subject of my future you may as well know what they are."

She then informed me, well-nigh bursting with pride and importance, that a Monsieur Pomard, a man considerably older than herself, who had the lucrative profession of fermier général to the monks at the abbey of St. Vincent in Le Mans (a fermier général being, in those days, a receiver of dues and taxes, of which he pocketed a large percentage), had been courting her, with Pierre's knowledge though hardly his approval, detesting, as he did, every fermier général on principle.

"And Monsieur Pomard is only waiting for your betrothal to be formally announced," said Edmé, "to speak to my mother on our behalf."

So . . . she had held to her vow of taking a husband of middle-age who, if not as rich as Croesus, was not far off it.

"You are certain," I asked, doubtfully, "that you will be doing right, and this is not just an attempt to copy me?"

She flared up at once, much put out at my suggestion.

"Naturally I am certain," she returned. "Monsieur Pomard is a man of great education, and it will be much more interesting living with him in Le Mans than with you three here, or with my mother in St. Christophe."

Well, that was for her to decide. It was not my business. And not long afterwards both betrothals were officially recognised, with my mother's full approval. Furthermore, she agreed that Edmé should not wait until she attained her majority, so that the two of us could have a double wedding, in the summer of '88.

"Far simpler," she declared, "to make one ceremony of it, and be dressed alike. In that way there will be no ill-feeling afterwards."

No doubt she was right, though both of us felt a certain deprivation . . .

There was much to do during the months preceding the wedding, our trousseaux to prepare, lists of guests to be drawn up, much going to and from le Chesne-Bidault, Le Mans and St. Christophe—for my mother had insisted that the double wedding should take place in her native village.

She was a firm believer in etiquette on these occasions; therefore both future bridegrooms were invited there frequently for consultation. I must confess that I did not greatly admire Edmé's choice—he was too rubicund and portly for my liking, as though he collected the wine for the abbey of St. Vincent in addition to the tithes and taxes—but he seemed good-humoured enough, and very devoted to her.

It was inevitable, in the circumstances, that my brother Michel was left on his own at le Chesne-Bidault more often than was good for him. He had few friends other than those amongst his fellow-craftsmen at the glass-house, for his stammer made him an awkward guest in strange company. He only felt at his ease in the narrow circle of the foundry, or among the charcoal-burners in the forest, or yet again amidst the strange collection of tinkers, pedlars, wandering gypsies and vagabonds who would roam the countryside in search of seasonal work.

I noticed a certain preoccupation on his part during the autumn of '87, particularly in November, when the three of us—François, Michel and myself—acted as godparents to the child of one of our workmen. He was one moment jocular and rowdy, unusual for him, and the next moment silent and seemingly ill-at-ease.

"What is the matter with Michel?" I asked François.

My future husband, in his turn, looked discomfited.

"Michel will settle down," he said, "when you and I are in the house to look after him."

I was far from reassured, and asked the same question of good Madame Verdelet, who had cooked for us for many years.

"Monsieur Michel is always out," she said abruptly. "That is to say, of an evening when he is not working on shift. He visits the charcoal-burners in the forest, the Pelagie brothers, and others. He had their good-for-nothing sister working here until I sent her packing."

I knew the Pelagies, a rough, wild couple, and the sister too, a bold, handsome girl, older than Michel.

"Things will be better," added Madame Verdelet, "when you are here for good, and take madame's place."

I sincerely hoped so. Meanwhile, it was useless to worry my mother. We gave a party at le Chesne-Bidault at the end of April, 1788, to all the workmen and their families who would not be able to travel to St. Christophe for the wedding, for only the senior craftsmen had been invited to the ceremony; with Monsieur Pomard's guests as well as ours, the numbers would have been too great.

Supper was set in the furnace-house for over a hundred of them, and there was singing to follow, as was the custom, and toasts, and speeches, with my mother presiding at what would be her last occasion to do so—for at any future event this would be my duty.

All went well. The cheers for François, and for Michel too, showed that our glass-house was a happy one, and the community well content. It was only when it was over, and everyone had gone home, that my mother produced a note she had received from the curé of le Plessis-Dorin, M. Cosnier, excusing himself from attending the supper. "In the circumstances," ran the note, "and with no disrespect to you, madame, I find myself unable to accept hospitality from your son."

My mother read this aloud, and then, turning to Michel, demanded an explanation.

"I should like to know," she asked, "in what way you have offended the curé, who is a very good friend of mine, and of all of us?"

I received a warning glance from François, and kept silent. Michel had turned pale, as he used to do in the old days when questioned by my father.

"You are w-w-welcome to his f-friendship," he said sullenly. "He's no f-friend of mine. He m-meddles in things that are n-not his concern."

"Such as what?" asked my mother.

"You had b-better go to the p-presbytery and find out," replied Michel, and with that he flung from the room.

My mother turned to François. "Have you anything to add?" she asked.

François looked uncomfortable. "I know there has been some trouble," he murmured. "More than that I cannot say."

"Very well," said my mother.

These were the words she always used in the old days when we had misbehaved as children and deserved punishment. No more was said that night, but in the morning my mother told me to accompany her to le Plessis-Dorin. The curé, Monsieur Cosnier, was in the presbytery awaiting us. As always in our community, word of our coming had preceded us.

"What is all this about Michel?" asked my mother, coming at once to the point.

For reply the curé opened his register, which he had ready for inspection, and pointed to one of the entries.

"You have only to read this, madame," he replied, "to understand."

The entry stood as follows: "On the 16th of April, 1788, Elizabeth Pelagie, born of an illegitimate relationship between Elizabeth Pelagie, servant, and Michel Busson-Challoir, her employer, was baptised by us. Godfather, Duclos, workman. Godmother, the daughter of Durocher, workman. Signed, Cosnier, curé."

My mother stood rigid. For a moment she was speechless. Then she turned to the curé. "Thank you," she said, "there is no need to discuss this further. Where are the mother and child?"

The curé hesitated before replying. "The child is dead," he then said. "Fortunately, perhaps, for its own sake. I understand the mother is no longer with her brothers the Pelagies, but has gone to relatives in another district."

We bade the curé good-day and walked back up the hill to le Chesne-Bidault. My mother said nothing until we were nearly home, then she paused for breath, midway up the hill, and I saw that she was deeply shocked.

"Why is it," she asked, "that two of your brothers should deliberately go against every principle I hold dear, and so destroy themselves in the process?"

I could not answer her. There seemed no reason for it. We had all of us been brought up in the same fashion.

"I do not believe," I ventured at last, "that anything they do wrong is done deliberately. Robert, Michel and Pierre, too, are rebels. It's as though they want to have done with tradition and authority, and all the things you and my father respected. Had you yourself been less forceful a person it might have been otherwise."

"Perhaps . . ." said my mother, "perhaps . . ."

Michel was on shift when we returned, but she had no compunction in sending for him forthwith, and speaking plainly.

"You have abused your position as master here, and disgraced your name," she told him. "That entry on the parish register of le Plessis-Dorin is there for all time. I don't know which has disgusted me more—your behaviour, or Robert's bankruptcy."

My brother did not defend himself. Nor did he accuse the Pelagies and their unfortunate sister. One man only had earned his hatred, the curé, Monsieur Cosnier.

"He refused the child b-burial," Michel said savagely, "and t-took it upon himself to s-send the g-girl from the district. It's his f-finish as far as I'm concerned, and that g-goes for every pr-priest in the county."

He went back on shift without another word, nor did he join us that night for the evening meal. The following day my mother and I returned to St. Christophe, and afterwards the preparation for the double wedding took up all our time. The disgrace had cast a shadow, though, upon rejoicing; it was as though the bloom had been brushed off anticipation.

It seemed strange, a few months later, to settle down at le Chesne-Bidault as wife of the joint-master, and take my mother's place in the community. I remember how she came to collect the last of her possessions, promising to be back every so often to see that all was well.

We stood at the entrance-gates of the glass-house, and watched her climb into one of the foundry vehicles that was to take her back to the Touraine. Cheerful, smiling, she kissed the three of us in turn, giving last instructions to François and Michel about a batch of glass destined for Lyon which, as it was to go to a trading-house well-known to her and my father, had particularly concerned her.

The workmen who were not on shift were all lined up in the road to see her go, along with their wives and children. Some of them had tears in their eyes. She leant out of the window and waved her hand. Then the driver whipped up his horse and she was gone, with the sound of the carriage wheels rumbling downhill to le Plessis-Dorin.

"It's the end of an era," said Michel, and glancing up at him I saw that he looked lost, like an abandoned child. I touched his arm, and the three of us moved back inside the gates of le Chesne-Bidault, to begin our life together.

It was not only the finish of the rule of the Reyne d'hongrie, who had held sway over our community of glass-houses for over forty years, but also—within a twelve-month, could we but know it—the end of the ancien régime in France, which had lasted for five centuries.

PART TWO

La Grande Peur

7

THE WINTER OF 1789 was the hardest within living memory. No one, not even the old people of the district, had ever known anything like it. The cold weather set in early, and, coming on top of a bad harvest, led to great distress among the tenant farmers and the peasants. We were hard hit at the foundry too, for conditions on the road became impossible, what with frost and ice, and then snow; and we were unable to deliver our goods to Paris and the other big cities. This meant that we were left with unsold merchandise on our hands, and little prospect of getting rid of it in the spring, for in the meantime the traders in Paris would be buying elsewhere—if, that is, they ordered at all. There was a general drop in demand for luxury commodities at this time, owing to the unrest throughout the country. I had heard my brothers in the past—especially Pierre—discussing with my mother the mounting frustration in the glass and other trades, with inland customs duties and various taxes all adding to the costs of production, but it was not until I became the wife of a master glass-maker that I began to realise the difficulties under which we worked.

We paid the proprietor of le Chesne-Bidault, Monsieur de Mangin of Montmirail, an annual lease of 1200 livres, which was not heavy, but we were responsible for the state of the buildings and for all repairs. We also had to pay manorial dues and tithes on top of this, and had the right to take only a certain portion of forest-timber for our furnace. We were fined if our animals grazed beyond the foundry limits; and if any of the workmen were found pilfering wood in those parts of the forest reserved for hunting we were obliged to pay an indemnity of 24 livres for each of them.

Wages had increased since my father's time because of the cost of living. The top craftsmen, the engravers and blowers, received about 60 livres a month, the less skilled men 20 to 30 livres, and the boys 15 to 20 livres, or less. Even so, life was hard for them, for they had to pay a head tax and a salt tax; but what came heaviest upon all our workmen and their families was the price of bread, which had reached as much as 11 sous for a 4 lb. loaf during recent months. Bread was their main fare—they could not afford meat—and a man earning at the rate of one livre or 20 sous a day, with a hungry family to feed, paid half his wages on bread alone.

I realised now how much my mother had done during her time for the wives and children in the country, and what a heartbreaking business it could be to try and prevent near starvation amongst them, while striving to keep the manufacturing costs as low as possible.

It was impossible to stop the men from taking wood from the forest that hard winter, or from poaching the deer. Indeed, we had no desire to do so, for the state of the roads, and the difficulty of getting into la Ferté-Bernard or Le Mans, made living equally difficult for us.

There was much bitterness throughout all France because of the high prices, but at least in the country we were spared the strikes and disturbances that were continually breaking out in Paris and in the big cities. Nevertheless, the general feeling of apprehension reached us even in the forest, where rumours were magnified because of our very isolation.

Pierre, Michel and my François had all become Freemasons during the past year, joining different Lodges at Le Mans—the Saint-Julien de l'Etroite Union, le Moira, and St. Hubert respectively. Here, before the hard winter made travel difficult, my two glass-masters would foregather with the progressive Manceaux thinkers of the day, many of them lawyers and professional men like my brother Pierre, or merchants and mastercraftsmen like themselves. There was a fair sprinkling, too, of the more enlightened members of the aristocracy and the clergy, but bourgeois or middle-class interests predominated.

I knew little about municipal affairs, and less of how the country was run as a whole—which was apparently the topic of conversation at all these gatherings—but I could see for myself that taxes and restrictions made trading increasingly difficult for all of us, that the high price of bread fell most heavily upon the poorer workmen, and that those who had the greatest amount of money—the nobility and the clergy—were excused from all forms of tax.

Meanwhile France, like my brother Robert some few years previously, was, according to the general opinion, on the verge of bankruptcy.

"I've been saying this for years," my brother Pierre would remark, when he came to visit us. "What we need is a written Constitution as they have in America, with equal rights for all, and no privileged classes. Our laws and legal system are out of date, along with our economy; and the King can do nothing about it. Feudalism has him in thrall as it has the whole country."

I was reminded of the days when he used to read Rousseau and so annoy my father. Now he was a greater enthusiast than ever, and burning to put Jean-Jacques's philosophy into practice.

"How," I asked, "would having a written Constitution make any of us the better off?"

"Because," answered Pierre, "by abolishing the feudal system the power of the privileged would be broken, and the money they take from all our pockets would go towards giving the country a sound economy. Prices would then come down, and your question would be answered."

This seemed to me all in the air, like so much of Pierre's talk. The system might one day change, but human nature remained the same, and there were always people who profited at the expense of others.

Just now we had a common hatred of the grain hoarders, those merchants and land-owners who withheld large stocks of grain and then released them upon the market when prices reached their peak. Sometimes bands of hungry peasants and unemployed workmen would raid the granaries or even seize the grain from the carts on the way to the markets, and we had every sympathy with them.

"V-violence is the only thing that w-works," Michel used to say. "S-string up a few g-grain merchants and l-land-owners, and the price of bread would s-soon fall."

Our business was almost at a standstill, and we were obliged to lay off workmen, some of whom had been with us for years. To save them from actual starvation we gave them unemployment pay of 12 sous a day, but there was no relaxation in the rents, taxes and dues which we had to pay.

Robert wrote from Paris, where they were having continual strikes and risings, and it seemed business was equally bad for him. The glass-house at St. Cloud had changed hands and been closed down shortly after his imprisonment, and he now depended entirely on what he could sell in the boutique in the Palais-Royal, which he supplied with goods made by himself, and a few pupils from a small laboratory he had set up in the rue Traversière, in the quartier St. Antoine.

In Paris he was close to the centre of political thought, and as a Freemason, and living in the Palais-Royal, he was forever quoting my one-time host, the duc d'Orléans, formerly duc de Chartres.

"The man's generosity is beyond all praise," wrote my brother. "During the worst of this winter, with the Seine solidly frozen for weeks, he has given away more than a thousand livres' worth of bread to the poor of Paris every day. Every woman in labour in our part of the Palais-Royal has been cared for at his expense. He has rented empty buildings in the St. Germain district and set up food kitchens for the homeless, where the poor wretches are served and fed by his own servants in livery. The duc d'Orléans is, without a doubt, the most loved person in the whole of Paris; which is very much resented at Court, where he is detested—they say the Queen won't speak to him. Next to the duc d'Orléans, Necker, the Minister of Finance, is the man of the hour, and it seems he has given two million livres out of his own funds to the Treasury. If the country can hold together until the States General are summoned in May, we may see great changes then, especially as Necker has succeeded in doubling the representation of the Third Estate, which will then outnumber in voting strength the aristocracy and the clergy. Meanwhile, here are several pamphlets which you might ask Pierre to distribute in Le Mans, and Michel and François in la Ferté-Bernard and Mondoubleau. They are being sent out from the duc d'Orléans, headquarters here at the Palais-Royal, and give all the latest political information."

So Robert too was following the fashion of the day and becoming involved in current topics. Ministerial intrigues had taken the place of Court scandal, and the question "What is the Third Estate?" was now a more burning one than "Who is the Queen's latest lover?"

Like many others of my generation, I had never heard of the States General, and it was Pierre again who had to explain to me that they were deputies representing the entire nation, divided into three separate bodies—the aristocracy, the clergy, and the Third Estate, the last comprising all the other classes in the kingdom. These bodies were to assemble in Paris to discuss the future of the country for the first time since 1614.

"Don't you understand," said Pierre, "that it is people like ourselves whom the Third Estate will represent? Deputies from towns and districts throughout the whole of France will go to Paris and speak for us. This has not happened for over a hundred and seventy years."

He was in a great state of excitement, and so apparently was everyone else in Le Mans, especially the lawyers and intellectuals among his friends.

"Did any good come from their meeting in 1614?" I asked.

"No," he admitted, "none of the representatives could agree. But this time it will be different. This time the Third Estate, thanks to Necker, will outnumber the others."

He, Michel and François read the pamphlets that Robert had sent with lively interest, and so, I gathered, did Edmé behind her husband's back—as a fermier général collecting taxes for the monks at St. Vincent, Monsieur Pomard's profession was one of those most attacked. The pamphlets also suggested that lists of grievances should be drawn up in every parish and handed to the deputies when they were elected. In this way the whole mass of the people would be represented, and their views made known when the States General met in Versailles.

The idea of a new constitution conveyed nothing to our workmen at le Chesne-Bidault. All they wanted was an end to the hated salt and head taxes, a promise of steady employment, and a drop in the price of bread. I tried to do as my mother had done, and visit the families and listen to their troubles; but the days were over when jugs of soup and wine and a few warm blankets from the master's house were accepted as a welcome luxury in times of sickness. These women did not have enough bread to feed their children; I was met with poverty, sickness and hunger in every dwelling. All I could do was to tell them repeatedly, day after day, that the winter would soon be over, trade would improve, prices would ease, and when the deputies got together with the King something would be done for all of us.

Conditions came hardest upon the old people, and the very young. There was hardly a dwelling in our community that remained untouched by death that winter. Lung disease, scourge of the glass-trade in all seasons, trebled its victims now amongst our older workmen, while sheer privation took its toll of young children and babies.

I think my most vivid memory of that winter was when Durocher, one of our finest workmen, opened his lodging door to me with his dead baby in his arms, and told me the ground was too hard for burial—he was going to take the little corpse to the forest and conceal it beneath a stack of frozen timber.

"And another thing, Madame Sophie," he said to me, his rugged face set in lines of despair. "I have always been an honest man, as you know, but today some of us from le Chesne-Bidault are going to seize the grain-carts on their way between Authon and Châteaudun, and if the drivers show fight we shall break their heads for them."

Durocher . . . whom my mother would have trusted with all the resources of the glass-house any day of the week.

"Please," I said to Michel, "do something to stop them. They will be recognised at once, and then reported. Durocher won't help his wife and children if he is flung into prison."

"They w-won't be reported," replied Michel. "The d-drivers won't dare to do so. We've earned a name for t-toughness these days at le C-Chesne-Bidault. If D-Durocher seizes the g-grain-carts, he does it with my b-blessing."

I looked at my husband François, who glanced away from me, and I saw that he had assumed his old rôle of follow-my-leader to my brother.

"It isn't that I don't sympathise with what Durocher wants to do," I told them, "but it's breaking the law. How can that help any of us?"

"These l-laws were designed to be b-broken," returned Michel. "Do you know what a b-bishop was reported as saying last week? That there would be enough b-bread for everyone if the p-peasants threw their children in the r-rivers. And that it d-didn't hurt anyone to live for a t-time on roots and grass."

"It's true," echoed François, seeing my look of disbelief. "It was the bishop of Rouen or Rennes, I forget which. These churchmen are the worst hoarders of grain. Everyone knows they keep sacks of it in their cellars."

"Everyone knows . . ." This was on the level of "they say" and Court gossip. It was regrettable that Michel and François should spread rumours in their turn.

As to the grain-waggons, Durocher and his companions did what they had intended to do. Nor were they betrayed to the authorities.

In the middle of April, with the winter at last behind us, I received a sudden plea from Cathie to go to Paris. She was expecting another baby at the end of the month, and wanted me to be with her. Her parents, it seemed, had both been ill during the winter, and did not feel equal to taking charge of young Jacques, who was now a sturdy lad approaching his eighth birthday. As to Robert, besides the boutique in the Palais-Royal, and his laboratory in the rue Traversière, he had become much involved in the entourage of the duc d'Orléans, and was forever at political meetings. I was four months pregnant myself, and had little desire to go to Paris; nevertheless there was something about Cathie's note that disturbed me, and I persuaded François to let me go.

My brother Robert met me at the terminus of the diligence in the rue Boulay, and making light of Cathie's condition he at once passed on to the one topic of the day—the meeting of the States General within a few weeks—and how a national crisis was approaching, and all Paris was in a political ferment.

"No doubt it is," I agreed, "but how about Cathie and your son?"

He was far too impatient to discuss such mundane matters as his wife's near confinement or his boy's birthday.

"You know what it is," he said, hailing a fiacre and putting my traps upon it. "If the duc d'Orléans was at the head of affairs there would be an end to the crisis." He appealed to the driver for confirmation. "You see?" he added. "Everyone agrees . . . I tell you, Sophie, I have my finger on the country's pulse, living at the Palais-Royal. We have the rooms over the boutique now, you know. There is nothing I don't hear."

And repeat, I thought to myself. And exaggerate a thousandfold.

"We are all patriots at the Palais-Royal," he continued, "and I get the news at first-hand from the Club de Valois round the corner. Not that I am a member myself, but I have many acquaintances who are."

He began to reel off a string of names of the highly-placed individuals entrusted with the duc d'Orléans' private and public affairs. Laclos—author of *Les Liaisons Dangereouses*, which my mother never allowed me to read—was apparently the prince's right-hand man, and directed all.

"There are hundreds of smaller fry," confided Robert, "closely bound up with the duke's interests. Laclos has only to say the word and . . ."

"And what?" I asked.

My brother smiled. "I am talking too much as usual," he said, folding his arms and cocking his hat sideways. "Suppose you tell me what they are saying in Le Mans instead."

I preferred to keep my own counsel. There was unrest enough in our part of the country already, without stirring up Robert's interest.

I found Cathie tired and strained, but pitifully glad to see me. Almost as soon as Robert had delivered me at the door he was off again, on what he termed lightheartedly "matters of State."

"I wish it were false," whispered Cathie, but could say no more just then, for my lively nephew Jacques burst in upon us—fair-haired, blue-eyed, my brother in miniature—and I had to exclaim at the playthings he had been given for his eighth birthday.

Later that evening Cathie told me her fears.

"Robert is forever with these agents and agitators of the duc d'Orléans," she said. "Their whole purpose is to spread rumours and make trouble. Robert accepts money from them, I know this for a fact."

"Surely," I argued, "the duc d'Orléans does not need to stir up trouble. He is too much loved by the people. And when the States General meet everything will be settled, so Pierre says."

Cathie sighed. "I don't understand the half of it," she admitted. "I believe, as you say, that the duc d'Orléans himself has no wish to make trouble. It's his entourage that is at fault. These past months, since Monsieur de Laclos came to the Palais-Royal, the atomosphere of the whole place has changed. The gardens and arcades, where everyone came to amuse themselves, are now full of whisperers, and groups of men talking in corners. I am certain most of them are spies."

Poor Cathie. Her condition made her fanciful. How could there be spies in the streets of Paris? The country was not at war. I tried to distract her by talking of the coming baby, and of Jacques's pleasure in having a young brother or sister, but it did little good.

"If only," she confessed, "we could be out of Paris, and living with you at le Chesne-Bidault. Your winter was hard, I realise that, but you do not live in constant terror of riots as we do."

I began to understand something of her fear during the succeeding week. Paris *had* changed since my last visit some four years previously. The faces of the people in the streets or in the shops were either sullen or withdrawn or tense like Cathie's; or yet again excited and somehow expectant like my brother's. And Cathie was right, there were whisperers everywhere. One came upon them in the arcades, or at street corners, or in small groups in the gardens of the Palais-Royal.

Once, I saw the duc d'Orléans himself, in his coach, leaving for the races at Vincennes with his mistress, Madame du Buffon, at his side. He had grown much fatter since our famous encounter at the theatre, and I was disappointed, as his coach turned out of the palace gates and he waved a pudgy hand at the cheering crowd, who were crying "Vive le duc d'Orléans, vive le père du peuple!" I had expected our leader, if he was to be our leader, to look more alert, more alive to the crowds about him, not lounging back on his seat, laughing at some remark made by his mistress.

Robert would say I was provincial . . . I determined to say no word in dispraise of his idol.

It so happened that my brother would have ignored any remark made by me that evening, for he returned to the boutique from his laboratory in the rue Traversière full of a speech made at the Electoral Assembly of his particular parish of St. Marguerite. A Monsieur Réveillon, a wealthy wallpaper manufacturer, had held forth about the high cost of production, and its relation to wages—he lamented the days, it seemed, when his workpeople had managed on 15 sous a day. Now, he had said, the higher wages interfered with production.

"It's very true," I told my brother. "We find the same at le Chesne-Bidault, but unless we increase wages our workmen will starve."

"Quite so," replied Robert, "but when these things are said in public they can sound unfortunate. Réveillon had best watch out for his windows."

He seemed highly amused at the thought of a fellow-merchant having the same trouble that he had experienced himself a few years back, and he went out again later that night to one of his mysterious gatherings—whether to one of the Clubs or to the Lodge of the Grand Orient we could not say. The next morning, when I went to market for Cathie, the talk was all of how some of the rich manufacturers in the quartier St. Antoine were going to cut their workmen's wages down to 10 sous a day, and one enormous fishwife, thrusting my purchase into my hand, declared loudly that, "It's people like them who are robbing honest folk, and they deserve to be hanged".

Regretting the days when wages were lower seemed a very different thing from cutting them down, and I wondered which was the true version of the story. I told Robert what I had heard, and he nodded approvingly. "It's all over Paris by this time," he said, "each version more garbled than the last. Someone told me Henriot, the powder manufacturer, expressed the same opinion as Réveillon. I wouldn't be in either of those fellows' shoes."

Cathie glanced across at me and sighed. "But Robert," she asked, "didn't you tell us that Monsieur Réveillon had merely lamented the old days, and said nothing about cutting down his workmen's wages?"

"Those were his words," shrugged my brother, "but of course anyone is free to put what emphasis he likes upon them."

Sunday was usually a busy day in the boutique, for the Parisians came to stroll in the arcades and in the gardens of the Palais-Royal, but it seemed to both Cathie and myself, on the Sunday of the 26th of April, that the crowds were more than usually thick, milling to and fro in front of the palace and down the rue St. Honoré towards the Tuileries. Robert's fine display of glass and porcelain lured no purchasers, and that evening he put up his shutters early. The following day, Monday, was a workers' rest-day, when Cathie and Robert usually took Jacques for an outing to another part of Paris, to see his Fiat grandparents, perhaps, or to walk in the Bois. Today, however, my brother told us at breakfast that we were to remain within doors, to keep the boutique shuttered, and on no account whatsoever to venture out into the streets.

Cathie turned pale and asked him the reason.

"There may be disturbances," he answered lightly, "and it is wiser to take precautions. I shall go to the laboratory and reassure myself that all is well there."

We implored him to stay with us rather than run the risk of coming to some harm in the crowds, but he would not listen, and insisted that nothing would happen to him. I could see, and so could Cathie, that he was tense with excitement; he had hardly swallowed his coffee before he was off, leaving the shuttered boutique below in charge of the apprentice boy Raoul.

The faemme de ménage, who usually helped Cathie with the house, had not come, which was another sign that something unusual was afoot. We went to the upper rooms above the boutique, and I tried to distract Jacques, who was protesting at being kept indoors on a holiday.

Presently Cathie, who had been in her bedroom, beckoned to me.

"I've been sorting through Robert's clothes," she whispered. "Look what I have found."

She showed me a great heap of small change of deniers, 12 of which went to the sou; on one side of them was the head of the duc d'Orléans, with the words "Mgr le duc d'Orléans, citoyen", and on the reverse "The hope of France".

"These are what Laclos and the rest of them wish to spread amongst the people," Cathie said. "Now I know why Robert's coat pockets were bulging this morning. Who is to benefit by this?"

We stared down at the money, and then Jacques called to us from the adjoining room. "There are crowds running," he said. "Can I open the window?"

We too heard the sound of running feet and opened the windows, but the stone-work and arches of the arcades blocked our view; all we knew was that the sound came from the place du Palais-Royal and the rue St. Honoré. Besides the running feet there was a murmur, growing even louder, swelling, like a river torrent, and it was something I had never heard before, the roar of a crowd in anger.

Before we could prevent him Jacques had rushed downstairs to tell Raoul, and the apprentice had drawn back the bolts of the door and gone to the place du Palais-Royal to find out what was happening. He was soon back, breathless and excited, saying someone in the crowd had told him the workmen were out in strength in the quartier St. Antoine; they were going to attack the property of some manufacturer who had threatened to cut wages.

"They will burn everything on sight," exclaimed the apprentice.

It was then that Cathie fainted, and when we had carried her upstairs and to her bed I perceived that worse was to follow; it was likely that her labour would start this very day, within a few hours, perhaps. I sent Raoul for the surgeon who was to attend her, and while we waited the roar of the crowd increased outside, all making their way towards St. Antoine. When Raoul returned, hours later, he informed us that the surgeon had been summoned with others to the district where the rioters were gathering, and at my wits' end—for Cathie's pains had started—I sent the lad out once more, to summon anyone from the streets who might have a knowledge of delivery in childbirth.

Poor Jacques was as scared as I was, and I put him to boiling water and tearing up old linen while I held Cathie's hand and tried to comfort her.

Ages passed, or so it seemed—in reality some forty minutes—and when Raoul next returned he had with him, to my horror, the stout fishwife from the market. She must have seen the expression on my face, for she laughed with rough good-nature, and introduced herself as "la femme Margot".

"There's not a surgeon anywhere in the quarter," she told us, "nor likely to be this side of midnight. They say the riot has spread from the rue de Montreuil down to the royal glass-foundry in the rue de Reuilly. They're carrying dummies made to look like Réveillon and Henriot the manufacturers, and serve them right—they ought to burn the men themselves, not the dummies. What's the trouble? A child on the way? I've delivered dozens."

She pulled the sheets aside to examine Cathie, who looked at me in anguish, but what were we to do? We were forced to accept the woman's help, for despite my own condition I was almost as ignorant as young Jacques. How I longed for my mother, or for any of our own workpeople from le Chesne-Bidault . . .

I now asked Raoul to go to the laboratory in the rue Traversière to fetch my brother, that is, if he could force his way through the crowds, and he dashed off, more excited to see what was afoot than filled with any concern for us. It was not until he had gone that our midwife announced cheerfully, "He'll never get there, he'll be swept off his feet."

I kept the windows open in the top rooms, and despite our distance from the troublous quarters we could hear the far-off roar of the crowds, and now and again the clatter of horses as the troops rode to disperse the rioters.

The day wore on, poor Cathie's sufferings increased, and there was still no sign of my brother. It was falling dusk when the market-woman called me into the bedroom and asked me to assist her. I bade Jacques brew coffee in the kitchen—the poor child was distraught from hearing his mother's cries—and between us the "femme Margot" and I brought Cathie's baby into the world, still-born, poor infant, the cord about its neck.

"A pity," muttered the midwife, "but the surgeon himself wouldn't have saved it. I've seen too many so. Feet first, they strangle themselves."

We made Cathie as comfortable as we could. I think she was too worn out to weep for her dead baby. I made much of Jacques, who, with a child's curiosity, kept wanting to peep at the dead infant, which we had placed in its basket and covered. And then we became aware suddenly that it was now quite dark, and the sound of the rioting had ceased.

"There's no more I can do," said the midwife. "I'd best get home myself and see if my good man has come back with a broken head. I'll look in tomorrow. Let her sleep. It's nature's best cure."

I thanked her, and pressed some money into her hand, which she refused to take. "No call for that," she said, "we're all equal in times of trouble. It's a pity about the baby. Still, she's young. There'll be others . . ."

I had never thought I could be sorry to see her go; but as I locked the door of the boutique below I felt strangely chilled.

Robert did not return that night. Jacques was soon asleep, and Cathie too, but I sat by the open window, listening for footsteps.

Early the next morning, Tuesday, the rioting began again. I must have snatched a few hours of sleep, when I was wakened once more by the tramping of feet, and shouting, and presently someone thundering on the door. I thought it might be Raoul, but it was a stranger.

"Open up . . . open up," he shouted. "Every working man is needed on the streets today. We're to carry the riot across the bridges to the left bank. Open up, open up . . ."

I shut the window, and heard him thundering next door, and so on, into the rue St. Honoré. He was soon followed by others, yelling and shouting, and as the day lengthened we could hear the crowds first in one quarter, then in another, with increasing sound of shooting, and the riding to and fro of the cavalry.

There was no sign of our midwife today. Either she had joined the crowds or was bolted within doors like ourselves, for no one seemed to be abroad who had not some part in the disturbances. Jacques, craning out of his own small window high in the roof, said he had seen men with bandaged heads carrying others who were bleeding freely—whether this was his imagination or not I could not say.

We had been two days now without fresh food, and our bread was finished, but I dared not leave the house to go to the market for fear of the riots. Cathie awoke and seemed hungry, which I thought a good sign. I made her some soup, but she was instantly sick when she had swallowed it, and complained of pain something similar to the labour pains of yesterday. The pain increased as the day wore on, and she seemed much weaker. I did not know what to do, for I saw that she was losing a lot of blood, and this did not seem to be right. I could only tear up more linen to stanch the flow.

Jacques, now that his mother no longer moaned as she had done the day before, was content to lean from the window, shouting to me now and again that the sound of the rioters was increasing or decreasing, as the case might be, and he would cry out, "I can hear the troops—I can hear the jangle of cavalry, and the horses. I wish I could see them". As each musket shot echoed in the distance, "Crack . . ." he kept shouting, in high delight, ". . . . crack . . . crack . . . crack . . ."

Cathie was now deathly pale. It was once more between seven and eight in the evening, and she had lain still without moving since three in the afternoon. Jacques became tired of his game of "Crack . . . crack . . ." and demanded his supper. I made some more soup, but we had no bread to dab into it, and he continued to complain of hunger. Then, for he was only eight years old and had been penned indoors since Sunday, he decided to run up and down the stairs between the boutique and the upper rooms where we were living, and this sound seemed to me now more deafening than the distant rioting and firing that came from St. Antoine.

There was an acrid smell upon the air of burning straw—houses must be ablaze somewhere, or else it was the powder in the soldiers' muskets—and all the while Jacques kept running up and down the stairs, jumping from one step to another, and it grew dusk once more in Cathie's room, and I knelt by her bed holding her limp hand in mine.

Once again we heard the footsteps of the stragglers returning to our quarter—those who had gone forth to watch the riots—and at last there came a rattle on the door. Jacques gave a great shout of excitement, "It's my father come home!" and ran down the stairs to let him in.

I rose from Cathie's bedside and lit the candles, and I heard Robert laughing and talking with the boy below. I went and stood at the head of the stairs with a candle in my hands, and looked down upon my brother.

"Did Raoul not bring you word yesterday?" I asked.

He glanced up the stairs, smiling, and began to climb towards me, with Jacques at his heels.

"Word?" he said. "Of course he did not bring me word! There have been 3,000 men or more between here and the rue Traversière for the past thirty-six hours. I did well to get back here tonight. Well, they've destroyed Réveillon's property, and Henriot's too, and done heaven knows how much damage besides—when a Paris crowd gets roused there are no half-measures. I watched most of it from my windows in the laboratory, and a fine sight it was too, with the crowd shouting, 'Vive le Tiers Etat!', 'Vive Necker!'—though what the Third Estate or the minister have to do with the riots I cannot say! Anyway, poor fellows, dozens of them paid for this with their lives when the military fired on them. At least twenty dead and more than fifty wounded, from what I saw, and that was only in the rue Traversière."

He had now reached the top of the stairs and stood beside me.

"Where's Cathie?" he asked. "Why the darkness?"

We went into the bedroom together. I took the candle to the bedside, and I said to him, "We've been alone here since last night. I have not known what to do."

I let the light shine down on Cathie's face, and it was waxen white. Robert bent over and took her hand, and then he said, "O! Mon Dieu . . . Mon Dieu . . . Mon Dieu . . ." three times, just like that, and turned to me. "She's dead, Sophie, can't you see?"

Outside there was still the sound of tramping feet as the last of the straggling crowd made their way home. A group of them were laughing and singing:

> *"Vive Louis Seize*
> *Vive ce roi vaillant,*
> *Monsieur Necker,*
> *Notre bon duc d'Orléans!"*

Jacques came running into the room and climbed the window-sill, calling "Crack . . . crack . . ." after the marching men. Then the sound of the singing died away down the rue St. Honoré.

8

MY FIRST INSTINCT was to take Jacques away from the unrest of Paris and home with me to le Chesne-Bidault, but Robert, after the first shock of Cathie's death, said he could not bear to part with the boy, and that the pair of them would lodge for the time with Monsieur and Madame Fiat, Cathie's parents, who now lived in the rue Petits Piliers in les Halles, within easy distance of the boutique at the Palais-Royal. The Fiats, having complained originally that they were too old to care for their grandchild during Cathie's confinement, were now bowed down by remorse, and as anxious to have Jacques with them now as they had been reluctant before. Nevertheless, it was with a heavy heart that I bade good-bye to the little fellow, and to my brother too, who still hardly realised the loss that had come upon him.

"I shall work hard," he told me, when he saw me to the diligence. "There is no other cure for grief." But I could not help wondering whether it was some ploy in the affairs of the duc d'Orléans that concerned him, rather than the creation of glass and porcelain in his laboratory.

As I journeyed south-west from the capital, the talk in the diligence was all of the Réveillon riots, and how curiously they had arisen. Not one of the manufacturer's own men had joined the riot, apparently—they were all workmen from rival found-ries, along with men from other trades, locksmiths, joiners, and dockers, while two had been arrested from the royal glass factory in the rue de Reuilly, only a short distance from my brother's laboratory in the rue Traversière.

I kept silent, but was all ears for information, especially when one fellow-traveller, well-dressed and with an air of authority, said he had had it from a cousin employed as an official in the Châtelet that many of those arrested were carrying coins with the effigy of the duc d'Orléans upon them.

"One does not know what to believe," echoed the traveller opposite me. "My brother-in-law tells me that members of the clergy, disguised as ordinary citizens, were bribing onlookers to join the riots."

This, I thought grimly, should be recounted to Michel . . .

The diligence put me down at la Ferté-Bernard, where I had an uncomfortable wait for a half-hour or so at the Petit Chapeau Rouge, as my conveyance had been ahead of time. This small hostelry was the meeting-place of all the vagabonds in our part of the country: hawkers, tinkers, pedlars and mountebanks of all description, who used to earn a precarious living by knocking on farmhouse doors and selling worthless articles, trinkets, almanachs, and so on.

I waited in the small room set aside for passengers on the diligence, but I could catch some of the talk behind, where the drinks were served, and it seemed that Paris had not been alone in having riots. There had been insurrections at Nogent too, and at Bellême. I caught a glimpse of one fellow who appeared to be blind—until he raised his black patch and I perceived that he could see as well as anyone else, but they would disguise themselves thus to win sympathy when begging. He kept hammering the floor with his stick and shouting, "They should seize all the grain-carts and hang the drivers; in that way we wouldn't starve."

I could not bear to think of good Durocher, and others of our workmen, being misled by men like these.

Presently François and Michel arrived to fetch me, and, like all stay-at-homes when a traveller returns, they were more interested in giving me their news than in hearing mine. Cathie's death, the Paris riots, these, after quick expressions of sympathy, were soon brushed aside, and I had to hear how many seasonal farm-labourers in outlying districts had been told there was no work for them, and were now going about in bands terrorising the neighbourhood. Farm animals were being mutilated in revenge, and early crops uprooted, and the wandering marauders were being joined by others from further west, from Brittany and the coast, as destitute as themselves.

"These men are brigands," declared François, "who think nothing of coming by night and rousing the entire household to obtain money. We shall soon have to establish a militia in every parish."

"Unless we j-join the brigands," said Michel. "Most of our fellows would d-do so, if I gave the word."

So I was back again to privation and distress and the poor state of trade; perhaps it was as well I had not brought young Jacques with me after all. Yet as I leant out of my window that night, and breathed the good sweet air, fragrant with blossom from the orchard below, I was thankful to be home again, under my own roof, and away from the fearful murmur of that Paris crowd, the memory of which would haunt me night after night during the months to come.

My brother Robert, when he wrote, said little of his own feelings or of his son's; once more it was the political pulse in the capital that preoccupied him. He had managed by some means or other to be on the fringe of the crowd when the States General assembled at Versailles on May the 5th, and so heard the first reports from eye-witnesses within. What troubled him most was that the deputies of the Third Estate were all dressed soberly in black, and, according to him, made a sorry showing beside the high dignitaries of the Church and the lavish costumes of the aristocracy.

"What is more, they were all penned up in an enclosure by themselves like a lot of cattle," he wrote, "while the aristocracy and the clergy surrounded the King. It was a deliberate affront to the bourgeoisie. The duc d'Orléans received a tumultuous welcome, and the King and Necker had a big ovation too, but the Queen was almost ignored, and they say she looked very pale and never smiled once. As to the speeches, they were disappointing. The Archbishop of Aix, speaking for the clergy, made a good impression, and even produced a wretched piece of black bread to show what appalling stuff the poorest people had to eat. But he was quite eclipsed by one of the deputies of the Third Estate, a young lawyer called Robespierre—I wonder if Pierre has heard of him?—who suggested that the Archbishop would do better if he told his fellow-clergy to join forces with the patriots who were friends to the people, and that if they wanted to help they might set an example by giving up some of their own luxurious way of living, and returning to the simple ways of the founder of their faith.

"I can imagine how Pierre would have applauded this speech! Depend upon it, we shall hear more of this fellow."

Meanwhile, we had the furnace going again, but not more than three days during the week, and some of our younger workmen took themselves off to look for employment elsewhere until trade should improve. I hated to see them drift away, for there was little likelihood of their finding anything beyond casual work on the land, hay-making and so on, and they would only add to the number of vagrants wandering the countryside.

The agonies of the winter were over, thank heaven, and our small community was not so sorely tried; but every day came news of more unrest and disturbance from all parts of the country, and it seemed to me that the meeting of the States General in Versailles had so far achieved nothing. Pierre, as usual, was full of optimism when he came to see us at the end of June. He brought with him his good-natured wife, and his two boys whom he was bringing up à la Jean-Jacques. They did not know their alphabet, ate with their fingers, and were as wild as hawks, but lovable enough.

I remember we were taking advantage of the weather that day, and carrying the hay to the barns beside the master's house.

"Agreed, there is deadlock at the moment," said Pierre, whistling to his boys to cease tumbling down the shocks of hay which had been so carefully stacked, "but the Third Estate have at least formed themselves into a National Assembly, a show of force has failed to disband them, and the King will be obliged to agree to a new Constitution. None of the deputies will return until this is achieved. You have heard the oath they swore on the 23rd? 'Never to separate until such time as the Constitution be firmly established.' What I would have given to have been there! This is the voice of the true France.''

He went on whistling to his boys, and they continued to ignore him.

"The King is ill-advised, more's the pity," said François. "If it were he alone, the Assembly would have no trouble. It's the Court party who do the damage, and the Queen especially.''

"B-b-bitch," exploded Michel.

How many other families, I wondered, were discussing this same subject, and echoing the same gossip, throughout the country this same day.

"Call her what you will," I said to Michel. "Do not forget she lost her little boy barely three weeks ago.''

It was true. I, like the rest of the women at the glass-house, had been shocked to hear of the Dauphin's death on the 2nd of June, a child only a few months younger than my nephew Jacques.

"If you think," I went on, "that a mother cares about politics at such a moment . . .''

"Then why doesn't she s-stop interfering," said Michel, "and let this c-country govern itself?''

I could not match his arguments, nor Pierre's either, when he began to side with Michel. It seemed to me presumption on our part to think we knew anything of what went on in high places. Here was Pierre laying down the law about what the King should say to the Assembly, or what the Assembly should say to the King, and yet he could not order his own unruly boys to come down from off the hay-shocks. My mother would have done so and boxed the ears of the pair of them.

Another letter came from Robert in the first week in July. There had been great excitement at the Palais-Royal. Supporters of the duc d'Orléans (who, incidentally, had taken his seat as an ordinary citizen of the Third Estate) had encouraged the crowd to free eleven guardsmen from the Abbaye prison—the guardsmen had been imprisoned in the first place for refusing to fire on demonstrators on the 23rd of June—and in many cafés and restaurants the French Guards were fraternizing with the unruly crowds, telling them, if trouble came, that they would never fire on fellow Frenchmen.

"They say," continued Robert, "that foreign troops have already entered the country to support the Court party, should they be needed, and many of the bridges are already guarded. The latest rumour is that the King's brother, the comte d'Artois, and the Queen have had a secret tunnel built under the Bastille which is to admit hundreds of troops and ammunition, and at a given word—if the National Assembly don't behave themselves—the troops will set light to a mine powerful enough to destroy them and almost all of Paris.''

If this was true, though I could hardly credit it, then there was only one thing to do, and that was for Robert to leave the capital at once, and bring Jacques with him, and the Fiats too, if they were willing to travel.

"W-what did I tell you?" said Michel grimly, after I had read the letter aloud to him and François. "That d-damned Court party and the aristocracy will do anything to b-break up the National Assembly. Why don't the people of P-Paris get out into the streets and f-fight? If it were happening in Le Mans, I'd soon be on the s-streets with the whole of le Chesne-Bidault b-behind me.''

I wrote at once to Robert, imploring him to leave Paris, though I had very little hope of his agreeing to do so. If he was still in the pay of Laclos or others of the duc d'Orléans' entourage, it would seem as if their supreme moment might be about to strike.

The hideous story of the Queen's plot to blow up the National Assembly, if not the whole of Paris, had reached Le Mans—Pierre was full of it when Michel and François went into town the following week. It appeared that one of the deputies had confirmed the tale in a letter to an Elector, the Electors being men of authority in every district who had voted for the deputies of the Third Estate. "Paris is surrounded by troops," Pierre told his brother and my husband, and for once his equanimity seemed shaken. "The wife of a deputy arrived back yesterday who had heard on the best authority that the Prince de Condé has only to give the word and 40,000 troops will occupy the capital, with orders to fire on anyone who supports the Assembly. If this happens there will be a massacre."

The story in its turn was contradicted by Edmé, whose husband, Monsieur Pomard, in his capacity as contractor to the Abbey of St. Vincent, had attended a dinner at the Oratoire given by the officers of the Dragons de Chartres to welcome back their colonel, the vicomte de Valence. According to the vicomte, morale in the capital had never been higher, and the duc d'Orléans and Necker were still the men of the hour.

"Of course," Edmé told Michel, "the vicomte de Valence is one of the duc d'Orléans' supporters. He is married to the daughter of the duke's ex-mistress, Madame de Genlis, and is the lover of the duke's stepmother. You can't be more involved in a family situation than that!"

Edmé had some of Robert's talent for searching out gossip, and when Michel repeated the tale I felt relieved that we lived in the country and not in Le Mans.

"I don't give a f-fig for the gossip," said Michel. "The point is that I trust n-none of the aristocracy, whether they support the d-duc d'Orléans or not. As to that ass P-Pomard, he'd best keep his mouth shut, along with the damned m-monks at St. Vincent."

My husband and brother returned home to le Chesne-Bidault with these various tales, and a parting shot from Pierre that if trouble broke out in Paris the patriots and Electors in Le Mans would form a committee and take over the municipality, with orders to every able-bodied citizen to enrol at the hotel de ville and form a people's militia.

"And there will be no trouble," he added significantly, "from the Dragons de Chartres."

Which, I thought to myself, bore out Edmé's gossip after all.

As it happened, we were more concerned at le Chesne-Bidault with the ripening corn in our farm acres than with the preparations for possible disturbances in Le Mans. The bands of vagrants roaming the countryside were trespassing on the farms by night and cutting the wheat and barley. Whether they intended to eat it or hoard it nobody knew—but we all feared for our crops, for should there be a disaster to this year's harvest then, without question, next winter we should starve.

Michel and François posted men as sentries every night to guard the fields, but even so we would go to bed uneasy, for the vagrants were said to be armed. They were also raiding timber stacks in the forests, to sell as fuel, no doubt, against the colder weather to come, and this was an equal threat to our livelihood; if our stocks of timber were purloined, we should not be able to keep the furnace fire alight. Already in the forest of Bonnétable this had happened. Pierre's wife came from Bonnétable; we had the story direct from her.

"There's n-nothing for it," said Michel, "but to have patrols of men, d-day and night, keeping watch b-between here and Montmirail."

He and François would take it in turn to go out on night patrol, and during those first ten days in July I would lie awake, alone and anxious if my husband had gone; but if he were by my side then I would worry about Michel, standing sentinel out there somewhere in the forest, watching and waiting for the brigands who did not come.

It must have been the Monday or Tuesday, the 13th or 14th of July, I forget which, when François brought the news from Mondoubleau that the Court party had persuaded the King to dismiss Necker from his post as Controller of Finance, and the minister had gone into exile. Paris was in a state of siege, customs barriers outside the city were being burnt down or overthrown, and the customs officers forced to fly for their lives—the people everywhere were out of control and raiding the ammunition depots for arms.

"The worst of it is," said François, "that the whole of the underworld of Paris has been let loose upon the countryside. Prisoners, beggars, thieves, murderers—all the unemployed of the capital—they are making south, leaving honest citizens to fight it out with the Court party and the aristocracy."

François had driven in from Mondoubleau in one of the foundry waggons, and both he and his horses were sweating with heat and exhaustion. In a moment he was surrounded by a group of workmen, with Michel amongst them.

"What is it? What has happened? Who told you of it?"

He repeated his tale, and almost immediately Michel started giving directions to the men to split into groups—all work at the foundry was to cease until further orders—and these groups were to go to le Plessis-Dorin, Montmirail, St. Avit, le Gault, and west to Vibraye, to inform the people in these communes what was happening in Paris, and to prepare against brigands. Another group would stay at le Chesne-Bidault in charge of the foundry. Either he or François would go to la Ferté-Bernard to seek further news when the change-coach arrived from Paris.

It was my business, naturally, to counsel the families, calling upon all of them in turn, warning them not to stir from the foundry precincts, nor to let the children wander out of earshot. As I repeated my warnings, and saw their anxiety, I myself felt seized with their apprehension; doubt and uncertainty were in the air, we none of us knew what might happen next, and the thought of the brigands penetrating so far south, burning and pillaging as they went, filled all of us with terror.

No more news came to us that night, other than what we had already heard through François from Mondoubleau. Two days passed without direct contact with Paris, save that there had been fighting in the streets and many killed—some said the Bastille had been blown up by gunpowder, others that the English Prime Minister Pitt had sent hundreds of troops into France to support the aristocracy and chase the brigands into the French countryside to disrupt communications.

On Saturday, the 18th of July, it was the turn of François to go into la Ferté-Bernard to obtain news from those who might be travelling by the diligence plying from Paris to Le Mans, descending at Bellême and changing coaches to la Ferté. The thought of staying alone at the master's house, guarded by a small group of workmen, with François away and Michel on patrol in the forest, was more than I could bear.

"I'm coming with you," I told my husband. "I'd rather face the dangers on the road than wait here, hour after hour, without even the roar of the furnace fire to keep me company."

He took one of the small covered carrioles and I climbed up on the seat beside him like a market-woman. If we were stopped by vagrants they would find nothing in the cart but ourselves, and the worst they could do would be to overturn it and force us to walk home.

We found la Ferté-Bernard in an uproar. No one was working, everyone was in the streets. The bells of Notre-Dame-des-Marais were sounding the tocsin. It was the first time in my life to hear church bells peal an alarm instead of a call to prayer, and the incessant sound was far more agitating and conducive to fear than a bugle call or a roll of drums.

We went to the Petit Chapeau Rouge to put up the carriole. Although there were no vagrants there, the crowds were thick in the street outside, and François agreed with me that many of them were not local townsfolk, but strangers.

Suddenly there was a movement amongst the crowd, which divided, and we saw the change-coach approaching through the town from Bellême. We ran towards it, ourselves part of the crowd, seized with the same passionate hunger for news, and then as the driver reined in his horses, and the coach shuddered to a standstill, the first passengers broke from within, to be immediately surrounded by a mob of questioners.

A slim figure caught my attention as he paused an instant before descending, giving his hand to a child.

"It's Robert," I cried, catching at François, "it's Robert and Jacques."

We pushed forward toward the coach, and at last succeeded in reaching the passengers beside it. There was my brother, calm, smiling, answering a dozen questions at once, while little Jacques sprang into my arms.

Robert nodded to us. "I'll be with you directly," he called. "First I have a letter here from the mayor of Dreux that I must deliver in person to the mayor of la Ferté-Bernard."

The crowd drew back, eyeing François and myself with a new respect because of our connection with this seemingly important traveller, and we followed in Robert's train, Jacques clutching my hand, while my brother and a group of men in authority walked to the hotel de ville.

We could get no sense out of Jacques. There had been fighting in Paris for two days, he said, there were men wounded and killed everywhere, and we had to listen to the news from other passengers, who were now telling the tale to the surrounding crowd.

The Bastille had been stormed and taken by the people of Paris. The Governor had been killed. The King's brother, the comte d'Artois, had fled, also the King's cousin, the Prince de Condé, and the de Polignacs, the friends of the Queen. The National Assembly was in control of the capital, with a citizen militia to protect it under the command of General la Fayette, hero of the American wars.

François turned to me, stupified.

"We've beaten them," he said. "It can't be possible. We've beaten them."

People around us began shouting and cheering, waving their arms and laughing, and from nowhere, it seemed, the driver of the coach, a great, red-faced fellow, began distributing amongst the crowd cockades of rose and blue, which he had brought with him from the diligence at Bellême. "Come on," he was shouting, "help yourselves. These are the colours of the duc d'Orléans, who with the help of the people of Paris has beaten the aristocracy," and everyone pushed forward to snatch the colours. The enthusiasm took hold of us. François, being tall, reached over the heads of several and secured a cockade, which he gave me, laughing, and I did not know whether to laugh or to cry as someone shouted "Vive le Tiers Etat . . . Vive l'Assemblée . . . Vive le du d'Orléans . . . Vive le Roi."

Then we saw Robert come out of the hotel de ville—he was still surrounded by Electors and other officials—but they none of them responded to the crowd. They were talking anxiously amongst themselves, and a murmur began to spread from one to the other of us waiting in the place beyond. "The danger isn't over yet . . . the fighting continues . . . "

Then the mayor of la Ferté came forward and held up his hand for silence, and we could just catch his words above the murmur of the crowd: "The National Assembly are in control of Paris, but an army of brigands, 6,000 strong, is said to have fled from the capital, fully armed. Every man must make himself available for a citizen's militia. Women and children and the infirm and elderly are to remain within doors."

Now joy had turned to panic, and the people strove this way and that to free themselves from the crowd, to offer their services, to go home, to get away, no one knew which—and the tocsin kept ringing from Notre-Dame-des-Marais so that the mayor's voice was drowned by the sound.

Robert pushed through from the hotel de ville towards us, and we made our way to the carriole at the Petit Chapeau Rouge. There were others trying to do the same thing, and much confusion, with the horses restless and stamping, and Robert kept calling out to everyone, "Warn the outlying parishes and communes to sound the alarm from the churches. Forewarned is forearmed. Vive le nation . . . Vive le duc d'Orléans." His words seemed to increase the confusion rather than allay it, and I heard people asking, "What has happened? Is the duc d'Orléans to be king?"

At last we were safely aboard the carriole, with François urging the horse forward and out of the town, and so down the road to Montmirail and the forest beyond.

By now it was dusk, and the road home seemed dark and forbidding. Poor Jacques, still clutching fast to my hand, kept saying, "What if the brigands come, what shall we do, will they kill us?"

Robert bade his boy be silent—I had never heard him so sharp with the child before—and then he told us how the Bastille had been stormed four days earlier. Some nine hundred persons had taken the fortress, and forced the Governor to surrender. "The people cut off his head with a butcher's knife later," whispered my brother. And yes, it was true, there had been a plot by the aristocracy to overthrow the National Assembly, but it had failed, and the comte d'Artois and all his friends and the Prince de Condé had fled to the frontier, "taking with them, so I hear," said Robert, "all the gold in the kingdom."

"But the brigands?" I asked, as fearful as Jacques. "What is the truth about the brigands."

"No one knows," replied my brother with strange satisfaction. "In Dreux they say that 6,000 were on their way from the other side of Paris, and had joined up with Pitt's mercenaries. That is why I spread the news in every town at which we stopped from Dreux to Bellême. The driver of the diligence has instructions to report it as he continues his journey to Le Mans."

I thought of Pierre and his wife and children, who might be at Bonnétable, through which the diligence would pass. Pierre would at once leave for Le Mans himself, to offer his services to the municipality, or rather to the committee which had vowed to take it over. Yet surely it was in the forest of Bonnétable that we had first heard of brigands?

"Robert . . . " I asked, taking my brother's arm, "what do you see for the future? Where will this all end?"

My brother laughed. "Don't talk about the end," he said. "This is only the beginning. This isn't just another Réveillon riot, you know. What has happened in Paris will happen throughout the country. This is revolution."

Revolution. I thought of my mother at St. Christophe. She was alone in her small farm-property, except for her servants and the cowman and his family near by. Who would look after my mother?

Robert shrugged aside my fears. "Don't concern yourself," he said. "They are all patriots in the Touraine. My mother will be the first to wear the blue and rose cockade."

"But the brigands?" I persisted.

"Ah yes," replied my brother, "I had forgotten the brigands. . ."

By now Jacques had fallen asleep on my shoulder, and I sat stiff and straight to support him during the remaining drive to le Chesne-Bidault. We had passed Montmirail, and were through the forest and nearly home, when a group of men sprang up from the side of the road and surrounded us.

Thank God—it was Michel and his patrol. For a moment we paused for Robert to seize his hand and give him the news; then, as we were about to proceed and turn down the road to the foundry, Michel said, "The brigands have been seen. One of the women was gathering sticks in a clearing, and she heard a movement and saw a dozen men, their faces blacked, crouching in the undergrowth. She ran back to the foundry to give warning. I sent word to the commune to give the alarm."

Even as he spoke, across the warm night air came the thin high summons from the church bell at le Plessis-Dorin.

9

I BELIEVE NONE of us slept that night except Jacques and Robert. Jacques dropped into the bed I had prepared for him with all the exhaustion of a child who had been more than ten hours on the road, and his father—after showing us the pistol concealed under his coat—observed that, as one who had watched the storming of the Bastille, it would take more than a dozen black-faced brigands to prevent him from sleeping. For myself, I dragged my way upstairs and undressed and got into bed, but the sleep for which I yearned would not come to me. I could hear François moving about below, giving orders to another patrol of workmen to relieve Michel and his band in the forest, and this going to and fro in the foundry yard disturbed the farm animals nearby. The cows lowed, the horses were restless in their stalls—for since the disturbances began we had not dared let any of the cattle graze by night.

Michel must have warned them at Montmirail and at Melleray, for the bells from these churches sounded the tocsin as well as from le Plessis. I could hear the peal coming from beyond the forest, the deeper note of Montmirail on the hill sounding more urgent and more ominous than the little reedy warning from our own parish.

I kept thinking of the brigands, thousands of them, so Robert said, from the prisons and the back streets of Paris, hungry, armed, and desperate, let loose on our countryside, some of them even now crouching in the forest where Michel and his band had been patrolling, biding their time to seize our crops, slaughter our beasts.

Presently François came upstairs and lay down by my side, but he did not undress, and he too laid a pistol on the chair beside him.

Perhaps I slept—I have no idea how long. I know I awoke heavy-eyed and weary. Nor did my condition make fatigue any easier to bear, for I was by now seven months gone with my first child.

I found Jacques awake and downstairs and demanding his breakfast from Madame Verdelet in the kitchen, and my two brothers, with my husband, in conference in the master's room. They fell silent at my entrance, and ironically I enquired whether I had disturbed a Freemasons' gathering.

"You don't know, Madame Duval," said my brother Robert with a smile, "how near you are to the truth. We should have posted a watch on the door as we do usually in our Lodges. No harm done, though. Our discussion is finished."

He got up from his chair and began parading the room in his usual restless fashion. I glanced at the others. My husband François looked thoughtful. Michel, on the contrary, was tense and excited, with his eyes on his eldest brother.

"Well, come on, let's g-get on with it," he said impatiently, "no point in s-sitting here. The s-sooner everything is organised the b-better for everyone."

Robert held up his hand. "Keep calm, keep calm," he replied. "I leave you and François to work out the business of your own patrols between you. As to myself and Jacques, all I ask is the loan of the carriole, which I will return to you here within a few days."

"Agreed," said Michel. "I'll s-see about it s-straight away." He seized the excuse to be off and out of the room, while I saw François watching me doubtfully.

"What has been decided?" I asked suspiciously. "You don't mean to take the child off again before he has recovered from his journey and his fright?"

"Jacques is as tough as I am," Robert said, "and none the worse for yesterday. It is my intention to take him today to my mother at St. Christophe . . ." St. Christophe, a journey of some 15 leagues or more, and heaven knew how many thousand brigands at loose about the countryside.

"Are you mad?" I protested. "When we none of us know the state of the roads between here and the Touraine?"

"The risk will be mine," said Robert, "and I foresee no difficulties. In any event, we shall be ahead of the brigands, and part of my purpose in travelling south will be to alert the countryside."

I thought so. The safety of his boy meant little at the present time. His mission was to sow disunity, and whether the object was to satisfy his own warped humour or to obey the orders given by the duc d'Orléans' entourage did not matter to me. I cared only for my nephew of eight years old.

"If," I said to my brother, "you intend passing coins with your patron's head upon them as an encouragement to violence, as you did before the Réveillon riots, that is your affair. But for mercy's sake don't drag your son into the business."

My brother raised his eyebrows. "The Réveillon riots?" he repeated. "What in the world has a workmen's rising, easily quelled, to do with the revolutin of the whole nation?"

"I don't know," I answered, "but do not tell me the two are disconnected, and that your friends have no interest in fermenting trouble."

Once again I saw my husband look uncomfortable—I was reminded of the time before our marriage when he hoped to shield Michel from disgrace—but Robert laughed, in his inimitable fashion, and patted my cheek.

"My sweet Sophie," he said, "don't confuse the duc d'Orléans, whose only desire is to serve the people, with princes like the comte d'Artois and the comte de Provence, the King's brothers, whose one interest is to hold fast to privilege and damn the bourgeoisie. They are the men who seek to spread disorder through France, not the duc d'Orléans."

"In that case," I said, "you must be accepting pay from their agents too."

Had I thrown a brick at his head he could not have looked more startled. He stared at me for a moment, but quickly recovered his composure and shrugged his shoulders.

"My little sister is overwrought," he said lightly, then turning to my husband he added, "If you know your business properly she would be hanging about your neck instead of arguing with her brother."

This put me on my mettle. François would never desert me in my hour of need as Robert had deserted Cathie.

"I stayed by your wife in a dangerous hour," I told my brother, "and I will stay by your son. If you insist on taking Jacques to St. Christophe today, then you can have me with you for the journey."

At this François came forward, protesting that I was in no fit state for a long day on bad roads. There was no need for panic, he said; the report about brigands being seen in the district the night before had been a false alarm. I should respect his wishes if I stayed at le Chesne-Bidault.

"And you," I asked him, "what are your plans for today?"

He hesitated. "The parishes in the district must be alerted," he said, after a moment. "Trouble may come tomorrow, or the day after. As Robert says, forwarned is forearmed."

"In other words," I said, "you and Michel have both agreed to play Robert's game. Instead of blowing glass, you will blow rumour across the countryside. In the circumstances, I should prefer to be with my mother at St. Christophe."

So . . . Robert must be pleased with himself. He had succeeded in causing trouble between husband and wife, besides sowing dissension between Paris and la Ferté-Bernard.

"Your first tiff?" he enquired. "No matter, a few days absent from one another in these early months works wonders. I shall be pleased to have you as nurse to Jacques, Sophie, providing you keep your mouth shut on the journey and leave me to do the talking."

We left as soon as I had gathered a few things together, summoned Jacques from playing in the furnace yard, and given directions to Madame Verdelet to see to things in my few days of absence.

She was much concerned at my going. "Is it because of the danger?" she asked.

"Are the brigands near us after all?"

I consoled her as well as I could, but as we drove away from the glass-house I saw many of the families watching me from their dwellings hard by, and I had an uneasy feeling that they believed I was deserting them.

As we passed through le Plessis-Dorin we saw the curé, Monsieur Cosnier, standing outside the church with a group of his parishioners. Robert drew rein to have a few moments' conversation with him.

"Is it true the brigands are within a few miles of us here?" asked the curé anxiously.

"No one knows," replied my brother. "It is essential to take every precaution. These vagabonds will stop at nothing. It might be safest to have all the women and children within the church, and then sound the tocsin without ceasing should you be attacked."

As we turned on to the Mondoubleau road I looked round behind our carriole and saw the curé giving directions to the excited group around him.

For myself, I could think of nothing more likely to cause panic and consternation amongst a crowd of women than to be shut up within a church without their menfolk, and to have the incessant clanging of that same church's bell sounding its warning from the belfry above their heads.

At Mondoubleau we fell in with one of our journeymen-carriers, who told us that word had come the night before via Cloyes and Châteaudun, from the diligence on the Paris route through Chartres to Blois, that brigands had been heard of in thousands, and it was all a plot of the aristocracy to break the power of the Third Estate. The tocsin was ringing here, just as it had been in our small parish of le Plessis-Dorin, and people were standing about in the streets in anxious groups, not knowing what to do.

"Is all safe at le Chesne-Bidault?" asked the journeyman, surprised, no doubt, to see me in the carriole beside my brother and nephew.

Before I could reassure him, Robert shook his head doubtfully and answered, "Brigands were seen in the forest there last night. We have put a strong guard round the foundry itself, for these villains are said to be burning everything on sight."

He spoke with such sincerity that I was instantly afraid: had my husband's words earlier that the reports were false been said to soothe me? Perhaps the foundry was in truth surrounded, and François had allowed me to go with Robert and Jacques to ensure my greater safety.

"You told me . . ." I began fearfully, but Robert whipped up the horse and we were once more on our way, leaving the honest journeyman staring after us in great perplexity.

"What is the truth?" I asked, in renewed agony of doubt—for had I, after all, done wrong in leaving my husband to his possible fate at le Chesne-Bidault? Were hordes of brigands even now setting fire to my home and everything I held dear?

"The truth?" repeated Robert. "Nobody ever knows the truth in this world."

He jerked the reins, whistling a tune between his teeth, and I was reminded of that time long ago when he had dispatched the consignment of glass to Chartres without my mother's knowledge, giving a masked ball on the proceeds. Was he playing upon my fear today, and the fear of hundreds like me, just as he had once played upon my mother's ignorance—and all to inflate his sense of power?

I glanced at him as he sat beside me, the reins in his hands, his eyes on the road, with the boy Jacques behind his back, and I realised a fact I had forgotten because of his eternally youthful appearance—that my eldest brother was now nearly forty years old. None of his trials and troubles had done anything for him except to make him, if it were possible, more of an adventurer than ever before: one who gambled, not only with his own and with other people's money, but with human failings as well.

"Take care," my father used to say, when first instructing Robert in the art of blowing glass. "Control is of supreme importance. One false movement and the expanding glass will be shattered." I remember the dawning excitement in my brother's eyes—could he, dared he, go beyond the limits proscribed? It was as though he longed for the explosion that would wreck his own first effort and his father's temper into the bargain. There comes this supreme moment to the glass-blower, when he can either breathe life and form into the growing bubble slowly taking shape before his eyes, or shatter it into a thousand fragments. The decision is the blower's, and the judgment too; the throwing of the judgment in the balance made the excitement—for my brother.

"At St. Calais," said Robert suddenly, his voice breaking in upon my thoughts, "we may be first with the news. In any event, it would be wise to call in at the hotel de ville."

I was sure then that I was right. Whether he was in the pay of the duc d'Orléans' entourage, of the King's brothers, even of the National Assembly itself, was not of primary importance to my brother. What had driven him from Paris to le Plessis-Dorin and on to the road today was that same desire for self-intoxication which had made him buy the glass-house of Rougemont twelve years before. He was drunk with a power that he did not possess.

We found St. Calais quiet. All seemed as usual. Yes, said a passer-by, there had been talk of disturbances in Paris, but nobody had heard of brigands. My brother left the reins in my hands and was absent for some twenty minutes at the hotel de ville.

Throughout the whole of that long, hot summer's day, as our road took us through one parish after another, with nearly all the inhabitants out working in the fields, there was no sign of agitation—only the dust we brought with us on our own wheels; yet whomsoever we passed, whether it was an aged man slumbering under the shade of a tree, or a woman standing at her door, Robert would hail them with the news that brigands were on their way south from Paris threatening the peace of the countryside.

At la Chartre, where we rested to bait our horse and to eat ourselves, we were met with an answering wave of rumour—Bretons in their thousands were marching inland from the coast. Here was a match for our own brigands, and I do not know who looked the more discomfited, Robert or myself. The brigands I had already doubted for some hours . . . but Bretons? Had we not already heard earlier in the year that in the west they were refusing to pay the salt tax, and many granaries had been pillaged and burnt? The tocsin was ringing in la Chartre, and there was all the confusion and commotion that we had witnessed the day before at la Ferté-Bernard.

"How did you hear the news here in la Chartre?" my brother asked at the inn, as we sat down to our first mouthful since leaving le Chesne-Bidault early that morning. The innkeeper, who hardly knew whether to serve us or barricade his house from the approaching Bretons, informed us that the change-coach from Le Mans had reported it soon after seven o'clock that morning.

"They had the news from the Paris diligence late last night," said the innkeeper. "Brigands are travelling south from the capital, Bretons are marching from the coast. Between the two we shall be annihilated."

The driver of that diligence, I thought, had done his work well. We had now come full circle. The original rumour, breathed upon the air at Dreux, had gathered momentum.

"Now," I said to my brother, "are you satisfied?" And I told the distraught innkeeper that we had come that day from beyond Mondoubleau and had seen no brigands on the road.

"Perhaps not, madame," answered the man. "Brigands or Bretons, they are all the same, and will show small mercy to folk like us. But it is not only strangers who are uttering threats, but our own peasants too. The same change-coach that brought the news this morning brought information also that the carriage of two deputies of the aristocracy had been flung into the river at Savigné-l'Evêque, and the deputies themselves would have lost their lives had not someone in the neighbourhood offered them asylum."

Savigné-l'Evêque was the final stopping-place, after Bonnétable, for the Paris diligence before Le Mans.

"What were the names of the deputies?" asked my brother.

"The comte de Montesson and the marquis de Vassé," replied the innkeeper.

Both names were familier to me by hearsay. They were deputies who had become unpopular in Le Mans because of their hostility to the Third Estate. Here, then, was an assault that could not be blamed on either brigands, Bretons, or the fertile imagination of the driver of the Paris diligence.

"Strange," murmured Robert. "The marquis de Vassé is a member of the Lodge of Parfait Estime. I should have thought . . . "

He left his sentence unfinished. Whether he meant to imply that Freemasons should come unscathed through times of trouble I did not know, but it occurred to me that both rumours and revolutions might be among those things which rebound very frequently upon the heads of those who start them.

Le Chartre, with its sounding tocsin and agitated crowds, was no place in which to linger, and we were soon on the road again, past Marçon and through Dissay, and the lush rolling countryside of my mother's Touraine opened out on either side of us, the ripe corn golden in the light of the setting sun. Here were no black-faced brigands or swarthy Bretons, but the bent bodies of the harvesters scything their wheat and barley—for they were earlier with the harvest here than we were in the forest.

We drove out of the village of St. Christophe to my mother's small farm property l'Antinière, lying in a hollow, surrounded by its orchard and few acres; and although it was by now late in the evening my mother and her helpers were still out in the fields. I recognised her tall figure on the skyline. My brother hallooed, and we saw her turn and gaze down the field to the carriole, then slowly she began to walk down the field toward us, her hand above her head in recognition.

"I did not know," exclaimed young Jacques, surprised, "that my grandmother worked in the fields like a peasant."

In a moment she was with us, and I had climbed down from the carriole and was in her arms crying—whether from fatigue or joy or relief I did not know. In her arms was security, all that was stable of our old world, which had been so disrupted; against her heart was refuge from my own fears of the present, my own doubts of the future.

"That's enough, now, that's enough," she said, holding me close, and then releasing me with a pat on the shoulder as if I were a child younger than Jacques. "If you have come all the way from le Chesne-Bidault you are hungry, thirsty, and tired. We will see what Berthe can produce for us in the house. Jacques, you have grown. Robert, you look more irresponsible than ever. What are you doing here, and what is it all about?"

Yes, she had heard of the disturbances in Paris. She had heard that the first two Orders were making trouble for the Third Estate.

"What can you expect from people like that?" she asked. "They have had things their own way too long, and find it unpleasant to be challenged by others."

No, she knew nothing of the storming of the Bastille on the 14 of July, nor had she been warned against brigands.

"If any black-faced vagrants show their faces in this neighbourhood, they will get more than they bargained for," she said.

She looked at the fork leaning against her barn, and I believe she would have faced an army with this weapon, turning it from her door armed with the fork only, and her own determination.

By the time we had finished our explanations, she and Berthe between them had laid the table in the kitchen and spread a meal before our eyes—a great side of home-cured pork, and cheese, and bread baked in the oven, and even a bottle of home-brewed wine to wash it all down.

"So . . ." said my mother, sitting in her customary place at the head of the table, making me fancy we were under her supervision once again at the glass-house. "The National Assembly have the situation in hand and the King has promised a new Constitution. Why, then, so much commotion? Everybody should be well pleased."

"You forget the first two Orders," replied Robert, "the aristocracy and the clergy. They will not accept this without a struggle."

"Let them struggle," said my mother. "Meantime we can gather in the harvest. Wipe your mouth, Jacques, after drinking."

Robert told her about the plots of the aristocracy, the six thousand brigands ravaging the countryside. My mother remained unmoved.

"We have come through the hardest winter in living memory," she said. "Naturally there are vagrants wandering about demanding work. I employed three myself last week, and fed them too. They appeared grateful. If the Paris prisons have been opened, as you say, then people like you have all the more reason to remain in the capital now they have gone. The place should be more tranquil."

Whatever were the rumours my brother had brought with him those many miles from Paris to la Ferté-Bernard and beyond, they had no effect upon the imperturbability of l'Antinière.

Robert had succeeded once in breaking down my mother's reserve, when he was imprisoned for fraud in La Force. He would not do so again, not even with the news of a revolution.

"As to you, Sophie," she said, fixing her eyes upon me in her usual direct fashion, "you have no business to be here at all with your baby due in eight weeks' time."

"I had hoped," I murmured, greatly daring, "that I might stay here with you and have the baby at l'Antinière."

"Out of the question," replied my mother. "Your place is with your husband at le Chesne-Bidault—besides, who would look after the families in your absence? I have never heard of such a thing. I will keep Jacques, if Robert wishes—the air is better here than in Paris, and I can feed him well, despite the hardships of the past months."

As always, she was in command of the situation and setting us to rights; even Robert was hard put to it to defend his action in leaving Paris. That he had done so for the greater security of his son did not impress my mother.

"I wonder you did not think of the security of your boutique," she remarked, "if the Palais-Royal is now the centre of activity you describe. I should fear for my stock. Have you left anyone in charge?"

She accepted with raised eyebrows his reply that the boutique was being looked after by friends.

"I am glad to hear it," she said. "It is in times of trouble that we depend upon our friends. A few years ago they were lacking when you most needed them. Perhaps this revolution will change all that."

"Since my patron the duc d'Orléans will probably mediate between the King and the people of Paris, and become lieutenant-general of the kingdom, I sincerely hope so," replied my brother.

They faced each other across the table, the pair of them, like a couple of fighting cocks, and I have little doubt they would have been at it until midnight had not a new sound, familiar now to me but new to my mother, caused her to lift her head and listen.

"Hark!" she said. "Who in the world would be ringing the church bell at this time of the evening?"

The tocsin was sounding across the fields from St. Christophe. Jacques, tired by now, and overwrought, burst into tears and ran to my side. "It's the brigands," he said, "the brigands have followed us from Paris."

Even Robert looked astonished. We had seen no one to speak to when we had driven through the village earlier. My mother rose to her feet and called out to the cowman in the yard outside.

"See that the animals are within and all secure," she said. "And you had better bolt your own door too before going to bed."

She turned herself, and bolted the door of the house behind her.

"Brigands or not," she said, "there is no sense in being unprepared. The curé would never have given orders for the church bell to ring an alarm had he not received a warning of some sort. Word must have come through Château-du-Loir from Le Mans."

I was wrong to have expected peace even at l'Antinière. The driver of that diligence had done his work too well. Rumour and revolution had caught up with us once more.

10

WE REMAINED AT St. Christophe with my mother on Monday and Tuesday, and on Wednesday the 22nd of July, no brigands having been seen in our immediate neighbourhood, my brother decided to delay our return no further; but, instead of retracing our route through la Chartre and St. Calais, to go west by way of Le Mans, and there obtain the latest news from Paris.

"If the Electors in Le Mans have formed a committee to take over the municipality, Pierre will somehow be connected with it, we can be sure of that," said Robert, "and they will be in touch with the capital. I suggest we waste no further time here but leave at once."

I was reluctant to do so, but I felt I had no choice. My mother plainly thought it my duty to go back to le Chesne-Bidault, and I would rather face a thousand brigands than her disapproval. I had no qualms for young Jacques, who was already my mother's shadow, and was so eager to be out in the fields helping with the harvest that he could barely spare the few minutes necessary to bid his father good-bye.

Whether, as Pierre used to say, we are watched over by the Great Architect of the Universe, or, as my mother taught me, by the Blessed Virgin and all the Saints, I shall always think it providential and merciful that whoever plans our destiny hides our future from us. None of us knew that the little boy of eight years old would be twenty-two before he saw his father again, and how bitter the encounter would be. As for my mother, this was the last time she was to hold her son in her arms.

"You have lost your Cathie," she said to him. "Hold fast to what is left."

"Nothing is left," my brother replied. "That is why I brought you my son."

He was not smiling now, and he looked his forty years. Could his air of detachment be a façade after all? None of us knew how much of his youth had gone into the grave with Cathie.

"I will take great care of him," said my mother. "I wish I could believe you will take equal care of yourself."

We mounted the carriole and drove up the hill from l'Antinière on to the road. Looking back, we saw grandmother and grandson standing there hand-in-hand waving to us, and it was as though they represented all that was steadfast and enduring in past and future, while our own generation—Robert's and mine—lacked stability, and was at the mercy of events which might prove too strong for all of us.

"We are only a short distance from Chérigny, where I was born," said Robert, pointing left with his whip. "The marquis de Cherbon left no heir. I forgot to ask my mother who owns it now."

"Our cousins, the Renvoisés, still maintain the foundry after a fashion," I told him. "We can go and call on them, if you like."

Robert shook his head. "No," he said, "what's past is past. But the thought of that château and all it stands for will be with me until I die."

He whipped the horse to a smarter pace, and even now, I thought, I do not know whether my brother speaks from envy or nostalgia, whether the château of Chérigny was something he wished to possess, or to destroy.

We came to the market-town of Château-du-Loir, and immediately we were in the midst of rumour and counter-rumour. There were crowds standing beneath the mairie, and people were shouting, "Vive la nation . . . vive le Tiers Etat" in a bewildered fashion, as though the very words themselves served as a charm to ward off danger.

It was a market-day, and there must have been some trouble, for stalls were overturned and chickens scattering in all directions, with several women weeping and one, bolder than her companions, shaking her fist at a group of men running towards the mairie.

Our carriole, strange to the town, became the centre of attention, and we were at once surrounded and asked our business, while one fellow seized hold of the horse's bridle, jerking it and forcing the poor animal backwards, shouting to us as he did so, "Are you for the Third Estate?"

"Certainly," answered my brother, "I'm cousin to a deputy. Let my horse alone." And he pointed to the rose and blue cockade that he had brought with him in the diligence from Paris, and had remembered to fix on the roof of the carriole.

"Put it in your hat, then, where everyone can see it," cried the man, and if Robert had not done so forthwith I believe they would have dragged him from his seat, though whether any of them knew the meaning of the word Third Estate, or what the colours stood for, was another matter. We were then asked why we travelled and whither we were bound—Robert had an answer for every question—but when he told them Le Mans another fellow in the crowd advised us to turn around and go back again to St. Christophe.

"Le Mans is surrounded on all sides by brigands," he told us. "They are ten thousand strong in the forest of Bonnétable. Every parish between here and the city has been alerted."

"We'll take the risk all the same," said Robert. "I am due to attend a meeting of Electors there this evening."

The word Electors had a great effect. The crowd fell back, and we were allowed to proceed. Someone called after us on no account to give a lift to any wandering friar who might be travelling on our road, as brigands disguised in monks' garb had been seen in all parts of the country. The old fear came upon me once again, and when we were away from the town and on the road to Le Mans I thought to see dark-robed friars behind each tree, or waiting in ambush beyond the rise of every hill.

"Why should the brigands dress as monks or friars? What would be the sense of it?" I asked my brother.

"Every sense in the world," he answered calmly. "A man so disguised could gain an entry into any house he cared, beg his bread, say his prayers, and then murder the inhabitants."

Perhaps, like poor Cathie three months before, my pregnancy made me more nervous and imaginative than I otherwise would be, but I longed with all my heart to be back again with my mother and Jacques. The nearer we came to Le Mans through the long day, the more evident it was that the inhabitants of every parish were in the grip of fear. Villages were either dead and silent, with closed doors, and faces staring down at us like ghosts from upper windows, or, as in Château-du-Loir, in a state of ferment, with the tocsin ringing and the people at once surrounding us to ask for news.

Twice, three times during the journey we perceived groups of men ahead of us on the road who at first sight appeared to be, must be, the dreaded brigands; and Robert, as a precaution, drew the carriole into the side under cover of the trees in the hope that we should escape notice. Each time we were observed and the groups came tearing down the road to question us, and they would prove to be bands of armed villagers, patrolling between parishes, much as Michel and François would be doing from le Chesne-Bidault. Each group had heard some fresh rumour—châteaux were being burnt to the ground and their owners forced to fly for their lives, the town of la Ferté-Bernard was in flames. The brigands were marching that day upon Le Mans, the comte d'Artois had not left the country after all but was advancing with twenty thousand English soldiers to lay waste the whole of France.

When late that afternoon we approached the outskirts of Le Mans, I was prepared to find the city razed to the ground, or the streets running blood—anything but the unnatural calm pervading, and our sudden unceremonious forced descent from the carriole.

We were stopped at the entrance to the city by sentries of the Dragons de Chartres and ourselves and the carriole searched, and we were only allowed to proceed into the centre of the town after Robert had given Pierre's name as surety. We were then ordered to go to the hotel de ville and report our arrival to the officials there.

"Organisation at last," murmured Robert in my ear. "But what else would one expect from their colonel, the comte de Valence, a personal friend of the duc d'Orléans?"

I did not care who was their colonel. The sight of men in uniform gave me confidence. Surely with this regiment in charge of the city's safety the brigands would not dare to advance further?

It was not so calm in the centre of the town. There were crowds everywhere in the streets, and an air of excitement. Most people were wearing a cockade of red, white and blue, and the rose and blue of Robert's emblem seemed out of place.

"Fashion has passed you by," I said to him. "The duc d'Orléans does not appear to be lieutenant-general of the kingdom after all."

For a moment my brother seemed disconcerted, but he quickly recovered.

"General La Fayette was giving cockades of red, white and blue to the citizen militia of Paris the day I left," he said. "No doubt these colours will be adopted by the whole country with the duc d'Orléans' approval."

The order that had impressed us at the gates of the city was lacking at the hotel de ville. Armed citizens, wearing the tricolour cockade, were doing their best to keep back the crowds, which took very little notice of them. There were the inevitable cries of, "Vive la nation . . . vive le Roi . . .", but not a single, "Vive le duc d'Orléans."

My brother, prudently, perhaps, removed the outmoded colours from his hat.

There were other vehicles drawn up at one corner of the place, and we left the carriole in charge of an old fellow who had roped off an enclosure with the words "Reservé aux Electors du Tiers Etat" written on a placard beside it. Robert's air of authority, and his distribution of largesse, left the man in little doubt that my brother was at least a deputy.

We fought our way through the crowd to the interior of the hotel de ville. Here were more armed citizens of the new militia, full of pride and self-importance, who directed us to a closed door behind which we waited for forty minutes or more, along with a small group of people as bewildered as ourselves. Then the door was opened, and we filed past a long table behind which were seated officials of various sorts— whether they were members of the new committee, and whether one of them was the mayor himself, I could not say—but all wore the cockade of red, white and blue. Our names and addresses and the particulars of our business in Le Mans were noted down and immediately filed by a harassed individual who seemed far less concerned with the fact that Robert hailed from Paris (and might conceivably be a brigand in disguise) than with the revelation that we had no idea to which company of the Citizens' Militia our brother Pierre belonged.

"But I have explained to you already," said Robert patiently. "We have been three days in the Touraine. We know nothing of the Citizens' Militia here in Le Mans."

Our interlocutor looked at us suspiciously. "At least you know in what quarter of the city your brother lives?"

We gave the addresses of Pierre's house and of his chambers, and this perplexed the man more than ever, for it seemed that recruits to the Citizens' Militia were drawn from both business addresses and places of residence, and Pierre might thus be in two places at once. Finally we were allowed to depart, having been issued with passes to show that we were brother and sister to Pierre Busson du Charme, member of the lodge of St. Julien de l'Etroite Union, which, when Robert remembered it, had an instant effect upon our official.

"Influence is all," whispered Robert in my ear, "even when a city is swept by revolution."

While we were surrounded by the militia and by officials we had been spared rumour, but once outside the hotel de ville we were caught up in it again. Brigands, thousands strong, were known to be in the forest of Bonnétable. There were also bands of marauders from the forest of Montmirail terrorising the countryside from la Ferté-Bernard to Le Mans. Hearing this, I was for returning home as soon as possible, despite the danger, but Robert steered me through the latest piece of news.

"First, you and I and the horse cannot go further this night," he said, "and secondly, Michel, François and the whole foundry are very well able to take care of themselves."

When we arrived at Pierre's house near the church of St. Pavin we found it full to its rooftop, not only with his boys, who were sporting miniature cockades and shouting "Vive la nation" at the top of their voices, but with clients out of their luck who had come to my lawyer brother for support—an elderly merchant retired from business, a widow and her daughter, and a young fellow who, unable to earn his living in any other way, was paid by Pierre to be companion to his sons. Pierre's youngest stood naked in his cot, which was draped in red, white and blue.

My brother himself was out on guard with his section of the Citizens' Militia, but his wife Marie soon had me upstairs and into the boys' room—the boys, I was thankful to note, dismissed to the attic—and I fell at once into an exhausted sleep, only to be awakened the next morning by the hated tocsin ringing from the church nearby.

The tocsin . . . were we ever to be rid of it? Must its summons continually haunt us by day and night, only to foster greater fear? I dragged myself from bed and went to the window; I could see people running in the street below. I went to the door and called my sister-in-law. I had no answer, save a wail from the youngest child in his cot. I dressed slowly and went downstairs. There was no one in the house but the widow and her daughter, left to mind the baby; everyone else had gone out into the streets.

"The brigands have come without a doubt," said the widow, rocking herself to and fro and, the cot as well, "but Monsieur Busson du Charme will repulse them. He is the only person in Le Mans with any integrity."

Since she had lost her all in a lawsuit which Pierre had defended, and as recompense he had offered the hospitality of his home for as long as she cared to remain there, it was small wonder the widow thought so well of him.

I went to brew myself some coffee, but the boys must have overturned the pan, for everything was scattered, nor could I find any bread. If my brother expected dinner on his return from guard there was precious little to feed him, here in his own kitchen.

People were still shouting in the street outside, and the tocsin was sounding. If this is revolution, I thought, we were better without one—then I remembered the winter, and the families at the foundry, and anything, even fear, was preferable to what we had endured.

It was midday before Marie and the boys returned, and all the excitement was because the officer in charge of the artillery had been seen mounting the guns on the walls of the city, and rumour had gone around that as he was a member of the aristocracy the guns would be turned upon the people.

"Every cart entering the city is now being searched for hidden weapons," exclaimed my sister-in-law. "The peasants from the countryside are having to turn out all their produce, and they have been rioting in the Place des Halles, which has added to the confusion."

"No matter," replied the widow, "your husband will see to everything."

Evidently she was as great an optimist as my brother Pierre himself, who, my sister-in-law informed me, could know nothing of what was going on in the town since his orders had been to guard the cathedral crypt. There was no sign of Robert, but it did not surprise me when one of the boys said that it had been his uncle's intention to speak with the officials at the hotel de ville. My eldest brother, true to type, believed in keeping his finger on the city's pulse . . .

My sister-in-law set to work to produce a meal for all of us from the produce upset in the market-place, and, as my brother Pierre insisted on every member of his household eating their vegetables raw and refraining from meat, this did not take long to do under the circumstances.

We then remained within doors waiting for our menfolk—for I was determined not to set foot outside if the peasants were still rioting—and, while the boys played leapfrog with the youth who was meant to tutor them, I nursed the youngest, my sister-in-law slept, and the widow told me the whole history of her lawsuit.

It was five or six o'clock before my brothers returned, and when they did they arrived together, Pierre resplendent with musket and tricolour cockade, and Robert also wearing the national colours. Both looked grave.

"What news?" "What has happened?"

The same words sprang to all our lips, even to the widow's.

"Two citizens of Le Mans butchered near Ballon," said Robert—Ballon was a commune some five leagues from the city. "The brigands cannot be blamed for it," he added. "These men were murdered by ruffians from a neighbouring parish. Couriers have just ridden into Le Mans with the news."

Pierre came forward to kiss me, for it was my first sight of him since our arrival in his house the night before, and he confirmed Robert's story.

"It was a silversmith by the name of Cureau, the wealthiest man in Le Mans," he told us, "detested by everyone and suspected of being a grain hoarder. However, that doesn't excuse his murder. He had been in hiding in the château of Nouans north of Mamers these past two days, and it was broken into early this morning by a band of excited peasants, who forced him and his son-in-law, one of the Montessons, a brother of the deputy who lost his carriage the other night, to return with them to Ballon. There they battered the wretched Cureau to death with an axe, shot Montesson, and paraded through the parish with the severed heads on pikes. There's no hearsay about this. One of the couriers saw it for himself."

My sister-in-law, usually so equable and calm, had turned very pale. Ballon was only a short distance from her own home at Bonnétable, where her father was a grain merchant.

"I know what you are thinking," said Pierre, putting his arm round her. "Your father has not been accused of hoarding . . . yet. And he is known to be a good patriot. In any event, once this news has spread, we must hope that every parish in the district will form its own militia to keep law and order. The priests are the trouble. Not a single curé can be trusted to keep his head in an emergency, but must run blabbing from parish to parish alarming the people."

I went and sat by my sister-in-law and took her hand. Although I knew nothing of the murdered men, the news of their butchery by local peasants from a nearby parish, and not by brigands, made their death all the more horrible. I thought of our workmen at the foundry, Durocher and others, who had gone out that night in the winter to attack the grain-carts. Could Durocher, blinded by resentment and hatred, be capable of committing murder too?

"You say they were peasants who did this terrible thing," I said to Pierre. "Were they out of work and starving—what did they hope to gain by it?"

"A momentary satisfaction," answered Pierre, "after months, years, centuries of oppression. No use shaking your head, Sophie. It's true. The point is that bloodshed of this sort is useless, and must be stopped, and the culprits punished. Otherwise we have anarchy."

He went to the kitchen to find the meal of fruit and raw vegetables that his wife had prepared for him, but his boys had been at it already and left him nothing. I thought of my father, and what would have happened if his sons had dared to interfere with the dinner kept hot for him when he came off shift. Pierre, however, did not seem to care.

"The boys are growing," he said, "and I am not. Besides, by going hungry I can learn something of what those poor devils went through before suffering brought them to the point of murder."

"The poor devils you are sorry for," observed Robert, "were neither hungry nor desperate, as it happened. I had it straight from an official at the hotel de ville who had spoken to one of the couriers. Two of the murderers were domestic servants—one of them servant to a colleague of yours, the notary at René, and exceedingly well-fed. Their excuse was that they were egged on to do it by vagabonds from the forest."

We were still talking of the murder when we went to bed that night, and in the morning the boys, who had been roaming the town though forbidden by their mother to do so, reported that people everywhere were discussing little else. The guard outside the hotel de ville had been doubled, not through fear of bandits, who were now said to be dispersing, but because the peasants outside the town were threatening all folk decently dressed and accusing them of belonging to the aristocracy.

Pierre's boys, brought up by their father to go barefoot, told me gleefully that they had amused themselves running through the streets shouting "A mort . . . à mort . . ." at the sight of every carriage, and had narrowly escaped arrest at the hands of the Citizens' Militia.

Pierre himself, and Robert also, were somewhere in the city, Pierre on guard, supposedly, and Robert, for all I knew, making further enquiries at the hotel de ville. I summoned up my courage and ventured forth, with the boys as escort, to pay a call on Edmé during the afternoon, but the crowds today, Friday the 24th, were even worse than on Wednesday when we had arrived, and despite the presence everywhere of the armed militia there seemed more disorder too. The national cockade, donned more for protection than for any other reason by the older generation of Manceaux (I was thankful for mine stuck prominently on my hat), appeared to be a symbol of defiance when worn by the young. Youths in groups of twenty or more paraded the streets carrying staves entwined with the tricolour, and at the sight of more timid wayfarers, the elderly, or women like myself, would dash toward us waving their banners and shouting, "Are you for the Third Estate? Are you for the nation?", at the same time yelling and shrieking like creatures possessed.

When we came to the Abbey of St. Vincent, beside which Edmé and her husband had their lodging, I was alarmed to see an even bigger crowd surrounding the walls and building. Some of the bolder spirits had swarmed upon the walls, and they were waving sticks and staves, encouraged by the crowd, and calling "Down with the grain hoarders! Down with those who starve the people!"

A few of the Citizens' Militia, posted by the Abbey doors, stood like ineffectual dummies unable to control their own muskets.

"You know what is going to happen," said Emile, Pierre's eldest boy. "The crowd will overwhelm the Militia, and break into the Abbey."

I had the same thought, and turned to make my way out of it all as soon as possible. The boys, being small and agile, ducked their heads and squeezed their way under arms and legs and so out to the fringe of the crowd behind us, but I was caught up in a surge towards the Abbey and then carried forward, helpless and impotent, part of the human tide.

The supreme fear of every pregnant woman of being overwhelmed and crushed was now mine in full measure. I was packed tight, jammed against my fellows. Some of them, like myself, had joined the crowd as onlookers, but most were aggressive, hostile toward the inmates of the Abbey, and in all probability, did they know his lodging, toward Edmé's husband, Monsieur Pomard, the contractor and tax-collector to the monks.

We swayed backwards and forwards outside the Abbey walls, and I knew that if I fainted, which I was near to doing, there would be no hope for me; I should be overborne and trampled underfoot.

"We'll have him out of it," they were shouting ahead of me. "We'll have him out and serve him as they served his fellows at Ballon," and I did not know whether it was the Abbot they cried for or my brother-in-law, for the words "grain hoarder" and "hunger-merchant" were yelled again and again. I remembered, too, that the unfortunates who had been butchered at Ballon were not aristocrats but bourgeois, incurring the enmity of the people because of their wealth, and the murderers themselves were not starving peasants but ordinary men like these now with me in the crowd, who, for a moment, had turned to devils.

I could feel hatred, like a tide, rise up from a hundred throats about me, and those who had been peaceable before were now infected. A woman and her husband who fives minutes earlier had been walking casually towards the Abbey, even as I had done with my nephews, were now shouting in anger, their arms raised above their heads, their faces distorted. "Grain hoarder," they yelled. "Fetch him out to us . . . grain hoarder."

Then, just as a new surge from the crowd behind us drove us towards the Abbey, a cry went up, "The Dragons . . . the Dragons are here . . ." and in the distance I could hear the clatter of hoofs coming in our direction and the high-pitched call from the officer in command. They were among us in an instant, scattering us to right and left, and the great burly form of the man beside me served, through no action of his own, as a barrier between me and the approaching horses. Somehow he thrust me sideways out of harm, but I could smell the warm horseflesh and see the raised sabre of the Dragon menacing the crowd, and down on her face under the horse's hoofs fell the woman who had been yelling just ahead of me. I shall never forget her scream, nor the shrill whinny of the horse as it reared, and stumbled upon her.

The people fell apart on either side, the Dragons in the midst of them, and I had blood on my dress—the woman's blood. I began to walk stiffly, hardly knowing what I did, towards the door of Edmé's lodging beside the Abbey. I knocked upon it and no one came. I went on knocking, and crying and calling, and a window opened on the floor above, and a man's face, white with terror, stared down upon me without recognition. It was my brother-in-law, Monsieur Pomard, and he straight-way shut the window once again and left me knocking on the door.

The shouting of the crowd, and the cries of the Dragons, and the singing in my ears all turned to one, and I sank down upon Edmé's doorstep in sudden darkness, nor did I feel the hands that touched me afterwards, and lifted me, and carried me inside. When I opened my eyes I was lying on a narrow bed in the small salon that I recognised to be my sister's, and Edmé herself was kneeling beside me. The unusual thing about her was that she was almost as dusty and torn as I was myself, with face begrimed and hair loose about her, but stranger still was the great band of tricolour ribbon she was wearing round her shoulders. Intuition told me what had happened. She too had been amongst the crowd, but not as a spectator. I closed my eyes.

"Yes, it's true," said Edmé, as if she had read my thoughts, "I was there. I was one of them. You don't understand the impulse. You are not a patriot."

I understood nothing except that I was a woman near her time, carrying a baby that might be born dead even as Cathie's had been, and I had narrowly escaped death myself through being caught up in a screaming mob which had no knowledge why it screamed.

"Your husband, Edmé," I said, "were they shouting for him?"

She laughed in scorn. "He thought they were," she answered. "That was why he stayed hidden there upstairs, and would not admit you. Thank heaven I found you, and forced him to come down and help me carry you inside. But this is his finish. I've done with him."

"What do you mean, you've done with him?"

She rose from her knees and stood at the end of the bed, her arms folded, and I thought how suddenly she had grown from a young girl into a woman, and a woman who believed it right to judge her husband, some twenty-five years older than herself.

"I've had proof these many months that he made his fortune from the percentage he took from the tithes and taxes," she said. "A year ago I might not have cared, but I do now. The whole world has changed in the last three months. I'm not going to go about being pointed at as the wife of a fermier général. That is why I joined the crowd outside. I was returning home and got caught up in it, and part of it, and I'm glad that I did. I belong with the people out there. Not here, in his grace-and-favour lodging."

She looked about her in disgust, and I wondered how much of her revulsion was due in truth to a surge of patriotism, and how much was resentment at having married an old man.

"Suppose the crowd had broken down the door and forced an entry?" I asked her. "What would you have done then?"

She evaded the question just as Robert would have done.

"The crowd, and I amongst them, wanted to break into the Abbey, not into the house," she answered. "Didn't you hear us shout for Besnard?"

"Besnard?" I repeated.

"The curé from Nouans, the parish near Ballon, where those grain hoarders were hiding yesterday," she said. "You heard how they were killed, I suppose, and a good riddance too. The curé, who defrauded the people just as they did, fled here to his friends the monks as soon as he had learnt what happened to Cureau and Montesson. Well, the Dragons saved his life today, but we'll get him in the end."

A year ago Edmé, my frivolous if intellectual little sister, had been a bride like me, her head full of her trousseau and the figure she would cut in bourgeois society. Now she was a revolutionary, more violent even than Pierre, talking of leaving her husband because she disapproved of his profession, and desiring the death of some parish priest she had never even met.

Suddenly her face clouded, and she looked at me suspiciously.

"I have not asked you yet what *you* are doing in Le Mans?" she enquired.

I told her briefly of Robert's arrival with Jacques the Saturday before and of our journey to St. Christophe, and how we were now with Pierre, awaiting our chance to return to le Chesne-Bidault. Edmé's face cleared.

"Since the 14th of July nobody has been able to tell for certain who is a patriot and who a spy," she said. "Even members of the same family lie to one another. I'm glad to hear Robert is one of us; knowing what little I do of his life in Paris, I should have feared the contrary. That's one good thing about your François and Michel. No one is likely to accuse either of them of being traitors to the nation after yesterday."

I rested on the bed, aware now of my intense exhaustion, and barely listening to her talk. Presently there came a knock at the door. It was Robert and Pierre, warned by the frightened boys of the fate that might have befallen me. Edmé's husband remained upstairs, and, although I heard his name several times in the murmured conversation between the three of them, neither of my brothers went up to talk to him.

They had a fiacre waiting outside the house, and when I felt well enough to move they helped me to it, for I preferred to be under Pierre's roof, despite the uproar and disorder, rather than Edmé's, in its present atmosphere of resentment and mistrust.

My brothers refrained from asking questions. They were too alarmed, I imagine, as to what might have happened in that crowd to fatigue me further, and as soon as we were safely inside the house I went to bed.

Lying awake, I went over in my mind the hideous events of the afternoon, and how nearly I had missed death. I longed for my home, and for my husband. I wondered if François and Michel were at le Chesne-Bidault or on patrol, and like a flash Edmé's words came back to me: "No one is likely to accuse of them of being traitors to the nation after yesterday."

Yesterday, the 23rd of July, had been the day on which Cureau the silversmith and his son-in-law Montesson had been butchered at Ballon; and those accused of the crime, according to the report current in the hotel de ville, had been egged on by vagabonds from the forest. Which forest? It was then that I remembered the rumour, one of many heard on the evening of our arrival on Wednesday, that the brigands were dispersing, but bands of marauders from the forest of Montmirail were terrorising the countryside from la Ferté-Bernard to Le Mans.

11

ROBERT TOOK ME home to le Chesne-Bidault on Sunday the 26th of July. We went by way of Coudrecieux and our old home of la Pierre, and then through the forest of Vibraye, but this time, though we stopped to talk to people on the way, no one had sighted brigands. They had dispersed, so we were told, they had scattered south to Tours, or westward to la Flèche and Angers, burning and pillaging as they went; yet no one could say for certain whose land had been laid waste, which property destroyed—all was hearsay, rumour, as it had been all along.

When we arrived at le Chesne-Bidault everything was quiet. The place had a deserted look, as though in our absence work had been abandoned. No smoke came from the furnace chimney, the sheds and store-rooms were locked, and the master's house itself was shuttered, with no sign of life within. We went round to the back, through the orchard, and hammered on the door there, and presently we heard the shutters open in the kitchen and Madame Verdelet, her face pale as a ghost, peered out at us from the chinks. She gave a gasp at sight of us, then came to the door and opened it, and immediately threw herself upon me, bursting into tears.

"They said you would not be back," she wept, taking my hand and holding it fast. "They said you would remain with madame at St. Christophe until the trouble was over, many weeks perhaps, until the baby was born. Praise be to the Blessed Virgin and all the Saints that you are safe."

I went inside and looked about me. Save for her own kitchen the house had an empty feeling, stale and close, and by the look of the big living-room—the master's room—no one had occupied the chairs since we left.

"Who told you," I asked, "that I should not be back?"

"Monsieur Michel and Monsieur François," she answered. "The day you left they told me to keep the house barred and shuttered, for fear of brigands—luckily I had food enough, and could manage—and a few of the men were left to guard the foundry, but the women were given the same orders as myself, to stay within doors, or at most not to stir beyond the foundry gates."

I glanced at Robert. He betrayed nothing in his face, but went about the room throwing open the shutters, letting light and air into the room.

"It's over now," he said. "The brigands have gone south. We shan't be troubled again."

I was far from reassured. Not that I any longer feared the brigands, but something worse, which I could not explain to Madame Verdelet.

"Where are Monsieur Michel and Monsieur François now?" I asked.

"I don't know, Mam'zelle Sophie," she said. "They, and most of the men with them, have been on patrol in the forest the whole week. The guards here told me there had been much fighting at la Ferté-Bernard and further west at Bonnétable, and perhaps our men have been mixed up in it. Nobody knows."

She was near to tears again, and I led her back into the kitchen to console her, and to start her in the preparation of a meal for us. Then with a heavy heart, remembering where duty lay and what my mother would have done, I went out across the foundry yard to the cottage to see the families.

One or two of them had witnessed our arrival, and now they came crowding out of their lodgings to greet me, most of them as bewildered and as fearful as Madame Verdelet had been. All I could do was to repeat Robert's statement; the brigands had dispersed, the worst was over, and we had met with no trouble on the road from Le Mans.

"If the danger is over, why don't our men return?" asked one of them. And this became the general cry. "Where are our men? What are they doing?" I could not answer them. I could only say they were still on patrol in the forest, or giving assistance, perhaps, to the Citizens' Militia in la Ferté-Bernard, if there had indeed been fighting there.

Madame Delalande, wife of one of our top craftsmen, stood watching me with folded arms.

"Is it true," she asked, "there have been two traitors killed by the people in Ballon?"

"I don't know about traitors," I answered carefully. "Two respectable citizens of Le Mans were murdered on Thursday. I can't tell you more than that."

"Grain hoarders," she retorted, "members of the aristocracy, and serve them right. These are the men who have been starving us all winter. They deserve to be torn to pieces, the whole lot of them."

This won approval from the rest of the women, and there was much murmuring and nodding of heads, and another of them called out that her husband had told her, before he went off on patrol, that there was a great plot amongst the aristocracy in the country to murder all the poor people. The rumour had started in Paris, and now it had spread to our district, and Monsieur Busson-Challoir and Monsieur Duval had gone off from the foundry to fight the aristocrats because of it.

"That's right," said Madame Delalande, "my André told me the same. And the King is on our side, and the duc d'Orléans, and they have promised that everything shall belong to the people in future, and nothing to the aristocrats. We can take their châteaux from them if we wish."

This last sounded to me as unlikely as the arrival of six thousand brigands in our homes, or a general massacre of all the poor people in France. "We shall learn the truth of what is happening in Paris before long," I said. "Meanwhile, whether the men are with us or not, our first thought should be for the harvest. The foundry acres are ready to cut, and we might make a start with it tomorrow. The more we gather in, the less likely we are to starve next winter."

This met with general approval, and I was able to get back to the master's house without further talk of fighting aristocrats or seizing châteaux which, though it might have won approval from Edmé, sounded to me as impracticable and useless as if we set forth there and then to Versailles demanding bread from the Queen herself.

I found Robert talking with the guard, which had shown up at last from within the furnace-house, where, I imagine, they had all been asleep. There were not more than a dozen of them, yawning and sheepish: Mouchard and Beriet the stokers, Duclos, one of the engravers who had been sick for some months anyway, Cazar, assistant to the flux-burner, and the rest ordinary workmen and apprentices.

The fire had been out since Michel gave the order, and no work had been done at the foundry. They had no idea where the masters had gone with the rest of the workmen. To la Ferté-Bernard or Authon. Whether to fight the brigands or the aristocrats they could not say. It was all the same anyway. Robert and I went into the house and sat down to the supper Madame Verdelet had prepared for us.

"Perhaps," I said to my brother, "you have some idea what has happened to François and Michel?"

Robert was too busy eating to answer at once. When he did so he wore the quizzical, half-mocking expression I knew so well.

"There is no reason to believe that anything has happened to them," he replied. "If they followed instructions they will have been on patrol in the forest, and kept away from the towns."

"Instructions? Whose instructions?"

He had made a slip, and realised it. He shrugged his shoulders and went on eating.

"Advice was the word I should have used," he said after a moment or two. "It was all decided upon before you and I left for St. Christophe. Any brigands advancing south from Paris could more easily be turned and scattered from the forests, where they would lose themselves, than upon the roads."

"If there were in truth any brigands to scatter," I answered.

He poured himself some wine and looked at me over the rim of his glass. "You heard the rumours like the rest of us," he said. "Brigands were seen in Dreux, in Bellême, in Chartres. The least anyone could do was to alert the people of the countryside."

I pushed my plate aside, sickened suddenly by food and all I had been through, with a vivid memory, for no good reason, of that screaming woman who had fallen beneath the horse outside the Abbey of St. Vincent. "You brought the rumour in the diligence from Paris," I said, "and no one else."

He wiped his mouth and stared at me. "The diligence I travelled in with Jacques was one of several," he said. "There must have been a dozen or more taking other routes out of the capital on the Saturday morning when we left. When we came away from the terminus in the rue du Boulay there was talk of little else but brigands, and what we might meet with on the road."

"I believe you," I said. "And were there in those other diligences agents like yourself, paid either by Laclos for the duc d'Orléans, or by some other source, for the very purpose of spreading rumour, and so causing fear and panic through the country?"

My brother smiled. He took up the knife and fork he had laid upon his plate. "My little sister," he said gently, "your travels have exhausted you, and you don't know what you are saying. I suggest you go to bed and sleep it off."

"Not until you tell me the truth," I answered, "and by whose instructions François and Michel took the workmen into the forest."

He did not answer. I watched him finish what he had on his plate, then we sat, the two of us, in silence, with no sound save the ticking of the old clock on the dresser, which took me back, as it always did, to childhood days at la Pierre, with my father at one end of the table, my mother at the other, my three brothers one side and Edmé and myself on the other, waiting for my father to give permission to speak.

"If I admitted to you, which I don't," he said at last, "that I had been paid to do just what you suggest—spread rumour to disrupt the countryside—you would never, for one moment, understand the reason for it. No woman would."

"Go on," I told him.

He got up and began to pace up and down the room, and it was as though something struggled within him for release that had been contained too long, since boyhood, perhaps, and had never yet found freedom.

"All my life," he said, "I have wanted to get out of here. Oh, not le Chesne-Bidault, not this particular glass-house—after all, I did as I pleased here for a time, when I ran the place for my father—but from the setting, from the confined space of the foundry, from any foundry. For one moment, in Rougemont, I thought I had succeeded—do you remember how you, and my father and mother, came to see us there? It was a proud day, nothing seemed beyond my grasp then; but the venture failed, as you know, and there have been other failures since. You will say, my father would have said, the fault is mine alone; but I'm not reconciled. Society failed me before I ever failed myself. Quévremont Delamotte at Villeneuve-St. Georges, Caumont, and others—the marquis de Vichy who promised me thirty thousand livres and withdrew his promise—those are the men who made success impossible, or have done so, until now."

He paused in his stride, and stood facing me across the table.

"Now the moment to revenge myself has come," he said. "No, revenge is too dramatic a word. Shall we say, meet life on equal terms at last? What has happened these past months, since May, and more especially these past two weeks, has overthrown society. I can't tell you, nobody can tell you, what the future will bring, which way the wind will blow. But for an opportunist—and there are hundreds, thousands, like me—this is the hour. I don't mind, none of us minds, what disruption may follow. If there is anything in this moment for us, then that is all that matters."

Once again, as he had done before, during the drive to St. Christophe, he looked his forty years, yet something else besides; someone who was staking all on a final throw, with a total disregard for possible disaster. If he lost, he would take care that those about him lost as well.

"Did Cathie's dying bring you down to this?" I asked him.

"Leave Cathie out of it," he said. "Those memories are dead."

Suddenly he looked lonely standing there, and vulnerable. My heart ached for him, and I was about to go to him, and put my arms about him, when he burst out laughing, resuming his old mask of gaiety.

"How serious we have become!" he exclaimed. "Instead of rejoicing that the world gets more exciting every day, which indeed it does, as the next few months will show. Go to bed, Sophie."

It was a warning against emotion, and I understood. I kissed him and went upstairs to bed, and the next day we were both of us out early in the fields with the men and the families, Robert in his shirt-sleeves like the rest, gleaning and stacking the wheat as though he had done nothing else his whole life long, laughing and joking, his usual airs and graces thrown aside. I found it hard to suit my mood to his for there was still no sign of François or Michel, and the long day passed without a sight of a stranger, or any fresh rumour from beyond the forest.

I went early to bed that night, and Robert too, exhausted with his labours in the fields. I awoke in the small hours, between three and four, when a false dawn throws a pallid light into a room. Some sound must have stirred me, though what it was I could not tell, but instinct whispered, "They are back."

I got out of bed and went to Pierre's old room, which looked out over the foundry yard by the furnace-house, and they were all there, some thirty or forty of them, moving about like ghosts in that grey light, yet murmuring low, as if hushed on purpose, still mindful that they were a forest ambush on patrol. Now and again one laughed, above the rest, as boys would laugh who had played some hoax or other. They had the back door of the furnace-house open and were passing in and out, bearing sacks on their shoulders.

I heard Robert's footstep along the passage outside Pierre's room, and his tread on the stairs—so he had been awakened, too—and in a few minutes he had unbarred the door below and gone out into the yard. Then I turned and went back to my room, thinking, in foolish fashion, that François would be up to join me within a moment or two, full of concern for me, and I planned to be somewhat cool to make him sorry; but I waited for nearly a half-hour, and he did not come.

Then anxiety got the better of my pride, and I put a wrapper on and went to the head of the stairs to listen. I could hear voices coming from the master's room, Michel's raised loud, as always when he was excited, and Robert's laugh. I went downstairs and opened the door.

The first thing I saw was François lying on the floor with pillows beneath him. Robert and Michel were sitting astride two chairs, Michel with a bandage about his head. I ran at once to my husband and knelt beside him to see where he was wounded. His eyes were closed and he was breathing heavily, but I could see no blood, no bandage.

"What's wrong, where is he hurt?" I asked my brothers.

They showed no concern, to my great astonishment and anger, and Robert made a grimace at Michel, half-laughing as he did so.

"N-nothing's wrong," said Michel, "he's d-drunk, that's all."

I looked down again at my husband, whom I had never seen the worse for drink in the few years I had known him, and I saw then that they were right—I could smell it on his breath. François was stupefied.

"Let him lie," said Robert. "No harm done. He'll sleep it off."

Then I saw the table, which they had dragged to one side of the room, and it was piled high with every sort of object from food to furniture. A great side of bacon lay on top of a satin stool, sacks of flour were wrapped about by brocaded curtains, a quantity of silver lay stacked beside bars of salt and jars of preserves.

They waited for me to speak. I could see their eyes upon me. I knew if I waited long enough Michel would break the silence.

"Well?" he said. "Aren't you going to s-say something?"

I went over to the table and touched the brocade curtains. They reminded me of those that used to hang in the grande salle at la Pierre.

"Why should I?" I replied. "You didn't find these in the forest. That's all there is to it. If you choose to close the foundry and find your living this way, it's your affair, not mine. But you might leave my husband behind next time you go fighting brigands."

I turned to go back upstairs, when Michel spoke again.

"Don't f-fool yourself, Sophie," he said. "François didn't need p-persuading, I assure you. And what you s-see on the table is nothing. We've got the f-furnace-house stacked high. I'll tell you one thing. Neither F-François nor I are prepared to see the men endure another w-winter like the last. That's final."

"You won't have to," I answered him. "If what Robert says is right, the whole world has changed. Paradise is round the corner. Meanwhile, I'd be obliged if the pair of you would carry François up to bed. Not to my room, but Pierre's."

I went away without looking back at them, and when I had shut the door of my room I heard them lumbering my husband up the stairs. He was protesting and mouthing nonsense in the way a drunk man will, and my brothers were hushing him to silence, laughing at the same time.

I lay back on my bed and watched the dawn come clear, and then after the first hush, and the stirring of birds under the window, heard the usual clatter and sound from the farm beyond the master's house, the cows lowing before milking, the dogs barking, and all that went to make the start of another summer's day.

It was a strange feeling, lying there in my mother's room, in the same room she had shared with my father, which I had made my own since my marriage, believing that François and I would, though in a different fashion, continue in their tradition. Now, overnight—or was it in truth much longer, the events of the past week linking back to Cathie's death and the riots in Paris, with the long winter overshadowing it all?— now, most unmistakably, I knew that a great gulf lay between our time and all that had gone before.

My brothers, my husband, even Edmé, my little sister, belonged to this moment, had waited for it, even, welcoming change as something they could themselves shape and possess, just as they moulded glass to a new form. What they had been taught as children did not matter any more. These things were past and done with; only the future counted, a future which must be different in every way from what we had known. Why, then, did I lag behind? Why must I be reluctant? I thought of the winter, and how the families and ourselves had suffered, and I knew what Michel meant when he said it must never happen again; yet, even so, everything within me baulked at what he had done.

I did not fool myself. The things that lay on the table below in the master's room were stolen property, looted in all probability from the château at Nouans where the wretched silversmith Cureau and his son-in-law had hidden before being dragged forth to Ballon to die. What I did not know, what I might never know, was whether my husband and my brother had been amongst those who butchered them.

I fell asleep at last, all feeling numb within me, and when I awoke it was to find François by my side, begging forgiveness, so greatly shamed for being drunk that he was blubbering like a child, and there was nothing for it but to hold him in my arms, and comfort him.

I was not going to question him, but he came out with it, eager, I think, to be rid of secrecy. I had guessed right; they had been to Nouans. The patrol had marched far beyond the limit set for them, rumours of a plot by the aristocracy drawing them on. Panic was great in the whole district south of Mamers, down to Ballon and Bonnét-able, no one knowing what was rumour, what was true—someone told them there were brigands dressed as friars, that same old story we had heard upon the road.

"It was this drove Michel mad," said François, "a tale of friars armed, finding their way into the villages, frightening the people. We heard that the curé Besnard of Nouans was a grain hoarder, and that he was absent in Paris getting arms and ammunition to bring back to the château to use against his parishioners. So we went there, to the château. A crowd had already broken into it, seizing the silversmith Cureau and his son-in-law as hostages. They took them off to Ballon. We did not follow them."

"You know what happened to them afterwards?" I asked.

He was silent a moment. "Yes," he said at last, "yes, we heard."

Then, raising himself up and leaning over me, he said, "The murder was none of our doing, Sophie. The people were mad. They had to have a victim. No single one of them was to blame, it was like a fever sweeping them."

The same fever that had swept the crowd outside the Abbey of St. Vincent, so that a woman was trampled to death. The same that had gripped my sister Edmé, so that, caught up in it, she forgot her husband and her home.

"François," I said, "if this goes on, murder, looting, taking life and property, it's an end to law and order, a return to barbarism. This is not building the new society Pierre talks about."

"It's one way of achieving it," he answered. "At least, so Michel says. Before you can build anything, you must first destroy—or, at least, sweep clean the ground. Those men who were . . . who died, Sophie, at Ballon, they were plotting against the people. They would not have hesitated to shoot them down had they possessed guns at the château. They deserved to die, as an example to the rest of their kind. Michel explained it all, the men were asking him."

Michel said . . . Michel explained . . . It was as it had always been. My husband followed his friend, followed his leader.

"So you took what you wanted from the château and came home?" I asked.

"You can put it that way," he replied. "Michel said that whoever had gone cold and hungry through the winter might make amends for it now. The men were nothing loath, you can imagine. We made camp in the forest for four nights, to let things quieten. We had plenty of food and wine with us, as you saw for yourself. That's when I . . ."

"Took what you did to quieten your conscience," I said to him.

After that we lay still for a while without speaking. We both had travelled far in time, if not in distance, during the week we had been away from one another. If this was indeed the new society, it would not be easy to adjust to it.

"Don't be too hard on me," he said presently. "I don't know what happened. We lit a fire there in the forest, and ate and drank, Michel and I beside the men. It was a strange feeling—nothing mattered but ourselves, we had no thought of yesterday or tomorrow. Michel kept saying, 'It's finished . . . it's finished . . . the old ways have gone forever. The country belongs to us.' It's as I said before, a sort of fever swept us . . ."

Then he fell asleep, lying there in the crook of my arm, and later, when he awoke once more, and we dressed and went downstairs, we found the master's room swept and tidied, the table in the middle of the floor again, and the only sign of change was that for our dinner that day we had fine silver set out, with monograms upon the forks, and spoons, and the canister for sugar.

"I wonder," I said to Madame Verdelet, to try her, "what my mother would say to this if she could see it."

We were examining the cupboards in the kitchen, where the rest of the silver was now neatly stored. Madame Verdelet picked up a great candlestick and breathed upon it, polished it awhile, then set it down again.

"She would do as I do," she replied, "accept such blessings, and ask no questions. It's as Monsieur Michel says, folk who own such treasures, and starve the poor who work for them, deserve to lose everthing they have."

It was a comforting philosophy, but I was not sure why the benefit should be ours. I only knew that as the days passed I became used to the sight of that monogrammed silver upon the dinner table, and a week later it was I myself who helped Madame Verdelet to cut up the brocaded curtains to fit the smaller windows of the master's room.

There was no more talk of brigands. The Great Fear that had swept the whole of France and ourselves after the Bastille fell petered out into oblivion. Born on rumour's breath, spread by all our fears, the panic went as swiftly as it came, but the impression it left upon our lives remained indelible.

Something within each one of us had been awakened that we had not known was there; some dream, desire or doubt, flickered into life by that same rumour, took root, and flourished. We were none of us the same afterwards. Robert, Michel, François, Edmé, myself, were changed imperceptibly. The rumour, true or false, had brought into the open hopes and dreads which, hitherto concealed, would now be part of our ordinary living selves.

The only one of us to rejoice wholeheartedly and stay uncorrupted by events was Pierre. It was he who came to tell us, in the second week in August, of the great decisions taken in Paris on the night of the 4th by the National Assembly. They had heard the news in Le Mans two days before, and he had taken the first chance to ride into the country and break it to us. The vicomte de Noailles, brother-in-law of General La Fayette, and one of the deputies of the aristocracy who held progressive views, had put forward a suggestion to the whole Assembly—that all the feudal rights should be abolished, that men should be declared equal whatever their birth or position. Titles were to be no more and men free to worship God how they pleased, office was to be open to all, privileges to go forever.

The Assembly had risen to their feet as one man to cheer the deputy's suggestion. Many were in tears. One after the other, those deputies of the aristocracy who shared the same views as de Noailles swore that the rights they had held for centuries were theirs no longer. A kind of magic, Pierre said, must have come upon the Assembly gathered there in Versailles. The aristocracy, the clergy, the Third Estate—all three were suddenly united.

"It's the end of all injustice and tyranny," said Pierre. "It's the beginning of a new France."

I remember that as he told us the news, standing there in the master's room, he suddenly burst into tears—Pierre, whom I never saw cry as a boy, except once, when a kitten died—and in a moment we were all of us crying and laughing and embracing one another. Madame Verdelet came in from the kitchen, and the niece who helped her. Michel rushed out into the foundry yard to ring the bell and summon all the workmen to tell them that he and François, Pierre and Robert, and all of them were brothers.

"The old laws are d-dead," he shouted. "All men are equal. Everyone is made new and b-born again."

There had been nothing like it, surely, since Pentecost. The happiness and desire for good that swept us all was like the hand of God upon each one of us. Robert, his eyes shining with excitement, told everyone that the duc d'Orléans must be behind it all—the vicomte de Noailles would never have thought of it by himself.

"Besides," he added in my ear, "de Noailles has no possessions to give up anyway. He's in debt to his eyebrows. If debts are to be abolished as well as privileges, we have reached the millennium."

He was already making plans to return to Le Mans with Pierre, and take the diligence there next day for Paris.

The foundry bell kept ringing; no tocsin this time, thank God, but a peal for joy. The men and their wives, and the children, began flooding into the house, shyly at first, then more boldly, as we welcomed them and shook their hands. There was no feast prepared, but somehow we found wine for all of them; and the children, losing their awkwardness, started calling and shouting, and chasing each other about the foundry yard.

"Today everything is permitted," said Michel. "The laws of adults are abolished along with f-feudal right."

I saw François look at him and smile, and for the first time I watched it without jealousy. The hand of God must have been upon me too.

I have no recollection of the weeks that followed. All I remember is that the harvest was safely gathered in, the foundry furnace was started once again, and Edmé came to be with me when my son was born on September the 26th.

He was a lovely boy, the first fruit, so Edmé said, of the revolution. Because he heralded good news, I called him Gabriel. He lived two weeks. . . . By then our mood of Pentecost had passed.

PART THREE

Les Enragés

12

MY OWN GRIEF has no part in this story. Many women lose their first child. My mother, in the days before I was born, lost two within as many years. I had seen it happen twice to Cathie, and with the last she herself went as well. Men call us the weaker sex. Perhaps it's true. Yet to carry life within us as we do, to feel it bud and flower and come from us fully formed as a living creature, separate though part of ourselves, and watch it fade and die—this asks for strength and spiritual endurance.

Men stand aloof, helpless at such times, their very gestures awkward and ill at ease, as though from the beginning—which indeed is true—their part in the whole business has been secondary.

As to the two masters of the glass-house, I leant most upon my brother Michel. He was roughly tender, practical as well, bearing away the cradle from my room so that I should not be reminded of my son. He told me too—I had once heard the story from my mother, long ago—of his first fears, when the infant brother and sister had died, that he might have contributed toward their death by plucking off their coverings for fun.

François made himself too humble for my comfort. He went about abashed, as though our child's loss had been his doing; and, to show this, whispered, or trod on tip-toe through the rooms. When he spoke to me, half cringing in doing so, it nearly drove me mad. He would see the irritation in my face, or hear it in my voice, and naturally, though I could not help it at the time, this contributed to his abject look, making me disfavour him the more. I had no pity, and did not let him near me for six months or longer, and then perhaps—who knows?—it was more from lassitude than inclination. They say it takes a woman her full time again to recover from the birth of a first child, if she should lose it.

Meanwhile, the Declaration of the Rights of Man made all men equal, if it did not make them brothers, and within a week of its passing into law there were riots in Le Mans, and disturbances in Paris too, with the price of bread as high as it had been before, and unemployment rife. Bakers were blamed in every city for charging too dearly for their 4 lb. loaf, and they in turn put the blame upon the grain merchants; all men were at fault save those who levelled the accusations.

The Manceaux were still divided as to whether the murderers of the silversmith and his son-in-law should be punished or let free, and there were insurrections about this as well, with people going out into the streets armed with knives and stones to use against the Citizens' Militia—now called the National Guard—and shouting, "Let the men of Ballon free"! I never heard if Edmé was amongst them.

The Abbey of St. Vincent had been taken over by the Dragons de Chartres, and as to Monsieur Pomard, Edmé's husband, his title of tax-collector to the monks was abolished, together with many other professions and privileges. He left the city, and where he disappeared to I do not know, for Edmé never followed him. The officers of the Dragons were quartered in her home, and she went to live with Pierre.

The municipality showed itself firm with the butchers of Ballon, and one ringleader was sentenced to death and another condemned to the galleys. The third, I believe, escaped. So the anarchy Pierre feared was stifled. The few times I went to Le Mans there was little to show for our fine new equality, except that the market-people were more pert, and those who had the material for it draped their stalls with tricolour.

In Paris they had survived another Bastille day, this time without bloodshed. A mob of people, half of them women—fishwives, Robert our informant called them, and I thought of Madame Margot who had helped me with Cathie that fatal day—had marched to Versailles on the 5th of October and camped there in the courtyard for the night, shouting for the royal family. They were thousands strong, prepared to do damage, too, and it was only the intervention of La Fayette and the National Guard that turned the day from near disaster to a triumph.

The King and Queen, with the two children and the King's sister, Madame Elizabeth, were persuaded, indeed forced, to leave Versailles and take up their residence at the Palace of the Tuileries in Paris, and the procession from the one place to the other was, so Robert wrote us, the most fantastic sight imaginable. The royal coach, escorted by La Fayette and a number of his National Guard recruited from the Paris sections, set out with a motley crowd of citizens some six or seven thousand strong, carrying crowbars, muskets, bludgeons, brooms, all shouting and singing at the tops of their voices, "Long live the Baker, and the Baker's brats".

"They were six hours on the road," wrote Robert, "and I watched the circus at the tail end of the journey, turning into the Place Louis XV. It was like a menagerie of ancient Rome, and the only things that were lacking were the lions. There were women, half-naked some of them, sitting astride guns as though they rode elephants, and they had torn branches from the trees on the way and decorated the guns with foliage. Crones from the faubourgs, fishwives from the Halles, street-girls with the paint still on their faces, and even respectable shopkeepers' wives prinked out in their holiday best with hats on—they might have been the mænads fêting Dionysus! No loss of life, except one unfortunate incident before the cohort left Versailles. One of the King's bodyguard, like an idiot, fired at a lad of the National Guard and killed him. The result of it, that same member of the bodyguard and his companion were torn to pieces. Their heads, on pikes, led the van as the procession marched for Paris."

Michel, to whom the letter was addressed, read it aloud. He and François thought it all good fun, but they had never seen, as I had, the faces of Parisians before a riot, nor smelt the stale air in the streets with the damage done.

I snatched the letter from my brother, for between his laughter and his stammer he made little sense. Robert went on to say that now the King was in Paris amongst his people things would settle down, bread would be more plentiful, and honest merchants like himself could sleep at night without fear of broken windows.

"I'm a member of the National Guard, of course," he said, "that is, for this section of the Palais-Royal. My duties are few. We simply patrol the street, fully armed, the cockade upon our hats as a badge of office. When scum approaches—and they swarm from every alley-way these days, as bold as cockroaches—we thrust our loaded muskets in their bellies, and they vanish. The women find us irresistible. One glance and they're hanging on us, strung about with ribboned tricolour. I'd be in high good humour but for the fact that trade is dead."

No word in all this of Laclos, or the duc d'Orléans. La Fayette was the man of the hour, or so it seemed. Then—and it was not Robert who wrote it, but Pierre, who had seen the news in a journal at Le Mans, and had it confirmed—we learnt that the duc d'Orléans, Laclos, his aide-de-camp Clarke, and his mistress Madame de Buffon had left Paris for Boulogne on the 14th of October en route for England. The excuse was a foreign mission.

"But," he added, "the comte de Valence, colonel of the Dragons de Chartres here in Le Mans, and a friend of the duc d'Orléans, has put it about that La Fayette and certain members of the Assembly believe the duc to have been behind the march on

Versailles, indeed encouraged the whole disturbance, and that it would be 'diploma-tic' for all concerned if the prince should disappear for a while. So the people's favourite has taken himself to London, and they say is enchanted to do so; the racing in England is so much better than in France!"

I remembered the carriage turning out of the Palais-Royal on its way to Vincennes, the two lovers lolling on the cushions, the wave of the languid hand. Had Robert staked his all on the wrong horse after all?

November passed, and we had no word from him. Michel and François were busy with the foundry work, which luckily was picking up, though slowly, for until all the new laws were passed nobody knew how they would affect our merchandise. Then, at the beginning of December, a letter came from Robert addressed to me.

"I'm in great trouble again," he wrote, "on the brink of the same disaster that overtook me in 1780, and in '85."

He must be referring, of course, to his bankruptcy. Perhaps to imprisonment too.

"I received a great shock, as you may well imagine," he continued, "when the duc d'Orléans and Laclos left Paris without a word of warning to those, like myself, who had faithfully served him during the past months. I forget who it was that said, 'Put not your faith in princes'. There may be, of course, some explanation, which no one has yet heard. Being an optimist, I live in hopes. Meanwhile, for my financial affairs, there is only one course to take. I can't tell you of it in a letter, or of another matter concerning my future. I want you to come to Paris. Please don't refuse me."

I kept the contents of this note to myself for twenty-four hours. It had been written to me, and made no mention to Pierre or Michel. My mother was too far away, otherwise I should have consulted her. Pierre was the most obvious counsellor, and he knew the law, but I was aware that he was much concerned at that time with matters of the municipality in Le Mans, and could ill afford to be absent. Besides, the very fact that he was a lawyer might make my eldest brother wary. Had he needed Pierre he would have sent for him. I turned the matter over in my mind, and in the end I took the letter to Michel.

"You must g-go, of course," he said, without any hesitation. "I'll m-make it all right with François."

"No need for that," I told him.

It was two months since Gabriel had died, and my husband was still out of favour with me. I knew it would pass, but for the moment I could hardly look at him. A few days without the guilty knowledge that I hurt him might be good for both of us. Then, with the memory of the last visit to Paris still vivid and unhappy, I said to Michel, "Come with me."

Apart from the apprentice years in le Berry, Michel had never left our glass-house country, or seen a larger city than Le Mans. In old days, I would never have suggested it; he looked, and was, a product of the foundry, black as a charcoal-burner and at times almost as uncouth. But now, with all men equal, since the Revolution had abolished distinction between persons, could not my youngest brother, if he had the mind to do so, elbow a Parisian off the pavement? Perhaps he had the same thought. He smiled at me, as he might have done years past when promoted to work on shift beside his elders.

"V-very well," he said. "I'd l-like to come."

We set forth for Paris within a day or two. The only concession Michel made to taste and fashion was to have his hair trimmed by the barber in Montmirail, and to buy a pair of shoes; as for the rest, his Sunday coat and breeches would have to serve.

"Had I known f-five months back I was to act as your escort," he told me slyly, "I'd have p-prised open the closets at the château de Nouans and d-dressed up like a peacock."

The first thing I noticed when the diligence drove into the capital was that there were fewer carriages in the streets, and the thoroughfares were bare of all but trading vehicles. Many of the bright cafés and small shops that I remembered had boards across the windows, with signs "To Sell" or "To Let" upon them, and although there were many people walking about there were fewer loiterers; most of them seemed intent upon their business, and were plainly dressed, as we were ourselves. True, it had been April when I last came to Paris, and the month was now December, bleak and wet, yet something had vanished from the scene, hard to define. The carriages and the folk who rode in them, gorgeously if sometimes absurdly attired, had made a kind of magic, and given a fairy-tale glitter to the capital. Now it seemed just like any other city, and Michel, peering through the windows of the diligence at the murky gloom about us, observed that no doubt the buildings were very fine, but it was not all that different from Le Mans.

There were no fiacres waiting in the rue du Boulay to take up passengers from the diligence, and the man who set our luggage down said the drivers did not find it paid them now to wait for travellers. Most of them had put themselves at the disposal of the deputies.

"That's where the money is these days," said the fellow, winking. "Hire yourself as a driver or courier to a member of the Assembly, and your worries are over. Nearly all the deputies are from the provinces, and as easy to fleece as unweaned lambs."

Michel shouldered our bags, and presently we found ourselves at the Cheval Rouge in the rue St. Denis. I did not wish to thrust ourselves upon Robert unprepared, and this was the only place I knew.

The patron was the son of the old people of my father's time, but he had some recollection of our name, and made us welcome. A deputy and his wife had the best room, the one my parents always had—the new patron made much of this, for they were evidently his most important clients—and later we passed them on the stairs, a plain-featured, stout little man swollen with self-importance like a pouter-pigeon, with a dim-faced wife who cooked most of their dinner in their rooms, because she did not trust the hotel chef. The deputy had been a notary somewhere in the Vosges, and until he was elected to the Assembly had never seen Paris in his life.

We were served with a meal of soup and beef, hardly as well-cooked as we should have had at home, and the patron, who came over to chat with us, told us there was no holding a servant since the day the Bastille fell. They lived in hourly expectation of being made masters, and would hardly settle in one place for more than a week.

"As long as the deputies remain in Paris I shall keep the hotel open," he said, "but when they disperse . . ." he shrugged his shoulders . . . "it may not pay me to remain. I might do better to buy a small place in the provinces. No one wants to come to Paris any more. Life is too dear, the times are too unsettled."

When we had finished, Michel took one look at the rain falling on the dark empty street and shook his head.

"The b-bright lights of the Palais-Royal can wait," he said. "If this is the capital, give me the f-furnace fire at le Chesne-Bidault."

I was up early next morning, and looking into his room saw he was still asleep, so I let him lie there, and scribbled him a note giving him directions how to find the Palais-Royal. Then I went off alone, for somehow I felt it best to see Robert by myself, and let him know that Michel had accompanied me.

Morning in the Paris streets was always busy, with people marketing and going to work. There was little difference here, the usual jostling and rudeness I remembered. A new factor was the presence of the National Guard patrolling the streets, walking in couples, giving a martial air to the scene about them. At least they were a protection against thieves, if nothing else.

The Palais-Royal, when I came to it, wore the usual forlorn appearance of any unlived-in château, and being so large a palace perhaps it showed the more. The windows were all shuttered, the big gates closed. Only the side gates were open to admit people to the gardens and arcades. Members of the National Guard did sentry duty, but they let me pass without question, and it seemed to me they served small purpose standing there.

It was early in the morning, and anyway too late in the season for garden loiterers; but whether it was the absence of the duc d'Orléans and his household in London, or simply, as my brother had warned me, that trade was bad, somehow the appearance of the Palais-Royal had changed. The arcades themselves had a drab winter look, the paving was full of puddles. It reminded me of a fairground after the fair has gone. Many of the boutiques were boarded up, with the tell-tale sign "For Sale" upon them, and those that were still in business displayed goods in their windows that must have been there for months. Some flair for the times, or spirit of imitation, had seized upon all the traders; faded tricolour ribbon draped every window, and prominent amongst the bric-à-brac on show were models of the Bastille, made in everything from wax to chocolate.

I arrived at No. 255 and saw with a pang of disillusion, though I had expected it, the notice "For Sale" hanging on the door. The windows, though unshuttered, were bare of goods.

How different from eight months past, when, despite the riots, the windows had been backed by velvet, and some half-dozen of Robert's most saleable "objets d'art" set in full view of the prospective buyer! "Never crowd a window," he used to say. "It puts the buyer off. One good piece on show suggests twenty more within. Dressing your window is an art like anything else. The rarer the bait, the more eager the customer." Now there was nothing to draw anyone. Not even a solitary cockade.

I rang the bell with small hope that it would be answered, for the rooms above looked as blank as those beneath. Presently I heard footsteps from inside, and someone unbolted the door and opened it.

"I'm sorry. The boutique is closed. Is there anything I can do for you?"

The voice was soft and low, the manner guarded. I was staring at a young woman of about Edmé's age, or younger, whose undoubted beauty but startled eyes suggested that a member of her own sex, dressed for a morning call, was the last person in the world she had expected to see.

"Monsieur Busson?" I enquired.

She shook her head. "He is not here," she answered. "He is living temporarily above his laboratory in the rue Traversiére. He may be here later in the morning if you care to call back. What name shall I say?"

I was about to tell her I was Monsieur Busson's sister, when caution held me back.

"I received a letter from him some days ago," I said, "asking if I should be in Paris, to look in on him upon a business matter. I only arrived last night, and came straight from the hotel."

She was still suspicious, and watched me, with her hand on the door. The curious thing was that she reminded me, in some indefinable way, of Cathie. Taller, slimmer, she had the same enormous eyes, though set in a sallow skin; and her hair fell about her shoulders as Cathie's had done when she was first married to my brother.

"Forgive my rudeness," I asked, "but what exactly is your own business here? Are you Monsieur Busson's concierge?"

"No," she said, "I'm his wife."

She must have noticed the change in my expression. I could feel it myself. My heart began thumping, and the colour rushed into my face.

"I beg your pardon," I said, "he never told me he had married again."

"Again?" She raised her eyebrows, and smiled for the first time. "I'm afraid you have made a mistake," she told me. "Monsieur Busson has never been married before. You are perhaps confusing him with his brother, who is proprietor of a great château between La Mans and Angers. He is a widower, I know."

Here was complete confusion. I felt giddy from shock. She must have sensed it, for she pulled a chair forward, and I sank into it.

"Perhaps you are right," I said to her. "There is sometimes confusion between brothers."

Now, looking up at her from the chair, I found her smile engaging. Less frankly warm than Cathie's, it was somehow youthful, artless.

"Have you been married long?" I asked her.

"About six weeks," she answered. "To tell you the truth, it is still a secret. I understand his family might make difficulties."

"His family?"

"Yes, this brother, the owner of the château, in particular. My husband is his heir, and was expected to marry someone of his own position. It happens that I am an orphan, without fortune. That is something the aristocracy can't forgive, even in these days."

I began to see it all. Robert had reverted to his old game of make-believe. Here was another practical joke, such as joining the Arquebusiers, and giving a masked ball to the ladies of Chartres. It would test all his ingenuity, though, to keep up with this deception.

"Where did you meet?" I asked her, curiosity now boundless.

"At the orphanage at Sèvres," she said. "There was a big glass manufactury there, as you probably know, which is now closed down. My husband unfortunately lost money in it at one time. Somehow he met the director of the orphanage over business—this was soon after the fall of the Bastille—and they made an arrangement about me. I had worked, you understand, for the director and his wife since growing up. Anyway, I came here to the boutique, and in a few weeks we were married."

She glanced down at her wedding-ring, and a second one besides, a fine ruby, which must have cost my brother a small fortune, unless he stole it.

"It doesn't daunt you," I asked, "to have a husband nearly twenty years older than yourself?"

"On the contrary," she told me, "it makes for experience."

This time her smile was more engaging still. I regretted Cathie, but I could hardly blame my brother.

"I wonder," I said, "that he cares to leave you alone at nights."

She seemed surprised. "With the windows shuttered and the door barred?" she queried.

"All the same . . ." I gestured, leaving my phrase unfinished.

"We see each other during the day," she murmured. "Business may be pressing, and his affairs in the hands of lawyers, but Robert can always find time for an hour or two with his wife."

It seemed to me that she had little to learn for one reared in an orphanage, however credulous she might be as to my brother's background.

"I'm sure he can," I answered, aware, with sudden humour, that my voice must be sounding as acid as my mother's would have done in the same circumstances. Then, after the light feeling of amusement, came a sudden shadow. Glancing up the stairs I was reminded, all too swiftly, of my last visit, of helping poor dear Cathie up to her room and to her bed, which she would never leave again save for her coffin. Here was her successor, complacent, dewy-eyed, knowing nothing of the predecessor who had trodden those same stairs before her not eight months since. My brother might be able to forget, but I could not.

"I must go," I said, rising from the chair, sick suddenly with distaste, and despising myself for it—God knows, I thought, if this helps Robert's loneliness then he is welcome. She asked what name she should give when her husband came, and I told her Duval, Madame Duval. We bade each other au revoir, and she shut the door of the boutique behind me.

It was raining again, and in the palace gardens the old leaves of autumn lay scattered that had been in bud when I last came. I hurried away, not wishing to linger in a place so haunted by poor Cathie's ghost and the young living Jacques, bowling his hoop before me. The shuttered windows of the Palais-Royal, and the yawning sentries of the National Guard, proclaimed another world from the one I had known in spring.

I retraced my steps, disheartened, to the Cheval Rouge, and found Michel on the doorstep, about to set forth in search for me. Instinct, I don't know why, made me hold the secret. I told him I had been to the boutique and found it shuttered, with no one there. He accepted this as natural. If Robert was near to bankruptcy once more, his boutique would be the first to go.

"C-come on, let's walk the streets," urged Michel, with all the impatience of a newcomer to the capital. "We can f-find Robert later."

To chase the glooms away I let myself be led by him, it hardly mattered where, over much of the same ground that I had already covered. Michel knew none of it. Finally we came to the Tuileries, where the King and Queen now lived. We stared at the great palace, or what we could see of it beyond the court, and watched the Swiss guard marching to and fro, and wondered, as many a provincial must have done before us, whether the King and Queen watched us from the windows.

"Imagine it," said Michel, "all those rooms to house f-four people. F-five, if you count the King's sister. What do you suppose they d-do all day?"

"Much as we do," I suggested. "Perhaps the King plays cards with his sister after dinner, and the Queen reads to the children."

"What?" said Michel. "With all the c-courtiers looking on?"

Who could say? The palace looked grey, forbidding, on this December day. I remembered the Queen stepping from her coach to go to the Opera that evening more than ten years ago, a procelain figurine that a breath could shatter, with the comte d'Artois giving her his arm, and the pageboys in attendance. Now he was an émigré, one might almost say a fugitive, and the Queen was hated, by all accounts, and forever plotting the downfall of the Assembly from behind those windows in the Tuileries. Whether this was true or not, one thing seemed certain; the days of opera-going and masked balls were over.

"It's dead," said Michel suddenly, "like looking at a s-sepulchre. Let's l-leave them there to rot."

We walked back by the quays, where at least, so Michel said, however stinking it might be, there was some sign of life and labour, with flat-bottomed timber barges warped against the river banks, and husky fellows shouting to one another. I need not have feared for my brother's provincial looks. There were few people in this part of Paris to put him to shame. Beggars were everywhere, and he would have had no money left to settle our account at the Cheval Rouge if I had let him give to all of them.

"If it was these folk who b-broke the Bastille down, you can hardly b-blame them," observed Michel. "If I'd been here I'd have razed the T-Tuileries to the g-ground as well."

He had a wish to see where the Bastille had stood, and we found our way there finally, and looked at the heap of rubble and blocks of stone that once had been a fortress. There were gangs of men with picks working on the site.

"That was the d-day!" said Michel. "What I would have g-given to have been amongst those who stormed it."

I am not so sure. The Réveillon riots, and the shouting before the Abbey of St. Vincent, had taught me all I wished to know of insurrection.

By this time it was long past noon, and both of us were hungry, and exhausted too. Like all strangers to the capital, we had walked too far, with little sense of direction. The Cheval Rouge could be east, or west, or just beside us, for all we knew. We found a small café nearby, not much of a place, and none too clean, but we dined there and ate well, and the lad who served us told Michel that we were in the Faubourg St. Antoine. I remembered then that it was somewhere here that Robert had his laboratory.

When we had finished eating I asked for the rue Traversiére, and the lad pointed with his finger. It was barely five minutes distant. Michel and I discussed what we should do, and we decided to go to the laboratory—I knew the number—and see if our brother was there. I warned Michel to wait outside. I wanted to talk to Robert first alone.

The rue Traversiére seemed endless, all warehouses and stores, and I was glad of Michel's company. It was full, too, of labourers who stared, and carters backing their great drays, cursing their horses.

"I can't m-make it out," said Michel suddenly. "You'd think Robert would have been content to stay at la B-Brûlonnerie. He's like Esau—selling his b-birthright for a mess of pottage. Not even that. Can you t-tell me what he's gained in life by this?"

He pointed at the grey-black building, the filthy street with the sewage running down it, the savage carter whipping his pair of horses.

"Nothing," I answered, "except the right to call himself Parisian. It may not mean much to us, but it does to him."

We came at last to No. 144. A dank, tall house, adjoining a little court. I made a sign to Michel to stay outside, and crossed the court and read a list of names scrawled upon an inner door. I at length descried the faded lettering "Busson", and an arrow pointing to the basement. I groped my way down the stairs, coming to a passage-way where crates were stacked, and beyond it to a large bare room, with a centre furnace—this must be the laboratory—unlighted, of course, and débris and dust upon the floor, the litter of weeks unswept.

Voices, and the sound of hammering, came from a small room nearby, the door half-open. I picked my way across the litter of the laboratory and there, in the small room, I saw my brother seated at a table covered with paper, all in great disorder, while a workman knelt on the floor hammering nails into a crate. Robert lifted his head as I entered, and for a second his expression had all the surprise and panic of an animal trapped. He instantly recovered, and sprang to his feet.

"Sophie!" he exclaimed. "Why, in the name of God, didn't you let me know you were in Paris?"

He took me in his arms and kissed me, telling the man to leave his work and go.

"How long have you been here, and how did you find this place? I apologise for the mess. I'm selling out, as you probably realise."

He gestured with a half-laugh, and shrugged his shoulders, watching me closely at the same time, and I had the impression that it was not the disorder for which he apologised, but the poor quarters themselves. The word "my laboratory", when he had used it in the past, had conjured to my mind a fine big place, well fitted-up and orderly; not this dim cellar, with a window-grating high in the wall to the street above.

"I came yesterday," I told him. "I'm putting up at the Cheval Rouge. This morning I called at the boutique in the Palais-Royal."

He drew a long breath, stared at me a moment, then burst into a laugh.

"Well?" he said. "So now you know my secret—one of them, that is. What did you think of her?"

"She's very pretty," I replied, "and also very young."

He smiled. "Twenty-two," he said. "Straight from that orphanage at Sèvres. She knows nothing of life, she can't even sign her name. But I found out all about her parentage from the people who had the orphanage, and it's nothing to be ashamed of. She was born in Doudan, her father a merchant in a small way, and the mother was a niece of the famous Jean Bart, the privateer. She has good blood in her."

Now it was my turn to smile. Did he really think I cared about her parentage? If he liked her well enough to marry her, this was all that mattered.

"You know more about her family than she does of yours," I remarked. "I never knew you had a brother who was proprietor of a château between Le Mans and Angers."

For a moment he was disconcerted. Then he laughed once more, and, dusting the one chair, made me sit down upon it.

"Ah well," he said, "she is so innocent, and it makes for excitement. I think she enjoys my love-making the more, believing me a seigneur hounded by misfortune. A glass-blower on the verge of bankruptcy is no great catch. Why break a young girl's dream?"

I looked about me at the tumbled papers and the disorder of the room.

"It's true, then?" I asked. "You've come to it again?"

He nodded. "I've given power of attorney to a friend of mine, a lawyer of the old Parliament, Monsieur Mouchoux de Bellemont," Robert answered. "He will deal with all my creditors, see to the sale of this place and the boutique too, and if he can salvage anything—which I doubt—place it to Pierre's credit in Le Mans. In any event, he will write to Pierre after I have gone, telling him all the circumstances, which are too involved to tell you now."

I stared at him. He was making a pretence of clearing the papers.

"Gone?" I asked. "Gone where?"

"To London," he said, after a moment's pause. "I'm emigrating. Clearing out of the country. There's nothing here for me any more. And they want engravers in crystal over there. I have work waiting for me with one of the foremost London glass-manufacturers."

I was dumbfounded. I had thought he might go out of Paris, to Normandy, perhaps, where there were several glass-houses, or even come back again to our neighbour-hood, where he was respected and known. But not to leave the country, not to emigrate like some scared member of the aristocracy who could not face up to the implication of the new régime . . .

"Don't do it, Robert," I said. "I beg of you, don't do it."

"Why not?" His voice was sharp. He gestured angrily, scattering some of the papers on the table on to the floor. "What is there to keep me here?" he cried. "Nothing but debts, more debts, and a certainty of prison. In England I can begin life anew, with nobody asking questions, and a young wife to give me courage. It's all settled, and no one will make me change my mind."

I saw nothing I could say would persuade him.

"Robert," I said gently, "Michel is with me. He's waiting in the street above."

"Michel?" Once again the trapped animal look came into his eyes. "Did he go with you to the Palais-Royal?" he asked.

"No, I went alone; nor did I tell him you had remarried."

"That wouldn't worry me, he would understand. But this, my going away . . ." He paused, staring straight in front of him. "Pierre would argue by the hour, yet have the consideration to see both sides of the question. Not Michel. He's a fanatic."

I felt depression come upon me. I had done wrong to bring Michel. Had I known of Robert's intention to emigrate I never would have done so. For my eldest brother had chosen the right word. Michel would never understand. He was indeed a fanatic.

"He'll have to know," I said. "I'd better fetch him."

He crossed over to the window-grating and shouted. "Michel?" he called. "Come along down, you rascal. Michel?"

I saw my brother's feet pass the grating above our heads and pause a moment. Then came his answering shout, and the feet moved away. Robert crossed into the laboratory, and in a few moments I heard them greet one another, and the sound of their laughter, and they came back to the little room together, arm-in-arm.

"Well, you've run me to earth like a baited badger," Robert was saying, "and there's nothing left of my equipment, as you can see. The place is cleared. But I've done good work here in my time."

I saw by Michel's puzzled look that he was as surprised as I had been to find Robert, his admired eldest brother, in a basement lair.

"I'm sure of it," he said politely. "No p-place looks its best when it's bare, and the fires are out."

Robert, to evade the issue, suddenly bent and picked up a package from the floor.

"Here is salvage anyway," he said, unwrapping the object and placing it on the table triumphantly. "The famous glass."

It was the goblet, engraved with the fleur-de-lys, that had been blown at la Pierre for Louis XV nearly twenty years before.

"I've copied it before and will do so again," said Robert. "A glass with this device will sell for double its value where I'm going."

"Where are you going?" asked Michel.

I had the hot feeling of unease that comes before disaster. Robert glanced at me, with mock-embarrassment, and said, "Tell him what you found today at the boutique."

"Robert has maried again," I said. "I wanted to have his permission before I told you."

A warm smile came over Michel's face, and he went and clapped his brother on the shoulder.

"I'm so very g-glad," he said, "the best thing you can do. S-Sophie was an idiot not to tell me. Who is she?"

Robert began his explanation of the orphanage, and Michel nodded his approval.

"She sounds a b-beauty," he said, "without any airs and g-graces. I expected you to remarry, but feared some haughty young woman with aristocratic prejudices. Well, if you've sold this, and your boutique too, where do you p-plan to live?"

"That's just it," said Robert. "I'm obliged to leave Paris. As I've already explained to Sophie, my creditors are after me, and I refuse to face another period in La Force."

He paused, and I saw he was thinking out how best to deliver his blow.

"I am all in f-favour of your leaving Paris," said Michel. "How you have stood the city all these years is b-beyond me. Come to us, mon vieux. If not to le Chesne-Bidault, at least within d-distance of it. Why, you might make some arrangement with the present t-tenant of la Pierre. Everything's changing hands. With so many f-frightened land-owners running from the country like rats, the opportunities are boundless. We'll f-find something for you, never fear. Forget your debts."

"It's no good," said Robert abruptly, "it's too late."

"Nonsense," replied Michel, "It's n-never too late. Trade has been bad these months, I know, but it's p-picking up every day. There's a great future ahead for all of us."

"No," said Robert, "France is finished."

Michel stared at him. He looked as though he had not heard aright.

"That's my opinion, anyway," said Robert, "so I'm clearing out, emigrating. I'm taking my young wife to London. They need engravers in crystal there, and, as I've just told Sophie, I have work waiting for me. It's been arranged by friends."

The silence hurt. I felt sick, looking at Michel's face. He had gone white, and his eyebrows, meeting in a straight line above the bridge of his nose as my father's had done, were pencil dark in contrast.

"By f-friends," he said at last, "you mean, by t-traitors."

Robert smiled, and took a step towards his brother.

"Come now," he said, "don't jump to conclusions. It just so happens that I have no great faith in what the present Assembly are going to do for trade or for anything else. These past few months in Paris have taught me much. It's all very well to be a patriot, but a man must see to his own future. And as things are at present, there's none for me here in France. That's why I'm quitting."

When Robert had gone bankrupt, the year my father died, Michel had been absent in le Berry. The family shame had somehow passed him by, leaving him untouched. If he considered it at all, I believe he understood Robert to have been unfortunate. At the time of the second trouble, in '85, Michel was too much concerned with the running of le Chesne-Bidault, and his growing friendship with François to worry overmuch about his eldest brother. Robert had always been extravagant, his fine friends had let him down. But this was different.

"Have you written to t-tell Pierre?" he asked.

"No," said Robert, "I shall do so before I leave. In any event the lawyer who has power of attorney for my affairs will write a full explanation to him."

"What about Jacques?" I asked.

"I've arranged for that as well. Pierre will act as guardian. I've suggested that Jacques should remain with my mother. I take it she will provide for him. It will be up to him to make his own way in life."

He might have been speaking about some crate to be dispatched. Not the future of his son. The unconcern in his voice was nothing new to me. This was the Robert with whom I had journeyed to St. Christophe, the man who had lost Cathie, the man who lived from day to day. It was a being unknown to his youngest brother. I could tell by Michel's eyes, that the illusion of a lifetime had been destroyed. Whatever tales Robert had told him when he was with us at le Chesne-Bidault after the Bastille fell, of patriotism, and of a new world dawning, were now shown up as fables. Robert himself had not believed a word of them.

Perhaps losing my first child had made me hard. Nothing Robert could say or do would ever again surprise me. If he chose to leave us this way, although my heart yearned after him it was his choice, not ours.

I had not realised Michel would take it the way he did. His faith was shattered. He put his hand up to loosen his cravat. I thought for a moment that he was going to choke; his face had turned from white to dullish grey.

"That's f-final, then," he said.

"That's final," Robert repeated.

Michel turned to me. "I'm g-going back to the Cheval Rouge," he said. "Come with me if you are ready to d-do so. I shall take the d-diligence in the morning. If you want to s-stay here, that's for you to decide."

Robert said nothing. He had turned pale too. I looked from one to the other. I loved them both.

"You can't part in this way," I said. "In the old days it was the three of you against my father when things went wrong. We have none of us ever quarrelled. Please, Michel."

Michel did not answer. He turned on his heel and began to walk away through the laboratory. I threw a helpless look at Robert, and went after him.

"Michel," I cried, "we may never see him again. Surely you will wish him luck, if nothing else?"

"Luck?" echoed Michel, over his shoulder. "He's g-got all the luck he needs in that glass he'll take with him. I thank God my f-father did not live to see this day."

I looked back again at Robert, who was staring after us, a strange, lost figure amidst the disorder of his papers in that bleak basement room.

"I'll come to you in the morning," I said. "I'll come to the Palais-Royal to say good-bye."

He gave a shrug, half amusement, half despair. "You'd be wiser to take the diligence and go home," he said.

I hesitated, then went quickly to him and put my arms round him. "If things go wrong in England," I told him, "I'll be waiting for you. Always, Robert."

He kissed me, a smile that meant nothing flickering for a moment on his face.

"You're the only one," he said, "the only one in the family to understand. I shan't forget."

Hand-in-hand we crossed the debris of the laboratory, and followed Michel up the stairs. The workman had disappeared. Michel was waiting for me in the little court.

"Look after le Chesne-Bidault," Robert said to him. "You're as fine a craftsman as my father, you know that. I'll take the glass with me to London, but I'll leave the family honour in your hands."

I felt that one gesture from Michel then might have made Robert stay. One smile, one clasp of the hand, and they could have fallen into argument, delayed decision, and somehow saved the day. Had it been Pierre standing there in the court, there would have been no bitterness. Illusions might be destroyed, compassion would remain. Michel had been cast in a different mould. Whoever hurt his pride hurt all. Forgiveness was not a word in his vocabulary. He stared across that small dank court at Robert, and there was so much anguish in his face that I could have wept.

"Don't t-talk to me of honour," he said. "You've never had any, I s-see it now. You're nothing but a traitor and a f-fraud. If this country fails in the future, it will be b-because of men like you. Like y-you." The old endearment, the "thou" between brothers, faltered on his tongue, and he turned, almost ran from the court and into street saying it still, stammering all the while, "Like y-you, like y-you."

The years vanished. He was a child again, wounded beyond his comprehension. I did not look back at Robert. I ran into the street after Michel, and walked beside him up the rue Traversiére until, by the mercy of heaven, we found a wandering fiacre, hailed it, and drove to the Cheval Rouge. Michel went straight to his room and locked the door.

Next morning we took the diligence together, saying nothing of Robert or of what had passed. It was only at the end of the day, with our journey nearly done, that Michel turned to me and said, "You can tell François what happened. I never want to speak of it again."

The brightness of the new world had faded for him too.

13

ROBERT'S EMIGRATION WAS a profound shock to the family. His marriage was accepted as natural, if somewhat hasty, but to abandon his country just at the moment when every man of intelligence and education was needed to prove the worth of the new régime was something only contemplated by cowards, aristocrats—and adventurers, like my brother.

Pierre, sticken at first almost as much as Michel, found fewer grounds for condemnation when the lawyer's papers arrived from Paris. There was little doubt that every sou obtained from the sale of the boutique in the Palais Royal, and the laboratory in the rue Traversiére, must go to pay Robert's creditors, and even so they would not be paid in full. Once again he had lived beyond his means, promising goods that he had never delivered, entering into negotiations with merchants the terms of which he could not fulfill. Had he not fled the country, months in prison would surely have been his fate.

"We could all have joined together to pay his debts," said Pierre. "If only he had consulted me, this tragedy would have been avoided. Now he has lost his name for ever. No one will believe us if we say he has gone to London for a few months to perfect his knowledge of English glass. An émigré is an émigré. They are all traitors to the nation."

Edmé, like Michel, refused to mention Robert's name again. "I have no eldest brother," she said. "As far as I am concerned he is dead."

Now that she had left her husband she passed her days helping Pierre in his work as notary, writing letters for him as a clerk would do, and seeing his clients for him too, when he was busy with the affairs of the municipality. She was as good as a man at the work, Pierre said, and finished it in half the time.

My mother did not concern herself much with the political implications of Robert's act. It was the fact that he had abandoned his son that grieved her most. Naturally she would keep Jacques, and bring him up in St. Christophe, until such time as Robert might return; for she refused to believe he would not return within the year.

"Robert failed in Paris," she wrote to us. "Why should he succeed any better in a strange country? He will come home once the novelty has worn off and he finds that his charm cannot fool the English people."

I had two letters from him soon after his arrival in London. All was couleur de rose. He and his young wife had found lodgings without difficulty, and he was already working as engraver to a large firm and, so he said, "made much of by his employers". He was picking up English fast. There was a coterie of Frenchmen and their wives settled in London in the same district as themselves—Pancras, he called it—so they were never at a loss for company.

"The duc d'Orléans has a house in Chapel Street," he wrote, "where Madame de Buffon keeps house for him. He spends most of his time at the races, but I am told on good authority that he is likely to be offered the crown of the Low Countries. If this should come about, it might very well make a difference to my plans."

It did not come about. The next we heard of the duc d'Orléans was when we read in the Le Mans journal that he had returned to Paris and presented himself to the Assembly to take the oath to the Constitution. This was in July of 1790, and for the whole of the month I expected to hear that Robert, faithful to the entourage, had returned to Paris too. I hoped in vain. A letter came at last, but brief, giving little news except that his wife, Marie-Françoise, was expecting her first child. As to the duc d'Orléans, there was no mention of his name.

Meanwhile, we ourselves had survived our first nine months under the new régime, and, although the paradise they promised us had not yet come about, business was brisk. We had no cause to complain.

There was no repetition of the previous winter's severity, nor of last year's famine, though prices were still high and people grumbled. What kept us all alert and interested were the decrees forthcoming from the Assembly, month by month, substituting new laws for the whole nation.

The old privileges abolished, there was not a man now in the kingdom who could not better his position and rise to high office if he had the wit and initiative to do so. The legal system was reformed, much to my brother Pierre's satisfaction, and a judge could no longer pronounce guilt—a civil trial must be held before a citizen jury. In the army, a common soldier could become an officer—and because of this many of the existing officers emigrated, and were no great loss.

The greatest shock to those who still held to the old ways was the reform of the clergy, but to men like my brother Michel it was the supreme achievement of that year of 1790. The religious orders were suppressed in February. That was only a beginning.

"No more f-fat friars and b-big-bellied monks," cried Michel gleefully, when we heard the news. "They'll have to work for their l-living in the future like the rest of us."

On the 14th of May a decree was passed giving all the church lands and property to the nation. Michel, who commanded the National Guard of le Plessis-Dorin—made up, it must be admitted, almost entirely of his own workmen from the foundry—had the supreme satisfaction of going to the presbytery and handing a copy of the decree in person to his old enemy the curé Cosnier.

"I could hardly c-contain myself," he told us afterwards, "from putting all the v-village cows and pigs into his strip of f-field, to prove that the land belonged to le P-Plessis-Dorin, and not to the Church."

Worse was to follow, though, for poor Monsieur Cosnier. Later in the year, in November, the Assembly declared that every priest must take an oath to serve the Civil Constitution of the Clergy, now part of the State—the Pope's authority was no more—and if a priest refused, then he would be replaced in office and forbidden to give the sacraments.

The curé Cosnier would not take the oath, and the curé Cosnier went. . . .

"I've waited t-two years for this," said Michel. "When the Assembly m-makes up its mind how and when to s-sell church lands, I shall be the f-first to buy them."

The Assembly above all needed money, to bolster the tumbling finances of the nation, and they issued bonds called assignats, representing church lands, to those patriots who wished to acquire them in return for ready cash. The more assignats a man held, the greater a patriot he appeared to be in the eyes of his fellow-countrymen, and later, when the actual land began to be distributed, he could either exchange the assignats for the land itself or for its equivalent in coinage.

It was a mark of civic pride to be known as an "acquirer of national property", and in our district of Mondoubleau, Loiret-Cher (for all the départements of France had been re-grouped and renamed under the new system), my brother Michel and my husband François headed the list of those patriots bearing the title.

It was in the February of '91 that Michel redeemed his assignats, buying up a bishop's château and the land belonging to it somewhere between Mondoubleau and Vendôme, which cost him some 13,000 livres—and all because of his hatred for the Church.

He had no intention of living there himself. He put a man in to farm the land, and he would go over there and walk about the acres, and stare at the place feeling, I suppose, that in some way he had revenged himself upon the curé Cosnier, and—in some curious fashion—upon his eldest brother too. Robert had squandered money he did not possess, defrauding his associates. Michel, in the name of the people, would somehow make good the loss.

I do not pretend to explain how his mind worked, but I do know that little by little, as Michel became an "acquirer of national property", so there developed in him, at the same time, a love of power for its own sake. I remember—and this was before he bought the land, and so must have been in the November of 1790—that I was visiting the Delalande family one afternoon, for their little girl was sick. I was about to leave, when Madame Delalande said to me, "So our men are off with the National Guard this evening to Authon."

It was the first I had heard of it, but I had no wish to appear ignorant before her, and answered, "I believe so".

She smiled, and added, "If they return fully loaded as they did a year ago, during the time of the forest patrols, we shall all benefit. They say the château de Charbonnières is a fine place, stacked to the roof with fine furniture. I've told my André to bring me back some bedding."

"The duty of the National Guard is to protect property, not to seize it," I answered coolly.

She laughed. "Our men interpret duty in their own fashion," she replied, "and anyway, everything belongs to the people these days. Monsieur Busson-Challoir says so himself."

I went back to the master's house, and as the three of us sat down to dinner I enquired about the expedition. François said nothing. As usual, he flashed a look at Michel.

"Yes, you heard right," said my brother shortly, "b-but it's not the château we're going after, it's the owner."

"The owner?" I repeated. "Isn't he Monsieur de Chamoy, who commands a garrison at Nancy, away on the frontier?"

"The same," answered Michel, "but a t-traitor, by all accounts. Anyway, I've had word he's in hiding at his château of Charbonnières, and the G-Guard under my command are going to get him."

It was not my business to interfere. If Monsieur de Chamoy was a traitor, it was the duty of the National Guard to apprehend him. I knew the château, only a short way away, within easy marching distance, this side of Authon, and I knew Monsieur de Chamoy too; he had bought glass from us in the old days, a pleasant, courteous man, rather a favourite with my mother. I thought it unlikely he would be a traitor. He was a serving officer, and he had not tried to emigrate.

"Don't forget your manners when you arrest him," I said. "The last time he came here was after our father died, and he called to offer sympathy."

"He won't get any s-sympathy from me if he t-tries to evade arrest," answered

Michel. "A cord round his wrists, and a kick on the s-seat of his breeches."

They set out as soon as it was dark, about seventy of them, fully armed, and when they did not return the following day I feared the worst—another butchery like Ballon, and this time our men the murderers. There was no question of brigands now, nor of grain hoarders, and the countryside was quiet.

I summoned Marcel Gautier, one of the younger workmen who, because of a sore foot, had not accompanied the others, and bade him drive me to Authon. I had acted godmother to his baby two months before, and he was willing to please me.

It was a raw, damp day, and we took the small carriole, in which Robert and I had driven to St. Christophe. When we arrived near the château of Charbonnières we found a junction of roads there barricaded, and some of our men on guard. No one was allowed through without permission, but they recognised me at once and let us pass. The National Guard was standing about in front of the château, André Delalande apparently in command, and one of the first things I saw, amongst the pile of loot in the carriage-way, was a great pile of bedding. He had remembered his wife's request.

He came up to the carriole, somewhat surprised, I think, to see me, but saluted and told me that the bird had flown—some spy had informed Monsieur de Chamoy of his danger, and he had fled before the National Guard arrived. Because of this, my brother and my husband had gone on to Authon to question the people there.

I bade Marcel turn the carriole round and continue to Authon, and as we wheeled in front of the château others of the Guard emerged, some half-dozen of them, bearing chairs and tables, and clothing too. Marcel took a sly look at me, but I said nothing.

The road entering Authon was cordonned off, but the sentries recognised the carriole once more and let us through. We drew up before the hotel de ville, where a small crowd had gathered in consternation. When I enquired the reason, I was told that the commandant of the National Guard had commanded a house-to-house search for Monsieur de Chamoy.

"He is not here," a woman cried from the crowd, "none of us have seen him in Authon. But it makes no difference. The Guard insist on turning every house upside down."

Indeed, I could see some of them at it as I watched. There was Durocher, who should have known better, pushing some shopkeeper before him with his musket, demanding admittance to the grocery beyond, with two small children running in front and crying.

I descended from the carriole and went up the steps into the hotel de ville. And there were François and Michel, seated at a table with two of the workmen on sentry-go behind their chairs, and standing to attention before them, grey with fear, a little man whom I took to be the mayor. No one noticed me as I stood by the door, for all eyes were directed at Michel.

"You understand I have my d-duty to do," he was saying. "If de Chamoy is f-found hiding in any house in Authon, you will be made responsible. Meanwhile, we shall remain here for at least f-forty-eight hours, to allow time for a thorough search to be made. We d-demand free quarters for ourselves and our men for that p-period. Is that clear?"

"Quite clear, mon commandant," said the mayor, bowing and trembling, and he turned to another frightened official at his side to give orders.

Michel murmured something to François at his side, and I saw my husband laugh, and sign some paper with his usual masonic flourish.

I could tell by their faces that they were in high good humour. To scare the mayor, to quarter themselves upon the little town, was like a boyhood prank all over again; Michel might have been playing Indians with Pierre in the forest long ago.

It was not a game, though, for the mayor. Nor for the towns-folk whose homes were broken into, and who were forced to feed our men.

Then François lifted his eyes and saw me. He turned bright scarlet and nudged Michel.

"W-what are you doing here?" asked my brother.

"I only wondered if you would be home for dinner," I replied.

Somebody tittered, one of the young workmen, I think, who had lately been recruited to the National Guard. Michel banged his hand on the table.

"S-silence," he shouted.

There was an instant hush. The mayor turned whiter than before. My husband kept his eyes fixed on the paper before him.

"Then you can go b-back at once to le Chesne-Bidault," said Michel. "The National Guard is here to s-serve the nation, and when the nation's b-business is settled, the Guard will return. Vaillot, Mouchard, escort Madame D-Duval outside."

The two guards walked on either side of me to the door, and I had the doubtful satisfaction of knowing that, if my intrusion had caused my brother and my husband to lose face, it had done little else besides; except, perhaps, to make them harsher with the mayor.

Marcel and I took the road back to the foundry, and as we left Authon I saw yet another detachment of the National Guard come out and scatter in the fields on either side of the road, hullooing to one another, probing the ditches with their muskets, for all the world like boar-hounds after prey.

"They'll get him if he's there," said Marcel with satisfaction, "and there won't be much left of him afterwards, not with our lads."

He clicked his tongue at the horse to go faster. This, I thought, was the man who had stood bare-headed at the font of le Plessis-Dorin not two months since, tears in his eyes, when his baby girl was christened.

"You hope they catch him, then?" I asked.

"Catch him and cook him, m'dame," he answered. "The sooner the country is rid of all his kind the better."

They never did find Monsieur de Chamoy. Indeed, he found his way back to Nancy, I believe, and on proving not to be a traitor was reinstated in the garrison there, though we did not hear this until later.

What degraded me in my own eyes was that, in driving back to Plessis, I thought I espied a humped figure in a ditch, and instead of keeping silent about it called out instantly to Marcel, in great excitement.

"There he is, crouching by the thorn bush yonder. After him . . ." I cried, almost seizing the reins out of my driver's hands to run the fugitive down. It was nothing but the stump of a long-dead tree, and my instinctive feeling of disappointment shocked me to silence.

This was only one of several expeditions on the part of the masters of le Chesne-Bidault and their workmen in the guise of the National Guard, and for his zeal and patriotism my brother Michel was made adjutant-general of the district of Mondoubleau. Sickened at first, I soon became resigned, accepting as natural these forays into the countryside, even feeling a thrill of pride when the women told me that "Messieurs Duval and Busson-Challoir were the most feared men between la Ferté-Bernard and Châteaudun". Michel was still the leader, but François increased in stature too, with a new air of authority about him which was more pleasing to me, his wife, than his old air of submission used to be.

He looked well, too, in his uniform of the National Guard, being tall and broad, and I liked to think he had only to march with a company of men to one of the communes in our district, for the inhabitants to be on their toes at sight of him.

My François, who, when I married him, was no more than a master glass-maker at a small foundry, now had the power to walk into a château and arrest the proprietor of it, should he be suspect—that same proprietor who, a few years back, would have shown him the door.

There was one occasion when the pair of them, my brother and my husband, with just a handful of the National Guard, arrested half the commune of St. Avit, seized two former members of the aristocracy, the brothers Belligny, and a third, Monsieur de Neveu, disarmed them, and packed them off under escort to Mondoubleau, on suspicion of being traitors to the nation. The municipality at Mondoubleau kept all three under arrest, for they dared not countermand the orders of the adjutant-general. A few days afterwards, visiting two or three of the families at le Chesne-Bidault, I saw they all had fine new knives and forks on display, some of them silver, with monograms upon them, and I thought no more of it than if they had been purchased in the market-place.

Custom, it is said, makes all things acceptable. Gradually I came to look upon any fair-sized property as something the owner had no right to possess, if he had been a member of the aristocracy under the old régime. Like Michel and François, I began to suspect these people of harbouring revenge, perhaps of storing arms, which one day they might decide to use upon us. The new laws, after all, had hit the aristocracy hard; it would not be surprising if they banded together in secret and worked for the overthrow of the new régime.

What Pierre thought of the forays I never heard. They were not discussed when we visited Le Mans, for he had so much news of his own to tell. He had become an ardent member of the Club des Minimes, a branch of the Jacobins Club in Paris, famous for its progressive views, started by those deputies of the Asssmbly who were forever agitating for further reforms to the Constitution. The sessions at the Club des Minimes were often stormy, and there was one toward the end of January of '91 when Pierre rose to his feet and made an impassioned speech against some three hundred priests and as many ex-nobles in Le Mans who, he swore, were moving heaven and earth to destroy the revolution.

I heard it all from Edmé when she came to stay for a few days at le Chesne-Bidault. "Pierre had it from me in the first place," she told me. "The wife of one of his clients, a Madame Foulard, came to me and said that when she went to Confession the priest ordered her to use her influence to prevent her husband from being a member of the Club des Minimes. If she did not so do, the priest said, he would refuse her Absolution."

I could hardly believe a priest would go thus far, but Edmé assured me that this was not the only case; she had heard the story repeated by other women.

"There's an ugly spirit of reaction in Le Mans," she said, "and I blame the officers of the Dragons de Chartres. There is a brigadier quartered in my old house at the Abbey of St. Vincent, and he told me that the officers have forbidden the men to fraternise with the National Guard. Pierre agrees with me. He says the Club des Minimes wants to get rid of the regiment altogether. They've served their original purpose, and too many of the officers have relations who are émigrés and have joined the Prince de Condé in Coblenz."

The Prince de Condé, the King's cousin, and the comte d'Artois were both in Prussia attempting to raise an army of volunteers from amongst the émigrés who had followed them into exile, and with the help of the Prussian prince, the duke of Brunswick, hoped in time to invade France and overthrow the new régime.

I had heard nothing from Robert for many months, and my fear was that he might have left England and gone, as so many had done, to Coblenz. Living, as he must be doing, amongst little groups of reactionaries who would not rest until the aristocracy and the clergy had been reinstated, he would inevitably become tainted with their ideas, and learn nothing of what had been achieved here at home for the good of the country.

Whenever I saw Pierre he would look at me first, before embracing me, and raise his eyebrows in a question, and I would shake my head. No more would be said unless we found ourselves alone. It was a stigma, a mark of shame, to have a relative who was an émigré.

Edmé was right, though, when she said that there were forces of reaction in Le Mans. This was very easily seen at the theatre—we were told that exactly the same thing happened in Paris—when allusions to liberty and equality in a play would be loudly applauded by all the patriots in the audience, but if the subject should turn upon loyalty to a throne or to princes there would be counter-cheers and applause from those who felt that our own King and Queen were facing difficulties in Paris.

I happened to be staying with Pierre early in February of '91—just about the time Michel bought his piece of church property beyond Mondoubleau, so neither he nor François could accompany me to Le Mans. I arrived on the Monday, and on the next day Pierre and Edmé returned home to dine, full of an uproar there had been at the salle de Comédie the night before. The band of the Dragons de Chartres, engaged as orchestra, had refused to play the popular song "Ça Ira", although requested to do so by a crowd of spectators in the cheap seats.

"The municipality are furious," announced Pierre, "and have already complained to the officer commanding the parade of the Dragons this morning. If you want to see some fun, Sophie, come to the theatre with Edmé and me on Thursday, when they are giving *Semiramis,* followed by a ballet. The band of the Dragons are to play, and if we don't have 'Ça Ira' I'll get up on the stage and sing it myself."

The song "Ça Ira" was the rage of Paris, and now everyone in the country was either whistling it or humming it, though it had been written as a carillon, and should have been played on bells. Heaven knows it was infectious. I had it from morning till night at the foundry with the apprentice boys in the yard, and even Madame Verdelet in the kitchen, though a good deal out of tune. I suppose it was the words that pleased the boys, and it must have been the words too that offended the conservative band of the Dragons de Chartres. If I remember rightly, the opening verse began thus:

> *"Ah! Ça ira! Ça ira! Ça ira!*
> *Les aristocrates à la lanterne,*
> *Ah! Ça ira! Ça ira! Ça ira!*
> *Les aristocrates on les pendra!"*

At first this song had been sung lightly, as a sort of jest—the Parisians had always been famous for their mockery—but as the weeks passed, and feeling grew against the émigrés and those at home who might be thinking of following their example, the words of this nonsense song began to hold more meaning. Michel had adopted it as his marching song for the National Guard at le Plessis-Dorin, and when he had his men formed up outside the foundry and they started out on some foray, legitimate or otherwise, I must confess that the words and the tune with it, shouted by some sixty fellows stamping their feet, would have made me bolt my door and hide had I been suspected of non-patriotism.

As it was . . . "Ah! Ça ira! Ça ira! Ça ira!" rattled round my head, as it did everyone else's. It became a kind of catch-phrase amongst us at le Chesne-Bidault and in Pierre's circle at Le Mans—whenever we heard of a new piece of legislation likely to offend the forces of reaction, or if at home one or the other of us had some plan which we were determined to put into practice, we said "Ça ira!" and there was no further argument.

On the night of Thursday the 10th of February Pierre, Edmé and I set forth for the salle de Comédie—Pierre's wife had remained with the children, and had tried to persuade me to do the same, for I was four months pregnant again and she feared a crush. It was lucky that Pierre had had the foresight to buy tickets, for the crowd was so great outside the building that we could barely force our way inside.

We had the best seats, stalls, near the orchestra, and the whole house was packed. The play—Voltaire's *Semiramis*—was well acted and passed off without incident, and it was in the entr'acte that Edmé nudged me, and murmured, "Watch out—they're going to begin."

Edmé, for a young woman of the provinces, was always ahead of fashion. Tonight, scorning the elaborate coiffure of the day, with hair piled on top of the head like a hay-stack decorated with ribbons, she wore a little jaunty Phrygian cap in velvet, set on the one side, for all the world like an errand lad in the street. How she thought of it I do not know, but it was certainly a forerunner of the "bonnet rouge" worn by the Paris crowds in later months.

We looked about us in the stalls and tried to guess which amongst the audience were reactionaries. Edmé insisted she could spot them at a glance. Pierre, who had risen from his seat to talk to friends, came back and whispered that the National Guard were gathered in force by the only entrance to the street.

Suddenly a stamping of feet began in the cheap seats behind us, and members of the National Guard, in uniform, standing by the gangways, called out: "Monsieur le chef d'orchestre! If you please, the people want to hear 'Ça Ira'."

The conductor took no notice. He lifted his baton, and the band of the Dragons began to play a brisk military march of no political implication.

The stamping of feet grew louder, with the slow clapping of hands, and voices started the inevitable rhythm of, "Ça ira! Ça ira! Ça ira!"

It had a menacing sound, sung thus, in a low chant to the stamping of feet, and against the discordant background of the military march. People stood up in the audience, shouting instructions at cross-purposes, some calling for "Ça Ira", others to let the Dragons continue their programme.

Finally members of the National Guard approached the rostrum, and the conductor was obliged to order his band to cease playing.

"These interruptions are a scandal to the city," he cried. "Let those who have no wish to listen to music leave the building."

There were cheers and counter-cheers, boos and stamping of feet.

The officer commanding the National Guard, a friend of Pierre's called out, "'Ça Ira' is a national tune. Every patriot in the house wants to hear it."

The conductor turned red and looked down into the audience. "There are also those present who do not," he answered. "The words of 'Ça Ira!' constitute an offence to all loyal subjects of the King."

Hoots and howls greeted his retort, Edmé beside me joining in, much to the embarrassment of her neighbours on the other side, and people from every section of the audience began to call out and wave their programmes in the air.

Then those officers of the Dragons who were amongst us in the stalls, and some of them in the boxes too, sprang to their feet and drew their swords and one of them, a captain, calling at the top of his voice, ordered any of the regiment present to fall in under the officers' box close to the stage, and see that no harm came to the musicians.

The National Guard were ranged opposite, fully armed. A shiver of apprehension could be felt amongst the audience, for if the two sides fell to fighting what would happen to all us seated there, unable to get out, with the exit barred?

It was my ill-luck, I thought, to be caught in crowds when I was pregnant, and yet this time, for some reason unknown to myself, I was without fear.

Like Edmé, I hated the sight of the supercilious Dragon officers, whom I would see strolling about the streets of Le Mans as if the place belonged to them. I glanced up at Pierre, who had donned his uniform of the National Guard for the occasion, and thought how well it became him. He was not yet forty, but his light hair had turned nearly white, which gave him greater distinction than before, and his blue eyes, so like my mother's, were blazing now in indignation.

"Let those amongst the audience who don't wish to hear 'Ça Ira!' stand up, and let us see them," he called out. "In that way we shall quickly discover who are the enemies of the people."

Shouts of approval greeted this suggestion, and I felt a glow of pride. Pierre, our impractical Pierre, was not going to be bullied by the Dragons.

A few half-hearted figures stumbled to their feet, only to be pulled down hastily by their companions, afraid no doubt of the epithet "aristocrat". Shouts and arguments filled the air, with the Dragons, sabres in hand, preparing to drive in amongst us all and cut us down.

The mayor of Le Mans, dressed in his municipal scarf, marched down the gangway to the stage, in company with another official, and in a firm voice he bade the officer commanding the Dragons to put up his sword and order his men to do likewise.

"Tell your musicians," he said, "to play 'Ça Ira!'"

"I am sorry," replied the officer—a Major de Rouillon, so someone whispered to Edmé—"but the song 'Ça Ira!' is not in the repertoire of the band of the Dragons de Chartres.:

Immediately a chorus of 'Ça Ira n'ira pas" came from every officer present, and from many of the audience too, while those opposed to the Dragons continued with the stamping of their feet and their own rendering of the song without music.

Finally, there was a compromise. Major de Rouillon agreed to allow his band to play the song if they could follow it up with the famous air "Richard, O mon roy; l'univers t'abandonne". This was known to be a great favourite during the days when the King and Queen held court at Versailles, and the implications were obvious. For the sake of peace, and in order to proceed with the ballet, which was the rest of the evening's entertainment, the mayor of Le Mans conceded.

I thought the singing of "Ça Ira!" would lift the roof. I even joined in myself, wondering inconsequentially what my mother would have said if she could see me. "Richard, O mon roy" sounded like a whisper in comparison, the only singers being the Dragons de Chartres themselves and one or two women in the stalls who wished to make a show of themselves.

We left before the ballet began—it would have been an anti-climax after the scene we had witnessed—and walked home from the salle de Comédie, the three of us, arms linked, Pierre between us sisters, singing—

> "Ah! Ça ira! Ça ira! Ça ira!
> Les aristocrates à la lanterne,
> Ah! Ça ira! Ça ira! Ça ira!
> Les aristocrates on les pendra!"

The next day there was a great demonstration in the city, the crowds demanding the expulsion of the Dragons de Chartres, and Pierre and Edmé began a house-to-house petition to obtain signatures for the same purpose. Le Mans was divided on the subject. Many citizens, in the municipality too, held the opinion that the Dragons had given good service to the city, and had guarded it through perilous times; the rest, Pierre, Edmé and all their circle, were insistent that a counter-revolutionary spirit was rife amongst the officers, and that the National Guard was sufficient to keep the peace.

For the moment the problem was shelved, but during my week's visit we had one more excitement, and this was election of the new bishop to the episcopal seat—Monseigneur Prudhomme de la Boussinière—who was obliged to swear his oath to the Constitution.

We went out into the streets to watch the procession, and cheer the bishop on his way to the cathedral to attend the Constitution Mass. He was escorted by a detachment of the National Guard—Pierre amongst them—and by the Dragons de Chartres as well, and this time there was no mistaking the roll of the drums, and whistle of the fife, as the band struck up "Ça Ira!"

At the end of the cortège marched a long line of ordinary citizens, armed with pistols for fear of trouble, and women carrying rods, threatening those amongst us who might hold old-fashioned views about the clergy.

As for the Dragons de Chartres, matters came to a crisis three months later in mid-May, when I was once more on a visit to Pierre, this time accompanied by both François and Michel. The ceremony of planting a May tree had taken place in the place des Jacobins a few days before our arrival, and, as a symbol of the times, it had been draped with the tricolour. The tree was sawn to pieces during the night, and the Dragons were at once suspected of this act of vandalism, the more so as a bunch of them, that same evening, had insulted an officer of the National Guard.

This time the whole populace of the city was roused. It might have been '89 all over again. Tremendous crowds assembled in the place des Jacobins shouting, "Vengeance! Vengeance! The Dragons must go!" People began flocking into Le Mans from the countryside beyond, for as always the news had spread, and suddenly, as though from nowhere, came hordes of peasants armed with pikes and forks and axes, threatening to burn the city to the ground unless the inhabitants themselves took action and forced the municipality to dismiss the Dragons.

This time I stayed within doors, remembering the horrors of that riot before the Abbey of St. Vincent nearly two years before, but leaning from the window of Pierre's house, with his excited boys beside me, I could hear the roar of the crowds. Nor did it make for ease of mind to know that Pierre, Michel, and Edmé, too, were there amongst them, shouting for vengeance in the place des Jacobins.

The National Guard, without orders from the municipality, had raised barricades in the streets, and mounted guns. If the officers commanding the Dragons had given but one hasty order to advance, the guns would have been fired against their men, and a bloody massacre would have followed.

The officers of the Dragons, all credit to them, kept their men in check. Meanwhile, the flustered officials of the municipality went from one headquarters to another, seeking advice from superior authority.

At eight o'clock in the evening the crowds were as thick and as menacing as ever, backed by the National Guard, and one and all shouted, despite the efforts of the officials to make them disperse, "No half-measures. The Dragons go tonight!"

Once more they took up the old cry "Ça ira!" The whole city must have rung with the song that night, and still the officials hesitated, fearing that if the regiment left the city the ordinary citizens must be at the mercy of all the riff-raff from outside.

Some time between eleven and midnight the decision must have been taken, although how and where I never heard; but at one in the morning, with the crowds still waiting in the streets, the Dragons de Chartres left the city. I had gone to bed, anxious for the safety of François and my brothers who were still in the streets. The shouting died away, and all was quiet. Then, just after the church nearby had struck one, I heard the sound of cavalry. There was something ominous, almost eerie, about that steady clip-clop in the darkness of the night, the jingle of the trappings and the harness, loud at first, then fading, then dying right away. Whether it would bring good or evil to the city, who could tell? Two years ago I should have trembled for my life at their departure. Now, lying awake, waiting for François and the others to return, I could only smile at the thought that a regiment of soldiers had been defeated by a citizens' militia without a shot being fired.

The departure of the Dragons de Chartres from Le Mans was a signal of victory for the Club des Minimes and others like it, and from that day forward their influence was paramount in the affairs of the city. Those officials of the municipality and others who had favoured the retention of the regiment lost office, and the National Guard itself was purged of anyone who might have sympathy with the old régime.

To mark the change the very names of the streets were altered, heraldic signs were pulled down, and at the same time the sale of church property began.

I saw the start of this before I left for home. Michel, hearing that workmen had begun demolishing one of the smaller churches in the city, and that the contents were on offer for anyone who cared to purchase them, suggested that we should step by out of curiosity.

It was a strange sight, and I did not care much for it. It seemed sacrilege to trade objects we had always looked on with respect. The actual demolition had barely started, but the church was stripped of its altar and screen and pulpit, which were being sold in lots to city tradesmen. At first bidding was slow, the people hesitant, no doubt, for the same reason as myself, staring with goggling eyes at such destruction. Then they became bolder, half-laughing with a certain awkwardness, and one big fellow, a butcher by trade, stepped forward with a roll of assignats and bought the altar-railings as a frontage to his shop. There was no more hesitation after this.

Statues, crucifixes, pictures, all were for sale and briskly purchased. I saw two women staggering under the load of a fine picture of the Ascension, and a little lad, clutching a crucifix, whirled it around his head for a weapon, as children will. I turned away and went out into the street, dismayed. I had a sudden vision of Edmé and myself as children in the chapel of la Pierre, and the good curé blessing us after our first Communion.

Presently I heard laughter behind me. It was Michel, François and Edmé, all bearing trophies from the sale. Michel had a vestment, a chasuble, flung over his shoulder like a cape.

"I've needed a new working blouse for some time past," he called. "Now I can set the tone at le Chesne-Bidault. Here, catch this."

He threw me an altar-cloth, which he intended, I suppose, for the master's table. As I held it with a burning face, the crowd around me watching curiously, I saw that François and Edmé had each one of them a chalice, and, with mock solemnity, gestured towards me as though to drink my health.

14

THE NEWS OF the flight of the royal family from Paris in '91 reached Le Mans on the afternoon of June 22nd. The shock was considerable. Panic seized the municipality, and leading citizens, believed to be in sympathy with the old régime, were at once arrested and held for questioning. Our old enemy rumour spread through the country-side once more. The King and Queen, so it was said, were on their way to the frontier to join forces with the Prince de Condé, and once in Prussia would summon vast armies to their side to invade France, and then reinstate the old way of life.

The flight, so Michel said, would be a signal for a mass exodus. All the faint-hearts and the disgruntled, who up till now had shown a façade of patriotism, would try a similar escape and so help to swell the growing crowd of émigrés. We talked of nothing else for two whole days. I remember how the women gathered round to have their say, and one and all were sure the King had gone reluctantly; it was all the Queen's doing, the King would never have thought of it but for her.

Then came the good news. The royal family had been arrested at Varennes near the frontier, and were on their way back to Paris under escort.

"That's their f-finish," said Michel. "No one will have any respect for them any more. The King's f-forfeited all honour. He ought to abdicate."

We believed for a time that this would happen. The duc d'Orléans' name was mentioned as possible Regent for the little Dauphin, and there was even talk of a Republic. Then somehow the scare died down, the Court resumed its life at the Tuileries, though heavily guarded, and later, in September, the King took his oath on the Constitution.

Feeling toward the royal family was never the same again. As Michel said, the King had forfeited respect. He was just a tool in the hands of the Queen and the Court party, whom the whole nation knew to be in secret correspondence with the princes and the émigrés abroad. Security tightened. A close watch was kept on those members of the aristocracy who remained in the country, and on the clergy who would not take the oath to the Constitution. Feeling ran so high in Le Mans that certain women, who refused to go to Mass when it was celebrated by the state priests, were publicly whipped in the place des Halles and forced to attend. This seemed to me excessive, but it did not do to express an opinion, and anyway my own life had more interest for me that summer.

My second baby, Sophie Magdaleine, was born on the 8th of July, and my mother and Jacques came up from St. Christophe for the event. It was a joy to have my mother with me once again, supervising the master's house as if she had never left it. Wisely, she kept her own counsel on the changes, though I know she noticed everything, from the brocade curtains to the monograms on the silver. Nor did she speak of the work in progress at the foundry, where the engraving upon the glass was designed to please a different clientèle from the one she had known. Gone were the fleur-de-lys, and the lettering interlaced. These emblems were out of fashion, even decadent. We now had torches upon our glass, representing liberty, with hands clasped in friendship, and the words "égalité" and "fraternité" scrawled at the base. I cannot say they were an improvement on the past, but they fetched a good price in Paris and Lyon, which was our main concern.

Sitting up in her old room, watching me nurse my baby, listening to the happy laughter of Jacques, now a sturdy boy of ten, playing with the Durocher children in the orchard, my mother smiled at me and said, "The world may alter, but there's a sight won't change."

I looked down at the baby at my breast, and stopped her feeding or she would have choked herself.

"One never knows," I answered. "The Assembly might pass a law condeming this as self-indulgence."

"It would not surprise me," said my mother, "what any of those people did. They're half of them only lawyers and little jumped-up clerks."

It was as well Pierre could not hear her, or Michel either. Anyone who spoke one word in criticism of the Assembly was a traitor in their eyes.

"Surely you are not against the revolution?" I asked her, greatly daring.

"I'm against nothing that benefits honest people," she answered. "If a man wishes to get on in life, he should be encouraged to do so. I don't see what that has to do with revolution. Your father became a rich man through his own efforts. He began at the bottom, like any apprentice boy."

"My father had talent," I argued. "Talented men will always make their way. The new laws are designed to help those who have nothing."

"Don't you believe it," replied my mother. "The peasants are no better off than they were in the past. It is the middle men who are climbing to the top today. Shopkeepers and the like. I would not grudge it them if they kept their manners."

Watching the baby feed, listening to the boys climbing the trees outside, the spirit of revolution seemed a world away.

"That child has had enough," said my mother suddenly. "She's feeding now from greed, like any adult. Put her in her cradle."

"She's a revolutionary," I answered. "Revolutionaries always demand more, and are never satisfied."

"That is my point," said my mother, taking Sophie Magdaleine from me and patting her back for wind. "She does not know what is good for her, any more than all the so-called patriots in the country. Someone should have the nerve, and the power, to say 'Enough'. But they're like a lot of sheep without a shepherd."

It was good to hear her talk. Good to listen to her practical strong sense. Revolutions might come and go, whispers and rumours blow about the countryside, society, as we had known it, tumble upside down; my mother remained herself, never reactionary, never pig-headed, only most blessedly sane. She stood by the cradle, gently rocking it, as she had done for all of us in days gone by, and said, "I wonder if your brother has a little one like this?"

She meant Robert, and I saw by the expression on her face how much she yearned for him.

"I expect he has, by now," I answered. "The last time he wrote they expected a child."

"I've heard nothing," she answered, "nothing for ten months. Jacques no longer asks after his father. It's a strange thought; if there is a brother or a sister for him in London, it will be English-born. Some little cockney, knowing nothing of his own country."

She stopped and made the sign of the cross over my baby, then murmured something about dinner for the men when they came off shift, and went downstairs. The room was full of shadows when she had gone, and I felt suddenly bereft. All we had lived through during the past two years seemed valueless. I was dispirited, lost, for no good reason.

When she went away again, back to St. Christophe, taking Jacques with her, it was as though peace and sanity departed too. François and Michel stood about the foundry yard in lifeless fashion, and for all three of us it seemed that our whole day had grown dim. During her brief visit my mother had managed, without anyone realising it, to establish her old authority. My menfolk came to the table groomed and clean, Madame Verdelet scrubbed the kitchen once a day, the workmen whipped off their caps and stood to attention when she spoke to them—and all of this by instinct, not through fear. There was not a soul in the foundry who did not have a regard for her.

"It's a q-queer thing," said Michel after she had gone, "but my mother achieves more with one l-look then we do with all our c-curses and cajolery. It's a pity they don't have women d-deputies. She'd be elected every t-time."

I don't know how it was, but during the four weeks of her stay with us my brother did not once call out the National Guard on an expedition, thought he had them parade for her benefit before the church at le Plessis-Dorin.

In September, after the elections were held, and the new deputies to the Legislative Assembly, as it was called, took their seats in Paris, we were able to talk with some authority on public matters—or pretended to do so, to impress Pierre and Edmé in Le Mans—because my husband's eldest brother, Jacques Duval of Mondoubleau, was elected one of the deputies for our département of Loir-et-Cher. Like all progressives, he was a member of the Club des Jacobins, and when he returned home from Paris François and Michel would either go to Mondoubleau to see him and hear the news, or he would spare the time to visit us at le Chesne-Bidault. He it was who told us of the divisions within the new Assembly, some favouring moderate measures, others, including himself, a more forward policy; and there was a continual jockeying for position amongst the leaders of each group.

There was still deep mistrust of the King, more so of the Queen, known to be corresponding with her brother the Emperor of Austria and urging him to make war upon France. It was felt by the progressive deputies, all of whom were members either of the Club des Jacobins or the Club des Cordeliers, that a far stricter watch should be kept on the aristocrats remaining in the country, and on the clergy who refused to take the oath. These people, my brother-in-law inferred, were a menace to security, provoking unrest and dissatisfacton in many parts of the country. As long as they remained at liberty they would hold up the work of the revolution, and stifle progress.

Jacques Duval became a close friend of Marat, editor of *L'Ami du Peuple,* one of the most widely read and popular newspapers in Paris, and he used to send this down to us every week, so that we could keep abreast of all that was said and done in the capital. I was not sure what to make of it myself; it was an inflammatory sheet, whipping its readers to violence, and urging them to take action against the "enemies of the people" if legislation should be slow. Michel and François read every word of it, and passed it on to the workmen too—a mistaken gesture. They had enough to do in the foundry as it was, keeping production going and fulfilling our orders, without roaming the countryside in quest of erring nobles and refractory priests.

For myself, I let them talk, and shut my ears to argument. My baby took up all my time. Those nine months that I was blest with her are bright now with her memory alone. Nothing else counted.

She caught a cold in spring that went to her chest, and although I nursed her day and night for almost a week, and sent for a doctor from Le Mans, we could not save her. She died on April the 22nd, 1792, two days after Prussia and Austria declared war on France; I remember we heard the news the same day we buried Sophie Magdaleine. I was quite numb with grief, and so were François and Michel and the people at the foundry, for the baby had been a radiant child, delighting all of us.

Like other persons suddenly bereaved, I heard of war with bitter satisfaction. Now I should not be the only one to suffer. Thousands would mourn. Let men fight and cut themselves to pieces. The quicker invasion came and we were all decimated, the sooner personal sorrow would be wiped out.

I think I hardly cared that spring what happened to the country, but, later, helpless misery at my baby's death turned to hatred of the enemy. Hatred of the Prussians and the Austrians who dared to interfere in France's affairs and make war upon us because they rejected our régime, but above all hatred of those émigrés who were now bearing arms against their country.

Any sympathy I might have had for them in the beginning had now vanished. They were traitors, every one of them. My brother Robert, who had not written to me for a year, might even now be amongst the number enrolled in the armies of the duke of Brunswick. The very thought of it made me sick. Now, when Michel and François set forth with the National Guard on a tour of inspection, I cheered them on, and had as great a satisfaction as any woman at the foundry when they returned from seizing property for the nation's benefit.

All the lands belonging to émigrés suffered the same treatment as those held by the Church, and it was about this time that we ourselves, François and I, bought the small property at Gué de Launay outside Vibraye, with an eye to the future and our middle age.

Everywhere châteaux were standing empty, their owners having fled. The le Gras de Luarts had gone from la Pierre, the de Cherbons from Chérigny. Our landlord, Philip de Mangin, had been evicted from the château of Montmirail, but his father-in-law, Jean de la Haye de Launay, did not come under suspicion, and was allowed to remain in residence.

Day after day we would hear of more rats running, most of them to join the army of the Prince de Condé under the duke of Brunswick, and as their names were listed on the sheet of émigrés, and their property was sequestered, we had the dubious satisfaction of knowing that should they ever return they would find their homes given to others, if not burnt down and pillaged, and every sou they possessed the property of the nation.

The Legislative Assembly was not hard enough on the traitors. François' brother, Jacques Duval, and many others who thought like him pressed for stronger measures; every suspect in the country to be rounded up and questioned, and if necessary kept in custody unless they could prove their innocence. The country was in mortal danger, with two armies invading it from the east; nor was this the only threat, for in Brittany and to the south-west in the Vendée there was known to be strong royalist feeling and much sympathy for the émigrés.

The war, of course, played havoc with the economy, and our own glass-trade was amongst the first to suffer. Many of the younger men obeyed the call to arms and joined the army, and we were left with the older workmen, and our furnace alight scarcely three days in the week.

Horses and vehicles were requisitioned for the troops, grain prices rose once more, and this time some deputies in the Assembly demanded the death penalty for hoarders, but the measure was not passed. The more the pity, I remember thinking, and looked back, without revulsion, to the killing of the silver-merchant and his son-in-law at Ballon. I had grown wiser in three years, or less compassionate. Being wife to an officer of the National Guard, and sister-in-law to a deputy, gave one a bias in favour of authority—if authority was on our side.

Jacques Duval's friend Marat, the journalist, was right when he denounced the timid members of the Assembly in his paper *L'Ami du Peuple*, and advocated the seizure of power by a strong group of proved patriots who would not hesitate to use stern measures to unite the country and put down opposition. There was one deputy in whom we all had confidence, the little lawyer Robespierre, who back in '89 had spoken with such fervour at Versailles. If anyone had the force and ability to control the situation, which rapidly worsened through the summer, here was the man to do it, said my brother-in-law.

Robespierre . . . known as "the Incorruptible" amongst his friends, for nothing and no one could deflect him from what he believed to be right and just. Others might look with leniency upon those who failed to prosecute the war, or remain friendly with the émigrés in case the tide turned and the enemy were successful, but not Robespierre. Again and again he warned the ministers who controlled policy in the Assembly that the King's position had become untenable; his obstinacy in refusing to sign decrees necessary for the safety of the country meant that he was playing for time, hoping that the forces of the duke of Brunswick would defeat the army of the French people. If the King would not co-operate with government, the King must be deposed. Government must be strong, or the nation would perish.

These were the arguments we heard during the feverish summer of '92, either through reading *L'Ami du Peuple* or direct from François' brother Jacques Duval. But the news that roused us most, and indeed every man and woman in the country, was when, on the 1st of August, the invading general, the duke of Brunswick, issued a manifesto threatening to deliver Paris to "military execution and total destruction" if "the slightest violence" was committed against the royal family. The royal family were not even in our thoughts. We were all too concerned with the imminent invasion and the danger to our homes to be concerned with them. The manifesto, intended to frighten us into submission, did just the opposite, and, far from making us feel tender toward the King and Queen, turned us, almost overnight, into republicans.

When, on the 10th of August, the Paris crowds rose en masse and marched on the Tuileries, destroyed the Swiss guards, and forced the royal family to take shelter behind the manège where the Assembly sat, our small community at le Chesne-Bidault had every sympathy with the people. Now, we felt, let the duke of Brunswick do his worst. We were ready for him. One triumph resulted from this fracas, and this was that the weak men within the Assembly were broken. The local government of Paris, the municipality, or Commune as it was called, now had control, and in September a new Assembly, to be known as the National Convention, would be elected by universal suffrage, which Robespierre had been demanding all along.

"At last," said my brother Pierre, "we shall have a strong government."

In fact, one of the first decrees passed, the day after the storming of the Tuileries, was an order giving every municipality throughout the country the right to arrest suspects on sight.

I think if Michel could have had his way every prison would have been at bursting-point. As it was he, and the National Guard, could now round up every non-juring priest for deportation, though in Paris the commune used harsher measures and imprisoned them.

The royal family were confined in the Temple, where the pernicious influence of the Queen could do no further damage, and letters to her nephew the emperor of Austria no longer find their way across the frontier.

Marat, in *L'Ami du Peuple,* declared that the only way to save the Revolution for the people was to slaughter the aristocrats en masse; yet if this happened the innocent might suffer with the guilty. Somehow, we no longer seemed to preach the brotherhood of man.

Meanwhile, both François and Michel were preoccupied with the primary elections to take place in the last week in August. Our département of Loir-et-Cher was divided into thirty-three cantons, and each canton comprised several parishes or communes. Every man over twenty-five was allowed to vote for an Elector or Electors in his canton, and these Electors in their turn voted for the deputies who would represent the people of the département in the Assembly.

Both my husband and my brother were to stand as Electors for the canton of Gault, and both were determined to see that no one who might have the slightest reactionary tendency should offer themselves as candidates beside them. They were supported in this by Jacques Duval, my husband's brother, who wrote to François from Paris urging the importance of a majority of progressives in the next Assembly—the National Convention. This, he said, could only come about if the Electors themselves were progressives, and could thus make sure that the right deputies were returned to power. He was not offering himself for re-election, for his health was bad. This was a great blow to François and Michel, for they felt that so close a relative holding a position in Paris of such importance, was not only a help to our own small business but a security should things go wrong.

"We must be f-firm on one thing," declared Michel, a week or so before the primary elections were to be held, "and that is to see that no p-priest or ex-m-member of the aristocracy is allowed to vote."

"What about priests who have already sworn the oath to the Constitution?" asked François.

"They can s-swear as hard as they like," replied my brother, "we'll k-keep them out. In any event, we'll march the National Guard around every parish first, and make sure the n-nominees for election have taken the oath."

It was on the Sunday preceding the elections, I remember, that he had the National Guard of le Plessis-Dorin, and others from a neighbouring parish, on parade in the foundry yard. They went off in strength, some eighty strong, under the command of André Delalande—whom Michel had promoted to commandant—to force any prospective Elector of doubtful patriotism to take the oath.

There was not a parish or a commune in the district that dared withstand this onslaught, though many protested at the treatment and said the National Guard had no right to enforce the oath upon loyal citizens.

"Loyal be d-damned," said Michel. "We'll soon s-see who's loyal when we come to c-count the votes."

The opening meeting to discuss the Elections was held in the church at Gault on the 26th of August. I was allowed to be present, though I kept myself well in the background. From the very start of the proceedings there was trouble. By right of age and precedence Monsieur Montlibert, mayor of Gault, was called to preside over the assembly, to the loud protests of my husband and brother.

"He is an aristocrat," cried my husband, "he has no business to be here."

"It's m-men like him," shouted my brother, "who have b-brought the country to its p-present state. He's t-turned coat once, he'll d-do it again."

Michel's stammer, of course, was a handicap at such a meeting, and his temper was not improved by the murmur of laughter that rose from the benches all about us in the church. I at once felt hot with shame, especially as at this moment the curé of Gault, and those of Oigny and St. Agil, entered from the sacristy. Both Michel and François began waving papers above their heads and shouting, "No priests in this assembly. . . . Tell them to get out. . . . No priests in here."

The curé of Gault, a mild enough looking man in all conscience, stood by the chancel steps. "Those members of the clergy who have taken the oath have every right to be admitted," he answered.

"We don't want f-fools like you," shouted Michel. "Go suck your s-soup."

There was a moment's horrified silence. Then an uproar broke out. Some older members present began to protest, but the younger ones yelled and jeered, and within a few minutes the three curés retreated with dignity, afraid, no doubt, that their presence would provoke violence.

I was scarlet with embarrassment, and wished that Michel and François would hold their peace. Finally a Monsieur Villette was nominated instead of the mayor and, mounting a chair, rebuked "certain of those present who would drive good patriots from this assembly."

"There is no law forbidding a constitutional priest from becoming an Elector, or from voting," he announced, "nor for expelling any ex-member of the aristocracy."

There were cheers at this, and counter-cheers, or rather boos, from my brother and my husband and those who sided with them. Nevertheless, a show of hands decided upon the expulsion of the so-called former aristocrats, and the mayor Montlibert, with his son and a few others, left the church.

There was no further trouble until the bulletins, on which each man voting for an Elector had to write his name, had been dropped in the box provided. Villette, the president, was about to take the box to the scrutators to be counted when I saw Michel nudge my husband. François sprang to his feet and seized the box from the president.

"Your duties are finished," he cried. "It is not the business of the president to concern himself with the bulletins. This is the function of the scrutators."

He at once bore off the box to the sacristy, where the scrutators were waiting, all of them members of the National Guard, and I wondered how many of the bulletins they counted would find their way first to my husband and my brother. I sat silent, aghast at what I saw. The words "Liberté, égalité, fraternité" seemed far remote from the proceedings here. No one protested. Even the president Villette looked stupefied, and did not move.

"They deserve all they get," I told myself, to quiet my conscience. "Half of those who vote can't read or write, and someone must do their thinking for them."

My husband returned and took his seat beside Michel. They consulted a moment, and then François called on Henri Darlanges, from the parish of la Grande-Borde, to stand up and show himself. There was a shuffle of feet, and a frightened individual stood to attention.

"We have information," said my husband, "that you are sheltering two men in your house, former members of the aristocracy without passports, who have arms hidden."

"Not a word of truth in it," answered the man, a prospective Elector. "You are welcome to search my house and the whole parish."

Further consultation between Michel and François resulted in a demand for the return of Monsieur Montlibert, the mayor of Gault, to the assembly. I could see that it was my brother who was issuing the orders, and my husband who acted as spokesman for him.

"Citizen mayor," said my husband, "you have heard this man Henri Darlanges deny all knowledge of strangers or hidden arms. As adjutant-general of the National Guard, Michel Busson-Challoir orders you to proceed at once to la Grande-Borde and search his house. The proceedings cannot continue here at Gault until this is done." When he had finished speaking the doors of the church were flung open and a great contingent of the National Guard marched in, about sixty of them, all workmen from le Chesne-Bidault.

I began to see what my menfolk were at. Suspicion, whether just or unjust, must be thrown on all prospective Electors of moderate views. Once tainted thus, no one would have the hardihood to vote for them. The way would be clear then for the progressives. "By what right . . . " began the mayor, but Michel, leaving his seat and walking over to Henri Darlanges, cut him short.

"By the right of f-force," he said. "Fall in behind the Guard." And then, to Darlanges beside him, "G-give me your keys."

The keys were handed over without a word. François snapped out an order. Then he, and Michel, with the mayor and Henri Darlanges between them, marched out of the church, escorted by the National Guard.

The meeting broke up in confusion. Prospective Electors stood by uncertain what to do, most of them too scared to take any action. I saw one woman outside the church burst into tears and run to her husband, asking if everyone was to be put in prison.

I went and sat in the mairie, not knowing where else to go, waiting upon events. Some of our own workmen, in uniform, were on sentry duty outside. None of the inhabitants of Gault dared approach us.

Presently the procession returned. Henri Darlanges had his hands roped behind his back, and so had two other men with him, his lodgers, it appeared, looking even more frightened than he did himself.

A mock trial was set in motion, and the mayor Montlibert forced to interrogate the prisoners. It was obvious, even to someone like myself who knew nothing of the law, that none of the men had done wrong. No arms had been found in the house. The men had no pretensions to being aristocrats. Monsieur Villette, who had presided over the proceedings in the church, spoke up in their defense.

"If you are in c-collusion with these men," said Michel, "have the c-courage to admit it, or keep silent."

I feared, from his gesture and his tone of voice, that the worst might happen and the wretched prisoners would be taken out into the street and hanged. They feared so too. I saw the expression in their eyes. Then Michel summoned the captain of his Guard, the workman André Delalande.

"Take these men into c-custody," he ordered, "and see that they are m-marched into Mondoubleau and handed over to the authorities f-first thing in the morning."

André saluted. The unfortunates were marched out of the mairie.

"That's all," said Michel, "no further questions. The meeting in the c-church will be resumed tomorrow morning."

The mayor Montlibert, the president Villette, and the other officials left the building without a word of protest. Then, and only then, did my brother wink at François.

"The scrutators are locked in the ch-church," he said, "and I have the keys, I suggest we walk across and f-find out if they are counting the votes correctly."

I returned alone that night to le Chesne-Bidault, except for six of the National Guard to act as escort. The next day I allowed the primary elections for the canton of Gault to continue without me. The proceedings, I was afterwards told, went smoothly enough until one official complained of the events of the preceding day, upon which he was informed if he gave further trouble the workmen of le Chesne-Bidault would be delighted to deal with him in their own fashion. The official was then silent.

I was not surprised, when the primary elections were over, to hear that both my husband and my brother had been elected for Gault. Whatever my own feelings in the matter, one thing was certain. Intimidation paid. "The destiny of the nation," said my brother-in-law, Jacques Duval, "depends upon the Elector's choice of deputies," and those who were returned for Loir-et-Cher were all progressives. There was not a moderate man amongst them.

The fall of Verdun on the 2nd of September put the whole country in a state of alarm. If the enemy advanced one step further we were ready for them. I was prepared to fight beside the men in the foundry yard.

"Danger is imminent," wrote Jacques Duval from Paris. "The tocsin has sounded here in the capital. Let it do so in each département throughout France, so that every citizen can rally to the nation's defence."

The very day he wrote that letter the prisons were broken into by the Paris crowds, and more than twelve hundred prisoners were slaughtered. We never heard who was to blame for it. Collective panic was the excuse given. Rumour, passing from one man to another, had whispered that the prisons held armed aristocrats, awaiting their moment to break free and destroy the citizens of Paris. The "brigands" of '89 had been resurrected.

On the 20th of September the Prussian and Austrian armies were repulsed at Valmy, and a few days later Verdun was retaken. The people's army had responded to the call.

The new Assembly—the National Convention—met for the first time on September the 21st. We hoisted the tricolour above the furnace-house at le Chesne-Bidault, and the workmen, all in their uniform of the National Guard, sang the marching song that had supplanted "Ça Ira"—the Marseillaise.

That evening, in the master's house, Michel, François and I set out the replicas of the original glass made twenty years ago for Louis XV at the château of la Pierre, and we toasted the new Republic.

15

"THE NATIONAL CONVENTION declares Louis Capet, last King of the French, guilty of conspiracy against the liberty of the nation, and of attempting to undermine the safety of the States.

"The National Convention decrees that Louis Capet shall suffer the death penalty."

There was not a home throughout the country, during January of '93, where the case was not argued, for or against the King. Robespierre had stated the matter with his usual clarity, when he declared in December before the Convention, "If the King is not guilty, then those who had dethroned him are."

There were no two ways about it. Either it was right to depose the monarch for summoning the aid of foreign powers against the State, or it was wrong. If right, then the monarch had been guilty of treason and must pay the penalty. If wrong, then the Natinal Convention must dissolve, ask pardon of the monarch, and capitulate to the enemy.

"You cannot go against Robespierre's logic," said my brother Pierre. "The Convention must either accuse the King, or accuse itself. If the King is absolved, it is tantamount to saying the Republic should never have been proclaimed, and the country must lay down its arms against Prussia and Austria."

"Who cares about l-logic?" answered Michel. "Louis is a t-traitor, we all know it. One sign of weakness on the p-part of the Convention, and every aristocrat and p-priest in the country will be rubbing their hands with j-joy. They should g-guillotine the lot."

"Why not send the royal family into exile? Wouldn't that be punishment enough?" I asked.

A groan went up from my two brothers, and my husband too.

"Exile?" exclaimed Pierre. "And let them use their influence to win more support for their cause? Imagine the Queen in Austria, for example! No, imprisonment for life is the only solution."

Michel gestured with his thumb towards the ground. "One answer, and one only," he said. "As long as those p-people live, above all that woman, they're a menace to s-security."

As it turned out, when judgement was passed against the King and he went to his death on the 21st of January, we were in trouble ourselves.

A court of enquiry was held at Gault by the département authorities on the holding of the primary elections, and the part my husband and my brother had played in them. It seemed that the mayor of Gault, and other officials, had forwarded a complaint to the Minister of the Interior, Monsieur Roland, who then ordered the investigation. It did not surprise me when the various citizens of Gault and other parishes appeared as witnesses for the prosecution.

The enquiry was held on the 22nd and 23rd of January (the day after the King was guillotined in Paris). Whether the authorities of our district in Loir-et-Cher held a secret sympathy or not for the fallen Louis I do not know, but they certainly came out strongly against violence, and both Michel and François were severely reprimanded.

"This Court finds that Messieurs Busson-Challoir and Duval acted illegally in expelling the ex-aristocrats and the clergy from the primary elections the preceding August, that they acted with excess towards the president of the assembly, that the workmen from the foundry of le Chesne-Bidault threatened many peaceable citizens, that public tranquillity was disturbed, and that in the eyes of the law and justice such conduct is reprehensible, and Messieurs Busson-Challoir and Duval should be denounced before the tribunal and suffer whatever penalty the law pronounces against those who disturb public order."

So ran the indictment, and it was only the intervention of my brother-in-law that saved François and Michel from serving a term in prison. A heavy fine got them out of their scrape, and Michel lost his status in the National Guard as adjutant-general for the district. The incident, far from subduing his patriotism, made him more fanatical than ever.

During that winter of '93, as we read our *Ami du Peuple* and learnt of the continuing division within the Convention, with ministers like Roland—who had instituted the enquiry against Michel and François—relaxing controls and allowing grain-prices to soar, despite the opposition of Robespierre and his Jacobin associates, who warned them of the dangers of inflation, it was only persuasion on the part of Pierre that prevented Michel from leaving us and throwing in his lot with the extremists in Paris.

There were continuous riots in the capital through February and March, the people complaining of the price of sugar, soap and candles. Once again the journalist Marat acted as their spokesman, suggesting that the only way to bring down prices was to hang a number of grocers over their own doorstep.

"By heaven, he's right," said my youngest brother. "I don't know why all P-Paris doesn't rise and make that f-fellow a dictator."

Certainly our Republic, which we had toasted so hopefully in September, was beset with enemies, both beyond our frontiers and within them.

After February I gave up all hope of hearing from my brother Robert again. the Convention had declared war against both England and Holland, and Robert, if he were still in London, would not only be an émigré but perhaps actively employed against his own country. If so, he would be as great a traitor as those thousands of our fellow-countrymen who, at this moment of extreme danger to the Republic from the Allies abroad, chose to launch a revolt in the west and plunge us all into the horrors of civil war.

The priests were behind the insurrection. Resentful of the loss of those privileges which they had held for centuries, and the seizure of their lands and property, they had been playing for months past upon the superstitions of the peasants, who, soon to welcome change, mistrusted the decrees passed by the Convention. Above all the peasants feared the military call-up passed the last week in February, which summoned to the colours every able-bodied unmarried man between the ages of eighteen and forty who could be spared from his ordinary work.

The King's execution and this conscription were the two final factors to rouse the peasants in the west, spurred on by the non-juring priests and disgruntled ex-aristocrats. The rebellion, once alight, spread like a forest fire, or, worse, like a disease, infecting all those malcontents who, for one reason or another, had lost faith in the revolution.

By April the Vendée, the Basse-Vendée, the Bocage, Anjou, the Loire-Inférieure, all were in revolt. Thousands of peasants, armed with any weapons from ancient muskets to hatchets and harvest sickles, pillaging as they went, led by men of indomitable courage who had nothing but their lives to lose, pressed forward across the Loire, meeting no resistance at first save from the terrified inhabitants of the villages and towns, which they promptly sacked. The republican armies were engaged on the frontier, repulsing the Allied invaders, and only a few companies of the National Guard were free to withstand this new and appalling onslaught from the west.

The rebels triumphed, encircling Nantes, pushing on to Angers and Saumur, driving prisoners and refugees before them, escorted on their march by waggon-loads of women and children, peasant families and the wives and mistresses of the former aristocrats, all living off the country, robbing and destroying as they went.

Heaven knows we hated the Allied invaders, and the émigrés who inspired them, but we hated the Vendéans, as the rebel army came to be called, even more. The hypocrisy of their war-cry "For Jesus" and of the banners of the Sacred Heart which they brandished, as though upon some new crusade, was only surpassed by their brutality in action. Slaughter on a scale far greater than any attempted by the Paris mob was the portion of those village patriots who dared to resist them. Women and children were not spared, men were thrown, while still alive, into ditches piled high with corpses. Clergy who had sworn the oath to the Contitution were tied to horses and dragged on the dusty roads to a terrible death. Here at last, in flesh and blood, with no rumour about them, were the "brigands" we had feared in '89. Wearing white ribands and white cockades, the royalist leaders urged their ignorant peasant armies forward, with the promise of more loot and further conquests, the priests in the rear summoning them to Mass before each battle. On their knees before the Crucifix at dawn, cutting their way through undefended villages at midday, drunk with slaughter and success by sundown, the conquering, ill-disciplined yet courageous rabble, calling themselves God's soliders, marched on through April and May to what seemed victory.

It was a struggle, as my brother Pierre said, between the Te Deum and the Marseillaise, and through that agonising summer of '93 the singers of the Marseillaise suffered one humiliating defeat after another.

The Convention in Paris, torn by dissension within their own ranks, gave contradictory orders to those generals, hastily recalled from the frontier, who now found themselves faced with the task of quelling the rebellion. It was not until the Republican armies had been regrouped, at the end of September, that the long series of Vendéan victories came to an end. Robespierre, now supreme in the Convention, and leading member of the Committee of Public Safety, was determined to crush the rebellion, and the generals were ordered to annihilate the rebels, giving no quarter, taking no prisoners.

On the 17th of October the Vendéans suffered a terrible defeat at Cholet, in Maine-et-Loire, where two of their chiefs, d'Elbée and Bonchamp, were severely wounded. It was the beginning of the end for the rebel army, though they did not know it; and instead of retreating across the Loire, and making a stand on their own ground, they pushed on towards the north, with the idea of taking Granville, the Channel port, for the English were said to be preparing a huge fleet to help them. The people of Granville, to their eternal credit, resisted the rebels, and in mid-November the long retreat back to the Loire began, with the republican armies closing in upon the Vendéans from every side.

Work had come almost to a standstill at le Chesne-Bidault, for although the rebels were well to the west of us, in Mayenne, we could never be certain, living as we did on the borders of Sarthe and Loir-et-Cher, that their leaders might not take it into their heads to strike across country into our own département. Michel and the workmen were in a constant state of alert, and in his capacity as captain of the National Guard of le Plessis-Dorin my brother was itching to be off with his men and in the thick of the fighting. Duty, however, constrained him to keep to the defence of the village, should it be threatened; and although I felt that he and his handful of workmen would do little against the Vendéan thousands, if they came our way, the very sight of them in their uniforms parading the foundry yard gave me confidence.

The preservation of life had become sweet to me once more, for my baby Zoë Suzanne, born on the 27th of May, was now six month old. Plump and healthy, she had shown more vigour from the first day than the two babies I had lost, and my mother, who had come up from St. Christophe to see us during the summer, predicted a normal childhood. Once the Vendéans had been defeated, we might all relax—those of us who were patriots. Robespierre's stern rule, though it sent hundreds to the guillotine, including the Queen and Robert's one-time patron, Philippe-Egalité, the duc d'Orléans, had not only saved the country from defeat but made day-to-day living easier for the people, with his Law of the Maximum limiting the price of food, essential goods and labour.

Our great concern during the autumn was for Pierre, his family and Edmé. The Vendéans, when they passed through Laval on their way north to the coast, were not nineteen leagues distant from Le Mans, and during the retreat, a month later, they traversed the same territory again. Mayenne, Laval, Sablé, la Flèche, each day we had the news of the progress south, the rebel army low in morale and riddled with dysentery, discipline lax, and considerably hampered by the numbers of women, children, nuns and priests who followed in its train.

On Tuesday the 13th Frimaire (the 3rd of December) we heard that they had reached Angers, and were preparing to lay siege to the city. Jacques Duval was living with us at the time, and he brought the news from Mondoubleau, where he had gone to consult with the authorities.

"All is well," he said. "Angers will resist, our army under Westermann is in pursuit, and we shall trap them before they can cross the Loire."

Angers was twenty-two leagues south-west of Le Mans, more than a day's march from the city, and a wave of thankfulness came over me for Pierre and Edmé, Marie and the boys.

"This will be their end," went on my brother-in-law. "They will be caught there in a pincer movement between our armies. We can deal with the stragglers and the deserters ourselves."

I saw Michel look across at François, and I guessed what was coming.

"If the National G-Guard of every parish went off in s-strength," he said, "we could cut them to p-pieces if they dared march east again."

He crossed to the window, and, opening it, shouted to André Delalande, who was crossing the foundry yard.

"S-sound the alert," he called. "Have every man p-parade within the hour with f-full equipment. We're off in pursuit of the s-sacré brigands."

It was shortly after two when they set forth, three hundred of them, carrying the tricolour and beating drums, with Michel at their head. Had my father been alive he would have been proud of that youngest son of his whom, more than thirty years ago, he used to blame for his sullen ways and his stammer.

We were at the mercy of rumour during the rest of the week, except for the news that the Vendéans had been thwarted in their attack on Angers. The city, gallantly defended, had not fallen, and the rebel leaders were now trying to decide where and when they could cross the Loire before the republican armies attacked them in the rear.

I might have known that hearsay is never to be trusted, that rumour, in the past, had spoken of brigands when brigands were not there. This time it was the other way about. Victory was claimed before victory was achieved.

"We've been without news of Pierre for long enough," I said to François the following Monday, when we awoke. "I propose to have Marcel drive me to Le Mans today and spend the night with them, and, if all is well, return tomorrow morning."

He at once demurred, as husbands will, saying that if any harm had come to Pierre we should have heard of it long since. The roads were still unsafe, the weather threatening. Let Marcel go with a message if need be, but I must stay at le Chesne-Bidault. In any event, the baby would be restless in the night without me.

"We have had no broken nights with Zoë since she was born," I told him, "and she can sleep in her cradle beside Madame Verdelet. I shall be gone for half a day and a night, no more than that, and if Edmé and Marie and the boys wish to do so, I shall bring them back here with me when I return."

Obstinacy, no doubt, made me hold to my plan. I had seen my brother Michel march off the week before in pursuit of the Vendéans, and his courage had made me bold. Besides, had not Jacques Duval assured me that the "brigands", as we so rightly called them, were routed, struggling, as best they could, to make their way across the Loire?

Perhaps, and this I hardly admitted even to myself, I also felt that François lagged behind Michel. My husband, unlike my brother, had not volunteered to accompany the National Guard on their expedition. He could learn that his wife did not share his scruples.

Marcel and I set forth as soon as we had breakfasted. François, seeing that nothing would make me change my mind, said at the last moment that he would drive me. I would have none of it, however, and bade him stay at home and mind his daughter.

"If we do see any brigands," I told him as I said good-bye, "we'll give a good account of ourselves"—patting the two muskets strapped to the roof of the carriole. My words were spoken in jest; I little thought how near they would come to the truth.

Once past Vibraye I saw that my husband had been right about one thing—the weather. It turned bitterly cold, and started to rain and sleet. I was warmly wrapped, nevertheless, my hands and feet were soon numb with the cold, and Marcel, peering into the driving rain ahead, looked disconcerted.

"You haven't chosen a good day for your venture, citoyenne," he said.

We had been careful, ever since the September decrees, to adopt the new courtesies. Monsieur and madame were things of the past, like the old calendar. I had to remind myself also that today was the 9th of December, 1793.

"Perhaps not," I answered, "but at least we have a roof to the carriole and keep dry, which is more than our National Guard can say, closing in upon the brigands, perhaps at this very moment."

Luckily for my peace of mind I saw them jubilant, not outnumbered and in full retreat, as was the truth.

We reached Le Mans by early afternoon, but because of the weather it was already almost dark, and there were sentries guarding the bridge across the Huisne.

They came forward to take our passports, and I saw that they were not members of the National Guard but ordinary citizens, with armbands, armed with muskets. I recognised the leader—he had been a client of Pierre's—and at sight of me he waved his men aside and came to the carriole himself.

"Citoyenne Duval?" he called out, in astonishment. "What in the world are you doing here at such a moment?"

"I've come to see my brother," I told him. "I've been anxious about him and his family for the past weeks, as you may imagine. Now the worst is over I've seized the first opportunity to come and visit him."

He stared at me as if I had lost my senses. "Over?" he repeated. "Haven't you heard the news?"

"News? What news?"

"The Vendéans have retaken la Flèche and may well march upon Le Mans tomorrow," he answered. "There are nearly 80,000 of them, desperate with hunger and disease, preparing to strike east, with some wild talk of taking Paris. Almost every man here in the garrison has gone south to try and stop them, but they won't have much hope, some 1,500 of them, against that band of brigands."

I had thought it was the icy wind that had turned him pale from the cold, but now I saw that it was fear as well.

"We heard there had been a victory at Angers," I said, my heart sinking. "What in the world are we to do? We've been half the day on the road from le Plessis-Dorin, and now it's almost dark."

"Go back there, if you have any sense," he answered, "or seek shelter for the night in some farmhouse out in the country."

I glanced at Marcel. The poor fellow was as white as the rest of them.

"The horse will never do the journey twice," I said, "nor will anyone in the country take us in, with this news. Doors and windows will be barred everywhere."

The citoyen Roger—I remembered his name, in a flash—stared up at me, the raindrops falling from his hat.

"I can't advise you," he said. "Thank God I'm unmarried. But if I had a wife I would not let her enter the city, not with this threat hanging over it."

My obstinacy was well-paid. What mockery it had been to leave le Chesne-Bidault without having waited for further news.

"If the brigands are coming," I said, "I'd rather face them with my brother in Le Mans than out here in the country beneath a hedge."

Pierre's client handed me back the passports and shrugged his shoulders.

"You won't find your brother in Le Mans," he replied. "The citoyen Busson du Charme will have left with the rest of the National Guard to defend the road to la Flèche. They had their orders at midday, just as we did."

To retreat now was impossible. The bleak countryside beyond the Huisne whence we had come, lashed with rain, grey in the gathering dusk, decided me. Also our dispirited horse, sagging between the shafts.

"We'll take our chance, citoyen," I said to Monsieur Roger. "Good luck to you and your men."

He saluted gravely and waved us on, and we entered a dead city, the houses shuttered, not a soul out in the streets. The hotel where we usually baited the horse was barricaded like the rest, and it was only after continued knocking that the landlord came, thinking we were the guard. Although he knew me, and the horse and carriole, he would not have stabled either had I not paid him triple his usual charge.

"If the brigands come, citoyenne, they'll burn the city down, you know that, don't you?" he said to me, on parting, and he showed me a pair of loaded pistols with which, so he assured me, he would shoot his wife and children rather than that they should fall into the hands of the Vendéans.

Marcel and I hurried through the streets to the quarter where Pierre lived, near the church of St. Pavin. As we walked, to be drenched by the rain within five minutes, I kept thinking of François and his brother, sitting contentedly at home at le Chesne-Bidault, knowing nothing of our plight. I thought of my baby too, sleeping peacefully in her cradle, and of poor Marcel's wife and children.

"I'm sorry, Marcel," I said to him, "you have me to blame for this adventure, no one else."

"Don't worry, citoyenne," he answered me. "The brigands may never come, and if they do we'll answer them with these."

He carried our two muskets over his shoulder, and I remembered the 80,000 Vendéans said to be starving in la Flèche.

Pierre's house was shuttered and barred like its neighbours, but here I had only to give two double knocks in quick succession, an old childhood signal, for the door to be opened forthwith and Edmé to be standing there. She might have been Michel in miniature, her brown hair ruffled, her eyes suspicious, a pistol in her hand which I had no doubt was loaded. At sight of me she put it down, and flung her arms about me.

"Sophie . . . Oh, Sophie . . . "

We clung to each other for a moment, and I heard my sister-in-law's anxious voice calling from the room beyond, "Who is it?" One of the younger boys was crying, a dog was barking, and I could imagine the pandemonium within.

I explained everything to Edmé in a moment, there in the entrance, then Marcel helped her bolt and bar the door once more.

"Pierre went off with the National Guard at noon," she said. "We haven't seen him since. He said to me 'Look after Marie and the children', and that's what I've done. We have food enough in the house for three or four days. If the brigands come, I'm ready for them."

She glanced at the muskets that Marcel had placed beside the door.

"Now we are well armed," she added, and, smiling at Marcel, "Do you mind serving under my command, citoyen?"

He was a lanky fellow of six foot or more, and he looked down at her sheepishly.

"You have only to give your orders, citoyenne," he answered.

I was reminded of our childhood at la Pierre, and how Edmé had preferred boys' games to dolls, forever asking Michel to shape swords and daggers. The chance to play the man had come for her at last.

"Troops cannot fight on an empty stomach," she said. "You'd both better come to the kitchen and fall to. It may have been foolish of you to leave le Chesne-Bidault, but I'll tell you one thing . . . I'm glad of reinforcements."

The boys now came running through from the inner room, Emile, the eldest, now thirteen, the youngest, Pierre-François, barely six, followed by a terrier bitch and a litter of puppies. My sister-in-law brought up the rear with the elderly widow and her daughter, permanent fixtures in this haphazard household, peering over her shoulder. I did not wonder that Edmé was glad of reinforcements. Her small community needed some defence.

We ate as best we could, bombarded on all sides by questions, none of which we could answer. The Vendéans were at la Flèche, that was all we knew. Whether they would now strike north, east, or west, nobody could say.

"One thing is certain," said Edmé. "If they try to take Le Mans, the city is virtually undefended. We have one battalion of Valenciennes quartered here, a detachment of cavalry, and our own National Guard; and they are now, all of them, somewhere on the road between the city and la Flèche."

This she told me later, when we were preparing for bed. She did not wish to alarm Pierre's wife, or the two boarders. She made me sleep on her bed, and she herself lay fully dressed on a mattress by the door. Marcel had elected to sleep in the entrance hall on a second mattress.

"If anything happens," said Edmé, "he and I are both prepared."

I saw she had a loaded musket beside her, and I had as much confidence in her capabilities to defend us as I would have had in Pierre himself.

We awoke to the same bleak sky and driving rain, and after breakfasting—eating as little as possible to save our rations—we sent Marcel out into the town to hear the latest news. He was gone more than an hour, and when he returned we could see at once by his face that the news was grave.

"The mayor and the municipality have already left for Chartres," he said. "All the public officials have gone with them, taking money, documents, papers, whatever mustn't fall into rebel hands. They've taken their families with them too. Whoever can find transport to get away has gone."

His words produced in me the old panic of '89. Then, the brigands had been legendary. Now they were real, not a half day's march from Le Mans.

"How many can the carriole hold?" I asked him.

He shook his head. "I called there not twenty minutes since, citoyenne," he answered. "The place was empty, and the stable too. That scoundrel of a landlord has taken carriole and horse to save himself and his family."

I turned desperately to Edmé. "What are we going to do?" I asked her.

She folded her arms and stood there, watching me.

"There's only one thing we can do," she answered. "Stay here, and fight it out."

Marcel moistened his lips with his tongue. I don't know who felt the more desperate, he or I.

"They were saying in the place des Halles that if the brigands enter the city no harm will come to those who don't resist them, citoyenne," he said. "It's food they want, nothing else. Women and children won't be made to suffer. They may take the men, though, and hang every one of them."

Edmé and I knew what he was after. He wanted permission to leave. He could still get away alone, and on foot. If he stayed with us, he might lose his life.

"Do as you wish, citoyen," said Edmé. "You don't belong here anyway. It's for the citoyenne Duval to say, not me."

I thought of the family waiting for him at le Chesne-Bidault, and I had not the heart to ask him to stay, though it meant leaving us defenceless.

"Go quickly, Marcel," I said. "If you reach home safely . . . you know what to tell them. Here, take your musket."

He shook his head. "I can travel quicker without it, citoyenne," he replied, and, bending low over my hands, he was gone the next moment.

"He meant," said Edmé, barring the door, "that he can run the faster. Are all the workmen at the foundry as chicken-hearted? If so, the place has changed. Can you fire a musket, Sophie?"

"No," I told her truthfully.

"Then I shall use the one and keep the second in reserve. Emile is old enough to use the pistol." She shouted for her nephew.

I had one of those strange aberrations of the mind when nothing that is happening seems true, and every action the sequence in a dream. I watched Edmé post the thirteen-year-old Emile at an upper window with the loaded pistol, while she herself, the muskets at her side, watched by the window of an adjoining room. Marie, the younger boys, the widow and her daughter were all locked up in the widow's apartment at the back of the house. The window there looked out upon rooftops but no street. It was the safest place.

"If they break down the door," said Edmé, "we can defend the stairs."

At this moment at le Chesne-Bidault Madame Verdelet would be giving Zoë Suzanne her mid-morning feed, lifting her from her cradle, propping her up in her high chair in the kitchen. Jacques Duval would be riding to Mondoubleau, perhaps, for news, and François employing the few men left about the foundry.

Just before midday I went down to the kitchen and prepared a meal which I carried up to the family in the back room. They had pushed the bed against the wall to give more floor space for the children's play. Marie, my sister-in-law, was mending the boys' socks. The widow was reading and her daughter threading beads on a string to amuse the youngest child. It was a calm, domestic scene, and the unusual peace more shocking to me than if the children had been crying and the others had shown fear.

I left them with their food and locked the door. Then I took a bowl of soup to Emile and a loaf of bread, which he ate as if half-starved.

"When will the brigands come?" he asked. "I want to fire this pistol."

The numb dream state that had been mine for the past few hours suddenly left me. What was happening was real. Edmé turned from her window on the street and looked at me.

"I don't want anything to eat," she said, "I'm not hungry."

Outside it was raining still.

16

I WAS SITTING at the top of the stairs, resting my head against the baluster, when Emile called out, "There are some strange looking people in the street. Some men who look like peasants, wearing sabots, and a lot of women, one of them with a baby. I think they must be lost."

I had been dozing, but his words startled me to action. I heard Edmé fumble with her musket, and I ran into Emile's room and stood beside him, peering through the chink of the shutters down into the street. When I saw them I knew. The Vendéans had entered the city. Here were some of the stragglers, who had found their way into our street, and were staring up at the houses for signs of life.

Instinct made me pull Emile back from the window.

"Stay quiet," I said, "don't let them see you."

He looked at me, puzzled, then suddenly he understood.

"Those ragged people down there?" he asked. "Are they the brigands?"

"Yes," I said. "Perhaps they'll go away. Keep still."

Edmé had crept into the room to join us. She had her musket with her. I questioned her with my eyes, and she nodded back at me.

"I won't fire," she said, "not unless we're attacked."

The three of us stood shoulder to shoulder looking down into the street. The first stragglers had gone ahead, and now others were coming, twenty, thirty, forty. Emile was counting them under his breath. They were not marching, there was no sort of order, these could not be the army proper, who would have gone by the main streets to the place des Halles. These were the followers-on, the rabble.

Now the numbers were growing larger, with more men than women, many of them armed with muskets and pikes, some barefoot but most in sabots. Some of them were wounded, and were supported by their fellows. Nearly all of them were ragged, emaciated, white with exhaustion, soaked and grimy with the mud and rain.

I do not know what I had expected, or Edmé and Emile either. The beating of drums, perhaps, firing, shouting, singing, the triumphant entry of a victorious army. Anything but silence, the slow clatter of sabots on the cobbles and the silence. The silence was the worst of all.

"What are they looking for? Where are they going?" whispered Emile.

We did not answer him. There was no answer to give. Like ghosts of dead men they passed beneath our windows and out of sight along the street, and as they passed more took their place, and then in the midst of them another band of women, and some half-dozen whimpering children.

"There won't be enough to feed them," said Edmé, "not in all Le Mans."

I noticed then that she had put down her musket. It was resting against the wall. The clock in the entrance below struck four.

"It will soon be dark," said Emile. "Where will all these people go?"

Suddenly we heard a clatter of hoofs, and shouting, and what appeared to be a small body of cavalry came down the street, led by an officer. He wore the hated white cockade in his hat and a white sash round his waist, and flourished a sabre in his hand. He yelled some order to the straggling wretches ahead, who turned and stared at him. He must have spoken to them in patois; we could not understand a word of it, but we could see by the way he pointed with his sabre that he was directing them to the house opposite.

Some of the people, dazed but obedient, began hammering at the doors. No one, as yet, touched ours. Another body of men, armed and on foot, came down the street. The mounted officer, at sight of them, shouted a command, directing them to the houses, and they scattered, taking a house apiece, hammering on the door, pushing the stragglers away. One of them came and knocked on our door too.

Then the mounted officer, raising himself and standing in his stirrups, shouted aloud, for all of us to hear.

"Not one of you who opens his door will be molested," he called. "There are some eighty thousand of us here in your city, and we must be fed and housed. Anyone who does not open his door will have that door marked, and the house burnt down within the hour. It is for you to decide."

He paused a moment, then, signalling to the mounted troops behind him, clattered off down the street. The armed foot soldiers and the peasants in the street went on knocking at the houses.

"What shall we do?" asked Edmé.

She had reverted to her rôle of younger sister. I watched the house opposite. One of our neighbours had opened the door, and three wounded men were being carried inside. Another door opened. One of the armed soldiers shouted to a woman with two children, and motioned her inside.

"If we don't open," I said to Edmé, "they'll mark the door and come back and burn the house."

"It could have been a threat," she answered. "They can't spare the time to go round marking every door."

We waited. More and more of them were coming down the street, and since the officer had passed, giving his orders to knock upon the doors, the silence had been broken. They were now calling and shouting to one another in confusion, and it was getting darker as each moment passed.

"I'll go down," I said. "I'll go down and open the door."

Neither my sister nor my nephew answered me. I went downstairs and unbolted the door. There were some half-dozen of them waiting, peasants by the look of them, and three women and two children, and another woman carrying a baby. One of the men was armed with a musket, the rest with pikes. The man with the musket asked me a question—he spoke so broadly that I couldn't understand him, but I caught the word "rooms". Could it be that he wanted to know how many rooms there were in the house?

"Six," I said, "we have six rooms above, and two below. Eight in all." I held up my fingers. I might have been the patron of a hotel touting for custom.

"Go on . . . go on . . ." he cried to those about him, driving them ahead, and they filed into the house, the women and the other peasants. Following them was a man who seemed to have but half a leg; he was carried by two others who, though they walked, looked almost as ill as he.

"That's it," said the peasant with the musket, prodding his fellows like so many cattle, "that's it . . . that's it . . ." and he pushed them forward to the salon and to Pierre's small library that opened out of it.

"They'll fix themselves," he said to me, "they'll need bedding . . ."

So much I understood, more from his gestures than his speech, and he pointed to his mouth and rubbed his belly.

"They're hungry. Doubled-up. What with that, and the sickness . . ." He grinned, showing toothless gums. "All day on the road," he said. "No good. Everybody tired."

The man with half a leg was being stretched out on Marie's settee by his two companions. The women had pushed past me to the kitchen and were opening the cupboards. "That's it, that's it . . ." repeated the man with the musket. "Someone will be along directly to see to the wounded man." He went out into the street, slamming the door behind him.

Edmé came down the stairs, followed by Emile. "How many are they?" she asked.

"I don't know," I answered. "I haven't counted."

We looked into the salon, and there were more than I thought. Eight men, one with the injured leg, and two who seemed sick. One of these was already grasping his stomach and retching. The stench coming from him was appalling.

"What's wrong with him?" asked Emile. "Is he going to die?"

The other sick man raised his head and stared at us.

"It's the sickness," he said, "half the army has it. We caught it in the north, in Normandy. The food and wine there poisoned us."

He seemed more educated than the others, and spoke a French I understood.

"It's dysentery," said Edmé. "Pierre warned us about it."

I looked at her, aghast. "We'll have to put them in a room apart," I said. "They had better go in the boys' room upstairs."

I bent down to the man whose French I understood.

"Follow me," I said. "You shall have a room to yourselves."

Once again I reminded myself of some hotel patron, and a wild desire to laugh rose in me, instantly checked when I perceived the full state of the man with dysentery, whom his companion was helping from the floor. He had been lying, poor wretch, in his own filth all about him, and he was too weak to walk.

"It's no use," said his companion, "he's too ill to move. If we could have the room yonder." He jerked his head at Pierre's library, and began to drag the sick man to it.

"Get a mattress," I said to Emile. "He'll have to have a mattress. The other one too. Bring down mattresses for both of them."

Surely, I thought, the sick man should be stripped of his things, and linen wrapped about him. The clothes he was wearing must be burnt . . . I went into the kitchen, and I saw that every cupboard had been flung open and every drawer turned out, and all the food remaining in the house piled high on the kitchen table. Two women were cutting up the bread, stuffing themselves as they did so, and feeding the children. The third woman stood by the stove, stirring the soup she had found there, suckling her baby at the same time. They took no notice of me when I entered, but went on talking to each other in their own patois.

I took some cloths and a pail of water into the salon to scrub the floor where the poor sick man had lain. And now the man with the injured leg was groaning; I could see the blood coming through his bandages. No one was looking after him. His companions had pushed past me and gone into the kitchen to search for food, and I could hear them cursing the women for feeding themselves before the rest.

There was a thumping on the floor from the back room above, and I called to Emile to tell his mother to keep the children quiet; the house was full of the Vendéans, some of them wounded and sick. He came running back again within the minute.

"The boys are hungry," he said, "they want to come down to supper."

"Tell them there is no supper," I said, wringing out the floor-cloth. "The Vendéans have taken it all."

Somebody thundered on the entrance door, and I thought it might be the man with the musket to see how his friends fared. But when Edmé went to open it six more of them pushed their way inside, five men and a woman, better dressed than our first peasants, and one of the men a priest.

"How many in the house?" demanded the priest.

He wore the Sacred Heart as an emblem on his breast, and a pistol thrust into his belt beside his rosary.

I shut my eyes and counted. "About twenty-four," I said, "counting ourselves. Some of your people are sick."

"Dysentery?" he asked.

"Two with dysentery," I answered, "one with a badly injured leg."

He turned to the woman beside him, who already held a handkerchief to her nose. She wore a bright green gown under a man's military cloak, and her feathered hat sat on a pile of curls.

"They've dysentery in the house," he said, "but it's the same everywhere. The house itself looks clean enough."

The woman shrugged her shoulders. "I must have a bed," she said, "and a room to myself. Surely the sick can all go in together?"

The priest pushed past me. "Have you a room upstairs for this lady?" he asked Edmé.

I saw Edmé staring at his Sacred Heart. "We have a room," she said. "Go upstairs and find it."

The priest and the woman went upstairs. The other four men had already passed through into the kitchen. In the salon the man with the injured leg began shouting aloud with pain. In a moment or two the priest came down the stairs.

"Madame will stay," he said. "She is very exhausted, and hungry. You will please take some food up to her at once."

"There is no food," I said. "Your people are eating it all in the kitchen."

He clicked his tongue in annoyance and thrust his way past me to the kitchen. The uproar ceased. I heard the priest's voice only, raised in anger.

"He's threatening them with hell," whispered Emile.

The cursing changed to intoning. They all began saying the Ave Maria, the women's voices the loudest. Then the priest returned to the entrance hall. He looked half-starved himself, but he had not eaten anything.

He stared at me a moment, then asked abruptly, "Where are the wounded?"

I took him to the salon. "One wounded," I said, "two in the further room with dysentery."

He muttered something in answer, and, unfastening his rosary, passed into the salon. I saw him glance down at the blood-stained bandage on the leg of the wounded man, but he did not examine the wound or touch the bandage. He held the rosary to the lips of the sufferer, saying, "Misereatur vestri omnipotens Deus."

I shut the door of the salon and left them alone.

I could hear the latest arrival, the woman, moving about in Pierre's and Marie's room above. I went up the stairs and opened the door. The woman had flung wide the cupboards and was turning Marie's clothes out on the floor. There was a fine shawl amongst the clothes, a gift to Marie from my mother. The woman put it round her shoulders.

"Make haste with the supper," she said. "I don't intend to wait all night."

She did not bother to turn her head to see who it was at the door.

"You'll be lucky if you get any," I told her. "The women who were here before you have eaten most of it."

She looked over her shoulder at the sound of my voice, which was new to her. She was handsome in a disagreeable way, and there was nothing of the peasant about her.

"You had better watch your tongue when you address me," she said. "One word to the men below, and I'll have you whipped for insolence."

I did not answer her. I went out and shut the door. It was her kind that the Committee of Public Safety in Paris were rounding up and sending to the Conciergerie en route for the guillotine. As wife or mistress of a Vendéan officer, she believed herself of consequence. It did not matter to me. I passed one of the peasant women on the stairs bearing up a tray of food to her. "She doesn't deserve it," I murmured. The woman stared.

When I went into the salon once again the man with half a leg was crying softly to himself. The blood had come right through his bandages and soaked the material on the settee. Someone had shut the door leading to the inner room where the dysentery patients lay. The priest had gone.

"We'd forgotten about the wine," said Edmé, coming through from the hall.

"Wine? What wine?" I asked.

"Pierre's wine," she said. "There were about a dozen bottles in the cellar. Those men have found it. They have all the bottles on the kitchen table, and are knocking the heads off them."

Emile had crept past me and was listening at the door of the inner room.

"I think one of those men must be dying in there," he whispered. "There's a queer groaning noise. Shall I open the door and see?"

It was suddenly too much. The moment and the hour. Nothing that any of us could do would be of use. I felt my legs tremble under me.

"Let's lock ourselves in one of the rooms upstairs," I said.

As we left the salon the man with half a leg began to groan again. Nobody heard him. They were all singing and laughing in the kitchen, and just before we locked ourselves in Edmé's room we heard a great crash of breaking glass.

Somehow we slept that night, waking every few hours and losing all count of time, disturbed by continual treading in the rooms beside us, and by crying—whether of our own younger children from the back of the house or the Vendéans we could not tell. Emile complained of hunger, though he had eaten well at midday. Edmé and I had taken nothing since early morning.

We must have fallen heavily asleep, all three of us, in the small hours, for we were awakened about seven to hear the sound of the cathedral bells. Emile jumped off the bed and ran to open the shutters. The bells were pealing as they did on Easter Day.

"It's the Vendéan priests," said Edmé after a moment. "They're going to celebrate their entry into the city by singing Mass in the cathedral. I hope they choke themselves."

The rain had ceased. A dreary, fitful sun was trying to force its way through the pallid sky.

"The street's empty," said Emile. "None of the shutters are open in the houses opposite. Shall I go downstairs and see what's happening?"

"No," I said, "no, I'll go."

I smoothed my hair and straightened my clothes, and unlocked the door. The house was silent, but for the sound of heavy snoring in the adjoining room. The door was half ajar. I glanced in. The woman with the baby was asleep on the bed, and a man beside her. One of the other children was lying on the floor.

I crept downstairs and looked into the salon. The room was in complete confusion, with broken bottles strewn about the floor and men sprawled anyhow. The man with half a leg was still lying on the couch, but twisted sideways, his arms above his head. He was breathing loudly, half-snoring with each breath he took. He was probably unconscious. The door through to Pierre's library was still shut, and I could not go and ask after the men with dysentery because of the others sleeping on the floor.

The kitchen was in the same confusion. Wreckage and destruction everywhere, broken bottles and spilt wine, and the filthy litter of spoilt food. Four of them were on the floor here too, one of them a woman, with a child across her knees. None of them woke when I entered, and I felt they would lie here all the day. One glance about me, and in the larder, was enough to tell me there was nothing to eat.

Once, long ago when we were children, a travelling menagerie had come to Vibraye, and my father had taken Edmé and me to see the animals. They were penned in cages, and after staring at them awhile we came away, because of the reeking smell. The kitchen smelt as the cages had done that day. I went back again upstairs, and beckoned Edmé and Emile, and we went through to the room at the back to see Marie and the others. We found them desperate with anxiety, not knowing how we had fared. The children were whining and restless, asking for their breakfast, and the poor dog frantic to go outside.

"Let me take her," said Emile, "they're all asleep. No one will say anything to me."

Edmé shook her head, and I guessed her thought. If a dog was loose in the street, even for a moment, some passer-by might seek to destroy it instantly for food. The larder in our house was empty, others in the city would be the same. There were some 80,000 Vendéans in Le Mans, and somehow, through the day, all of their number must be fed . . .

"Have you anything to give our children?" I asked. My sister-in-law had four loaves left, and some apples, and a jug of milk half turned. The widow had three pots of blackcurrant preserve. They had water enough to brew coffee, and with this they must be satisfied. There was plenty of wood to keep the fire going.

The three of us drank coffee, knowing it might be all we should get that day, and then we locked their door and went back to our own room. We went on sitting there through the morning, keeping a watch on the window in turn, and about noon Emile, who was on guard, reported movement from the house opposite. Two Vendéans came out and stretched themselves, and presently a third, and then a fourth, and they talked amongst themselves awhile on the step, and then began walking up the street.

There was movement in our house too. We heard the door open below, and two of our "lodgers" went into the street, with the woman and the child who had been lying in the kitchen. They walked up the street after the others.

"They're hungry," said Emile. "They're going off to see if they can do better somewhere else."

"It's like watching a play," said Edmé, "and not knowing the ending. A play where the actors don't pretend any more, but come alive."

Suddenly we saw a carriage come up the street, driven by a man in uniform, wearing a white cockade. The carriage stopped before our door.

"It's that priest," said Edmé. "He's had a lift to save his feet."

She was right. The priest of the night before got out of the carriage and knocked on the door of our house. We heard someone open the door and admit him. There was a murmur of voices from below, and presently a stumping up the stairs, and knocking on the room at the end of the landing, Pierre's and Marie's room where the woman in the green dress had gone.

"What's he going to do in there?" whispered Emile.

Edmé murmured something under her breath and Emile, half-choking, stuffed his fist into his mouth.

In about five minutes' time the window of Pierre's room was flung open and we heard the priest shouting down to the soldier in uniform. The soldier shouted back, and then one of the peasants below went and held his horse, and the soldier entered the house and came upstairs.

"Two of them?" whispered Emile, his voice high with hysteria.

Presently there was a sound of dragging and thumping from the room to the stairs, and peering from our window we saw that the priest and the soldier were hauling Marie's clothes-press into the street, helped by one of the peasants, and between the three of them they lifted it into the carriage.

"Oh no . . ." said Edmé. "No . . . no . . ."

I held her wrist. "Be quiet," I said. "We can't do anything."

Now the woman in the green dress was throwing things out of the window, shoes belonging to Marie, and a fur cape and several dresses, and, not content, she followed up with the blankets from the bed and the quilted bedspread that had been Pierre's and Marie's from their wedding-day. The woman found nothing else to her fancy, for soon we heard her coming down the stairs, and she went out into the street and stood talking for a moment to the priest and the soldier. Her voice carried, and it was not difficult to understand her.

"What has been decided?" she asked, and the soldier and the priest argued together, but it was impossible to hear them, though the soldier pointed toward the centre of the town.

"If the Prince Tallemont is for evacuating the city you can rest assured that is what we shall do," said the woman.

There was further argument and further talk, and then she and the priest climbed into the carriage and the soldier took the reins and they drove away.

"The priest didn't go in to look at the wounded man, or the men with the dysentery," said Emile. "All he could think about was letting that woman have my mother's clothes."

The priest's example must have fired the peasants, who had awakened from their drunken sleep below, for there now started a great racket throughout the house, up and down the stairs and in the salon and the kitchen, and the men began carrying things out into the street as well—pots and pans, and coats belonging to Pierre from the closet in the entrance hall.

I was reminded, all too suddenly, of the workmen from le Chesne-Bidault and their forays to Authon and St. Avit. What had been done to others was now done to us.

"Only surely," I said to myself, "it was not quite the same. Surely Michel and the workmen set about it differently?"

Perhaps not. Perhaps, in fact, it had been just the same. And there had been women and a young boy watching the National Guard from the windows of the château Charbonnières just as we now watched the Vendéans.

"We can't prevent them," I said to Edmé. "Don't let's look any more."

"I can't stop myself," said Edmé. "The more I watch, the more I hate. I didn't know it was possible to hate so much."

She stared down at the street below, and Emile called out in bewilderment and anger when he recognised familiar objects carried from the house.

"There's the clock from the salon," he said, "the one with the chimes. And my father's fishing-rod—what can they want with that? They've stripped the curtains from the window and rolled them into a bundle, and that woman with the children is making one of the men carry them on his shoulder. Why can't we shoot at them?"

"Because," said Edmé, "they're too many for us. Because, perhaps for this day only, luck is on their side."

I saw her glance at the two muskets still standing in the corner of the room, and I could guess how much it cost her to keep her hands off them.

"That's the finish," said Emile suddenly, his eyes filling with tears. "The woman has found Dadá in the cupboard below the stairs. She has given it to her child, and he's walking off with it."

Dadá was the wooden horse that had been Emile's childhood toy, prized all his thirteen years, and now the loved property of his youngest brother. Clocks, clothes, bed-linen, the theft of these I had accepted with resignation, but the bearing away of Dadá was the final outrage.

"Stay here," I said, "I'll get it back for you."

I unlocked the door and ran downstairs, and into the street after the woman and the boy. Neither Edmé nor Emile had told me, though, that the peasants had been piling their loot into a cart, and now, as I came out into the street, they had climbed up into the cart and were driving off. There were three or four of them in the cart, sitting on top of the stuff they had packed on to it, and the woman was there, and the boy clutching Dadá.

"We don't mind you taking the other things" I cried, "it's the horse. The horse belongs to the children in the house."

They stared down at me, astonished. I don't think they understood me. The woman nudged her companions, and broke into a silly cackle of laughter. She shouted something, which made all of them laugh, but what it was I could not say.

"I'll find your boy another toy if we could have back the horse," I said.

Then the man who was driving cut down at me with his whip, flaying my face. The shock of the pain made me cry out, and I backed away from the cart, and a moment later they were driving down the street. I heard the window above being opened, and Edmé called down to me, her voice half-strangled and unlike herself, "I'll shoot them for that . . . I'll shoot them for that."

"No," I shouted, "no, they'll kill you . . ."

I ran up the stairs and into the room, and as I entered it I heard the explosive shot of the musket. She had missed, of course, and the shot had hit a house at the end of the street. The peasants, startled, looked up at the sky and all about them, then drove on, turned the corner of the street and disappeared. They had not seen from where the shot had come.

"That was madness," I told Edmé. "If they had seen you, they would have sent soldiers back to shoot us all."

"I wish they would," said Edmé, "I wish they would . . ."

I looked at myself in the mirror on the wall. There was a great weal on my face where the man had lain his whip, and it was bleeding, too. I did not mind the pain, but the shock of what had happened made me feel faint. I put my handkerchief to my face and sat on the bed, trembling.

"Are you hurt?" asked Emile anxiously.

"No," I said, "no, it's not that."

It was what one person could do to another. The man driving the cart, not knowing me, cracking my face with his whip. It was Edmé, shooting wildly from the window. It was the crowd, in '89, before the Abbey of St. Vincent. It was the two men being butchered at Ballon . . .

"I'm going to see what's happening below," said Edmé.

I went on sitting on the bed, holding the handkerchief to my face.

When she came up again, and Emile with her—I had not noticed he had followed her—she said that the man with half a leg was delirious, moaning and thrashing about, his bandages loose.

"There's blood all over the settee and on the floor," said Emile.

"He'll die if a doctor does not see him," said Edmé.

I stared at her. "Perhaps we should try and clean the wound?" I said.

"Why should we?" she answered. "The sooner he dies the better. It would be one Vendéan the less."

She went over again to the window and stared down into the street.

Presently, when I felt better, I went downstairs myself to look at the injured man. There was no one else in the salon, all the others had gone. The man was muttering and moaning, and the blood had soaked right through the bandages to the couch and on to the floor. I went through the salon and opened the door of the inner room. The stench was unbearable. Instinctively, I clapped my handkerchief over my nose and mouth. One man lay on his back dead. I knew he was dead because of the stiffness. The other, the one who had spoken courteously the day before, lifted his head from his mattress as I entered.

"My friend is dead," he murmured. "I am going to die too. If you could ask the priest to come . . ."

I went out and shut the door. I went back to the wounded man and stared down at his bandage. At least, if I cut away the bandages and put a clean cloth on the wound, it might help to stanch the blood. I might have known, though, that the Vendéans would have stripped the linen closet too. It was empty. I found a white petticoat in Pierre's and Marie's room which the woman in the green dress had picked up and thrown aside. This I tore into strips to make a clean bandage for the wounded man.

When I tried to take away the soaked old bandage I found it stuck to the gaping wound beneath, and I was too sick to try and cut it away, so I put the new bandage on top of the old. Somehow, to my ignorant eye, it looked better, cleaner. I tried to give the man some water to drink, but he was too delirious to take it, and swept the cup aside.

"They'll have to have a priest," I remember thinking. "We can't do any more for these men. They must have a priest."

Edmé and Emile were still above, and the rest of the family shut away in the room at the back. Nothing any longer went by rule—I did not even know the time of day. I went out into the street to find a priest. The first I saw was in so great a hurry to attend a meeting of the Vendéan chiefs that he made a cross in the air above his head, after expressing his regrets, and went his way.

The second, when I told him men were dying, replied, "There are thousands dying, all asking to be shriven. Yours must await their turn. What is your address?" I gave it to him, and he too went his way.

Curiosity—for no one took any notice of me—made me walk as far as the municipality, and I saw, without surprise, that the Vendéans were serving it much as they had served us. Numbers of them were flinging things out of the windows into the street below, not to bear off as trophies, but for destruction. They had a fire burning before the building, and were feeding it with tables, chairs and rugs.

The crowds assembled were like nothing I had ever seen in Paris, before '89 or after it. There were peasants barefoot, with sabots looped from a string round their necks, their women hanging on to them, and soldiers too, wearing the white cockade, and ladies of the former aristocracy wrapped in military coats, their ringlets falling from beneath enormous hats. It was a masquerade of olden times, a scene from an opera. Had I not known their origin I should have said that these people had dressed up for the occasion, instead of fighting their way from the coast across the Loire to Normandy and back.

Suddenly there appeared two Vendéan chiefs riding in the midst of them, and the crowd fell apart, making way. They were fantastic, like engravings out of history, with great white plumes soaring from their hats after the style of Henri IV, and the broad white sash encircling their waists. Their breeches were the colour of chamois, their boots were buskin, and their swords were curved like scimitars.

No wonder that the peasants about me curtseyed, making the sign of the Cross at their approach.

"It's the Prince Tallemont," said a woman near to me. "It's he who wants us to march to Paris."

I continued walking, looking for a priest to come to the dying men, but everywhere people were piling carts and horses with the loot they had taken from the houses and the shops, and whoever I asked brushed my question aside, repeating the saying of the second priest that many people were dying, there was no time to attend to all of them, and anyway the city was to be evacuated the next day.

Here at least was something to cling to, even if we were left with dying men. I went back to the house without a priest, and we waited there through the rest of the day, but no one came, not even our peasant lodgers. They must have found food and better quarters elsewhere.

When, just before dusk, I went into the little room through the salon, I saw that the man with the dysentery who had asked for the priest was dead. I found something to cover both their bodies, and shut the door. The man with half a leg was no longer delirious. He stared at me with hollow eyes, and begged for water. I gave him some, and when I asked after his wound he said it no longer pained him, but he had stomach cramps. He began to roll from side to side, gasping with this new pain, and then I saw that he too had dysentery. There was nothing I could do. I stayed with him a moment and left the water by his side, then shut the door and went upstairs.

Soon darkness came, and the long night. Nothing happened. Nobody came. Next day bugles sounded the alert, echoing from every quarter of the city, and, just as we had done the day before at the sound of the church bells, so we rushed again to the window, and flung aside the shutters.

"It's the call to arms," shouted Emile. "They're leaving us . . . they're going."

The Vendéans were running out of the houses opposite, some of them still barefoot, clutching their weapons. We could hear artillery in the distance.

"It's our army," said Edmé, "it's Westermann and the republicans at last."

Emile wanted to run out into the streets at once, and we had to hold him back.

"They're not here yet, Emile," I told him. "There may be heavy fighting in the city. We don't know which way the battle will go."

"I can at least help it to go our way," said Edmé, and she reached for the musket and took careful aim out of the window. This time, when she fired, she had an easier target, for she picked off a Vendéan standing in the middle of the road, uncertain which way to run. He fell instantly, his left leg kicking like a hare. Then he lay still.

"I've hit him," said Edmé, her voice unsteady. "I've killed him."

The three of us stared down at the doubled-up body in the street.

"There's another," cried Emile, jumping up and down. "Hit that one coming out of the door."

Edmé did not do anything. She just stared out of the window. The Vendéans came pouring out of the houses to the summons of the bugle. They took no notice of the man Edmé had shot. They shouted to one another distraught, asking which way to go. I heard one of them say, "The blues are attacking the city. The blues must have captured the bridge." They all started running up the street to the sound of the bugle, panic-stricken, in no sort of order, and out of the houses came the women too, some of them with children, running this way and that, like frightened geese. Then one of them saw the man Edmé had shot. She ran to his side and turned him over.

"It's Jean-Louis," she cried, "he's dead. Someone has shot him."

She began to scream, rocking backwards and forwards, and the child with her stared, his finger in his mouth. One of the peasants came and led them both away, the woman protesting, looking back over her shoulder.

"I'll go and tell them all in the back room," said Emile excitedly. "I'll go and tell them tante Edmé has shot a brigand."

He ran from the room, calling his news loudly. Edmé leant the musket against the window.

"I don't know why it had to be that one," she said, her voice unsteady still. "He wasn't doing anything. If it could have been the man who cracked his whip. . . ."

"It never is," I said. "It's never the right man. That's why it's so useless."

I turned away from the window, and went downstairs into the salon. The man with half a leg had fallen off the couch on to the floor. He was still breathing. He was not dead.

There was a great hubbub above. Emile had unlocked the door and told everyone that the brigands were running away, and Edmé had shot one who was lying dead in the street. The younger boys wanted to see. Even the dog came tearing down the stairs, barking excitedly to go out.

"No," I said, "go back, everybody. Nothing is over yet. They're fighting in the streets."

I saw the shocked white face of the widow staring down at the wounded man from the head of the staircase.

"Go back," I said. "Please all of you go back."

I shut the dog in the kitchen—the scraps and litter on the floor would quieten her. I could hear Edmé persuading the others to go back into their room until the fighting was over.

Through the rest of the day, all through the night, the battle continued, and next morning, about seven, we heard musket shots near to us in the street, and the sound of cavalry too.

Inevitably we went to our vantage point beside the window, and we saw that the Vendéans had come back to our street once more, but this time not as conquerors. They were running for their lives seeking shelter. Men, women, children, they were running down the street, their mouths open wide in terror, their arms outstretched, and our hussars were after them, cutting them down with their sabres, sparing no one. The women were screaming, and the children too, but our hussars were yelling and shouting in triumph.

"Get them . . . get them . . . get them . . ." cried Edmé savagely, and she picked up the musket once more and fired it blindly into the retreating crowd. Somebody fell, to be trampled in his turn by others.

The National Guard came running down the street behind the hussars, and they were shooting too, and suddenly I saw Pierre, carrying no weapon, his right arm in a sling, his uniform stripped and torn, and he was shouting at the top of his voice "No . . . no . . . stop the slaughter of the women and children. . . . Stop the slaughter. . . ."

Emile leant out of the window, laughing excitedly. "We're here, Papa," he called. "Look at us, we're here, we're safe."

Edmé picked off another Vendéan who had sheltered in a doorway, and the man's companion, firing blindly in self-defence, returned the shot, not looking, then ran on down the street.

The shot struck Emile full in the face and he fell backwards into my arms, choking, his face bespattered with blood.

He uttered no other sound, but from the street below came the screams of the Vendéan women as they were cut down by our hussars.

Pierre did not see the shot that killed his son. He was still standing in the street, crying out to his companions of the National Guard, who took no notice of him, "Stop the slaughter! Stop the hussars from killing those women and children."

I knelt on the floor, clasping Emile to me, rocking backwards and forwards as I had seen the Vendéan woman do earlier in the day when she found the dead man in the street.

"Oh, Lamb of God," I said, "oh, Lamb of God who takest away the sins of the world, have mercy upon us. Have mercy upon us, have mercy upon us. . . ."

Somewhere, at the far end of the street, I heard a burst of cheering, and our men singing the Marseillaise.

17

ALL RESISTANCE HAD ended before midday on Friday, the 13 of December, and the defeated rebel army fled in disorder south toward the Loire, leaving no Vendéans in Le Mans save those hundreds of women and children, the sick and the wounded, and their own dead.

If I do not speak of those first days following upon the battle it is because memory, mercifully blunted, contains few images. Our own grief for Emile, and the attempt to console his stricken mother and bring some sort of order back to the house, filled our hours. I remember that Pierre, when he knew that nothing could be done for his son, knelt by the side of the wounded man below and tended him until he died; and the knowledge that my brother could somehow assuage his own sorrow thus gave me courage to endure the days ahead.

The victory, though complete, held such an aftermath of horror that much of it is best forgotten. Our soldiers, outraged at their earlier defeats, returned measure for measure, not only when in pursuit of the fleeing enemy, but upon those Vendéan women and children remaining in the city.

The officials of the municipality had not yet returned from Chartres, and a body of citizens, my brother Pierre amongst them, formed a temporary administration to try and restore order. But they were not helped in their work by a large number of the population whose houses had been pillaged just as ours had been, and who saw, in those wretched prisoners left behind by the retreating rebels, a ready target for their feelings of revenge.

I thanked God I was not present when some twenty-two women and children who had been found straying on the roads outside the city were brought back and set upon in the place des Jacobins by a crowd of Manceaux, who, so Edmé informed me afterwards, tore them to pieces, aided by the hussars. Such scenes could not quieten grief, or bring back the dead. They only added to the burden of sorrow. One of the sights that most sickened me, during the Saturday when I was in the town trying to buy bread for the household, was seeing a heap of bodies being tossed into a cart, preparatory to burial, like a load of dung, and on the top of them, spreadeagled, green skirts about her head, our red-haired lodger.

Michel appeared for a brief moment, on the Friday. It showed how all of us had lost count of the days in that he saw nothing strange in my presence in the city, or even questioned me. He and his men—he had lost some twenty of them in the skirmishes with the Vendéans—had been lying in wait somewhere in the countryside the past few days, biding their time to join the republican armies. Now, with the Vendéans totally routed and in full retreat, he was returning in haste to Mondoubleau to tell the authorities of the rebel defeat.

"Nearly one hundred thousand of the brigands crossed the Loire two months ago," said Michel. "They may count themselves lucky if four thousand stragglers live to cross it once again. Those who do reach home will regret it. Our armies have orders from the Convention to raze every village to the ground. There will be no Vendée left."

It was a legacy of hatred to confer upon the west. Even those Vendéans who had not marched with the others, but had stayed peaceably in their homes, were as guilty as the rest. Not one of them was held innocent, no matter the age, no matter the sex. The oldest man must suffer with the youngest child. These were the orders.

Happily some of our generals, amongst them Kléber, who was to win greater fame in later years, protested against the severity of the decrees passed on to him, and the worst atrocities did not take place under his command. Others of the leaders were less humane. Like my brother Michel, they believed that the only way to crush a revolt for all time was to leave no one alive who could rebel.

I stayed a week with Pierre and his unhappy family, doing what I could to help in the house. Then François came from le Chesne-Bidault to fetch me home, and we took the two youngest boys back with us, and the terrier and puppies. My sister-in-law, still prostrate, would not leave Pierre, and Edmé stayed behind to look after the pair of them.

My brother's chambers had been broken into by the Vendéans and more ruthlessly pillaged than his house. His furniture, his files, the documents of all his clients had been senselessly destroyed by a band of intruders who must have burnt whatever they could lay their hands on for the joy of seeing the flames.

Pierre's one concern was for the property of his clients. Some, poorer than their fellows, whose homes had been broken into in similar fashion and who had lost almost all they possessed, were not deprived for long. The necessities of life became theirs again; furniture, food, bedding was supplied by Pierre out of his own funds.

It was not until long afterwards that I heard the tale from Edmé. He all but beggared himself in the process, without a word to anyone but her, and was forced to sell his practice, a year later, and accept payment from the municipality as a public notary. I think, if anyone lived up to the principles of equality and brotherhood that had first inspired our revolution, it was my brother Pierre.

The "original" who, according to my father, would never make anything of his life, who refused to earn his living—returning from Martinique at seventeen with a trunk-load of coloured waistcoats and a parrot on either shoulder—was now, at forty-one, not only a leading patriot but one of the best-loved citizens in Le Mans.

Not so my brother Michel. Idolised by a section of his workmen, who admired his leadership and courage, and had shared in his exploits during the past few years, he was feared by a large number of them, and criticised for the ruthless discipline which he imposed upon the National Guard. The families of those who had lost their lives in the last campaign against the Vendéans murmured that their men had been sacrificed in vain. They had been enrolled to defend their parish, not to march for two days and attack against overwhelming odds.

The part Michel had played, and my husband too, in the primary elections to the Convention a year before was not forgotten amongst the various communes in our district. Busson-Challoir and Duval, so it was said, were favoured persons, not only because of their relationship to an ex-deputy but because their high position as "acquirers of national wealth". This title, so popular in '91, had lost much of its prestige by '94. The poor were still poor, and those who had enriched themselves by the purchase of church lands were looked upon as profiteers, despite the initial act of patriotism.

If the civil war against the Vendéans was over, an aftermath of discontent remained, and this was very evident in our own neighbourhood and amongst our own workpeople. The millennium had not come about. Living was still dear. And, worst of all, conscription was taking away the youngest and strongest members of each family, very often the bread-winner.

"Why do our lads have to go?" This was the eternal question asked by the wives and mothers in our community. "Why don't they call up the officials first, and the acquirers too? Let them go off, and our lads follow afterwards."

As the wife and sister of both officials and acquirers I was hard put to it for an answer, except that the country, like the foundry, must be administered by men who were trained and capable. This reply would be received with a stare, or a grumble that the revolution had benefited those people who had been doing well in the first place, but as far as the workmen and peasants were concerned nothing had changed. Such statements were not true, but they made me feel uncomfortable all the same.

Another difficulty was that the Law of the Maximum, passed by Robespierre and the Convention the preceding autumn, put a limit, not only on the price of food and goods, but upon wages as well. This caused great discontent amongst workmen everywhere, and at our own foundry Michel and François were accused as if they were to blame for the decree, and not the Convention.

"Citoyen Busson-Challoir and Citoyen Duval can buy national property, but our wages must stay as they are," I would be told.

Throughout the winter and spring of '94 this spirit of dissatisfaction grew. News of the daily executions in Paris, not only of the former aristocrats but of the Girondin deputies who had helped to govern us the year before, and indeed of anyone who dared to lift a voice against the inner circle of the Convention, Robespierre, St. Just, and a few others, filtered through to us in the country.

Danton's death shocked all of us, even Michel. Here was one of our greatest patriots sent to the guillotine in his turn.

"We can't g-give an opinion," said my brother angrily, angry, I think, because his faith in the Convention had been shaken. "Danton must have been c-conspiring against the nation, or he would n-never have been condemned."

The war against the Allies progressed with successive victories for our republican armies, yet the numbers sent to the guillotine increased. François admitted to me that he believed Robespierre and the Revolutionary Tribunal had gone too far, but he dared not say so before Michel.

The excesses, and the severities, brought their own reaction throughout the country as a whole, and in our region too. Petty pilfering began in our own foundry, refusals to work, threats uttered against Michel.

"If this sort of thing continues," François told me, "either we must break up the partnership and Michel will have to go; or we shall have to surrender the lease, and leave le Chesne-Bidault."

The lease was due for renewal on All Saints' Day in November, or, as we now called it, the 11th Brumaire, and the decision what to do must be left over until then. Meanwhile, we should hope to see trade and tempers improved during the summer.

What distressed me most was that the goodwill amongst us all seemed lost. Hostility, for no good reason, could be sensed in the workmen's lodgings and on the furnace floor, and I could feel it with the women too. The camaraderie, instilled into the workmen when Michel first took over as master of the foundry, had vanished, and whether it was conscription, or the toll of the civil war, or the limit of their wages, nobody could say—these are things that are never put into words. Madame Verdelet, my usual informant, told me that the people were "fed up". This was the expression used.

"They've had enough," she said, "enough of the revolution, enough of fighting and restrictions, enough of change. It was better, so the older ones say, when your mother was in charge here and everyone felt settled. Now, nobody knows what tomorrow will bring."

Tomorrow, so far as the government was concerned, brought a struggle for power within the Convention itself, a treacherous assault upon Robespierre and his colleagues. On the 10th Thermidor, July 28th, the leader whose integrity and convictions we so much respected, however ruthless his methods, was sent to the guillotine within twenty-four hours of his arrest. The people of Paris, whom he had protected against invasion without and rebellion within for so many months, made no effort to save him.

The death of Robespierre and his friends was a signal for the relaxation of the many rules and restrictions without which the nation could never have survived. The moderates were back again. The Law of the Maximum was repealed. Prices and wages soared. Those with royalist sympathies began to talk openly of a return, before long, to the ways of the old régime and the restoration of the monarchy. The Jacobins everywhere lost their positions of authority, and this was reflected in the municipalities of the various districts throughout the country. "Progressives" were out of favour, not only with officials but amongst the workpeople too, and men like my brother Michel, who had openly supported the rigorous measures of Robespierre, were called the "enragés"—terrorists—and in some cases were arrested simply for this reason.

The halt in the forward movement of the revolution, and the fall from power of the Jacobins, profoundly shocked Michel. Just as his faith in human nature had been shattered when my brother Robert emigrated, so now his belief in the revolution received a similar blow. His pride suffered too. Michel Busson-Challoir had become someone of consequence in the district during the past few years, a figure to be reckoned with, possessing considerable power over his neighbours. Now, because of a switch in government policy, all this must be abandoned. He was suddenly no one—a master glass-blower whose business was not even flourishing, and about whom his own workmen muttered spiteful slander behind his back. As the date for the renewal of the lease approached I guessed, with a heavy heart, how it would go.

"We're not only losing money," said François, "we're losing the confidence of the trade as well. If we try to continue, under present circumstances, we shall end as bankrupt as your brother Robert, though for different reasons."

"What's the answer, then?" I asked. "Where are we to go?"

I could tell by my husband's face that he was not sure of my agreement with his plans.

"My brother Jacques has been suggesting for months that I should go into business with him at Mondoubleau," he said. "We could share his house—there is plenty of room. Then, in a few years' time, we could retire to our little property at le Gué de Launay."

"What about Michel?"

"Michel must fend for himself. We've already discussed it. He talks of going to Vendôme. There are several ex-Jacobins living there with whom he is in touch, though they are lying low at the present time. Whether he thinks of forming some sort of society with them or not, I cannot say. Michel is not very communicative these days."

Once, had he admitted so much, François would have said this with a sigh. Now he picked up our daughter Zoë, some fifteen months old, and jigged and danced her on his knee without further thought of his associate and comrade. Time had come between them. Or perhaps the Vendéans. When my brother marched his workmen off to war the year before, leaving my husband at home, something had been shattered.

"If this is how it has to be," I said to François now, "nothing I can say or do will make any difference. I'll come with you to Mondoubleau. But let it be, as you say, for a few years only."

I went out and stood in the orchard. It was a good year for apples, and our old trees were laden. We had the ladder up against one of them and a basket, half-filled, below. In my mother's day the little apple-house at the far end of the orchard would be stacked from one year's end to the other, and the apples for the house chosen in strict rotation, so that the ones which kept the longest would be eaten when the fresh fruit on the trees was ready to pick again.

Le Chesne-Bidault had been my home for over sixteen years. I had come here with my parents, my brothers and sister, when I was a girl of fifteen. I had continued to live here as a bride. Now, with my thirty-first birthday approaching, only a few days after the date when the lease for le Chesne-Bidault would be rejected, I must prepare myself to pack up our possessions and say good-bye. I stood there, tears pricking behind my eyes, and someone came softly behind me and put his arm through mine. It was my brother Michel.

"Don't fret," he said. "We've had the b-best of it. Nothing perfect ever l-lasts. I learnt that l-long ago."

"We've been happy here, the three of us," I said, "though I spoilt it for you at times by jealousy."

"I never n-noticed it," he answered.

I wondered, thinking how much my husband must have borne in silence in order to spare his friend. Men have strange loyalties to one another.

"Perhaps," I said, "when times become more settled again, and trade improves, we can start up all over again somewhere else."

He shook his head. "No, Sophie," he said, "once we've made the b-break, it's b-better to abide by it. François will soon s-settle down, either in Mondoubleau or le G-Gué de Launay, and help you raise your f-family. As for myself, I'm a l-lone wolf, and always have been. It might have been b-better had I been killed in a scrap against the b-brigands. The people of the district would have given me a hero's b-burial."

I understood his bitterness. He was now thirty-eight, the best of his life behind him. Trained in glass, he knew no other trade. He had thrown himself whole-heartedly into the revolution, and his fellow-revolutionaries had abandoned him. I could foresee no happy future for him in Vendôme.

When the time to leave came, I went before the others. I could not bear to see my home stripped bare. Some of our possessions went to le Gué de Launay, to be cared for by our tenant until we lived there; the rest we gave to Pierre. Saying good-bye to the families was like saying good-bye to my own youth, and to part of life that was now shut away forever. The older ones that I knew were sad. The others seemed indifferent. If they could earn a living under the new leaseholder, a relative of the proprietor at Montmirail, it mattered little to them who lived in the master's house.

As I was driven away, with Zoë in my arms, I looked back over my shoulder to wave at François and Michel; the last thing I saw was the foundry chimney piercing the sky, a wreath of smoke above it. And that, I thought, is the break up of our family; the Bussons, father and sons, existed no more. The tradition was broken. What my father created had come to an end. My sons, if I should ever bear them, would be Duvals, bred to a different trade in a different age. Michel would never marry. Pierre's boys, brought up in haphazard fashion without education, would not turn to glass. The art would be lost, the knowledge that my father bequeathed to his sons wasted. I remembered Robert, an alien and an émigré. I wondered if he were dead, and if that second wife of his had borne him children.

My daughter Zoë put her hand up to my face and laughed, and I shut the past behind me, looking forward, with some misgiving, to a house in Mondoubleau that would not be my own.

Nearly a twelvemonth passed before the four of us, Pierre, Michel, Edmé and myself, were reunited once again, and, when we were, it was not a moment for rejoicing, but for sharing a common grief.

It was on the 5th Brumaire, of the Year III (the 26th of October, 1795, by the old calendar), when we were sitting down to dinner—François, my brother-in-law, and I, with Zoë promoted to a high chair at the table and my infant son Pierre-François asleep in his cradle above—that we heard the peal of the entrance bell, and then the sound of voices. François rose to his feet to investigate. Within a few minutes he was back again, his face grave, his eyes searching mine.

"It's young Marrion," he said, "from St. Christophe."

Marrion was the farmer my mother employed at l'Antinière to look after the farm and her few acres. There were two of them, father and son. Instantly I knew the worst, and it felt like a cold hand touching my heart.

"She's dead," I said.

François came at once to my side and put his arms about me.

"Yes," he said, "it happened yesterday, very suddenly. She was driving out from St. Christophe to l'Antinière to shut up the house for the winter, young Marrion with her, and they were just turning down from the road to the farm when she collapsed. He called to his father, and between them they carried her inside and laid her down on the bed. She complained of violent pain, and was sick. Marrion sent his son for the doctor at St. Paterne, but the boy had hardly left the house when she died."

Alone there, with the farmer. Not one of us with her. And, knowing my mother, I could see what must have happened. She must have felt unwell earlier in the day, but told no one of it. Determined to keep to her routine of closing the farmhouse in the early autumn and spending the winter months in her other small house in St. Christophe—or Rabriant, as it had been renamed in '92, when the saints were out of favour—she had set out from the village to put everything in order.

Shock numbed my emotion, and it was still too soon for tears. I went into the kitchen, where young Marrion was having his dinner, and questioned him.

"Yes," he agreed, "the citoyenne Busson looked pale when she left the village, but nothing would deter her from driving out to l'Antinière. She said she must look round just once, before the weather turned. She was obstinate, you understand. I said to my father afterwards—it's as though she knew."

Yes, I thought, she knew. Instinct warned her that it was to be for the last time. But instinct came too late. There was no time to look about her, only time to lie down upon her bed, and die.

Young Marrion told us there was to be an autopsy. The health officer for the district was to go out to l'Antinière this very afternoon to discover the cause of death.

It was too late for us to drive down to St. Christophe that evening. We decided to send word to Pierre and Edmé at Le Mans, and to make a start early the next day.

Someone, young Marrion said, had already gone from the village to tell my brother Michel at Vendôme.

It was one of those soft golden days that come sometimes in late autumn when the four of us gathered together at l'Antinière. Tomorrow the skies would cloud over and the wind come from the west, bringing the rain as it always did, stripping the last leaves from the trees and making the country all about us dreary. Today everything was mellow, tender, and the yellow-washed farmhouse in the fold of the hills hazy under the sun.

It was the sort of day my mother loved. I stood on the rise of the hill above the farmstead, on the very spot where she had been taken ill, young Marrion told me, and I had the strange impression that she was with me, holding my hand as she used to do when I was small. Death, instead of severing all ties, made family feeling stronger.

The health officer was waiting in the house, Michel at his side. My brother had grown thinner and paler since he had left le Chesne-Bidault. Presently Pierre and Edmé joined us, and my sister, who had never shed one tear during our three days of terror in Le Mans two years before, now burst out crying at the sight of me.

"Why didn't she send for us?" she asked. "Why didn't she tell us she was ill?"

"It was not her way," answered Pierre. "I was here only a few weeks past, but she never complained. Even young Jacques noticed nothing wrong."

Jacques was with one of our cousins, the Labbés, in St. Christophe, pending the decision about his future. It did not surprise me when Pierre instantly volunteered to be his guardian.

We stood in silence by my mother's body, while the health officer explained to us that the autopsy had shown the cause of death to be inflammation of the stomach, but of how long duration he could not say. He and his colleague had performed the autopsy in the farmer's lodging close by, and it was there that my mother's body lay, waiting burial. The officer had placed his official seals on the doors of l'Antinière itself, but he removed them now so that we could go inside and see for ourselves that nothing had been touched.

I had not cried before, but I did so now. The imprint of my mother was on everything we touched. Much she had given away to all four of us already, keeping for herself those things that reminded her most of my father and the life they had shared together.

St. Christophe might become Rabriant, Madame Busson a "citoyenne", kings, queens and princes go to their death and the whole country change; but my mother had held fast to her own timeless world. There was the old chest with the marble top, the walnut desk, the dozen silver plates she had served grand dinners upon when company came to the château of la Pierre. She had kept the eighteen goblets and the twenty-four crystal salt-cellars blown by Robert in his first days as a master, and in the writing-desk amongst her papers we found the closely-written copy of his procès for bankruptcy.

More intimate, as though she were with us still, was her easy chair before the fireplace, the card-table on which she played a solitary piquette, the music-stand— memory of days long past when we had our own choir at la Pierre and the workmen came to sing on feast-days—the dog-basket for Nou-Nou, the spaniel dead these many years, the parrot-cage for Pelée, one of the two parrots Pierre had brought home from Martinique in '69.

We went upstairs to the bedroom, and it was full of her presence—the bed with the green hangings which she had shared with my father, the tapestry on the wall, the fire-screen by the writing table. The clock on the chimney-piece, beside a silver goblet, my father's gold-topped cane and his golden snuff-box, given him by the marquis de Cherbon when he left Chérigny for la Pierre, her taffeta-silk umbrella, her bedside lamp . . .

"There is no such thing as time," whispered Edmé. "I'm back again at la Pierre. I'm three years old, and the bell is sounding in the foundry for the men to come off shift."

I think what moved us most was her wardrobe and the linen stacked neatly on the shelves within it. Linen that we had forgotten all about but that she had kept and treasured all these years, making do herself with a few worn sheets, the rest of it put away untouched that it might now form part of our inheritance. Embroidered sheets and napkins, table-cloths by the dozen. Petticoats, handkerchiefs, muslin bonnets of long out-dated fashion but exquisitely laundered and fresh, some hundred and twenty of them, laid on a shelf with roseleaves.

These things, so unexpected and incongruous in our troublous times, were an indictment of our age that reverenced nothing past and hated all things old.

"If you have finished your inspection of the citoyenne Busson's effects," said the health officer from behind us, "the authorities will make a proper inventory in due course. Meantime I must replace the seals."

We came out of our childhood world and were back again in Brumaire, Year III. Yet it seemed to me that I felt my mother's hand on both our shoulders as Edmé and I turned and left her room.

We buried her in the churchyard at St. Christophe beside her parents, Pierre Labbé and his wife Marie Soiné.

The five of us had an equal share in the inheritance, with the citoyen Lebrun, public notary for the département, representing young Jacques, in place of my émigré brother. These shares, drawn up into five lots, consisted of the various properties owned by my mother in the parish of St. Christophe. So that no one of us should own more than the other, the value of each of them was taken into account: whoever should find himself owner of Pierre Labbé's house in St. Christophe, for instance, would pay cash to whichever of us might hold the smaller properties. Then the notaries shuffled the names of the lots in a hat, and we all of us drew in turn.

Michel, who had no need of it, had the luck of the draw, finding himself possessor of my grandfather's house. He at once offered it to Pierre, who had drawn a small farm outside the village, and my brother from Le Mans, with three hearty boys of his own, a newly adopted nephew, and another baby expected within the month, was glad of the exchange. It was shortly after this that he left Le Mans and brought his family to live in St. Christophe, for unrest had started again in the west and there was constant fighting against the royalist irregular armies, or "chouans", as they were called, and Pierre dared not expose his family a second time to the horrors of civil war.

I drew the small farm la Grandinière and Edmé la Goupillière, and the notary public held l'Antinière for Jacques. We contined to lease the properties, for the dwelling-houses were no use to any of us.

The personal effects were put up for sale amongst the four of us, and we bid for those things each one of us valued the most. I know that Edmé and I shared out the linen, that Pierre, because of his growing family, bid for all the chairs, for the dog kennel and the parrot's cage that had no parrot in it, and Michel to my pleasure and my astonishment too, paid nearly 4000 livres for my father's golden snuff-box and his gold-topped cane.

"They're the f-first things I remember," he said afterwards. "Father would take the cane to Coudrecieux to church on S-Sundays, and when Mass was over stand outside ch-chatting to the curé, offering him snuff from that same snuff-box. It was the f-finest sight I've ever seen."

He pocketed the box, and smiled. Could it be, I wondered, that Michel, the son who had fought against parental authority from the beginning, was the one who all these years had loved my father most?

He looked across at Edmé, the other member of the family with no husband to consider. "What are your p-plans?" he asked her.

She shrugged her shoulders. The prospect of moving to St. Christophe did not attract her. If Pierre really intended to give up his position as public notary in Le Mans and live out there in a village, there would be no work for her. Domestic duties and a pack of boys might satisfy her sister-in-law, but Edmé Busson Pomard liked to use her brains.

"I have no plans," she answered, "unless you know of a new revolutionary party I could join."

Our mother's death, as it happened, had coincided with a fresh change of government in Paris. A royalist insurrection in the capital had been crushed a few weeks back by General Bonaparte, and on the very day my mother died the Convention wound up its sessions, and a Directoire of five ministers was given executive power. How they would govern the country nobody knew. The only men with any authority were the generals, Bonaparte above all, and they were too busy winning victories against our enemies abroad to sit in Paris.

"There're plenty of J-Jacobins in Vendôme," said Michel. "Hésine is there—he's to be c-commissaire under the Directoire. His idea is to work for the b-bringing back of Robespierre's Constitution of '93, and put an end to all these m-moderates and chouans. I know him well."

I could see a new light in Edmé's eyes. Robespierre had been her God, the Constitution laid down in '93 her breviary.

"He's going to p-publish a newspaper in Vendôme," Michel continued, "called *L'Echo des Hommes Libres*. Babeuf, the extremist, will write for it. He believes that all wealth, all p-property should be shared. Some men c-call it Communism. It s-sounds like a new faith, and one that I could believe in."

Suddenly he went to Edmé and held out his hands.

"Come to V-Vendôme, Aimée," he said, using the old pet name of childhood days. "Let's l-live together, and share our inheritance, and go on w-working for the revolution. I don't mind if they call me a t-terrorist, or an extremist, or a s-sacré Jacobin. That's what I always have b-been, and always will be."

"Me too," said Edmé.

They burst out laughing, and hugged each other like two children.

"It's a q-queer thing," said Michel, turning to me. "It must be something to do with l-living in a community all my life, but I'm lost without my own p-people about me. If Aimée comes to V-Vendôme it will be like living in the f-foundry once again."

I was happy for the two of them. The future, which had seemed so bleak and dreary for both, now had a purpose. It was strange that my mother's death should have brought them together, the two who were lonely, the two most like in feature to my father.

"If our politics don't succeed," said Edmé, "we'll take another foundry and go into partnership. I can do a man's work. You've only to ask Pierre."

"I've always known it," replied Michel, quickly jealous. "I d-don't have to ask anyone."

He frowned for a moment, as if struck by a sudden thought, and heaven knows from what hidden depths within him came his next suggestion.

"We might rent the f-foundry at Rougemont," he said, "and reinstate it in its old g-glory. Not for ourselves, but to share the p-profits with the workmen."

He did not choose la Brûlonnerie or Chérigny, or even la Pierre. He chose Rougemont, the foundry that had first brought ruin to Robert, and I knew that once again, without understanding why Michel sought to atone for his brother's fault.

"That's the answer," he repeated. "If our political c-comrades fail us we'll go into partnership, Aimée, and d-develop Rougemont together."

As it turned out, it was not so much that Michel's comrades failed him as that their ideas of a people's sovereignty, with all things shared in common, displeased the corrupt Directoire to such an extent that some eighteen months later Gracchus Babeuf, the originator of these ideas, was condemned to death, and Hésine, the editor of *L'Echo des Hommes Libres,* imprisoned.

How Michel and Edmé escaped imprisonment themselves I never discovered. That both of them were deeply implicated in all that concerned Hésine and his associates was common knowledge in Vendôme, but François and I, with our growing family, were more concerned to keep out of politics and trouble than risk everything for a lost cause.

We settled in our small property at le Gué de Launay, outside Vibraye, in November 1799, just after Bonaparte's coup d'état in Paris and his subsequent appointment as First Consul. It was in this same year that Michel and Edmé, pooling their joint inheritance from my mother, entered into partnership at Rougemont.

The project was doomed to failure—we all of us knew it. Pierre, living in St. Christophe, his brood of boys enriched at last by the birth of a daughter named—so characteristic of Pierre—Pivione Belle-de-Nuit, warned both of them that any attempt to resurrect a glass-house the size of Rougemont, which had completely fallen into disrepair, would have small hope of success unless backed by vast capital sums.

Michel and Edmé would not listen to Pierre, or to anyone. A glass-house, where the workmen and the masters shared the profits, was their dream, and they pursued their dream for nearly three years, until, in March, 1802, they were forced to abandon it. Like other ideals, before and since, like the revolution itself and its spirit of equality and brotherly love, the attempt to put it into practice failed.

"He has ruined himself, and he has ruined your sister too," said my husband François, now the mayor of Vibraye and father of two sons, Pierre-François and Alphonse-Cyprien, besides our daughter Zoë. "Michel will be obliged to take some beggarly employment as manager of a small foundry, and Edmé either housekeep for him, or exist on a few acres in St. Christophe. They have thrown everything away, and are left without fortune or future."

François had been successful; they had failed. Despite the happiness we enjoyed, François and myself, with our little property and our growing sons and daughter, there was something about our smug complacency that made me secretly ashamed.

It was a few months after this, when the First Consul had signed the Treaty of Amiens, so bringing about a truce at last between France and England, that I was in our garden with the children, seeing to the bedding out of some plants in front of the windows of the salon, when my eldest son, Pierre-François, came running up from the drive with his sister to tell me that a man was looking through the entrance gate, asking for Madame Duval.

"What sort of man?" I asked.

We still had vagrants on the road from time to time, deserters from the remnant of the chouan armies, and as we lived some little distance out of Vibraye I did not care much for strangers when François was absent.

My daughter Zoë, now about nine years old, spoke for her brother.

"I can tell you he wasn't a beggar, mama," she said. "He took off his hat when he spoke to me, and bowed."

The gardener was within hailing distance should I need him, and I walked down the drive, followed by the children.

The stranger was tall and lean, and his clothes hung about him as though he had lost weight through recent illness. They had a foreign cut about them, as did his dusty, squared-toed shoes. Spectacles concealed his eyes, and I could tell by the unnatural brightness of his reddish hair that it was dyed. I guessed him to be a travelling salesman, from the bag he had set down by the gate, who hoped to persuade me to buy trash.

"I'm sorry," I said, intending to drive him off by my severity, "but we have everything we need here for the household. . . ."

"I'm glad of that," he answered, "for I can contribute nothing. I have only one clean shirt in my bag, and my father's goblet, unbroken."

He took off his spectacles and held out his arms.

"I told you I'd never forget you, Sophie," he said. "I've come home to you, just as I promised."

It was my brother Robert.

PART FOUR

The Emigré

18

THE FIRST SHOCK, so Robert said, came just five months after their arrival in England. Everything had gone well during the early months. His employers at the Whitefriars Glass Manufactury, known to him of old during the days when he had held the position of first engraver in crystal at the foundry in St. Cloud, and to whom he had written asking for work before leaving France in December '89, welcomed him with courtesy and kindness, and had arranged lodging for him and his wife in Whitefriars close by.

The knowledge that he was free of debt, had no responsibility, and was in every sense starting life anew with his young wife, with whom he was much in love, made Robert ignore the small pin-pricks and irritants almost inevitably inherent in the position of anyone starting out to make a living for himself in a strange country. The language, the customs, the food, even the climate, which would probably have daunted Pierre and Michel, more tenacious in their way of life than their elder brother, he accepted as amusing, and a challenge to his own powers of assimilation. It delighted him to plunge immediately into English colloquialisms with a total disregard for grammar, to slap his fellow-workmen on the back, English fashion, to drink his grog and his ale, and to show himself in every way perfectly at home and quite unlike the frizzed and perfumed Frenchmen lampooned in the English newspapers.

Marie-Françoise, left alone most of the day in the lodgings, and obliged to do the household shopping without a word of English, was more overcome. But youth, good health, and a wide-eyed admiration for everything her husband said and did soon found her echoing his phrases, praising the Londoners for their good humour, and declaring that she saw more life on Thames-side than she had ever done in twenty-one years in Paris—which, as almost all of them had been spent in an orphanage in St. Cloud, was not surprising.

As far as his work was concerned—he was employed as engraver in crystal— Robert soon discovered that he had nothing to learn from his associates. Equally, he could not boast of any superiority in technique. The standard at the glass-works in Whitefriars was high. It had been founded as long ago as 1680, and the flint glass made there was famous throughout Europe. There was no question of a Frenchman crossing the Channel to teach his trade to English craftsmen; the contrary was the more likely, and Robert was quick enough to tone down any little hint of patronage that might have risen to the surface in his first attitude of bonhomie to all.

A lively interest, though much ignorance, about recent affairs in France was shown by the cockneys, both at the glass-works in Whitefriars and amongst his fellow-lodgers; and here Robert was pleased to show himself supreme authority, once he had mastered enough English to make himself understood.

"It takes more than a few months to set right the abuses of five hundred years," he would declare, whether it was in a chop-house near Thames-side or in his landlady's front parlour. "Our feudal system was as out of date as your moated castles and barons would be today. Give us time, and we may accomplish great things. Providing our

King adapts himself to the mood of the people. If not"—here, he told me, he would pause significantly—"if not, then we may replace him with an abler and more popular prince."

He was referring, naturally, to his patron the duc d'Orléans, whose arrival in England the previous October had contributed largely to Robert's own decision to try his luck across the Channel.

He soon found, however, that Chapel Street was very different from the Palais-Royal. The arcades of the latter had been my brother's home and place of business; he had been free to come and go at will, to exchange gossip and chat with the throng of minor officials, busy-bodies, secretaries and personal aides that went to make up the entourage of the duc d'Orléans. At the Palais-Royal a whisper to the right person, a hint about favours given and received, would bring results. The very sense of being on the fringe of a society close to the most popular man in Paris had added enormously to Robert's self-esteem.

There was none of this in London. Laclos, Captain Clarke, the duc d'Orléans' valet and one or two others, including, of course, his mistress Madame de Buffon, were the only members of his personal circle whom the prince had brought with him to England. The servants in the furnished house in Chapel Street were English. Stately footmen answered the front door and stared blankly at any intruder upon the step. There was none of the coming and going, the free enter-as-you-will atmosphere of the Palais-Royal; and Robert, when he called for the first time soon after his arrival in London, was allowed to leave his card with the footman but was not invited within.

He called again, with the same result. The third time he wrote a personal letter to Laclos, and after a week or more received a laconic reply to the effect that, should the duc d'Orléans or his staff require any private business done for them during their temporary sojourn in England, Monsieur Busson would be informed.

Here was a rebuff, but Robert was undaunted. He took to frequenting the ale-houses in the immediate neighbourhood of Chapel Street, in the hope of meeting with someone or other, whether it was the valet or the barber, who might give him more definite news of the duc d'Orléans' intentions. He had some small success in learning that his patron was privately sounding the English Cabinet as to their objections or approval should he accept, if it were offered to him, the crown of Belgium. This, my brother insisted, was more than rumour. Full of optimism, as usual, he returned to Marie-Françoise with much talk of Brussels as a possible future home instead of London.

"If the duc d'Orléans becomes Philippe I, King of the Belgians," Robert told his young wife, "he will need a very large staff indeed. There is no question but that I shall obtain some sort of position."

"But can you leave the Whitefriars foundry so abruptly?" she asked. "Have you not signed papers agreeing to be employed by them for several months?"

He waved her question aside. "If I wish to leave Whitefriars I can do so tomorrow," he told her. "I only took on the work to tide over these present months. As soon as the duc d'Orléans has need of me he will send for me, and if it's a case of going to Brussels, to Brussels we shall go. There would be great possibilities in serving a new monarch, and our future would be assured."

The duc d'Orléans' expectations, and my brother's with them, were doomed to disappointment. The trouble in the Pays-Bas was short-lived, and the Austrians re-entered Brussels at the end of February.

Once again Robert presented his card in Chapel Street, and once again he was told that his prince and patron was at the races. The loss of a possible crown did not appear to have interfered with the duc d'Orléans' routine. The big shock came when, just as suddenly as he had left Paris for London the preceding year, so without warning, on the 8th of July, 1790, the duc d'Orléans quitted London for Paris, with, it would seem, nothing achieved politically between the two countries and little to show for his nine months' sojourn but plenty of entertainment and the sale of a number of race-horses. My brother was not even aware of the prince's decision to return home until he saw the news in a London newspaper.

He rushed to Chapel Street forthwith, and found the usual aftermath of departure— sheets already on the furniture, and the servants who had not already been paid off sweeping away the straw from packing-cases and grumbling at the master and mistress whom they had so lately served.

No, he learnt, there was no question of their return. The duc d'Orléans had left London for good.

This sudden departure had a profound effect upon my brother. He now realised, with a sense of finality, that neither the duc d'Orléans, nor any of his close associates, had any influence out of France, and that even in his own country the likelihood of the prince being appointed Regent or holding high office in the National Assembly was now remote. The temperament of the duc d'Orléans himself lacked fire and energy. He was not "cut out", as the English put it, to become a true leader of the French people.

Robert's adulation, almost idolatry, for his so-called patron turned to contempt. The qualities of amiability and generosity, so praised before, were now despised. The duc d'Orléans was a weakling, flattered by a self-seeking entourage, and those men he should have depended upon—amongst whom my brother included himself—had been spurned, their faith abused.

Robert, a confessed bankrupt in Paris, and likely to be imprisoned for debt if he set foot in the capital again, could not return to his own country. He must continue to build up what reputation he could for himelf in London, and stay content as an engraver in crystal to his employers in Whitefriars.

As the months passed, and his young wife became pregnant, London no longer seemed an enchanted city full of promise. Promotion might come to his English fellow-craftsmen, but as a foreigner Robert must count himself lucky to be employed at all.

The first-born of his second marriage, a son whom they named Robert, was born in the late spring of '91, shortly before the flight of Louis XVI and Marie Antoinette to Varennes which shocked and outraged us all so much at home. In London, Robert said, the people were equally shocked, but for a different reason. Sympathy was for the injured French monarch and his Queen, forced to seek asylum beyond the frontier; and when they were apprehended and brought back to Paris there was scarcely a man in London who did not praise the dignity and resignation of the royal family, and hurl abuse against the French Assembly.

"It was impossible," Robert told me, "not to see the venture with their eyes. The account of the flight was in all their newspapers. People talked of nothing else in the ale-houses and at work, and, knowing where I came from, they accused all French-men of treating their king like a common criminal. I knew nothing of the true circumstances. What could I do but agree? The Assembly, I explained, had got into the hands of hotheads and irresponsibles who were only seeking their own advantage, to which the cockneys countered, 'The more fools the French people to allow themselves to be so led. Such a state of affairs would never be permitted in England. In England there was too much common sense. The French were a nation of hysterics.' This was the attitude."

Almost immediately after the flight to Varennes came the flood of émigrés to England, all telling the same tale of goods sequestered, châteaux seized, clergy and aristocracy molested, a general persecution of all who had held any sort of position under the old régime. The English, always eager to hear anything to the detriment of their old enemy across the Channel, magnified each story of distress into wholesale condemnation of the revolution that had apparently convulsed all France.

"You must understand," said Robert, "that already in '91 the émigrés were painting a picture of desolation. It was not just Paris that had become impossible, but the entire country. There was no law, no order, no food; false money was floated to disguise economic failure, and the peasants were setting fire to every village. When you were peacefully giving birth to your daughter at le Chesne-Bidault, the one you have told me later died, and François and Michel were buying church lands and enriching themselves for the future, I saw the foundry in flames, and all of you in prison. My country, and you with it, had been seized by bandits. That was how we learnt to look at it from London."

These first émigrés, during the summer and autumn of '91, and on into the winter of '92, were mostly members of the former aristocracy and the clergy who could not, or would not, adapt themselves to the new régime. Fresh from his rebuff by Laclos and the Orléans faction, my brother hastened to make himself agreeable to the enemies of his former patron—persons close to Court circles, devoted to the King and Queen and to the King's two brothers, the comte de Provence and the comte d'Artois. As an émigré himself of more than two years' standing, Robert had some advantage over the newcomers. He could speak English, he knew the ways and customs, he was adept at acting as intermediary in negotiations between his bewildered compatriots on the one hand and the jocular cockneys on the other.

As courier, as inspector of furnished houses and apartments, as the friend-in-need who could arrange purchases at low prices without any difficulty, my brother was in his element. Marquises, countesses and duchesses, exhausted from fearful Channel crossings by way of Brittany or Jersey, would be enchanted to find a fellow-countryman who could so swiftly put them at their ease after their trials. His sympathy, his charm and his delightful manner made the ordeal of arriving in a strange country far easier to bear. Some small recompense might be forthcoming, of course, after they had settled down; meanwhile, possibly the people at the Embassy would take care of it. As to private arrangements, matters of percentages and so on, between the courier and the various London tradesmen and the vendors of furnished apartments, that was a matter with which the new émigrés need not concern themselves.

It soon became evident that to combine the work of an engraver in crystal at Whitefriars with his new status as courier to the élite of the former Parisian society would be difficult, if not an impossible, task. My brother, with his gambler's instinct, chose to sever his connection with the Whitefriars foundry and throw in his lot entirely with the newcomers, or, as he put it to his employers, with his distressed fellow-countrymen. This was, like almost all Robert's ventures, a mistake, and one which—within a few years—he was profoundly to regret.

"I chanced my luck," he said, "and my luck lasted just as long as the funds the émigrés brought with them. When, instead of finding themselves in London for six months or a year, fêted by the English and treated as heroes and heroines, they discovered that they were paupers forced to accept English charity without any prospect of returning to their own country, their luck ran out, and so did mine. I was not to know in '91 that in January '93 the Assembly in Paris would give place to the Convention, that the King would be condemned to death, and that the Allies, in whom all us in England had put our faith, would be repulsed by that citizen army we had been laughing at for months."

The émigrés, my brother amongst them, who had lived in almost daily expectation of a triumphant Allied invasion—the entry of the duke of Brunswick's forces into Paris, followed by the overthrow of the Convention, the restoration of Louis and the mass punishment of every revolutionary leader—found, to their horror and consternation, that none of this came about. The Republic, threatened on all sides, stood firm. The King went to the guillotine. Any émigré who dared to set foot in France would suffer the same fate, as a traitor to his country; and unless they chose to join their fellow-royalists in the Prince de Condé's army, the émigrés must accept their status as refugees in a country that, by the spring of '93, was actively at war with their own.

"The honeymoon was over," said Robert. "Not my own—that had ended after the first year—but the honeymoon of the French émigrés with the English people. We had not only killed our King—we were accused of this just as though we had voted for his death in the Convention—but we were members of the enemy. Any one amongst us might have been a spy. The favours, the generosity, the courtesy, the welcome, all this went after the declaration of war. We were no longer part of London society, except those notables who really had a foothold amongst the first English families. The rest of us, as I have said, were refugees, with little money left, no prospect of employment, obliged to give an account of ourselves whenever questioned, and treated as a general nuisance by all concerned."

The manufacturers of Whitefriars Glass regretted that they already had more than enough engravers in crystal on their books, and Robert's place had long ago been filled. In any event, times had changed. French craftsmen were no longer popular with the English workmen.

"I walked the streets as many of us did, looking for work," confessed Robert. "My English helped, and after several weeks I managed to obtain a place as packer in a glass and china warehouse, in Long Acre—the sort of work I used to give to porters when I had my laboratory in the rue Traversière. In the evenings I taught English at a school in Sommerstown, Pancras, founded by one of our émigré priests, the Abbé Carron. We had moved lodgings several times, and were by this time housed at 24, Cleveland Street, with a crowd of other émigrés. The parish of Pancras was full of French families; it was almost like living in the Bonne-Nouvelle or the Poissonnière, and we had our own schools, and our own chapel in Conway Street, off Fitzroy Square."

Marie-Françoise, despite her lack of education—she still could not sign her own name—adapted herself to changing circumstances as gallantly as Cathie would have done, perhaps more so, for her upbringing in an orphanage had made her hardy, and used to restrictions.

"She kept reminding me of Cathie," Robert admitted "not only in her looks but in her ways as well. Sometimes—and you won't understand this, Sophie—I would find myself living a fantasy, a recreation of the past, and Cleveland Street became St. Cloud at the time when Cathie and I were living there together. In '93, when our second son was born, we called him Jacques. It made the fantasy more real."

He never told Marie-Françoise about her predecessor, nor of the other Jacques, some twelve years old by now, living with his grandmother at St. Christophe. The lie that Robert was a bachelor, without ties, started as a jest, had developed into a supreme deception, and along with it grew a mounting fabrication of untruths, with so many devious strings that they could not be unravelled.

"I myself began to believe what I had told her," Robert said, "and those fantasies were a consolation in times of trouble. The château between Le Mans and Angers to which I was heir, owned by an elder brother who detested me, became as real to me, and to her, and presently to our growing children, as if it had existed in reality. It was a mixture of Chérigny and la Pierre, the places where I was happiest as a boy, and of course had its glass-house beside it, for otherwise I could not explain my work as an engraver."

As the tide of emigration increased, with not only the aristocracy and the clergy seeking the safety of the English shores, but merchants and traders and members of the bourgeoisie as well, so my brother's fantasy took shape. In their parish of Pancras, or "Little Paris", as they called it, it seemed imperative to him, as one of the first-comers, to hold his status as a fervent loyalist to the King who had been dethroned, and later to the comte de Provence, whom the émigrés called Louis XVIII. His old patron the duc d'Orléans, self-styled Philippe Egalité when he took his seat in the Convention, and one of the deputies who voted for his cousin's death, was perhaps the most hated man in Pancras. Robert was careful to impress upon his wife that she must never mention his earlier connection with the Orléans entourage and the Palais-Royal.

"In any event," he told her, "I only moved on the fringe of that society. I was not deeply involved. Their politics were suspect from the start."

This was a volte-face which must have surprised even Marie-Françoise, and to make up for it he would embroider afresh upon his own past, dwelling upon the beauty of his birthplace, the tranquillity, the peace, all of which had been denied him so long because of the hostility of the mythical brother.

It was providential that nobody with any knowledge of Busson l'Aîné, the bankrupt of Villeneuve-St. Georges and the debtor and fraud of La Force prison, should be amongst those who had fled from France to England. As it was, Busson l'Aîné was no sort of designation for one who declared himself a member of the aristocracy, and Robert, following the example of his true brothers, Pierre and Michel, who had many years before taken the names of du Charme and Challoir to distinguish themselves from him, decided that it would increase his stature in the eyes of his fellow émigrés, and amongst the Londoners as well, if he too took a suffix.

He chose the name of his birthplace, the farmhouse Maurier, and on moving to 24, Cleveland Street, at the end of '93 signed himself thus—Busson du Maurier. His wife, and his neighbours also, understood "le Maurier" to be a château. As the months passed, and tales of "Robespierre's Terror" were wafted by spies across the Channel, with all the exaggerated horrors of innocents mounting the guillotine in thousands not only in Paris but in the provinces as well, my brother suited his fantasy to the times, and suddenly declared to his wife, and an admiring audience of horrified émigrés, that the château had been attacked by an army of peasants, all within it murdered, and the château itself burnt to the ground.

"I had to do it," Robert said. "It was becoming an encumbrance. And a danger too. I had not realised there was a real château Maurier in the parish of la Fontaine St. Martin, near la Flèche, belonging to the family d'Orveaux. One of this family, an officer who later joined the Prince de Condé's army at Coblenz, appeared in London, and on hearing my name called to claim relationship. I had the greatest difficulty in shaking him off. He might have exposed me. Luckily, we moved in different circles, and a few weeks later I heard that he had left the country."

The myth of belonging to the former aristocracy, the fantasy of the burnt-down château, these extravagances may have flattered my brother's egoism during the early wartime years when the émigrés of Pancras saw themselves doomed to many months of exile. But as one year passed and then another, with no sign of a break in hostilities, and the French armies winning victory after victory, the plight of the refugees in London worsened, and their sufferings became very real indeed.

"Our daughter Louise was born in '95," said Robert, "and another boy, Louis-Mathurin, in November of '97. That made four young mouths to feed, six counting ourselves, and seven with the young servant that Marie-Françoise had to help her with the children. We had the whole of the second floor of our lodging-house, and the old couple below us, the Dumants, used to complain of the children's noise. I would leave the house early, to go to my work in Carter's warehouse in Long Acre. I was away all day and—as I told you—would teach in the Abbé Carron's school in the evenings. Even so, I did not earn enough to keep us all or pay the rent. We had to accept assistance. There was a fund, an allocation for us émigrés, arranged between the English Treasury and our own officials. I was given £7 a month, starting in September of '97, just two months before young Louis-Mathurin was born. But it did not go far, and at times I was almost desperate."

My brother had an advantage over many of his fellow-émigrés in that he had been born to a trade, and had worked in glass from the age of fourteen. As foreman in the warehouse in Long Acre his talents were wasted, but at least he knew what he was about. Others were less fortunate. Counts and countesses, who had never worked in their lives, were now glad to pick up a few extra shillings by tailoring and dress-making, and one of the most popular "trades" in Pancras and Holborn was the fashioning of straw-hats by the émigrés for those Londoners who cared to patronise them.

"It became quite the thing," Robert said, "to walk from Oxford Street to Holborn to see where straw was cheapest. The pavements would be crowded by the marquis de this and the baron de that, all with bundles of straw under their arms to take back to their wives, who waited with bunches of ribbons and velvet flowers to decorate the finished article, after their husbands had twisted the straw into shape.

"Marie-Françoise was no modiste. Her talent lay in laundering, something she had learnt at the orphanage in St. Cloud. There was a wealthy middle-aged spinster called Miss Black, who lived round the corner from us in Fitzroy Square—she stood as godmother to Louis-Mathurin—and all her finery came to Cleveland Street to be washed and pressed and mended. Marie-Françoise did it herself, and then sent it back in a basket by the maidservant—it did not do for Madame Busson du Maurier to be seen carrying laundry in the street. The worst of it was, when I came to be away from her and the children for seven months, from July '98 to February '99, she had to arrange for friends to collect our allowance from the authorities, as she understood nothing of finance, and still could not sign her name. This added to her troubles."

When my brother reached thus far in his story he became purposely vague. He talked of "other business" that had concerned him during these months of absence, and avoided questions. No, he had not left the country, he had remained in London, although at another address. It had nothing to do with the war or with espionage or with any matter concerning the émigrés. I let it go, trusting he would tell me in his own good time. It was not until one evening a few days later, after he had shown the family goblet to my daughter Zoë and the boys, and I had put it away in a cabinet for safekeeping, that I learnt the truth.

"Those seven months," he said, "when I was absent from Cleveland Street, came about for the sake of that same glass."

He paused, watching my eyes.

"You had it copied," I suggested, "or worked on copies yourself, and this meant taking up employment in some foundry the other side of London?"

He shook his head. "Nothing so simple," he said. "The fact is, I was so pushed for money that I sold the glass to George Carter, my employer at the warehouse in Long Acre, and regretted doing so the instant I had sold it. It was no use buying it back, for the money he had given me in exchange went immediately on food, rent and other necessities for the children. There was only one thing to do, and with the keys of the warehouse in my possession it was the simplest thing in the world to achieve. I knew where the glass was packed, ready to dispatch to some firm in the north of England, in Staffordshire, and I returned to Long Acre one evening when the building was locked for the night, and let myself in. It took me only a matter of minutes to secure the glass, nail down the packing-case as though nothing had been disturbed, and let myself out again. Unfortunately I had mistimed the hours of the night-watchman. I understood that he came on duty at eleven o'clock. Instead, it was half-past ten. I walked straight into him as I left the building."

"'Anything wrong?' he asked.

"'Nothing at all,' I assured him. 'I had some business to do for Mr. Carter.'

"The fellow knew me, and accepted my tale, but when I went to the warehouse next morning I was summoned into the office by George Carter himself, and he had the empty packing-case on the floor beside him.

"'This is your work, isn't it?' he said.

"It was no use denying it. The glass had gone. I had the keys of the building. The night-watchman had seen me.

"'I shall summon you for trespass and theft,' he said, 'and to ensure that there is no chance of your giving me the slip I have the Sheriff's officer waiting to apprehend you. You will either return the glass or pay me the sum of £135 that I gave you for it.'

"I told him I would keep the glass and return the £135 as soon as I could raise it amongst my friends.

"'Your friends?' he said. 'What friends? A bunch of émigrés like yourself, fed and clothed by the charity of the English government. I'm afraid I haven't much respect for you or your friends, Mr. Busson Morier. If you can't produce the glass today, or its value in cash, you will be taken into custody and committed for trial. As to your wife and children, your so-called friends must take care of them.'

"There was no question of raising the money, no question of returning the glass. I could not even raise the money for bail, for not one amongst us could muster more than twenty pounds. The worst part about it was returning to Cleveland Street and breaking the news to Marie-Françoise.

"'Why not give him back the glass?' she asked me, bewildered that I would rather be arrested for debt and theft than surrender it. 'Robert, you must, for my sake and for the children's.'

"I would not agree. Call it sentiment and pride, and cursed obstinacy, but I kept seeing my father's face and the day he put the glass into my hands, and God knows I had let him down often enough in after years. I saw Michel, and you, Sophie, and Pierre, and my mother, and dear dead Cathie, and I knew that whatever happened to me I must not let the glass go."

Robert looked across the salon at the glass, safe at long last in the cabinet at le Gué de Launay.

"My father was right, you know," he said. "I misused my talents, so the glass brought me ill-luck. Endeavouring to sell it was the final insult to his memory, and to a perfect work of art. I had time enough to think about that during seven months in jail."

He smiled, and despite the lined face, the spectacles, and the dyed hair there was something of the old Robert in that smile.

"I should have been deported," he said, "but the Abbé Carron intervened. It was he who had my sentence reduced to seven months, and finally raised the money for my release in February of '99, about the time your General Bonaparte was winning victories against the Turks, with all of you applauding him here at home. Winter in Cleveland Street was bad enough, with the children ill with whooping-cough, and Marie-Françoise pregnant again and doing the laundry for Miss Black in Fitzroy Square. Yet to live as an alien debtor was harder still, confined in a cell about six by four, knowing that it was my own pride and my own folly that had brought me there."

My brother glanced about him, at the familiar furniture he had known at l'Antinière and le Chesne-Bidault.

"First La Force in Paris," he said, "and then King's bench in London. I've become an authority on prisons on both sides of the Channel. Something, I might add, I have no desire to hand down to my children. Nor will they ever know of it. Marie-Françoise will see to that. When I returned to Cleveland Street we told them that I had been on business in the country, and they were still too young to question further. She will bring them up to believe that their father was just, upright, a devoted royalist, and indeed the very soul of honour. She believes it herself, and is hardly likely to tell them otherwise."

He smiled again, as though this new image of himself was an excellent jest, as worthy in its way as that of the impoverished member of the former aristocracy.

"You talk," I said, "as if Marie-Françoise were already a widow, and you in your grave."

He stared at me a moment, then took off his spectacles and wiped them.

"She is a widow, Sophie," he said. "Officially I'm dead. The sick man with whom I voyaged across the Channel died just before we reached Le Havre. He died with my papers upon him. The authorities will notify our committee in London, who will break the news to Marie-Françoise. Bereft, with six children to rear and educate, the Abbé Carron and his helpers will do far more for her than I ever could. Don't you see, Sophie, it was the only way out? Shall we call it—my final gamble?"

19

I WAS THE only one to know my brother's secret, and I kept it even from my husband. François believed, and so did the others when they came to hear of his return, that Robert was a widower once more, his second wife having died in childbirth, as Cathie had done, during his first years as an émigré in London. It was bad enough that he had emigrated, thus forfeiting all respect and honour; but to have been imprisoned in London for debt, and to have left his wife and six young children to the mercy of others, was something that I knew very well my husband would not stomach, or my two brothers either.

Robert's action in allowing another man to be buried as himself was, I felt certain, a criminal one which—if it should be discovered—would mean yet a further term in prison, perhaps for years. I could not condone his crime, neither could I condemn him. His lined face, the pouches beneath his eyes, even the tremor of his hands, a disability that had come upon him after leaving King's Bench prison, proved to me how much he had suffered.

The dyed hair, an attempt to make himself look young but failing in its purpose, made me the more compassionate. I saw him as he was, a broken man, yet remembered the lovable boy, my mother's first-born. For the sake of her memory alone I could not betray him.

"What do you intend to do?" I asked him when he had been at home with us little more than a week, and François and I were still the only ones to know of his return. "Did you have anything in mind when you left London?"

"Nothing," he confessed, "only a profound desire to get away from England and come home. You don't know what it is, Sophie, to have mal du pays. I did not once. London, for the first few years, was almost as much of an adventure as Paris used to be when I lived there with Cathie. It was only when the war started and the people turned against us, followed by the horror of those seven months in prison, that I came to long for my own country—not Paris, but this."

We were in the garden at the time. It was summer, and the trees about us were in full leaf. Rain, during the night, had made the earth smell rich, and raindrops glistened on the petals of my roses and on the long grass below the gravel walk.

"Looking out through the bars of King's Bench at that sooty London sky," he said, "I would dream myself back at la Pierre and become a boy again. You remember when I was sworn in as master, and we processed from the glass-house to the château, and my mother wore her brocade gown and had powder on her hair? Looking up at her that day was the proudest moment of my life, and the time when she came to visit me at Rougemont. Where do they go, Sophie, those younger selves of ours? How do they vanish and dissolve?"

"They don't," I said. "They're with us always, like little shadows, ghosting us through life. I've been aware of mine, often enough, wearing a pinafore over my starched frock, chasing Edmé up and down the great staircase in la Pierre."

"Or in the forest," he said. "It was the forest I missed most. And the smell of charcoal from the foundry fire."

When Robert was released from prison no one would employ him, nor did he blame the Londoners for this. Why should they give work to an enemy alien, and a convicted thief? The Abbé Carron put him to sort library books in the schools, and this, with the allowance from the Treasury, kept Robert and his family from greater poverty still. Another baby, a girl, to whom he gave Cathie's second name Adelaide, was born when he was still in prison, and a son, Guillaume, eighteen months later.

"I tried to keep the children French," my brother told me, "but, although they lived in what was virtually a French colony, they were hybrids from the start. Robert became Bobbie, Jacques James, Louis-Mathurin liked his name to be pronounced Lewis when he was little more than four years old. And Marie-Françoise, her looks gone and her hopes for my ultimate success blighted forever, turned to religion for comfort. She was always on her knees, either in our lodgings, or around the corner in the French chapel in Conway Street. She had to cling to something, and I had failed her."

It was too late to reinstate himself in the eyes of his fellow-émigrés. They pitied him but they despised him too. Anyone who could sink to trespass and theft when existing on foreign charity could never again rise to a position of trust amongst them. My brother's one salvation was that the Abbé Carron did not despise him too.

"As Marie-Françoise and the children became more reconciled, or it would be more truthful to say more resigned, to our drab, hopeless future," Robert said, "so I yearned the more for France, for home. I began to feel a contempt for our émigré princes, for the comte d'Artois holding a petty court in Edinburgh, and for our king in Poland. Secretly I rejoiced in Bonaparte's victories—he was the leader we had needed all the time. The country which I had believed finished when I came to London was by now the strongest in Europe, and the most feared. Had I been younger, and more courageous, I believe I should have escaped somehow and crossed the seas to follow him."

As soon as the Treaty of Amiens was signed, and the amnesty granted to returning émigrés, my brother determined to come home. He had no thought then of deserting his wife and children. His idea was to seek me out, take counsel with Pierre and Michel, obtain some promise of employment, and then return to London to fetch his family home.

"Even as I said good-bye to them," he told me, "there, in our cramped lodging in Cleveland Street, I reverted to the old fantasy of the burnt-down château, of the splendours lost and gone. 'We'll rebuild,' I assured them, 'on the site of le Maurier, in the park, and found another glass-house where you, Bobbie and James, and Louis-Mathurin can work.' I half believed it myself as I told them this, and, although inwardly I knew it could never be, it might still be possible, I thought, when the time came, to create some sort of a home for them and so make up for the deception.

"'I'll see you,' I told them, 'in six months or less. In just as long as it will take me to arrange matters on the other side.' And, God forgive me, when I left Cleveland Street and mounted the coach for Southampton I felt all the burden and the trouble of the years slide away from me. Their faces dimmed almost as soon as I sniffed the salt air of the Channel, and once aboard the packet I had only one thought in my mind, and that was to feel French soil under my feet once more."

Even then Robert still looked upon his journey as an experiment. He had no other purpose but to explore the possibilities of settling in France again. It was not until the evening before landing that temptation, swift and instant, came to him when, in the small cabin that he was sharing, his fellow-passenger was seized with a sudden heart attack and died before a doctor's help could be sought.

"He lay there in my arms," he said to me, "this sick man, an émigré like all of us on the boat, known to nobody except by his papers. To change those papers, replacing them with my own, was a moment's work. To call for help, to report the death, to acquaint the port officials when the boat docked and to leave the burial arrangements to them, all that was easy. I left Le Havre a free man, Sophie. Free to pick up my old life again without ties or responsibilities. Not perhaps as a master glass-maker, but as something else, it does not matter what. I'm ambitious no longer, I only want to make up for the years I've missed. Above all, I want to see my son."

This was what he had been leading up to from the first. Once he had settled down under our roof at le Gué de Launay, his story told, his secret shared with me, it was Jacques who was foremost in his mind. His mother's death he had expected. Grief for her soon passed. Jacques had become the symbol of everything precious in that old life laid aside.

"I've already told you," I said, playing for time, "Jacques is a conscript in the republican army. He was called to the colours in April, on his twenty-first birthday, and he is attached to an infantry regiment, I don't know where. Not even Pierre could give you his exact whereabouts at the present time."

"But tell me about him," protested my brother. "How has he developed, whom is he like? Does he often talk of me?"

The first two questions were easy enough to answer.

"He has your eyes," I answered, "and your colouring. That much you know. He has Cathie's build, he is small, below middle height. As to his nature, I've always found him affectionate and loyal. He is much attached to Pierre and to Pierre's boys."

"Is he intelligent and quick?"

"I would not call him quick. Conscientious would be the better word. He's taken to life in the army, judging by his letters home, and the officers speak well of him."

Robert nodded, pleased. I knew that for him Jacques was still a merry boy of eight, clamouring to help with the harvest in the fields of l'Antinière that summer of '89.

"If he is like Cathie in nature we shall get on famously," he said. "Surely now we are at peace they might let him home on leave, on compassionate grounds, to see his father?"

I was silent. Had my brother's desire to see his son blunted perception?

"You forget," I said after a moment, "that the republican army has been fighting England, the Allies and you émigrés for nine years. A sudden peace may suit the Consul and his government, but it doesn't make the soldiers who fought the battles the less bitter. You can hardly expect the commanding officer of Jacques's regiment to send a conscript home because of you."

Now it was his turn for silence. "You're very right," he said at length. "Now that I'm home I forget I was ever away. I must be patient, that is all."

He sighed and turned to go indoors, and I noticed, not for the first time, how humped his shoulders had become in these last years; he had the stoop of an old man, and he was not yet fifty-three.

"Besides," I called after him, "it would not do to call attention to your presence here, since you are officially dead."

He gestured, as if this did not concern him.

"Dead to those in London, perhaps," he said, "and to the port officials at Le Havre. Nobody else is likely to interest himself in another broken-down émigré come to end his days amongst his family."

The meeting with Jacques was thus postponed, for I was not lying when I told Robert that neither Pierre nor I knew where the battalion was stationed. Jacques might be anywhere—Italy, Egypt, Turkey—and the signing of peace treaties would not guarantee his return home.

"If I can't see my son," said Robert, "I can at least see my brothers. Are you not going to write to them and tell them that the prodigal has returned?"

Once again, I felt that he lacked perception. My welcome, because I loved him, was no surety for the feelings of the rest of us. François was noticeably cool, which Robert accepted because he had never known him well. As for my children, they were too young to form opinions, and seeing my fondness for this sudden long-lost uncle they took their lead from me.

But Edmé and Michel. . . . That was another matter. The pair of them, their inheritance and savings sunk in the Rougemont foundry and so lost, as I have said, were at present living on the borders of Sarthe and Orne, not far from Alençon. Michel had a position as manager of a small foundry there, and Edmé kept house for him. How long this would continue we did not know. Michel already showed signs of bronchial trouble, the dread disease of every glass-blower, which would, before very long, put an end to active work, if not to his life as well. I had seen too much of it in old days amongst our craftsmen at le Chesne-Bidault not to recognise the symptoms—the unhealthy pallor, the shortness of breath, the tight dry cough. Once the disease took hold, the end came quickly. It did not bear thinking about. I used to put it from my mind, and so did Edmé, but we were not deceived.

A letter, warning us of their approaching visit, came in the last days of July. Edmé had heard tell of a good doctor in Le Mans who was knowledgeable about chest diseases. The summer weather, with the warm winds blowing grass and pollen, had increased the severity of Michel's cough and his shortness of breath. Edmé had persuaded him to take a few days' absence from work, and they were to proceed to Le Mans, and would spend the night with us on their return.

"What shall I do?" I asked François. "Shall I be blunt with them and tell the truth? That Robert has come home?"

"They won't come here if you do," he answered. "I have not forgotten, if you have, what Michel said about his émigré brother. He told me once that Robert would be better dead, and that was the end of it. Certainly warn them, so that they may make a change in plans. I don't want a fight under my own roof. As it is, I find myself in considerable embarrassment because of your brother's presence here. It's hardly becoming in the mayor of Vibraye to house an émigré, relative or not. I think you don't always realise what is due to my position."

I realised too well. The years that had dealt so kindly with my husband's face and fortune had not graced him with humility or compassion. I loved him still, but he was a world away from the young man in the uniform of the National Guard singing "Ça Ira", who used to follow Michel on forays in '91.

"I'll write to Edmé," I said, "and to Michel too. It's best that they should know Robert is here, and so keep away."

The letter was dispatched. A week passed, and also the date that Edmé and Michel were due to visit the doctor in Le Mans. I expected to hear the result of the visit on their return to Alençon, with comment, perhaps, on Robert's presence. I did not expect the sound of wheels on our gravel drive one afternoon, and the sight of the hired 'chaise outside the windows, with first Michel and then Edmé descending from it.

Robert, who was reading, laid down his book and spectacles.

"Were you expecting visitors," he enquired, "or does monsieur le maire perform his duties at home as well as at Vibraye?"

There was little love lost between him and my husband, but the pinprick did not rouse me on this day. I was too much concerned about the others.

"It's Edmé and Michel," I said quickly. "I'll greet them, you stay here."

His face lit up, and he rose to his feet. Then, seeing my expression, his smile vanished. Slowly he sat down again.

"I understand," he said, "you don't have to tell me."

He was not so lacking in perception after all. François, perhaps, had been more explicit than I had realised.

I went out of the salon and into the entrance hall. Edmé was there before me. Michel was still without, paying off the driver.

"You didn't expect us," she said at once. "You were right, we had decided otherwise. Then, after seeing the doctor, Michel changed his mind."

I looked at her. The question was in my eyes.

"Yes," she answered, "what we feared. He can't get better. . . ."

She showed no emotion on her face. Only her voice betrayed her.

"It may be six months," she said, "or even less. He took it well. He insists that he will go on working until the end, and it's better so."

She said no more, for at this moment Michel came into the hall. I was startled by the alteration in his appearance since I had seen him last, a few months back. His face was grey and pinched, and he walked with little shuffling steps. When he spoke the breath came short, as though the effort hurt him.

"We can p-put up at Vibraye if you have no room for us," he said. "My f-fault, as Aimée will have told you. I ch-changed my mind."

I put my arms round him. The square stalwart figure had become suddenly small.

"You know there's room for you," I answered, "tonight and always, should you want it."

"Only t-tonight," he said. "Tomorrow I must get b-back to work again. Is Robert here?"

I glanced at Edmé and she nodded, then dropped her eyes.

"Where are the children?" she asked. "Shall I go and find them?"

My sister, no great lover of young people under the age of twelve, must have needed the excuse. Michel might have changed his mind about coming to le Gué de Launay, but she had not.

"As you please," I told her. "They are somewhere in the garden. Come, Michel."

I put my arm through his and opened the door of the salon. On the instant I was back again to that moment, thirteen years before, when he and I had walked out of the laboratory in the rue Traversière.

Robert, standing by the window of my salon, nervous, watchful, ready to match his mood to his brother's whatever it should be, whether mocking or aggressive, was not prepared, in fact, for what he saw. The angry fanatic with his shock of dark unruly hair had gone forever. The sick man, who stood with his arm in mine, had lost his fire.

"Hullo, mon b-brave," said Michel.

This was all. He shuffled towards Robert, holding out his arms. I went out of the room, leaving them alone, and shut myself upstairs until my tears had dried.

François was kept in Vibraye that day until after we had dined, and I was glad of it, for it meant that the four of us could be together. It was only Pierre we lacked to make my family complete.

Edmé, cool at first, holding out a stiff formal hand to Robert, which he kissed in mock solemnity, then flung aside to take her in his arms, soon found it hard to withstand the old gaiety, the old forgotten charm. She followed Michel's lead, through love of him, I think, more than anything else, knowing as I did that the occasion was almost certainly unique, never to be repeated. As to Michel, whether his own death sentence had blotted out resentment I do not know; but remembering how he had felt, and spoken too, during the years since Robert left us, it was a miracle this day to see how he had mellowed.

They say death does this to us once we are warned. Unconsciously, we strive not to waste time. Pettiness falls away, with all those things of little value in our lives. Could we but have known sooner, we tell ourselves, it would have been otherwise; no anger, no destruction, above everything no pride.

At dinner Robert kept us entertained with stories of cockney London, mocking the city that had sheltered him, along with its inhabitants and his own fellow-émigrés, in merciless disregard of any help they may have give him. But as we moved back into the salon afterwards he suddenly said, "But why, mon vieux, are you killing yourself as manager in a scrubby little foundry near Alençon when you might have taken the lease of some place like la Pierre? You could surely have done so, with our mother's inheritance, and what you had made besides out of church lands?"

My heart sank. This topic might lead us to the drama I had dreaded before they came. There was no time, though, to leave the room on some excuse. Robert had firmly shut the door behind him as we entered.

Michel walked slowly to the hearth-rug, and stood with his hands berhind his back. He had taken wine at dinner, and two spots of colour showed on his grey, sick face.

"I had n-no alternative," he replied at last. "Aimée and I went into p-partnership together in the Year VII. We lost everything we p-possessed."

Robert raised his eyebrows.

"Then I'm not the only gambler in the family after all," he said. "What in the world induced you to take the risk?"

Michel paused a moment. "Y-you did," he said.

Robert, bewildered, looked from him to Edmé.

"I did?" he asked. "How could I have possibly done such a thing when you were over here and I in London?"

"You m-misunderstand me," answered MIchel. "It was the th-thought of you which induced me, that's all. I wanted to succeed where you had f-failed. I did not d-do so. I think the answer is that we both of us, you and I, l-lack not only our father's t-talent, but his courage as well. I shall leave no children, but your J-Jacques may pass on both qualities to p-posterity."

Not necessarily Jacques, I thought. There were the children abandoned in London, who might do the same.

"Where did you lose your money?" asked Robert.

"At R-Rougemont," answered Michel.

I shall never forget the look on Robert's face. Incredulity passed to admiration, then to pity, then to shame.

"I'm sorry," he said. "I would have warned you had I known."

"Don't be sorry," answered Michel. "It was all experience. I've learnt my l-limitations, and the country's too."

"The country's?"

"Yes. Our p-plan was to share our p-profits with the workmen. Perhaps you haven't heard of Gracchus B-Babeuf, who killed himself rather than be g-guillotined? He believed that all wealth and p-property should be shared amongst the people. He was a f-friend of mine."

Our émigré, spectacles in hand, stared back at his youngest brother open-mouthed. It was not just thirteen years that stood between them, but a century of ideas as well. King's Bench prison might have taught him some humility, but his world was still the world of '89; Michel's and Edmé's belonged to a future we should never live to see.

"In other words," said Robert slowly, "you gambled on a dream."

"P-put it that way if you like," replied Michel.

Robert crossed to the window and looked out over the ogarden. The children were chasing butterflies on the lawn.

"Come to think of it," he added, "my gamble was also a dream. But a different one from yours."

We were all of us silent for a while, until Michel's cough, stabbing the air, made us suddenly conscious of what lay ahead for him. He sat down, gasping, waving his hand to draw attention away from himself.

"Don't be alarmed," he said, "it c-comes and goes. Sophie gave me too good a d-dinner." Then, smiling at his brother, he asked, "What happened to the g-glass?"

"The glass?"

Robert, startled into the present, was nonplussed for a moment only. Then, with a glance at me, he went to the cabinet. "It's here," he said, "the only thing I brought home with me from England. I nearly lost it once, but that's another story."

He opened the cabinet and took out the glass and showed it to Michel. "Not a scratch upon it, as you see," he said, "but I won't let you handle it, you say it brings bad luck."

"Not any l-longer," answered Michel, "my luck ran out some t-time ago. I'd like to hold it now."

He put out his hands and took the glass and turned it this way and that. The light from the window caught the engraven fleur-de-lys.

"They were c-craftsmen, I'll say that for them, both my f-father and my uncle," Michel said. "I've t-tried to copy this a hundred times, and always f-failed. Is Sophie going to keep it?"

"Until Jacques takes it from her," Robert answered.

"He won't d-do that," said Michel, "he belongs to B-Bonaparte. Jacques will f-follow the First Consul to the S-Siberian steppes and beyond. You ought to have bred more s-sons. I'm sorry your s-second marriage ended as disastrously as the f-first."

Robert did not answer. He took the glass from Michel and put it back in the cabinet. I was still the only one to know his secret.

"Too late for you and me to enter into p-partnership, mon vieux," said Michel, "the p-plain fact being that I may not live six months. But I'd welcome your c-company, even though you are a s-sacré émigré. You don't m-mind, do you, Aimée?"

"Not if you want him with you," answered Edmé.

"You can come back to S-Sophie and the comfort of the mayor's establishment after I'm g-gone," continued Michel. "How about it?"

This time it was Robert who was thinking of the parting at the laboratory in the rue Traversière. What bitterness he may have suffered then was now forgotten, extinguished forever by his brother's words. They made a strange contrast: Robert, the one-time dandy, now stooping, with his clothes hanging about him, his dyed hair streaked with grey, spectacles on nose; and Michel, no more a terrorist of the district of Mondoubleau ready to fight the world, but a dying man, facing his last battle.

If they had known then, I kept repeating to myself, if they had known then, would they have acted differently, would they have never quarrelled? Why the loneliness, the resentment, the anguish in between?

"I'll come with you," said Robert. "I'd be proud to do so. As to your six months' sentence, we might wager on that too. I give you at least a year. If I win, so much the better for both of us. If I lose, I shan't have to pay my debt!"

One thing was certain. Neither the London rain and fog, nor the gloom of King's Bench prison, nor Michel's approaching death, could quench my eldest brother's sense of fun or his gambling instinct.

20

MY ELDEST BROTHER lost his wager. Michel died seven months later, in February, 1803—thank God, without much pain. He was working until the day before he died, and the end came suddenly, after a paroxysm of coughing. He was talking to Edmé one moment, and the next was dead. We brought his body back to Vibraye and buried him in the cemetery there, where I shall lie one day, and my sons as well.

None of us could have wished him to live longer. His strength had gone, and he would never have taken to an invalid's life, humped in an easy chair. His last months were made the easier by the presence of Robert, who, Edmé said, was gentler with Michel than she was herself. He made his bed for him, helped him to dress, and sat by him at night when his cough worsened; and all of it was done with ease and gaiety.

"I grudged his coming," Edmé admitted, "but after two weeks relied on him completely. Without him I think I could hardly have faced the end."

So the youngest of my brothers was the first to go, and, never having lost my faith, I liked to think of him when he was no longer with us, walking in some celestial glass-house with my father, reconciled at last, his stammer gone. Sentiment can turn after-life into a fairy tale for children, and I prefer this to Edmé's theory of oblivion.

She herself was so much moved by Michel's death that she lost all purpose for a while. He had been that purpose for more than seven years, and without him her roots were severed. They had shared the same beliefs, the same fanaticism for so long, and even in failure, when their dreams had shattered, their mutual loss became their consolation.

"She should marry again," said François bluntly. "A home and a husband would soon put her to rights."

I thought how lacking in intuition men could be in persuading themselves that mending some stranger's socks, and attending to his comfort, could content a woman of thirty-eight like my sister Edmé, who, with her quick brain and passion for argument, would—had she lived in another age—have fought for her beliefs like Joan of Arc.

For Edmé the revolution had come to an end too soon. Bonaparte's victorious armies might be a cause for pride, but in her view, and in Michel's also while he lived, the glory was all an empty mockery to make the generals shine—the mass of the people did not participate. The new aristocrats were the First Consul's friends, be-feathered and be-ribboned, jockeying for favours just as the courtiers had done once at Versailles. Only the names had changed.

"I've outlived my time," she used to say. "I should have gone to the guillotine with Robespierre and St. Just, or else died for their ideals in the streets of Paris. Everything since has been corruption."

A few weeks with us at le Gué de Launay were enough. She was plainly restless, bored. She packed her things and went off to Vendôme in search of any of the former clique of "Babouviste" adherents who might still be living there, and when next we heard from her she was writing articles for Hésine, Babeuf's friend and associate, who was once more at liberty, and agitating against the conscription laws.

I always said she should have been born a man. Her brains and her tenacity were wasted in a woman.

When the spring came Robert and I went down to St. Christophe to see Pierre, who, of course, had come earlier to Vibraye for Michel's funeral, so the pair of them had already seen each other. I had had no fears about this encounter. Pierre had welcomed the émigré as though he had never been away, and immediately presented him with that share of my mother's inheritance which he had carefully kept apart from the portion of it that had gone to Jacques. The rent from the small farm property, with the produce from the vines, though not in any sense a considerable sum, was at least enough to keep my eldest brother in the future, with enough over for investment.

"The question is," said Pierre, "what do you want to do with it?"

"I propose to do nothing," answered Robert, "until I can discuss the matter with Jacques. I don't understand this business of conscription. Isn't it possible to buy him out of the army?"

"No," said Pierre, "and even if it was . . ."

He left his sentence unfinished and glanced at me. I knew very well what he was thinking. Jacques, whether a soldier or civilian, was nearly twenty-two, and believed his father dead, or so we supposed.

"I think you should know," said Pierre, "that Jacques has never mentioned your name to me in all the years he has lived with us here at St. Christophe. My boys have told me the same. He may have talked about you to my mother, when he lived with her, but never to us."

"Perhaps not," Robert replied. "It does not mean he never thought about me."

I could tell that Pierre was disturbed for both their sakes. There was nothing he would have liked more than to bring father and son together, but Robert refused to see that the position was unusual. It was not as though he had returned as a colonialist might do after long absence. He had deserted his son, deserted his country, and lived as an émigré in England for thirteen years. He must not expect to find on his return the same affectionate lad that he remembered.

"What about his other grandparents?" persisted Robert. "Has he lost touch with them? I suppose so."

"On the contrary," said Pierre, "he writes to them very regularly, and sees them too, or did until he was conscripted. It was part of the arrangement I made for him when I became his guardian. I understand that when the old Fiats die everything they have will go to Jacques. It may not amount to much—the house in Paris and the old man's savings—but it will certainly be something, and a pleasant addition to a conscript's pay."

Robert was silent. After a while he said, "I hardly think the Fiats have any great opinion of me."

"Would you expect otherwise?" asked Pierre.

"No, no, very naturally not. Is it possible they may have poisoned Jacques's mind against me?"

"Possible," answered Pierre, "but improbable. They are a good old couple, and more likely left your name alone. The word émigré would hardly be used in front of Jacques."

Robert's face set in hard lines, unlike his usual expression. It was strange that he should learn from Pierre what he had not heard from Michel.

"Were we so much despised?" he asked.

"Frankly, yes," said Pierre, "and don't forget you were one of the first to go. In your case there was no persecution."

"Only the threat of a prison sentence," answered Robert.

"Which again is hardly likely to win admiration from your son," said Pierre.

Pierre, himself the most compassionate and forgiving of men, had the faculty of seeing straight where this whole question of emigration was concerned, and he wished to spare his brother humiliation. He did not reckon with Robert's powers of fantasy, nor suspect, as I did, with my knowledge of the London years, that Robert could fabricate whole images to quieten his conscience.

The test came sooner than we had expected. We were in the last days of our visit when Pierre-François, aged sixteen, Pierre's third boy and namesake to my own son, came running into the house, breathless and excited, to say that the 4th battalion of the 93rd regiment of foot had been reported in Tours.

"They've halted there, on their way north to the coast," he said, "and likely to be in the garrison three days. Without a doubt Jacques will ask permission to come and see us, if only for an hour or two."

Jacques was attached to the 5th company of this battalion, and if the report was true, if they were indeed in Tours, it was likely that he would be granted leave of absence.

"We must set out for Tours immediately," said Robert, in a fever to see his son. "What is the sense of waiting here?"

"Let us first discover if the report is correct," answered Pierre. "It is doubtless the 93rd regiment, but not necessarily the 4th battalion."

He went off to track the rumour to its source, while Robert, more restless and impatient than he had ever been since his return from England, and reminding me of old days, paced up and down the untidy living-room of Pierre's house, littered as it always was with puppies, kittens, pet-hedgehogs in homemade cages, books—too many for the bursting shelves—heaped in corners, and the startling, very lifelike drawings by Pierre's daughter, the enchanting, seven-year-old Pivoine Belle-de-Nuit, already a favourite with her uncle.

"If Pierre causes me to miss Jacques now I shall never forgive him," said Robert. "Tours is barely an hour-and-a-half from here. It is now two. We could hire a conveyance and be there by four o'clock."

I sympathised with his agony, but with Pierre's caution too. We none of us wanted the disappointment of a fruitless journey, nor, on arriving in Tours, the possibility of Robert's entering into heated argument with Jacques's officers.

"You can trust Pierre to do what is right," I said. "You must know that by now."

For answer he pointed at the disorder of the room. "I'm not so sure," he answered. "What is all this due to but muddled thinking? Those lads of his may be fine fellows, able to put a kitten's paw in splints, but they can barely write their own language. I suppose my son has suffered the same lack of education because of Pierre's theories."

I let him rave. Anxiety was the reason for it. He knew as well as I did that Pierre's ideas on the upbringing of children mattered not at all, his integrity was what counted. But for Pierre's foresight, Robert himself would now be penniless.

"I'm sorry," he said after a while, "I'm not blaming Pierre. I don't think he understands what this meeting means to me."

"He understands very well," I told him. "That's why he is taking such pains about it."

Pierre returned within the hour. The report was true all right. The 4th battalion had arrived in Tours.

"I suggest," said Pierre, looking at his watch, "that we wait to see if Jacques travels on the diligence from Tours to Château-du-Loir, which is due here at five o'clock. If he is upon it, and I think he very well may be, then we shall see him in two hours. One thing I beg of you. Let me meet the boy alone, and tell him you are here."

"For the love of God, why?" Robert, at the end of his patience, shouted his question, to the alarm of little Belle-de-Nuit, scribbling by the window.

"Because," said Pierre patiently, "this will be an emotional moment for you both. You don't want people watching you in the street."

The next two hours were a strain upon us all. If Jacques was not on the diligence Robert's disappointment would be intense, and a fresh plan must be made. If Jacques was upon it. . . I was not sure of the answer, nor was Pierre.

Five minutes before the hour Pierre walked to the mairie, where the diligence was due to unload its passengers. He went alone. Pierre-François and the other boy, Joseph, remained in the house with their mother and Bell-de-Nuit, at Pierre's express orders. The children ran upstairs to watch the expected arrival from the upper windows. Robert and I sat in the living-room, or rather I sat, whilst my brother paced the floor. My sister-in-law, from discretion, kept to the kitchen.

Presently I was aware of Belle-de-Nuit standing in the doorway, a puppy under either arm.

"Papa and Jacques are walking up and down outside," she said. "They've been doing so for ten minutes or more. I don't think Jacques wants to come inside the house."

Robert was making for the entrance immediately, but I seized his arm.

"Wait," I said, "perhaps Pierre will explain."

A moment later Pierre came into the room. His eyes sought mine and I understood the message. Then he turned to Robert.

"Jacques is here," he said briefly. "He has only an hour, and must take the returning diligence to Tours. I have broken the news to him that you are with us."

"Well?" My eldest brother's anxiety was pitiful to watch.

"It's as I feared. He was very much shaken, and only consents to see you for my sake."

Pierre went out into the entrance hall and called for Jacques. Robert himself moved forward, hesitated, then waited, uncertain what to do. His son came into the room and stood beside his uncle at the door. Jacques had grown no taller since I saw him last, but was broader, more thick-set; no doubt he had filled out with army rations. He looked well in his uniform, if a trifle overburdened with it, and a little clumsy. I thought what a different figure he cut from his father in old days as an officer in the Arquebusiers, who took greater interest in the fit of his coat than he ever did in soldierly activities.

He stood there staring at his father, pale and unsmiling. I wondered which of the two suffered the most—Jacques, at the sight of his elderly father, nervously twisting his spectacles in his right hand, or Robert, at the sight of his hostile son.

"You've not forgotten me, have you?" Robert said at last, summoning a smile.

"No," said Jacques, his young voice harsh and abrupt. "It might be better if I had."

Pierre beckoned to me from the door.

"Come, Sophie," he called, "let's leave them together."

I was about to cross the room, but Jacques held up his hand.

"No, uncle," he said, "stay where you are, and tante Sophie too. I should prefer it. I have nothing to say to this man."

It would have been kinder had he walked up to his father and hit him across the face. I saw the agony of disbelief in Robert's eyes, then the recognition of defeat. Undaunted, he made a final effort to overcome the situation with bravado.

"Oh, come, my boy," he said, "it's too late for drama. Life's too short for that. You're a fine man, and I'm proud of you. Come and shake hands with your old father, who's loved you devotedly all these years."

Pierre laid his hand on the boy's arm, but Jacques shook it off.

"I'm sorry, uncle," he said, "I've done what you asked. I've come into the room. He sees that I exist. That is enough. Now I would like to go and see tante Marie and my cousins."

He turned on his heel, but Pierre still barred the way.

"Jacques," he said softly, "have you no pity?"

Jacques swung round and looked at all of us in turn.

"Pity?" he asked. "Why should I have pity? He didn't have any pity for me nearly fourteen years ago, when he deserted me. All he could think of was getting out of the country as quickly as possible, fearful for his own skin. Now, because of the amnesty, he thinks it's safe to return. Well, that's his affair, but I wonder he had the face to do so. You can pity him if you like. I can only despise him."

It is a disadvantage to see the past as clearly as the present, and to carry a picture in the forefront of one's mind which is as vivid today as on the day it happened. For my part, I was sitting in the carriole leaving l'Antinière, and Jacques was a sunburnt little lad in a blue smock, kissing his father good-bye.

"That's enough, then," said Robert quietly. "Let him go."

Pierre stood aside, and Jacques went out of the room. I heard little Belle-de-Nuit call him from the stairs, and her brothers too, and one of the puppies began barking excitedly. They took him into their world, and the three of our generation were left alone.

"I was afraid of it," said Pierre, whether to Robert or to me I do not know. Deep in thought, he repeated it once more. "I was afraid of it."

Presently Robert went upstairs to his room and shut the door. He stayed there until the time came for Jacques to mount the diligence for Tours. Then he stood on the landing, in the hope that his son might relent and come up to bid him good-bye. We pleaded with Jacques, but he was firm. Neither Pierre, nor Marie, nor I could make him change his mind. He had spent his hour of absence sitting with his cousins in the playroom above, telling them, so we learnt afterwards, of his experiences as a conscript, and, judging by their laughter, making a joke of it. Never once did he speak about his father, and they, taking their lead from him, let it alone.

As he set forth for the diligence accompanied by Pierre-François and Joseph, having kissed us all, and we heard the door into the street slam behind him, the sound echoed from above. It was Robert, who had waited until the last moment, shutting his bedroom door.

That night I spilt his secret, and told Pierre about the family left in England. He heard the whole wretched tale through without comment, and, when I had finished, thanked me for having told him.

"There's only one thing to do now," he said, "and that is to bring his wife and children over here. Whether he goes to fetch them, or I go, is immaterial. Without them he will become a broken man, because of what Jacques has done to him today."

The relief of having unburdened myself to Pierre was very great. We talked at length about the procedure necessary to bring Robert's wife and children from London across the Channel. She believed herself a widow, and would be receiving assistance from the authorities in England. No one must know in that country that Robert was not dead, for the penalty, as I had imagined, would be severe. Pierre, for all his knowledge of the law, was uncertain how it would be applied. The fraud was a peculiar one, and he would have to take counsel, discreetly, amongst his legal friends.

"Surely the best way to set about it," I said, "is for you, or for me, to write to Marie-Françoise, offering her a home over here, and saying that we have Robert's inheritance to offer her?"

"And if she doesn't want to come?" replied Pierre. "What then? She may prefer to live in London amongst those émigrés who have no wish to return. It would be better for one of us to go in person and persuade her. If she once knows Robert is alive, there will be no question but that she will come."

I remembered how Robert had told me that his wife had turned very religious during his term of imprisonment. It might be that she would have scruples about keeping the fraud secret, and would want to tell the Abbé Carron, who had been so good to them.

There seemed no end to all these problems, but I knew Pierre was right. The only way for Robert to make restoration for the past, and for what he had done to Jacques, was to become reunited once more with his second family. He had commited the same crime twice. There was no other word to describe it. It was only a matter of time before guilt for the first crime would merge into guilt for the second, and when that happened . . . Pierre looked at me expressively.

"What are you afraid of?" I asked him.

"I'm afraid he might kill himself," answered Pierre.

He went upstairs to his brother, and stayed with him for a long time. When he came down again Pierre told me that Robert had agreed to do anything that was suggested. Jacques was lost to him, doubtless forever. He realised now the irreparable damage he had done to a sensitive boy. The idea that it was still possible to become reunited with the children left in England would prove his salvation.

"Can you delay your return home for a few days?" asked Pierre.

I told him I could. Charlotte, niece of dear old Madame Verdelet who used to cook for us at le Chesne-Bidault, was quite capable of looking after my family for a little longer.

"In that case," answered Pierre, "I shall go to Paris tomorrow. I shall learn there what are the possibilities of one or other of us travelling to England. Meanwhile, stay here with Robert. Don't let him out of your sight."

He was away the next morning before Robert had even risen, and during the days that followed I did as Pierre told me, and, with the boys and Belle-de-Nuit, kept Robert company.

He was strangely quiet and contrite, and had become, during the twenty-four hours since Jacques had departed, a much older man.

The shock had been profound, not only to his emotions but to his self-esteem. During those long hours alone in his bedroom, after Pierre had spoken with him, I think he must have realised, at last, just what had happened in the years between. The stigma of having been an émigré, and all that it must have meant to Jacques, the son of an émigré, brought up in a household of patriots, was now made clear. We—Pierre, Michel and I, and Edmé to a lesser degree—had been able to accept him; our middle years made it easier for us. The young are less forgiving.

While we waited for Pierre's return from Paris Robert talked, at first with some hesitation, later with eagerness, of the possibility of seeing Marie-Françoise and the children once again,

"She will soon get over the deception," he said. "I can make up some story or other of the papers becoming mixed, it's of no great consequence. And once here, with the money from the inheritance, we can find a place to settle. The children, anyway, will speak both languages, always an advantage for their future careers. My little girl Louise is almost the same age as Belle-de-Nuit. They will be great companions."

He took his niece on his knee as he said this, and she, being an affectionate child, clung closely to him.

"Yes," he said, "yes, I see now I was mad to do what I did. It would have been so simple to come to you, as I planned first, and make arrangements to bring them over. At the time, of course, I knew nothing of the inheritance, I did not even know that I should find any of you alive. I acted on impulse. I've done so all my life."

I encouraged him to think and to plan for the future. It seemed the only way to pass the time, and it prevented him from brooding over Jacques.

After five or six days he had almost recovered his spirits, and was becoming restless for Pierre's return. At last, just a week after he had left us, and we were in the dining room, about to sit down to dinner, Belle-de-Nuit called out, "I can hear my

Papa in the hall." She struggled to get down from her chair, but Robert was there before her. I heard him greet Pierre, there was a quick exchange of questions and answers, and then silence. I felt that something was wrong. I got up and left the table, and went into the hall.

Pierre was standing with his hand on Robert's shoulder.

"There is nothing to be done," he was saying. "Hostilities have broken out again between the English and ourselves, and the Channel ports are closed to traffic. I understand now why Jacques's battalion was marching north. They say Bonaparte is preparing to invade England."

The truce that had lasted for fourteen months had ended, and the war, which had started up anew, was to continue for another thirteen years. Pierre's plan had been formed too late. Robert had lost not only his eldest son, but all chance of reunion with his second wife and family. He was never to see them, or to hear of them, again.

21

WE HAD BECOME SO used to Bonaparte's success that we looked upon the renewal of war between France and England as a temporary set-back to our personal hopes and plans. It would all be over in a few months. Bonaparte would invade England, march upon London, and force the English government to accede to his terms, whatever they should be. As to the émigrés living under English protection, they would very naturally be sent home to their own country; therefore Robert's desire to be reunited with Marie-Françoise and the children could not be long deferred. Since we reasoned thus, the outbreak of war was less of a shock than a frustration, or so I argued, supported by Pierre. It was Robert himself, calmer and more resigned than we expected, who warned us not to expect an early victory.

"You forget," he said. "I've lived amongst these people for thirteen years. A continental war may not rouse them, but if you threaten their own shores they'll turn tenacious. Do not count on any quick result, and if Bonaparte launches an invasion, it may misfire."

The months that followed proved my brother right. The great army gathered at Boulogne waited in vain for a chance to cross the Channel, and when summer turned to autumn, with the onset of bad weather, their hopes of success faded, and so did ours.

Robert, who was living with us once more at le Gué de Launay, admitted to me one evening during the worst of the winter, in February, 1804, that even when spring came he did not believe Bonaparte would risk invasion.

"The chances of a defeat at sea would be too great," he said. "I think we must make up our minds to a long-drawn-out war between ourselves and England, no matter what success Bonaparte may have elsewhere. This means, from my own point of view, that I must stop thinking of Marie-Françoise and the children. I'm dead to them, and have to face the fact they are dead to me."

He spoke without bitterness, but with decision, and I realised that he must have been turning the matter over in his mind for some while.

"Put it that way if you will," I told him, "but not if it's just to quieten your conscience. They are alive in London, growing year by year, just as Pierre-François , Alphonse-Cyprien and Zoë are growing here, and Pierre's brood at St. Christophe. Accept the fact that they are living and you cannot help them. It will be easier for you to hold to the truth if you have the courage."

"It isn't a question of courage," he answered. "I mean they are dead to me emotionally. It's a strange thing, but I can't even conjure up their faces any more.

They've become like shadows. When I think of Louise, who was always my favourite, her features turn into those of little Belle-de-Nuit. Perhaps it is because they are the same age."

Here was a perplexity. I know that if I had been separated from my children, no matter for how long, their faces, and their voices too, would become more vivid. I wondered whether the disastrous encounter with Jacques had shocked some part of Robert's brain, affecting his memory. Or could it be that he conveniently forgot all things that troubled him? I doubted if the thought of Jacques had bothered him much in London, and the decision to name his second boy Jacques could have been pure perversity, and part of the fantasy-life. I could not help remarking, though, his genuine affection for my children, and for Pierre's also. He had a natural way about him, gay and light-hearted, that won their response, despite his age, and I noticed that my two sons would run to him with some problem of grammar or arithmetic sooner than to their father. After all, it was Robert who had tried to teach me Latin in the old days at le Chesne-Bidault before he married, and during those last few years in London he had helped the Abbé Carron with the émigré pupils in the Pancras school.

"You've wasted your time as a master-engraver," I said one day, after I had found him with my two boys on either side of him, with a volume of Latin grammar in his hands. "You ought to have been an instructor in a school."

He laughed and put the book aside. "I was glad enough of the work in London for the money it brought in," he said. 'Here it passes the time and stops me thinking, which—you will agree—is an achievement."

Once more he spoke without bitterness, but although I knew he was content with my company, and happy to be amongst us, I sensed the void within. A year ago he had been building in imagination a future with Jacques; now that was over, but the days had to be filled all the same. My brother was fifty-four. His inheritance from our mother was untouched. Somehow he must maintain himself and have a raison d'être.

"You have only to say the word," Pierre wrote to him, "and I will join forces with you in any undertaking you care to suggest, with one exception. The glass-trade must be barred to us. For one thing, we haven't the resources. For another, your creditors in Paris have forgotten you, but any attempt to bring your name forward again in circles familiar to the trade might fetch them about your ears. Here, in the Touraine, you are unknown." We were many years distant from Busson l'Aîné and his influential friends.

In early May Pierre told us that Jacques had written him to say his grandmother, Madame Fiat, had died, and he was on leave in Paris receiving the inheritance due to him. His grandfather, old Fiat, was also ailing, and Jacques confirmed that when he died the house and its contents would belong to him.

"Which means," said Robert, "that Jacques now knows himself to be independent. He will be able to sell the house and invest the proceeds, leaving the capital untouched until he quits the army."

"In other words," I replied, "he will never need your help. When you saw him last year you could not be sure. Now you know."

"He would not have come to me direct," said Robert, "but he might have approached Pierre. Even that last hope is now denied me."

It was not until news came that Jacques's regiment had embarked at Toulon for service in the Mediterranean, and was likely to be out of the country for at least two years, that Robert finally decided what he wanted to do with his own inheritance. He asked Pierre to come to le Gué de Launay for a family conference, and when the three of us were together—François preferring to take no part in the discussion, and Edmé too deeply involved with her Jacobin friends in Vendôme to attend—he put his proposal to us.

"I want to devote my life, what remains of it," he said, "to the young. I want to try and do, heaven knows in a much smaller way, what I watched the Abbé Carron achieve in London. He chose a crowd of fatherless boys and girls from the poorest amongst the émigrés, housed them, fed them and clothed them, and gave them an education into the bargain. It could be that this is what he is still doing for my family there. In any event, I want to do it here."

I think we were too surprised at first to make any comment. My remarks to Robert that he had wasted his talents as an engraver had been spoken in jest. I had never for one moment considered they would bear fruit. As to Pierre, he had his own strange ideas on education; let a child alone and it would teach itself was the method he had employed with his own boys, much to the disruption of his household, good-humoured though it was. Now, with Robert's pronouncement exploding amongst us like a cannon-ball, I wondered what the effect would be on Pierre. An occasion for argument, perhaps, with the theories of Jean-Jacques claiming us until midnight. Instead, Pierre's enthusiasm took me by surprise. He leapt to his feet and clapped his brother on the shoulder.

"You've got it," he almost shouted. "You've got it absolutely. I can think of at least six boys straight off, sons of my old clients in Le Mans, who would come to us as pupils. I could teach them philosophy, botany and law, and leave the rest to you. We would charge practically nothing, of course; we don't want to make money out of them. Just enough to cover the cost of food and rent. Sophie, you will give us Pierre-François and Alphonse-Cyprien. I'm not so sure about my own three, they'd be better working on a farm. But it will mean letting the house in St. Christophe and moving to Tours. Tours must be our centre. I wonder if we can persuade Edmé to quit Vendôme and give lectures on political freedom? Perhaps not, her ideas are too advanced, and we must do nothing to offend the Code Civil."

Pierre's enthusiasm was infectious. He had all of us inspired. Two days later he left for Tours in search of suitable quarters for the proposed pension, and, more important still, to obtain permission from the authorities for "les frères Busson" to found a "maison d'éducation" for fatherless children. Even François, who had prophesied some fresh speculation on Robert's part with its inevitable loss, had to agree that the new idea was commendable, if hardly profitable, but insisted that our own boys, having a father living, could not qualify for positions in the school.

It took six months or more before the pension was ready to receive its first pupils, and when it opened in early December, 1804, at No. 4, rue des Bons Enfants, Tours, I remember that our own family celebrations coincided with that of the whole nation. The city was beflagged, the crowds were out in the streets, for Napoleon Bonaparte, the First Consul, had been crowned Emperor.

How much the general excitement contributed to my two brothers' sense of dedication I did not know, but the occasion was a moving one. As they stood side by side, welcoming their twenty pupils, in the square oak-beamed room on the first floor of the ancient house in the centre of Tours which they had taken for their pension, it seemed to me that the wheel had somehow come full circle, and the Busson brothers were together again in a community. This community life was what they had known as children in the glass-houses of Chérigny and la Pierre; it was something to which they had been born and bred, and although here in Tours there was no foundry chimney, no furnace, no product made with hands, fundamentally the spirit was the same.

My brothers were the masters, imparting knowledge and a way of life to these children, just as my father and my uncles had bequeathed the knowledge of their craft to my brothers when they were apprentices at la Pierre. Here, in the rue des Bons Enfants, were no molten glass, no rods, no pipes; the glass-blowers did not stand before the fire, blow-pipe in hand, breathing life into the slowly expanding vessel. Instead there were children, their personalities malleable, awaiting development, and my brothers must guide them as surely and as steadily as they had once shaped liquid glass, bringing to fullness and maturity a rounded and balanced human being.

Pierre had the ideals and the selflessness to put those ideas into practice, Robert the powers of persuasion, the necessary charm and inventive ability to turn a history lesson into an adventure.

I watched the eager expectant faces of those orphaned boys, and the one girl amongst them, little Belle-de-Nuit, twenty-one in all staring at my brothers, who, each of them in turn, made a short speech of welcome. Pierre, his blue eyes, so like my mother's, afire with enthusiasm, and his white hair en brosse, bore small resemblance to those professors of education whom I had seen elsewhere in Tours.

"I am here," he said, "not to teach you, but to be taught. I've forgotten all I ever learnt, except a smattering of the law, which I applied in my own fashion when I was a notary in Le Mans. I know nothing about buying and selling, and if you ask my brother about this it won't help—he lost everything he possessed in speculation. What I do remember is where to look for wild strawberries in early summer, and the most likely trees to climb to find the nests of buzzards—for this, you must go to the forest, and we will do it together. Buzzards are predators, that is to say, they rob the nests of other birds and eat their young. This is anti-social, and for this reason they are mobbed by their fellows. People who follow their example in the world suffer likewise. We might also examine together the life-cycle of butterflies and moths. You are all of you, at this period of your life, grubs and caterpillars; the fascination of growing up is to see what you become.

"I don't intend to make any rules here that I won't keep myself. If you make any amongst yourselves I will keep them too. My wife has one request, that you don't throw your food upon the floor. Food, mixed with dirt, encourages rats, and rats breed plague. Nobody wants plague in Tours. This evening, if any of you care to listen, I shall be reading the first few chapters of Rousseau's *Emile* aloud. If nobody turns up it does not matter. I enjoy the sound of my voice, and shall not be offended. Afterwards, I shall start building an aviary for two birds with broken wings that my daughter, Pivione Belle-de-Nuit, brought with her from St. Christophe, and helpers will be welcomed. Now, perhaps you will have the courtesy to hear my brother. He is the elder by three years, and has all the brains."

Pierre sat down, amid bewildered though polite applause, and François, at my side, whispered that the pension would surely be closed down by the authorities within the year.

Robert rose to his feet, his hair, newly dyed for the occasion, contrasting a little oddly, if spectacularly, with his new plum-coloured coat. He carried a sheaf of papers to steady the tremor in his hands.

"There was once a lad," he said, "who went to Martinique to seek his fortune. He returned empty-handed, having given away whatever he possessed, save for an embroidered waistcoat and two parrots. That lad, now middle-aged, has just been speaking to you. He knows little more of life now than he did then. If you want to learn how to gamble for vast sums and lose them within the year I can teach you, but don't expect either my brother or myself to bail you out of prison afterwards.

"The English poet Shakespeare said that life is 'a tale told by an idiot, full of sound and fury, signifying nothing'. But he put these words into the mouth of a Scottish chief who had murdered the king sheltering beneath his roof, so it need not apply to you at the moment—unless you rise up and murder my brother and myself in our beds. Life, on the contrary, is at its most intense when it is silent; the silence of a prison cell, for instance, which gives every opportunity for thought, or when sitting beside the dead body of a loved one to whom you never bade good-bye.

"The sound and the fury, nevertheless, you will experience all in good time as obedient conscripts fighting for the greater glory of the Emperor and France. But whilst you are here, at No. 4, rue des Bons Enfants—which name, by the way, is quite fortuitous, for we came upon the street by chance—I shall endeavour to imbue your reluctant souls with a desire for stillness. Restless as a caged lion myself, I can never stay motionless for more than five seconds at a time; hence my respect for those who can. I was forced to remain still at certain periods of my life, which I may tell you about one day—it will depend upon how much I have had to drink.

"'Pitchers have ears'—another quotation from Shakespeare, *Richard III* this time, for I am an English scholar—and if you keep yours alert you may hear a great deal to your ultimate advantage, on the wiles of men and princes. For I speak as one who saw the heyday of Louis XV and his unfortunate descendant, and now bows the knee to the Emperor Napoleon. History, literature, Latin, grammar, arithmetic, I'm a qualified professor in all five subjects—in my own opinion, if not in my brother's—and before you go out from here in a few years' time to shed your blood on the battlefields of Europe, I suggest you obtain some sort of grounding in these matters, along with gathering wild strawberries with my associate, so that dying you may murmur, 'Virtuti nihil obstat et armis,' which may be some consolation in the circumstances.

"In my own youth I held to the precept, 'Video meliora proboque, deteriora sequor', which is the reason my hands tremble today and I dye my hair—I do not ask you to follow my example.

"Meanwhile, my life is yours. This is your home. Trample on both to your hearts' content, and be happy."

Robert shuffled his papers, replaced his spectacles, and gave a signal for dismissal. The children, conditioned after the first speech to applause, clapped their hands loudly, led by Belle-de-Nuit. Only my husband, the mayor of Vibraye, shocked beyond measure, stared firmly at his feet.

"I think it only fair to tell you," he said to my brothers as soon as the children had clattered down the stairs and across the small inner court to their own quarters, "that, despite our relationship, I shall have to erase the name of the pension from my list of recommendations. These children won't have a chance under your care. They will grow up either scoundrels or buffoons."

"We are most of us either the one or the other," replied Robert. "In which category do you class yourself?"

This was no moment for a family quarrel, and I laid my hand on François' arm.

"Come," I said, "you must see the dormitory where the boys will sleep. Pierre has contrived it with great cunning, and partitioned it into two."

My tact was wasted, for at this moment Edmé, who had come over from Vendôme for the occasion, approached us.

"I liked both your speeches," she said in her usual forthright fashion, "but you neither of you said anything about tyranny. Surely one of the first lessons a boy should learn is how to distinguish between the oppressors and the leaders of the people? Nor did you as much as mention the Rights of Man."

Pierre looked astonished. "But I gave an explicit description of tyranny when I spoke about buzzards," he said. "And as to the Rights of Man, I intend to hammer the point home when we find our first clutch of eggs and leave them intact. Birds have their rights as well as human beings. Little by little these children will discover the facts for themselves."

Edmé appeared relieved, though not entirely convinced, and as we made a tour of the house I saw her frowning at the enthusiastic "Vive l'Empereur" that one of the students had already scrawled in enormous letters over the entrance to their dormitory.

"That," she observed quietly, "should be removed straight away."

"What would you put in its place?" questioned Robert. "Children, like adults, need a symbol."

"'Vive la nation' would be preferable," she said.

"Too impersonal," answered Robert. "You can't have the nation seated on a white horse, with the tricolour in the background against a stormy sky. When these lads scrawl 'Vive l'Empereur', that is what they see. Neither you nor I will ever dissuade them."

Edmé sighed. "Not you, perhaps," she replied, "but if I was allowed to speak to them for twenty minutes about conscription, and what it will mean for them, they would never scrawl 'Vive l'Empereur' again."

I could not help being relieved, for the sake of both my brothers, that my sister had not been invited to lecture at the pension in the rue des Bons Enfants, for if she did the place would close, not in a year as François prophesied, but within three months.

As it turned out, the pension Busson remained open for nearly seven years, though not quite as my brothers intended it. The laws on education became much stricter as the months passed, all part of the Code Civil, which the local authorities throughout the country were bound to enforce. Boys were obliged to attend the State schools and be taught by qualified teachers, and so the unorthodox and original theories of my brothers were never fully put into practice. The pension remained a pension for fatherless boys, a place in which to eat and sleep, but they went daily to the State schools.

As time went by, and the children grew older and left, their places were taken by those homeless or down-on-their-luck individuals so dear to my brother Pierre. Needless to say, they never paid for their bed or board, but looked to him for charity. The pension, started with such high hopes, deteriorated into a kind of lodging-house where all were welcome, with Pierre acting host, and Robert endeavouring to make up for his brother's lack of money sense by coaching private pupils before they sat for examination.

The decline, so François said, was only to be expected; indeed, it was a wonder the place was kept going at all. It saddened me to see the house grow shabby from want of care, the walls unpainted, the stairs unscrubbed; and when I went to stay in the rue des Bons Enfants, as I did from time to time, I would miss the laughter and the clatter of those children of the first year, when the pension opened. Instead I would hear a rasping cough from some semi-invalid in the room adjoining, or meet a grumbling individual as I walked down the stair to the inner court where the children had once played.

Neither Robert nor Pierre seemed aware of dilapidation or decay. They had chosen to live thus, and it seemed to suit them. The light of both their lives was Belle-de-Nuit, whose radiant presence turned the otherwise drab pension to a place of joy.

This enchanting child, doomed—though thank heaven neither her father nor her uncle lived to see it happen—to die of tuberculosis before she was twenty years old, had all the family gifts and none of their faults. Selfless like Pierre, she possessed more application and discernment. Intelligent like Edmé, she was without rancour, and envied no one. Her talent for drawing was such that had it matured she could have excelled as a professional artist. As it is, I keep the best of her drawings, filed away in my cabinet in le Gué de Launay.

She was the only one of Pierre's children to profit by Robert's teaching. The boys, after military service, drifted into various trades, Joseph starting up as a saddler in Château-du-Loir and Pierre-François, my own son's namesake, becoming a hairdresser in Tours.

"The inevitable result of deliberate neglect," François used to say. "Those boys, with proper upbringing, might have entered a profession."

Even so, what talent they possessed came from their hands. I have seen leather-work stitched by Jospeph with all the loving care that a fine engraver would put upon his glass, and wigs dressed by Pierre-François that the Empress herself would not have scorned to wear. Nothing is degraded that is bequeathed with love. My father handed down a passion for craftsmanship to the grandsons he never saw.

"Let each one work to the best of his ability," Pierre used to say. "I don't care what they do as long as they do it to extreme."

He spoke his own epitaph. Fishing one Sunday on the banks of the Loire, he saw a dog leap from the opposite shore to retrieve a stick, thrown by its master. The dog faltered in mid-stream and pawed the water, frightened, at which my brother flung off his coat and plunged in after him. The dog, seeing his rescuer, gained courage and turned for the shore, but Pierre, shocked by the sudden cold and hampered by his clothes, was seized with cramp, and sank. The owner of the dog gave the alarm and a boat was launched, but it was too late. Pierre's body was recovered three days afterwards.

The impulse which brought him death, and so much grief to his family, had its consequences, one of which might never have occurred had he lived. Because of it, I like to think that this impulse was not in vain.

The tragedy happened in April, 1810, a few days before Pierre's fifty-eighth birthday and Jacques's twenty-ninth, and during the time when the Emperor was holding the celebrations in Paris for his second marriage, to Marie-Louise of Austria. Jacques's regiment had formed part of the Grande Armée since 1807, he had campaigned in most of the countries in Europe, and his company was amongst those doing duty in the capital for the marriage celebrations.

I wrote to him instantly, upon learning of the accident, so that he could send a message of sympathy to his aunt and cousins. I did not imagine for a moment that he would obtain leave of absence.

François and I and our daughter Zoë, now seventeen, went down to Tours for the funeral, and we delayed our return for a day or two, with the intention of taking my sister-in-law Marie and Belle-de-Nuit back with us.

The child, who was now fourteen and had adored her father, had stifled her own grief in attending to her mother. It was during their preparations for departure, when I was with her in her room, that she suddenly turned to me and said, "I don't know if I did wrong, tante Sophie, but I wrote to Jacques to tell him what has happened."

"So did I," I reassured her. "No doubt you will be hearing from him, and your mother too."

She looked at me in her steadfast way, then said, "I've asked him to come here. I told him he was needed."

This news disturbed me. We did not want a repetition of the encounter of seven years past. Pierre's death had greatly shocked my brother, and he was in no state to suffer a second rebuff.

"It wasn't wise, Belle-de-Nuit," I said. "You know Jacques does not care to speak to his father, or to see him. That is why he refuses to come on leave to Tours unless your uncle is away."

"I know that very well," she answered, "and it was always Papa's wish to bring them together. It seemed to me that the time had come to try just that. We will see."

I did not know whether to warn Robert or to say nothing. I felt certain Jacques would not be able to get leave of absence because of the celebrations, but I was wrong. I never discovered what special pleading Belle-de-Nuit put into her letter, but it brought a response, which mine would never have done. That evening, I was descending the old staircase into the inner court, with Robert by my side, and as I paused a moment, my hand on the carved balustrade, I heard Belle-de-Nuit's cry of welcome in the archway leading to the street beyond.

Instinct told me who it was, and I made to turn.

"What's the matter?" Robert asked. "If it's another caller, the child will deal with him."

They came through the archway together, Belle-de-Nuit in her black mourning dress and Jacques in his uniform of caporal fusilier. The boy had developed into a man, still short but broad and thick-set, with powerful shoulders, and I should hardly have recognised him but for his blue eyes and his shock of fair hair.

The pair of them stared up at us, and I saw that Robert beside me had turned white. He must have shared my instinct, for he turned to make his way back up the stairs once more, stumbling as he did so.

"No, uncle, don't go." Belle-de-Nuit's voice rang clear like a command. "Jacques has permission from his company commander for two days," she said, "after which they will rejoin the battalion for service in Spain. He has come to say good-bye to you."

Robert hesitated. His hand on the balustrade trembled.

"I was decorated last year at Wagram," said Jacques. "If it would interest you, I should like to show you the medal."

The voice was no longer harsh and arrogant. It held respect, and a certain shyness too. Robert turned again, and looked down the stairs at his son. His hair was no longer dyed these days. It had gone white, as Pierre's had done, and he looked all of his sixty years.

"I heard about the decoration," he said. "I should like to see your medal more than anything else in the world."

Jacques started up the stairway towards us. I kissed him quickly, and then joined Belle-de-Nuit in the court below. Our presence was not needed at this encounter. Looking back over my shoulder, I saw father and son silhouetted a moment at the turn of the stairs; then Robert put his arm through Jacques's and led him up to his room beyond.

The rest of us left the next day for le Gué de Launay, and Jacques spent the remaining twenty-four hours of his leave alone with his father. I could only guess what the reconciliation meant to both of them.

There is little left to tell about my brother Robert. Despite my entreaties that he should give up the pension and come to live at le Gué de Launay, he would not be persuaded. I think he felt that Pierre would have expected him to stay.

"I shall keep the place open," he told me, "just as long as I can afford to do so."

But once Pierre's widow had departed back to St. Christophe with Belle-de-Nuit, unable to face life at the pension without him, the little joy remaining went out of the poor shabby building, and with it my brother's will to live.

He became very frail and shaky during the succeeding winter, and, like Michel before him, complained in his letters of shortness of breath. He continued to coach pupils before examinations, for young faces were his one delight, reminding him, not only of Jacques and Belle-de-Nuit, but of that family of his across the Channel, of whose existence I alone knew.

He spoke of them to me the last time I saw him, which was in May of 1811, little more than twelve months after Pierre's death.

"If he still lives," Robert said to me, "my second Jacques will now be eighteen years old, Louise, like Belle-de-Nuit, approaching sixteen, and Louis-Mathurin in his fourteenth year. I wonder if they have become entirely English, disliking all things French, even their own language."

"I doubt it," I said, "and one day, ten, twenty, thirty years hence, they will come home."

"Perhaps," he answered, "but not to me."

He waved good-bye to me from the upper window of his room at No. 4, rue des Bons Enfants, for I would not let him walk with me to the diligence that would take me back to Vibraye, in case it strained his heart.

I left him with an unhappy feeling of premonition. There were not more than half-a-dozen persons living in the pension, none of whom knew him well, or would be able to take care of him if he became ill.

A month later, on the 2nd of June, at about three o'clock in the afternoon, he was climbing the stairway from the inner court to the landing above when a clot of blood must have blocked a vein of his heart, for he fell, and was found there by two of the lodgers, dying, a moment or two afterwards.

They carried him to his room and laid him on his bed and stood there waiting, uncertain whom to send for or what to do. He tried to speak but could not, and they thought he wanted air, and opened the window. It troubles me still, after thirty years, to know that my brother was with strangers when he died.

Epilogue

Madame Duval laid down her pen on the 6th of November, 1844, the day before her eighty-first birthday. It had taken her a little over four months to write the story of her family, and during the telling of her tale she had lived again, in memory, many incidents she had thought forgotten. Their faces were very clear to her: her father Mathurin and her mother Magdaleine, her three brothers, Robert, Pierre, Michel, and her sister Edmé.

She had outlived them all, even her nephew Jacques, who, severely wounded in January, 1812, had died the following June, shortly after leaving hospital, thus surviving his father by only twelve months.

Edmé, poor Edmé, whose dreams of a life where there should be a "communauté des biens", equality and happiness for all, were shattered forever by the restoration of the monarchy, continued to lead a lonely and frustrated existence in Vendôme, telling all who cared to listen to her of the great days of the Revolution and the Constitution of '93. Passionate for reform, forever scribbling ideas for a future political system that no editor in Vendôme dared to print, she died in her early fifties, "sans fortune et sans famille", a republican to the end.

François Duval had the satisfaction of seeing his son, Pierre-François, succeed him as mayor of Vibraye in 1830, and his daughter, Zoë, married to Doctor Rosiau, former mayor of Mamers, before he was laid to rest in Vibraye cemetery, near to his one-time partner and comrade, Michel Busson-Challoir.

The glass-houses founded and developed by Mathurin Busson nearly a century before had continued to flourish, though no member of his family had any connection with them.

On her eighty-first birthday, despite the lateness of the season and the threat of rain, Madame Duval induced her son, the mayor, to drive her the short distance to la Pierre, so that she might descend from the carriage awhile, and look through the park gates at the château and the foundry beside it.

The château was shuttered, its owners away in Paris, but smoke came from the foundry chimney, and the familiar bitter tang of charcoal filled the air. Workmen were wheeling barrows to and from the sheds to the furnace-house, a two-horse waggon waited to be loaded, and three apprentice-boys, laughing and joking to one another, came out of one of the sheds bearing a crate between them.

Across the greensward were the workmen's cottages, and one or two women stood in the open doorways, staring at the carriage. They had taken advantage of the meagre sun to spread their linen on the grass to dry. The foundry bell sounded for the midday change of shift, and the men came out of the furnace-house and from the sheds, and gathered in little groups. Like the women, they stared at the waiting carriage.

"Haven't you seen enough?" asked Pierre-François Duval, mayor of Vibraye. "We are drawing attention to ourselves, standing about like this."

"Yes," answered his mother, "I have seen enough."

She got back into the carriage, and looked for a moment through the open window.

Nothing had changed. It was still a community, a little body of craftsmen and workmen with their families, indifferent, even hostile, to the world outside, making their own rules, abiding by their own customs. What they created with their hands would go out across France, through Europe, to America; and surely each object would carry upon it some stamp of the first masters who long before had worked here with pride and love, passing on the old traditions to their successors.

Madame Duval's last glimpse of her childhood home la Pierre showed the furnace-house, with the buildings grouped about it, caught momentarily in the pale glimmer of a November sun, the whole shrouded and protected by the tall forest trees whose strength and durability fed the furnace fire.

That night she made a package of all the papers she had written, tied them with ribbon, and gave them to her son for dispatch to her nephew Louis-Mathurin in Paris.

"Even if he does not read any of it aloud," she said to herself, "or suppresses those parts that show his family, and especially his father Robert, to disadvantage, it will not matter. I shall have done my duty and told the truth. Most important of all, his son George, the boy he called Kicky, will keep the glass."

She went over to the window and opened it, listening to the rain falling upon the garden below. Even here, in her own house at le Gué de Launay, it seemed to her that the community she loved was not far distant. The men would be going on night-shift at la Pierre and at le Chesne-Bidault, and the women preparing coffee; and even if she herself no longer lived amongst them, the spirit of the past was with her still.

The House on the Strand

For my predecessors
at Kilmarth

1

THE FIRST THING I noticed was the clarity of the air, and then the sharp green colour of the land. There was no softness anywhere. The distant hills did not blend into the sky but stood out like rocks, so close that I could almost touch them, their proximity giving me that shock of surprise and wonder which a child feels looking for the first time through a telescope. Nearer to me, too, each object had the same hard quality, the very grass turning to single blades, springing from a younger, harsher soil than the soil I knew.

I had expected—if I expected anything—a transformation of another kind: a tranquil sense of well-being, the blurred intoxication of a dream, with everything about me misty, ill-defined; not this tremendous impact, a reality more vivid than anything hitherto experienced, sleeping or awake. Now every impression was heightened, every part of me singularly aware: eyesight, hearing, sense of smell, all had been in some way sharpened.

All but the sense of touch: I could not feel the ground beneath my feet. Magnus had warned me of this. He had told me, "You won't be aware of your body coming into contact with inanimate objects. You will walk, stand, sit, brush against them, but will feel nothing. Don't worry. The very fact that you can move without sensation is half the wonder."

This, of course, I had taken as a joke, one of the many bribes to goad me to experiment. Now he was proved right. I started to go forward, and the sensation was exhilarating, for I seemed to move without effort, feeling no contact with the ground.

I was walking downhill towards the sea, across those fields of sharp-edged silver grass that glistened under the sun, for the sky—dull, a moment ago, to my ordinary eyes—was now cloudless, a blazing ecstatic blue. I remembered that the tide had been out, the stretches of flat sand exposed, the row of bathing huts, lined like dentures in an open mouth, forming a solid background to the golden expanse. Now they had gone, and with them the rows of houses fronting the road, the docks, all of Par—chimneys, rooftops, buildings—and the sprawling tentacles of St. Austell enveloping the countryside beyond the bay. There was nothing left but grass and scrub, and the high distant hills that seemed so near; while before me the sea rolled into the bay, covering the whole stretch of sand as if a tidal wave had swept over the land, swallowing it in one rapacious draught. To the northwest the cliffs came down to meet the sea, which, narrowing gradually, formed a wide estuary, the waters sweeping inward, following the curve of the land and so vanishing out of sight.

When I came to the edge of the cliff and looked beneath me, where the road should be, the inn, the café, the almshouses at the base of Polmear hill, I realised that the sea swept inland here as well, forming a creek that cut to the east, into the valley. Road and houses had gone, leaving only a dip between the land which rose on either side of the creek. Here the channel ran narrowly between banks of mud and sand, so that at low tide the water would surely seep away, leaving a marshy track that could be forded, if not on foot, at least by a horseman. I descended the hill and stood beside the creek, trying to pinpoint in my mind the exact course of the road I knew, but already the old sense of orientation had gone: there was nothing to serve as guide except the ground itself, the valley and the hills.

The waters of the narrow channel rippled swift and blue over the sand, leaving on either side a frothy scum. Bubbles formed, expanded and vanished, and all the ordinary timeless waste came drifting with the tide, tresses of dark seaweed, feathers, twigs, the aftermath of some autumnal gale. I knew, in my own time, it was high summer, however dull and overcast the day, but all about me now was the clearer light of approaching winter, surely an early afternoon when the bright sun, already flaming in the west, would turn the sky dark crimson before the night clouds came.

The first live things swam into vision, gulls following the tide, small waders skimming the surface of the stream, while high on the opposite hill, sharply defined against the skyline, a team of oxen ploughed their steady course. I closed my eyes, then opened them again. The team had vanished behind the rise of the field they worked, but the cloud of gulls, screaming in their wake, told me they had been a living presence, no figment of a dream.

I drank deep of the cold air, filling my lungs. Just to breathe was a joy never yet experienced for its own sake, having some quality of magic that I had not sensed before. Impossible to analyse thought, impossible to let my reason play on what I saw: in this new world of perception and delight there was nothing but intensity of feeling to serve as guide.

I might have stood forever, entranced, content to hover between earth and sky, remote from any life I knew or cared to know; but then I turned my head and saw that I was not alone. The hooves had made no sound—the pony must have travelled as I had done, across the fields—and now that it trod upon the shingle the clink of stone against metal came to my ears with a sudden shock, and I could smell the warm horseflesh, sweaty and strong.

Instinct made me back away, startled, for the rider came straight towards me, unconscious of my presence. He checked his pony at the water's edge and looked seaward, measuring the tide. Now, for the first time, I experienced not only excitement but fear as well, for this was no phantom figure but solid, real, the shape of foot in stirrup, hand on rein, all too perilously close for my comfort. I did not fear being ridden down: what jolted me to a sudden sense of panic was the encounter itself, this bridging of centuries between his time and mine. He shifted his gaze from the sea and looked straight at me. Surely he saw me, surely I read, in those deep-set eyes, a signal of recognition? He smiled, patted his pony's neck, then, with a swift kick of heel to flank, urged the beast across the ford, straight through the narrow channel, and so to the other side.

He had not seen me, he could not see me; he lived in another time. Why, then, the sudden shift in the saddle, the swing round to look back over his shoulder to where I stood? It was a challenge. "Follow if you dare!"—compelling, strange. I measured the depth of water across the ford, and, though it had reached the pony's hocks, plunged after him, careless of a wetting, realising when I reached the other side that I walked dry-shod, without sensation.

The horseman rode uphill, I following, the track he took muddied and very steep, swinging abruptly to the left when it traversed the higher ground. This, I remembered, pleased with the recognition, was the same course that the lane took today—I had driven up it only that morning. Here resemblance ended, for no hedges banked the track as they did in my own time. Plough lands lay to right and left, bare to the winds, and patches of scrubby moor with clumps of furze. We came abreast the team of oxen, and for the first time I could see the man who drove them, a small, hooded figure humped over a heavy wooden plough. He raised a hand in greeting to my horseman, shouted something, then plodded on, the gulls crying and wheeling above his head.

This greeting of one man to another seemed natural, and the sense of shock that had been part of me since I first saw the horseman at the ford gave place to wonder, then acceptance. I was reminded of my first journey as a child in France, travelling by sleeper overnight, throwing open the carriage window in the morning to see foreign fields fly by, villages, towns, figures labouring the land humped like the ploughman now, and thinking, with childish wonder, "Are they alive like me, or just pretending?"

My excuse for wonder was greater now than then. I looked at my horseman and his pony, and moved within touching, smelling distance. Both exhaled a pungency so strong that they seemed of the essence of life itself. The sweat streaks on the pony's flanks, the shaggy mane, the fleck of froth at the bit's edge; and that broad knee in the stockinged leg, the leather jerkin laced across the tunic, that movement in the saddle, those hands upon the reins, that face itself, lantern-jawed and ruddy, framed in black hair which fell below his ears—this was reality, I the alien presence.

I longed to stretch out my hand and lay it on the pony's flank, but I remembered Magnus's warning. "If you meet a figure from the past, don't for heaven's sake touch him. Inanimate objects don't matter, but if you try to make contact with living flesh the link breaks, and you'll come to with a very unpleasant jerk. I tried it: I know."

The track led across the plough lands and then dipped, and now the whole altered landscape spread itself before my eyes. The village of Tywardreath, as I had seen it a few hours earlier, had utterly changed. The cottages and houses that had formed a jigsaw pattern, spreading north and west from the church, had vanished: there was a hamlet here now, boxed together by a child, like the toy farm I used to play with on my bedroom floor. Small dwellings, thatch-roofed, squat, clustered round a sprawling green on which were pigs, geese, chickens, two or three hobbled ponies, and the inevitable prowling dogs. Smoke rose from these humble dwellings, but not from any chimneys, from some hole in the thatch. Then grace and symmetry took charge again, for below the cluster was the church. But not the church that I had known a few hours earlier. This one was smaller and had no tower, and forming part of it, or so it seemed, ran a long, low building of stone, the whole encompassed by stone walls. Within this enclosure were orchards, gardens, outbuildings, a wooded copse, and beneath the copse the land sloped to a valley, and up that valley came the long arm of the sea.

I would have stood and stared, the setting had such beauty and simplicity, but my horseman travelled on, and compulsion to follow sent me after him. The track descended to the green, and now the village life was all about me; there were women by the well at the near corner of the green, their long skirts caught up round the waist, their heads bound with cloth covering them to the chin, so that nothing showed but eyes and nose. The arrival of my horseman created disturbance. Dogs started barking, more women appeared from the dwellings that now, on closer inspection, proved to be little more than hovels, and there was a calling to and fro across the green, the voices, despite the uncouth clash of consonants, ringing with the unmistakable Cornish burr.

The rider turned left, dismounted before the walled enclosure, flung his reins over a staple in the ground, and entered through a broad, brass-studded doorway. Above the arch there was a carving showing the robed figure of a saint, holding in his right hand the cross of St. Andrew. My Catholic training, long forgotten, even mocked, made me cross myself before that door, and as I did so a bell sounded from within, striking so profound a chord in my memory that I hesitated before entering, dreading the old power that might turn me back into the childhood mould.

I need not have worried. The scene that met my eyes was not that of orderly paths and quadrangles, quiet cloisters, the odour of sanctity, the silence born of prayer. The gate opened upon a muddied yard, round which two men were chasing a frightened boy, flicking at his bare thighs with flails. Both, from their dress and tonsure, were monks, and the boy a novice, his skirt secured above his waist to make their sport more piquant.

The horseman watched the pantomime unmoved, but when the boy at last fell, his habit about his ears, his skinny limbs and bare backside exposed, he called, "Don't bleed him yet. The Prior likes sucking pig served without sauce. The garnish will come later when the piglet turns tough." Meanwhile the bell for prayer continued, without effect upon the sportsmen in the yard.

My horseman, his sally applauded, crossed the yard and entered the building that lay before us, turning into a passageway which seemed to divide kitchen from refectory, judging by the smell of rancid fowl, only partly sweetened by turf smoke from the fire. Ignoring the warmth and savour of the kitchen to the right, and the colder comfort of the refectory with its bare benches on his left, he pushed through a centre door and up a flight of steps to a higher level, where the passage was barred by yet another door. He knocked upon it, and without waiting for an answer walked inside.

The room, with timbered roof and plastered walls, had some semblance of comfort, but the scrubbed and polished austerity, a vivid memory of my own childhood, was totally absent. This rush-strewn floor was littered with discarded bones half-chewed by dogs, and the bed in the far corner, with its musty hangings, appeared to serve as a general depository for dumped goods—a rug made from a sheep's coat, a pair of sandals, a rounded cheese on a tin plate, a fishing rod, with a greyhound scratching itself in the midst of all.

"Greetings, Father Prior," said my horseman.

Something rose to a sitting posture in the bed, disturbing the greyhound, which leapt to the floor, and the something was an elderly, pink-cheeked monk, startled from his sleep.

"I left orders I was not to be disturbed," he said.

My horseman shrugged. "Not even for the Office?" he asked, and put out his hand to the dog, which crept beside him, wagging a bitten tail.

The sarcasm brought no reply. The Prior dragged his coverings closer, humping his knees beneath him. "I need rest," he said, "all the rest possible, to be in a fit state to receive the Bishop. You have heard the news?"

"There are always rumours," answered the horseman.

"This was not rumour. Sir John sent the message yesterday. The Bishop has already set out from Exeter and will be here on Monday, expecting hospitality and shelter for the night with us, after leaving Launceston."

The horseman smiled. "The Bishop times his visit well. Martinmas, and fresh meat killed for his dinner. He'll sleep with his belly full, you've no cause for worry."

"No cause for worry?" The Prior's petulant voice touched a higher key. "You think I can control my unruly mob? What kind of impression will they make upon that new broom of a Bishop, primed as he is to sweep the whole Diocese clean?"

"They'll come to heel if you promise them reward for seemly behaviour. Keep in the good graces of Sir John Carminowe, that's all that matters."

The Prior moved restlessly beneath his covers. "Sir John is not easily fooled, and he has his own way to make, with a foot in every camp. Our patron he may be, but he won't stand by me if it doesn't suit his ends."

The horseman picked up a bone from the rushes, and gave it to the dog. "Sir Henry, as lord of the manor, will take precedence over Sir John on this occasion," he said. "He'll not disgrace you, garbed like a penitent. I warrant he is on his knees in the chapel now."

The Prior was not amused. "As the lord's steward you should show more respect for him," he observed, then added thoughtfully, "Henry de Champernoune is a more faithful man of God than I."

The horseman laughed. "The spirit is willing, Father Prior, but the flesh?" He fondled the greyhound's ear. "Best not talk about the flesh before the Bishop's visit." Then he straightened himself and walked towards the bed. "The French ship is lying off Kylmerth. She'll be there for two more tides if you want to give me letters for her."

The Prior thrust off his covers and scrambled from the bed. "Why in the name of blessed Antony did you not say so at once?" he cried, and began to rummage amongst the litter of assorted papers on the bench beside him. He presented a sorry sight in his shift, with spindle legs mottled with varicose veins, and hammer-toed, singularly dirty feet. "I can find nothing in this jumble," he complained. "Why are my papers never in order? Why is Brother Jean never here when I require him?"

He seized a bell from the bench and rang it, exclaiming in protest at the horseman, who was laughing again. Almost at once a monk entered: from his prompt response he must have been listening at the door. He was young and dark, and possessed a pair of remarkably brilliant eyes.

"At your service, Father," he said in French, and before he crossed the room to the Prior's side exchanged a wink with the horseman.

"Come, then, don't dally," fretted the Prior, turning back to the bench.

As the monk passed the horseman he murmured in his ear, "I'll bring the letters later tonight, and instruct you further in the arts you wish to learn."

The horseman bowed in mock acknowledgment, and moved towards the door. "Goodnight, Father Prior. Lose no sleep over the Bishop's visit."

"Goodnight, Roger, goodnight. God be with you."

As we left the room together the horseman sniffed the air with a grimace. The mustiness of the Prior's chamber had now an additional spice, a whiff of perfume from the French monk's habit.

We descended the stairs, but before returning through the passageway the horseman paused a moment, then opened another door and glanced inside. The door gave entrance to the chapel, and the monks who had been playing pantomime with the novice were now at prayer. Or, to describe it more justly, making motion of prayer. Their eyes were downcast, and their lips moved. There were four others present whom I had not seen in the yard, and of these two were fast asleep in their stalls. The novice himself was huddled on his knees, crying silently but bitterly. The only figure with any dignity was that of a middle-aged man, dressed in a long mantle, his grey locks framing a kindly, gracious face. With hands clasped reverently before him, he kept his eyes steadfast on the altar. This, I thought, must be Sir Henry de Champernoune, lord of the manor and my horseman's master, of whose piety the Prior had spoken.

The horseman closed the door and went out into the passage, and so from the building and across the now empty yard to the gate. The green was deserted, for the women had left the well, and there were clouds in the sky, a sense of fading day. The horseman mounted his pony and turned for the track through the upper plough lands.

I had no idea of time, his time or mine. I was still without sense of touch, and could move beside him without effort. We descended the track to the ford, which he traversed now without wetting his pony's hocks, for the tide had ebbed, and struck upwards across the further fields.

When we reached the top of the hill and the fields took on their familiar shape I realised, with growing excitement and surprise, that he was leading me home, for Kilmarth, the house which Magnus had lent me for the summer holidays, lay beyond the little wood ahead of us. Some six or seven ponies were grazing close by, and at sight of the horseman one of them lifted his head and whinnied; then with one accord they swerved, kicked up their heels, and scampered away. He rode on through a clearing in the wood, the track dipped, and there immediately below us in the hollow lay a dwelling, stone-built, thatched, encircled by a yard deep in mud. Piggery and byre formed part of the dwelling, and through a single aperture in the thatch the blue smoke curled. I recognised one thing only, the scoop of land in which the dwelling lay.

The horseman rode down into the yard, dismounted and called, and a boy came out of the adjoining cow house to take the pony. He was younger, slighter than my horseman, but had the same deep-set eyes, and must have been his brother. He led the pony off, and the horseman passed through the open doorway into the house, which seemed at first sight to consist of one room only. Following close behind, I could distinguish little through the smoke, except that the walls were built of the mixture of clay and straw that they call cob, and the floor was plain earth, without even rushes upon it.

A ladder at the far end led to a loft, only a few feet above the living space, and looking up I could see straw pallets laid upon the planking. The fire, stacked with turf and furze, lay in a recess let into the wall, and a stew pot simmered above the smoke, slung between iron bars fixed to the earthen floor. A girl, her lank hair falling below her shoulders, was kneeling by the fire, and as the horseman called a greeting she looked up at him and smiled.

I was close upon his heels, and suddenly he turned, staring straight at me, shoulder to shoulder. I could feel his breath upon my cheek, and I put out one hand, instinctively, to fend him off. I felt a sudden sharp pain on my knuckles and saw that they were bleeding, and at the same time I heard a splintering of glass. He was not there any longer, neither he, nor the girl, nor the smoking fire, and I had driven my right hand through one of the windows of the disused kitchen in Kilmarth's basement, and was standing in the old sunken courtyard beyond.

I stumbled through the open door of the boiler room, retching violently, not at the sight of blood but because I was seized with an intolerable nausea, rocking me from head to foot. Throbbing in every limb, I leant against the stone wall of the boiler room, the trickle of blood from my cut hand running down to my wrist.

In the library overhead the telephone began to ring, sounding, in its insistency, like a summons from a lost, unwanted world. I let it ring.

2

IT MUST HAVE taken the best part of ten minutes for the nausea to pass. I sat on a pile of logs in the boiler room waiting. The worst thing about it was the vertigo: I dared not trust myself to stand. My hand was not badly cut, and I soon staunched the blood with my handkerchief. I could see the splintered window from where I sat, and the fragments of glass on the patio beyond. Later on I might be able to reconstruct the scene, judge where my horseman had been standing, measure the space of that long-vanished house where there were now patio and basement: but not now. Now I was too exhausted.

I wondered what sort of figure I must have cut, if anyone had seen me walking over the fields and across the road at the bottom of the hill, and climbing the lane to Tywardreath. That I had been there I was certain. The state of my shoes, the torn cloth of one trouser leg, and my shirt clammy cold with sweat—this had not come about from a lazy amble on the cliffs.

Presently, the nausea and vertigo having passed, I walked very slowly up the back stairs to the hall above. I went into the lobby where Magnus kept his oilskins and boots and all the rest of his junk, and stared at myself in the looking-glass above the wash-basin. I looked normal enough. A bit white about the gills, nothing worse. I needed a stiff drink more than anything. Then I remembered that Magnus had said: "Don't touch alcohol for at least three hours after taking the drug, and then go slow." Tea would be a poor second-best, but it might help, and I went into the kitchen to make myself a cup.

This kitchen had been the family dining room when Magnus was a boy; he had converted it during recent years. While I waited for the kettle to boil I looked out of the window at the courtyard below. It was a paved enclosure, surrounded by old, moss-encrusted walls. Magnus, in a burst of enthusiasm at some time, had attempted to turn it into a patio, as he called it, where he could flop about nude if a heat wave ever materialised. His mother, he told me, had never done anything about the enclosure because it led out from what were then kitchen quarters.

I looked upon it now with different eyes. Impossible to recapture what I had so lately seen—that muddied yard, with the cowhouse adjoining, and the track leading to the wooded grove above. Myself following the horseman through the trees. Was the whole thing hallucination engendered by that hell-brew of a drug? As I wandered, mug in hand, through to the library, the telephone started to ring again. I suspected it might be Magnus, and it was. His voice, clipped and decisive as always, stood me in greater stead than the drink I could not have, or the mug of tea. I flung myself down in a chair and prepared for a session.

"I've been ringing you for hours," he said. "Had you forgotten you promised to put through a call at half-past three?"

"I had not forgotten," I told him. "The fact is, I was otherwise engaged."

"So I imagined. Well?"

The moment was one to savour. I wished I could keep him guessing. The thought gave me a pleasing sensation of power, but it was no use. I knew I had to tell him.

"It worked," I said. "Success one hundred percent."

I realised, from the silence at the other end of the line, that this piece of information was totally unexpected. He had visualised failure. His voice, when it came, was pitched in a lower key, almost as though he were talking to himself.

"I can hardly believe it," he said. "How absolutely splendid . . ." And then, taking charge, as always, "You did exactly as I told you, followed the instructions? Tell me everything, from the beginning . . . Wait, though, are you all right?"

"Yes," I said, "I think so, except that I feel bloody tired, and I've cut my hand, and I was nearly sick in the boiler room."

"Minor matters, dear boy, minor matters. There's often a feeling of nausea afterwards, it soon passes. Go on."

His impatience fed my own excitement, and I wished he had been in the room beside me instead of three hundred miles away.

"First of all," I said, enjoying myself, "I've seldom seen anything more macabre than your so-called lab. Bluebeard's chamber would be an apter description for it. All those embryos in jars, and that revolting monkey's head . . ."

"Perfectly good specimens and extremely valuable," he interrupted, "but don't get side-tracked. I know what they are for: you don't. Tell me what happened."

I took a sip of my rapidly cooling tea, and put down the mug.

"I found the row of bottles," I continued, "all in the locked cupboard. Neatly labelled, A, B, C. I poured exactly three measures from A into the medicine glass, and that was that. I swallowed it, replaced the bottle and glass, locked the cupboard, locked the lab, and waited for something to happen. Well, nothing did."

I paused, to let this information sink in. No comment from Magnus.

"So," I went on, "I went into the garden. Still no reaction. You told me the time factor varied, that it could be three minutes, five, ten, before anything happened. I expected to feel drowsy, although you hadn't specifically mentioned drowsiness, but as nothing seemed to be happening I thought I would go for a stroll. So I climbed over the wall by the summerhouse into the field, and began to walk in the direction of the cliffs."

"You damn fool," he said. "I told you to stay in the house, at any rate for the first experiment."

"I know you did. But, frankly, I wasn't expecting it to work. I planned to sit down, if it did, and drift off into some delightful dream."

"Damn fool," he said again. "It doesn't happen that way."

"I know it doesn't, now," I said.

Then I described my whole experience, from the moment the drug took effect to the smashing of glass in the kitchen. He did not interrupt me at all except to murmur, when I paused for breath and a sip of tea, "Go on . . . go on . . ."

When I had finished, including the aftermath in the boiler room, there was complete silence, and I thought we had been cut off. "Magnus," I said, "are you there?"

His voice came back to me, clear and strong, repeating the same words that he had used at the start of our telephone session.

"How splendid," he said. "How absolutely splendid."

Perhaps . . . The truth was that I was completely drained, exhausted, having been through the whole process twice.

He began to talk rapidly, and I could just imagine him sitting at that desk of his in London, one hand holding the receiver, the other reaching out for his inevitable doodling pad and pencil.

"You realise," he said, "that this is the most important thing that has happened since the chemical boys got hold of teonanacatl and ololiuqui? These only push the brain around in different directions—quite chaotic. This is controlled, specific. I knew I was on to something potentially tremendous, but I couldn't be sure, having only tried it on myself, that it wasn't hallucinogenic. If this was so, you and I would have had similar physical reactions—loss of touch, greater intensity of vision, and so on—but not the same experience of altered time. This is the important thing. The tremendously exciting thing."

"You mean," I said, "that when you tried it on yourself you also went back in time? You saw what I did?"

"Precisely. I didn't expect it any more than you did. No, that's not true, because an experiment I was working on then made it remotely possible. It has to do with DNA, enzyme catalysts, molecular equilibria and the like—above your head, dear boy, I won't elaborate—but the point that interests me at the moment is that you and I apparently went into an identical period of time. Thirteenth or fourteenth century, wouldn't you say, judging from their clothes? I too saw the chap you describe as your horseman—Roger, didn't the Prior call him?—the rather slatternly girl by the fire, and someone else as well, a monk, which immediately suggested a tie-up with the mediaeval priory that was once part of Tywardreath. The point is this: Does the drug reverse some chemical change in the memory systems of the brain, throwing it back to a particular thermodynamic situation which existed in the past, so that the sensations elsewhere in the brain are repeated? If it does, why does the molecular brew return to that particular moment in time? Why not yesterday, five years ago, or a hundred and twenty years? It could be—and this is the thing that excites me—it could be that there is some very potent link connecting the taker of the drug with the first human image recorded in the brain, while under the drug's influence. In both our cases we saw the horseman. The compulsion to follow him was particularly urgent. You felt it, so did I. What I don't yet know is why he plays Virgil to our Dante in this particular Inferno, but he does, there's no escaping him. I've made the 'trip'—to use the student's phraseology—a number of times, and he's invariably there. You'll find the same thing happens on your next adventure. He always takes charge."

The assumption that I was to continue acting as guinea pig for Magnus did not surprise me. It was typical of our many years of friendship, both at Cambridge and afterwards. He called the tune, and I danced, in God only knew how many disreputable escapades in our undergraduate life together, and later when we went our separate ways, he to his career as biophysicist and thence to a professorship at London University, I to the tamer routine of a publisher's office. My marriage to Vita three years ago had made the first break between us, possibly a salutary one for us both. The sudden offer of his house for the summer holidays, which I had accepted gratefully, being between jobs—Vita was urging me to accept a directorship in a flourishing New York publishing firm run by her brother, and I needed time to decide—now appeared to have strings attached. The long, lazy days with which he had baited me, lying about in the garden, sailing across the bay, were beginning to take on another aspect.

"Now look here, Magnus," I said, "I did this for you today because I was curious, and also because I was on my own, and whether the drug had any effect or not didn't matter one way or the other. It's quite out of the question to go on. When Vita and her children arrive I shall be tied up with them."

"When do they come?"

"The boys break up in about a week. Vita's flying back from New York to fetch them from school and bring them down here."

"That's all right. You can achieve a lot in a week. Look, I must go. I'll ring you at the same time tomorrow. Goodbye."

He had gone. I was left holding the receiver, with a hundred questions to ask and nothing resolved. How damnably typical of Magnus. He had not even told me if I must expect some side effect from his hell-brew of synthetic fungus and monkeys' brain cells, or whatever the solution was that he had extracted from his range of loathsome bottles. The vertigo might seize me again, and the nausea too. I might suddenly go blind, or mad, or both. To hell with Magnus and his freak experiment . . .

I decided to go upstairs and take a bath. It would be a relief to strip off my sweaty shirt, torn trousers, the lot, and relax in a tub of steaming water primed with bath oil—Magnus was nothing if not fastidious in his tastes. Vita would approve of the bedroom suite he had put at our disposal, his own, in point of fact, bedroom, bathroom, dressing room, the bedroom with a stunning view across the bay.iu13I lay back in the bath, letting the water run until it reached my chin, and thought of our last evening in London, when his dubious experiment had been proposed. Previously he had merely suggested that, if I wanted somewhere to go during the boys' school holidays, Kilmarth was mine for the taking. I had telephoned Vita in New York, pressing the offer. Vita, not altogether enthusiastic, being a hothouse plant like many American women, and usually preferring to take a vacation under a Mediterranean sky with a casino handy, demurred that it always rained in Cornwall, didn't it, and would the house be warm enough, and what should we do about food? I reassured her on all these points, even to the daily woman who came up every morning from the village, and finally she agreed, chiefly, I think, because I had explained there was a dishwasher and an outsize fridge in the lately converted kitchen. Magnus was much amused when I told him.

"Three years of marriage," he said, "and the dishwasher means more to your conjugal life than the double bed I'm throwing in for good measure. I warned you it wouldn't last. The marriage, I mean, not the bed."

I skated over the somewhat thorny topic of my marriage, which was going through a period of reaction after the first impulsive, passionate twelve months, for if it was thorny this was largely because I wanted to remain in England and Vita wanted me to settle in the States. In any event, neither my marriage nor my future job concerned Magnus, and he passed on to talk about the house, the various changes he had made since his parents had died—I had stayed there several times when we were at Cambridge—and how he had converted the old laundry in the basement to a laboratory, just for the fun of it, so that he could amuse himself with experiments that would have no connection with his work in London.

On this last occasion he had prepared the ground well with an excellent dinner, and I was under the usual spell of his personality, when he suddenly said, "I've had what I think is a success with one particular piece of research. A combination of plant and chemical into a drug which has an extraordinary effect upon the brain."

His manner was casual, but Magnus was always casual when he was making some statement that was important to him.

"I thought all the so-called hard drugs had that effect," I said. "The people who take them, mescalin, LSD, or whatever, pass into a world of fantasy filled with exotic blooms and imagine they're in Paradise."

He poured more brandy into my glass. "There was no fantasy about the world I entered," he said. "It was very real indeed."

This piqued my curiosity. A world other than his own egotistical centre would have to possess some special attraction to draw him into it.

"What sort of world?" I asked.

"The past," he answered.

I remember laughing as I cupped the brandy glass in my hand. "All your sins, do you mean? The evil deeds of a misspent youth?"

"No, no," he shook his head impatiently, "nothing personal at all. I was merely an observer. No, the fact was . . ." he broke off, and shrugged his shoulders. "I won't tell you what I saw: it would spoil the experiment for you."

"Spoil the experiment for me?"

"Yes. I want you to try the drug yourself, and see if it produces the same effect."

I shook my head. "Oh, no," I told him, "we're not at Cambridge any more. Twenty years ago I might have swallowed one of your concoctions and risked death. Not any longer."

"I'm not asking you to risk death," he said impatiently. "I'm asking you to give up twenty minutes, possibly an hour, of an idle afternoon, before Vita and the children arrive, by trying an experiment on yourself that may change the whole conception of time as we know it at present."

There was no doubt that he meant every word he said. He was no longer the flippant Magnus of Cambridge days; he was a professor of biophysics, already famous in his particular field, and, although I understood little if anything of his life's work, I realised that if he really had hit upon some remarkable drug he might be mistaken in its importance, but he was not lying about his own evaluation of it.

"Why me?" I asked. "Why not try it on your disciples in London University under proper conditions?"

"Because it would be premature," he said, "and because I'm not prepared to risk telling anyone, not even my disciples, as you choose to call them. You are the only one to know that I'm even thinking along these particular lines, which is way outside the stuff I usually do. I stumbled on this thing by chance, and I've got to find out more about it before I'm even remotely satisfied that it has possibilities. I intend to work on it when I come down to Kilmarth in September. Meanwhile, you're going to be alone in the house. You could at least try it once, and report back. I may be entirely wrong about it. It may have no effect upon you except to turn your hands and feet temporarily numb and make your brain, such as you possess, dear boy, rather more alert than it is at present."

Of course in the end, after another glass of brandy, he had talked me into it. He gave me detailed instructions about the lab, he gave me the keys to the lab itself and to the cupboard where he kept the drug, and described the sudden effect it might have—no intervening stage, but direct transition from one state to another—and he said something about the aftereffects, the possibility of nausea. It was only when I asked him directly what I was likely to see that he became evasive.

"No," he said, "it might predispose you, unconsciously, to see what I saw. You've got to make this experiment with an open mind, unprejudiced."

A few days later I left London and drove to Cornwall. The house was aired and ready—Magnus had briefed Mrs. Collins from Polkerris, the small village below Kilmarth—and I found vases filled with flowers, food in the fridge, and fires in the music room and the library, although it was mid-July; Vita could not have done better herself. I spent the first couple of days enjoying the peace of the place, and the comfort, too, which, if I remembered rightly, had been lacking in former times when Magnus's delightful and somewhat eccentric parents were in command. The father, Commander Lane, had been a retired naval man with a passion for sailing a ten-ton yacht in which we were invariably seasick, the mother a vague, haphazard creature of great charm who pottered about in an enormous broad-brimmed hat whatever the weather, indoors and out, and spent her time snipping the dead heads off roses, which she grew with passion but with singular lack of real success. I laughed at them and loved them, and when they died within twelve months of one another I was almost more distressed than Magnus was himself.

It all seemed a long time ago now. The house was a good deal changed and modernized, yet somehow their engaging presence lingered still, or so I had thought, those first few days. Now, after the experiment, I was not so sure. Unless, having seldom penetrated the basement in those early holidays, I had been unaware that it held other memories.

I got out of the bath and dried myself, put on a change of clothes, lit a cigarette, and went downstairs to the music room, so-called in lieu of the more conventional "drawing room" because Magnus's parents excelled at playing and singing duets. I wondered if it was still too soon to pour myself the drink I badly needed. Better be safe than sorry—I would wait another hour.

I switched on the radiogram and picked a record at random from the top of the stack. Bach's Brandenburg Concerto No, 3 might restore my poise and equanimity. Magnus must have mixed up his records the last time he was down, however, for it was not the measured strains of Bach that fell upon my ears, as I lay stretched on the sofa before the log fire, but the insidious, disquieting murmur of Debussy's *La Mer*. Odd choice for Magnus when he had been down at Easter. I thought he eschewed the romantic composers. I must have been mistaken, unless his taste had changed through the years. Or had his dabbling in the unknown awakened a liking for more mystical sounds, the magical conjuring of sea upon the shore? Had Magnus seen the estuary sweeping deep into the land, as I had done this afternoon? Had he seen the green fields sharp and clear, the blue water prodding the valley, the stone walls of the Priory graven against the hill? I did not know: he had not told me. So much unasked on that abortive telephone conversation. So much unsaid.

I let the record play to the end, but far from calming me it had the opposite effect. The house was strangely silent now the music had stopped, and with the rise and fall of *La Mer* still lingering in my head I walked through the hall to the library and looked out of the wide window to the sea. It was slate grey, whipped darker in places by a westerly wind, yet calm, with little swell. Different from the more turbulent blue sea of afternoon glimpsed in that other world.

There are two staircases descending to the basement at Kilmarth. The first, leading from the hall, goes direct to the cellars and the boiler-room, and thence to the door into the patio. The second is reached by passing through the kitchen, and so down to the back entrance, the old kitchen, scullery, larder and laundry. It was the laundry, reached by the second staircase, that Magnus had converted to a laboratory.

I went down these stairs, turned the key of the door, and entered the laboratory once again. There was nothing clinical about it. The old sink still stood upon the stone-flagged floor beneath a small barred window. Beside it was an open fireplace, with a cloam oven, used in old days for baking bread, cut into the thickness of the wall. In the cobwebbed ceiling were rusty hooks, from which in former times salted meat and hams must have hung.

Magnus had ranged his curious exhibits along the slatted shelves fixed to the walls. Some of them were skeletons, but others were still intact, preserved in a chemical solution, their flesh bleached pale. Most were hard to distinguish—for all I knew they could have been kittens in embryo form, or even rats. The two specimens I recognised were the monkey's head, the smooth skull perfectly preserved, like the bald pate of a tiny unborn child, with eyes closed, and, next to it, a second monkey's head from which the brain had been removed, and which now lay in a jar nearby, pickled and brown. There were other jars and other bottles that held fungi, plants and grasses, grotesquely shaped, with spreading tentacles and curling leaves.

I had mocked him, over the telephone, calling the laboratory Bluebeard's chamber. Now, as I looked round it again, the memory of my afternoon still vivid in my mind, the small room seemed to hold a different quality. I was reminded not so much of the bearded potentate in the Eastern fairy tale as of an engraving, long forgotten, that had scared me as a child. It was called *The Alchemist*. A figure, naked save for a loincloth, was crouching by a walled oven like the one here in the laundry, kindling a fire with bellows, and to his left stood a hooded monk and an abbot, carrying a cross. A fourth man, in mediaeval hat and cloak, leant upon a stick conferring with them. There had been bottles, too, upon a table, and open jars containing eggshells, hairs and thread-like worms, and in the centre of the room a tripod with a rounded flask balanced upon it, and in the flask a minute lizard with a dragon's head.

Why only now, after some five-and-thirty years, did the memory of that dread engraving return to haunt me? I turned away, locking the door of Magnus's laboratory, and went upstairs. I could not wait any longer for that much-needed drink.

3

IT RAINED THE following day, one of those steady mizzles that accompany a drifting fog from the sea, preventing any enjoyment out of doors. I awoke feeling perfectly normal, having slept surprisingly well, but when I drew back the curtains and saw the state of the weather I went back to bed again, despondent, wondering what I was going to do with myself all day.

This was the Cornish climate about which Vita had expressed her doubts, and I could imagine her reproaches if it happened when the holidays were in full swing, my young stepsons staring aimlessly out of the window, then forced into wellingtons and macs and sent, protesting, to walk along the sands at Par. Vita would wander from music room to library altering the position of the furniture, saying how much better she could arrange the rooms if they were hers, and when this palled she would telephone one of her many friends from the American Embassy crowd in London, themselves outward bound for Sardinia or Greece. These symptoms of discontent I was spared for a while longer, and the days ahead of me, wet or fine, were at least free, my own time for my own movements.

The obliging Mrs. Collins brought me up my breakfast and the morning paper, commiserated with me about the weather, saying that the Professor always found plenty to do in that funny little old room of his down under, and informed me that she would roast one of her own chickens for my lunch. I had no intention of going "down under," and opened the morning paper and drank my coffee. But the doubtful interest of the sports page soon palled, and my attention wandered back to the all-absorbing question of exactly what had happened to me the previous afternoon.

Had there been some telepathic communication between Magnus and myself? We had tried this at Cambridge, with cards and numbers, but it had never worked, except once or twice by pure coincidence. And we had been more intimate in those days than we were now. I could think of no means, telepathic or otherwise, by which Magnus and I could have undergone the same experience, separated by an interval of some three months—it was Easter, apparently, when he had tried the drug himself—unless that experience was directly connected with previous happenings at Kilmarth. Part of the brain, Magnus had suggested, was susceptible to reversal, restoring conditions, when under the influence of the drug, to an earlier period in its chemical history. Yet why that particular time? Had the horseman planted so indelible a stamp on his surroundings that any previous or later period was blotted out?

I thought back to the days when I had stayed at Kilmarth as an undergraduate. The atmosphere was casual, happy-go-lucky. I remembered asking Mrs. Lane once whether the house was haunted. My question was an idle one, for certainly it did not have a haunted atmosphere—I asked simply because it was old.

"Good heavens, no!" she exclaimed. "We're far too wrapped up in ourselves to encourage ghosts. Poor things, they'd wither away from tedium, unable to draw attention to themselves. Why do you ask?"

"No reason," I assured her, afraid I might have given offence. "Only that most old houses like to boast a spook."

"Well, if there is one at Kilmarth we've never heard it," she said. "The house has always seemed such a happy one to us. There's nothing particularly interesting about its history, you know. It belonged to a family called Baker in sixteen hundred and something, and they had it until the Rashleighs rebuilt the place in the eighteenth century. I can't tell you about its origins, but someone told us once that it has fourteenth century foundations."

That was the end of the matter, but now her remarks about early fourteenth century foundations returned to me. I thought about the basement rooms and the courtyard leading out of them, and Magnus's curious choice of old laundry for his laboratory. Doubtless he had his reasons. It was well away from the lived-in part of the house, and he would not be disturbed by callers or Mrs. Collins.

I got up rather late and wrote letters in the library, did justice to Mrs. Collins' roast chicken, and tried to keep my thoughts on the future and what I was going to decide about that offer of a New York partnership. It was no use. The whole thing seemed remote. Time enough when Vita arrived and we could discuss it together.

I looked out of the music-room window and watched Mrs. Collins walk up the drive on her way home. It was still drizzling, and a long, uninviting afternoon lay ahead. I don't know when it was that the idea came to me. Perhaps I had been harbouring it unconsciously since I awoke. I wanted to prove that there had been no telepathic communication between Magnus and myself when I had taken the drug the day before in the laboratory. He had told me he had made his first experiment there, and so had I. Perhaps some thought process had passed between us at the moment when I actually swallowed the stuff, so influencing my train of ideas and what I saw, or imagined I saw, during the course of the afternoon. If the drug was taken elsewhere, not in that baleful laboratory with its suggestive likeness to an alchemist's cell, might not the effect be different? I should never know unless I tried it out.

There was a small pocket flask in the pantry cupboard—I had noticed it the evening before—and I got it out now, and rinsed it under the cold tap. This did not commit me to anything one way or another. Then I went downstairs to the basement, and, feeling like the shadow of my boyhood self when I had sneaked a bar of forbidden chocolate during Lent, I turned the key in the door of the laboratory.

It was a simple matter to disregard the specimens in their jars and reach for the neat little row of labelled bottles. As yesterday, I measured the drops from bottle A, but into the pocket flask this time. Then I locked the laboratory door behind me, went across the yard to the stable block, and fetched the car.

I drove slowly up the drive, turned left out of the lane to the main road, and went down Polmear hill, pausing when I reached the bottom to survey the scene. Here, where the almshouses and the inn stood now, had been yesterday's ford. The lie of the land had not altered, despite the modern road, but the valley where the tide had swept inward was now marsh. I took the lane to Tywardreath, thinking, with some misgiving, that if I had in fact taken this same route yesterday, under the influence of the drug, I could have been knocked down by a passing car without hearing it.

I drove down the steep, narrow lane to the village and parked the car a little above the church. There was still a light rain falling, and nobody was about. A van drove up the main Par road and disappeared. A woman came out of the grocer's shop and walked uphill in the same direction. No one else appeared. I got out of the car, opened the iron gates into the churchyard, and stood in the church porch to shelter from the rain. The churchyard itself sloped away in a southerly direction until it terminated at the boundary wall, and beneath it were farm buildings. Yesterday, in that other world, there were no buildings, only the blue waters of a creek filling the valley with the incoming tide, and the Priory buildings had covered the space the churchyard held today.

I knew the lie of the land better now. If the drug took effect I could leave the car where it was and walk home. There was no one around. Then, like a diver taking a plunge into some arctic pool, I took out the flask and swallowed the contents. The instant I had done so panic seized me. This second dose might have a quite different effect. Make me sleep for hours. Should I stay where I was, or should I be better off in the car? The church porch gave me claustrophobia, so I went out and sat down on one of the tombstones, not far from the pathway but out of sight of the road. If I stayed quite still, without moving, perhaps nothing would happen. I began to pray, "Don't let anything happen. Don't let the drug have any effect."

I went on sitting for about five minutes, too apprehensive about the possible effects of the drug to mind the rain. Then I heard the church clock strike three, and glanced down at my watch to check the time. It was a few minutes slow, so I altered it, and almost immediately I heard shouting from the village, or cheering, perhaps—a curious mélange of the two—and a cracking sound like wheels. Oh God, what now I thought, a travelling circus about to descend the village street? I shall have to move the car. I got up and started to walk along the path to the churchyard gate. I never arrived, because the gate had gone, and I was looking through a rounded window set in a stone wall, the window facing a cobbled quadrangle bounded by shingle paths.

The entrance gate at the far end of the quadrangle was open wide, and beyond it I could see a mass of people assembled on the green, men, women, children. The shouting was coming from them, and the creaking sounds were the wheels of an enormous covered waggon drawn by five horses, the second leader and the horse between the shafts carrying riders upon their backs. The wooden canopy surmounting the waggon was painted a rich purple and gold, and as I watched the heavy curtains concealing the front of the vehicle were drawn aside, the shouting and the applause from the crowd increased, and the figure which appeared in the aperture raised his hands in blessing. He was magnificently dressed in ecclesiastical robes, and I remembered that Roger and the Prior had spoken of an imminent visit by the Bishop of Exeter, and how apprehensive the Prior had been—doubtless with reason. This must be His Grace in person.

There was a sudden hush, and everyone went down upon their knees. The light was dazzling, the feeling had gone from my limbs, and nothing seemed to matter any more. I did not care—the drug could work on me as it wished; my only desire was to be part of the world about me.

I watched the Bishop descend from his covered vehicle, and the crowd pressed forward. Then he entered the gate into the quadrangle, followed by his train. From some door beneath me I saw the Prior advance to meet him at the head of his flock of monks, and the entrance gates were closed against the crowd.

I looked over my shoulder and saw that I was standing in a vaulted chamber filled with a score or more of people, waiting to be presented, to judge by their hushed sense of expectancy. From their clothes they belonged to the gentry, and so presumably were permitted entrance to the Priory.

"Mark it well," said the voice in my ear, "she'll not wear paint on her face on this occasion."

My horseman, Roger, stood beside me, but his remarks were addressed to a companion, a man of about his own age or somewhat older, who put his hand before his mouth to stifle laughter.

"Painted or plain, Sir John will have her," he answered, "and what better moment than the eve of Martinmas, with his own lady safely brought to bed eight miles away at Bockenod?"

"It could be contrived," agreed the other, "but with some risk, for she cannot depend upon Sir Henry's absence. He will scarcely sleep at the Priory tonight, with the Bishop in the guest chamber. No, let them wait awhile longer, if only to whet appetite."

Scandal had not changed much through the centuries then, and I wondered why this back-chat should intrigue me now, which, if it had been exchanged by my contemporaries at some social event, would have made me yawn. Perhaps, because I was eavesdropping in time and within monastic walls, the gossip held more spice. I followed the direction of their gaze to the small group near to the door, the selected few, no doubt, to be presented. Which was the gallant Sir John—the same who liked a foot in both camps, if I remembered the Prior's comment rightly—and which the favoured lady of his choice, shorn of her paint?

There were four men, three women and two youths, and the fashion of the women's headgear made it difficult to distinguish their features from a distance, swathed as they were in coif and wimple. I recognised the lord of the manor, Henry de Champernoune, the dignified, elderly man who had been at his prayers in the chapel yesterday. He was dressed more soberly than his friends, who wore tunics of varying colours hanging to mid-calf, with belts slung low beneath the hip, and pouch and dagger in the centre. All of them were bearded and had their hair curled to a frizz, which must have been the prevailing fashion.

Roger and his companion had been joined by a newcomer in clerical dress, a rosary hanging from his belt. His red nose and slurred speech suggested a recent visit to the Prior's buttery.

"What is the order of precedence?" he mumbled. "As parish priest and chaplain to Sir Henry surely I should form part of his entourage?"

Roger laid a hand on his shoulder and swung him round to face the window. "Sir Henry can do without your breath, and his Grace the Bishop likewise, unless you wish to forfeit your position."

The newcomer protested, clinging nevertheless to the protection of the wall, then lowered himself on to the bench beside it. Roger shrugged his shoulder, turning to the companion at his side.

"It surprises me that Otto Bodrugan dares show his face," said his friend. "Not two years since he fought for Lancaster against the King. They say he was in London when the mob dragged Bishop Stapledon through the streets."

"He was not," replied Roger. "He was with many hundreds of the Queen's party up at Wallingford."

"Nevertheless, his position is delicate," said the other. "If I were the Bishop I should not look kindly upon the man reputed to have condoned the murder of my predecessor."

"His Grace has not the time to play politics," retorted Roger. "He will have his hands full with the diocese. Past causes are no concern of his. Bodrugan is here today by reason of the demesnes he shares with Champernoune, because his sister Joanna is Sir Henry's lady. Also, out of his obligation to Sir John. The two hundred marks he borrowed are still unpaid."

Commotion at the door made them move forward for a better view, small fry on the lower rungs of this particular ladder. The Bishop entered, the Prior beside him, sprucer and cleaner than when he had sat up in his tumbled bed with the scratching greyhound. The gentlemen made obeisance, the ladies curtseyed, and the Bishop extended his hand for each to kiss, while the Prior, flustered by the ceremonial, presented them in turn. Playing no part in their world I could move about at will, so long as I touched none of them, and I drew closer, curious to discover who was who in the company.

"Sir Henry de Champernoune, lord of the manor of Tywardreath," murmured the Prior, "lately returned from a pilgrimage to Campostella."

My elderly knight stepped forward, bending low with one knee on the ground, and I was struck once more by his air of dignity and grace, coupled with humility. When he had kissed the extended hand he rose, and turned to the woman at his side.

"My wife Joanna, your Grace," he said, and she sank to the ground in an endeavour to equal her husband in humility, bringing off the gesture well. So this was the lady who would have painted her face but for the Bishop's visitation. I decided she had done well enough to let it alone. The wimple that framed her features was adornment enough, enhancing the charms of any woman, plain or beautiful. She was neither the one nor the other, but it did not surprise me that her fidelity to her conjugal vows had been in question. I had seen eyes like hers in women of my own world, full and sensual: one flick of the male head, and she'd be game.

"My son and heir, William," continued her husband, and one of the youths came forward to make obeisance.

"Sir Otto Bodrugan," continued Sir Henry, "and his lady, my sister Margaret."

It was evidently a closely knit world, for had not my horseman Roger remarked that Otto Bodrugan was brother to Joanna, Champernoune's wife, and so doubly connected with the lord of the manor? Margaret was small and pale, and evidently nervous, for she stumbled as she made her curtsey to His Grace, and would have fallen had not her husband caught her. I liked Bodrugan's looks: there was a panache about him, and he would, I thought, be a good ally in a duel or escapade. He must have had a sense of humour, too, for instead of colouring or looking vexed at his wife's gaffe he smiled and reassured her. His eyes, brown like those of his sister Joanna, were less prominent than hers, but I felt that he had his full share of her other qualities.

Bodrugan in his turn presented his eldest son Henry, and then stepped back to give way to the next man in the line. He had clearly been itching to put himself forward. Dressed more richly than either Bodrugan or Champernoune, he wore a self-confident smile on his lips.

This time it was the Prior who made the introduction. "Our loved and respected patron, Sir John Carminowe of Bockenod," he announced, "without whom we in this Priory would have found ourselves hard-pressed for money in these troublous times."

Here then was the knight with a foot in either camp, one lady in confinement eight miles away, the other present in this chamber but not yet bedded. I was disappointed, expecting a roisterous type with a roving eye. He was none of these, but small and stout, puffed up with self-importance like a turkey-cock. The lady Joanna must be easily pleased.

"Your Grace," he said in pompous tones, "we are deeply honored to have you here amongst us," and bent over the proffered hand with so much affectation that had I been Otto Bodrugan, who owed him two hundred marks, I would have kicked him on the backside and compounded the debt.

The Bishop, keen-eyed, alert, was missing nothing. He reminded me of a general inspecting a new command and making mental notes about the officers: Champernoune past it, needs replacing; Bodrugan gallant in action but insubordinate, to judge from his recent part in the rebellion against the King; Carminowe ambitious and overzealous—apt to make trouble. As for the Prior, was that a splash of gravy on his habit? I could swear the Bishop noticed it, as I did; and a moment later his eye travelled across the heads of the lesser fry and fell upon the almost recumbent figure of the parish priest. I hoped, for the sake of the Prior's charges, that the inspection would not be continued later in the Priory kitchen, or, worse, still, in the Prior's own chamber.

Sir John had risen from his knees, and was making introductions in his turn.

"My brother, your Grace, Sir Oliver Carminowe, one of His Majesty's Commissioners, and Isolda his lady." He elbowed forward his brother, who, from his flushed appearance had hazy eye, looked as if he had been passing the hours of waiting in the buttery with the parish priest.

"Your Grace," he said, and was careful not to bend his knee too low for fear of swaying when he stood upright. He was a better-looking fellow than Sir John, despite the tippling: taller, broader, with a ruthless set about the jaw, not one to fall foul with in an argument.

"She's the one I'd pick if fortune favoured me."

The whisper in my ear was very near. Roger the horseman was at my side once more; but he was not addressing me but his companion. There was something uncanny in the way he led my thoughts, always at my elbow when I least supposed him there. He was right, though, in his choice, and I wondered if she too was aware of his attention, for she stared straight at us as she rose from her curtsey, and the kissing of the Bishop's hand.

Isolda, wife to Sir Oliver Carminowe, had no wimple to frame her features, but wore her golden hair in looped braids, with a jewelled fillet crowning the small veil upon her head. Nor did she wear a cloak over her dress like the other women, and the dress itself was less wide in the skirt, more closely fitting, the long, tight sleeves reaching beyond her wrist. Possibly, being younger than her companions, not more than twenty-five or twenty-six, fashion played a stronger part in her life; if so, she did not seem conscious of the fact, wearing her clothes with casual grace. I have never seen a face so beautiful or so bored, and as she swept us with her eyes—or rather, Roger and his companion—without the faintest show of interest, the slight movement of her mouth a moment later betrayed the fact that she was stifling a yawn.

It is the fate of every man, I suppose, at some time or other to glimpse a face in a crowd and not forget it, or perhaps, by a stroke of luck, to catch up with the owner at a later date, in a restaurant, at a party. To meet often breaks the spell and leads to disenchantment. This was not possible now. I looked across the centuries at what Shakespeare called "a lass unparalleled," who, alas, would never look at me.

"How long, I wonder," murmured Roger, "will she stay content within the walls of Carminowe and keep a guard upon her thoughts from straying?"

I wished I knew. Had I been living in his time I would have handed in my resignation as steward to Sir Henry Champernoune and offered my services to Sir Oliver and his lady.

"One mercy for her," replied the other, "she does not have to provide her husband with an heir, with three stout stepsons filling the breach. She can do as she pleases with her time, having produced two daughters whom Sir Oliver can trade and profit by when they reach marriageable age."

So much for woman's value in other days. Goods reared for purchase, then bought and sold in the marketplace, or rather manor. Small wonder that, their duty done, they looked round for consolation, either by taking a lover or by playing an active part in the bargaining over their own daughters and sons.

"I tell you one thing," said Roger. "Bodrugan has an eye to her, but while he's under this obligation to Sir John he has to watch where he steps."

"I lay you five denarii to nought she will not look at him."

"Taken. And if she does I'll act as go-between. I play the role often enough between my lady and Sir John."

As eavesdropper in time my role was passive, without commitment or responsibility. I could move about in their world unwatched, knowing that whatever happened I could do nothing to prevent it—comedy, tragedy, or farce—whereas in my twentieth century existence I must take my share in shaping my own future and that of my family.

The reception appeared over, but the visit was not yet through, for a bell summoned one and all to vespers and the company divided, the more favoured to the Priory chapel, the lesser ranks to the church, which was at the same time part of the chapel, an arched doorway, with a grille, dividing the one from the other.

I thought I might dispense with vespers, though by standing close to the grille I could have watched Isolda, but my inevitable guide, craning his neck with the same thought in mind, decided that he had been idle long enough, and, signalling to his companion with a quick jerk of the head, made his way out of the Priory building and across the quadrangle to the entrance gate. Someone had flung it open once again, and a cluster of people, lay brothers and servants, were standing there, laughing, as they watched the Bishop's attendants struggle to turn the clumsy vehicle towards the Priory yard. The wheels were stuck between muddied road and village green, but this was by no means the only fun to be observed, for the green itself was crowded with men, women and children. Some sort of market seemed to be in progress, for there were little booths and stalls set up, some fellow was beating a drum and another squeaked on a fiddle, while a third nearly split my ears with two horns as long as himself, which he managed by sleight of hand to play simultaneously.

I followed Roger and his friend across the green. They paused every moment to greet acquaintances, and I realised that this was no sudden jollification put on for the Bishop's benefit but some butcher's paradise, for newly slaughtered sheep and pigs, still dripping blood, were hanging upon posts at every booth. The dwellings bordering the green boasted a like display. Each householder, knife in hand, was hard at work stripping the pelt off some old ewe, or slitting a pig's throat, and one or two fellows, higher perhaps on the feudal ladder, brandished the heads of oxen, the widespread horns winning shouts of applause and laughter from the crowd. Torches flared as the light faded, slaughterers and strippers taking on a demonic aspect, working fast and furiously to have their task accomplished before night came, and because of it the excitement mounted, and the musician with the horn in either hand, wandering in and out amongst the crowd, lifted his instruments high to make a greater blast upon the air.

"God willing, they'll have their bellies lined this winter," observed Roger. I had forgotten him in all the tumult, but he was with me still.

"I take it you have every beast counted?" asked his friend.

"Not only counted but inspected before slaughter. Not that Sir Henry would know or care if he was lacking a hundred head of cattle, but my lady would. He's too deep in his prayers to watch his purse, or his belongings."

"She trusts you, then?"

My horseman laughed. "Faith! She's obliged to trust me, knowing what I do of her affairs. The more she leans upon my counsel, the sounder she sleeps at night."

He turned his head as a new commotion fell upon our ears, this time from the Priory stableyard, where the Bishop's equipage had finally been housed, taking the place of smaller vehicles, similarly furnished with wooded canopy and sides, and bearing coats-of-arms. Half-chariot, half-waggonette, they seemed a clumsy method of carrying ladies of rank about the countryside, but this was evidently their purpose, for three of them emerged from the rear premises, creaking and groaning with every turn of the wheel, and stood in line before the Priory entrance.

Vespers was over, and the faithful who had attended were emerging from the church, to mingle with the crowd upon the green. Roger made his way into the quadrangle, and so to the Priory building itself, where the Prior's guests were gathering before departure. Sir John Carminowe was in the forefront, and beside him Sir Henry's lady, Joanna de Champernoune. As we approached he murmured in her ear, "Will you be alone if I ride tomorrow?"

"Perhaps," she said. "Better still, wait until I send word."

He bent to kiss her hand, then mounted the horse which a groom was holding, and cantered off. Joanna watched him go then turned to her steward.

"Sir Oliver and Lady Isolda lodge with us tonight," she said. "See if you can hasten their departure. And find Sir Henry too. I wish to be away."

She stood there in the doorway, foot tapping impatiently upon the ground, the full brown eyes surely brooding upon some scheme which would further her own ends. Sir John must be hard-pressed to keep her sweet. Roger entered the Priory, and I followed him. Voices came from the direction of the refectory, and, enquiring from a monk who was standing by, he was told that Sir Oliver Carminowe was taking refreshment with others of the company, but that his lady was in the chapel still.

Roger paused a moment, then turned towards the chapel. I thought at first that it was empty. The candles on the altar had been extinguished, and the light was dim. Two figures stood near to the grille, a man and a woman. As we came closer I saw that they were Otto Bodrugan and Isolda Carminowe. They were speaking low and I could not hear what they said, but the weariness had gone from her face, and the boredom too, and suddenly she looked up at him and smiled.

Roger tapped me on the shoulder. "It's much too dark to see. Shall I switch on the lights?"

It was not his voice. He had gone, and so had they. I was standing in the southern aisle of the church, and a man wearing a dog collar under his tweed jacket was by my side.

"I saw you just now in the churchyard," he said, "looking as if you couldn't make up your mind whether to come in out of the rain. Well, now you have, let me show you round. I'm the vicar of St. Andrew's. It's a fine old church and we're very proud of it."

He put his hand on a switch and turned on all the lights. I glanced down at my watch, without nausea, without vertigo. It was exactly half-past three.

4

THERE HAD BEEN no perceptible transition. I had passed from one world to the other instantaneously, without the physical side effects of yesterday. The only difficulty was mental readjustment, requiring an almost intolerable degree of concentration. Luckily the vicar preceded me up the aisle, chatting as we went, and if there was anything strange in my expression he was too polite to comment.

"We get a fair number of visitors in the summer," he said, "people staying at Par, or they come over from Fowey. But you must be an enthusiast, hanging about the churchyard in the rain."

I made a supreme effort to pull myself together. "In point of fact," I said, surprised to find that I could even speak, "it was not really the church itself or the graves that interested me. Someone told me there had been a Priory here in former days."

"Ah, yes, the Priory," he said. "That's been gone a long time, no trace of it left, unfortunately. The buildings all fell in after the dissolution of the monasteries in 1539. Some say the site was where Newhouse Farm is now, just below us in the valley, and others that it occupied the present churchyard itself, south of the porch, but nobody really knows."

He led me to the north transept and showed me the tombstone of the last Prior, who had been buried before the altar in 1538, and pointed out the pulpit and some pew-ends, and all that was left of the original rood screen. Nothing of what I observed bore any resemblance to the small church I had so lately seen, with the grille in the wall dividing it from the Priory chapel; nor, as I stood here now beside the vicar, could I reconstruct from memory anything of an older transept, an older aisle.

"Everything's changed," I said.

"Changed?" he repeated, puzzled. "Oh, no doubt. The church was largely restored in 1880, possibly not altogether successfully. Are you disappointed?"

"No," I assured him hastily, "not at all. It's only that . . . Well, as I was saying, my interest goes back to very early days, long before the dissolution of the monasteries."

"I understand." He smiled in sympathy. "I've often wondered myself what it all looked like in former times, with the Priory close by. It was a French house, you know, attached to the Benedictine Abbey of St. Serguis and Bacchus in Angers, and I believe most of the monks were French. I wish I could tell you more about it, but I've only been here a few years, and I'm afraid I'm no historian."

"Neither am I," I told him, and we retraced our steps toward the porch.

"Do you know anything," I asked, "about the lords of the manor in early times?"

He paused to switch off the lights. "Only what I have read in the *Parochial History*," he said. "The manor is mentioned in Domesday as Tiwardrai—the House

on the Strand—and it belonged to the great family of Cardinham until the last heiress
Isolda sold it to the Champernounes, in the thirteenth century, and when they died out
it passed to other hands."

"Isolda?"

"Yes, Isolda de Cardinham. She married someone called William Ferrers of Bere
in Devon, but I'm afraid I don't remember the details. You would find out more about
it in the St. Austell public library than from me." He smiled again, and we passed
through the door to the churchyard. "Are you staying in the neighbourhood or passing
through?" he asked.

"Staying. Professor Lane has lent me his house for the summer."

"Kilmarth? I know it, of course, but I've never been inside. I don't think Professor
Lane gets down very often, and he doesn't come to church."

"No," I replied, "probably not."

"Well," he said, as we parted at the gate, "if you feel like coming either to a service
or just to wander around, it will be nice to see you."

We shook hands, and I walked up the road to where I had parked the car. I
wondered whether I had been impossibly rude. I had not even thanked him for his
courtesy, or introduced myself. Doubtless he considered me just another summer
visitor, more boorish than usual, and a crank into the bargain. I got into the car, lit a
cigarette, and sat there to collect my thoughts. The fact that there had been no
physical reaction to the drug whatsoever was an astonishing relief. Not a suspicion of
dizziness or nausea, and my limbs did not ache as they had done the day before, nor
was I sweating.

I wound down the car window and looked up the street, then back again to the
church. None of it fitted. The green where the people had so lately crowded must have
covered all the present area, and beyond it too, where the modern road turned uphill.
The Priory yard, where the bishop's equipage nearly came to grief, would have been
in that hollow below the gents' hairdresser, boundering the east wall of the churchyard, and the Priory itself, according to one theory mentioned by the vicar, filled
the entire space that the southern portion of the churchyard held today. I closed my
eyes. I saw the entrance, the quadrangle, the long narrow building forming kitchens
and refectory, monks' dormitory, chapter house, where the reception had been held,
and the Prior's chamber above. Then I opened them again, but the pieces did not fit,
and the church tower threw my jigsaw puzzle out of balance. It was no good—nothing
tallied save the lie of the land.

I threw away my cigarette, started the car, and took the road past the church. A
curious feeling of elation came to me as I swept downhill past the valley stream, and
so to the low-lying, straggling shops of Par. Not ten minutes since the whole of this
had been under water, the sloping Priory lands lapped by the sea. Sandbanks had
bordered the wide sweep of the estuary where those bungalows stood now, and
houses and shops were all blue channel with a running tide. I stopped the car by the
chemist's and bought some toothpaste, the feeling of elation increasing as the girl
wrapped it up. It seemed to me that she was without substance, the shop as well, and
the two other people standing there, and I felt myself smiling furtively because of
this, with an urge to say, "You none of you exist. All this is under water."

I stood outside the shop, and it had stopped raining. The heavy pall that had been
overhead all day had broken at last into a patchwork sky, squares of blue alternating
with wisps of smoky cloud. Too soon to go back home. Too early to ring Magnus.
One thing I had proved, if nothing else: this time there had been no telepathy between
us. He might have had some intuition of my movements the preceding afternoon, but
not today. The laboratory in Kilmarth was not a bogey hole conjuring up ghosts, any
more than the porch in St. Andrew's church had been filled with phantoms. Magnus
must be right in his assumption that some primary chemical process was reversible,
the drug inducing this change; and conditions were such that the senses, reacting to
the situation as a secondary effect, swung into action, capturing the past.

I had not awakened from some nostalgic dream when the vicar tapped me on the shoulder, but had passed from one living reality to another. Could time be all-dimensional—yesterday, today, tomorrow running concurrently in ceaseless repetition? Perhaps it needed only a change of ingredient, a different enzyme, to show the future, myself a bald-headed buffer in New York with the boys grown-up and married, and Vita dead. The thought was disconcerting. I would rather concern myself with the Champernounes, the Carminowes, and Isolda. No telepathic communication here: Magnus had mentioned none of them, but the vicar had, and only after I had seen them as living persons.

Then I decided what to do: I would drive to St. Austell and see if there was some volume in the public library that would give proof of their identity.

The library was perched above the town, and I parked the car and went inside. The girl at the desk was helpful. She advised me to go upstairs to the reference library, and search for pedigrees in a book called *The Visitations of Cornwall*.

I took the fat volume from the shelves and settled myself at one of the tables. First glance in alphabetical order was disappointing. No Bodrugans and no Champernounes. No Carminowes either. And no Cardinhams. I turned to the beginning once again, and then, with quickening interest, realised that I must have muddled the pages the first time, for I came upon the Carminowes of Carminowe. I let my eye travel down the page, and there Sir John was, married to a Joanna into the bargain—he must have found the similarity of names of wife and mistress confusing. He had a great brood of children, and one of his grandsons, Miles, had inherited Boconnoc. Boconnoc . . . Bockenod . . . a change in the spelling, but this was my Sir John without a doubt.

On the succeeding page was his elder brother Sir Oliver Carminowe. By his first wife he had had several children. I glanced along the line and found Isolda his second wife, daughter of one Reynold Ferrers of Bere in Devon, and below, at the bottom of the page, her daughters, Joanna and Margaret. I'd got her—not the Vicar's Devon heiress, Isolda Cardinham, but a descendant.

I pushed the heavy volume aside, and found myself smiling fatuously into the face of a bespectacled man reading the *Daily Telegraph*, who stared at me suspiciously, then hid his face behind his paper. My lass unparalleled was no figure of the imagination, nor a telepathic process of thought between Magnus and myself. She had lived, though the dates were sketchy: it did not state when she was born or when she died.

I put the book back on the shelves and walked downstairs and out of the building, the feeling of elation increased by my discovery. Carminowes, Champernounes, Bodrugans, all dead for six hundred years, yet still alive in my other world of time.

I drove away from St. Austell thinking how much I had accomplished in one afternoon, witnessing a ceremony in a Priory long since crumbled, coupled with Martinmas upon the village green. And all through some wizard's brew concocted by Magnus, leaving no side effect or aftermath, only a sense of well-being and delight. It was as easy as falling off a cliff. I drove up Polmear hill doing a cool sixty, and it was not until I had turned down the drive to Kilmarth, put away the car and let myself into the house that I thought of the simile again. Falling off a cliff . . . Was this the side effect? This sense of exhilaration, that nothing mattered? Yesterday the nausea, the vertigo, because I had broken the rules. Today, moving from one world to another without effort, I was cock-a-hoop.

I went upstairs to the library and dialled the number of Magnus's flat. He answered immediately.

"How was it?" he asked.

"What do you mean, how was it? How was what? It rained all day."

"Fine in London," he replied. "But forget the weather. How was the second trip?"

His certainty that I had made the experiment again irritated me. "What makes you think I took a second trip?"

"One always does."

"Well, you're right, as it happens. I didn't intend to, but I wanted to prove something."

"What did you want to prove?"

"That the experiment was nothing to do with any telepathic communication between us."

"I could have told you that," he said.

"Perhaps. But we had both experimented first in Bluebeard's chamber, which might have had an unconscious influence."

"So . . ."

"So, I poured the drops into your drinking flask—forgive me for making myself at home—drove to the church, and swallowed them in the porch."

His snort of delight annoyed me even more.

"What's the matter?" I asked. "Don't tell me you did the same?"

"Precisely. But not in the porch, dear boy, in the churchyard after dark. The point is, what did you see?"

I told him, winding up with my encounter with the vicar, the visit to the public library, and the absence, or so I had thought, of any side effects. He listened to my saga without interruption, as he had done the day before, and when I had concluded he told me to hang on, he was going to pour himself a drink, but he reminded me not to do likewise. The thought of his gin and tonic added fuel to my small flame of irritation.

"I think you came out of it all very well," he said, "and you seem to have met the flower of the county, which is more than I have ever done, in that time or this."

"You mean you did not have the same experience?"

"Quite the contrary. No chapter house or village green for me. I found myself in the monks' dormitory, a very different kettle of fish."

"What went on?" I asked.

"Exactly what you might suppose when a bunch of mediaeval Frenchmen got together. Use your imagination."

Now it was my turn to snort. The thought of fastidious Magnus playing peeping Tom amongst that fusty crowd brought my good humour back again.

"You know what I think?" I said. "I think we found what we deserved. I got His Grace the Bishop and the County, awaking in me all the forgotten snob appeal of Stonyhurst, and you got the sexy deviations you have denied yourself for thirty years."

"How do you know I've denied them?"

"I don't. I give you credit for good behaviour."

"Thanks for the compliment. The point is, none of this can be put down to telepathic communication between us. Agreed?"

"Agreed."

"Therefore we saw what we saw through another channel—the horseman, Roger. He was in the chapter house and on the green with you, and in the dormitory with me. His is the brain that channels the information to us."

"Yes, but why?"

"Why? You don't think we are going to discover that in a couple of trips? You have work to do."

"That's all very well, but it's a bit of a bore having to shadow this chap, or have him shadow me, every time I may decide to make the experiment. I don't find him very sympathetic. Nor do I take to the lady of the manor."

"The lady of the manor?" He paused a moment, I supposed for reflection. "She's possibly the one I saw on my third trip. Auburn-haired, brown eyes, rather a bitch?"

"That sounds like her. Joanna Champernoune," I said.

We both laughed, struck by the folly and the fascination of discussing someone who had been dead for centuries as if we had met her at some party in our own time.

"She was arguing about manor lands," he said. "I did not follow it. Incidentally, have you noticed how one gets the sense of the conversation without conscious translation from the mediaeval French they seem to be speaking? That's the link again, between his brain and ours. If we saw it before us in print, old English or Norman-French or Cornish, we shouldn't understand a word."

"You're right," I said. "It hadn't struck me. Magnus . . ."

"Yes?"

"I'm still a bit bothered about side effects. What I mean is, thank God I had no nausea or vertigo today, but on the contrary a tremendous sense of elation, and I must have broken the speed limit several times driving home."

He did not reply at once, and when he did his tone was guarded. "That's one of the things," he said, "one of the reasons we have to test the drug. It could be addictive."

"What do you mean exactly, addictive?"

"What I say. Not just the fascination of the experience itself, which we both know nobody else has tried, but the stimulation to the part of the brain affected. And I've warned you before of the possible physical dangers—being run over, that sort of thing. You must appreciate that part of the brain is shut off when you're under the influence of the drug. The functional part still controls your movements, rather as one can drive with a high percentage of alcohol in the blood and not have an accident, but the danger is always present, and there doesn't appear to be a warning system between one part of the brain and another. There may be. There may not. All this is part of what I have to find out."

"Yes," I said. "Yes, I see." I felt rather deflated. The sense of exhilaration which I had experienced while driving back had certainly been unusual. "I'd better lay off," I said, "give it a miss, unless the circumstances are absolutely right."

Again he paused before he answered. "That's up to you," he said. "You must judge for yourself. Any more questions? I'm dining out."

Any more questions . . . A dozen, twenty. But I should think of them all when he had rung off. "Yes," I said. "Did you know before you took your first trip that Roger had once lived here in this house?"

"Absolutely not," he replied. "Mother used to talk about the Bakers of the seventeenth century, and the Rashleighs who followed them. We knew nothing about their predecessors, although my father had a vague idea that the foundations went back to the fourteenth century; I don't know who told him."

"Is that why you converted the old laundry into Bluebeard's chamber?"

"No, it just seemed a suitable place, and the cloam oven is rather fun. It retains the heat if you light the fire, and I can keep liquids there at a high temperature while I'm working at something else alongside. Perfect atmosphere. Nothing sinister about it. Don't run away with the idea that this experiment is some sort of a ghost hunt, dear boy. We're not conjuring spirits from the vasty deep."

"No, I realise that," I said.

"To reduce it to its lowest level, if you sit in an armchair watching some old movie on television, the characters don't pop out of the screen to haunt you, although many of the actors are dead. It's not so very different from what you were up to this afternoon. Our guide Roger and his friends were living once, but are well and truly laid today."

I knew what he meant, but it was not as simple as that. The implications went deeper, and the impact too, the sensation was not so much that of witnessing their world as of taking part in it.

"I wish," I said, "we knew more about our guide. I daresay I can dig up the others in the St. Austell library—I've found the Carminowes already, as I told you, John, and his older brother Oliver, and Oliver's wife Isolda—but a steward called Roger is rather a long shot, and is hardly likely to figure in any pedigree."

"Probably not, but you can never tell. One of my students has a buddy who works in Public Record Office and the British Museum, and I've got the business in hand. I haven't told him why I am interested, just that I want a list of taxpayers in the parish of Tywardreath in the fourteenth century. He should be able to find it, I gather, in the Lay Subsidy Roll for 1327, which must be pretty near the period we want. If something turns up I'll let you know. Any news of Vita?"

"None."

"Pity you didn't arrange to fly the boys over to her in New York," he said.

"Too damned expensive. Besides, that would have meant I had to go too."

"Well, keep them all at bay for as long as you can. Say something has gone wrong with the drains—that will daunt her."

"Nothing daunts Vita," I told him. "She'd bring some plumbing expert down from the American Embassy."

"Well, press on before she arrives. And while I think of it, you know the sample marked B in the lab, alongside the A solution you're using?"

"Yes."

"Pack it carefully and send it up to me. I want to put it under test."

"Then you *are* going to try it out in London?"

"Not on myself, on a healthy young monkey. He won't see his mediaeval forebears, but he might get the staggers. Goodbye."

Magnus had hung up on me again in his usual brusque fashion, leaving me with the inevitable sense of depletion. It was always so, whenever we met and talked, or spent an evening together. First the stimulation, sparks flying and the moments speeding by, then suddenly he would be gone, hailing a taxi and disappearing—not to be seen again for several weeks—while I wandered aimlessly back to my own flat.

"And how was your Professor?" Vita would ask in the ironic, rather mocking tone she assumed when I had passed an evening in Magnus's company, an emphasis on the "your" which never failed to sting.

"In the usual form," I would answer. "Full of wild ideas I find amusing."

"Glad you had fun," was the reaction, but with a biting edge that implied the reverse of pleasure. She told me once, after a somewhat longer session than usual, when I had come home rather high about two A.M., that Magnus sapped me, and that when I returned to her I looked like a pricked balloon.

It was one of our first rows, and I did not know how to deal with it. She wandered around the sitting room punching cushions and emptying her own ash trays, while I sat on the sofa looking aggrieved. We went to bed without speaking, but the next morning, to my surprise and relief, she behaved as if nothing had happened, and positively glowed with feminine warmth and charm. Magnus was not mentioned, but I made a mental note not to dine with him again unless she had a date herself elsewhere.

Today I did not feel like a pricked balloon when he rang off—the expression was rather offensive, come to think of it, suggesting the fetid air of somebody's breath exploding—merely denuded of stimulation, and a little uneasy too, because why did he suddenly want a test done on the bottle marked B? Did he want to make certain of his findings on the unfortunate monkey before putting me, the human guinea pig, to a possibly sharper test? There was still sufficient solution in bottle A, to keep me going . . .

I was brought up sharply in my train of thought. Keep me going? It sounded like an alcoholic preparing for a spree, and I remembered what Magnus had said about the possibilities of the drug being addictive. Perhaps this was another reason for trying it out on the monkey. I had a vision of the creature, bleary-eyed, leaping about his cage and panting for the next injection.

I felt in my pocket for the flask, and rinsed it out very thoroughly. I did not replace it on the pantry shelf, however, for Mrs. Collins might take it into her head to move it somewhere else, and then if I happened to want it I should have to ask her where it was, which would be a bore. It was too early for supper, but the tray she had laid with ham and salad, fruit and cheese looked tempting, and I decided to carry it into the music room and have a long evening by the wood fire.

I took a stack of records at random and piled them one on top of the other on the turntable. But, no matter what sounds filled the music room, I kept returning to the scenes of this afternoon, the reception in the Priory chapter house, the stripping of carcasses on the village green, the hooded musician with his double-horn wandering amongst the children and barking dogs, and above all that lass with braided hair and jewelled fillet who, one afternoon six hundred years ago, had looked so bored until, because of some remark which I could not catch, spoken by a man in another time, she had lifted her head and smiled.

5

THERE WAS AN airmail letter from Vita on my breakfast tray next morning. It was written from her brother's house on Long Island. The heat was terrific, she said, they were in the pool all day, and Joe was taking his family to Newport on the yacht he had chartered midweek. What a pity we had not known his plans earlier on. I could have flown the boys over and we could all have spent the summer vacation together. As things were, it was too late to change anything. She only hoped the Professor's house would turn out to be a success—and how was it, anyway? Did I want her to bring a lot of food down from London? She was flying from New York on Wednesday, and hoped there would be a letter waiting for her at the flat in London.

Today was Wednesday. She was due in at London airport around ten o'clock this evening, and she would not find a letter in the flat because I had not expected her until the weekend.

The thought of Vita arriving in the country within a few hours came as a shock. The days I had thought my own, with complete freedom to plan as I wished, would be upset by telephone calls, demands, questions, the whole paraphernalia of life *en famille*. Somehow, before the first telephone call came through, I must be ready with a delaying device, some scheme to keep her and the boys in London for at least another few days.

Magnus had suggested drains. Drains it well might be, but the trouble was that when Vita finally arrived she would naturally start asking Mrs. Collins about it, and Mrs. Collins would stare at her in blank surprise. The room's not ready? This would reflect on Mrs. Collins, and bode ill for future relations between the two women. Electricity failure? But it hadn't, any more than the drains. Nor could I pretend to be ill, for this would bring Vita down immediately to move me, wrapped in blankets, to hospital back in London; she was suspicious of all medical treatment unless it was top grade. Well, I must think of something, if only for Magnus's sake; it would be letting him down if the experiment was brought to an abrupt conclusion after only two attempts to prove success.

Today was Wednesday. Say experiment on Wednesday, give it a miss on Thursday, then experiment on Friday, a miss on Saturday, experiment on Sunday, and, if Vita was adamant about coming down on Monday, then Monday she must come. This plan allowed for three "trips" (the LSD phraseology was certainly apt) and, providing nothing went wrong and I chose my moment well, did nothing foolish, the side effects would be nil, just as they had been yesterday, apart from the sense of exhilaration, which I should immediately recognise and accept as a warning. In any event I felt no exhilaration now; Vita's letter was doubtless the cause of the slight despondency that appeared to be my form today.

Breakfast over, I told Mrs. Collins that my wife was arriving in London tonight, and would probably be coming down with her boys next week, on Monday or Tuesday. She immediately produced a list of groceries and other things which would be needed. This gave me an opportunity to drive down to Par to collect them, and at the same time think out the text of a letter to Vita which she would get the following morning.

The first person I saw in the grocer's was the vicar of St. Andrews', who crossed the shop to say good morning. I introduced myself, belatedly, as Richard Young, and told him that I had taken his advice and gone to the county library at St. Austell after leaving the church.

"You must be a real enthusiast," he smiled. "Did you find what you wanted?"

"In part," I replied. "The heiress Isolda de Cardinham proved elusive in the book of pedigrees, although I found a descendant, Isolda Carminowe, whose father was a Reynold Ferrers of Bere in Devon."

"Reynold Ferrers rings a bell," he said. "The son, I believe I'm right in saying, of Sir William Ferrers who married the heiress. Therefore your Isolda would be their granddaughter. I know the heiress sold the manor of Tywardreath to one of the Champernounes in 1269, just before she married William Ferrers, for one hundred pounds. Quite a sum in those days."

I made a rapid calculation in my head. My Isolda could hardly have been born before 1300. She had not looked more than about twenty-eight at the Bishop's reception, which would date that event around 1328.

I followed the vicar round the shop as he made his purchases. "Do you still celebrate Martinmas at Tywardreath?" I asked.

"Martinmas?" he echoed, looking bewildered—he was hesitating between a choice of biscuits. "Forgive me, I don't quite follow you. It was a well-known feast in the centuries before the Reformation. We keep St. Andrew's Day, of course, and generally hold the church fete in the middle of June."

"Sorry," I murmured, "I've got my dates rather mixed. The truth is, I was brought up a Catholic, and went to school at Stonyhurst, and I seem to remember we used to attach a certain importance to St. Martin's Even . . ."

"You are prefectly right," he interrupted, smiling. "November 11th, Armistice Day, has rather taken its place, hasn't it? Or rather, Armistice Sunday. But now I understand your interest in the Priory, if you're a Catholic."

"Non-practising," I admitted, "but you have a point. Old customs cling. Do you ever have a fair on the village green?"

"I'm afraid not," he said, plainly puzzled, "and to the best of my knowledge there has never been a village green at Tywardreath. Excuse me . . ."

He leant forward to receive the purchases dropped in his basket, and the assistant turned his attention to me. I consulted the list given me by Mrs. Collins, and the vicar, with a cheery good morning, went his way. I wondered if he thought me mad, or merely one of Professor Lane's more eccentric friends. I had forgotten St. Martin's Eve was November 11th. An odd coincidence of dates. Slaughter of oxen, pigs and sheep, and in the world of today a commemoration of uncounted numbers slain in battle. I must remember to tell Magnus.

I carried my load of groceries outside, dumped them in the boot of the car, and drove out of Par by the church road to Tywardreath. But instead of parking outside the gents' hairdresseres, as I had done the day before, I drove slowly up the hill through the centre of the village, trying to reconstruct that nonexistent village green. It was hopeless. There were houses to the right and left of me, and at the top of the hill the road branched right to Fowey, while to the left the signpost said To Treesmill. Somewhere, from the top of this hill, the Bishop and his cortège had driven yesterday, and the covered waggonettes of Carminowes, Champernounes, and Bodrugans, their coats-of-arms emblazoned on the side. Sir John Carminowe would have taken the right-hand fork—if it existed—to Lostwithiel and his demesne of Bockenod, where his lady awaited her confinement. Today Bockenod was Boconnoc, a vast estate a few miles from Lostwithiel; I had passed one of the lodge gates on my drive down from London. Where, then, did the lord of the manor, Sir Henry de Champernoune, have his demesne? His wife Joanna had told her steward, my horseman Roger, "The Bodrugans lodge with us tonight." Where would the manor house have stood?

I stopped the car at the top of the hill and looked about me. There was no house of any great size in the village of Tywardreath itself; some of the cottages could be late eighteenth century, but none belonged to an earlier period. Reason told me that manor houses were seldom destroyed, unless by fire, and even if they were burnt to the ground, or the walls crumbled, the site would be put to another purpose within a few years, and a farmhouse erected on the spot to serve the one-time manor lands. Somewhere, within a radius of a mile or two of Priory and church, the Champernounes would have built their own dwelling, or the original manor house would have awaited them when the first Isolda, the Cardinham heiress, sold them the manor lands in 1269. Somewhere—down that left-hand fork, perhaps, where the signpost read To TREESMILL—the foot-tapping Joanna, impatient to be home, had driven in her painted waggonette from the Priory reception, accompanied by her sad-faced lord Sir Henry, and their son William, and followed by her brother Otto Bodrugan and his wife Margaret.

I glanced at my watch. It was past twelve, and Mrs. Collins would be waiting to put away groceries and cook my lunch. Also I had to write to Vita.

I settled to the letter after lunch. It took an hour or so to compose, nor was I satisfied with the result, but it would have to serve.

"Darling," I said, "I had not realised, until your letter came this morning, that you were actually flying back today, so you won't get this before tomorrow. If I've muddled things, forgive me. The fact is there has been a tremendous amount to do here to get the place straight for you and the boys, and I've been hard at it ever since I arrived. Mrs. Collins, Magnus's daily, has been wonderful, but you know what a bachelor household is, and Magnus himself has not been down since Easter, so things were a bit sketchy. Also, and this is the real crux, Magnus asked me to go through a lot of his papers, and so on—he keeps a mass of scientific stuff in his laboratory which must not be touched—and all this has to be put away safely. He asked me to see to it as a personal favour, and I can't let him down, because after all we are getting the house rent-free, and it's some sort of return. I ought to be clear of this chore by Monday, but want the next few days to get on with it, and the weekend too. Incidentally, the weather has been foul. It rained without ceasing all yesterday, so you aren't missing anything, but the locals say it will improve next week.

"Don't worry about food, Mrs. C. has everything under control, and she's a very good cook, so you won't have to worry on that score. Anyway, I'm sure you can occupy the boys until Monday, there must be museums and things they haven't seen, and you will want to meet people, so, darling, I suggest we plan for next week, and by then there should be no problems.

"I'm so glad you enjoyed yourself with Joe and family. Yes— perhaps, in retrospect, it might have been a good idea to have flown the boys out to New York, but it's easy to be wise after the event. I hope you're not too tired, darling, after the flight. Ring me when you get this.

"YOUR LOVING DICK."

I read the letter through twice. It seemed better the second time: it rang true. And I did have to sort things for Magnus. When I lie I like to base the lie on a foundation of fact, for it appeases not only conscience but a sense of justice. I stamped the envelope and put it in my pocket, and then I remembered that Magnus wanted bottle B from the laboratory sent up to him in London. I rummaged about, found a small box, paper and string, and went down to the lab. I compared bottle B with bottle A, but there seemed to be no difference between the two. I was still casrrying the flask of yesterday in my jacket pocket, and it was a simple matter to measure a second dose from A into the flask. I could use my judgment when, and if, I decided to take it.

Then I locked the lab and went upstairs, and had a look at the weather through the library window. It was not raining, and the sky was clearing out to sea. I packed up bottle B with great care, then drove down to Par to register it and to drop Vita's letter in the box, wondering, not so much what she would say when she read it, as how the monkey would react to his first trip into the unknown. My mission accomplished, I drove up through Tywardreath and took the left-hand fork to Treesmill.

The narrow road, with fields on either side of it, ran steeply to a valley, and before the final descent sloped sharply to a hump-backed bridge beneath which the main railway line ran between Par and Plymouth. I braked by the bridge and heard the hoot of the diesel express as it emerged from the tunnel out of sight to my right, and in a few moments the train itself came rattling down the line, passed under the bridge, and curved its way through the valley down to Par. Memories of undergraduate days came back to me. Magnus and I had always travelled down by train, and directly the train came out of the tunnel between Lostwithiel and Par we used to reach for our suitcases. I had been aware, then, of steep fields to the left of the carriage window and a valley to the right, full of reeds and stumpy willows, and suddenly the train would be at the station, the large black board with the white lettering announcing PAR CHANGE FOR NEWQUAY, and we should have arrived.

Now, watching the express disappear round the bend in the valley, I observed the terrain from another angle, and realised how the coming of the railway over a hundred years ago must have altered the sloping fields, the line literally dug out of the hillside. There had been other disturbers of the peace besides the railway. Quarries had scarred the opposite side of the valley on the high ground where the tin and copper mines had flourished a century ago—I remembered Commander Lane telling us once at dinner how hundreds of men had been employed in the mines in Victorian days, and when the slump came chimneys and engine houses were left to crumble into decay, the miners emigrating, or seeking work in the newer industry of china clay.

This afternoon, the train out of sight and the rattle spent, all was quiet once again, and no thing moved in the valley except a few cows grazing in the swampy meadow at the base of the hill. I let the car descend gently to the end of the road before it rose sharply again to climb the opposite hill out of the valley. A sluggish stream ran through the meadow where the cows were grazing, spanned by a low bridge, and above the stream, to the right of the road, were old farm buildings. I lowered the window of the car and looked about me. A dog ran from the farm, barking, followed by a man carrying a pail. I leant out the window and asked him if this was Treesmill.

"Yes," he said. "If you continue straight on you'll come to the main road from Lostwithiel to St. Blazey."

"In point of fact," I answered, "I was looking for the mill itself."

"Nothing left of it," he said. "This building here was the old mill house, and all that's left of the stream is what you see. The main stream was diverted many years ago, before my time. They tell me that before they built this bridge there was a ford here. The stream ran right across this road, and most of the valley was under water."

"Yes," I said, "yes, that's very possible."

He pointed to a cottage the other side of the bridge. "That used to be a pub in old days," he said, "when they were working the mines up at Lanescot and Carrogett. It would be full of miners on a Saturday night, so they tell me. Not many people alive who know much about the old days now."

"Do you know," I asked him, "if there is any farmhouse here in the valley that might have been a manor house in days gone by?"

He considered a moment before replying. "Well," he said, "there's Trevenna up back behind us, on the Stonybridge road, but I've never heard it was old, and Trenadlyn beyond that, and of course Treverran up the valley nearer the railway tunnel. That's an old house all right, fine old place, built hundreds of years ago."

"How long ago?" I enquired, interest rising.

He considered again. "There was a piece about Treverran in the paper once," he said. "Some gentleman from Oxford went to look at it. I believe it was 1705 they said it was built."

My interest ebbed. Queen Anne houses, tin and copper mines, the pub across the road, all these were centuries later than my time. I felt as an archaeologist must feel who discovers a late Roman villa instead of a Bronze Age camp.

"Well, thanks very much," I said, "good day to you," and turned the car and drove back up the hill. If the Champernounes had descended this road in 1328, their covered waggonettes would have been baulked by the millstream at the bottom, unless an older bridge than the one I had seen once forded it. Halfway up the hill I turned left into a side lane, and presently saw the three farmsteads the man had mentioned. I reached for my road map. This side road that I was on would join the main road at the top of the hill—the long tunnel must run deep underground beneath the road, a fine feat of engineering—and yes, the farm on my right was Trevenna, the one in front of me Trenadlyn, and the third, near to the railway line itself, would be Treverran. So what, I asked myself? Drive to each in turn, knock upon the door, and say, "Do you mind if I sit down for half-an-hour, give myself what the drug addicts call 'a fix' and see what happens?"

Archaeologists had the best of it. Someone to finance their digs, enthusiastic company, and no risk of a lunatic asylum at the end of the day. I turned, drove back along my side road, and up the steep hill towards Tywardreath. A car, towing a caravan, was trying to edge its way into the entrance of a bungalow halfway up the hill, effectively blocking my passage. I braked, almost in the ditch, and let the driver proceed with his manoeuvres. He shouted his apologies, and finally succeeded in getting both car and caravan parked beside the bungalow.

He climbed out of his car and walked towards me, apologising once again. "I think you can get past now," he said. "I'm sorry for the holdup."

"That's O.K.," I told him, "I'm in no hurry. You did a fine job getting your caravan clear of the road."

"Oh well, I'm used to it," he said. "I live here, and the caravan gives us extra room when we have summer visitors."

I glanced at the name on the gate. "Chapel Down," I said. "That's unusual."

He grinned. "That's what we thought when we built the bungalow," he said. "We decided to keep the name of the actual plot of ground. It's been Chapel Down for centuries, and the fields across the road are both called Chapel Park."

"Anything to do with the old Priory?" I asked.

He did not register. "There were a couple of cottages here once," he said, "some sort of Methodist meeting house, I believe. But the field names go back a lot further than that."

His wife came out of the bungalow with a couple of children, and I started up the car. "All clear ahead," he called, and I pulled away from the ditch and drove up the hill until the curve in the road hid the bungalow from sight. Then I pulled across to a lay by on the right, where there was a pile of stones and timber.

I had reached the summit of the hill, and beyond the lay by the road curved down to Tywardreath, the first houses already in sight. Chapel Down . . . Chapel Park . . . Could there have been a chapel here in former days, long since demolished, either on the site of the caravan owner's bungalow or near the lay by, where a modern house fronted the road?

Below the house a gate led into a field, and I climbed over it, circuiting the field and keeping close to the hedge until the sloping ground hid me from sight. This was the field the caravan owner said was Chapel Park. It had no distinctive feature that I could see. Cows were grazing at the far end. I scrambled through the hedge at the bottom, and found myself on the precipitous grassland a few hundred feet above the railway, looking straight into the valley.

I lit a cigarette and surveyed the scene. No chapels tucked away, but what a view, Treesmill Farm away to my right, the other farms beyond, all sheltered from prevailing wind and weather, immediately below me the railway, and beyond it the strange sweep of the valley, no pattern of fields, nothing but a tapestry of willow, birch, and alder. A paradise, surely, for birds in spring, and a good place for boys to hide from the parental eye—but boys never went birds-nesting nowadays, at least my stepsons didn't.

I sat down against the hedge to finish my cigarette, and as I did so became aware of the flask in my breast pocket. I took it out and looked at it. It was a handy size, and I wondered if it had belonged to Magnus's father; it would have been just right for a nip of rum in his sailing days, when the breeze freshened. If only Vita had disliked flying and had chosen to come by sea it would have given me several more days . . . A rattle beneath me made me look down to the valley. A solitary diesel engine was coming up the line, going hell for leather without its load of carriages, and I watched it worm its way, like a fat, swift-moving slug, above the willows and the birches, pass under the bridge above Treesmill, and disappear finally into the gaping jaws of the tunnel a mile distant. I unscrewed the flask and downed its contents.

All right, I told myself, so what? I'm bloody-minded. And Vita's still in mid-Atlantic. I closed my eyes.

6

THIS TIME, SITTING motionless with my back against the hedge and my eyes shut, I would try and pinpoint the moment of transition. On the previous occasions I had been walking, the first time across fields, the second up the churchyard path, when the vision altered. Now it would surely happen otherwise, because I was concentrating on the moment of impact. The sense of well-being would come, like a burden being lifted, and with it the sensation of lightness as feeling went from my body. No panic today, and no dismal falling rain. It was even warm, and the sun must be breaking through the clouds—I could sense the brightness through my closed eyelids. I took a last pull at the fag-end of my cigarette and let it drop.

If this drowsy content lasted much longer I might even fall asleep. Even the birds were rejoicing in the burst of sunshine; I could hear a blackbird singing in the hedge somewhere behind me, and more delightfully still a cuckoo called from the valley, distant at first, then near at hand. I listened to the call, a favourite sound, connected in my mind with every sort of carefree boyhood ramble thirty years ago. There, he called again, immediately overhead.

I opened my eyes and watched him wing his strange, unsteady flight across the sky, and as he did so I remembered that it was late July. The cuckoo's brief English summer ceased in June, along with the blackbird's song, and the primroses that were blooming in the bank beside me would have withered by mid-May. This warmth and brightness belonged to another world, an earlier spring. It had happened, despite concentration, in a moment of time that had not registered in my brain. All the sharp green colour of that first day was spread about me on the sloping hill below, and the valley with its tapestry of birch and willow lay submerged beneath a sheet of water, part of a great winding estuary that cut into the land, bordered by sandbanks where the water shallowed. I stood up, and saw how the river narrowed to mingle with the tumbling mill stream below Treesmill, the farmhouse altered in shape, narrow, thatched, the hills opposite thickly forested with oak, the foliage young and tender because of spring.

Immediately beneath me, where the field had shelved precipitously to the railway cutting, the ground took on a gentler slope, in the midst of which a broad track ran to the estuary, the track terminating in a quay beside which boats were anchored, the channel there being deep, forming a natural pool. A larger vessel was moored in midstream, her sail partly stowed. I could hear the voices of the men aboard her singing, and as I watched a smaller boat alongside pushed off to ferry someone ashore, and the voices were suddenly hushed, as the passenger in the small boat lifted his hand for silence. Now I looked around me, and the hedge had gone, the hill behind me was thickly wooded like the hills opposite, and to my left, where there had been scrub and gorse, a long stone wall encircled a dwelling house; I could see the rooftop above the surrounding trees. The path from the quay led straight uphill to the house.

I drew nearer, watching the man below descend from the boat at the quay, then proceed to climb the road towards me. As he did so the cuckoo called again, flying overhead, and the man looked up to watch it, pausing for breath as he climbed, his action so ordinary, so natural, that it endeared him to me for no reason except that he lived, and I was a ghost in time. A time, moreover, that was not constant, for yesterday it had been Martinmas, and now, by the cuckoo's call and the primroses in flower, it must be spring.

He came close, breasting the hill, and as I recognised him, though his expression was graver, more solemn than that of the preceding day, the analogy came to me that these faces were like the diamonds, hearts, and spades in some well-thumbed pack of cards shuffled by a patience player; however they were sorted, they still formed themselves into a combination that the player could not guess at. I did not know, nor they, how the game would go.

It was Otto Bodrugan climbing the hill, followed by his son Henry, and, when he raised his hand in greeting, so instinctive was the gesture that I raised mine in answer, and even smiled; but I should have known the futility of my action, for father and son brushed past me towards the entrance gate of the house, and Roger the steward came forward to greet them. He must have been standing there watching them approach, but I had not seen him. Gone was the festive air of yesterday, the mocking smile of the would-be go-between; he wore a dark tunic, as did Bodrugan and his son, and his manner was as grave as theirs.

"What news?" asked Bodrugan.

Roger shook his head. "He is sinking fast," he said. "There is little hope for him. My lady Joanna is within, and all the family. Sir William Ferrers is already come from Bere, accompanied by the lady Matilda. Sir Henry does not suffer, we have seen to that—or, to speak more plainly, Brother Jean has done so, for he had been at the bedside night and day."

"And the cause?"

"Nothing but the general weakness of which you know, and a sudden chill with that late frost we had. He wanders in his mind, speaking of his grievous faults and asking pardon. The parish priest heard his confession, but, not content with that, he begged to be shriven by Brother Jean as well, and has received the last rites."

Roger stood aside to let Bodrugan and his son pass through the entrance gates, and now the extent of the building came into view, stone-walled with tiled roof, fronting upon a court, an outside staircase leading to an upper chamber, the steps similar to those serving a farmhouse granary today. There were stables at the rear, and beyond the walls the track wound uphill towards Tywardreath, the thatched cottages of the serfs who tilled the surrounding lands scattered on either side of it.

Dogs ran barking across the court at our approach, crouching low, ears flat, as Roger shouted at them, and a scared-faced servant emerged from a corner of the building to drive them off. Bodrugan and his son Henry crossed the threshold, with Roger in attendance, and I his shadow close behind. We had entered a long, narrow hall, extending the full width of the house, small casement windows giving upon the court on the eastern side and looking down to the estuary on the west. There was an open hearth at the far end, the banked turf barely smoking, and across the width of the room was a trestle table, with benches alongside. The hall was dark, partly because of the small windows and the smoke that lingered in the atmosphere, partly because the walls were plastered a deep vermilion, giving the whole a rich and sombre air.

There were three youngsters straddling the benches, two boys and a girl, their sprawling attitude of dejection suggesting a numb bewilderment at the approach of death rather than actual sorrow. I recognised the eldest, William Champernoune, who had been presented to the Bishop; he was the first to rise now and come forward to greet his uncle and cousin, while the younger two, after momentary hesitation, followed his example. Otto Bodrugan bent to embrace all three, and then, as children will at the sudden entrance of adults in a moment of stress, they seized the opportunity to escape from the room, taking their cousin Henry with them.

Now I had leisure to observe the other occupants of the room. Two of them I had not seen before—a man and a woman, the man light-haired, bearded, the woman stout, with a sharp expression which boded ill for those who crossed her. She was already dressed in black, ready for calamity when it came, her white coif contrasting with her dark gown. This must be Sir William Ferrers, who, so Roger had said, had come posthaste from Devon, and his wife Matilda. The third occupant of the room, who was sitting on a low stool, was no stranger; it was my girl Isolda. She had made her own gesture to impending mourning by wearling lilac; but the silver sheen of the dress glistened, and a lilac ribbon, looping her braided hair away from her face, had been placed there with care. The prevailing mood seemed to be one of tension, and Matilda Ferrers wore an expression of high dudgeon which spoke of trouble.

"We expected you long since," was her immediate reproof to the new arrival, Otto Bodrugan, as he advanced towards her chair. "Does it take so many hours to sail across the bay, or did you delay purposely that your men might amuse themselves fishing?"

He kissed her hand, ignoring the reproach, and exchanged a glance with the man behind her chair. "How are you, William?" he said. "One hour from my anchorage to this, which was fair going, with the wind abeam. It would have taken longer had we ridden."

William nodded, with an imperceptible shrug, used to his lady's temper. "I thought as much," he murmured. "You could not have come sooner, and in any event there is nothing you can do."

"Nothing he can do?" echoed Matilda. "Except support us all when the moment comes, and add his voice to ours. Dismiss the French monk from the bedside and that drunken parish priest from the kitchen. If he cannot use a brother's authority and persuade Joanna to listen to reason, nobody can."

Bodrugan turned to Isolda. He barely brushed her hand in greeting, nor did she look up at him and smile. The constraint between them surely was due to caution: one word of too great intimacy would draw comment.

November . . . May . . . Six months must have passed, in my leap through time, since the reception at the Priory for the Bishop's visitation.

"Where is Joanna?" asked Bodrugan.

"In the chamber above," replied William, and now I saw the family likeness to Isolda. This was William Ferrers, her brother, but at least ten, perhaps fifteen years older, his face lined, his light hair turning grey. "You are aware of the trouble," he continued. "Henry will have no one near him but the French monk Jean, receives no treatment but from his hands, and refuses the surgeon who came with us from Devon and stands in high repute. Now, the treatment having failed, he is fallen into a coma and the end is near, probably within a few hours."

"If such is Henry's wish and he is not suffering, what is there to complain of?" asked Bodrugan.

"Because it is ill done!" exclaimed Matilda. "Henry has even expressed a wish to be buried in the Priory chapel, which should be withstood on every account. We all know the reputation of the Priory, the lax behaviour of the Prior, the lack of discipline amongst the monks. Such a resting place for someone of Henry's standing would make fools of all of us in the eyes of the world."

"Whose world?" asked Bodrugan. "Does yours embrace the whole of England, or only Devon?"

Matilda crimsoned. "We know well enough where your allegiance lay seven years past," she said, "supporting an adulterous Queen against her son, the lawful King. Doubtless all things French have your attachment, from invading forces, should they cross the Channel, to dissolute monks serving a foreign Order."

Her husband William laid a restraining hand upon her shoulder. "We gain nothing by opening old wounds," he said. "Otto's part in that rebellion does not concern us now. However . . ." he glanced at Bodrugan, "Matilda has a point. It might not be politic for a Champernoune to be interred amongst French monks. It would be more fitting if you would let him lie at Bodrugan, seeing that Joanna holds much of your manor in fee as her marriage portion. Or I should be most happy for him to be buried at Bere, where we are rebuilding the church at the present time. After all, Henry is my cousin: the connection is almost as close as your own."

"Oh, for the love of God," Isolda broke in impatiently, "let Henry lie where he will. Must we conduct ourselves like butchers haggling over a sheep's carcass before the beast is slain?"

It was the first time I had heard her voice. She spoke in French, like the rest, with the same nasal intonation, but perhaps because she was younger than they, and I was prejudiced, I found the quality more musical, holding a ring of clarity theirs did not possess. Matilda at once burst into tears, to the consternation of her husband, while Bodrugan strode over to the window and stared moodily at the view beyond. As for Isolda, who had caused the commotion, she tapped her foot impatiently, an expression of disdain upon her face.

I glanced at Roger standing beside me. He was making a supreme effort to control a smile. Then he stepped forward, his attitude one of respect towards all present, and observed to no one in particular, but I suspected to catch Isolda's eye, "If you wish, I will tell my lady of Sir Otto's arrival."

Nobody answered, and Roger, taking silence for acquiescence, bowed and withdrew. He climbed the stairway to the upper chamber, I following close upon his heels as if some thread bound us together. He entered without knocking, pushing aside the heavy hangings that masked the entrace to the room, which was half the size of the hall beneath, most of the space taken up by a draped bed at the further end. The small, pane-less windows gave little light, the aperture tight closed by oiled parchment, while the lighted candles standing on the trestle table at the bed's foot threw monstrous shadows on ochre-coloured walls.

There were three people in the room, Joanna, a monk, and the dying man. Henry de Champernoune was propped up in the bed by a great bolster that thrust him forward, forcing his chin upon his breast, and a white cloth was bound round his head turban fashion, giving him an incongruous likeness to an Arab sheik. His eyes were closed, and judging by the pallor of his face he was on the point of death. The monk was bending to stir something in a bowl on the trestle table, and he lifted his head as we entered. It was the young man with the brilliant eyes who had served the Prior as secretary or clerk on my first visit to the Priory. He said nothing but continued stirring, and Roger turned to Joanna, who was seated at the other end of the room. She was perfectly composed, without a sign of grief on her face, and was engaged in drawing threads of coloured silk through a frame to form a pattern.

"Are they all here?" she asked, without turning her eyes from the frame.

"Those who were bidden," answered the steward, "and already at odds with one another. Lady Ferrers first scolded the children for speaking too loud, and has now fallen out with Sir Otto, while Lady Carminowe, by her looks, wishes herself elsewhere. Sir John has not yet come."

"Nor likely to," replied Joanna. "I left the matter to his discretion. If he is premature in condolence it might be thought overzealous on his part, and his sister Lady Ferrers will be the first to make mischief out of it."

"She is making mischief already," replied the steward.

"I'm aware of it. The sooner the business is over the better for all of us."

Roger crossed to the foot of the bed and looked down upon the helpless occupant. "How long now?" he asked the monk.

"He will not wake again. You may touch him if you will, he cannot feel it. We are only waiting for the heart to cease, and then my lady can announce his death."

Roger shifted his gaze from the bed to the small bowls on the trestle table. "What did you give him?"

"The same as before, meconium, the juice of the whole plant, in equal parts with henbane to the strength of a dram."

Roger looked at Joanna. "It would be as well if I removed these, lest there should be discussion as to the treatment. Lady Ferrers spoke of her own surgeon. They hardly dare go against your wishes, but there could be trouble."

Joanna, still employing herself with her skeins of silk, shrugged her shoulders.

"Take the ingredients if you will," she said, "though we have disposed of the liquids down the drain. The vessels you may remove if you consider it safer, but I hardly think Brother Jean has anything to fear. His discretion has been absolute."

She smiled at the young monk, who responded with one glance from his expressive eyes, and I wondered if he too, like the absent Sir John, had found favour during the weeks of her husband's illness. Between them, Roger and the monk, they made a package of the bowls, wrapping them in sacking, and all the while I could hear the murmur of voices from the hall below, suggesting that Lady Ferrers had recovered from her fit of crying and was in full spate again.

"How is my brother Otto taking it?" asked Joanna.

"He made no comment when Sir William suggested that interment in Bodrugan chapel would be preferable to the Priory. I think he is hardly likely to interfere. Sir William proposed his own church at Bere as an alternative."

"To what purpose?"

"For self-aggrandisement, perhaps—who knows? I would not recommend it. Once they had Sir Henry's body in their hands there could be meddling. Whereas in the Priory chapel . . ."

"All would be well. Sir Henry's wishes observed, and ourselves at peace. I look to you to see there is no trouble with the tenants, Roger. The people have no great love of the Priory."

"There'll be no trouble if they are treated well at the funeral feast," he answered. "A promise of mitigation of fines at the next court and a pardon for all misdemeanours. That should content them."

"Let us hope so." She pushed aside her frame and rising from her chair, went to the bed. "Is he living still?" she asked.

The monk took the lifeless wrist in his hand and felt the pulse, then lowered his head to listen to his patient's heart.

"Barely," he answered. "You may light the candles if you will, and by the time the family has been summoned he will have gone."

They might have been talking of some wornout piece of furniture that had lost its use, instead of a woman's husband on the point of death. Joanna returned to her chair, took up a piece of black veiling, and began to drape it round her head and shoulders. Then she seized a looking-glass made of silver from the table near at hand.

"Should I wear it thus," she asked the steward, "or covering my face?"

"More fitting to be covered," he told her, "unless you can weep at will."

"I have not wept since my wedding day," she answered.

The monk Jean crossed the dying man's hands upon his breast and fastened a linen bandage about his jaw. He stood back to observe his work, and as a finishing touch placed a crucifix between the folded hands.

Meanwhile Roger was rearranging the trestle table. "How many candles do you require?" he asked.

"Five on the day of death," replied the monk, "in honour of the five wounds of Our Lord Jesus Christ. Have you a black coverlet for the bed?"

"In the chest yonder," said Joanna, and while monk and steward draped the bed with its black pall she looked in the mirror for the last time, before covering her face with the veil.

"If I may presume," murmured the monk, "it would make the better impression if my lady knelt beside the bed and I stationed myself at the foot. Then when the family comes into the chamber I can recite the Prayers for the Dead. Unless you prefer the perish priest to do so."

"He is too drunk to mount the stairs," said Roger. "If Lady Ferrers has one glimpse of him it will be his finish."

"Then leave him alone," said Joanna, "and let us proceed. Roger, will you descend and summon them? William first, for he is the heir."

She knelt beside the bed, head bowed in grief, but raised it before we left the room, saying over her shoulder to the steward, "It cost my brother Sir Otto near on fifty marks at Bodrugan when my father died, not counting the beasts that were slaughtered for the funeral feast. We must not be outdone. Spare no expense."

Roger drew aside the hangings by the door, and I followed him on to the steps outside. The contrast between the bright day without and the murky atmosphere within must have struck him as forcibly as it did me, for he paused at the top of the steps and looked down over the surrounding walls to the gleaming waters of the estuary below. The sails of Bodrugan's ship were furled loosely in the yard as she lay at anchor, and a fellow in a small boat astern sculled to and fro in search of fish. The youngsters from the house had wandered down the hillside to stare at their uncle's boat. Henry, Bodrugan's son, was pointing out something to his cousin William, and the dogs leapt about them, barking once again.

I realised at that moment, more strongly than hitherto, how fantastic, even macabre, was my presence amongst them, unseen, unborn, a freak in time, witness to events that had happened centuries past, unremembered, unrecorded; and I wondered how it was that standing here on the steps, watching yet invisible, I could so feel myself involved, troubled, by these loves and deaths. The man who was dying might have been a relative from my own lost world of youth—my father, even, who had died in spring when I was about the age of young William down there in the field. The cable from the Far East—he had been killed fighting the Japanese—arrived just as my mother and I had finished lunch, staying in an hotel in Wales for the Easter holidays. She went up to her bedroom and shut the door and I hung about the hotel drive aware of loss but unable to cry, dreading the sympathetic glance of the girl at the reception desk if I went indoors.

Roger, carrying the piece of sacking containing the bowls stained by herb juices, descended to the court, and went through an archway at the farther end leading to a stable yard. What servants made up the household seemed to be gathered there, but the steward's approach they broke up their gossip and scattered, all but one lad whom I had seen that first day and recognised, by his likeness to the horseman, as Roger's brother. Roger summoned him to his side with a jerk of his head.

"It is over," he said. "Ride to the Priory at once and inform the Prior, that he may give order for tolling the bell. Work will cease when the men hear the summons, and they will start to come in from the fields, and assemble on the green. Directly you have delivered your message to the Prior ride on home and place this package in the cellar, then wait for my return. I have much to do, and may not be back tonight."

The boy nodded, and disappeared into the stables. Roger passed through the archway into the court once more. Otto Bodrugan was standing at the entrance to the house. Roger hesitated a moment, then crossed the court to him.

"My lady asks you to go to her," he said, "with Sir William and Lady Ferrers and the Lady Isolda. I will call William and the children."

"Is Sir Henry worse?" asked Bodrugan.

"He is dead, Sir Otto. Not five minutes since, without recovering consciousness, peacefully, in his sleep."

"I am sorry," said Bodrugan, "but it is better so. I pray God we may both go as peacefully when our time comes, though undeservedly." Both men crossed themselves. Automatically I did the same. "I will tell the others," he continued. "Lady Ferrers may go into hysterics, but no matter. How is my sister?"

"Calm, Sir Otto."

"I expected it."

Bodrugan paused before turning into the house. "You are aware," he said, and there was something hesitant in his manner, "that William, being a minor, will forfeit his lands to the King until he attains his majority?"

"I am, Sir Otto."

"The confiscation would be little more than a formality in ordinary circumstances," Bodrugan went on. "As William's uncle by marriage, and therefore his legal guardian, I should be empowered to administer his estates, with the King as overlord. But the circumstances are not ordinary, owing to the part I took in the so-called rebellion." The steward maintained discreet silence, his face inscrutable. "Therefore," said Bodrugan, "the escheator acting for the minor and the King is likely to be one held in greater esteem than myself—his cousin Sir John Carminowe in all probability. In that event, I don't doubt he will arrange matters smoothly for my sister."

The irony in his voice was unmistakable.

Roger inclined his head without replying, and Bodrugan went into the house. The steward's slow smile of satisfaction was instantly suppressed as the young Champernounes, with their cousin Henry, entered the court, laughing and chatting, having momentarily forgotten the imminence of death. Henry, the eldest of the party, was the first to sense, intuitively, what must have happened. He called the younger pair to silence, and motioned William to come forward. I saw the expression on the boy's face change from carefree laughter to apprehension, and I guessed how sudden dread must have turned his stomach sick.

"Is it my father?" he asked.

Roger nodded. "Take your brother and sister with you," he said, "and go to your mother. Remember, you are the eldest; she will look to you for support in the days to come."

The boy clutched at the steward's arm. "You will remain with us, will you not?" he asked. "And my uncle Otto too?"

"We shall see," answered Roger. "But you are the head of the family now."

William made a supreme effort at self-control. He turned and faced his young brother and sister and said, "Our father is dead. Please to follow me," and walked into the house, head erect, but very pale. The children, startled, did as they were told, taking their cousin Henry's hand, and glancing at Roger I saw, for the first time, something of compassion on his face, and pride as well; the boy he must have known from cradle days had not disgraced himself. He waited a few moments, then followed them.

The hall appeared deserted. A tapestry hanging at the far end near the hearth had been drawn aside, showing a small stairway to the upper room, by which Otto Bodrugan and the Ferrers must have ascended, and the children too. I could hear the shuffle of feet overhead, then silence, followed by the low murmur of the monk's voice, *"Requiem aeternam dona eis Domine: et lux perpetua luceat eis."*

I said the hall appeared deserted, and so it was, but for the slender figure in lilac: Isolda was the only member of the group who had not gone to the room above. At sight of her Roger paused on the threshold, before moving forward with deference.

"Lady Carminowe does not wish to pay tribute with the rest of the family?" he asked.

Isolda had not noticed him standing there by the entrance, but now she turned her head and looked at him direct, and there was so much coldness in her eyes that standing where I was, beside the steward, they seemed to sweep me with the same contempt as they did him.

"It is not my practice to make a mockery of death," she said.

If Roger was surprised he gave no sign of it, but made the same deferential gesture as before. "Sir Henry would be grateful for your prayers," he said.

"He has had them with regularity for many years," she answered, "and with increasing fervour these past weeks."

The edge in her voice was evident to me, and must have been doubly so to the steward. "Sir Henry has ailed ever since making the pilgrimage to Campostella," he replied. "They say Sir Ralph de Beaupré suffers today from the same sickness. It is a wasting fever, there is no cure for it. Sir Henry had so little regard for his own person that it was hard to treat him. I can assure you that everything possible was done."

"I understand Sir Ralph Beaupré retains full possession of his faculties despite his fever," Isolda replied. "My cousin did not. He recognised none of us for a month or more, yet his brow was cool, the fever was not high."

"No two men are alike in sickness," Roger answered. "What will save the one will trouble the other. If Sir Henry wandered in his mind it was his misfortune."

"Made the more effective by the potions given him," she said. "My grandmother, Isolda de Cardinham, had a treatise on herbs, written by a learned doctor who went to the Crusades, and she bequeathed it to me when she died, because I was her name-sake. I am no stranger to the seed of the black poppy and the white, water hemlock, mandragora, and the sleep they can induce."

Roger, startled out of his attitude of deference, did not answer her at once. Then he said, "These herbs are used by all apothecaries for easing pain. The monk, Jean de Meral, was trained in the parent-house at Angers and is especially skilled. Sir Henry himself had implicit faith in him."

"I don't doubt Sir Henry's faith, the monk's skill, or his zeal in employing that skill, but a healing plant can turn malign if the dose is increased," replied Isolda.

She had made her challenge, and he knew it. I remembered that trestle table at the foot of the bed, and the bowls upon it, now carefully wrapped in sacking and carried away.

"This is a house of mourning," said Roger, "and will continue so for several days. I advise you to speak of this matter to my lady, not to me. It is none of my business."

"Nor mine either," replied Isolda. "I speak through attachment to my cousin, and because I am not easily fooled. You might remember it."

One of the children started crying overhead, and there was a sudden lull in the murmur of prayers, the sound of movement, and the scurrying of footsteps down the stairs. The daughter of the house—she could not have been more than ten—came running into the room, and flung herself into Isolda's arms.

"They say he is dead," she said, "yet he opened his eyes and looked at me, just once, before closing them again. No one else saw, they were too busy with their prayers. Did he mean that I must follow him to the grave?"

Isolda held the child to her protectively, staring over her shoulder at Roger all the while, and suddenly she said, "If anything evil has been done this day or yesterday, you will be held responsible, with others, when the time comes. Not in this world, where we lack proof, but in the next, before God."

Roger moved forward, with some impulse, I think, to silence her or take the child from her, and I stepped into his path to prevent him, but stumbled, catching my foot in a loose stone. And there was nothing about me but great mounds of earth and hillocks of grass, gorse bushes and the root of a dead tree, and behind me a large pit, circular in shape like a quarry, full of old tins and fallen slate. I caught hold of a twisted stem of withered gorse, retching violently, and in the distance I could hear the hoot of a diesel engine as it rattled below me in the valley.

7

THE QUARRY WAS steep, carved out of the hillside, spread about with holly and clumps of ivy, the debris of years scattered amongst the earth and stones, and the path leading out of it ran into a small pit, and then another, and yet a third, all heaped about with banks and ditches and knolls of tufted grass. The gorse was everywhere, masking the view, and because of my vertigo I could not see but kept stumbling against the banks, with one thought paramount in my mind—that I must get out of this waste land and find the car. It was imperative to find the car.

I caught hold of a thorn tree and held on to it to steady myself, and there were more old cans at my feet, a broken bedstead, a tyre, and still more clumps of ivy and holly. Feeling had returned to my limbs, but as I staggered up the mound above me the dizziness increased, the nausea too, and I slithered down into another pit and lay there panting, my stomach heaving. I was violently sick, which gave momentary relief, and I got up again and climbed another mound. Now I saw that I was only a few hundred yards from the original hedge where I had smoked my cigarette—the mounds and the quarry beyond had been hidden from me then by a sloping bank and a broken gate. I looked down once more into the valley, and saw the tail end of the train disappearing round the corner to Par station. Then I climbed through a gap in the hedge and began to walk uphill across the field and back to the car.

I reached the lay by just as another violent attack of nausea came upon me. I staggered sideways amongst the heap of cement and planks and was violently sick again, while ground and sky revolved around me. The vertigo I had experienced that first day in the patio was nothing to this, and as I crouched on the heap of cement waiting for it to pass I kept saying to myself, "Never again . . . never again . . ." with all the fervour and weak anger of someone coming round from an anaesthetic, the revulsion beyond control.

Before I collapsed I had been aware, dimly, that there was another car in the lay by besides my own, and after what seemed an eternity, when the nausea and the vertigo ceased, and I was coughing and blowing my nose, I heard the door of the other car slam, and realised that the owner had come across and was staring down at me.

"Are you all right now?" he asked.

"Yes," I said, "yes, I think so."

I rose unsteadily to my feet, and he put out a hand to help me. He was about my own age, early forties, with a pleasant face and a remarkably strong grip.

"Got your keys?"

"Keys . . ." I fumbled in my pocket for the car keys. Christ! What if I had dropped them in the quarry or amongst those mounds—I should never find them again. They were in my top pocket, with the flask; the relief was so tremendous that I felt steadier at once, and walked without assistance to the car. Another fumble, though: I could not fit the key into the lock.

"Give it to me, I'll do it," said my Samaritan.

"It's extremely kind of you. I do apologise," I said.

"All in the day's work," he answered. "I happen to be a doctor."

I felt my face stiffen, then quickly stretch into a smile intended to disarm. Casual courtesy from a passing motorist was one thing; professional attention from a medico another. As it was he was staring at me with interest, and small blame to him. I wondered what he was thinking.

"The fact is," I said, "I must have walked up the hill a bit too fast. I felt giddy when I reached the top, and then was sick. Couldn't stop myself."

"Oh, well," he said, "it's been done before. I suppose a lay by is as good a place as any to throw up in. You'd be surprised what they find down here in the tourist season."

He was not fooled, though. His eyes were particularly penetrating. I wondered if he could see the shape of the flask bulging the top pocket of my jacket.

"Have you far to go?" he asked.

"No," I said, "a couple of miles or so, no more."

"In that case," he suggested, "wouldn't it be more sensible if you left your car here and let me drive you home? You could always send for it later."

"It's very kind of you," I said, "but I assure you I'm perfectly all right now. It was just one of those passing things."

"H'm," he said, "rather violent while it lasted."

"Honestly," I said, "there's nothing wrong. Perhaps it was something I had for lunch, and then walking uphill . . ."

"Look," he interrupted, "you're not a patient of mine, I'm not trying to prescribe. I'm only warning you that it might be dangerous to drive."

"Yes," I said, "it's very good of you and I'm grateful for your advice." The thing was, he could be right. Yesterday I had driven to St. Austell and back home with the greatest ease. Today it might be different. The vertigo might seize me once again. He must have seen my hesitation, for he said, "If you like I'll follow you, just to see you're O.K."

I could hardly refuse—to have done so would have made him the more suspicious. "That's very decent of you," I told him. "I only have to go to the top of Polmear hill."

"All on the way home," he smiled. "I live in Fowey."

I climbed rather gingerly into my car and turned out of the lay by. He followed close behind, and I thought to myself that if I drove into the hedge I was done for. But I navigated the narrow lane without difficulty, and heaved a sigh of relief as I emerged on to the main road and shot up Polmear hill. When I turned right, to go to Kilmarth, I thought he might follow me to the house, but he waved his hand and continued along the road to Fowey. It showed discretion, at any rate. Perhaps he thought I was staying in Polkerris or one of the nearby farms. I passed through the gate and down the drive, put the car away in the garage, and let myself into the house. Then I was sick again.

The first thing I did when I recovered, still feeling pretty shaky, was to rinse out the flask. Then I went down to the laboratory and stood it in the sink to soak. It was safer there than in the pantry. It was not until I went upstairs once more, and flung myself into an armchair in the music room, exhausted, that I remembered the bowls wrapped in sacking. Had I left them in the car?

I was about to get up and go down to the garage to look for them, because they must be cleansed even more thoroughly than the flask and put away under lock and key, when I realised with a sudden wave of apprehension, just as though something were being vomited from my brain as well as my stomach, that I had been on the point of confusing the present with the past. The bowls had been given to Roger's brother, not to me.

I sat very still, my heart thumping in my chest. There had been no confusion before. The two worlds had been distinct. Was it because the nausea and the vertigo had been so great that the past and the present had run together in my mind? Or had I miscounted the drops, making the draught more potent? No way of telling. I clutched the sides of the armchair. They were solid, real. Everything about me was real. The drive home, the doctor, the quarry full of old cans and crumbling stones, they were real. Not the house above the estuary, nor the people in it, nor the dying man, nor the monk, nor the bowls in sacking—they were all products of the drug, a drug that turned a clear brain sick.

I began to be angry, not so much with myself, the willing guinea pig, as with Magnus. He was unsure of his findings. He did not know what he had done. No wonder he had asked me to send up bottle B to try out the contents on the laboratory monkey. He had suspected something was wrong, and now I could tell him what it was. Neither exhilaration nor depression, but confusion of thought. The merging of two worlds. Well, that was enough. I had had my lot. Magnus could make his experiments on a dozen monkeys, but not on me.

The telephone started ringing, and, startled out of my chair, I went across to the library to answer it. Damn his telepathic powers. He would tell me he knew where I had been, that the house above the estuary was familiar ground, there was no need to worry, it was all perfectly safe providing I touched no one; if I felt ill or confused it was a side effect of no consequence. I would put him right.

I seized the telephone and someone said, "Hold on a moment, please, I have a call for you," and I heard the click as Magnus took over.

"Damn and blast you," I said. "This is the last time I behave like a performing seal."

There was a little gasp at the other end, and then a laugh. "Thanks for the welcome home, darling."

It was Vita. I stood stupefied, holding on to the receiver. Was her voice part of the confusion?

"Darling?" she repeated. "Are you there? Is something wrong?"

"No," I said, "nothing's wrong, but what's happened? Where are you speaking from?"

"London airport," she answered. "I caught an earlier plane, that's all. Bill and Diana are collecting me and taking me out to dinner. I thought you might call the flat later tonight and wonder why I didn't answer. Sorry if I took you by surprise."

"Well, you did," I said, "but forget it. How are you?"

"Fine," she said, "just fine. What about you? Who did you think I was when you answered me just now? You didn't sound too pleased."

"In point of fact," I told her, "I thought it was Magnus. I had to do a chore for him . . . I've written you all about it in my letter, which you won't get until tomorrow morning."

She laughed. I knew the sound, with the slight "I thought as much" inflection. "So your Professor has been putting you to work," she said. "That doesn't surprise me. What's he been making you do that has turned you into a performing seal?"

"Oh, endless things, sorting out junk, I'll explain when I see you. When do the boys get back?"

"Tomorrow," she said. "Their train arrives at a hideous hour in the morning. Then I thought I'd pack them in the car and come on down. How long will it take?"

"Wait," I said, "that's just it. I'm not ready for you. I've told you so in my letter. Leave it until after the weekend."

There was silence on the other end. I had dropped the usual clanger.

"Not ready?" she repeated. "But you must have been there all of five days? I thought you'd fixed up with some woman to come in and cook and clean, make beds and so on. Has she let us down?"

"No, it's not that," I told her. "She's first rate, couldn't be better. Look, darling, I can't explain over the telephone, it's all in my letter, but, frankly, we weren't expecting you until Monday at the earliest."

"We?" she said. "You don't mean the Professor is there too?"

"No, no . . ." I could feel irritation rising in both of us. "I meant Mrs. Collins and myself. She only comes in the morning, she has to bicycle up from Polkerris, the little village at the bottom of the hill, and the beds aren't aired or anything. She'll be terribly put out if everything isn't absolutely straight, and you know what you are, you'll take a dislike to the place if it isn't shining."

"What absolute nonsense," she said. "I'm fully prepared to picnic, and so are the boys. We can bring food with us, if that's worrying you. And blankets too. Are there enough blankets?"

"Masses of blankets," I said, "masses of food. Oh, darling, don't be obstructive. If you come down right away it won't be convenient, and that's the plain truth of it. I'm sorry."

"O.K." The lilt in the "K" had the typical upward ring of Vita temporarily defeated in argument but determined to win the final battle. "You'd better find yourself an apron and a broom," she added as a parting shot. "I'll tell Bill and Diana you've turned domestic and are going to spend the evening on your hands and knees. They'll love it."

"It's not that I don't want to see you, darling," I began, but her "Bye," still with the upward inflection, told me I had done my worst, and she had hung up on me and was now making her way to the airport restaurant to order a Scotch on the rocks and smoke three cigarettes in quick succession before the arrival of her friends.

Well, that was that . . . What now? My anger against Magnus had been deflected to Vita, but how could I know she was going to catch an earlier plane and ring me unexpectedly? Anyone in the same situation would have been caught on the wrong foot. But that was the rub. My situation was not the same as anyone else's: it was unique. Less than an hour ago I had been living in another world, another time, or had imagined myself to be doing so, through the effect of the drug.

I began to walk from the library through the small dining room across the hall to the music room and back again, like someone pacing the deck of a ship, and it seemed to me that I was not sure of anything any more. Neither of myself, nor of Magnus, nor of Vita, nor of my own immediate world, for who was to say where I belonged—here in this borrowed house, in the London flat, in the office I had left when quitting my job, or in that singularly vivid house of mourning which lay buried beneath centuries of rubble? Why, if I was determined not to see that house again, had I dissuaded Vita from coming down tomorrow? The excuses had been immediate, a reflex action. Nausea and vertigo had gone. Accepted. They might strike again. Accepted also. The drug was dangerous, its implications and its side effects unknown. This, too, accepted. I loved Vita, but I did not want her with me. Why?

I seized the telephone once more and dialled Magnus. No answer. No answer, either, to my self-imposed question. That doctor with his intelligent eyes might have given me one. What would he have told me? That a hallucinatory drug could play curious tricks with the unconscious, bringing the supressions of a lifetime to the surface, so let it alone? A practical answer, but it did not suffice. I had not been moving amongst childhood ghosts. The people I had seen were not shadows from my own past. Roger the steward was not my alter ego, nor Isolda a dream fantasy, a might-have-been. Or were they?

I tried Magnus two or three times later, but there was never a reply, and I spent a restless evening, unable to settle to newspapers, books, records or TV. Finally, fed up with myself and the whole problem, to which there seemed no solution, I went early to bed, and slept, to my astonishment when I awoke next morning, amazingly well.

The first thing I did was to ring the flat, and I caught Vita just as she was tearing off to meet the boys.

"Darling, I'm sorry about yesterday . . ." I began, but there was no time to go into it, she told me, she was late already.

"Well, when shall I ring you?" I asked.

"I can't give you a time," she answered. "It depends upon the boys, what they want to do, whether there'll be a mass of shopping. They'll probably need jeans, swimming trunks, I don't know. Thanks for your letter, by the way. Your Professor certainly keeps you employed."

"Never mind Magnus . . . How was your dinner with Bill and Diana?"

"Fun. Lots of scandal. Now I must go, or I'll keep the boys hanging about at Waterloo Station."

"Give them my love," I shouted, but she had gone. Oh well, she sounded happy enough. The evening with her friends and a good night's rest must have changed her ideas, and my letter too, which she seemed to have accepted. What a relief . . . Now I could relax once more. Mrs. Collins knocked on the door and came in with my breakfast tray.

"You're spoiling me," I said. "I ought to have been up an hour ago."

"You're on holiday," she said. "There's nothing to get up for, is there?"

I thought about this as I drank my coffee. A revealing remark. Nothing to get up for . . . No more hopping into the underground from West Kensington to Convent Garden, the familiar office window, the inevitable routine, discussions about publicity, jackets, new authors, old authors. All finished, through my resignation. Nothing to get up for. But Vita wanted it to start all over again on her side of the Atlantic. Darting down the subway, elbowing strangers on sidewalks, an office building thirty stories high, the inevitable routine, discussions about publicity, jackets, new authors, old authors. Something to get up for . . .

There were two letters on my breakfast tray. One was from my mother in Shropshire saying how lovely it must be in Cornwall and she envied me, I must be getting so much sun. Her arthritis had been bad again and poor old Dobsie was getting very deaf. (Dobsie was my stepfather, and I didn't wonder he was deaf; it was probably a defence mechanism, for my mother never drew breath.) And so on and so on, her large, looped handwriting covering about eight pages. Pangs of conscience, for I had not seen her for a year, but to give her her due she never reproached me, was delighted when I married Vita, and always remembered the boys at Christmas with what I considered an unnecessarily thumping tip.

The other envelope was long and slim, and contained a couple of typewritten documents and a note scribbled by Magnus.

"Dear Dick," it read, "my disciple's long-haired friend who spends his time browsing around the BM and the PRO had produced the enclosed when I arrived at my desk this morning. The copy of the Lay Subsidy Roll is quite informative, and the other, mentioning your lord of the manor, Champernoune, and the to-do about removing his body may amuse you.

"I shall think about you this afternoon and wonder if Virgil is leading Dante astray. Do remember not to *touch* him; reaction can be progressively unpleasant. Keep your distance and all will be well. I suggest you stay put on the premises for your next trip.

"YOURS, MAGNUS."

I turned to the documents. The research student had scribbled at the top of the first, "From Bishop Grandisson of Exeter. Original in Latin. Excuse my translation." It read as follows:

"Grandisson. A.D. 1329. Tywardreath Priory.

"John, etc, to his beloved sons men of a religious order, the Lords, the Prior and Convent of Tywardreath, greetings, etc. By the laws of the sacred Canons it is known that we are warned that the bodies of the Faithful, once delivered for burial by the Church, may not be exhumed except by those same laws. It has lately come to our ears that the body of the Lord Henry of Champernoune, Knight, rests buried in your consecrated church. Certain men, however, directing their minds' eyes in wordly fashion upon the transitory pomps of this life rather than on the welfare of the said Knight's soul and the discharging of due rites, are busying themselves about the exhumation of the said body, in circumstances not permitted by our laws, and about removing it to another place without our licence. Wherefore strictly enjoining upon you the virtue of obedience we give orders that you, in resistance to such reckless daring, must not allow the exhumation of the said body or its removal to be undertaken in any way, when we have not been consulted, nor have the reasons for such exhumation or removal, if there were any, been examined, discussed, or approved; even as you wish to escape divine retribution or that of ourselves. While we for our part lay an inhibition on all and each of our subjects, and no less upon others through whom it is hoped apparently to perpetrate a crime of this kind, so that they should not, under pain of excommunication, afford any help, counsel or favour for such an exhumation or removal of this kind which is in question. Given at Paignton on the 27th of August."

Magnus had added a footnote. "I like Bishop Grandisson's forthright style. But what is it all about? A family squabble, or something more sinister, of which the Bishop himself was ignorant?"

The second document was a list of names, headed "Lay Subsidy Roll, 1327, Paroch Tiwardrayd. Subsidy of a twentieth of all moveable goods . . . upon all the Commons who possess goods of the value of ten shillings or upwards." There were forty names in all, and Henry de Champernoune headed the list. I ran my eye down the rest. Number twenty-three was Roger Kylmerth. So it wasn't hallucination—he had really lived.

8

When I had dressed I went to the garage and fetched the car, and skirting Tywardreath took the road to Treesmill. I purposely avoided the lay by and drove down the hill into the valley, but not before the fellow at the bungalow Chapel Down, who was busy washing his caravan, waved a hand in greeting. The same thing happened when I stopped the car below the bridge near Treesmill Farm. The farmer of yesterday morning was driving his cows across the road, and paused to speak to me. I thanked my stars neither of them had been at the lay by later in the day.

"Found your manor house yet?" he asked.

"I'm not sure," I told him. "I thought I'd take another look round. That's a curious sort of place halfway up the field there, covered in gorse bushes. Has it got a name?"

I could not see the site from the bridge, but pointed roughly in the direction of the quarry where yesterday, in another century, I had followed Roger into the house where Sir Henry Champernoune lay dying.

"You mean up Gratten?" he said. "I don't think you'll find anything up there except old slate and rubble. Fine place for slate, or was. Mostly rubbish now. They say when the houses were built in Tywardreath in the last century they took most of the stones and slates from that place. It may be true."

"Why Gratten?" I asked.

"I don't know exactly. The ploughed field at the back is the Gratten, part of Mount Bennett farm. The name has something to do with burning, I believe. There's a path opposite the turning to Stonybridge will lead you to it. But you'll find nothing to interest you."

"I don't suppose I shall," I answered, "except the view."

"Mostly trains," he laughed, "and not so many of them these days."

I parked the car halfway up the hill, opposite the lane, as he suggested, then struck across the field towards the Gratten. The railway and the valley were beneath me, to my right, the ground descending very steeply to a high embankment beside the railway, then sloping away more gradually to swamp and thicket. Yesterday, in that other world, there had been a quayside midway between the two, and in the centre of the wooded valley, where trees and bush were thickest, Otto Bodrugan had anchored his craft midchannel, the bows of the boat swinging to meet the tide.

I passed the spot below the hedge where I had sat and smoked my cigarette. Then I went through the broken gate, and stood once more amongst the hillocks and the mounds. Today, without vertigo or nausea, I could see more clearly that these knolls were not the natural formation of uneven ground, but must have been walls that had been covered for centuries by vegetation, and the hollows which I had thought, in my dizziness, to be pits were simply the enclosures that long ago had been rooms within a house.

The people who had come to gather slates and stones for their cottages had done so for good reason. Digging into the soil that must have covered the foundations of a building long vanished would have given them much of the material they needed for their own use, and the quarry at the back was part of this same excavation. Now, the quest ended, the quarry remained a tip for useless junk, the discarded tins rusted with age and winter rains.

Their quest had ended, while mine had just begun, but, as the farmer down at Treesmill had warned me, I should find nothing. I knew only that yesterday, in another time, I had stood in the vaulted hall that formed the central feature of this long-buried house, had mounted the outer stairway to the room above, had seen the owner of the dwelling die. No courtyard now, no walls, no hall, no stable quarters in the rear; nothing but grassy banks and a little muddy path running between them.

There was a patch of even ground, smooth and green, fronting the site, that might have been part of the courtyard once, and I sat down there looking into the valley below as Bodrugan had done from the small window in the hall. Tiwardrai, the House on the Strand . . . I thought how, when the tide ebbed in early centuries, the twisting channel would stay blue, revealing sandy flats on either side of it, these flats a burnished gold under the sun. If the channel was deep enough, Bodrugan could have raised anchor and made for sea later that night; if not, he would have returned on board to sleep amongst his men, and at daybreak, perhaps, come out on deck to stretch himself and stare up at the house of mourning.

I had put the documents that had come by post this morning into my pocket, and now I drew them out and read them through again.

Bishop Grandisson's order to the Prior was dated August, 1329. Sir Henry Champernoune had died in late April or early May. The Ferrers pair were doubtless behind the attempt to remove him from his Priory tomb, with Matilda Ferrers the more pressing of the two. I wondered who had carried the rumour to the Bishop's ears, so playing on ecclesiastical pride, and ensuring that the body would escape investigation? Sir John Carminowe, in all probability, acting hand in glove with Joanna—whom he had, no doubt, long since successfully taken to bed.

I turned to the Lay Subsidy Roll, and glanced once again through the list of names, ticking off those that corresponded to the place-names on the road map I had brought from the car. Ric Trevynor, Ric Trewiryan, Ric Trenathelon, Julian Polpey, John Polorman, Geoffrey Lampetho . . . all, with slight variations in the spelling, were farms marked on the road map beside me. The men who dwelt in them then, dead for over six hundred years, had bequeathed their names to posterity; only Henry Champernoune, lord of the manor, had left a heap of mounds as legacy, to be stumbled upon by myself, a trespasser in time. All dead for nearly seven centuries, Roger Kylmerth and Isolda Carminowe amongst them. What they had dreamt of, schemed for, accomplished, no longer mattered, it was all forgotten.

I got up and tried to find, amongst the mounds, the hall where Isolda had sat yesterday, accusing Roger of complicity in crime. Nothing fitted. Nature had done her work too well, here on the hillside and below me in the valley, where the estuary once ran. The sea had withdrawn from the land, the grass had covered the walls, the men and women who had walked here once, looking down upon blue water, had long since crumbled into dust.

I turned away, retracing my steps across the field, low-spirited, reason telling me that this was the end of the adventure. Emotion was in conflict with reason, however, destroying peace of mind, and for better, for worse, I knew myself involved. I could not forget that I had only to turn the key of that laboratory door for it to happen once again. The choice, perhaps, put to Man from the beginning, whether or not to eat of the Tree of Knowledge. I got into the car and drove back to Kilmarth.

I spent the afternoon writing a full account of yesterday to Magnus, and told him also that Vita was in London. Then I drove to Fowey to post the letter, and arranged to hire a sailing boat after the weekend, when Vita and the boys were down. She would not experience the flat calm of Long Island Sound, or the luxury of her brother Joe's chartered yacht, but the gesture showed my will to please, and the boys would enjoy it.

I rang nobody that evening and nobody rang me, with the result that I slept badly, continually waking and listening to silence. I kept thinking of Roger Kylmerth in his sleeping quarters over the kitchen of the original farmstead, and wondering whether his brother had thoroughly scoured out the bowls six hundred and forty years ago. He must have done so, for Henry Champernoune to lie undisturbed in the Priory chapel until that chapel had crumbled into dust as well.

No breakfast in bed the following morning, for I was too restless. I was drinking my coffee on the steps outside the french window of the library when the telephone rang. It was Magnus.

"How are you feeling?" he asked at once.

"Jaded," I told him. "I slept badly."

"You can make up for it later. You can sleep all afternoon in the patio. There are several lilos in the boiler room, and I envy you. London is sweltering in a heat wave."

"Cornwall isn't," I replied, "and the patio gives me claustrophobia. Did you get my letter?"

"I did," he said. "That's why I rang. Congratulations on your third trip. Don't worry about the aftermath. It was your own fault, after all."

"It may have been," I said, "but the confusion was not."

"I know," he agreed. "The confusion fascinated me. Also the jump in time. Six months or more between the second and third trips. You know what? I've a good mind to get away in a week or so and join you so that we can go on a trip together."

My first reaction was one of excitement. The second, a zoom to earth. "It's out of the question. Vita will be here with the boys."

"We can get rid of them. Pack them off to the Scillies, or for a long day at the Land's End, scattering banana skins. That'll give us time."

"I don't think so," I said. "I don't think so at all." He did not know Vita well. I could imagine the complications.

"Well, its not urgent," he said, "but it could be a lot of fun. Besides, I'd like to have a look at Isolda Carminowe."

His flippant voice restored my jagged nerves. I even smiled. "She's Bodrugan's girl, not ours," I told him.

"Yes, but for how long?" he queried. "They were always changing partners in those days. I still don't see where she fits in amongst the rest."

"She and William Ferrers seem to be cousins to the Champernounes," I explained.

"And Isolda's husband Oliver Carminowe, absent at yesterday's death bed, is brother to Matilda and Sir John?"

"Apparently."

"I must write all this down and get my slave to check for futher details. I say, I was right about Joanna being a bitch." Then, abruptly changing his tone, "So you're satisfied now that the drug works, and what you saw was not hallucination?"

"Almost," I replied, with caution.

"Almost? Don't the documents prove it, if nothing else?"

"The documents help to prove it," I countered, "but don't forget you read them before I did. So there is still the possibility that you were exercising some kind of telepathic influence. Anyway, how's the monkey?"

"The monkey." He paused a moment. "The monkey's dead."

"Thanks very much," I said.

"Oh, don't worry—it wasn't the drug. I killed him on purpose; I have work to do on his brain cells. It will take some time, so don't get impatient."

"I'm not in the least impatient," I replied, "merely appalled at the risk you appear to be taking with *my* brain."

"Your brain's different," he said. "You can take a lot more punishment yet. Besides, think of Isolda. Such a splendid antidote to Vita. You might even find that . . ."

I cut him short. I knew exactly what he had been going to say. "Leave my love life out of this," I said. "It doesn't concern you."

"I was only about to suggest, dear boy, that moving between two worlds can act as a stimulant. It happens every day, without drugs, when a man keeps a mistress round the corner and a wife at home . . . That was a major find on your part, by the way, landing on the quarry above Treesmill valley. I'll put my archaeological friends on to digging the site when you and I have finished with it."

It struck me, as he spoke, how our attitude to the experiment differed. His was scientific, unemotional, it did not really concern him who was broken in the process so long as what he was attempting to prove was proved successfully; whereas I was already caught up in the mesh of history; the people who to him were puppets of a bygone age were alive for me. I had a sudden vision of that long-buried house reconstructed on concrete blocks, admission two shillings, car park at Chapel Down . . .

"Then Roger never led you there?" I asked.

"To Treesmill valley? No," he answered. "I strayed from Kilmarth once only, and that was to the Priory, as I told you. I preferred to remain on my own ground. I'll tell you all about it when I come down. I'm off to Cambridge for the weekend, but remember you have all Saturday and Sunday for self-indulgence. Increase the dose a little—it won't hurt you."

He rang off before I could ask him for his telephone number, should I want it over the weekend. I had hardly put down the receiver before the telephone rang again. This time it was Vita.

"You were engaged a long while," she said. "I suppose it was your Professor?"

"As a matter of fact it was," I told her.

"Loading you up with weekend chores? Don't exhaust yourself, darling." Acidity, then, was the morning mood. She must blow it off on the boys, I could not cope.

"What are you planning for today?" I asked, ignoring her previous remark.

"Well, the boys are going swimming at Bill's club. That's a must. We've a heat wave here in London. How's it with you?"

"Overcast," I said without glancing at the window. "A trough of low pressure crossing the Atlantic will reach Cornwall by midnight."

"It sounds delightful. I hope your Mrs. Collins is getting on with airing the beds."

"Everything's under control," I told her, "and I've hired a sailing boat for next week, quite a big one, with a chap in charge. The boys will love it."

"What about Mom?"

"Mom will love it too, if she takes enough seasick pills. There's also a beach below the cliffs here, only a couple of fields to cross. No bulls."

"Darling"—the acidity had turned sweet, or at any rate mellow—"I believe you are looking forward to our coming after all."

"Of course I am," I said. "Why should you think otherwise?"

"I never know what to think when your Professor's been at you. There's some sort of hoodoo between us when he's around . . . Here are the boys," she went on, her voice changing. "They want to say hullo."

My stepsons' voices, like their appearance, were identical, though Teddy was twelve and Micky ten. They were said to resemble their father, killed in an air crash a couple of years before I met Vita. Judging by the photograph they carried round with them, this was true. He had, they had, the typical Teuton head, hair cropped close, of many American young. Blue eyes, innocent, set in a broad face. They were nice kids. But I could have done without them.

"Hi, Dick," they said, one after the other.

"Hi," I repeated, the phrase as alien to my tongue as if I had been speaking Tongalese.

"How are you both?" I asked.

"We're fine," they said.

There was a long pause. They couldn't think of anything more to say. Neither could I. "Looking forward to seeing you next week," I told them.

I heard a lot of whispering, and then Vita was back on the line again. "They're raging to swim. I shall have to go. Take care of yourself, darling, and don't overdo it with your pail and broom."

I went and sat in the little summerhouse that Magnus's mother had erected years ago, and looked down across the bay. It was a happy spot, peaceful, sheltered from all winds except a south-westerly blow. I could see myself spending a lot of time here during the holidays, if only to get out of bowling to the boys; they were sure to bring cricket stumps with them, and a bat, and a ball which they would continually hit over the wall into the field beyond.

"Your turn to get it!"

"No, it's not, it's yours!"

Then Vita's voice chiming in from behind the hydrangea bushes. "Now, now, if you're going to quarrel there won't be any cricket at all, and I mean it," with a final appeal to me. "Do something, darling, you're the only adult male."

But at least today, in the summerhouse, looking up the bay as a ray of sun touched the horizon, there was peace at Kylmerth. Kylmerth . . . I had pronounced the word in thought as originally spelt, and quite unconsciously. Confusion of thought becoming habit? Too tired for introspection, I got up again and wandered aimlessly about the grounds, clipping at hedges with an old hook I found in the boiler house. Magnus had been right about the lilos. There were three of them, the kind you inflate with a *pump*. I'd set to work on them in the afternoon, if I had the energy.

"Lost your appetite?" asked Mrs. Collins, when I had laboured through my lunch and asked for coffee.

"Sorry," I said, "no reflection on your cooking. I'm a bit out of sorts."

"I thought you looked tired. It's the weather. Turned very close."

It was not the weather. It was my own inability to settle, a sort of restlessness that drove me to physical action, however futile. I strolled down across the fields to the sea, but it looked exactly the same as it had from the summerhouse, flat and grey, and then I had all the effort of walking up again. The day dragged on. I wrote a letter to my mother, describing the house in boring detail just to fill the pages, reminding me of the duty letters I used to write from school: "I'm in another dormitory this term. It holds fifteen." Finally, physically and mentally exhausted, I went upstairs at half-past seven, threw myself fully clothed upon the bed, and was asleep within minutes.

The rain awoke me. Nothing much, just a pattering sound on the open window, with the curtain blowing about. It was quite dark. I switched on the light; it was four-thirty. I had slept a solid nine hours. My exhaustion had vanished and I felt ravenous, having had no supper.

Here was the pay-off for living alone: I could eat and sleep entirely as and when I pleased. I went downstairs to the kitchen, cooked myself sausages, eggs and bacon, and brewed a pot of tea. I felt fighting fit to begin a new day, but what could I possibly do at five o'clock in this grey, cheerless dawn? One thing, and one thing only. Then take the weekend to recover, if recovery was needed . . .

I went down the backstairs to the basement, switching on all the lights and whistling. It looked better lit up, much more cheerful. Even the laboratory had lost its alchemistic air, and measuring the drops into the medicine glass was as simple as cleaning my teeth.

"Come on, Roger," I said, "show yourself. Let's make it a tête-à-tête."

I sat on the edge of the sink and waited. I waited a long time. The thing was, nothing happened. I just went on staring at the embryos in the bottles as it grew gradually lighter outside the barred window. I must have sat there for about half-an-hour. What a frightful swindle! Then I remembered that Magnus had suggested increasing the dose. I took the dropper, very cautiously let another two or three more drops fall on to my tongue, and swallowed it. Was it imagination, or was there a taste to it this time—bitter, a little sour?

I locked the door of the laboratory behind me, and went down the passage into the old kitchen. I switched off the light, for it was already grey, with the first dawn in the patio outside. Then I heard the back door creak—it had a habit of grating on the stone flag beneath—and it blew wide open in the sudden draught. There was the sound of footsteps and a man's voice.

"God!" I thought. "Mrs. Collins has turned up early—she said something about the husband coming to mow the grass."

The man pushed past the door, dragging a boy behind him, and it was not Mrs. Collins' husband, it was Roger Kylmerth, and he was followed by five other men, carrying flares, and there was no longer any dawn light coming from the patio, only the dark night.

9

I HAD BEEN standing against the old kitchen dresser, but there was no dresser behind me now, only the stone wall, and the kitchen itself had become the living quarters of the original house, with the hearth at one end and the ladder leading to the sleeping room beside it. The girl I had seen kneeling by the hearth that first day came running down the ladder at the sound of the men's footsteps, and at sight of her Roger shouted, "Go back out of it! What we have to say and do does not concern you."

She hesitated, and the boy, the brother, was there too, looking over her shoulder. "Out of it," shouted Roger, "the pair of you," and they backed away again, up the ladder, but from where I stood I could see them crouching there, out of sight of the group of men, who entered the kitchen behind the steward.

Roger set his flare upon a bench, lighting the room, and I recognised the boy he was holding—it was the young novice I had seen on my first visit to the Priory, the lad who had been forced to run round the stableyard to make sport for his fellow monks, and later had wept at his prayers in the Priory chapel.

"I'll make him talk," said Roger, "if the rest of you cannot. It will loosen his tongue to have a taste of Purgatory to come."

Slowly he rolled up his sleeves, taking his time, his eyes upon the novice all the while, and the boy backed away from the bench, seeking shelter amongst the other men, who thrust him forward, laughing. He had grown taller since I had seen him last, but it was the same lad, there was no mistaking him, and the look of terror in his eyes suggested that the rough handling he dreaded this time was not sport.

Roger seized him by his habit and pushed him on his his knees beside the bench. "Tell us all you know," he said, "or I'll singe the hair off your head."

"I know nothing," cried the novice. "I swear by the Mother of God . . . ."

"No blasphemy," said Roger, "or I'll set fire to your habit too. You've played spy long enough, and we want the truth."

He took hold of the flare and brought it within an inch or so of the boy's head. The boy crouched lower and began to scream. Roger hit him across the mouth. "Come on, out with it," he said.

The girl and her brother were staring from the ladder, fascinated, and the five men drew nearer to the bench, one of them touching the boy's ear with his knife. "Shall I prick him and draw blood," he suggested, "then singe his pate afterwards where the flesh is tender?"

The novice held up his hands for mercy. "I'll tell all I know," he cried, "but it's nothing, nothing . . . only what I overheard Master Bloyou, the Bishop's emissary, say to the Prior."

Roger withdrew the flare, and set it back upon the bench. "And what did he say?"

The terrified novice glanced first at Roger and then at his companions. "That the Bishop was displeased with the conduct of some of the brethren, Brother Jean in particular. That he, with others, acts against the Prior's will, and squanders the property of the monastery in dissolute living. That they are a scandal to the whole Order, and a pernicious example to many outside it. And that the Bishop cannot close his eyes to the situation any longer, and has given Master Bloyou all power to enforce the canon law, with the aid of Sir John Carminowe."

He paused for breath, seeking reassurance in their faces, and one of the men, not the fellow with the knife, moved away from the group.

"By the faith, it's true," he muttered, "and who are we to deny it? We know well enough that the Priory, and all within it, are a scandal. If the French monks went back where they belong, we'd be well rid of them."

A murmur of agreement rose from the others, and the man with the knife, a great hulking chap, losing interest in the novice, turned to Roger.

"Trefrengy has a point," he said sullenly. "It stands to reason we valley men this side of Tywardreath would stand to gain if the Priory closed its doors. We'd have a claim to the surrounding land, on which they grow fat, instead of being pushed to graze our cattle amongst reeds."

Roger folded his arms, spurning the still frightened novice with his foot. "Who speaks of closing the Priory doors?" he asked. "Not the Bishop up in Exeter, he speaks for the Diocese only, and can recommend the Prior to discipline the monks, but nothing further. The King is overlord, as you are perfectly aware, and every one of us who are tenants under Champernoune has had fair treatment, and received benefits from the Priory into the bargain. More than that. None of you have held back from trading with the French ships when they cast anchors in the bay. Is there anyone amongst you who has not had his cellars filled because of them?"

Nobody answered. The novice, believing himself safe, began to crawl away, but Roger caught at him once again and held him.

"Not so fast," he said, "I haven't finished with you. What else did Master Henry Bloyou tell the Prior?"

"No more than I have said," stammered the boy.

"Nothing concerning the safety of the realm itself?"

Roger made as though to seize the flare from the bench, and the novice, trembling, put up his hands in self-defence.

"He spoke of rumours from the north," he faltered, "that trouble is still brewing between the King and his mother Queen Isabella, and might break out into open strife before long. If so, he wondered who in the west would be loyal to the young King, and who would declare for the Queen and her lover Mortimer."

"I thought as much," said Roger. "Now crawl into a corner and stay mute. If you blab a word of this outside these walls I'll slit your tongue for you."

He turned and faced the five men, who stared back at him uncertainly, this latest information having shocked them into silence.

"Well?" asked Roger. "What do you make of it? Are you all dumb?"

The fellow called Trefrengy shook his head. "It's none of our business," he said.

"The King can quarrel with his mother if he wants. It does not concern us."

"You think not?" queried Roger. "Not even if the Queen and Mortimer should keep the power within their own hands still? I know of some in these parts who would prefer it so, and would be recompensed for declaring for the Queen when the battle was done. Yes, and pay liberally if others would do the same."

"Not young Champernoune," said the man with the knife. "He's underage and tied to his mother's apron strings. As for you, Roger, you'd never risk rebellion against a crowned king—not holding your position."

He laughed derisively and the others joined in, but the steward, looking at each in turn, remained unmoved.

"Victory is assured if action is swift and power seized overnight," he said. "If that is what the Queen and Mortimer intend we shall all of us be on the winning side if we keep sweet with their friends. There could be some division of manor lands, who knows? And instead of grazing your cattle amongst reeds, Geoffrey Lampetho, you might have the advantage of the hills above."

The man with the knife shrugged his shoulders. "Easy said," he observed, "but who are these friends, so ready with their promises? I know of none."

"Sir Otto Bodrugan, for one," said Roger quietly.

A murmur rose amongst the men, the name Bodrugan was repeated, and Henry Trefrengy, who had spoken against the French monks, shook his head once more.

"He's a fine man, none better," he said, "but the last time he rebelled against the Crown, in 1322, he lost, and was fined a thousand marks for his pains."

"He was recompensed four years later when the Queen made him Governor of Lundy Island," replied Roger. "The lea of Lundy makes good anchorage for vessels carrying arms, and men as well, who can lie in safety there until they're needed on the mainland. Bodrugan is no fool. What is easier for him, holding lands in Cornwall and in Devon, and Governor of Lundy into the bargain, than to raise the men and ships that the Queen needs?"

His argument, smooth, persuasive, seemed to make impact, especially upon Lampetho. "If there's profit in it for us I'd wish him well," he said, "and rally to his side when the deed is done. But I won't cross the Tamar for any man, Bodrugan or another, and you can tell him so."

"You may tell him yourself," said Roger. "His vessel lies below, and he knows I await him here. I tell you, friends, Queen Isabella will show her gratitude to him, and to others, who knew which side to favour."

He went to the foot of the ladder. "Come down, Robbie," he called. "Take a light across the field and see if Sir Otto is on his way," and turning to the others, "I'm ready to strike a blow for him if you are not."

His brother came down the ladder, and, seizing one of the flares, ran out into the yard beyond the kitchen.

Henry Trefrengy, more cautious than his companions, stroked his chin. "What lies in it for you, Roger, by siding with Bodrugan? Will the Lady Joanna join forces with her brother against the King?"

"My lady has no part in any of it," replied Roger shortly. "She is away from home, at her other property of Trelawn, with her own children and Bodrugan's wife and family. None of them have any knowledge of what is at stake."

"She won't thank you when she hears of it," replied Trefrengy, "nor Sir John Carminowe either. It is common knowledge they only wait for Sir John's lady to die so that they can marry."

"Sir John's lady is healthy and likely to continue so," answered Roger, "and when the Queen makes Bodrugan Keeper of Restormel Castle and overseer of all the Duchy lands, my lady may lose her interest in Sir John and look upon her brother with more affection than she does now. I don't doubt I shall be recompensed by Bodrugan, and forgiven by my lady." He smiled, and scratched his ear.

"By the faith," said Lampetho, "we all know you lay your plans to suit yourself.

Whoever wins the day will find you at his elbow. Bodrugan or Sir John at Restormel Castle, and you will be standing at the drawbridge, holding a well-lined purse."

"I don't deny it," said Roger, smiling still. "If you possessed the same ability for thought you would do likewise."

Footsteps sounded from the yard beyond, and he crossed to the door and flung it open. Otto Bodrugan stood on the threshold, with young Robbie behind him.

"Enter, sir, and welcome. We are all friends," said Roger, and Bodrugan came into the kitchen, looking sharply about him, surprised, I think, to see the little group of men who, embarrassed by his sudden arrival, drew back against the wall. His tunic was laced to the throat, with a padded leather jerkin over all, belted with purse and dagger, and a travelling cloak, fur-trimmed, hung from his shoulders. He made a contrast to the others in their homespun cloth and hoods, and it was evident from his air of confidence that he was used to commanding men.

"I am very glad to see you," he said at once, advancing to each in turn. "Henry Trefrengy, isn't it? And Martin Penhelek. John Beddyng I know too—your uncle rode north with me in '22. The others I have not met before."

"Geoffrey Lampetho, sir, and his brother Philip," said Roger. "They farm the valley adjoining Julian Polpey's land, beneath the Prior mannor."

"Is Julian not here, then?"

"He awaits us at Polpey."

Bodrugan's eye fell upon the novice, still crouching beside the bench. "What is the monk doing here amongst you?"

"He brought us information, sir," said Roger. "There has been some trouble at the Priory, a matter of discipline in the house amongst the brothers, of no concern to us, but disturbing in that the Bishop has lately sent Master Bloyou from Exeter to enquire into the business."

"Henry Bloyou? A close friend to Sir John Carminowe and Sir William Ferrers. Is he still at the Prior?"

The novice, anxious to please, touched Bodrugan's knee. "No, sir, he has gone. He left yesterday for Exeter, but promised to return shortly."

"Well, get to your feet, lad, no harm shall come to you." Bodrugan turned to the steward. "Have you been threatening him?"

"Not a hair of his head," protested Roger. "He is only frightened that the Prior might learn of his presence here, despite my promise to the contrary."

Roger signalled to Robbie to take the novice to the upper room, and the pair of them disappeared up the ladder, the novice in as much hurry to be gone as a kicked doe. When the two had gone Bodrugan, standing before the hearth, his hands on is belt, looked keenly at each one of the men.

"What Roger has been telling you about our chances I do not know," he said, "but I can promise you a better life when the King is in custody." No one answered. "Has Roger informed you that most of the country will declare for Queen Isabella in a few days' time?" he asked them.

Henry Trefrengy, who seemed to be spokesman, was bold enough to speak. "He told us so, yes," he said, "but little detail of it."

"It is a question of the timing," replied Bodrugan. "Parliament now sits at Nottingham, and it is planned to seize the King—with all care for his safety, naturally—until he comes of age. In the meantime Queen Isabella will continue as Regent, with Mortimer to aid her. He may lack popularity with some, but he is a strong man, and capable, and a very good friend of many Cornishmen. I am proud to count myself amongst them."

Silence again. Then Geoffrey Lampetho stepped forward. "What would you have us do?" he asked.

"Come north with me, if you will," answered Bodrugan, "but if not, and God knows I cannot make you, then promise to swear allegiance to Queen Isabella when word comes from Nottingham that we hold the King."

"That's spoken fairly," said Roger. "For my part I say yes, and gladly, and will ride with you."

"And so will I," said another man, the man called Penhelek.

"And I too," cried the third, John Beddyng.

Only the Lampetho brohers and Trefrengy were reluctant.

"We'll swear allegiance when the moment comes," said Geoffrey Lampetho, "but we'll swear it at home, not across the Tamar."

"Also fairly spoken," said Bodrugan. "If the King had the power himself we should be at war with France within ten years, fighting across the Channel. By supporting the Queen now we strike a blow for peace. I have the promise of at least a hundred men from my own lands, from Bodrugan, from Tregrehan and farther west, and from Devon too. Shall we go and see how Julian Polpey stands?"

There was a general stir amongst the men as they made towards the door.

"The tide is flooding across the ford," said Roger. "We must cross the valley by Trefrengy and Lampetho. I have a pony for you, sir. Robbie?" He called his brother from the room above. "Have you the pony saddled for Sir Otto? and mine as well? Make haste, then . . ." And as the boy came down the ladder he whispered in his ear, "Brother Jean will send for the novice later. Keep him until then. As for myself, I cannot say when I shall return."

We found ourselves in the stableyard, a huddle of ponies and men, and I knew I must go too, for Roger was mounting his pony beside Bodrugan, and wherever he went I was compelled to follow. The clouds were racing across the sky, the wind was blowing, and the stamping of ponies and the jingle of harness rang in my ear. Never before, neither in my own world nor on the previous occasions when I had strayed into the other, had I felt such a sense of unity. I was one of them, and they did not know it. This, I think, was the essence of what it meant to me. To be bound, yet free; to be alone, yet in their company; to be born in my own time yet living, unknown, in theirs.

They rode up the track through the little copse bordering Kilmarth, and at the top of the hill, instead of following the route of the modern road I knew, they struck across the summit and then plunged steeply towards the valley. The track was rough, making the ponies stumble from time to time, and twisting too. The descent seemed almost as sharp as a cliff face, but, disembodied as I felt myself to be, I was no judge of height or depth, and my only guides were the men upon their ponies. Then, through the darkness, I saw the gleam of water, and presently we plumbed the valley's depth and reached a wooden bridge bordering a stream, across which the ponies walked dry-shod in single file, and the path wound to the left, following the water's course, until the stream itself widened to a broad creek that opened out in the far distance to the sea itself. I knew I must be on the opposite side of the valley from Polmear hill, but because I was abroad in their world and it was night, the judging of distance was impossible; I could only follow the ponies, my eyes firmly fixed on Roger and Bodrugan.

The path led us past farm-buildings, where the Lampetho brothers dismounted, the elder, Geoffrey, shouting that he would follow later, and we went on again, the track rising to higher ground but still bordering the creek. There were further farm buildings ahead above the sand dunes where the river met the sea; even in the darkness I could see the gleam of the white rollers as they broke in the distance and then ran upon the shore. Someone came to meet us, there were barking dogs and flares, and we were in yet another stableyard, similar to the one at Kilmarth, with outbuildings surrounding it. As the men dismounted from their ponies the door of the main building opened, and I recognised the man who had come forward to greet us. It was Roger's companion on the day of the Bishop's reception at the Priory, the same who had walked with him afterwards on the village green.

Roger, the first to dismount, was the first at his friend's side, and even in the dim light of the lantern by the house door I could see his expression change as the man whispered hurriedly in his ear, pointing to the further side of the farm buildings.

Bodrugan hesitated for a moment, then quickly said, "As you will," and put out his hand to the owner of the house. "I had hoped," he said, "we would muster arms and men at Polpey, Julian. My ship is anchored below Kylmerth, you must have seen her. There are several aboard, ready to disembark."

Julian Polpey shook his head. "I'm sorry, Sir Otto, they will not be needed, nor yourself either. Word came not ten minutes ago that the whole scheme has been defeated before it took final shape. A very special messenger has brought you the news herself, disregarding if I may say so, her own safety."

I could hear Roger, over my shoulder, telling the men to mount their ponies and ride back to Lampetho, where he would presently join them. Then, handing his pony's reins to the servant standing by, he joined Polpey and Bodrugan as they made their way past the outbuildings to the farther side of the house.

"It is Lady Carminowe," said Bodrugan to Roger, his glad confidence vanished, his face sharp with anxiety. "She has brought bad news."

"Lady Carminowe?" exclaimed Roger, incredulous, then with sudden understanding, and lowering his voice, "you mean lady Isolda?"

"She is on her way to Carminowe," said Bodrugan, "and, guessing my movements, has broken her journey here at Polpey."

We came to the other side of the house, which fronted upon the lane leading to Tywardreath. A covered vehicle was drawn up outside the gate, similar to the waggonettes I had seen at the Priory at Martinmas, but this was smaller, drawn by two horses only.

As we approached the curtain was held aside from the small window, and Isolda leant from it, the dark hood that covered her head falling back upon her shoulders. "Thank God I am in time," she said. "I come straight from Bockenod. Both John and Oliver are there, and believe me halfway to Carminowe to rejoin the children. The worse has happened for your cause, and what I feared. News came before I left that the Queen and Mortimer have been seized at Nottingham Castle and are prisoners. The King is in full command, and Mortimer is to be taken to London for trial. Here is an end, Otto, to all your dreams."

Roger exchanged a glance with Julian Polpey, and as the latter, from discretion, moved away into the shadows I could see the conflict of emotion on Roger's face. I guessed what he was thinking. Ambition had led him astray, and he had backed a losing cause. It now remained for him to urge Bodrugan to return to his ship, disband his men and speed Isoloda on her journey, while himself, having explained his volte face to Lampetho, Trefrengy and the rest as best he could, reinstated himself as Joanna Champernourne's trusted steward.

"You have risked discovery in coming here," said Bodrugan to Isolda. Nothing in his face betrayed how much he had lost.

"If I have done so," she replied, "you know the reason why."

I saw her look at him, and he at her. We were the only witnesses, Roger and I. Bodrugan bent forward to kiss her hand, and as he did so I heard the sound of wheels from the lane, and I thought, "She came too late to warn him after all. Oliver, the husband, and Sir John have followed her."

I wondered that neither of them heard the wheels, and then I saw they were not with me any longer. The waggonette had gone, and the mail van from Par had come up the lane and stopped beside the gate.

It was morning. I was standing inside the drive leading to a small house across the valley from Polmear hill. I tried to hide myself in the bushes bordering the drive, but the postman had already got out of his van and was opening the gate. His stare combined recognition and astonishment, and I followed the direction of his eyes down to my legs. I was soaking wet from crutch to foot: I must have waded through bog and marsh. My shoes were waterlogged and both trouser legs were torn. I summoned a painful smile.

He looked embarrassed. "You're in a proper mess," he said. "It's the gentleman living up Kilmarth, isn't it?"

"Yes," I replied.

"Well, this is Polpey, Mr. Graham's house. But I doubt if they're up yet, it's only just turned seven. Were you intending to call on Mr. Graham?"

"Good heavens, no! I got up early, went for a walk, and somehow lost my way."

It was a thumping lie, and sounded like one. He seemed to accept it, though.

"I have to deliver these letters, and then I'll be going up the hill to your place," he said. "Would you care to get in the van? It would save you a walk."

"Thanks a lot," I said. "I'd be most grateful."

He disappeared down the drive and I climbed into his van. I looked at my watch. He was right, it was five past seven. Mrs. Collins was not due for at least another hour and a half, and I should have plenty of time for a bath and a change.

I tried to think where I had been. I must have crossed the main road at the top of the hill, then walked downhill across country and through the marshy ground at the bottom of the valley. I had not even known that this house was called Polpey.

No nausea, though, thank God, no vertigo. As I sat there, waiting for him to return, I realised that the rest of me was wet as well, jacket, head, for it was raining—and had probably been raining when I left Kilmarth almost an hour and a half ago. I wondered whether I should enlarge upon my story to the postman or let it go. Better let it go . . ."

He came back and climbed into the van. "Not much of a morning for your walk. It's been raining hard since midnight."

I remembered then that it had been the rain which woke me up originally: blowing the curtain at the bedroom window.

"I don't mind the rain," I told him. "I get short of exercise in London."

"Same as me," he said cheerfully, "driving this van. But I'd rather be snug in my bed this weather than take a walk across the marsh. Still, there it is, it wouldn't do if we were all the same."

He called at the Ship Inn at the bottom of the hill and at one of the cottages nearby, and as the van raced up the main road I looked leftward over my shoulder to the valley, but the high hedge hid it from view. God only knew what swampy meadowland and marsh I must have traversed. My shoes were oozing water on the floor of the van.

We left the main road and turned right down the drive to Kilmarth.

"You're not the only early bird," he said as the sweep in front of the house came into sight. "Either Mrs. Collins has had a lift up from Polkerris or you have visitors."

I saw the large open boot of the Buick packed tight with luggage. The horn was blowing continuously, and the two children, with macs held over their heads to protect them from the rain, were running up the steps through the front garden to the house.

The shock of disbelief turned to the dull certainty of impending doom.

"It's not Mrs. Collins," I said, "it's my wife and family. They must have driven down from London through the night."

10

THERE WAS NO question of driving past the garage to the back entrance. The postman, grinning, stopped his van and opened the door for me to get out, and anyway the children had already seen me, and were waving.

"Thanks for the lift," I said to him, "but I could do without the reception," and I took the letter that he held out to me and advanced to meet my fate.

"Hi, Dick," called the boys, tearing back down the steps. "We rang and rang, but we couldn't make you hear. Mom's mad at you."

"I'm mad at her," I told them. "I didn't expect you."

"It's a surprise," said Teddy. "Mom thought it would be more fun. Micky slept at the back of the car, but I didn't. I read the map."

The blowing of the horn had ceased. Vita emerged from the Buick, immaculate as always, wearing just the right sort of clothes for Piping Rock on Long Island. She had a new hairdo, more wave in it, or something; it looked all right but it made her face too full.

Attack is the best form of defence, I thought. Let's get it over. "Well, for God's sake," I said, "you might have warned me."

"The boys gave me no peace," she said. "Blame it on them."

We kissed, then both stood back, eyeing each other warily like sparring partners before a shadow feint.

"How long have you been here?" I asked.

"About half an hour," she said. "We've been all round, but we couldn't get in. The boys even tried throwing earth at the windows, after they'd rung the bell. What's happened? You're soaked to the skin."

"I was up very early," I said. "I went for a walk."

"What, in all this rain? You must be crazy. Look, your trousers are torn, and there's a great rent in your jacket."

She seized hold of my arm and the boys crowded round me, gaping. Vita began to laugh. "Where on earth did you go to get in a state like this?" she asked.

I shook myself clear. "Look," I said, "we'd better unload. It's no good doing it here—the front door is locked. Hop in the car and we'll go round to the back."

I led the way with the boys, and she followed in the car. When we reached the back entrance I remembered that it was locked too from the inside—I had left the house by the patio.

"Wait here," I said, "I'll open the door for you," and with the boys in close attendance I went round to the patio. The boilerhouse door was ajar—I must have passed through it when I followed Roger and the rest of the conspirators. I kept telling myself to keep calm, not to get confused; if confusion started in my mind it would be fatal.

"What a funny old place. What's it for?" asked Micky.

"To sit in," I said, "and sun-bathe. When there is any sun."

"If I were Professor Lane I'd turn it into a swimming pool," said Teddy. They trooped after me into the house, through the old kitchen to the back door. I unlocked it, and found Vita waiting impatiently outside.

"Get in out of the rain," I said, "while the boys and I fetch in the suitcases."

"Show us round first," she said plaintively. "The luggage can wait. I want to see everything. Don't tell me *that* is the kitchen through there?"

"Of course it isn't," I said. "It's an old basement kitchen. We don't use any of this."

The thing is, I had never intended to show them the house from this angle. It was the wrong way round. If they had arrived on Monday I should have been waiting for them on the steps by the porch, with the curtains drawn back, the windows open, everything ready. The boys, excited, were already scampering up the stairs.

"Which is our room?" they shouted. "Where are we to sleep?"

Oh God, I thought, give me patience. I turned to Vita who was watching me with a smile.

"I'm sorry, darling," I said, "but honestly . . ."

"Honestly what?" she said. "I'm as excited as they are. What are you fussing about?"

What indeed! I thought, with total inconsequence, how much better organised this would have been if Roger Kylmerth, as steward, had been showing Isolda Carminowe the layout of some manor house.

"Nothing," I said, "come on . . ."

The first thing Vita noticed when we reached the modern kitchen on the first floor was the debris of my supper on the table. The remains of fried eggs and sausages, the frying pan not cleaned, standing on one corner of the table, the electric light still on.

"Heavens!" she exclaimed. "Did you have a cooked breakfast before your walk? That's new for you!"

"I was hungry," I said. "Ignore the mess, Mrs. Collins will clear all that. Come through to the front."

I hurried past her to the music room, drawing curtains, throwing back shutters, and then across the hall to the small dining room and the library beyond. The pièce de résistance, the view from the end window, was blotted out by the mizzling rain.

"It looks different," I said, "on a fine day."

"It's lovely," said Vita. "I didn't think your Professor had such taste. It would be better with that divan against the wall and cushions on the window seat, but that's easily done."

"Well, this completes the ground floor," I said. "Come upstairs."

I felt like a house agent trying to flog a difficult let, as the boys raced ahead up the stairs, calling to each other from the rooms, while Vita and I followed. Everything had already changed, the silence and the peace had gone, henceforth it would be only this, the takeover of something I had shared, as it were, in secret, not only with Magnus and his dead parents in the immediate past, but with Roger Kylmerth six hundred years ago.

The tour of the first floor finished, the sweat of unloading all the luggage began, and it was nearly half-past eight when the job was done, and Mrs. Collins arrived on her bicycle to take charge of the situation, greeting Vita and the boys with genuine delight. Everyone disappeared into the kitchen. I went upstairs and ran the bath, wishing I could lie in it and drown.

It must have been half an hour later that Vita wandered into the bedroom. "Well, thank God for her," she said. "I shan't have to do a thing, she's extremely efficient. And must be sixty at least. I can relax."

"What do you mean, relax?" I called from the bathroom.

"I imagined something young and skittish, when you tried to put me off from coming down," she said. She came into the bathroom as I was rubbing myself with the towel. "I don't trust your Professor an inch, but at least I'm satisfied on that account. Now you're all cleaned up you can kiss me again, and then run me a bath. I've been driving for several hours and I'm dead to the world."

So was I, but in another sense, I was dead to her world. I might move about in it, mechanically, listening with half an ear as she peeled off her clothes and flung them on the bed, put on a wrapper, spread her lotions and creams on the dressing table, chatting all the while about the drive down, the day in London, happenings in New York, her brother's business affairs, a dozen things that formed the pattern of her life, our life; but none of them concerned me. It was like hearing background music on the radio. I wanted to recapture the lost night and the darkness, the wind blowing down the valley, the sound of the sea breaking on the shore below Polpey farm, and the expression in Isolda's eyes as she looked out of that painted waggon at Bodrugan.

" . . . And if they do amalgamate it wouldn't be before the fall anyway, nor would it affect your job."

"No."

Response was automatic to the rise and fall of her voice, and suddenly she wheeled round, her face a mask of cream under the turban she always wore in the bath, and said, "You haven't been listening to a word I said!"

The change of tone shocked me to attention. "Yes, I have," I told her.

"What, then? What have I been talking about?" she challenged.

I was clearing my things out of the wardrobe in the bedroom, so that she could take over. "You were saying something about Joe's firm," I answered, "a merger of some sort. Sorry, darling, I'll be out of your way in a minute."

She seized the hanger bearing a flannel suit, my best, out of my hand, and hurled it on the floor.

"I don't want you out of the way," she said, her voice rising to a pitch I dreaded. "I want you here and now, giving me your full attention, instead of standing there like a tailor's dummy. What on earth's the matter with you? I might be talking to someone in another world."

She was so right. I knew it was no use counterattacking; I must grovel, and let her tide of perfectly justifiable irritation pass over my head.

"Darling," I said, sitting down on the bed and pulling her beside me, "let's not start the day wrong. You're tired, I'm tired; if we start arguing we'll wear ourselves out and spoil things for the boys. If I am vague and inattentive, you must blame it on exhaustion. I took that walk in the rain because I couldn't sleep, and instead of pulling me together it seems to have slowed me up."

"Of all the idiotic things to do . . . You might have known . . . and anyway, why couldn't you sleep?"

"Forget it, forget it, forget it."

I rose from the bed, seized armfuls of clothes and bore them through to the dressing room, kicking the door to with my foot. She did not follow me. I heard her turn the taps off and get into the bath, slopping the water so that some of it ran into the overflow.

The morning drifted on. Vita did not appear. I opened the bedroom door very softly just before one, and she was fast asleep on the bed, so I closed it again and lunched downstairs alone with the boys. They chatted away, perfectly content with a "yes" or "perhaps" from me, invariably undemanding when Vita was absent. It continued to rain steadily, and there was no question of cricket or the beach, so I drove them into Fowey and let them loose to buy ice creams, peppermint rock, Western paperbacks, and jigsaw puzzles.

The rain petered out about four, giving place to a lustreless sky and a pallid, constipated sun, but this was enough for the boys, who rushed on to the Town Quay and demanded to be waterborne. Anything to please, and postpone the moment of return, so I hired a small boat, powered by an outboard engine, and we chug-chugged up and down the harbour, the boys snatching at passing flotsam as we bobbed about, all of us soaked to the skin.

We arrived home about six o'clock, and the children rushed to sit down to the enormous spread of tea that the thoughtful Mrs. Collins had provided for them. I staggered into the library to pour myself a stiff whisky, only to find a revitalized Vita in possession, smiling, the furniture all moved around, the morning mood, thank heaven, a thing of the past.

"You know, darling," she said, "I think I'm going to like it here. Already it's begining to look like home."

I collapsed into an armchair, drink in hand, and watched through half-closed eyes as she pottered about the room rearranging Mrs. Collins' brave efforts with the hydrangeas. My strategy henceforth would be to applaud everything, or, when occasion demanded silence, to stay mute, play each moment as it came by ear.

I was on my second whisky, and off my guard, when the boys burst into the library.

"Hi, Dick," shouted Teddy, "what's this horrible thing?"

He had got the embryo monkey in its jar. I leapt to my feet. "Christ!" I said. "What the hell have you been up to?" I seized the jar from his hand and made for the door. I remembered only then that when I had gone out from the lab in the small hours, after taking my second dose, I hadn't pocketed the key but had left it in the lock.

"We weren't doing anything," said Teddy, aggrieved, "we were only looking through the empty rooms below." He turned to Vita. "There's a little dark room full of bottles, just like the stinks lab at school. Come and look, Mom, quick—there's something else in one of the jars like a dead kitten . . ."

I was out of the library in a flash, and down the small stairway in the hall leading to the basement. The door of the lab was wide open, and the light was on. I looked quickly around. Nothing had been touched except the jar holding the monkey. I switched off the light and stepped into the passage, locking the door behind me and pocketing the key. As I did so the boys came running through the old kitchen, Vita at their heels. She looked concerned.

"What did they do?" she asked. "Have they broken something?"

"Luckily, no," I said. "It was my fault for leaving the door unlocked."

She was peering over my shoulder down the passage. "What is through there anyway?" she asked. "That object Teddy brought up looked perfectly ghastly."

"I dare say," I answered. "It happens that this house belongs to a professor of biophysics, and he uses the small room behind there as a laboratory. If I ever catch either of the boys near that room again there'll be murder."

They stalked off, muttering, and Vita turned to me. "I must say," she said, "I think it's rather extraordinary of the Professor to keep a room like that, with all sorts of scientific things in it, and not make certain it's kept properly locked."

"Now don't you start," I said. "I am responsible to Magnus, and I can assure you it won't happen again. If you had only come next week instead of turning up this morning at an unearthly hour, when nobody expected you, it would never have happened."

She stared at me, startled. "Why, you're shaking!" she said. "Anyone would think there were explosives in there."

"Perhaps there are," I said. "Anyway, let's hope those kids have learnt their lesson."

I switched off the basement lights and walked upstairs. I was shaking, and small wonder. A nightmare of possibilities crowded my mind. They might have opened the bottles containing the drug, they might have poured the contents into the medicine glass, they might even have emptied the bottles into the sink. I must never again let that key out of my sight. I kept touching it in my pocket. Perhaps I could get an impression made of it, and keep both; it would be safer. I went into the music room and stood there, staring at nothing, thrusting my fingertip into the little hole in the key.

Vita had gone upstairs to the bedroom. Presently, I heard the telltale click of the telephone from the bell in the hall. It meant she was speaking from the extension upstairs. I went and washed my hands in the downstairs lavatory, and then wandered into the libaray. I could hear Vita talking from the bedroom overhead. Listening to conversations on the telephone is not a habit of mine, but now some furtive instinct made me cross to the instrument in the library and pick up the receiver.

" . . . So I just don't know what to make of it," Vita was saying. "I've never heard him speak sharply to the boys before. They're quite upset. He doesn't look awfully well. Very hollow-eyed. He says he's been sleeping badly."

"High time you got down there," came the answer. I recognised the drawl; it was her friend Diana. "A husband on the loose is a husband on the prowl, I've told you so before. I've had experience with Bill."

"Oh, Bill," said Vita. "We all know Bill can't be trusted out of your sight. Well, I don't know . . . Let's hope it will be fine and we can all be out a lot. I believe he's arranged to hire some boat."

"That sounds healthy enough."

"Yes . . . Well, let's hope that Professor of his hasn't been putting Dick up to something. I don't trust that man. Never have, and never will. And I know he dislikes me."

"I can guess why that is," laughed Diana.

"Oh, don't be idiotic. He may be like that, but Dick certainly isn't. Very much the reverse."

"Maybe that's his attraction for the Professor," said Diana.

I replaced the receiver very gently. The trouble was, with women, they had one-track minds, and to their narrow view everything male, be it man, dog, fish or slug, pursued but a single course, and that the dreary road to copulation. I sometimes wondered if they ever thought of anything else.

Vita and her friend Diana nattered on for at least another fifteen minutes, and when she came downstairs, fortified by feminine advice, she made no reference to my scene in the basement, but, humming gaily and wearing an apron of bizarre design—it looked as if it had apples and serpents all over it—set about cooking us steaks for supper heaped about with parsley butter.

"Early bed for all," she announced as the boys, heavy-eyed and silent, yawned their way through the meal—the seven-hour journey in the car and the jaunt in the harbour was catching up with them. After supper she installed herself on the sofa in the library, and set about mending the rents in my trousers torn in the valley. I sat down at Magnus's desk murmuring something about unpaid bills, but in reality looking once again through the Lay Subsidy Roll for Tywardreath Parish for 1327. Julian Polpey was there, Henry Trefrengy, Geoffrey Lampetho. The names had meant nothing when I first read through the list, but they could have registered unconsciously in my mind. The figures might still be phantom figures that I had followed to the valley, passing the farms that still bore their names today.

I noticed an unopened letter on my desk. It was the one the postman had given me that morning; in my flurry at the family's arrival I had laid it down. It was just a scrap, typewritten, from the research student in London.

"Professor Lane thought you might like this note on Sir John Carminowe," it read. "He was the second son of Sir Roger Carminowe of Carminowe. Enrolled in the military 1323. Became a knight 1324. Summoned to attend Great council at Westminister. Appointed Keeper of Tremerton and Restormel castles April 27th, 1331, and on October 12th of the same year, keeper of the King's forests, parks, woods and warrens, etc., and of the King's game in the county of Cornwall, so that he had to answer yearly for the profit of the pannage and herbage within the said forests, parks and woods, by the hand of the steward there, and deputy keepers under him."

The student had written in brackets, "Copied from Calendar of Fine Rolls 5th year Edward III." He had added a further note beneath, "October 24th. Patent Rolls, for same year (1331), mentions a licence for Joanna, late wife of Henry de Champernoune, tenant-in-chief, to marry whomsoever she will of the King's allegiance. Pay fine of 10 marks."

So . . . Sir John had got what he wanted and Otto Bodrugan had lost, while Joanna, in anticipation of Sir John's wife dying, had a marriage licence handy in some bottom drawer. I filed the paper with the Lay Subsidy Roll, and getting up from the desk went to the bookshelves, where I remembered seeing the numerous volumes of the Encyclopedia Britannica, legacy of Commander Lane. I pulled out Volume 8, and turned to Edward III.

Vita stretched herself on the sofa, yawning, her repeated sighs following one another in swift succession. "Well, I don't know about you," she said, "but I'm off to bed."

"I'll be up in a moment," I told her.

"Still hard at work for your Professor?" she asked. "Take that volume to the light, you'll ruin your eyes."

I did not answer.

> Edward III (1312-1377), king of England, eldest son of Edward II and Isabella of France, was born at Windsor on the 13th of November 1312 . . . On the 13th of January 1327 parliament recognised him as king, and he was crowned on the 29th of the same month. For the next four years Isabella and her paramour Mortimr governed in his name, though nominally his guardian was Henry, Earl of Lancaster. In the summer of 1327 he took part in an abortive campaign against the Scots, and was married to Philippa at York on the 24th of January 1328. On the 15th of June 1330 his eldest child, Edward the Black Prince, was born."

Nothing there about a rebellion. But here was the clue.

> "Soon after, Edward made a successful effort to throw off his
> degrading dependence on his mother and Mortimer. In October
> 1330 he entered Nottingham Castle by night, through a subterra-
> nean passage, and took Mortimer prisoner. On the 29th of Novem-
> ber the execution of the favourite at Tyburn completed the young
> king's emancipation. Edward discreetly drew a veil over his
> mother's relations with Mortimer, and treated her with every
> respect. There is no truth in the stories that henceforth he kept her in
> honourable confinement, but her political influence was at an end."

Bodrugan's too, what he possessed in Cornwall. Sir John, only a year later
appointed Keeper in Tremerton and Restormel castles, a good King's man, was in
command, with Roger, playing it safe, imposing silence on his valley friends, the
October night forgotten. I wondered what had happened after that meeting at Polpey's
farm when Isolda risked so much to warn her lover, whether Bodrugan, brooding on
what might-have-been, returned to his estates and thought about his love, and
whether she, when her husband Oliver was absent, met him perhaps in secret. I had
been standing beside them both less than twenty-four hours ago. Six centuries ago . . .
    I put the volume back on the shelf, switched off the lights and went upstairs. Vita
was already in bed, the curtains pulled back so that when she sat up she could look
through the wide windows to the sea.
    "This room is heaven," she said. "Imagine what it will be like with a full moon.
Darling, I'm going to love it here, I promise you, and it's so wonderful to be together
again."
    I stood for a moment at the window, staring out across the bay. Roger, from his
sleeping quarters above the original kitchen, had the same dark expanse of sea and
sky for company, and as I turned away, toward the bed, I remembered Magnus's
mocking remark on the telephone the day before, "I was only about to suggest, dear
boy, that moving between two worlds can act as stimulant." It was not true, in fact,
the contrary.

11

THE NEXT DAY being Sunday, Vita announced her intention over breakfast of taking
the boys to church. She did this sort of thing from time to time during the holidays.
Two or three weeks would go by with never a mention of devotional duty, and then
suddenly, without giving any reason, and generally when they were otherwise
happily employed, she would burst into their room saying, "Come on, now, I'll give
you just five minutes to get ready."
    "Ready? What for?" they would query, looking up from fitting together a model
airplane or something momentarily engrossing their attention.
    "Church, of course," she would answer, sweeping from the room again, deaf to
their wails of protestation. It was always a let-out for me. Pleading my Catholic
upbringing, I would lie late in bed, reading the Sunday papers. Today, despite
sunshine flooding our room as we awoke, and the beaming smile of Mrs. Collins as
she bore in our tray of toast and coffee, Vita looked preoccupied, and said she had had
a restless night. I at once felt guilty, having slept like a log myself, and I thought how
this thing of how well or how badly one had slept was really the great test of marital
relationship; if one partner came off poorly during the night hours the other was
immediately to blame, and the following day would come apart in consequence.

This particular Sunday was to be no exception to the rule, and when the boys came into the bedroom to say good morning, dressed in jeans and T shirts, she immediately exploded.

"Off with those things at once and into your flannel suits!" she said. "Have you forgotten it's Sunday? We're going to church."

"Oh, Mom . . . No!"

I admit, I felt for them. Sunshine, blue sky, the sea below the fields. They must have had one thought in mind, to get down to it and swim.

"No arguing now," she said, getting out of bed. "Go off and do as I say." She turned to me. "I take it there is a church somewhere in the vicinity, and you can at least drive us there?"

"You have a choice of churches," I said, "either Fowey or Tywardreath. It would be easier to take you to Tywardreath." As I said the word I smiled, for the very name had a special significance, but to me alone, and continued casually, "As a matter of fact, it's quite interesting historically. There used to be a priory where the churchyard is today."

"You hear that, Teddy?" said Vita. "There used to be a priory where we are going to church. You always say you like history. Now hurry along."

I have seldom seen a sulkier pair of figures. Shoulders hunched, mouths drooping. "I'll take you swimming later," I shouted as they left the room.

It suited me to drive the party to Tywardreath. Morning service would be at least an hour, and I could drop them off at the church, and then park the car above Treesmill and stroll across the field to the Gratten. I did not know when I might get another chance to revisit the site, and the quarry with its surrounding grassy banks held a compulsive fascination.

As I drove Vita and the reluctant boys, dressed in their Sunday suits, down Polmear hill I glanced over to the right at Polpey, wondering what would have happened if the present owners had discovered me lurking in the bushes instead of the postman, or, worse, what might well have happened had Julian Polpey bidden Roger and his guests inside. Should I have been found attempting to break into the downstairs rooms? This struck me as amusing, and I laughed aloud.

"What's so funny?" asked Vita.

"Only the life I lead," I answered. "Driving you all to church today, and yesterday taking that early morning walk. You see the marsh down there? That's where I got so wet."

"I'm not surprised," she said. "What an extraordinary place to choose for walking. What did you think you were going to find?"

"Find?" I echoed. "Oh, I don't know. A damsel in distress, perhaps. You never know your luck."

I shot up the lane to Tywardreath elated, the very fact that she knew nothing of the truth filling me with a ridiculous sense of delight, like hoodwinking my mother in the past. It was a basic instinct fundamental to all males. The boys possessed it too, which was the reason I backed them up in those petty crimes of which Vita disapproved, eating snacks between meals, talking in bed after lights out.

I dropped them at the church gate, the boys still wearing their hard-done-by expressions.

"What are you going to do while we are in church?" Vita asked.

"Just walk around," I said.

She shrugged her shoulders, and turned through the gate into the churchyard. I knew that shrug; it implied that my easygoing morning mood was not in tune with hers. I hoped Matins would bring consolation.

I drove off to Treesmill, parked the car, and struck off across the field to the Gratten. The morning was superb. Warm sunshine filled the valley. A lark soared overhead bursting his heart in song. I wished I had brought sandwiches and could have had the whole long day ahead of me instead of one stolen hour.

I did not enter the quarry with its trailing ivy and old tin cans, but stretched myself full-length on a grassy bank in one of the small hollows, wondering how the place would look by night when the sky was full of stars, or rather how it had looked once, when water filled the valley below. Lorenzo's scene with Jessica came to my mind.

> *"In such a night,*
> *Troilus methinks mounted the Trojan walls,*
> *And sighed his soul toward the Grecian tents,*
> *Where Cressid lay that night . . .*
> > *"In such a night*
> > *Stood Dido with a willow in her hand*
> > *Upon the wild sea-banks, and wav'd her love*
> > *To come again to Carthage.*
> > > *"In such a night,*
> > > *Medea gather'd the enchanted herbs*
> > > *That did renew old Aeson . . ."*

Enchanted herbs was apt. The point was that, when Vita and the boys were getting ready for church, I had gone down to the lab and poured four measures into the flask. The flask was in my pocket. God knew when I should get the chance again . . .

It happened very quickly. But it was not night, it was day, and a day in summer, too, though late afternoon, judging from the western sky, which I could see from the casement window in the hall. I was leaning against a bench at the far end, with a view of the entrance court with its surrounding walls. I recognised it at once—I was in the manor house. Two children were playing in the courtyard, girls, aged around eight and ten possibly—it was difficult to tell, with the close-fitting bodices and ankle-length skirts—but the long golden hair falling down their backs, and the small clear-cut features so much alike, proclaimed them miniature editions of their mother. No one but Isolda could have produced such a pair, and I remembered Roger saying to his companion Julian Polpey at the Bishop's reception that she had grown stepsons amongst the first wife's brood, but only two daughters of her own.

They were playing some chequer game upon the flags, on a square marked out for them, with pieces like ninepins dotted about, and as they moved the pieces shrill arguments broke out between them as to whose turn was next. The younger reached forward to seize a wooden pin and hide it in her shirt, and this in turn led to cries and slaps and the pulling of hair. Roger emerged into the court suddenly, from the hall where he had been standing watching them, and thrusting himself between them squatted on his haunches, taking the hand of each in turn.

"You know what comes about when women scold?" he said to them. "Their tongues turn black and curl into their throats, choking them. It happened to my sister once, and she would have died had I not reached her side in time to pluck it back. Open your mouths."

The children, startled, opened their mouths wide, thrusting out their tongues. Roger touched each in turn with his fingertip, and waggled it.

"Pray God that does the trick," he said, "but it may not last unless you let your tempers cool. There now, shut your mouths, and only open them for your next meal, or to let kind words fly. Joanna, you're the elder, you should teach Margaret better manners than to hide a man under her skirt." He pulled out the ninepin from the younger girl's dress and set it down upon the flags. "Come now," he said, "proceed. I'll see that you play fair."

He stood up, legs wide apart, and let them move their pieces round him, which they did at first with some hesitation, then with greater confidence, and soon with peals of delighted laughter as he rocked sideways, stumbling, knocking the pieces down, so that all had to be set straight once more with Roger helping. Presently a woman— their nurse, I supposed—called them from a second doorway beyond the hall, and the pieces were taken up and given solemnly to Roger, who as he took them, promising to play again next day, winked at the nurse, advising her to examine both their tongues later, and let him know if they showed signs of turning black.

He put the pieces down near the entrance and came into the hall, while the children disappeared into the back regions with their nurse; and it seemed to me for the first time that he had showed some human quality. His steward's role, calculating, cool, very possibly corrupt, had been momentarily put aside, and with it the irony, the cruel detachment I associated with all his actions hitherto.

He stood in the hall, listening. There was no one there but our two selves, and looking about me I sensed that the place had somehow changed since that day in May when Henry Champernoune had died; it no longer had the feeling of permanent occupancy, but more of a house where the owners came and went, leaving it empty in their absence. There was no sound of barking dogs, no sign of servants, other than the children's nurse, and it came to me suddenly that the lady of the house herself, Joanna Champernoune, must be away from home with her own brood of sons and daughter, perhaps in that other manor of Trelawn, which the steward had mentioned to Lampetho and Trefrengy in the Kilmarth kitchen on the night of the abortive rebellion. Roger must be in charge, and Isolda's children and their nurse were here to break their journey between one house and another.

He crossed over to the window, through which the late sunlight came, and looked out. Almost at once he flattened himself against the wall as though someone from ouside might catch sight of him, and he preferred to remain unseen. Intrigued, I also ventured to the window, and immediately guessed the reason for his manoeuvre. There was a bench beneath the window, with two people sitting on it, Isolda and Otto Bodrugan, and because of the angle of the wall, which jutted outward, giving the bench shelter, anyone who sat there would have privacy unless he was spied upon from this one window.

The grass beneath the bench sloped to a low wall, and beyond the wall the fields descended to the river where Bodrugan's ship was anchored. I could see the mast-head, but not the deck. The tide was low, the channel narrow, and on either side of the blue ribbon of water were sand flats, crowded with every sort of wading bird, dipping and bobbing around the pools where the tide had ebbed. Bodrugan held Isolda's hands in his, examining the fingers, and in a foolish sort of love-play bit each one of them in turn, or rather made pretence of biting them, grimacing as he did so as though they tasted sour.

I stood by the window watching them, oddly disturbed, not because I, like the steward, was playing spy, but because I sensed in some fashion that the relationship between these two, however passionate it might be at other times, was at this moment innocent, without guile and altogether blessed, and it was the kind of relationship that I myself would ever know. Then suddenly he released both hands, letting them drop on to her lap.

"Let me stay another night and not sleep aboard," he said. "In any event the tide may serve me ill, and I may find myself hard aground if I make sail."

"Not if you choose your moment," she replied. "The longer you remain here the more dangerous for us both. You know how gossip travels. To come here anyway was madness, with the vessel well-known."

"There's nothing to that," he said. "I come frequently to the bay and to this river, either on business or for my own pleasure, fishing between here and Chapel Point. It was pure chance that brought you here as well."

"It was not," she said, "and you know it very well. The steward brought you my letter telling you I should be here."

"Roger is a trusty messenger," he answered. "My wife and children are at Trelawn, and so is my sister Joanna. The risk was worth the taking."

"Worth taking, yes, this once, but not for two nights in succession. Nor do I trust the steward as you do, and you know my reasons."

"Henry's death, you mean?" He frowned. "I still think you judged unfairly there. Henry was a dying man. We all knew it. If those potions made him sleep the sooner, free from pain and with Joanna's knowledge, why should we shake our heads?"

"Too easy done," she said, "and with intent. I'm sorry for it, Otto, but I cannot forgive Joanna, even if she is your sister. As for the steward, doubtless she paid him well, and his monk accomplice."

I glanced at Roger. He had not moved from his shadowed corner by the window, but he could hear them as well as I did, and judging by the expression in his eyes he hardly relished what she said.

"As to the monk," added Isolda, "he is still at the Priory, and adds something to his influence every day. The Prior is wax in his hands, and his flock do as they are bidden by Brother Jean, who comes and goes as he pleases."

"If he does so," said Bodrugan, "it is no concern of mine."

"It could become so," she told him, "if Margaret comes to have as much faith in his herbal knowledge as Joanna. You know he has treated your family lately?"

"I know nothing of the sort," he answered. "I have been at Lundy, as you know, and Margaret finds both the island and Bodrugan too exposed, and prefers Trelawn." He rose from the bench and began pacing up and down the grass walk in front of her. Love-making was over, with the problems of domestic life upon them once again. They had my sympathy. "Margaret is too much a Champernoune, like poor Henry," he said. "A priest or a monk could persuade her to abstinence or perpetual prayer if he had the mind to do so. I shall look into it."

Isolda also rose from the bench, and standing close to Bodrugan looked up at him, with her hands upon his shoulders. I could have touched them both had I leant from the window. How small they were, inches below adult height today, yet he broadly built and strong, with a fine head and a most likable smile, and she as delicately formed as a porcelain shepherdess, hardly taller than her own daughters. They held each other, kissing, and once again I felt this strange disturbance, a sense of loss, utterly unlike anything I might experience in my own time, had I seen two lovers from a window . . . Intense involvement, and intense compassion too. Yes, that was the word, compassion. And I had no way of explaining my sense of participation in all they did, unless it was that stepping backwards, out of my time to theirs, I felt them vulnerable, and more certainly doomed to die than I was myself, knowing indeed that they had both been dust for more than six centuries.

"Have a care for Joanna, too," said Isolda. "She is no nearer being married to John now than she was two years ago, and has altered for the worse in consequence. She might even serve his wife as she served her husband."

"She would not dare, nor John," answered Bodrugan.

"She would dare anything if it suited her. Harm you likewise, if you stood in her way. She has one thought in mind, to see John Keeper of Restormel and Sheriff of Cornwall, and herself his wife, queening it over all the crown lands as Lady Carminowe."

"If it should come about I can't prevent it," protested Bodrugan.

"As her brother you could try," said Isolda, "and at least prevent that monk from trailing at her heels with his poisonous draughts."

"Joanna was always headstrong," replied her lover. "She has always done as she pleased. I cannot be on watch continually. I might say a word to Roger."

"To the steward? He is as thick with the monk as she," said Isolda scornfully. "I warn you again, don't trust him, Otto. Neither on her account, nor on ours. He keeps our few meetings secret for the time because it pleases him."

Once again I glanced at Roger, and saw the shadow on his face. I wished someone would call him from the room so that he could no longer play eavesdropper. It would put him against her to hear his faults so plainly stated and with such dislike.

"He stood by me last October and will do so again," said Bodrugan.

"He stood by you then because he reckoned he had much to gain," replied Isolda.

"Now you can do little for him, why should he risk losing his position? One word to Joanna, and thence to John, and thence to Oliver, and we'd be lost."

"Oliver is in London."

"London today, perhaps. But malice travels with every wind that blows. Tomorrow Bere or Bockenod. The next day Tregest or Carminowe. Oliver cares not a jot if I live or die, he has women wherever he goes, but his pride would never brook a faithless wife. And that I know."

A cloud had come between them, and in the sky too, gathering above the hills beyond the valley. All the brightness of the summer day had gone. Innocence had vanished, and with it the serenity of their world. Mine too. Separated by centuries, I somehow shared their guilt.

"How late is it?" she asked.

"Near six, by the sun," he answered. "Does it matter?"

"The children should be away with Alice," she said. "They may come running to find me, and they must not see you here."

"Roger is with them," he told her, "he will take care they leave us alone."

"Nevertheless, I must bid them goodnight, or they will never mount their ponies."

She began to move away along the grass, and as she did so the steward also slipped from his dark corner and crossed the hall. I followed, puzzled. They could not be staying in the house after all but somewhere else, at Bockenod, perhaps. But the Boconnoc I knew was a longish ride for children on ponies in late afternoon; they would hardly reach it before dusk.

We went through the hallway to the open court beyond, and through the archway to the stables. Roger's brother Robbie was there, saddling the ponies, helping the little girls to mount, laughing and joking with the nurse who, propped high on her own steed, had some trouble in making it stand still.

"He'll go quietly enough with two of you on his back," called Roger. "Robbie shall sit on the pony with you and keep you warm. Before you or behind you, state your preference. It's all the same to him, isn't it, Robbie?"

The nurse, a country girl with flaming cheeks, gawked delightedly, protesting she could ride very well alone, and there was further giggling, instantly silenced with a frown from Roger as Isolda came into the stableyard. He moved to her side, head bent in deference.

"The children will be safe enough with Robbie," he said, "but I can escort them if you prefer it."

"I do prefer it," she said briefly. "Thank you."

He bowed, and she crossed the yard to the children, who were already mounted, managing their ponies with the greatest ease.

"I shall stay here awhile," she told them, kissing each in turn, "and return later. No whipping of the ponies on the road, mind, to make them go the faster. And do as Alice bids you."

"We'll do as *he* bids," said the youngest, pointing her small whip at Roger, "or he'll twist our tongues to see if they turn black."

"I don't doubt it," answered Isolda, "that, or some other method of enforcing silence."

The steward smiled in some confusion, but she did not look at him and he went forward, seizing the children's bridles in either hand, and began to lead the ponies toward the archway, jerking his head to Robbie to do likewise with the nurse's mount. Isolda came with us as far as the entrance gate, and then I was torn between compulsion and desire. Compulsion to follow the little party led by Roger, desire to look at Isolda as she stood alone, waving to her children, unconscious that I stood beside her.

I knew I must not touch her. I knew if I did it would have no more effect upon her than a draught of air—not even that, for in her world I never had existed, nor ever could exist, for she was living and I a ghost without shape or form. If I gave myself the sudden useless pleasure of brushing her cheek there would be no contact, she would instantly dissolve, and I should be left with all the agony of vertigo, nausea and inevitable remorse. Luckily I was spared the choice. She waved her hand once more, looking straight into my eyes and through me, then turned and crossed the court back to the house.

I followed the riding party down the field. Isolda and Bodrugan would be alone for a few more hours. Perhaps they would make love. I hoped, with a sort of desperate sympathy, that they would. I had the feeling time was running out for them, and for me as well.

The track led downwards to the ford where the millstream, coursing through the valley, met the salt water from the creek. Now, the tide low, the ford was passable, and when the children came to it Roger released the bridles, and clapping his hand on the hindquarters of either pony set them to gallop through the splash, the children screaming with delight. He did the same to the third pony, bearing Robbie and the nurse, who let out a shriek that must have been heard on either side of the valley. The blacksmith from the forge across the stream—the fire's glow and the anvil beside it, and a couple of horses waiting to be shod showed that this must be the smithy—came out from his shed grinning, and seizing a pair of bellows from the lad at his side pointed them at the nurse, so that the blast caught her petticoats, already spattered with the mill stream.

"Take the poker red from the fire to warm her up," shouted Roger, and the blacksmith made pretence of brandishing an iron bar, sparks flying in all directions, while Robbie, half-strangled by the hysterical nurse and doubled up with laughter, dug his heels into the pony's side to make him jump the more. The spectacle brought out the miller and his mate from the mill this side of the stream. I saw that they were monks, and there was a cart drawn up in the yard beside the building, tended by two others, who were filling it with grain. They paused in their work, grinning like the blacksmith, and one of them put his two hands to his mouth and hooted in imitation of an owl, while his companion flapped his arms rapidly above his head as wings.

"Make your choice, Alice," called Roger. "Fire and wind from Rob Rosgof in the forge, or shall the brothers tie you by your kirtle to the water wheel?"

"The water wheel, the water wheel," screamed the children from the further side of the ford, believing, in their excitement, that Alice was to be dowsed. Then suddenly, as swiftly as it had started, the sport was over. Roger waded through the splash with the water mid-thigh, and, seizing the children's ponies once again, took the right-hand track up the valley, with Robbie and the nurse in close pursuit.

I was preparing to follow him across the ford when one of the labouring monks in the mill-yard let out another shout—at least, I took it to be the monk, and turned to see what he was about, but instead a small car, with an irate driver at the wheel, had braked sharply behind me.

"Why don't you buy yourself a deaf aid?" he yelled, swerving past me, almost plunging into the ditch as he did so. I stood blinking after the car as it shot away, and the people in the back seat, three abreast, dolled for a Sunday outing, stared through the rear window in shocked surprise.

Time had done its trick, too swift, too soon. There was no running mill stream and no water splash, no forge the further side; I was standing in the middle of the Treesmill road at the bottom of the valley.

I leant against the low bridge spanning the marsh. A near miss; it might have landed the whole party in the ditch and myself as well. I couldn't apologise, for the car had already disappeared up the opposite hill. I sat still for a while waiting for any reaction, but none came. My heart was beating rather faster than usual, but that was natural, due to the shock of the car. I was lucky to escape. No blame to the driver, all my fault.

I began to walk up the hill to the turning where I had parked my own car, and sat in the driving seat for another short spell, feaing confusion. I must not turn up at the church unless my mind was perfectly clear. The image of Roger escorting the children on their ponies up the track through the valley was still vivid, but I knew it for what it was, part of the other world already vanished. The house above the sandflats had reverted to the Gratten quarry, grass-covered, empty, except for the gorse bushes and the tin cans. Bodrugan and Isolda were no longer making love. Present reality was with me once again.

I looked at my watch, and stared in disbelief. The hands showed half-past one. Matins at St. Andrew's had been over for an hour and a half, possibly longer.

I started up the car, guilt-stricken. The drug had played me false, spinning out the time in some incredible way. I couldn't have been more than half-an-hour at most up at the house, with another ten minutes, possibly, following Roger and the children to the ford. The whole episode had passed swiftly and I had done nothing but listen at the window, watch the children mount their ponies, and so away. As I drove up the hill I was more bothered about the action of the drug than the prospect of meeting Vita with another trumped-up excuse about walking and losing my way. Why the time lag, I asked myself? I remembered then that when I went into the past I never looked at my watch—the impulse to do so never came; therefore there was no means of knowing how time passed: their sun was not my sun, nor their sky mine. There was no check, no possibility of measuring the time limit of the drug. As always, when the thing went wrong, I blamed Magnus. He should have warned me.

I drew up at the church, but of course nobody was there. Vita must have waited with the boys, fuming with rage, then begged a lift home from someone, or else found a taxi.

I drove to Kilmarth trying to think of some better excuse than losing my way and my watch having stopped. Petrol. Could I have run out of petrol? A puncture. What about a puncture? Oh, bloody hell, I thought . . .

I rattled down the drive and swerved to a standstill before the house, then walked through the front garden, up the steps and into the hall. The dining-room door was closed. Mrs. Collins, with an anxious face, emerged from the passage to the kitchen.

"I think they've finished," she said apologetically, "but I've kept yours hot. It won't be spoilt. Did you have a breakdown?"

"Yes," I said, with gratitude.

I opened the door of the dining room. The boys were clearing away, but Vita was still seated at the table, drinking coffee.

"God damn that blasted car . . ." I began, and the boys turned round, staring, uncertain whether to giggle or slink away. Teddy showed sudden tact, and with a glance at Micky they hurriedly left the room, Teddy bearing out the laden tray.

"Darling," I went on, "I'm most frightfully sorry. I wouldn't have had this happen for the world. You've no idea . . ."

"I've a very good idea," she said. "I'm afraid we've rather spoilt your Sunday."

Her irony was lost on me. I hesitated, wondering whether to continue or not with my brilliant story of a breakdown on the road.

"The vicar was extremely kind," she went on. "His son drove us back in their car. And when we arrived Mrs. Collins gave me this." She pointed to a telegram beside her plate. "It arrived just after we left for church, she said. Thinking it must be important, I opened it. From your Professor, naturally."

She handed me the telegram. It had been wired from Cambridge.

HAVE A GOOD TRIP THIS WEEKEND, it read. HOPE YOUR GIRL TURNS UP. SHALL BE THINKING OF YOU. GREETINGS. MAGNUS.

I read it twice, then looked at Vita, but she had already turned towards the library, blowing clouds of cigarette smoke over her shoulder, as Mrs. Collins came into the dining room bringing me an enormous plate of hot roast beef.

12

IF MAGNUS HAD wanted to drop a deliberate brick it could not have been better timed, but I absolved him. He believed Vita to be in London and myself alone. Nevertheless, the wording was unfortunate, to say the least. Catastrophic would be more apt. It must have conjured an instant vision to Vita of my sneaking off with shaving kit and toothbrush to meet some floozie in the Scilly Isles. My innocence would be difficult to prove. I followed her into the library.

"Now, listen," I said, firmly shutting the folding doors between the two rooms in case Mrs. Collins overheard me, "that telegram is a complete joke—a leg-pull on the part of Magnus. Don't make an absolute idiot of yourself by taking it seriously."

She turned round and faced me, her posture the classical one of outraged wife, one hand on hip, the other brandishing her cigarette held at an angle, eyes narrowed in a frozen face.

"I'm not interested in the Professor or his jokes," she said. "You share so many of them, and keep me out, that I'm past caring. If that telegram was a joke good luck to you both. I repeat, I'm sorry I spoilt the weekend. Now you had better go and eat your lunch before it gets cold."

She picked up the Sunday paper and pretended to look at it. I snatched it away. "Oh, no, you don't," I said, "you just pay attention to me." Taking her cigarette I squashed it in the ash tray. Then I seized both her wrists and swung her round.

"You know perfectly well that Magnus is my oldest friend," I said. "What's more he's lent us this house rent free, and thrown Mrs. Collins in for good measure. In return for this I've been doing bits and pieces of research for him in connection with his work. The telegram was just his way of wishing me luck."

My words made no impression. Her face was frozen stiff. "You're not a scientist," she said. "What sort of research can you possibly do? And where were you going?"

I dropped her wrists and sighed, as one whose patience is becoming rapidly exhausted by a wilfully misunderstanding child.

"I wasn't going anywhere," I insisted, emphasis on the anywhere. "I had vaguely planned to drive along the coast and visit one or two sites he happens to be interested in."

"How extremely plausible," she said, "I can't think why the Professor doesn't have a teach-in here, with you as his chief assistant. Why don't you suggest it? I'd be in the way, of course, and would make myself scarce. But he'd probably like to keep the boys."

"Oh, for God's sake," I said, opening the door to the dining room, "you're behaving like every well-worn joke about wives I've ever heard. The simplest thing to do will be to ring up Magnus first thing tomorrow morning and tell him you're filing a divorce suit because you suspect me of wanting to meet-up with some scrubber at Land's End. He'll howl his head off."

I went into the dining room and sat down at the table. The gravy was beginning to congeal, but no matter. I filled a tankard with beer to wash down the beef and two veg before tackling apple tart. Mrs. Collins, tactfully silent, brought in coffee and stood it on the hot plate, then disappeared. The boys, at a loose end, were kicking the gravel on the path in front of the house. I got up, and called to them from the window.

"I'll take you swimming later," I shouted. They brightened visibly, and came running up the steps to the porch. "Later," I said. "Let me have my coffee first, and see what Vita wants to do." Their faces fell. Mom would be a nonstarter, and possibly throw cold water on the plan. "Don't worry," I said. "I promise I'll take you."

Then I went into the library. Vita was lying on the sofa, her eyes closed. I knelt beside her, and kissed her. "Stop being bloody-minded," I said. "There's only one girl in this world for me, and you know it. I'm not going to take you upstairs to prove it because I've told the boys I'd take them swimming, and you don't want to spoil their day for them, do you?"

She opened one eye. "You've succeeded in spoiling mine," she said.

"Balls!" I told her. "And what about my lost weekend with that floozie? Shall I tell you what I'd planned to do with her? A strip-tease show at Newquay. Now shut up." I kissed her again with vigour. Response was negligible, but she did not push me away.

"I wish I understood you," she said.

"Thank God you don't," I said. "Husbands loathe wives who understand them. It makes for monotony. Come and swim. There's a perfectly good empty beach below the cliffs. It's blazing hot, and it isn't going to rain."

She opened both eyes. "What were you actually doing this morning while we were in church?" she asked.

"Mooching about in a derelict quarry," I told her, "less than a mile from the village. It has connections with the old Priory, and Magnus and I happen to be interested in the site. Then I couldn't start the car, which I'd parked rather awkwardly in a ditch."

"It's news to me that your Professor is an historian as well as a scientist," she said.

"Good news, don't you think? Makes a change from all those embryos in bottles. I encourage it."

"You encourage him in everything," she said, "that's why he makes use of you."

"I'm adaptable by nature, always have been. Come on, those boys are itching to be off. Go and make yourself beautiful in a bikini, but put something over it, or you'll startle the cows."

"Cows?" she almost shrieked. "I'm not going in any field with cows, thank you very much."

"They're tame ones," I said, "fed on a certain sort of grass so that they can't move out of a slow amble. Cornwall's famous for them."

I think she believed me. Whether she believed my story about the quarry was another matter. She was pacified, for the moment. Let it rest . . .

We spent a long, lazy afternoon on the beach. Everybody swam, and afterwards, while the boys scrambled about in pools hunting for non-existent prawns, Vita and I stretched ourselves full-length on a spit of yellow sand, letting it trickle through our fingers. Peace reigned.

"Have you thought about the future at all?" she asked suddenly.

"The future?" I repeated. In point of fact, I was staring across the bay wondering if Bodrugan had made it that night with a rising tide, after he and Isolda had said goodbye. He had mentioned Chapel Point. In old days, Commander Lane had taken us sailing across the bay from Fowey to Mevagissey, and had pointed out Chapel Point jutting out on the port side before we entered Mevagissey harbour. Bodrugan's house must have lain somewhere close at hand. Perhaps the name existed still. I could find it on the road map if it was still there.

"Yes," I said, "I have. If it's fine tomorrow we'll go sailing. You couldn't possibly be seasick if it's as calm as it is today. We'll sail right across the bay and anchor off that headland over there. Take lunch, and go ashore."

"Very nice," she agreed, "but I didn't mean the immediate future. I meant the long-term one."

"Oh, that," I said. "No, darling, frankly I have not. So much to do getting settled in here. Don't let's be premature."

"That's all very well," she said, "but Joe can wait forever. I think he was hoping to hear from you fairly soon."

"I know that. But I've got to be absolutely sure. It's all right for you, it's your country. It isn't mine. Pulling up roots won't be easy."

"You've pulled them up already, chucking that London job. To be blunt, you have no roots. So there's no argument," she said.

She was right, for all practical purposes.

"You'll have to do something," she went on, "whether it's in England or the States. And to turn down Joe's offer when no one has offered you anything comparable in this country seems utterly crazy. I admit I'm prejudiced," she added, putting her hand in mine, "and would adore to settle back home. But only if you want it too."

I did not want it, that was the crux. Nor did I want a similar job, literary agency or publishing, in London. It was the end of the road, the end, temporarily, of a particular moment in time, my time. And I could not plan ahead, not yet.

"Don't go on about it now, darling," I said. "Let's take each moment as it comes. Today, tomorrow . . . I'll think constructively about the whole thing soon, I promise you."

She sighed, and let go of my hand, reaching in the pocket of her towelling wrap for a cigarette. "As you say," she said, the upward inflection on the "say" proclaiming her origins on the western Atlantic seaboard. "But don't blame me if you find yourself left high and dry by brother Joe."

The boys came running across the beach with various trophies to show us, starfish, mussels, and an oversize, long-dead crab that stank to heaven. The moment of truth had passed. It was time to gather up our things and face the trek uphill back to Kilmarth. As I brought up the rear I looked over my shoulder across the bay. The coast was clearly defined, and the white houses on the edge of Chapel Point, some eight miles distant, were caught by the western sun.

> *"In such a night*
> *Otto methinks mounted Bodrugan walls,*
> *And sighed his soul towards the Treesmill creek*
> *Where Isold lay that night . . ."*

But did she? Surely she must have followed the children later, after Otto sailed. But where to? Bockenod, where her husband's brother, the self-important Sir John, lived? Too far. Something was missing. She had mentioned another name. Treg something. I must look on the map. The trouble was that almost every other farmhouse in Cornwall began with Tre. It had not been Trevenna, Treverran or Trenadlyn. So where was it that Isolda and her two children had lain their heads that night?

"I don't see myself doing this often," complained Vita. "My heaven, what a hill! It's like the ski slopes of Vermont. Let me take your arm."

The thing was, they had crossed the water splash below the mill and taken a track to the right. And then I had not seen them any more, because of that car coming up behind me. They could have gone in any direction. And Roger was on foot. When the tide came in the ford would be fully covered. I tried to remember if there was a boat beneath the blacksmith's forge to ferry him back.

"After all this exercise and air I ought to sleep tonight," said Vita.

"Yes," I replied.

There had been a boat. High and dry on the edge of the creek. At high water this would be used for carrying passengers to and fro between the blacksmith's forge and Treesmill.

"You couldn't care less, could you," she asked, "what sort of a night I have, and whether I'm dead on my feet right now?"

I stopped and stared at her. "I'm sorry, darling," I said, "of course I care." Why revert suddenly to that business of a sleepless night?

"You were miles away in thought—I can always tell," she said.

"Four miles at the most," I told her. "If you really want to know, I was thinking about a couple of children riding ponies I saw this morning. I wondered where they were going."

"Ponies?" We continued walking, Vita a dead weight on my arm. "Well, that's the most sensible thought you've had yet," she said. "The boys love riding. Maybe the ponies were let out on hire?"

"I doubt it," I said. "I imagine they came from some farm."

"Well, you could make enquiries. Nice-looking children?"

"Enchanting. Two little girls, and a youngish woman who looked as if she might be their nurse, and a couple of men."

"All riding ponies?"

"One man was walking, holding the children's bridles."

"Then it must be a riding school," she said. "Do find out. It would make something for the boys to do other than swimming or sailing."

"Yes," I said.

How convenient it would be if I could summon Roger from the past and bid him saddle two of the Kilmarth ponies for Teddy and Micky, then send them off with Robbie for a gallop on Par sands! Roger would handle Vita to perfection. Her slightest whim obeyed. Juice of henbane whistled up from Brother Jean at the Priory to induce a restful night, and if that failed . . . I smiled.

"What's the joke?"

"No joke." I pointed to the fading foxgloves, a purple mass thrusting tall stems through the hedge encircling the paddocks below Kilmarth. "If you have a heart attack, no problem. Digitalis comes from foxgloves. You've only to say the word and I'll crush the seeds.

"Thanks a lot. No doubt your Professor's laboratory is full of them along with other poisonous seeds and goodness knows what sinister mixtures.

How right she was. An error, though, to let her dwell on Magnus. "Here we are," I said. "Through that gate and into the garden. I'll mix you a long, cool drink, and the boys as well. Then I'll cope with the supper. Plenty of cold beef and salad."

Let cheerfulness prevail. Memories of my misspent morning fade into an urge to please. Attentive husband, smiling stepfather; keep the whole thing going to bedtime and beyond.

As it turned out, beyond took care of itself. The swim, the long climb and the soporific Cornish air had done their trick. Vita, yawning her head off at a television play, was in bed by ten, and fast asleep when I crept in stealthily beside her an hour later. Tomorrow would be fine, judging by the sky, and we would sail to Chapel Point. Bodrugan existed still. I had found it on the road map after supper.

There was just enough breeze to take us out of Fowey harbour. Our skipper, Tom, a stalwart fellow with a ready smile, busied himself with the sails, aided or hindered by the boys, while I stationed myself at the tiller. I knew just enough about it not to bring the boat up into the wind and set the sails flapping, but neither Vita nor the boys knew this, and were suitably impressed by my air of efficiency. Soon we had mackerel lines astern, the boys hauling them in with shouts of excitement as soon as they felt the slightest tug, caused by the ripple of tide or a piece of weed, while Vita stretched herself at my side. Her jeans became her, like all Americans, she had a stunning figure—and so did her scarlet sweater.

"This is heaven," she said, snuggling close and leaning her head against my shoulder. "So clever of you to arrange it, I give you full marks for once. The water couldn't be smoother."

The trouble was, it didn't stay heaven for long. I remembered of old, after passing the Cannis buoy and the Gribbin Head, a westerly wind met the tide with a smacking force, increasing the boat's speed—always a joy to the helmsman with his heart in his job, like Commander Lane—but causing the craft to heel over, so that the passenger sitting on the leeward side found himelf within a few inches of the sea. In this case the passenger was Vita.

"Hadn't you better let the man steer?" she said nervously, after the boat had curtseyed three times like a rockinghorse—my fault, too close to the wind—then lay firmly on her side with the lea rail awash.

"Not a bit of it," I said cheerfully. "Crawl under the boom and sit on the weather side."

She groped to her feet, and caught her head an almighty tonk on the boom. As I bent to help her unravel a rope from her ankle, which took my eye off my work as helmsman, I shipped a short sea across the bows, thus drenching the whole party, myself included.

"A drop of salt water hurts nobody," I shouted, but the boys, clinging to the weather rail, were not so sure, and with their mother made a dive for the shelter of the small cabin, which, lacking headroom, forced them to crouch like hunchbacks on the tiny locker seat, where they rose and fell with every curtsey of the overlively craft.

"Nice fresh breeze," said our skipper Tom, grinning all over his face. "We'll be at Mevagissey in no time at all."

I bared my teeth in imitation of his confidence, but the three white faces upturned to me in the cockpit lacked enthusiasm, and I had the impression that none of them shared the skipper's opinion about the breeze.

He offered me a cigarette, but it proved an error after three puffs, and I let it fall over the side when he was not looking, while he proceeded to light up a particularly noxious pipe. Some of the smoke found its way down to the cabin and circled there in rings.

"The lady would feel the motion less if she sat in the cockpit," suggested Tom, "and the lads as well."

I looked at the boys. The boat was steady enough now, but penned in the dark cabin they felt every thump, and an ominous yawn appeared on Micky's face. Vita, her eyes glazed, appeared hypnotized by Tom's oilskin, which was hanging on a hook by the cabin door, swaying to and fro with the boat's motion like a hanging man.

Tom and I exchanged glances, seized by a sudden freemasonry, and while he took over the tiller and knocked out his pipe I pulled the family up into the cockpit, where Vita and her youngest were promptly sick. Teddy survived, possibly because he kept his head averted.

"We'll soon be under the lea of Black Head," said Tom. "They won't feel any motion in there."

His touch on the tiller was like magic. Or perhaps it was pure chance. The rocking-horse motion moved to a gentle lilt, the white faces lost their pallor, teeth ceased their chattering, and the pasties baked by Mrs. Collins were torn from their napkins in the basket and fallen upon by all of us, even Vita, with the ferocity of carrion crows. We passed Mevagissey and came to anchor on the western side of Chapel Point. There was not a tremor in sea or sky, and the sun blazed down.

"Rather extraordinary," observed Vita, now stripped of her sweater, which she bunched under her head as a pillow, "that as soon as Tom took charge of the boat it scarcely moved at all and the wind dropped."

"Not really," I said. "We were coming closer to land, that's all."

"I know one thing," she said, "and that is that he's going to steer the boat home."

Tom was helping the boys into the dinghy. They had bathing shorts and towels under their arms. Tom had fishing lines, baited with worm.

"If you want to stay aboard, sir, with the lady, I'll see the lads come to no harm," he said. "This beach is quite safe for bathing."

I did not want to stay aboard with the lady. I wanted to climb up through the fields and find Bodrugan.

Vita sat up, and removing her dark glasses looked around her. It was half-tide and the beach looked tempting, but I saw, with delight, that it was temporarily in the possession of half-a-dozen cows, who were mooning about aimlessly, spattering the sand in the inevitable fashion.

"I'll stay aboard," said Vita firmly, "and if I want to swim I'll swim from the boat."

I yawned, my immediate reaction when feeling guilty. "I'll go ashore and stretch my legs," I said. "It's too early to swim anyway, after a pasty lunch."

"Do as you like," she said. "It's perfect here. Those white houses on the point look enchanting. We might be in Italy."

I let her think it, and climbed into the dinghy with the others. "Land me over there, in the left-hand corner," I said to Tom.

"What are you going to do?" asked Teddy.

"Walk," I said firmly.

"Can't we stay in the dinghy and fish for pollack?"

"Of course you can. Much the best plan," I told him.

I sprang ashore amongst the cows, free of encumbrance. The boys were equally glad to be rid of me. I stood for a moment, watching them pull away. Vita waved a languid hand from the anchored boat. Then I turned, and struck uphill.

The path ran parallel with a stream and curved, passing a cottage on the right-hand side, and then the sea was out of sight. The track continued up the hill, leading to a gate between old walls, and on the left-hand side what appeared to be the ruins of a mill. I ventured through the gate, and Bodrugan farm was all about me, a big pond to my left that must have fed the mill stream, and to my right the gracious, slate-hung farmhouse of today, early eighteenth century, perhaps, curiously like Magnus's Kilmarth, and beside it and beyond great stone-walled barns of a much earlier date that surely must have stood upon the site of Otto's fourteenth century home. Two children were playing under the windows of the farmhouse, but they took no notice of me and I ventured on, crossing the wide sweep where cows were grazing, and stepped inside the high-roofed barn the farther side.

This served as granary today, and must have done for centuries, but six hundred years ago perhaps a dining hall stood here, and other rooms, while the long, low barn across the way could have been the chapel. The whole demesne was vast, far larger than the space covered by those mounds and banks that once had formed the home of the Champernounes, below the Gratten; and I realised now why Joanna, born and bred a Bodrugan in this place, may have thought the house above the Treesmill creek a poor exchange when she married Henry Champernoune.

I came out of the barn and followed the low stone walls surrounding the entire farm, then, striking off to the hills on the opposite slope, came once more in sight of the sea. Here, on top of the high field, was a mound that must once have formed a keep or outpost, commanding the bay, and I wondered how often Otto rode here from his house, and looked out from the keep past Black Head to the cliffs in the far distance that gradually descended to Tywardreath bay and to the winding estuary with its narrow arms, the first running to the Lampetho valley, the second to the Priory walls, the third to Treesmill and the Champernoune demesne. He would have seen all of this on a clear day, even perhaps the humped dwelling of Kylmerth, and the little straggling copse beyond.

This would have been the moment to have the flask in my pocket, and have seen Otto leaning from the round tower of his keep, and beneath him, in the sheltered cove where the boys fished today, his ship at anchor, ready to make sail. Or travel even further back in time and watch him ride away to that first rebellion against Edward the Second in 1322, younger and hotheaded, to be fined a thousand marks when the rebellion failed. Champion of lost causes, seeker after forbidden fruit; how often, I wondered, did he steal across that bay, leaving his dim-faced wife Margaret, Henry Champernoune's sister, snugly secure inside Bodrugan house, or in their other property of Trelawn, wherever that might be, in which the Champernounes also seemed to have rights?

I clumped back to the beach, hot and curiously tired. It was odd, but it seemed more of an effort to face the family now, without having swallowed the drug and moved in the other world, than it would had I actually taken a trip in time. I felt thwarted, drained of energy, and filled with a strange sense of apprehension. Imagination was not enough; I craved the living experience which had been denied me, and which I could have possessed had I taken a few drops from the flask safely locked away in the old laundry at Kilmarth. I might have witnessed scenes, on that old site above the cliff, or by the farmstead itself, that now I should never know, and the frustration was absolute.

The cows had gone from the beach. The boys had returned to the anchored boat and were sitting in the cockpit having tea, their swimming trunks strung up on the mast to dry. Vita was standing in the bows taking snapshots. A contented party, everybody happy, myself the odd man out.

I wore bathing trunks under my trousers, and stripping off my clothes I entered the water. It struck chill, after the walk, and seaweed floated on the surface like tresses from the drowned Ophelia's hair. I turned over on my back and stared at the sky, still filled with this strange feeling of despondency, almost of doom. It would need a tremendous effort to respond to the family greeting, join in the general chatter, smile and joke.

Tom had seen me, and was bringing the dinghy ashore to fetch my clothes. I swam out to the boat and managed somehow to clamber aboard, with the aid of a rope's end and the willing hands of Vita and the boys.

"Look, three pollack," shouted Micky. "Mom says she'll cook them for supper. And we've found a lot of shells."

Vita came forward with the remains of the tea from the thermos jug. "You look all in," she said. "Did you walk far?"

"No," I said, "only across the fields. There was a castle of sorts there once, but nothing's left of it."

"You should have stayed on the boat," she said. "The bathing was heaven. Here, rub yourself with this towel, you're shivering. I hope you haven't taken a chill. Such a mistake to plunge into cold water when you've been perspiring."

Micky thrust a damp doughnut into my hand tasting of cotton wool, and I swallowed lukewarm tea. Then Tom climbed aboard, bearing my clothes, and before long it was up anchor and away, with Tom at the tiller. I put on another jersey and went and sat up in the bows, where Vita presently joined me.

The little popple in mid-bay sent her back to the cockpit, to wrap herself in Tom's oilskin, and I stared ahead toward the distant prospect of Kilmarth, screened by its belt of trees. In old days, sailing nearer to the coast, Bodrugan would have had a closer view, as he steered his ship towards the estuary that covered Par sands then, and Roger, had he been watching from the fields, could have signalled to him that all was well. I wondered whose fever was the greater, Bodrugan's as he rounded the sloping headland to the channel, knowing she waited for him in that empty house behind the low stone walls, or Isolda's, when she sighted the masthead and saw the first flutter of the dark sail. Now, with the sun astern, we passed the Cannis buoy and made for Fowey, entering the harbour, to the great excitement of the boys, just as a large vessel, her decks white with china clay and escorted by two tugs, left it outward bound.

"Can we come again tomorrow?" they clamoured, as I paid off Tom and thanked him for our sail.

"We'll see," I said, uttering the inevitable adult formula that must be so infuriating to the young. See what, they might have asked? If the mood suits and there is harmony in the grown-up world? The success or failure of their day depended upon the state of truce between their mother and myself.

My immediate problem, when we got back to Kilmarth, was to telephone Magnus before he telephoned me, which he was bound to do, now the weekend was over. I hung about the library furtively, waiting for a good moment, and then the boys came in and switched on the TV, so I had to go upstairs to the bedroom. Vita was downstairs in the kitchen seeing about supper: it was now or never. I dialled his number and he answered immediately.

"Look," I said quickly, "I can't talk long. The worst has happened. Vita and the boys arrived unexpectedly on Saturday morning. They caught me almost in *flagrant delit*. You understand? And your telegram was an equal calamity. Vita opened it.

Since then the situation has been decidedly tricky, and that's putting it mildly."

"Oh, dear . . ." said Magnus, in the tone of an elderly maiden aunt confronted with a mild household problem.

"It's not 'Oh, dear' at all, it's hell and damnation," I exploded, "and the end of the road, as far as any more trips are concerned. You realise that, don't you?"

"Keep calm, dear boy, keep calm. You say she arrived and actually caught you en route?"

"No, I was returning from one. Seven in the morning. I won't go into it now."

"Was it valuable?" he asked.

"I don't know what you call valuable," I said. "It concerned a near rebellion against the Crown. Otto Bodrugan was there, and Roger, of course. I'll write you fully about it tomorrow, and Sunday's trip as well."

"So you *did* risk it again, despite the family? How splendid."

"Only because they went to church, and I was able to slip off to the Gratten. And there is a time problem, Magnus, I can't account for it. The trip seemed to last half an hour to forty minutes at the most, but in actual fact I was 'out' for about two and a half hours."

"How much did you take?"

"The same as Friday night—a few more drops than on the first two or three trips."

"Yes, I see."

He was silent a minute, considering what I had told him.

"Well?" I asked. "What's the significance?"

"I'm not sure," he said. "I'll have to work on it. Don't worry, it won't be serious, at this stage. How are you feeling in yourself?"

"Well . . . healthy enough physically, we've been sailing all day. But it's a hell of a strain, Magnus."

"I'll see how the week goes and then try and get down. I shall have some results from the lab up here in a few days and we can discuss them. Meanwhile, go easy on the trips."

"Magnus . . ."

He had rung off, which was as well. I thought I could hear Vita coming up the stairs. In a sense, I was relieved this time at the thought of seeing him, even if it meant difficulties with Vita. He would adopt his special brand of charm and smooth them away, and the responsibility would be his, not mine. Besides, I was worried about the drug. This sense of depression, of foreboding, might be a side effect.

I looked in the shaving mirror in the bathroom. There was something odd about my right eye, it looked bloodshot, and there was a faint red streak across the white. A blood vessel burst, perhaps, which was nothing, but I did not remember it having happened before. I hoped Vita would not notice it.

Supper passed off all right, with the boys chatting happily about their day and enjoying the pollack they had caught (the most tasteless of all fish, to my mind, but I did not damp their ardour). Just as we were clearing away the telephone rang.

"I'll get it," said Vita quickly, "it could be for me."

At least it would not be Magnus. The boys and I loaded the dishwasher and had set it going when Vita came back into the kitchen. She had a face I knew. Determined, rather defiant.

"That was Bill and Diana," she said.

"Oh, yes?"

The boys disappeared to the library to watch TV. I poured out coffee for us both.

"They're flying to Dublin from Exeter," she said. "They're in Exeter now." Then, before I could make some adequate reply, she said hurriedly, "They're just crazy to see the house, so I suggested they put off their flight for forty-eight hours or so, and come down to us for lunch tomorrow and to stay the night. They jumped at the idea."

I put down my cup of coffee untasted, and slumped in the kitchen chair.

"Oh, my God!" I said.

13

THERE ARE FEW strains more intolerable in life than waiting for the arrival of unwelcome guests. I had said no more in protest after my first groan of despair, but we had spent the hours until bedtime in separate rooms, Vita in the library watching television with the boys, myself in the music room listening to Sibelius.

Now, the next morning, Vita was sitting on what she liked to call the terrace, outside the french windows of the music room, listening for the blare of their horn, while I paced up and down inside, primed with my first gin and tonic, my eye on the clock, wondering which state was the worst—this of anticipating the dire moment of a car coming down the drive, or the full flush of their having settled in, cardigans strewn on chairs, cameras clicking, voices loud and long, the smell of Bill's inevitable cigar. The second, perhaps, was better, the heat of battle rather than the bugle's call.

"Here they come," yelled the boys, tearing down the steps, and I advanced through the french window like one facing up to mortar shells.

Vita, as a hostess, was magnificent: Kilmarth was transformed instantly into some American embassy overseas, lacking only a flagstaff bearing the Stars and Stripes. Food borne in by the willing and triumphant Mrs. Collins graced the dining-room table. Liquor flowed, cigarette smoke filled the air, we lunched at two and rose at half-past three. The boys, fobbed off with the promise of swimming later, vanished to play cricket in the orchard. The girls, disguised in uniform dark glasses, dragged lilos out of earshot to indulge in gossip. Bill and I installed ourselves on the patio intending, or so I hoped, to sleep, but sleep was intermittent; like all diplomats, he enjoyed hearing his own voice. He held forth on world policy and policy nearer home, and then, with elaborate unconcern and obviously briefed by Diana, touched on my future plans.

"I hear you're going into partnership with Joe," he said. "That's wonderful."

"It's not settled," I replied. "There's a lot still to be discussed."

"Oh, naturally," he said. "You can't just decide on a flick of a coin, but what an opportunity! His firm is on the crest of the wave right now, and you'd never regret it. Especially as I gather you've nothing really to lose this side. No special ties." I did not answer. I was determined not to be led into a lengthy discussion. "Of course, Vita would make a home anywhere," he went on. "She has the knack. And with an apartment in New York and a weekend place in the country, you'd lead a very full life together, with plenty of opportunities for travel thrown in."

I grunted, and tilted an old panama hat of Commander Lane's over my right eye, which was still bloodshot. Unremarked, so far, by Vita.

"Don't think I'm butting in," he said, lowering his voice, "but you know how the girls talk. You've got Vita worried. She told Diana you've blown cool over the idea of coming to the States, and she can't figure out why. Women always think the worst." He then launched into a long, and to my mind loaded, story about a girl he had met in Madrid when Diana was in the Bahamas with her parents. "She was only nineteen," he said. "I was crazy about her. But of course we both knew it couldn't last. She had a job in the Embassy there, and Diana was due back in London when her vacation was over. I was so wild about that kid I felt like cutting my throat when we said goodbye. However, I survived and so did she, and I haven't seen her since."

I lit a cigarette to counteract the clouds of smoke from his blasted cigar. "If you think," I said, "that I've got a girl round the corner you couldn't be more wrong."

"Well, that's fine," he said, "just fine. I wouldn't blame you if you had, as long as you kept it quiet from Vita."

There was a long pause while he tried, I suppose, to think of another tactic, but he must have decided that discretion was the better part of valour, for he went on abruptly, "Didn't those boys say something about wanting to swim?"

We wandered off to find our wives. Their session was apparently still in full swing. Diana was one of those overripe blondes who are said to be grand fun at a party and a tigress in the home. I had no desire to try her out in either capacity. Vita told me she was the loyalest of friends, and I believed her. The session ceased immediately we appeared, and Diana changed down into second gear, her invariable custom at the approach of masculine company.

"You've got a tan, Dick," she said. "It suits you. Bill turns lobster red at the first touch of the sun."

"Sea air," I told her. "Not synthetic like your own."

She had a bottle of sun oil beside her with which she had been lubricating her lily-white legs.

"We're going down to the beach to swim," said Bill. "Rouse yourself, pug-face, it will take off some of that surplus fat."

The usual badinage ensued, the interplay of married couples before their kind. Lovers never did this, I thought; the game was played in silence, and was in consequence the more delightful.

Carrying towels and snorkels, we made the long trek to the beach. The tide was low, and to enter the water the intending swimmer had to pick his way over seaweed and uneven slabs of rock. It was an experience new to our guests, but they took it in good part, splashing about like dolphins in the shallows, proving my favourite maxim that it is always easier to entertain, albeit unwillingly, out-of-doors.

The evening to come would be the real test of hospitality, and so it proved. Bill had brought his own bottle of bourbon (a gift to the house), and I cleared the fridge of ice so that he could consume it on the rocks. The muscadet which we drank with supper, on top of the bourbon, made too rich a mixture, and with the dishwasher throbbing away in the kitchen we staggered into the music room after dinner considerably the worse for wear. I did not have to worry about my bloodshot eye. Both Bill's looked as if he had been stung by bees, while our wives had the high flush of barmaids lounging in some disreputable sailors' joint.

I went over to the gramophone and put on a stack of records—the choice did not matter, so long as the sound served the purpose of keeping the party quiet. Vita was a moderate drinker as a general rule, but when she had had one too many I found her embarrassing. Her voice took on a strident tone, or alternatively turned silky sweet. Tonight the sweetness was for Bill, who, nothing loath, lolled beside her on one sofa, while Diana, patting the empty place next to her on the second, pulled me to it with a meaning smile.

I realised, with distaste, that these manoeuvres had been worked out by the two women earlier on, and we were set for one of those frightful evenings of swapping partners, not for the ultimate act itself, but as a preliminary try-out, like a curtain-raiser before a two-act play. I could not have been more bored. The only thing I wanted to do was to go to bed, and, by God, to go alone.

"Talk to me, Dick," said Diana, so close that I had to turn my head sideways like a ventriloquist's doll. "I want to know all about your brilliant friend Professor Lane."

"A detailed account of his work?" I asked. "There was a very informative article about certain aspects of it in the *Biochemical Journal* a few years ago. I've probably got a copy in the flat in London. You must read it some time."

"Don't be idiotic. You know perfectly well I wouldn't understand a word. I want to know what he's like as a man. What are his hobbies, who are his friends?"

Hobbies . . . I considered the word. It conjured a vision of an absent-minded buffer chasing butterflies.

"I don't think he has any hobbies," I told her, "beyond his work. He's fond of music, particularly church music, Gregorian chants and plainsong."

"Is that what you have in common, a liking for music?"

"It started that way. We happened to meet in the same pew one evening at King's College when a carol service was in progress."

In point of fact we had not gone for the carols but to stare at one particular choir-boy with a golden aureole of hair like the infant Samuel. But though the meeting was accidental it was the first of many. Not that my tastes inclined to choir-boys, but the combination of holy innocence with adeste fideles and a halo of curls was so aesthetically pleasing to our twenty years that we were subsequently enraptured for several days.

"Teddy told me there was a room locked up in the basement here full of monkeys' heads," she said. "How deliciously creepy."

"One monkey's head, to be exact," I replied, "and a number of other specimens in jars. Highly toxic, and not to be disturbed."

"You hear that, Bill?" said Vita from the opposite sofa. I noticed, with aversion, that he had his arm round her and her head was on his shoulder. "This house is built on dynamite. One false movement, and we'd be blown skyhigh."

"Any movement?" queried Bill, with an offensive wink at me. "What happens if we get a little closer? If dynamite sends us both up to the floor above it's O.K. by me, but I'd best ask Dick's permission first."

"Dick's staying right here," said Diana, "and should the monkey's head explode you two can rise, and Dick and I'll descend. That way we'll all be happy, but in different worlds. Isn't that so, Dick?"

"Oh, absolutely," I agreed. "And in any event I've had enough of this particular world. So if you three like to triple-up on one piece of furniture, go ahead and enjoy yourselves. There's a quarter of bourbon left in the bottle, and it's all yours. I'm for bed."

I got up and left the room. Now that I had broken up the foursome the petting party would automatically stop, and they would all three sit for another hour or more solemnly discussing the various facets of my character, how I had or had not changed, what could be done about me, what the future held.

I undressed, plunged my head into cold water, flung the curtains wide, climbed into bed and fell instantly asleep.

The moon awakened me. It came through a chink of the curtains, which Vita had drawn, and sent a shaft of light on to my pillow. She lay on her own side of the bed and was snoring, a thing she rarely did, and with her mouth wide open. It must have been that last quarter of bourbon. I glanced at my watch: it was half-past three. I got out of bed, went through to the dressing room, and pulled on a pair of jeans and a sweater.

I stood at the head of the stairs and listened at the guest-room door. Not a sound. Silence, too, along the passage where the boys slept. I went downstairs, down the back way to the basement, and so to the lab. I was perfectly sober, cool and collected, neither elated nor depressed; I had never felt more normal in my life. I was determined to take a trip, and that was that. Pour four measures in the flask, get the car out of the garage, coast downhill to Treesmill valley, park the car, and walk to the Gratten. The moon was bright, and when it paled in the western sky the dawn would come. If time played tricks with me and the trip lasted until breakfast, what did it matter? I would return when I was ready to return. And Vita and her friends could lump it.

On such a night . . . a rendezvous with whom? The world of today asleep, and my world not awakened, or not as yet, until the drug possessed me. Tywardreath was a ghost village as I skirted it, but in my secret time I knew I traversed the green, and the Priory stood conspicuous though aloof behind stone walls. I crept down the Treesmill road and the moonlight flooded the valley, shining on the grey-lidded hutches of the mink farm on the farther side. I parked the car close to the ditch, and climbed the gate across the field. Then I made my way to the pit near the quarry which I knew formed the site of part of the original hall, and in the darkness there, close to a tree stump, in a square patch of moonlight, swallowed the contents of the flask. Nothing happened at first, except a humming in my ears which I had not experienced before. I leant against the bank and waited.

Something stirred, a rabbit, perhaps, in the hedge, and the humming in my ears increased. A piece of corrugated iron behind me in the quarry rattled and fell. The humming became universal, part of the world around me, changing from the sound in my own ears to the rattle of the casement in the great hall, and the roaring of the wind without. The rain was teeming down from a grey sky, falling slantwise across the parchment panes, and moving forward I looked out and saw that the water in the estuary below was turbulent and high, short-crested seas racing with the tide. What trees there were on the opposite slopes bent in unison, the autumn leaves scattering with the force of the wind, and a flock of starlings flying north formed into a clamouring mass and disappeared. I was not alone. Roger was by my side, peering down into the creek also, his face concerned, and when a greater draught of wind rattled the casement he fastened it tight, shaking his head and murmuring, "Pray God he does not venture here in this."

I glanced round, and saw that a curtain had been drawn across the hall, dividing it in two, and voices came from behind it. I followed Roger as he crossed the hall and drew the curtain aside. I thought for a moment that time had played another trick, taking me into a past I had witnessed already, for there was a pallet bed against one wall, with someone lying on it, while Joanna Champernoune was seated at the foot, and the monk Jean close to the pillow. But drawing closer I saw that the sick man was not her husband but his namesake, Henry Bodrugan, Otto's eldest son and her own nephew, and standing well withdrawn, with his handkerchief covering his mouth, was Sir John Carminowe. The young man, evidently in a high fever, kept trying to raise himself, calling for his father, as the monk wiped the sweat from his forehead and tried to ease him back on to his pillow.

"Impossible to leave him here, with the servants at Trelawn and no one to care for him," said Joanna. "And even if we tried to move him there we could not do so before nightfall, in such a gale. Whereas we could have him beneath your own roof, at Bockenod, within an hour."

"I dare not risk it," said Sir John. "If it should prove to be smallpox, as the monk fears, none of my family have had it. There is no other course but to leave him here in Roger's care."

He looked at the steward, his eyes apprehensive above the handkerchief, and I thought what a poor figure he must cut before Joanna, showing such fear that he might catch the disease himself. Gone was the cocksure bearing I had seen at the Bishop's reception. He had increased in weight, and his hair was turning grey. Roger, respectful as ever before his masters, inclined his head, but I noticed a look of scorn in his lowered eyes.

"I am willing to do whatever my lady commands me," he said. "I had smallpox as a child, my father died of it. My lady's nephew is young and strong, he should recover. Nor can we be certain yet of the disease. Many a fever starts in the same fashion. In twenty-four hours he could be himself once more."

Joanna rose from her chair and approached the bed. She still wore her widow's headdress, and I remembered the note scribbled by the student at the Public Record Office from the Patent Rolls dated October 1331: "Licence for Joan late wife of Henry de Champernoune to marry whomsoever she will of the King's allegiance." If Sir John was still her choice of suitor, then the marriage had not yet taken place . . .

"We can only hope so," she said slowly, "but I am of the monk's opinion. I have seen smallpox before. I too had the disease as a child, and Otto with me. If it were possible to send word to Bodrugan, Otto himself would come and fetch him home." She turned to Roger. "How is the tide?" she asked. "Is the ford covered?"

"It has been covered for an hour or more, my lady," he replied, "and the tide is still flooding. There is no possibility of traversing the ford before the water ebbs, or I would ride to Bodrugan myself and tell Sir Otto."

"Then there is nothing for it but to leave Henry in your care," said Joanna, "despite the lack of servants in the house." She turned to Sir John. "I will come with you to Bockenod, and proceed to Trelawn at daybreak and warn Margaret. She is the one who should be at her son's bedside."

The monk, despite his preoccupation with young Henry, had been listening to every word. "There is another course open to us, my lady," he said. "The guest chamber at the Priory is vacant, and neither I nor my fellow brethren fear smallpox. Henry Bodrugan would fare better under our roof than here, and I would make it my business to watch him night and day."

I saw the expression of relief on Sir John's face, and on Joanna's too. Whatever happened they would be quit of responsibility.

"We should have decided upon this sooner," said Joanna, "then we could all have been on our way hours since, before this gale. What do you say John? Is not this the only remedy?"

"It would seem so," he said hastily, "that is, if the steward can arrange for his removal to the Priory. We dare not take him in your chariot for fear of infection."

"Infection for whom?" laughed Joanna. "You mean for yourself? You can ride as escort, surely, with your handkerchief over your face as you have it now? Come, we have delayed long enough."

The decision taken, she had no further thought for her nephew but went to the door of the great hall, escorted by Sir John, who flung it open, only to stagger back with the force of the wind.

"You'd be well advised," she said with irony, "to travel in comfort at my side, despite that sick boy, rather than feel the wind on your back when we reach high ground."

"I have no fear for myself," he began, and then, seeing the steward close behind him, added, "You understand, my wife is delicate, and my sons also. The risk would be too great."

"Too great indeed, Sir John. You show prudence."

Prudence my arse, I thought, and so did Roger, judging from his expression, and Joanna's too.

The lumbering chariot was drawn up outside the further gate, and crossing the court in the blustering wind we escorted the widow to it, whilst Sir John mounted his horse. Then we returned once more to the hall. The monk was piling covers about the half-conscious Henry.

"They are ready and waiting," said Roger. "We can bear the mattress between us. Now we are alone, what hope have you of his recovery?"

The monk shrugged. "As you said yourself, he is young and strong, but I have seen weaklings live and stalwarts die. Let him remain at the Priory under my care, and I will try certain remedies."

"Watch your skill on this occasion," said Roger. "If you should fail you would have to answer for it to his father, and in that event the Prior himself could not protect you."

The monk smiled. "From what I understand, Sir Otto Bodrugan will have trouble enough protecting himself," he answered. "You know Sir Oliver Carminowe lay at Bockenod last night and left at dawn, telling none of the servants of his destination? If he has ridden in secret along the coast it would be for one thing only, to seek out his lady's lover and destroy him."

"Let him try," scoffed Roger. "Bodrugan is the better swordsman."

Once again the monk shrugged. "Possibly," he said, "but Oliver Carminowe used other methods when he fought his enemies in Scotland. I would not give much for Bodrugan's chances should he be caught in ambush."

The steward signalled him to silence as young Henry opened his eyes. "Where is my father?" he asked. "Where are you taking me?"

"Your father is home, sir," said Roger. "We are sending for him, he will come to you in the morning. This night you are to rest at the Priory in the care of brother Jean. Then, if you feel stronger and as your father so decides, you can be moved either to Bodrugan or to Trelawn."

The young man looked from one to the other in bewilderment. "I have no wish to stay at the Priory," he said. "I would rather go home tonight."

"It is not possible, sir," replied Roger gently. "It is blowing a full gale and the horses cannot travel far. My lady is waiting for you in the chariot, and will take you to the Priory. You will be safely in bed in the guest chamber there within half-an-hour."

They bore him on the mattress, still protesting weakly, through the hall and across the court to the waiting vehicle, stretching him full length at his aunt's feet. Then the monk climbed in beside him. Joanna looked at her steward through the open window. The veil had blown back from her face, and I noticed how her features had coarsened since I saw her last. Her mouth was slacker, and there were pouches under her full eyes.

She leant close to the window, so that her nephew could not hear. "There have been rumours," she said softly, "of possible trouble between Sir Oliver and my brother. Whether Sir Oliver is in the neighborhood or not I cannot say. But it is one of the reasons I want to be away, and quickly."

"As you will, my lady," answered the steward.

"Neither Sir John nor I wish to take part in the dispute," she said. "It is not our quarrel. If they come to blows my brother can take care of himself. My strict charge upon you is that you side with neither, but concern yourself solely with my affairs. Is that understood?"

"Perfectly, my lady."

She nodded briefly, then turned her attention to young Henry at her feet. Roger signalled to the driver, and the heavy vehicle pursued its course up the muddied road towards the Priory, followed by Sir John on horseback and an attendant servant, both riders bent low on their saddles, lashed by the wind and rain. As soon as they had topped the brow and disappeared, Roger walked swiftly through the archway into the stableyard and called for Robbie. His brother came at once, leading a pony, his mat of unruly hair falling over his face.

"Ride like the devil to Tregest," Roger said, "and warn Lady Isolda to stay within doors. Bodrugan was to have sailed here to the creek tonight, but he will never venture in this gale. Whether Sir Oliver is with her or not—and I doubt it—she must get my message without fail."

The boy leapt on to the pony's back and was away, streaking across the field, but in an easterly direction, our side of the valley, and I remembered that Roger had said the ford was impassable because of the tide. He would have to cross the stream higher up the valley, if the place called Tregest lay the other side. The name conveyed nothing. I knew there was no Tregest on the ordinance map today.

Roger made his way across the court and through the gate in the wall to the sloping hill above the creek. Here the strength of the wind nearly blew him off his feet, but he continued downhill towards the river, into the driving rain, taking the rough track that led to the quayside at the bottom. His expression was anxious, even haggard, quite different from his usual air of self-possession, and as he walked, or rather ran, he kept looking towards the river mouth where it entered the wide Par estuary. The sense of foreboding that had been mine when I returned from the expedition across the bay was with me once again, and I felt that it was with him too, that somehow we shared a common bond of anxiety and fear.

There was some shelter when we came to the quay because of the hill behind us, but the river itself was in turmoil, the wavelets short and steep, bearing upon their crests every sort of autumn debris, floating branches, logs and seaweed, which, as they were driven towards the quay or passed it in midchannel, were skimmed by a flock of screaming gulls endeavouring with outstretched wings to stem the wind.

We must have seen the ship simultaneously, our eyes turned seaward, but not the brave craft I had admired at anchor on a summer's afternoon. She staggered like a drunken thing, her mast broken, the yards upon it hanging halfway to the deck, and the sails dropping around the yards like shrouds. The rudder must have gone too, for she was out of control, at the mercy of both wind and tide that bore her forward but broadside on, her bows turned towards the shallower sands where the seas broke shortest. I could not see how many were on board, but there were three at least, and they were endeavouring to launch from the deck a little boat that was caught up in the tangle of sail and fallen yards. Roger cupped his hands to his mouth and shouted, but they could not hear him, because of the wind. He sprang on to the quay wall and waved his arms, and one of those aboard—it must have been Otto Bodrugan—saw him and waved in answer, pointing to the opposite shore.

"This side the channel," shouted Roger, "this side the channel," but his voice was lost in the wind. They did not hear him, for they were still working hard to launch the boat from the ship's side.

Doubtless Bodrugan knew the channel well, and if they launched the smaller boat they would have little difficulty in getting ashore, despite the short seas breaking above the sand flats on either side. It was not like open sea, rock-bound and dangerous, and, although the river was broadest where the craft drifted, she could at worst only run aground and wait for the falling tide.

Then I saw the reason for Roger's fear, and why he strove to attract Bodrugan and his sailors to the quay. A line of horsemen was riding on the opposite hill, some dozen of them, in single file. Because of the contours of the land the men aboard were not aware of their presence, the clump of trees masking them from the vessel.

Roger continued to shout and wave, but those on board took it as encouragement for the successful launching of the small boat, and replied in like fashion. Then, as the vessel drifted on upchannel, they managed to lower the boat over the side, all three men dropping into it a moment afterwards. They had a hawser fastened from the ship's bows to the stern of the small boat, and while two of the men bent to the oars and pulled towards the opposite shore the third, Bodrugan, crouched in the stern, holding fast to the hawser in an attempt to turn the vessel in the same direction as themselves.

They were too intent upon their task to pay further attention to Roger, and as they drew slowly nearer to the opposite shore I saw the horsemen on the hill dismount by the belt of trees. Taking advantage of the cover they crept down towards the creek, where the land dipped suddenly to the water's edge, forming a spit of sand. Roger shouted for the last time, waving his arms in desperation, and forgetting my phantom status I did the same, without sound, more powerless as an ally than any spectator at a football game cheering a losing side, and as the small boat drew nearer to the shore so their enemies, screened by the belt of trees, came closer to the spit of sand.

Suddenly the hawser parted as the larger vessel ran aground, and Bodrugan, flung off his feet, tumbled amongst his men and the small boat upset, throwing all three of them into the water. They were already so close to the opposite shore that the river had no great depth where they received their ducking, and Bodrugan was the first to stand, the water up to his chest, while the others floundered beside him, and Bodrugan answered Roger's final warning yell with a triumphant cry.

It was his last. The band of men were upon him and his companions before they had time to turn their heads or defend themselves, a dozen against three, and before the driving rain that burst upon us, heavier than ever, blotted them from view I saw, with sick revulsion, that instead of dragging their victims up the spit of sand to finish them there, by sword or dagger, they were thrusting them face-downwards in the water. One was already still, the other struggling, but it took eight men to hold Bodrugan down. Roger started to run along the river's edge towards the mill, cursing, gasping, and I knew it was useless, that we ran in vain, for long before he could summon help it would be over.

We came to the ford below the mill, and, just as he had told Joanna earlier, the water ran swiftly here, and deep, almost to the door of the forge itself. Once against Roger put his hands to his mouth.

"Rob Rosgof," he yelled, "Rob Rosgof," and the frightened figure of the blacksmith appeared at the door, with his wife beside him.

Roger pointed downstream, but the man gestured with both his hands in denial, shaking his head, then jerked his thumb up the hill behind him, this play without words suggesting he had known of the ambush and could do nothing, and he dragged his wife with him inside the forge and barred the door. Roger turned in despair to the mill, and the three monks I had seen there on the Sunday morning, when Isolda's children crossed the ford, came through the yard to meet him.

"Bodrugan and his men have been driven ashore," cried Roger. "His vessel's aground, and an ambush lay in wait to destroy them. They are dead men, all three, against a dozen fully armed."

I hardly know which showed the more strongly upon his face, his anger, or his grief, or his powerlessness to help.

"Where is Lady Champernoune?" asked one of the monks. "And Sir John Carminowe? We saw the carriage at the house all afternoon."

"Her nephew, Bodrugan's son, is sick," answered Roger. "They have taken him to the Priory, and they themselves are now on the road to Bockenod. I have sent Robbie to Tregest to warn the household there, and I pray God none of them ventures forth, or their lives could be in danger too."

We stood there, below the mill-yard, uncertain whether to go or stay, and all the time straining our eyes towards the river, where the curving banks above the creek hid the stranded vessel and the murderous scene on the spit of sand.

"Who led the ambush?" asked the monk. "Bodrugan had enemies once, but that is long past, with the King firmly established on the throne."

"Sir Oliver Carminowe, who else?" answered Roger. "They fought on opposing sides in the rebellion of '22, and today he does murder in another cause."

No sound but the wind, and the turmoil of the river as it coursed between the narrowing banks, with the gulls skimming the surface, screaming. Then one of the monks pointed to the bend in the creek and cried, "They've launched the boat, they're coming up with the tide!"

It was not a boat, at least not the whole of it, but what seemed in the distance to be part of the planking stripped from its side, and set afloat upstream as jetsam, circling slowly as it drifted with the current. Something was lashed to it that now and again bobbed to the surface, then disappeared, only to reappear again. Roger looked at the monks and I at him, and with one accord we ran down to the edge of the creek where the eddy carried the driftwood and the scum, and all the while, as we waited, the planking rose and fell with the force of the tide, and the thing that was lashed upon it rose as well. Then there was shouting from the opposite bank, and through the belt of trees rode the horsemen, their leader ahead. They cantered down to the road by the forge, and the shouting ceased, and they stood there watching in silence.

We plunged into the river to drag the plank ashore, the monks with us, and as we did so the leading horseman shouted, "A birthday package for my wife, Roger Kylmerth. See that she receives it with my compliments, and when she has done with it tell her that I await her at Carminowe."

He burst out laughing, and his men with him, and then they turned their horses up the hill and rode away.

Roger and the first monk drew the plank ashore. The others crossed themselves and began to pray, and one of them went down upon his knees at the water's edge. There was no knife wound upon Bodrugan, no sign of violence. The water streamed from his mouth and his eyes were open. They had drowned him before they lashed him to the plank.

Roger untied the hawser strands and bore him in his arms, with the water dripping from his hair, towards the mill. "Merciful God," he said, "how am I to tell her?"

There was no need. As we turned towards the mill we saw the ponies, Robbie upon his own, Isolda mounted on a second, her hair loose upon her shoulders, wet and lank, her cloak billowing out behind her like a cloud. Robbie at a glance saw what had happened, and put out his hand to seize her bridle and turn her pony back, but in a moment she had dismounted and came running down the hill towards us.

"Oh, my love," she said, "oh, no . . . oh, no . . . oh, no . . ." her voice, that had started clear and strong, trailing off into a single cry.

Roger laid his burden on the ground and ran towards her, and so did I. As we took hold of her outstretched hands she slipped out of our grasp and fell, and instead of holding on to her cloak I was scrambling amongst bales of straw piled against a corrugated tin shed across the road from Treesmill farm.

14

I LAY THERE waiting for the nausea and the vertigo to pass. I knew it had to be endured, and the quieter I remained the quicker it would go. It was already light, and I had sense enough to glance at my watch. It was twenty-past five. If I gave myself a quarter of an hour, without moving, all should be well. Even if people at Treesmill farm were already astir no one was likely to cross the road and come to the shed, which was hard against the wall of an old valley orchard, the stream a few yards away from where I lay, all that remained of the tidal creek.

My heart was thumping, but it gradually eased, and the dreaded vertigo was not as bad as that previous time when I had come to at the Gratten, and had the encounter with the doctor at the lay by at the top of the hill.

Five minutes, ten, fifteen . . . then I struggled to my feet, and slipping from the orchard walked very slowly up the hill. So far so good. I climbed into the car and sat another five minutes, then started the engine and drove equally carefully back to Kilmarth. Plenty of time to put away the car and lock up the flask in the lab, then the wisest thing to do would be to go straight to bed and try to get some rest.

There was nothing more I could do, I told myself. Roger would take Isolda back to that Tregest place, wherever it was, and poor Bodrugan's body would be safe in the care of those monks. Someone would have to carry the news to Joanna at Bockenod. Roger would take care of that, I felt sure. I now had a regard, even an affection for him, he was so obviously moved by Bodrugan's appalling death, and we had shared the horror of it together. I was right to have had that sense of foreboding on the beach below Chapel Point before sailing to Fowey with Vita and the boys. Vita and the boys . . .

I drove into the garage just as I remembered them, and with the memory came full understanding. I had driven home in one world with my brain still in the other. I had driven home, part of my brain completely sensible to the fact that I had the wheel in my hands and belonged to the present, while the rest of me was still in the past, believing Roger on the way to Tregest with Isolda.

I began to sweat all over. I sat quite still in the car, my hands trembling. It must not happen again. I must take a grip on myself. It was just on six o'clock in the morning. Vita and the boys, and those damned guests of ours, were all asleep upstairs, and Roger and Isolda and Bodrugan had been dead for more than six centuries. I was in my own time . . .

I let myself in at the back door and put the flask away. It was fully light by now, but the house was silent still. I crept upstairs and into the kitchen, and put on the electric kettle to make myself a cup of tea. Tea was the answer, a steaming cup. The purr of the kettle was oddly comforting, and I sat down at the table, remembering suddenly how much we had all had to drink the night before. The kitchen still smelt of the lobster we had eaten, and I got up and opened the window.

I was in the middle of my second cup when I heard a creak on the stairs, and I was about to streak down to the basement and remain *perdu* when the door opened and Bill came into the room. He grinned sheepishly.

"Hullo," he said. "Two minds with but a single thought. I woke up, thought I heard a car, and suddenly had the most fearful thirst. Is that tea you're drinking?"

"Yes," I said. "Have a cup. Is Diana awake?"

"No," he replied, "and if I know my wife after a binge, not likely to, either. We were all pretty well stoned, weren't we? I say, no hard feelings?"

"No, none," I told him.

I poured him out a cup of tea, and he sat down at the table. He looked a mess, and his pyjamas, a livid pink, did not tone with his grey complexion.

"You're dressed," he said. "Have you been up long?"

"Yes," I said. "I've been out, as a matter of fact—I couldn't sleep."

"Then it was your car I heard coming down the drive?"

"It must have been," I said.

The tea was doing me good, but it was making me sweat as well. I could feel the sweat pouring down my face.

"You look a bit off," he said critically. "Are you all right?"

I took my handkerchief out of my coat pocket and wiped my forehead. My heart had started thumping again. Must be something to do with the tea.

"As a matter of fact," I said slowly, and I could hear myself slurring my words, as if the tea had been a strong dose of alcohol that had temporarily knocked me off balance, "I was an unseen witness to an appalling crime. I just can't forget it."

He put down his cup and stared at me. "What on earth?" he began.

"I felt I needed some air," I said, speaking very fast, "so I took the car down to a place I know, about three miles from here, near the estuary, and a boat went aground. It was blowing damned hard, and the chap aboard with his crew had to take to the dinghy. They made the opposite shore all right and then this appalling thing happened . . ." I poured myself another cup of tea, despite my trembling hands. "These thugs," I said, "these bloody thugs on the opposite shore—the chap from the boat didn't have a chance. They didn't knife him or anything, they forced his head under water and let him drown."

"My God!" said Bill. "My God, how terrible. Are you sure?"

"Yes," I said, "I saw it. I saw the poor devil drown . . ." I got up from the table and began walking up and down the kitchen.

"Well, what are you going to do?" he asked. "Hadn't you better ring the police?"

"Police?" I said. "It's not a job for the police. It's this chap's son I'm thinking of. He's ill, and someone will have to tell him, and the other relatives."

"But, good God, Dick, it's your duty to inform the police! I can see you don't want to be involved, but this is murder, surely? And you say you know the chap who was drowned, and his son?"

I stared at him. Then I pushed aside my cup of tea. It had happened, oh, sweet Christ, it had happened. The confusion. The confusion between worlds . . . The sweat was running down the whole of my body.

"No," I said, "I don't know him personally. I've seen him about, he keeps a yacht the other side of the bay, I've heard people talk about the family. You're right, I *don't* want to be involved. And anyway I wasn't the only witness. There was another chap watching, and he saw the whole thing. I'm pretty sure he will report it—in fact, he's probably done so already."

"Did you speak to him?" asked Bill.

"No," I said, "no, he didn't see me."

"Well, I don't know," said Bill. "I still think you ought to telephone the police. Would you like me to do it for you?"

"No, on no account. And, Bill, not a word of this to Diana or Vita. Swear it."

He looked very troubled. "I understand that," he said. "It would upset them terribly. My God, you must have had one hell of a shock."

"I'm all right," I told him, "I'm all right." I sat down again at the kitchen table.

"Here, have some more tea?" he suggested.

"No," I said, "no, I don't want anything."

"It just goes to prove what I'm always saying, Dick. The crime figures are mounting steadily, in every civilized country in the world. The authorities have just got to take things in hand. I mean, who would believe it happening here, off the map, down in Cornwall? A set of thugs, you say? Any idea where they came from? Were they local men?"

I shook my head. "No," I said, "I don't think so. I've no idea who they were."

"And you're quite certain this other fellow saw, and was going to report to the police?"

"Yes, I saw him running. He was making straight for the nearest farmhouse. They'll have a telephone there."

"I hope to heaven you're right," he said.

We sat for a while in silence. He kept sighing, and shaking his head. "What an experience for you. What a damned awful experience."

I put my hands in my pockets so that he should not see them shaking. "Look, Bill," I said, "I think I'll go upstairs and lie down. I don't want Vita to know I've even been out. Or Diana either. I want this thing to remain absolutely private between ourselves. There's nothing you or I can do now. I want you to forget it."

"O.K.," he said, "about not saying anything. But I shan't forget what you've told me. And I'll listen for it on the news. By the way, we shall have to leave after breakfast if we're to catch that plane from Exeter. Is that all right by you?"

"Of course," I said. "I'm only sorry to have spoilt your morning."

"My dear Dick, I'm the one to be sorry, and for you. Yes, I should go upstairs, and try to get some sleep. And look here, don't bother to get up and say goodbye. You can always plead a hangover." He smiled, and held out his hand. "We loved yesterday," he said, "and a thousand thanks for everything. I only hope nothing else comes up to spoil your holiday. I'll write you from Ireland."

"Thanks, Bill," I said, "thanks a lot."

I went upstairs, undressed in the dressing room, then retched violently for about five minutes down the lavatory. The sound must have woken Vita, for I heard her calling from the bedroom.

"Is that you?" she said. "What's the matter?"

"All that muscadet on top of bourbon," I said. "Sorry, I can hardly stand. I'm going to turn in on the divan here. It's still quite early—about half-past six."

I closed the dressing-room door and threw myself on the divan bed. I was back in the world of today, but God alone knew how long it would stay that way. One thing was certain. As soon as Bill and Diana had gone I should have to telephone Magnus.

The unconscious is a curious thing. I was deeply disturbed over this total confusion of thought that might have made me blab the truth to Bill about the experiment itself; but five minutes or so after I had lain down on the divan I was asleep and dreaming, not, strangely enough, about Bodrugan and his appalling fate, but of a cricket match at Stonyhurst when one of the team got hit on the head with a cricket ball and died of haemorrhage of the brain twenty-four hours later. I had not thought about the incident for at least twenty-five years.

When I awoke just after nine I was perfectly lucid and clear in the head, apart from a hell of a genuine hangover, and my right eye was more bloodshot than ever. I bathed and shaved, and could hear sounds of movement from our guests in the room next door. I waited until I heard Bill and Diana go downstairs, then I put a call through to Magnus. No luck. He was not at the flat. So I left a message with his secretary at the university saying I wanted to speak to him very urgently, but it might be better if I put the call through to him rather than he to me. Then I stuck my head out of the dressing-room window overlooking the patio, and shouted to Teddy to bring me up a cup of coffee. I would appear in the hall to bid our guests godspeed five minutes before departure, and not a moment before.

"What's wrong with your eye? You hit the floor or something?" asked my elder stepson as he brought in my coffee.

"No," I told him. "I think it's a backlash from the wind on Monday."

"You were up early anyway," he said. "I heard you talking to Bill in the kitchen."

"I was making tea," I said. "We both of us had too much to drink at dinner."

"Guess that's what turned your eye all streaks and not the sea," he said, looking so like his mother in one of her more perceptive moods that I turned away, and then remembered that his room was above the kitchen and he could conceivably have overhead our conversation.

"Anyway," I asked before he left the dressing room, "what were we talking about?"

"How should I know?" he replied. "Do you think I'd pull up the floorboards to listen?"

No, I reflected, but his mother might, if she heard a discussion going on between her husband and her guest at six A.M.

I finished dressing, drank down my coffee, and appeared at the top of the stairs just in time to help Bill down with the suitcases. He greeted me with a conspiratorial glance of enquiry—the girls were below us in the hall—and murmured, "Get any sleep?"

"Yes," I said, "yes, I'm fine." I saw him staring at my eye. "I know," I said, touching it, "no explanation for that. Must have been the bourbon. By the way," I added, "Teddy heard us talking this morning."

"I know," he said, "I heard him tell Vita. Everything's O.K. Don't worry." He patted me on the shoulder, and we clumped downstairs.

"Heavens!" cried Vita. "What have you done to your eye?"

"Bourbon allergy," I said, "combined with shellfish. It happens to some people."

Both girls insisted on examining me, suggesting alternative remedies from penicillin ointment to TCP.

"It can't be the bourbon," said Diana. "I don't want to be personal, but I noticed it yesterday as soon as we arrived. I said to myself, 'Whatever's Dick done to his eye?'"

Enough was enough. I put a hand on each of their shoulders and pushed them through the porch. "Neither one of you would win a beauty prize this morning," I said, "and it wasn't the bourbon that woke me at dawn, but Vita snoring. So shut up."

We had to install ourselves on the steps for the inevitable picture-taking by Bill, and it was nearly half-past ten before they were finally off. Once again Bill's handclasp was that of a conspirator.

"Hope we get this fine weather in Ireland," he said. "I'll watch the papers and listen to the radio forecasts to see what's happening here in Cornwall." He looked at me, nodding imperceptibly. He meant that his eyes and ears would be alert for the first mention of a dastardly crime.

"Send us postcards," said Vita. "Wish we were coming with you."

"You always can," I said, "when you get fed-up here."

It was not perhaps the most encouraging of remarks, and when we had finished waving and turned back toward the house Vita wore an abstracted air. "I really believe," she said, "you'd be glad if the boys and I had gone off with them. Then you'd have this place to yourself again."

"Don't talk nonsense," I said.

"Well, you made your feelings pretty clear last night, flinging off to bed directly we'd finished dinner."

"I flung off to bed, as you call it, because it bored me stiff to see you lolling about in Bill's arms and Diana waiting to do the same in mine. I'm just no good at party games, and you ought to know it by now."

"Party games!" she laughed. "What utter nonsense! Bill and Diana are my oldest friends. Where's your much-vaunted British sense of humour?"

"Not in tune with yours," I said. "I've a cruder sense of fun. If I pulled a mat from under your feet and you slipped up, I'd have hysterics."

We wandered back into the house, and just at that moment the telephone rang. I went into the library to answer it, and Vita followed me. I was afraid it might be Magnus, and it was.

"Yes?" I said guardedly.

"I got your message," he said, "but I've a very full day. Is it an awkward moment?"

"Yes," I said.

"You mean Vita is in the room?"

"Yes."

"I understand. You can answer yes or no. Anything turned up?"

"Well, we've had visitors. They arrived yesterday, and have just left."

Vita was lighting up a cigarette. "If it's your Professor—and I can't think who else it would be—give him my regards."

"I will. Vita sends her regards," I told Magnus.

"Return them. Ask her if it would be convenient for me to come for the weekend, arriving Friday evening."

My heart leapt. Whether with excitement or the reverse I couldn't say. In any case with relief. Magnus would take over.

"Magnus wants to know if he can come on Friday for the weekend," I said to her.

"Surely," she answered. "It's his house, after all. You'll have more fun entertaining your friend than you had putting up with mine."

"Vita says of course," I repeated to Magnus.

"Splendid. I'll let you know the train later. About your urgent call. Does it concern the other world?"

"Yes," I said.

"You went on a trip?"

"Yes."

"With ill-effect?"

I paused a moment, with a glance at Vita. She had made no attempt to leave the room. "As a matter of fact I'm feeling pretty lousy," I said. "Something I ate or drank disagreed with me. I've been violently sick and have a peculiar bloodshot eye. It may be due to drinking bourbon before lobster."

"Combined with taking a trip, you may well be right," he answered. "What about confusion?"

"That also. I could hardly think straight when I awoke."

"I see. Anyone notice?"

I took another glance at Vita. "Well, we were all pretty high last night," I said, "so the males of the party woke early. I had suffered a very vivid nightmare, and told Vita's friend Bill about it over a morning cup of tea."

"How much did you tell?"

"About the nightmare? Just that. It was very real, you know what nightmares are. I thought I saw someone set on by thugs and drowned."

"Serves you right," said Vita. "And it sounds more like the two helpings of lobster than the bourbon."

"Was it one of our friends?" asked Magnus.

"Yes," I answered. "You know that chap who used to keep a boat years ago over at Chapel Point, and was always sailing round to Par? Well, the nightmare was about him. I dreamt his ship was dismasted in a storm, and when he finally came ashore he was murdered by a jealous husband who thought he was after his wife."

Vita laughed. "If you ask me," she said, "a dream of that sort means an uneasy conscience. You thought I was getting off with Bill and your vivid nightmare resulted from that. Here, let me talk to your Professor." She crossed the room and seized the receiver from me. "How are you, Magnus?" she said, her voice full of calculated charm. "I shall be delighted to see you here in your own home next weekend. Maybe you'll put Dick in a better temper. He's very sour right now." She smiled, her eyes on me. "What's wrong with his eye?" she repeated. "I haven't the slightest idea. He looks as if he's lost a prize fight. Yes, of course I'll do my best to keep him quiet until you arrive, but he's very stubborn. Oh, by the way, you'll be able to tell me. My boys adore riding, and Dick says he saw some children on ponies having a lot of fun on Sunday morning when we were in church. I wondered if there were riding-stables somewhere the other side of the village there—what-do-you-call-it—Tywardreath. You don't know? Well, never mind, Mrs. Collins might tell me. What? Hold on, I'll ask him . . ." She turned to me. "He says were the children the two little girls of someone called Oliver Carminowe and his wife? Old friends of his."

"Yes," I said. "I'm almost sure they were. But I don't know where they live."

She turned back to the telephone. "Dick thinks yes, though I don't see why he should know if he hasn't met them. Oh well, if the mother is attractive he's probably seen her around some place, and that's how he knows who they were." She pulled a face at me. "Yes, you do that," she added, "and if you get in touch with them next weekend we might ask them round for drinks, and Dick can get an introduction to her. See you Friday, then."

She handed the receiver back to me. Magnus was laughing at the other end of the line.

"What's this about getting in touch with the Carminowes?" I asked.

"I got out of that rather neatly, don't you think?" he countered. "In any event, it's what I intend to do, if we can get rid of Vita and the boys. In the meantime I'll get my lad in London to check up on Otto Bodrugan. So he came to a sticky end, and it upset you?"

"Yes," I said.

"Roger was there, of course? Did he have a hand in it?"

"No."

"Glad to hear it. Look, Dick, this is important. Absolutely no more trips unless we take one together. No matter how big the temptation. You must sweat it out. Is that agreed?"

"Yes," I said.

"As I told you before, I shall have the first results from the lab by the time I see you. In the meantime, abstention. Now I must go. Take care of yourself."

"I'll try," I said. "Goodbye."

It was like cutting off the only link between both worlds.

"Cheer up, darling," said Vita. "Less than three days and he'll be here. Won't that be wonderful? Now what about going upstairs to the bathroom and doing something about that eye?"

Later on, the eye bathed and Vita having disappeared into the kitchen to tell Mrs. Collins about Magnus coming for the weekend, and doubtless to discuss his gastronomic tastes, I got out my road map and had another look for Tregest. It just was not there. Treesmill was marked, as I knew, and Treverran, Trenadlyn, Trevenna—the last three on the Lay Subsidy Roll as well—but that was all. Perhaps Magnus would find the answer from his London student.

Presently Vita wandered back into the library. "I asked Mrs. Collins about the Carminowes," she said, "but she'd never heard of them. Are they very great friends of Magnus's?"

It startled me for a moment to hear her speak the name. I knew I must be careful, or the confusion might start up again.

"I think he's rather lost sight of them," I replied. "I doubt if he's seen them for some time. He doesn't get down very often."

"They're not in the telephone directory—I've looked. What does Oliver Carminowe do?"

"Do?" I repeated. "I don't really know. I think he used to be in the army. Has some sort of government job. You'll have to ask Magnus."

"And his wife's very attractive?"

"Well, she was," I said. "I've never spoken to her."

"But you've seen her since you got down here?"

"Only in the distance," I said. "She wouldn't know me."

"Was she around in the old days when you used to stay here as an undergraduate?"

"She could have been," I said, "but I never met her, or the husband. I know very little about them."

"But you knew enough to recognise her children when you saw them the other day?"

I felt myself getting tied up in knots. "Darling," I said, "what is all this? Magnus occasionally mentions names of friends and acquaintances, and the Carminowes were amongst them. That's all there is to it. Oliver Carminowe was married before and Isolda is his second wife, and they have two daughters. Satisfied?"

"Isolda?" she said. "What a romantic name."

"No more romantic than Vita," I replied. "Can't we give her a rest?"

"It's funny," she said, "that Mrs. Collins has never heard of them. She's such a mine of information on local affairs. But in any case there's a perfectly good stables up the road from here at Menabilly Barton, she tells me, so I'm going to fix something up with the people there."

"Thank God for that," I said. "Why not fix it right away?"

She stared at me a moment, then turned round and went out of the room. I surreptitiously got out my handkerchief and wiped my forehead, which was sweating again. It was a lucky thing the Carminowes were extinct, or she would have run them to earth somehow and invited a bewildered descendant to lunch next Sunday.

Two, nearly three days to go before Magnus came to my rescue. It was difficult to fob Vita off once her interest was aroused, and it was typical of his malicious sense of fun to have mentioned the name.

The rest of Wednesday passed without incident, and thank heaven I had no return of confusion. It was such a relief to be without our guests that little else mattered. The boys went riding and enjoyed themselves, and, although Vita may have suffered from anticlimax and a normal reaction from a hangover, she had the good sense not to say so, nor did she make any further reference to our party the preceding night. We went to bed early and slept like logs, awaking on Thursday to a day of steady rain. It did not worry me, but Vita and the boys were disappointed, having planned another expedition in the boat.

"I hope it's not going to be a wet weekend," said Vita. "What in the world shall I do with the boys if it is? You won't want them hanging about the house all day when the Professor is here."

"Don't worry about Magnus," I told her. "He'll be full of suggestions for them and for us. Anyway, he and I may have work to do."

"What sort of work? Surely not shutting yourselves up in that peculiar room in the basement?"

She was nearer the truth than she imagined. "I don't know exactly," I said vaguely. "He has a lot of papers tucked away, and he may want to go through them with me. Historical research, and so on. I've told you about this new hobby."

"Well, Teddy might be interested in that, and so should I," she said. "It would be fun if we all took a picnic to some historical site or other. What about Tintagel? Mrs. Collins says everyone should see Tintagel."

"Not exactly Magnus's line of country, and anyway too full of tourists," I said. "We'll see what he wants to do when he arrives."

I wondered how the hell we should be shut of them if Magnus wanted to visit the Gratten. Anyway, it would be his problem, not mine.

Thursday dragged, and a dreary walk along Par sands did little to alleviate it. Magnus had told me to sweat it out, and by the evening I knew what he meant. Sweat was the operative word, and in the physical sense. I had seldom if ever been troubled by this common affliction of mankind. At school, yes, after violent exercise, but not to the extent suffered by some of my companions. Now, after any minor exertion, or even perhaps when sitting still, I would sweat from every pore, the perspiration having a peculiar acid tang to it that I fervently hoped nobody would be aware of but myself.

The first time it happened, after the walk along Par sands, I thought it was merely connected with the exercise I had taken, and I had a bath before dinner, but during the course of the evening, when Vita and the boys were watching television and I was sitting comfortably in the music room listening to records, it started again. A clammy feeling of sudden chill, then the sweat pouring from my head, neck, armpits, trunk, lasting for perhaps five minutes before it passed, but my shirt was wringing wet by the time the attack was over. Laughable, like seasickness, when it happens to anyone but oneself, this side effect, which was obviously a new reaction from the drug, threw me into sudden panic. I switched off the gramophone and went upstairs to wash and change for the second time, wondering what on earth would happen if I suffered a further attack later when I was in bed with Vita.

Nervous apprehension did not make for an easy night, and Vita was in one of her conversational moods that lasted through undressing and continued until we were lying side by side. I could not have been more nervous had I been a bridegroom on the first night of honeymoon, and I found myself edging away to my side of the bed, giving vent to prodigious yawns as a sign that excessive fatigue had overtaken me. We turned out the bedside lights, and I went through a kind of pantomime of heavy breathing on the verge of sleep which may or may not have fooled Vita, but after one or two attempts to coil close—which I ignored—she turned over on her side and was soon asleep.

I lay awake thinking of the hell I would give Magnus when he arrived. Nausea, vertigo, confusion, a bloodshot eye, and now acid sweat, and all for what? A moment in time, long past, that had no bearing on the present, that served no purpose in his life or mine, and could as little benefit the world in which we lived as a scrapbook of forgotten memories lying idle in a dusty drawer. So I argued, up to midnight and beyond, but common sense has a habit of vanishing when the demon of insomnia rides us in the small hours, and as I lay there, counting first two, and then three, on the illuminated face of the travelling clock beside the bed, I remembered how I had walked about that other world with a dreamer's freedom but with a waking man's perception. Roger had been no faded snapshot in time's album; and even now, in this fourth dimension into which I had stumbled inadvertently but Magnus with intent, he lived and moved, ate and slept, beneath me in his house Kylmerth, enacting his living Now which ran side by side with my immediate Present, and so the two merged.

Am I my brother's keeper? Cain's cry of protest against God suddenly had new meaning for me as I watched the hands of the clock move towards ten past three. Roger was my keeper, I was his. There was no past, no present, no future. Everything living is part of the whole. We are all bound, one to the other, through time and eternity, and, our senses once opened, as mine had been opened by the drug, to a new understanding of his world and mine, fusion would take place, there would be no separation, there would be no death . . . This would be the ultimate meaning of the experiment, surely, that by moving about in time death was destroyed. This was what Magnus so far had not understood. To him, the drug released the complex brew within the brain that served up the savoured past. To me, it proved that the past was living still, that we were all participants, all witnesses. I was Roger, I was Bodrugan, I was Cain; and in being so was more truly myself.

I felt myself on the brink of some tremendous discovery when I fell asleep.

15

I DID NOT wake up until after ten, and when I did Vita was standing by the bed with the breakfast tray of toast and coffee.

"Hullo," I said. "I must have overslept."

"Yes," she said, and then, looking at me critically, "Are you feeling all right?"

I sat up in bed and took the tray from her. "Perfectly," I said. "Why?"

"You were restless during the night," she told me, "and perspired a great deal. Look, your pajama top is quite damp."

It was, and I threw it off. "Extraordinary thing," I said. "Be an angel and get me a towel."

She brought me one from the bathroom, and I rubbed myself down before reaching for the coffee.

"Something to do with all that exercise on Par beach with the boys," I said.

"I wouldn't have thought so," she replied, staring at me, puzzled, "and anyway you took a bath afterwards. I've never known you perspire from exercise before."

"Well, it happens to people," I said. "It's my age group. The male menopause perhaps, striking me down in my prime."

"I hope not," she said. "How very unpleasant."

She wandered over to the dressing table and surveyed herself in the mirror as if that might hold the answer to the problem. "It's odd," she went on, "but both Diana and I remarked on the fact that you weren't looking yourself despite that suntan from sailing." She wheeled round suddenly, facing me. "You must admit you're not a hundred percent," she went on. "I don't know what it is, darling, but it worries me. You're moody, distrait, as if you had something on your mind all the time. Then that funny bloodshot eye . . ."

"Oh, for heaven's sake," I interrupted, "give it a miss, can't you? I admit I was foul-tempered when Bill and Diana were here, and I apologise. We all had too much to drink, and that was that. Must we do a post-mortem on every hour?"

"There you go again," she said. "Always on the defensive. I hope the arrival of your Professor straightens you out."

"It will," I answered, "providing this inquisition on our behaviour doesn't continue through the entire weekend."

She laughed, or rather her mouth twitched in the way wives' mouths are wont to twitch when they desire to inflict a wound upon the husband. "I would not dare presume to conduct an inquisition on the Professor. His state of health and his behaviour are no concern of mine, but yours are. I happen to be your wife, and I love you."

She left the room and went downstairs, and this, I thought, as I buttered my piece of toast, is a good beginning to the day—Vita offended, myself with the sweating sickness, and Magnus due to arrive some time in the evening.

There was a card on the breakfast tray from him, as it happened, hidden by the toast rack. I wondered if Vita had obscured it deliberately. It said he would be catching the 4:30 from London, arriving at St. Austell around ten. This was a relief. It meant that Vita and the boys could go to bed, or at any rate only stay up for the courtesy of greeting the new arrival, and then Magnus and I could talk in comfort on our own. Cheered, I got up, and bathed and dressed with a determination to improve upon the morning's mood and abase myself before Vita and the boys.

"Magnus won't be here until after ten," I shouted down the stairs, "so there's no food problem. He'll dine on the train. What does everybody want to do?"

"Go sailing," cried the boys, who were hanging about in the hall in the customary aimless fashion of all children who are incapable of organising their own day.

"No wind," I said, with a rapid glance out of the window on the stairs.

"Then hire a motorboat," said Vita, emerging from the direction of the kitchen.

I decided to appease them all, and we set forth from Fowey with a picnic lunch and our skipper Tom in charge, this time not in the sailing boat but in an ex-lifeboat of his own conversion with an honest chug-chug engine that forged along at about five knots and not a centimetre faster. We went east, out of the harbour, and anchored off Lanlivet Bay, where we picnicked, swam, and took our ease, everybody happy. Half-a-dozen mackerel caught on the homeward journey proved a further delight for Teddy and Micky, and a sop to Vita's culinary plans for the evening meal. The expedition had proved an unqualified success.

"Oh, do say we can come again tomorrow," pleaded the boys, but Vita, with a glance at me, told them it would depend upon the Professor. I saw their faces fall, and guessed their feelings. What could be more boring than to have to adjust themselves to this possibly stuffy friend of their stepfather's whom instinct told them their mother did not care for anyway?

"You can go with Tom," I said, "even if Magnus and I have other plans." In any event, I thought, a let-out for us, and Vita would hardly allow them to go alone, even in Tom's charge.

We arrived back at Kilmarth about seven o'clock, Vita going immediately to the kitchen to see about the mackerel, while I had a bath and changed. It was not until about ten to eight that I wandered down the front stairs into the dining room and saw the piece of paper in Mrs. Collins' handwriting propped up against the place where I usually sat. It read: "Telegram came over the phone to say Professor Lane is catching the 2:30 train from London instead of the 4:30. Arriving St. Austell 7:30."

God! Magnus must have been kicking his heels at St. Austell station for the last twenty minutes . . . I tore into the kitchen.

"Crisis!" I shouted. "Look at this! I've only just seen it. Magnus caught an earlier train. Why the hell didn't he telephone? What a bloody mess-up!"

Vita, distraught, looked at the half-fried mackerel. "He'll be here for dinner, then? Good heavens, I can't give him this! I must say it shows very little consideration for us. Surely . . ."

"Of course Magnus will eat mackerel," I shouted, already halfway down the back stairs. "Brought up on it, very probably. And we've cheese and fruit. What are you fussing about?"

I tore out to the car, in half-agreement with her immediate reaction that to change his time of arrival, knowing we could easily be out for the day, showed small consideration for his hosts. But that was Magnus. An earlier train had suited his plans and he had caught it. If I arrived late to meet him he would probably take a taxi and pass me en route with a callous wave of the hand.

Ill luck dogged me to St. Austell. Some fool had driven his car into the side of the road, and there was a long queue of traffic waiting to get past. It was a quarter to nine before I drew up at St. Austell station. No sign of Magnus, and I did not blame him. The platform was empty, and everywhere seemed to be shut up. Finally I routed out a porter on the other side of the station. He looked vague, and told me that the seven-thirty had been on time.

"I dare say," I replied. "That's not the point. The point is I was meeting someone off it, and he isn't here."

"Well, sir," he grinned, "he probably got tired of waiting and took a taxi."

"If he'd done that," I said, "he would have telephoned, or left a message with the chap in the booking office. Were you here when the train came in?"

"No," he said. "The booking office will be open again in time for the next down train, due at a quarter to ten."

"That's no good to me," I told him, exasperated. Poor devil, it wasn't his fault.

"I tell you what, sir," he said, "I'll open it up and see if your friend left a message."

We went back to the station and laboriously, or so it seemed to me, he fitted a key in the lock and opened the office door. I followed close behind. The first thing I noticed was a suitcase standing against the wall with the initials MAL upon it.

"That's it," I said, "that's his case. But why did he leave it here?"

The porter went to the desk and picked up a piece of paper. "Suitcase with initials MAL handed in by guard on seven-thirty train," he read, to be delivered to gentleman named Mr. Richard Young. You Mr. Young?"

"Yes," I said, "but where's Professor Lane?"

The porter studied the piece of paper. "Owner of suitcase, Professor Lane, gave message to guard that he had changed his mind and decided to get out at Par and walk from there. Told guard Mr. Young would understand." He handed me the scrap of paper, and I read it for myself.

"I don't understand," I said, more exasperated than ever. "I didn't think the London trains stopped at Par these days."

"They don't," replied the porter. "They stop at Bodmin Road, and anyone wanting Par changes there, and gets the connection. That's what your friend must have done."

"What a bloody silly thing to do," I said.

The porter laughed. "Well, it's a fine evening for a walk," he said, "and there's no accounting for tastes."

I thanked him for his trouble and went back to the car, throwing the suitcase on the back seat. Why the hell Magnus should take it into his head to alter every one of our arrangements beat me. He must be at Kilmarth by this time, sitting down to his mackerel supper, making a joke of the affair to Vita and the boys. I drove back at breakneck speed and arrived home just after half-past nine, furiously angry. Vita, changed into a sleeveless frock and with fresh make-up on, appeared from the music room as I ran up the steps.

"Whatever happened to you both?" she said, the hostess smile of welcome fading as she saw I was alone. "Where is he?"

"You mean to say he hasn't turned up yet?" I cried.

"Turned up?" she repeated, bewildered. "Of course he hasn't turned up. You met the train, didn't you?"

"Oh, Jesus! What the hell is going on? Look," I said wearily, "Magnus wasn't at St. Austell, only his suitcase. He left a message with the guard on the 7:30 train that he'd be getting out at Par and walking here. Don't ask me why. One of his bloody silly ideas. But he should have been here by now."

I went into the music room and poured myself a drink and Vita followed, the boys running down to the car to fetch the suitcase.

"Well really," she said, "I expected more consideration from your Professor, I must say. First he changes trains, then he changes connections, and finally he doesn't bother to turn up at all. I expect he found a taxi at Par and has gone off to have dinner somewhere."

"Maybe," I said, "but why not telephone to say so?"

"He's your friend, darling, not mine. You're supposed to know his ways. Well, I'm not going to wait any longer, I'm starving."

The uncooked mackerel was put aside for Magnus's breakfast, though I was pretty sure orange juice and black coffee would be his choice, and Vita and I sat down to a hasty snack of game pie, which she remembered she had brought down from London and had put at the back of the fridge. Meanwhile Teddy rang, or tried to ring, Par station, with no result. They did not answer.

"You know what," he said, "the Professor may have been kidnapped by some organisation in search of secret documents."

"Very likely," I said. "I'll give him half-an-hour longer and then ring Scotland Yard."

"Or had a heart attack," suggested Micky, "flogging up Polmear hill. Mrs. Collins told me her grandfather died walking up it thirty years ago when he missed the bus."

I pushed aside my plate and swallowed the last drop of whisky.

"You're perspiring again, darling," said Vita. "I can't say I blame you. But don't you think it might be a good idea if you went up and changed your shirt?"

I took the hint and left the dining room, pausing at the top of the stairs to glance into the spare room. Why the hell hadn't Magnus telephoned to say what he was doing, or at least written a note instead of giving the guard a verbal message that had probably been garbled anyway? I drew the curtains and switched on the bedside light, which made the room look more snug. Magnus's suitcase was lying on the chair at the bottom of the bed, and I tried the hasps. To my surprise it opened.

Magnus, unlike myself, was a methodical packer. Sky-blue pyjamas and paisley dressing gown reposed beneath a top layer of tissue paper, with blue leather bedroom slippers in their own cellophane container alongside. A couple of suits, a change of underwear beneath. Well, it was not an hotel or a stately home; he could do his own unpacking. The only gesture from host to guest—or was it the other way round?—would be to place the pyjamas on the pillow and drape the dressing gown over the chair.

I took both out of the case, and saw that there was a long, buff-coloured envelope immediately beneath them, and typed upon it the words:

"Otto Bodrugan. Writ and Inquisition. 10.Oct.5
Edward III. (1331)"

The student must have been at work again. I sat down on the edge of the bed and opened the envelope. It was a copy of a document giving the names of the various manors and lands owned by Otto Bodrugan at the time of his death. The manor of Bodrugan was amongst them, but he apparently paid rent for it to Joanna, "Relict of Henry de Campo Arnulphi" (which must be Champernoune). A further paragraph followed: "Henry his son, aged twenty-one years and more, was his next heir, who died three weeks after his said father, so that he had no seisin in the inheritance aforesaid, nor did he know of his father's death. William son of the aforesaid Otto, and brother of the said Henry, aged twenty years on the morrow of the feast of St. Giles last, is his next heir."

It was a strange sensation, sitting there on the bed, reading something I already knew. The monks had done their best, or perhaps their worst, for young Henry at the Priory, and he had not survived. I was glad he had never been told of his father's death.

There was another long list of properties which Henry, if he had lived, would have inherited from Otto, and then a further note, taken from the Calendar of Fine Rolls.

"Oct.10. Westminster. 1331. Order to the escheator on this side Trent to take into the King's hand the lands late of Otto de Bodrugan, deceased, tenant-in-chief".

The student had scribbled PTO at the bottom of the page, and turning over I found a half-page attached, also taken from the Calendar of Fine Rolls, and dated Nov. 14th, 1331, from Windsor.

"Order to the escheator on this side Trent to take into the King's hand the lands late of John de Carminowe, deceased, tenant in chief. The like to the same touching the lands of Henry son of Otto de Bodrugan."

So Sir John must have caught the infection he had so greatly feared and died immediately, and Joanna had lost her choice of a second husband . . .

I forgot the present, forgot the mix-up at the station, and sat there on the spare-room bed thinking about the other world, wondering what advice, if any, Roger had given to the disappointed Joanna Champernoune. The two Bodrugan deaths, with the successor her nephew and a minor, must have given her every hope of greater power over the Bodrugan lands, and just as the power was within her grasp she found the tables turned, and the Keeper of Restormel and Tremerton castles gone as well. I felt almost sorry for her. And for Sir John, who, luckless fellow, had held his hand-kerchief to his mouth in vain. Who would take his place as keeper of castles, woods and parks in the county of Cornwall? Not his brother Oliver, I hoped, the bloody murderer . . .

"What are you going to do?" Vita called up the stairs.

Do? What could I do? Oliver had ridden off with his gang of thugs leaving Roger to take care of Isolda. I still did not know what had happened to Isolda . . .

I heard Vita coming up the stairs, and instinctively I put the papers back in the envelope and stuffed them in my pocket, closing the suitcase. I must switch myself back to the present. This was not the moment to become confused.

"I was just getting out Magnus's pyjamas and dressing gown," I said as she came into the room. "He'll be pretty well fagged out when he does turn up."

"Why not run his bath for him as well?" she countered. "And lay a tray for early morning tea? I didn't notice you being so attentive a host to Bill and Diana."

I ignored the sarcasm and went along to my dressing room. The murmur of the television came from the library below. "Time those boys went to bed," I said, without conviction.

"I promised them they could wait up for the Professor," said Vita, "but really I think you're right, there's not much point in their hanging about any longer. Don't you think you ought to drive down to Par? He might be in some pub getting blind to the world."

"Magnus isn't the type to hang about in pubs."

"Well then, he must have come across old friends and has been taking dinner off them instead of us."

"Very unlikely. And damn rude not to telephone," I replied. We went together down the stairs and into the hall, and I added, "Anyway, he doesn't have any local friends, to my knowledge."

Vita suddenly gave a little cry. "I know," she said, "he's met the Carminowes! They haven't got a telephone. That's what's happened. He must have run into them at Par, and they took him back to dine with them."

I stared at her, my brain confused. What on earth was she talking about? And suddenly I knew. Suddenly the message from the guard came clear and full of meaning. "Owner of suitcase, Professor Lane, gave message to guard that he had changed his mind and decided to get out at Par, and walk from there. Told guard Mr. Young would understand."

Magnus had taken the local connection from Bodmin Road to Par because it would travel more slowly through the Treesmill valley than the express. He knew, from my description, that he had only to look left and up, after passing above Treesmill Farm, to see the Gratten. Then, because it was still light when the train arrived at Par, he would have walked up the Tywardreath Road and cut across the fields to inspect the site.

"God!" I exclaimed. "What a fool I've been! It never entered my head. Of course that's it."

"You mean he's gone to see the Carminowes?" said Vita.

I suppose I was tired. I suppose I was excited. I suppose I was relieved. All three in one, and I could not bother to explain or think up some different lie. The most natural thing to say just tripped off my tongue.

"Yes," I replied. I ran down the steps and across the front path to the car.

"But you don't know where they live!" called Vita.

I did not answer. I waved my hand and leapt into the car, and in a moment I was tearing up the drive and out on to the road.

It was quite dark, with only a waning moon that did not help, but I took the short cut up the lane skirting the village, meeting no one on the way, and parked in the lay by near the house called Hill Crest. If Magnus found the car before I found him he would recognise it, and wait for me. It was hard going across the field to the Gratten, stumbling about amongst the banks and mounds, and I shouted for him, once I was well out of earshot of the house, but he did not answer. I covered the site thoroughly, but there was no sign of him. I walked along the lower path to the valley itself, and down to Treesmill Farm, but he was not there either. Then I walked up the road to the top of the hill and back to the car. It was as I had left it, empty. I drove down into the village, and walked round the churchyard. The hands on the clock face said after half-past eleven; I had been searching for Magnus for over an hour.

I went to the telephone box near the hairdresser and dialled Kilmarth. Vita answered immediately. "Any luck?" she asked.

My heart sank. I had hoped he might have arrived home. "No, not a trace of him."

"What about the Carminowes? Did you find their house?"

"No," I said, "no, I think we were on the wrong track there. It was stupid of me. Actually, I've no idea where they live."

"Well, someone must know," she said. "Why don't you ask the police?"

"No," I said, "it wouldn't do any good. Look, I'll drive down the village to the station and then come slowly home. There's nothing more I can do."

But Par station appeared to be closed for the night, and though I circled Par itself twice there was no sign of Magnus.

I began to pray, "Oh, God, let me see him walking up Polmear hill!" I knew just how he would look, my headlights picking him up at the side of the road, the tall angular figure with a loping stride, and I would hoot loudly and he would stop, and I would say to him, "What the bloody hell . . ."

He was not there, though. There was no one there. I turned down the Kilmarth drive, and walked slowly up the steps and into the house. Vita was waiting for me by the porch. She looked distressed.

"Something must have happened to him," she said. "I do think you ought to ring up the police."

I brushed past her and went upstairs. "I'll unpack his things," I said. "He may have left a note. I don't know . . ."

I took his clothes out of the suitcase and hung them in the wardrobe, and put his shaving tackle in the bathroom. I kept telling myself that any moment I should hear a car coming down the drive, a taxi, and Magnus would jump out of it, laughing, and Vita would call up the stairs to me, "He's here, he's arrived!"

There was no note. I felt in all the pockets. Nothing. Then I turned to the dressing gown, which I had unpacked already. My hand closed upon something round in the left-hand pocket, and I drew it out. It was a small bottle, which I recognised at once. It bore a label: B. It was the bottle I had posted to him the week before, and it was empty.

16

I went along to my dressing room, found my own suitcase, put the bottle in one of the pockets and the documents about Bodrugan as well, locked the case and joined Vita downstairs.

"Did you find anything?" she asked.

I shook my head. She followed me into the music room and I poured myself a whisky. "You'd better have one too," I said.

"I don't feel like it," she answered. She sat down on the sofa and lit a cigarette. "I'm quite certain we ought to ring the police."

"Because Magnus has taken it into his head to roam the countryside?" I queried. "Nonsense, he knows what he's doing. He must know every inch of the district for miles around."

The clock in the dining room struck midnight. If Magnus had left the train at Par, he had been walking for four and a half hours . . .

"You go to bed," I said. "You look exhausted. I'll stay down here in case he comes. I can lie on the sofa if I feel like it. Then as soon as it's light, if I'm awake and he hasn't arrived, I'll go out in the car and have another search."

It was true, she looked all-in: I was not trying to get rid of her. She stood up uncertainly, and wandered towards the door. Then she looked back at me, over her shoulder.

"There's something odd about all this," she said slowly. "I have a feeling you know more than you say." I had no ready answer. "Well, try and get some sleep," she went on. "Something tells me you're going to need it."

I heard the bedroom door shut, and stretched myself out on the sofa with my hands behind my head, trying to think. There were only two solutions. The first, as I had originally imagined, that Magnus had decided to find the Gratten site, and had either lost his way or ricked his ankle, and so decided to wait where he was until daylight; or the second . . . and the second was the one I feared. Magnus had gone on a trip. He had poured the contents of bottle B into some container that could be carried in a coat pocket, and had got out of the train at Par and walked—to the Gratten, to the church, anywhere in the district, and then swallowed the drug and waited . . . waited for it to take effect. Once this had happened he would not be responsible for his actions. If time took him into that other world that we both knew he would not necessarily witness what I had witnessed, the scene could be different, the point in time earlier or later, but the penalty for touching anyone, as he well knew, would be the same for both of us; nausea, vertigo, confusion. Magnus had not, as far as I knew, touched the drug for at least three or four months; he, the inventor, was not prepared and might not have the stamina to endure it as I, the guinea pig, could.

I closed my eyes and tried to picture him walking away from the station, up the hill and across the fields to the Gratten, and swallowing the drug, laughing to himself. "I've stolen a march on Dick!" Then the leap backwards in time, and the estuary below, the walls of the house about him, Roger close at hand—leading him where? To what strange encounter on the hills or beside the strand? To what month, what year? Would he see, as I had seen, the faltering ship, dismasted, enter the creek, the horsemen riding on the opposite hill? Would he see Bodrugan drowned? If so, his actions might not be the same as mine. Knowing his taste for the dramatic, he might have flung himself headlong into the river and struck out for that opposite shore—and there would have been no river, only the smothered valley, the scrub, the marsh, the trees. Magnus could be lying there now, in that impassable waste land, shouting for help, and none to hear. There was nothing I could do. Nothing until daylight came.

I did sleep, after a fashion, waking with a jerk from some distorted dream that instantly faded, to fall off again once more. A deeper sleep must have come with the first light, for I remember looking at my watch at half-past five and telling myself another twenty minutes would not hurt, and then when I opened my eyes again it was ten past seven.

I made a cup of tea, then crept upstairs and washed and shaved. Vita was already awake. She did not even question me. She knew Magnus had not come.

"I'm going to Par station," I said. "They'll know if he handed the ticket in. Then I'll try and trace his movements from there. Somebody must have seen him."

"It would be so much simpler," she insisted, "if you went direct to the police."

"I will go to them," I said, "if no one can tell me anything at the station."

"If you don't," she called as I left the room, "I shall ring them up myself."

I drew a blank at the station: a chap wandering about told me the booking office would not be open for half an hour. I filled in the time by walking up to the bridge that spanned the railway line and gave a view of the valley. Once this would have been wide estuary; Bodrugan's ship, dismasted by the gale, would have drifted past this very spot, driven by wind and tide, seeking shelter up the creek and finding death instead. Today, part reedy marsh, part scrub, it was still easy enough to trace the original course of the river from the winding valley itself. A man, sick or in some way hurt, might lie beneath those stubby, close-packed trees for days, for weeks, and no one know of it. Even the marsh ground on which the station stood, the wide, flat expanse between Par and neighbouring St. Blazey, was still waste land to a large extent; even here there were large tracks where no one wandered. Except, perhaps, a traveller in time whose mind trod a vessel's deck upon blue water while his body stumbled amongst scrub and ditch.

I returned to the station and found the booking office open, and for the first time proof that Magnus had arrived. The clerk had not only taken his ticket but remembered the holder of it. Tall, he said, going grey, hatless, wearing a sports jacket and dark trousers, with a pleasant smile, and carrying a stick. No, the clerk had not seen which way he had gone after leaving the station.

I got into the car and drove halfway up the hill, to where a footpath went off to the left. Magnus could have taken it, and I did the same, striking across country to the Gratten. It was warm and misty, foretelling a hot day. The farmer the land belonged to must have opened a gate somewhere since the preceding night, because cows wandered on the hillside now, amongst the gorse bushes and the mounds, following me in curiosity to the entrance of the overgrown quarry itself.

I searched it thoroughly, every corner, every dip, but found nothing. I looked down into the valley below, across the intervening railway line, to the sweeping mass of trees and bushes covering the one-time river bed. They might have been woven tapestry, coloured with silken threads in every shade of golden green. If Magnus was there, nothing would ever find him but tracker dogs.

Then I knew I must do what I should have done earlier, what I should have done last night. I must go to the police. I must go, as any other man would go whose guest had failed to arrive over twelve hours earlier, though his ticket had been given up at the station at the correct time.

I remembered there was a police station at Tywardreath, and I wound my weary way back again and drove straight there. I felt inadequate, guilty, like all persons who have been lucky enough never to have found themselves involved with the police, beyond minor traffic offences, and my story, as I told it to the sergeant, sounded shamefaced, somehow, irresponsible.

"I want to report a missing person," I said, and instantly had a vision of a poster with the haunted face of a criminal staring from it, and the word WANTED in enormous letters underneath. I pulled myself together, and told the exact story of all that had happened the preceding day.

The sergeant was helpful, sympathetic and extremely kind. "I haven't had the pleasure of meeting Professor Lane personally," he said, "but we know all about him, of course. You must have had a very anxious night."

"Yes," I said.

"There's been no report to us of any accident," he said, "but of course I will check with Liskeard and St. Austell. Would you like a cup of tea, Mr. Young?"

I accepted the offer gratefully, while he got busy on the telephone. I had the sick feeling at the pit of my stomach that people get waiting outside a hospital ward during an emergency operation performed on someone they love. It was out of my hands. There was nothing I could do. Presently he came back.

"There's been no report of any accident," he said. "They're alerting the patrol cars in the district, and the other police stations. I think the best thing you can do, sir, is to go back to Kilmarth and wait there until you hear from us. It could be that Professor Lane twisted an ankle and spent the night at one of the farms, but they're mostly on the telephone these days, and it's strange he shouldn't have rung you up to let you know. No previous history of loss of memory, I suppose?"

"No," I told him, "never. And he was very fit when I dined with him in London a few weeks ago."

"Well, don't worry too much, sir," he said, "there'll probably be some simple explanation at the end of it."

I went back to the car, the sick feeling with me still, and drove down to the church. I could hear the organ—they must have been having choir practice. I went and sat on one of the graves near the wall above the orchard—Priory orchard once. Where I sat would have been the monks' dormitory, looking south over the Priory creek; and close at hand was the guest chamber where young Henry Bodrugan had died of smallpox. In that other time he could be dying still. In that other time the monk, Jean, could be mixing some hell-brew that finished off the business, then sending word to Roger that he must carry the news to the mother and the aunt, Joanna Champernoune. Ill tidings were all about me, in the other world and in my own. Roger, the monk, young Bodrugan, Magnus; we were all links in an interwoven chain, bound one to the other through the centuries.

> *"In such a night*
> *Medea gather'd the enchanted herbs*
> *That did renew old Aeson."*

Magnus could have sat here and taken the drug. He could have gone to any of the places where I had been. I drove down to the farm where Julian Polpey had lived six centuries ago, and where the postman had found me a week ago, and walked down the farm track to Lampetho. If I had traversed the marsh at night, my body in the present, my brain in the past, Magnus could have done the same. Even now, with no water and no tide filling the inlet, only meadow marsh and reeds, the route was familiar, like some scene from a forgotten dream. The track petered out, though, into marsh, and I could see no way forward, no means of crossing the valley to the other side. How I had done it myself at night, following, in that earlier world, Otto and the other conspirators, God only knew. I retraced my footsteps past Lampetho Farm, and an old man came out of one of the buildings, calling to his dog, who ran towards me, barking. He asked if I had lost my way and I told him no, and apologised for trespassing.

"You didn't by any chance see anyone walking this way last night?" I asked. "A tall man, grey-haired, carrying a stick?"

He shook his head. "We don't get many visitors coming here," he said. "Doesn't lead anywhere, just to this farm. Visitors stay mostly on Par beach."

I thanked him and walked back to the car. I was not convinced, though. He could have been indoors between half-past eight and nine; Magnus could be lying in the marsh below his farm . . . But surely someone would have seen him? The effect of the drug, if he had taken it, would have worn off hours ago; if he had taken it at half-past eight, or nine, he would have come to by ten, by eleven, by midnight.

There was a police car drawn up outside the house when I arrived, and as I entered the hall I heard Vita say, "Here's my husband now."

She was in the music room with a police officer' and a constable.

"I'm afraid we've no definite news for you, Mr. Young," the Inspector said, "only a slight clue, which may lead us to something. A man answering to the description of Professor Lane was seen last evening between nine and half-past walking along the Stonybridge lane above Treesmill past Trenadlyn Farm."

"Trenadlyn Farm?" I repeated, and the surprise must have shown in my face, for he said quickly, "You know it, then?"

"Why, yes," I said, "it's much higher up the valley than Treesmill, it's the small farm right on the lane itself."

"That's right. Have you any idea why Professor Lane should have been walking in that particular direction, Mr. Young?"

"No," I said with hesitation. "No . . . There was nothing to take him there. I would have expected him to be walking lower down the valley, nearer to Treesmill."

"Well," the Inspector replied, "our information is that a gentleman was seen walking past Trenadlyn between nine and half-past. Mrs. Richards, wife of Mr. Richards who owns the farm, saw him from her window, but her brother, who farms

Great Treverran, higher up the lane saw no one. If Professor Lane was walking to Kilmarth it seems a long way round, even for someone who wanted exercise after sitting in a train."

"Yes, I agree. Inspector," I went on hesitantly, "Professor Lane is very interested in historical sites, and this may have been the reason for his walk. I think he was looking for an old manor house which he believes stood there once. But it couldn't have been either of the farms you mentioned, or he would have called at one of them."

I knew now why Magnus—and it must have been Magnus, from the woman's description—was walking past Trenadlyn on the Stonybridge lane. It was the route Isolda had taken on horseback with Robbie, when the two of them had come riding down to Treesmill to the creek, to find Bodrugan murdered, drowned. It was the only route to the unknown Tregest when the ford across Treesmill was impassable through flood or high tide. Magnus, when he passed Trenadlyn farm, was walking in time. He could have been following Roger, and Isolda too.

Vita, unable to contain herself, turned to me impulsively. "Darling, all this historical business is beside the point. Please don't be angry with me for butting in, but I feel it's essential." She turned to the Inspector. "I'm quite sure, and so was my husband last night, that the Professor was going to call on some old friends of his, people called Carminowe. Oliver Carminowe is not on the telephone, but he does live somewhere in that district, where the Professor was last seen. It's quite obvious to me that he was on his way to call on them, and the sooner somebody contacts them the better."

There was a momentary silence after her outburst. Then the Inspector glanced at me. His expression changed from concern to surprise, even disapproval.

"Is that so, Mr. Young? You said nothing about the possibility of Professor Lane visiting friends."

I felt my mouth flicker in a weak smile. "No, Inspector," I said, "of course not. There was no question of the Professor visiting anyone. I'm afraid my wife had her leg pulled over the telephone by the Professor, and I very foolishly did nothing to put her wise, but kept up the joke. There are no such people as Carminowe. They don't exist."

"Don't exist?" echoed Vita. "But you saw the children riding ponies on Sunday morning, two little girls with their nurse, you told me so."

"I know I did," I said, "but I can only repeat I was pulling your leg."

She stared at me in disbelief. I could tell, from the expression in her eyes, that she thought I was lying to get Magnus and myself out of an awkward situation. Then she shrugged her shoulders, flicked a rapid glance at the Inspector and lit a cigarette. "What a very stupid joke," she said, and added, "I beg your pardon, Inspector."

"Don't apologise, Mrs. Young," he said, rather more stiffly, I thought, than before. "We all get our legs pulled from time to time, especially in the police force." He turned again to me. "You're quite certain about that, Mr. Young? You know of no one whom Professor Lane might have been calling upon after he arrived at Par station?"

"Absolutely not," I said. "As far as I know we are his only friends here, and he was definitely coming to spend the weekend with us. The house belongs to him, as you know. He's lent it to us for the summer holidays. Quite frankly, Inspector, I was not really concerned about Professor Lane until this morning. He knows the district well, for his father, Commander Lane, had this house before him. I was sure he couldn't lose himself, and that he'd turn up with some plausible explanation of where he had been all night."

"I see," said the Inspector.

Nobody said anything for a moment, and I had the impression that he doubted my story, just as Vita did, and that they both thought Magnus had been bound on some doubtful assignation and I was covering up for him. Which, indeed, was true.

"I realise now," I said, "that I should have got in touch with you last night.

Professor Lane must have twisted his ankle, probably shouted for help, and nobody heard. There wouldn't have been much traffic up that side road once it was dark."

"No," the Inspector agreed, "but the people from Trenadlyn and Treverran would have been astir early this morning, and should have seen or heard something of him by now, if he had had some mishap on the road. More likely he walked up to the main road, and then he could have taken either direction, on towards Lostwithiel or back to Fowey."

"The name Tregest doesn't convey anything to you?" I asked cautiously.

"Tregest?" The Inspector thought a moment, then shook his head. "No, I can't say it does. Is it the name of a place?"

"I believe there was a farm of that name once, somewhere in the district. Professor Lane could have been trying to find it, in connection with his historical research." Then I suddenly had another idea. "Trelawn," I said, "where exactly is Trelawn?"

"Trelawn?" repeated the Inspector, surprised. "That's an estate a few miles from Looe. Must be eighteen miles or more from here. Professor Lane would surely not start to try to walk there around nine o'clock at night?"

"No," I said, "no, of course not. It's just that I'm trying to think of old houses of historical interest."

"Yes, but, darling," interrupted Vita, "as the Inspector says, Magnus would hardly start looking for something of that sort, miles away, without telephoning us first. That's what I can't understand, why he didn't attempt to telephone."

"He didn't telephone, Mrs. Young," said the Inspector, "because he apparently thought Mr. Young would know where he was going."

"Yes," I said, "and I didn't know. I don't know now. I only wish to God I did."

The telephone rang with startling suddenness, like an echo to our thoughts. "I'll get it," said Vita, who was nearest to the door. She crossed the hall to the library, and we stood there in the music room saying nothing, listening to her voice.

"Yes," she said briefly, "he is here. I'll get him."

She came back into the room and told the Inspector that the call was for him. We waited for what seemed an interminable three or four minutes, while he answered in monosyllables, his voice muffled. I looked at my watch. It was just on half-past twelve. I had not realised it was so late. When he returned he looked directly at me, and I saw from the expression on his face that something had happened.

"I'm very sorry, Mr. Young," he said, "I'm afraid it's bad news."

"Yes," I said, "tell me."

One is never prepared. One always believes, in moments of acute stress, that things will turn out all right, that even now, with Magnus missing for so long, it would surely be to say that someone had picked him up with loss of memory and taken him to hospital.

Vita came and stood beside me, her hand in mine.

"That was a message from Liskeard police station," said the Inspector. "Word has come through that one of our patrols has found the body of a man resembling Professor Lane near the railway line just this side of Treverran tunnel. He seems to have received a blow on the head from a passing train, unobserved by the driver or the guard. He managed, apparently, to crawl into a small disused hut just above the line, and then he collapsed. It looks as if he must have been dead for some hours."

I went on standing there, staring at the Inspector. Shock is a peculiar thing, numbing emotion. It was as though life itself had ebbed away, leaving me a shell, like Magnus. I was only aware of Vita holding my hand.

"I understand," I said, but it was not my voice. "What do you want me to do?"

"They are on their way to the mortuary in Fowey now, Mr. Young," he said. "I hate to trouble you at such a moment, but I think it would be best if we took you there right away to identify the body. I should like to think, for both your sakes, yours and Mrs. Young's, that it is not Professor Lane, but in the circumstances I can't offer you much hope."

"No," I said, "no, of course not."

I let go of Vita's hand and walked toward the door and out of the house into the hot sunlight. Some Scouts were putting up tents in the field beyond the Kilmarth meadow. I could hear them shouting and laughing, and hammering the pegs into the ground.

17

THE MORTUARY WAS a smallish, red-brick building not far from Fowey station. There was nobody there when we arrived: the second patrol car was still on its way. When I got out of the car the Inspector looked at me a moment, and then he said, "Mr. Young, there may be some delay. I'd like to offer you a cup of coffee and a sandwich at the café just up the road."

"Thank you," I said, "but I'm all right."

"I can't insist," he continued, "but it really would be wise. You'll feel the better for it."

I gave in, and allowed him to lead me along to the café, and we each had some coffee, and I had a ham sandwich too. As we sat there I thought of the times in the past, as undergraduates, when Magnus and I had travelled down by train to Par to stay with his parents at Kilmarth. The rattle in the darkness and the echo of sound in the tunnel, and suddenly that welcome emergence into the light, with green fields on either side. Magnus must have made that journey every school holiday as a boy. Now he had met his death by the entrance to that same tunnel.

It would make sense to no one. Not to the police, or to his many friends, or to anyone but myself. I should be asked why a man of his intelligence had wandered close to a railway line on a summer's evening at dusk, and I should have to say that I did not know. I did know. Magnus was walking in a time when no railway line existed. He was walking in an age when the hillside was rough pasture, even scrub. There was no gaping tunnel mouth yawning from the hillside in that other world, no metal lines, no track, only the bare grassland, and perhaps a man astride a pony, leading him on . . .

"Yes?" I said.

The Inspector was asking me if Professor Lane had any relatives.

"I'm sorry," I said, "I didn't hear what you said. No, Commander and Mrs. Lane have been dead for a number of years, and there were no other children. I've never heard him mention cousins or anyone."

There must be a lawyer somewhere who dealt with his affairs, a bank which managed his finances: now I came to think of it I did not even know his secretary's name. Our relationship, binding, intimate, did not concern itself with day-to-day matters, with ordinary concerns. There must be someone other than myself who would know about all this.

Presently the constable came to tell the Inspector that the second patrol car had arrived, and the ambulance too, and we walked back to the mortuary. The constable murmured something which I did not hear, and the Inspector turned to me.

"Dr. Powell from Fowey happened to be a Tywardreath police station when the message came through from our patrol," he said, "and he agreed to make a preliminary examination of the body. Then it will be up to the Coroner's pathologist to conduct the post-mortem."

"Yes," I said. Post-mortem . . . inquest . . . the whole paraphernalia of the law.

I went into the mortuary. The first person I saw was the doctor I had met at the lay by, who had watched me recovering from my attack of vertigo over ten days ago. I saw the instant recognition in his eyes, but he did not let on when the Inspector introduced us.

"I'm sorry about this," he said, and then, abruptly, "If you haven't seen anyone before who's been badly smashed up in an accident, let alone a friend, it's not a pleasant sight. This man has had a great gash on the head."

He took me to the stretcher lying on the long table. It was Magnus, but he looked different—smaller, somehow. There was a sort of cavity caked with blood above his right eye. There was dried blood on his jacket, which was torn, and a tear in one of his trouser legs.

"Yes," I said, "yes, that is Professor Lane."

I turned away, because Magnus himself wasn't there. He was still walking in the fields above the Treesmill valley, or looking about him, in greater wonder, in some other undiscovered world.

"If it's any consolation to you," said the doctor, "he couldn't have lived very long after receiving a blow like that. God knows how he managed to crawl the few yards to the hut—he wouldn't have been conscious of his movements, he would have died literally a few moments afterwards."

Nothing was a consolation, but I thanked him all the same. "You mean," I said, "he would not have lain there, wondering why nobody came?"

"No," he answered, "definitely not. But I'm sure the Inspector will let you have the full details, as soon as we know the extent of the injuries."

There was a walking stick lying at the end of the table. The sergeant pointed it out to the Inspector. "The stick was lying halfway down the embankment, sir," he said, "a short distance from the hut."

The Inspector looked enquiringly at me, and I nodded. "Yes," I said, "it's one of many he had. His father collected walking sticks; there are about a dozen in his flat in London."

"I think the best thing to do now is for us to run you straight back to Kilmarth, Mr. Young," said the Inspector. "You'll be kept fully informed, of course. You realise that you will be required to give evidence at the inquest."

"Yes," I said. I wondered what would happen to Magnus's body after the post-mortem. I wondered if it was going to lie there through the weekend. Not that it mattered. Not that anything mattered.

As the Inspector shook hands he said that they would probably come out on Monday and ask me a few more questions, in case I could add to my original statement. "You see, Mr. Young," he explained, "there might be a question of amnesia, or even suicide."

"Amnesia," I repeated. "That's loss of memory, isn't it? Most unlikely. And suicide, definitely no. The Professor was the last man in the world to do such a thing, and he had no cause. He was looking forward to the weekend, and was in very good spirits when I spoke to him on the telephone."

"Quite so," said the Inspector. "Well, that's just the sort of statement the Coroner will want to have from you."

The constable dropped me at the house, and I walked very slowly through the garden and up the steps. I poured out the equivalent of a triple whisky, and flung myself on the divan bed in the dressing room. I must have passed out shortly afterwards, for when I woke up it was late afternoon or early evening, and Vita was sitting on the chair nearby with a book in her hands, the last of the sun coming through the western window that gave on to the patio.

"What's the time?" I asked.

"About half-after six," she said, and came and sat on the bed beside me.

"I thought it wisest to let you lie," she went on. "The doctor who saw you at the mortuary telephoned during the afternoon, and asked if you were all right, and I told him you were sleeping. He said to let you sleep as long as possible, it was the best thing that could happen." She put her hand in mine and it was comforting, like being a child again.

"What did you do with the boys?" I asked. "The house seems very quiet."

"Mrs. Collins was wonderful," she said. "She took them down to Polkerris to spend the day with her. Her husband was going to take them fishing after lunch and bring them back about seven. They'll be home any moment now."

I was silent a moment, and then I said, "This mustn't spoil their holiday, Magnus would have hated that."

"Don't bother about them or me," she said. "We can take care of ourselves. What worries me is the shock it's been for you."

I was thankful she did not pursue the subject, go over the whole business again—why it had happened, what Magnus had been doing, why he did not notice the approaching train, why the driver had not seen him; it would have led us nowhere.

"I ought to get on the telephone," I said. "The people at the university should be told."

"The nice Inspector is taking care of all of that," she said. "He came back again, quite soon after you must have gone upstairs. He asked to see Magnus's suitcase. I told him you'd unpacked it last night and hadn't found anything. He didn't either. He left the clothes hanging in the closet."

I remembered the bottle in my own suitcase, and the papers about Bodrugan. "What else did he want?"

"Nothing. Just said to leave everything to them, and he'd be in touch with you on Monday."

I put out my arms and pulled her down to me. "Thanks for everything, darling," I said. "You're a great comfort. I can't really think straight yet."

"Don't try," she whispered. "I wish there was more I could say, or do."

We heard the boys talking together in their room. They must have come in by the back entrance. "I'll go to them," said Vita, "they'll want some supper. Would you like me to bring yours up here?"

"No, I'll come down. I'll have to face them some time."

I went on lying there awhile, watching the last of the sun filtering through the trees. Then I had a bath and changed. Despite the shock and the turmoil of the day my bloodshot eye was back to normal. The trouble may have been coincidental, nothing to do with the drug. In any event it was something, now, that I should never know.

Vita was giving the boys their supper in the kitchen. I could hear what they were saying as I hovered in the hall, bracing myself before I went in.

"Well, I bet you anything you like it turns out to be foul play." Teddy's rather high-pitched, nasal voice came clearly through the open kitchen door. "It stands to reason the Professor had some secret scientific information on him, probably to do with germ warfare, and he'd arranged to meet someone near that tunnel, and the man he met was a spy and knocked him on the head. The police down here won't think of that, and they'll have to bring in the Secret Service."

"Don't be idiotic, Teddy," said Vita sharply. "That's just the sort of frightful way rumours spread. It would upset Dick terribly to hear you say things like that. I hope you didn't suggest such a thing to Mr. Collins."

"Mr. Collins thought of it first," chimed in Mickey. "He said you never knew what scientists were up to these days, and the Professor might have been looking for a site for a hush-hush research station up the Treesmill valley."

This conversation had the instant effect of pulling me together. I thought how Magnus would have loved it, played up to it, too, encouraged every exaggeration. I coughed loudly and went towards the kitchen, hearing Vita say "Ssh . . ." as I passed through the door.

The boys looked up, their small faces taking on the expression of shy discomfort that children wear when suddenly confronted with what they fear to be an adult plunged in grief.

"Hullo," I said. "Had a good day?"

"Not bad," mumbled Teddy, turning red. "We went fishing."

"Catch anything?"

"A few whiting. Mom's cooking them now."

"Well, if you've any to spare, I'll stand in the queue. I had a cup of coffee and a sandwich in Fowey, and that's been my lot for the day."

They must have expected me to stand with bowed head and shaking shoulders, for they cheered visibly when I attacked a large wasp on the window with the fly swatter, saying "Got him!" with enormous relish as I squashed it flat. Later, when we were eating, I said to them, "I may be a bit tied up next week because they'll have to hold an inquest on Magnus, and there'll be various things to attend to, but I'll see to it that you go out with Tom in one of his boats from Fowey, engine or sailing, whichever you like best."

"Oh, thanks awfully," said Teddy, and Micky, realising that the subject of Magnus was no longer taboo, paused, his mouth full of whiting, and enquired brightly, "Will the Professor's life story be on TV tonight?"

"I shouldn't think so," I replied. "It's not as if he were a pop singer or a politician."

"Bad luck," he said. "Still, we'd better watch just in case."

There was nothing, much to the disappointment of both boys, and secretly, I suspected, of Vita too, but to my own considerable relief. I knew the next few days would bring more than enough in the way of publicity, once the press got hold of the story, and so it proved. The telephone started ringing first thing the following morning, although it was Sunday, and either Vita or I spent most of the day answering it. Finally we left it off the hook, and installed ourselves on the patio, where reporters, if they rang the front-door bell, would never find us.

The next morning she took the boys into Par to do some shopping, leaving me to my mail, which I had not opened. The few letters I had were nothing to do with the disaster. Then I picked up the last of the small pile and saw, with a queer stab of the heart, that it was addressed to me in pencil, bore an Exeter postmark, and was in Magnus's handwriting. I tore it open.

"Dear Dick," I read, "I'm writing this in the train, and it will probably be illegible. If I find a post box handy on Exeter station I'll drop it in. There is probably no need to write at all, and by the time you receive it on Saturday morning we shall have had, I trust, an uproarious evening together with many more to come, but I write as a safety measure, in case I pass out in the carriage from sheer exuberance of spirits. My findings to date are pretty conclusive that we are on to something of prime importance regarding the brain. Briefly, and in layman's language, the chemistry within the brain cells concerned with memory, everything we have done from infancy onwards, is reproducible, returnable, for want of a better term, in these same cells, the exact content of which depends upon our hereditary make-up, the legacy of parents, grandparents, remoter ancestors back to primeval times. The fact that I am a genius and you are a lay-about depends solely upon the messages transmitted to us from these cells and then distributed through the various other cells and throughout our body, but, our various characteristics apart, the particular cells I have been working upon—which I will call the memory box—store not only our own memories but habits of the earlier brain pattern we inherit. These habits, if released to consciousness, would enable us to see, hear, become cognoscent of things that happened in the past, not because any particular ancestor witnessed any particular scene, but because with the use of a medium—in this case a drug—the inherited, older brain pattern takes over and becomes dominant. The implications from a historian's point of view don't concern me, but, biologically, the potential uses of the hitherto untapped ancestral brain are of enormous interest, and open immeasurable possibilities.

"As to the drug itself, yes, it's dangerous, and could be lethal if taken to excess, and should it fall into the hands of the unscrupulous it might bring even more havoc upon our already troubled world. So, dear boy, if anything happens to me, destroy what remains in Bluebeard's chamber. My staff—who, however, know nothing of the implications of my discovery, for I have been working on this on my own—have similar instructions here in London, and can be trusted implicitly. As to yourself, if I don't see you again, forget the whole business. If we meet this evening as arranged, and take a walk and perhaps a trip together, as I hope we shall, I intend to have a close look, if I have the luck, at the beautiful Isolda, who, from the evidence in the document at the top of my suitcase, appears to have lost her lover just as you said, and must be in dire need of consolation. Whether Roger Kylmerth can supply it we may discover at the same time. No time to say any more, we are drawing into Exeter. Abientôt, in this world, or the other, or hereafter.

"MAGNUS."

If we had not gone sailing on the Friday I should have found the telephone message about the earlier train in time . . . If I had made straight for the Gratten after leaving St. Austell station, instead of going home . . . Too many "ifs," and none of them working out. Even this letter, coming now like a message from the dead, should have reached me on Saturday morning instead of today, Monday. Not that it would have done any good. Nor did it say anything about Magnus's real intentions. Even then, as he posted it, he may not have made up his mind. The letter was a safety measure, as he said, in case anything went wrong. I read it through again, once, twice, then put my lighter to it and watched it burn.

I went down to the basement and through the old kitchen to the lab. I had not entered it since early Wednesday morning, after returning from the Gratten, when Bill had come downstairs and found me making tea in the kitchen. The rows of jars and bottles, the monkey's head, the embryo kittens and the fungus plants held no menace for me now, nor had they done so since the first experiment. Now, with their magician gone, never to return, they had a wasted, almost a forlorn appearance, like puppets and props from a conjurer's bag of tricks. No ebony wand would bring these things to life, no cunning hand extract the juices, pick the bones and set them fermenting in some bubbling cauldron brew.

I took the jars which held various liquids and poured the contents down the sink. Then I washed the jars out and put them back on the shelf. They could have been used for preserving fruit or jam, for all anybody would ever know; there were no distinctive marks upon them—only labels which I stripped off and pocketed. Then I fetched an old sack which I remembered seeing in the boiler house, and set about unscrewing the remaining jars and bottles that contained the embryos and the monkey's head. I put them all in the sack, having first poured down the sink the liquid that had preserved them, taking care that none of it touched my hands. I did the same with the various fungi, putting them also in the sack. Only two small bottles remained, bottle A, containing the remains of the drug I had been using myself to date, and bottle C, untouched. Bottle B I had sent to Magnus, and it was lying empty in my suitcase upstairs. I did not pour the contents of either down the sink. I put them in my pocket. Then I went to the door and listened. Mrs. Collins was moving about between the kitchen and the pantry—I could hear her radio going.

I swung the sack over my shoulder and locked the door of the lab. Then I went out through the back door and climbed up to the kitchen garden behind the stable block, and into the wood at the top of the grounds. I went to where the undergrowth was thickest, straggling laurels, rhododendrons that had not bloomed for years, broken branches of dead trees, brambles, nettles, the fallen leaves of successive autumn gales, and I took one of the dead branches and scraped a pit in the wet, dank earth and emptied the sack into it, smashing the monkey's head with a jagged stone so that it no longer bore any resemblance to a living thing, only fragments, only jelly, and the embryos slithered amongst the fragments, unrecognisable, like the stringy entrails flung to a seagull when a fish is gutted. I covered them, and the sack, with the rotting leaves of years, and the brown earth, and a heap of nettles, and the sentence came into my mind, "Ashes to ashes, dust to dust," and in a sense it was as if I were burying Magnus and his work as well.

I went back into the house, through the basement, and up the little side stairway to the front, thus avoiding Mrs. Collins, but she must have heard me entering the hall, for she called, "Is that you, Mr. Young?"

"Yes," I said.

"I looked for you everywhere—I couldn't find you. The Inspector from Liskeard was on the telephone."

"I was in the garden," I told her. "I'll ring him back."

I went upstairs to the dressing room, and put bottles A and C in my suitcase along with the empty bottle B, locked it once again, put the key on my ring, washed, and went downstairs to the library. Then I put a call through to the police station at St. Austell.

"I'm sorry, Inspector," I said, when they got him on the line. "I was in the garden when you telephoned."

"That's all right, Mr. Young," he said. "I thought you would like to know the news to date. Well, we've made some headway. It was a freight train that caused the accident, that seems to be clearly established. It passed through Treverran tunnel, going up the line, at approximately ten minutes to ten. The driver saw no one near the line as he approached the tunnel, but these freight trains are sometimes of considerable length, and this one carried no guard in the rear, so that once the engine had entered the tunnel there would be no one to observe whether anybody came on to the line and was struck by one of the passing waggons."

"No," I said, "no, I appreciate that. And you think this is what happened?"

"Well, Mr. Young, everything points to it. It would seem as though Professor Lane must have continued up the lane past Trenadlyn Farm, but before he got to the main road he turned off into a field they call Higher Gum, well above Treverran, and crossed it in a diagonal direction towards the railway. It is possible, by climbing through the wire and scrambling up a bank, to get onto the line, but anyone doing so could not have failed to notice the freight train. It was dark, of course, but there is a signal just outside the tunnel, and a freight train is far from silent, quite apart from the warning hoot of the diesel engine, which is routine procedure before entering the tunnel."

Yes, but six centuries ago there were no signals, no wire, no lines, no warning hoots sounding on the air . . .

"You mean," I said, "that anyone would have to be blind or stone-deaf not to be aware of a train coming up that valley, even when it is some distance off?"

"Well yes, Mr. Young. Of course, it is possible to stand at the side of the line as the train goes by—there is plenty of room on either side of the double tracks—and it would seem that this was what Professor Lane did. We have found marks on the ground where he slipped, and up the bank where he dragged himself to the hut."

I thought a moment, and then I said, "Inspector, would it be possible for me to go and see the exact spot myself?"

"As a matter of fact, Mr. Young, it was what I was going to suggest, but I was not sure how you would feel about it. It could be helpful, not only to you but to us."

"Then I'm ready whenever you are."

"Shall we say eleven-thirty outside the police station at Tywardreath?"

It was already eleven. I was backing my car out of the garage when Vita came down the drive in the Buick with the boys. They scrambled out, clutching baskets filled with provisions.

"Where are you going?" asked Vita.

"The Inspector wants me to see the spot near the tunnel where they found Magnus," I told her. "They think they know what did it—a freight train that passed there around ten minutes to ten. The driver would already have been in the tunnel when Magnus walked, or slipped, into one of the rear waggons."

"Run along," said Vita sharply to both boys, who were hovering. "Take those things up to Mrs. Collins," and when they were out of earshot, "But why should Magnus have been on the line? It makes no sense at all. You know what people are going to say? I heard it in one of the shops, and I felt dreadful . . . That it must have been suicide."

"Complete and utter drivel," I said.

"Well, I know . . . But when anyone is well-known, and there is a disaster, there's always such talk. And scientists are supposed to be peculiar anyway, borderline cases."

"So are we all," I said, "ex-publishers, policemen, the lot. Don't wait lunch—I don't know when I'll be back."

The Inspector took me to the site he had described over the telephone on the lane above Treverran Farm. On the way he told me that they had got in touch with the senior man on Magnus's staff, who had been unable to throw any light on the disaster.

"He was very upset, naturally," the Inspector went on. "He knew Professor Lane was intending to spend the weekend with you, and was looking forward to it. He concurred with you in stating that the Professor was in perfect health and excellent spirits. Incidentally, he did not seem to be aware of his interest in historical sites, but agreed that it could undoubtedly be a private hobby."

We took the Treesmill road out of Tywardreath and turned right at the Stonybridge lane, past Trenadlyn and Treverran, and drew up near the top of the lane, parking beside a gate leading into a field.

"What is difficult to understand," observed the Inspector, "is why, if Treverran Farm was the place that interested Professor Lane, he did not call there, instead of walking across these fields some distance above the farm."

I threw a quick glance around me. Treverran was to the left, above the valley but in a dip, with the railway running below it; and beyond the railway line itself the land sloped down again. Centuries ago the contour of the land would have been the same, but a broad stream would have run through the valley below Treverran Farm, more than a stream, a river, which in high autumn spate would flood the low-lying ground before it entered the waters of Treesmill creek.

"Is there a stream there still?" I asked, pointing to the valley base.

"Still?" repeated the Inspector, puzzled. "There is a ditch at the bottom of the hill, below the railway—you might call it a stream, rather sluggish—and the ground is marshy."

We walked down the field. The railway was already in sight, and just to the right of us was the ominous tunnel mouth.

"There might have been a road here once," I said, "descending to the valley, and a ford across the stream to the other side."

"Possibly," the Inspector said. "Not much sign of one now, though."

Magnus wanted to ford the stream. Magnus was following someone on horseback who was going to ford the stream. Therefore he moved swiftly. And it was not a summer's evening at dusk on a clear night: it was autumn, and the wind was blowing, and the rain was coming in gusts across the hills . . .

We descended the field to the railway embankment, close to the tunnel. A short distance to the left there was an archway under the line, forming a passage between one field and another. A number of cattle were standing here, under the arch, seeking shelter from the flies.

"You see," said the Inspector, "there's no need for the farmer or anyone to cross the line to get to the opposite field. They can go through the passageway there, where those cattle are standing."

"Yes," I said, "but the Professor might not have noticed it, if he was walking higher up the field. It would be more direct to cross the line itself."

"What, climb the embankment, get through the wire, and scramble down the bank on to the line?" he said. "And in the darkness too? I shouldn't care to try it myself."

In point of fact, it was what we did right then, in broad daylight. He led the way, I followed, and once over the wire he pointed to the disused hut, covered with ivy, a few yards higher up the embankment, just above the line.

"The undergrowth is beaten down because we were here yesterday," he told me, "but Professor Lane's tracks were plain enough, where he dragged himself clear of the line and up to the hut; semiconscious as he must have been, it showed almost superhuman strength and tremendous courage."

Which world had surrounded Magnus, the present or the past? Had the freight train rattled towards the tunnel unobserved, as he scrambled down the bank on to the line? With the engine already in the tunnel did he make to cross the line, which in his vision was grass-meadow still, sloping down to the stream below, and so was struck by the swinging waggon? In either world, it was the coup de grâce. He could not have known what hit him. The instinct for survival made him crawl towards the hut, and then, please God, merciful oblivion, no sudden loneliness, no knowledge of imminent death.

We stood there, staring into the empty hut, and the Inspector showed me the spot on the earthen floor where Magnus had died. The place was impersonal, without atmosphere, like some forgotten toolshed with the gardener long gone.

"It hasn't been used for years," he said. "The gangs working on the line used to brew tea here, and eat their pasties. They use the other hut lower down now, and that not often."

We turned away, retracing our footsteps along the overgrown bank to the strands of sagging wire through which we had climbed. I looked across to the opposite hills, some of them thickly wooded. There was a farm to the left, with a smaller building above it, and away to the north another cluster of buildings. I asked their names. The farm was Colwith, and the smaller building had been a schoolhouse once. The third, almost out of sight, was another farm, Strickstenton.

"We're on the borders of three parishes here," the Inspector said, "Tywardreath, St. Sampsons or Golant, and Lanlivery. Mr. Kendall of Pelyn is a big landowner hereabouts. Now that's a fine old manor house for you, Pelyn, just down the main road on the way to Lostwithiel. Been in the family for centuries."

"How many centuries?"

"Well, Mr. Young, I'm no expert. Four, maybe?"

Pelyn could not turn itself into Tregest. None of the names fitted Tregest. Somewhere here, though, within walking distance, Magnus had been following Roger to Oliver Carminowe's dwelling, whether it was manor house or farm.

"Inspector," I said, "even now, despite all you've shown me, I believe Professor Lane intended to find the head of the stream somewhere in the valley, and cross it to the other side."

"With what object, Mr. Young?" He looked at me, not unsympathetic but frankly curious, trying to see my point of view.

"If you get bitten by the past," I said, "whether you're a historian, or an archaeologist, or even a surveyor, it's like a fever in the blood; you never rest content until you've solved the problem before you. I believe that Professor Lane had one object in mind, and that was why he decided to get off at Par rather than St. Austell. He was determined to walk up this valley, for some reason which we shall probably never discover, despite the railway-line."

"And stood there, with the train passing, and then walked into the rear?"

"Inspector, I don't know. His hearing was good, his eyesight was good, he loved life. He didn't walk into the back of the train deliberately."

"I hope you'll convince the Coroner, Mr. Young, for Professor Lane's sake. You almost convince me."

"Almost?" I asked.

"I'm a policeman, Mr. Young, and there's a piece missing somewhere; but I agree with you, we shall probably never find it."

We retraced our steps up the long field to the gate at the top of the hill. As we drove back I asked him if he had any idea how long it would be before the inquest was held.

"I can't tell you exactly," he answered. "A number of factors are involved. The Coroner will do his best to expedite matters, but it may be ten days or a fortnight, especially as the Coroner is bound to sit with a jury, in view of the unusual circumstances of the death. By the way, the pathologist for the area is on holiday, and the Coroner asked Dr. Powell if he would perform the autopsy, as he had already examined the body. The doctor agreed. We should have his report some time today."

I thought of the many times Magnus had dissected animals, birds, plants, bringing to his work a cool detachment which I admired. He suggested once that I should watch him remove the organs of a newly slaughtered pig. I stood it for five minutes, and then my stomach turned. If anyone had to dissect Magnus now, I was glad it was Dr. Powell.

We arrived at the police station just as the constable came down the steps. He said something to the Inspector, who turned to me.

"We've finished the examination of Professor Lane's clothes and effects," he said. "We are prepared to hand them over to you if you are willing to accept the responsibility."

"Certainly," I replied. "I doubt if anyone else will claim them. I'm hoping to hear from his lawyer, whoever he may be."

The constable returned in a few minutes with a brown paper parcel. The wallet was separate, lying on the top, and a paperback he must have bought to read in the train, *Some Experiences of an Irish R.M.* by Somerville and Ross. Anything less conducive to a sudden brainstorm or attempted suicide I could not imagine.

"I hope," I said to the Inspector, "you've noted down the title of the book for the Coroner's attention."

He assured me gravely that he had already done so. I knew I should never open the paper parcel, but I was glad to have the wallet and the stick.

I drove back to Kilmarth feeling tired, dispirited, no nearer to a conclusion. Before I turned off the main road I stopped on the crown of Polmear hill to let a car pass. I recognised the driver—it was Dr. Powell. He pulled in at the side of the road by the grass verge, and I did the same. Then he got out and came to my window.

"Hullo," he said. "How are you feeling?"

"All right," I told him. "I've just been out to Treverran tunnel with the Inspector."

"Oh, yes," he said. "Did he tell you I'd done the post-mortem?"

"Yes," I said.

"My report goes to the Coroner," he went on, "and you'll know about it in due course. But, unofficially, you would probably like to know that it was the blow on the head that killed Professor Lane, causing extensive haemorrhage to the brain. There were other injuries too, due to falling; there's no doubt he must have walked slap into one of the waggons on the freight train."

"Thank you," I said. "It's good of you to tell me personally."

"Well," he said, "you were his friend, and the most directly concerned. Just one other thing. I had to send the contents of the stomach away for analysis. A matter of routine, actually. Just to satisfy the Coroner and jury he wasn't loaded with whisky or anything else at the time."

"Yes," I said, "yes, of course."

"Well, that's about it," he said. "I'll see you in Court."

He returned to his own car, and I went slowly down the drive to Kilmarth. Magnus drank sparingly in the middle of the day. He could conceivably have had a gin-and-tonic on the train. Possibly a cup of tea during the afternoon. This much, I supposed, would show up in analysis. What else?

I found Vita and the boys already at lunch. There had been a series of telephone calls throughout the morning, including one from Magnus's lawyer, a man called Dench, and Bill and Diana from Ireland, who had heard the news over the radio.

"It's going to be endless," said Vita. "Did the Inspector say anything about the inquest?"

"Probably not for ten days or a fortnight," I told her.

"Not much holiday for us," she sighed.

The boys went out of the room to collect their next course, and she turned to me, her face anxious. "I didn't say anything in front of them," she said in a low voice, "but Bill was aghast at the news, not just because it was such a tragedy anyway, but because he wondered if there was anything awful behind it. He wasn't specific, but he said you'd know what he meant."

I laid down my knife and fork. "Bill said what?"

"He was rather mysterious," she said, "but is it true you told him about some gang of thugs in the neighbourhood who were going about attacking people? He hoped you had told the police."

It only needed that, and Bill's ham-fisted misplaced efforts to help, to put us all in trouble.

"He's crazy," I said shortly. "I never told him anything of the sort."

"Oh," she said, "oh, well . . ." and then she added, her face still troubled, "I do hope you *have* told the Inspector everything you know."

The boys came back into the dining room and we finished the meal in silence. Afterwards I took the paper parcel, the wallet and the walking stick up to the spare room. Somehow they seemed to belong there, with the rest of the things hanging in the wardrobe. I would use the stick myself; it was the last thing that Magnus had ever held in his hands.

I remembered the collection at the flat. There had been a gun stick and a sword stick, a stick with a telescope at one end, and another with a bird's head on the handle. This one was comparatively simple, with the usual silver knob on top, engraved with Commander Lane's initials. He had been the originator of the craze for family walking sticks, and vaguely I had a recollection of him showing me this particular example, long ago, when I was staying at Kilmarth. It contained some gadget, I had forgotten what, but by pressing the knob down a spring was released. I tried it; nothing happened. I tried it again and then twisted the knob, and something clicked. I unwound the knob and it came away in my hands, and revealed a minute silver-lined measure, just large enough to hold a halfdram of spirit or other liquid. The measure had been wiped clean, probably by a tissue thrown away or buried, when Magnus set off upon his last walk, but I knew now, with absolute certainty, what it must have contained.

18

THE LAWYER, HERBERT Dench, telephoned again during the afternoon, and expressed great shock at his client's sudden death. I told him that the inquest was not likely to be for ten days or a fortnight, and suggested that he should leave the funeral arrangements to me, coming down himself on the morning of the cremation. This suited him, greatly to my relief, for he sounded what Vita called a "stuffed shirt," and with luck would have the tact to return by an afternoon train, which meant that he wouldn't be on our hands for more than a couple of hours or so.

"I would not trespass upon your time at all, Mr. Young," he said, "were it not out of respect for the late Professor Lane and the unhappy circumstances of his death, and for the fact that you are a beneficiary under his will."

"Oh," I said, rather taken aback, "I had not realised . . ." and hoped it would be the walking sticks.

"It is something I would prefer not to discuss over the telephone," he added.

It was not until I had put down the receiver that I realised I was in a somewhat awkward position, living in Magnus's house rent-free by verbal agreement. It might be the lawyer's intention to kick us out in the shortest possible time, immediately after the inquest, perhaps. The thought stunned me. Surely he would not do such a thing? I would offer to pay rent, of course, but he might bring up some objection, and say the place must be shut up, or handed over to agents prior to a sale. I was depressed and shaken enough, without the prospect of a sudden move to make things worse.

I spent the rest of the afternoon on the telephone, arranging about the funeral, after checking with the police that it was in order to go ahead, and finally ringing back the lawyer to tell him what I had arranged. None of it seemed to have anything to do with Magnus. What the undertaker did, what happened in the meantime to his body, the whole paraphernalia of death before committal to the flames, did not concern the man who had been my friend. It was as though he had become part of that separate world I knew, the world of Roger, of Isolda.

Vita came into the library when I had finished telephoning. I was sitting at Magnus's desk by the window, staring out to sea.

"Darling," she said, "I've been thinking," and she came and stood behind me, putting her hands on my shoulders. "When the inquest is over, don't you think it would be best if we went away? It would be rather awkward for us to go on staying here, and sad for you, and in a way the whole point of it has gone, hasn't it?"

"What point?" I asked.

"Well, the loan of the house, now Magnus is dead. I can't help feeling an interloper, and that we've really no right to be here. Surely it would be much more sensible if we spent the rest of the holidays somewhere else? It's only the beginning of August. Bill was saying over the telephone how lovely Ireland is; they've found a delightful hotel in Connemara, some old castle or other, with its own private fishing."

"I bet he has," I said. "Twenty guineas a night, and full of your compatriots."

"Don't be unfair! He was just trying to be helpful. He took it for granted you would want to get away from here."

"Well, I don't," I said. "Not unless the lawyer kicks us out, and that's a different matter."

I told her that the cremation was fixed for Thursday, and that Dench would be coming down, and perhaps some of Magnus's staff as well. The prospect of guests for lunch or dinner, or even the night, took her mind off the longer-term suggestion of Ireland, but as it turned out we were spared the worst of it, for Dench and Magnus's senior assistant, John Willis, elected to travel down together through the Wednesday night, attend the cremation, accept our hospitality for lunch, and return to London by a night train. The boys were sent off for the whole of Thursday for a fishing expedition in charge of the obliging Tom.

I remember little of the cremation service, beyond thinking how Magnus might have devised a simpler method of disposing of the dead by chemicals instead of by fire. Our companions in mourning, Herbert Dench and John Willis, were quite unlike what I had imagined. The lawyer was big, hearty, unpompous, ate an enormous lunch, and regaled us while we consumed our funeral meats with stories of Hindu widows committing suttee on their husbands' pyres. He had been born in India, and swore he had witnessed such a sacrifice as a babe in arms.

John Willis was a little mouse-like man, with intent eyes behind horn-rimmed spectacles, who would not have looked out of place behind a bank's grille; I could not picture him at Magnus's elbow, ministering to live monkeys or dissecting their brain cells. He barely uttered. Not that this signified, for the lawyer spoke enough for all.

Lunch over, we walked through to the library, and Herbert Dench bent to his dispatch case for a formal reading of the will, in which apparently John Willis figured as well as I. Vita, tactfully, was about to withdraw, but the lawyer told her to stay.

"No necessity for that, Mrs. Young," he said cheerfully. "It's very short and to the point."

He was right. Legal language apart, Magnus had left whatever financial assets he possessed at the time of his death to his own college for the advancement of biophysics. His flat in London and his personal effects there were to be sold, and the money given to the same cause, with the exception of his library, which he bequeathed to John Willis in gratitude for ten years of professional co-operation and personal friendship. Kilmarth, with all its contents, he left to me, for my own use or to dispose of, as I wished, in memory of years of friendship dating back to undergraduate days, and because the former occupants of the house would have wished it so. And that was all.

"I take it," said the lawyer, smiling, "that by the former occupants he is referring to his parents, Commander and Mrs. Lane, whom I believe you knew?"

"Yes," I said, bewildered, "yes, I was very fond of them both."

"Well, there we are. It's a delightful house. I hope you will be very happy here."

I looked at Vita. She was lighting a cigarette, her usual defence in a moment of sudden shock. "How . . . how extraordinarily generous of the Professor," she said. "I really don't know what to say. Of course it's up to Dick whether he intends to keep it or not. Our future plans are in a state of flux at present."

There was a moment's awkward silence, as Herbert Dench looked from one to the other of us.

"Naturally," he said, "you will have a great deal to discuss together. You realise, of course, that the house and contents will have to be valued for probate. I would appreciate it if I could see over it, by the way, if it wouldn't be too much trouble?"

"Why, of course."

We all rose to our feet, and Vita said, "The Professor had a laboratory in the basement, a most alarming place—at least, so my small sons thought. I suppose the things there would hardly go with the house but should be returned to his laboratory in London? Perhaps Mr. Willis would know what they are."

Her face was all innocence, but I had the impression that her mention of the laboratory was deliberate, and she wanted to know what was there.

"A laboratory?" queried the lawyer. "Did the Professor do any work down here?" He addressed himself to Willis.

The little mouse-like man blinked behind his horn-rimmed spectacles. "I very much doubt it," he said with diffidence, "and, if he did, it would be of little scientific importance, and have no connection with his work in London. He may have made a few experiments, just to amuse himself on a rainy day—certainly nothing more, or he would have mentioned it to me."

Good man. If he knew anything he was not going to commit himself. I could see that Vita was on the point of saying I had told her the contents of the laboratory were of inestimable value, so I suggested that we should inspect the laboratory before visiting the rest of the house.

"Come along," I said to Willis, "you're the expert. The room used to be an old laundry in Commander Lane's day, and Magnus kept a lot of bottles and jars in it."

He looked at me, but said nothing. We all trooped down to the basement, and I opened the door.

"There you are," I said. "Nothing very exciting. Just a lot of old jars, as I told you."

Vita's face was a study as she looked around her. Amazement, disbelief, and then a swift glance of enquiry at me. No monkey's head, no embryo kittens, only the empty rows of bottles. She had the supreme intelligence to remain silent.

"Well, well," said the lawyer, "the valuer might put a price of sixpence apiece on the jars. What do you say, Willis?"

The biophysicist ventured a smile. "I would think," he said, "that Professor Lane's mother may have preserved fruit here in former days."

"A still room, didn't they call them?" laughed the lawyer. "The still-room maid would make preserves for the whole year. Look at the hooks in the ceiling! They probably hung the meat here too. Great sides of ham. Well, Mrs. Young, this will be your province, not your husband's. I recommend an electric washing-machine in the corner to save your laundry bills. Expensive to install, but it will pay for itself in a couple of years, with a young family."

He turned, still laughing, back into the passage, and we followed. I locked the door behind me. Willis, who was hovering in the rear bent to pick up something from the stone floor. It was a label from one of the jars. He gave it to me without a word, and I put it in my pocket. Then we tramped upstairs to inspect the remainder of the house, Herbert Dench making the remarkable suggestion that if we wanted to turn the property into an investment we might split the whole place up into flatlets for summer visitors, keeping for our own use the bedroom suite with the view of the sea. He was still extrolling the idea to Vita as we wandered round the garden. I saw Willis glance at his watch.

"You must have had about enough of us," he said. "I told Dench on the way down that we would call in at Divisional Headquarters at Liskeard and answer any questions the police might want to put to us. If you'd telephone for a taxi we could go there straight away, and have dinner in Liskeard later before catching the night train."

"I'll drive you myself," I said. "Hold on, there's something I want to show you." I went upstairs, and after a few minutes came back with the walking stick. "This was near Magnus's body. It belongs with the others in the London flat. Do you think they will let me keep it?"

"Surely," he said, "and the other sticks too. I'm so glad you've got this house, by the way, and I hope you won't part with it."

"I don't intend to."

Vita and Dench were still a short distance off on the terrace.

"I think," said Willis quietly, "we had better tell more or less the same story at the inquest. Magnus was an enthusiastic walker, and if he wanted some exercise after hours in the train it was typical of him."

"Yes," I said.

"Incidentally, a young friend of mine, a student, has been looking up historical stuff for Magnus at the B.M. and the Public Record Office. Do you want him to continue?"

I hesitated. "It might be useful. Yes . . . If he turns anything up ask him to send it to me here."

"I'll do that."

I noticed for the first time an expression of loss, of emptiness, behind the horn-rimmed spectacles.

"What are your own plans?" I asked.

"I shall go on just the same, I suppose," he said. "Try to carry on something of Magnus's work. But it will be tough going. As boss and colleague he will be irreplaceable. You probably realise that."

"I do."

The others came up, and nothing further was said between Willis and myself. After a cup of tea, which none of us wanted but Vita insisted on getting, Willis suggested the move to Liskeard. I knew now why Magnus had chosen him as senior member of his staff. Professional competence apart, loyalty and discretion were the qualities behind that mouse-like appearance.

Once we were in the car, Dench asked if we might cover part of the route Magnus had taken on the Friday night. I drove them along the Stonybridge lane past Treverran

Farm and up to the gate near the top of the hill, and pointed across the fields down to the tunnel.

"Incredible," Dench murmured, "quite incredible. And dark, too, at the time. I don't like it, you know."

"How do you mean?" I asked.

"Well, if it doesn't make sense to me it won't to the Coroner, or to the jury. They're bound to see something behind it."

"What sort of thing?"

"Some sort of compulsion to get to that tunnel. And once he found it we know what happened."

"I don't agree," said Willis. "As you say, it was dark at the time, or nearly dark. The tunnel wouldn't have shown up from here, or the line either. I believe he had the idea to go down into the valley, perhaps take a look at that farmhouse from the other side, and when he got to the bottom of the field the railway viaduct interfered with his view. He scrambled up the bank to find out the lie of the land, and the train hit him."

"It's possible. But what an extraordinary thing to do."

"Extraordinary to the legal mind," said Willis, "but not to Professor Lane. He was an explorer in every sense of the word."

After I had landed them safely at the police headquarters I turned back for Home . . . The word had a new significance. It was my home now. The place belonged to me, as it had once belonged to Magnus. The strain that had been upon me through the day began to lift, and the weight of depression, too. Magnus was dead; I should never see him again, never hear his voice, rejoice in his company or be aware of his presence in the background of my life, but the link between us would never be broken because the home that had been his was mine. Therefore I could not lose him. Therefore I should not be alone.

I passed the entrance to Boconnoc, which in that other time had been Bockenod, before descending the hill to Lostwithiel, and thought of poor Sir John Carminowe, already infected with the dreaded smallpox, riding beside Joanna Champernoune's clumsy chariot on that windy October night in 1331, to die a month later, having enjoyed his position as Keeper of Restormel and Tremerton castles for barely seven months. On the other side of Lostwithiel I took the road to Treesmill, so that I could have a closer view of the farms situated on the opposite side of the valley from the railway. Strickstenton was on the left-hand side of the narrow road, and, from the brief glimpse I had from the car, of considerable age, and what a tourist brochure would describe as "picturesque." The pasture land belonging to it sloped downwards to a wood.

Once I was out of sight of the house I got out of the car and looked across to the railway on the other side of the valley. The tunnel showed up plainly, and even as I watched a train emerged like a straggling snake, yellow-headed, evil, and wound its way below Treverran Farm and disappeared down to the lower valley. The freight train that had killed Magnus had appeared from the opposite direction, climbing the rising ground and vanishing into the tunnel, a reptile seeking cover in the underworld, as Magnus, who had neither seen nor heard it, dragged himself, dying, to the hut above. I drove on down the twisting lane, noting on my left the turning which, I judged, led past Colwith Farm to the bottom of the valley and what remained of the original river stream. At some time, before the railway cut into the land, there would have been a track leading from Great Treverran across the valley to its smaller neighbour, Little Treverran. Either farm might be the Tregest of the Carminowes.

I went on down to Treesmill, and up the hill to the call box in Tywardreath. I dialled the Kilmarth number, and Vita answered.

"Darling," I said, "it seems rather rude to leave Dench and Willis on their own in Liskeard, so I think I'll hang around until they have finished with the police, and then have dinner with them."

"Oh well," she said, "if you must. But don't be late. No need to wait for the train."

"Probably not," I told her. "It depends how much there is to discuss."

"All right. I'll expect you when I see you."

I rang off, and returned to the car. Then I drove back again to Treesmill and up the twisting lane, and this time took the turning that led to Colwith. The lane went on, past the farm, as I had thought it would, becoming steeper, and finally petered out in a small water splash at the bottom of the hill. To the left, across a cattle grid, was a narrow entrance to Little Treverran. The buildings themselves were out of sight, but a board with lettering on it said: W. P. KELLY. WOODWORKER.

I risked the water splash and parked the car, out of sight of the lane, in the field beyond, close to a line of trees and only a few hundred yards from the railway.

I looked at my watch. It was a little after five. I opened the boot of the car and took out the walking stick, which I had primed, in the dressing room, with the last of bottle A, before showing it to John Willis in the library.

19

IT WAS SNOWING. The soft flakes fell upon my head and my hands, and the world all about me was suddenly white, no lush green summer grass, no line of trees, and the snow fell steadily, blotting the hills from sight. There were no farm buildings anywhere near me—nothing but the black river, about twenty foot broad where I was standing, and the snow, which had drifted high on either bank, only to slither into the water as the mass caved in from the weight, revealing the muddied earth beneath. It was bitter cold; not the swift, cutting blast that sweeps across high ground, but the dank chill of a valley where winter sunshine does not penetrate, nor cleansing wind. The silence was the more deadly, for the river rippled past me without sound, and the stunted willows and alder growing beside it looked like mutes with outstretched arms, grotesquely shapeless because of the burden of snow they bore upon their limbs. And all the while the soft flakes fell, descending from a pall of sky that merged with the white land beneath.

My mind, usually clear when I had taken the drug, was stupefied, baffled; I had expected something akin to the autumn day that I remembered from the previous time, when Bodrugan had been drowned, and Roger carried the dripping body in his arms towards Isolda. Now I was alone, without a guide; only the river at my feet told me I was in the valley.

I followed its course upstream, groping like a blind man, knowing by instinct that if I kept the river on my left I must be moving north, and that somewhere the strip of water would narrow, the banks would close, and I should find a bridge or ford to take me to the other side. I had never felt more helpless or lost. Time, in this other world, had hitherto been calculated by the height of the sun in the sky, or, as when I traversed the Lampetho valley at night, by the stars overhead; but now, in this silence and beneath the falling snow, there was no means of gauging whether it was morning or afternoon. I was lost, not in the present, with familiar landmarks close at hand, the reassuring presence of the car, but in the past.

The first sound broke the silence, a splash in the river ahead, and moving swiftly I saw an otter dive from the further bank and swim his way upstream. As he did so a dog followed him, and then a second, and immediately there were some half-dozen of them yelping and crying at the river's brink, splashing their way into the water in chase of the otter. Someone shouted, the shout taken up by another, and a group of men came running towards the river through the falling snow, shouting, laughing, encouraging the dogs, and I saw they were coming from a belt of trees just beyond me, where the river curved. Two of them scrambled down the bank into the water, thrashing it with their sticks, and a third, holding a long whip, cracked it in the air, stinging the ear of one of the dogs still crouching on the bank, which plunged after its companions.

I drew nearer, to watch them, and saw how the river narrowed a hundred yards or so beyond, while on the left, at the entrance to a copse of trees, the land fell away and the stream formed a sheet of water like a miniature lake, a film of ice upon its surface.

Somehow the men and the dogs, between them, drove the hunted otter into the gulley that fed the lake, and in a moment they were upon him, the dogs crying, the men thrashing with their sticks. The dogs floundered as the ice cracked, the surface crimsoned, and blood spattered the film of white above black water as the otter, seized between snapping jaws, was dragged from the hole he sought, and torn to pieces where the ice held firm.

The lake can have held little depth, for the men, hallooing and calling to the dogs, strode forward on to it, careless of the crack appearing suddenly from one end to the other. Foremost among them was the man with the long whip, who stood out from his fellows because of his height, and his dress as well, a padded surcoat buttoned to the throat and a high beaver hat upon his head, shaped like a cone.

"Drive them clear," he shouted, "to the bank on the further side. I'd as soon lose the lot of you as one of these," and bending suddenly, amongst the pack of yelping hounds, he lifted what remained of the otter from the midst of them, and flung it across the lake to the snow-covered verge. The dogs, baulked of their prey, struggled and slid across the ice to retrieve it where it now lay, while the men, less nimble than the animals, and hampered by their clothing, floundered and splashed in the breaking ice, shouting, cursing, jerkins and hoods caked white with the falling snowflakes.

The scene was part brutal, part macabre, for the man with the conical hat, once he knew his hounds were safe, turned his attention, laughing, to his companions in misfortune. While he himself was wet now to the thigh, he at least had boots to protect his feet, while his attendants, as I supposed they were, had some of them lost their shoes when the ice broke, and were thrashing about with frozen hands in useless search of them. Their master, laughing still, regained the bank, and, lifting his conical hat a moment, shook the snowflakes clear before replacing it once more. I recognised the ruddy face and the long jaw, although he was some twenty feet away. It was Oliver Carminowe.

He was staring hard in my direction, and although reason told me he could not see me, and I had no part in his world, the way he stood there, motionless, his head turned towards me, disregarding his grumbling attendants, gave me a strange feeling of unease, almost of fear.

"If you want to have speech with me, come across and say so," he called suddenly. The shock of what I thought discovery sent me forward to the lake's edge, and then, with relief, I saw Roger standing beside me to become, as it were, my spokesman and my cover. How long he had been there I did not know. He must have walked behind me along the river bank.

"Greetings to you, Sir Oliver!" he cried. "The drifts are shoulder-high above Treesmill, and your side of the valley too, so Rob Rosgof's widow told me at the ferry. I wondered how you fared, and the lady Isolda too."

"We fare well enough," answered the other, "with food enough to last a siege of several weeks, which God forbid. The wind may change within a day or two and bring us rain. Then, if the road does not flood, we shall leave for Carminowe. As to my lady, she stays in her chamber half the day sulking, and gives me little of her company." He spoke contemptuously, watching Roger all the while, who moved nearer to the river bank. "Whether she follows me to Carminowe is her concern," he continued. "My daughters are obedient to my will, if she is not. Joanna is already promised to John Petyt of Ardeva, and, although a child still, prinks and preens before the glass as if she were already a bride of fourteen years and ripe for her strapping husband. You may tell her godmother Lady Champernoune so, with my respects. She may wish a like fortune for herself before many years have passed." He burst out laughing, and then, pointing to the hounds scavenging beneath the trees, said, "If you have no fear of fording the river where the plank has rotted, I will find an otter's paw which you may present to Lady Champernoune with my compliments. It may remind her of her brother Otto, being wet and bloody, and she can nail it on the walls of Trelawn as a memento to his name. The other paw I will deliver to my own lady for a similar purpose, unless the dogs have swallowed it."

He turned his back and walked towards the trees, calling to his hounds, while Roger, moving forward up the river bank, and I beside him, came to a rough bridge, made out of lengths of log bound together, the whole slippery with the fallen snow, and partly sagging in the water. Oliver Carminowe and his attendants stood watching as Roger set foot upon the rotting bridge, and when it collapsed beneath his weight and he slipped and fell, soaking himself above his thighs, they roared in unison, expecting to see him turn again and claw the bank. But he strode on, the water coming nearly to his waist, and reached the other side, while I, dry shod, followed in his wake. He walked directly to the edge of the copse where Carminowe stood, whip in hand, and said, "I will deliver the otter's paw, if you will give it to me."

I thought he would receive a lash from the whip across his face, and I believe he expected the same himself, but Carminowe, smiling, his whip raised, lashed suddenly amongst the dogs instead, and whipping them from the torn body of the otter took the knife from his belt, and cut off two of the remaining paws.

"You have more stomach than my steward at Carminowe," he said. "I respect you for that, if for nothing else. Here, take the paw, and hang it in your kitchen at Kylmerth, amongst the silver pots and platters you have doubtless stolen from the Priory. But first walk up the hill with us and pay your respects to the lady Isolda in person. She may prefer a man, once in a while, to the tame squirrel she occupies her days with."

Roger took the paw from him and put it in his pouch, saying nothing, and we entered the copse and began threading our way through the snow-laden trees, walking steadily uphill, but whether to right or left I had no idea, having lost all sense of direction, knowing only that the river was behind us and the snow was falling still.

A track packed high with snow on either side led to a stone-built house, tucked snugly against the hill; and, while Carminowe's attendants still straggled in our rear, he himself kicked open the door before us and we entered a square hall, to be greeted at once by the house dogs, fawning upon him, and the two children, Joanna and Margaret, whom I had last seen riding their ponies across the Treesmill ford on a summer's afternoon. A third, somewhat older than the others, about sixteen, whom I took for one of Carminowe's daughters by his first marriage, stood smiling by the hearth, nor did she embrace him, but pouted with a sort of petulant grace when she saw he was not alone.

"My ward, Sybell, who seeks to teach my children better manners than their mother," Carminowe said.

The steward bowed and turned to the two children, who, after having kissed their father, came to welcome him. The elder, Joanna, had grown, and showed some sign of dawning self-consciousness, as her father had said, by blushing, and tossing her long hair out of her eyes, and giggling, but the younger, with still some years to go before she too ripened for the marriage market, struck out her small hand to Roger and smote him on the knee.

"You promised me a new pony when last we met," she said, "and a whip like your brother Robbie's. I'll have no truck with a man who fails to keep his word."

"The pony awaits you, and the whip too," answered Roger gravely, "if Alice will bring you across the valley when the snow melts."

"Alice has left us," replied the child. "We have her to mind us now," and she pointed a disdainful finger at the ward Sybell, "and she's too grand to ride pillion behind you or Robbie."

She looked so much like her mother as she spoke that I loved her for it, and Roger must have seen the likeness too, for he smiled and touched her hair, but her father, irritated, told the child sharply to hold her tongue or he would send her supperless to bed.

"Here, dry yourself by the fire," he said abruptly, kicking the dogs out of the way, "and you, Joanna, warn your mother the steward has crossed the valley from Tywardreath and has a message from his mistress, if she cares to receive him."

He took the remaining otter's paw from his surcoat and dangled it in front of Sybell. "Shall we give it to Isolda, or will you wear it to keep you warm?" he teased. "It will soon dry, furry and soft, inside your kirtle, the nearest thing to a man's hand on a cold night."

She shrieked in affectation and backed away, while he pursued her, laughing, and I saw by the expression in Roger's eyes that he had fully grasped the relationship between guardian and ward. The snow might remain upon the hills for days or weeks; there was little at the moment to tempt the master of this establishment back to Carminowe.

"My mother will see you, Roger," said Joanna, returning to the hall, and we crossed a passageway into the room beyond.

Isolda was standing by the window, watching the falling snow, while a small red squirrel, a bell around its neck, squatted upon its haunches at her feet, pawing at her gown. As we entered she turned and stared, and although to my prejudiced eyes she looked as beautiful as ever I realised, shocked, that she had become much thinner, paler, and there was a white streak in the front of her golden hair.

"I am glad to see you, Roger," she said. "There have been few encounters between our households of late, and we are seldom here at Tregest these days, as you know well. How is my cousin? You have a message from her?"

Her voice that I remembered, clear and hard, defiant, almost, had become flat, toneless. Then, sensing that Roger wished to speak to her in private, she told her daughter Joanna to leave them alone.

"I bear no message, my lady," said Roger quietly. "The family are at Trelawn, or were, when I last had word. I came out of respect for you, Rob Rosgof's widow having told me you were here, and were not well."

"I'm as well as I ever shall be," she answered, "and whether here or at Carminowe the days are much the same."

"That's ill-spoken, my lady," said Roger. "You showed more spirit once."

"Once, yes," she replied, "but I was younger then . . . I came and went as I pleased, for Sir Oliver was more frequently at Westminster. Now, whether from malice through not obtaining Sir John's position as Keeper of the King's forests and parks in Cornwall, as he hoped, he wastes his days keeping women instead. The present fancy is hardly more than a child. You have seen Sybell?"

"I have, my lady."

"It's true she is his ward. If I should die it would be convenient to both of them, for he could marry her and install her at Carminowe in all legality."

She stooped to pick up the pet squirrel at her feet, and, smiling for the first time since we had come into the small room, which was as sparsely furnished as a nun's cell, she said, "This is my confidante now. He takes hazel nuts from my hand and regards me wisely all the while with his bright eyes." Then, serious once more, she added, "I am kept prisoner, you know, both here and when we are at Carminowe. I am prevented even from sending word to my brother Sir William Ferrers at Bere, who is told by his wife that I have gone out of my mind and am therefore dangerous. They all believe it. Sick in body, indeed, I have been, and in pain, but so far it has not sent me mad."

Roger moved silently to the door, opened it, and listened. There was still the sound of laughter from the hall: the otter's paw continued to cause diversion. He closed the door again.

"Whether Sir William believes it or not I cannot say," he said, "but talk of your illness there has been, and for some months. That is why I have come, my lady, to prove it a lie for myself, and now I know it to be so."

Isolda, with the squirrel in her arms, might have been her small daughter Margaret as she looked at the steward steadily, weighing in the balance his trustworthiness.

"I did not like you once," she said. "You had too shrewd an eye, casting about you for your own advantage, and, because it suited you to serve a woman rather than a man, you let my cousin Sir Henry Champernoune die."

"My lady," said Roger, "he was mortally sick. He would have died anyway within a few weeks."

"Perhaps, but the way he went showed undue haste. It taught me one thing—to beware of potions brewed by a French monk. Sir Oliver will seek to rid himself of me by other methods, a dagger's thrust or strangulation. He won't wait for nature to put an end to me." She dropped the squirrel on the floor and, moving to the window, looked out once more at the still falling snow. "Before he does," she said, "I'll rather take myself outdoors and perish. With the country covered as it is today I'd freeze the sooner. How about it, Roger? Carry me in a sack upon your back and cast me somewhere at the cliff's edge? I'd thank you for it."

She meant it as a joke if somewhat twisted, but crossing to the window beside her he stared up at the pall of sky and pursed his lips in a soundless whistle.

"It could be done, my lady," he said, "if you had the courage."

"I have the courage if you have the means," she replied.

They stared at one another, an idea suddenly taking root in both their minds, and she said swiftly, "If I went from here, and thence to my brother's at Bere, Sir Oliver would not dare to follow me, for he could never sustain his lies about my sick mind. But in this weather the roads would be impassable. I could not reach Devon."

"Not immediately," he said, "but once the roads are fit it could be done."

"Where would you hide me?" she asked. "He has only to cross the valley to search the Champernoune demesne above Treesmill."

"Let him do so," answered Roger. "He would find it barred and empty, with my lady at Trelawn. There are other hiding places, if you cared to trust yourself to me."

"Such as where?"

"My own house, Kylmerth. Robbie is there, and my sister Bess. It's nothing but a rough farm, but you are welcome to it, until the weather mends."

She said nothing for a moment, and I could see, by the expression in her eyes, that she still had some lingering doubt of his integrity.

"It's a question of choice," she said. "To stay here a prisoner, at the mercy of my husband's whim, who can hardly wait to rid himself of a wife who is a lasting reproach, and an encumbrance too, or throw myself on your hospitality, which you may deny when it pleases you to do so."

"It will not please me," he answered, "nor will it ever be denied, until you say the word yourself."

She looked out once again at the falling snow and the slowly darkening sky, which foretold not only worsening weather to come but the approach of evening and all the hazards of a winter's night.

"I am ready," she said, and throwing open a chest against the wall drew out a hooded cloak, a woollen kirtle, and a pair of leather shoes that must surely never have seen service out of doors except thrust into a covering bag when she rode sidesaddle.

"My own daughter Joanna, who overtops me now, climbed from this same window a week ago," she said, "after a wager with Margaret that she had grown too fat. I am thin enough, in all conscience. What do you say? Do I lack spirit now?"

"You never lacked it, my lady," he answered, "only the spur to prick you to endeavour. You know the wood below your pasture land?"

"I should," she said. "I rode in it most days when I was free to do so."

"Then lock your door, after I have left the room, climb from the window, and make your way to it. I will see that the track is deserted and the household all within, and will tell Sir Oliver that you dismissed me and wish to be alone."

"And the children? Joanna will be aping Sybell, as she has done continually these past weeks, but Margaret . . ." she paused, her courage ebbing. "Once I lose Margaret, there is nothing left."

"Only your will to live," he said. "If you keep that, you keep all things. And your children too."

"Go quickly," she said, "before I change my mind."

As we left the room I heard her lock the door, and looking at Roger I wondered if he knew what he had done, urging her to risk her life and her future in an escapade that must surely fail. The house had grown silent. We walked along the passage to the hall and found it empty, except for the two children and the dogs. Joanna was pirouetting before the looking glass, her long hair dressed in braids with a ribbon threaded through it which had, a short time before, been on Sybell's head; while Margaret sat astride a bench, her father's conical hat upon her head and his long whip in her hand. She looked at Roger severely when he entered.

"Observe now," she said, "I am obliged to make do with a bench for a horse and borrowed plumage for equipment. I'll not remind you of your failings again, my master."

"Nor shall you have to," he told her. "I know my duty. Where is your father?"

"He's above," answered the child. "He cut his finger severing the otter's paw, and Sybell is dressing it for him."

"He'll not thank you to disturb him," said Joanna. "He likes to sleep before he dines, and Sybell sings to him. It makes him drop off the sooner and wake with better appetite. Or so he says."

"I do not doubt it," replied Roger. "In that event, please thank Sir Oliver for me and bid him goodnight. Your mother is tired and does not wish to see anyone. Perhaps you will tell him so?"

"I may," said Joanna, "if I remember."

"I'll tell him," said Margaret, "and wake him too, if he does not descend by six o'clock. Last night we dined at seven, and I can't abide late hours."

Roger wished them both goodnight and, opening the hall door, stepped outside, closing it softly behind him. He stole round to the back of the house and listened. There were sounds coming from the kitchen quarters, but windows and doors were fastened tight, and the shutters barred. The hounds were yelping from outbuildings in the rear. It would be dark within half an hour or even less; already the copse below the field was dim, shrouded by the pall of snow, and the opposite hills were bleak and bare under the grey sky. The tracks we had made ascending to the house were almost blotted out by the fresh-fallen snow, but beside them were new prints, closer together, like those of a child who, hurrying for shelter, runs like a dancer upon her toes. Roger covered them with his own long stride, disturbing the ground, kicking the snow in front of him as he walked rapidly downhill towards the copse; and now if anyone should venture forth before darkness came they would see nothing but the tracks he had made himself, and those would be blotted too within the hour.

She was waiting for us by the entrance to the wood, carrying her pet squirrel, her cloak drawn close around her and her hood fastened under her chin. But her long gown, which she had tried to fasten up under the belted cloak, had slipped down again below her ankles and hung about her feet like a dripping valance. She was smiling, the smile her daughter Margaret would have worn had she too set forth on some adventure, with the promise of a pony at the end of it instead of a bleak unknown.

"I dressed my pillow in my night attire," she said, "and heaped the covers over it. It may fool them for a while, should they break down the door."

"Give me your hand," he said. "Disregard your skirts and let them trail. Bess will find warm clothes for you at home."

She laughed and put her hand in his, and as she did so I felt as if it were in mine as well, and that the pair of us were lifting, dragging her through the fallen snow, and he was no longer a steward bound in the service of another woman and I a phantom from a later world, but both of us were men sharing a common purpose and a common love that neither of us, in his time or mine, would ever dare make plain.

When we came to the river and the rotten bridge that lay half-broken in midstream he said to her, "You must trust me once again and let me carry you across, as I would your daughter."

"But if you let me fall," she answered, "I will not clout you about the head, as Margaret would."

He laughed, and bore her safely to the other side, once more soaking himself nearly to the waist. We went on walking through the little line of stunted, shrouded trees, the silence all about us no longer ominous, as it had been when I walked alone, but hushed with a sort of magic, and a strange excitement too.

"The snow will be thicker in the valley around Treverran," he said, "and if Ric Treverran should see us he might not hold his tongue. Have you breath enough left to strike out into the open and climb the hill to the track above? Robbie awaits me there with the ponies. You shall choose which of us you please to ride behind. I am the more cautious."

"Then I choose Robbie," she said. "Tonight I bid farewell to caution, and forever."

We turned left and began to climb the hill out of the valley, the river behind us, the snow reaching above the knees of my companions with every step, making progress laborious and slow.

"Wait," he said, letting go her hand, "there may be a drift ahead before we strike the path," and he plunged upwards, sweeping the snow aside with both his hands, so that for a moment, as he walked on alone to higher ground, I was left with her, and could stare for a brief instant at the small, pale, resolute face beneath the hood.

"All's well," he called. "The snow is firmer here. I'll come and fetch you."

I watched him turn and advance, half-sliding, down the slope towards her, and it seemed to me suddenly that two men were moving there, not one, and both of them were holding out their hands to help her climb. It must be Robbie, having heard his brother's voice, who had come down from the track above.

Some instinct warned me not to move, not to climb, but to let her go alone and grasp their hands. She went from me and I lost sight of her, and of Roger, and of the third shadowy figure too, in a sudden great pall of snow that blotted all of them from sight. I stood there, shaking, the strands of wire between me and the line, and it was not snow that blanketed the opposite hills and the high bank, but the grey canvas hangings looped to the waggons of the freight train as it rattled and lumbered through the tunnel.

20

SELF-PRESERVATION IS common to all living things, linked perhaps to that older brain which Magnus said forms part of our natural inheritance. Certainly in my own case instinct transmitted a danger signal: had it not done so I should have died as he did, through the same cause. I remember stumbling blindly away from the railway embankment to the protection of the passageway where the cattle had sheltered, and I heard the waggons thunder over my head as they passed down the line into the valley. Then I crossed a hedge and found myself in a field behind Little Treverran, home of the woodworker, and so on to the field where I had left the car.

There was no nausea, no vertigo, the instinct to "awake" had spared me this as well as my life, but as I sat huddled behind the wheel, still shaking all over, I wondered whether, had Magnus and I ventured forth together on that Friday night, there would have been what the reporters like to term a double tragedy. Or would both of us have survived? It would never now be proved, the opportunity for us to wander together in another time had gone forever. One thing I knew, which no one else would ever know, and that was why he had died. He had stretched out his hand to help Isolda in the snow. If instinct had warned him otherwise he had disregarded it, unlike myself, and therefore showed the greater courage.

It was after half-past seven when I started the car, and as I drove over the water splash I still did not know how far I had walked during the excursion to the other world, or which farm or former site had proved to be Tregest. Somehow it no longer mattered. Isolda had escaped, and on that winter's night of 1332, or '33, perhaps even later, had been bound for Kilmarth; whether she reached it or not I might discover. Not now, nor tomorrow, but one day . . . My immediate purpose must be to conserve my strength and mental alertness for the inquest, and above all watch out for the aftereffects of the drug. It would not do to appear in Court with a couple of bloodshot eyes and an inexplicable sweating sickness, especially with Dr. Powell's experienced eye upon me.

I had no desire for food, and when I arrived home at about half-past eight, having parked the car at the top of the hill to while away the time, I called to Vita that we had all dined early at the hotel in Liskeard, and I was dead-beat and wanted to go to bed. She and the boys were eating in the kitchen, and I went straight upstairs without disturbing them, and put away the walking stick in the dressing-room cupboard. I knew now, to the fullest extent, what it felt like to lead what is called a "double life." The walking stick, the bottles locked in the suitcase, were like keys to some woman's flat, to be used when opportunity offered; but more tempting still, and more insidious, was the secret knowledge that the woman herself might be under my own roof, even now, tonight, in her own time.

I lay in bed, my hands behind my head, wondering how Robbie and the wild-haired sister Bess received their unexpected visitor. First warm clothes for Isolda, and food before the smoky hearth, the youngsters tongue-tied in her presence, Roger playing host; then groping her way to bed up that ladder to one of the straw-filled mattresses, hearing the cattle moving and stamping in the byre beneath her. Sleep might come early, through exhaustion, but it would more likely be late, because of the strangeness of everything about her, and because she would be thinking about her children, wondering whether she would see them again.

I shut my eyes, trying to picture that dark, cold loft. It would correspond in position, surely, to the small back bedroom above the basement, used in other days by Mrs. Lane's unfortunate cook, and filled today with discarded trunks and cardboard boxes. How near to Roger in the kitchen below, how unattainable, both then and now!

"Darling . . ."

It was Vita bending over me, fantasy and confusion combining to make her other than she was, and when I pulled her down beside me it was not the living woman and my wife whom I held but the phantom one I sought and who I knew, in reality and the present, never could respond. Presently, when I opened my eyes—for I must have dozed off for a while—she was sitting on the stool before the dressing table, smothering her face with cream.

"Well," she said smiling, looking at me in the glass, "if that's the way you celebrate your inheritance of this place I'm all for it."

The towel, wrapped turban-fashion round her head, and the mask of cream gave her a clown-like appearance, and suddenly I felt revolted by the puppet world in which I found myself, and desired no part in it, neither now, nor tomorrow, nor at any time. I wanted to vomit. I got out of bed and said, "I'm going to sleep in the dressing room."

She stared at me, her eyes like holes in the mask. "What on earth's the matter?" she said. "What have I done?"

"You've done nothing," I told her. "I want to sleep alone."

I went through the bathroom to the dressing room and she followed me, the silly shift she wore in bed flouncing round her knees, grotesquely ill-suited to the turban; and it struck me for the first time that the varnish on her fingernails made her hands like claws.

"I don't believe you've been with those men at all," she said. "You left them in Liskeard and have been drinking at some pub. That's it, isn't it?"

"No," I answered.

"Something's happened, all the same. You've been somewhere else, you're not telling me the truth; everything you say and do is one long lie. You lied about the laboratory to the lawyer and that Willis man, you lied to the police about the way the Professor died. For God's sake what's behind it? Did you have some secret pact between you both that he would kill himself, and you knew about it all the time?"

I put my hands on her shoulders and began to push her out of the room. "I've not been drinking. There was no suicide pact. Magnus died accidentally, walking into a freight train as it was going into a tunnel. I stood by the line an hour ago and nearly did the same. That's the truth, and if you won't accept it it's just too bad. I can't make you."

She stumbled against the bathroom door, and as she turned to look at me I saw a new expression on her face, not anger, but amazement, and disgust as well.

"You went and stood there again," she said, "by the place where he was killed? You deliberately went and stood there and watched a train go by that might have killed you too?"

"Yes."

"Then I'll tell you what I think. I think it's unhealthy, morbid, crazy, and the worst thing about it is that you were capable, after such an experience, of coming back here and making love to me. That I'll never forgive, or forget. So for heaven's sake sleep in the dressing room. I prefer it that way."

She slammed the bathroom door, and I knew this time it was not another of her gestures, made on impulse, but something fundamental, springing from the core of innermost feeling shocked beyond measure. I understood, even honoured her for it, and was torn by a strange, inarticulate pity, but there was nothing I could say, nothing I could do.

We met next morning not as husband and wife on edge after yet one more marital tiff, but as strangers who, through force of circumstance, were obliged to share a common roof—dress, eat, walk from room to room, make plans for the day, exchange pleasantries with the children, who were bred of her body and not mine, thus making the division yet more complete. I sensed her profound unhappiness, was aware of every sigh, every dragging step, every weary inflection in her voice, and the boys, sharp like little animals to the atmospheric change of mood, watched both of us with gimlet eyes.

"Is it true," asked Teddy warily, catching me alone, "that the Professor has left the house to you?"

"It is," I answered. "Unexpected but very kind of him."

"Will it mean we shall come here every holiday?"

"I don't know, it depends on Vita," I said.

He began fiddling with things on tables, picking them up and putting them back again, then kicking aimlessly at the backs of chairs.

"I don't believe Mom likes it here," he said.

"Do you?" I asked.

"It's all right," he shrugged.

Yesterday, because of fishing and the genial Tom, enthusiasm. Today, with the adult mood at odds, apathy and insecurity. My fault, of course. Whatever happened in this house had been, would be, my fault. I could not tell him so, or ask forgiveness.

"Don't worry," I said. "It will sort itself out. You'll probably spend the Christmas holidays in New York."

"Whew . . . How super!" he exclaimed, and ran out of the room on to the terrace, calling to Micky, who was outside, "Dick says we may spend next holidays back home."

The cheer that echoed from his young brother summed up their joint attitude to Cornwall, England, Europe, doubtless to their stepfather as well.

We got through the weekend somehow, though the weather broke, making it the more difficult, and while the boys played a form of racquets in the basement—I could hear the balls thudding against the walls below—and Vita wrote a ten-page letter to Bill and Diana in Ireland, I made an inspection of all Magnus's books, from the nautical tales of Commander Lane's day to his own more personal choice, touching each one with possessive pride. The third volume of *The Parochial History of the County of Cornwall* (L to N—no sign of the other volumes) was tucked behind *The Story of the Windjammers,* and I pulled it out and ran my eye over the index of parishes. Lanlivery was there, and in the chapter allotted to it pride of place was given to Restormel Castle. Alas for Sir John; his seven months' tenure as Keeper was not mentioned. I was just about to replace the book, with the intention of reading it in full another time, when a line at the top of the page caught my attention.

> "The manor of Steckstenton or Strickstenton, originally Tregesteynton, belonged to the Carminowes of Boconnoc, and passed from them to the Courtenays, and eventually to the representatives of the Pitt family. The estate of Strickstenton is the property of N. Kendall, Esq."

Tregesteynton . . . the Carminowes of Boconnoc. I had got it at last, but too late. Had I known ten days ago, had we both known, Magnus could have crossed the valley lower down, at Treesmill, and need not have died. As to the original manor house, the site of it had surely been below the present farmhouse, or, trespassing there in time last Thursday evening, I must have been seen by the present owners.

Strickstenton . . . Tregesteynton. One thing was certain: I could bring the name up in Court if the Coroner questioned me.

The date of the inquest was fixed for Friday morning—earlier than had been expected. Dench and Willis would do as they had done before—travel down by a night train and return after it was over. I was congratulating myself, as I was shaving on the day of the inquest, that I had suffered no side effects from the drug, no sweats, no bloodshot eyes, and despite the estrangement with Vita had passed the few days in comparative peace, when suddenly, for no reason, the razor dropped from my hand into the washbasin. I tried to pick it up, and my fingers would not co-ordinate; they were numb, with a sort of cramp. There was no feeling in them, no pain—they just did not function. I told myself it was nerves, due to the forthcoming ordeal, yet later at breakfast, as I reached for a cup of coffee without thinking, the cup slipped out of my hand, spilling the contents and smashing itself on the tray.

We were breakfasting in the dining room to be on time for the inquest, and Vita was sitting opposite me.

"Sorry," I said. "What a bloody clumsy thing to do."

She stared at my hand, which had started to tremble, the tremor seeming to run up the wrist to the elbow. I could not control it. I thrust my hand into my jacket pocket and kept it close to my side, and the tremor eased.

"What's wrong?" she asked. "Your hand is all shaking."

"It's cramp," I said. "I must have lain on it during the night."

"Well, blow on it or something," she said. "Stretch the fingers, and bring the circulation back."

She began mopping up the tray, and poured me a fresh cup of coffee. I drank it with my left hand, but appetite had gone. I was wondering how I was going to drive the car, with one hand trembling or useless. I had told Vita that I preferred to attend the inquest alone, for there was no reason for her to come with me, but when the moment drew near to leave my hand was still useless, although the tremor had ceased. "Look, I think you'll have to take me into St. Austell," I said. "My right hand has still got this infernal cramp."

The warm sympathy which would have been hers a week ago was lacking. "I'll drive you, of course," she replied, "but it's rather odd, isn't it, suddenly to have cramp? You've never had it before. You had better keep your hand in your pocket, or the Coroner will think you have been drinking."

It was not a remark calculated to put me at my ease, and the very business of having to sit as passenger, humped beside Vita as she drove instead of being at the wheel myself, did something to my self-respect. I felt inadequate, frustrated, and began to lose the thread of the answers to the Coroner which I had so carefully rehearsed.

When we arrived at the White Hart and met Dench and Willis Vita, quite unnecessarily, apologised for her presence by saying, "Dick's disabled. I had to act as chauffeur," and the whole silly business was then explained. There was little time for talking, and I walked with the others to the building where the inquest was to be held, feeling a marked man, while the Coroner, doubtless a mild enough individual in private life, took on, in my eyes, the semblance of a judge of the Criminal Court, with the jury, one and all, adepts at finding a prisoner guilty.

The proceedings started with the police evidence about the finding of the body. It was straightforward enough, but as I listened to the story I thought how strangely it must fall on other ears, and how suggestive of someone who had temporarily lost his reason and been bent on his own destruction. Dr. Powell was then called to give evidence. He read his statement in that clear, no-nonsense-about-it voice which suddenly reminded me of one of the younger Rugger-playing priests at Stonyhurst.

"This was the well-preserved body of a man of about forty-five years of age. When first examined at 1P.M. on Saturday August 3rd death had occurred about fourteen hours previously. The autopsy, performed the following day, showed superficial bruises and abrasions of the knees and chest, deeper and more severe bruising of the upper arm and shoulder, and extensive laceration of the right side of the scalp. Underlying this was a depressed fracture of the right parietal region of the skull, accompanied by lacerations of the brain and bleeding from the right middle meningeal artery. The stomach was found to contain about one pint of mixed food and fluid, which on subsequent analysis contained nothing abnormal and no alcohol. Blood samples examined were also normal, and the heart, lungs, liver and kidneys were all normal and healthy. In my opinion, death was due to a cerebral haemorrhage following a severe crushing blow on the head."

I relaxed in my seat, tension momentarily lifted, wondering if John Willis did the same, or whether he had never had cause for concern.

The Coroner than asked Dr. Powell if the brain injuries were consistent with what might be expected if the deceased had come in violent contact with a passing vehicle such as the waggon of a freight train.

"Yes, definitely," was the reply. "A point of some importance is that death was not instantaneous. He had strength enough to drag himself a few yards to the hut. The head blow was sufficient to cause severe concussion, but actual death from haemorrhage probably took place five to ten minutes afterwards."

"Thank you, Dr. Powell," said the Coroner, and I heard him call my name. I stood up, wondering if the fact that my right hand was in my pocket gave me too casual an appearance, or whether, in point of fact, anyone noticed it at all.

"Mr. Young," said the Coroner, "I have your statement here, and propose reading it to the jury. Stop me if there is anything you wish to correct."

The statement, as read by him, made me sound callous, as if I had been more preoccupied in missing my dinner than anxious for the safety of my guest. The jury would get the impression of a loafer, spinning away the small hours with a cushion behind his head and a bottle of whisky at his elbow.

"Mr. Young," said the Coroner, when he had finished, "it did not occur to you to contact the police on the Friday night. Why?"

"I thought it unnecessary," I replied. "I kept expecting Professor Lane to turn up."

"You were not surprised at his getting off the train at Par and taking a walk instead of meeting you at St. Austell as arranged?"

"I was surprised, yes, but it was quite in character. If he had some objective in view he followed it through. Time and punctuality meant nothing to him on these occasions."

"And what do you think was the particular objective Professor Lane had in view on the night in question?" asked the Coroner.

"Well, he had become interested in the historical associations of the district, and the sites of manor houses. We had planned to visit some of them during the weekend. When he did not turn up I assumed he must have decided to take a walk to some particular site which he had not told me about. Since I made my statement to the police I believe I have located the site he had in mind."

I thought there might be a stir of interest amongst the jury but they remained unmoved.

"Perhaps you will tell us about it," said the Coroner.

"Yes, of course," I answered, self-confidence returning, and inwardly blessing the *Parochial History*. "I believe now, which I did not know at the time, that he was trying to locate the one-time manor of Strickstenton in Lanlivery parish. This manor belonged at one time to a family called Courtenay"—I was careful not to mention the Carminowes, because of Vita—"who also used to own Treverran too. The quickest way between these houses, as the crow flies, would be to cross the valley above the present Treverran Farm, and walk through the wood to Strickstenton."

The Coroner asked for an ordnance map, which he examined carefully. "I see what you mean, Mr. Young," he said. "But surely there is a passageway under the railway which Professor Lane would have taken in preference to crossing the line itself?"

"Yes," I said, "but he had no map. He might not have known it was there."

"So he cut across the line, despite the fact that it was by then quite dark, and a freight train was coming up the valley?"

"I don't think the darkness worried him. And obviously he didn't hear the train—he was so intent on his quest."

"So intent, Mr. Young, that he deliberately climbed through the wire and walked down the steep embankment as the train was passing?"

"I don't think he walked down the bank. He slipped and fell. Don't forget it was snowing at the time."

I saw the Coroner staring at me, and the jury too. "I beg your pardon, Mr. Young," said the Coroner, "did I hear you say it was snowing?"

I took a moment or two to recover, and I could feel the sweat breaking out on my forehead. "I'm sorry," I said. "That was misleading. The point was that Professor Lane had a particular interest in climatic conditions during the Middle Ages; his theory was that winters were much harder in those days than they are now. Before the railway cutting was built through the hillside above the Treesmill valley the ground would have sloped down continuously all the way to the bottom, and drifts would have lain there heavily, making communication between Treverran and Strickstenton virtually impossible. I believe, from a scientific rather than a historical point of view, he was thinking so much about this, and the general incline of the land about him, and how it would be affected by snowfall, that he became oblivious of everything else."

The incredulous faces went on staring at me, and I saw one man nudge his companion, signifying that either I was a raving lunatic or the Professor had been.

"Thank you, Mr. Young, that is all," said the Coroner, and I sat down, pouring with sweat and a tremor shooting down my arm from elbow to wrist.

He called John Willis, who proceeded to give evidence that his late colleague had been in the best of health and spirits when he saw him before the weekend, that he was engaged in work of great importance to the country which he was not at liberty to speak about, but that naturally this work had no connection with his visit to Cornwall, which was in the nature of a private visit and in pursuance of a personal hobby, mainly historical.

"I must add," he said, "that I am in complete agreement with Mr. Young as to his theory of how Professor Lane met his death. I am not an antiquarian, nor a historian, but certainly Professor Lane held theories about the extent of snowfall in previous centuries," and he proceeded, for about three minutes, to launch into jargon so incomprehensible and above my head and the heads of everybody present that Magnus himself could not have surpassed it had he been giving an imitation, after a thundering good dinner, of the sort of stuff published in the more obscure scientific journals.

"Thank you, Mr. Willis," murmured the Coroner when he had finished. "Very interesting. I am sure we are all grateful for your information."

The evidence was concluded. The Coroner, summing up, directed that, although the circumstances were unusual, he found no reason to suppose that Professor Lane had deliberately walked on to the line as the train approached. The verdict was Death by Misadventure, with a rider to the effect that British Railways, Western Region, would do well to make a more thorough inspection of the wiring and danger notices along the line.

It was all over. Herbert Dench turned to me with a smile, as we left the building, and said, "Very satisfactory for all concerned. I suggest we celebrate at the White Hart. I don't mind telling you I was afraid of a very different verdict, and I think we might have had it but for your and Willis's account of Professor Lane's extraordinary preoccupation with winter conditions. I remember hearing of a similar case in the Himalayas . . ." and he proceeded to tell us, as we walked to the hotel, of a scientist who for three weeks lived at some phenomenal altitude in appalling conditions to study the atmospheric effect upon certain bacteria. I did not see the connection but was glad of the respite, and when we reached our destination went straight to the bar and got quietly and very inoffensively drunk. Nobody noticed, and what is more the tremor in my hand ceased immediately. Perhaps after all it had been nerves.

"Well, we musn't keep you from enjoying your delightful new home," the lawyer said, when we had consumed a brief but hilarious lunch. "Willis and I can walk up to the station."

As we moved towards the door of the hotel I said to Willis, "I can't thank you enough for your evidence. What Magnus would have called a remarkable performance."

"It made its impact," he admitted, "though you had me somewhat shaken. I wasn't prepared for snow. Still, it goes to prove what my boss always said: the layman will accept anything if it is put forward in an authoritative enough fashion." He blinked at me behind his spectacles and added quietly, "You did make a clean sweep of all the jam jars, I take it? Nothing left that could do you or anyone else any damage?"

"Buried," I replied, "under the debris of years."

"Good," he said. "We don't want any more disasters."

He hesitated, as if he might have been going to say something else, but the lawyer and Vita were waiting for us by the hotel entrance, and the opportunity was lost. Farewells were said, hands shaken, and we all dispersed. As we made our way to the car-park Vita remarked in wifely fashion, "I noticed your hand recovered as soon as you reached the bar. Be that as it may, I intend to drive."

"You're welcome," I said, borrowing her country's curious phraseology, and, tilting my hat over my eye as I got into the car, I prepared myself for sleep. My conscience pricked me, though. I had lied to Willis. Bottles A and B were empty, true enough, but the contents of bottle C were still intact, and lay in my suitcase in the dressing room.

21

THE EFFECTS OF conviviality in the White Hart subsided after a couple of hours, leaving me in a truculent mood and determined to be master in my own house. The inquest was over, and despite my gaffe about the snow, or perhaps because of it, Magnus's good name remained untarnished. The police were satisfied, local interest would die down, and there was nothing more I had to fear except interference from my own wife. This must be dealt with, and speedily. The boys had gone off riding and were not yet home. I went to look for Vita and found her eventually, tape measure in hand, standing on the landing outside the boys' room.

"You know," she said, "that lawyer was perfectly right. You could get half-a-dozen small apartments into this place—more if you used the basement too. We could borrow the money from Joe." She flicked the tape measure back into its case and smiled. "Have you any better ideas? The Professor didn't leave you the money to keep up his house, and you haven't a job, unless you cross the ocean and Joe gives you one. So . . . How about being realistic for a change?"

I turned and walked downstairs to the music room. I expected her to follow me, and she did. I planted myself before the fireplace, the traditional spot sacrosanct from time immemorial to the master of the house, and said, "Get this straight. This is my house, and what I do with it is my affair. I don't want suggestions from you, lawyers, friends, or anyone else. I intend to live here, and if you don't care to live here with me you must make your own arrangements."

She lighted a cigarette and blew a great puff of smoke into the air. She had gone very white. "This is the showdown, is it?" she asked. "The ultimatum?"

"Call it what you like," I told her. "It's a statement of fact. Magnus has left me this house, and I propose to make a life for myself here, and for you and the boys if you want to share it. I can't speak plainer than that."

"You mean you have given up all idea of taking the directorship Joe offered you in New York?"

"I never had the idea. You had it for me."

"And how do you think we are going to live?"

"I haven't the slightest idea," I said, "and at the moment I don't care. Having worked in a publishing firm for over twenty years I know something about the game, and might even turn author myself. I could start by writing a history of this house."

"Good heavens!" She laughed, and extinguished her barely lighted cigarette in the nearest ash tray. "Well, it might keep you occupied if nothing else. And what would I do with myself in the meantime? Join the local sewing society, or something?"

"You could do what other wives do, adapt."

"Darling, when I agreed to marry you and live in England you had a perfectly worth-while job in London. You've thrown it up for no reason at all, and now want to settle down here at the back of beyond, where neither of us knows a soul, hundreds of miles from all our friends. It's just not good enough."

We had reached an impasse; and I disliked being called darling when we were locked in argument instead of an embrace. Anyway, the situation bored me; I had said my say, and argument led nowhere. Besides, I had an intense desire to go up to the dressing room and examine bottle C. If I remembered rightly it looked slightly different from bottles A and B. Perhaps I ought to have given it to Willis to try out on his laboratory monkeys; but if I had taken him into my confidence he might never have sent it back.

"Why don't you take your tape measure," I suggested, "and think up some bright ideas for curtains and carpets, and send them to Bill and Diana for their opinion in Ireland?"

I did not mean to be sarcastic. She could do what she liked, within reason, with Magnus's furnishings and bachelor taste. Rearranging rooms was one of her favourite things: it kept her happy for hours.

My effort to appease rebounded. Her eyes filled, and she said, "You know I'd live anywhere if only I thought you loved me still."

I can take anger any day and feel justified in returning blow for blow. Not unhappiness, not tears. I held out my arms and she came at once, clinging to me for comfort like a wounded child.

"You've changed so these last weeks," she told me. "I hardly recognise you."

"I haven't changed," I said. "I do love you. Of course I love you."

Truth is the hardest thing to put across, to other people to oneself as well. I did love Vita, for moments shared during months and years, for all those ups and downs of married life that can be precious, exasperating, monotonous and dear. I had learnt to accept her faults, and she mine. Too often, wrangling, the insults hurled were never meant. Too frequently, used to each other's company, we had left the sweeter things unsaid. The trouble was, some inner core within had been untouched, lain dormant, waiting to be stirred. I could not share with her or anyone the secrets of my dangerous new world. Magnus, yes . . . but Magnus was a man, and dead. Vita was no Medea with whom I could gather the enchanted herbs.

"Darling," I said, "try and bear with me. It's a moment of transition for me, not a parting of the ways. I just can't see ahead. It's like standing on a spit of shore with an incoming tide, waiting to take the plunge. I can't explain."

"I'll take any plunge you want, if you'll take me with you," she answered.

"I know," I said, "I know . . ."

She wiped her eyes and blew her nose, the temporarily blotched features oddly touching, making me feel the more inadequate.

"What's the time? I shall have to pick up the boys," she said.

"No, we'll go together," I told her, glad of an excuse to prolong the entente, to justify myself not only in her eyes but in my own as well. Cheerfulness broke in; the atmosphere, that had been so heavy with resentment and unspoken bitterness, cleared, and we were almost normal again. That night I returned from self-banishment in the dressing room, not without regret, but I felt it politic; besides, the divan bed was hard.

The weather was fine, and the weekend passed with sailing, swimming, picnics with the boys, and as I resumed my role of husband, stepfather, master of the house, I planned in secret for the week ahead. I must have one day to myself alone. Vita herself, in all innocence, supplied the opportunity.

"Did you know Mrs. Collins has a daughter in Bude?" she said on Monday morning. "I told her we'd take her over there one day this week, drop her off with the daughter, and pick her up again later in the afternoon. So how about it? The boys are keen to go, and so am I."

I pretended to damp the idea. "Awful lot of traffic," I said. "The roads will be jammed. And Bude packed with tourists."

"We don't mind that," said Vita. "We can make an early start, and it's only about fifty miles."

I assumed the look of a hard-pressed family man with a backlog of work on hand he was given no time to clear. "If you don't mind, I'd rather you left me out of it. Bude on a mid-August afternoon is not my idea of a perfect way of life."

"O.K. . . . O.K. . . . We'll have more fun without you."

We settled for Wednesday. No tradesmen called that day, so it suited me. If they left at half-past ten and picked up Mrs. Collins again around five o'clock, they'd be home by seven at the latest.

Wednesday dawned fine, luckily, and I saw the party off in the Buick soon after half-past ten, knowing that I had at least eight hours ahead of me, hours for experiment and recovery too. I went up to the dressing room and took bottle C out of my suitcase. It was the same stuff all right, or appeared to be, but there was a brownish sediment at the bottom, like cough mixture put away after the winter and forgotten until the cold weather comes again. I took out the stopper and smelt the contents: they had no more colour and smell than stale water—less, in fact. I poured four measures into the top of the walking stick, and then decided to screw it up for future use, and pour a fresh dose into the medicine glass, which was still lying on a shelf with the jars in the old laundry.

It was an odd sensation, standing there once more, knowing that the basement all around me and the house above were empty of their present occupants, Vita, the boys, while waiting in the shadows were possibly the people of my secret world.

When I had swallowed the dose I went and sat in the old kitchen, expectant and alert as a theatregoer who has just slipped into his stall before the curtain rises on the eagerly awaited third act of a play.

In this case either the players were on strike or the management at fault, for the curtain of my private theatre never rose, the scene remained unchanged. I sat down there in the basement for an hour, and nothing happened. I went out on to the patio, thinking the fresh air might do the trick, but time stayed obstinately at Wednesday morning in mid-August; I might have swallowed a draught from the kitchen tap for all the effect bottle C had upon mind or stomach.

At twelve o'clock I returned to the lab and poured a few more drops into the medicine glass. This had done the trick once before, and without any ill-effect.

I returned to the patio and stayed until after one o'clock, but still nothing happened, so I went upstairs and had some lunch. It must mean that the contents of bottle C had lost their strength, or Magnus had somehow missed out on the special ingredients and bottle C was worthless. If this was so, I had made my last trip. The curtain had risen on my journey across the Treesmill stream in the snow, only to fall by the railway tunnel at the close of the third act. I had come to journey's end.

The realisation was so devastating that I felt stunned. I had lost not only Magnus but the other world. It lay here, all around me, but out of reach. The people of that world would travel on in time without me, and I must keep to my own course, fulfilling God only knew what monotonous day-by-day. The link between the centuries had gone.

I went down to the basement once more and out into the patio, thinking that by walking on the stone flags and touching the walls some force would come through to me, that Roger's face would look out at me from the hatch door to the boiler room, or Robbie would emerge from the stables under the loft leading his pony. I knew they must be there, and I could not see them. Isolda too, waiting for the snows to melt. The house was inhabited not by the dead but by the living, and I was the restless wanderer, I was the ghost.

This urge to see, to listen, to move amongst them was so intense that it became intolerable; it was as though my brain had been set alight by some tremendous fire. I could not rest. I could not set myself to any humdrum task in the house or garden; the whole day had gone to waste, and what had promised to be hours of magic were slipping by unused.

I got out the car and drove to Tywardreath, the sight of the solid parish church a mockery to my mood. It had no right to be there in its present form. I wanted to sweep it away, leaving only the south aisle and the Priory chapel, see the Priory walls enclosing the churchyard. I drove aimlessly to the lay by at the top of the hill beyond the Treesmill turning and parked, thinking that, if I walked down the road and crossed the fields to the Gratten, memory of what I had once seen would fill the vacuum.

I stood by the car, reaching for a cigarette, but it had not touched my lips before a jolt shook me from head to foot, as though I had stepped on a live cable. There was no serene transition from present to past but a sensation of pain, with flashes before my eyes and thunder in my ears. "This is it," I thought. "I'm going to die." Then the flashes cleared, the thunder died away, and there was a mass of people lining the summit of the hill where I stood, crowding and pressing towards a building across the road. More people came from the direction of Tywardreath, men, women, children, some walking, some running. The building was the magnet, irregular in shape, with leaded windows, and what appeared to be a small chapel beside it. I had seen the village once before, at Martinmas, but that was from the green beyond the Priory walls. Now there were no booths, no travelling musicians, no slaughtered beasts. The air was crisp and cold, the ditches banked with frozen snow that had turned grey and hard from lying during weeks. Small puddles in the road had turned to craters of sheeted ice, and the ploughlands across the ditches were black with frost. Men, women and children alike were wrapped and hooded against the cold, their features sharp like the beaks of birds, and the mood I sensed was neither jocular nor gay but somehow predatory, the mob mood of people bent upon a spectacle that might turn sour. I drew nearer to the building, and saw that a covered chariot was drawn up by the chapel entrance, with servants standing by the horses' heads. I recognised the Champernoune coat-of-arms, and the servants too, while Roger himself stood within the chapel porch, his arms folded.

The door of the main building was shut, but as I stood there watching it opened, and a man, better dressed than those lining the route, emerged with a companion. I knew them both, for I had seen them last on the night when Otto Bodrugan had urged them to join in his rebellion against the King: they were Julian Polpey and Henry Trefrengy. They came down the pathway, and threading their way through the crowd paused near to where I stood.

"God preserve me from a woman's spite," said Polpey. "Roger has held the office for ten years, and now to be dismissed without reason being given, and the stewardship handed to Phil Hornwynk . . ."

"Young William will reinstate him when he comes of age, no doubt of that," replied Trefrengy. "He has his father's sense of justice and fair play. But I could smell the change coming these past twelve months or more. The plain truth is that she lacks not only a husband but a man as well, and Roger has had his bellyful and will oblige no more."

"He finds his oats elsewhere."

The last speaker, Geoffrey Lampetho from the valley, had shouldered his way through the crowd to join them. "Rumour has it there's a woman under his roof. You should know, Trefrengy, being his neighbour."

"I know nothing," answered Trefrengy shortly. "Roger keeps his counsel, I keep mine. In hard weather such as this wouldn't any Christian give shelter to a stranger on the road?"

Lampetho laughed, digging him with his elbow. "Neatly said, but you can't deny it," he said. "Why else does my Lady Champernoune come here from Trelawn, disregarding the state of the roads, unless to snuff her out? I was in the geld house here before you to pay my rents, and she sat in the inner room while Hornwynk collected. All the paint in the world couldn't hide the black look on her face: dismissing Roger from his stewardship won't see the end of it. Meantime, sport for the populace of another kind. Will you stay to watch the fun?"

Julian Polpey shook his head in disgust. "Not I," he answered. "Why should we in Tywardreath have some custom foisted upon us from elsewhere, making us barbarians? Lady Champernoune must be sick in mind to think of it. I'm for home."

He turned and disappeared into the crowd, which was now thick not only upon the summit of the hill where the house and chapel stood, but halfway down the track to Treesmill. One and all wore this curious air of expectancy upon their faces, half-resentful, half-eager, and Geoffrey Lampetho, pointing this out to his companion, laughed again.

"Sick in mind maybe, but it salves her conscience to have another widow act as scapegoat, and sweetens Quadragessima for us. There's nothing a mob likes more than witnessing public penance."

He turned his head, like the rest, towards the valley, and Henry Trefrengy edged forward past the Champernoune servants to the chapel entrance where Roger stood, while I followed close behind.

"I'm sorry for what has happened," he said. "No gratitude, no recompense. Ten years of your life wasted, gone for nothing."

"Not wasted," answered Roger briefly. "William will come of age in June and marry. His mother will lose her influence, and the monk as well. You know the Bishop of Exeter has expelled him finally, and he must return to the Abbey at Angers, where he should have gone a year ago?"

"God be praised!" exclaimed Trefrengy. "The Priory stinks because of him, the parish too. Look at the people yonder . . ."

Roger stared over Trefrengy's head at the gaping crowd. "I may have acted hard as steward, but to make sport of Rob Rosgof's widow was more than I could stomach," he said. "I stood against it, and this was another reason for my dismissal. The monk is responsible for all of this, to satisfy my lady's vanity and lust."

The entrance to the chapel darkened, and the small, slight figure of Jean de Meral appeared in the open doorway. He put his hand on Roger's shoulder.

"You used not to be so squeamish once," he said. "Have you forgotten those evenings in the Priory cellars, and in your own as well? I taught you more than philosophy, my friend, on those occasions."

"Take your hand off me," replied Roger curtly. "I parted company with you and your brethren when you let young Henry Bodrugan die under the Priory roof, and could have saved him."

The monk smiled. "And now, to show sympathy with the dead, you harbour an adulterous wife under your own?" he asked. "We are all hypocrites, my friend. I warn you, my lady knows your wayfarer's identity, and it is partly on her account that she is here in Tywardreath. She has certain proposals to put before the lady Isolda when this business with Rosgof's widow has been settled."

"Which business, please God, will be struck from the manor records in years to come, and rebound upon your head instead, to your everlasting shame," said Trefrengy.

"You forget," murmured the monk, "I am a bird of passage, and in a few days' time shall have spread my wings for France."

There was a sudden stir amongst the crowd, and a man appeared at the door of the adjoining building, which Lampetho had named the geld house. Stout, florid-faced, he held a document in his hand. Beside him, wrapped in a cloak from head to foot, was Joanna Champernoune.

The man, whom I took to be the new steward Hornwynk, advanced to address the crowd, unrolling the document in his hand.

"Good people of Tywardreath," he proclaimed, "whether freeman, customary tenant or serf, those of you who pay rent to the manor court have done so here today at the geld house. And since this manor of Tywardreath was once held by the Lady Isolda Cardinham of Cardinham, who sold it to our late lord's grandfather, it has been decided to introduce here a practice established in the manor of Cardinham since the Conquest." He paused a moment, the better to impress his words upon his listeners. "The practice being," he continued, "that any widow of a customary tenant, holding lands through her late husband, who has deviated from the path of chastity, shall either forfeit her lands or make due penance for their recovery before the lord of the manor and the steward of the manor court. Today before the Lady Joanna Champernoune, representing the lord of the manor William, a minor, and myself, Philip Hornwynk, steward, Mary, widow of Robert Rosgof, must make such penance if she desires the restoration of her lands."

A murmur rose from the crowd, a strange blend of excitement and curiosity, and a sudden sound of shouting came from the road leading down to Treesmill.

"She'll never face them," said Trefrengy. "Mary Rosgof has a son at home who would rather surrender his farmland ten times over than have his mother shamed."

"You are mistaken," answered the monk. "He knows her shame will prove his gain in six months' time, when she is brought to bed of a bastard child, and he can turn both out of doors and keep the lands himself."

"Then you've persuaded him," said Roger, "and lined his purse in so doing."

The shouting and the cries increased, and as the people pressed forward I saw a procession ascend the hill from Treesmill, lumbering towards us at a jog-trot. Two lads raced ahead, brandishing whips, and behind them came five men escorting what at first sight I took to be a small moorland pony with a woman mounted on its back. They drew closer, and the laughter amongst the spectators turned to jeers, as the woman sagged upon her steed and would have fallen, had not one of the men escorting her held her fast, flourishing a hay fork in his other hand. She was not mounted upon a pony at all but on a great black sheep, his horns be-ribboned with crepe, and the two fellows on either side had thrust a halter over his head to lead him, so that, startled and terrified of the crowd about him, he ducked and stumbled in a vain endeavour to throw his passenger from his back. The woman was draped in black to match her steed, with a black veil covering her face, her hands bound in front of her with leather thongs; I could see her fingers clutching at the thick dark wool on the sheep's neck.

The procession came stumbling and lurching to the geld house, and as it drew to a standstill before Hornwynk and Joanna, the escort jerking the halter, the man with the hay fork dragged off the woman's veil to disclose her features. She could not have been more than thirty-five, her eyes as terror-stricken as the sheep that bore her, while her dark hair, roughly scissored, stood out from her head like a cropped thatch. The jeering turned to silence as the woman, trembling, bowed her head before Joanna.

"Mary Rosgof, do you admit your fault?" called Hornwynk.

"I do in all humility," she answered, her voice low.

"Speak louder for all to hear, and state its nature," he cried.

The wretched woman, her pale face flushing, raised her head and looked toward Joanna.

"I lay with another man, my husband not six months dead, thus forfeiting the lands I held in trust for my son. I crave indulgence of my lady and the manor court, and beg for the restoration of my lands, confessing my incontinence. Should I give birth to a base-born child, my son will take possession of the lands and do with me as he pleases."

Joanna beckoned the new steward to her side, and he bent low as she whispered something in his ear. Then he turned once more and addressed the penitent.

"My gracious lady cannot condone your fault, which is of a nature abhorrent to all people, but since you have admitted it in person, and before the manor court and others of this parish, she will, in great clemency, restore the forfeited lands you rent from her."

The woman bowed her head and murmured gratitude, then asked with swimming eyes if there was further penance she must do.

"Aye," returned the steward. "Descend from the sheep that carried you in your shame, proceed to the chapel here, crawling on your knees, and confess your sin before the altar. Brother John will hear your confession."

The two men who held the sheep pulled the woman from its back, forcing her to her knees, and as she dragged herself along the path towards the chapel, hampered by her skirts, a groan arose from the watching crowd, as if this total degradation could in some way appease their own sense of shame. The monk waited until she had crawled to his feet, then turned into the chapel, where she followed him. Her escort, at a sign from Hornwynk, set the sheep free, whereupon it ran in terror amongst the crowd, scattering them to either side, and a great shout of hysterical laughter burst forth, as they drove it back along the road to Treesmill, pelting it with pieces of packed snow, sticks, anything they could find. With the sudden release from tension everyone was in a moment laughing, joking, running, seized by a holiday mood, what was happening making a break between winter and the Lenten season just begun. Soon they had all dispersed, and no one was left before the geld house but Joanna herself, Hornwynk the steward, and Roger and Trefrengy standing to one side.

"So be it," said Joanna. "Tell my servants I am ready to leave. There is nothing further to keep me here in Tywardreath save a certain business which I can attend to on the road home."

The steward went down the path to prepare for her departure, the servants opening the carriage door in readiness, and Joanna, pausing, looking across the path at Roger.

"The people were well satisfied if you are not," she said, "and will pay their rents the sooner for it in the future. The custom has its merits if it inspires fear, and may well spread to other manors."

"God forbid," answered Roger.

Geoffrey Lampetho had been right about the paint on her face, or perhaps the atmosphere inside the geld house had been close. It ran in streaks now on either cheek, which, with increasing weight, were a puffy puce. She seemed to have aged, since I saw her last, a good ten years. The splendour had gone from her brown eyes, turning them hard like agate.

She put out her hand now and touched Roger's arm. "Come," she said, "we have known one another too long for lies and subterfuge. I have a message for the Lady Isolda from her brother Sir William Ferrers, which I have promised to deliver to her in person. If you bar your door to me now I can summon fifty men from the manor to break it down."

"And I another fifty between here and Fowey to withstand them," answered Roger. "But you may follow me to Kylmerth if you wish, and beg an interview. Whether it will be granted or not I cannot say."

Joanna smiled. "It will," she said, "it will," and taking her skirts in her hands she swept down the path towards the carriage, followed by the monk. Once it would have been Roger who helped her mount the steps into the waiting vehicle; today it was the new steward Hornwynk, flushed with self-esteem and bowing low, while Roger, crossing to a gate behind the chapel, where his pony was tethered, leapt upon its back, and kicking his heels into its side rode out into the road. The lumbering chariot rumbled after him, Joanna and the monk inside it, and the few stragglers at the top of the hill stared to watch it pass down the icy road to the village green and the Priory walls beyond. A bell sounded from the Priory chapel and the vehicle began to draw away from me, and Roger too, and I started running, fearing to lose both. Then a pounding in my heart began, and a singing in my ears, and I saw the carriage lurch to a standstill; the window was lowered, and Joanna herself looked out of it, waving her hand and beckoning to me. I stumbled to the window, breathless, the singing increasing to a roar. Then it ceased, absolutely, and I was swaying on my feet, with the clock in St. Andrews' church striking seven, and the Buick had drawn up on the road ahead of me, with Vita waving from the window, and the surprised faces of the boys and Mrs. Collins looking out.

22

THEY WERE ALL talking at once, and the boys were laughing. I heard Micky say, "We saw you running down the hill, you looked so funny . . ." and Teddy chimed in, "Mom waved and called, but you didn't hear at first, you seemed to look the other way." Vita was staring at me from the open window by the driving seat. "You'd best get in," she said, "you can hardly stand," and Mrs. Collins, red in the face and flustered, opened the door for me the other side. I obeyed mechanically, forgetting my own car parked in the lay by, and squeezed in beside Mrs. Collins, as we continued along the lane skirting the village towards Polmear.

"A good thing we drove this way," said Vita. "Mrs. Collins said it was quicker than going down through St. Blazey and Par."

I could not remember where they had been or what they were doing, and although the singing in my ears had stopped my heart was thumping still, and vertigo was not far away.

"Bude was super," said Teddy. "We had surfboards, but Mom wouldn't let us go out of our depth. And the ocean was rolling in, huge great waves, much better than here. You ought to have come with us."

Bude, that was right. They had gone to spend the day at Bude, leaving me alone in the house. But what was I doing wandering in Tywardreath? As we passed the almshouses at the bottom of Polmear hill and I looked across to Polpey and the Lampetho valley, I remembered how Julian Polpey had not waited for the loathsome spectacle outside the geld house but had walked home, and Geoffrey Lampetho had been one of those amongst the crowd who had pelted the sheep with stones.

It was over and done with, finished. It was not happening any more. Mrs. Collins was saying something to Vita about dropping her at the top of Polkerris hill, and the next thing I knew was that she had disappeared and Vita had drawn up outside Kilmarth.

"Run along in," she said sharply to the boys. "Put your swimming trunks in the hot cupboard and start laying the supper," and when they had vanished up the steps into the house she turned to me and said, "Can you make it?"

"Make what?" I was still dazed, and could not follow her.

"Make the steps," she said. "You were rocking on your feet when we came on you just now. I felt terrible in front of Mrs. Collins and the boys. However much have you had to drink?"

"Drink?" I repeated. "I haven't drunk a thing."

"Oh, for heaven's sake," she said, "don't start lying. It's been a long day, and I'm tired. Come on, I'll help you into the house."

Perhaps this was the answer. Perhaps it was best she should think I had been sitting in some pub. I got out of the car, and she was right—I was still rocking on my feet, and I was glad of her arm to steady me up the garden and into the house.

"I'll be all right," I said. "I'll go and sit in the library."

"I'd rather you went straight to bed," she said. "The boys have never seen you like this. They're bound to notice."

"I don't want to go to bed. I'll just sit in the library and shut the door. They needn't come in."

"Oh well, if you insist on being obstinate . . ." She shrugged in exasperation. "I'll tell them we'll eat in the kitchen. For heaven's sake don't join us—I'll bring you something later."

I heard her walk through the hall to the kitchen, and slam the door. I flopped on a chair in the library and closed my eyes. A strange lethargy crept over me; I wanted to sleep. Vita was right, I should have gone to bed, but I hadn't the energy even to get up out of the chair. If I stayed here quietly, in the stillness and the silence, the feeling of exhaustion, of being drained, would pass away. Tough luck on the boys, if there was some programme they hoped to watch on TV, but I would make it up to them tomorrow, take them sailing, go to Chapel Point. I must make up to Vita too; this business would set us back again, the sweat of reconciliation would have to start all over again.

I awoke with a sudden jerk, to find the room in darkness. I glanced at my watch, and it was almost half-past nine. I had slept for nearly two hours. I felt quite normal, hungry too. I went through the dining room into the hall, and heard the sound of the gramophone coming from the music room, but the door was shut. They must have finished eating ages ago, for the lights were turned out in the kitchen. I rummaged in the fridge to find eggs and bacon to fry, and I had just put the frying pan on the stove when I heard someone moving about in the basement. I went to the top of the back stairs and called, thinking it was one of the boys, who might report to me on Vita's mood. Nobody answered.

"Teddy?" I shouted. "Micky?"

The footsteps were quite definite, passing across the old kitchen and then on towards the boiler room. I went down the stairs, fumbling for the lights, but they were not in the right place, I couldn't find the switch, and I had to grope my way to the old kitchen by feeling for the walls. Whoever it was ahead of me had passed through the boiler room on to the patio, for I could hear him stamping about there, and he was drawing water from the well that lay in the near corner and was covered up and never used. And now there were further footsteps, but not from the patio, from the stairs, and turning round I saw that the stairs had gone and the footsteps were coming from the ladder leading to the floor above. It was no longer dark, but the murky grey of a winter afternoon, and a woman was coming down the ladder, bearing a lighted candle in her hands. The singing started in my ears, the bursting thunder clap of sound, and the drug was taking effect all over again *without having been renewed*. I did not want it now, I was afraid, for it meant that past and present were merging, and Vita and the boys were with me, in my own time, in the front part of the house.

The woman brushed past me, shielding the candle's flame from the draught. It was Isolda. I flattened myself against the wall, holding my breath, for surely she must dissolve if I as much as moved, and what I was seeing was a figment of the imagination, an aftermath of what had been that afternoon. She set the candle down on a bench, lighting another that stood beside it, and began humming under her breath, an odd sweet snatch of song, and all the time I could hear the distant throbbing of the radiogram from the music room on the ground floor of the house.

"Robbie," she called softly, "Robbie, are you there?"

The boy came in from the yard through the low arched doorway, setting his pail of water on the kitchen floor.

"Is it freezing still?" she asked.

"Aye," he said, "and will do until full moon is past. You must stay a few days yet, if you can bear with us."

"Bear with you?" she smiled. "Rejoice in you, rather, and willingly. I wish my daughters were as well-mannered as you and Bess, and minded what I tell them as you mind your brother Roger."

"If we do it's from respect for you," he answered. "We got hard words from him, and a belting too, before you came." He laughed, shaking the thick hair out of his eyes, and lifting the pail poured the water into a pitcher on the trestle table. "We eat well, too," he added. "Meat every day instead of salted fish, and the pig I slaughtered yesterday would have stayed in his sty until Quadragesima was done had you not graced our table. Bess and I would have you live with us forever and not leave us when the weather mends."

"Ah, I understand," said Isolda, mocking. "It isn't for myself you like me here but for the ease of living."

He frowned, uncertain what she meant, then his face cleared, and he smiled again. "Nay, that's untrue," he said. "We feared when you first came that you'd play the lady and we couldn't please you. It's not so now, you could be one of us. Bess loves you, and so do I. As for Roger, God knows he has sung your praises to us these past two years or more."

He flushed, suddenly awkward, as if he had said too much, and she put out her hand to him and touched his arm.

"Dear Robbie," she said gently, "I love you too, and Bess, and the warm welcome you have given me these past weeks. I shall never forget it."

The sound of footsteps made me raise my head to the loft above, but it was only the girl descending the ladder, certainly cleaner than when I saw her last, her long hair combed and smooth, her face well scrubbed.

"I can hear Roger riding through the copse," she called. "See to the pony, Robbie, when he comes, while I set the table."

The boy went out into the yard and his sister heaped fresh turf upon the hearth, and furze as well. The furze flickered and caught, throwing great tongues of flame upon the smoky walls, and as Bess looked over her shoulder, smiling at Isolda, I knew how it must have been here for the four of them, night after night, during the time of frost, seated at the trestle table with the candles set amongst the pewter plates.

"Here's your brother now," said Isolda, and she went and stood by the open door as he rode into the yard and flung himself off the pony, throwing the reins to Robbie. It was not yet dark, and the yard, so much wider than the patio I knew, stretched to the wall above the fields, so that through the open gate I could see the fields sloping to the sea beyond and the wide expanse of bay. The mud in the yard was frosted hard, the air was sharply cold, and the small trees in the copse stood black and naked against the sky. Robbie led the pony to his shed beside the byre, as Roger crossed the yard towards Isolda.

"You bring bad news," said Isolda. "I can tell it from your face."

"My lady knows you are here," said Roger. "She is on her way to see you, with a message from your brother. If you wish it I can turn the chariot back from the top of the hill. Robbie and I will have no trouble with her servants."

"No trouble now, perhaps," she answered, "but later she could do harm to you, to Robbie and Bess, to this whole place. I would not have that happen for the world."

"I would sooner she razed the house to the ground than cause you suffering," he said.

He stood there, looking down at her, and I knew instinctively that they had reached a point in their relationship, through proximity and sympathy during the past days, when his love for her could no longer smoulder and be contained, but must burn up and reach the sky, or else be quenched.

"I know you would, Roger," she said, "but any further suffering that may come my way I can bear alone. If I have brought dishonour on two houses, my husband's and Otto Bodrugan's, which doubtless will be said about me down the years, I'll not do the same to yours."

"Dishonour?" He spread out his hands and looked about him at the low walls encircling the yard, the narrow thatched dwelling where the ponies and the cows were housed. "This was my father's farm and will be Robbie's when I die, and had you sheltered here for one night only and not fifteen, you would have lent it grace enough to last through centuries."

She must have sensed the depth of feeling in his voice, and possibly the passion too, for a sudden shadow came across her face, a wariness, as if prompted by an inner voice that murmured, "Thus far, and no further." Moving to the open gate she put her hand upon it, and looked out over the fields to the bay beyond.

"Fifteen nights," she repeated, "and on each one of them, since I have been with you, and in the daytime too, I have stood looking out across the sea to Chapel Point, remembering that his ship would anchor there, below Bodrugan, and this was the bay he sailed when he came to find me in the Treesmill creek. Part of me died with him, Roger, the day they drowned him, and I think you know it."

I wondered what Roger's dream had been, and whether, as we all do, he had created a fantasy that their lives would somehow fuse; not in marriage; not as lovers, even, but in some sort of drifting intimacy, intuitive and silent, that no one else would ever share. Whether it were so or not, the dream was shattered; by speaking Bodrugan's name she had made this plain.

"Yes," he said, "I have always known it. If I have given you cause to believe otherwise, forgive me."

He lifted his head and listened. She did the same, and beyond the dark copse above the farm came the sound of voices and trampling of feet, and then the figures of three of the Champernoune servants emerged through the naked trees.

"Roger Kylmerth?" one of them called. "Your road is too rough to drive the chariot down to your dwelling, and my lady waits within it on the hill."

"Then she must stay there," answered Roger, "or come on foot, with your assistance. It's one and the same to us."

The men hesitated a moment, conferring under the trees, and Isolda, at a sign from Roger, turned quickly and passed across the yard into the house. Roger whistled, and Robbie came out of the door where the ponies were stabled.

"Lady Champernoune is above, and some of her servants," said Roger quietly. "She could have summoned others between here and Tywardreath, and we may have trouble. Stay within call should I need you."

Robbie nodded, and went back into the stables. It was growing darker every moment, colder, too, the trees in the copse etched more sharply against the sky. Presently I saw the lights of the first flares on the crest of the hill; Joanna was descending, three of the servants with her, and the monk as well. They came slowly and in silence, Joanna's dark cloak and the monk's habit blending as though the two were one; and standing beside Roger, watching their progress, it seemed to me that the group had something sinister about it; the hooded figures could have been walking in procession through a churchyard to a waiting grave.

When they arrived at the open gate Joanna paused and looked about her, then she said to Roger, "In all the ten years you served my household you never thought to bid me welcome here."

"No, my lady," he replied, "you neither asked for refuge nor desired it. Consolation was ever ready for you under your own roof."

The irony did not touch her, or if it did she chose to ignore it, and Roger led the way towards the house.

"Where must my servants wait?" she asked. "Have the courtesy to direct them to your kitchen."

"We ourselves live in the kitchen," he told her, "and Lady Carminowe will receive you there. Your men will find it warm enough in the byre amongst the cows, or with the ponies, whichever they please."

He stood aside to let her pass with the monk, and followed after, and as we crossed the threshold I saw that the trestle table had been pulled close to the hearth, the tallow candles set upon it, and Isolda sat alone at the head of the table. Bess must have gone to the room above.

Joanna stared about her, at a loss, I think, to find herself in such surroundings. God knows what she had expected—some greater attempt at comfort, perhaps, with furnishings pilfered from her own abandoned manor house.

"So . . ." she said at last, "this is the retreat, and snug enough, no doubt, on a winter's night, apart from the smell of beasts across the yard. How do you do, Isolda?"

"I do very well, as you see," Isolda answered. "I have lived better here, and had more kindness, in two weeks than in as many months or years spent at Tregesteynton or Carminowe."

"I don't doubt it," said Joanna. "Contrast ever whetted appetite grown stale. You had a fancy for Bodrugan Castle once, but had Otto lived you would have become as weary there and of him as you have of other properties and other men, including your own husband. Well, this is a rich reward. Tell me, do both brothers share you here before the hearth?"

I heard Roger draw in his breath, and he moved forward, as though to place himself between the two women, but Isolda, her small face pale in the flickering light of two candles, only smiled.

"Not as yet," she said. "The elder is too proud, the younger too shy. My protestations of affection fall upon deaf ears. What do you want with me, Joanna? Have you brought a message from William? If so, speak plainly and have done with it."

The monk, who was still standing by the door, took a letter from his habit to give to Joanna, but she waved it aside.

"Read it to Lady Carminowe," she said. "I have no desire to strain my eyes in this dim light. And you may leave us," she added to Roger. "Family matters are no longer your concern. You meddled with them enough when you were my steward."

"This is his house, and he has the right to be here," said Isolda. "Besides, he is my friend, and I prefer him to stay."

Joanna shrugged, and sat down at the lower end of the table opposite Isolda.

"If Lady Carminowe permits," said the monk smoothly, "this is the letter from her brother, Sir William Ferrers, which came to Trelawn a few days since, Sir William thinking his messenger would find her there with Lady Champernoune. It reads thus:

'Dearest Sister, the news of your flight from Tregesteynton has only reached us here at Bere within the past week, because of the hard weather and the state of the roads. I am at a loss to understand either your action or your great imprudence. You must know that by deserting your husband and your children you forfeit all claims on his and their affection, and, I am bound to say, on mine as well. Whether Oliver, in Christian charity, will receive you at Carminowe again I cannot say, but I misdoubt it, fearing your pernicious influence upon his daughters, and for my own part I could not offer you protection at Bere, for Matilda, as Oliver's sister, has too much sympathy for her brother to offer hospitality to his erring wife. Indeed, she is in so sore a state since hearing you have deserted him that she could not countenance your presence amongst us with our five sons. It seems, therefore, there is only one course open to you, which is to seek refuge in the nunnery of Cornworthy here in Devon, the Prioress being known to me, and to remain there in seclusion until such time as Oliver, or some other member of the family, may be willing to receive you. I have every confidence that our kinswoman, Joanna, will permit her servants to escort you to Cornworthy.

'Farewell, in the power of Christ,
'Your sorrowful brother,
'WILLIAM FERRERS'"

The monk folded the letter and passed it across the table to Isolda. "You may see for yourself, my lady," he murmured, "that the letter is in Sir William's own handwriting, and bears his signature. There is no deception."

She barely glanced at it. "You are very right," she said, "there is no deception."

Joanna smiled. "If William had known you were here and not at Trelawn, I doubt if he would have written so generously, nor would the Prioress at Cornworthy be willing to open her convent doors. However, you may count on me to keep it secret, and arrange your escort into Devon. Two days under my roof to make the necessary preparations, a change of attire, which I can see you need, and you can be on the road." She leant back in her chair, a look of triumph on her face. "I am told the air is mild at Cornworthy," she added. "The nuns there live to a great age."

"Then let us dwell behind convent walls together," replied Isolda. "Widows, when their sons marry, as your William does next year, must needs find new shelter, along with erring wives. We will be sisters in misfortune."

Proud and defiant, she stared at Joanna down the length of the trestle table, and the candlelight, throwing shadows on the wall, distorted both their figures, turning Joanna, because of her hooded cloak and widow's veil, to the likeness of some monstrous crab.

"You forget," she said, playing with her multitude of rings, slipping them from one finger to another, "I have a licence to remarry, and can do so whenever I choose to pick a new husband from a chain of suitors. You are still bound to Oliver, and furthermore disgraced. There is a second course open to you other than the nunnery at Cornworthy, if you prefer it, and that is to remain as drab here to my one-time steward, but I warn you the parish might serve you as they served my tenant this day in Tywardreath, and have you riding to do penance in the manor chapel on the back of a black ram."

She broke into a peal of laughter, and, turning to the monk who was standing behind her chair, she said, "What do you say, Frère Jean? We could mount the one on a ram and the other on a ewe, and have them jog-trot together or forfeit the Kylmerth land."

I knew it must happen, and it did. Roger seized the monk and threw him back against the wall. Then, bending to Joanna, he jerked her to her feet.

"Insult me as you please, not Lady Carminowe," he said. "This is my house, and you shall leave it."

"I will do so," she replied, "when she has made her choice. I have three servants only in your cow house in the yard, but a score or more waiting by my carriage on the hill, only too willing to pay off ancient grudges."

"Then summon them," said Roger, freeing her. "Robbie and I can defend our home against every one of your tenants, the whole parish if you will."

His voice, raised in anger, had penetrated to the sleeping room above, and Bess came running down the ladder, pale and anxious, to take her stand behind Isolda's bench.

"Who's this?" asked Joanna. "A third for the sheepfold? How many other slatterns do you harbour in your loft?"

"Bess is Roger's sister, and so my own," answered Isolda, putting her arm round the frightened girl. "And now, Joanna, call your servants so that this household can be rid of you. God knows we've borne your insults long enough."

"We?" queried Joanna. "Then you count yourself one of them?"

"Yes, while I receive their hospitality," said Isolda.

"So you do not intend to travel with me to Trelawn?"

Isolda hesitated, glancing first at Roger, then at Bess. But before she could reply the monk stepped out of the shadows on the wall and stood beside them.

"There is a third choice yet for Lady Carminowe," he murmured. "I sail from Fowey, within twenty-four hours, to the parent house of St. Sergius and Bacchus at Angers. If she and the girl care to accompany me to France, I know very well I could find asylum for them there. No one would molest them, and they would be safe from all pursuit. Their very existence would be forgotten once they were in France, and Lady Carminowe herself be at liberty to start life anew in pleasanter surroundings than behind convent walls."

The proposal was so obvious a trick to get both Bess and Isolda out of Roger's care and into his own charge, to dispose of them as he wished, that I expected even his patroness to round upon him. Instead, she smiled, and shrugged her shoulders.

"Upon my word, Frère Jean, you show true Christian feeling," she said. "What do you say, Isolda? Now you have three alternatives: seclusion at Cornworthy, life in a pigsty at Kylmerth, or the protection of a Benedictine monk across the water. I know which I would choose."

She glanced about her as she had first done when she entered the house, and moving round the room touched the smoke-grimed walls, grimacing, then examined her fingers, wiping them with the handkerchief she carried, and finally paused by the ladder leading to the loft above, her foot upon one rung.

"One pallet amongst four, and louse-ridden?" she asked. "If you travel into Devon or to France, Isolda, I'll thank you to sprinkle your gown with vinegar first."

The singing started in my ears, and the thunder. Their figures began to fade. All but

Joanna's, standing there at the foot of the ladder. She stared towards me, her eyes opening wide, and I did not care what happened afterwards, I wanted to put my hands round her throat and choke her before she vanished, like the others, out of sight. I crossed the room and stood beside her, and she did not fade. She began to scream, as I shook her backwards and forwards, my hands round her plump, white neck.

"Damn you," I shouted, "damn you . . . damn you . . ." and the screaming was all around me, and above as well. I loosened my grip and looked up, and the boys were crouching there on the landing at the top of the back stairs, and Vita had fallen against the banister beside me, and was staring at me, whitefaced, terrified, her hands to her throat.

"Oh, my God" I said. "Vita . . . darling . . . Oh, my God . . ."

I fell forwards on to the banister rail beside her, retching, seized by the uncontrollable, blasted vertigo, and she dragged herself away up the stairs to safety beside the boys, and they all started screaming once again.

23

THERE WAS NOTHING I could do. I lay there on the stairs, clinging to the handrail, arms and legs splayed out grotesquely, with walls and ceiling reeling above my head. If I shut my eyes the vertigo increased, with streaks of golden light stabbing the darkness. Presently the screaming stopped; the boys were crying, and I could hear the crying die away as they ran into the kitchen overhead, slamming both the doors.

Blinded by dizziness and nausea, I started to crawl upstairs, step by step, and when I had reached the top stood upright, swaying, and felt my way across the kitchen to the hall. The lights were on, the doors were open. Vita and the boys must have run up to the bedroom and locked themselves in. I staggered into the lobby and reached for the telephone, floor and ceiling blurring to become one. I sat there, holding the receiver in my hand, until the floor steadied, and the telephone directory, instead of being a jumble of black dots, straightened into words. I found Dr. Powell's number at last and dialled it, and when he answered the tension inside me broke, and I felt the sweat pouring down my face.

"It's Richard Young from Kilmarth," I said. "You remember, the friend of Professor Lane."

"Oh yes?" He sounded surprised. After all, I was not one of his patients, and I must only be a face amongst hundreds of summer visitors.

"The most frightful thing has happened," I said. "I had a sort of blackout and tried to strangle my wife. I may have hurt her, I don't know."

My voice was calm, without emotion, yet all the time my heart was pounding, and the realisation of what had happened was clear and strong. There was no confusion. No merging of two worlds.

"Is she unconscious?" he asked.

"No," I said, "no, I don't think so. She's upstairs, with the boys. They must have locked themselves in the bedroom. I'm speaking to you from the lobby downstairs."

He was silent, and for one terrible moment I was afraid he was going to tell me it was none of his business and I had better call the police. Then, "All right, I'll be along straight away," he said, and rang off.

I put down the receiver and wiped the sweat off my face. The vertigo had subsided, and I was able to stand without swaying. I walked slowly upstairs and through the dressing room to the bathroom door. It was locked.

"Darling," I called, "don't worry, it's O.K. I've just telephoned the doctor. He's coming out at once. Stay there with the boys until you hear his car." She did not answer, and I called louder. "Vita," I shouted, "Teddy, Micky, don't be frightened, the doctor's coming. Everything's going to be all right."

I went back downstairs and opened the front door, and stood waiting there on the steps. It was a fine night, the sky ablaze with stars. There was no sound anywhere; the campers in the field across the Polkerris road must have turned in. I looked at my watch. It was twenty to eleven. Then I heard the sound of the doctor's car coming along the main road from Fowey, and I began to sweat again, not from fear but from relief. He turned down the drive and came to a standstill in the sweep before the house. I went through the garden to meet him.

"Thank God you've come," I said.

We went into the house together, and I pointed up the stairs. "First room at the top, on the right. That's my dressing room, but she's locked the bathroom beyond. Tell them who you are. I'll wait for you down here."

He ran upstairs, two steps at a time, and I kept thinking that the silence from above meant that Vita was dying, that she was lying on the bed, and the boys were crouching beside her, too terrified to move. I went into the music room and sat down, wondering what would happen if he told me Vita was dead. All of it was happening. All of it was true.

He was up there a long time, and presently I heard the sound of shifting furniture; they must be dragging the divan bed through the bathroom to the bedroom, and I could hear the doctor talking, and Teddy too. I wondered what the hell they were doing. I went and listened at the foot of the stairs, but they had gone through to the bedroom again and shut the door. I sat on in the music room, waiting.

He came down just after the clock in the hall struck eleven. "Everything's under control," he said. "No panic stations. Your wife's all right, and so are your stepsons. Now what about you?"

I tried to stand up, but he pushed me back into the chair.

"Have I hurt her?" I asked.

"Slight bruising on the neck, nothing more," he said. "It may look a bit blue tomorrow, but it won't show if she wears a scarf."

"Did she tell you what happened?"

"Supposing you tell me."

"I'd rather hear her version first," I said.

He took a cigarette out of a packet and lighted it. "Well," he said, "I gather you didn't want any dinner, for reasons known best to yourself, and she spent the evening in here with the boys, while you were in the library. Then they decided to go to bed, and she found you had gone to the kitchen and switched on the lights. There was bacon on the stove burnt to a frazzle, the stove still on, but nobody there. So she went down to the basement. It seems you were standing there, near the old kitchen, so she said, waiting for her to come downstairs, and as soon as you saw her you went straight across to the foot of the stairs and began swearing at her, and then you put your hands round her throat and tried to throttle her."

"That's right," I said.

He looked at me sharply. Perhaps he thought I would deny it. "She insists you were fighting drunk and didn't know what you were doing," he said, "but it was a pretty grim experience for all of them, and she and those boys were scared out of their wits. More so, as I gather you're not a drinking type."

"No," I said, "I'm not. And I wasn't drunk."

He did not answer for a moment. Then he came and stood in front of me, and taking some sort of flash thing from the bag he had with him he examined my eyes. Afterwards he felt my pulse.

"What are you on?" he asked abruptly.

"On?"

"Yes, what drug. Tell me straight, and I'll know how to treat you."

"That's just it," I said. "I don't know."

"Was it something Professor Lane gave you?"

"Yes," I replied.

He sat down on the arm of the sofa beside my chair. "By mouth or by injection?"

"By mouth."

"Was he treating you for something specific?"

"He wasn't treating me for anything. It was an experiment. Something I volunteered to do for him. I've never taken drugs in my life before I came down here."

He went on looking at me with his shrewd eyes, and I knew there was nothing for it but to tell him everything.

"Was Professor Lane on the same drug when he walked into that freight train?" he asked.

"Yes."

He got off the sofa and began walking up and down the room, fiddling with things on tables, picking them up and putting them down again, as Magnus himself used to do when coming to a decision.

"I ought to get you into hospital for observation," he said.

"No," I said, "for God's sake . . ." I got up from my chair. "Look," I said, "I've got the stuff in a bottle upstairs. It's all there is left. One bottle. He told me to destroy everything I found here in his lab, and I did—it's all buried in the wood above the garden. I only kept the one bottle, and I used some of it today. It must be different in some way—stronger, I don't know—but you take it away, have it analysed, anything. Surely you realize, after what has happened tonight, I couldn't touch the stuff again? Christ! I might have killed my wife."

"I know," he said. "That's why you ought to be in hospital."

He did not know. He did not understand. How could he understand?

"Look," I said, "I never saw Vita, my wife, standing at the foot of the stairs. It wasn't her I tried to strangle. It was another woman."

"What woman?" he asked.

"A woman called Joanna," I said. "She lived six hundred years ago. She was down there, in the old farmhouse kitchen, and the others were with her too, Isolda Carminowe, and the monk Jean de Meral, and the man the farm belonged to, who used to be her steward, Roger Kylmerth."

He put out his hand and held my arm. "All right," he said, "steady on, I follow you. You took the drug, and then you went downstairs and saw these people in the basement?"

"Yes," I said, "but not only here. I've seen them in Tywardreath as well, at the old manor house below the Gratten, and at the Priory too. That's what the drug does. It takes you back into the past, straight into an older world."

I could hear my voice rising in excitement, and he kept a firm grip on my arm. "You don't believe me!" I persisted. "How can you possibly believe me? But I swear to you I've seen them, heard them talking, watched them moving, I've even seen a man, Isolda's lover Otto Bodrugan, murdered down in Treesmill creek."

"I believe you all right," he said. "Now supposing we go together and you hand over that remaining bottle?"

I led him upstairs to the dressing room, and took the bottle out of the locked suitcase. He did not examine it, he just put it in his bag.

"Now I'll tell you what I'm going to do," he said. "I'm going to give you a pretty hefty sedative that will put you out until tomorrow morning. Is there some other room than this where you can sleep?"

"Yes," I said. "There's the spare room along the landing here."

"Right," he said. "Collect a pair of pyjamas and let's go."

We went together into the spare room, and I undressed and got into bed, feeling suddenly humble and subdued, like a child without responsibility.

"I'll do anything you say," I told the doctor. "Put me right out, if you like, so that I never wake again."

"I shan't do that," he answered, and for the first time smiled. "When you open your eyes tomorrow I shall probably be the first object you see."

"Then you won't pack me off to hospital?"

"Probably not. We'll talk about it in the morning."

He was getting a syringe out of his bag. "I don't mind what you tell my wife," I said, "as long as you don't tell her about the drug. Let her go on thinking I was crazy drunk. Whatever happens she mustn't know about the drug. She disliked Magnus—Professor Lane—and if she knew about this she'd dislike his memory even more."

"I dare say she would," he answered, wiping my arm with spirit before plunging his needle in, "and you could hardly blame her."

"The thing was," I said, "she was jealous. We'd known one another for so many years, he and I; we were at Cambridge together. I used to come and stay here in the old days, and Magnus seemed to take charge. We were always together, the same things intrigued us, the same things made us laugh, Magnus and I . . . Magnus and I . . ."

The depth of an abyss or the long sweet sleep of death, I did not mind. Five hours, five months, five years . . . in point of fact, so I learnt later, it was five days. The doctor always seemed to be there, when I opened my eyes, giving me another jab, or else sitting at the end of the bed swinging his legs, listening while I talked. Sometimes Vita looked in at the door with an uncertain smile, then disappeared. She and Mrs. Collins between them must have made my bed, washed me, fed me—though I have no recollection of eating anything at all. Memory of those days is blotted out. I could have cursed, raved, torn the bedding, or merely slept. I understand I slept, and also talked. Not to Vita, not to Mrs. Collins, but to the doctor. However many sessions it took between jabs I have no idea, nor do I know just what I said, but I gather I spilt, as the saying goes, the beans from start to finish, with the consequence that in the middle of the following week, when I was more or less back to normal and sitting around in a chair upstairs instead of lying in bed, body and mind felt not only rested but completely purged.

I told him so, over coffee which Vita had brought and left with us, and he laughed, saying a thorough clear-out never did any harm, and it was amazing the amount of stuff people locked away in attics and cellars they had forgotten about, which would be all the better if the light got through to it.

"Mind you," he added, "purging the soul comes easier to you than to others, because of your Catholic background."

I stared. "How did you know I was a Catholic?" I asked.

"It all came out in the wash," he said.

I felt strangely shocked. I had imagined that I had told him everything from start to finish about the experiment with the drug, and had described to him, in detail, the happenings of the other world. The fact that I had been born and bred a Catholic had no bearing on this at all.

"I'm a very bad Catholic," I said. "I couldn't wait to get away from Stonyhurst, and I haven't been to Mass for years. As to Confession . . ."

"I know," he said, "all in the attic or underground. Along with your dislike of monks, stepfathers, widows who remarry, and other little things along the same line."

I poured myself another cup of coffee, and one for him as well, throwing in too much sugar and stirring furiously.

"Look here," I said, "you're talking nonsense. I never give a thought to monks, widows or stepfathers—with the exception of myself—in my ordinary present-day life. The fact that these people existed in the fourteenth century, and I was able to see them, was entirely due to the drug."

"Yes," he said, "entirely due to the drug." He did his abrupt thing of getting up and walking round the room. "That bottle you gave me, I did what you ought to have done after the inquest. I sent it up to Lane's chief assistant, John Willis, with a brief word that you had been in trouble with it, and could I have a report as soon as possible? He was good enough to ring me up on the telephone as soon as he had my letter."

"Well?" I asked.

"Well, you're a very lucky man to be alive, and not only alive but here in this house and not in a loony-bin. The stuff in that bottle contained probably the most potent hallucinogen that has ever been discovered, and other substances as well which he isn't even sure of yet. Professor Lane was apparently working on this alone: he never took Willis fully into his confidence."

A lucky man to be alive, possibly. Lucky not to be in a loony-bin, agreed. But much of this I had told myself already, when I first started the experiment.

"Are you trying to tell me," I asked, "that everything I've seen has been hallucination, dug up from the murky waste of my own unconscious?"

"No, I'm not," he said. "I think Professor Lane was on to something that might have proved extraordinarily significant about the workings of the brain, and he chose you as guinea pig because he knew you would do whatever he told you, and that you were a highly suggestible subject into the bargain." He wandered over to the table and finished his cup of coffee. "Incidentally, everything you've told me is just as secret as if you had spilt it into the Confessional. I had an initial struggle with your wife to keep you here, instead of sending you in an ambulance to some top chap in Harley Street who would have bunged you straight into a psychiatric home for six months. I think she trusts me now."

"What did you tell her?" I asked.

"I said you had been on the verge of a nervous breakdown, and suffering from strain and delayed shock owing to the sudden death of Professor Lane. Which, you may agree, is perfectly true."

I got up rather gingerly from my chair and walked over to the window. The campers had gone from the field across the way, and the cattle were grazing once again. I could hear our own boys playing cricket by the orchard.

"You may say what you like," I said slowly, "suggestibility, breakdown, Catholic conscience, the lot, but the fact remains that I've been in that other world, seen it, known it. It was cruel, hard, and very often bloody, and so were the people in it, except Isolda, and latterly Roger, but, my God, it held a fascination for me which is lacking in my own world of today."

He came and stood beside me at the window. He gave me a cigarette, and we both smoked awhile in silence.

"The other world," he said at last. "I suppose we all carry one inside us, in our various ways. You, Professor Lane, your wife, myself, and we'd see it differently if we all made the experiment together—which God forbid!" He smiled, and flicked his cigarette out of the window. "I have a feeling my own wife might take a dim view of an Isolda if I took to wandering about the Treesmill valley looking for her. Which is not to say I haven't done so through the years, but I'm too down to earth to go back six centuries on the off-chance that I might meet her."

"My Isolda lived," I said stubbornly. "I've seen actual pedigrees and historical documents to prove it. They all lived. I've got papers downstairs in the library that don't lie."

"Of course she lived," he agreed, "and what is more had two small girls called Joanna and Margaret, you told me about them. Little girls are more fascinating sometimes than small boys, and you have a couple of stepsons."

"And what the hell is that supposed to mean?"

"Nothing," he said, "just an observation. The world we carry inside us produces answers, sometimes. A way of escape. A flight from reality. You didn't want to live either in London or in New York. The fourteenth century made an exciting, if somewhat gruesome, antidote to both. The trouble is that daydreams, like hallucinogenic drugs, become addictive; the more we indulge, the deeper we plunge, and then, as I said before, we end in the loony-bin."

I had the impression that everything he said was leading up to something else, to some pratical proposition that I must take a grip on myself, get a job, sit in an office, sleep with Vita, breed daughters, look forward contentedly to middle-age, when I might grow cacti in a greenhouse.

"What do you want me to do?" I asked. "Come on, out with it."

He turned round from the window and looked me straight in the face.

"Frankly, I don't mind what you do," he said. "It's not my problem. As your medical advisor and father confessor for less than a week, I'd be glad to see you around for several years to come. And I'll be delighted to prescribe the usual antibiotics when you catch the flu. But for the immediate future I suggest that you get out of this house pretty quick before you have another urge to visit the basement."

I drew a deep breath. "I thought so," I said. "You've been talking to Vita."

"Naturally I've talked to your wife," he agreed, "and apart from a few feminine quirks she's a very sensible woman. When I say get out of the house I don't mean forever. But for the next few weeks at least you'd be better away from it. You must see the force of that."

I did see it, but like a cornered rat I struggled for survival, and played for time.

"All right," I said. "Where do you suggest we go? We've got those boys on our hands."

"Well, they don't worry you, do they?"

"No . . . No, I'm very fond of them."

"It doesn't matter where, providing it's out of the pull of Roger Kylmerth."

"My alter ego?" I queried. "He and I are not a scrap alike, you know."

"Alter egos never are," he said. "Mine is a long-haired poet who faints at the sight of blood. He's dogged me ever since I left medical school."

I laughed, in spite of myself. He made everything seem so simple. "I wish you had known Magnus," I said. "You remind me of him in an odd sort of way."

"I wish I had. Seriously, though, I mean what I say about your getting away. Your wife suggested Ireland. Good walking country, fishing, crocks of gold buried under the hills . . ."

"Yes," I said, "and two of her compatriots who are touring around in the best hotels."

"She mentioned them," he said, "but I gather they've gone—got fed up with the weather and flown to sunny Spain instead. So that needn't worry you. I thought Ireland a good idea because it only means a three-hour drive from here to Exeter, and then you can fly direct. Hire a car the other side, and you're away."

He and Vita had the whole thing taped. I was trapped; there was no way out. I must put a brave face on it and admit defeat.

"Supposing I refuse?" I asked. "Get back into bed and pull the sheet over my head?"

"I'd send for an ambulance and cart you off to hospital. I thought Ireland was a better idea, but it's up to you."

Five minutes later he had gone, and I heard his car roaring up the drive. The sense of anticlimax was absolute: the purge had been very thorough. And I still did not know how much I had told him. Doubtless a hotch-potch of everything I had ever thought or done since the age of three, and, like all doctors with leanings towards psychoanalysis, he had put it together and summed me up as the usual sort of misfit with homosexual leanings who had suffered from birth with a mother complex, a stepfather complex, an aversion to copulation with my widowed wife, and a repressed desire to hit the hay with a blonde who had never existed except in my own imagination.

It all fitted, naturally. The Priory was Stonyhurst, Brother Jean was that silken bastard who taught me history, Joanna was my mother and poor Vita rolled into one, and Otto Bodrugan the handsome, gay adventurer I really longed to be. The fact that they all had lived, and could be proved to have lived, had not impressed Dr. Powell. It was a pity he had not tried the drug himself, instead of sending bottle C to John Willis. Then he might have thought again.

Well, it was over now. I must go along with his diagnosis, and his holiday plans as well. God knows it was the least that I could do, after nearly killing Vita.

Funny he hadn't said anything about side effects, or delayed action. Perhaps he had discussed this with John Willis, and John Willis had given the O.K. But then Willis didn't know about the bloodshot eye, the sweats, the nausea and the vertigo. Nobody did, though Powell may have guessed, especially after our first encounter. Anyway, I felt normal enough now. Too normal, if the truth be told. Like a small boy spanked who had promised to amend his ways.

I opened the door and called for Vita. She came running up the stairs at once, and I realised, with a sense of shame and guilt, what she must have been through during the past week. Her face was drained of colour and she had lost weight. Her hair, usually immaculate, was swept back with a hasty comb behind her ears, and there was a strained, unhappy look in her eyes that I had never seen before.

"He told me you had agreed to come away," she said. "It was his idea, not mine, I promise you. I only want to do what's best for you."

"I know that," I said. "He's absolutely right."

"You're not angry, then? I was so afraid you'd be angry."

She came and sat beside me on the bed, and I put my arm round her.

"You must promise me one thing," I said, "and that is to forget everything that's happened up to now. I know it's practically impossible, but I do ask you."

"You've been ill. I know why, the doctor explained it all," she said. "He told the boys too, and they understand. We none of us blame you for anything, darling. We just want you to get well and to be happy."

"They're not frightened of me?"

"Heavens, no. They were very sensible about it. They've both been so good and helpful, Teddy especially. They're devoted to you, darling, I don't think you realise that."

"Oh, yes, I do," I said, "which makes it all the worse. But never mind that now. When are we supposed to be off?"

She hesitated. "Dr. Powell said you'd be fit to travel by Friday, and he told me to go ahead and get the tickets."

Friday . . . The day after tomorrow.

"O.K." I said, "if that's what he says. I suppose I'd better move about a bit to get myself in trim. Sort out some things to pack."

"As long as you don't overdo it. I'll send Teddy up to help you." She left me with the best part of a week's mail, and by the time I'd been through it, and chucked most of it into the wastepaper basket, Teddy had appeared at the door.

"Mom said you might like some help with your packing," he said shyly.

"Good lad, I would. I hear you've been head of the house for the past week, and doing a fine job."

He flushed with pleasure. "Oh, I don't know. I haven't done much. Answered the phone a few times. There was a man called up yesterday, asked if you were better and sent his regards. A Mr. Willis. He left his number, in case you wanted to ring him. And he left another number too. I wrote them both down."

He brought out a shiny black notebook and tore out a page. I recognised the first number—it was Magnus's lab—but the other one baffled me.

"Is this second one his home number, or didn't he say?" I asked.

"Yes, he did say. It's someone called Davies, who works at the British Museum. He thought you might like to get in touch with Mr. Davies before he went on holiday."

I put the torn page in my pocket, and went along with Teddy to the dressing room. The divan bed had gone, and I realised what the dragging sound had signified the night the doctor came: the bed had been moved into the double room and put under the window.

"Micky and I have been sleeping in here with Mom," said Teddy. "She felt she wanted company."

It was a delicate way of putting that she wanted protection. I left him in the dressing room pulling things out of the wardrobe, and picked up the telephone receiver beside the bed.

The voice that answered me, precise and rather reserved, assured me the owner's name was Davies.

"I'm Richard Young," I told him, "a friend of the late Professor Lane. You know all about me, I believe."

"Yes, indeed, Mr. Young, I hope you are better. I heard through John Willis that you'd been laid up."

"That's right. Nothing serious. But I'm going away, and I gather you are too, so I wondered if you had anything for me."

"Unfortunately nothing very much, I'm afraid. If you'll excuse me a moment, I'll just get my notes and read them out to you."

I waited, while he put down the receiver. I had the uncomfortable feeling that I was cheating, and that Dr. Powell would have disapproved.

"Are you there, Mr. Young?"

"Yes, I'm here."

"I hope you won't be disappointed. They are only extracts from the Registers of Bishop Grandisson of Exeter, one dated 1334, the second 1335. The first relates to Tywardreath Priory, and the second to Oliver Carminowe. The first is a letter from the Bishop at Exeter to the Abbot of the sister house at Angers, and reads as follows:

"John, etc, Bishop of Exeter, sends greetings with true kindness of thought in the Lord. Inasmuch as we expel from our fold the diseased sheep which is wont to spread its disorder, lest it should infect our other healthy sheep, so in the case of Brother Jean, called Meral, a monk of your monastery at present living in the Priory of Tywardreath in our diocese, which is ruled by a Prior of the Order of St. Benedict, on account of his outrageous abandonment of all shame and decent behaviour, in spite of frequent kindly admonitions—and because, alas, as I am ashamed to say (not to mention his other notorious offences), he has nevertheless become more hardened in his wickedness—we have therefore, with all zeal and reverence for your order and for yourself, arranged to send him back to you to be subjected to the discipline of the monastery for this evil behaviour. May God Himself maintain you in the rule of this flock in length of days and health."

He cleared his throat. "The original is in Latin, you understand. This is my translation. I couldn't help thinking, as I copied it out how the phrasing would have appealed to Professor Lane."

"Yes," I said, "it would."

He cleared his throat again. "The second piece is very short, and may not interest you. It is only that on April 21st, 1335, Bishop Grandisson received Sir Oliver Carminowe and his wife Sybell, who had been clandestinely married without banns or licence. They confirmed that they had erred through ignorance. The Bishop relaxed the sentences imposed upon them and confirmed the marriage, which seems to have taken place at some previous date, not stated, in Sir Oliver's private chapel at Carminowe, in the parish of Mawgan-in-Meneage. Proceedings were taken against the priest who married them. That's all."

"Does it say what had happened to the previous wife, Isolda?"

"No. I presume she died, possibly a short while before, and this other marriage was clandestine because it took place so soon after her death. Perhaps Sybell was pregnant, and a private ceremony seemed necessary to save face. I'm sorry, Mr. Young, but I haven't been able to turn up anything else."

"Don't worry," I said. "What you've told me is very valuable. Have a good holiday."

"Thank you. The same to you."

I put down the receiver. Teddy was calling to me from the dressing room. "Dick?"

"Yes?"

He came through from the bathroom with Magnus's walking stick in his hands. "Will you be taking this with you?" he asked. "It's too long to fit into your suitcase."

I had not seen the stick since I had poured into it the colourless liquid from bottle C nearly a week ago. I had forgotten all about it.

"If you don't want it," said Teddy, "I'll put it back in the cupboard where I found it."

"No," I said, "give it to me. I do want it."

He pretended to take aim at me, smiling, holding it balanced like a spear, then lobbed it gently in the air. I caught it and held it fast.

24

WE SAT IN the lounge at Exeter airport waiting for our flight to be called. Take-off was twelve thirty. The Buick was parked behind the airport, to remain there until our return, whenever that should be. I got sandwiches for all of us, and while we ate them cast an eye over our fellow travellers. There were flights that afternoon for the Channel Isles as well as Dublin, and the lounge facing the airfield was filled with people. There were a number of priests returning from some convocation, a party of schoolchildren, family parties such as our own, and the usual sprinkling of holiday types. There was also a hilarious sextet who, from their conversation, were on their way to, or from, a riotous wedding.

"I hope," said Vita, "we aren't going to find ourselves beside that lot on the plane."

The boys were already doubled up with laughter, for one of the group had donned a false nose and a moustache, which he kept dipping into his glass of Guinness, to emerge beaded with froth.

"The thing to do," I said, "is to leap to our feet as soon as our flight is called, so that we can get right up to the front, well away from them."

"If that man with the false nose tries to sit beside me, I shall scream," said Vita.

Her remark set the boys off again, and I congratulated myself on having ordered generous rations of cider for them and brandy and soda—our holiday drink—for Vita and myself, because it was that, more than the wedding party, which was making the boys giggle and causing Vita to squint as she peered in her powder compact. I kept a close watch on the plane on the runway, until I saw that it was loaded. They were pulling the baggage trucks away, and a hostess was walking across the tarmac to our door.

"Damn," I said. "I knew it was a mistake to swill all that coffee and brandy. Look, darling, I must rush to the gents. If they call the flight go ahead and get seats in front, as I said. If I'm caught up in the mob I'll find myself a seat at the back and change places after take-off. As long as you three are together you'll be all right. Here—you take your boarding cards and I'll hang on to mine, just in case."

"Oh, Dick, honestly!" exclaimed Vita. "You might have gone before. How typical of you!"

"Sorry," I said. "Nature calls . . ."

I walked rapidly across the lounge as I saw the hostess enter the door, and waited inside the Gents. I heard the flight number called over the loudspeaker, and after a few minutes, when I came out again, our party was walking with the hostess across to the aircraft, Vita and the boys in the van. As I watched, they disappeared into the plane, followed by the schoolchildren and the priests. It was now or never. I went rapidly out of the main door of the airport building, and crossed over to the car-park. In a moment I had started the Buick and pulled out of the airport entrance. Then I drew into the side of the road and listened. I could hear the sound of the engines before the plane taxied to the start, which must mean that everyone was now aboard. If the engines ceased it would mean my plan had gone for nothing, and the hostess had discovered that I was missing. It was twelve thirty-five exactly. Then I heard the engines increase in pitch and in a few minutes, unbelievably, my heart pounding, I saw the silver streak of the aircraft speed along the runway and take off, gain height and flatten out, and then it was away amongst the clouds and out of sight, and I was sitting there, at the wheel of the Buick, on my own.

They were due to touch down at Dublin at one-fifty. I knew exactly what Vita would do. She would put through a call from the airport to Dr. Powell in Fowey, and find him out. He would be out because it was his half-day. He had told me so, when I had rung up after breakfast to say goodbye. He had said that, if it was fine, he was going to take his family over to the north coast to surf, and he would be thinking about us, and would I please send him a postcard from Ireland saying "Wish you were here."

I started to sing, as I turned into the main road and touched seventy. This was how a criminal must feel when he had just robbed a bank and got away with the loot in a stolen van. A pity I had not the whole day before me to explore at leisure, drive over to Bere and look up Sir William Ferrers and his wife Matilda perhaps. I had found the spot on the map—it was only just across the Tamar in Devon—and I wondered if their house was standing still. Probably not, or, if it was, it had turned itself into a farm like Carminowe. I had located Carminowe on my map at the same time, when Teddy was up in my dressing room packing my case, and had also found reference to it in the old volume of *Parochial History* that had given me Tregesteynton. Carminowe was in Mawgan-in-Meneage, near the Looe Pool, and the writer said that the ancient mansion and chapel had fallen into decay in the reign of James I, along with the old burial ground.

I took the Launceston road after leaving Okehampton, for it was faster than the way we had come, and as I crossed from Devon into Cornwall, heading for Bodmin moor like a homing pigeon, I sang louder still, for even if Vita had beaten me to it, and was about to land in Dublin, I was safe from pursuit; she could not reach me now. This was my last trip, my final fling; and whatever became of me in the process I could not hurt either her or the boys, for they would be safe on Irish soil.

> "In such a night
> Stood Dido with a willow in her hand
> Upon the wild sea-banks, and wav'd her love
> To come again to Carthage."

The trouble was, Isolda's lover had died in Treesmill creek upon the strand, and I doubted if either the threat of convent walls, or Joanna's taunts, or the monk's promise of safe passage to some doubtful refuge in Angers would have made her turn to Roger in the end. The future was bleak, six hundred years ago, for wives who left their husbands, especially when the husband had an eye to a third bride. It would have suited Oliver Carminowe, and the Ferrers family too, if Isolda had simply disappeared, which she might well have done had she entrusted herself to Joanna's care; but to remain under Roger's roof was at best only a stop-gap measure, and could not have continued long.

As I drove across Bodmin moor, rejoicing that each mile brought me nearer home, exhilaration was tempered by the knowledge that not only must this be the last trip to the other world, but that when I entered it I had no choice of date or season. The thaw could have come and Lent be over, high summer have taken its place, Isolda herself, having made her choice, be languishing behind those convent walls somewhere in Devon, in which case she would have moved out of Roger's life, and mine as well. I wondered, had Magnus lived, whether he could have perfected the timing factor, thus leaving the awakening from present to past to the participant's own choice; so that today, by some infinitesimal alteration of the dose, I could have summoned up at will those figures in the basement where I had left them last. Never, in the few weeks of experiment, had it happened that way. There had always been a jump in time. Joanna's carriage would no longer be waiting on the top of the hill above Kylmerth, Roger, Isolda and Bess would have left the farmhouse kitchen. That single draught in the walking stick could guarantee re-entry to my world, but not what I should find there when I did.

The halt-sign brought me up with a jerk on to the main Lostwithiel-St. Blazey road. I had driven the last twenty miles like an automaton, and I remembered the side turning that would take me past Tregesteynton to the Treesmill valley. I drove down it with a strange nostalgic sense, and as I passed the present farmhouse of Strickstenton, and a black-and-white collie darted out on to the road barking, I thought of small Margaret, Isolda's younger child, who had wanted a riding whip like Robbie's, and Joanna, the elder, preening in the looking-glass while her father chased Sybell up the stairs with the otter's paw.

I came down into the valley, and so intense was my identification with the past that I had forgotten, momentarily, that the river would no longer be there, and I looked for Rosgof's cottage by the side of the ford opposite the mill; but of course there was no river and no ford, only the road turning left and a few cows grazing in the marshy field.

I wished I was in the Triumph, for the Buick was too big and conspicuous. On sudden impulse I parked by the bridge below the mill, and, walking a short way up the lane, climbed over the gate into the field leading to the Gratten. I knew I must stand there once more amongst the mounds before returning home, for once back at Kilmarth the future would be uncertain; the last experiment might land me in some trouble unforeseen. I wanted to carry in my mind the image of the Treesmill valley as it looked today under the late August sun, letting imagination and memory do the rest, bringing back the winding river and the creek, and the anchorage below the long-vanished house. They had been harvesting in the Chapel Park fields behind the Gratten, but here where I walked beneath the hedge it was all grass, and cows were grazing. I came to the first of the gorse bushes, climbing to the top of the high bank surrounding the site, and then looked down to the apron of grass which had once been a path under the hallway window, where Isolda and Bodrugan had sat holding hands.

A man was lying there, smoking a cigarette, his coat propped under his head as pillow. I stared hard, unbelieving, thinking that guilt and an uneasy conscience must have conjured his image out of the air; but I was not mistaken. The man who was lying there was very real, and it was Dr. Powell.

I stood there a moment watching him, then deliberately, without malice but with total resolution, I unscrewed the top of Magnus's stick and took out the little measure. I swallowed my last dose, and replaced the measure once again inside the stick. Then I walked down the mound and joined him.

"I thought," I said, "you had gone surfing on the north coast?"

He sat up instantly, and I experienced, for the first time since knowing him, the immensely satisfying feeling that I had caught him unawares and at a disadvantage.

He recovered quickly, the look of astonishment giving place to an engaging smile. "I changed my mind," he said calmly, "and let the family go off without me. You seem to have done the same."

"So Vita beat me to it after all. She didn't lose much time," I told him.

"What's your wife got to do with it?"

"Well, she telephoned you from Dublin, didn't she?"

"No," he said.

Now it was my turn to look astonished and stare at him. "Then what the hell are you doing here waiting for me?"

"I wasn't waiting for you. Rather than brave the Atlantic breakers I decided to explore your piece of territory. A hunch that has apparently paid off. You can show me round."

My one-upmanship began to fade, my self-confidence desert me. He seemed to be playing my own game and getting away with it.

"Look," I said, "don't you want to know what happened at the airport?"

"Not particularly," he replied. "The plane took off, I know, because I rang through to Exeter and checked. Whether you were on it or not they couldn't tell me, but I knew that if you weren't you would head back for Kilmarth, and if I turned up there for a cup of tea I'd find you in the basement. Meanwhile, burning curiosity drove me to while away half an hour or so down here."

His cocksure attitude infuriated me, but I was even more angry with myself. If I had taken the other road, if I had not come through the Treesmill valley and allowed momentary sentiment to sway me, I should have been safely back at Kilmarth with at least half an hour or more in hand before he breezed in to take possession.

"All right," I said, "I know I've played a dirty trick on Vita and the boys, and she's probably ringing you from Dublin airport now and getting no reply. What staggers me is that you let me go knowing what might happen. It's almost as much your fault as mine."

"Oh, I agree," he answered. "I'm equally to blame, and we'll both apologise when we get her on the telephone. But I wanted to give you a chance, just to see if you could make it, instead of going by the rules."

"And what do the rules say?"

"Put your addict inside, once he's well and truly hooked."

I looked at him thoughtfully, and leant on Magnus's walking stick for support. "You know very well," I said, "I gave bottle C to you, and that was the last; and you must have given the house a pretty thorough search when I was lying prone upstairs all the week."

"I did," he replied, "and searched it again today. I told Mrs. Collins I was looking for buried treasure, and I think she believed me. Suspicious sort of chap, aren't I?"

"Yes. And you found nothing, because there was nothing there."

"Well, you may count yourself damn lucky that there wasn't. I've got Willis's final report in my pocket."

"What does it say?"

"Only that the drug contains a substance of some toxicity that could seriously affect the central nervous system, possibly leading to paralysis. No need to elaborate."

"Show it to me now."

He shook his head, and suddenly he was not there any more, and the walls were all around me, and I was standing in the hall of the Champernoune manor house looking out of the casement window at the rain. Panic gripped me, for it was not meant to happen, at least not yet; I had counted on being home, behind my own four walls, with Roger acting as my usual guide-protector. He was not here, and the hall was empty, and had been altered since I had seen it last. There seemed to be more furniture, more hangings, and the curtain masking the doorway to the stair above was drawn aside. Someone was crying in the bedroom overhead, and I could hear the sound of heavy footsteps pacing the floor. I looked out of the casement window once again, and saw through the falling rain that it must be autumn, for the clump of trees on the opposite hill where Oliver Carminowe had concealed himself and his men, as they lay in ambush waiting for Bodrugan, was golden brown as it had been then. But today no wind blew, tossing the leaves on to the ground below; the steady mizzle made them hang dispirited, and a shroud of mist clung above Lanescot and the river's mouth.

The crying turned to a high-pitched laugh, and down the stairs came a cup and ball, rolling one behind the other, until they reached the floor of the hall itself, when the ball rolled slowly under the table. I heard a man's voice call anxiously, "Mind how you go, Elizabeth!" as someone, still laughing, came clumping down the stairs in search of the toy. She stood a moment, her hands clasped in front of her, her long dress trailing, an absurd little bonnet askew on her auburn hair. Her likeness to Joanna Champernoune was startling, then tragic, for this was an idiot girl, about twelve years old, with a full loose mouth, and eyes set high in her head. She nodded, laughing, then picked up the ball and cup and began to throw them in the air, screaming with delight. Suddenly, tiring of the game, she tossed them aside and started to spin round in circles until she became giddy, when she fell on to the floor and sat there motionless, staring at her shoes.

The man's voice from above called out again, "Elizabeth . . . Elizabeth," and the girl struggled clumsily to her feet and smiled, gazing at the ceiling. Footsteps came slowly down the stairs and the man appeared, wearing a long loose robe to his ankles, and a nightcap. I thought, for a moment, I had travelled back in time and it was Henry Champernoune who stood there, weak and pale in his final illness, but it was Henry's son William, an adolescent when I saw him last, squaring up to take his place as head of the family when Roger broke the news of his father's death. Now he looked thirty-five or even more, and I realised, with a shock of dismay, that time had leapt ahead of me at least twelve years, and all the intervening months and years were buried in a past I should never know. The frozen winter of 1335 meant nothing to this William, who had been a minor and unmarried then. He was now master of his own house, although battling, it would seem, against sickness, and enmeshed as well in the inescapable net of some family flaw.

"Come, daughter, come, love," he said gently, holding out his arms, and she put her finger in her mouth and sucked it, shaking her shoulders, then, with a sudden change of mind, darted to the floor and picked up her cup and ball again and gave it to him.

"I'll toss it for you above, but not down here," he said. "Katie has been sick as well, and I must not leave her."

"She'll not have my toy, I won't let her," said Elizabeth, nodding her head up and down, and she put out her hand and tried to snatch it back.

"What? Not let your sister share it when she gave it to you? That's not my Lizzie speaking, surely? Lizzie's flown up the chimney and a bad girl has taken her place."

He clicked his tongue in reproof, and at the sound of it her full mouth drooped, her eyes filled with tears, and she flung her arms about him, crying bitterly, clinging to his long robe.

"There, there," he said. "Father did not mean it, Father loves his Liz, but she must not tease him, he is still weak and sick, and poor Katie too. Come, now, upstairs, and she can watch us from her bed, and when you toss the ball high she'll be the better for it, and maybe smile."

He took her hand and led her towards the stairs, and as he did so someone came through the door leading to the kitchen quarters. William heard the footsteps and turned his head.

"See that all the doors are fastened before you go," he said, "and bid the servants keep them so, and open them to no one. God knows I hate to give the order, but I daren't do otherwise. Sick stragglers bide their time, and wait for darkness before they walk abroad and knock on men's doors."

"I know it. There have been many so in Tywardreath, and death has spread because of it."

There was no doubt about the speaker who stood at the open door. It was Robbie, a taller, broader Robbie than the lad I knew, and his chin was bearded now like his brother's.

"Watch how you go upon the road, then," answered William. "The same poor demented wanderers might attempt to strike you down, thinking, because you ride, you have some magic property of health denied to them."

"I'll ride with care, Sir William, have no fear. I would not leave you for the night except for Roger. Five days since I was home, and he's alone."

"I know, I know. God keep you both, and watch over all of us this night."

He led his daughter up the stairs to the room above, and I followed Robbie to the kitchen quarters. Three servants sat there in dejected fashion, hugging the hearth, one with his eyes closed and his head resting against the wall. Robbie gave him William's message, and he echoed, "God be with us" without opening his eyes.

Robbie shut the door behind him and walked across the stable court. His pony was tied to the stall inside the shed. He mounted and began riding slowly up the hill through the mizzling rain, passing the small cottages that formed part of the demesne, lining the muddied track. All the doors were fastened tight, and smoke came from the roofs of only two, the others seeming deserted. We reached the brow of the hill, and Robbie, instead of turning to the right on the road to the village, paused by the geld house on the left, and, dismounting, tied his pony to the gate and walked up the path to the chapel alongside. He opened the door and entered, I following after. The chapel was small, hardly more than twenty feet in length and fifteen broad, with a single window facing east behind the altar. Robbie, making the sign of the Cross, knelt down before it, and bowed his head in prayer. There was an inscription in Latin beneath the window, which I read:

"Matilda Champernoune built this chapel in memory of her husband William Champernoune, who died in 1304." A stone before the chancel steps was inscribed with her own initials and the date of her death, which I could not decipher. A similar stone, to the left, bore the initials H.C. There were no stained glass windows, no effigies or tombs built against the walls: this was an oratory, a memorial chapel.

When Robbie rose from his knees and turned away I saw another stone before the chancel steps. The lettering read I.C.; the date was 1335. As I followed Robbie out into the rain and down towards the village, I knew of only one name that would fit, and it was not Champernoune.

Desolation was all about me, here by the geld house and in the village too. No people on the green, no animals, no barking dogs. The doors of the small dwellings huddled close around the green were closed, like those on the demesne itself. A single goat, half-starved by its appearance, with ribs protruding from its lean body, was tethered by a chain near to the well, cropping the rough grass.

We climbed the hill-track above the Priory, and looking down on to the enclosure I could see no sign of life from behind the walls. No smoke came from the monks' quarters, nor from the chapter house; the whole place seemed abandoned, and the ripening apples in the orchard had been left to cluster on the trees unplucked. And when we passed the plough lands on the high ground I saw that the soil had not been turned, and some of the corn was not even harvested but lay rotting on the earth, as if some cyclone in the night had swept it down. As we came to the pasture land on the lower slopes the Priory cattle, roaming loose, came lowing after us in desperation, as though in hope that Robbie, on his pony, might drive them home.

We crossed the ford with ease, for the tide was ebbing fast and the sands lay uncovered, flat and dirty brown under the rain. A thin wreath of smoke came from Julian Polpey's roof—he at least must have survived calamity—but Geoffrey Lampetho's dwelling in the valley looked as bare and deserted as those on the village green. This was not the world I knew, the world I had come to love and long for because of its magic quality of love and hate, its separation from a drab monotony; this was a place resembling, in its barren desolation, all the most hideous features of a twentieth-century landscape after disaster, suggesting a total abandonment of hope, the aftertaste of atomic doom.

Robbie rode uphill above the ford, and passing through the copse of straggling trees came down to the wall encircling Kylmerth yard. No smoke curled up from the chimney. He flung himself from his pony, leaving it to wander loose towards the byre, and running across the yard he opened the door.

"Roger!" I heard him call, and "Roger!" once again. The kitchen was empty, the turf no longer smouldered on the hearth. The remains of food lay untouched upon the trestle table, and as Robbie climbed the ladder to the sleeping loft I saw a rat scurry across the floor and disappear.

There can have been no one in the loft, for Robbie came down the ladder instantly, and opened the door beneath it which gave access to the byre, revealing at the same time a narrow passage ending in a store room and a cellar. Slits in the thickness of the wall allowed streaks of light to penetrate the gloom, and this was the only source of air as well. There was little draught to cleanse the atmosphere of sweet mustiness pervading, due to the rotting apples laid in rows against the wall. An iron cauldron, unsteady on three legs, and rusted from disuse, stood in the far corner, and beside it pitchers, jars, a three-pronged fork, a pair of bellows. This store room was a strange choice for a sick man to make his bed. He must have dragged his pallet from the sleeping loft and placed it here beside the slit in the wall, and then, from increasing weakness or lack of will, lain through the days and nights until today.

"Roger . . ." whispered Robbie, "Roger!"

Roger opened his eyes. I did not recognise him. His hair was white, his eyes sunk deep in his head, his features thin and drawn; and under the white furze that formed his beard the flesh was discoloured, bruised, with the same discoloured swellings behind his ears. He murmured something, water, I think it was, and Robbie rose from his side and ran into the kitchen, but I went on kneeling there beside him, staring down at the man I had last seen confident and strong.

Robbie returned with a pitcher of water, and, putting his arms round his brother, helped him to drink. But after two mouthfuls Roger choked, and lay back again on his pallet, gasping.

"No remedy," he said. "The swelling's spread to my throat and blocked the windpipe. Moisten my lips only, that's comfort enough."

"How long have you lain here?" asked Robbie.

"I cannot tell. Four days and nights, maybe. Not long after you went I knew it had me, and I brought my bed to the cellar so that you could sleep easy above when you returned. How is Sir William?"

"Recovered, thanks be to God, and young Katherine too. Elizabeth still escapes infection, and the servants. More than sixty died this week in Tywardreath. The Priory is closed, as you know, and the Prior and brethren gone to Minster."

"No loss," murmured Roger. "We can do without them. Did you visit the chapel?"

"I did, and said the usual prayer."

He moistened his brother's lips with water once again, and in rough but tender fashion tried to soften the swellings beneath his ears.

"I tell you, there's no remedy," said Roger. "This is the end. No parish priest to shrive me, no communal grave amongst the rest. Bury me at the cliff's edge, Robbie, where my bones will smell the sea."

"I'll go to Polpey and fetch Bess," said Robbie. "She and I can nurse you through this together."

"No," said Roger, "she has her own children to care for now, and Julian too. Hear my confession, Robbie. There's been something on my conscience now these thirteen years."

He struggled to sit up but had not strength enough, and Robbie, the tears running down his cheeks, smoothed the matted hair out of his brother's eyes.

"If it concerns you and Lady Carminowe, I don't need to hear it, Roger," he said. "Bess and I knew you loved her, and love her still. So did we. There was no sin in that for any of us."

"No sin in loving, but in murder, yes," said Roger.

"Murder?"

Robbie, kneeling by his brother's side, stared down at him, bewildered, then shook his head. "You're wandering, Roger," he said softly. "We all know how she died. She had been sick for weeks before she came here, and hid it from us; and then when they tried to carry her away by force she gave her promise she would follow in a week, and so they let her stay."

"And would have gone, but I prevented it."

"How did you prevent it? She died before the week had passed, here, in the room above, with Bess's arms about her, and yours too."

"She died because I would not let her suffer pain," said Roger. "She died because, had she kept her bargain and travelled to Trelawn and thence into Devon, there would have been weeks of agony ahead, even months, agony that our own mother knew and endured when we were young. So I let her go from us in sleep, knowing nothing of what I had done, and you and Bess in the same ignorance."

He put out his hand and felt for Robbie's, holding it tight. "Did you never wonder, Robbie, when in the old days I stayed at the Priory late at night, or on occasion brought de Meral here to the cellar, what it was I did?"

"I knew the French ships landed merchandise," said Robbie, "and you conveyed it to the Priory. Wine and other goods which the Prior lacked. And the monks lived well because of it."

"They taught me their secrets too," said Roger. "How to make men dream and conjure visions, rather than pray. How to seek a paradise on earth that would last for a few hours only. How to make men die. It was only after young Bodrugan perished in de Meral's care that I sickened of the game, taking no further part in it. But I had learnt the secret well, and so made use of it, when the time came. I gave her something to ease pain and let her slip away. It was murder, Robbie, and a mortal sin. And no one knows of it but you."

The effort of speaking had drained him of all strength, and Robbie, lost and frightened suddenly in the presence of death, let go his hand, and, stumbling to his feet, went blindly along the passage to the kitchen, in search, I think, of some additional covering to draw over his brother. I went on kneeling there, in the cellar, and Roger opened his eyes for the last time and stared at me. I think he asked for absolution, but there was no one there, in his own time, to grant it, and I wondered if, because of this, he had travelled through the years in search of it. Like Robbie, I was helpless, and six centuries too late.

"Go forth, O Christian soul, out of this world, in the name of God the Father Almighty, who created thee; in the name of Jesus Christ, the Son of the living God, who suffered for thee; in the name of the Holy Ghost, who sanctified thee . . ."

I could not remember any more, and it did not matter, because he had already gone. The light was coming through the chinks of the shuttered window in the old laundry, and I was kneeling there, on the stone floor of the lab, amongst the empty bottles and the jars. There was no nausea, no vertigo, no singing in my ears. Only a great silence, and a sense of peace.

I raised my head and saw that the doctor was standing by the wall and watching me.

"It's finished," I said. "Roger's dead, he's free. It's all over."

The doctor put out his hand and took my arm. He led me out of the room and up the stairs, and through to the front part of the house and into the library. We sat down together on the window seat, staring out across the sea.

"Tell me about it," he said.

"Don't you know?"

I had thought, seeing him in the lab, that he must have shared the experience with me, then I realised it was impossible.

"I waited with you on the site," he told me, "then walked with you up the hill, and followed behind you in the car. You stopped for a moment in a field above Tywardreath, near where the two roads join, then down through the village and along the side lane to Polmear, and so back here. You were walking quite normally, rather faster, perhaps, than I would have cared to do myself. Then you struck to the right through the wood, and I came down the drive. I knew I should find you below."

I got up from the window seat and went to the bookshelf, and took down one of the volumes of the *Encyclopaedia Britannica*.

"What are you looking for?" he asked.

I turned the pages until I found the reference I sought.

"The date of the Black Death," I said, "1348. Thirteen years after Isolda died." I put the book back upon the shelf.

"Bubonic plague," he observed. "Endemic in the Far East—they've had a number of cases in Vietnam."

"Have they?" I said. "Well, I've just seen what it did in Tywardreath six hundred years ago."

I went back to the window seat and picked up the walking stick. "You must have wondered how I managed that last trip," I said. "This is how." I unscrewed the top and showed him the small measure. He took it from me and held it upside down. It was fully drained.

"I'm sorry," I said, "but when I saw you sitting there below the Gratten I knew I had to do it. It was my last chance. And I'm glad I did, because now the whole thing is done with, finished. No more temptation. No more desire to lose myself in the other world. I told you Roger was free, and so am I."

He did not answer. He was still staring at the empty measure.

"Now," I said, "before we put through a call to Dublin airport and ask if Vita is there, supposing you tell me what else was written in that report John Willis sent you?"

He picked up the stick, and replacing the measure screwed on the top and gave it back to me.

"I burnt it," he said, "with the flame from my lighter, when you were on your knees in the basement reciting that prayer for the dying. Somehow it seemed to me the right moment, and I preferred to destroy it rather than have it lying in the surgery amongst my files."

"That's no answer," I told him.

"It's all you're going to get," he replied.

The telephone started ringing from the lobby in the hall. I wondered how many times it had rung before.

"That will be Vita," I said. "Now for the countdown. I'd better get on my knees again. Shall I tell her I got locked in the gents and I'll join her tomorrow?"

"It would be wiser," he said slowly, "if you told her you hoped to join her later, perhaps in a few weeks' time."

"But that's absurd," I frowned. "There's nothing to hold me back. I've told you it's all over and I'm free."

He did not say anything. He just sat there staring at me.

The telephone went on ringing, and I crossed the room to answer it, but a silly thing happened as I picked up the receiver. I couldn't hold it properly; my fingers and the palm of my hand went numb, and it slipped out of my grasp and crashed to the floor.

Don't Look Now
And Other Stories

Don't Look Now

"DON'T LOOK NOW," John said to his wife, "but there are a couple of old girls two tables away who are trying to hypnotize me."

Laura, quick on cue, made an elaborate pretence of yawning, then tilted her head as though searching the skies for a nonexistent aircraft.

"Right behind you," he added. "That's why you can't turn round at once—it would be much too obvious."

Laura played the oldest trick in the world and dropped her napkin, then bent to scrabble for it under her feet, sending a shooting glance over her left shoulder as she straightened once again. She sucked in her cheeks, the first telltale sign of suppressed hysteria, and lowered her head.

"They're not old girls at all," she said. "They're male twins in drag."

Her voice broke ominously, the prelude to uncontrolled laughter, and John quickly poured some more chianti into her glass.

"Pretend to choke," he said, "then they won't notice. You know what it is, they're criminals doing the sights of Europe, changing sex at each stop. Twin sisters here on Torcello. Twin brothers tomorrow in Venice, or even tonight, parading arm-in-arm across the Piazza San Marco. Just a matter of switching clothes and wigs."

"Jewel thieves or murderers?" asked Laura.

"Oh, murderers, definitely. But why, I ask myself, have they picked on me?"

The waiter made a diversion by bringing coffee and bearing away the fruit, which gave Laura time to banish hysteria and regain control.

"I can't think," she said, "why we didn't notice them when we arrived. They stand out to high heaven. One couldn't fail."

"That gang of Americans masked them," said John, "and the bearded man with a monocle who looked like a spy. It wasn't until they all went just now that I saw the twins. Oh God, the one with the shock of white hair has got her eye on me again."

Laura took the powder compact from her bag and held it in front of her face, the mirror acting as a reflector.

"I think it's me they're looking at, not you," she said. "Thank heaven I left my pearls with the manager at the hotel." She paused, dabbing the sides of her nose with powder. "The thing is," she said after a moment, "we've got them wrong. They're neither murderers nor thieves. They're a couple of pathetic old retired schoolmistresses on holiday, who've saved up all their lives to visit Venice. They come from some place with a name like Walabanga in Australia. And they're called Tilly and Tiny."

Her voice, for the first time since they had come away, took on the old bubbling quality he loved, and the worried frown between her brows had vanished. At last, he thought, at last she's beginning to get over it. If I can keep this going, if we can pick up the familiar routine of jokes shared on holiday and at home, the ridiculous fantasies about people at other tables, or staying in the hotel, or wandering in art galleries and churches, then everything will fall into place, life will become as it was before, the wound will heal, she will forget.

"You know," said Laura, "that really was a very good lunch. I did enjoy it."

Thank God, he thought, thank God . . . Then he leaned forward, speaking low in a conspirator's whisper. "One of them is going to the loo," he said. "Do you suppose he, or she, is going to change her wig?"

"Don't say anything," Laura murmured. "I'll follow her and find out. She may have a suitcase tucked away there, and she's going to switch clothes."

She began to hum under her breath, the signal, to her husband, of content. The ghost was temporarily laid, and all because of the familiar holiday game, abandoned too long, and now, through mere chance, blissfully recaptured.

"Is she on her way?" asked Laura.

"About to pass our table now," he told her.

Seen on her own, the woman was not so remarkable. Tall, angular, aquiline features, with the close-cropped hair which was fashionably called Eton crop, he seemed to remember, in his mother's day, and about her person the stamp of that particular generation. She would be in her middle sixties, he supposed, the masculine shirt with collar and tie, sports jacket, gray tweed skirt coming to midcalf. Gray stockings and laced black shoes. He had seen the type on golf courses and at dog shows—invariably showing not sporting breeds but pugs—and if you came across them at a party in somebody's house they were quicker on the draw with a cigarette lighter then he was himself, a mere male, with pocket matches. The general belief that they kept house with a more feminine, fluffy companion was not always true. Frequently they boasted, and adored, a golfing husband. No, the striking point about this particular individual was that there were two of them. Identical twins cast in the same mold. The only difference was that the other one had whiter hair.

"Supposing," murmured Laura, "when I find myself in the toilette beside her she starts to strip?"

"Depends on what is revealed," John answered. "If she's hermaphrodite, make a bolt for it. She might have a hypodermic syringe concealed and want to knock you out before you reach the door."

Laura sucked in her cheeks once more and began to shake. Then, squaring her shoulders, she rose to her feet. "I simply must not laugh," she said, "and whatever you do, don't look at me when I come back, especially if we come out together." She picked up her bag and strolled self-consciously away from the table in pursuit of her prey.

John poured the dregs of the chianti into his glass and lit a cigarette. The sun blazed down upon the little garden of the restaurant. The Americans had left, and the monocled man, and the family party at the far end. All was peace. The identical twin was sitting back in her chair with her eyes closed. Thank heaven, he thought, for this moment at any rate, when relaxation was possible, and Laura had been launched upon her foolish, harmless game. The holiday could yet turn into the cure she needed, blotting out, if only temporarily, the numb despair that had seized her since the child died.

"She'll get over it," the doctor said. "They all get over it, in time. And you have the boy."

"I know," John had said, "but the girl meant everything. She always did, right from the start, I don't know why. I suppose it was the difference in age. A boy of school age, and a tough one at that, is someone in his own right. Not a baby of five. Laura literally adored her. Johnnie and I were nowhere."

"Give her time," repeated the doctor, "give her time. And anyway, you're both young still. There'll be others. Another daughter."

So easy to talk . . . How replace the life of a loved lost child with a dream? He knew Laura too well. Another child, another girl, would have her own qualities, a separate identity, she might even induce hostility because of this very fact. A usurper in the cradle, in the cot, that had been Christine's. A chubby, flaxen replica of Johnnie, not the little waxen dark-haired sprite that had gone.

He looked up, over his glass of wine, and the woman was staring at him again. It was not the casual, idle glance of someone at a nearby table, waiting for her companion to return, but something deeper, more intent, the prominent, light blue eyes oddly penetrating, giving him a sudden feeling of discomfort. Damn the woman! All right, bloody stare, if you must. Two can play at that game. He blew a cloud of cigarette smoke into the air and smiled at her, he hoped offensively. She did not register. The blue eyes continued to hold his, so that finally he was obliged to look away himself, extinguish his cigarette, glance over his shoulder for the waiter and call for the bill. Settling for this, and fumbling with the change, with a few casual remarks about the excellence of the meal, brought composure, but a prickly feeling on his scalp remained, and an odd sensation of unease. Then it went, as abruptly as it had started, and stealing a furtive glance at the other table he saw that her eyes were closed again, and she was sleeping, or dozing, as she had done before. The waiter disappeared. All was still.

Laura, he thought, glancing at his watch, is being a hell of a time. Ten minutes at least. Something to tease her about, anyway. He began to plan the form the joke would take. How the old dolly had stripped to her smalls, suggesting that Laura should do likewise. And then the manager had burst in upon them both, exclaiming in horror, the reputation of the restaurant damaged, the hint that unpleasant consequences might follow unless . . . The whole exercise turning out to be a plant, an exercise in blackmail. He and Laura and the twins taken in a police launch back to Venice for questioning. Quarter of an hour . . . Oh, come on, come on . . .

There was a crunch of feet on the gravel. Laura's twin walked slowly past, alone. She crossed over to her table and stood there a moment, her tall, angular figure interposing itself between John and her sister. She was saying something, but he couldn't catch the words. What was the accent, though—Scottish? Then she bent, offering an arm to the seated twin, and they moved away together across the garden to the break in the little hedge beyond, the twin who had stared at John leaning on her sister's arm. Here was the difference again. She was not quite so tall, and she stooped more—perhaps she was arthritic. They disappeared out of sight, and John, becoming impatient, got up and was about to walk back into the hotel when Laura emerged.

"Well, I must say, you took your time," he began, then stopped, because of the expression on her face.

"What's the matter, what's happened?" he asked.

He could tell at once there was something wrong. Almost as if she were in a state of shock. She blundered toward the table he had just vacated and sat down. He drew up a chair beside her, taking her hand.

"Darling, what is it? Tell me—are you ill?"

She shook her head, and then turned and looked at him. The dazed expression he had noticed at first had given way to one of dawning confidence, almost of exaltation.

"It's quite wonderful," she said slowly, "the most wonderful thing that could possibly be. You see, she isn't dead, she's still with us. That's why they kept staring at us, those two sisters. They could see Christine."

Oh God, he thought. It's what I've been dreading. She's going off her head. What do I do? How do I cope?

"Laura, sweet," he began, forcing a smile, "look, shall we go? I've paid the bill, we can go and look at the cathedral and stroll around, and then it will be time to take off in that launch again for Venice."

She wasn't listening, or at any rate the words didn't penetrate.

"John, love," she said, "I've got to tell you what happened. I followed her, as we planned, into the *toilette* place. She was combing her hair and I went into the loo, and then came out and washed my hands in the basin. She was washing hers in the next basin. Suddenly she turned and said to me, in a strong Scots accent, 'Don't be unhappy anymore. My sister has seen your little girl. She was sitting between you and your husband, laughing.' Darling, I thought I was going to faint. I nearly did.

Luckily, there was a chair, and I sat down, and the woman bent over me and patted my head. I'm not sure of her exact words, but she something about the moment of truth and joy being as sharp as a sword, but not to be afraid, all was well, but the sister's vision had been so strong they knew I had to be told, and that Christine wanted it. Oh John, don't look like that. I swear I'm not making it up, this is what she told me, it's all true."

The desperate urgency in her voice made his heart sicken. He had to play along with her, agree, soothe, do anything to bring back some sense of calm.

"Laura, darling, of course I believe you," he said, "only it's a sort of shock, and I'm upset because you're upset . . ."

"But I'm not upset," she interrupted. "I'm happy, so happy that I can't put the feeling into words. You know what it's been like all these weeks, at home and everywhere we've been on holiday, though I tried to hide it from you. Now it's lifted, because I know, I just know, that the woman was right. Oh Lord, how awful of me, but I've forgotten their name—she did tell me. You see, the thing is that she's a retired doctor, they come from Edinburgh, and the one who saw Christine went blind a few years ago. Although she's studied the occult all her life and been very psychic, it's only since going blind that she has really seen things, like a medium. They've had the most wonderful experiences. But to describe Christine as the blind one did to her sister, even down to the little blue-and-white dress with the puff sleeves that she wore at her birthday party, and to say she was smiling happily . . . Oh darling, it's made me so happy I think I'm going to cry."

No hysteria. Nothing wild. She took a tissue from her bag and blew her nose, smiling at him. "I'm all right, you see, you don't have to worry. Neither of us need worry about anything anymore. Give me a cigarette."

He took one from his packet and lighted it for her. She sounded normal, herself again. She wasn't trembling. And if this sudden belief was going to keep her happy he couldn't possibly begrudge it. But . . . but . . . he wished, all the same, it hadn't happened. There was something uncanny about thought-reading, about telepathy. Scientists couldn't account for it, nobody could, and this is what must have happened just now between Laura and the sisters. So the one who had been staring at him was blind. That accounted for the fixed gaze. Which somehow was unpleasant in itself, creepy. Oh hell, he thought, I wish we hadn't come here for lunch. Just chance, a flick of a coin between this, Torcello, and driving to Padua, and we had to choose Torcello.

"You didn't arrange to meet them again or anything, did you?" he asked, trying to sound casual.

"No, darling, why should I?" Laura answered. "I mean, there was nothing more they could tell me. The sister had had her wonderful vision, and that was that. Anyway, they're moving on. Funnily enough, it's rather like our original game. They *are* going round the world before returning to Scotland. Only I said Australia, didn't I? The old dears . . . anything less like murderers and jewel thieves!"

She had quite recovered. She stood up and looked about her. "Come on," she said. "Having come to Torcello we must see the cathedral."

They made their way from the restaurant across the open piazza, where the stalls had been set up with scarves and trinkets and postcards, and so along the path to the cathedral. One of the ferryboats had just decanted a crowd of sightseers, many of whom had already found their way into Santa Maria Assunta. Laura, undaunted, asked her husband for the guidebook, and, as had always been her custom in happier days, started to walk slowly through the cathedral, studying mosaics, columns, panels from left to right, while John, less interested, because of his concern at what had just happened, followed close behind, keeping a weather eye alert for the twin sisters. There was no sign of them. Perhaps they had gone into the Church of Santa Fosca closeby. A sudden encounter would be embarrassing, quite apart from the effect it might have upon Laura. But the anonymous, shuffling tourists, intent upon culture, could not harm her, although from his own point of view they made artistic appreciation impossible. He could not concentrate, the cold clear beauty of what he saw left him untouched, and when Laura touched his sleeve, pointing to the mosaic of the Virgin and Child standing above the frieze of the Apostles, he nodded in sympathy yet saw nothing, the long, sad face of the Virgin infinitely remote, and turning on sudden impulse stared back over the heads of the tourists toward the door, where frescoes of the blessed and the damned gave themselves to judgment.

The twins were standing there, the blind one still holding onto her sister's arm, her sightless eyes fixed firmly upon him. He felt himself held, unable to move, and an impending sense of doom, of tragedy, came upon him. His whole being sagged, as it were, in apathy, and he thought, This is the end, there is no escape, no future. Then both sisters turned and went out of the cathedral and the sensation vanished, leaving indignation in its wake, and rising anger. How dare those two old fools practice their mediumistic tricks on him? It was fraudulent, unhealthy; this was probably the way they lived, touring the world making everyone they met uncomfortable. Give them half a chance and they would have got money out of Laura—anything.

He felt her tugging at his sleeve again. "Isn't she beautiful? So happy, so serene."

"Who? What?" he asked.

"The Madonna," she answered. "She has a magic quality. It goes right through to one. Don't you feel it too?"

"I suppose so. I don't know. There are too many people around."

She looked up at him, astonished. "What's that got to do with it? How funny you are. Well, all right, let's get away from them. I want to buy some postcards anyway." Disappointed, she sensed his lack of interest, and began to thread her way through the crowd of tourists to the door.

"Come on," he said abruptly, once they were outside, "there's plenty of time for postcards, let's explore a bit," and he struck off from the path, which would have taken them back to the center where the little houses were, and the stalls, and the drifting crowd of people, to a narrow way amongst uncultivated ground, beyond which he could see a sort of cutting, or canal. The sight of water, limpid, pale, was a soothing contrast to the fierce sun above their heads.

"I don't think this leads anywhere much," said Laura. "It's a bit muddy, too, one can't sit. Besides, there are more things the guidebook says we ought to see."

"Oh, forget the book," he said impatiently, and, pulling her down beside him on the bank above the cutting, put his arms round her.

"It's the wrong time of day for sight-seeing. Look, there's a rat swimming there the other side." He picked up a stone and threw it in the water, and the animal sank, or somehow disappeared, and nothing was left but bubbles.

"Don't," said Laura. "It's cruel, poor thing," and then suddenly, putting her hand on his knee, "Do you think Christine is sitting here beside us?"

He did not answer at once. What was there to say? Would it be like this forever?

"I expect so," he said slowly, "if you feel she is."

The point was, remembering Christine before the onset of the fatal meningitis, she would have been running along the bank excitedly, throwing off her shoes, wanting to paddle, giving Laura a fit of apprehension. "Sweetheart, take care, come back . . . "

"The woman said she was looking so happy, sitting beside us, smiling," said Laura. She got up, brushing her dress, her mood changed to restlessness. "Come on, let's go back," she said.

He followed her with a sinking heart. He knew she did not really want to buy postcards or see what remained to be seen; she wanted to go in search of the women again, not necessarily to talk, just to be near them. When they came to the open place by the stalls he noticed that the crowd of tourists had thinned, there were only a few stragglers left, and the sisters were not amongst them. They must have joined the main body who had come to Torcello by the ferry service. A wave of relief seized him.

"Look, there's a mass of postcards at the second stall," he said quickly, "and some eye-catching head scarves. Let me buy you a head scarf."

"Darling, I've so many!" she protested. "Don't waste your lire."

"It isn't a waste. I'm in a buying mood. What about a basket? You know we never have enough baskets. Or some lace. How about lace?"

She allowed herself, laughing, to be dragged to the stall. While he rumpled through the goods spread out before them, and chatted up the smiling woman who was selling her wares, his ferociously bad Italian making her smile the more, he knew it would give the body of tourists more time to walk to the landing stage and catch the ferry service, and the twin sisters would be out of sight and out of their life.

"Never," said Laura, some twenty minutes later, "has so much junk been piled into so small a basket," her bubbling laugh reassuring him that all was well, he needn't worry anymore, the evil hour had passed. The launch from the Cipriani that had brought them from Venice was waiting by the landing stage. The passengers who had arrived with them, the Americans, the man with the monocle, were already assembled. Earlier, before setting out, he had thought the price for lunch and transport, there and bck, decidedly steep. Now he grudged none of it, except that the outing to Torcello itself had been one of the major errors of this particular holiday in Venice. They stepped down into the launch, finding a place in the open, and the boat chugged away down the canal and into the lagoon. The ordinary ferry had gone before, steaming toward Murano, while their own craft headed past San Francesco Del Deserto and so back direct to Venice.

He put his arm around her once more, holding her close, and this time she responded, smiling up at him, her head on his shoulder.

"It's been a lovely day," she said. "I shall never forget it, never. You know, darling, now at last I can begin to enjoy our holiday."

He wanted to shout with relief. It's going to be all right, he decided, let her believe what she likes, it doesn't matter, it makes her happy. The beauty of Venice rose before them, sharply outlined against the glowing sky, and there was still so much to see, wandering there together, that might now be perfect because of her change of mood, the shadow having lifted, and aloud he began to discuss the evening to come, where they would dine—not the restaurant they usually went to, near the Venice Theatre, but somewhere different, somewhere new.

"Yes, but it must be cheap," she said, falling in with his mood, "because we've already spent so much today."

Their hotel by the Grand Canal had a welcoming, comforting air. The clerk smiled as he handed over their key. The bedroom was familiar, like home, with Laura's things arranged neatly on the dressing table, but with it the little festive atmosphere of strangeness, of excitement, that only a holiday bedroom brings. This is ours for the moment, but no more. While we are in it we bring it life. When we have gone it no longer exists, it fades into anonymity. He turned on both taps in the bathroom, the water gushing into the bath, the steam rising. Now, he thought afterward, now at last is the moment to make love, and he went back into the bedroom, and she understood, and opened her arms and smiled. Such blessed relief after all those weeks of restraint.

"The thing is," she said later, fixing her earrings before the looking glass, "I'm not really terrible hungry. Shall we just be dull and eat in the dining room here?"

"God, no!" he exclaimed. "With all those rather dreary couples at the other tables? I'm ravenous. I'm also gay. I want to get rather sloshed."

"Not bright lights and music, surely?"

"No, no . . . some small, dark intimate cave, rather sinister, full of lovers with other people's wives."

"H'm," sniffed Laura, "we all know what *that* means. You'll spot some Italian lovely of sixteen and smirk at her through dinner, while I'm stuck high and dry with a beastly man's broad back."

They went out laughing into the warm soft night, and the magic was about them everywhere. "Let's walk," he said, "let's walk and work up an appetite for our gigantic meal," and inevitably they found themselves by the Molo and the lapping gondolas dancing upon the water, the lights everywhere blending with the darkness. There were other couples strolling for the same sake of aimless enjoyment, backward, forward, purposeless, and inevitable sailors in groups, noisy, gesticulating, and dark-eyed girls whispering, clicking on high heels.

"The trouble is," said Laura, "walking in Venice becomes compulsive once you start. Just over the next bridge, you say, and then the next one beckons. I'm sure there are no restaurants down here, we're almost at those public gardens where they hold the Biennale. Let's turn back. I know there's a restaurant somewhere near the Church of San Zaccaria, there's a little alleyway leading to it."

"Tell you what," said John, "if we go down here by the Arsenal, and cross that bridge at the end and head left, we'll come upon San Zaccaria from the other side. We did it the other morning."

"Yes, but it was daylight then. We may lose our way, it's not very well lit."

"Don't fuss. I have an instinct for these things."

They turned down the Fondamenta del l'Arsenale and crossed the little bridge short of the Arsenal itself, and so on past the church of San Martino. There were two canals ahead, one bearing right, the other left, with narrow streets beside them. John hesitated. Which one was it they had walked beside the day before?

"You see," protested Laura, "we shall be lost, just as I said."

"Nonsense," replied John firmly. "It's the left-hand one, I remember the little bridge."

The canal was narrow, the houses on either side seemed to close in upon it, and in the daytime, with the sun's reflection on the water and the windows of the houses open, bedding upon the balconies, a canary singing in a cage, there had been an impression of warmth, of secluded shelter. Now, ill-lit, in darkness, the windows of the houses shuttered, the water dank, the scene appeared altogether different, neglected, poor, and the long narrow boats moored to the slippery steps of cellar entrances looked like coffins.

"I swear I don't remember this bridge," said Laura, pausing, and holding onto the rail, "and I don't like the look of that alleyway beyond."

"There's a lamp halfway up," John told her. "I know exactly where we are, not far from the Greek quarter."

They crossed the bridge, and were about to plunge into the alleyway, when they heard the cry. It came, surely, from one of the houses on the opposite side, but which one it was impossible to say. With the shutters closed, each of them seemed dead. They turned, and stared in the direction from which the sound had come.

"What was it?" whispered Laura.

"Some drunk or other," said John briefly, "come on."

Less like a drunk than someone being strangled, and the choking cry suppressed as the grip held firm.

"We ought to call the police," said Laura.

"Oh, for heaven's sake," said John. Where did she think she was—Piccadilly?

"Well, I'm off, it's sinister," she replied, and began to hurry away up the twisting alleyway. John hesitated, his eye caught by a small figure which suddenly crept from a cellar entrance below one of the opposite houses, and then jumped into a narrow boat below. It was a child, a little girl—she couldn't have been more than five or six-wearing a short coat over her minute skirt, a pixie hood covering her head. There were four boats moored, line upon line, and she proceeded to jump from one to the other with surprising agility, intent, it would seem, upon escape. Once her foot slipped and he caught his breath, for she was within a few feet of the water, losing balance; then she recovered, and hopped onto the farthest boat. Bending, she tugged at the rope, which had the effect of swinging the boat's after-end across the canal, almost touching the opposite side and another cellar entrance, about thirty feet from the spot where John stood watching her. Then the child jumped again, landing upon the cellar steps, and vanished into the house, the boat swinging back into midcanal behind her. The whole episode could not have taken more than four minutes. Then he heard the quick patter of feet. Laura had returned. She had seen none of it, for which he felt unspeakably thankful. The sight of a child, a little girl, in what must have been near danger, her fear that the scene he had just witnessed was in some way a sequel to the alarming cry, might have had a disastrous effect on her overwrought nerves."

"What are you doing?" she called. "I daren't go on without you. The wretched alley branches in two directions."

"Sorry," he told her, "I'm coming."

He took her arm and they walked briskly along the alley, John with an apparent confidence he did not possess.

"There were no more cries, were there?" she asked.

"No," he said, "no, nothing. I tell you, it was some drunk."

The alley led to a deserted campo behind a church, not a church he knew, and he led the way across, along another street and over a farther bridge.

"Wait a minute," he said, "I think we take this righthand turning. It will lead us into the Greek quarter, the Church of San Georgio is somewhere over there."

She did not answer. She was beginning to lose faith. The place was like a maze. They might circle round and round forever, and then find themselves back again, near the bridge where they had heard the cry. Doggedly he led her on, and then, surprisingly, with relief, he saw people walking in the lighted street ahead, there was a spire of a church, the surroundings became familiar.

"There, I told you," he said, "that's San Zaccaria, we've found it all right. Your restaurant can't be far away." And anyway, there would be other restaurants, somewhere to eat, at least here was the cheering glitter of lights, of movement, canals beside which people walked, the atmosphere of tourism. The letters RISTORANTE in blue lights, shone like a beacon down a left-hand alley.

"Is this your place?" he asked.

"God knows," she said. "Who cares? Let's feed there anyway."

And so into the sudden blast of heated air and hum of voices, the smell of pasta, wine, waiters, jostling customers, laughter. "For two? This way, please." Why, he thought, was one's British nationality always so obvious? A cramped little table and an enormous menu scribbled in an indecipherable mauve ink, with the waiter hovering, expecting the order forthwith.

"Two very large Camparis, with soda," John said. "*Then* we'll study the menu."

He was not going to be rushed. He handed the bill of fare to Laura and looked about him. Mostly Italians—that meant the food would be good. Then he saw them. At the opposite side of the room. The twin sisters. They must have come into the restaurant hard upon Laura and his own arrival, for they were only now sitting down, shedding their coats, the waiter hovering beside the table. John was seized with the irrational thought that this was no coincidence. The sisters had noticed them both, in the street outside, and had followed them in. Why, in the name of hell, should they have picked on this particular spot, in the whole of Venice, unless . . . unless Laura herself, at Torcello, had suggested a further encounter, or the sister had suggested it to her? A small restaurant near the Church of San Zaccaria, we go there sometimes for dinner. It was Laura, before the walk, who had mentioned San Zaccaria . . .

She was still intent upon the menu, she had not seen the sisters, but any moment now she would have chosen what she wanted to eat, and then she would raise her head and look across the room. If only the drinks would come. If only the waiter would bring the drinks, it would give Laura something to do.

"You know, I was thinking," he said quickly, "we really ought to go to the garage tomorrow and get the car, and do that drive to Padua. We could lunch in Padua, see the cathedral and touch St. Anthony's tomb and look at the Giotto frescoes, and come back by way of those various villas along the Brenta that the guidebook recommends so highly."

It was no use, though. She was looking up, across the restaurant, and she gave a little gasp of surprise. It was genuine. He could swear it was genuine.

"Look," she said, "how extraordinary! How really amazing!"

"What?" he said sharply.

"Why, there they are. My wonderful old twins. They've seen us, what's more. They're staring this way." She waved her hand, radiant, delighted. The sister she had spoken to at Torcello bowed and smiled. False old bitch, he thought. I know they followed us.

"Oh, darling, I must go and speak to them," she said impulsively, "just to tell them how happy I've been all day, thanks to them."

"Oh, for heaven's sake," he said. "Look, here are the drinks. And we haven't ordered yet. Surely you can wait until later, until we've eaten?"

"I won't be a moment," she said, "and anyway I want scampi, nothing first. I told you I wasn't hungry."

She got up, and, brushing past the waiter with the drinks, crossed the room. She might have been greeting the loved friends of years. He watched her bend over the table, shake them both by the hand, and because there was a vacant chair at their table she drew it up and sat down, talking, smiling. Nor did the sisters seemed surprised, at least not the one she knew, who nodded and talked back, while the blind sister remained impassive.

All right, thought John savagely, then I *will* get sloshed, and he proceeded to down his Campari and soda and order another, while he pointed out something quite unintelligible on the menu as his own choice, but remembered scampi for Laura. "And a bottle of soave," he added, "with ice."

The evening was ruined anyway. What was to have been an intimate and happy celebration would now be heavy-laden with spiritualistic visions, poor little dead Christine sharing the table with them, which was so damned stupid when in earthly life she would have been tucked up hours ago in bed. The bitter taste of his Campari suited his mood of sudden self-pity, and all the while he watched the group at the table in the opposite corner, Laura apparently listening while the more active sister held forth and the blind one sat silent, her formidable sightless eyes turned in his direction.

She's phoney, he thought, she's not blind at all. They're both of them frauds, and they could be males in drag after all, just as we pretended at Torcello, and they're after Laura.

He began on his second Campari and soda. The two drinks, taken on an empty stomach, had an instant effect. Vision became blurred. And still Laura went on sitting at the other table, putting in a question now and again, while the active sister talked. The waiter appeared with the scampi, and a companion beside him to serve John's own order, which was totally unrecognisable, heaped with a livid sauce.

"The signora does not come?" inquired the first waiter, and John shook his head grimly, pointing an unsteady finger across the room.

"Tell the signora," he said carefully "her scampi will get cold."

He stared down at the offering placed before him, and prodded it delicately with a fork. The pallid sauce dissolved, revealing two enormous slices, rounds, of what appeared to be boiled pork, bedecked with garlic. He forked a portion to his mouth and chewed, and yes, it was pork, steamy, rich, the spicy sauce having turned it curiously sweet. He laid down his fork, pushing the plate away, and became aware of Laura, returning across the room and sitting beside him. She did not say anything, which was just as well, he thought, because he was too near nausea to answer. It wasn't just the drink, but reaction from the whole nightmare day. She began to eat her scampi, still not uttering. She did not seem to notice he was not eating. The waiter, hovering at his elbow, anxious, seemed aware that John's choice was somehow an error, and discreetly removed the plate. "Bring me a green salad," murmured John, and even then Laura did not register surprise, or, as she might have done in more normal circumstances, accuse him of having had too much to drink. Finally, when she had finished her scampi, and was sipping her wine, which John had waved away, to nibble at his salad in small mouthfuls like a sick rabbit, she began to speak.

"Darling," she said, "I know you won't believe it, and it's rather frightening in a way, but after they left the restaurant in Torcello the sisters went to the cathedral, as we did, although we didn't see them in that crowd, and the blind one had another vision. She said Christine was trying to tell her something about us, that we should be in danger if we stayed in Venice. Christine wanted us to go away as soon as possible."

So that's it, he thought. They think they can run our lives for us. This is to be our problem from henceforth. Do we eat? Do we get up? Do we go to bed? We must get in touch with the twin sisters. They will direct us.

"Well?" she said. "Why don't you say something?"

"Because," he answered, "you are perfectly right, I don't believe it. Quite frankly, I judge your old sisters as being a couple of freaks, if nothing else. They're obviously unbalanced, and I'm sorry if this hurts you, but the fact is they've found a sucker in you."

"You're being unfair," said Laura. "They are genuine, I know it. I just know it. They were completely sincere in what they said."

"All right. Granted. They're sincere. But that doesn't make them well-balanced. Honestly, darling, you meet that old girl for ten minutes in a loo, she tells you she sees Christine sitting beside us, well, anyone with a gift for telepathy could read your unconscious mind in an instant, and then, pleased with her success, as any old psychic expert would be, she flings a further mood of ecstasy and wants to boot us out of Venice. Well, I'm sorry, but to hell with it."

The room was no longer reeling. Anger had sobered him. If it would not put Laura to shame he would get up and cross to their table, and tell the old fools where they could get off.

"I knew you would take it like this," said Laura unhappily. "I told them you would. They said not to worry. As long as we left Venice tomorrow everything would come all right."

"Oh, for God's sake," said John. He changed his mind and poured himself a glass of wine.

"After all," Laura went on, "we have really seen the cream of Venice. I don't mind going on somewhere else. And if we stayed—I know it sounds silly, but I should have a nasty nagging sort of feeling inside me, and I should keep thinking of darling Christine being unhappy and trying to tell us to go."

"Right," said John with ominous calm, "that settles it. Go we will. I suggest we clear off to the hotel straight away and warn the reception we're leaving in the morning. Have you had enough to eat?"

"Oh, dear," sighed Laura, "don't take it like that. Look, why not come over and meet them, and then they can explain about the vision to you? Perhaps you would take it seriously then. Especially as you are the one it most concerns. Christine is more worried over you than me. And the extraordinary thing is that the blind sister says you're psychic and don't know it. You are somehow *en rapport* with the unknown, and I'm not."

"Well, that's final," said John. "I'm psychic, am I? Fine. My psychic intuition tells me to get out of this restaurant now, at once, and we can decide what we do about leaving Venice when we are back at the hotel."

He signaled to the waiter for the bill and they waited for it, not speaking to each other, Laura unhappy fiddling with her bag, while John, glancing furtively at the twins' table, noticed that they were tucking into plates piled high with spaghetti, in very unpsychic fashion. The bill disposed of, John pushed back his chair.

"Right. Are you ready?" he asked.

"I'm going to say good-bye to them first," said Laura, her mouth set sulkily, reminding him instantly, with a pang, of their poor lost child.

"Just as you like," he replied, and walked ahead of her, out of the restaurant without a backward glance.

The soft humidity of the evening, so pleasant to walk about in earlier, had turned to rain. The strolling tourists had melted away. One or two people hurried by under umbrellas. This is what the inhabitants who live here see, he thought. This is the true life. Empty streets by night, and the dank stillness of a stagnant canal beneath shuttered houses. The rest is a bright facade put on for show, glittering by sunlight.

Laura joined him and they walked away together in silence, and emerging presently behind the ducal palace came out into the Piazza San Marco. The rain was heavy now, and they sought shelter, still walking, with the few remaining stragglers under the colonnades. The orchestras had packed up for the evening. The tables were bare. Chairs had been turned upside down.

The experts are right, he thought. Venice is sinking. The whole city is slowly dying. One day the tourists will travel here by boat to peer down into the waters, and they will see pillars and columns and marble far, far beneath them, slime and mud uncovering for brief moments a lost underworld of stone. Their heels made a ringing sound on the pavement and the rain splashed from the gutterings above. A fine ending to an evening that had started with brave hope, with innocence.

When they came to their hotel Laura made straight for the lift, and John turned to the desk to ask the nightporter for the key. The man handed him a telegram at the same time. John stared at it a moment. Laura was already in the lift. Then he opened the envelope and read the message. It was from the headmaster of Johnnie's preparatory school.

JOHNNIE UNDER OBSERVATION SUSPECTED
APPENDICITIS IN CITY HOSPITAL HERE.
NO CAUSE FOR ALARM BUT SURGEON THOUGHT
WISE ADVISE YOU.

CHARLES HILL

He read the message twice, then walked slowly toward the lift, where Laura was waiting for him. He gave her the telegram. "This came when we were out," he said. "Not awfully good news." He pressed the lift button as she read the telegram. The lift stopped at the second floor, and they got out.

"Well, this decides it, doesn't it?" she said. "Here is the proof. We have to leave Venice because we're going home. It's Johnnie who's in danger, not us. This is what Christine was trying to tell the twins."

The first thing John did the following morning was to put a call through to the headmaster at the preparatory school. Then he gave notice of their departure to the reception manager, and they packed while they waited for the call. Neither of them referred to the events of the preceding day, it was not necessary. John knew the arrival of the telegram and the foreboding of danger from the sisters was coincidence, nothing more, but it was pointless to start an argument about it. Laura was convinced otherwise, but intuitively she knew it was best to keep her feelings to herself. During breakfast they discussed ways and means of getting home. It should be possible to get themselves, and the car, onto the special car train that ran from Milan through to Calais, since it was early in the season. In any event, the headmaster had said there was no urgency.

The call from England came while John was in the bathroom. Laura answered it. He came into the bedroom a few minutes later. She was still speaking, but he could tell from the expression in her eyes that she was anxious.

"It's Mrs. Hill," she said. "Mr. Hill is in class. She says they reported from the hospital that Johnnie had a restless night, and the surgeon may have to operate, but he doesn't want to unless it's absolutely necessary. They've taken X-rays and the appendix is in a tricky position, it's not awfully straightforward."

"Here, give it to me," he said.

The soothing but slightly guarded voice of the headmaster's wife came down the receiver. "I'm so sorry this may spoil your plans," she said, "but both Charles and I felt you ought to be told, and that you might feel rather easier if you were on the spot. Johnnie is very plucky, but of course he has some fever. That isn't unusual, the surgeon says, in the circumstances, sometimes an appendix can get displaced, it appears, and this makes it more complicated. He's going to decide about operating this evening."

"Yes, of course, we quite understand," said John.

"Please do tell your wife not to worry too much," she went on. "The hospital is excellent, a very nice staff, and we have every confidence in the surgeon."

"Yes," said John, "yes," and then broke off because Laura was making gestures beside him.

"If we can't get the car on the train, I can fly," she said. "They're sure to be able to find me a seat on a plane. Then at least one of us would be there this evening."

He nodded agreement. "Thank you so much, Mrs. Hill," he said, "we'll manage to get back all right. Yes, I'm sure Johnnie is in good hands. Thank your husband for us. Good-bye."

He replaced the receiver and looked around him at the tumbled beds, suitcases on the floor, tissue paper strewn. Baskets, maps, books, coats, everything they had brought with them in the car. "Oh, God," he said, "what a bloody mess. All this junk." The telephone rang again. It was the hall porter to say he had succeeded in booking a sleeper for them both, and a place for the car, on the following night.

"Look," said Laura, who had seized the telephone, "could you book one seat on the midday plane from Venice to London today, for me? It's imperative one of us gets home this evening. My husband could follow with the car tomorrow."

"Here, hang on," interrupted John. "No need for panic stations. Surely twenty-four hours wouldn't make all that difference?"

Anxiety had drained the color from her face. She turned to him, distraught.

"It mightn't to you, but it does to me," she said. "I've lost one child, I'm not going to lose another."

"All right, darling, all right . . . " He put his hand out to her, but she brushed it off, impatiently, and continued giving directions to the porter. He turned back to his packing. No use saying anything. Better for it to be as she wished. They could, of course, both go by air, and then when all was well, and Johnnie better, he could come back and fetch the car, driving home through France as they had come. Rather a sweat, though, and a hell of an expense. Bad enough Laura going by air and himself with the car on the train from Milan.

"We could, if you like, both fly," he began tentatively, explaining the sudden idea, but she would have none of it. "That really *would* be absurd," she said impatiently. "As long as I'm there this evening, and you follow by train, it's all that matters. Besides, we shall need the car, going backward and forward to the hospital. And our luggage. We couldn't go off and just leave all this here."

No, he saw her point. A silly idea. It was only, well, he was as worried about Johnnie as she was, though he wasn't going to say so.

"I'm going downstairs to stand over the porter," said Laura. "They always make more effort if one is actually on the spot. Everything I want tonight is packed. I shall only need my overnight case. You can bring everything else in the car." She hadn't been out of the bedroom five minutes before the telephone rang. It was Laura. "Darling," she said, "it couldn't have worked out better. The porter has got me on a charter flight that leaves Venice in less than an hour. A special motor launch takes the party direct from San Marco, in about ten minutes. Some passenger on the charter flight had canceled. I shall be at Gatwick in less than four hours."

"I'll be down right away," he told her.

He joined her by the reception desk. She no longer looked anxious and drawn, but full of purpose. She was on her way. He kept wishing they were going together. He couldn't bear to stay on in Venice after she had gone, but the thought of driving to

Milan, spending a dreary night in a hotel there alone, the endless dragging day which would follow, and the long hours in the train the next night, filled him with intolerable depression, quite apart from the anxiety about Johnnie. They walked along to the San Marco landing stage, the Molo bright and glittering after the rain, a little breeze blowing, the postcards and scarves and tourist souvenirs fluttering on the stalls, the tourists themselves out in force, strolling, contented, the happy day before them.

"I'll ring you tonight from Milan," he told her. "The Hills will give you a bed, I suppose. And if you're at the hospital they'll let me have the latest news. That must be your charter party. You're welcome to them!"

The passengers descending from the landing stage down into the waiting launch were carrying hand luggage with Union Jack tags upon them. They were mostly middle-aged, with what appeared to be two Methodist ministers in charge. One of them advanced toward Laura, holding out his hand, showing a gleaming row of dentures when he smiled. "You must be the lady joining us for the homeward flight," he said. "Welcome aboard, and to the Union of Fellowship. We are all delighted to make your acquaintance. Sorry we hadn't a seat for hubby too."

Laura turned swiftly and kissed John, a tremor at the corner of her mouth betraying inward laughter. "Do you think they'll break into hymns?" she whispered. "Take care of yourself, hubby. Call me tonight."

The pilot sounded a curious little toot upon his horn, and in a moment Laura had climbed down the steps into the launch and was standing amongst the crowd of passengers, waving her hand, her scarlet coat a gay patch of color amongst the more sober suiting of her companions. The launch tooted again and moved away from the landing stage, and he stood there watching it, a sense of immense loss filling his heart. Then he turned and walked away, back to the hotel, the bright day all about him desolate, unseen.

There was nothing, he thought, as he looked about him presently in the hotel bedroom, so melancholy as a vacated room, especially when the recent signs of occupation were still visible about him. Laura's suitcases on the bed, a second coat she had left behind. Traces of powder on the dressing table. A tissue, with lipstick smear, thrown in the wastepaper basket. Even an old toothpaste tube squeezed dry, lying on the glass shelf above the washbasin. Sounds of the heedless traffic on the Grand Canal came as always from the open window, but Laura wasn't there anymore to listen to it, or to watch from the small balcony. The pleasure had gone. Feeling had gone.

John finished packing, and, leaving all the baggage ready to be collected, he went downstairs to pay the bill. The reception clerk was welcoming new arrivals. People were sitting on the terrace overlooking the Grand Canal reading newspapers, the pleasant day waiting to be planned.

John decided to have an early lunch, here on the hotel terrace, on familiar ground, and then have the porter carry the baggage to one of the ferries that steamed between San Marco and the Porta Roma, where the car was garaged. The fiasco meal of the night before had left him empty, and he was ready for the trolley of hors d'oeuvres when they brought it to him, around midday. Even here, though, there was change. The headwaiter, their especial friend, was off duty, and the table where they usually sat was occupied by new arrivals, a honeymoon couple, he told himself sourly, observing the gaiety, the smiles, while he had been shown to a small single table behind a tub of flowers.

She's airborne now, John thought, she's on her way, and he tried to picture Laura seated between the Methodist ministers, telling them, no doubt, about Johnnie ill in hospital, and heaven knows what else besides. Well, the twin sisters anyway could rest in psychic peace. Their wishes would have been fulfilled.

Lunch over, there was no point in lingering with a cup of coffee on the terrace. His desire was to get away as soon as possible, fetch the car, and be en route for Milan. He made his farewells at the reception desk, and, escorted by a porter who had piled his baggage onto a wheeled trolley, he made his way once more to the landing stage of San Marco. As he stepped onto the steam ferry, his luggage heaped beside him, a crowd of jostling people all about him, he had one momentary pang to be leaving Venice. When, if ever, he wondered, would they come again? Next year . . . in three years . . . Glimpsed first on honeymoon, nearly ten years ago, and then a second visit *en passant,* before a cruise, and now this last abortive ten days that had ended so abruptly.

The water glittered in the sunshine, buildings shone, tourists in dark glasses paraded up and down the rapidly receding Molo; already the terrace of their hotel was out of sight as the ferry churned its way up the Grand Canal. So many impressions to seize and hold, familiar loved facades, balconies, windows, water lapping the cellar steps of decaying palaces, the little red house where d'Annunzio lived, with its garden—our house, Laura called it, pretending it was theirs—and too soon the ferry would be turning left on the direct route to the Piazzale Roma, so missing the best of the Canal, the Rialto, the farther palaces.

Another ferry was heading downstream to pass them, filled with passengers, and for a brief foolish moment he wished he could change places, be amongst the happy tourists bound for Venice and all he had left behind him. Then he saw her. Laura, in her scarlet coat, the twin sisters by her side, the active sister with her hand on Laura's arm, talking earnestly, and Laura herself, her hair blowing in the wind, gesticulating, on her face a look of distress. He stared, astounded, too astonished to shout, to wave, and anyway they would never have heard or seen him, for his own ferry had already passed and was heading in the opposite direction.

What the hell had happened? There must have been a holdup with the charter flight and it had never taken off, but in that case why had Laura not telephoned him at the hotel? And what were those damned sisters doing? Had she run into them at the airport? Was it coincidence? And why did she look so anxious? He could think of no explanation. Perhaps the flight had been canceled. Laura, of course would go straight to the hotel, expecting to find him there, intending, doubtless, to drive with him after all to Milan and take the train the following night. What a blasted mix-up. The only thing to do was to telephone the hotel immediately his ferry reached the Piazzale Roma and tell her to wait, he would return and fetch her. As for the damned interfering sisters, they could get stuffed.

The usual stampede ensued when the ferry arrived at the landing stage. He had to find a porter to collect his baggage, and then wait while he discovered a telephone. The fiddling with change, the hunt for the number, delayed him still more. He succeeded at last in getting through, and luckily the reception clerk he knew was still at the desk.

"Look, there's been some frightful muddle," he began, and explained how Laura was even now on her way back to the hotel—he had seen her with two friends on one of the ferry services. Would the reception clerk explain and tell her to wait? He would be back by the next available service to collect her. "In any event, detain her," he said. "I'll be as quick as I can." The reception clerk understood perfectly and John rang off.

Thank heaven Laura hadn't turned up before he had put through his call, or they would have told her he was on his way to Milan. The porter was still waiting with the baggage, and it seemed simplest to walk with him to the garage, hand everything over to the chap in charge of the office there, and ask him to keep it for an hour, when he would be returning with his wife to pick up the car. Then he went back to the landing station to await the next ferry to Venice. The minutes dragged and he kept wondering all the time what had gone wrong at the airport and why in heaven's name Laura hadn't telephoned. No use conjecturing. She would tell him the whole story at the hotel. One thing was certain. He would not allow themselves to be saddled with the sisters and become involved with their affairs. He could imagine Laura saying that they also had missed a flight, and could they have a lift to Milan?

Finally the ferry chugged alongside the landing stage and he stepped aboard. What an anticlimax, thrashing back past the familiar sights to which he had bidden a nostalgic farewell such a short while ago! He didn't even look about him this time, he was so intent on reaching his destination. In San Marco there were more people than ever, the afternoon crowds walking shoulder to shoulder, every one of them on pleasure bent.

He came to the hotel, and pushed his way through the swing door, expecting to see Laura, and possibly the sisters, waiting in the lounge on the left-hand side of the entrance. She was not there. He went to the desk. The reception clerk he had spoken to on the telephone was standing there, talking to the manager.

"Has my wife arrived?" John asked.

"No, sir, not yet."

"What an extraordinary thing. Are you sure?"

"Absolutely certain, sir. I have been here ever since you telephoned me at a quarter to two. I have not left the desk."

"I just don't understand it. She was on one of the vaporetos passing by the Accademia. She would have landed at San Marco above five minutes later and come on here."

The clerk seemed nonplussed. "I don't know what to say. The signora was with friends, did you say?"

"Yes. Well, acquaintances. Two ladies we had met at Torcello yesterday. I was astonished to see her with them on the vaporetto, and of course I assumed that the flight had been canceled, and she had somehow met up with them at the airport and decided to return here with them, to catch me before I left."

Oh hell, what was Laura doing? It was after three. A matter of moments from San Marco landing stage to the hotel.

"Perhaps the signora went with her friends to their hotel instead. Do you know where they are staying?"

"No," said John, "I haven't the slightest idea. What's more I don't even know the names of the two ladies. They were sisters, twins, in fact—looked exactly alike. But, anyway, why go to their hotel and not here?"

The swing door opened but it wasn't Laura. Two people staying in the hotel.

The manager broke into the conversation, "I tell you what I will do," he said. "I will telephone the airport and check about the flight. Then at least we will get somewhere." He smiled apologetically. It was not usual for arrangements to go wrong.

"Yes, do that," said John. "We may as well know what happened there."

He lit a cigarette and began to pace up and down the entrance hall. What a bloody mix-up. And how unlike Laura, who knew he would be setting off for Milan directly after lunch—indeed, for all she knew he might have gone before. But surely, in that case, she would have telephoned at once, on arrival at the airport, had takeoff been canceled? The manager was ages telephoning, he had to be put through on some other line, and his Italian was too rapid for John to follow the conversation. Finally he replaced the receiver.

"It is more mysterious than ever, sir," he said. "The charter flight was not delayed, it took off on schedule with a full complement of passenger. As far as they could tell me, there was no hitch. The signora must simply have changed her mind." His smile was more apologetic than ever.

"Changed her mind," John repeated. "But why on earth should she do that? She was so anxious to be home tonight."

The manager shrugged. "You know how ladies can be, sir," he said. "Your wife may have thought that after all she would prefer to take the train to Milan with you. I do assure you, though, that the charter party was most respectable, and it was a Caravelle aircraft, perfectly safe."

"Yes, yes," said John impatiently, "I don't blame your arrangements in the slightest. I just can't understand what induced her to change her mind, unless it was meeting with these two ladies."

The manager was silent. He could not think of anything to say. The reception clerk was equally concerned. "It is possible," he ventured, "that you made a mistake, and it was not the signora that you saw on the vaporetto?"

"Oh, no," replied John, "it was my wife, I assure you. She was wearing her red coat, she was hatless just as she left here. I saw her as plainly as I can see you. I would swear to it in a court of law."

"It is unfortunate," said the manager, "that we do not know the name of the two ladies, or the hotel where they were staying. You say you met these ladies at Torcello yesterday?"

"Yes . . . but only briefly. They weren't staying there. At least, I am certain they were not. We saw them at dinner in Venice later, as it happens."

"Excuse me . . ."Guests were arriving with luggage to check in, the clerk was obliged to attend to them. John turned in desperation to the manager. "Do you think it would be any good telephoning the hotel in Torcello in case the people there knew the name of the ladies, or where they were staying in Venice?"

"We can try," replied the manager. "It is a small hope, but we can try."

John resumed his anxious pacing, all the while watching the swing door, hoping, praying, that he would catch sight of the red coat and Laura would enter. Once again there followed what seemed an interminable telephone conversation between the manager and someone at the hotel in Torcello.

"Tell them two sisters," said John, "two elderly ladies dressed in gray, both exactly alike. One lady was blind," he added. The manager nodded. He was obviously giving a detailed description. Yet when he hung up he shook his head. "The manager at Torcello says he remembers the two ladies well," he told John, "but they were only there for lunch. He never learned their names."

"Well, that's that. There's nothing to do now but wait."

John lit his third cigarette and went out onto the terrace, to resume his pacing there. He stared out across the canal, searing the heads of the people on passing steamers, motorboats, even drifting gondolas. The minutes ticked by on his watch, and there was no sign of Laura. A terrible forboding nagged him that somehow this was prearranged, that Laura had never intended to catch the aircraft, that last night in the restaurant she had made an assignation with the sisters. Oh God, he thought, that's impossible, I'm going paranoiac . . . Yet why, why? No, more likely the encounter at the airport was fortuitous, and for some incredible reason they had persuaded Laura not to board the aircraft, even prevented her from doing so, trotting out one of their psychic visions, that the aircraft would crash, that she must return with them to Venice. And Laura, in her sensitive state, felt they must be right, swallowed it all without question.

But granted all these possibilities, why had she not come to the hotel? What was she doing? Four o'clock, half-past four, the sun no longer dappling the water. He went back to the reception desk.

"I just can't hang around," he said. "Even if she does turn up, we shall never make Milan this evening. I might see her walking with these ladies, in the Piazza San Marco, anywhere. If she arrives while I'm out, will you explain?"

The clerk was full of concern. "Indeed, yes," he said. "It is very worrying for you, sir. Would it perhaps be prudent if we booked you in here tonight?"

John gestured, helplessly. "Perhaps, yes, I don't know. Maybe . . ."

He went out of the swing door and began to walk toward the Piazza San Marco. He looked into every shop up and down the colonnades, crossed the piazza a dozen times, threaded his way between the table in front of Florian's, in front of Quadri's, knowing that Laura's red coat and the distinct appearance of the twin sisters could easily be spotted, even amongst this milling crowd, but there was no sign of them. He joined the crowd of shoppers in the Merceria, shoulder to shoulder with idlers, thrusters, window-gazers, knowing instinctively that it was useless, they wouldn't be here. Why should Laura have deliberately missed her flight to return to Venice for such a purpose? And even if she had done so, for some reason beyond his imagining, she would surely have come first to the hotel to find him.

The only thing left to him was to try to track down the sisters. Their hotel could be anywhere amongst the hundreds of hotels and pensions scattered through Venice, or even across the other side at the Zattere, or farther again on the Giudecca. These last possibilities seemed remote. More likely they were staying in a small hotel or pension somewhere near San Zacarria handy to the restaurant where they had dined last night. The blind one would surely not go far afield in the evening. He had been a fool not to have thought of this before, and he turned back and walked quickly away from the brightly lighted shopping district toward the narrower, more cramped quarter where they had dined last evening. He found the restaurant without difficulty, but they were not yet open for dinner, and the waiter preparing tables was not the one who had served them. John asked to see the *patrone,* and the waiter disappeared to the back regions, returning after a moment or two with the somewhat disheveled-looking proprietor in shirt-sleeves, caught in a slack moment, not in full *tenue.*

"I had dinner here last night," John explained. "There were two ladies sitting at that table there in the corner." He pointed to it.

"You wish to book that table for this evening?" asked the proprietor.

"No," said John. "No, there were two ladies there last night, two sisters, *due sorelle,* twins, *gemelle,"* —what was the right word for twins? "Do you remember? Two ladies, *sorelle, vecchie . . . "*

"Ah," said the man, *"si, si signore, la povera signorina."* He put his hands to his eyes to feign blindness. "Yes, I remember."

"Do you know their names?" asked John. "Where they were staying? I am very anxious to trace them."

The proprietor spread out his hands in a gesture of regret. "I am ver' sorry, signore, I do not know the names of the signorine, they have been here once, twice perhaps, for dinner, they do not say where they were staying. Perhaps if you come again tonight they might be here? Would you like to book a table?"

He pointed around him, suggesting a whole choice of tables that might appeal to a prospective diner, but John shook his head.

"Thank you, no. I may be dining elsewhere. I am sorry to have troubled you. If the signorine should come"—he paused—"possibly I may return later," he added. "I am not sure."

The proprietor bowed, and walked with him to the entrance. "In Venice the whole world meets," he said smiling. "It is possible the signore will find his friends tonight. *Arrive derci, signore."*

Friends? John walked out into the street. More likely kidnappers . . . Anxiety had turned to fear, to panic. Something had gone terribly wrong. Those women had got hold of Laura, played upon her suggestibility, induced her to go with them, either to their hotel or elsewhere. Should he find the consulate? Where was it? What would he say when he got there? He began walking without purpose, finding himself, as they had done the night before, in streets he did not know, and suddenly came upon a tall building with the word QUESTURA above it. This is it, he thought. I don't care, something has happened, I'm going inside. There were a number of police in uniform coming and going, the place at any rate was active, and, addressing himself to one of them behind a glass partition, he asked if there was anyone who spoke English. The man pointed to a flight of stairs and John went up, entering a door on the right where he saw that another couple were sitting, waiting, and with relief he recognized them as fellow countrymen, tourists, obviously a man and his wife, in some sort of predicament.

"Come and sit down," said the man. "We've waited half an hour but they can't be much longer. What a country! They wouldn't leave us like this at home."

John took the proffered cigarette and found a chair beside them.

"What's your trouble?" he asked.

"My wife had her handbag pinched in one of those shops in the Merceria," said the man. "She simply put it down one moment to look at something, and you'd hardly credit it, the next moment it had gone. I say it was a sneak thief, she insists it was the girl behind the counter. But who's to say? These Ities are all alike. Anyway, I'm certain we shan't get it back. What have you lost?"

"Suitcase stolen," John lied rapidly. "Had some important papers in it."

How could he say he had lost his wife? He couldn't even begin . . .

The man nodded in sympathy. "As I said, these Ities are all alike. Old Musso knew how to deal with them. Too many communists around these days. The trouble is, they're not going to bother with our troubles much, not with this murderer at large. They're all out looking for him."

"Murderer? What murderer?" asked John.

"Don't tell me you've not heard about it?" The man stared at him in surprise. "Venice has talked of nothing else. It's been in all the papers, on the radio, and even in the English papers too. A grizzly business. One woman found with her throat slit last week—a tourist too—and some old chap discovered with the same sort of knife wound this morning. They seem to think it must be a maniac because there doesn't seem to be any motive. Nasty thing to happen in Venice in the tourist season."

"My wife and I never bother with the newspapers when we're on holiday," said John. "And we're neither of us much given to gossip in the hotel."

"Very wise of you," laughed the man. "It might have spoiled your holiday, especially if your wife is nervous. Oh well, we're off tomorrow anyway. Can't say we mind, do we, dear?" He turned to his wife. "Venice has gone downhill since we were here last. And now this loss of the handbag really is the limit."

The door of the inner room opened, and a senior police officer asked John's companion and his wife to pass through.

"I bet we don't get any satisfaction," murmured the tourist, winking at John, and he and his wife went into the inner room. The door closed behind them. John stubbed out his cigarette and lighted another. A strange feeling of unreality possessed him. He asked himself what he was doing here, what was the use of it? Laura was no longer in Venice but had disappeared, perhaps forever, with those diabolical sisters. She would never be traced. And just as the two of them had made up a fantastic story about the twins, when they first spotted them in Torcello, so, with nightmare logic, the fiction would have basis in fact: the women were in reality disguised crooks, men with criminal intent who lured unsuspecting persons to some appalling fate. They might even be the murderers for whom the police sought. Who would ever suspect two elderly women of respectable appearance living quietly in some second-rate pension or hotel? He stubbed out his cigarette, unfinished.

This, he thought, is really the start of paranoia. This is the way people go off their heads. He glanced at his watch. It was half-past six. Better pack this in, this futile quest here in police headquarters, and keep to the single link of sanity remaining. Return to the hotel, put a call through to the prep school in England, and ask about the latest news of Johnnie. He had not thought about poor Johnnie since sighting Laura on the vaporetto.

Too late, though. The inner door opened, the couple were ushered out.

"Usual claptrap," said the husband sotto voice to John. "They'll do what they can. Not much hope. So many foreigners in Venice, all of 'em thieves! The locals all above reproach. Wouldn't pay 'em to steal from customers. Well, I wish you better luck."

He nodded, his wife smiled and bowed, and they had gone. John followed the police officer into the inner room.

Formalities began. Name, address, passport. Length of stay in Venice, etc., etc. Then the questions, and John, the sweat beginning to appear on his forehead, launched into his interminable story. The first encounter with the sisters, the meeting at the restaurant, Laura's state of suggestibility because of the death of their child, the telegram about Johnnie, the decision to take the chartered flight, her departure, and her sudden inexplicable return. When he had finished he felt as exhausted as if he had driven three hundred miles nonstop after a severe bout of flu. His interrogator spoke excellent English with a strong Italian accent. "You say," he began, "that your wife was suffering the aftereffects of shock. This had been noticeable during your stay here in Venice?"

"Well, yes," John replied, "she had really been quite ill. The holiday didn't seem to be doing her much good. It was only when she met these two women at Torcello yesterday that her mood changed. The strain seemed to have gone. She was ready, I suppose, to snatch at every straw, and this belief that our little girl watching over her had somehow restored her to what appeared normality."

"It would be natural," said the police officer, "in the circumstances. But no doubt the telegram last night was a further shock to you both?"

"Indeed, yes. That was the reason we decided to return home."

"No argument between you? No difference of opinion?"

"None. We were in complete agreement. My one regret was that I could not go with my wife on this charter flight."

The police officer nodded. "It could well be that your wife had a sudden attack of amnesia and meeting the two ladies served as a link, she clung to them for support. You have described them with great accuracy, and I think they should not be too difficult to trace. Meanwhile, I suggest you should return to your hotel, and we will get in touch with you as soon as we have news."

At least, John thought, they believed his story. They did not consider him a crank who had made the whole thing up and was merely wasting their time.

"You appreciate," he said, "I am extremely anxious. These women may have some criminal design upon my wife. One has heard of such things . . ."

The police officer smiled for the first time. "Please don't concern yourself," he said. "I am sure there will be some satisfactory explanation."

All very well, thought John, but in heaven's name, what?

"I'm sorry," he said, "to have taken up so much of your time. Especially as I gather the police have their hands full hunting down a murderer who is still at large."

He spoke deliberately. No harm in letting the fellow know that for all any of them could tell there might be some connection between Laura's disappearance and this other hideous affair.

"Ah, that," said the police officer, rising to his feet. "We hope to have the murderer under lock and key very soon."

His tone of confidence was reassuring. Murderers, missing wives, lost handbags were all under control. They shook hands, and John was ushered out of the door and so downstairs. Perhaps, he thought, as he walked slowly back to the hotel, the fellow was right. Laura had suffered a sudden attack of amnesia, and the sisters happened to be at the airport and had brought her back to Venice, to their own hotel, because Laura couldn't remember where she and John had been staying. Perhaps they were even now trying to track down his hotel. Anyway, he could do nothing more. The police had everything in hand, and, please God, would come up with the solution. All he wanted to do right now was to collapse upon a bed with a stiff whisky and then put through a call to Johnnie's school.

The page took him up in the lift to a modest room on the fourth floor at the rear of the hotel. Bare, impersonal, the shutters closed, with a smell of cooking wafting up from a courtyard down below.

"Ask them to send me up a double whisky, will you?" he said to the boy, "and a ginger ale," and when he was alone he plunged his face under the cold tap in the washbasin, relieved to find that the minute portion of visitor's soap afforded some measure of comfort. He flung off his shoes, hung his coat over the back of a chair, and threw himself down on the bed. Somebody's radio was blasting forth an old popular song, now several seasons out-of-date, that had been one of Laura's favorites a couple of years ago. "I love you, baby . . . " They had taped it and used to play it back in the car. He reached out for the telephone, and asked the exchange to put through the call to England. Then he closed his eyes, and all the while the insistent voice persisted, "I love you, baby . . . I can't get you out of my mind."

Presently there was a tap at the door. It was the waiter with his drink. Too little ice, such meager comfort, but what desperate need. He gulped it down without the ginger ale, and in a few moments the ever-nagging pain was eased, numbed, bringing, if only momentarily, a sense of calm. the telephone rang, and now, he thought, bracing himself for ultimate disaster, the final shock, Johnnie probably dying, or already dead. In which case nothing remained. Let Venice be engulfed . . .

The exchange told him that connection had been made, and in a moment he heard the voice of Mrs. Hill at the other end of the line. They must have warned her that the call came from Venice, for she knew instantly who was speaking.

"Hullo?" she cried. "Oh, I am so glad you rang. All is well. Johnnie has had his operation, the surgeon decided to do it at midday rather than wait, and it was completely successful. Johnnie is going to be all right. So you don't have to worry anymore, and will have a peaceful night."

"Thank God," he answered.

"I know," she said, "we are all so relieved. Now I'll get off the line and you can speak to your wife."

John sat up on the bed, stunned. What the hell did she mean? Then he heard Laura's voice, cool and clear.

"Darling? Darling, are you there?"

He could not answer. He felt the hand holding the receiver go clammy cold with sweat. "I'm here," he whispered.

"It's not a very good line," she said, "but never mind. As Mrs. Hill told you, all is well. Such a nice surgeon, and a very sweet Sister on Johnnie's floor, and I really am happy about the way it's turned out. I came straight down here after landing at Gatwick—the flight O.K., by the way, but such a funny crowd, it'll make you hysterical when I tell you about them—and I went to the hospital, and Johnnie was coming round. Very dopey, of course, but so pleased to see me. And the Hills are being wonderful, I've got their spare room, and it's only a short taxi drive into the town and the hospital. I shall go to bed as soon as we've had dinner, because I'm a bit fagged, what with the flight and the anxiety. How was the drive to Milan? And where are you staying?"

John did not recognize the voice that answered as his own. It was the automatic response of some computer.

"I'm not in Milan," he said, "I'm still in Venice."

"Still in Venice? What on earth for? Wouldn't the car start?"

"I can't explain," he said. "There was a stupid sort of mix-up . . ."

He felt suddenly so exhausted that he nearly dropped the receiver, and, shame upon shame, he could feel tears pricking behind his eyes.

"What sort of mix-up?" Her voice was suspicious, almost hostile. "You weren't in a crash?"

"No . . . no . . . nothing like that."

A moment's silence, and then she said, "Your voice sounds very slurred. Don't tell me you went and got pissed."

Oh Christ . . . if she only knew! He was probably going to pass out any moment, but not from the whisky.

"I thought," he said slowly, "I saw you, in a vaporetto, with those two sisters."

What was the point of going on? It was hopeless trying to explain.

"How could you have seen me with the sisters?" she said. "You knew I'd gone to the airport. Really, darling, you are an idiot. You seem to have got those two poor old dears on the brain. I hope you didn't say anything to Mrs. Hill just now."

"No."

"Well, what are you going to do? You'll catch the train at Milan tomorrow, won't you?"

"Yes, of course," he told her.

"I still don't understand what kept you in Venice," she said. "It all sounds a bit odd to me. However . . . thank God Johnnie is going to be all right and I'm here."

"Yes," he said, "yes."

He could hear the distant boom-boom sound of a gong from the headmaster's hall. "You had better go," he said. "My regards to the Hills, and my love to Johnnie."

"Well, take care of yourself, darling, and for goodness sake don't miss the train tomorrow, and drive carefully."

The telephone clicked and she had gone. He poured the remaining drop of whisky into his empty glass, and, sousing it with ginger ale, drank it down at a gulp. He got up, crossed the room, threw open the shutters, and leaned out of the window. He felt light-headed. His sense of relief, enormous, overwhelming, was somehow tempered with a curious feeling of unreality, almost as though the voice speaking from England had not been Laura's after all but a fake, and she was still in Venice, hidden in some furtive pension with the two sisters.

The point was, he *had* seen all three of them on the vaporetto. It was not another woman in a red coat. The women *had* been there, with Laura. So what was the explanation? That he was going off his head? Or something more sinister? The sisters, possessing psychic powers of formidable strength, had seen him as their two ferries had passed, and in some inexplicable fashion had made him believe Laura was with them. But why, and to what end? No, it didn't make sense. The only explanation was that he had been mistaken, the whole episode an hallucination. In which case he needed psychoanalysis, just as Johnnie had needed a surgeon.

And what did he do now? Go downstairs and tell the management he had been at fault and had just spoken to his wife, who had arrived in England safe and sound from her charter flight? He put on his shoes and ran his fingers through his hair. He glanced at his watch. It was ten minutes to eight. If he nipped into the bar and had a quick drink it would be easier to face the manager and admit what had happened. Then, perhaps, they would get in touch with the police. Profuse apologies all round for putting everyone to enormous trouble.

He made his way to the ground floor and went straight to the bar, feeling self-conscious, a marked man, half-imagining everyone would look at him, thinking, *There's the fellow with the missing wife*. Luckily the bar was full and there wasn't a face he knew. Even the chap behind the bar was an underling who hadn't served him before. He downed his whisky and glanced over his shoulder to the reception hall. The desk was momentarily empty. He could see the manager's back framed in the doorway of an inner room, talking to someone within. On impulse, cowardlike, he crossed the hall and passed through the swing door to the street outside.

I'll have some dinner, he decided, and then go back and face them. I'll feel more like it once I've some food inside me.

He went to the restaurant nearby where he and Laura had dined once or twice. Nothing mattered anymore, because she was safe. The nightmare lay behind him. He could enjoy his dinner, despite her absence, and think of her sitting down with the Hills to a dull, quiet evening, early to bed, and on the following morning going to the hospital to sit with Johnnie. Johnnie was safe too. No more worries, only the awkward explanations and apologies to the manager at the hotel.

There was a pleasant anonymity sitting down at a corner table alone in the little restaurant, ordering *vitello allo* Marsala and half a bottle of Merlot. He took his time, enjoying his food but eating in a kind of haze, a sense of unreality still with him, while the conversation of his nearest neighbors had the same soothing effect as background music.

When they rose and left, he saw by the clock on the wall that it was nearly half-past nine. No use delaying matters any further. He drank his coffee, lighted a cigarette, and paid his bill. After all, he thought, as he walked back to the hotel, the manager would be greatly relieved to know that all was well.

When he pushed through the swing door, the first thing he noticed was a man in police uniform, standing talking to the manager at the desk. The reception clerk was there too. They turned as John approached, and the manager's face lighted up with relief.

"*Eccolo!*" he exclaimed, "I was certain the signore would not be far away. Things are moving, signore. The two ladies have been traced, and they very kindly agreed to accompany the police to the Questura. If you will go there at once, this *agente di polizia* will escort you."

John flushed. "I have given everyone a lot of trouble," he said. "I meant to tell you before going out to dinner, but you were not at the desk. The fact is that I have contacted my wife. She did make the flight to London after all, and I spoke to her on the telephone. It was all a great mistake."

The manager looked bewildered. "The signora is in London?" he repeated. He broke off, and exchanged a rapid conversation in Italian with the policeman. "It seems that the ladies maintain they did not go out for the day, except for a little shopping in the morning," he said, turning back to John. "Then who was it the signore saw on the vaporetto?"

John shook his head. "A very extraordinary mistake on my part which I still don't understand," he said. "Obviously, I did not see either my wife or the two ladies. I really am extremely sorry."

More rapid conversation in Italian. John noticed the clerk watching him with a curious expression in his eyes. The manager was obviously apologizing on John's behalf to the policeman, who looked annoyed and gave tongue to this effect, his voice increasing in volume, to the manager's concern. The whole business had undoubtedly given enormous trouble to a great many people, not least the two unfortunate sisters.

"Look," said John, interrupting the flow, "will you tell the *agente* I will go with him to headquarters and apologize in person both to the police officer and to the ladies?"

The manager looked relieved. "If the signore would take the trouble," he said. "Naturally, the ladies were much distressed when a policeman interrogated them at their hotel, and they offered to accompany him to the Questura only because they were so distressed about the signora."

John felt more and more uncomfortable. Laura must never learn any of this. She would be outraged. He wondered if there were some penalty for giving the police misleading information involving a third party. His error began, in retrospect, to take on criminal proportions.

He crossed the Piazza San Marco, now thronged with after-dinner strollers and spectators at the cafés, all three orchestras going full blast in harmonious rivalry, while his companion kept a discreet two paces to his left and never uttered a word.

They arrived at the police station and mounted the stairs to the same inner room where he had been before. He saw immediately that it was not the officer he knew but another who sat behind the desk, a sallow-faced individual with a sour expression, while the two sisters, obviously upset—the active one in particular—were seated on chairs nearby, some underling in uniform standing behind them. John's escort went at once to the police officer, speaking in rapid Italian, while John himself, after a moment's hesitation, advanced toward the sisters.

"There has been a terrible mistake," he said. "I don't know how to apologize to you both. It's all my fault, mine entirely, the police are not to blame."

The active sister made as though to rise, her mouth twitching nervously, but he restrained her.

"We don't understand," she said, the Scots inflection strong. "We said good-night to your wife last night at dinner, and we have not seen her since. The police came to our pension more than an hour ago and told us your wife was missing and you had filed a complaint against us. My sister is not very strong. She was considerably disturbed."

"A mistake. A frightful mistake," he repeated.

He turned toward the desk. The police officer was addressing him, his English very inferior to that of the previous interrogator. He had John's earlier statement on the desk in front of him, and tapped it with a pencil.

"So?" he queried. "This document all lies? You not speaka the truth?"

"I believed it to be true at the time," said John. "I could have sworn in a court of law that I saw my wife with these two ladies on a vaporetto in the Grand Canal this afternoon. Now I realize I was mistaken."

"We have not been near the Grand Canal all day," protested the sister, "not even on foot. We made a few purchases in the Merceria this morning, and remained indoors all afternoon. My sister was a little unwell. I have told the police officer this a dozen times, and the people at the pension would corroborate our story. He refused to listen."

"And the signora?" rapped the police officer angrily. "What happened to the signora?"

"The signora, my wife, is safe in England," explained John patiently. "I talked to her on the telephone just after seven. She did join the charter flight from the airport, and is now staying with friends."

"Then who you see on the vaporetto in the red coat?" asked the furious police officer. "And if not these signorine here, then what signorine?"

"My eyes deceived me," said John, aware that his English was likewise becoming strained. "I think I see my wife and these ladies but not, it was not so. My wife in aircraft, these ladies in pension all the time."

It was like talking stage Chinese. In a moment he would be bowing and putting his hands in his sleeves.

The police officer raised his eyes to heaven and thumped the table. "So all this work for nothing," he said. "Hotels and pensiones searched for the signorine and a missing signora *inglese,* when here we have plenty, plenty other things to do. You maka a mistake. You have perhaps too much vino at *mezzo giorno* and you see hundred signore in red coats in hundred vaporetti." He stood up, rumpling the papers on the desk. "And you, signorine," he said, "you wish to make complaint against this person?" He was addressing the active sister.

"Oh no," she said, "no, indeed. I quite see it was all a mistake. Our only wish is to return at once to our pension."

The police officer grunted. Then he pointed at John. "You very lucky man," he said. "These signorine could file complaint against you—very serious matter."

"I'm sure," began John, "I'll do anything in my power . . ."

"Please don't think of it," exclaimed the sister, horrified. "We would not hear of such a thing." It was her turn to apologize to the police officer. "I hope we need not take up any more of your valuable time," she said.

He waved a hand of dismissal and spoke in Italian to the underling. "This man walk with you to the pension," he said. "*Buona sera,* signorine," and, ignoring John, he sat down again at his desk.

"I'll come with you," said John. "I want to explain exactly what happened."

They trooped down the stairs and out of the building, the blind sister leaning on her twin's arm, and once outside she turned her sightless eyes to John.

"You saw us," she said, "and your wife too. But not today. You saw us in the future."

Her voice was softer than her sister's, slower, she seemed to have some slight impediment in her speech.

"I don't follow," replied John, bewildered.

He turned to the active sister and she shook her head at him, frowning, and put her fingers on her lips.

"Come along, dear," she said to her twin. "You know you're very tired, and I want to get you home." Then, sotto voce to John, "She's psychic. Your wife told you, I believe, but I don't want her to go into trance here in the street."

God forbid, thought John, and the little procession began to move slowly along the street, away from police headquarters, a canal to the left of them. Progress was slow, because of the blind sister, and there were two bridges to cross over two canals. John was completely lost after the first turning, but it couldn't have mattered less. Their police escort was with them, and anyway, the sisters knew where they were going.

"I must explain," said John softly. "My wife would never forgive me if I didn't," and as they walked he went over the whole inexplicable story once again, beginning with the telegram received the night before and the conversation with Mrs. Hill, the decision to return to England the following day, Laura by air, and John himself by car and train. It no longer sounded as dramatic as it had done when he had made his statement to the police officer, when, possibly because of his conviction of something uncanny, the description of the two vaporettos passing one another in the middle of the Grand Canal had held a sinister quality, suggesting abduction on the part of the sisters, the pair of them holding a bewildered Laura captive. Now that neither of the women had any further menace for him he spoke more naturally, yet with great sincerity, feeling for the first time that they were somehow both in sympathy with him and would understand.

"You see," he explained, in a final endeavor to make amends for having gone to the police in the first place, "I truly believed I had seen you with Laura, and I thought . . ." he hesitated, because this had been the police officer's suggestion and not his, "I thought that perhaps Laura had some sudden loss of memory, had met you at the airport, and you had brought her back to Venice to wherever you were staying."

They had crossed a large campo and were approaching a house at one end of it, with a sign PENSIONE above the door. Their escort paused at the entrance.

"Is this it?" asked John.

"Yes," said the sister. "I know it is nothing much from the outside, but it is clean and comfortable, and was recommended by friends." She turned to the escort. "*Grazie,*" she said to him, "*grazie tanto.*"

The man nodded briefly, wished them "*Buona notte,*" and disappeared across the campo.

"Will you come in?" asked the sister. "I am sure we can find you some coffee, or perhaps you prefer tea?"

"No, really," John thanked her, "I must get back to the hotel. I'm making an early start in the morning. I just want to make quite sure you do understand what happened, and that you forgive me."

"There is nothing to forgive," she replied. "It is one of the many examples of second sight that my sister and I have experienced time and time again, and I should very much like to record it for our files, if you permit it."

"Well, as to that, of course," he told her, "but I myself find it hard to understand. It has never happened to me before."

"Not consciously, perhaps," she said, "but so many things happen to us of which we are not aware. My sister felt you had psychic understanding. She told your wife. She also told your wife, last night in the restaurant, that you were to experience trouble, that you should leave Venice. Well, don't you believe now that the telegram was proof of this? Your son was ill, possibly dangerously ill, and so it was necessary for you to return home immediately. Heaven be praised your wife flew home to be by his side."

"Yes, indeed," said John, "but why should I see her on the vaporetto with you and your sister when she was actually on her way to England?"

"Thought transference, perhaps," she answered. "Your wife may have been thinking about us. We gave her our address, should you wish to get in touch with us. We shall be here another ten days. And she knows that we would pass on any message that my sister might have from your little one in the spirit world."

"Yes," said John awkwardly, "yes, I see. It's very good of you." He had a sudden rather unkind picture of the two sisters putting on headphones in their bedroom, listening for a coded message from poor Christine. "Look, this is our address in London," he said. "I know Laura will be pleased to hear from you."

He scribbled their address on a sheet torn from his pocket diary, even, as a bonus thrown in, the telephone number, and handed it to her. He could imagine the outcome. Laura springing it on him one evening that the "old dears" were passing through London on their way to Scotland, and the least they could do was to offer them hospitality, even the spare room for the night. Then a séance in the living room, tambourines appearing out of thin air.

"Well, I must be off," he said, "good-night, and apologies, once again, for all that has happened this evening." He shook hands with the first sister, then turned to her blind twin. "I hope," he said, "that you are not too tired."

The sightless eyes were disconcerting. She held his hand fast and would not let it go. "The child," she said, speaking in an odd staccato voice, "the child . . . I can see the child . . ." and then, to his dismay, a bead of froth appeared at the corner of her mouth, her head jerked back, and she half collapsed in her sister's arms.

"We must get her inside," said the sister hurriedly. "It's all right, she's not ill, it's the beginning of a trance state."

Between them they helped the twin, who had gone rigid, into the house, and sat her down on the nearest chair, the sister supporting her. A woman came running from some inner room. There was a strong smell of spaghetti from the back regions. "Don't worry," said the sister, "the signorina and I can manage. I think you had better go. Sometimes she is sick after these turns."

"I'm most frightfully sorry . . ." John began, but the sister had already turned her back, and with the signorina was bending over her twin, from whom peculiar choking sounds were proceeding. He was obviously in the way, and after a final gesture of courtesy, "Is there anything I can do?" which received no reply, he turned on his heel and began walking across the square. He looked back once, and saw they had closed the door.

What a finale to the evening! And all his fault. Poor old girls, first dragged to police headquarters and put through an interrogation, and then a psychic fit on top of it all. More likely epilepsy. Not much of a life for the active sister, but she seemed to take it in her stride. An additional hazard, though, if it happened in a restaurant or in the street. And not particularly welcome under his and Laura's roof should the sisters ever find themselves beneath it, which he prayed would never happen.

Meanwhile, where the devil was he? The campo, with the inevitable church at one end, was quite deserted. He could not remember which way they had come from police headquarters, there had seemed to be so many turnings. Wait a minute, the church itself had a familiar appearance. He drew nearer to it, looking for the name which was sometimes on notices at the entrance. San Giovanni in Bragora, that rang a bell. He and Laura had gone inside one morning to look at a painting by Cima da Conegliano. Surely it was only a stone's throw from the Riva degli Schiavoni and the open wide waters of the San Marco lagoon, with all the bright lights of civilization and the strolling tourists? He remembered taking a small turning from the Schiavoni and they had arrived at the church. Wasn't there the alleyway ahead? He plunged along it, but halfway down he hesitated. It didn't seem right, although it was familiar for some unknown reason.

Then he realized that it was not the alley they had taken the morning they visited the church, but the one they had walked along the previous evening, only he was approaching it from the opposite direction. Yes, that was it, in which case it would be quicker to go on and cross the little bridge over the narrow canal, and he would find the Arsenal on his left and the street leading down to the Riva degli Schiavoni to his right. Simpler than retracing his steps and getting lost once more in the maze of back streets.

He had almost reached the end of the alley, and the bridge was in sight, when he saw the child. It was the same little girl with the pixie hood who had leaped between the tethered boats the preceding night and vanished up the cellar steps of one of the houses. This time she was running from the direction of the church the other side, making for the bridge. She was running as if her life depended on it, and in a moment he saw why. A man was in pursuit, who, when she glanced backward for a moment, still running, flattened himself against a wall, believing himself unobserved. The child came on, scampering across the bridge, and John, fearful of alarming her further, backed into an open doorway that led into a small court.

He remembered the drunken yell of the night before which had come from one of the houses near where the man was hiding now. This is it, he thought, the fellow's after her again, and with a flash of intuition he connected the two events, the child's terror then and now, and the murders reported in the newspapers, supposedly the work of some madman. It could be coincidence, a child running from a drunken relative, and yet, and yet . . . His heart began thumping in his chest, instinct warning him to run himself, now, at once, back along the alley the way he had come, but what about the child? What was going to happen to the child?

Then he heard her running steps. She hurtled through the open doorway into the court in which he stood, not seeing him, making for the rear of the house that flanked it, where steps led presumably to a back entrance. She was sobbing as she ran, not the ordinary cry of a frightened child but a panic-stricken intake of breath of a helpless being in despair. Were there parents in the house who would protect her, whom he could warn? He hesitated a moment, then followed her down the steps and through the door at the bottom, which had burst open at the touch of her hands as she hurled herself against it.

"It's all right," he called. "I won't let him hurt you, it's all right," cursing his lack of Italian, but possibly an English voice might reassure her. But it was no use—she ran sobbing up another flight of stairs, which were spiral, twisting, leading to the floor above, and already it was too late for him to retreat. He could hear sounds of the pursuer in the courtyard behind, someone shouting in Italian, a dog barking. This is it, he thought, we're in it together, the child and I. Unless we can bolt some inner door above he'll get us both.

He ran up the stairs after the child, who had darted into a room leading off a small landing, and followed her inside and slammed the door, and, merciful heaven, there was a bolt which he rammed into its socket. The child was crouching by the open window. If he shouted for help, someone would surely hear, someone would surely come before the man in pursuit threw himself against the door and it gave, because there was no one but themselves, no parents, the room was bare except for a mattress on an old bed, and a heap of rags in one corner.

"It's all right," he panted, "it's all right," and held out his hand, trying to smile.

The child struggled to her feet and stood before him, the pixie hood falling from her head onto the floor. He stared at her, incredulity turning to horror, to fear. It was not a child at all but a little thickset woman dwarf, about three feet high, with a great square adult head too big for her body, gray locks hanging shoulder length, and she wasn't sobbing anymore, she was grinning at him, nodding her head up and down.

Then he heard the footsteps on the landing outside and the hammering on the door, and a barking dog, and not one voice but several voices, shouting, "Open up! Police!" The creature fumbled in her sleeve, drawing a knife, and as she threw it at him with hideous strength, piercing his throat, he stumbled and fell, the sticky mess covering his protecting hands. And he saw the vaporetto with Laura and the two sisters steaming down the Grand Canal, not today, not tomorrow, but the day after that, and he knew why they were together and for what sad purpose they had come. The creature was gibbering in its corner. The hammering and the voices and the barking dog grew fainter, and, Oh, God, he thought, what a bloody silly way to die . . .

The Breakthrough

MY PART IN the affair started on September 18, when my chief sent for me and told me he was transferring me to Saxmere on the east coast. He was sorry about it, he said, but I was the only one with the necessary technical qualifications for the particular work they had on hand. No, he couldn't give me any details; they were an odd lot down there, and shut themselves up behind barbed wire at the slightest provocation. The place had been a radar experimental station a few years back, but this was finished, and any experiments that were going on now were of an entirely different nature, something to do with vibrations and the pitch of sound.

"I'll be perfectly frank with you," said my chief, removing his horn-rimmed spectacles and waving them in the air apologetically. "The fact is that James MacLean is a very old friend of mine. We were at Cambridge together and I saw a lot of him then and afterward, but our paths diverged, and he tied himself up in experimental work of rather a dubious nature. Lost the government a lot of money, and didn't do his own reputation much good either. I gather that's forgotten, and he's been reinstated down at Saxmere with his own hand-picked team of experts and a government grant. They're stuck for an electronics engineer—which is where you come in. MacLean has sent me an S.O.S. for someone I can vouch for personally—in other words, he wants a chap who won't talk. You'd do me a personal favor if you went."

Put like this, there was little I could do but accept. It was a damned nuisance, all the same. The last thing in the world I wanted to do was to leave Associated Electronics Ltd., and its unique facilities for research, and drift off to the east coast to work for someone who had blotted his copybook once and might do so again.

"When do you want me to go?" I asked.

The chief looked more apologetic than ever.

"As soon as you can make it. The day after tomorrow? I'm really very sorry, Saunders. With any luck you'll be back by Christmas. I've told MacLean I'm lending you to him for this particular project only. No question of a long-term transfer. You're too valuable here."

This was the sop. The pat on the back. A.E.L. would forget about me for the next three months. I had another question, though.

"What sort of a chap is he?"

"MacLean?" My chief paused before replacing his horn-rims, always a signal of dismissal. "He's what I'd call an enthusiast, the kind that don't let go. A fanatic in his way. Oh, he won't bore you. I remember at Cambridge he spent most of his time bird watching. He had some peculiar theory then about migration, but he didn't inflict it on us. He nearly chucked physics for neurology, but thought better of it—the girl he later married persuaded him. Then came the tragedy. She died after they'd only been married a year."

My chief replaced his spectacles. He had no more to say or, if he had, it was beside the point. As I was leaving the room he called after me, "You can keep that last piece of information to yourself. About his wife, I mean. His staff down there may not know anything about it."

It was not until I had actually packed up at the A.E.L. and left my comfortable digs, and the train was drawing out of Liverpool Street station, that the full force of my situation hit me. Here I was, lumbered with a job I didn't want in an outfit I knew nothing about, and all as a personal favor to my chief, who obviously had some private reason for obliging his one-time colleague. As I stared moodily out of the carriage window, feeling more bloody minded every minute, I kept seeing the expression on my successor's face when I told him I was going to Saxmere.

563

"That dump?" he said. "Why, it's a joke—they haven't done any serious research there for years. The Ministry has given it over to the crackpots, hoping they'll blow themselves to pieces."

A few discreet off-hand inquiries in other quarters had brought the same answer. A friend of mine with a sense of humor advised me over the telephone to take golf clubs and plenty of paperbacks. "There's no sort of organization," he said. "MacLean works with a handful of chaps who think he's the Messiah. If you don't fall into line he ignores you, and you'll find yourself doing nothing but sitting on your fanny."

"Fine. That suits me. I need a holiday," I lied, hanging up with feelings of intense irritation against the world in general.

It was typical, I suppose, of my approach to the whole business that I hadn't checked thoroughly on timetables, and therefore an added annoyance to find that I had to get out at Ipswich, wait forty minutes, and board a slow train to Thirlwall, which was the station for Saxmere. It was raining when I finally descended upon the empty, windswept platform, and the porter who took my ticket told me that the taxi which usually waited for this particular train had been snapped up five minutes before.

"There's a garage opposite the Three Cocks," he added. "They might still be open and could run you over to Saxmere."

I walked past the booking office carrying my bags and blaming myself for my bad staff work. As I stood outside the station wondering whether to brave the doubtful hospitality of the Three Cocks—it was close on seven, and even if a car was not available I could do with a drink—a very ancient Morris came swerving into the station yard and pulled up in front of me. The driver got out and made a dive for my bags.

"You are Saunders, I take it?" he asked, smiling. He was young, not more than about nineteen, with a shock of fair hair.

"That's right," I said. "I was just wondering where the hell I'd raise a taxi."

"You wouldn't," he answered. "On a wet night the Yanks swipe the lot. Anything on wheels that will take 'em out of Thirlwall. Hop in, will you?"

I'd forgotten that Thirlwall being a U.S. air base, and made a mental note to avoid the Three Cocks in my leisure hours. American personnel on the loose are not among my favorite companions.

"Sorry about the rattle," apologized the driver as we swerved through the town to the accompaniment of what sounded like a couple of petrol cans rolling under the back seat. "I keep meaning to fix it, but never find time. My name's Ryan, by the way, Ken Ryan, always known as Ken. "We don't go in for surnames at Saxmere."

I said nothing. My Christian name is Stephen, nor had anyone ever shortened it to Steve. My gloom increased and I let a cigarette. Already the houses of Thirlwall lay behind us, and our road, having traversed a mile or two of flat countryside consisting of turnip fields, suddenly shot up onto a sandy track across a heath, over which we proceeded in a series of bumps until my head nearly hit the roof.

My companion apologized once more.

"I could have taken you in by the main entrance," he said, "but this way is so much shorter. Don't worry, the springs are used to it."

The sandy track topped a rise and there below us, stretching into infinity, lay acre upon acre of wasteland, marsh and reed, bounded on the left by sand dunes with the open sea beyond. The marshes were intersected here and there by dykes, beside which stood clumps of forlorn rushes bending now to the wind and rain, the dykes in their turn forming themselves into dank pools, one or two of them miniature lakes, ringed about with reeds.

Our road, the surface of which was now built up with clinkers and small stones, descended abruptly to this scene of desolation, winding like a narrow ribbon with the marsh on either side. In the far distance a square tower, gray and squat, stood out against the skyline, and as we drew nearer I could see beyond the tower itself the curving spiral of the one-time radar installation, brooding over the wasteland like a giant oystershell. This, then, was Saxmere. My worst forbodings could not have conjured up a more forbidding place.

My companion, sensing probably from my silence that I lacked enthusiasm, gave me a half glance.

"It looks a bit grim in this light," he said, "but that's the rain. The weather's pretty good on the whole, though the wind is keen. We get some stunning sunsets."

The laugh with which I greeted his remark was intended to be ironic, but it missed its mark, or was taken as encouragement, for he added, "If you're keen on birds you've come to the right spot. Avocets breed here in the spring, and last March I heard the bittern boom."

I choked back the expletive that rose to my lips—his phraseology struck me as naïve—and while admitting indifference to all objects furred or feathered I expressed surprise that anything in such a dreary locality should have a desire to breed at all. My sarcasm was lost, for he said, quite seriously, "Oh, you'd be surprised," and ground the Morris to a halt before a gate set in a high wired fence.

"Have to unlock this," he told me, jumping out of the car, and I saw that now we had come to Saxmere itself. This area ahead was bounded on all sides by this same fence, some ten feet in height, giving the place the look of a concentration camp. This agreeable vista was enhanced by the sudden appearance of an Alsatian dog, who loped out of the marshes to the left, and stood wagging its tail at young Ken as he unlocked the gate.

"Where are the tommy guns?" I asked when he climbed back into the driving seat. "Or does the dog's handler watch us unseen from some concrete dugout in the marsh?"

This time he had the grace to laugh as we passed through the barricade. "No guns, no handlers," he said. "Cerberus is as gentle as a lamb. Not that I expected to find him here, but Mac will have him under control."

He got out once more and locked the gate, while the dog, his head pointing across the marsh, took no more notice of us. Then all at once, pricking his ears, he dived into the reeds, and I watched him running along a narrow muddied track in the direction of the tower.

"He'll be home before we are," said Ken, letting in the clutch, and the car swerved to the right along a broad asphalt road, the marsh giving place now to scrub and shingle.

The rain had stopped, the clouds had broken into splintered fragments, and the squat tower of Saxmere stood out bold and black against a copper sky. Did this, I wondered, herald one of the famous sunsets? If so, no member of the staff appeared to be taking advantage of it. Road and marsh alike were deserted. We passed the fork to the main entrance and turned left toward the disused radar installation and the tower itself, grouped about with sheds and concrete buildings. The place looked more like a deserted Dachau than ever.

Ken drove past the tower and the main buildings, taking a side road running seaward, at the end of which was a row of prefabricated huts.

"Here we are," he said, "and what did I tell you? Cerberus has beaten us to it."

The dog emerged from a track on the left and ran off behind the huts.

"How is he trained?" I asked. "A hi-fi whistle?"

"Not exactly," answered my companion.

I got out of the car and he heaved my bags from the rear seat.

"These are the sleeping quarters, I suppose?"

I glanced about me. The prefabs at least looked wind and watertight.

"It's the whole works," replied Ken. "We sleep, feed, and do everything here."

He ignored my stare and led the way ahead. There was a small entrance hall, and a corridor beyond running right and left. Nobody was about. The walls of both hall and corridor were a dull gray, the floor covered with linoleum. The impression was that of a small-town country surgery after hours.

"We feed at eight, but there's loads of time," said Ken. "You'd like to see your room and have a bath, perhaps."

I had no particular desire for a bath, but I badly needed a drink. I followed him down the left-hand corridor, and he opened a door and switched on the light, then crossed the floor and pulled aside the curtains.

"Sorry about that," he said. "Janus likes to bed us down early before going through to the kitchen. Winter or summer, these curtains are drawn at six-thirty, and the covers removed from the beds. He's a stickler for routine."

I looked around. Whoever designed the room must have had a hospital training all right. It had the bare essentials. Bed, washbasin, chest of drawers, wardrobe, one chair. The window gave onto the entrance front. The blankets on the bed were folded hospital fashion, and a military hospital at that.

"O.K.?" asked Ken. He looked puzzled. Possibly my expression surprised him.

"Fine," I answered. "Now what about a drink?"

I followed him up the corridor once more, across the entrance hall, and on through a swing door at the far end. I heard the light clack-clack of Ping-Pong balls, and braced myself for frivolity. The room we entered was empty. The sportsmen, whoever they were, were playing in the room beyond. Here there were easy chairs, a table or two, an electric fire, and a bar in the far corner, behind which my youthful companion installed himself. I noticed, with misgiving, two enormous urns.

"Coffee or cocoa?" he asked. "Or do you prefer something cool? I can recommend the orange juice with a splash of cola."

"I'd like a Scotch," I said.

He looked distressed. His expression became that of an anxious host whose guest demands fresh strawberries in midwinter.

"I'm frightfully sorry," he said, "we none of us touch alcohol. Mac won't have it served, it's one of his things. But of course you can bring your own supply and drink in your room. What a fool I was not to have warned you. We could have stopped at Thirwall and brought you back a bottle from the Three Cocks."

His distress was so genuine that I controlled the flood-gates of emotion that threatened to burst from me, and told him I would settle for orange juice. He looked relieved, and splashed the nauseous liquid into a tall glass, deftly sousing it with soda.

I felt the time had come for further explanation, not only about him, the acolyte, but about the rest of the establishment. Was the order Benedictine or Franciscan? And at what hour would the bell sound for vespers and compline?

"Forgive my igonorance," I said, "but my briefing before leaving A.E.L. was somewhat short. I don't know the first thing about Saxmere, or what you do here."

"Oh, don't worry," he answered, smiling. "Mac will explain all that."

He poured some juice into his own glass and said, "Cheers." I ignored the toast and listened to the echo of the Ping-Pong balls.

"You told me," I continued, "that all the work was done in this building where we are now."

"That's right," he said.

"But where do all the personnel hang out?" I persisted.

"Personnel?" he echoed, frowning. "There are no personnel. That's to say, there's only Mac, Robbie, Janus—I suppose you'd count Janus—and myself. And now of course you."

I put down my glass and stared. Was he having me on? No, he seemed perfectly serious. Tossing down his orange juice like a cupbearer of the gods quaffing ambrosia, he watched me from behind the bar.

"It's O.K., you know," he said. "We're a very happy party."

I did not doubt it. What with cocoa, Ping-Pong, and the booming bittern, this team of sportsmen would make the members of a Women's Institute seem like trolls.

My baser instinct made me yearn to prick the youngster's pride.

"And what," I asked, "is your position on the staff? Ganymede to the professor's Jove?"

To my intense surprise he laughed, and with an ear cocked to the farther room, where the sound of balls had ceased, set two more glasses down upon the bar and filled them both with juice.

"How smart of you to guess," he answered. "That's roughly the idea . . . to snatch me from this earth to a doubtful heaven. No, seriously, I'm Mac's guinea pig, along with Janus's daughter and Cerberus the dog."

At that moment the door opened and two men came into the room.

Instinctively I recognized MacLean. He was fiftyish, craggy, tall, with the pale, rather light blue eyes which I associate with drunkards, criminals, and fighter pilots—in my view the three frequently combine. His lightish hair receded from a high forehead, and the prominent nose was matched by a thrusting chin. He wore baggy corduroy trousers and an immense pullover with a turtleneck.

His companion was sallow, bespectacled, and squat. Shorts and a baggy shirt gave him a boy scout appearance, nor did the circular sweat stains under his armpits enchance his charm.

MacLean advanced toward me holding out his hand, the broad smile of welcome suggesting I had already become one of his small band of brothers.

"I'm so very glad to see you," he said. "I do hope Ken has been looking after you all right. Such a wretched evening for your first glimpse of Saxmere, but we'll do better for you tomorrow, won't we, Robbie?"

His voice, his manner, was that of an old-fashioned host. I might have been a late arrival at a country-house shoot. He put his hand on my shoulder and urged me toward the bar.

"Orange juice for all, please, Ken," he said, and, turning to me, "We've heard tremendous things about you from A.E.L. I can't tell you how grateful I am to them—to John in particular—for allowing you to come. And above all to yourself. We'll do everything we can to make your visit memorable. Robbie, Ken, I want you to drink to—it's Stephen isn't it? Shall we say Steve?—and to the success of our joint efforts."

I forced a smile, and felt it become a fixture on my face. Robbie, the boy scout, blinked at me from behind his spectacles.

"Your very good health," he said. "I'm the Johannis factotum here. I do everything from exploding gasses to taking Ken's temperature, as well as exercising the dog. When in trouble send for me."

I laughed, then swiftly realized that the falsetto, music-hall comedian voice was in fact his own, and not assumed for the occasion.

We crossed the corridor to a room facing the front, plain and bare like the one we had left, with a table set for four. A long-faced, saturnine fellow, with close-cropped grizzled hair, stood by the sideboard.

"Meet Janus," Mac said to me. "I don't know how they feed you at A.E.L., but Janus sees we none of us starve."

I favored the steward with a cheerful nod. He replied to it with a grunt, and I instantly doubted his willingness to run errands for me to the Three Cocks. I waited for MacLean to say grace, which would somehow have seemed in character, but none was forthcoming, and Janus set before him an enormous old-fashioned soup tureen shaped like a jerry, from which my new chief ladled a steaming, saffron-colored brew. It was surprisingly good. The grilled Dover sole that followed was better still, and the cheese soufflé feather light. The meal took us some fifty minutes to consume, and by the end of it I was ready to make peace with my fellow men.

Young Ken—whose conversation during dinner had consisted of a series of private jokes with Robbie, while MacLean discoursed on mountain climbing in Crete, the beauty of flamingoes on the wing in the Camargue, and the peculiar composition of Piero della Francesca's *Flagellation of Christ*—was the first to rise from the table and ask leave to be dismissed.

MacLean nodded. "Don't read too late," he said. "Robbie will turn your light out if you do. Nine-thirty's the limit."

The youngster smiled, and bade the three of us goodnight. I asked whether Ken was in training to race the dog around the marsh and back.

"No," answered MacLean abruptly, "but he needs a lot of sleep. Let's to billiards."

He led the way from the dining room back to the so-called bar, while I prepared myself for half an hour or so in the room beyond—nothing loath, for I rather fancied myself with a cue—but as we passed through, and I saw nothing but a Ping-Pong table and a dart board, Robbie, noticing my puzzled expression, boomed in my ear, "A quote from Shakespeare, the 'Serpent of old Nile.' Mac means he wants to brief you." He pushed me gently forward and then vanished. I followed my leader through yet another door, soundproofed this time, and we entered the chill atmosphere of what appeared to be half working lab, half clinic, streamlined and severe. It even had an operating-table under a center light, and instruments and jars behind glass panels on the walls.

"Robbie's department," said MacLean. "He can do anything here from developing a virus to taking out your tonsils."

I made no comment, having small desire to offer myself up as a potential victim to the boy scout's doubtful ministrations, and we passed from the laboratory to the room adjoining.

"You'll feel more at home here," observed MacLean, and as he switched on the lights I saw that we had reached the electronics department. The first installation to which we came appeared similar to the one we had built for the G.P.O. some years ago—that is to say, a computer capable of speech, though its vocabulary was limited and the actual "voice" was far from perfect. MacLean's box of tricks, however, had various accessories, and I went up to examine them closely.

"He's neat, don't you think?" said MacLean, rather like a proud father showing off his new-born infant. "I call him Charon One."

We all have pet names for our inventions, and Hermes had seemed particularly appropriate for the winged messenger we had developed for the G.P.O. Charon, if I remembered rightly, was the ferryman who conveyed the spirits of the dead across the Styx. I suppose this was MacLean's own brand of humor.

"What does it do?" I asked cautiously.

"It has several functions," answered MacLean, "which I'll explain later, but your main concern will be the voice mechanism."

He went through a starting-up procedure, much as we had done at A.E.L., but the result was very different. The voice reproduction was perfect, and he had got rid of all the hesitation.

"I'm using the computer for certain experiments in the field of hypnosis," he went on. "These involve programming it with a series of questions. The answeres are then fed back into the computer, and are themselves used to modify the questions that follow. What do you think of that?"

"It's fantastic!" I answered. "You've gone miles beyond what anybody else is doing."

I was indeed flabbergasted, and wondered just how he had done it—as well as keeping it all so secret. We thought we had achieved all that could be done in this particular field at A.E.L.

"Yes," said Mac, "your experts will hardly improve upon it. Charon One will have many uses, especially in the medical world. I won't go into any more details tonight, except to say that it is primarily connected with an experiment I'm working on which the Ministry knows nothing whatever about."

He smiled, and here we go, I thought, now we're coming to the "experiments of a dubious nature" which my chief had warned me about. I said nothing, and MacLean moved to a different installation.

"This," he said, "is what really concerns the government, and the military chaps in particular. You know, of course, that blast is difficult to control. An airplane breaking the sound barrier may shatter windows indiscriminately, but not one particular window, or one particular target. Charon Two can do just that." He crossed the room to a cabinet, took out a glass jar, and placed it on the working bench by the wall. Then he threw a switch on his second installation, and the glass shivered to fragments.

"Rather neat, don't you think?" said MacLean. "But of course the point is the long-range use, should you wish to inflict serious damage on specific objects at a distance. I personally don't—blast doesn't interest me—but the Services would find it effective on occasion. It's just a case of a special method of transmission. But my particular concern is high-frequency response between individuals, and between people and animals. I'm keeping this quiet from my masters, who give me a grant." He put his fingers on another control on the second installation. "You won't see anything with this one," he said. "It's the call note with which I control Cerberus. Human beings can't pick it up. He'll be out in the grounds somewhere."

We waited in silence, and a few minutes later I heard the sound of a dog scratching at the farther door. MacLean let him in. "All right. Good boy. Lie down." He turned to me, smiling. "Nothing really in that—he was only the other side of the building—but we've got him to obey orders from long distances. It could be quite useful in an emergency." He glanced at his watch. "I wonder if Mrs. J. will forgive me," he murmured. "It's only a quarter-past nine after all. And I do so enjoy showing off." His schoolboy grin was suddenly infectious.

"What are you going to do?" I asked.

"Bring her small daughter to the telephone, or wake her up if she's asleep."

He made another adjustment to the apparatus, and once again we waited. In about two minutes the telephone rang. MacLean crossed the room to answer it. "Hullo?" he said. "Sorry, Mrs. J. Just an experiment. I'm sorry if I've woken her up. Yes, put her on. Hullo, Niki. No, it's all right. you can go back to bed. Sleep tight." He replaced the receiver, then bent down to pat Cerberus stretched at his feet.

"Children, like dogs, are particularly easy to train," he said. "Or put it this way—their sixth sense, the one that picks up these signals, is highly developed. Niki has her own call note, just as Cerberus does, and the fact that she suffers from retarded development makes her an excellent subject."

He patted his box of tricks in much the same fashion that he had patted his dog. Then he glanced up at me and smiled.

"Any questions?"

"Obviously," I replied. "the first being, what is the exact object of the exercise? Are you trying to prove that certain high-frequency signals have potentialities not only for destruction but also for controlling the receptive mechanism in an animal, and also the human brain?"

I forced a composure I was far from feeling. If these were the sort of experiments that were going on at Saxmere, small wonder the place had been shrugged aside as a crackpot's paradise.

MacLean looked at me thoughtfully. "Of course Charon Two could be said to prove exactly that," he said, "though this is not my intention. The Ministry may possibly be very disappointed in consequence. No, I personally am trying to tackle something more far-reaching." He paused, then put his hand on my shoulder. "We'll leave Charons One and Two for tonight. Come outside for a breath of air."

We left by the door which the dog had scratched at. It led to another corridor, and finally to an entrance at the back of the building. MacLean unbolted the door and I followed him through. The rain had ceased and the air was clean and cold, the sky brilliant with stars. In the distance, beyond the line of sand dunes, I could hear the roar of sea breaking upon shingle.

MacLean inhaled deeply, his face turned seaward. Then he looked upward at the stars. I lit a cigarette and waited for him to speak.

"Have you any experience of poltergeists?" he asked.

"Things that go bump in the night?" I said. "No, I can't say I have." I offered him a cigarette, but he shook his head.

"What you watched just now," said MacLean, "the glass shivering to pieces, is the same thing. Electrical force, released. Mrs. J. had trouble with crashing objects long before I developed Charon. Saucepans, and so on, hurling themselves about at the coast-guard's cottage where they live. It was Niki, of course."

I stared at him, incredulous. "You mean the child?"

"Yes."

He thrust his hands in his pockets and began pacing up and down. "Naturally, she was quite unaware of the fact," he continued. "So were her parents. It was only psychic energy exploding, extra strong in her case because her brain is undeveloped, and since she is the only survivor of identical twins the force was doubled."

This was rather too much to swallow, and I laughed. He swung round and faced me.

"Have you a better solution?" he asked.

"No," I admitted, "but surely . . ."

"Exactly," he interrupted. "Nobody ever has. There are hundreds, thousands of cases of these so-called phenomena, and almost every time they are reported there is evidence to show that a child, or someone who is regarded as of substandard intelligence, was in the locality at the time." He resumed his walk and I beside him, the dog at our heels.

"So what?" I said.

"So that," he went on, "it suggests we all possess an untapped source of energy within us that awaits release. Call it, if you like, Force Six. It works in the same way as the high-frequency impulse which I released just now from Charon. Here is the explanation of telepathy, precognition, and all the so-called psychic mysteries. The power we develop in any electronic device is the same as the power that the Janus child possesses, with one difference, to date—we can control the one but not the other."

I saw this meaning, but not where the discussion was leading us. God knows life is complicated enough without seeking to probe the unconscious forces that may lie formant within man, especially if the connecting link must first be an animal, or an idiot child.

"All right," I said, "so you tap this Force Six, as you call it. Not only in Janus's daughter, but in all animals, in backward children, and finally in the human race. You have us breaking glasses, sending saucepans flying, exchanging messages by telepathic communication, and so on and so forth, but wouldn't it add immeasurably to our difficulties, so that we ended up in the complete chaos from which we presumably sprang?"

This time it was MacLean who laughed. Our walk had taken us to a ridge of high ground, and we were looking across the sand dunes to the sea beyond. The long shingle beach seemed to stretch into eternity, as drear and featureless as the marsh behind it. The sea broke with a monotonous roar, sucking at the dragging stones, only to renew the effort and spend itself once more.

"No doubt it would," he said, "but that's not what I'm after. Man will find a proper use for Force Six in his own good time. I want to make it work for him after the body dies."

I threw my cigarette onto the ground and watched it glow an instant before it flickered to a wet stub.

"What on earth do you mean?" I asked him.

He was looking at me, trying to size up my reaction to his words. I could not make up my mind if he was mad or not, but there was something vaguely endearing about him as he stood there, hunched, speculative, like an overgrown schoolboy in his corduroy bags and his old turtlenecked sweater.

"I'm quite serious," he said. "The energy is there, you know, when it leaves the body on point of death. Think of the appalling wastage through the centuries—all that energy escaping as we die, when it might be used for the benefit of mankind. It's the oldest of theories, of course, that the soul escapes through the nostrils or the mouth—the Greeks believed in it, so do certain African tribes today. You and I are not concerned with souls, and we know that our intelligence dies with our body. But not the vital spark. The life-force continues as energy, uncontrolled, and up to the present . . . useless. It's above us and around us as we stand talking here."

Once again he threw back his head and looked at the stars, and I wondered what deep inner loneliness had driven him to this vain quest after the intangible. Then I remembered that his wife had died. Doubtless this theoretical bunk had saved him.

"I'm afraid it will take you a lifetime to prove," I said to him.

"No," he answered. "At the most a couple of months. You see, Charon Three, which I didn't show you, has a built-in storage unit, to receive and contain power, or, to be exact, to receive and contain Force Six when it is available." He paused. The glance he threw at me was curious, speculative. I waited for him to continue. "The groundwork has all been done," he said. "We are geared and ready for the great experiment, when Charons One and Three will be used in conjunction, but I need an assistant, fully trained to work both installations, when the moment comes. I'll be perfectly frank with you. Your predecessor here at Saxmere wouldn't cooperate. Oh yes, you had one. I asked your chief at A.E.L. not to tell you—I preferred to tell you myself. Your predecessor refused his cooperation for personal reasons which I respect."

I stared. I was not surprised at the other fellow refusing to cooperate, but I did not see where ethics came into it.

"He was a Catholic," explained MacLean. "Believing as he did in the survival of the soul and its sojourn in prugatory, he couldn't stomach my idea of imprisoning the life-force and making it work for us herc on earth. Which, as I have told you, is my intention."

He turned away from the sea and began walking back the way we had come. The lights were all extinguished in the low line of prefabs where presumably we were to eat, work, sleep, and have our being during the eight weeks that lay ahead. Behind them loomed the square tower of the disused radar station, a monument to the ingenuity of man.

"They told me at A.E.L. you had no scruples," went on MacLean. "Neither have the rest of us at Saxmere, though we like to think of ourselves as dedicated men. As young Ken puts it himself, it comes to the same thing as giving your eyes to a hospital, or your kidneys to cold storage. The problem is ours, not his."

I had a sudden recollection of the youngster at the bar, pouring out the orange juice and calling himself a guinea pig.

"What's Ken's part in all this, then?" I asked.

MacLean paused in his walk and looked straight at me.

"The boy has leukemia," he said. "Robbie gives him three months at the outside. There'll be no pain. He has tremendous guts, and believes wholeheartedly in the experiment. It's very possible the attempt may fail. If it fails, we lose nothing—his life is forfeit anyway. If we succeed . . ." He broke off, catching his breath as though swept by a sudden deep emotion. "If we succeed, you see what it will mean?" he said. "We shall have the answer at last to the intolerable futility of death."

When I awoke next morning to a brilliant day and looked from my bedroom window along the asphalt and to the disused radar tower, brooding like a sentinel over empty sheds and rusted metal toward the marsh beyond, I made my decision then and there to go.

I shaved, bathed, and went along to breakfast determined to be courteous to all, and to ask for five minutes alone with MacLean immediately afterward. I would catch the first available train and with luck be in London by one o'clock. If there was any unpleasantness with A.E.L. my chief would take the rap for it, not I.

The dining room was empty except for Robbie, who was attacking an enormous plateful of soused herrings. I bade him a brief good-day and helped myself to bacon. I looked round for a morning paper but there was none. Conversation would be forced upon me.

"Fine morning," I observed.

He did not answer immediately. He was engaged in dissecting his herring with the finesse of an expert. Then his falsetto voice came at me across the table.

"Are you proposing to back out?" he asked.

His question took me by surprise, and I disliked the note of derision.

"I'm an electronic engineer," I answered. "I'm not interested in psychical research."

"No more were Lister's colleagues concerned with discovering antisepsis," he rejoined. "What fools they were made to look later."

He forked a half herring into his mouth and proceeded to chew it, watching me from behind his bifocal specs.

"So you believe all this stuff about Force Six?" I said.

"Don't you?" he parried.

I pushed aside my plate in protest.

"Look here," I said. "I can accept this work MacLean has done on sound. He has found the answer to voice production which we failed to do at A.E.L. He has eveloped a system by which high-frequency waves can be picked up by animals, and also, it seems, by one idiot child. I give him full marks for the first, am doubtful about the potential value of the second, and as to his third project—capturing the life-force, or whatever he calls it, as it leaves the body—if anyone talked to the Ministry about that one, your boss would find himself inside."

I resumed my bacon feeling I had put Robbie in his place. He finished his herrings, then started on the toast and marmalade.

"Ever watched anyone die?" he asked suddenly.

"As a matter of fact, no," I answered.

"I'm a doctor, and it's part of my job," he said, "in hospitals, in homes, in refugee camps after the war. I suppose I've witnessed scores of deaths during my professional life. It's not a pleasant experience. Here at Saxmere it's become my business to stand by a very plucky, likeable lad, not only during his last hours, but during the few weeks that remain to him. I could do with some help."

I got up and took my plate to the sideboard. Then I returned and helped myself to coffee.

"I'm sorry," I said.

He pushed the toast rack toward me but I shook my head. Breakfast is not my favorite meal, and this morning I lacked appetite. There was a sound of footsteps outside on the asphalt, and a head looked in at the window. It was Ken.

"Hullo," he said, with a grin, "what a wonderful morning. If Mac doesn't need you in the control room I'll show you round. We could take a walk up to the coast-guard cottages and over Saxmere cliff. Are you game?" He took my hesitation for assent. "Splendid! It's no use asking Robbie. He'll spend the morning in the lab gloating over specimens of my blood."

The head vanished, and I heard him call to Janus through the kitchen window alongside. Neither Robbie nor I spoke. The sound of munching toast became unbearable. I stood up.

"Where will I find MacLean?" I asked.

"In the control room," he answered, and went on eating.

It was best done at once. I went the way I had been shown the night before, through the swing door to the lab. Somehow the operating table under the center light held more significance this morning, and I avoided looking at it. I went through the door at the far end, and saw MacLean standing by Charon One. He beckoned me over.

"There's a slight fault in the processing unit," he said. "I noticed it last night. I'm sure you'll be able to fix it."

This was the moment to express my regrets and tell him I had decided against joining his team and intended to return to London immediately. I did no such thing. Instead I crossed the floor to the computer and stood by while he explained the circuits. Professional pride, professional jealousy, if you will, coupled with intense curiosity to know why this particular apparatus was superior to the one we had built at A.E.L., proved too much for me.

"There are some overalls on the wall," said MacLean. "Put 'em on, and we'll fix the fault between us."

From then onward I was lost, or perhaps it would be more correct to say that I was won. Not to his lunatic theories, not to any future experiment with life and death; I was conquered by the supreme beauty and efficiency of Charon One itself. Beauty may be an odd word to use where electronics are concerned. I did not find it so. Herein lay all my passion, all my feelings; from my boyhood I had been involved with the creation of these things. This was my life's work. I was not interested in the uses to which the machines I had helped to develop and perfect were ultimately put. My part was to see that they fulfilled the function for which they were designed. Until arriving at Saxmere I had had no other object, no other aim in life, but to do what I was fitted to do, and do it well.

Charon One awakened something else in me, an awareness of power. I had only to handle those control to know that what I wanted now was to have detailed knowledge of all the working parts, and then be given charge of the whole layout. Nothing else mattered. By the end of that first morning I had not only located the fault, a minor one, but had set it right. MacLean had become Mac, the shortening of my name to Steve was something that no longer jarred, and the whole fantastic setup had ceased either to irritate or to dismay; I had become one of the team.

Robbie showed no surprise when I turned up at lunchtime, nor did he allude to our conversation at breakfast. In the late afternoon, with Mac's permission, I took my suggested walk with Ken. It was impossible to connect approaching death with this irrepressible youngster, and I put it from my mind. It could be that both Mac and Robbie were wrong about it. Anyway, it was not, thank God, my problem.

He showed no sign of fatigue and led the way, laughing and chatting, across the sand dunes to the sea. The sun was shining, the air felt cold and clean, even the long stretch of shore that had seemed drear the night before had now a latent charm. The heavy shingle gave place to sand, crisp under our feet; Cerberus, who accompanied us, bounded ahead. We threw sticks for him to retrieve from the pallid, almost effortless sea which gently, without menace, broke beside us as we walked. We did not discuss Saxmere, or anything connected with it; instead Ken regaled me with amusing gossip about the U.S. base at Thirwall, where he had apparently worked as one of the ground staff before Mac arranged his transfer ten months before.

Suddenly Cerberus, barking puppy fashion for another stick, turned and stood motionless, ears pricked, head to wind. Then he started loping back the way we had come, his lithe black-and-tan form soon lost to sight against the darker shingle and the dunes beyond.

"He's had a signal from Charon," said Ken.

The night before, watching Mac at the controls, the dog's scratching at the door seemed natural. Here, some three miles distant on the lonely shore, his swift departure was uncanny.

"Effective, isn't it?" said Ken.

I nodded; but somehow, because of what I'd seen, my spirits left me. Enthusiasm for the walk had waned. It would have been different had I been alone. Now, with the boy beside me, I was, as it were, confronted with the future, the project Mac had in mind, the months ahead.

"Want to turn back?" he asked me.

His words reminded me of Robbie's at breakfast, though he meant them otherwise. "Just as you like," I said indifferently.

He swung left and we clambered, slipping and sliding with every step, up the steep slope to the cliffs above the beach. I was breathless when I reached the top. Not Ken. Smiling, he lent a hand to pull me up. Heather and scrub lay all about us, and the wind was in our faces, stronger than it had been below. About a quarter of a mile distant, stark and white against the skyline, stood a row of coastguard cottages, bleak windows all aflame with the setting sun.

"Come and pay your respects to Mrs. J.," suggested Ken.

Reluctantly I followed, detesting unpremeditated visits, no matter where. The unprepossessing Janus household did not attract me. As we drew near I saw that only the far cottage was inhabited. The others had the forlorn, lost look of buildings untenanted for years. Two had their windows broken. Gardens, untended, sprawled. Posts, sagging drunkenly from the damp earth, trailed pieces of barbed wire from their rotting stumps. A small girl was leaning over the gate of the occupied cottage. Dark, straight hair framed her pinched face, her eyes were lusterless, and she was wanting a front tooth.

"Hullo, Niki," called Ken.

The child stared, then slowly removed herself from the gate. Morosely, she pointed to me. "Who's that?" she asked.

"His name is Steve," Ken answered her.

"I don't like his shoes," said the child.

Ken laughed and opened the gate, and as he did so the child attempted to climb upon him. Gently he put her aside, and walking up the path to the open door called, "Are you there, Mrs. J.?"

A woman appeared, pallid and dark like her child. Her anxious face broke into a smile at the sight of Ken. She bade us enter, apologizing for the disarrray. I was introduced as Steve, and we hovered uncomfortably in the front room where the child's toys were strewn about the floor.

"We've had tea," Ken said, in reply to Mrs. J.'s question, but, insisting that the kettle had just boiled, the woman vanished to the adjoining kitchen, to reappear at once with a large brown teapot and two cups and saucers. There was nothing for it but to swallow the stuff under her watchful eyes, while the child, edging against Ken all the while, stared balefully at my inoffensive canvas shoes.

I gave full marks to my young companion. He exchanged pleasantries with Mrs. Janus, and patted the unendearing Niki. I remained silent throughout, and wondered why the child's likeness, framed in place of honor over the fireplace, should be so much more pleasing than the child herself.

"It's very cold here in the winter, but a bracing cold," said Mrs. Janus, fixing me with her own mournful eyes. "I always say I prefer the frost to the damp."

I agreed, and shook my head at the offer of more tea. At this moment the child stiffened. She stood rigid a moment, her eyes closed. I wondered if she were going to throw a fit. Then very calmly she announced, "Mac wants me."

Mrs. Janus, with a murmur of apology, went into the hall and I heard her dial. Ken was watching the child, himself unmoved. I felt slightly sick. In a moment I heard Mrs. Janus speaking over the telephone and she called, "Niki, come here and speak to Mac."

The child ran from the room, and for the first time since our arrival showed animation. She even laughed. Mrs. Janus returned and smiled at Ken.

'I think Mac really wants a word with you," she said.

Ken got up and went into the hall. Alone with the child's mother, I did not know what to say. At last, in desperation, nodding at the photograph above the fireplace, I said, "What a good likeness of Niki. Taken a few years ago, I suppose?"

To my dismay, the woman's eyes filled with tears.

"That's not Niki, that's her twin," she answered. "That's our Penny. We lost her soon after they had both turned five."

My awkward apology was cut short by the entrance of the child herself. Ignoring my shoes, she came straight to me, put her hand on my knee and announced, "Mac says Cerberus is back. And you and Ken can go home."

"Thank you," I said.

As we walked away from the cottages, over scrub and heather, and took a short cut back to Saxmere through the marsh, I asked Ken whether the call signal from Charon invariably had the effect I had seen, that of awakening latent intelligence in the child.

"Yes," he said. "We don't know why. Robbie thinks the ultra-shortwave may have therapeutic value in itself. Mac doesn't agree. He believes that when he puts out the call it connects Niki with what he calls Force Six, which in her case is doubled because of the dead twin."

Ken spoke as if this fantastic theory was perfectly natural.

"Do you mean," I asked, "that, when the call goes through, the dead twin somehow takes over?"

Ken laughed. He walked so fast it was hard to keep up with him.

"Ghoulies and ghosties?" he queried. "Good Lord, no! There's nothing left of poor Penny but electric energy, still attached to her living twin. That's why Niki makes such a useful guinea pig."

He glanced across at me, smiling.

"When I go," he said, "Mac plans to tap my energy too. Don't ask me how. I just don't know. But he's welcome to have a crack at it."

We went on walking. The sour smell of stagnant water rose from the marsh on either side of us. The wind strengthened, flattening the reeds. The tower of Saxmere loomed ahead, hard and black against a russet sky.

I had the voice production unit functioning to my satisfaction within the next few days. We fed it with tape, programmed in advance as we had done at A.E.L., but the vocabulary was more extensive, consisting of a call signal—"This is Charon speaking . . . this is Charon speaking"—followed by a series of numbers, spoken with great clarity. Then came questions, most of them quite simple, such as, "Are you O.K.?" "Does anything bother you?" proceeding to statements of fact such as, "You are not with us. You are at Thirlwall. It is two years back. Tell us what you see," and so on. My job was to control the precision of the voice, the program was Mac's responsibility, and, if the questions and statements appeared inane to me, doubtless they made sound sense to him.

On Friday he told me that he considered Charon was ready for use the next day, and Robbie and Ken were warned for 11 a.m. Mac himself would be at the controls, and I was to watch. In the light of what I had already witnessed, I should have been fully prepared for what happened. Oddly enough, I was not. I took up my station in the adjoining lab, while Ken stretched himself out on the operating table.

"It's all right," he said to me with a wink. "Robbie isn't going to carve me up."

There was a microphone in position above his head, with a lead going through to Charon One. A yellow light for STANDBY flashed on the wall. It changed to red. I saw Ken close his eyes Then a voice came from Charon. "This is Charon speaking . . . This is Charon speaking." The series of numbers followed, and, after a pause, the question, "Are you O.K.?"

When Ken replied, "Yes, I'm O.K." I noticed that his voice lacked its usual buoyancy; it was flatter, pitched in a lower key. I glanced at Robbie; he handed me a slip of paper on which were written the words "He's under hypnosis."

The penny dropped, and I realized for the first time the full importance of the sound unit and the reason for perfecting it. Ken had been conditioned to hypnosis by the electronic voice. The questions on the program were not haphazard, they were taped for him. The implications of this were even more shocking to me than when I had seen the dog and the child obey the call signal from a distance. When Ken, jokingly, had spoken of "going to work," this was what he had meant.

"Does anything bother you?" asked the voice.

There was a long pause before the answer, and when it came the tone was impatient, almost fretful.

"It's the hanging about. I want it to happen quickly. If it could be over and done with, then I wouldn't give a damn."

I might have been standing by a confessional, and I understood now why my predecessor had turned in his job. I saw Robbie's eyes upon me; the demonstration had been staged not only to show Ken's cooperation under hypnosis, proved no doubt dozens of times already, but to test my nerve. The ordeal continued. Much of what Ken said made painful hearing. I don't want to repeat it here. It revealed the unconscious strain under which he lived, never outwardly apparent either to us or to himself.

The program Mac used was not one I had heard before, and it ended with the words, "You'll be all right, Ken. You aren't alone. We're with you every step of the way. O.K.?"

A faint smile passed over the quiet face.

"O.K."

Then the numbers were repeated, in swifter sequence, ending with the words, "Wake up, Ken!"

The boy stretched himself, opened his eyes, and sat up. He looked first at Robbie, then at me, and grinned.

"Did old Charon do his stuff?" he asked.

"One hundred percent," I answered, my voice falsely hearty.

Ken slid off the operating table, his work for the morning done. I went through to Mac, standing by the controls.

"Thanks, Steve," he said. "You can appreciate the necessity for Charon One now. An electronic voice, plus a planned program, eliminates emotion on our part, which will be essential when the time comes. That's the reason Ken has been conditioned to the machine. He responds very well. But better, of course, if the child is with him."

"The child?" I repeated.

"Yes," he answered. "Niki is an essential part of the experiment. She is conditioned to the voice too, and the pair of them chat away together as gay as crickets. They know nothing about it afterward, naturally. He paused, watching me closely, as Robbie had done. "Ken will almost certainly go into coma at the end. The child will be our only link with him then. Now, I sugget you borrow a car, drive into Thirlwall, and buy yourself a drink."

He turned away, craggy, imperturbable, suggesting a benevolent bird of prey.

I didn't go into Thirlwall. I walked out across the sand dunes to the sea. There was nothing calm about it today. Turbulent and gray, it sank into troughs before breaking on the shingle with a roar. Miles away along the beach a group of U.S. Air Corps cadets were practising bugle calls. The shrill notes, the discordant sounds, drove toward me down the wind. For no reason at all the half-forgotten lines of a Negro spiritual kept repeating themselves over and over in my mind.

> *He has the whole world in his hands,*
> *He has the whole world in his hands . . .*

The demonstration was repeated, with varying programs, every three days during the weeks that followed. Mac and I took it in turn at the controls. I soon grew accustomed to this, and the bizarre sessions became a matter of routine.

It was, as Mac had said, less painful when the child was present. Her father would bring her to the lab and leave her with us, Ken already in position and under control. The child would sit in a chair beside him, also with a microphone above her head to record her speech. She was told that Ken was asleep. Then, in her turn, she would receive the signal from Charon, and a different series of numbers from Ken, after which she would be under control. The program, of course, was different when the two were working together. Charon would take Ken back in time, to a period when he was the same age as Niki, saying, "You are seven years old. Niki has come to play with you. She is your friend," and a similar message would be given to the child: "Ken has come to play with you. He is a boy of your age."

The two would then chat together, without interruption from Charon, with the quite fantastic result—this had been built up during the past months, I gathered—that the pair were now close friends "in time," hiding nothing from each other, playing imaginary games, exchanging ideas. Niki, backward and morose when conscious, was lively and gay under control. The taped conversations were checked after each session, to record the increasingly closer rapport between the two, and to act as guide for further programs. Ken, when conscious, looked upon Niki as Janus's backward child, a sad little object of no interest. He was totally ignorant of what happened when under control. I was not so sure about Niki. Intuition seemed to draw her to him. She would hang about him, if given the chance.

I asked Robbie what the Janus parents felt about the sessions.

"They'd do anything for Mac," he told me, "and they believe it may help Niki. The other twin was normal, you see."

"Do they realize about Ken?"

"That he's going to die?" replied Robbie. "They've been told, but I doubt if they understand. Who would, looking at him now?"

We were at the bar, and from where we stood we could see Ken and Mac engaged in a game of Ping-Pong in the room beyond.

Early in December we had a scare. A letter came from the Ministry asking how the Saxmere experiments were going; and could they send someone down to have a look around? We had a consultation, the upshot of which was that I undertook to go up to London to choke them off. By this time I was wholeheartedly behind Mac in all he was doing, and during my brief stay in town I succeeded in satisfying the authorities in question that a visit at this moment would be premature, but we hoped to have something to show them before Christmas. Their interest, of course, lay in Charon Two's potentialities for blast; they knew nothing of Mac's intended project.

When I returned, alighting at Thirlwall station in a very different mood from that of three months past, the Morris was waiting for me, but without Ken's cheerful face at the wheel. Janus had replaced him. He was never a talkative bloke, and he answered my question with a shrug.

"Ken's got a cold," he said. "Robbie's keeping him in bed as a precaution."

I went straight to the boy's room on arrival. He looked a bit flushed, but was in his usual spirits, full of protests against Robbie.

"There's absolutely nothing the matter," he said. "I got wet feet stalking a bird down in the marsh."

I sat with him awhile, joking about London and the Ministry, then went to report to Mac.

"Ken has some fever," he said at once. "Robbie's done a blood test. It's not too good." He paused. "This could be it."

I felt suddenly chilled. After a moment I told him about London. He nodded briefly.

"Whatever happens," he said, "we can't have them here now."

I found Robbie in the lab, busy with slides and a microscope. He was preoccupied, and hadn't much time for me.

"It's too soon to say yet," he said. "Another forty-eight hours should show one way or the other. There's an infection in the right lung. With leukemia that could be fatal. Go and keep Ken amused."

I took the portable gramophone along to the boy's bedroom. I suppose I put on about a dozen records, and he seemed quite cheerful. Later he dozed off and I sat there, wondering what to do. My mouth felt dry, and I kept swallowing. Something inside me kept saying, "Don't let it happen."

Conversation at dinner was forced. Mac talked about undergraduate days at Cambridge, while Robbie reminisced over past Rugby games—he'd played scrum half for Guy's. I don't think I talked at all. I went along afterward to say good-night to Ken, but he was already alseep. Janus was sitting with him. Back in my room I flung myself on my bed and tried to read, but I couldn't concentrate. There was fog at sea, and every few minutes the fog horn boomed from the lighthouse along the coast. There was no other sound.

Next morning Mac came to my room at a quarter to eight.

"Ken's worse," he said. "Robbie's going to try a blood transfusion. Janus will assist." Janus was a trained orderly.

"What do you want me to do?" I asked.

"Help me get Charons One and Three ready for action," he said. "If Ken doesn't respond, I may decide to put phase one of Operation Styx into effect. Mrs. J. has been warned we may need the child."

As I finished dressing I kept telling myself that this was the moment we had been training for all through the past two and a half months. It didn't help. I swallowed some coffee and went to the control room. The door to the lab was closed. They had Ken in there, giving him the blood transfusion. Mac and I worked over both Charons, seeing that everything functioned perfectly, and that there could be no hitch when the time came. Programs, tapes, microphones, all were ready. After that it was a matter of standing by until Robbie came through with his report. We got it at about half-past twelve.

"Slight improvement." They had taken him back to his room. We all had something to eat while Janus continued his watch over Ken. Today there was no question of forced conversation. The work on hand was the concern of all. I felt calmer, steadier. The morning's work had knocked me into shape. Mac proposed a game of Ping-Pong after lunch, and whereas the night before I would have felt aghast at the suggestion, today it seemed the right thing to do. Looking from the window, between games, I saw Niki wandering up and down with Mrs. Janus, a strange, lost-looking little figure, filling a battered doll's pram with sticks and stones. She had been on the premises since ten o'clock.

At half-past four Robbie came into the sports room. I could tell by his face that it was no good. He shook his head when Mac suggested another transfusion. It would be a waste of time, he told us.

"He's conscious?" asked Mac.

"Yes," answered Robbie. "I'll bring him through when you're ready."

Mac and I went back to the control room. Phase two of Operation Styx consisted of bringing the operating table in here, placing it between the three Charons, and connecting up with an oxygen unit alongside. The microphones were already in position. We had done the maneuver often before, in practise runs, but today we beat our fastest time by two minutes.

"Good work," said Mac.

The thought struck me that he had been looking forward to this moment for months, perhaps for years. He pressed the button to signal that we were ready, and in less than four minutes Robbie and Janus arrived with Ken on the trolley, and lifted him onto the table. I hardly recognised him. The eyes, usually so luminous, had almost disappeared into the sunken face. He looked bewildered. Mac quickly attached electrodes, one against each temple and others to his chest and neck, connecting him to Charon Three. Then he bent over the boy.

"It's all right," he said. "We've got you in the lab to do a few tests. Just relax, and you'll be fine."

Ken stared up at Mac, and then he smiled. We all knew that this was the last we should see of his conscious self. It was, in fact, good-bye. Mac looked at me, and I put Charon One into operation, the voice ringing clear and true. "This is Charon calling . . . This is Charon calling." Ken closed his eyes. He was under hypnosis. Robbie stood beside him, finger on pulse. I set the program in motion. We had numbered it X in the files, because it was different from the others.

"How do you feel, Ken?"

Even with the microphone close to his lips we could barely hear the answer. "You know damn well how I feel."

"Where are you, Ken?"

"I'm in the control room. Robbie's turned the heating off. I've got the idea now. It's to freeze me, like butcher's meat. Ask Robbie to bring back the heat . . ." There was a long pause, and then he said, "I'm standing by a tunnel. It looks like a tunnel. It could be the wrong end of a telescope, the figures look so small . . . Tell Robbie to bring back the heat."

Mac, who was beside me at the controls, made an adjustment, and we let the program run without sound until it reached a certain point, when it was amplified once more to reach Ken.

"You are five years old, Ken. Tell us how you feel."

There was a long pause, and then, to my dismay, though I suppose I should have been prepared for it, Ken whimpered, "I don't feel well. I don't want to play."

Mac pressed a button, and the door at the far end opened. Janus pushed his daughter into the room, then closed the door again. Mac had her under control with her call sign at once, and she did not see Ken on the table. She went and sat down in her chair and closed her eyes.

"Tell Ken you are here, Niki."

I saw the child clutch the arms of her chair.

"Ken's sick," she said. "He's crying. He doesn't want to play."

The voice of Charon went ruthlessly on.

"Make Ken talk, Niki."

"Ken won't talk," said the child. "He's going to say his prayers."

Ken's voice came faintly through the microphone to the loud speakers. The words were gabbled, indistinct:

> *"Gen'ral Jesus, mekan mild,*
> *Look'pon little child,*
> *Pity my simple city,*
> *Sofa me to come to thee . . ."*

There was a long pause after this. Neither Ken nor Niki said anything. I kept my hands on the controls, ready to continue the program when Mac nodded. Niki began drumming her feet on the floor. All at once she said, "I shan't go down the tunnel after Ken. It's too dark."

Robbie, watching his patient, looked up. "He's gone into coma," he said.

Mac signaled to me to set Charon One in motion again.

"Go after Ken, Niki," said the voice.

The child protested. "It's black in there," she said. She was nearly crying. She hunched herself in her chair and went through crawling motions. "I don't want to go," she said, "It's too long, and Ken won't wait for me."

She started to tremble all over. I looked across at Mac. He questioned Robbie with a glance.

"He won't come out of it," Robbie said. "It may last hours."

Mac ordered the oxygen apparatus to be put into operation, and Robbie fixed the mask on Ken. Mac went over to Charon Three and switched on the monitor display screen. He made some adjustments, and nodded at me. "I'll take over," he said.

The child was still crying, but the next command from Charon One gave her no respite, "Stay with Ken," it said. "Tell us what happens."

I hoped Mac knew what he was doing. Suppose the child went into a coma too?

Could he bring her back? Hunched in her chair, she was as still as Ken, and about as lifeless. Robbie told me to put blankets round her and feel her pulse. It was faint, but steady. Nothing happened for over an hour. We watched the flickering and erratic signals on the screen, as the electrodes transmitted Ken's weakening brain impulses. Still the child did not speak.

Later, much later, she stirred, then moved with a strange twisting motion. She crossed her arms over her breast, humping her knees. Her head dropped forward. I wondered if, like Ken, she was engaged in some childish prayer. Then I realized that her position was that of a fetus before birth. Personality had vanished from her face. She looked wizened, old.

Robbie said, "He's going."

Mac beckoned me to the controls, and Robbie bent over Ken with fingers on his pulse. The signals on the screen were fainter, and faltering, but suddenly they surged in a strong upward beat, and in the same instant Robbie said, "It's all over. He's dead."

The signal was rising and falling steadily now. Mac disconnected the electrodes and turned back to watch the screen. There was no break in the rhythm of the signal, as it moved up and down, up and down, like a heartbeat, like a pulse.

"We've done it!" said Mac. "Oh, my God . . . we've done it!"

We stood there, the three of us, watching the signal that never for one instant changed its pattern. It seemed to contain, in its confident movement, the whole of life.

I don't know how long we stayed there—it could have been minutes, hours. At last Robbie said, "What about the child?"

We had forgotten Niki, just as we had forgotten the quiet, peaceful body that had been Ken. She was still lying in her strange, cramped position, her head bowed to her knees. I went to the control of Charon One to operate the voice, but Mac waved me inside.

"Before we wake her, we'll see what she has to say," he said.

He put through the call signal very faintly, so as not to shock her to consciousness too soon. I followed with the voice, which repeated the final program command.

"Stay with Ken, Tell us what happens."

At first there was no response. Then slowly she uncoiled, her gestures odd, uncouth. Her arms fell to her side. She began to rock backward and forward as though following the motion on the screen. When she spoke her voice was sharp, pitched high.

"He wants you to let him go," she said, "that's what he wants. Let go . . . let go . . . let go . . ." Still rocking, she began to gasp for breath, and, lifting her arms, pummeled the air with her fists.

"Let go . . . let go . . . let go . . . let go . . ."

Robbie said urgently, "Mac, you've got to wake her."

On the screen the rhythm of the signal had quickened. The child began to choke. Without waiting for Mac, I set the voice in motion.

"This is Charon speaking . . . This is Charon speaking . . . Wake up, Niki."

The child shuddered, and the suffused color drained from her face. Her breathing became normal. She opened her eyes. She stared at each of us in turn in her usual apathetic way, and proceeded to pick her nose.

"I want to go to the toilet," she said sullenly.

Robbie led her from the room. The signal, which had increased its speed during the child's outburst, resumed its steady rise and fall.

"Why did it alter speed?" I asked.

"If you hadn't panicked and woken her up, we might have found out," Mac said. His voice was harsh, quite unlike himself.

"Mac," I protested, "that kid was choking to death."

"No," he said, "no, I don't think so."

He turned and faced me. "Her movements simulated the shock of birth," he said. "Her gasp for air was the first breath of an infant, struggling for life. Ken, in coma, had gone back to that moment, and Niki was with him."

I knew by this time that almost anything was possible under hypnosis, but I wasn't convinced.

"Mac," I said, "Niki's struggle came *after* Ken was dead, *after* the new signal appeared on Charon Three. Ken couldn't have gone back to the moment of birth—he was already dead, don't you see?"

He did not answer at once. "I just don't know," he said at last. "I think we shall have to put her under control again."

"No," said Robbie. He had entered the lab while we were talking. "That child has had enough. I've sent her home, and told her mother to put her to bed."

I had never heard him speak with authority before. He looked away from the lighted screen back to the still body on the table. "Doesn't that go for the rest of us?" he said. "Haven't we all had enough? You've proved your point, Mac. I'll celebrate with you tomorrow, but not tonight."

He was ready to break. So, I think, were we all. We had barely eaten through the day, and when Janus returned he set about getting us a meal. he had taken the news of Ken's death with his usual calm. The child, he told us, had fallen asleep the moment she was put to bed.

So . . . it was all over. Reaction, exhaustion, numbness of feeling, all three set in, and I yearned, like Niki, for the total release of sleep.

Before dragging myself to bed, some impulse, stronger than the aching fatigue that overwhelmed me, urged me back to the control room. Everything was as we had left it. Ken's body lay on the table, covered with the blanket. The screen was lighted still, and the signal was pulsing steadily up and down. I waited a moment, then I bent to the tape-control, setting it to play back that last outburst from the child. I remembered the rocking head, the hands fighting to be free, and switched it on.

"He wants you to let him go," said the high-pitched voice, "that's what he wants. Let go . . . let go . . . let go . . ." Then came the gasp for breath, and the words were repeated. "Let go . . . let go . . . let go . . . let go . . ."

I switched it off. The words did not make sense. The signal was simply electrical energy, trapped at the actual moment of Ken's death. How could the child have translated this into a cry for freedom, unless . . .

I looked up. Mac was watching me from the doorway. The dog was with him. "Cerberus is restless," he said. "He keeps padding backward and forward in my room. He won't let me sleep."

"Mac," I said, "I've played that recording again. There's something wrong."

He came and stood beside me. "What do you mean, something wrong? The recording doesn't affect the issue. Look at the screen. The signal's steady. The experiment has been a hundred percent successful. We've done what we set out to do. The energy is there."

"I know it's there," I replied, "but is that all?"

I set the recording in motion once again. Together we listened to the child's gasp, and the words "Let go . . . let go . . ."

"Mac," I said, "when the child said that, Ken was already dead. Therefore, there could be no further communication between them."

"Well?"

"How then, after death, can she still identify herself with his personality—a personality that says 'Let go . . . let go . . .' unless . . ."

"Unless what?"

"Unless something has happened that we know to be impossible, and what we can see, imprisoned on the screen, is the essence of Ken himself?"

He stared at me, haggard, unbelieving, and together we looked once more at the signal, which suddenly took on new meaning, new significance, and as it did so became the expression of our dawning sense of anguish and fear.

"Mac," I said, "what have we done?"

Mrs. Janus telephoned in the morning to say that Niki had woken up and was acting strangely. She kept throwing herself backward and forward. Mrs. Janus had tried to quieten her, but nothing she said did any good. No, she had no temperature, she was not feverish. It was this queer rocking movement all the time. She would not eat any breakfast, she would not speak. Could Mac put through the call signal? It might quieten her.

Janus had answered the phone, and we were in the dining room when he brought us his wife's message. Robbie got up and went to the telephone. He came back again almost immediately.

"I'll go over," he said. "What happened yesterday—I should never have allowed it."

"You knew the risk," answered Mac. "We've all known the risk from the very start. You always assured me it would do no harm."

"I was wrong," said Robbie. "Oh, not about the experiment . . . God knows you've done what you wanted to do, and it didn't affect poor Ken one way or the other. He's out of it all now. But I was wrong to let the child become involved."

"We shouldn't have succeeded without her," replied Mac.

Robbie went out and we heard him start up the car. Mac and I walked along to the control room. Janus and Robbie had been there before us, and had taken Ken's body away. The room was stripped once more to the essentials of normal routine with one exception. Charon Three, the storage unit, still functioned as it had done the previous day and through the night, the signal keeping up its steady rise and fall. I found myself glancing at it almost furtively, in the irrational hope that it would cease.

Presently the telephone buzzed, and I answered it. It was Robbie.

"I think we ought to get the child away," he said at once. "It looks like catatonic schizophrenia, and whether she becomes violent or not Mrs. J. can't cope with it. If Mac will say the word, I could take her up myself to the psychiatric ward at Guy's."

I beckoned to Mac, explaining the situation. He took the receiver from me.

"Look, Robbie," he said, "I'm prepared to take the risk of putting Niki under control. It may work, or it may not."

The argument continued. I could tell from Mac's gesture of frustration that Robbie would not play. He was surely right. Some irreparable damage might have been done to the child's mind already. Yet, if Robbie did take her up to the hospital, what possible explanation could he give?

Mac waved me over to replace him at the telephone.

"Tell Robbie to stand by," he said.

I was his subordinate, and could not stop him. He went to the transmitter on Charon Two and set the control. The call signal was in operation. I lifted the receiver and gave Robbie Mac's message. Then I waited.

I heard Robbie shout to Mrs. Janus, "What's the matter?"—then the sound of the receiver being dropped.

Nothing for a moment or two but distant voices, Mrs. Janus, I think, pleading, and then an appeal to Robbie, "Please, let her try . . ."

Mac went over to Charon One and made some adjustments. Then he waved to me to bring the telephone as near to him as it would go, and reached out for the receiver.

"Niki," he said, "do you hear me? It's Mac."

I stood beside him, to catch the whisper from the receiver.

"Yes, Mac."

She sounded bewildered even frightened.

"Tell me what's wrong, Niki."

She began to whimper. "I don't know. There's a clock ticking somewhere. I don't like it."

"Where's the clock, Niki?"

She did not answer. Mack repeated his question. I could hear Robbie protest. He must have been standing beside her.

"It's all round," she said at last. "It's ticking in my head. Penny doesn't like it either."

Penny. Who was Penny? Then I remembered. The dead twin.

"Why doesn't Penny like it?"

This was intolerable. Robbie was right. Mac should not put the child through this ordeal. I shook my head at him. He took no notice, but once again repeated his question. I could hear the child burst into tears.

"Penny . . . Ken . . ." she sobbed, "Penny . . . Ken."

Instantly Mac switched to the recorded voice of Charon Two giving the order on yesterday's program: "Stay with Ken. Tell us what happens."

The child gave a piercing cry, and she must have fallen, because I heard Robbie and Mrs. Janus exclaim and the telephone crash.

Mac and I looked at the screen. The rhythm was getting faster, the signal moving in quick jerks. Robbie, at his end, picked up the receiver.

"You'll kill her, Mac," he called. "For Christ's sake . . ."

"What's she doing?" said Mac.

"The same as yesterday," called Robbie. "Backward, forward, rocking all the time. She's suffocating. Wait . . ."

Once again he must have let the receiver go. Mac switched back to the call signal. The pulsing on the screen was steadying. Then, after a long interval, Robbie's voice came through again.

"She wants to speak," he said.

There was a pause. The child's voice, expressionless and dull, said, "Let them go."

"Are you all right now, Niki?" asked Mac.

"Let them go," she repeated.

Mac deliberately hung up. Together we watched the signal resume its normal speed.

"Well?" I said. "What does it prove?"

He looked suddenly old, and immeasurably tired, but there was an expression in his eyes that I had never seen before: a curious, baffled incredulity. It was as though everything he possessed—senses, body, brain—protested and denied the thoughts within.

"It could mean you were right," he said. "It could mean survival of intelligence after the body's death. It could mean we've broken through."

The thought, staggering in its implications, turned us both dumb. Mac recovered first. He went and stood beside Charon Three, his gaze fixed upon the picture.

"You saw it change when the child was speaking," he said. "But Niki by herself could not have caused the variation. The power came from Ken's Force Six, and from the dead twin's too. The power is capable of transmission through Niki, but through no one else. Don't you see . . ." He broke off, and swung round to face me, a new excitement dawning. "Niki is the only link. We must get her here, program Charon, and put furthr questions to her. If we really have got intelligence plus power under control . . ."

"Mac," I interrupted, "do you want to kill that child, or, worse, condemn her to a mental institution?"

In desperation he looked once more toward the screen. "I've got to know, Steve," he said. "I've got to find out. If intelligence survives, if Force Six can triumph over matter, then it's not just one man who has beaten death but all mankind from the beginning of time. Immortality in some form or other becomes a certainty, the whole meaning of life on earth is changed."

Yes, I thought, changed forever. The fusion of science and religion in a partnership at first joyous, then the inevitable disenchantment, the scientist realizing, and the priest with him, that, with eternity assured, the human being on earth is more easily expendable. Despatch the maimed, the old, the weak, destroy the very world itself, for what is the point of life if the promise of fulfillment lies elsewhere?

"Mac," I said, "you heard what the child said. The words were, 'Let them go.'"

The telephone rang again. This time it was not Robbie but Janus, from our own extension in the hall. He apologized for disturbing us, but two gentlemen had arrived from the Ministry. He had told them we were in conference, but they said the business was urgent. They had asked to see Mr. MacLean at once.

I went into the bar, and the official I had seen in London was standing there with a companion. This first chap expressed apologies, and said the fact was that my predecessor at Saxmere had been to see them, and admitted that his reason for leaving was because he was doubtful of the work MacLean had in progress. There was some experiment going on of which he did not think the Ministry was aware. They wished to speak to MacLean at once.

"He will be with you shortly," I said. "In the meantime, if there is anything you want to know, I can brief you."

They exchanged glances, and then the second chap spoke.

"You're working on vibrations, aren't you," he asked, "and their relation to blast? That was what you said in London."

"We are," I replied, "and have had some success. But, as I warned you, there is still a lot to do."

"We're here," he said, "to be shown what you've achieved."

"I'm sorry," I answered, "the work has been held up since I returned. We've suffered an unfortunate loss on the staff. Nothing to do with the experiment, or the research connected with it. Young Ken Ryan died yesterday from leukemia."

Once again there was the swift exchange of glances.

"We heard he was not well," said the first man. "Your predecessor told us. In fact, we were given to understand that the experiment in progress was, without the Ministry being informed, connected with this boy's illness."

"You've been misinformed," I said. "His illness had nothing to do with the experiment. The doctor will be back shortly. He can give you the medical details."

"We should like to see MacLean," persisted the second chap, "and we should like to see the electronics department."

I went back to the control room. I knew that nothing I had said would prevent them from having their way. We were in for it.

MacLean was standing by Charon Two doing something to the controls. I looked quickly from him to Charon Three alongside. The screen was still glowing, but the signal had vanished. I did not say anything, I just stared at him.

"Yes," he said, "it's dismantled. I've disconnected everything. The force is lost."

My instantaneous feeling of relief turned to compassion, compassion for the man whose work for months, for years, had gone within five minutes. Destroyed by his own act.

"It isn't finished," he said, meeting my eyes. "It's only begun. Oh, one part of it is over. Charon Three is useless now, and what happened will only be known to the three of us—for Robbie must share our knowledge. We were on the verge of a discovery that no one living would believe. But only on the verge. It could well be that both of us were wrong, that what the child told us last night, and again this morning, was simply some distortion of her unconscious mind—I don't know. I just don't know . . . But, because of what she said, I've released the energy. The child is free. Ken is free. He's gone. Where, to what ultimate destination, we shall probably never know. But—and this includes you, Steve, and Robbie, if he will join us—I am prepared to work to the end of my days to find out."

Then I told him what the officials from the Ministry had said. He shrugged his shoulders.

"I'll tell them all our experiments have failed," he said, "that I want to pack in the job. Henceforth, Steve, we'll be on our own. It's strange—somehow I feel nearer to Ken now than I ever did before. Not only Ken, but everyone who has gone before." He paused, and turned away. "The child will be all right," he said. "Go to her, will you, and send Robbie to me? I'll deal with those sleuths from the Ministry."

I slipped out of the door at the back and started walking across the marsh toward the coast-guard cottages. Cerberus came with me. He was no longer panting, restless, as he had been the night before, but bounded ahead in tearing spirits, returning now and again to make sure that I was following him.

It seemed to me that I had no feeling left, either for what had happened or for what was yet to come. Mac had destroyed, with his own hands, the single thread of evidence that had brought us, through the whole of yesterday, to this morning's dawn. The ultimate dream of every scientist, to give the first answer to the meaning of death, had belonged to us for a brief few hours. We had captured the energy, the energy had ignited the spark, and from that point on there had appeared to loom world after world of discovery.

Now . . . now, my faith was waning. Perhaps we had been wrong, tricked by our own emotions and the suffering of a frightened, backward child. The ultimate questions would never receive their answer, either from us or from anyone.

The marsh fell back on either side of me, and I climbed the scrubby hill to the coast-guard cottages. The dog ran on ahead, barking. Away to the right, outlined on the cliff edge, the damned U.S. cadets were blowing their bugles once again. The raucous, discordant screeches tore the air. They were trying, of all things, to sound the reveille.

I saw Robbie come out of the Januses' cottage, and the child was with him. She seemed all right. She ran forward to greet the dog. Then she heard the sound of the reveille, and lifted her arms. As the tempo increased she swayed to the rhythm, and ran out toward the cliffs with her arms above her head, laughing, dancing, the dog barking at her feet. The cadets looked back, laughing with her; and then there was nothing else but the dog barking, the child dancing, and the sound of those thin, high bugles in the air.

Not After Midnight

I AM A schoolmaster by profession. Or was. I handed in my resignation to the headmaster before the end of the summer term in order to forestall inevitable dismissal. The reason I gave was true enough—ill-health, caused by a wretched bug picked up on holiday in Crete, which might necessitate a stay in hospital of several weeks, various injections, etc. I did not specify the nature of the bug. He knew, though, and so did the rest of the staff. And the boys. My complaint is universal, and has been so through the ages, an excuse for jest and hilarious laughter from earliest times, until one of us oversteps the mark and becomes a menace to society. Then we are given the boot. The passerby averts his gaze, and we are left to crawl out of the ditch alone, or stay there and die.

If I am bitter, it is because the bug I caught was picked up in all innocence. Fellow sufferers of my complaint can plead predisposition, poor heredity, family trouble, excess of the good life, and throwing themselves on a psychoanalyst's couch, spill out the rotten beans within and so effect a cure. I can do none of this. The doctor to whom I endeavored to explain what had happened listened with a superior smile, and then murmured something about emotionally destructive identification coupled with repressed guilt, and put me on a course of pills. They might have helped me if I had taken them. Instead I threw them down the drain and became more deeply imbued with the poison that seeped through me, made worse, of course, by the fatal recognition of my condition by the youngsters I had believed to be my friends, who nudged one another when I came into class, or, with stifled laughter, bent their loathsome little heads over their desks—until the moment arrived when I knew I could not continue, and took the decision to knock on the headmaster's door.

Well, that's over, done with, finished. Before I take myself to hospital or, alternatively, blot out memory, which is a second possibility, I want to establish what happened in the first place. So that, whatever becomes of me, this paper will be found, and the reader can make up his mind whether, as the doctor suggested, some want of inner balance made me an easy victim to superstitious fear, or whether, as I myself believe, my downfall was caused by an age-old magic, insidious, evil, its origins lost in the dawn of history. Suffice to say that he who first made the magic deemed himself immortal, and with unholy joy infected others, sowing in his heirs, throughout the world and down the centuries, the seeds of self-destruction.

To return to the present. The time was April, the Easter holidays. I had been to Greece twice before, but never Crete. I taught classics to the boys at the preparatory school, but my reason for visiting Crete was not to explore the sites of Knossos or Phaestus but to indulge a personal hobby. I have a minor talent for painting in oils, and this I find all-absorbing, whether on free days or in the school holidays. My work has been praised by one or two friends in the art world, and my ambition was to collect enough paintings to give a small exhibition. Even if none of them sold, the holding of a private show would be a happy achievement.

Here, briefly, a word about my personal life. I am a bachelor. Age forty-nine. Parents dead. Educated Sherbourne and Brasenose, Oxford. Profession, as you already know, schoolmaster. I play cricket and golf, badminton, and rather poor bridge. Interests, apart from teaching, art, as I have already said, and occasional travel, when I can afford it. Vices, up to the present, literally none. Which is not being self-complacent, but the truth is my life has been uneventful by any standard. Nor has this bothered me. I am probably a dull man. Emotionally I have had no complications. I was engaged to a pretty girl, a neighbor, when I was twenty-five, but she married somebody else. It hurt at the time, but the wound healed in less than a year. One fault, if fault it is, I have always had, which perhaps accounts for my hitherto monotonous life. This is an aversion to becoming involved with people. Friends I possess, but at a distance. Once involved, trouble occurs, and too often disaster follows.

I set out for Crete in the Easter hodlidays with no encumbrance but a fair-sized suitcase and my painting gear. A travel agent had recommended a hotel overlooking the Gulf of Mirabello on the eastern coast, after I had told him I was not interested in archaeological sights but wanted to paint. I was shown a brochure which seemed to meet my requirements. A pleasantly situated hotel close to the sea, and chalets by the water's edge where one slept and breakfasted. Clientele well-to-do, and although I count myself no snob I cannot abide paper bags and orange peel. A couple of pictures painted the previous winter—a view of St. Paul's Cathedral under snow, and another one of Hampstead Heath, both sold to an obliging female cousin—would pay for my journey, and I permitted myself an added indulgence, though it was really a necessity—the hiring of a small Volkswagen on arrival at the airport of Herakleion.

The flight, with an overnight stop in Athens, was pleasant and uneventful, the forty-odd miles' drive to my destination somewhat tedious, for being a cautious driver I took it slowly, and the twisting road, once I reached the hills, was decidedly hazardous. Cars passed me, or swerved toward me, hooting loudly. Also, it was very hot, and I was hungry. The sight of the blue Gulf of Mirabello and the splendid mountains to the east acted as a spur to sagging spirits, and once I arrived at the hotel, set delightfully in its own grounds, with lunch served to me on the terrace despite the fact that it was after two in afternoon—how different from England!—I was ready to relax and inspect my quarters. Disappointment followed. The young porter led me down a garden path flagged on either side by brilliant geraniums to a small chalet bunched in by neighbors on either side, and overlooking, not the sea, but a part of the garden laid out for mini-golf. My next-door neighbors, an obviously English mother and her brood, smiled in welcome from their balcony, which was strewn with bathing suits drying under the sun. Two middle-aged men were engaged in mini-golf. I might have been in Maidenhead.

"This won't do," I said, turning to my escort. "I have come here to paint. I must have a view of the sea."

He shrugged his shoulders, murmuring something about the chalets beside the sea being fully booked. It was not his fault, of course. I made him trek back to the hotel with me, and addressed myself to the clerk at the reception desk.

"There has been some mistake," I said. "I asked for a chalet overlooking the sea, and privacy above all."

The clerk smiled, apologized, began ruffling papers, and the inevitable excuses followed. My travel agent had not specifically booked a chalet overlooking the sea. These were in great demand, and were fully booked. Perhaps in a few days there might be some cancellations, one never could tell, in the meantime he was sure I would be very comfortable in the chalet that had been allotted to me. All the furnishings were the same, my breakfast would be served me, etc. etc.

I was adamant. I would not be fobbed off with the English family and the mini-golf. Not after having flown all those miles at considerable expense. I was bored by the whole affair, tired, and considerably annoyed.

"I am a professor of art," I told the clerk. "I have been commissioned to execute several paintings while I am here, and it is essential that I should have a view of the sea, and neighbors who will not disturb me."

(My passport states my occupation as professor. It sounds better than schoolmaster or teacher, and usually arouses respect in the attitude of reception clerks.)

The clerk seemed genuinely concerned, and repeated his apologies. He turned again to the sheaf of papers before him. Exasperated, I strode across the spacious hall and looked out of the door on to the terrace down to the sea.

"I cannot believe," I said, "that every chalet is taken. It's too early in the season. In summer, perhaps, but not now." I waved my hand toward the western side of the bay. "That group over there," I said, "down by the water's edge. Do you mean to say every single one of them is booked?"

He shook his head and smiled. "We do not usually open these until midseason. Also, they are more expensive. They have a bath as well as a shower."

"How much more expensive?" I hedged.

He told me. I made a quick calculation. I could afford it if I cut down on all other expenses. Had my evening meal in the hotel, and went without lunch. No extras in the bar, not even mineral water.

"Then there is no problem," I said grandly. "I will willingly pay more for privacy. And, if you have no objection, I should like to choose the chalet which would suit me best. I'll walk down to the sea now and then come back for the key, and your porter can bring my things."

I gave him no time to reply, but turned on my heel and went out onto the terrace. It paid to be firm. One moment's hesitation, and he would have fobbed me off with the stuffy chalet overlooking the mini-golf. I could imagine the consequences. The chattering children on the balcony next door, the possibly effusive mother, and the middle-aged golfers urging me to have a game. I could not have borne it.

I walked down through the garden to the sea, and as I did so my spirits rose. For this, of course, was what had been so highly colored on the agent's brochure, and why I had flown so many miles. No exaggeration, either. Little white-washed dwellings, discreetly set apart from one another, the sea washing the rocks below. There was a beach, from which people doubtless swam in high season, but no one was on it now, and, even if they should intrude, the chalets themselves were well to the left, inviolate, private. I peered at each in turn, mounting the steps, standing on the balconies. The clerk must have been telling the truth about none of them being let before full season, for all had their windows shuttered. Except one. And directly I mounted the steps and stood on the balcony, I knew that it must be mine. This was the view I had imagined. The sea beneath me, lapping the rocks, the bay widening into the gulf itself, and beyond the mountains. It was perfect. The chalets to the east of the hotel, which was out of sight anyway, could be ignored. One, close to a neck of land, stood on its own like a solitary outpost with a landing stage below, but this would only enhance my picture when I came to paint it. The rest were mercifully hidden by rising ground. I turned, and looked through the open windows to the bedroom within. Plain whitewashed walls, a stone floor, a comfortable divan bed with rugs upon it. A bedside table with a lamp and telephone. But for these last it had all the simplicity of a monk's cell, and I wished for nothing more.

I wondered why this chalet, and none of its neighbors, was unshuttered, and stepping inside I heard from the bathroom beyond the sound of running water. Not further disappointment, and the place booked after all? I put my head round the open door, and saw that it was a little Greek maid swabbing the bathroom floor. She seemed startled at the sight of me. I gestured, pointed, said, "Is this taken?" She did not understand, but answered me in Greek. Then she seized her cloth and pail and, plainly terrified, brushed past me to the entrance, leaving her work unfinished.

I went back into the bedroom and picked up the telephone, and in a moment the smooth voice of the reception clerk answered.

"This is Mr. Grey," I told him. "Mr. Timothy Grey. I was speaking to you just now about changing my chalet."

"Yes, Mr. Grey," he replied. He sounded puzzled. "Where are you speaking from?"

"Hold on a minute," I said. I put down the receiver and crossed the room to the balcony. The number was above the open door. It was sixty-two. I went back to the telephone. "I'm speaking from the chalet I have chosen," I said. "It happened to be open—one of the maids was cleaning the bathroom, and I'm afraid I scared her away. This chalet is ideal for my purpose. It is number sixty-two."

He did not answer immediately, and when he did he sounded doubtful. "Number sixty-two?" he repeated. And then, after a moment's hesitation, "I am not sure if it is available."

"Oh, for heaven's sake . . ." I began, exasperated, and I heard him talking in Greek to someone beside him at the desk. The conversation went back and forth between them; there was obviously some difficulty, which made me all the more determined.

"Are you there?" I said. "What's the trouble?"

More hurried whispers, and then he spoke to me again. "No trouble, Mr. Grey. It is just that we feel you might be more comfortable in number fifty-seven, which is a little nearer to the hotel."

"Nonsense," I said, "I prefer the view from here. What's wrong with number sixty-two? Doesn't the plumbing work?"

"Certainly the plumbing works," he assured me, while the whispering started again. "There is nothing wrong with the chalet. If you have made up your mind I will send down the porter with your luggage and the key."

He rang off, possibly to finish his discussion with the whisperer at his side. Perhaps they were going to step up the price. If they did, I would have further argument. The chalet was no different from its empty neighbors, but the position, dead center to sea and mountains, was all I had dreamed and more. I stood on the balcony, looking out across the sea and smiling. What a prospect, what a place! I would unpack and have a swim, then put up my easel and do a preliminary sketch before starting serious work in the morning.

I heard voices, and saw the little maid staring at me from halfway up the garden path, cloth and pail still in hand. Then, as the young porter advanced downhill bearing my suitcase and painting gear, she must have realized that I was to be the occupant of number sixty-two, for she stopped him midway, and another whispered conversation began. I had evidently caused a break in the smooth routine of the hotel. A few moments later they climbed the steps to the chalet together, the porter to set down my luggage, the maid doubtless to finish her swabbing of the bathroom floor. I had no desire to be on awkward terms with either of them, and, smiling cheerfully, placed coins in both their hands.

"Lovely view," I said loudly, pointing to the sea. "Must go for a swim," and made breast-stroke gestures to show my intent, hoping for the ready smile of the native Greek, usually so responsive to goodwill.

The porter evaded my eyes and bowed gravely, accepting the tip nevertheless. As for the little maid, distress was evident in her face, and, forgetting about the bathroom floor, she hurried after him. I could hear them talking as they walked up the garden path together to the hotel.

Well, it was not my problem. Staff and management must sort out their troubles between them. I had got what I wanted, and that was all that concerned me. I unpacked and made myself at home. Then, slipping on bathing-trunks, I stepped down to the ledge of rock beneath the balcony, and ventured a toe into the water. It was surprisingly chill, despite the hot sun that had been upon it all day. Never mind. I must prove my mettle, if only to myself. I took the plunge and gasped, and being a cautious swimmer at the best of times, especially in strange waters, swam round and round in circles rather like a sea-lion pup in a zoological pool.

Refreshing, undoubtedly, but a few minutes were enough, and as I climbed out again onto the rocks I saw that the porter and the little maid had been watching me all the time from behind a flowering bush up the garden path. I hoped I had not lost face. And anyway, why the interest? People must be swimming every day from the other chalets. The bathing suits on the various balconies proved it. I dried myself on the balcony, observing how the sun, now in the western sky behind my chalet, made dappled patterns on the water. Fishing boats were returning to the little harbour port a few miles distant, the chug-chug engines making a pleasing sound.

I dressed, taking the precaution of having a hot bath, for the first swim of the year is always numbing, and then set up my easel and became absorbed. This was why I was here, and nothing else mattered. I worked for a couple of hours, and as the light failed, and the color of the sea deepened and the mountains turned a softer purple blue, I rejoiced to think that tomorrow I should be able to seize this afterglow in paint instead of charcoal, and the picture would begin to come alive.

It was time to stop. I stacked away my gear, and before changing for dinner and drawing the shutters—doubtless there were mosquitoes, and I had no wish to be bitten—watched a motorboat with gentle purring engine draw in softly to the eastward point with the landing stage away to my right. Three people aboard, fishing enthusiasts no doubt, a woman amongst them. One man, a local, probably, made the boat fast, and stopped on the landing stage to help the woman ashore. Then all three stared in my direction, and the second man, who had been standing in the stern, put up a pair of binoculars and fixed them on me. He held them steady for several minutes, focusing, no doubt, on every detail of my personal appearance, which is unremarkable enough, heaven knows, and would have continued had I not suddenly become annoyed and withdrawn into the bedroom, slamming the shutters too. How rude can you get, I asked myself? Then I remembered that these western chalets were all unoccupied, and mine was the first to open for the season. Possibly this was the reason for the intense interest I appeared to cause, beginning with members of the hotel staff and now embracing guests as well. Interest would soon fade. I was neither pop star nor millionaire. And my painting efforts, however pleasing to myself, were hardly likely to draw a fascinated crowd.

Punctually at eight o'clock I walked up the garden path to the hotel and presented myself in the dining room for dinner. It was moderately full and I was allotted a table in the corner, suitable to my single status, close to the screen dividing the service entrance from the kitchens. Never mind. I preferred this position to the center of the room, where I could tell immediately that the hotel clientele were on what my mother used to describe as an "all fellows to football" basis.

I enjoyed my dinner, treated myself—despite my deluxe chalet—to half a bottle of domestic wine, and was peeling an orange when an almighty crash from the far end of the room disturbed us all. Waiters hurried to the scene. Heads turned, mine amongst them. A hoarse American voice, hailing from the Deep South, called loudly, "For God's sake clear up this God-darn mess!" It came from a square-shouldered man of middle age whose face was so swollen and blistered by exposure to the sun that he looked as if he had been stung by a million bees. His eyes were sunk into his head, which was bald on top, with a grizzled thatch on either side, and the pink crown had the appearance of being tightly stretched, like the skin of a sausage about to burst. A pair of enormous ears the size of clams gave further distortion to his appearance, while a drooping wisp of moustache did nothing to hide the protruding underlip, thick as blubber and about as moist. I have seldom set eyes on a more unattractive individual. A woman, I suppose his wife, sat beside him, stiff and bolt upright, apparently unmoved by the debris on the floor, which appeared to consist chiefly of bottles. She was likewise middle-aged, with a mop of tow-colored hair turning white, and a face as sunburned as her husband's, but mahogany brown instead of red.

"Let's get the hell out of here and go to the bar!" The hoarse strains echoed across the room. The guests at the other tables turned discreetly back to their own dinners, and I must have been the only one to watch the unsteady exit of the bee-stung spouse and his wife—I could see the deaf-aid in her ear, hence possibly her husband's rasping tones—as he literally rolled past me to the bar, a lurching vessel in the wake of his steady partner. I silently commended the efficiency of the hotel staff, who made short work of clearing the wreckage.

The dining-room emptied. "Coffee in the bar, sir," murmured my waiter. Fearing a crush and loud chatter, I hesitated before entering, for the camaraderie of hotel bars has always bored me, but I hate going without my afternoon coffee. I need not have worried. The bar was empty, apart from the white-coated server behind the bar, and the American sitting at a table with his wife. Neither of them was speaking. There were three empty beer bottles already on the table behind the bar. I sat myself on a stool and ordered coffee.

The bartender, who spoke excellent English, asked if I had spent a pleasant day. I told him yes, I had had a good flight, found the road from Herakleion hazardous, and my first swim rather cold. He explained that it was still early in the year. "In any case," I told him, "I have come to paint, and swimming will take second place. I have a chalet right on the waterfront, number sixty-two, and the view from the balcony is perfect."

Rather odd. He was polishing a glass, and his expression changed. He seemed about to say something, then evidently thought better of it, and continued with his work.

"Turn that Goddamn record off!"

The hoarse, imperious summons filled the empty room. The barman made at once for the gramaphone in the corner and adjusted the switch. A moment later the summons range forth again.

"Bring me another bottle of beer!"

Now, had I been the bartender I should have turned to the man and, like a parent to a child, insisted that he say please. Instead, the brute was promptly served, and I was just downing my coffee when the voice from the table echoed through the room once more.

"Hi, you there, chalet number sixty-two. You're not superstitious?"

I turned on my stool. He was staring at me, glass in hand. His wife looked straight in front of her. Perhaps she had removed her deaf-aid. Remembering the maxim that one must humor madmen and drunks, I replied courteously enough.

"No," I said, "I'm not superstitious. Should I be?"

He began to laugh, his scarlet face creasing into a hundred lines.

"Well, God-darn it, I would be," he answered. "The fellow from that chalet was drowned only two weeks ago. Missing for two days, and then his body brought up in a net by a local fisherman, half eaten by octupuses."

He began to shake with laughter, slapping his hand on his knee. I turned away in disgust, and raised my eyebrows in inquiry to the bartender.

"An unfortunate accident," he murmured. "Mr. Gordon was such a nice gentleman. Interested in archaeology. It was very warm the night he disappeared, and he must have gone swimming after dinner. Of course the police were called. We were all most distressed here at the hotel. You understand, sir, we don't talk about it much. It would be bad for business. But I do assure you the bathing is perfectly safe. This is the first accident we have ever had."

"Oh, quite," I said.

Nevertheless, it was rather off-putting, the fact that the poor chap had been the last to use my chalet. However, it was not as though he had died in the bed. And I was not superstitious. I understood now why the staff had been reluctant to let the chalet again so soon, and why the little maid had been upset.

"I tell you one thing," boomed the revolting voice. "Don't go swimming after midnight, or the octupuses will get you too." This statement was followed by another outburst of laughter. Then he said, "Come on, Maud. We're for bed," and I heard him noisily shove the table aside.

I breathed more easily when the room was clear and we were alone.

"What an impossible man," I said. "Can't the management get rid of him?"

The bartender shrugged. "Business is business. What can they do? The Stolls have plenty of money. This is their second season here, and they arrived when we opened in March. They seem to be crazy about the place. It's only this year, though, that Mr. Stoll has become such a heavy drinker. He'll kill himself if he goes on at this rate. It's always like this, night after night. Yet his day must be healthy enough. Out at sea fishing from early morning until sundown."

"I dare say more bottles go over the side than he catches fish," I observed.

"Could be," the bartender agreed. "He never brings his fish to the hotel. The boatman takes them home, I dare say."

"I feel sorry for the wife."

The bartender shrugged. "She's the one with the money," he replied sotto voice, for a couple of guests had just entered the bar, "and I don't think Mr. Stoll has it all his own way. Being deaf may be convenient to her at times. But she never leaves his side, I'll grant her that. Goes fishing with him every day . . . Yes, gentlemen, what can I get for you?"

He turned to his new customers and I made my escape. The cliché that it takes all sorts to make a world passed through my head. Thank heaven it was not my world, and Mr. Stoll and his deaf wife could burn themselves black under the sun all day at sea as far as I was concerned, and break beer bottles every evening into the bargain. In any event, they were not neighbors. Number sixty-two may have had the unfortunate victim of a drowning accident for its last occupant, but at least this had ensured privacy for its present tenant.

I walked down the garden path to my abode. It was a clear starlit night. The air was balmy, and sweet with the scent of the flowering shrubs planted thickly in the red earth. Standing on my balcony, I looked out across the sea toward the distant shrouded mountains and the harbor lights from the little fishing port. To my right winked the lights of the other chalets, giving a pleasing, almost fairy impression, like a clever backcloth on a stage. Truly a wonderful spot, and I blessed the travel agent who had recommended it.

I let myself in through my shuttered doorway and turned on the bedside lamp. The room looked welcoming and snug; I could not have been better housed. I undressed, and before getting into bed remembered I had left a book I wanted to glance at on the balcony. I opened the shutters and picked it up from the deck chair where I had thrown it, and once more, before turning it, glanced out at the open sea. Most of the fairy lights had been extinguished, but the chalet that stood on its own on the extreme point still had its light burning on the balcony. The boat, tied to the landing stage, bore a riding light. Seconds later I saw something moving close to my rocks. It was the snorkel of an underwater swimmer. I could see the narrow pipe, like a minute periscope, move steadily across the still, dark surface of the sea. Then it disappeared to the far left out of sight. I drew my shutters and went inside.

I don't know why it was, but the sight of that moving object was somehow disconcerting. It made me think of the unfortunate man who had been drowned during a midnight swim. My predecessor. He, too, perhaps, had sallied forth one balmy evening such as this, intent on underwater exploration, and by so doing lost his life. One would imagine the unhappy accident would scare off other hotel visitors from swimming alone at night. I made a firm decision never to bathe except in broad daylight, and—chickenhearted, maybe—well within my depth.

I read a few pages of my book, then, feeling ready for sleep, turned to switch out my light. In doing so I clumsily bumped the telephone, which fell to the floor. I bent over, picked it up, luckily no damage done, and saw that the small drawer that was part of the fixture had fallen open. It contained a scrap of paper, or rather a card, with the name Charles Gordon upon it, and an address in Bloomsbury. Surely Gordon had been the name of my predecessor? The little maid, when she cleaned the room, had not thought to open the drawer. I turned the card over. There was something scrawled on the other side, the words "Not after midnight." And then, maybe as an after-thought, the figure thirty-eight. I replaced the card in the drawer and switched off the light. Perhaps I was overtired after the journey, but it was well past two before I finally got off to sleep. I lay awake for no rhyme or reason, listening to the water lapping against the rocks beneath my balcony.

I painted solidly for three days, never quitting my chalet except for the morning swim and my evening meal at the hotel. Nobody bothered me. An obliging waiter brought my breakfast, from which I saved rolls for midday lunch, the little maid made my bed and did her chores without disturbing me, and when I had finished my impressionistic scene on the afternoon of the third day I felt quite certain it was one of the best things I had ever done. It would take pride of place in the planned exhibition of my work. Well-satisfied, I could now relax, and I determined to explore along the coast the following day, and discover another view to whip up inspiration. The weather was glorious. Warm as a good English June. And the best thing about the whole site was the total absence of neighbors. The other guests kept to their side of the domain, and, apart from bows and nods from adjoining tables as one entered the dining room for dinner, no one attempted to strike up acquaintance. I also took good care to drink my coffee in the bar before the obnoxious Mr. Stoll had left his table.

I realized now that it was his boat which lay anchored off the point. They were away too early in the morning for me to watch their departure, but I used to spot them returning in the late afternoon; his square, hunched form was easily recognizable, and the occasional hoarse shout to the man in charge of the boat as they came to the landing stage. Theirs, too, was the isolated chalet on the point, and I wondered if he had picked it purposely in order to soak himself into oblivion out of sight and earshot of his nearest neighbors. Well, good luck to him, as long as he did not obtrude his offensive presence upon me.

Feeling the need of gentle exercise, I decided to spend the rest of the afternoon taking a stroll to the eastern side of the hotel grounds. Once again I congratulated myself on having escaped the cluster of chalets in this populated quarter. Mini-golf and tennis were in full swing, and the little beach was crowded with sprawling bodies on every available patch of sand. But soon the murmur of the world was behind me, and, screened and safe behind the flowering shrubs, I found myself on the point near to the landing stage. The boat was not yet at its mooring, nor even in sight out in the gulf. A sudden temptation to peep at the unpleasant Mr. Stoll's chalet swept upon me. I crept up the little path, feeling as furtive as a burglar on the prowl, and stared up at the shuttered windows. It was no different from its fellows, or mine for that matter, except for a telltale heap of bottles lying on the corner of the balcony. Brute . . . Then something else caught my eye. A pair of frog feet, and a snorkel. Surely, with all that liquor inside him, he did not venture his carcass under water? Perhaps he sent the local Greek whom he employed as crew to seek for crabs. I remembered the snorkel on my first evening, close to the rocks, and the riding light in the boat.

I moved away, for I thought I could hear someone coming down the path and did not want to be caught prying, but before doing so I glanced up at the number of the chalet. It was thirty-eight. The figure had no particular significance for me then, but later on, changing for dinner, I picked up the tiepin I had placed on my bedside table, and on sudden impulse opened the drawer beneath the telephone to look at my predecessor's card again. Yes, I thought so. The scrawled figure *was* thirty-eight. Pure coincidence, of course, and yet . . . "Not after midnight." The words suddenly had meaning. Stoll had warned me about swimming late on my first evening. Had he warned Gordon too? And Gordon had jotted down the warning on this card with Stoll's chalet number underneath? It made sense, but obviously poor Gordon had disregarded the advice. And so, apparently, did one of the occupants of chalet thirty-eight.

I finished changing, and instead of replacing the card in the telephone drawer put it in my wallet. I had an uneasy feeling that it was my duty to hand it in to the reception desk in case it threw any light on my unfortunate predecessor's demise. I toyed with the thought through dinner, but came to no decision. The point was, I might become involved. And as far as I knew the case was closed. There was little point in my suddenly coming forward with a calling card lying forgotten in a drawer that probably had no significance at all.

It so happened that the people seated to the right of me in the dining room appeared to have gone, and the Stolls' table in the corner now came into view without my being obliged to turn my head. I could watch them without making it too obvious, and I was struck by the fact that he never once addressed a word to her. They made an odd contrast. She stiff as a ramrod, prim looking, austere, forking her food to her mouth like a Sunday school teacher on an outing, and he, more scarlet than ever, like a great swollen sausage, pushing aside most of what the waiter placed before him after the first mouthful, and reaching out a pudgy, hairy hand to an ever-emptying glass.

I finished my dinner and went through to the bar to drink my coffee. I was early, and had the place to myself. The bartender and I exchanged the usual pleasantries and then, after an allusion to the weather, I jerked my head in the direction of the dining room.

"I noticed our friend Mr. Stoll and his lady spent the whole day at sea as usual," I said.

The bartender shrugged. "Day after day, it never varies," he replied, "and mostly in the same direction, westward out of the bay into the gulf. It can be squally, too, at times, but they don't seem to care."

"I don't know how she puts up with him," I said. "I watched them at dinner—he didn't speak to her at all. I wonder what the other guests make of him."

"They keep well clear, sir. You saw how it was for yourself. If he ever does open his mouth it's only to be rude. And the same goes for the staff. The girls dare not go in to clean the chalet until he's out of the way. And the smell!" He grimaced, and leaned forward confidentially. "The girls say he brews his own beer. He lights the fire in the chimney, and has a pot standing, filled with rotting grain, like some sort of pig swill! Oh, yes, he drinks it right enough. Imagine the state of his liver, after what he consumes at dinner and afterward here in the bar!"

"I suppose," I said, "that's why he keeps his balcony light on so late at night. Drinking pig swill until the small hours. Tell me, which of the hotel visitors is it who goes underwater swimming?"

The bartender looked surprised. "No one, to my knowledge. Not since the accident, anyway. Poor Mr. Gordon liked a night swim, at least so we supposed. He was one of the few visitors who ever talked to Mr. Stoll, now I think of it. They had quite a conversation here one evening in the bar."

"Indeed?"

"Not about swimming, though, or fishing either. They were discussing antiquities. There's a fine little museum here in the village, you know, but it's closed at present for repairs. Mr. Gordon had some connection with the British Museum in London."

"I wouldn't have thought," I said, "that would interest friend Stoll."

"Ah," said the bartender, "you'd be surprised. Mr. Stoll is no fool. Last year he and Mrs. Stoll used to take the car and visit all the famous sites, Knossos, Mallia, and other places not so well-known. This year it's quite different. It's the boat and fishing every day."

"And Mr. Gordon," I pursued, "did he ever go fishing with them?"

"No, sir. Not to my knowledge. He hired a car, like you, and explored the district. He was writing a book, he told me, on archaeological finds in eastern Crete, and their connection with Greek mythology."

"Mythology?"

"Yes, I understood him to tell Mr. Stoll it was mythology, but it was all above my head, you can imagine, nor did I hear much of the conversation—we were busy that evening in the bar. Mr. Gordon was a quiet sort of gentleman, rather after your own style, if you'll excuse me, sir, seeming very interested in what they were discussing, all to do with the old gods. They were at it for over an hour."

H'm . . . I thought of the card in my wallet. Should I, or should I not, hand it over to the reception clerk at the desk? I said good-night to the bartender and went back through the dining room to the hall. The Stolls had just left their table and were walking ahead of me. I hung back until the way was clear, surprised that they had turned their backs upon the bar and were making for the hall. I stood by the rack of postcards, to give myself an excuse for loitering, but out of their range of vision, and watched Mrs. Stoll take her coat from a hook in the lobby near the entrance, while her unpleasant husband visited the cloakroom, and then the pair of them walked out of the front door, which led direct to the car park. They must be going for a drive. With Stoll at the wheel in his condition?

I hesitated. The reception clerk was on the telephone. It wasn't the moment to hand over the card. Some impulse, like that of a small boy playing detective, made me walk to my own car, and when Stoll's taillight was out of sight—he was driving a Mercedes—I followed in his wake. There was only the one road, and he was heading east toward the village and the harbor lights. I lost him, inevitably, on reaching the little port, for, instinctively making for the quayside opposite what appeared to be a main café, I thought he must have done the same. I parked the Volkswagen, and looked around me. No sign of the Mercedes. Just a sprinkling of other tourists like myself, and local inhabitants, strolling, or drinking in front of the café.

Oh well, forget it, I'd sit and enjoy the scene, have a lemonade. I must have sat there for over half-an-hour, savoring what is known as "local color," amused by the passing crowd, Greek families taking the air, pretty, self-conscious girls eyeing the youths, who appeared to stick together, practising a form of segregation, a bearded Orthodox priest who smoked incessantly at the table next to me, playing some game of dice with a couple of very old men, and of course the familiar bunch of hippies from my own country, considerably longer-haired than anybody else, dirtier, and making far more noise. When they switched on a transitor and squatted on the cobbled stones behind me, I felt it was time to move.

I paid for my lemonade, and strolled to the end of the quay and back—the line upon line of fishing boats would be colorful by day, and possibly the scene worth painting—and then I crossed the street, my eye caught by a glint of water inland, where a side road appeared to end in a cul-de-sac. This must be the feature mentioned in the guidebook as the Bottomless Pool, much frequented and photographed by tourists in the high season. It was larger than I had expected, quite a sizable lake, the water full of scum and floating debris, and I did not envy those who had the temerity to use the diving board at the farthest end of it by day.

Then I saw the Mercedes It was drawn up opposite a dimly-lit café, and there was no mistaking the hunched figure at the table, beer bottles before him, the upright lady at his side, but to my surprise, and I may add disgust, he was not imbibing alone but appeared to be sharing his after dinner carousal with a crowd of raucous fishermen at the adjoining table.

Clamor and laughter filled the air. They were evidently mocking him, Greek courtesy forgotten in their cups, while strains of song burst forth from some younger member of the clan, and suddenly he put out his hand and swept the empty bottles from his table onto the pavement, with the inevitable crash of broken glass and the accompanying cheers of his companions. I expected the local police to appear at any moment and break up the party, but there was no sign of authority. I did not care what happened to Stoll—a night in jail might sober him up—but it was a wretched business for his wife. However, it wasn't my affair, and I was turning to go back to the quay when he staggered to his feet, applauded by the fishermen, and, lifting the remaining bottle from his table, swung it over his head. Then, with amazing dexterity for one in his condition, he pitched it like a discus-thrower into the lake. It must have missed me by a couple of feet, and he saw me duck. This was too much. I advanced toward him, livid with rage.

"What the hell are you playing at?" I shouted.

He stood before me, swaying on his feet. The laughter from the café ceased as his cronies watched with interest. I expected a flood of abuse, but Stoll's swollen face creased into a grin, and he lurched forward and patted me on the arm.

"Know something?" he said. "If you hadn't been in the way I could have lobbed it into the center of the Goddamn pool. Which is more than any of these fellows could. Not a pure-blooded Cretan amongst them. They're all of them Goddamn Turks."

I tried to shake him off, but he clung onto me with the effusive affection of the habitual drunkard who had suddenly found, or imagines he has found, a lifelong friend.

"You're from the hotel, aren't you?" he hiccoughed. "Don't deny it, buddy boy, I've got a good eye for faces. You're the fellow who paints all day on his Goddamn porch. Well, I admire you for it. Know a bit about art myself. I might even buy your picture."

His bonhomie was offensive, his attempt at patronage intolerable.

"I'm sorry," I said stiffly, "the picture is not for sale."

"Oh, come off it," he retorted. "You artists are all the same. Play hard to get until someone offers 'em a darn good price. Take Charlie Gordon now . . ." He broke off, peering slyly into my face. "Hang on, you didn't meet Charlie Gordon, did you?"

"No," I said shortly, "he was before my time."

"That's right, that's right," he agreed, "poor fellow's dead. Drowned in the bay there, right under your rocks. At least, that's where they found him."

His slit eyes were practically closed in his swollen face, but I knew he was watching for my reaction.

"Yes," I said, "so I understand. He wasn't an artist."

"An artist?" Stoll repeated the word after me, then burst into a guffaw of laughter. "No, he was a connoisseur, and I guess that means the same Goddamn thing to a chap like me. Charlie Gordon, connoisseur. Well, it didn't do him much good in the end, did it?"

"No," I said, "obviously not."

He was making an effort to pull himself together, and, still rocking on his feet, he fumbled for a packet of cigarettes and a lighter. He lit one for himself, then offered me the packet. I shook my head, telling him I did not smoke. Then, greatly daring, I observed, "I don't drink either."

"Good for you," he answered astonishingly, "neither do I. The beer they sell here is all piss anyway, and the wine is poison." He looked over his shoulder to the group at the café, and with a conspiratorial wink dragged me to the wall beside the pool.

"I told you all those bastards are Turks, and so they are," he said, "wine-drinking, coffee-drinking Turks. They haven't brewed the right stuff here for over five thousand years. They knew how to do it then."

I remembered what the bartender had told me about the pig swill in his chalet. "Is that so?" I enquired.

He winked again, and then his slit eyes widened, and I noticed that they were naturally bulbous and protuberant, a discolored muddy brown with the whites red-flecked. "Know something?" he whispered hoarsely. "The scholars have got it all wrong. It was beer the Cretans drank here in the mountains, brewed from spruce and ivy, long before wine. Wine was discovered centuries later by the Goddamn Greeks."

He steadied himself, one hand on the wall, the other on my arm. Then he leaned forward and was sick into the pool. I was very nearly sick myself.

"That's better," he said, "gets rid of the poison. Doesn't do to have poison in the system. Tell you what, we'll go back to the hotel and you shall come along and have a nightcap at our chalet. I've taken a fancy to you, Mr. What's-your-name. You've got the right ideas. Don't drink, don't smoke, and you paint pictures. What's your job?"

It was impossible to shake myself clear, and I was forced to let him tow me across the road. Luckily the group at the café had now dispersed, disappointed, no doubt, because we had not come to blows, and Mrs. Stoll had climbed into the Mercedes and was sitting in the passenger seat in front.

"Don't take any notice of her," he said. "She's stone-deaf unless you bawl at her. Plenty of room at the back."

"Thank you," I said, "I've got my own car on the quay."

"Suit yourself," he answered. "Well, come on, tell me, Mr. Artist, what's your job? An academician?"

I could have left it at that, but some pompous strain in me made me tell the truth, in a foolish hope that he would then consider me too dull to cultivate.

"I'm a teacher," I said, "in a boys' preparatory school."

He stopped in his tracks, his wet mouth open wide in a delighted grin. "Oh, my God," he shouted, "that's rich, that's really rich. A Goddamn tutor, a nurse to babes and sucklings. You're one of us, my buddy, you're one of us. And you've the nerve to tell me you've never brewed spruce and ivy!"

He was raving mad, of course, but at least this sudden burst of hilarity had made him free my arm, and he went on ahead of me to his car, shaking his head from side to side, his legs bearing his cumbersome body in a curious jog-trot, one-two . . . one-two . . . like a clumsy horse.

I watched him climb into the car beside his wife, and then I moved swiftly away, to make for the safety of the quayside, but he had turned his car with surprising agility, and had caught up with me before I reached the corner of the street. He thrust his head out of the window, smiling still.

"Come and call on us, Mr. Tutor, any time you like. You'll always find a welcome. Tell him so, Maud. Can't you see the fellow's shy?"

His bawling word of command echoed through the street. Strolling passersby looked in our direction. The stiff, impassive face of Mrs. Stoll peered over her husband's shoulder. She seemed quite unperturbed, as if nothing was wrong, as if driving in a foreign village beside a drunken husband was the most usual pastime in the world.

"Good evening," she said in a voice without any expression. "Pleased to meet you, Mr. Tutor. Do call on us. Not after midnight. Chalet thirty-eight . . ."

Stoll waved his hand, and the car went roaring up the street to cover the few kilometers to the hotel.

It would not be true to say the encounter cast a blight on my holiday and put me off the place. A half-truth, perhaps. I was angry and disgusted, but only with the Stolls. I awoke refreshed after a good night's sleep to another brilliant day, and nothing seems so bad in the morning. I had only the one problem, which was to avoid Stoll and his equally half-witted wife. They were out in their boat all day, so this was easy. By dining early I could escape them in the dining room. They never walked about the grounds, and meeting them face to face in the garden was not likely. If I happened to be on my balcony when they returned from fishing in the evening, and he turned his field glasses in my direction, I would promptly disappear inside my chalet. In any event, with luck, he might have forgotten my existence, or, if that was too much to hope for, the memory of our evening's conversation might have passed from his mind. The episode had been unpleasant, even, in a curious sense, alarming, but I was not going to let it spoil the time that remained to me. I had come here to paint and relax, and was determined to go on doing so.

The boat had left its landing stage by the time I came onto my balcony to have breakfast, and I intended to carry out my plan of exploring the coast with my painting gear, and once absorbed in my hobby could forget all about them. And I would not pass on to the management poor Gordon's scribbled card. I guessed now what had happened. The poor devil, without realizing where his conversation in the bar would lead him, had been intrigued by Stoll's smattering of mythology and nonsense about ancient Crete, and, as an archaeologist, had thought further conversation might prove fruitful. He had accepted an invitation to visit chalet thirty-eight—the uncanny similarity of the words on the card and those spoken by Mrs. Stoll still haunted me—though why he had chosen to swim across the bay instead of walking the slightly longer way by the rock path was a mystery. A touch of bravado, perhaps? Who knows? Once in Stoll's chalet he had been induced, poor victim, to drink some of the hell-brew offered by his host, which must have knocked all sense and judgment out of him, and when he took to the water once again, the carousal over, what followed was bound to happen. I only hoped he had been too far gone to panic, and sank instantly. Stoll had never come forward to give the facts, and that was that. Indeed, my theory of what had happened was based on intuition alone, coincidental scraps that appeared to fit, and prejudice. It was time to dismiss the whole thing from my mind and concentrate on the day ahead.

Or rather, days. My exploration along the coast westward, in the opposite direction from the harbor, proved even more successful than I had anticipated. I followed the winding road to the left of the hotel, and having climbed for several kilometers descended again from the hills to sea level, where the land on my right suddenly flattened out to what seemed to be a great stretch of dried marsh, sun-baked, putty-colored, the dazzling blue sea affording a splendid contrast as it lapped the stretch of land on either side. Driving closer I saw that it was not marsh at all but salt flats, with narrow causeways running between them, the flats themselves contained by walls intersected by dykes to allow the seawater to drain, leaving the salt behind. Here and there were the ruins of abandoned windmills, their rounded walls like castle keeps, and in a rough patch of ground a few hundred yards distant, and close to the sea, was a small church—I could see the minute cross on the roof shining in the sun. Then the salt flats ended abruptly, the land rose once more to form the long, narrow isthmus of Spinalongha beyond.

I bumped the Volkswagen down to the track leading to the flats. The place was quite deserted. This, I decided, after viewing the scene from every angle, would be my pitch for the next few days. The ruined church in the foreground, the abandoned windmills beyond, the salt flats on the left, and blue water rippling to the shore of the peninsula on my right.

I set up my easel, planted my battered felt hat on my head, and forgot everything but the scene before me. Those three days on the salt flats—for I repeated the expedition on successive days—were the high spot of my holiday. Solitude and peace were absolute. I never saw a single soul. The occasional car wound its way alng the coast road in the distance and then vanished. I broke off for sandwiches and lemonade, which I'd brought with me, and then, when the sun was hottest, rested by the ruined windmill. I returned to the hotel in the cool of the evening, had an early dinner, and then retired to my chalet to read until bedtime. A hermit at his prayers could not have wished for greater seclusion.

The fourth day, having completed two separate paintings from different angles, yet loath to leave my chosen territory, which had now become a personal stamping ground, I stacked my gear in the car and struck off on foot to the rising terrain of the peninsula, with the idea of choosing a new site for the following day. Height might give an added advantage. I toiled up the hill, fanning myself with my hat, for it was extremely hot, and was surprised when I reached the summit to find how narrow was the peninsula, no more than a long neck of land with the sea immediately below me. Not the calm water that washed the salt-flats I had left behind, but the curling crests of the outer gulf itself, whipped by a northerly wind that nearly blew my hat out of my hand. A genius might have caught those varying shades on canvas—turquoise blending into Aegean blue with wine-deep shadows beneath—but not an amateur like myself. Besides, I could hardly stand upright. Canvas and easel would have instantly blown away.

I climbed downward toward a clump of broom affording shelter, where I could rest for a few minutes and watch that curling sea, and it was then that I saw the boat. It was moored close to a small inlet where the land curved and the water was comparatively smooth. There was no mistaking the craft: it was theirs all right. The Greek they employed as crew was seated in the bows, with a fishing line over the side, but from his lounging attitude the fishing did not seem to be serious, and I judged he was taking his siesta. He was the only occupant of the boat. I glanced directly beneath me to the spit of sand along the shore, and saw there a rough stone building, more or less ruined, built against the cliff face, possibly used at one time as a shelter for sheep or goats. There was a haversack and a picnic basket lying by the entrance, and a coat. The Stolls must have landed earlier from the boat, although nosing the bows of the craft onto the shore must have been hazardous in the running sea, and were now taking their ease out of the wind. Perhaps Stoll was even brewing his peculiar mixture of spruce and ivy, with some goat dung added for good measure, and this lonely spot on the isthmus of Spinalongha was his "still."

Suddenly the fellow in the boat sat up, and winding in his line he moved to the stern and stood there, watching the water. I saw something move, a form beneath the surface, and then the form itself emerged, headpiece goggles, rubber suiting, Aqualung and all. Then it was hidden from me by the Greek bending to assist the swimmer to remove his top gear, and my attention was diverted to the ruined shelter on the shore. Something was standing in the entrance. I say "something" because, doubtless owing to a trick of light, it had at first the shaggy appearance of a colt standing on its hand legs. Legs and even rump were covered with hair, and then I realized that it was Stoll himself, naked, his arms and chest as hairy as the rest of him. Only his swollen scarlet face proclaimed him for the man he was, with the enormous ears like saucers standing out from either side of his bald head. I had never in all my life seen a more revolting sight. He came out into the sunlight and looked toward the boat, and then, as if well pleased with himself and his world, strutted forward, pacing up and down the spit of sand before the ruined shelter with that curious movement I had noticed earlier in the village, not the rolling gait of a drunken man but a stumping jog trot, arms akimbo, his chest thrust forward, his backside prominent behind him.

The swimmer, having discarded goggles and Aqualung, was now coming into the beach with long leisurely strokes, still wearing flippers—I could see them thrash the surface like a giant fish. Then, flippers cast aside on the sand, the swimmer stood up, and despite the disguise of the rubber suiting I saw, with astonishment, that it was Mrs. Stoll. She was carrying some sort of bag around her neck, and, advancing up the sand to meet her strutting husband, she lifted it over her head and gave it to him. I did not hear them exchange a word, and they went together to the hut and disappeared inside. As for the Greek, he had gone once more to the bows of the boat to resume his idle fishing.

I lay down under cover of the broom and waited. I would give them twenty minutes, half-an-hour, perhaps, then make my way back to the salt flats and my car. As it happened, I did not have to wait so long. It was barely ten minutes before I heard a shout below me on the beach, and peering through the broom I saw that they were both standing on the spit of sand, haversack, picnic basket, and flippers in hand, and Stoll himself dressed. The Greek was already starting the engine, and immediately afterward he began to pull up the anchor. Then he steered the boat slowly inshore, touching it beside a ledge of rock where the Stolls had installed themselves. They climbed aboard, and in another moment the Greek had turned the boat and it was heading out to sea away from the sheltered inlet and into the gulf. Then it rounded the point and was out of my sight.

Curiosity was too much for me. I scrambled down the cliff onto the sand and made straight for the ruined shelter. As I thought, it had been a haven for goats; the mudded floor reeked, and their droppings were everywhere. In a corner, though, a clearing had been made, and there were planks of wood, forming a sort of shelf. The inevitable beer bottles were stacked beneath this, but whether they had contained the local brew or Stoll's own poison I could not tell. The shelf itself held odds and ends of pottery, as though someone had been digging in a rubbish dump and had turned up broken pieces of discarded household junk. There was no earth upon them, though; they were scaled with barnacles, and some of them were damp, and it suddenly occurred to me that these were what archaeologists called "sherds," and came from the seabed. Mrs. Stoll had been exploring, and exploring underwater, whether for shells or for something of greater interest I did not know, and these pieces scattered here were throw-outs, of no use, and so neither she nor her husband had bothered to remove them. I am no judge of these things and after looking around me, and finding nothing of further interest, I left the ruin.

The move was a fatal one. As I turned to climb the cliff I heard the throb of an engine, and the boat had returned once more, to cruise along the shore, so I judged from its position. All three heads were turned in my direction, and inevitably the squat figure in the sterm had field glasses poised. He would have no difficulty, I feared, in distinguishing who it was that had just left the ruined shelter and was struggling up the cliff to the hill above.

I did not look back but went on climbing, my hat pulled down well over my brows in the vain hope that it might afford some sort of concealment. After all, I might have been any tourist who had happened to be at that particular spot at that particular time. Nevertheless, I feared recognition was inevitable. I tramped back to the car on the salt flats, tired, breathless, and thoroughly irritated. I wished I had never decided to explore the farther side of the peninsula. The Stolls would think I had been spying upon them, which indeed was true. My pleasure in the day was spoiled. I decided to pack it in and go back to the hotel. Luck was against me, though, for I had hardly turned onto the track leading from the marsh to the road when I noticed that one of my tires was flat. By the time I had put on the spare wheel—for I am ham-fisted at all mechanical jobs—forty minutes had gone by.

My disgruntled mood did not improve, when at last I reached the hotel, to see that the Stolls had beaten me to it. Their boat was already at its moorings beside the landing stage, and Stoll himself was sitting on his balcony with field glasses trained upon my chalet. I stumped up the steps feeling as self-conscious as someone under a television camera and went into my quarters, closing the shutters behind me. I was taking a bath when the telephone rang.

"Yes?" Towel round the middle, dripping hands, it could not have rung at a more inconvenient moment.

"That you, Mr. Tutor-boy?"

The rasping, wheezing voice was unmistakable. He did not sound drunk, though.

"This is Timothy Grey," I replied stiffly.

"Grey or Black, it's all the same to me," he said. His tone was unpleasant, hostile. "You were out on Spinalongha this afternoon. Correct?"

"I was walking on the peninsula," I told him. "I don't know why you should be so interested."

"Oh, stuff it up," he answered, "you can't fool me. You're just like the other fellow. You're nothing but a Goddamn spy. Well, let me tell you this. The wreck was clean-picked centuries ago."

"I don't know what you're talking about," I said. "What wreck?"

There was a moment's pause. He muttered something under his breath, whether to himself or to his wife I could not tell, but when he resumed speaking his tone had moderated, something of pseudo-bonhomie had returned.

"O.K. . . . O.K. . . . Tutor-boy," he said. "We won't argue the point. Let us say you and I share an interest. Schoolmasters, university professors, college lecturers, we're all alike under the skin, and above it too sometimes." His low chuckle was offensive. "Don't panic, I won't give you away," he continued. "I've taken a fancy to you, as I told you the other night. You want something for your God-darn school museum, correct? Something you can show the pretty lads and your colleagues too? Fine. Agreed. I've got just the thing. You call round here later this evening, and I'll make you a present of it. I don't want your Goddamn money . . ." He broke off, chuckling again, and Mrs. Stoll must have made some remark, for he added, "That's right, that's right. We'll have a cosy little party, just the three of us. My wife's taken quite a fancy to you too."

The towel round my middle slipped to the floor, leaving me naked. I felt vulnerable for no reason at all. And the patronizing, insinuating voice infuriated me.

"Mr. Stoll," I said, "I'm not a collector for schools, colleges, or museums. I'm not interested in antiquities. I am here on holiday to paint, for my own pleasure, and quite frankly I have no intention of calling upon you or any other visitor at the hotel. Good evening."

I slammed down the receiver and went back to the bathroom. Infernal impudence. Loathsome man. The question was, would he now leave me alone, or would he keep his glasses trained on my balcony until he saw me go up to the hotel for dinner, and then follow me, wife in tow, to the dining room? Surely he would not dare to resume the conversation in front of waiters and guests? If I guessed his intentions right, he wanted to buy my silence by fobbing me off with some gift. Those day-long fishing expeditions of his were a mask for underwater exploration—hence his allusion to a wreck—during which he hoped to find, possibly had found already, objects of value that he intended to smuggle out of Crete. Doubtless he had succeeded in doing this the preceding year, and the Greek boatman would be well-paid for holding his tongue. This season, however, it had not worked to plan. My unfortunate predecessor at chalet sixty-two, Charles Gordon, himself an expert in antiquities, had grown suspicious. Stoll's allusion—"You're like the other fellow. Nothing but a Goddamn spy"—made this plain. What if Gordon had received an invitation to chalet thirty-eight, not to drink the spurious beer but to inspect Stoll's collection and be offered a bribe for keeping silent? Had he refused, threatening to expose Stoll? Did he really drown accidentally, or had Stoll's wife followed him down into the water in her rubber suit and mask and slippers, and then, once beneath the surface? . . .

My imagination was running away with me. I had no proof of anything. All I knew was that nothing in the world would get me to Stoll's chalet, and indeed, if he attempted to pester me again, I should have to tell the whole story to the management.

I changed for dinner, then opened my shutters a fraction and stood behind them, looking out toward his chalet. The light shone on his balcony, for it was already dusk, but he himself had disappeared. I stepped outside, locking the shutters behind me, and walked up the garden to the hotel. I was just about to go through to the reception hall from the terrace when I saw Stoll and his wife sitting on a couple of chairs inside, guarding, as it were, the passageway to lounge and dining room. If I wanted to eat I had to pass them. Right, I thought. You can sit there all evening waiting. I went back along the terrace, and, circling the hotel by the kitchens, went round to the car park and got into the Volkswagen. I would have dinner down in the village, and damn the extra expense. I drove off in a fury, found an obscure taverna well away from the harbor itself, and instead of the three-course hotel meal I had been looking forward to on my *en pension* terms—for I was hungry after my day in the open and meager sandwiches on the salt flats—I was obliged to content myself with an omelette, an orange, and a cup of coffee.

It was after ten when I arrived back in the hotel. I parked the car, and, skirting the kitchen quarters once again, made my way furtively down the garden path to my chalet, letting myself in through the shutters like a thief. The light was still shining on Stoll's balcony, and by this time he was doubtless deep in his cups. If there was any trouble with him the next day I would definitely go to the management.

I undressed and lay reading in bed until after midnight, then, feeling sleepy, switched out my light and went across the room to open the shutters, for the air felt stuffy and close. I stood for a moment looking out across the bay. The chalet lights were all extinguished except for one. Stoll's, of course. His balcony light cast a yellow streak on the water beside his landing stage. The water rippled, yet there was no wind. Then I saw it. I mean, the snorkel. The little pipe was caught an instant in the yellow gleam, but before I lost it I knew that it was heading in a direct course for the rocks beneath my chalet. I waited. Nothing happened, there was no sound, no further ripples on the water. Perhaps she did this every evening. Perhaps it was routine, and while I was lying on my bed reading, oblivious of the world outside, she had been treading water close to the rocks. The thought was discomforting, to say the least of it, that regularly after midnight she left her besotted husband asleep over his hell brew of spruce and ivy and came herself, his underwater partner, in her black-seal rubber suit, her mask, her flippers, to spy upon chalet sixty-two. And on this night in particular, after the telephone conversation and my refusal to visit them, coupled with my new theory as to the fate of my predecessor, her presence in my immediate vicinity was more than ominous, it was threatening.

Suddenly, out of the dark stillness to my right, the snorkel-pipe as caught in a finger-threat of light from my own balcony. Now it was almost immediately below me. I panicked, turned, and fled inside my room, closing the shutters fast. I switched off the balcony light and stood against the wall between my bedroom and bathroom, listening. The soft air filtered through the shutters beside me. It seemed an eternity before the sound I expected, dreaded, came to my ears. A kind of swishing movement from the balcony, a fumbling of hands, and heavy breathing. I could see nothing from where I stood against the wall, but the sounds came through the chinks in the shutters, and I knew she was there. I knew she was holding onto the hasp, and the water was dripping from the skin-tight rubber suit, and that even if I shouted "What do you want?" she would not hear. No deaf-aids under water, no mechanical device for soundless ears. Whatever she did by night must be done by sight, by touch.

She began to rattle on the shutters. I took no notice. She rattled again. Then she found the bell, and the shrill summons pierced the air above my head with all the intensity of a dentist's drill upon a nerve. She rang three times. Then silence. No more rattling of the shutters. No more breathing. She might yet be crouching on the balcony, the water dripping from the black rubber suit, waiting for me to lose patience, to emerge.

I crept away from the wall and sat down on the bed. There was not a sound from the balcony. Boldly I switched on my bedside light, half expecting the rattling of the shutters to begin again, or the sharp ping of the bell. Nothing happened, though. I looked at my watch. It was half-past twelve. I sat there hunched on my bed, my mind that had been so heavy with sleep now horribly awake, full of foreboding, my dread of that sleek black figure increasing minute by minute so that all sense and reason seemed to desert me, and my dread was the more intense and irrational because the figure in the rubber suit was female. What did she want?

I sat there for an hour or more until reason took possession once again. I got up from the bed and went to the shutters and listened. There wasn't a sound. Only the lapping of water beneath the rocks. Gently, very gently, I opened the hasp and peered through the shutters. Nobody was there. I opened them wider and stepped on to the balcony. I looked out across the bay, and there was no longer any light shining from the balcony of number thirty-eight. The little pool of water beneath my shutters was evidence enough of the figure that had stood there an hour ago, and the wet footmarks leading down the steps toward the rocks suggested she had gone the way she came. I breathed a sigh of relief. Now I could sleep in peace.

It was only then that I saw the object at my feet, lying close to the shutter's base. I bent and picked it up. It was a small package, wrapped in some sort of waterproof cloth. I took it inside and examined it, sitting on the bed. Foolish suspicions of plastic bombs came to my mind, but surely a journey underwater would neutralize the lethal effect? The package was sewn about with twine, criss-crossed. It felt quite light. I remembered the old classical proverb, "Beware of the Greeks when they bearing gifts." But the Stolls were not Greeks, and, whatever lost Atlantis they might have plundered, explosives did not form part of the treasure trove of that vanished continent.

I cut the twine with a pair of nail scissors, then unthreaded it piece by piece and unfolded the waterproof wrapping. A layer of finely-meshed net concealed the object within, and, this unraveled, the final token itself lay in my open hand. It was a small jug, reddish in color, with a handle on either side for safe holding. I had seen this sort of object before—the correct name, I believe, is rhyton—displayed behind glass cases in museums. The body of the jug had been shaped cunningly and brilliantly into a man's face, with upstanding ears like scallop shells, while protruding eyes and bulbous nose stood out above the leering, open mouth, the moustache drooping to the rounded beard that formed the base. At the top, between the handles, were the upright figures of three strutting men, their faces similar to that upon the jug, but here human resemblance ended, for they had neither hands nor feet but hooves, and from each of their hairy rumps extended a horse's tail.

I turned the object over. The same face leered at me from the other side. The same three figures strutted at the top. There was no crack, no blemish that I could see, except a faint mark on the lip. I looked inside the jug and saw a note lying on the bottom. The opening was too small for my hand, so I shook it out. The note was a plain white card, with words typed upon it. It read: "Silenos, earth-born satyr, half-horse, half-man, who, unable to distinguish truth from falsehood, reared Dionysus, god of intoxication, as a girl in a Cretan cave, then became his drunken tutor and companion."

That was all. Nothing more. I put the note back inside the jug, and the jug on the table at the far end of the room. Even then the lewd, mocking face leered back at me, and the three strutting figures of the horse-men stood out in bold relief across the top. I was too weary to wrap it up again. I covered it with my jacket and climbed back into bed. In the morning I would cope with the laborious task of packing it up and getting my waiter to take it across to chalet thirty-eight. Stoll could keep his rhyton—heaven knew what the value might be—and good luck to him. I wanted no part of it.

Exhausted, I feel asleep, but, oh God, to no oblivion. The dreams which came, and from which I struggled to awaken, but in vain, belonged to some other unknown world horribly intermingled with my own. Term had started, but the school in which I taught was on a mountain top hemmed in by forest, though the school buildings were the same and the classroom was my own. My boys, all of them familiar faces, lads I knew, wore vine leaves in their hair, and had a strange, unearthly beauty both endearing and corrupt. They ran toward me, smiling, and I put my arms about them, and the pleasure they gave me was insidious and sweet, never before experienced, never before imagined, the man who pranced in their midst and played with them was not myself, not the self I knew, but a demon shadow emerging from a jug, strutting in his conceit as Stoll had done upon the spit of sand at Spinalongha.

I awoke after what seemed like centuries of time, and indeed broad daylight seeped through the shutters, and it was a quarter to ten. My head was throbbing. I felt sick, exhausted. I rang for coffee, and looked out across the bay. The boat was at its moorings. The Stolls had not gone fishing. Usually they were away by nine. I took the jug from under my coat, and with fumbling hands began to wrap it up in the net and waterproof packing. I had made a botched job of it when the waiter came onto the balcony with my breakfast tray. He wished me good morning with his usual smile.

"I wonder," I said, "if you would do me a favor."

"You are welcome, sir," he replied.

"It concerns Mr. Stoll," I went on. "I believe he has chalet thirty-eight across the bay. He usually goes fishing every day, but I see his boat is still at the landing-stage."

"That is not surprising." The waiter smiled. "Mr. and Mrs. Stoll left this morning by car."

"I see. Do you know when they will be back?"

"They will not be back, sir. They have left for good. They are driving to the airport en route for Athens. The boat is probably vacant now if you wish to hire it."

He went down the steps into the garden, and the jar in its waterproof packing was still lying beside the breakfast tray.

The sun was already fierce upon my balcony. It was going to be a scorching day, too hot to paint. And anyway, I wasn't in the mood. The events of the night before had left me tired, jaded, with a curious sapped feeling due not so much to the intruder beyond my shutters as to those interminable dreams. I might be free of the Stolls themselves, but not of their legacy. I unwrapped it once again and turned it over in my hands. The leering, mocking face repelled me; its resemblance to the human Stoll was not pure fancy but compelling, sinister, doubtless his very reason for palming it off on me—I remembered the chuckle down the telephone—and if he possessed treasures of equal value to this rhyton, or even greaer, then one object the less would not bother him. He would have a problem getting them through Customs, especially in Athens. The penalties were enormous for this sort of thing. Doubtless he had his contacts, knew what to do.

I stared at the dancing figures near the top of the jar, and once more I was struck by their likeness to the strutting Stoll on the shore of Spinalongha, his naked, hairy form, his protruding rump. Part man, part horse, a satyr . . . "Silenos, drunken tutor to the god Dionysus."

The jar was horrible, evil. Small wonder that my dreams had been distorted, utterly foreign to my nature. But not perhaps to Stoll's? Could it be that he, too, had realized its bestiality, but not until too late? The bartender had told me that it was only this year he had gone to pieces, taken to drink. There must be some link between his alcoholism and the finding of the jar. One thing was very evident, I must get rid of it—but how? If I took it to the management questions would be asked. They might not believe my story about its being dumped on my balcony the night before; they might suspect that I had taken it from some archaeological site, and then had second thoughts about trying to smuggle it out of the country or dispose of it somewhere on the island. So what? Drive along the coast and chuck it away, a rhyton centuries old and possibly priceless?

I wrapped it carefully in my jacket pocket and walked up the garden to the hotel. The bar was empty, the bartender behind his counter polishing glasses. I sat down on a stool in front of him and ordered a mineral water.

"No expedition today, sir?" he inquired.

"Not yet," I said. "I may go out later."

"A cool dip in the sea and a siesta on the balcony," he suggested, "and by the way, sir, I have something for you."

He bent down and brought out a small screw-topped bottle filled with what appeared to be bitter lemon.

"Left here last evening with Mr. Stoll's compliments," he said. "He waited for you in the bar until nearly midnight, but you never came. So I promised to hand it over when you did."

I looked at it suspiciously. "What is it?" I asked.

The bartender smiled. "Some of his chalet home brew," he said. "It's quite harmless, he gave me a bottle for myself and my wife. She says it's nothing but lemonade. The real smelling stuff must have been thrown away. Try it." He had poured some into my mineral water before I could stop him.

Hesitant, wary, I dipped my finger into the glass and tasted it. It was like the barley-water my mother used to make when I was a child. And equally tasteless. And yet . . . it left a sort of aftermath on the palate and the tongue. Not as sweet as honey nor as sharp as grapes, but pleasant, like the smell of raisins under the sun, curiously blended with the ears of ripening corn.

"Oh well," I said, "here's to the improved health of Mr. Stoll," and I drank my medicine like a man.

"I know one thing," said the bartender, "I've lost my best customer. They went early this morning."

"Yes," I said, "so my waiter informed me."

"The best thing Mrs. Stoll could do would be to get him into hospital," the bartender continued. "Her husband's a sick man, and it's not just the drink."

"What do you mean?"

He tapped his forehead. "Something wrong up here," he said. "You could see for yourself how he acted. Something on his mind. Some sort of obsession. I rather doubt we shall see them again next year."

I sipped my mineral water, which was undoubtedly improved by the barley taste. "What was his profession?" I asked.

"Mr. Stoll? Well, he told me he had been professor of classics in some American university, but you never could tell if he was speaking the truth or not. Mrs. Stoll paid the bills here, hired the boatman, arranged everything. Though he swore at her in public he seemed to depend on her. I sometimes wondered, though . . ."

He broke off.

"Wondered what?" I inquired.

"Well . . . she had a lot to put up with. I've seen her look at him sometimes, and it wasn't with love. Women of her age must seek some sort of satisfaction out of life. Perhaps she found it on the side while he indulged his passion for liquor and antiques. He had picked up quite a few items in Greece, and around the islands and here in Crete. It's not too difficult to know the ropes."

He winked. I nodded, and ordered another mineral water. The warm atmosphere in the bar had given me a thirst.

"Are there any lesser known sites along the coast?" I asked. "I mean, places they might have gone ashore to from the boat?"

It may have been my fancy, but I thought he avoided my eye.

"I hardly know, sir," he said. "I dare say there are, but they would have custodians of some sort. I doubt if there are any places the authorities don't know about."

"What about wrecks?" I pursued. "Vessels that might have been sunk centuries ago, and are now lying on the sea bottom?"

He shrugged his shoulders. "There are always local rumours," he said casually, "stories that get handed down through generations. but it's mostly superstition. I've never believed in them myself, and I don't know anybody with education who does."

He was silent for a moment, polishing a glass. I wondered if I had said too much. "We all know small objects are discovered from time to time," he murmured, "and they can be of great value. They get smuggled out of the country, or if too much risk is involved they can be disposed of locally to experts and a good price paid. I have a cousin in the village connected with the local museum. He owns the café opposite the Bottomless Pool. Mr. Stoll used to patronize him. Papitos is the name. As a matter of fact, the boat hired by Mr. Stoll belongs to my cousin. He lets it out on hire to the visitors here at the hotel."

"I see."

"But there . . . you are not a collector, sir, and you're not interested in antiques."

"No," I said, "I am not a collector."

I got up from the stool and bade him good morning. I wondered if the small package in my pocket made a bulge.

I went out of the bar and strolled onto the terrace. Nagging curiosity made me wander down to the landing stage below the Stolls' chalet. The chalet itself had evidently been swept and tidied, the balcony cleared, the shutters closed. No trace remained of the last occupants. Before the day was over, in all probability, it would be opened for some English family who would strew the place with bathing suits.

The boat was at its moorings, and the Greek hand was swabbing down the sides. I looked out across the bay to my own chalet on the opposite side and saw it, for the first time, from Stoll's viewpoint. As he stood there, peering through his field glasses, it seemed closer to me than ever before that he must have taken me for an interloper, a spy—possibly, even, someone sent out from England to inquire into the true circumstances of Charles Gordon's death. Was the gift of the jar, the night before departure, a gesture of defiance? A bribe? Or a curse?

Then the Greek fellow on the boat stood up and faced toward me. It was not the regular boatman, but another one. I had not realized this before when his back was turned. The man who used to accompany the Stolls had been younger, dark, and this was an older chap altogether. I remember what the bartender had told me about the boat belonging to his cousin, Papitos, who owned the café in the village by the Bottomless Pool.

"Excuse me," I called, "are you the owner of the boat?"

The man climbed onto the landing stage and stood before me.

"Nicolai Papitos is my brother," he said. "You want to go for trip round the bay? Plenty good fish outside. No wind today. Sea very calm."

"I don't want to fish," I told him. "I wouldn't mind an outing for an hour or so. How much does it cost?"

He gave me the sum in drachmae, and I did a quick reckoning and made it out to be not more than two pounds for the hour, though it would doubtless be double that sum to round the point and go along the coast as far as that spit of sand on the peninsula of Spinalongha. I took out my wallet to see if I had the necessary notes, or whether I should have to return to the reception desk and cash a travelers' check.

"You charge to hotel," he said quickly, evidently reading my thoughts. "The cost go on your bill."

This decided me. Damn it all, my extras had been moderate to date.

"Very well," I said, "I'll hire the boat for a couple of hours."

It was a curious sensation to be chug-chugging across the bay as the Stolls had done so many times, the line of chalets in my wake, the harbor astern on my right, and the blue waters of the open gulf ahead. I had no clear plan in mind. It was just that, for some inexplicable reason, I felt myself drawn toward that inlet near the shore where the boat had been anchored on the previous day. "The wreck was picked clean centuries ago . . ." Those had been Stoll's words. Was he lying? Or could it be that day after day, through the past weeks, that particular spot had been his hunting ground, and his wife, diving, had brought the dripping treasure from its seabed to his grasping hands? We rounded the point, and inevitably, away from the sheltering arm that had hitherto encompassed us, the breeze appeared to freshen, the boat became more lively as the bows struck the short curling seas.

The long peninsula of Spinalongha lay ahead of us to the left, and I had some difficulty in explaining to my helmsman that I did not want him to steer into the comparative tranquillity of the waters bordering the salt flats, but to continue along the more exposed outward shores of the peninsula bordering the open sea.

"You want to fish?" he shouted above the roar of the engine. "You find very good fish in there," pointing to my flats of yesterday.

"No, no," I shouted back, "farther on, along the coast."

He shrugged. He couldn't believe I had no desire to fish, and I wondered, when we reached our destination, what possible excuse I could make for heading the boat inshore and anchoring, unless—and this seemed plausible enough—I pleaded that the motion of the boat was proving too much for me.

The hills I had climbed yesterday swung into sight above the bows, and then, rounding a neck of land, the inlet itself, the ruined shepherd's hut close to the shore.

"In there," I pointed. "Anchor close to the shore."

He stared at me, puzzled, and shook his head. "No good," he shouted, "too many rocks."

"Nonsense," I yelled. "I saw some people from the hotel anchored here yesterday."

Suddenly he slowed the engine, so that my voice rang out foolishly on the air. The boat danced up and down in the troughs of the short seas.

"Not a good place to anchor," he repeated doggedly. "Wreck there, fouling the ground."

So there was a wreck . . . I felt a mounting excitement, and I was not to be put off.

"I don't care anything about that," I replied, with equal detrmination, "but this boat did anchor here, just by the inlet, I saw it myself."

He muttered something to himself, and made the sign of the cross.

"And if I lose the anchor?" he said. "What do I say to my brother Nicolai?"

He was nosing the boat gently, very gently, toward the inlet and then, cursing under his breath, he went forward to the bows and threw the anchor overboard. He waited until it held, then returned and switched off the engine.

"If you want to go in close, you must take the dinghy," he said sulkily. "I blow it up for you, yes?"

He went forward once again, and dragged out one of those inflatable rubber affairs they use on air-sea rescue craft.

"Very well," I said, "I'll take the dinghy."

In point of fact, it suited my purpose better. I could paddle close inshore, and would not have him breathing over my shoulder. At the same time, I couldn't forbear a slight prick to his pride.

"The man in charge of the boat yesterday anchored further in without mishap," I told him.

My helmsman paused in the act of inflating the dinghy.

"If he like to risk my brother's boat that is his affair," he said shortly. "I have charge of it today. Other fellow not turn up for work this morning, so he lose his job. I do not want to lose mine."

I made no reply. If the other fellow had lost his job it was probably because he had pocketed too many tips from Stoll.

The dinghy inflated and was in the water; I climbed into it gingerly and began to paddle myself toward the shore. Luckily there was no run upon the spit of sand, and I was able to land successfully and pull the dinghy after me. I noticed that my helmsman was watching me with some interest from his safe anchorage, then, once he perceived that the dinghy was unlikely to come to harm, he turned his back and squatted in the bows of the boat, shoulders humped in protest, meditating, no doubt, upon the folly of English visitors.

My reason for landing was that I wanted to judge, from the shore, the exact spot where the boat had anchored yesterday. It was as I thought. Perhaps a hundred yards to the left of where we had anchored today, and closer inshore. The sea was smooth enough, I could navigate it perfectly in the rubber dinghy. I glanced toward the shepherd's hut, and saw my footprints of the day before. There were other footprints too. Fresh ones. The sand in front of the hut had been disturbed. It was as though something had lain there, and then been dragged to the water's edge where I stood now. The goatherd himself, perhaps, had visited the place with his flock earlier that morning.

I crossed over to the hut and looked inside. Curious . . . The little pile of rubble, odds and ends of pottery, had gone. The empty bottles still stood in the far corner, and three more had been added to their number, one of them half full. It was warm inside the hut, and I was sweating. The sun had been beating down on my bare head for nearly an hour—like a fool I had left my hat back in the chalet, not having prepared myself for this expedition—and I was seized with an intolerable thirst. I had acted on impulse, and was paying for it now. It was, in retrospect, an idiotic thing to have done. I might become completely dehydrated, pass out with heatstroke. The half-bottle of beer would be better than nothing.

I did not fancy drinking from it after the goatherd, if it was indeed he who had brought it here; these fellows were none too clean. Then I remember the jar in my pocket. Well, it would at least serve a purpose. I pulled the package out of its wrappings and poured the beer into it. It was only after I had swallowed the first draught that I realized it wasn't beer at all. It was barley-water. It was the same home-brewed stuff that Stoll had left for me in the bar. Did the locals, then, drink it too? It was innocuous enough, I knew that; the bartender had tasted it himself, and so had his wife.

When I had finished the bottle I examined the jar once again. I don't know how it was, but somehow the leering face no longer seemed so lewd. It had a certain dignity that had escaped me before. The beard, for instance. The beard was shaped to perfection around the base—whoever had fashioned it was a master of his craft. I wondered whether Socrates had looked thus when he strolled in the Athenian agora with his pupils and discoursed on life. He could have done. And his pupils may not necessarily have been the young men whom Plato said they were, but of a tenderer age, like my lads at school, like those youngsters of eleven and twelve who had smiled upon me in my dreams last night.

I felt the scalloped ears, the rounded nose, the full soft lips of the tutor Silenos upon the jar, the eyes no longer protruding but questioning, appealing, and even the naked horsemen on the top had grown in grace. It seemed to me now they were not strutting in conceit but dancing with linked hands, filled with a gay abandon, a pleasing, wanton joy. It must have been my fear of the midnight intruder that had made me look upon the jar with such distaste.

I put it back in my pocket, and walked out of the hut and down the spit of beach to the rubber dinghy. Supposing I went to the fellow Papitos, who had connections with the local museum, and asked him to value the jar? Supposing it was worth hundreds, thousands, and he could dispose of it for me, or tell me of a contact in London? Stoll must be doing this all the time, and getting away with it. Or so the bartender had hinted . . . I climbed into the dinghy and began to paddle away from the shore, thinking of the difference between a man like Stoll, with all his wealth, and myself. There he was, a brute with a skin so thick you couldn't pierce it with a spear, and his shelves back at home in the States loaded with loot. Whereas I . . . Teaching small boys on an inadequate salary, and all for what? Moralists said that money made no difference to happiness, but they were wrong. If I had a quarter of the Stolls' wealth I could retire, live abroad, on a Greek island, perhaps, and winter in some studio in Athens or Rome. A whole new way of life would open up, and just at the right moment, too, before I touched middle-age.

I pulled out from the shore and made for the spot where I judged the boat to have anchored the day before. Then I let the dinghy rest, pulled in my paddles, and stared down into the water. The color was pale green, translucent, yet surely fathoms deep, for as I looked down to the golden sands beneath, the seabed had all the tranquillity of another world, remote from the one I knew. A shoal of fish, silver-bright and gleaming, wriggled their way toward a tress of coral hair that might have graced Aphrodite, but was seaweed moving gently in whatever currents lapped the shore. Pebbles that on land would have been no more than rounded stones were brilliant here as jewels. The breeze that rippled the gulf beyond the anchored boat would never touch these depths, but only the surface of the water, and as the dinghy floated on, circling slowly without pull of wind or tide, I wondered whether it was the motion in itself that had drawn the unhearing Mrs. Stoll to underwater swimming. Treasure was the excuse, to satisfy her husband's greed, but down there, in the depths, she would escape from a way of life that must have been unbearable.

Then I looked up at the hills above the retreating spit of sand, and I saw something flash. It was a ray of sunlight upon glass, and the glass moved. Someone was watching me through field glasses. I rested upon my paddles and stared. Two figures moved stealthily away over the brow of the hill, but I recognized them instantly. One was Mrs. Stoll, the other the Greek fellow who had acted as their crew. I glanced over my shoulder to the anchored boat. My helmsman was still staring out to sea. He had seen nothing.

The footprints outside the hut were now explained. Mrs. Stoll, the boatman in tow, had paid a final visit to the hut to clear the rubble, and now, their mission accomplished, they would continue their drive to the airport to catch the afternoon plane to Athens, their journey made several miles longer by the detour along the coast road. And Stoll himself? Asleep, no doubt, at the back of the car upon the salt flats, awaiting their return.

The sight of that woman once again gave me a profound distaste for my expedition.

I wished I had not come. And my helmsman had spoken the truth: the dinghy was now floating above rock. A ridge must run out here from the shore in a single reef. The sand had darkened, changed in texture, become gray. I peered closer into the water, cupping my eyes with my hands, and suddenly I saw the vast encrusted anchor, the shells and barnacles of centuries upon its spikes, and as the dinghy drifted on the bones of the long-buried craft itself appeared, broken, sparless, her decks, if decks there had been, long since dismembered or destroyed.

Stoll had been right: her bones had been picked clean. Nothing of any value could now remain upon that skeleton. No pitchers, no jars, no gleaming coins. A momentary breeze rippled the water, and when it became clear again and all was still I saw the second anchor by the skeleton bows, and a body, arms outstretched, legs imprisoned in the anchor's jaws. The motion of the water gave the body life, as though, in some desperate fashion, it still struggled for release, but, trapped as it was, escape would never come. The days and nights would follow, months and years, and slowly the flesh would dissolve, leaving the frame impaled upon the spikes.

The body was Stoll's head, trunk, limbs grotesque, inhuman, as they swayed backward and forward at the bidding of the currents.

I looked up once more to the crest of the hill, but the two figures had long since vanished, and in an appalling flash of intuition a picture of what had happened became vivid: Stoll, strutting on the spit of sand, the half-bottle raised to his lips, and then they struck him down and dragged him to the water's edge, and it was his wife who towed him, drowning, to his final resting place beneath the surface, there below me, impaled on the crusted anchor. I was sole witness to his fate, and no matter what lies she told to account for his disappearance I would remain silent; it was not my responsibility, guilt might increasingly haunt me, but I must never become involved.

I heard the sound of something choking beside me—I realize now it was myself, in horror and fear—and I struck at the water with my paddles and started pulling away from the wreck back to the boat. As I did so my arm brushed against the jar in my pocket, and in sudden panic I dragged it forth and flung it overboard. It did not sink immediately but remained bobbing on the surface, then slowly filled with that green translucent sea, pale as the barley liquid laced with spruce and ivy. The eyes in the swollen face stared up at me, and they were not only those of Silenos the satyr tutor, and of the drowned Stoll, but my own as well, as I should see them one day reflected in a mirror. They seemed to hold all knowledge in their depths, and all despair.

A Borderline Case

HE HAD BEEN asleep for about ten minutes. Certainly no longer. Shelagh had brought up some of the old photograph albums from the study to amuse her father, and they had been laughing and going through them together. He seemed so much better. The nurse had felt free to go off duty for the afternoon and take a walk, leaving her patient in the care of his daughter, while Mrs. Money herself had slipped off in the car to the village to have her hair done. The doctor had reassured them all that the crisis was past; it was just a matter of rest and quiet, and taking things easy.

Shelagh was standing by the window looking down into the garden. She would remain at home, of course, as long as her father wanted her—indeed, she could not bear to leave him if there was any doubt about his condition. It was only that if she turned down the offer the Theatre Group had made to her of playing the lead in their forthcoming series of Shakespeare plays, the chance might not come her way again. Rosalind . . . Portia . . . Viola—Viola surely the greatest fun of all. The yearning heart concealed beneath a cloak of dissimulation, the whole business of deception whetting appetite.

Unconsciously she smiled, pushing her hair behind her ears, tilting her head, one hand on her hip, aping Cesario, and she heard a sudden movement from the bed and saw her father struggling to sit upright. He was staring at her, an expression of horror and disbelief upon his face, and he cried out, "Oh, no . . . Oh, Jinnie . . . Oh, my God!" and as she ran to his side, saying to him, "What is it, darling, what's wrong?" he tried to wave her aside, shaking his head, and then he collapsed backward on his pillows, and she knew that he was dead.

She ran out of the room, calling for the nurse, then remembered that she had gone for a walk. She could have gone across the fields, anywhere. Shelagh rushed downstairs to find her mother, but the house was empty, and the garage doors were wide open—her mother must have gone somewhere in the car. Why? What for? She had never said she was going out. Shelagh seized the telephone in the hall with shaking hands and dialed the doctor's number, but when the answering click came it was not the doctor himself but his recorded voice, toneless, automatic, saying, "This is Dr. Dray speaking. I shall not be available until five o'clock. Your message will be recorded. Please start now . . . " and there was a ticking sound, just as when one rang to know the time and the voice said, "At the third stroke it will be two, forty-two, and twenty seconds . . . ."

Shelagh flung down the receiver and began to search the telephone directory feverishly for the number of Dr. Dray's partner, a young man lately joined the practice—she did not even know him—and this time a live voice answered, a woman. There was the sound of a child crying in the distance and a radio blaring, and she heard the woman shout impatiently at the child to be quiet.

"This is Shelagh Money speaking, of Whitegates, Great Marsden. Please ask the doctor to come at once, I think my father has just died. The nurse is out and I'm alone in the house. I can't get Dr. Dray."

She heard her own voice break, and the woman's reply, swift, sympathetic, "I'll contact my husband immediately," made further explanation impossible. She couldn't speak, but turned away blindly from the telephone and ran up the stairs again into the bedroom. He was lying as she had left him, the expression of horror still on his face, and she went and knelt beside him and kissed his hand, the tears pouring down her cheeks. "Why?" she asked herself. "What happened? What did I do?" Because when he cried out, using her pet name Jinnie, it was not as if he had been seized with sudden pain on waking from sleep. It did not seem like that at all, but more as though his cry was one of accusation, that she had done something so appalling that it suspended all belief. "Oh, no . . . Oh, Jinnie . . . Oh, my God!" Then trying to ward her off as she ran to his side, and dying instantly.

I can't bear it, I can't bear it, she thought; what did I do? She got up, still blinded by tears, and went and stood by the open window and looked back over her shoulder to the bed, but it was no longer the same. He was not staring at her anymore. He was still. He had gone. The moment of truth had vanished forever, and she would never know. What had happened was *Then,* was already past, in some other dimension of time, and the present was *Now,* part of a future he could not share. This present, this future, was all blank to him, like the empty spaces in the photograph album beside the bed, waiting to be filled. Even, she thought, if he had read my mind, which he often did, he would not have cared. He knew I wanted to play those parts with the Theatre Group, he encouraged me, he was delighted. It was not as though I were planning to go off at any moment and leave him . . . Why the expression of horror, of disbelief? Why? Why?

She stared out of the window, and the carpet of autumn leaves scattered here and there on the lawn was suddenly blown in a gust of wind up into the air like birds and tossed in all directions, only to drift apart, and tumble, and fall. The leaves that had once budded tight and close upon the parent tree, to glisten thick and green through-out the summer, had no more life. The tree disowned them, and they had become the sport of any idle wind that chanced to blow. Even the burnished gold was reflected sunlight, lost when the sun had set, so that in shadow they became crinkled, barren, dry.

Shelagh heard the sound of a car coming down the drive, and she went out of the room and stood at the top of the stairs. It was not the doctor, though, it was her mother. She came through the front door to the hall, peeling off her gloves, her hair bunched high on her head, gleaming and crisp from the drier. Unconscious of her daughter's eyes, she hovered a moment before the mirror, patting a stray curl into place. Then she took her lipstick from her bag and made up her mouth. A door banging in the direction of the kitchen made her turn her head.

"That you, Nurse?" she called. "How about tea? We can all have it upstairs."

She looked back into the mirror, cocking her head, then dabbed off the surplus lipstick with a tissue.

The nurse appeared from the kitchen. She looked different out of uniform. She had borrowed Shelagh's duffle-coat for her walk and her hair, usually so trim, was disheveled.

"Such a lovely afternoon," she said. "I've been for quite a tramp across the fields. It was so refreshing. Blown all the cobwebs away. Yes, let's have tea, by all means. How's my patient?"

They are living in the past, Shelagh thought, in a moment of time that does not exist anymore. The nurse would never eat the buttered scones she had anticipated, glowing from her walk, and her mother, when she glanced into the mirror later, would see an older, more haggard face beneath the piled-up coiffure. it was as if grief, coming so unexpectedly, had sharpened intuition, and she could see the nurse already installed by the bedside of her next patient, some querulous invalid, unlike her father, who teased and made jokes, while her mother, dressed suitably in black and white (black alone she would consider too severe), replied to the letters of condolence, those from the more important people first.

Then they both become aware of her, standing at the top of the stairs.

"He's dead," Shelagh said.

Their upturned faces stared at her in disbelief, as his had done, but without the horror, without the accusation, and as the nurse, recovering first, brushed past her up the stairs, she saw her mother's carefully preserved and still lovely face disintegrate, crumple, like a plastic mask.

You must not blame yourself. There was nothing you could have done. It was bound to happen, sooner or later . . . Yes, thought Shelagh, but why not later rather than sooner, because when one's father dies there is so much that has been left unsaid. Had I known, that last hour sitting there, talking and laughing about trivial things, that there was a clot forming like a time bomb close to his heart, ready to explode, I would surely have behaved differently, held onto him, at least thanked him for all my nineteen years of happiness and love. Not flipped over the photographs in the album, mocking bygone fashions, nor yawned halfway through, so that, sensing boredom, he let the album drop to the floor and murmured, "Don't bother about me, pet, I'll have a kip."

It's always the same when you come face to face with death, the nurse told her, you feel you could have done more. It used to worry me a lot when I was training. And of course with a close relative it's worse. You've had a great shock, you must try and pull yourself together for your mother's sake . . . My mother's sake? My mother would not mind if I walked out of the house this moment, Shelagh was on the point of saying, because then she would have all the attention, all the sympathy, people would say how wonderfully she was bearing up, whereas with me in the house sympathy will be divided. Even Dr. Dray, when he finally arrived in the wake of his partner, patted her on the shoulder before her mother and said, "He was very proud of you, my dear, he was always telling me so." So death, Shelagh decided, was a moment for compliments, for everyone saying polite things about everybody else which they would not dream of saying at another time. Let me run upstairs for you . . . Let me answer the telephone . . . Shall I put on the kettle? An excess of courtesy, like mandarins in kimonos bowing, and at the same time an attempt at self-justification for not having been there when the explosion happened.

The nurse (to the doctor's partner): "I would never have gone for a walk if I hadn't been quite sure he was comfortable. And I believed that both Mrs. Money and her daughter were in the house. Yes, I had given him the tablets . . . " etc. etc.

She is in the witness box, on trial, thought Shelagh, but so are we all.

Her mother (also to the doctor's partner): "It had entirely slipped my memory that Nurse was going out. There has been so much to think of, so much anxiety, and I thought it would relax me to pay a quick visit to the hairdresser, and he had seemed to much better, really his old self. I would never have dreamed of leaving the house, leaving his room, if I had thought for one moment . . ."

"Isn't that the trouble?" Shelagh burst in. "We never *do* think, any of us. You didn't, Nurse didn't, Dr. Dray didn't, and above all I didn't because I'm the only one who saw what happened, and I shall never forget the look on his face as long as I live."

She stormed along the passage to her own room, sobbing hysterically in a way she had not done for years—the last time was when the post van smashed into her first car when it was parked in the entrance drive, all that twisted metal, the lovely plaything ruined. *That* will teach them a lesson, she told herself, that will shake them out of this business of trying to behave so well, of being noble in the face of death, of making out that it's a merciful release and everything is really for the best. None of them really minding, caring, that someone has gone forever. But *forever* . . .

Later that evening, everyone gone to bed, death being so exhausting to all but the departed, Shelagh crept along the landing to her father's room and found the photograph album, tactfully tidied away on a corner table by the nurse, and carried it back with her to her own bedroom. Earlier, during the afternoon, the photographs had been without significance, familiar as old Christmas cards hoarded in a drawer, but now they were a kind of obituary, like stills flashed in tribute on a television screen.

The befrilled baby on a rug, mouth agape, his parents playing croquet. An uncle, killed in the First World War. Her father again, no longer a baby on a rug but in breeches, holding a cricket bat too big for him. Homes of grandparents long dead. Children on beaches. Picnics on moors. Then Dartmouth, photographs of ships.

Rows of lined-up boys, youths, men. As a child it had been her pride to point to him at once. "There you are, that's you," the smallest boy at the end of the line, then in the next photograph slimmer and standing in the second row, then growing quite tall and suddenly handsome, a child no longer, and she would turn the pages rapidly because the photographs would be of places, not of people—Malta, Alexandria, Portsmouth, Greenwich. Dogs that had been his which she had not known. "There's dear old Punch . . . " (Punch, he used to tell her, always knew when his ship was due home, and waited at an upstairs window.) Naval officers riding donkeys . . . playing tennis . . . running races, all this before the war, and it had made her think. Unconscious of their doom, the little victims play, because on the next page it became suddenly sad, the ship he had loved blown up, and so many of those laughing young men lost. "Poor old Monkey White, he would have been an admiral had he lived." She tried to imagine the grinning face of Monkey White in the photo turned into an admiral, bald-headed, perhaps, stout, and something inside her was glad that he had died, although her father said he was a loss to the Service. More officers, more ships, and the great day when Mountbatten visited the ship, her father in command, meeting him as he was piped aboard. The courtyard at Buckingham Palace. Standing rather self-consciously before the press photographer, displaying medals.

"Not long now before we come to you," her father used to say as he turned the page to the full-blown and never-to-him-admitted rather silly photograph of her mother in an evening dress which he so much admired, wearing her soulful look that Shelagh knew well. It embarrassed her, as a child, to think that her father had fallen in love, or, if men must love, then it should have been someone else, someone dark, mysterious, and profoundly clever, not an ordinary person who was impatient for no reason and cross when one was late for lunch.

The naval wedding, her mother smiling in triumph—Shelagh knew that look too; she wore it when she got her way about anything, which she generally did—and her father's smile, so different, not triumphant, merely happy. The frumpish bridesmaids wearing dresses that made them fatter than they were—she must have chosen them on purpose not to be outdone—and the best man, Nick, not nearly so good-looking as her father. He was better in one of the earlier groups on the ship, but here he looked supercilious, bored.

The honeymoon, the first house, and then her own appearance, the childhood photographs that were part of her life: on her father's knee, on his shoulders, and right through childhood and adolescence until last Christmas. It could be my obituary, too, she thought; we've shared this book together, and it ends with his snapshot of me standing in the snow and mine of him, smiling at me through the study window.

In a moment she would cry again, which was self-pity; if she cried it must not be for herself but for him. When was it, that afternoon, that he had sensed her boredom and pushed the album aside? It was while they were discussing hobbies. He had told her she was physically lazy, didn't take enough exercise.

"I get all the exercise I need in the theater," she said, "pretending to be other people."

"It's not the same," he said. "You should get away from people sometimes, imaginary and real. I tell you what. When I'm up and about again and in the clear we'll go over to Ireland and fish, the three of us. It would do your Mum a power of good, and I haven't fished for years."

Ireland? Fish? Her instinct was selfish, one of dismay. It would interfere with her Theatre Group plans. She must joke him out of it.

"Mum would hate every minute," she said. "She would much rather go to the south of France to stay with Aunt Bella." (Bella was her mother's sister. Had a villa at Cap d'Ail.)

"I dare say"—he smiled—"but that wouldn't be my idea of convalescence. Have you forgotten I'm half Irish? Your grandfather came from County Antrim."

"I've not forgotten," she said, "but Grandfather's been dead for years, and lies buried in a Suffolk churchyard. So much for your Irish blood. You haven't any friends over there, have you?"

He did not answer immediately, and then he said, "There's poor old Nick."

Poor old Nick . . . Poor old Monkey White . . . Poor old Punch . . . She was momentarily confused between friends and dogs she had never known.

"Do you mean your best man at the wedding?" She frowned. "Somehow I thought he was dead."

"Dead to the world," he said shortly. "He was badly smashed up in a car crash some years ago, and lost an eye. Lived like a recluse ever since."

"How sad. Is that why he never sends you a Christmas card?"

"Partly . . . Poor old Nick. Gallant as they come, but mad as a hatter. A borderline case. I wouldn't recommend him for promotion, and I'm afraid he bore me a grudge ever afterward."

"That's hardly surprising, then. I'd feel the same if I'd been somebody's close friend and they turned me down."

He shook his head. "Friendship and duty are two separate things," he said, "and I put duty first. You are another generation, you wouldn't understand. I was right in what I did, I'm sure of that, but it wasn't very pleasant at the time. A chip on the shoulder can turn a man sour. I'd hate to think myself responsible for what he may have got mixed up in."

"What do you mean?" she asked.

"Never mind," he said, "none of your business. Anyway, it's over and done with long ago. But I sometimes wish . . ."

"What do you wish, darling?"

"That I could shake the old boy by the hand once more and wish him luck."

They turned over a few more pages of the album, and it was soon afterward that she yawned, glancing idly about the room, and he sensed her boredom and said he would have a kip. No one could die of a heart attack because his daughter was bored . . . But supposing he had had a nightmare in which she had figured? Supposing he had thought himself back in that sinking ship during the war, with poor old Monkey White, and Nick, and all those drowning men, and somehow she had been with him in the water? Everything became jumbled up in dreams, it was a known thing. And all the time that clot getting bigger, like an excess of oil in the workings of a clock. At any moment the hands would falter, the clock stop ticking.

Somebody tapped at her bedroom door. "Yes?" she called.

It was the nurse. Still professional, despite her dressing gown.

"Just wondered if you were all right," she whispered. "I saw your light under the door."

"Thanks. I'm O.K."

"Your mother's fast asleep. I gave her a sedative. She was fussing about tomorrow being Saturday, and the difficulty of getting an announcement in the *Times* and *Telegraph* before Monday. She's being so plucky."

Was there hidden reproach in her voice because Shelagh had not thought of taking charge of these things herself? Surely tomorrow would have done? Aloud she said, "Can nightmares kill?"

"What do you mean, dear?"

"Could my father have had a terrible nightmare and died of shock?"

The nurse advanced to the bed and straightened the eiderdown. "Now, I told you earlier, and the doctors said the same, it would have happened anyway. You really must not keep on going over it in your mind. It doesn't help. Let me get you a sedative too."

"I don't want a sedative."

"You know, dear, forgive me, but you're being just a little bit childish. Grief is natural, but to worry about him in this way is the last thing your father would have wanted. It's all over now. He's at peace."

"How do you know he's at peace?" Shelagh exploded. "How do you know he's not hovering beside us at this minute in an astral body absolutely furious that he's dead, and saying to me, 'That bloody nurse gave me too many pills?'"

Oh no, she thought, I didn't mean that, people are too vulnerable, too naked. The poor woman, shaken out of professional calm, sagged in her dressing gown, drooped before her eyes, and with a tremulous voice said, "What a terribly unkind thing to say! You know I did no such thing."

Impulsively Shelagh leaped out of bed and put her arms round the nurse's shoulders.

"Forgive me," she pleaded, "of course you didn't. And he liked you very much. You were a wonderful nurse to him. What I mean was"—she searched in her mind for some explanation—"what I meant was that we don't know what happens when a person dies. They might be waiting in some queue at St. Peter's gate with all the other people who have died that day, or else pushing into some awful purgatorial nightclub with the ones who were destined for hell, or just drifting in a kind of fog until the fog clears and everything becomes clear. All right, I will have a sedative, you have one too, then we'll both be fresh for the morning. And please don't think any more about what I said."

The trouble is, she thought, after she had taken her sedative and gone back to bed, words leave a wound, the wound leaves a scar. The nurse will never give out pills to patients again without a doubt somewhere at the back of her mind as to whether she is doing the right thing. Like the question mark in her father's conscience about not passing poor old Nick for promotion and so giving him his chip on the shoulder. It was bad to die with something on your conscience. One ought to have some warning, so that one could send a telegram to anyone who might have been wronged, saying, "Forgive me," and then the wrong would be canceled, blotted out. This was why, in the old days, people flocked round a dying person's bed, hoping, not to be left something in the will, but for mutual forgiveness, a cessation of ill-feeling, a smoothing out of right and wrong. In fact, a sort of love.

Shelagh had acted on impulse. She knew she always would. It was part of her character, and had to be accepted by family and friends. It was not until she was on her way, though, driving north from Dublin in the hired car, that her journey, hastily improvised, took on its real meaning. She was here on a mission, a sacred trust. She was carrying a message from beyond the grave. It was absolutely secret, though, and no one must know about it, for she was sure that if she had told anyone questions would have been asked, arguments raised. So, after the funeral, complete silence about her plans. Her mother, as Shelagh guessed she would, decided to fly to Aunt Bella at Cap d'Ail.

"I feel I must get right away," she had said to her daughter. "You may not realize it, but Dad's illness was a fearful strain. I've lost half a stone. I feel that all I want to do is to close my eyes and lie on Bella's sun-drenched balcony, and try to forget the misery of the past weeks."

It was like an advertizement for some luxury soap. Pamper yourself. A naked woman deep in a bath of bubbling foam. In point of fact, the first shock over, her mother looked better already, and Shelagh knew that the sun-drenched balcony would soon fill up with Aunt Bella's very mixed bunch of friends—socialites, bogus artists, boring old homos, what her father used to call "phoney riffraff," but they amused her mother. "What about you? Why don't you come too?"—the suggestion halfhearted but nevertheless made.

Shelagh shook her head. "Rehearsals start next week. I thought, before going to London, I'd push off alone in the car somewhere. No sort of plan. Just drive."

"Why not take a friend?"

"Anyone would get on my nerves at the moment. I'm better alone."

No further contact between them on anything more than the practical level. Neither said to the other, "How unhappy are you really? Is this the end of the road for me, for you? What does the future hold?" Instead there were discussions about the gardener and his wife coming to live in, visits from lawyers left until after her mother returned from Cap d'Ail, letters to be forwarded, etc., etc. . . . Without emotion, like two secretaries, they sat side by side reading and replying to the letters of condolence. You take A to K. I'll take L to Z. And more or less the same message to each: "Deeply touched . . . Your sympathy so helpful . . ." It was like sending out the Christmas cards every December, but the wording was different.

Looking through her father's old address book, she came across the name Barry. Commander Nicolas Barry, D.S.O., R.N. Retd., Ballfane, Lough Torrah, Eire. Both name and address had a line through them, which generally meant that the person had died. She glanced at her mother.

"I wonder why that old friend of Dad's, Commander Barry, hasn't written?" she asked casually. "He isn't dead, is he?"

"Who?" Her mother looked vague. "Oh, you mean Nick? I don't think he's dead. He was in some frightful car crash years ago. But they were out of touch before that. He hasn't written to us for years."

"I wonder why."

"I don't know. They had some row, I never heard what about. Did you see this very sweet letter from Admiral Arbuthnot? We were all together in Alexandria."

"Yes, I saw it. What was he like? Not the admiral—Nick."

Her mother leaned back in her chair, considering the matter.

"Frankly, I never could quite make him out," she said. "He'd either be all over one and the greatest fun, especially at parties, or ignoring everybody and making sarcastic remarks. He had a wild streak in him. I remember him coming to stay soon after Dad and I were married—he was best man, you know, at the wedding—and he turned all the furniture upside down in the drawing room and got very tight. Such a silly thing to do. I was livid."

"Did Dad mind?"

"I don't think so, I can't remember. They knew each other so well, served together, been at Dartmouth as boys. Then Nick left the Navy and went back to live in Ireland, and they somehow drifted apart. I had the impression actually that he had the sack, but I never liked to ask. You know what an oyster Dad was about Service matters."

"Yes . . ."

(Poor old Nick. A chip on the shoulder. I'd like to shake him by the hand again and wish him luck . . .)

She saw her mother off at the airport a few days afterward, and made her own plans for departure to Dublin. The night before she left, searching amongst her father's papers, she found a scrap of paper with a list of dates, scribbled in pencil, and the name Nick alongside with a question mark, but no word of explanation as to what the dates referred to. June 5, 1951. June 25, 1953. June 12, 1954. October 17, 1954. April 24, 1955. August 13, 1955. The list bore no relevance to the rest of the papers in the file, and must have been slipped in there by accident. She copied them down, and put them in an envelope inside her tourist guide.

Well, that was that, and here she was, on the road to . . . to do what? To apologize, in her deceased father's name, to a retired naval commander passed over for promotion. Wild in his youth? The greatest fun at parties? The image conjured up was not one to whip the appetite, and she began to picture a middle-aged buffer with a hyena laugh who put booby traps on the top of every door. Perhaps he had tried it on the First Sea Lord and received the boot for his pains. A car accident turned him into a recluse, an embittered one-time clown (but gallant, her father said, which meant what—plunging into oil-infested waters to rescue drowning sailors in the war?) who sat gnawing his fingernails in some old Georgian mansion or mock castle, drinking Irish whisky and regretting all those apple-pie beds. Some seventy-odd miles from Dublin on a balmy October afternoon, though, with the countryside becoming greener, lusher, yet somehow sparsely inhabited, the glint of water more frequent away to the west, and suddenly a myriad pools and lakes with tongues of land thrusting between them, the prospect of ringing the bell of a Georgian mansion faded. Here there were no high walls encircling stately demesnes, only wet fields beyond the road, and surely no means of access to the silver-splintered lakes beyond.

The description of Ballyfane in the official guide had been laconic. "Situated west of Lough Torrah with numerous smaller loughs close to the village." The Kilmore Arms had six bedrooms, but there was no mention of mod. cons. If the worst came to the worst she could telephone Nick—his old friend's daughter stranded in the neighborhood, could he suggest a comfortable hotel within ten miles, and she hoped to call upon him in the morning. A butler would answer, an old retainer. "The Commander would be pleased if you would accept his hospitality here at Ballyfane Castle." Irish wolfhounds baying and her host himself appearing on the steps, leaning on a stick . . .

A church tower appeared over the crest of the road, and here was Ballyfane itself, a village street straggling up a rise flanked by a few sombre houses and shops, names like Driscoll and Murphy painted on boards above doors. The Kilmore Arms could have done with a coat of whitewash, but marigolds in a window box making a valiant attempt at a second flowering suggested someone with an eye for color.

Shelagh parked her Austin Mini and surveyed the scene. The door of the Kilmore Arms was open. The entrance hall that also served as a lounge was bare and neat. Nobody was in sight, but a handbell standing on the counter to the left of the entrance seemed there for a purpose. She rang it briskly, and as a sad-faced man emerged from an inner room, limping and wearing spectacles, she had a fearful feeling that it was Nick himself, having fallen on hard times.

"Good afternoon," she said. "I was wondering if I could have tea?"

"You can," he told her. "A full tea or just the pot?"

"Well, full, I think," she replied, with a vision of hot scones and cherry jam, flashing him the smile she generally reserved for the stage doorkeeper.

"It will take about ten minutes," he said. "The diningroom is to the right, just three steps down. Have you come far?"

"From Dublin," she said.

"It's a pleasant drive. I was in Dublin myself a week ago," he told her. "My wife, Mrs. Doherty, has relatives there. She's away sick at present."

She wondered whether she should apologize for giving trouble, but he had already disappeared to get the tea, and she went down the steps into the dining room. Six tables laid ready, but she had the impression nobody had eaten there for days. A clock on the wall ticked loudly, breaking the silence. Presently a little maid emerged from the back regions, breathing heavily, bearing a tray that had upon it a large pot of tea and, not the scones and cherry jam she had anticipated, but a plate with two fried eggs and three fat slices of bacon, as well as a heap of fried potatoes. A full tea . . . She would have to eat it, or Mr. Doherty would be offended. The maid vanished, and a black and white cat that had made its appearance with the tea arched itself against her legs, purring loudly. Furtively she fed it the bacon and one of the eggs, then tackled the remainder. The tea was piping hot and strong, and she could feel it searing her inside as she swallowed it.

The little maid emerged once more. "Is the tea to your liking?" she asked anxiously. "I could fry you another egg if you're still hungry."

"No," said Shelagh, "I've done very well, thank you. Could I see your telephone directory? I want to look up the number of a friend."

The directory was produced and she thumbed the pages. Barrys galore, but none in this district. No commander. No Nicolas Barry, R.N., Retd. The journey had been in vain. Her mood of high expectancy, of daring, turned to despondency.

"How much do I owe for the tea?" she asked.

The little maid murmured a modest sum. Shelagh thanked her, paid, and went out into the hall and through the open doorway to the street. The post office was on the opposite side. One last inquiry and then, if that was unlucky too, she would turn the car round again and make for some hotel back on the road to Dublin, where she could at least relax in a steaming bath and spend the night in comfort. She waited patiently while an old woman bought stamps and a man inquired about parcels to America. Then she turned to the postmaster behind the grille.

"Excuse me," she asked, "I wonder if you can help me? Do you happen to know if Commander Barry lives anywhere in the district?"

The man stared. "He does," he said. "He's lived here these twenty years."

Oh joy! Oh, the relief! The mission was on again. All was not lost.

"The thing is," Shelagh explained, "I couldn't find his name in the telephone directory."

"That isn't surprising," the man said. "There is no telephone on Lamb Island."

"Lamb Island? repeated Shelagh. You mean he lives on an island?"

The man stared as if she had asked a stupid question. "It's on the southern side of Lough Torrah," he said, "about four miles from here as the crow flies. You can't reach it except by boat. If you want to get in touch with Commander Barry you'd best write for an appointment. He doesn't see many people."

The chip on the shoulder . . . The recluse . . .

"I see," said Shelagh. "I hadn't realised. Can one get a glimpse of the island from the road?"

The man shrugged. "There's a turning down to the lough a mile or so out of Ballyfane," he told her, "but it's no more than a rough track. You can't take a car there. If you have stout shoes it's an easy enough walk. Best done in daylight. You would miss your way if it came on for dusk, and the mist rises too over the lake."

"Thank you," said Shelagh, "thank you very much."

She went out of the post office with the feeling that the postmaster was staring after her. What now? Better not risk it this evening. Better endure the doubtful comforts of the Kilmore Arms and indigestion. She returned to the hotel and came face to face with Mr. Doherty on the doorstep.

"I suppose," she said, "you couldn't let me have a room for the night?"

"I could indeed, you'd be very welcome," he told her. "It's quiet now, but in the tourist season you'd be surprised—we've seldom an empty bed. I'll bring in your baggage. Your car will come to no harm there in the street."

Anxious to please, he limped to the boot of the car, brought out her suitcase, conducted her inside the Kilmore Arms, and led the way upstairs, showing her into a small double room overlooking the street.

"I'll only charge you for the one bed," he said. "Twenty-two shillings and your breakfast. There's a bathroom across the passage."

Oh well, it was rather fun—and mod. cons. after all. Later on the locals would come into the bar and break into song. She would drink Guinness out of an enormous tankard and watch them, join in herself, perhaps.

She inspected the bathroom. It reminded her of digs on tour. One tap dripping, leaving a brown stain, and when she turned it on the water gushed forth like the Niagara Falls. Still, it was hot. She unpacked her night things, bathed, dressed again, and went downstairs. Voices drifted down the passage. She followed the sound and came to the bar. Mr. Doherty himself stood behind the counter. The voices ceased as she entered, and everyone stared. Everyone being about half-a-dozen men, and amongst them she recognized the postmaster.

"Good evening," she said brightly.

A mumbled response from all, but uninterested. They went on talking amongst themselves. She ordered whisky from Mr. Doherty and felt suddenly self-conscious, perched there on the stool, which was perfectly ridiculous because she was used to going into every sort of bar on tour, and there was nothing very singular about this one anyway.

"Is it your first visit to Ireland?" asked Mr. Doherty, still anxious to please, pouring out the whisky.

"Yes, it is," she told him. "I'm rather ashamed I've never been over before. My grandfather was Irish. I'm sure the scenery is lovely around here. I must do some exploring tomorrow, down by the lake."

She glanced across the bar, and was aware of the postmaster's eye upon her.

"You'll be with us for a few days, then?" asked Mr. Doherty. "I could arrange some fishing for you, if that's what you like."

"Oh, well . . . I'm not sure. It rather depends."

How loud and English her voice sounded on the air, reminding her of her mother. Like a socialite out of a glossy magazine. And the local chatter had momentarily ceased. The Irish bonhomie she had visualized was absent. Nobody here was going to seize a fiddle and dance a jig and burst into song. Perhaps girls who stayed the night in pubs on their own were suspect.

"Your dinner is ready when you are," said Mr. Doherty.

She took the cue and slipped from the barstool and so on into the dining room, feeling about ten years old. Soup, fish, roast beef—the trouble they had taken, when all she needed was a wafer slice of ham, but impossible to leave anything on her plate. Trifle to finish with, doused in sherry.

Shelagh looked at her watch. It was only half-past eight.

"Will you take your coffee in the lounge?"

"Thank you, yes."

"There's a television set. I'll switch it on for you."

The little maid drew up an armchair close to the television, and Shelagh sat down to the coffee she did not want while an American comedy, vintage 1950, flickered from the box. The murmur of voices droned on from the direction of the bar. Shelagh poured the coffee back into the pot and crept upstairs to fetch her coat. Then, leaving the television blaring in the empty lounge, she went out into the street. There was nobody about. All Ballyfane was already in bed or safe within doors. She got into the car and drove away through the empty village, back along the road she had traveled earlier that afternoon. A turning, the postmaster had said, a mile or so out of Ballyfane. This must be it, here on the left. A crooked signpost with the lettering FOOTPATH TO LOUGH TORRAH showed up in the glare of her headlights. The footpath, narrow and twisting, led downhill. Silly to attempt it without a torch, and the moon, three-quarters full, giving only a fitful gleam behind banks of racing cloud. Still . . . she could go part of the way, if only for the benefit of the exercise.

She left the car close to the signpost and began to walk. Her shoes, luckily flat, squelched in the mud. As soon as I catch a glimpse of the lake, she thought, I'll turn back, and then be up early tomorrow and come here again, bring a packed lunch, decide upon my plan of attack. The footpath was opening out between the banks, and suddenly before her was the great sheet of water, encircled by jutting lips of land, and in the center was the island itself, shrouded in trees. It had an eerie, sombre quality, and the moon, breaking through the clouds, turned the water silver, while the island remained black, humped like the back of a whale.

Lamb Island . . . inconsequentially it made her think of legends, not of Irish chiefs long dead or tribal feuds, but of sacrifices to ancient gods before the dawn of history. Stone altars in a glade. A lamb with its throat cut lying amidst the ashes of a fire. She wondered how far it was from the shore. A half mile perhaps? Distances were hard to judge by night. A stream on her left ran down into the lake, fringed by reeds. She advanced toward it, picking her way carefully amongst the pebbles and the mud, and then she saw the boat, tied to a stump, and the figure of a man standing beside it. He was staring in her direction. Foolish panic seized her, and she backed away. It was no good, though. He walked swiftly up the mud and stood beside her.

"Were you looking for someone? he said.

He was a young man, strongly built, wearing a fisherman's jersey and dungarees.

He spoke with the local accent.

"No," Shelagh answered, "no, I'm a visitor to the district. It was a lovely evening and I thought I'd take a walk."

"A lonely spot for a walk. Have you come far?"

"Only from Ballyfane," she told him. "I'm staying at the Kilmore Arms."

"I see," he said. "You're here for the fishing, maybe. The fishing is better the other side of Ballyfane."

"Thank you. I'll remember that."

There was a pause. Shelagh wondered if she should say any more or whether she should turn and go, bidding him a cheerful good-night. He was looking beyond her shoulder toward the footpath, and she heard the sound of somebody else's footsteps squelching through the mud. Another figure loomed out of the shadows and advanced toward them. Shelagh saw that it was the postmaster from Ballyfane. She was not sure whether to be sorry or relieved.

"Good evening again," she said, her voice a shade too hearty. "You see I didn't wait until morning after all, I found my way successfully, thanks to your advice."

"So," replied the postmaster, "I noticed your car up there on the road parked by the turning, and thought it best to follow in case you came to harm."

"That was kind of you," said Shelagh. "You shouldn't have bothered."

"No bother at all. Better be sure than sorry." He turned to the young man in the fisherman's jersey. "It's a fine night, Michael."

"It is, Mr. O'Reilly. This young lady tells me she's here for the fishing. I've explained she'll have better sport the other side of Ballyfane."

"That's true, if it's fishing she's after," said the postmaster, and he smiled for the first time, but unpleasantly, too knowing. "The young lady was in the post office this evening asking for Commander Barry. She was surprised he was not on the telephone."

"Fancy that, now," said the young man, and disconcertingly he produced a torch from his pocket and flashed it in her face. "Excuse the liberty, miss, but I haven't had the pleasure of meeting you before. If you'd care to tell me your business with the Commander I will pass on the message."

"Michael here lives on Lamb Island," said the postmaster. "He's by way of being a watchdog to the Commander, and keeps unwelcome visitors at bay, you might say."

He said this with the same knowing smile which she found so unpleasant, and she wished she could be away and out of it, back in the neat little bedroom at the Kilmore Arms, not here beside the sinister lake with these two strange men.

"I'm afraid I can't give a message," she said. "It's a private matter. Perhaps it would be better if I wrote to Commander Barry from the hotel. He isn't expecting me, you see. It's all rather difficult."

Her loss of composure was evident to the two men. She saw them exchange glances. Then the young man jerked his head at the postmaster and drew him aside, and they spoke together out of earshot. Her uneasiness increased.

The young man turned back to her. "I tell you what I'll do," and he was smiling now, but a shade too broadly. "I'll run you over to the island in the boat, and the Commander shall decide for himself whether he wants to see you or not."

"Oh, no . . ." said Shelagh, backing away, "not tonight. It's much too late. I'll come back in the morning, and you can run me across then."

"It would be better to get it over with tonight," said Michael.

Get it over with? What did he mean? A few months ago she had boasted to some friends after a first-night party that she had never been frightened of anything in her life, except drying up. She was frightened now.

"They'll be waiting up for me at the hotel," she said quickly. "If I don't return soon Mr. Doherty will get in touch with the police."

"Don't fret yourself," said the postmaster. "I have a friend standing by up the road. He'll drive your car back to the Kilmore Arms and we'll make it all right between us with Tim Doherty."

Before she could protest further they had seized her arms and were marching her between them down to the boat. It can't be true, she thought, it can't be happening, and a strangled sob escaped her, like that of a terrified child.

"Ah, sshh now," said Michael, "no one's going to touch a hair of your head. You said yourself it's a fine night. It's finer still on the water. You may see the fish jumping."

He helped her into the boat and pushed her firmly on the stern seat. The postmaster remained onshore. That's better, she thought, at least there's only one of them.

"So long, Mr. O'Reilly," Michael called softly, starting the engine, then loosening the painter from the mooring post.

"So long, Michael my boy," called the postmaster.

The boat glided away from the reeds onto the open lough, the chug-chug of the little engine quiet, subdued. The postmaster waved his hand, then turned back and started walking up the shore toward the footpath.

The journey from mainland to island took barely five minutes, but seen from the lake the mainland appeared dark, remote, the hills in the distance an ominous smudge. The comforting lights of Ballyfane were out of sight. She had never felt so vulnerable, so alone. Michael said nothing until the boat drew in alongside a small landing stage built out from the narrow shore. The trees clustered thickly to the water's edge. He tied up the boat, then held out his hand to her.

"Now then," he said when he had helped her onto the landing stage, "the truth is that the Commaner is away at a meeting the other side of the lough, but he should be back by midnight or thereabouts. I'll take you up to the house and the steward will look after you."

The steward . . . The Ballyfane Castle or the Georgian mansion had returned to the land of fantasy whence they had sprung, but steward had a medieval ring to it, Malvolio with a tapering staff, stone steps leading to an audience chamber. Wolf-hounds guarding doors. A faint measure of confidence returned to her. Michael was not going to strangle her under the trees.

Surprisingly, the house was revealed after little more than a hundred yards, set in a clearing amidst the trees. A long, low, one-storied building, built surely of timber put up in sections, like pictures of relief hospitals erected by missionaries in jungles for sick natives. A veranda ran the whole length of it, and as Michael led her up the steps and paused before a door marked GALLEY ENTRANCE a dog barked from within, not the deep-throated baying of a wolfhound but shriller, sharper, and Michael laughed, turned to her, and said, "They don't need me as watchdog when Skip's around. She'd smell strangers twenty miles away."

The door opened. A short, stocky, middle-aged man stood before them dressed in the uniform of a naval steward.

"A small problem for you, Bob," said Michael. "The young lady here was wandering down by the lough just now in the darkness and all, and it appears she was inquiring of Mr. O'Reilly for the Commander."

The steward's face remained impassive, but his eyes traveled down from Shelagh's face to her clothes, and her jacket pockets in particular.

"There's nothing on her," said Michael, "and she must have left her handbag in the car beside the road. The young lady is staying up at the Arms, but we thought it best to bring her straight here. You never can tell."

"Please come inside miss," said the steward to Shelagh, his voice courteous but firm. "You're from England, I take it."

"Yes," she replied. "I flew over to Dublin today, and drove straight here. My business with Commander Barry is a personal matter, and I don't want to discuss it with anyone else."

"I see," said the steward.

The little dog, a schipperke, with pricked ears and bright, intelligent eyes, was sniffing daintily at Shelagh's ankles.

"Would you give me your coat?" asked the steward.

A strange request. She was wearing a short tweed jacket and matching skirt. She handed over the jacket, and he examined the pockets and placed it over the back of the chair. Then—and this was disconcerting—he ran his hands in a brisk professional way over her body, while Michael watched with interest.

"I don't know why you're doing this," she said. "You've hijacked me, not the other way round."

"It's a way we have with visitors we don't know," said the steward. "It saves argument in the long run." He jerked his head at Michael. "You did right to bring the young lady along. I'll explain matters to the Commander when he returns."

Michael grinned, winked at Shelagh, raised his hand in a mock salute, and went out, shutting the door behind him.

"Will you come with me, please?" said the steward.

Reluctant to see the last of Michael, who seemed suddenly an ally, not a prospective rapist, Shelagh threw a quick look round the kitchen, picked up her jacket, and followed Bob the steward (not Malvolio after all) along a corridor to a room at the farther end. The steward threw open the door and ushered her in.

"Cigarettes on the table by the fire," he said. "Ring the bell if there is anything you require. Would you care for coffee?"

"Please," said Shelagh. If she was going to sit up all night coffee would help.

The room was spacious, comfortable, a blue carpet fitted wall to wall. A settee, a couple of deep armchairs, a large flat-topped desk near the window. Pictures of ships on the wall. A log fire burning brightly in the hearth. The setting reminded her of something. She had seen some place like it in the past, reminding her of childhood days. Then she remembered. It was a duplicate of the captain's cabin in *Excalibur,* her father's cabin. Layout, furnishings, were identical. The familiar surroundings were uncanny, it was like stepping back into the past.

She wandered round the room, trying to take it in. She crossed to the window and drew aside the curtains, half-expecting to see the deck outside, and beyond, in the distance, other ships at anchor in Portsmouth harbor. There was no deck, though, no ships. Only the long veranda, the shrouded trees, and the pathway to the lough, the silver water shining beneath the moon. The door opened once again, and the steward brought in coffee on a silver tray.

"The Commander won't be long now," he said. "I've just had word his launch left fifteen minutes ago."

Launch . . . They had more than one boat, then. And just had word. There had been so sound of a telephone ringing, and anyway, the house wasn't on the phone. He went out and closed the door. She began to panic once again, realized she was lost without her bag, left in the car. No comb, no lipstick. She hadn't touched her face since before going down to the bar at the Kilmore Arms. She peered into the mirror hanging on the wall beyond the desk. Hair dank, face white and pinched, she looked frantic. She wondered whether it would be best for him to find her sitting in one of the armchairs, drinking her coffee, seemingly relaxed, or standing rather boyishly before the fireplace, hands in her jacket pockets. She needed direction, she needed someone like Adam Vane to tell her what to do, how to place herself before the curtain rose.

She turned round from the mirror, facing the desk, and saw the photograph in the blue leather frame. The photograph of her mother as a bride, her veil thrown back, the irritating smile of triumph on her face. There was something wrong, though. The groom standing beside her was not Shelagh's father. It was Nick, the best man, hair *en brosse,* supercilious, bored. She looked closer, baffled, and realized that the photgraph had been cleverly faked. Nick's head and shoulders had been transposed onto her father's figure, while her father's head, sleek-haired, smiling happily, had been shifted to the lanky figure behind, standing between the bridesmaids. It was only because she knew the original photograph on her father's desk at home, and had a copy herself somewhere, stuck away in a drawer, that she recognized the transposition instantly. A stranger would think the photograph genuine. But why on earth?

Whom did Nick want to deceive, unless it was himself?

Shelagh moved away from the desk, uneasy. People who were mentally sick deceived themselves. What was it her father had said? Nick had always been a border-line case . . . She had been frightened before, standing on the shore by the lake, questioned by the two men, but that had been physical fear, a natural reaction in the face of possible brutality. This was different—a feeling of revulsion, a strange apprehension. The room that had seemed warm and familiar became kinky, queer. She wanted to get out of it.

She went to the French window and pulled aside the curtains. The window was locked. No key, no way of escape. Then she heard the sound of voices in the hall, and this is it, she thought, I've got to face it. I must lie, make up my lines, improvise. I'm alone here but for the steward, with someone who is sick, who is mad. The door opened, and he came into the room.

Surprise was mutual. He had caught her, literally, on the wrong foot, hovering between armchair and coffeetable, semibent, an awkward position, no sort of poise. She straightened herself and stared. So did he. He was not in the least like the best man in the authentic wedding group, except for the figure, lanky and tall. The hair was no loner *en brosse* because there was little of it, and the small black patch over the left eye suggested Moshe Dayan. The right eye was very bright and blue. The mouth thin. As he stood there, staring, the little dog pranced in behind him. He called over his shoulder to the steward. "See that Operation B goes forward as of now, Bob," he said, without taking his eye off Shelagh, and "Aye, aye, sir," replied the steward from the corridor.

The door closed, and Nick came into the room and said, "I see Bob brought you some coffee. Is it cold?"

"I don't know," Shelagh replied. "I haven't drunk any yet."

"Add some whisky to it, you'll feel better."

He opened a wall cupboard and brought out a tray with decanter, soda syphon, and glasses upon it. He put it on the table between the two chairs, then flung himself down on the one opposite her, the dog on his lap. Shelagh poured some whisky into her cup of coffee, aware that her hand trembled. She was sweating, too. His voice was clear, rather clipped, authoritative, reminding her of a director who used to teach at drama school and had half his students in tears. All except her. She had walked out of class one morning, and he had had to apologize.

"Come on, relax," said her host. "You're as taut as a bowstring. I apologize for the abduction, but it was your own fault for wandering down by the lake late in the evening."

"The signpost said footpath to Lough Torrah," she replied. "I didn't see a notice forbidding trespassers, or warning people away. They ought to advise visitors at the airport never to wander after sundown, but I suppose they can't, it would hit the tourist trade for six."

Stuff that up, she thought, and tossed down her whisky-laced coffee. He smiled, but not with her, at her, and began to stroke the smooth, sleek coat of the little dog. The one eye was disconcerting. She had the impression that the left eye was still there behind the patch.

"What's your name?"

Her reply was instinctive. "Jinnie," she told him, and added, "Blair."

Jennifer Blair was her stage name. Shelagh Money had never sounded right. But nobody except her father had ever called her Jinnie. It must have been nerves that had made her blurt it out now.

"H'm," he said. "Jinnie. Rather nice. Why did you want to see me, Jinnie?"

Improvisation. Play it by ear, Adam Vane always said. This is the situation, take it from here. Starting now . . .

There was a cigarette box on the table, and a lighter. She leaned forward and took a cigarette from the box. He did not attempt to light it for her.

"I'm a journalist. My editors want to run a new series in the spring about the effects of retirement on Service men. Whether they like it, whether they're bored. Their hobbies, and so on. You know the kind of thing. Well, four of us were given the assignment. You were on my list, and here I am."

"I see."

She wished he would take that eye off her for one moment. The little dog, in ecstasy at the stroking hand, was now lying on its back, paws in the air.

"What made you think I should be of any interest to your readers?"

"That wasn't really my problem," she told him. "Other people do the checkups in the office. I was merely given brief particulars. Service career, good war record, retired, lives at Ballyfane, and told to take it from there. Bring back a story. Human interest, and all that . . ."

"Curious," he said, "that your bosses should have picked on me when there are many far more distinguished persons living over here in retirement. Generals, rear-admirals, scores of 'em."

She shrugged her shoulders. "If you ask me," she said, "they pick the names out of a hat. And someone, I forget who, said you were a recluse. They love that sort of thing. Find out what makes him tick, they told me."

He poured himself a drink, then leaned back again in his chair.

"What's the name of your paper?" he asked.

"It isn't a newspaper, it's a magazine. One of the new glossies, very up and coming, published every fortnight. *Searchlight*. You may have seen it."

"*Searchlight* was, in point of fact, a recent publication. She had skimmed through it in the aircraft coming over.

"No, I've not seen it," he told her "but then, living as a recluse, that's hardly surprising, is it?"

"No. No, I suppose not."

The eye was watchful. She blew a cloud of smoke into the air.

"So it was professional curiosity that took you wandering to the lake by night, rather than wait until daylight to approach me?"

"Naturally. And the fact that you live on an island. Islands are always mysterious. Especially by night."

"You're not easily scared?"

"I was scared when your henchman Michael and the rather unpleasant postmaster seized me by the arms and forced me into the boat."

"What did you think they were going to do?"

"Assault, rape, murder, in that order."

"Ah, that's what comes of reading the English newspapers and writing for glossy magazines. We're a peaceable lot in Ireland, you'd be surprised. We shoot each other up, but that's traditional. Rape is uncommon. We seldom seduce our women. They seduce us."

Now it was Shelagh who smiled, in spite of herself. Confidence was returning. Parry and thrust. She could keep this sort of thing going for hours.

"May I quote you on that?" she asked.

"I'd rather you didn't. Bad for the national image. We like to think of ourselves as devils. We get more respect that way. Have some more whisky."

"Thank you, I will."

If this was rehearsal, she thought, the director would tell me to change position. Pour myself another drink from the decanter and stand up, look about the room. No, on second thoughts, better stay put.

"Now it's your turn to answer questions," she said. "Does your boatman make a habit of hijacking tourists?"

"No. You are the first. You should be flattered."

"I told him," she went on, "and the postmaster as well, that it was too late for an evening call, and I'd come back in the morning. They wouldn't listen. And when I got here your steward searched me—frisked me, I believe they call it."

"Bob's very thorough. It's an old naval custom. We used to frisk the local girls when they came aboard. It was part of the fun."

"Liar," she said.

"No, I assure you. They've put a stop to it now, I'm told. Like the daily tots of rum. Another reason why youngsters won't join the Navy anymore. You can quote me on that, if you like."

She watched him over the rim of her glass. "Do you regret leaving the Service?"

"Not in the slightest. I had all I wanted from it."

"Except promotion?"

"Oh, to hell with promotion. Who wants to command a ship in peacetime when a vessel is obsolete before she's even launched? Nor did I fancy sitting on my backside in the Admiralty or some establishment ashore. Besides, I had more worthwhile things to do here at home."

"Such as?"

Finding out about my own country. Reading history. Oh, not Cromwell and all that—the ancient stuff, which is much more fascinating. I've written thousands of words on the subject which will never get printed. Articles appear sometimes in scholarly journals, but that's about all. I don't get paid for them. Not like you, writing for magazines."

He smiled again. It was rather a good smile. Not good in the accepted sense of the word, but in hers. Whipping up, in fact, challenging. ("He used to be such fun at parties.") Had the moment come? Did she dare?

"Tell me," she asked, "I know it's personal, but my readers will want to know. I couldn't help noticing that photograph on your desk. You've been married, then?"

"Yes," he said, "the one tragedy of my life. She was killed in a car crash a few months after we were married. Unluckily I survived. That's when I lost my eye."

Her mind went blank. Improvise . . . improvise.

"How terrible for you," she murmured. "I'm very sorry."

"That's all right. It happened years ago. I took a long time to get over it, of course, but I learned to live with the situation, to adapt. There was nothing else I could do. I'd retired from the Navy by then, which admittedly didn't help matters. However, there it was, and, as I told you, it happened a long time ago."

Then he really believed it? He really believed he had been married to her mother, and she had been killed in a car crash? Something must have happened to his brain when he lost the eye, something had gone wrong. And when had he tampered with the photograph? Before the accident or afterward? And why? Doubt and mistrust returned. She was just beginning to like him, to feel at ease with him, and now her confidence was shattered. If he was insane, how must she handle him, what must she do? She got up and stood by the fireplace, and how odd, she thought, the movement is natural, it's not acting, not a stage direction, the play is becoming real.

"Look," she said, "I don't think I want to write this article after all. It isn't fair to you. You've been through too much. I hadn't realized. And I'm sure my editor would agree. It's not our policy to probe into a person's suffering. *Searchlight* isn't that sort of magazine."

"Oh, really?" he replied. "How disappointing. I was looking forward to reading all about myself. I'm rather conceited, you know."

He began stroking the dog again, but his eye never left her face.

"Well," she said, searching for words, "I could say a bit about your living here alone on the island, fond of your dog, keen on ancient history . . . and so on."

"Wouldn't that be rather dull and hardly worth printing?"

"No, not at all."

Suddenly he laughed, put the dog on the floor, and stood up on the hearthrug beside her. "You'd have to do rather better than this to get away with it," he said. "Let's discuss it in the morning. You can tell me then, if you like, who you really are. If you're a journalist, which I doubt, you weren't sent here to write about my hobbies and my pet dog. Funny, you remind me of someone, but I can't for the life of me think who it is."

He smiled down at her, very confident of himself, not at all mad, reminding her . . . of what? Being in her father's cabin on board *Excalibur?* Being swept up in the air by her father, screaming with delight and fear? Or, the smell of eau-de-cologne that he used, and this man, too, not like the stinking aftershave they all swamped themselves with today . . .

"I'm always reminding people of somebody else," she said. "No personality of my own. You remind me of Moshe Dayan."

He touched his eyeshade. "Just a gimmick. If he and I sported them pink, we'd be ignored. The fact that it's black transforms it. Has the same effect on women that black stockings have on men."

He walked across the room and threw open the door. "Bob?" he called.

"Sir," came the reply from the kitchen.

"Operation B under way?"

"Sir. Michael coming alongside now."

"Right!" He turned to Shelagh. "Let me show you the rest of the house."

She inferred, from the nautical language, that Michael was standing by to escort her by boat to the mainland. Time enough when she got back to the Kilmore Arms to decide whether to return in the morning and brazen it out, or forget all about the mission and beat it for home. He escorted her down the corridor, throwing open one door after the other, with names upon them. CONTROL ROOM . . . SIGNALS . . . SICK BAY . . . CREW'S QUARTERS . . . This must be it, she told herself. He had a fantasy of living on board ship. This is how he has come to terms with life, with disappointment, with injury.

"We're highly organized," he told her. "I've no use for the telephone—communication with the mainland is by shortwave radio. If you live on an island you've got to be self-sufficient. Like a ship at sea. I've built all this up from scratch. There wasn't even a log house when I came to Lamb Island, and now it's a complete flagship. I could control a fleet from here."

He smiled at her in triumph, and he *is* mad, she thought, raving mad, but for all that attractive—very, in fact. It would be easy to be taken in, to believe everything he said.

"How many of you live here?"

"Ten, including myself. These are my quarters."

They had reached a door at the end of the corridor. He led the way through it to a separate wing. There were three rooms and a bathroom. One door had COMMANDER BARRY written upon it.

"I'm in here," he said, throwing open the door, revealing a typical captain's cabin, with a bed, though, not a bunk. The layout was familiar, giving her a sudden poignant nostalgia.

"Guest rooms next door," he said. "Numbers One and Two. Number One has a better view of the lake."

He advanced into the room and drew aside the curtains. The moon had risen high by now, and shone down upon the sheet of water beyond the trees. It was very peaceful, very still. There was nothing sinister about Lamb Island now. The situation was reversed, and it was the distant mainland that seemed shrouded, drear.

"Even I should become a recluse if I lived here," she said, and then, turning from the window, added, "I mustn't keep you up. Perhaps Michael is waiting to take me back."

He had switched on the bedside lamp. "You're not going back. Operation B has been put into effect."

"What do you mean?"

The single eye was upon her, discomfiting, amused. "When I was told that a young woman wanted to see me, I decided upon a plan of action. Operation A meant that whoever it was signified nobody of interest, and could be returned to Ballyfane. Operation B meant that the visitor would be my guest, and her luggage fetched from the Kilmore Arms and matters explained to Tim Doherty. He's very discreet."

She stared at him, her sense of unease returning. "You didn't give yourself much time to consider. I heard you give orders about Operation B as soon as you came into the room down there."

"That's right. I'm in the habit of coming to quick decisions. Here is Bob with your things now."

There was a cough, a quiet knock on the door. The steward came in bearing her luggage. Everything had evidently been put back into her suitcase, all the small litter from her bedroom at the hotel. He also had her maps and her handbag from the car. Nothing had been forgotten.

"Thank you, Bob," Nick said. "Miss Blair will ring down for breakfast when she wants it."

The steward placed her things on a chair, murmured, "Good-night, miss," and withdrew. So that is that, thought Shelagh, and where do we go from here? He was still watching her, the smile of amusement on his face. When in doubt, she told herself, yawn. Be casual. Pretend this sort of thing happens every night of your life. She picked up her bag and found her comb, ran it through her hair, humming a tune under her breath.

"You should never have retired," she said. "Such a waste of your organizing powers. You ought to be commanding the Mediterranean Fleet. Planning an exercise, or something."

"That's exactly what I am doing. You'll get your orders when this ship is at action stations. Now I've got some work to do, so I'll leave you. By the way . . ." he paused, his hand on the door, "you don't have to lock this, you're perfectly safe."

"I wouldn't dream of locking it," she replied. "As a journalist I'm used to shakedowns in the most unlikely places, and prowling about unknown corridors in the middle of the night."

Punch line, she thought. That will teach you. Now disappear and turn all your furniture upside down . . .

"Ah," he said, "so that's your form. It's not a case of you locking your door but of me locking mine. Thanks for the warning."

She heard him laughing as he went down the corridor. Curtain. Damn. He had had the last word.

She went to her suitcase and threw it open. The few clothes, night things, makeup, neatly packed. Her handbag untouched. A lucky thing the papers for the hired Austin were all in her stage name. Nothing to connect her with Shelagh Money. The only thing that had been shaken and folded differently was the map and the tourist guide. Well, that didn't matter. She had marked Ballyfane and Lough Torrah with blue pencil, but a journalist would have done that anyway. Something was missing though—the copper-colored paper clip had gone. She shook the tourist guide, but nothing fell out. The envelope was no longer there. The envelope containing the slip of paper with the dates upon it, which she had copied from the file in her father's study.

When Shelagh awoke the sun was streaming into the room. She glanced at her traveling clock beside the bed. A quarter past nine. She had slept soundly for nearly ten hours. She got out of bed and went to the window, drawing the curtains aside. Her room appeared to be at the extreme end of the building, and immediately beyond her window a grass bank sloped toward the trees, and through the trees themselves a narrow clearing led down to the lake. The glimpse she could catch of the lake showed the water to be sparking blue, the surface that had been so still last evening now turned to wavelets, whipped by a scudding breeze. Nick had told the steward she would ring down for her breakfast, and she picked up the telephone by the bed. Bob's voice came at once.

"Yes, miss. Orange juice? Coffee? Rolls? Honey?"

"Please . . ."

Service, she thought. I shouldn't be getting this at the Kilmore Arms. Bob brought the tray to her bedside within four minutes. The morning paper was also upon it, neatly folded.

"The Commander's compliments, miss," he said. "He hopes you slept well. If there is anything else you require you have only to tell me."

I'd like to know if it was Mr. Doherty at the Kilmore Arms or Mr. O'Reilly from the post office who took the envelope from the tourist guide, she was thinking. Or could it be you, Malvio? Nobody would have bothered about it if I hadn't scribbled on the envelope, "N. Barry. Dates possibly significant."

"I have everything I need, thank you, Bob," she said.

When she had breakfasted, dressed herself in sweater and jeans, and made up her eyes with rather greater care than she had done the day before, she was ready to face whatever surprises Nick had in store for her. She walked down the corridor, passed through the swing door, and came to the living room. The door was open, but he was not there. Somehow she had expected to see him at his desk. She went across to it, glancing furtively over her shoulder, and stared at the photograph once again. Nick was much better now than then, she thought. As a young man he must have been irritating, over-pleased with himself, and she had a feeling that his hair had been red. The whole truth was, she supposed, that they had both been in love with her mother, and when her father won this had helped to turn Nick sour. Started the chip. Odd that her mother had not mentioned the fact. She generally preened her feathers about old admirers. Disloyal, Shelagh knew, but what had both men seen in her except that very obvious pretty-pretty face? Far too much lipstick, like they wore in those days. And a bit of a snob, always name-dropping. She and her father used to wink at each other if she did it in front of other people. A discreet cough warned her that the steward was watching her from the corridor beyond.

"The Commander is in one of the wood clearings, miss, if you were looking for him. I can point you the way."

"Oh, thank you, Bob."

They went out together, and he said, "You'll find the Commander working down on the site about ten minutes' walk away."

The site . . . Felling trees, perhaps. She set off through the woods, the foliage thick and green on either side of the path, dense as a miniature forest, without a glimpse of the lake to be seen. If one strayed from the path, she thought, and wandered amongst the trees, one would be lost instantly, striking for the lake and not finding it, moving round and round in circles. The wind sighed in the branches above her head. No birds, no movement, no lapping water near at hand. A person could be buried here in all the undergrowth and never found. Perhaps she should turn back, retrace her steps to the house, tell the steward she preferred to wait indoors for Commander Barry. She hesitated, but it was already too late. Michael was advancing through the trees toward her. He carried a spade in his hand.

"The Commander is waiting for you, miss, He wants to show you the grave. We've just uncovered it."

Oh God, what grave, for whom? She felt the color drain from her face. Michael was not smiling. He jerked his head toward a small clearing just ahead. Then she saw the others. There were two other men besides Nick. They were stripped to the waist, bending over something in the ground. She felt her legs weaken under her, and her heart began thumping in her breast.

"Miss Blair is here, sir," said Michael.

Nick turned and straightened. He was dressed like the others, in singlet and jeans. He did not carry a spade, but had a small axe in his hand.

"So," he said, "the moment has arrived. Come over here and kneel down."

He placed his hand on her shoulder, and drew her toward the crater that opened wide before her. She could not speak. She could only see the brown earth piled on either side of the crater, the tumbled leaves, the branches tossed aside. Instinctively, as she knelt, she buried her face in her hands.

"What *are* you doing?" He sounded surprised. "You can't see with your eyes covered. This is a great occasion, you know. You're probably the first Englishwoman to be present at the uncovering of a megalithic tomb in Ireland. Court cairns, we call them. The boys and I have been working on this one for weeks."

The next thing she knew was that she was sitting humped against a tree with her head between her legs. The world stopped spinning, gradually became clear. She was sweating all over.

"I think I'm going to be sick," she said.

"Go ahead," he replied. "Don't mind me."

She opened her eyes. The men had all disappeared and Nick was crouching beside her.

"That's what comes of only having coffee for breakfast," he told her. "Quite fatal starting the day on an empty stomach."

He rose to his feet and wandered back to the crater.

"I've tremendous hopes of this find. It's in a better state of preservation than many others I've seen. We only stumbled upon it by chance a few weeks ago. We've uncovered the forecourt and part of what I think is a gallery for the burial place itself. It's not been disturbed since about 1500 B.C.. Can't have the outside world getting wind of it, or we shall have all the archaeological chaps over here wanting to take photographs, and that would put the fat in the fire all right. Feeling better?"

"I don't know," she said weakly. "I think so."

"Come and have a look, then."

She dragged herself to the crater and peered into the depths. A lot of stones, a sort of rounded arch affair, a kind of wall. Impossible to show enthusiasm, her misunderstanding and fear had been too great.

"Very interesting," she said, and then to her shame, far worse than being sick, she burst into tears. He stared at her, momentarily nonplussed, then taking her by the hand began walking briskly through the wood without speaking, whistling between his teeth, until within a few minutes the trees had cleared and they were standing by the side of the lake.

"Ballyfane is over to the west. You can't see it from here. The lake broadens to the north on this side, and winds in and out against the mainland like a patchwork quilt. In winter the duck fly in and settle amongst the reeds. I never shoot them, though. In summer I come and swim here before breakfast."

Shelagh had recovered. He had given her time to pull herself together, which was all that mattered, and she was grateful to him.

"I'm sorry," she said, "but frankly, when I saw Michael with the spade and he said something about a grave, I thought my last moment had come."

He stared at her, astonished. Then he smiled. "You're not so hard-bitten as you like to pretend. That swagger of yours is all bluff."

"Partly," she admitted, "but it's a new situation to me, being dumped on an island with a recluse. I see now why I was hijacked. You don't want anyone leaking about your megalithic find to the Press. O.K., I won't. That's a promise."

He did not answer immediately. He stood there, stroking his chin.

"H'm," he said after a moment. "Well, that's very sporting of you. Now, I'll tell you what we'll do. We'll go back to the house, get Bob to make up a packed lunch, and I'll take you for a tour of the lake. And I promise not to push you overboard."

He's only mad, she thought, "nor-nor-west." He's sane in every respect save for the photograph. But for that . . . but for the photograph she would come clean at once and tell him the truth about herself, about her reason for coming to Ballyfane. Not yet, though.

Nothing could be more different, Shelagh decided several hours later, than the Nick described by her father, with a chip on the shoulder, a grudge against the world, soured by disappointment, than this man who put himself out to entertain her, to see that she enjoyed every moment of the hours spent in his company. The twin-engined launch, with a small cabin forward—not the little chug-chug craft in which Michael had brought her to the island the day before—glided smoothly across the lake, dodging in and out amongst the tongues of land, while he pointed out to her, from the helmsman's seat, the various points of interest on the mainland. The distant hills to the west, a ruined castle, the tower of an ancient abbey. Never once did he allude to the reason for her visit, nor press her for information about her own life. Seated side by side in the small cabin, they ate hard-boiled eggs and cold chicken, and she kept thinking how her father would have loved it, how this would have been just his way of spending a day had he lived to take that holiday. She could picture him and Nick together, chaffing, slanging away at each other, showing off, in a curious sort of way, because she was there. Not her mother, though. She would have wrecked the whole thing.

"You know," she said in a burst of confidence, the effect of a tot of whisky before the Guinness, "the Commander Barry I imagined wasn't a scrap like you."

"What did you imagine?" he asked.

"Well, because of your being this recluse they told me about, I pictured someone living in a castle filled with old retainers and baying wolfhounds. Rather a buffer. Either grim and very rude, shouting at the retainers, or terribly hearty, playing practical jokes."

He smiled. "I can be very rude when I choose, and I often shout at Bob. As to practical jokes . . . I've played them in my time. Still do. Have another Guinness?" She shook her head and leaned back against the bulkhead. "The trouble was," he said, "the sort of jokes I played were mostly to amuse myself. They've gone out of fashion, anyway. I don't suppose you, for instance, ever put white mice in your editor's desk?"

For editor's desk substitute star's dressing room, she thought.

"Not white mice," she replied, "but I once put a stink bomb under my boss's bed. He hopped out of it pretty quick, I don't mind telling you."

Manchester it was, and Bruce never forgave her, either. What he thought was boiling up to be a discreet affair between them vanished in smoke.

"That's what I meant," he said. "The best of jokes are only fun for oneself. A bit of a gamble, though, to pick on your boss."

"Self-protection," she told him. "I was bored at the thought of getting into bed with him."

He started to laugh, then checked himself. "Forgive me, I'm being hearty. Do you have a lot of trouble with your editors?"

She pretended to reflect. "It all depends. They can be rather demanding. And if you're ambitious, which I am, it earns you promotion. The whole thing's a chore, though. I'm not really permissive."

"Meaning what?"

"Well, I don't strip down at the flick of a hat. It has to be someone I like. Am I shocking you?"

"Not in the least. A buffer like myself likes to know how the young live."

She reached for a cigarette. This time he lighted it for her.

"The thing is," she said, and she might have been talking to her father after Sunday supper, with her mother safe in the other room, only actually this was more fun, "the thing is, I find sex overrated. Men make such a fuss, put one off, all that groaning. Some even cry. The only reason one does it is to claim a scalp, like playing Red Indians. The whole thing's a dead loss, in my opinion. But there, I'm only nineteen.

Plenty of time to ripen up."

"I wouldn't count on it. Nineteen is getting on a bit. It's later than you think." He rose from the locker, strolled over to his helmsman's seat and switched on the engine. "It gives me enormous satisfaction," he added. "to think of all those heads you've scalped, and the groaning that goes on in Fleet Street. I must warn my friends amongst the Press that they had better watch out."

She looked up at him, startled. "What friends?"

He smiled. "I have my contacts." He turned the launch back in the direction of Lamb Island, and it's only a matter of time, she told herself, before he checks my Press credentials, discovers they don't exist. As for Jennifer Blair, he'd have to contact a fair number of theater managers before one of them said, "You mean that brilliant young actress the Stratford people have been trying to get hold of for next season?"

Too soon by far he was bringing the launch alongside the landing-stage-cum-boathouse of his domain, cunningly masked by the thickly planted trees, Michael there to receive them, and she remembered her fright of the morning, the partly uncovered megalithic cairn in the heart of the wooded island.

"I've spoiled your day," she said to Nick. "You were all of you working on that site, and would have gone on with it but for me."

"Not necessarily. Relaxation takes varying forms. The digging can wait. Any news, Michael?"

"Some signals received, sir, up at the house. Everything in order."

Metamorphosis was complete by the time they reached the house. The companion had become brusque, alert, intent upon matters other than herself. Even the little dog who leaped into his arms as soon as she heard her master's voice was swiftly put down again.

"Everyone in the control room for briefing in five minutes, Bob," he said.

"Sir."

Nick turned to Shelagh. "You must amuse yourself, if you don't mind. Books, radio, T.V., records, all in the room we were in last night. I shall be busy for several hours."

Several hours . . . It was only just after six. Would his business whatever it was, take him until nine or ten? She had hoped for something different, a long intimate evening stretched out in front of the fire when anything might happen.

"O.K.," she said with a shrug. "I'm in your hands. I'd like to know, by the way, how long you intend to keep me here. I have certain commitments back in London."

"I bet you have. But the scalping will have to wait. Bob, see that Miss Blair has some tea."

He disappeared along the corridor, the dog at his heels. She flung herself down on the settee, sulking. What a bore! Especially when the day had gone so well. She had no desire to read or listen to records. His taste would be like her father's old Peter Cheyneys and John Buchans; he used to read them over and over again. And music of the lighter sort, probably *South Pacific*.

The steward brought in her tea, and this time there were cherry jam and scones, freshly baked, what's more. She wolfed the lot. Then she pottered round the room, inspecting the shelves. No Peter Cheyney, no John Buchan, endless books on Ireland, which she expected anyway, Yeats forever, Synge, A.E., a volume on the Abbey Theatre. That might be interesting, but, I'm not in the vein, she thought, I'm not in the vein. The records were mostly classical, Mozart, Haydn, Bach, stacks of the damn things. All right if he'd been in the room and they could have listened together. The photograph on the desk she ignored. Even to glance at it produced intense irritation. How could he? What had he seen in her? Indeed, what had her father seen, for that matter? But for Nick, obviously more intellectual than her father had ever been, to go round the bend about somebody like her mother, granting she had been pretty in her day, passed all comprehension.

I know what I'll do, thought Shelagh, I'll go and wash my hair.

It was frequently a remedy when all else failed. She walked along the corridor, passing the door with the words CONTROL ROOM upon it. She could hear the murmur of voices from within. Then Nick laughed, and she hurried past in case the door opened and she was caught trying to eavesdrop. The door did open, when she was safely on her way, and glancing back over her shoulder she saw a boy come out, one of those who had been helping to uncover the cairn that morning. She remembered his mop of light hair. He couldn't be more than eighteen. They were all young, now she came to think of it. All except Nick himself, and Bob. She passed through the swing door to her own room and sat down on her bed, stunned by a new idea that had suddenly come to her.

Nick was a homo. They were all homos. That was why Nick had been sacked from the Navy. Her father had found out, couldn't pass him for promotion, and Nick had borne a grudge ever afterward. Perhaps, even the dates she had copied from the list referred to times when Nick had got into trouble. The photograph was a blind—homos often tried to cover themselves by pretending they were married. Oh, not Nick . . . It was the end. She couldn't bear it. Why must the only attractive man she had ever met in her life have to be like that? Goddamn and blast them all, stripped to the waist there down by the megalithic tomb. They were probably doing the same in the control room now. There was no point in anything anymore. No sense in her mission. The sooner she left the island and flew back home the better.

She turned on the taps in her washbasin, and plunged her head into the water furiously. Even the soap—Aegean Blue—was far too exotic for a normal man to have under his roof. She dried her hair, twisting the towel round it turban fashion, tore off her jeans, and put on another pair. They didn't look right. She dragged on her traveling skirt instead. "That will show him I've no desire to go around aping boys."

There was a tap at her door.

"Come in," she said savagely.

It was Bob. "Excuse me, miss; the Commander would like to see you in the control room."

"I'm sorry, he'll have to wait. I've just washed my hair."

The steward coughed. "I wouldn't advise you, miss, to keep the Commander waiting."

He could not have been more courteous, and yet . . . There was something implacable about his square, stocky frame.

"Very well," said Shelagh. "The Commander must put up with my appearance, that's all."

She stalked along the corridor after him, the twisted turban giving her the appearance of a Bedouin sheik.

"Beg pardon," murmured the steward, and tapped on the door of the control room. "Miss Blair to see you, sir," he announced.

She was ready for anything. Young men sprawling in the nude on bunks. Joss sticks burning. Nick, as master of ceremonies, directing unspeakable operations. Instead, she saw the seven young men seated round a table, Nick at the head of it. An eighth man was sitting in the corner with headphones over his ears. The seven at the table stared at her, then averted their gaze. Nick raised his eyebrows briefly, then picked up a piece of paper. She recognized it as the list with the dates upon it that had been missing from her tourist guide. "I apologize for interrupting the *haute coiffure*," he said, "but these gentlemen and I would like to know the significance of these dates that you were carrying in your tourist guide."

Obey the well-tried maxim. Attack is the best form of defence.

"That is exactly what I would have asked you, Commander Barry, had you granted me an interview. But I dare say you would have avoided the question. They obviously have great significance for you, otherwise your gentlemen friends would never have pinched them in the first place."

"Fair enough," he said. "Who gave you the list?"

"It was with the other papers which the office gave me when I was put onto this job. They were just part of the briefing."

"You mean the editorial office of *Searchlight?'*

"Yes."

"Your assignment was to write an article about a retired naval officer—myself—and describe how he filled his time, hobbies, etc.?"

"That's right."

"And other members of the staff were to write similar articles about other ex-Service officers?"

"Yes. It sounded a bright idea. Something new."

"Well, I'm sorry to spoil your story, but we've checked with the editor of *Searchlight,* and not only have they no intention of publishing such a series of articles, but they don't possess a Miss Jennifer Blair even amongst the most junior members of their staff."

She might have known it. His contacts amongst the Press. Pity she wasn't a journalist. Whatever it was he was trying to hide would win her a fortune if it was published in one of the Sunday newspapers.

"Look," she said, "this is a delicate matter. Could I possibly speak to you alone?"

"Very well," Nick said, "if you prefer it."

The seven rose to their feet. They were a tough-looking bunch. She supposed that was the way he liked it.

"If you don't mind," Nick added, "the wireless operator has to stay at his post. Messages are continually coming through. He won't hear anything you say."

"That's all right," she said.

The seven young men shuffled from the room, and Nick leaned back in his chair. The bright blue eye never wavered from her face.

"Take a seat and fire away," he said.

Shelagh sat down in one of the vacant seats, conscious suddenly of the twisted towel round her head. It could hardly add to her dignity. Never mind. It was his dignity she hoped to shatter now. She would tell the truth up to a certain point, then improvise, wait for his reaction.

"The *Searchlight* editor was perfectly right," she began, drawing a deep breath. "I've never worked for them, or for any other magazine. I'm not a journalist, I'm an actress, and few people on the stage have heard of me either, as yet. I'm a member of a young theater group. We travel a lot, and we've just succeeded in getting our own theater in London. If you want to check up on that you can. It's the New World Theatre, Victoria, and everybody there knows Jennifer Blair. I'm booked to play the lead in their forthcoming series of Shakespearean comedies."

Nick smiled. "That's more like it. Congratulations."

"You can keep them for the opening night," she replied, "which will be in about three weeks' time. The director and the rest of the group know nothing about this business, they don't even know I'm here in Ireland. I'm here as the result of a bet."

She paused. This was the tricky part.

"A boy friend of mine, nothing to do with the theater, has naval connections. That list of dates came into his hands, with your name scribbled beside it. He knew it must signify something, but didn't know what. We got slightly lit up one evening after dinner, and he bet me twenty-five quid, plus expenses, that I wasn't a good enough actress to pose as a journalist and bounce you into an interview just for the hell of it. Done, I told him. And that's why I'm here. I must admit I hadn't expected to be hijacked onto an island as part of the experience. I was slightly shaken last night to find the list had been pinched from my tourist guide. So, I told myself, then the dates *did* stand for something which wouldn't bear reporting. They were all in the 'fifties, around the time you retired from the Navy, according to the naval list which I ran to earth in a public library. Now, candidly, I don't give a damn what those dates signify, but, as I said before, they obviously mean a lot to you, and I wouldn't mind betting something pretty shady, too, not to say illegal."

Nick tilted his chair, rocking it gently to and fro. The eye shifted, examined the ceiling. He was evidently at a loss for an answer, which suggested her arrow had scored a bull's-eye.

"It depends," he said softly, "what you call shady. And illegal. Opinions differ. You might be considerably shocked by actions for which my young friends and myself find perfect justification."

"I'm not easily shocked," said Shelagh.

"No, I gathered that. The trouble is, I have to convince my associates that such is indeed the case. What happened in the 'fifties does not concern them—they were children at the time—but what we do jointly today concerns all of us very much indeed. If any leak of our actions reached the outside world we should, as you rightly surmise, find ourselves up against the law."

He got up and began to straighten the papers on his table. So, Shelagh thought, whatever illegal practices her father had suspected Nick of, he was still engaged in them, here in Ireland. Smuggling archaeological finds to the U.S.A.? Or had her hunch this evening been correct? Could Nick and his bunch of friends be homosexual? Eire made so much fuss about morality that anything of the kind might well be gainst the law. It was obvious that he wouldn't let on about it to her.

Nick went and stood beside the man with the headphones, who was writing something on a pad. Some message, she supposed. Nick read it, and scribbled something himself in answer. Then he turned back to Shelagh.

"Would you like to see us in action?" he asked.

She was startled. She had been prepared for anything when she came into the control room, but to be asked point blank . . .

"What do you mean?" she asked defensively.

Her turban had slipped onto the floor. He picked it up and handed it to her.

"It would be an experience," he said, "you are never likely to have again. You won't have to take part in it. The display will be at a distance. Very stimulating. Very discreet."

He was smiling, but there was something disconcerting in the smile. She backed away from him toward the door. She had a sudden vision of herself seated somewhere in the woods, by that prehistoric grave, perhaps, unable to escape, while Nick and the young men performed some ancient and unspeakable rite.

"Quite honestly . . ." she began, but he interrupted her, still smiling.

"Quite honestly, I insist. The display will be an education in itself. We shall proceed part of the way by boat, and then take to the road."

He threw open the door. The men were lined up in the corridor, Bob amongst them.

"No problem," he said. "Miss Blair will give no trouble. Action stations."

They began to file away down the corridor. Nick took Shelagh by the arm and propelled her toward the swing door leading to his own quarters.

"Get your coat, and a scarf, if you have one. It may be cold. Look sharp."

He disappeared into his own room. When she came out again into the corridor he was waiting for her, wearing a high-necked jersey and a windcheater. He was looking at his watch.

"Come on," he said.

The men had all vanished, except the steward. He was standing at the entrance to the galley door, the little dog in his arms.

"Good luck, sir," he said.

"Thank you, Bob. Two lumps of sugar for Skip, no more."

He led the way down the narrow path through the woods to the boathouse. The engine of the launch was humming gently. There were only two men on board, Michael and the young man with the mop of hair. "Sit in the cabin and stay there," Nick told Shelagh. He himself moved to the controls. The launch began to slip away across the lake, the island disappearing astern. Shelagh soon lost direction, seated as she was inside the cabin. The mainland was a distant blur, coming close at times and then receding, but none of it taking shape under the dark sky. Sometimes, as she peered through the small porthole, they passed so near to a bank that the launch almost brushed the reeds, and then a moment afterward there was nothing but water, black and still, save for the white foam caused by the bow's thrust. The engine was barely audible. Nobody spoke. Presently the gentle throbbing ceased—Nick must have nosed his craft into shallow water beside a bank. He lowered his head into the cabin and held out his hand to her.

"This way. You'll get your feet wet, but it can't be helped."

She could see nothing around her but water and reeds and sky. She stumbled after him on the soggy ground, clinging to his hand, the fair boy just ahead, the mud oozing through her shoes. They were leading her onto some sort of track. A shape loomed out of the shadows. It looked like a van, and a man she did not recognize was standing beside it. He opened the van door. Nick got in first, dragging Shelagh after him. The fair boy went round to the front beside the driver, and the van lurched and lumbered up the track until, topping what seemed to be a rise, it came to a smooth surface that must be road. She tried to sit upright, and banged her head against a shelf above her. Something rattled and shook.

"Keep still," said Nick. "We don't want all the bread down on top of us."

"Bread?"

It was the first word she had spoken since leaving the island. He flicked on a lighter, and she saw that the partition between themselves and the driver was shut. All around them were loaves of bread, neatly stacked upon shelves, and cakes, pastries, confectionery, and tinned goods as well.

"Help yourself," he told her. "It's the last meal you'll get tonight."

He put out his arm and seized a loaf, then broke it in two. He flicked off the lighter, leaving them in darkness again. I couldn't be more helpless, she thought, if I were riding in a hearse.

"Have you stolen the van?" she asked.

"Stolen it? Why the hell should I steal a van? It's on loan from the grocer in Mulldonagh. He's driving it himself. Have some cheese. And a spot of this." He put a flask to her lips. The neat spirit nearly choked her, but gave warmth and courage at the same time. "Your feet must be wet. Take your shoes off. And fold up your jacket under your head. Then we can really get down to it."

"Down to what?"

"Well, we've a drive of some thirty-six miles before we reach the border. A smooth road all the way. I propose to scalp you."

She was traveling by sleeper back to boarding school in the north of England. Her father was waving good-bye to her from the platform. "Don't go," she called out, "don't ever leave me." The sleeper dissolved, became a dressing room in a theater, and she was standing before the looking glass dressed as Cesario in *Twelfth Night*. Sleeper and dressing room exploded . . .

She sat up, bumped her head on the rack of loaves. Nick was no longer with her. The van was stationary. Something had awakened her, though, from total blackout— they must have burst a tire. She could see nothing in the darkness of the van, not even the face of her watch. Time did not exist. It's body chemistry, she told herself, that's what does it. People's skins. They either blend or they don't. They either merge and melt into the same texture, dissolve and become renewed, or nothing happens, like faulty plugs, blown fuses, switchboard jams. When the thing goes right, as it had for me tonight, then it's arrows splintering the sky, it's forest fires, it's Agincourt. I shall live till I'm ninety-five, marry some nice man, have fifteen children, win stage awards and Oscars, but never again will the world break into fragments, burn before my eyes. I've bloody had it . . .

The van door opened and a rush of cold air blew in upon her. The boy with the mop of hair was grinning at her.

"The Commander says if you're fond of fireworks come and take a look. It's a lovely sight."

She stumbled out of the van after him, rubbing her eyes. They had parked beside a ditch, and beyond the ditch was a field, a river surely running through it, but the foreground was dark. She could distinguish little except what seemed to be farm buildings around a bend in the road. The sky in the distance had an orange glow, as if the sun, instead of setting hours ago, had risen in the north, putting all time to odds, while tongues of flame shot upward, merging with pillars of black smoke. Nick was standing by the driver's seat, the driver himself alongside, both of them staring at the sky. A muffled voice was speaking from a radio fixed near to the dashboard.

"What is it?" she asked. "What's happening?"

The driver, a middle-aged man with a furrowed face, turned to her, smiling.

"It's Armagh burning, or the best part of it. But there'll be no damage done to the cathedral. St. Patrick's will stand when the rest of the town is black."

The young man with the mop of hair had bent his ear to the radio. He straightened himself, touched Nick on the arm.

"First explosion has gone off at Omagh, sir," he said. "We should have the report on Strabane in three minutes' time. Enniskillen in five."

"Fair enough," replied Nick. "Let's go."

He bundled Shelagh back into the van and climbed in beside her. The van sprang into action, did a U-turn, and sped along the road once more.

"I might have known it," she said, "I should have guessed. But you had me fooled with your cairns in the wood and all that cover-up."

"It isn't a cover-up, I've a passion for digging. But I love explosions too."

He offered her a nip from the flask but she shook her head.

"You're a murderer. Helpless people away there burning in their beds, women and children dying perhaps in hundreds."

"Dying nothing," he replied. "They'll be out in the streets applauding. You mustn't believe Murphy. He lives in a dream world. The town of Armagh will hardly feel it. A warehouse or two may smoulder, with luck the barracks."

"And the other places the boy mentioned?"

"A firework display. Very effective."

It was all so obvious now, thinking back to that last conversation with her father. He had been onto it all right. Duty before friendship. Loyalty to his country first. No wonder the pair of them had stopped exchanging Christmas cards.

Nick took an apple from the shelf above and began to munch it.

"So . . ." he said, "You're a budding actress."

"Budding is the operative word."

"Oh come, don't be modest. You'll go far. You tricked me almost as neatly as I tricked you. All the same, I'm not sure I quite swallow the one about the friend with naval connections. Tell me his name."

"I won't. You can kill me first."

Thank heaven for Jennifer Blair. She would not have stood a chance as Shelagh Money.

"Oh well," he said, "it doesn't matter. It's all past history now."

"Then the dates did make sense to you?"

"Very good sense, but we were amateurs in those days. June 5, 1951, a raid on Ebrington Barracks, Derry. Quite a success. June 25, 1953, Felstead School Officers' Training Corps, Essex. Bit of a mix-up. June 12, 1954, Gough barracks, Armagh. Nothing much gained, but good for morale. October 17, 1954, Omagh Barracks. Brought us some recruits. April 24, 1955, Eglington Naval Air Base at Derry. H'm. . . . No comment. August 13, 1955, Arborfield Depot, Berkshire. Initial success, but a proper cockup later. After that, everyone had to do a lot of homework."

There was an Italian opera by Puccini with a song in it, "O! My Beloved Father." It always made her cry. Anyway, she thought, wherever you are, darling, in your astral body, don't blame me for what I've done, and may very well do again before the night is over. It was one way to settle your last request, though you wouldn't have approved of the method. But then, you had high ideals and I have none. And what happened in those days was not my problem. My problem is much more basic, much more direct. I've fallen hook, line, and sinker for your one-time friend.

"Politics leave me cold," she said. "What's the point of banging off bombs and upsetting everyone's lives? You hope for a united Ireland?"

"Yes," he replied, "so do we all. It will come eventually, though it may be dull for some of us when it does. Take Murphy, now. No excitement in driving a grocer's van around the countryside and being in bed by nine. This sort of keeps him young. If that's to be his future in a united Ireland he'll die before his seventieth birthday. I said to him last week when he came to the island for briefing, 'Johnnie's too young'— Johnnie's his son, the boy sitting beside him in front now—'Johnnie's too young," I told him. "Maybe we shouldn't let him risk his life yet awhile.' 'Risk be damned,' says Murphy. 'It's the only way to keep a lad out of trouble, with the world in the state it is today.'"

"You're all of you raving mad," said Shelagh. "I'll feel safer when we're back across your side of the border."

"My side of the border?" he repeated. "We never crossed it. What do you take me for? I've done some damn-fool things in my time, but I wouldn't bounce about in a grocer's van in hostile territory. I wanted you to see the fun, that's all. Actually, I'm only a consultant these days. 'Ask Commander Barry,' somebody says, 'he may have a suggestion or two to make,' and I come in from clearing cairns or writing history, and get cracking on the shortwave. It keeps me young in heart, like Murphy." He began pulling down some of the loaves from the rack and settling them under his head. "That's better. Gives me support for my neck. I once made love to a girl with my backside against a heap of handgrenades, but I was younger then. Girl never fluffed. Thought they were turnips."

Oh, no, she thought. Not again. I can't take any more just yet. The battle's over, won, I'll sue for peace. All I want to do now is to lie like this, with my legs thrown across his knees and my head on his shoulder. This is safety.

"Don't," she said.

"Oh, really? No stamina?"

"Stamina nothing, I'm suffering from shock. I shall smolder for days, like your barracks in Armagh. By the way, I belong by rights to the Protestant north. My grandfather was born there."

"Was he, indeed? That explains everything. You and I have a love-hate relationship. It's always the same with people who share a common border. Attraction and antagonism mixed. Very peculiar."

"I dare say you're right."

"Of course I'm right. When I lost my eye in the car crash I had letters of sympathy from dozens of people across the border who would gladly have seen me dead."

"How long were you in hospital?"

"Six weeks. Plenty of time to think. And plan."

Now, she thought. This is the moment. Go carefully, watch your step.

"That photograph," she said, "that photograph on your desk. It's a phoney, isn't it?"

He laughed. "Oh well, it takes an actress to spot deception. A throwback to the days of practical jokes. It makes me smile whenever I look at it, that's why I keep in on my desk. I've never been married, I invented that tale on the spur of the moment for your benefit."

"Tell me about it."

He shifted position to ensure greater comfort for both of them.

"The real bridegroom was Jack Money, a very close friend. I saw he died the other day, I was sorry for it. We'd been out of touch for years. Anyway, I was his best man. When they sent me a print of the wedding group I switched the heads round and sent a copy to Jack. He laughed his head off, but Pam, his wife, was not amused. Outraged, in fact. He told me she tore the thing up and threw the pieces in the wastepaper basket."

She would, thought Shelagh, she would. I bet she didn't even smile.

"I got my own back, though," he said, moving one of the loaves from under his head. "I dropped in on them one evening unexpectedly. Jack was out at some official dinner. Pam received me rather ungraciously, so I mixed the martinis extra strong, and had a rough-and-tumble with her on the sofa. She giggled a bit, and then passed out cold. I upset all the furniture to look as if a cyclone had hit the house, and carried her up to her bed and dumped her there. On her own, I may add. She'd forgotten all about it by the morning."

Shelagh lay back against his shoulder and stared at the roof of the van.

"I knew it," she said.

"Knew what?"

"That your generation did perfectly revolting things. Far worse than us. Under your best friend's roof. It makes me sick to think of it."

"What an extraordinary statement," he said, astonished. "No one was ever the wiser, so what the hell? I was devoted to Jack Money, although he did bog my chances of promotion shortly afterward, but for a different reason. He only acted according to his lights. Thought I might put a spoke in the slowly grinding wheels of naval intelligence, I presume, and he was bloody right."

Now I can't tell him. It's just not on. Either I go back to England battered and defeated, or I don't go at all. He's deceived my father, deceived my mother (serve her right), deceived the England he fought for for so many years, tarnished the uniform he wore, degraded his rank, spends his time now, and has done for the past twenty years, trying to split this country wider apart than ever, and I just don't care. Let them wrangle. Let them blow themselves to pieces. Let the whole world go in smoke. I'll write him a bread-and-butter letter from London saying, "Thanks for the ride," and sign it Shelagh Money. Or else . . . or else I'll go down on all fours like the little dog who follows him and leaps on his lap, and beg to stay with him forever.

"I start rehearsing Viola in a few days' time," she said. "My father had a daughter loved a man . . ."

"You'll do it very well. Especially Cesario. 'Concealment like a worm in the bud will feed on your damask cheek.' You may pine in thought, but I doubt with a green and yellow melancholy."

Murphy did another U-turn and the loaves rattled. How many miles to Lough Torrah? Don't let it end.

"The trouble is," she said, "I don't want to go home. It's not home to me anymore. Nor do I care two straws for the Theatre Group, *Twelfth Night,* or anything else. You can have Cesario."

"I can indeed."

"No . . . What I mean is, I'm willing to chuck the stage, give up my English status, burn all my bloody boats, and come and throw bombs with you."

"What, become a recluse?"

"Yes, please."

"Absurd. You'd be yawning your head off after five days."

"I would not . . . I would not . . ."

"Think of all that applause you'll be getting soon. Viola-Cesario is a cinch. I tell you what. I won't send you flowers for your opening night, I'll send you my eyeshade. You can hang it up in your dressing room to bring you luck."

I want too much, she thought. I want everything. I want day and night, arrows and Agincourt, sleeping and walking, world without end, amen. Someone warned her once that it was fatal to tell a man you loved him. They kicked you out of bed forthwith. Perhaps Nick would kick her out of Murphy's van.

"What I really want," she said, "deep down, is stillness, safety. The feeling you'd always be there. I love you. I think I must have loved you without knowing it all my life."

"Ah!" he said. "Who's groaning now?"

The van drew up, stopped. Nick crawled forward, threw open the doors. Murphy appeared at the entrance, his furrowed face wreathed in smiles.

"I hope I didn't shake you about too much," he said. "The side roads are not all they should be, as the Commander knows. The main thing is that the young lady should have enjoyed her outing."

Nick jumped down onto the road. Murphy put out his hand and helped Shelagh to alight.

"You're welcome to come again, my dear, anytime you like. It's what I tell the English tourists when they visit us. Things are more lively here than what they are across the water."

Shelagh looked around her, expecting to see the lake, and the bumpy track near the reads where they had left Michael with the boat. Instead, they were standing in the main street of Ballyfane. The van was parked outside the Kilmore Arms. She turned to Nick, her face a question mark. Murphy was knocking on the hotel door.

"Twenty minutes' more driving time, but worth it," said Nick. "At least for me, and I hope for you as well. Farewells should be sharp and sweet, don't you agree? There's Doherty at the door, so cut along in. I have to get back to base."

Desolation struck. He could not mean it. He surely did not expect her to say good-bye here on the side of the street, with Murphy and his son hovering, and the landlord at the entrance of the hotel?

"My things," she said, "my case. They're on the island, in the bedroom there."

"Not so," he told her "Operation C brought them back to the Kilmore Arms while we were junketing about on the border."

Desperately she fought for time, pride nonexistent.

"Why?" she asked. "Why?"

"Because that's the way it is, Cesario. I sacrifice the lamb that I do love to spite my own raven heart, which alters the text a bit."

He pushed her in front of him toward the door of the hotel.

"Look after Miss Blair, Tim. The exercise went well, by all accounts. Miss Blair is the only casualty."

He had gone, and the door had closed behind him. Mr. Doherty looked at her with sympathy.

"The Commander is a great one for hustle. It's always the same. I know what it is to be in his company, he seldom lets up. I've put a thermos of hot milk beside your bed."

He limped up the stairs before her, and threw open the door of the bedroom she had quitted two nights earlier. Her suitcase was on the chair. Bag and maps on the dressing table. She might never have left it.

"Your car has been washed and filled up with petrol," he continued. "A friend of mine has it in his garage. He'll bring it round for you in the morning. And there's no charge for your stay. The Commander will settle for everything. Just you get to bed now and have a good night's rest."

A good night's rest . . . A long night's melancholy. "Come away, come away, death, and in sad cypress let me be laid." She threw open the window and looked out upon the street. Drawn curtains and blinds, shuttered windows. The black-and-white cat mewing from the gutter opposite. No lake, no moonlight.

"The trouble with you is, Jinnie, you won't grow up. You live in a dream world that doesn't exist. That's why you opted for the stage." Her father's voice, indulgent but firm. "One of these days," he added, "you'll come to with a shock."

It was raining in the morning, misty, gray. Better, perhaps, like this, she thought, than golden bright like yesterday. Better to go off in the hired Austin with windscreen wipers slashing from side to side, and then with luck I might skid and crash in a ditch, be carried to hospital, become delirious, clamor for him to come. Nick kneeling at the bedside, holding her hand and saying, "All my fault, I should never have sent you away."

The little maid was waiting for her in the dining room. Fried egg and bacon. A pot of tea. The cat, come in from the gutter, purred at her feet. Perhaps the telephone would ring, and a message would flash from the island before she left. "Operation D put into effect. The boat is waiting for you." Possibly, if she hovered about in the hall, something would happen. Murphy would appear in his van, or even the postmaster O'Reilly with a few words scribbled on a piece of paper. Her luggage was down, though, and the Austin was in the street outside. Mr. Doherty was waiting to say goodbye.

"I hope I shall have the pleasure," he said, "of welcoming you to Ballyfane again. You'd enjoy the fishing."

When she came to the signpost pointing to Lake Torrah she stopped the car and walked down the muddied track in the pouring rain. One never knew, the boat might be there. She came to the end of the track and stood there a moment, looking out across the lake. It was shrouded deep in mist. She could barely see the outline of the island. A heron rose from the reeds and flapped its way over the water. I could take off all my things and swim, she thought. I could just about make it, exhausted, almost drowned, and stagger through the woods to the house and fall at his feet on the veranda. "Bob, come quick! It's Miss Blair. I think she's dying . . ."

She turned, and walked back up the track and got into the car. Started the engine, and the windscreen wipers began thrashing to and fro.

> *When that I was and a little tiny boy,*
> *With hey, ho, the wind and the rain,*
> *A foolish thing was but a toy,*
> *For the rain it raineth every day.*

It was still raining when she arrived at Dublin airport. First she had to get rid of the car, then book a seat on the first available plane to London. She did not have long to wait—there was a flight taking off within the next half hour. She sat in the departure lounge with her eyes fixed on the door leading back to the reception hall, for even now a miracle might take place, the door swing open, a lanky figure stand there, hatless, black patch over his left. He would brush past the officials, come straight toward her. "No more practical jokes. That was the last. Come back with me to Lamb Island right away."

Her flight was called, and Shelagh shuffled through with the rest, her eyes searching her fellow travelers. Walking across the tarmac she turned to stare at the spectators waving good-bye. Someone tall in a mackintosh held a handkerchief in his hand. Not him—he stooped to pick up a child . . . Men in overcoats taking off hats, putting despatch cases on the rack overhead, any one of them could have been, was not, Nick. Supposing, as she fastened her safety belt, a hand came out from the seat in front of her, on the aisle, and she recognized the signet ring on the little finger? What if the man humped there in the very front seat—she could just see the top of his slightly balding head—should suddenly turn, black patch foremost, and stare in her direction, then break into a smile?

"Pardon."

A latecomer squeezed in beside her, treading on her toes. She flashed him a look. Black squash hat, spotty faced, pale, the fag end of a cigar between his lips. Some woman, somewhere, had loved, would love, this unhealthy brute. Her stomach turned. He opened a newspaper wide, jerking her elbow. Headlines glared.

"Explosions Across the Border. Are There More to Come?"

A secret glow of satisfaction warmed her. Plenty more, she thought, and good luck to them. I saw it, I was there, I was part of the show. This idiot sitting beside me doesn't know.

London Airport. Customs check. "Have you been on holiday, and for how long?" Was it her imagination, or did the Customs officer give her a particularly searching glance? He chalked her case and turned to the next in line.

Cars shot past the bus as it lumbered through the traffic to the terminal. Aircraft roared overhead, taking other people away and out of it. Men and women with drab, tired expressions waited on pavements for red to change to green. Shelagh was going back to school with a vengeance. Not to peer at the notice board in the drafty assembly hall, shoulder to shoulder with giggling companions, but to examine another board, very similar, hanging on the wall beside the stage door. Not, "Have I *really* got to share a room with Katie Matthews this term? It's too frantic for words," and smiling falsely, "Hullo, Katie, yes, wonderful hols, super," but wandering instead into that rather poky cubby hole they called the dressing room at the bottom of the stairs, and finding that infuriating Olga Brett hogging the mirror, using Shelagh's or one of the other girl's lipstick instead of her own, and drawling, "Hullo, darling, you're late for rehaearsal, Adam is tearing his hair out in handfuls, but literally . . ."

Useless to ring up home from the air terminal and ask Mrs. Warren, the gardener's wife, to make up her bed. Home was barren, empty, without her father. Haunted, too, his things untouched, his books on the beside table. A memory, a shadow, not the living presence. Better go straight to the flat, like a dog to a familiar kennel smelling only of its own straw, untouched by its master's hands.

Shelagh was not late at the first rehearsal on the Monday morning, she was early.

"Any letters for me?"

"Yes, Miss Blair, a postcard."

Only a postcard? She snatched it up. It was from her mother at Cap d'Ail. "Weather wonderful. Feeling so much better, really rested. Hope you are too, darling, and that you had a nice little trip in your car wherever it was. Don't exhaust yourself rehearsing. Aunt Bella sends her love and so do Reggie and May Hillsborough, who are here on their yacht at Monte Carlo. Your loving Mum." (Reggie was the fifth Viscount Hillsborough.)

Shelagh dropped the postcard into a wastepaper basket and went down onto the stage to meet the group. A week, ten days, a fortnight, nothing came. She had given up hope. She would never hear from him. The theater must take over, become meat and drink, love and sustenance. She was neither Shelagh nor Jinnie, she was Viola-Cesario, and must move, think, dream in character. Here was her only cure, stamp out all else. (She tried to get Radio Eire on her transistor but did not succeed. The voice of the announcer might have sounded like Michael's, like Murphy's, and roused some sort of feeling other than a total void.) So on with the damned motley, and down despair.

> *Olivia:* Where goes Cesario?
> *Viola:* After him I love,
>   More than I love these eyes, more than my life . . .

Adam Vane, crouching like a black cat at the side of the stage, his horn-rimmed glasses balanced on his straggling hair, "Don't pause, dear, that's very good, very good indeed."

On the day of the dress rehearsal she left the flat in good time, picking up a taxi en route for the theater. There was a jam at the corner of Belgrave Square, cars hooting, people hanging about on the pavement, mounted policemen. Shelagh opened the glass panel between herself and the driver.

"What's going on?" she asked. "I'm in a hurry, I can't afford to be late."

He grinned back at her over his shoulder. "Demonstration," he said, "outside the Irish Embassy. Didn't you hear the one o'clock news? More explosions on the border. It looks as if it's brought the London-Ulster crowd out in force. They must have been throwing stones at the embassy windows."

Fools, she thought. Wasting their time. Good job if the mounted police ride them down. She never listened to the one o'clock news, and she hadn't even glanced at the morning paper. Explosions on the border, Nick in the control room, the young man with the headphones over his ears, Murphy in the van, and I'm here in a taxi driving to my own show, my own fireworks, and after it's over my friends will crowd round me saying, "Wonderful, darling, wonderful!"

The holdup had put her timing out. She arrived at the theater to find the atmosphere a mixture of excitement, confusion, last-minute panic. Never mind, she could cope. Her first scene as Viola over, she tore back to the dressing room to change to Cesario. "Oh, get out, can't you? I want the place to myself." That's better, she thought, now I'm in control I'm the boss around this place, or very soon will be. Off with Viola's wig, a brush to her own short hair. On with the breeches, on with the hose. Cape set on my shoulders. Dagger in my belt. Then a tap at the door. What the hell now?

"Who is it?" she called.

"A packet for you, Miss Blair. It's come express."

"Oh, throw it down."

Last-minute touch to eyes, then stand back, take a last look, you'll do, you'll do. They'll all be shouting their heads off tomorrow night. She glanced away from the mirror, down to the packet on the table. A square-shaped envelope. It bore the postmark Eire. Her heart turned over. She stood there a moment holding it in her hands, then tore the envelope open. A letter fell out, and something hard, between cardboard. She seized the letter first.

> DEAR JINNIE,
>
> I'm off to the U.S. in the morning to see a publisher who has finally shown interest in my scholarly works, stone circles, ring forts, Early Bronze Age in Ireland, etc., etc. but I spare you . . . I shall probably be away for some months, and you can read in your glossy magazines about a one-time recluse spouting his head off in universities to the American young. In point of fact it suits me well to be out of the country for a while, what with one thing and another, as they say.
>
> I have been burning some of my papers before leaving, and came across the enclosed photograph amongst a pile of junk in the bottom drawer of my desk. I thought it might amuse you. You may remember I told you that it was myself! *Twelfth Night* was the bond. Good luck, Cesario, and happy scalping.
>
> LOVE, NICK

America . . . From her viewpoint it might just as well be Mars. She took the photograph out of its cardboard covers and looked at it, frowning. Another practical joke? But she had never had a photograph taken of herself as Viola-Cesario, so how could he have possibly faked this? Had he snapped her when she wasn't aware of it, then placed the head on other shoulders? Impossible. She turned it over. He had written across the back, "Nick Barry as Cesario in *Twelfth Night*. Dartmouth. 1929."

She looked at the photograph again. Her nose, her chin, the cocky expression, head tip-tilted in the air. Even the stance, hand on hip. The thick cropped hair. Suddenly she was not standing in the dressing room at all but in her father's bedroom, beside the window, and she heard him move, and she turned and looked at him. He was staring at her, an expression of horror and disbelief upon his face. It was not accusation she had read in his eyes, but recognition. He had awakened from no nightmare, but from a dream that had lasted twenty years. Dying, he discovered truth.

They were knocking at the door again. "Curtain coming down on Scene Three in four minutes' time, Miss Blair."

She was lying in the van, his arms around her. "Pam giggled a bit, then passed out cold. She'd forgotten all about it by the morning."

Shelagh raised her eyes from the photograph she was holding in her hand and stared at herself in the mirror.

"Oh, no . . ." she said. "Oh, Nick . . . Oh, my God!"

Then she took the dagger from her belt and stabbed it through the face of the boy in the photograph, ripping it apart, throwing the pieces into the wastepaper basket. And when she went back onto the stage it was not from the Duke's palace in Illyria that she saw herself moving henceforth, with painted backcloth behind her and painted boards beneath her feet, but out into a street, any street, where there were windows to be smashed and houses to burn, and bricks and petrol in hand, where there were causes to despise and men to hate, for only by hating can you purge away love, only a sword, by fire.

The Way of the Cross

THE REV. EDWARD Babcock stood beside one of the lounge windows of the hotel on the Mount of Olives looking across the Kedron Valley to the city of Jerusalem on the opposite hill. Darkness had come so suddenly, between the time of arrival with his small party, the allotting of rooms, unpacking, a quick wash; and now, with hardly a moment to get his bearings and study his notes and guidebook, the little group would be on him, primed with questions, each requiring some measure of individual attention.

He had not chosen this particular assignment: he was deputizing for the vicar of Little Bletford, who had succumbed to an attack of influenza and had been obliged to stay on board the S. S. *Ventura* in Haifa, leaving his small party of seven parishioners without a shepherd. It had been felt that, in the absence of their own vicar, another clergyman would be the most suitable person to lead them on the planned twenty-four-hour excursion to Jerusalem, and so the choice had fallen on Edward Babcock. He wished it had been otherwise. It was one thing to visit Jerusalem for the first time as a pilgrim amongst other pilgrims, even as an ordinary tourist, and quite another to find himself in charge of a group of strangers who would be regretting the unavoidable absence of their own vicar, and would in addition expect him to show qualities of leadership, or, worse, the social bonhomie that was so evident a characteristic of the sick man. Edward Babcock knew the type only too well. He had observed the vicar on board, forever moving amongst the more affluent of the passengers, hobnobbing with the titled, invariably at his ease. One or two even called him by his Christian name, notably Lady Althea Mason, the most prominent of the group from Little Bletford, and the doyenne, apparently, of Bletford Hall. Babcock, used to his own slum parish on the outskirts of Huddersfield, had no objection to Christian names—the members of his own Youth Club referred to him as Cocky often enough over a game of darts, or during one of the informal chats which the lads appeared to enjoy as much as he did himself—but snobbery was something he could not abide; and if the ailing vicar of Little Bletford thought that he, Babcock, was going to abase himself before a titled lady and her family, he was very much mistaken. Babcock had instantly summed up Lady Althea's husband, Colonel Mason, a retired army officer, as one of the old-school-tie brigade, and considered that their spoiled grandson Robin, instead of attending some private preparatory school, would have done better rubbing shoulders with the kids on a local Council estate.

Mrs. and Mrs. Foster were of a different caliber, but equally suspect in Babcock's eyes. Foster was managing director of an up-and-coming plastics firm, and from his conversation on the bus journey from Haifa to Jerusalem he seemed to think more of the possibilities of doing business with the Israelis than he did of visiting the holy places. His wife had countered the business chat by holding forth about the distress and starvation amongst Arab refugees, which, she insisted, was the responsibility of the whole world. She might have contributed toward this, thought Babcock, by wearing a less expensive fur coat, and giving the money to the refugees.

Mr. and Mrs. Smith were a young honeymoon couple. This had made them a special object of attention, giving rise to the usual indulgent glances and smiles—even a few ill-judged jokes from Mr. Foster. They would have done better, Babcock couldn't help telling himself, to have stayed in the hotel on the shores of Galilee and got to know each other properly, rather than trail around Jerusalem, the historical and religious importance of which they couldn't possibly grasp in their present mood.

The eighth, and oldest, member of the party was a spinster, and it had been her life's dream to come to Jerusalem under the auspices of the vicar of Little Bletford.

The substitution of the Rev. Edward Babcock for her beloved vicar, whom she alluded to as Father, had evidently spoiled her idyll.

So, thought the shepherd of the flock, glancing at his watch, the position is not an enviable one, but it is a challenge, and one that I must face. It is also a privilege.

The lounge was filling up, and the clamor of the many tourists and pilgrims who were already taking their places in the dining room beyond rose in the air with discordant sound. Edward Babcock looked out once more toward the light of Jerusalem on the opposite hill. He felt alien, alone, and curiously nostalgic for Huddersfield. He wished his crowd of friendly, though often rowdy, lads from the Youth Club could have been standing at his side.

Althea Mason was sitting on the stool before the dressing table arranging a piece of blue organza round her shoulders. She had chosen the blue to match her eyes. It was her favorite color, and she always managed to wear it somewhere on her person, no matter the circumstances, but this evening it looked particularly well against the darker shade of her dress. With the string of pearls, and the small pearl earrings, the effect was just right. Kate Foster would be overdressed as usual, of course—all that costume jewelry was in such bad taste, and the blue rinse to the hair added to her years, if she only realized it. It was a fact of life that however much money a woman had—or a man either, for that matter—it never could make up for lack of breeding. The Fosters were amiable enough, and everyone said Jim Foster would stand for Parliament one of these days, which one did not begrudge him—after all, it was a known thing that his firm gave large sums to the Conservative Party—but there was just a little touch of ostentation, of vulgarity, which betrayed his origins. Althea smiled. Her friends always told her she was shrewd, a keen judge of human nature.

"Phil?" she called over her shoulder to her husband. "Are you ready?"

Colonel Mason was in the bathroom filing his nails. A minute speck of grime had wedged itself beneath his thumbnail and was almost impossible to extract. He resembled his wife in one particular only, in that he was careful about his appearance. A man must be well-groomed. A lack of polish to the shoes, an unbrushed shoulder, a dingy fingernail, these things were taboo. Besides, if he and Althea were well turned out it set an example to the rest of the party, and above all to their grandson Robin. True, he was only nine years old, but a boy was never too young to learn, and heaven knows he was quick enough in the uptake. He would make a fine soldier one of these days—that is, if his scruffy scientist of a father ever allowed him to join the army. Seeing that the grandparents were paying for the boy's education, they should be allowed a say in his future. Curious thing that the younger men of today were glib enough when they talked of ideals and how everyone must progress in a changing world, but when the crunch came they were very ready to let the older generation pay the piper. Take this cruise, for instance. Robin was with them because it suited the parents' plans. Whether it suited himself and Althea was another matter. It so happened that it did, for he and Althea were devoted to the child, but that was not the point: it occurred too often during school holidays to be a coincidence.

"Coming," he called, and straightening his tie went through to the bedroom. "All very comfortable, I must say," he observed. "I wonder if the rest of our party have it as good. Of course, none of this existed when I was here twenty years ago."

Oh dear, thought Althea, are we going to have nonstop comparison with his time in the army and during the British occupation? Phil was not above demonstrating strategic positions with saltcellars to Jim Foster during dinner.

"I did stipulate a view over Jerusalem for all of us," she said, "but whether the others realize that they have me to thank for the whole idea I can't make out. They've taken it very much for granted. Such a pity dear Arthur can't be with us. It really is a tragedy that he had to stay on board. He would have brought such life into it all. I don't think I take very much to young Babcock."

"Oh, I don't know," replied her husband. "Seems a nice enough chap. Bit of an ordeal for him, coping at a moment's notice. We must make allowances."

"He should have refused, if he wasn't equal to it," said Althea. "I must say I am continually amazed at the type of young man entering the Church today. Certainly not out of the top drawer. Have you noticed his accent? Still, one never knows what to expect in this day and age."

She stood up for a final glance in the mirror. Colonel Mason cleared his throat and glanced at his watch. He hoped Althea would not put on her superior manner in front of the luckless parson.

"Where's Robin?" he asked. "We ought to be getting on down."

"I'm here, Grandfather."

The boy had been standing behind the drawn curtains all the time, looking at the view of the city. Funny little chap. Always appearing out of nowhere. Pity he had to wear those spectacles. Made him the spit image of his father.

"Well, my boy," said Colonel Mason, "what do you make of it all? I don't mind telling you Jerusalem wasn't lighted up like that twenty years ago."

"No," replied his grandson, "I don't suppose it was. Nor two thousand years ago either. Electricity has made an enormous difference to the world. I was saying to Miss Dean as we came along in the bus that Jesus would be very surprised."

H'm . . . No answer to that one. Extraordinary things children said. He exchanged looks with his wife. She smiled indulgently, and patted Robin's shoulder. She liked to think that nobody but herself understood what she was fond of calling his little ways.

"I hope Miss Dean wasn't shocked."

"Shocked?" Robin put his head on one side and considered the matter. "I'm sure she wasn't," he replied, "but I was rather shocked myself when we saw that car that had broken down by the side of the road, and we drove past it without stopping."

Colonel Mason closed the bedroom door behind them, and all three walked along the corridor.

"Car?" he asked. "What car? I don't remember seeing one."

"You were looking the other way, Grandfather," said Robin. "You were pointing out to Mr. Foster a place where there had been machine guns in your day. Perhaps nobody saw the broken-down car but myself. The guide was busy showing us the site of the Good Samaritan Inn. The car was a few yards farther along the road."

"The driver had probably run out of petrol," said Althea. "I dare say somebody came along shortly. It seemed a busy road."

She caught sight of her reflection in the long mirror at the end of the corridor, and adjusted the piece of blue organza.

Jim Foster was having a quick one in the bar. Or two, to be exact. Then when the others appeared he would stand everybody drinks, and Kate would have to lump it. She would scarcely have the nerve to tick him off in front of everyone with threats of a coronary and the number of calories contained in a double gin. He looked round at the chattering throng. God, what a mob! The chosen people in full possession, and good luck to them, especially the women, although the young ones were better looking in Haifa. Nobody worth crossing the room for here. This lot was probably from New York's East Side anyway, and not indigenous. The hotel was lousy with tourists, and it would be worse tomorrow in Jerusalem proper. He had a good mind to cry off the sightseeing and hire a car to take himself and Kate down to the Dead Sea, where there was this talk of installing a plant for making plastics. The Israelis had hit on a new method of processing, and you could bet your life that if they were onto something they believed in, it would prosper. Bloody sin to come all this way and not be able to talk with authority about the site when he got home. Sheer waste of expense account. Hullo, here came the honeymooners. No need to ask what they had been doing since disembarking from the bus! Though on second thoughts you never could be sure. Bob Smith looked a bit strained. Perhaps the bride, like all redheads, as insatiable. A drink would put new strength into both of them.

"Come on, the bridal pair," he called. "The choice of drinks is yours, the damage mine. Let's all relax."

Gallantly he slid off his stool and offered it to Jill Smith, taking care to allow his hand to remain just one instant beneath her small posterior as she mounted his vacated seat.

"Thanks ever so, Mr. Foster," said the bride, and to prove that she had not lost her self-possession, and was aware that his lingering hand was intended for a compliment, she added, "I don't know about Bob, but I'd like champagne."

The remark was made with such defiance that the bridegroom flushed scarlet. Oh hell, he thought. Mr. Foster will fluff. He can't help fluffing from Jill's tone that . . . that it's not working out, that I just can't somehow get going. It's a nightmare, I don't know what's wrong, I shall have to ask a doctor, I . . .

"Whisky, please, sir," he said.

"Whisky it shall be," smiled Jim Foster, "and for heaven's sake don't either of you call me anything but Jim."

He commanded a champagne cocktail for Jill, a double whisky for Bob, and a large gin and tonic for himself, and as he did so his wife, Kate, pushed through the crowd hovering at the bar and heard him give the order.

I knew it, thought Kate. I knew that was the reason he came downstairs before I had finished dressing, so that he could get to the bar before me. And he's got his eye on that chit of a girl, what's more. Hasn't the decency to leave anything young and female alone, even on her honeymoon. Thank heaven she had put a stop to his idea of meeting up with business friends in Tel Aviv and letting her come to Jerusalem alone. She was not going to let him get away with that one, thank you very much. If only Colonel Mason wasn't such an old bore and Lady Althea such a colossal snob, the visit to Jerusalem could be so rewarding, especially to anyone with a spark of intelligence and an interest in world affairs. But what did they care? They hadn't even bothered to come to the talk she had given in Little Bletford on the world refugee problem a few weeks ago, making the excuse that they never went out in the evenings, which was quite untrue. If Lady Althea thought more about other people and less about the fact that she was the only surviving daughter of a peer who had never even risen to his feet in the House of Lords, and was said to be dotty anyway, Kate would have more respect for her. As it was . . . She looked about her, indignation rising. All these tourists drinking and enjoying themselves, and spending the money that might have gone to Oxfam or some other worthwhile charity, it made her feel quite ashamed to be amongst them. Well, if there was nothing active she could do to help world causes at the moment, she could at least break up Jim's little party and put him in his place. She advanced toward the bar, her high color clashing with her magenta blouse.

"Now, Mr. Smith," she said, "don't encourage my husband. He's been told by his doctor to cut down on drinking and smoking, or he'll have a coronary. It's no use making that face at me, Jim, you know it's true. As a matter of fact, we'd all of us be better without alcohol. Statistics prove that the damage to the liver through even quite a modest intake is incalculable."

Bob Smith replaced his glass on the bar counter. He was just beginning to feel more sure of himself. Now Mrs. Foster had gone and spoiled it all.

"Oh, don't mind me," she said, "nobody ever listens to a word I say, but one of these days the world will wake up to the fact that by drinking only pure fruit juices the human being can stand ten times the stress and strain of modern life. We should all live longer, look younger, achieve greater things. Yes, I'd like a grapefruit juice, please. Plenty of ice."

Pheugh! It was stuffy. She could feel the flush rising from her neck right up to her temples, and then descending in a slow-moving wave. What a fool she was . . . She had forgotten to take her hormones.

Jill Smith watched Kate Foster over the rim of her champagne glass. She must be older than he was. Looked it, anyway. You never could tell with middle-aged people, and men were most deceptive. She had read somewhere that men went on doing it until they were nearly ninety, but women lost interest after the change of life. Perhaps Mrs. Foster was right about fruit juice being good for you. Oh, why did Bob have to wear that spotted tie? It made him look so pasty. And he had such a schoolboy appearance beside Mr. Foster. Fancy telling them to call him Jim! He was touching her arm again. Honestly! The fact that she was on her honeymoon didn't seem to put men off but rather egged them on, if he was anything to go by. She nodded when he suggested another glass of champagne.

"Don't let Mrs. Foster hear you," she whispered. "She would say it would damage my liver."

"My dear girl," he murmured, "a liver as young as yours will stand years of punishment. Mine is already pickled."

Jill giggled. The things he said! And drinking down her second champagne cocktail she forgot about the unhappy scene in the bedroom upstairs, with Bob, white and tense, telling her she wasn't responding properly and it was not his fault. Staring defiantly at Bob, who was agreeing politely with Mrs. Foster about starvation in the Middle East and Asia and India, she leaned pointedly against Jim Foster's arm and said, "I don't know why Lady Althea picked on this hotel. The one the purser recommended was right in Jerusalem, and it runs a tour of the city by night, ending up in a nightclub, drinks included."

Miss Dean peered about her shortsightedly. How was she going to find the rest of the party amongst such a crowd of strangers? If only dear Father Garfield had been with them, he would never have left her to fend for herself. That young clergyman who was replacing him had barely said two words to her, and she felt sure he wasn't an Anglican. Probably disapproved of vestments, and had never intoned in his life. If she could catch sight of Lady Althea or the Colonel it would be something, although Lady Althea, bless her, was inclined to be just a little snubby sometimes, but then she must have a lot on her mind. It was so good of her to take all the trouble she had done with the tour. Jerusalem . . . Jerusalem . . . Well, the daughters of Jerusalem would certainly weep if they could see this big agnostic crowd on the Mount of Olives. It really did not seem right to have a modern hotel on such a hallowed spot, where Our Lord had wandered so frequently with his disciples on his way to Jerusalem from Bethany. How she had missed Father when the bus paused for a few minutes in the village and the guide had pointed out the ruined church beneath which, so he said, the home of Mary and Martha and Lazarus had stood two thousand years ago! Father would have brought it so vividly to life. She could have pictured the modest but comfortable home, the well-swept kitchen, Martha in charge and Mary not too helpful, probably, with clearing the dishes, reminding her, when she read the passage in the Gospel, of her own younger sister Dora, who never did a hand's turn if there was a good program on television. Not that one could compare Mary at Bethany listening to Our Lord's wonderful sermons with someone like Malcolm Muggeridge asking the question why, but after all, as Father always said, one should try and relate the past to the present, and then one would come to a better understanding of what everything meant.

Ah, there was Lady Althea coming along the corridor now. How distinguished she looked, so English, so refined amongst the rest of the people here in the hotel, who seemed mostly foreigners, and the Colonel at her side every inch the soldier and gentleman. Little Robin was such an original child. Fancy him making that remark about Our Lord being surprised if he could see electric light. "But He invented it, dear," she had told him. "Everything that has ever been invented or discovered was Our Lord's doing." She was afraid it had not sunk into his little mind. No matter. There would be other opportunities to make the right impression upon him.

"Well, Miss Dean," said the Colonel, advancing toward her, "I hope you feel rested after the long bus ride, and have a good appetite for dinner?"

"Thank you, Colonel, yes, I am quite refreshed, but a little bewildered. Do you think we shall have English food, or will it be that greasy foreign stuff? I have to be careful with my inside."

"Well, if my experience in the Near East is anything to go by, avoid fresh fruit and melon. Likewise salad. They never wash them properly. Had more tummy trouble amongst the troops in the old days with fruit and salad than anything else."

"Oh, Phil, what nonsense." Lady Althea smiled. "You're living in the past. Of course everything is washed in an up-to-date place like this. Don't take any notice of him, Miss Dean. We shall all be served a five-course dinner, and you must do justice to everything they put on your plate. Just picture your sister Dora sitting down to a boiled egg at home, and think how she would envy you."

Now that, thought Miss Dean, was kindly meant but uncalled for. Why should Lady Althea imagine that she and Dora never had more than a boiled egg for supper? It was true they ate sparsely in the evening, but that was because they both had small appetites. It was nothing to do with the way they lived or what they could afford. Now, if Father had been here he would have known just how to answer Lady Althea. He would have told her—laughingly, of course, for he was so courteous—that he had been better fed by the two Miss Deans in Syringa Cottage than anywhere else in Little Bletford.

"Thank you, Colonel," she said, adressing herself pointedly to him, "I shall follow your advice about the fruit and salad. As to the five-course menu, I shall reserve judgment until I see what they have to offer."

She hoped she would be sitting next to the Colonel at dinner. He was so considerate. And he knew Jerusalem of old—he was quite an authority.

"Your grandson," she said to him, "makes friends very easily. He is not at all shy."

"Oh, yes," replied Colonal Mason, "Robin's an excellent mixer. Part of my training, I like to think. He reads a lot too. Most children never open a book."

"Your son-in-law is a scientist, is he not?" said Miss Dean. "Scientists are such clever men. Perhaps the little boy takes after his father."

"H'm, I don't know about that," said the Colonel.

Silly old fool, he thought. Doesn't know what she's talking about. Robin was a Mason all right. Reminded him of himself at the same age. He used to be a great reader too. And imaginative.

"Come on, Robin," he called, "your grandmother wants her dinner."

"Really, Phil," said Lady Althea, half amused but not entirely so, "you make me sound like the wolf in Red Riding Hood."

She walked leisurely through the lounge, aware of the many heads that were turned in her direction, not because of her husband's remark, which few people had heard, but because she knew that, despite her sixty-odd years, she was the best-looking and most distinguished woman present. She looked around for the party from Little Bletford, deciding as she did so how she would seat them at dinner. Oh, there they were, in the bar—all, that is to say, except Babcock. She despatched her husband in search of him, and moving into the restaurant summoned the headwaiter with an imperious finger.

Her seating plan worked out very well, and everyone appeared satisfied. Miss Dean did justice to the five-course dinner and the wine, though possibly it was a little tactless to lift her glass as soon as it was filled and say to her left-hand neighbor, the Rev. Babcock, "Let us wish dear Father a speedy recovery, and I am sure he knows how sorely we all miss him here this evening."

It was not until they were embarking upon the third course that she realized the full import of her words, and remembered that the young man talking to her was not a social worker in the midlands at all but a clergyman himself, acting as deputy for her own beloved vicar. The glass of sherry in the bar had made her lightheaded, and the fact that Rev. Babcock did not wear a clergyman's collar had somehow confused the whole situation.

"Be very careful what you eat," she said to him, hoping to make amends for any small hurt her words had caused. "The Colonel says that fruit and salad are not advisable. The native people do not rinse them thoroughly. I think roast lamb would be a wise choice."

Edward Babcock stared at her use of the word native. Did Miss Dean imagine herself in the wilds of Africa? Just how out of touch with the world of today could you get, he wondered, living in a village in southern England?

"In my rough-and-ready fashion," he told her, helping himself to ragout of chicken, "I believe we do more good in the world by seeing how the other half lives than by just usticking to our own routine. We have quite a number of Pakistanis and Jamaicans in our club, amongst our own local lads, and they take it in turn to prepare a meal in the canteen. We get some surprises, I don't mind telling you! But it's a case of share and share alike, and the boys enjoy it."

"Quite right, padre, quite right," said the Colonel, who had heard the tail end of this remark. "It's absolutely essential to promote a spirit of goodwill in the mess. Morale goes to pieces if you don't."

Jim Foster pushed Jill Smith's foot under the table. The old boy was off again. Where did he think he was—Poona? Jill Smith retaliated by bumping her knee against his. They had reached the stage of mutual for-want-of-anything-better attraction when bodily contact brings warmth, and the most harmless remark made by others suggests a double meaning.

"Depends what you share and who you share it with, don't you agree?" he murmured.

"Once married, a girl has no choice," she murmured back. "She has to take what her husband gives her."

Then, noticing Mrs. Foster staring at her across the table, she opened her eyes, wide and innocent, and bumped Jim Foster's knee once more to cement duplicity.

Lady Althea, glancing round the restaurant at the occupants of the other tables, wondered if the Jerusalem had been such a good choice after all. Nobody of much interest here. Perhaps there would be a better class of people in the Lebanon. Still, it was only for twenty-four hours, and then they would rejoin the boat and go on to Cyprus. She would be content that Phil and darling Robin were enjoying themselves. She must tell Robin not to sit with his mouth open. He was such a good-looking child, and it made him appear half-witted. Kate Foster was surely feeling the heat, she had become very flushed.

"But you *should* have signed the petition against the manufacture of nerve gas," Kate was saying to Bob Smith. "I got more than a thousand names on my appeal list, and it's up to every one of us to see that this frightful business is stopped. How will you like it," she demanded, banging on the table, "when your children are born deaf, maimed, and blind, because of this terrible chemical that will pollute succeeding generations unless you all unite to prevent its manufacture?"

"Oh, come," protested the Colonel, "the authorities have everything under control. And the stuff isn't lethal. We must have a certain amount in stock in case of riots. Somebody has to deal with the scallywags of the world. Now, in my humble opinion . . ."

"Never mind your humble opinion, Phil, dear," interrupted his wife. "I think we are all getting a little too serious, and we haven't come to Jerusalem to discuss nerve gas, or riots, or anything of the sort. We are here to take back pleasant memories of one of the most famous cities in the world."

Silence was instant. She smiled upon them all. A good hostess knew when to change a party's mood. Even Jim Foster, momentarily quelled, remove his hand from Jill Smith's knee. The question was, who would be the first to speak and set the ball rolling in a new direction? Robin knew that his moment had arrived. He had been awaiting his opportunity all through dinner. His scientist father had told him never to introduce a subject or speak about it unless he were sure of his facts, and he had taken good care to be well-primed. He had consulted the courier-guide in the foyer before dinner, and he knew that his facts were correct. The grown-ups would be obliged to listen. The very thought of this was delicious, giving him a tremendous sense of power. He leaned forward across the table, his spectacles slightly out of balance, his head on one side.

"I wonder if any of you know," he said, "that today is the thirteenth day of Nisan?" Then he leaned back in his chair for his words to take effect.

The adults at the table stared back at him, nonplussed. What on earth was the child talking about? His grandfather, trained to be prepared for the unexpected, was the first to reply.

"The thirteenth day of Nisan?" he repeated. "Now, my lively lad, stop trying to be clever and tell us what you mean."

"I'm not trying to be clever, Grandfather," replied Robin, "I'm just stating a fact. I'm going by the Hebrew calendar. Tomorrow, the fourteenth day of Nisan, at sunset, is the start of Pesach, the Feast of Unleavened Bread. The guide told me. That's why there are so many people staying here. They've come on pilgrimage from all over the world. Well, everybody knows—at least Mr. Babcock does, I'm sure—that according to St. John and many other authorities Jesus and this disciples ate the Last Supper on the thirteenth day of Nisan, the day before the Feast of Unleavened Bread, so it seemed to me rather appropriate that we should all just have finished our supper here this evening. Jesus was doing precisely the same thing two thousand years ago."

He pushed his spectacles back on his forehead and smiled. The effect of his words was not so stunning as he had hoped. No burst of applause. No exclamations of wonder at his general knowledge. Everyone looked rather cross.

"H'm," said Colonel Mason, "this is your province, padre."

Babcock did a rapid calculation. He was used to problems being fired at him on the Any Questions program he gave quarterly at the Youth Club, but he wasn't prepared for this one.

"You have evidently read your Gospels thoroughly, Robin," he said. "Matthew, Mark, and Luke appear to disagree with John as to the exact date. However, I must admit I had not checked up on the fact that tomorrow is the fourteenth day of Nisan, and so the Jewish holiday begins at sunset. It was rather remiss of me not to have talked to the guide myself."

His statement did not do much to clear the air. Miss Dean was frankly bewildered.

"But how can this be the day of the Last Supper?" she asked. "We all celebrated Easter early this year. Surely Easter Day was the twenty-ninth of March?"

"The Jewish calendar is different from ours," said Babcock. "Pesach, or Passover, as we term it, does not necessarily coincide with Easter."

Surely he was not expected to enter into a theological discussion because a small boy enjoyed showing off?

Jim Foster clicked his fingers in the air. "That explains why I couldn't get Rubin on the telephone, Kate," he said. "They told me the office in Tel Aviv would be shut until the twenty-first. A public holiday."

"I hope the shops and bazaars will be open," Jill exclaimed. "I want to buy souvenirs for the family and friends back home."

After a moment's thought Robin nodded his head. "I think they will," he said, "at least until sunset. You could give your friends some unleavened bread." An idea suddenly struck him, and he turned delightedly to the Rev. Babcock. "Seeing that it's the evening of the thirteenth day of Nisan," he said, "oughtn't we all to walk down the hill to the Garden of Gethsemane? It's not very far away. I asked the guide. Jesus and the disciples crossed the valley, but we needn't do that. We could just imagine we had gone back two thousand years and they were going to be there."

Even his grandmother, who generally applauded his every action, looked a little uncomfortable.

"Really, Robin," she said, "I don't think any of us are quite prepared to set forth after dinner and stumble about in the dark. We aren't taking part in your end-of-term play, remember." She turned to Babcock. "They put on a very sweet little nativity play last Christmas," she said. "Robin was one of the Three Wise Men."

"Oh yes," he countered, "my Huddersfield lads staged a nativity play at the club. Set the scene in Vietnam. I was very impressed." Robin was gazing at him with more than usual intensity, and he made a supreme effort to meet the challenge. "Look," he said, "if you really want to walk down the hill to Gethsemane, I'm willing to go with you."

"Splendid!" said the Colonel. "I'm game. A breath of fresh air would do us all good. I know the terrain—you won't be lost with me in charge."

"How about it?" murmured Jim Foster to his neighbor Jill. "If you hold on tight I won't let you go."

A delighted smile spread over Robin's face. Things were going his way after all. No risk now of having to shake hands all round and being packed off early to bed.

"You know," he said, touching the Rev. Babcock's arm, his voice sounding very loud and clear, "if we were really the disciples and you were Jesus, you would have to line us all up in a row against the wall there and start to wash our feet. But my grandmother would probably say that was going a bit too far."

He stood aside, bowing politely, to let the grown-up people pass. He was destined for Winchester, and he remembered the motto, Manners Makyth Man.

The air was sharp and clean, like a sword's blade. No wind—the air alone made the cutting edge. The stony path led downward, steep and narrow, bound on either side by walls. On the right the sombre cluster of cypress trees and pines masked the seven spires of the Russian cathedral and the smaller humped dome of the Dominus Flevit Church. In the daytime the onion spires of St. Mary Magdalene would gleam golden under the sun, and across the valley of Kedron the city walls which encompassed Jerusalem, with the Dome of the Rock prominent in the foreground and the city itself spreading ever farther west and north, would not fail to awaken some response in every pilgrim heart, as it had done through the centuries, but tonight . . . Tonight, thought Edward Babcock, with the pale yellow moon coming up behind us and the dark sky above our heads, even the low hum of the traffic beneath us on the main road to Jericho seems to blend and merge into the silence. As the steep path descended, so the city rose, and the valley separating it from the Mount of Olives down which they walked became somber, black, like a winding riverbed. Mosques, domes, spires, towers, the rooftops of a myriad human dwellings fused together, blotted against the sky, and only the walls of the city remained, steadfast on the opposite hill, a threat, a challenge.

I'm not ready for this, he thought. It's too big, I can't take it, I shan't be able to explain what it means, not even to this small handful of people who are with me. I ought to have stayed in the hotel reading up my notes and studying the map so as to be able to speak with some sort of authority tomorrow. Or, better still, have come here on my own.

It was wrong of him, uncharitable, but the perpetual chatter of the Colonel at his side got on his nerves, made him edgy, irritable. Who cared what his regiment had been doing in '48? It was out of keeping with the scene spread out before them.

"And so," the Colonel was saying, "the mandate was handed over to the U.N. in May, and we were all out of the country by July 1. To my mind we should have stayed. The whole thing has been a bloody nuisance ever since. No one will ever settle down in this part of the world, and they'll still be fighting over Jerusalem when you and I have been in our graves for years. Beautiful spot, you know, from this distance. Used to be pretty scruffy inside the Old City."

The pine trees to their right were motionless. Everything was still. To their left the hillside appeared bare, uncultivated, but Babcock could be mistaken: moonlight was deceptive, those white shapes that seemed to be rocks and boulders could be tombs.

Once there would have been no somber pines, no cypresses, no Russian cathedral, only the olive trees with silver branches sweeping the stony ground, and the sound of the brook trickling through the valley below.

"Funny thing," said the Colonel, "I never did any proper soldiering once I left this place behind me. Served for a time back home, at Aldershot, but what with reorganization in the army, and one thing and another, and my wife wasn't too fit at the time, I decided to pack it in and quit. I should have been given command of my regiment if I had stayed, and gone to Germany, but Althea was all against it, and it didn't seem fair to her. Her father left her the Hall, you know, in Little Bletford. She had been brought up there, and her life centered in it. Still is, in fact. She does a great deal locally."

Edward Babcock made an effort to attend, to show some sign of interest. "You regret leaving the army?"

The Colonel did not answer immediately, but when he did the usual tone of brisk self-confidence had gone; he sounded puzzled, strained.

"It was my whole life," he said. "And that's another funny thing, padre—I don't think I've ever realized it before tonight. Just standing here, looking at that city across the valley, makes me remember."

Something moved in the shadows below. It was Robin. He had been crouching against the wall. He had a map in his hand and a small torch.

"Look, Mr. Babcock," he said, "that's where they must have come, from the gate in the wall over to the left. We can't see it from here, but it's marked on the map. Jesus and his disciples, I mean, after they had had their supper. And the gardens and trees were probably all up this hill then, not just down at the bottom where the church stands today. In fact, if we go on a bit farther and sit down by that wall, we can picture the whole thing. The soldiers and the high priests' attendants coming down with flares from the other gate, perhaps where that car is showing now. Come on!"

He began running down the hill in front of them, flicking his small torch to and fro, until he disappeared round a turn of the wall.

"Watch your step, Robin," called his grandfather. "You might fall. It's jolly steep down there." Then he turned to his companion. "He can read a map as well as I can myself. Only nine years old."

"I'll go after him," said Babcock. "See he doesn't get into trouble. You wait here for Lady Althea."

"You needn't worry, padre," replied the Colonel. "The boy knows what he's doing."

Babcock pretended not to hear. It was an excuse to be alone, if only for a few minutes, otherwise the scene beneath him would never make the deep impression he desired, so that he could describe it later to all the lads, when he returned to Huddersfield.

Colonel Mason remained motionless beside the wall. The slow, careful footsteps of his wife and Miss Dean descending the path behind him were only a short distance away, and Althea's voice carried on the still cold air.

"If we don't see them we'll turn back," she was saying, "but I know what Phil can be like when he's in charge of an expedition. He always thinks he knows the way, and only too often he doesn't at all."

"I can hardly credit that," said Miss Dean, "as a military man."

Lady Althea laughed. "Dear Phil," she said. "He likes everyone to think he might have become a general. But the truth is, Miss Dean, he would never have made the grade. I had it on the highest authority from one of his brother officers. Oh, they were all fond of him, but the dear old boy would never have gone any further, not in the army as it is today. That's why we all persuaded him to retire when he did. I sometimes wish he would be just a little more active where local affairs are concerned, but there it is, I have to act for us both. And he has done wonders in the garden."

"That lovely herbaceous border!" said Miss Dean.

"Yes, and the rock plants too. They make quite a show the whole year through."

The slow footsteps passed without stopping, neither woman looking to right or left, so intent were they upon the rough path under their feet. For one moment their two figures were sharply outlined against the trees beyond, then they turned the corner as Robin had done, and Babcock, and disappeared.

Colonel Mason let them go without calling them back. Then he turned up the collar of his coat, for it seemed suddenly colder, and began to retrace his steps slowly toward the hotel above. He had nearly made the ascent when he bumped into two other members of the party coming down.

"Hullo," said Jim Foster, "you crying off already? I thought you'd be in Jerusalem by now!"

"Turned very cold," said the Colonel shortly. "Not much sense in stumping on down to the bottom. You'll find the others scattered about the hillside."

He climbed on past them toward the hotel with a hasty good-night.

"Now, if he runs into my wife up there and tells her you and I are together we shall be in trouble," said Jim Foster. "Willing to risk it?"

"Risk what?" asked Jill Smith. "We're not doing anything."

"Now that, my girl, is what I call a direct invitation. Never mind, Kate can console your husband in the bar. Watch your step, this path is steep. The slippery slope to ruin for the pair of us. Don't leave go of my arm."

Jill threw off her head scarf and drew a deep breath, clinging tightly to her companion.

"Look at all the city lights," she said. "I bet there's plenty going on up there. Makes me feel envious. We seem to be stuck at the back of beyond up here."

"Don't worry. You'll see it all tomorrow, led by his reverence. But I doubt if he'll take you into a discotheque, if that's what you're after."

"Well, naturally we must see the historical part first—that's why we're here, isn't it? But I want to go to the shopping center too."

"Suks, my girl, suks. Lot of little trinket booths in back alleys with dark-eyed young salesmen trying to pinch your bottom."

"Oh, you think I'd let them, do you?"

"I don't know. But I wouldn't blame them for trying."

He glanced back over his shoulder. No sign of Kate. Perhaps she had decided against joining the expedition after all. The last he had seen of her was the back of her figure making for the lift en route for their room. As for Bob Smith, if he couldn't keep an eye on his bride that was his lookout. The clump of trees on the other side of the wall farther down the path looked enticing. Just the right spot for a little harmless fun.

"What do you make of marriage, Jill?" he asked.

"It's too early to say," she answered, instantly on the defensive.

"Of course it is. Silly question. But most honeymoons are a flop. I know mine was. It took Kate and me months to get adjusted. That Bob of yours is a great fellow, but he's still very young. All bridegrooms suffer from nerves, you know, even in these enlightened days. Think they know it all, but they damn well don't, and the poor girls suffer for it in consequence." She did not answer, and he steered her toward the trees. "It's not until a man has been married for some time that he knows how to make his wife respond. It's technique, like everything else in life—not a question of letting nature take its course. And all women vary. Their moods, their likes and dislikes. Am I shocking you?"

"Oh no," she said, "not at all."

"Good. I wouldn't want to shock you. You're far too sweet and precious for that. I don't see any sign of the others, do you?"

"No."

"Let's go and lean against the wall down there and look at the city lights.

Wonderful spot. Wonderful evening. Does Bob ever tell you how lovely you are? Because it's true, you know . . ."

Kate Foster, who had been upstairs to take her hormone pills, came down to the lounge to look for her husband. When she couldn't find him she went into the bar, and saw Bob Smith all alone, drinking a double whisky.

"Where is everybody?" she asked. "Our lot, I mean," for the room was till crowded.

"Gone out, I think," he answered.

"What about your wife?"

"Oh yes, she went. She followed Lady Althea and Miss Dean. Mr. Foster was with her."

"I see."

She did see, too. Only too well. Jim had deliberately given her the slip when she went upstairs.

"Well, it won't do you any good sitting there drinking that poison," she said. "I suggest you get your coat and come with me and join the rest of the party. No sense in mooning here on your own."

Perhaps she was right. Perhaps it *was* wet and ineffectual to sit drinking all alone when by rights Jill should have been with him. But the way she had smiled at Foster was more than he could stand, and he had thought, by staying here, that it would be a sort of lesson to her. In fact, he had only been punishing himself. Jill probably couldn't care less.

"All right," he said, sliding off the stool, "we'll go after them. They can't have gone far."

They set off together down the path that led to the valley, a strangely ill-assorted couple, Bob Smith long and lanky, a mop of dark hair nearly touching his shoulders, hands thrust deep in the pockets of his coat, and Kate Foster in her mink jacket, gold earrings dangling beneath blue-rinsed hair.

"If you ask me," she said, as she stumped down the path in her unsuitable shoes, "this whole outing to Jerusalem has been a mistake. Nobody is really interested in the place. Except perhaps Miss Dean. But you know what Lady Althea is, she had everything arranged with the vicar, and has to play lady of the manor whether she's in England, on board ship, or in the Middle East. As for Babcock, he's worse than useless. We'd have been better without him. And as for you two . . . Well, it's hardly the best start for married life to let your wife do just as she pleases all the time. You want to show a little authority."

"Jill's very young," he said, "barely twenty."

"Oh, youth . . . Don't talk to me about youth. You all have it too good these days. In our country, anyway. Very different for some of the youngsters in this part of the world—I'm thinking of the Arab countries in particular—where husbands keep a tight watch on their brides to make sure they don't get into trouble."

I don't know why I'm saying all this, she thought, it won't sink in. They none of them think of anyone but themselves. If only I didn't feel things so acutely, it does no good, I make myself ill with worry about everything—the state of the world, the future, Jim . . . Where on earth has he got to with that girl? My heart keeps missing a beat. I wonder if those pills suit me?

"Don't walk so fast," she said. "I can't keep up with you."

"I'm sorry, Mrs. Foster. I thought I saw two figures in the distance over by those trees."

And if it is them, he wondered, what of it? I mean, what can I do? I can't make a scene just because Jill chose to wander out of the hotel with another member of the party. I shall have to hang about and say nothing, and then wait until we're back at the hotel and give her hell. If only this bloody woman would stop talking for one moment. . . .

The two figures turned out to be Lady Althea and Miss Dean.

"Have you seen Jim?" Kate Foster called.

"No," replied Lady Althea. "I was just wondering what's happened to Phil. I wish our menfolk wouldn't tear off in this way. It's so inconsiderate. I do think Babcock at least should have waited for us."

"So different from dear Father," murmured Miss Dean. "He would have had it all so well-organized, and known just what to show us. As it is, we don't know whether the Garden of Gethsemane is farther on along this path or all around us as we stand here."

The trees beyond the wall were so very dark, and the path seemed to get stonier and stonier. If Father had been with them she could have leaned on his arm. Lady Althea was being very kind, but it wasn't the same.

"I'll go on," said Bob. "You three stay here."

He strode ahead of them down the path. If the rest of the party were all together, they couldn't be far away. The Colonel would be in charge, he would keep an eye on Jill.

There was a break in the trees about a hundred yards ahead, and open ground, with clumps of small olives and rough unbroken soil, nothing looking like a garden, what a bloody silly expedition anyway, and all to do over again tomorrow. Then he saw a figure, only one, though, humped against a piece of rock. It was Babcock. For one embarrassed moment Bob thought he was praying, and then he saw that he was bent over a notebook, scribbling with the aid of a torch. He lifted his head at the sound of Bob's footsteps and waved the torch.

"Where are the others?" called Bob.

"The Colonel's up behind you on the road," returned Babcock, "and the boy's down there, where he can get a better view of Gethsemane. But the garden itself is shut. It doesn't really matter, though. You can get the atmosphere from here." He smiled in a rather shamefaced fashion as Bob approached him. "If I don't write down what I see, I shan't remember it. Robin lent me his torch. I want to lecture about this when I get home. Well, not a straight lecture. Just my impressions to the lads."

"Have you seen Jill?" asked Bob.

Babcock stared. Jill . . . Oh yes, his young wife.

"No," he said. "Isn't she with you?"

"You can see she isn't with me," Bob almost shouted in exasperation. "And there are only Mrs. Foster and Lady Althea and Miss Dean up the road."

"Oh," said Babcock. "Well, I'm afraid I can't help you. The Colonel is around somewhere. I came on alone with the boy."

Bob could feel the anger mounting within him. "Look here," he said, "I don't mean to be rude, but just who is in charge of this outfit?"

The Rev. Babcock flushed. There was no call for Bob Smith to get so excited.

"There's no question of anybody being in charge," he said. "The Colonel and Robin and I left the hotel on our own. If the rest of you chose to follow on and got lost, I'm afraid it's your own affair."

He was used to rough talk from the lads, but this was different. Anyone would think he was a paid courier.

"I'm sorry," said Bob. "The fact is . . ." The fact was he had never felt more helpless, more alone. Weren't parsons supposed to help one in trouble? "The fact is, I'm worried stiff. Everything's gone wrong. I had one hell of a row with Jill before dinner, and I can't think straight."

Babcock put down his notebook and extinguished his torch. No more impressions of Gethsemane tonight. Well, it couldn't be helped.

"I'm sorry to hear that," he said, "but it happens all the time, you know. Young married couples have arguments, and they feel it's the end of the world. You'll both look at it differently in the morning."

"No," said Bob, "that's just it. I don't think we shall. I keep wondering if we haven't made a terrible mistake in getting married."

His companion was silent. The poor chap was over-tired, probably. Had let things get on top of him. It was difficult to give advice when one didn't know either of them. If things hadn't been going too well, the vicar of Little Bletford should have spotted it and had a word with them both. He probably would have, if he had been here, and not on the boat in Haifa.

"Well," he said, "marriage is give and take, you know. It's not just . . . how shall I put it? It's not just a physical relationship."

"It's the physical side of it that's gone wrong," said Bob Smith.

"I see."

Babcock wondered if he should advise the lad to see a doctor when he got home. There was nothing much that could be done about it here tonight.

"Look," he said, "don't worry too much. Take it easy. Be as gentle as you can with your wife, and perhaps . . ."

But he couldn't continue, for at that moment a small figure darted up from the trees below. It was Robin.

"The actual Garden of Gethsemane looks very small," he called. "I feel sure Jesus and the disciples wouldn't have sat down there. They would more likely have climbed up here, amongst all the olive trees that were growing in those days. What puzzles me, Mr. Babcock, is why the disciples kept falling asleep, if it was as cold as it is tonight. Do you suppose the climate has changed in two thousand years? Or could the disciples have had rather too much wine at supper?"

Babcock handed Robin back his torch and pushed him gently along the homeward path. "We don't know, Robin, but we have to remember they had all a long and very exhausting day."

That's not the right answer, he thought, but it's the best I can do. And I haven't helped Bob Smith either. Nor was I particularly sympathetic to the Colonel. The trouble is, I don't know any of these people. Their own vicar would have known how to deal with them. Even if he had given them quite the wrong answers they would have been satisfied.

"There they are," said Robin, "standing in a huddle up the road and stamping their feet. That's the most sensible way to try and keep awake."

It was Lady Althea who was stamping her feet. She had wisely changed into sensible shoes before setting forth. Kate Foster was not so well-shod, but she scored over Lady Althea by being well wrapped up in her mink jacket. Miss Dean was a little apart from them both. She had found a break in the wall, and was sitting on a pile of crumbling stones. She had become rather weary of listening to her two companions, who could discuss nothing except the whereabouts of their respective husbands.

I'm glad I never married, she thought. There always seems to be such endless argument going on between husband and wife. I dare say some marriages are ideal, but very few. It was very sad for dear Father losing his wife all those years ago, but he has never tried to replace her. She smiled tenderly, thinking of the manly smell in the vicar's study. He smoked a pipe, and whenver Miss Dean called, which she generally did twice a week to bring flowers to brighten up his bachelor solitude, or with a special cake she had baked, or a jar of homemade jam or marmalade, she would give a quick look through the open door of the study to see if his housekeeper had tidied it properly, brought some sort of order to the chaos of books and papers. Men were such boys, they needed looking after. That was why Mary and Martha invited Our Lord so often to Bethany. They probably fed Him well after those long walks across the hills, mended His clothes—darned his socks, she was about to say, but of course men didn't wear socks in those days, only sandals. What a blessed honor it must have been to soak the travel-stained garments in the washtub . . .

Miss Dean became aware of some sort of scuffle in the trees behind her. Could the menfolk have climbed over the stones and wandered into what seemed like private property? Then she heard a man laugh, and a woman whisper, "Shshsh . . ."

"It's all right," murmured the man, "it's only Miss Dean. Sitting all on her own lamenting the absence of her beloved vicar."

"If she only knew," came the answering murmur, "that he hides whenever he sees her walking up the vicarage drive. She's the thorn in his flesh, he told Mum once. Pursued him for years, despite her age."

There was a sound of stifled laughter, and then suddenly Jim Foster coughed loudly and emerged from the cluster of dark trees, Jill Smith at his heels.

"Well, well, Miss Dean," he said, "what a surprise. We've been looking for the rest of the party. Ah, isn't that Kate standing up the road with Lady Althea? And some more of them coming from the opposite direction? Rendezvous all round." He held out his hand to Jill and helped her over the stones. "Now, Miss Dean, what about you? Will you take my arm?"

"Thank you, Mr. Foster," she said quietly, "I can manage on my own."

Jill Smith threw a quick look down the path. Bob was there, and the Rev. Babcock and young Robin. Robin was chattering and waving a torch. It would look better if she stayed with Miss Dean. She nudged Jim Foster with her elbow, and immediately he understood and began walking alone up the path to where Kate and Lady Althea were standing.

"Hullo, hullo there," he called, "we all seem to have been going round in circles. I can't think how I came to miss you."

The tight-lipped expression on his wife's face made him hesitate a moment, then he smiled, and strolled up to her casually, self-confident.

"Sorry old girl," he said. "Been here long?"

He put his arm around her shoulders and kissed her lightly on the cheek.

"Twenty minutes at least," she replied. "More like half an hour."

The three of them turned their heads as Robin came running toward them flicking the light of his torch in all their faces.

"Oh, Mr. Foster," he called delightedly, "that looked so sinister as you kissed Mrs. Foster. You could have been Judas. Mr. Babcock and I have had a tremendous time. We've been right down to Gethsemane and back on our own."

"In that case, where were you?" Kate turned to her husband.

"Oh, Mr. Foster and Mrs. Smith were under the trees through the gap in that wall," said Robin, "and I'm afraid they can't have had a very good view of Jerusalem. I flashed my torch on you once, Mr. Foster, but your back was turned."

Thank God for that, thought Jim Foster. Because if it hadn't been turned . . .

"What I want to know is what in the world has become of Phil?" asked Lady Althea.

"Oh, he returned to the hotel," said Jim Foster, relieved that attention had switched from him. "I passed him as I was coming down. Said he was cold and had had enough of it."

"*Cold?*" queried Lady Althea. "Phil's never cold. What an extraordinary thing for him to say."

Slowly the little party began to wind their way back up the path toward the hotel on the summit. They walked in couples, Lady Althea and Robin in the lead, the Fosters following closely behind in silence, and some distance in the rear the young Smiths, hotly arguing.

"Naturally I preferred to go out rather than sit with you soaking in the bar," Jill was saying. "I felt thoroughly ashamed of you."

"Ashamed?" Bob answered. "That's fine, coming from you. How do you think I felt when Mrs. Foster asked me to help find her husband? I knew very well where he was. And so do you."

The Rev. Babcock held back with Miss Dean. It would only distress her to hear the young couple quarreling. They must really work things out between them. There was nothing in the world he could do. Miss Dean herself, generally such a chatterbox, was strangely silent.

"I'm so sorry," he began awkwardly, "that things haven't turned out quite as you had hoped. I know I make a poor substitute for your vicar. Never mind, you'll be able to describe everything to him when we return on board. It's been a wonderful experience for all of us to have walked above the Garden of Gethsemane by night."

Miss Dean did not hear him. She was many hundreds of miles away. She was walking up the vicarage drive, a basket over her arm, and suddenly she saw a figure dart from behind the curtain in the study window and efface itself against the wall. When she rang the bell nobody answered.

"Are you feeling all right, Miss Dean?" asked the Rev. Babcock.

"Thank you," she said, "I'm perfectly well. It's just that I'm very tired."

Her voice faltered. She must not disgrace herself. She must not cry. It was just that she felt an overwhelming sense of loss, of betrayal . . .

"I can't imagine," said Lady Althea to Robin, "why your grandfather went back to the hotel. Did he tell you he felt cold?"

"No," replied Robin. "He was talking to Mr. Babcock about old days, and how he would have been given command of his regiment, but he had to leave the army because you weren't very well at the time, and your life was centered on Little Bletford. He didn't say anything about being cold, though. He just sounded rather sad."

Left the army because of her? How could he have said such a thing, and to a stranger like Babcock? It wasn't true. It was very unjust. Phil had never for one moment hinted, all that time ago, that . . . Or had he? Were things said and she hadn't listened, had brushed them away? But Phil had always appeared so content, so busy with the garden, and arranging his military papers and books in the library . . . Doubt, guilt, bewilderment swept over her in turn. It had all happened so long ago. Why should Phil have suddenly felt resentful tonight? Babcock must have said something to put Phil out, made some tactless remark.

One by one they climbed the hill, went into the hotel, hovered for a moment in the entrance to bid one another good-night. Each member of the little party looked tired, strained. Robin could not understand it. He had enjoyed himself immensely, despite the cold. Why did everyone seem to be in such a bad mood? He kissed his grandmother good-night, promised not to read late, and waited by the door of his bedroom for Mr. Babcock to enter the room next door.

"Thank you for a splendid evening," he said. "I hope you liked it as much as I did."

The Rev. Babcock summoned a smile. The boy was not so bad really. He couldn't help his precocity, spending most of his time with adults.

"Thank you, Robin," he said. "It was your idea, you know. I would never have thought of it on my own." And then, quite spontaneously, he heard himself adding, "I blame myself for not having made the walk more interesting for the rest of the party. They're all a bit lost without your vicar."

Robin considered the matter, head cocked on one side. He liked being treated as an adult, it gave him status. He must say something to put poor Mr. Babcock at his ease, and his mind harked back to the conversation between his grandparents earlier that evening before dinner.

"It must be difficult to be a clergyman in this day and age," he said. "Quite an ordeal, in fact."

The Rev. Babcock looked surprised. "Yes, it is. At least sometimes."

Robin nodded gravely. "My grandfather was saying people must make allowances, and my grandmother remarked that so many clergymen were not out of the top drawer nowadays. I'm not sure what the means exactly, but I suppose it's to do with passing exams. I hope you sleep well, Mr. Babcock."

He clicked his heels and bowed, as his grandmother had taught him to do, and went into his bedroom, shutting the door behind him. He crossed the floor and drew aside the curtains. The lights were still burning bright in the city of Jerusalem.

On that other thirteenth day of Nisan the disciples would all be scattered by now, he thought, and only Peter left, stamping about to keep warm by the charcoal fire in the courtyard. That shows it was a cold night.

He undressed and got into bed, then switched on his bedside light and spread the map of Jerusalem over his knees. He compared it with a second map that his father had borrowed for him, showing the city as it was around 30 A.D. He studied both maps for about half an hour, then, remembering the promise to his grandmother, switched off the light.

The priests and scholars have got it all wrong, he thought. They've made Jesus go out of the wrong gate. Tomorrow I shall discover Golgotha for myself.

"Visitors to the Holy City of Jerusalem, this way please." "You wish for a guide? English-speaking? German? American?" "The Church of St. Anne on your right, birthplace of the Virgin Mary." "Walk to your left and enter the superb Haram Esh Sharif, see the Dome of the Rock, the Dome of the Chain, the Al Aqsa Mosque." "This way, please, to the Jewish Quarter, the site of the Temple, the Wailing Wall." "Pilgrims to the Holy Sepulchre proceed by the Via Dolorosa straight ahead. Straight ahead for the Via Dolorosa, the Way of the Cross . . ."

Edward Babcock, standing just inside St. Stephen's Gate with his small party, was besieged on all sides by guides of every nationality. He waved them aside. He carried a street map of his own, and a sheaf of scribbled instructions handed him at the last moment by the courier at the hotel.

"Let us all try and keep together," he said, turning this way and that in search of his own little group amongst the pushing crowd. "If we don't keep together we shan't see anything. The first thing to remember is that the Jerusalem we are going to visit has been built upon the foundations of the one that was known to Our Lord. We shall be walking, and standing, many feet above where He walked and stood. That is to say . . ."

He consulted his notes again, and the Colonel seized him by the arm.

"First things first," he said briskly. "Deploy your troops where they can take advantage of the ground. I suggest we lead off with the Church of St. Anne. Follow me."

The signal was obeyed. The little flock trailed after the temporary shepherd to find themselves within a large courtyard, the Church of St. Anne on their right.

"Built by the Crusaders," declaimed the Colonel. "Finished in the twelfth century. They knew what they were doing in those days. One of the finest examples of Crusader architecture you'll ever see." He turned to the Rev. Babcock. "I know it of old, padre," he added.

"Yes, Colonel."

Babcock heaved a sigh of relief, and stuffed his notes in his pocket. He needn't refer to them for the moment anyway, and the Colonel, who had seemed below his usual form when they had met at breakfast, had now regained something of his old zest and confidence. The group followed their leader dutifully around the almost empty church. They had seen one already, the Franciscan Church of All Nations in the Garden of Gethsemane, and, although this second one was very different, the compulsion to silence was the same, the shuffling footsteps, the wandering eyes, the inability to distinguish one feature from another, the sensation of relief when the inspection was over and it was possible to go out once more into the bright sunlight.

"If you've seen one, you've seen the lot," Jim Foster whispered to Jill Smith, but she avoided his eye and he turned away, shrugging his shoulders. Guilty conscience? Oh well, if that was to be the mood she must get on with it. She had sung a very different tune last night . . .

Lady Althea, adjusting a blue chiffon scarf around her head so that it fell loosely about her shoulders, observed her husband closely. He seemed to be himself again. She had been relieved to find him in bed and asleep when she had entered their bedroom the night before. Nor had she questioned him. Better to let things alone . . . She had caught sight of friends driving away from the Church of All Nations, Lord and Lady Chaseborough, who were apparently staying at the King David Hotel, and they had agreed to meet by the Dome of the Rock at eleven o'clock. Such a surprise. If only she had known they were coming to Jerusalem she would have arranged to stay at the King David Hotel too. Never mind. At least she would get a glimpse of them, be able to exchange news of mutual friends.

"There's something going on at the far end of this courtyard," said Robin. "Look, Grandfather, quite a big queue. Shall we join them? It looks like some sort of excavation."

"Pool of Bethesda," replied the Colonel. "They've done a lot of work there since my day. I doubt if there's much to see. Part of the city drain."

But Robin was already running ahead to join the queue. His attention had been drawn to a screaming child, carried in the arms of her father, who was pushing his way to the head of the queue.

"What on earth are they doing with that child?" asked Kate Foster.

Babcock had been glancing at his notes again. "The site of the old sheep market. You remember Chapter Five of St. John's Gospel, Mrs. Foster, and the Pool of Bethesda, where the infirm waited to be healed, and how the angel came at certain times to trouble the water? Our Lord healed the man who had been lame for thirty-eight years." He turned to the Colonel. "I think we should just take a look at it."

"Come along then, follow me," said the Colonel, "but I warn you, it's only part of the old sewer system. We had trouble with it in '48."

Miss Dean was still standing outside the Church of St. Anne. She felt confused by all the chatter and bustle. What did the Rev. Babcock mean by saying they would be walking several feet above where Our Lord had trodden? The church here was very beautiful, no doubt, but the Colonel said even this had been built on the foundations of an earlier one, which in its turn had been erected over the simple dwelling of St. Joachim and St. Anne. Was she to understand that the parents of Our Lady had lived underground? In that curious sort of grotto they had visited before coming out of the church? She had hoped to be inspired by it, but instead she was disenchanted. She had always had such a happy picture of St. Joachim and St. Anne living in a pleasant whitewashed house with flowers growing in a small garden, and their blessed daughter learning to sew by her mother's side. There had been a calendar once with just such a painting upon it; she had treasured it for years until Dora took it off the wall and threw it away.

She looked around her, trying to conjure up the garden that no longer existed, but there were too many people present, none of them behaving with the slightest reverence, and one young women was actually sucking an orange and giving pieces to the small child trailing at her skirt, then scattering the peel on the ground. Oh dear, sighed Miss Dean, how Our Lady would have hated litter . . .

The pressure was intense around the steps descending to the Pool of Bethesda, and an official was standing with his hand on the rail, directing the people to go down one by one. The little girl in her father's arms was screaming louder than ever.

"Why is she making such a fuss?" asked Robin.

"I don't think she wants to go to the pool," replied Babcock in some hesitation. He averted his eyes. The child was obviously spastic, and the father, with his anxious wife by his side, was apparently intent upon dipping her in the pool, hoping for a miracle.

"I think," said the Colonel, sizing up the situation, "we'd be well-advised to push on to the Praetorium before the crowds get worse."

"No, wait a minute," said Robin. "I want to see what happens to the little girl."

He leaned over the rail and stared down into the pool with interest. It was certainly not much of a place, the water dark and rather slimy, the steps slippery-looking, too. Grandfather must be right, and it formed part of the city drain. The man who had been lame for thirty-eight years was lucky when Jesus came along and healed him instantly, rather than waiting for someone to lift him into the pool. Perhaps Jesus realized the water was bad. There they go, he said to himself, as the father, ignoring the child's terrified screams, slowly descended the steps. Freeing one hand, he dipped it in the pool and sloshed the water three times over his daughter, wetting her face, her neck, her arms. Then, smiling in triumph at the curious watchers above, he ascended the steps to safety, his wife smiling with him, mopping the child's face with a towel. The child herself, bewildered, distraught, rolled her frightened eyes over the heads of the crowd. Robin waited to see if the father would put her down, cured. Nothing happened, though. She began screaming again, and the father, making soothing sounds, bore her away from the top of the steps and was lost in the crowd.

Robin turned to the Rev. Babcock. "No luck, I'm afraid. There wasn't a miracle. I didn't really think there would be, but of course you never know."

The rest of the little party had moved away, embarrassed, distressed, unwilling witnesses of what appeared to be an excess of faith. All but Miss Dean, who, still standing before the Church of St. Anne, had seen nothing of the incident. Robin ran toward her.

"Miss Dean," he called, "you haven't seen the Pool of Bethesda."

"The Pool of Bethesda?"

"Yes, you know. It comes in St. John. The pool where the angel troubled the water and the lame man was healed. Except that Jesus healed him, not the pool."

"Yes, of course," said Miss Dean. "I remember well. The poor fellow had no one to carry him down, and he used to wait day after day."

"Well," said Robin proudly, "it's over there. I've just seen a little girl carried down to it. But she wasn't cured."

The Pool of Bethesda . . . what a strange and curious coincidence. She had turned to that very chapter in the Gospel the night before on returning to the hotel, and the whole scene was vivid in her recollection. It had made her think of Lourdes, of all the poor sick people who traveled there every year, and some of them indeed were cured, doctors and priests were quite confounded, there was never a medical explanation. Of course some came back without being cured, but then it could be that they did not have sufficient faith.

"Oh, Robin," she said, "I would like to see it. Will you show it me?"

"Well," he replied, "actually it's a bit disappointing. Grandfather says it's a drain. He remembers it in '48. And the rest of us are going on to the Praetorium where Jesus was scourged by the soldiers."

"I don't think I could bear to go there," said Miss Dean, "especially if it's underground, like everything else."

Robin, intent upon the next adventure, was not going to waste time showing the Pool of Bethesda to Miss Dean.

"The pool is over there," he said. "There's a man who stands at the top of the steps. See you later."

His grandmother was waving to him in the distance. Lady Althea was impatient to meet her friends at the Dome of the Rock.

"Do go back and tell Miss Dean to hurry up, Robin," she called.

"She doesn't want to see the Praetorium," he replied.

"Neither do I," said his grandmother. "I'm meeting the Chaseboroughs instead. Miss Dean will really have to take care of herself. Darling, you had better run ahead and join Grandfather. He's just passing under the archway now."

Everything was so disorganized owing to Babcock's lack of experience that it was a case of each one for himself, she decided. If Miss Dean failed to join up with the rest of the party, she could always go and sit in the hotel bus that was parked just round the corner outside St. Stephen's Gate. If the crowds were too impossible, the Chaseboroughs might invite herself and Phil and Robin back to lunch at the King David Hotel. She watched Robin until he had caught up with his grandfather, and the pair of them were lost in the throng of sightseers and pilgrims, then she followed the sign pointing toward the Dome of the Rock.

"Via Dolorosa . . . the Way of the Cross . . ."

The Colonel pushed ahead, ignoring the eager guides. The street was very narrow, flanked by high walls, the walls themselves spanned by archways covered in vine leaves. Walking was difficult, indeed impossible. Some of the pilgrims were already on their knees.

"What's everybody kneeling for?" asked Robin.

"First Station of the Cross," said the Colonel. "In point of fact, we're on the site of the Praetorium, padre. This was all part of the old Antonia Fortress. We can get a better idea of it inside the Convent of the Ecce Homo."

He was not so sure, though. Things seemed to have altered since '48. Men were seated at a table taking tickets. He had a murmured consultation with Babcock.

"How many of us are there?" he asked, searching the eyes of strangers.

He could see none of his party except himself, Robin, and the padre. The place seemed to be full of nuns. The pilgrims were being divided into groups.

"Better do what they tell us," he muttered to Babcock. "Call themselves the Soueurs de Sion, can't understand a word they say."

They were descending to a lower level, and this, thought Robin, must be what Miss Dean didn't want to do. It's not particularly frightening, though. Not nearly as bad as the Ghost Train at a fair.

The nun in charge of their party was explaining that they were descending to the Lithostratus or, as the Hebrews had it, the Gabbatha, the stone-paved judgment place of Pilate. The pavement had only recently been discovered, she told them, and perhaps the most striking proof that it was indeed the site of the place where the Seigneur had been held by Pilate, and scourged and mocked, was furnished by the curious markings on the flagstones themselves, the crisscross lines and pits which, experts told them, the Roman soldiers used for games of chance. Here in this corner they would have sat, dicing, guarding their prisoner, and we now know, too, she said, that it was a Roman custom to play a game called The King, when a condemned prisoner was crowned king during his last few hours, and treated with mock ceremony.

The gaping pilgrims stared about them. The place was low, vaulted, like an immense cellar, the flagstones hard and rugged beneath their feet. The whispering voices died away. The nun herself was silent.

Perhaps, thought Robin, the soldiers didn't actually mock Jesus at all. It was just a game, which they let him join in. He might even have thrown dice with them. The crown and the purple robe were just dressing up. It was the Romans' idea of fun. I don't believe when a prisoner is condemned to death the people guarding him are beastly. They try and make the time go quickly, because they feel sorry for him.

He could imagine the soldiers squatting on the flagstones, and with them, chained to a fellow prisoner, a thief, was a young man, smiling, who threw his dice with greater skill than his jailers, and so won the prize and was elected king. The laughter that greeted his skill was not mockery, it was applause.

That's it, thought Robin. People have been teaching it all wrong through the years. I must tell Mr. Babcock.

He looked about him, but he could see none of his party except his grandfather, who was standing very still, staring toward the far end of the vaulted room. People began to drift away but the Colonel did not move, and Robin, content to squat on the flagstones and trace the curious lines and markings with his finger, waited until his grandfather was ready.

We only acted under instructions, the Colonel told himself. They came direct from High Command. Terrorism was rife at the time, the Palestine police force couldn't deal with it, we had to take control. The Jews were laying mines at street corners, the situation was deteriorating daily. They had blown up the King David Hotel in July. We had to arm the troops, and protect them and the civilian population against terrorist attack. The trouble was, there was no political policy back at home, with a

Labour Government in power. They told us to go soft, but how can you go soft when people on the spot are being killed? The Jewish Agency insisted that they were against terrorism, but it was all talk and no action. Well, then we picked up this Jewish boy and flogged him. He was a terrorist, right enough. Caught him in the act. Nobody likes inflicting pain . . . There were reprisals afterward, of course. One of our officers and three N.C.O.'s kidnapped and flogged. Hell of a row about it at home. I don't know why standing here should bring the whole scene back so vividly. I haven't thought of it since. Suddenly he remembered the expression on the boy's face. The look of panic. And his mouth twisting as the lashes fell. He was very young. The boy was standing there in front of him once again, and his eyes were Robin's eyes. They did not accuse him. They simply stared at him in dumb appeal. Oh God, he thought, oh God, forgive me. And his years of service fell away, became as nothing, were wasted, useless.

"Come on, let's go," he said abruptly, but even as he turned on his heel and walked across the flagged stones he could hear the sound of the blows, could see the Jewish boy writhe and fall. He pushed his way through the crowd up into the open air, Robin at his heels, and so out into the street, looking neither to right nor to left.

"Hold on, Grandfather,' called Robin. "I want to know exactly where Pilate stood."

"I don't know," said the Colonel. "It doesn't matter."

Another queue was already forming to descend to the paved Gabbatha, and here outside the pilgrims were thicker than ever. A new guide was standing at his elbow, who plucked at his sleeve and said, "This way, the Via Dolorosa. Straight on for the Way of the Cross."

Lady Althea, wandering within the Temple area, was doing her best to shake off Kate Foster before they met the Chaseboroughs.

"Yes, yes, very impressive," she said vaguely as Kate pointed out the various domes, and began reading something out of a guidebook about Mameluke Sultan Quait Bai, who had built a fountain over the Holy of Holies. They wandered from one edifice to another, mounted row upon row of steps, descended them again, saw the rock where Isaac was sacrificed by Abraham and Mohammed rose to heaven, and still no sign of her friends. The sun, directly overhead, blazed down upon them.

"I think I've had enough," she said. "I really don't think I want to fag right over there and see the inside of that mosque."

"You'll be missing the finest sight in the whole of Jerusalem," retorted Kate. "The stained-glass windows of the Al Aqsa Mosque are world famous. I'm only hoping they weren't damaged in the bomb explosions one read about."

Lady Althea sighed. Middle East politics bored her, except when they were being discussed in an authoritative manner by a member of Parliament over dinner. There was so little to distinguish between Jews and Arabs anyway. They all threw bombs.

"Go and look at your mosque," she said. "I'll wait for you here."

She watched her companion disappear and then, loosening her chiffon scarf, strolled back again toward the flight of steps leading to the Dome of the Rock. The one great advantage in being in this Temple area was that there were fewer crowds than in that narrow, stifling Via Dolorosa. So much more space in which to move about. She wondered what Betty Chaseborough would be wearing—she had only caught sight of her white hat in the car. Pity she had let her figure go these last few years.

Lady Althea installed herself against one of the triple pillars above the flight of steps. They surely would not miss her here. She felt rather empty; coffee and breakfast seemed a long time ago. She opened her bag, remembering the piece of ring-shaped bread that Robin had pressed her into buying from some vendor who had been standing with a donkey outside the Church of All Nations. "It's not unleavened bread," he had told her, "but the next best thing to it." She smiled. His little ways were so amusing.

She bit into the bread—it was a lot harder than it looked—and as she did so she saw Eric Chaseborough and his wife emerging with a group of sightseers from some building Kate had said was Solomon's stables. She waved her hand to attract their attention, and Eric Chaseborough waved his hat in reply. Lady Althea dropped the piece of bread back into her bag, and was instantly aware, from the odd sensation in her mouth, that something was terribly wrong. She thrust her tongue upward. It pricked against two sharp points. She looked down again at the piece of bread, and there, impaled in the ring, were her two front teeth, capped by her dentist just before she left London. She seized her hand-mirror in horror. The face that was hers belonged to her no longer. The woman who stared back at her had two small filed pegs stuck in her upper gums where the teeth should have been. They looked like broken matchsticks, discolored, black. All trace of beauty had gone. She might have been some aged peasant who, old before her time, stood begging at a street corner.

Oh no . . . she thought, oh no, not here, not now! And in an agony of shame and humiliation she tried to cover her mouth with her blue chiffon scarf as the Chaseboroughs, smiling, advanced toward her.

"Run you to earth at last," called Eric Chaseborough, but she could only shake her head, gesticulating, trying to wave them off.

"What's the matter with Althea? Is she feeling ill?" asked his wife.

The tall, elegant figure backed away from them, groping with her scarf, and as they hurried to her side the chiffon fell back, revealing the tragedy, and the owner of the scarf, endeavoring to mumble between closed lips, pointed to the impaled teeth on the piece of bread within her bag.

"Oh, I say," murmured Eric Chaseborough, "bad luck. What a wretched thing to happen."

He looked about him helplessly, as if, amongst the people mounting the steps, there might be someone who could give them the address of a dentist in Jerusalem.

His wife, sensing the humiliation of her friend, held on to her arm.

"Don't worry," she said, "It doesn't show. Not if you keep your scarf over your mouth. You're not in pain?"

Lady Althea shook her head. Pain she could have borne, but not this loss of pride, this misery of shame, the knowledge that in that one moment of biting the bread she had thrown away all grace, all dignity.

"The Israelis are very up-to-date," said Eric Chaseborough. "There's sure to be a first-class man who can fix you up. The reception clerk at the King David will be able to tell us."

Lady Althea shook her head, thinking of those endless appointments in Harley Street, the careful probing, the high-speed drill, the hours of patience to keep beauty intact. She thought of the lunch ahead, herself eating nothing, while her friends tried to behave as if all was quite usual. The vain search for a dentist who could at best patch up the ravages that had taken place. Phil's gasp of astonishment. Robin's curious gaze. The averted eyes of the rest of the party. The remainder of the tour a nightmare.

"There's someone coming up the steps who seems to know you," murmured Eric Chaseborough.

Kate Foster, having inspected the Al Aqsa Mosque, had resolutely turned her back on the entrance to the Wailing Wall—too many Orthodox Jews pressing forward over the enormous space where their government had had the ruthless audacity to bulldoze Jordanian dwellings and condemn more Jordanians to desert tents—and return toward the Dome of the Rock. There she caught sight of Lady Althea being supported between strangers. She hurried to her rescue.

"What on earth's wrong?" she inquired.

Lord Chaseborough introduced himself and explained the situation.

"Poor Althea is very distressed," he murmured. "I'm not quite sure what's the best thing to do."

"Lost her front teeth?" said Kate Foster. "Well, it's not the end of the world, is it?"

She stared in some curiosity at the stricken woman who, proud and confident, had strolled by her side such a short while ago. "Let's have a look."

Lady Althea, her hand trembling, lowered the chiffon scarf, and with a tremendous effort tried to smile. To her consternation, and that of her sympathetic friends, Kate Foster burst out laughing.

"Well I must say," she exclaimed, "you couldn't have made a cleaner job of it if you'd been in a prizefight."

It seemed to Lady Althea, as she stood there above the steps, that all the people pressing forward were staring, not at the Dome of the Rock, but at her alone, and were nudging one another, whispering, smiling; for she knew, from her own experience of mocking others, that there is nothing more likely to unite a crowd of strangers in a wave of laughter than the sight of someone who, with dignity shattered, becomes suddenly grotesque.

"Straight on for the Via Dolorosa . . . Straight on for the Way of the Cross."

Jim Foster, dragging Jill Smith by the hand, was held up at every turn by kneeling pilgrims. Jill had expressed a wish to visit the markets, or the suks, or whatever they called themselves, and to the suks she should go. Besides, he could buy something for Kate, and make his peace with her.

"I think I ought to wait for Bob," said Jill, hanging back.

But Bob was nowhere to be seen. He had followed Babcock to the Praetorium, "You didn't want to wait for him last night," replied Jim Foster.

Amazing how a girl could change gears between midnight and noon. She might have been a different creature altogether. Last night under the trees, at first protesting, then moaning with pleasure at his touch, and now prickly, offhand, it was almost as if she wanted nothing more to do with him. Well, fine, O.K., let it be so. But it was a bit of a slap in the face all the same. A guilty conscience was one thing, a brush-off another. He wouldn't put it past her to have run bleating to her fool of a husband last night, telling him she had been the victim of assault. Though Bob Smith would never have the nerve to do anything about it. Well, it was probably the last thrill she would get out of sex, poor girl. Something to remember all her life.

"Come on," he urged, "if you want that brass bangle."

"We can't" she whispered. "That clergyman there is praying."

"*We Adore thee, O christ, and we bless thee.*"

The priest, just ahead of them, was on his knees, his head bowed.

"*Because by the Holy Cross thou hast redeemed the world.*"

The response came from the group of pilgrims kneeling behind him.

I shouldn't have let him, thought Jill Smith. I shouldn't have let Jim Foster do what he did last night. It wasn't right. I feel terrible when I think of it. And we came here to see the holy places, and all these people praying around us, and Jesus Christ dying for our sins. I feel awful, I feel really bad. On my honeymoon, too. What would everyone say if they knew? They'd say I was nothing but a scrubber, a slut, and it's not as if I were in love with him, I'm not, I love Bob. I just don't know what came over me to let Jim Foster do what he did.

The pilgrims rose to their feet and passed on up the Via Dolorosa, and thank goodness it didn't seem so holy once they had gone. The street was full of ordinary people, women with baskets on their heads, and they were coming to stalls full of vegetables, butchers' shops with carcasses of lambs hanging up on hooks, and traders shouting and calling their wares, but it was all so close and huddled together you could hardly move, you could hardly breathe.

The street was dividing, and there were booths and shops on either side, and flights of steps to the right flanked by stalls piled with oranges, grapefruit, enormous cabbages, onions, and beans. "We're in the wrong suk," said Jim Foster impatiently. "Nothing but blasted food-stuffs here."

Through an archway he espied a row of booths hung with belts and scarves, and next to it a stall where an old man was displaying cheap jewelry. "Here, this is more like it," he said, but a donkey loaded with melons barred his path, and a woman with a basket on her head tripped over his foot.

"Let's go back," said Jill. "We're getting hopelessly lost."

A young man sidled up to her, a sheaf of pamphlets in his hand.

"You wish to visit Holy Land Hill for superb panoramic view?" he inquired. "Also see the Artist Colony and Night-club?"

"Oh, please go away," said Jill. "I don't want to see any of them."

She had let go of Foster's hand, and now he was the other side of the street, beckoning to her. This might be the moment to give him the slip and try to retrace her steps and find Bob, yet she was scared at the thought of being on her own in these narrow, bewildering streets.

Jim Foster, standing by the booth which sold jewelry, picked up one object after another and threw it down again. Complete junk. Nothing worth buying. Medallions with the Dome of the Rock, and headscarves printed all over with donkeys. Hardly do to buy one of those for Kate—she might think it was a joke in bad taste. He turned round to look for Jill, forgetting that he still held one of the despised medallions in his hand. He could just see her disappearing down the street. Bloody girl, what was the matter with her? He started to cross the road, when an angry voice shouted after him from the stall.

"Three dollars for the medallion. You owe me three dollars!"

He looked back over his shoulder. The vendor behind the stall was red with anger.

"Here, take it. I don't want the damn thing," said Jim, and threw the medallion back onto the stall.

"You pick it up, you buy," shouted the man, and he began jabbering to his neighbor, and the pair of them started shaking their fists, attracting the attention of other vendors in the market, and other purchasers. Jim hesitated a moment, then panicked. You never knew what might happen with a Middle East crowd. He walked quickly away, and as the uproar rose behind him, and heads turned, he quickened his pace and began to run, elbowing people aside, head down, and the crowds intent upon their shopping, or merely strolling, stepped back upon one another, causing more upheaval. "What is it? Is he a thief? Has he planted a bomb?"

Murmurs were all behind him, and as Jim mounted a flight of steps he saw two Israeli policemen coming down, and he turned again, and tried to carve his way through the crowd below in the narrow street. His breath came quickly, there was a pain under his left rib like a knife, and the sensation of panic increased, for perhaps the Israeli policemen had questioned someone in the crowd and even now were pursuing him, believing him to be a thief, an anarchist, anything . . . How could he clear himself? How could he explain?

He fought his way through the crowd, losing all control, all sense of direction, and came out into a broader street, and now there was no escape because the way was barred by a throng of pilgrims walking with linked arms, and he had to fall back against a wall. They seemed to be all men, wearing dark trousers and white shirts. They didn't look like pilgrims, for they were laughing and singing. He was borne along with them, like a piece of flotsam on the crest of a wave, unable to turn back, and he found himself in the center of a great open space, in the midst of which young men similarly dressed were dancing, hand in hand, shoulder to shoulder.

The pain under his left rib was intense. He could move on farther. If he could only sit down for one moment, but there was no space. If he could only lean against something . . . against that enormous, lemon-colored wall. He couldn't reach it, though, he could only stand and stare, for the way to it was barred by a line of black-hatted men with curling hair, who were bowing and praying and beating their breasts. They are all Jews, he thought, I am alien, I'm not one of them, and his sense of panic returned, of fear, of desolation, for what if the two Israeli policemen were even now close to him on the fringe of the crowd, and forced their way to his side, and instead of bowing and praying before the Wailing Wall, the line of men turned and looked upon him in accusation, and a cry arose from the whole lot of them calling, "Thief . . . thief?"

Jill Smith had only one thought in mind, and that was to put as great a distance as possible between herself and Jim Foster. She didn't want to have anything more to do with him. She would have to be polite, of course, as long as they were all together, but they were due to leave Jerusalem later in the day, and once they were on board ship again none of them need have any close contact. Thank heaven she and Bob were going to live several miles from Little Bletford.

She walked quickly back along the narrow crowded street, away from the market quarter and the shops, passing tourists, sightseers, pilgrims, priests, but still no sign of Bob, nor of any of their party. There were signposts everywhere to the Holy Sepulchre, but she ignored them. She did not want to go inside the Holy Sepulchre. It didn't seem right. It didn't seem, well, clean. It would be hypocritical and false to go amongst all those people praying. She wanted to find some place where she could sit and think and be alone. The walls of the Old City seemed to be closing in upon her, and perhaps if she continued walking she would be free of them, find more air, and there would be less noise, less hustle.

Then she saw a gate in the distance, at the far end, but it was not St. Stephen's Gate, by which they had entered earlier. The letters said SHECHEM and another sign read DAMASCUS. It did not matter to her what it was called, as long as it led her out of the city.

She passed under the great archway, and there were cars and buses parked in rows outside, just as there had been at St. Stephen's Gate, and more tourists than ever coming down across the broad thoroughfare into the city. And there, standing in the midst of them, looking as lost and bewildered as she probably did herself, was Kate Foster. Too late to turn back—Kate had seen her. Reluctantly Jill went toward her.

"Have you seen Jim?" asked Kate.

"No," she replied. "I lost him in all those narrow streets. I'm looking for Bob."

"Well, you'll never find him," said Kate. "I've never met with such total disorganization. The crowds are absolute murder. None of our party has kept together. Lady Althea has gone back to the hotel practically having a nervous breakdown. She's lost her teeth."

"She's *what?*" asked Jill.

"Lost her front teeth. They came out on a piece of bread. She looks an absolute fright."

"Oh dear, how dreadful for her, I am sorry," said Jill.

A car was hooting at them and they moved to the side of the street, walking out of the stream of traffic but in no particular direction.

"The friends who were with her kept talking about finding a dentist, but how do you know where to get hold of one in such a place of turmoil? Then luckily we ran into the Colonel near St. Stephens Gate, and he took over."

"What did he do ?"

"Found a taxi at once and bundled her into it. She was nearly in tears, but he sent her friends packing and got in beside her, and if you ask me, though she usually spends her time snubbing him, she was never more relieved to see anyone in her life. I wish I could find Jim. What was he doing when you saw him last?"

"I'm not sure," faltered Jill. "I think he wanted to buy you a present."

"I know Jim's presents," said Kate. "I always get one when he has a guilty conscience. God! I could do with a cup of tea. Or at least somewhere to sit where I could take the weight off my feet."

They went on walking, looking aimlessly about them, and came to a sign with the words GARDEN OF THE RESURRECTION upon it.

"I don't suppose," said Jill, "we could get a cup of tea there?"

"You never know," replied Kate. "All these tourist centers carry ridiculous names. It's like Stratford-on-Avon. Everything is either Shakespeare or Ann Hathaway. Here it's Jesus Christ."

They found themselves descending into an enclosure surrounded by rock, with paved ways all about it, and an official in the center handed them a pamphlet. It said something about the Garden of Joseph of Arimathea.

"No tea here," said Kate. "No, thank you, we don't want a guide."

"We can at least," murmured Jill, "sit down on that little wall. They surely won't make us pay for that."

The official moved away, shrugging his shoulders. The garden would soon be full of pilgrims showing greater interest. Kate was studying the pamphlet.

"It's a rival site to the Holy Sepulchre," she said. "I suppose they like to spread the tourists around. That curious little tumbledown place built against the rock must be the tomb."

They walked across the peered into the opening in the wall.

"It's empty," said Jill.

"Well, it would be, wouldn't it?" answered Kate.

It was peaceful, anyway. They could sit down beside it and rest. The garden was practically empty, and Kate supposed it was still too early in the day for the usual hordes to stamp all over it. She glanced sideways at her companion, who looked tired and strained. Perhaps she had misjudged her after all. It was probably Jim who had made the running the night before.

"If you take my advice," she said shortly, "you'll start your family right away. We waited, with the result we've had no children. Oh yes, I tried everything. Opening the fallopian tubes, the lot. It didn't work. The doctors told me they thought Jim was probably sterile, but he wouldn't take a test. Now, of course, it's all too late. I'm plum in the middle of change of life."

Jill did not know what to say. Everything Kate Foster told her made her feel more guilty.

"I'm so sorry," she said.

"No use being sorry. I've got to put up with it. Be thankful you're young, and have all your life before you. Sometimes I feel there's absolutely nothing left, and that Jim wouldn't give a damn if I died tomorrow."

To Kate's dismay, Jill Smith suddenly burst into tears.

"What on earth's wrong?" Kate asked.

Jill shook her head. She couldn't speak. How could she explain the wave of guilt, of remorse, that was sweeping over her?

"Please forgive me," she said. "The thing is, I don't feel very well. I've been tired and out of sorts all day."

"Got the curse?"

"No . . . no . . . it's just that sometimes I wonder if Bob really loves me, if we're suited. Nothing seems to go right with us."

Oh, what was she saying, and as if Kate Foster could possibly care anyway?

"You probably married too young," said her companion. "I did too. Everyone marries too young. I often think single women have a far better time."

What was the use, though? She had been married to Jim for over twenty years, and despite all the anxiety and stress he caused her, she could never consider parting from him. She loved him, he depended upon her. If he became ill he would look to her before anyone else.

"I hope he's all right," she said suddenly.

Jill looked up from blowing her nose. Did she mean Bob, or Jim?"

"What do you mean?" she asked.

"Jim hates crowds, always has done, that's why as soon as I saw the mob of pilgrims in that narrow street I wanted him to come with me to the Mosque area, where I knew it would be quieter, but he would go tearing off with you in the opposite direction. Jim panics in crowds. Gets claustrophobia."

"I didn't realize," said Jill, "he never said . . ."

Perhaps Bob also panicked in crowds. Perhaps Bob, and Jim, too, were at this moment trying to fight their way out of that terrible mass of people, those clamoring street vendors, those chanting pilgrims.

She looked around her at the silent garden, at the scattered shrubs somebody had planted, at the dreary little empty tomb. Even the official had moved out of sight, leaving them alone.

"It's no use staying here," she said. "They'll never come."

"I know," said Kate, "but what are we to do? Where can we go?"

The thought of plunging back into the hated city was appalling, but there was no alternative. On, on, searching the faces of the passersby for their husbands and never finding them, always coming upon strangers, people who did not know, did not care.

Miss Dean waited until the stream of visitors to the Church of St. Anne and to the Pool of Bethesda had cleared, and then she walked very slowly toward the entrance to the pool and the flight of steps descending to it. A strange and rather wonderful idea had come into her head. She had been hurt, deeply hurt, by what she had overheard the night before. A thorn in his flesh. Jill Smith had told Mr. Foster that Father had said to her mother that she, Mary Dean, was a thorn in his flesh. Had pursued him for years. It was a lie, of course. Father would never say such a thing. Mrs. Smith had told a deliberate lie. Nevertheless, the fact that such a thing could be said, that possibly stories were told about her all over Little Bletford, had given her so much pain and distress that she had hardly slept. And to have overheard this above the Garden of Gethsemane of all places . . .

Then that dear little Robin, who seemed to be the only one in the party who ever read his Gospel, had explained to her that she was standing close to the Pool of Bethesda itself, and that a child had already been carried down to the pool to be cured of some disease. Well, perhaps the cure was not instantaneous, perhaps it would take some hours, or even days, for the miracle to show. Miss Dean had no disease, she was perfectly healthy, and strong. But if she could fill her small eau-de-cologne bottle with some of the water from the pool, and take it back with her to Little Bletford, and give it to Father to put in the holy water stoup in the entrance of the church, he would be overcome by her thought, by her gesture of faith. She could picture his expression when she handed the bottle to him. "Father, I have brought you water from the Pool of Bethesda." "Oh, Miss Dean, what a tender, wonderful thing to have done!"

The trouble was, it might be forbidden by the authorities to take water from the pool, whoever the authorities were, but the man standing near the entrance doubtless represented th em. Therefore—and it was in a good cause, a holy cause—she would wait until he had moved away, and would then descend the steps and fill the little bottle with water. Deceitful, perhaps, but deceitful in the name of the Lord.

Miss Dean bided her time, and presently—and the Lord must have been on her side—the man moved a short distance away toward a group of people who were obviously questioning him about some excavations farther on. This must be her chance.

She moved gingerly toward the steps, placed her hand carefully on the handrail, and began to descend. Robin was right in a sense. It did look rather like a drain, but there was plenty of water, and it was in a deep sort of chasm, and after what the Rev. Babcock had told them about everything being underground then there was no doubt about this being the genuine place. She felt truly inspired. Nobody descending to the pool but herself. She reached the slab at the bottom of the steps, and glancing above her to make quite sure nobody had followed and she was not observed, she took out her handkerchief, knelt upon it, and emptied the eau-de-cologne onto the stone beside her. It seemed rather a waste, but in a way it was a kind of offering.

She leaned over the pool and allowed the water to flow into the empty bottle. Then she stood up and replaced the cork, but as she did so her foot slipped on the damp stone slab, and the bottle fell out of her hand into the water. She gave a little cry of dismay and tried to retrieve it, but already it was out of reach and she herself was falling, falling, into the dark, deep waters of the pool.

"Oh, dear Lord," she called. "Oh, dear Lord, help me!"

Thrusting outward with her arms, she tried to reach the slippery wet slab on which she had stood, but the water was entering her open mouth, was choking her, and there was nothing and no one around her but the stagnant water, and the great high walls, and the patch of blue sky above her head.

The Rev. Babcock had been almost as moved by the pavement floor below the Ecce Homo Convent as the Colonel, although his reason was less personal. He, too, saw a man being scourged, guarded by soldiers, but it was happening two thousand years ago, and the man who was suffering was God. It made him feel utterly unworthy, and at the same time privileged, to have stood on hallowed ground. He wished he could in some way prove himself, and leaving the Praetorium, and watching the stream of pilgrims proceed slowly up the Via Dolorosa, halting at successive Stations of the Cross, he knew that no gesture of his, now or in the future, could atone for what had happened in that first century A.D. He could only bow his head and follow, with equal humility, those pilgrims who went before.

"Oh Lord," he prayed, "let me drink the cup that you have drunk, let me share your suffering."

He felt someone pluck him by the arm. It was the Colonel. "Will you carry on?" he asked. "I'm going to take my wife back to the hotel. She's had a slight accident."

Babcock expressed concern.

"No, it's nothing really," the Colonel reassured him. "An unfortunate mishap to her front teeth. She's rather upset, and I want to get her away from the crowds."

"Of course. Please express my sympathy. Where are the others?"

The Colonel looked over his shoulder. "I can only see two of them, our Robin and young Bob Smith. I've told them not to lose sight of you."

He turned back toward St. Stephen's Gate and disappeared.

Babcock resumed his slow progress toward Calvary, hemmed in on either side by the devout. We're really a cross section of the Christian world, he thought, every nationality, men, women, children, all walking where our Master walked before. And in His day, too, the curious stared, pausing about their daily business to watch the condemned pass by. In His day, too, the traders and shopkeepers sold their wares, women brushed past, or halted in doorways with baskets on their heads, youths shouted from stalls, dogs chased cats under benches, old men argued, children cried.

Via Dolorosa . . . the Way of the Cross.

Left, then right again, and now, on the turn, the band of pilgrims beside whom he walked mingled with another group in front, and yet a second and third dovetailed into them. Babcock, turning for one backward glance, could see no sign of Robin or Bob Smith, no sign of any of his flock. His pilgrim partners were now, immediately in front of him, a company of nuns, and behind him, bearded and black-robed, a group of Greek Orthodox priests. To move either to right or left was out of the question. He hoped he was not too conspicuous as the one lone figure bunched between them, the singing nuns ahead, the chanting priests in the rear.

The nuns were saying the Hail Mary in Dutch. At least, he thought it was Dutch, but it could have been German. They went down on their knees when they came to the Fifth and Sixth Stations, and Babcock, fumbling for his little pilgrim's handbook, reminded himself that the Fifth was the spot where the Cross had been laid upon Simon of Cyrene, and the Sixth where the face of Our Lord had been wiped by Veronica. He wondered whether he should kneel with the nuns, or stand with the Greek Orthodox priests. He decided to kneel with the nuns. It showed greater reverence, greater humility.

On, on ever upward, ever climbing, the dome of the Church of the Holy Sepulchre rearing above him, and now a final pause because they had arrived in the paved court before the great basilica itself, and in a moment the nuns, he himself, and the priests would be passing through the imposing door to the final Stations, within the church itself.

It was then that Babcock became aware, though not for the first time—he had known a momentary queasiness within the Ecce Homo Convent—that all was far from well with his own inside. A sharp pain gripped him, passed, then gripped him again. He began to sweat. He looked to right and left, but there was no means of extricating himself from the pilgrims who surrounded him. The chanting continued, the door of the church was before him, and despite his efforts to turn and go back the priests barred his way. He *must* go on and into the church, there was no other way.

The Church of the Holy Sepulchre enveloped him. He was aware of darkness, scaffolding, steps, the smell of many bodies and much incense. What can I do, he asked himself in agony, where can I go, the lingering taste of last night's chicken ragout rising from his belly to confound him, and as he stumbled up the steps to the Chapel of Golgotha in the wake of the nuns, with altars to right and left of him, candles, lights, crosses, votive offerings in profusion all about him, he saw nothing, heard nothing, he could only feel the pressure within his body, the compelling summons of his bowels, which no prayer, no willpower, no divine mercy from on high could overcome.

Bob Smith, bunched in behind the Greek Orthodox priests some distance in the rear, with Robin at his side, had been the first to observe the signs of distress on Babcock's face. He had noticed that when Babcock knelt for the final time, before being swept through the door of the church, he was looking very white, and was wiping his forehead with his handkerchief.

I wonder, he thought, if he's feeling ill. Faint, or something. He turned to Robin. "Look," he said, "I'm a bit worried about the parson. I don't think we ought to let him out of our sight."

"All right," said Robin. "Why don't you follow him? Perhaps he feels awkward walking with all those nuns."

"I don't think it's that," replied Bob. "I think he may be feeling ill."

"Perhaps," said Robin, "he wants to go to the toilet. I wouldn't mind going myself, as a matter of fact."

He looked about him for a practical solution. Bob Smith hesitated.

"Why don't you stay here," he suggested, "and wait for us to come out? That is, unless you're terribly keen to se inside the Holy Sepulchre."

"I'm not at all keen," said Robin. "I don't believe it's the correct site anyway."

"Right, then. I'll see if I can find him inside."

Bob pushed through the door, and like Babcock before him was met with darkness, scaffolding, chanting pilgrims, priests, a flight of steps and chapels on either side. Most of the pilgrims were descending, the nuns amongst them, closely followed by the priests. The figure of Babcock, so conspicuous in their midst winding his way up the Via Dolorisa, was no longer to be seen.

Then Bob Smith spied him, huddled against the base of the wall in the second chapel, his face buried in his hands, a sacristan—Greek, Coptic, Armenia, Bob didn't know which—crouching by his side. The sacristan raised his head as Bob approached.

"An English pilgrim," he whispered, "taken very unwell. I will go to find help."

"That's O.K.," said Bob. "I know him. He belongs to our party. I'll manage." He bent down and touched Babcock on the arm. "Don't worry," he said. "I'm here."

Babcock motioned with his hand. "Ask him to go away," he whispered. "The most frightful thing has happened."

"Yes," said Bob, "it's all right. I understand."

He gestured to the sacristan, who nodded, and crossed the chapel to prevent the incoming batch of pilgrims from approaching, and Bob helped Babcock to his feet.

"It could happen to any one of us," he said. "It must be happening all the time. I remember once at the Cup Final . . ."

He didn't finish his sentence. His unfortunate companion was too distressed, too doubled up with weakness, with shame. Bob took his elbow and helped him down the steps, and out of the church to the court beyond.

"You'll be better in a moment," he said, "in the fresh air."

Babcock clung to him. "It was the chicken," he said, "that chicken I had last night for dinner. I particularly didn't touch any fruit or salad, Miss Dean warned me against them. I thought chicken would be safe."

"Don't worry," said Bob. "You just couldn't help it. Do you think . . . do you think the worst is over?"

"Yes, yes, it's over."

Bob looked about him, but there was no sign of Robin. He must have gone into the church after all. What the hell should he do? The child ought not to be left to himself, but then no more should Babcock. He might be taken ill again. Bob should escort him back to the bus at St. Stephen's Gate. He would return for Robin.

"Look," he said, "I feel you should get back to the hotel as soon as possible, to change and lie down. I'll come with you as far as the bus."

"I'm so grateful," murmured his companion, "so terribly grateful."

He no longer cared if he had become conspicuous. It no longer mattered whether people turned and stared. As they retraced their steps downhill, back along the Via Dolorosa, past more chanting pilgrims, more tourists, more crying vendors of vegetables, onions, and the carcasses of lambs, he knew that he had indeed descended to the depths of humiliation, that by his final act of human weakness he had suffered a shame that only a man could suffer, and to which perhaps his Master had also succumbed, in his loneliness, in his fear, before being nailed to his criminal's cross.

When they came to St. Stephen's Gate the first thing they saw was an ambulance drawn up alongside their bus, and a crowd of people, strangers, grouped round it. An official, white in the face, was directing them to move away. Bob's first thought was for Jill. Something had happened to Jill . . . Then Jim Foster, limping, his hair disheveled, appeared from the midst of them.

"There's been an accident," he sid.

"Are you hurt?" asked Bob.

"No . . . no, nothing wrong with me, I got caught up in some sort of demonstration and managed to get away . . . It's Miss Dean. She fell into that drain they call the Pool of Bethesda."

"Oh, God in heaven . . ." exclaimed Babcock, and he looked despairingly from Jim Foster back to Bob. "This is all my fault, I should have been taking care of her. I didn't know. I thought she was with the rest of you." He moved forward to the ambulance, then remembered his own plight and spread out his hands in a gesture of despair. "I don't think I can go to her," he said. "I'm not in a fit state to see anyone . . ."

Jim Foster was staring at him, then glanced inquiringly at Bob Smith.

"He's not in good shape," murmured Bob. "He was taken ill a short while ago, up at the church. A bad tummy upset. He ought to get back to the hotel as soon as possible."

"Poor devil," replied Jim Foster under his breath, "what an awful thing. Look"— he turned to Babcock—"get up into the bus right away. I'll tell the driver to take you straight to the hotel. I'll go with Miss Dean in the ambulance."

"How bad is she?" asked Babcock.

"They don't seem to know," said Jim Foster. "It's shock chiefly. I imagine. She was pratically unconscious when the guide fellow pulled her out of the water. Luckily he was only at the top of the steps. Meanwhile, I can't think what has happened to either Bob's wife or mine. They're somewhere back in that infernal city."

He took hold of Babcock by the arm and steered him toward the bus. Funny thing how other people's misfortunes made you forget your own. The panic he himself had experienced had vanished at his first sight of the ambulance as he stumbled down through St. Stephen's Gate, giving way to a deeper anxiety that Kate might be the victim the stretcher-bearers were carrying to it. But it was only Miss Dean. Poor wretched Miss Dean. Thank heaven, not Kate.

The bus rumbled off with the pale, unhappy Babcock staring at them from one of the windows.

"Well, he's on his way, that's one thing," said Jim Foster. "What a calamity, what a situation. I wish the Colonel was here to handle it."

"I'm worried now about Robin," said Bob Smith. "I told him to wait for us outside the Church of the Holy Sepulchre, and he was missing when we came out."

"Missing? In that mob?" Jim Foster stared, aghast.

Then, with unspeakable relief, he saw his wife, with Jill beside her, coming through St. Stephen's Gate. He ran across to her.

"Thank heaven you've come," he said. "We've got to get Miss Dean to hospital. She's in the ambulance already. I'll explain everything on the way. There's been a series of mishaps all round. Babcock ill, Robin missing, it's been a disastrous day."

Kate seized his arm. "But you?" she said. "Are you all right?"

"Yes, yes . . . of course I'm all right."

He dragged her toward the ambulance. He did not even look at Jill. Bob hesitated, wondering what he ought to do. Then he turned, and saw Jill standing beside him.

"Where have you been?" he asked.

"I don't know," she said wearily. "In a sort of garden. I was looking for you but I couldn't find you. Kate was with me. She was worried about her husband. He can't stand crowds."

"Nor can any of us," he said, "but we'll have to face them again. Young Robin is lost, and I must go and find him. There's nobody else left."

"I'll come with you."

"Are you sure? You look absolutely done in."

The Fosters were climbing into the ambulance. The siren wailed, and the spectators moved away. Jill thought of that endless winding street they called the Via Dolorosa, the chanting pilgrims, the chattering vendors, the repetition of a scene she never wanted to see again, the clatter, the noise.

"I can face it," she sighed. "It won't seem so long if we're together."

Robin was enjoying himself. Being on his own always gave him a sense of freedom, of power. And he had become very bored trailing along in the path of the pilgrims, with people going down on their knees every other moment. It wasn't even as if they were walking the right way. The city had been pulled down and rebuilt so many times that it was altogether different from what it had been two thousand years ago. The only way to reconstruct it would be to pull it down again, and then dig and dig and dig and reveal all the foundations. He might well become an archaeologist when he grew up, if he didn't become a scientist like his father. The two professions were rather similar, he decided. He certainly would not become a clergyman like Mr. Babcock, Not in this day and age.

He wondered how long they would stay inside the church. Hours, probably. It was full to the brim with priests and pilgrims wanting to pray, and they would all bump into each other. This made him laugh, and laughing made him want to go to the toilet—his grandmother hated the word toilet, but everyone used it at school—and so, as there wasn't a real one handy, he went and relieved himself against the wall of the church. Nobody saw. Then he sat down on a step, opened his two maps, and spread them across his knees. The thing was, Jesus had either been held in the Antonia Fortress or in the Citadel. Probably both. But which one had He been held in last, before He had to carry His cross with the two other prisoners, and set out for Golgotha? The description in the Gospels did not make it clear. He was brought before Pilate, but Pilate could just as well have been in the one place as in the other. Pilate delivered Jesus to the high priests to be crucified, but where were the high priests waiting for Him? That was the point. It could have been at Herod's Palace, where the Citadel stood now, and in that case Jesus and the two thieves would all have left the city by the Genath Gate. He looked from one map to the other: the Genath Gate was now called Jaffa Gate, or in Hebrew, Yafo—it depended which language you spoke.

Robin looked at the church door. They would be ages yet. He decided to walk to the Jaffa Gate and see how it was for himself. It wasn't very far, and with the help of the modern map he wouldn't lose the way. It took him less than ten minutes to reach the gate, and here he paused to take stock of his surroundings. People were passing in and out, and there were cars drawn up outside, as there had been by St. Stephen's Gate at the opposite end of the walled city. The trouble was, of course, that instead of the bare hillside and gardens, which was how it would have been two thousand years ago, there was now a main road, and the modern city spreading itself everywhere. He consulted his old map once again. There used to be a fortress tower called Psephinus, standing proud and mighty by the north-west corner of the city, and this was the tower that the Emperor Titus rode to inspect, when he camped with his Roman legions before capturing and sacking Jerusalem in A.D. 70. There was something built on the present site called the Collège des Frères. Wait a moment, though. Was it the Collège des Frères or a hotel called the Knight's Palace? Either way, it was still inside the walls of the city and somehow that was not right, even with the walls having been rebuilt.

I'll imagine, he told himself, that I'm Jesus, and I've just come out of the Genath Gate, and all this is bare hillside and sloping gardens, and they don't crucify a person in a garden, but a decent distance away, especially before the Feast of the Passover, otherwise the people would make a disturbance, and there had been enough riots already. So Jesus and the two other condemned prisoners were made to walk a fair way, that's why they made Simon the farm laborer—and Cyrene means farm laborer in Aramaic, the headmaster told me so—carry the cross. He was just coming in from work in the fields. Jesus couldn't manage it, being weak from all that scourging. And they took him and the others out to some rough scrubby ground overlooked by the Psephinusu tower, where the soldiers would have had a guard posted, so that if there should have been an attempt at rescue the attempt would fail.

Pleased with his deduction, Robin turned to the right out of the Jaffa Gate and walked along the main road until he judged that he was the right distance from the long-vanished tower of Psephinus. He found that he had reached a junction with main roads going in all directions and traffic roaring by, and the great building across the other side of the central square was the town hall, according to his modern map.

So this is it, he thought. This is scrubby ground, with fields where the town hall stands, and the farm laborer is sweating, and so are Jesus and the others. And the sun is overhead in a blazing sky, as it is now, and when the crosses are set up the men nailed on them won't see the fields behind them, they'll be looking at the city.

He shut his eyes a moment, and turned, and looked back at the city and the walls, and they were a golden color, very fine and splendid. For Jesus, who had spent most of his life wandering about the hills and lakes and villages, it would have seemed the finest and most splendid city in the world. But after staring at it for three hours, in pain, it would not seem so splendid—in fact, it would be a relief to die.

A horn blared, and he stepped out of the way of the incoming traffic. If he didn't watch out he would die, too, and there wouldn't be much sense in that.

He decided to walk back to the city through the New Gate, which was just along to the right. Some men were repairing a place in the road, and they looked up as Robin approached. They shouted, pointing to the traffic, and although Robin got the message and skipped to safety beside them, he could not understand what they were saying. It could be Yiddish, or possibly Hebrew, but he wished it could have been Aramaic. He waited until the man with the drill ceased his ear-splitting probe, and then he called to them.

"Does anyone speak English?" he asked.

The man with the drill smiled and shook his head, then called out to one of his companions, who was bending over a piece of piping. The man looked up. He was young, like the rest, and had very white teeth and black curly hair.

"I speak English, yes," he said.

Robin peered down into the pit beneath. "Can you tell me, then," he asked, "if you have found anything interesting down there?"

The young man laughed, and picked up a small animal by its tail. It looked like a dead rat.

"Tourist souvenir?" he suggested.

"No skulls? No bones?" Robin asked hopefully.

"No." The laborer smiled. "For that we have to drill very deep, below the rock. Here, you can catch?" He threw a small piece of rock up to Robin from the pit in which he stood. "Keep it," he said. "The rock of Jerusalem. It will bring you luck."

"Thank you very much," said Robin.

He wondered whether he should tell them that they were standing within a hundred yards or so, perhaps, of a place where three men had been crucified two thousand years ago, and then he decided they would not believe him; or, if they did, it would not impress them very much. For Jesus was not important to them, not like Abraham or David, and, anyway, so many men had been tortured and killed around Jerusalem since then that the young man might very well say, with justice, so what? It would be more tactful to wish them a happy holiday instead. It was the fourteenth day of Nisan, and at sundown all work would cease. He put the small piece of work in his pocket.

"I hope you have a very pleasant Pesach," he said.

The young man stared. "You Jewish?"

"No," answered Robin, uncertain whether the question related to his nationality or to his religion. If the latter, he would have to reply that his father was an atheist, and his mother went to church once a year on Christmas Day. "No, I come from Little Bletford in England, but I do know that today is the fourteenth day of Nisan and that you have a public holiday tomorrow."

This, in fact, was the reason for so much traffic, he supposed, and the reason why the city itself had been so crowded. He hoped the young man was suitably impressed by his knowledge.

"It's your Feast of Unleavened Bread," he told him.

The young man smiled again, showing his row of white teeth, and, laughing, he called something over his shoulder to his companion with the drill, who shouted in reply, before applying his drill to the surface of the road again. The ear-splitting sound began once more, and the young man cupped his hands to his mouth and called up to Robin. "It is also the Festival of our Freedom," he shouted. "You are young, like us. Enjoy it too."

Robin waved his hand and began walking toward the New Gate, his hand clenched tightly round the piece of rock in his pocket. The Festival of our Freedom . . . It sounded better than the Passover. More modern, more up-to-date. More suitable for, as his grandmother would say, this day and age. And whether it meant freedom from bondage, as it did in the Old Testament, or freedom from the rule of the Roman Empire, which the Jews hoped for at the time of the Crucifixion, or freedom from hunger and poverty and homelessness, which the young men digging in the road had won for themselves today, it was all one and the same thing. Everyone, everywhere, wanted freedom from something, and Robin decided that it would be a good idea if Pesach and Easter could be combined throughout the world, and then all of us, he thought, could join in celebrating the Festival of our Freedom.

The bus took the road north from the Mount of Olives before sundown. There had been no further drama. Bob and Jill Smith, having searched the precincts of the Holy Sepulchre in vain, had turned their steps in the direction of the New Gates and had come across Robin, perfectly composed, entering the city behind a group of singing pilgrims from the coast. The bus had been late departing because of Miss Dean. The ambulance had taken her to hospital, where she had been detained for a number of hours suffering from shock, but luckily with no external or internal injuries. She had been given an injection and a sedative, and then the doctor had pronounced her fit to travel, with strict injunctions that she should be put straight to bed directly they were back on board in Haifa. Kate Foster had become nurse in charge of the patient.

"It is so kind of you," Miss Dean had murmured, "so very kind."

It was decided by all not to mention her unfortunate accident. Nor did Miss Dean allude to it herself. She sat silently, with a rug over her knees, between the Fosters. Lady Althea was silent too. Her blue chiffon scarf masked the lower part of her face, giving her the appearance of a Moslem woman who had not relinquished the veil. If anything, it added to her dignity and grace. She, too, had a rug over her knees, and the Colonel held her hand beneath it.

The young Smiths held hands more openly, Jill sporting a new bangle, an inexpensive one that Bob had bought for her as they passed near one of the suks on their return earlier in the day after finding Robin.

Babcock sat beside Robin. Like Miss Dean, he also wore a change of clothing—a pair of trousers borrowed from Jim Foster which were a shade too large for him. No one passed any remarks, and for this he was unspeakably thankful. Nor did anyone look back at the city of Jerusalem as the bus skirted Mount Scopus—that is to say, no one but Robin. The ninth hour of the fourteenth day of Nisan had come and gone, and the thieves, or the insurrectionists, whichever they were, had been taken down from their crosses. Jesus, too, his body perhaps in a grave deep in the rock below where the young laborers had been drilling. Now the young men could go home, and wash, and meet their families, and look forward to the public holiday. Robin turned to the Rev. Babcock at his side.

"It's rather a shame," he said, "that we couldn't have stayed two more days."

Babcock, who wished for nothing more than to be safely back on board ship so that he could shut himself in his cabin and try to forget his shame in the church of the Holy Sepulchre, marveled at the resilience of the young. The boy had been dragging round the city all day, and had nearly lost himself into the bargain.

"Why, Robin?" he asked.

"Well, you never know," Robin replied. "Of course, it's not very probable in this day and age, but we might have seen the Resurrection."